PRACTICAL
POLISH-ENGLISH
ENGLISH-POLISH
DICTIONARY

HIPPOCRENE PRACTICAL DICTIONARY

PRACTICAL POLISH-ENGLISH ENGLISH-POLISH DICTIONARY

by

Iwo Cyprian Pogonowski

REVISED EDITION
1991

HIPPOCRENE BOOKS

New York

HIPPOCRENE PRACTICAL DICTIONARY

Fourth revised edition, 1991

Copyright © 1991, 1983, 1979 by Iwo Cyprian Pogonowski
All rights reserved

Hippocrene Books, Inc.
171 Madison Avenue
New York, New York 10016

Printed in the United States or America

Library of Congress Cataloging in Publication Data

Pogonowski, Iwo Cyprian, 1921–
  Dictionary, Polish-English, English-Polish

  1. Polish language—Dictionaries—English.
  2. English language—Dictionaries—Polish.
  I. Title.
PG6640.P54   491.8'5321   82-9211
                   AACR2

ISBN 0-87052-083-0

TO MY WIFE MAGDALENA

ACKNOWLEDGMENTS AND WORDS OF APPRECIATION

To Ms.Melanie Tomaszkiewicz for help in preparation of the phonetic guide.
To Ms.Teresa Widomska for typing and proof-reading.
To Mr.Robert Czarnek, Mr.Emil J.Skibiński, Mr.Jerzy A. Starczewski,Drs. Kazimierz Sowiński, Wiesław Zdaniewski and Zdzisław Mach for proof-reading and checking of the spelling against
current standard dictionaries.
To Ms.Janina Czarnek and Mr. Zdzisław Mach for help in preparation of information on the Polish cuisine.
To Dr.Magdalena J. Pogonowska for help in editing "SAY IT IN
POLISH!"conversations for travelers to Poland.

CONTENTS - SPIS TREŚCI

INTRODUCTION

The Polish-English part of this dictionary contains about 16,000 entries. The large Polish-English dictionaries usually contain some 180,000 entries, which give basic forms only and do not include ending changes, etc. discussed below. The term dictionary entry is used here as defined by the U.S. Bureau of Federal Supply, which indicates that each word variant explained constitutes an entry.

The word choice and translation are updated for current usage in America and Poland. Characteristic idiomatic usages are included. Each entry includes a pronunciation guide for sound and stress. A stress mark is placed over the stressed vowel.

The pronunciation guide, following the listing of all entries in this dictionary, gives also an illustrated discussion of Polish and English sounds and an explanation of the phonetic symbols. For practical reasons, the number of phonetic symbols are expressed in Latin letters only. Special care is given to explain and illustrate the pronunciation of Polish consonants and vowels which do not occur in the English language and vice versa. The information presented stresses whenever possible the familiar pronunciation and meaning in common usage in both languages.

Linguists define the language as a raw material for the creative activity of speaking. It is a rule-governed creativity in which we are creating and understanding sentences within rules of grammar. A grammatical rule is a description of a pattern habitually followed in a given language; changes in pattern render changes in meaning. This is true, of course, in both Polish and English languages.

An active language changes at varying rates but always at a rate faster than its changes in rules of grammar. Grammar has greater stability than syntax and vocabulary. Every language offers a special way of seeing and interpreting. Languages within the same Indo-European group are not simply equivalent.

The abundance of Polish grammatical forms that do not occur in English should be noticed. A multitude of inflectional forms of Polish nouns and adjectives is reflected in their structure and spelling. Changes in endings of nouns and adjectives correspond to their function in a sentence, their gender and number. Thus, Polish declension requires seven ending changes in nouns and adjectives for both singular and plural, in each gender. Polish personal verb forms correspond by gender and number to the subject of the sentence; thus, nine verb endings occur in the present tense alone. Impersonal forms and various moods expand this number. Both the perfect and imperfect of Polish verbs are indicated by structural variation (In informal Polish, the distinction between perfect and imperfect forms is not always carefully observed.). Verbs "dać" and "dawać" and "zabrać" and "zabierać" illustrate the structural difference between perfect and imperfect forms characteristic of the Polish language.

If every possible structural form of every Polish noun, adjective, verb, adverb, etc. inclusive of all ending changes was a dictionary entry, the number of Polish words listed would be in millions. The number of Polish words is further increased by multitudes of augmentative and diminutive forms which give expression to emotional values by word structure. These augmentative and diminutive forms serve to make the meaning of nouns and adjectives precise by often achieving broadening and clarifying. Augmentative and diminutive forms in Polish are often used to express feelings and attitudes both positive and negative. A comparison of a Polish, German and English word may be useful in order to illustrate the relative usage of augmentatives and diminutives. The use of the German word offers a chance to see the transition between Slavic and Germanic languages. In German diminutives and augmentatives we see the influence of the languages of the Elbe River Slavs, the Polabians, the Lusatians and the Czechs as well as the influence of the Polish language./Also see page VII/.

Language:	Basic word:	Augmentative Form:	Diminutive Form:
ENGLISH	BOY	BIG BOY	LITTLE BOY
GERMAN	KNABE	KNAB	KNABCHEN, KNABLEIN
POLISH	CHŁOPIEC	CHŁOPAK CHŁOPACZYSKO CHŁOPCZYSKO ETC.	CHŁOPCZYK CHŁOPACZEK CHLOPTAS CHŁOPACZYNA ETC.

It should be noticed that in this example the Polish word "chlopiec" is a diminutive form derived from the Polish word "chlop" which among other meanings stands for a grown man. In the Polish language there is a middle voice of verb inflection not used in English. The middle voice represents the subject as acting on and for itself in a way different than the usual active and passive form common to both the Polish and English languages. The middle voice in Polish describes self-reflectiveness not directly describable in English. The Polish middle voice occurs within the reflexive form of verb followed by "się." The gender of nouns in Polish is structurally indicated in conjugation of verbs (See p.VIII). The designation of gender of the Polish nouns is influenced by the sound of the ending. Thus, inanimate things in the Polish, as in most Indo-European languages, often are of masculine or feminine grammatically designated gender. The Polish word "robota," for example, meaning "work," is of feminine gender because of

the ending "a"; a derivative noun "robot" which means a mechanical man or brain is of masculine gender indicated by ending
sound of the letter "t." The profound differences between the
Polish and English language make literal translation of common
expressions usually impossible which is the main cause of the
difficulty of learning Polish by English speakers and vice
versa. The relative difficulty of learning a foreign language
depends on the characteristics of one's own language as illustrated on Table 1, (page VI) showing the relative difficulty
of languages for English speakers based on the experience of
the Foreign Service Institute (1973).

The Slavic languages, including Polish, are a family of languages evolved directly from the original Indo-European language by relatively undisturbed evolution. Any two of the
fourteen Slavic languages are sufficiently similar to allow
their speakers to communicate quite effectively if each speaks
his own language slowly and explains to the other the words
that are not common to both languages. All the Slavic languages have almost the same flexional characteristics with the
exception of Bulgarian, which like English lost the decle-
sions. It happened in Bulgaria after the imposition of Greek
in place of the Old Slavic liturgical language and during the
lengthy Turkish occupation. Polish speakers have to learn to
express meaning by word structure within the grammatical rules
of flexional changes. The English and Bulgarian speakers a-
chieve logical clarity of meaning by order or position of
words. Thus, English and Bulgarian are defined as isolating
or position languages. Polish speaker learning English en-
counters much simpler grammatical forms and basic concepts in
the English language than does his English counterpart in Polish. Assuming the same intensity of foreign language teaching program Polish speakers learn English about 20 to 30% faster than vice versa. The English language is mixed so much
that it does not have a close sister language. However, what
remained in English of the Old Anglo-Saxon grammar, is of Germanic character, even though, to the English speakers today,
the Old Anglo-Saxon is a foreign language. Also Germanic is
the majority of the high-frequency vocabulary in the modern
English. Thus, English is usually classified by the linguists
as a Germanic language, even though, the Romance languages,
including Latin, contribute to English about half of its vocabulary. Both, Romance and Germanic languages have much simpler grammar than do the Slavic languages with exception of
Bulgarian. The Polish language belongs to the inflective
group of languages and it utilizes the active voice to a
greater extent than does the English language. Numerous dia-
critical markings in Polish give good correlation of sound to
spelling. The difficulties of correlating sound to spelling
in English result mainly from the fact that two different
sound correlations to the Latin alphabet occurred in Britain,
first to the Anglo-Saxon and then to the French (brought with
the Norman invasion). Polish pronunciation is rather stable
and clear. English vowels are relatively less stable and un-

dergo variations under stress. On the other hand, the voiced consonants that occur at the end of an English word are often pronounced clearly. The word "love," for example, has a clear "v" at the end and not an "f" as it would be pronounced in Polish. In Polish, all consonants that occur at the end of a Polish word are voiceless. The word "woz," for example, is pronounced with an "s" at the end: "voos." Typically, rules of grammar and phonetics in English start with words "often," "sometimes," etc. while in Polish similar rules are stated: "always, with very few exceptions." The foreign words enrich English vocabulary and remain relatively unchanged. In Polish the foreign borrowings are assimilated into declension of nouns (single and plural) and adjectives (both subject to expansion in to augmentative and diminutive forms) and conjugation of verbs (each in perfect and imperfect form) and grammatical forms derived from verbs. The English language is much simpler in this respect because each noun without any change in spelling potentially may be used as a verb and sometimes as an adjective. In Polish the vigorous growth of abstract and scientific terms was based mainly on the indigenous words with parallel foreign borrowings. The Polish language achieves the size of its vocabulary by use of prefixes and suffixes to a much greater extent than does the English language. For example the mystical ancient Indo-European root-word "god," common to both Polish and English is expanded in Polish to over 3,000 structurally different words. Meanings of these words include weather, agreements, disagreements, harmony, adventure, comfort, discomfort, toilet (wy-god-ka), injury, dignity, decency, indecency, mystical union, time measurement, reconciliation, hiring etc.(VII).Total vocabulary in English and Polish is about one half a million words. However the make up of each vocabulary is different. English has some 120,000 root-words or about double the 60,000 root-words that are characteristic of an inflective language such as Polish. A practical dictionary is based on the frequency of use of words. Table II (p. VI) includes the plot of high frequency words as a percent of the words printed on an average English page. Thus knowing 1,000 most frequently used words one would know about 70% of words on an average page; and knowing 5,000 would give 86% and knowing 10,000 would give one about 92% of words on an average English page. The size of a person's vocabulary and the degree of comprehension of a native language learned with age and education is shown approximately on Table III (p. VI).

It is interesting to note that throughout Europe, including Poland, many professional and business people with rudimentary knowledge of English prefer to read factual reports in English, rather than in their native language. English is recognized by them as a methodical, energetic, businesslike and sober language, that is somewhat short on finery and elegance, but flexible and unrestrained by strict rules of grammar and lexicion. Centuries of colonial expansion brought English to all corners of the world where hundreds of millions use it.

English today is a dominant world language, while less than sixty million people know the Polish language. However, the Polish language with its logic, finery and elegance will continue to give a good start to abstract thinkers such as mathematicians, logicians, philosophers, anthropologists, novelists and poets and thus contribute to the pluralistic culture of the world.

TABLE I   RELATIVE DIFFICULTY OF LANGUAGES FOR ENGLISH SPEAKERS
Class time for average student to reach between minimal and working professional proficiency according to Foreign Service Institute (1973).
24 weeks=720 hours: Afrikaans;Danish;Dutch;French;German;Haitian;
Creole;Italian;Norwegian;Spanish;Swedish;Swahili.
38 weeks=1140hours: Bulgarian;Dari:Farsi:Greek:Hindi:Indonesian;
Malay;Urdu.
44 weeks=1320hours: Amharic;Bengali;Burmese;Czech;Finnish;Hebrew;
Hungarian;Cambodian-Khmer;Lao;Nepali:Philipino;Polish;Russian;Ser-
bo-Croatian;Sinhala;Thai;Tamil;Turkish;Vietnamese.
65 weeks=1950hours: Arabic;Chinese;Japanese;Korean.

TABLE II   HIGH FREQUENCY ENGLISH WORDS VS. PERCENTAGE OF WORDS ON
               AN AVERAGE PRINTED PAGE according to H.Kučera and W.N.
Francis"Computational Analysis of Present-day American English"1967.
PERCENTAGE OF WORDS UNDERSTOOD ON AN AVERAGE PRINTED PAGE :

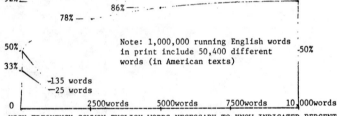

Note: 1,000,000 running English words
in print include 50,400 different
words (in American texts)

HIGH FREQUENCY COMMON ENGLISH WORDS NECESSARY TO KNOW INDICATED PERCENT

TABLE III APPROXIMATE GROWTH OF VOCABULARY AND UNDERSTANDING OF
              WORDS WITH AGE AND EDUCATION IN A NATIVE LANGUAGE
Compare with estimated median vocabulary size for each age group by
K.C.Diller "The Language Teaching Controversy" 1978.

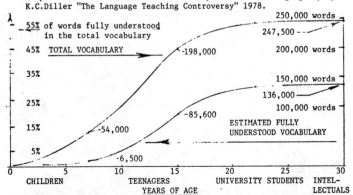

EXAMPLE OF NOUN AND ADJECTIVE DECLENSION IN POLISH LANGUAGE

DOBRY DOM = GOOD HOME, GOOD HOUSE

SINGULAR:

NOMINATIVUS	= MIANOWNIK	DOBRY DOM	GOOD HOME
GENETIVUS	= DOPEŁNIACZ	DOBREGO DOMU	OF A GOOD HOME
DATIVUS	= CELOWNIK	DOBREMU DOMOWI	FOR A GOOD HOME
ACCUSATIVUS	= BIERNIK	DOBRY DOM	A GOOD HOME
INSTRUMENTALIS	=NARZĘDNIK	DOBRYM DOMEM	BY A GOOD HOME
LOCATIVUS	= MIEJSCOWNIK	W DOBRYM DOMU	IN A GOOD HOME
VOCATIVUS	= WOŁACZ	O DOBRY DOMU!	OH! GOOD HOME

PLURAL:

NOMINATIVUS	= MIANOWNIK	DOBRE DOMY (2,3,4)	GOOD HOMES
		DOBRYCH DOMOW (5...)	GOOD HOMES
GENETIVUS	= DOPEŁNIACZ	DOBRYCH DOMOW	OF GOOD HOMES
DATIVUS	= CELOWNIK	DOBRYM DOMOM	FOR GOOD HOMES
ACCUSATIVUS	= BIERNIK	DOBRE DOMY (2,3,4)	GOOD HOMES
		DOBRYCH DOMOW (5...)	GOOD HOMES
INSTRUMENTALIS	=NARZĘDNIK	DOBRYMI DOMAMI	BY GOOD HOMES
LOCATIVUS	= MIEJSCOWNIK	W DOBRYCH DOMACH	IN GOOD HOMES
VOCATIVUS	= WOŁACZ	O DOBRE DOMY!(2,3,4)	OH!GOOD HOMES
		O (PIĘC) DOBRYCH	OH! (FIVE)
		DOMOW! (5...)	GOOD HOMES

NOTE: (2,3,4) = Small Polish plural of two, three and four.
    (5...) = Large Polish plural of five and more.

DIMINUTIVES: SING.: DOBRY DOMEK - PLUR.: DOBRE DOMKI (2,3,4)
                                            DOBRYCH DOMKOW (5...)
             DOBRY DOMECZEK   DOBRE DOMECZKI (2,3,4)
                              DOBRYCH DOMECZKOW (5...)
AUGMENTATIVES: SING.:DOBRE DOMISKO PLUR.:DOBRE DOMISKA(2,3,4)
                                       DOBRYCH DOMISK (5...)

EXAMPLE OF CONJUGATION OF A VERB IN THE POLISH LANGUAGE

CZYTAC (chi-tach) = TO READ

- PAST TENSE -

PERFECT FORM = SINGLE TIME COMPLETED OCCURENCE

MASCULINE	"I"	(JA)	CZYTAŁEM	I READ
FEMININE	"I"	(JA)	CZYTAŁAM	
MASCULINE	"YOU"	(TY)	CZYTAŁES	YOU READ
FEMININE	"YOU"	(TY)	CZYTAŁAS	
		(ON)	CZYTAŁ	HE READ
		(ONA)	CZYTAŁA	SHE READ
		(CNO)	CZYTAŁO	IT READ
MASCULINE	"WE"	(MY)	CZYTALISMY	WE READ
FEMININE	"WE"	(MY)	CZYTAŁYSMY	
MASC.PLUR.	"YOU"	(WY)	CZYTALISCIE	YOU READ
FEM. PLUR.	"YOU"	(WY)	CZYTAŁYSCIE	
		(ONI)	CZYTALI	THEY READ
FEM.& NEUTER		(ONE)	CZYTAŁY	

CZYTYWAC (chi-ti-vach)=TO READ (OFTEN)

IMPERFECT FORM = MULTIPLE INCOMPLETE OCCURENCE IN THE PAST

MASCULINE	"I"	(JA)	CZYTYWAŁEM	I USED TO READ
FEMININE	"I"	(JA)	CZYTYWAŁAM	
MASCULINE	"YOU"	(TY)	CZYTYWAŁES	YOU USED TO READ
FEMININE	"YOU"	(TY)	CZYTYWAŁAS	
		(ON)	CZYTYWAŁ	HE USED TO READ
		(ONA)	CZYTYWAŁA	SHE USED TO READ
		(ONO)	CZYTYWAŁO	IT USED TO READ
MASCULINE	"WE"	(MY)	CZYTYWALISMY	WE USED TO READ
FEMININE	"WE"	(MY)	CZYTYWAŁYSMY	
MASC.PLUR.	"YOU"	(WY)	CZYTYWALISCIE	YOU USED TO READ
FEM. PLUR.	"YOU"	(WY)	CZYTYWAŁYSCIE	
		(ONI)	CZYTYWALI	THEY USED TO READ
FEM.& NEUTER		(ONE)	CZYTYWAŁY	

EXAMPLES OF WORDS DERIVED FROM THE VERB "CZYTAC"= TO READ

DOCZYTAC, DOCZYTAC SIE, DOCZYTYWAC, DOCZYTYWAC SIE,
NACZYTAC SIE, NACZYTYWAC SIE, OCZYTAC SIE, ODCZYTAC,
ODCZYTYWAC, POCZYTAC, POCZYTAC SOBIE, POCZYTYWAC, POCZY-
TYWAC SOBIE, PRZECZYTAC, ROZCZYTAC SIE, ROZCZYTYWAC SIE,
WCZYTAC SIE, WCZYTYWAC SIE, WYCZYTAC, WYCZYTYWAC, ZACZY-
TYWAC, SIE, ZACZYTAC SIE describe all the possible ways
and conditions of reading with the exception of "rereading" which can not be translated into Polish in one word.
Besides the twenty three verbs are nouns: CZYTANKA, CZY-
TELNICTWO, CZYTELNIK, CZYTELNIA, CZYTELNOSC, ODCZYT, POCZY-
TALNOSC, NIEPOCZYTALNOSC, POCZYTNOSC, and adjectives as:
CZYTELNY, NIECZYTELNY, OCZYTANY, NIEOCZYTANY, POCZYTALNY,
NIEPOCZYTALNY, POCZYTNY etc.

Angielsko-polska część słownika zawiera około 15,000 haseł. Jak wiadomo pojęcia i myśli formuje się w poszczególnych językach w różny sposób. Nawet języki należące do tej samej grupy / jak np polski i angielski do grupy indoeuropejskiej/ nie są równoznaczne.

Bogactwo polskich form gramatycznych nie ma odpowiednika w angielskim. Odmiana rzeczowników i przymiotników przez siedem przypadków oraz czasowników przez wszystkie możliwe osoby z odpowiednimi zmianami końcówek, typowymi dla języka polskiego, nie istnieje w angielskim. Język angielski bogatszy jest w wyrażenia zwyczajowo-idiomatyczne; więcej też jest w nim przyimków i zaimków.

Język polski zawiera liczne formy gramatyczne poszczególnych słów i gdyby wprowadzić każdą z nich jako odrębne hasło słownika to takich haseł byłoby kilka milionów.

Polska forma zwrotna zawiera określenia pośrednie między formami czynną i bierną charakterystycznymi dla obu języków. Tej formy nie można dosłownie przetłumaczyć na angielski. Na przykład powiedzenie "wzruszyłem się" nie znaczy dokładnie "I am touched", co równa się polskiemu "jestem wzruszony". "I touched myself" natomiast wcale nie znaczy "wzruszyłem się".

Inną cecha charakterystyczną języka polskiego jest odróżnienie małej liczby mnogiej /2,3 i 4/ od dużej /5 i więcej/: tego rozróżnienia nie ma w języku angielskim.

Ogólnie biorąc język polski ma więcej form rzeczownikowych, przymiotnikowych oraz czasownikowych. W angielskim natomiast prawie każdy rzeczownik bez zmiany pisowni może być użyty jako czasownik a nieraz także jako przymiotnik. Polskie zasady gramatyczne można wyrazić słowami "zawsze z kilkoma wyjątkami", angieskie zasady gramatyczne i fonetyczne są bardziej płynne - mówi się w nich: "często", "czasem" i "nieraz". W angielskim przeważają wyrażenia i fonetyka zwyczajowe.

W części angielsko-polskiej słownika oznaczono formy gramatyczne poszczególnych haseł: rzeczowniki, przymiotniki, czasowniki, przysłówki, zaimki, przyimki i częste zwroty.

Angielskie czasowniki nieregularne podano w trzech podstawo-

wych formach /infinitive, past and past participle = bezokolicznik, czas przeszły i imiesłów czasu przeszłego/.

Hasła wybrano z uwzględnieniem słownictwa używanego obecnie
w Polsce i w Ameryce; są wśród nich ważniejsze wyrażenia poto-
czne.

Podano wymowę i akcent.

BIBLIOGRAPHICAL NOTE

The spelling used in this dictionary was checked against standard current dictionaries.

The semantic aspects of phrases was analysed in accordance with Korzybski's General Semantics. Alfred Korzybski, Polish philosopher, mathematician and engineer founded in 1938 the Institute of General Semantics in Lakeland, Connecticut. The works of Jens Otto Jespersen were used as references for linguistic comments.

POLISH-ENGLISH

a (a) (as "a" in car) conj. and; or; but; then: at that time

a to (a to) conj. and so

abażur (a-bá-zhoor) m. lamp shade; a device to screen light

abdykować (ab-di-kó-vaćh) v. abdicate, abdicate the throne

abecadło (a-be-tsá-dwo) n. A.B.C., alphabet

abonament (a-bo-ná-ment) m. subscription; season ticket

abonent (a-bó-nent) m. subscriber, holder of a season ticket

abonować (a-bo-nó-vaćh) v. subscribe to a periodical etc.

absencja (ab-sén-tsya) f. absence, non-attendance

abstrakcja (ab-strák-tsya) f. abstraction; abstract

absurd (áb-soord) m. absurdity

aby (á-bi) conj. to; in order to, in order that, only to

ach ! (akh) excl.: oh ! ah!

aczkolwiek (ach-kól-vyek) conj. though; although, albeit, tho

adapter (a-dáp-ter) m. record player, adapter; pick-up

administracja (ad-mee-ńees-tráts-ya) f. administration; (management) authorities

admirał (ad-mée-raw) m. admiral

adres (ád-res) m. address

adwokat (ad-vó-kat) m. lawyer

afera (a-fé-ra) f. swindle

aferzysta (a-fe-zhís-ta) m. swindler: confidence man

afisz (á-feesh) m. poster

afiszować (a-fee-shó-vaćh) v. advertise; flaunt: parade

agrafka (a-gráf-ka) f. safety pin; hist.: buckle; brooch

agrest (ág-rest) m. gooseberry

aha ! (akh-á!) excl.:oh yes...

a jakże ! (a-yák-zhe) excl. oh yes...! yes indeed!

akacja (a-káts-ya) f. acacia; locust tree: black locust

akcja (ák-tsya) f. action; share; plot; campain

akord (ák-ort) m. chord; piece work ; contract work

AK (a-ká) f. Polish Home Army (W.W.II) (Armia Krajowa)

akowiec (a-kóv-yets) m. soldier of the Polish Home Army (W.W.II)

aksamit (ak-sá-meet) m. velvet

akt (akt) m. deed; act; certificate; painting of a nude

akta (ák-ta) pl. documents; deeds; dossier; files; records

aktualny (ak-too-ál-ni) m. timely; current; up to date

akumulator (a-koo-moo-lá-tor)m. battery: storage battery

akuszerka (a-koo-shér-ka) f. midwife: accoucheuse

akwarela (ak-va-ré-la) f. water-color; painting in water color

albo (á-lbo) conj. or; else

albowiem (al-bó-vyem) conj. for; as; since;because; on account of

ale (á-le) conj. however; but; still; yet; not at all; n.defect

aleja (a-lé-ya) f. avenue: alley

ależ (á-lesh) conj. why (yes)

alfa (ál-fa) f. alpha

alfabet (al-fá-bet) m. alphabet

alfons (ál-fons) m. pimp; cadet

alimenty (a-lee-mén-ti) pl. alimony for separated wife

alkohol (al-kó-khol) m. alcohol

alpejski (al-peý-skee) adj. m. Alpine: of the Alps

aluzja (a-looz-ya) f. hint: allusion: insinuation: dig

ałun (á-woon) m. alum

amant (á-mant) m. lover: beau

ambasada (am-ba-sá-da) f. embassy; ambassador and his staff

ambicja (am-beéts-ya) f. ambition: aspiration: self esteem

ambona (am-bó-na) f. pulpit

Amerykanin (A-me-ri-ká-ńeen) m. American: man native of America

Amerykanka (A-me-ri-kán-ka) f. American: American women

amerykański (a-me-ri-kań-skee) adj. m. American; of America

amnestia (am-nést-ya) f.amnesty

amory (a-mó-ri) pl. flirtation; courting; love affairs

amortyzacja (a-mor-ti-záts-ya) f. depreciation; amortization

amperomierz (am-pe-ró-myesh) m. ammeter: meter of amperes

amputować (am-poo-tó-vach) v.
amputate; to cut off

amunicja (a-moo-ńeets-ya) f.
ammunition: munitions

analfabeta (a-nal-fa-bé-ta) m.
illiterate: an ignorant

analiza (a-na-lee-za) f. analysis ; parsing

analogia (a-na-lóg-ya) f. analogy; parallelism; parity

ananas (a-na-nas) m. pineapple;
rascal ; rogue; blighter

andrus (an-droos) m. rough kid

andrut (ánd-root) m. wafer

anegdota (a-neg-dó-ta) f.
anecdote; story; theme

aneksja (a-neks-ya) f. annexation; rape of a country

anemia (a-ném-ya) f. anemia

angażować (an-ga-zhó-vach) v.
engage; undertake; hire;bind

angielski (an-ǵél-skee) adj.
m. English; English language

ani (á-ńee) conj. neither; nor;
no; not; or; not even

anielski (a-ńél-skee) adj. m.
angelic: cherubic; angelical

animusz (a-ńee-moosh) m.
courage; verve; vigor; zest

anioł (a-ńow) m. angel

aniżeli (a-ńee-zhé-lee) part.
rather; than; rather than

ankieta (an-ḱé-ta) f. poll;
inquiry; questionnaire

anons (a-nons) m. advertisement in a newspaper; ad

antybiotyki (an-ti-bee-yó-ti-
kee) pl. antibiotics

antyk (án-tik) antique

antypatyczny (an-ti-pa-tich-
ni) adj. m. repugnant

apartament (a-par-tá-ment) m.
residence: suite of rooms

aparat (a-pá-rat) m. apparatus;
appliance; camera; gadget;gear

apel (áp-el) m. appeal; roll-
call; appeal; muster; parade

apetyt (a-pé-tit) m. appetite

apostolski (a-pos-tól-skee)
adj. m. apostolic; missionary

aprobować (a-pro-bó-vach) v.
approve; endorse; sanction

aprowizacja (a-pro-vee-záts-ya)
f. food supply; provisions

apteczka (ap-téch-ka) f. first
aid kit; medicine chest

apteka (ap-té-ka) f. pharmacy

arbiter (ar-bée-ter) m. umpire;
arbitrator; moderator; mediator

arbuz (ár-boos) m. watermelon

architekt (ar-khee-tekt) m.
architect

arcydzieło (ar-tsi-dźhé-wo) n.
masterpiece

arena (a-ré-na) f. arena; stage

areszt (á-resht) m. arrest; jail

argument (ar-góo-ment) m.
argument; reason; contention

arkusz (ár-koosh) m. sheet

armata (ar-má-ta) f. cannon

armator (ar-má-tor) m. shipowner; skipper; charterer

armia (árm-ya) f. army; array

arogancja (a-ro-gán-tsya) f.
arrogance; insolence; conceit

arteria(ar-tér-ya) f. artery

artykuł (ar-tí-koow) m. article

artretyzm (ar-tré-tizm) m.
arthritis; gout

artyleria (ar-ti-lér-ya) f.
artillery; gunnery; ordnance

artysta (ar-ti-sta) m. artist

arytmetyka (a-rit-mé-ti-ka) f.
arithmetic

as (as) m. ace ; A flat

asceta (as-tsé-ta) m. ascetic

asekuracja (a-se-koo-ráts-ya)
f. insurance; assurance

aspiryna (as-pee-ri-na) f.
aspirin

astma (ást-ma) f. asthma

asygnata (a-sig-ná-ta) f.
order (of payment)

asymilować (a-si-mee-ló-vach)
v. assimilate; absorb; liken

asystować (a-sis-tó-vach) v.
accompany; attend; court; assist

atak (á-tak) m. attack; charge
(fit); spasm; offensive

atlas (at-las) m. atlas

atleta (at-lé-ta) m. athlete

atłas (át-was) m. satin

atmosfera (at-mos-fé-ra) f.
atmosphere: air; climate; tone

atom (á-tom) m. atom
atol (á-tol) m. atoll
atomowy (a-to-mó-vi) adj. m. atomic
atrakcja (a-trák-tsya) f. attraction; high light
atrament (a-trá-ment) m. ink
atut (á-toot) m. trump
audycja (aw-díts-ya) f. broadcast; program; pop
aukcja (áwk-tsya) f. auction
autentyczny (aw-ten-tích-ni) adj. m. authentic; genuine
auto (áw-to) n. motor car
autor (áw-tor) m. author
autostrada (aw-to-strá-da) f. superhighway; freeway
awans (á-vans) m. promotion; advancement; preferment
awantura (a-van-tóo-ra) f. brawl; fuss; row: scandal
azot (á-zot) m, nitrogen
aż (ásh) part. as much; up to; til ; until; as far as
ażeby (a-zhé-bi) conj. that; in order that; so that
ażurowy (a-zhoo-ró-vi) adj. m. lace-like; transparent
ba (bá) excl. hey ?; nay; indeed..; and even; what more
baba (bá-ba) f. woman (old, simple; grandmother; rammer
babiarz (báb-yash) m. lady chaser: ladies' man
babie lato (bá-bye lá-to) n. Indian Summer ; lass; chick; cake
babka (báb-ka) f. grandmother
babrać (báb-rach) v. smear; stain; dabble; soil: fumble
bachor (bá-khor) m. kid; brat
baczność (bách-noshch) f. attention; care
bać się (bach shäh) v. fear
badacz (bá-dach) m. researcher
badać (bá-dach) v. investigate; examine; research ; explore
badyl (bá-dil) m. stem: weed
badylarz (ba-dí-lash) m. marketing gardener (slang)
bagatela (ba-ga-té-la) f. trifle ; easy matter
bagaż (bá-gash) m. luggage

bagażowy (ba-ga-zhó-vi) m. porter; adj. m. baggage-; luggage-
bagnet (bág-net) m. bayonet
bagno (bág-no) m. swamp; morass
bajka (báy-ka) f. fairy-tale; gossip; scandal; story; fable
bajoro (ba-yó-ro) n. muddy pool
bak (bak) m. gasoline tank; side whisker ; bacteria;
bakterie (bak-tér-ye) pl.germs
bal (bal) m. ball; bale; log
balet (bá-let) m. ballet
balia (bál-ya) f. wash tub
balkon (bál-kon) m. balcony
balustrada (ba-loos-trá-da) f. railing; hand rail: guard rail
bałagan (ba-wá-gan) m. mess; disorder; disarray; confusion
bałamucić (ba-wa-moo-tseech) v. lead astray; loiter; flirt; coax
bałwan (báw-van) m. snowman; ass; breaking wave crest; blockhead; fool; nitwit; fetish; idol; lump
banał (bá-naw) m. stock phrase; tag; banality; truism; triviality
banan (bá-nan) m. banana
banda (bán-da) f. band; gang
bandaż (bán-dash) m. bandage
bandera (ban-dé-ra) f. flag
bandyta (ban-dí-ta) m. bandit
bank (bank) m. bank; pool
bankiet (bán-ket) m. banquet
banknot (bánk-not) m. banknote
bankrut (bánk-root) m. bankrupt
babtysta (bap-tís-ta) m. baptist
bar (bar) m. bar; barium
barman (bár-man) m. barman
barak (bá-rak) m. barrack
baran (bá-ran) m. ram;tup; idiot
baraszkować (ba-rash-kó-vach) v. frolic: gambol; romp; caper
barbarzyńca (bar-ba-zhiń-tsa) m. barbarian: savage; vandal
barczysty (bar-chís-ti) m. broad-shouldered; square built
bardziej (bar-dźhey)adv.more; (emphatic "bardzo"); worse
bardzo (bár-dzo) adv. very
bariera (bar-yé-ra) f. rail; barrier; obstacle
barki (bár-kee) pl. shoulders
barłóg (bár-woog) m. litter bed

barszcz (barshch) m. beet soup
barwa (bár-va) f. color; hue
bary (bá-ri) pl. large
 shoulders: parallel bars
barykada (ba-ri-ká-da) f.
 barricade; barrier
baryłka (ba-riw-ka) f. barrel
basen (bá-sen) m. pool; tank
bastard (bás-tard) m. bastard
baśń (baśñ) f. fable; myth
bat (bat) m. whip; lash
bateria (ba-tér-ya) f. battery
bawełna (ba-véw-na) f. cotton
bawialnia (ba-vyál-ña) f.
 sitting room; parlor
bawić (bá-veech) v. amuse;
 entertain; recreate; stay
bawidamek (ba-vee-dá-mek) m.
 ladies man; gallant
bawoł (bá-voow) m. buffalo
baza (bá-za) f. base; basis
bazgrać (báz-grach) v. scribble;
 scrawl; scratch; daub; splotch
bażant (ba-zhant) m. pheasant
bąbel (bówn-bel) m. blister
bądą (bównch) v. be this
bądź (bównch) conj. either-or
bąk (bównk) m. horse fly;
 blunder; vulg. ; fart
bąkać(bówn-kach) v. mumble;
 hint; mutter; hum
bebechy (be-bé-khi) pl. guts
beczka (béch-ka) f. barrel
bednarz (béd-nash) m. cooper
befsztyk (bef-shtik) m. beefsteak
beksa (bék-sa) f. cry baby
beletrystyka (be-le-tris-ti-
 ka) f. fiction; letters
belka (bél-ka) f. beam; bar
bełkot (béw-kot) m. mumbling
benzyna (ben-zína) f. gasoline
berbeć (bér-bech) m. small kid;
 toddler ; brat; dot
berek (be-rek) m. tag play
beret (bé-ret) m. beret ; cap
besztać (bésh-tach) v. scold;
 rebuke ; chide; rebuke:trounce
bestia (bés-tya) f. beast
beton (bé-ton) m. concrete
bety (bé-ti) pl. bedding
bez (bes) prep. without

bez (beṣ) m. lilac;prep.without
bez-(beṣ) prefix = suffix less
beza (be-za) f. meringue
bezbarwny (bez-bárw-ni) adj.
 m. colorless: plain; drab; dull
bezbłędny (bez-bwánd-ni) adj.
 m. faultless; correct; perfect
bezbolesny (bez-bo-lés-ni) adj.
 m. painless
bezbronny (bez-brón-ni) adj.
 m. defenseless: helpless;unarmed
bezcelowy (bez-tse-ló-vi) adj.
 m. aimless; pointless; useless
bezcenny (bez-tsén-ni) adj.m.
 priceless; invluable; inestimable
bezchmurny (bez-khmoo-rni)
 adj. m. cloudless; serene; clear
bezdomny (bez-dóm-ni) adj. m.
 homeless; houseless; shelterless
bezdzietny (bez-dzhét-ni) adj
 m. childless; without offspring
bezdźwięczny (bez-dzhvánch-ni)
 adj. m. soundless; voiceless
bezecny (be-zéts-ni) adj. m.
 wicked; infamous; ignominious
bezgotówkowy (bez-go-toov-kó-
 vi) adj. m. without cash
bezgrzeszny (bez-gzhésh-ni)
 adj. m. sinless;inocent; chaste
bezkonkurencyjny (bez-kon-koo-
 ren-tsíy-ni) adj. m. unrivaled
bezkrwawy (bez-krvá-vi) adj.
 m. bloodless; free of bloodshed
bezkształtny (bez-kshtáwt-ni)
 adj. m. shapeless; formless
bezład (béz-wat) m. disorder
bezmiar (béz-myar) m. immen-
 sity; boundlessnesŝ; vastness
bezmyślność (bez-míshl-nośhch)
 f. thoughtlessness; wantonness
beznadziejny (bez-na-dzhéy-ni)
 adj. m. hopeless; desperate
bez ogródek (bez o-gróo-dek)
 adv. bluntly; unequivocally
bezokolicznik (bez-o-ko-leech-
 ñeek) m. infinitive (mood)
bezowocny (bez-o-vóts-ni) m.
 fruitless; vain; unsuccessful
bezpieczeństwo (bez-pye-cheń-
 stvo) m. security; safety
bezpłatnie (bez-pwát-ñe) adv.
 free of charge; gratuitously

bezpłciowy (bez-pwchó-vi) adj.
m. sexless; neutral; insipid
bezpodstawny (bez-pod-stáv-ny)
adj. m. groundless; baseless
bezposrednio (bez-po-shred-ńo)
adv. directly; directly
bezprawny (bez-práv-ni) adj.
m. lawless; illegal; illicit
bezprzedmiotowy (bez-przed-myo-
tó-vi) adj. m.   aimless
bezprzykładny (bez-pzhi-kwád-
ni) adj. m. unprecedented
bezradny (bez-rád-ni) adj. m.
helpless; baffled; at a loss
bezręki (bez-ráń-kee) adj.m.
armless; handless (cripple)
bezrobotny (bez-ro-bó-tni)
adj. m. unemployed
bezrolny (bez-ról-ni) adj.m.
landless; with no land
bezsenny (bez-sén-ni) adj. m.
sleepless; restless; wakeful
bezsens (béz-sens) m. nonsense
bezsilny (bez-sheel-ni) adj.
m. powerless; weak; helpless
bezskuteczny (bez-skoo-téch-
ni) adj. m. to no avail;
futile; ineffective; nugatory
bezsporny (bez-spór-ni) adj.
m. incontestable; undebatable
bezsprzeczny (bez-spzhech-ni)
adj. m. indisputable; evident
bezstronność (bez-stron-nośhćh)
f. impartiality; fairness
beztroski (bez-trós-kee) adj.
m. carefree; careless;jaunty
bezustanny (bez-oos-tán-ni)
adj. m. ceaseless; endless
bezużyteczny (bez-oo-zhi-téch-
ni) adj. m. useless; idle
bezwartościowy (bez-var-tośh-
ćhó-vi) adj. m. worthless
bezwarunkowy (bez-va-roon-kó-vi)
adj. m. unconditional; utter
bezwładność (bez-vwád-nośhćh)
f. inertia; torpor; decline
bezwstydny (bez-vstid-ni) adj.
m. shameless; lewd; flagrant
bezwyznaniowy (bez-viz-na-ńo-
vi) adj. m. nonsectarian
bezwzględny (bez-vzgláńd-ni)
adj. m. ruthless; despotic
bezzębny (bez-záńb-ni) adj. m.
toothless; edentate

bezzwłoczny (bez-zvwóch-ni)
adj. m. immediate; prompt
bezzwrotny (bez-zvrót-ni) adj.
m. not to be refunded
beż (besh) m. beige
bęben (báń-ben) m. drum; kid;
brat; barrel; cylinder;tumbler
bęcwał (báńts-vaw) m. nincompoop; dullard; chickle head
bękart (báń-kart) m. bastard
biadać (bya-dáćh) v. moan
białaczka (bya-wách-ka) f.
leukemia
białko (bya-wko) n. egg white;
protein; white of the eve
biały (bya-wi) adj. m. white
biba (bee-ba) f. drinking spree
biblia (béeb-lya) f. Bible
biblioteka (beeb-lyo-té-ka) f.
library; bookcase; book series
bibuła (bee-boo-wa) f. blotting
paper; illegal political
publication; literary trash
bicz (beech) m. whip; whiplash
bić (beéch) v. beat; defeat(etc)
biec (byets) v. run; trot; flow
bieda (bye-da) f. poverty; want;
trouble; distress; evil days
biedny (byed-ni) adj. m. poor
bieg (byeg) m. run; race; course
biegle (bye-gle) adv. fluently
biegun (bye-goon) m. pole;
rocker; spindle; trunnion
biegunka (bye-goon-ka) f.
diarrhea; dysentery
biel (byel) f.whiteness; white
bielizna (bye-leéz-na) f. linen
bielmo (byel-mo) n. cataract
bierny (byer-ni) adj. m. passive
bieżący (bye-zhówń-tsi) adj. m.
current; flowing; running
bieżnia (byezh-ña) f. runway;
track; racecourse; tyre tread
bigos (bee-gos) m. hashed meat
and cabbage (Polish style)
bijatyka (bee-ya-tí-ka) f.
fight; brawl; tussle; scrimmage
bila (bee-la) f. billiard ball
bilans (bee-lans) m. balance
sheet; balance; rest; outcome
bilet (bee-let) m. note; ticket
biodro (byód-ro) n. hip; huckle
biszkopt (beesh-kopt) m.
biscuit; sponge cake; cracer

bitny (beet-ni) adj. m. valiant
bitwa (beet-va) f. battle;fight
biuro (byóo-ro) n. office
biust (byoost) m. bust; breast
biustonosz (byoos-tó-nosh) m.
  brassiere; bra; bust bodice
biżuteria (bee-zhoo-tér-ya) f.
  jewelry; jewels
blacha (blá-kha) f. sheet
  metal; cook top; tinware
blady (blá-di) adj. m. pale
blaga (blá-ga) f. lie; bluff
blankiet (blán-ket) m. blank
  form; printed form: blank
blask (blask) m. flush; luster
bliski (blees-kee) adj. m.
  near; imminent; near by;close
blizna (bleez-na) f. scar
bliźni (bleézh-ñee)m. fellow
man; twin; identical; neighbor
blokować (blo-kó-vach) v.block;
  blockade; obstruct; stall
blondynka (blon-dín-ka) f.
  blonde (girl); fair haired girl
bluzka (blooz-ka) f. blouse
bluźnić (bloozh-ñeech) v. curse;
  blaspheme; talk nonsense
błahość (bwá-khoshch) f. trifle
błagać (bwá-gach) v. beseech
błazen (bwa-zen) m. clown;
  buffoon ⌠mistake; lapse
błąd (bwownt) m. error; slip-up;
błąkać się (bwówn-kach śhań)v.
  wander; stray; roam; rove
błękit (bwan-keet) m. blue;
  azure; blue pigment; sky
błocić (bwo-cheech) v. get
  muddy; soil with mud; spatter
błogi (bwo-gee) adj. m.bliss-
  ful; delightful; sweet
błogosławić (bwo-go-swa-veech)
  v. bless; praise; exalt; thank
błona (bwona) f. membrane; coat;
  film; tunic; velum; web
błonie (bwo-ñe) n. meadow;
  plain; public grassy land
błotnik (bwót-ñeek) m.(car)
  fender; mudguard; splash board
błoto (bwo-to) n. mud; muck
błysk (bwisk) m. flash; flare
bo (bo) conj. because; for; or;
  as; since; or else; but then

bochenek (bo-khé-nek) m. loaf
bocian (bó-chan) m. stork
boczny (bóch-ny) adj. m. lateral; side; collateral (line)
boczyć się (bó-chych śhań) v.
  sulk; be angry; look askance
bodaj (bó-day) part. may be;
  should be...; would be...;
bodziec (bó-dżhets) m. stimulus
bogactwo (bo-gáts-tvo) n.riches;
  wealth; means; fortune; plenty
bogaty (bo-gá-ti) adj. m. rich
bogobojny (bo-go-bóy-ni) adj.
  m. pious; devout; church going
bohater (bo-kha-ter) m. hero
boisko (bo-ees-ko) n. stadium;
  field; threshing floor;gridiron
bojaźń (bó-yaźhñ) f. fear; fright
boja (bó-ya) f. buoy ; beacon
bojkot (bóy-kot) m. boycott
bojownik (bo-yóv-ñeek) m.
  fighter; militant; champion
bok (bok) m. side; flank
boks (boks) m. boxing; stall
boleć (bo-lech) v. pain; ache
bolesny (bo-lés-ni) adj. m. sore;
  painful; sad; woeful; dismal
bomba (bóm-ba) f. bomb; sphere
bombowiec (bom-bó-vyets) m.
  bomber ; bombing plane
borykać się (bo-rí-kach śhań)
  v. cope; struggle; wrestle
bosak (bó-sak) m. boat hook
boso (bó-so) adv. barefoot
bosy (bó-si) adj. m. barefoot
bowiem (bó-vyem) conj. for;
  because; since; as; hence
boży (bo-zhi) adj. m. God's
Bóg (book)m. God
bój (booy) m. fight; battle
ból (bool) m. pain; ache; sore
bór (boor) m. forest; wood
bóść (booshch) v. gore; sting
bóżnica (boozh-ñee-tsa) f.
  synagogue; house of prayer
bractwo (bráts-tvo) n. fraternity; brotherhood; guild
brać (brach) v. take; hold etc.
brak (brak) m. lack; need;want;
  scarcity; shortage;absence;fault
brama (brá-ma) f. gate; gateway;
  front door; wicket

bransoletka (bran-so-lét-ka) f.
  bracelet; wristlet; bangle
brat (brat) m. brother; mate
bratać (bra-tać) v. unite;
  fraternize; chum up
bratanek (bra-tá-nek) m. nephew
bratanica (bra-ta-ńee-tsa) f.
  niece
brednie (bréd-ńe) n. nonsense
brew (brev) f. eyebrow
brewerie (bre-vér-ye) n. brawl
brezent (bré-zent) m. tarpau-
  lin; canvas
brnąć (brnówńch) v. wade
broczyc (bró-chich) v. bleed
broda (broda) f. beard; chin
brodzić (bró-dźheech)v. wade
broić (bró-eech) v. make
  mischief; frolic; romp;gambol
brom (brom) m. bromine
brona (bró-na) f. harrow
bronić (bró-ńeech) v. defend
bronz (brons) m. bronze
broń (broń) f. weapon; arms
broszka (brósh-ka) f. brooch
broszura (bro-shóo-ra) f.
  pamphlet; folder; booklet
browar (bró-var) m. brewery
bród (broot) m. ford
brud (broot) m. dirt; filth
bruk (brook) m. pavement
brukiew (bróo-kyev) f. turnip
brulion (bróol-yon) m. rough
  draft; notebook; exercise book
brunatny (broo-ná-tni) adj. m.
  brown; tawny; tan colored
brunetka (broo-nét-ka) f.
  brunette
brutal (bróo-tal) m. brute
bruzda (bróoz-da) f. furrow;
  groove; deep wrinkle; streak
brwi (brvee) pl. eye brows
brykać (brí-kach) v. prance
bryła (brí-wa) f. lump; mass
bryzg (brizk) m. splash
bryzgać (bríz-gach) v. splash
brzeg (bzhek) m. shore; margin
brzemię (bzhe-myáń) n. burden
brzęk (bzháńk) m. clink; chink;
  rattle; ping; buzz; hum:drone
brzuch (bzhookh) m. belly; abdomen; stomach; tummy; guts

brzydki (bzhid-kee) adj. m.
  ugly; unsightly; hideous; foul
brzydzić się (bzhi-dźheech śháń)
  v. feel disgust; loathe; abhor
brzytwą (bzhít-va) f. razor
buchać (boo-khach) v. squirt;
  spout;burst forth; flare; blaze
bucik (boo-cheek) m. shoe; boot
buda (boo-da) f. shed (stall)
budowa (boo-dó-va) f. construction: erection; framework
budowla (boo-dov-la) f. building (large); edifice;structure
budynek (boo-dí-nek) m. building; edifice; house
budzić (boo-dźheech)v. wake up
budzik (boo-dźheek)m. alarm
  clock; alarum clock
budżet (boo-jet) m. budget
bujać (boo-yach) v. rock; lie
bufor (boo-for) m. buffer
bułka (boow-ka) f. roll (breakfast); bread roll; loaf
bunt (boont) m. mutiny
bura (boo-ra) f. reprimand
burak (boo-rak) m. beet
burda (boo-r-da) f. scuffle;row;
  brawl; disturbance; rough neck
burmistrz (boor-meestsh) m.
  mayor
bursztyn (boor-shtin) m. amber
burta (boor-ta) f. ship's side
bury (boo-ri)adj. m. dark gray
burza (boo-zha) f. tempest;
  storm; wind storm; rain storm
burżuazja (boor-zhoo-áz-ya) f.
  bourgeoisie; middle class
busola (boo-só-la) f. compass
but (boot) m. boot; shoe; sabot
buta (boo-ta) f. arrogance
butelka (boo-tél-ka) f. bottle
butny (boot-ni) adj. m. arrogant; insolent; overbearing
buzia (boo-zha) f. face; mouth
by (bi) conj. in order that;
  (conditional)as if; at least
byczy (bí-chi) adj. m. 1. bull's
  2. very good; glorious
być (bich) v. be; exist; live
bydlę (bíd-laň) n. beast; brute
byle (bí-le) conj. in order to;
  so as to; pron. any; slap-dash

były (bí-wi) adj. m. former

bynajmniej (bi-náy-mney) adv. by no means,; not at all

bystrość (bíst-roshch) f. swiftness; shrewdness

byt (bit) m. existence

bytność (bit-nośhch) f. stay

bywać (bí-vach) v. frequent

bywalec (bi-vá-lets) m.patron frequenter; man of the world

bzdura (bzdoó-ra) f. nonsense

bzik (bźheek)adj. m. crank; loony; crazy; m. fad; craze

bzykać (bzí-kach) v. buzz

cackać się (tsáts-kach shañ)v. fondle; pamper; humor;coddle

cacko (tsáts-ko) n. jewel; trinket; plaything;toy;beauty

cal (tsal) m. inch

całka (tsáw-ka) f. integral

całkiem (tsáw-kem) adv.quite; entirely; completely; totally

całkowity (tsaw-ko-veé-ti) adj. m. total; complete

cało (tsá-wo) adv. (in one piece) safely; safe and sound

całować (tsa-wó-vach) v. kiss; embrace; give a kiss

całus (tsa-woos) m. kiss

cap (tsap) m. billy goat

caber (tsówn-ber) m. rump; fillet

cążki (tsównzh-kee) pl. small tongs; pliers; pincers

ceber (tse-ber) m. bucket

cebula (tse-boó-la) f. onion

cech (tsekh) m. trade; guild

cecha (tsé-kha) f. feature; mark; trait; stamp; character

cechować (tse-khó-vach) v. mark; characterize; calibrate

cedr (tsedr) m. cedar

cedzić (tse-dźheećh)v. strain; filter; percolate;sip;trickle

cegielnia (tse-gél-ña) f. brickyard; brick factory

cegła (tség-wa) f. brick

cel (tsel) m. purpose; aim

cela (tsé-la) f. cell

celnik (tsél-ñeek) m. customs inspector: customs officer

celować (tse-ló-vach) v. aim; excel; exceed

celuloza (tse-loo-ló-za) f. cellulose

cembrować (tsem-bró-vach) v. case(well); timber (a shaft)

cement (tsé-ment) m. cement

cena (tsé-na) f. price; value

cenić (tsé-ñeech) v. value;rate; esteem; prize; evaluate

cennik (tsén-ñeek) m. price list; price catalogue

centnar (tsént-nar) m. hundred-weight

centrala (tsen-trá-la) f. head office ; main office; exchange

centrum (tsént-room) n. center

centryfuga (tsen-tri-foó-ga) f. centrifuge; separator

centymetr (tsen-ti-metr) m. centimeter ___blockhead

cep (tsep) m. flail; darn; mend

cera (tsé-ra) f. complexion

ceramiczny (tse-ra-meéch-ni) adj. m. ceramic; earthenware

cerata (tse-rá-ta) f. oilcloth

ceregiele (tse-re-ge-le) n. fuss; petty formalities

certować sie(tser-to-vach shan)v. pretend;stand on ceremony;fuss

cewka (tsév-ka) f. spool

cęgi (tsáñ-gee) pl. tongs

cętka (tsáñt-ka) f. dot

chałat (khá-wat) m. lab.coat

chałastra (kha-wás-tra) f. mob

chałupa (kha-woó-pa) f. hut

cham (kham) m. roughneck; boor

charakter (kha-rák-ter) m. disposition; character

charczeć (khár-chech) v. wheeze; snort; be hoarse

chata (khá-ta) f. hut; cabin

chcieć (khćheech) v. want

chciwiec (khćhee-vyets) m. greedy man; grasping man

chełpic się (khew-peech shañ) v. boast; brag; bluster:vaunt

chemia (khém-ya) f. chemistry

chemiczny (khe-meéch-ni) adj.m. chemical

cherlak (khér-lak) m. weakling

chęć (khañch) f. wish; desire

chędogi (kháñ-do-gi) adj. m. neat; clean; tidy; orderly

chichot (khee-khot) m. giggle;
laughter ; chuckle; titter

chimera (khee-me-ra) f. whim

chinina (khee-ñee-na) f. quinine

chiński (kheeñ-skee) adj.m.
Chinese

chirurg (khee-roorg) m. surgeon ; sawbones (slang)

chlapać (khla-pach) v. splash

chleb (khleb) m. bread

chlew (khlev) m. pigsty;pigpen

chlor (khlor) m. chlorine

chluba (khloo-ba) f.glory,pride

chlubić się (khloo-beech shañ)
v. boast; flatter oneself

chlusnąć (khloos-nownch) v.
splash; fling; spout; spurt

chłeptać (khwep-tach) v. lap up

chłodzić (khwo-dźheech)v. cool

chłonąć (khwo-nownch) v. absorb;
devour: drink in; inhale

chłop (khwop) m. peasant; man

chłosta (khwos-ta) f. lashing

chłód (khwoot) m. cold; freshness; coolness; iciness;shiver

chłystek (khwis-tek) m. squirt

chmara (khma-ra) f. swarm

chmiel (khmyel) m. hop; hops

chmura (khmoo-ra) f. cloud

chociaż (kho-chash) conj.albeit;
even if; though, tho'; while

chociaż = chocby = chociażby

choć (khoch) conj. at least

chodnik (khod-ñeek) m. sidewalk; pathway; stair carpet

chodzić (kho-dźheech) v. go;
walk; move; creep; pace;attend

choina (kho-ee-na) f. fir

cholera (kho-le-ra) f. cholera
excl.:damn ! hell! the devil!

cholewa (kho-le-va) f. boot

chorągiew (kho-rown-gev) f.
flag; standard; ensign

choroba (kho-ro-ba) f. sickness

chory (kho-ri) adj. m. sick;
ill; ailing; infirm; unwell

chować (kho-vach) v. hide

chód (khoot) m. gait; walk

chór (khoor) m. choir

chów (khoof) m. breeding

chrabąszcz (khra-bownshch) m.
beetle;May —bug

chrapać (khra-pach) v. snore

chroniczny (khro-ñeech-ni) adj.
m. chronic

chronić (khro-ñeech) v. shelter;
protect; quard; shield; fence

chrust (khroost) m. kindling

chrupać (khroo-pach) v. crunch

chrypka (khrip-ka) f. hoarse-
ness; sore throat

Chrystus (khris-toos) m. Christ

chrzan (khzhan) m. horseradish

chrząstka (khzhownst-ka) f.
cartilage; gristle; copula

chrząszcz (khshownshch) m.
May bug; beetle; cockchafer

chrzcić (khzhchcheech) v. baptize

chrzest (khzhest) m. baptism

chrześcijanin (khzhe-shchee-
ya-ñeen) m. Christian

chrzęst (khzhañst) m. clatter

chrzęścić (khzhañ-shcheech) v.
clank; jangle; grate; crunch

chuchać (khoo-khach) v. puff

chuchro (khookh-ro) m. weakling

chuć (khooch) f. lust

chudnąć (khood-nownch) v.lose
weight; grow thin; lose flesh

chuligan (khoo-lee-gan) m.
hoodlum; ruffian; roughneck

chustka (khoost-ka) f. handkerchief; kerchief; scarf

chwacki (khvats-kee) adj. m.
brave; plucky; gallant; rakish

chwalić (khva-leech) v. praise

chwała (khva-wa) f. praise;
glory; splendor; pride

chwast (khvast) m. weed

chwiać (khvyach) v. waver

chwila (khvee-la) f. moment

chwycić (khvi-cheech) v. grasp

chwyt (khvit) m. grasp; grip

chyba (khi-ba) part. maybe

chybotać (khi-bo-tach) v. rock

chybić (khi-beech) v. miss

chylić (khi-leech) v. bow

chyłkiem (khiw-kem) adj.
stealthily; on the sly

chytry (khit-ri) adj. m. sly

chyży (khi-zhi) adj. m. swift

ci (chee) pron. these; they;
part.: for you

ciało (cha-wo) n. body; substance; frame; anatomy;corpse
ciarki (char-kee) pl. shudder
ciasnota (chas-nó-ta) f.
tightness; narrow-mindedness
ciastko (chast-ko) n . cake;pie
ciasto (chás-to) n, dough
ciąć (chownch) v. cut; clip
ciągnac (chowng-nownch)v.pull
ciągnik (chowng-ñeek) m. tractor; agrimotor; crawler
ciąża (chown-zha) f. pregnancy
ciążenie (chown-zhe-ñe) v.
gravitation;tendency
cichaczem (chee-kha-chem) adv.
stealthily ; on the quiet
cichnąć (cheekh-nownch) v.
quiet down; subside; abate
cicho (chee-kho) adv. silently;
noiselessly ; softly;privately
cichy (chee-khi) adj. m. quiet;
still; low;gentle; calm; serene
ciec (chets) v. leak; flow
ciecz (chech) f. liquid
ciekaw (che-kav) adj. m. cute:
curious ;interesting;prying
cielak (che-lak) m. calf
cielesny (che-lés-ni) adj. m.
carnal; bodily; sexual
ciemię (che-myań) n. crown of
the head ; septum of the skull
ciemiężenie (che-myań-zhe-ñe)
n. oppression ; subjugation
ciemnia (chém-ña) f. dark room
ciemno (chém-no) adv. darkly
ciemny (chém-ni) adj. m. dark
cieniowac (che-ño- vach) v.
shade ; modulate; grade
cienisty (che-ñees-ti) adj.
m. shady ; shade giving
cienki (chen-kee) adj. m. thin
cień (cheń) m. shade ; shadow
cieplarnia (che-plár-ña) f.
greenhouse ; hothouse; stove
ciepło (che-pwo) adv. warm
cieplawy (che-pwa-vi) adj.
m. lukewarm ; tepid
ciepły (chep-wi) adj. m. warm
cierń (cherń) m. thorn; pricle
cierpiący (cher-pyówn-tsi)
adj. m. suffering ; ailing;ill
cierpieć (cher-pyech) v.suffer;
anguish; be troubled; endure

cierpki (cherp-kee) adj. m.
tart; acid;surly;acrid;sour
cierpliwość (cher-plee-vośhch)
f. patience; endurance
cierpliwy (cher-plee-vi) adj.
m. enduring; patient; forbearing
cierpnąć (cherp-nównch) v.
grow numb; creep; go to sleep
ciesielstwo (che-shel-stvo) n.
carpentry (in construction)
cieszyć (che-shich) v. cheer
cieśla (chesh-la) m. carpenter
(constr.) ;wood worker;shipwright
cietrzew (che-tzhev) m. black-
cock; black grouse; grey hen
cieśnina (chesh-ñee-na) f. strait
cięcie (chań-che) n. cut; gash
cięciwa (chań-chee-va) f. chord;
bow string; string; subtense
cięgi (chań-gee) pl. lashing
cięty (chań-ti) adj. m. sharp-
tongued; biting;dogged;incisive
ciężar (chań-zhar) m. weight;
burden; gravity; onus; duty;task
ciężec (chań-zhech) v. grow
heavy; become a burden;encumber
ciężki (chańzh-kee) adj. m.
heavy; weighty; bulky; oppressive
ciężko (chańzh-ko) adv. heavily
ciocia (cho-cha) f. auntie;aunt
cios (chos) m. blow; stroke;
hit; shok; ashlar; block; joint
cioteczny brat (cho-tech-ni
brat) m. cousin
ciotka (chót-ka) f. aunt
ciosac (cho-sach) v. hew; chop out
cis (chees) m. yew
cisawy (chees-ávi) adj. m.
chesnut (horse)
ciskac (chees-kach) v. fling;cast;
throw; hurl: sling; plunk;let fly
cisnąc (chees-nównch) v. press;
squeeze; bear; urge; pinch;crowd
cisza (chee-sha) f. calm; silence
ciśnienie (cheesh-ñé-ñe) n.
pressure ; blood pressure; thrust
ciuch (chookh) m. used clothing
ciułać (choo-wach) v. hoard
ciurkiem (choor-kem) adv. in
a trickle; with big drops
ciupa (choo-pa) f. jail; clink
ciupasem (choo-pá-sem) adv.
under convoy under armed convoy

ciżba (chéezh-ba) f. crowd

ckliwy (tsklee-vi) adj. m.
qualmy; sickly; faint;sloppy

clic (tsleech) v. collect
custom duty;lay a custom duty

cło (tswo) n. customs

cmentarz (tsmén-tash) m. cemetery; burial ground

cmokać (tsmo-kach) v. smack

cnota (tsnó-ta) f. virtue

co (tso) pron. part. what;which

codzień (tsó-dżheń)adv. daily

cofać się (tsó-fach shaň) v.
back up; remove; withdraw

cokolwiek (tso-kól-vyek) pron.
anything; whatever; somewhat

comber (tsom-ber) m. saddle
(of mutton);rump;loin; haunch

coraz (tso-raz) adv. ever

coś (tsosh) pron. something

córka (tsoor-ka) f. daughter

cóż (tsoosh) pron. what then

cuchnąć (tsóokh-nównch) v.
stink foul; smell foul

cucić (tsoo-cheech) v. revive

cud (tsoot) m. wonder; miracle

cudzołożyć (tsoo-dzo-wó-zhich)
v. commit adultery

cudzoziemiec (tsoo-dzo-zhé-
myets) m. alien; foreigner

cudzy (tsoo-dzi) adj. m.
someone else's; alien;foreign

cudzysłów (tsoo-dzi-swoof)m.
quotation marks

cukier (tsoo-ker) m. sugar

cuma (tsoo-ma) f. mooring

cwał (tsvaw) m. full gallop

cwaniak (tsva-ňak) m. city
slicker; sly dog;crafty guy

cwany (tsva-ni) adj. m. sly;
cunning; crafty; artful

cyc (tsits) m. nipple (vulg.)

cyfra (tsif-ra) f. number

cygan (tsi-gan) m. gipsy;
cheat; Gypsy;swindler; liar

cykl (tsikl) m. cycle

cylinder (tsi-leen-der) m.
cylinder; barrel; top hat

cyna (tsi-na) f. tin

cynamon (tsi-ná-mon)m.cinnamon

cynober (tsi-nó-ber) m.vermilion

cyngiel (tsin-gel) m. trigger

cynik (tsi-ňeek) m. cynic

cynk (tsink) m. zinc; tutenag

cypel (tsi-pel) m. cape; tip

cyprys (tsi-pris) m. cypress

cyrk (tsirk) m. circus

cyrkiel (tsir-kel) m. compass

cysterna (tsis-ter-na) f.
cistern; tank car; vat

cytadela (tsi-ta-de-la) f.
citadel; fortress

cytata (tsi-ta-ta) f. quotation

cytryna (tsi-tri-na) f. lemon

cywil (tsi-veel) m. civilian

cyzelować (tsi-ze-ló-vach) v.
engrave; carve; elaborate

czad (chat) m. carbon monoxide

czaić się (cha-eech shaň) v.
lie in wait; lurk; stalk;crouch

czajnik (cháy-ňeek) m. tea-pot

czajka (cháy-ka) f. gull

czako (cha-ko) f. shako

czapka (cháp-ka) f. cap; pileus

czapla (cháp-la) f. heron

czaprak (cháp-rak) m. horse
blanket; caparison: trappings

czar (char) m. spell; charm

czarno (chár-no) adv. blackly

czart (chart) m. devil; deuce

czas (chas) m. time; duration

czaszka (chásh-ka) f. skull

czaty (cha-ti) pl. watch;
lookout; wait; ambush

cząstka (chownst-ka) f. particle

czcić (chcheech) v. adore;
worship; idolize; venerate

czcigodny (chchee-god-ni) adj.
m. honorable; revered; venerable

czcionka (chchyon-ka) f. type;
character; letter in print

czczo (chcho) adv. empty (stomach); emptily; vainly; idly

czego (che-go) conj. why? what?

czek (chek) m. check (in banking)

czekać (che-kach) v. wait;
expect; waste time; be in store

czekanie (che-ka-ňe) n. wait

czekan (che-kan) f. pickhammer

czekolada (che-ko-la-da) f.
chocolate; slab of chocolate

czeladnik (che-lad-ňeek) m.
apprentice; journeyman

czelność (chél-noshch) f. impudence ; effrontery; nerve
czeluść (che-looshch) f. abyss;
gulf; precipice; depths to what?
czemu (ché-moo) part. why?what
czepek (ché-pek) m. bonnet;
hood ; night cap; caul;calyptra
czepiać się (chep-yach sháń)
v. cling; hang on; peck at
czereda (che-ré-da) f. gang;
throng ; crowd; swarm; pack
czerep (ché-rep) m. shell;
skull; fragment; splinter;shard
czereśnia (che-résh-ńa) f.
cherry,; cherry tree; gean
czernić (chér-ńeech) v, black-
en ; black; paint black
czerń (cherń) f. black color
czerpać (chér-pach) v. scoop;
draw; ladle; derive (benefit)
czerstwy (chérs-tvi) adj. m.
stale; robust(man); firm
czerw (cherv) m. worm; grub
czerwienić sie (cher-vyé-
ńeech sháń) v. blush (redden)
czerwony (cher-vó-ni) adj. m.
red; scrlet; crimson; ruddy
czesać (ché-sach) v. comb ;brush
czeski (chés-kee) adj. m. Czech
czesne (chés-ne) n. tuition
cześć (cheshch) f. honor; cult;
respect ; adoration;good name
często (cháns-to) adv. often
częstokroć (chán-sto-kroch)
adv. often ; repeatedly
częstość (cháns-toshch) f.
frequency ; recurrence
częstotliwość (chan-sto-tlee-
woshch) f. frequency;recurrence
częstować (chán-stó-vach) v.
treat to something ; regale
częsty (cháns-ty) adj. m.
frequent ; repeated often
częsciowy (chán-shchó-vi) adj.
m. partial ; fragmentary
część (cháńshch) f. part:share
czkawka (chkáv-ka) f. hiccups
człon (chwon) m. element; segment ; link ; member; clause
członek (chwo-nek) m. limb;
member; man's sex organ
człowiek (chwo-vyek) m. man;
individual; chap; somebody

czmychnąć (chmikh-nównch) v.
bolt; steal out; whisk away
czochrać (chókh-rach) v. tousle; ripple; hackle ;scratch
czołg (chowg) m. tank (military) ; reptile
czołgać (chow-gach) v. crawl
czoło (chó-wo) n. forehead
czop (chop) m. peg, plug; pin
czosnek (chós-nek) m. garlic
czterdzieści (chter-dżhésh-
chee) num. forty
czternaście (chter-násh-che)
num. fourteen
czteropiętrowy (chte-ro-pyań-
tró-vi) adj. m. four stories
high : four storeyed
cztery (chté-ri) num. four
czub (choop) m. tuft; crest
czucie (choo-che) n. feeling;
smelling ; sense perception
czuć (chooch) v. feel; smell
czujka (chooy-ka) f. sentry
czułość (choo-woshch) f.
tenderness ; affection; caress
czuły (choo-wi) adj. m. tender;
affectionate; sensitive;keen
czupurny (choo-poor-ni) adj. m.
pugnacious; boastful;defiant
czuwać (choo-vach) v. watch;
nurse ; look-out ; stay up;tend
czwartek (chvar-tek) m. Thursday
czwarty (chvár-ti) num. fourth
czworobok (chvo-ro-bok) m.
quadrilateral; square;tetragon
czworokąt (chvo-ró-kownt) m.
quadrangle; quad; tetragon
czwórka (chvoór-ka) f. four-
some: crew of four; good mark
czy (chi) conj. if; whether
czychać (chí-khach) v. lurk
czyj (chiy) pron. whose
czyjś (chiysh) pron. somebody's
anybody's; someone else's
czyli (chi-lee) conj. or;
otherwise; that is to say
czym...tym (chim...tim) adv.
the sooner... the; the more
the...: the less... the...
czyn (chin) m. act. deed
czynsz (chinsh) m. rent
czynić (chí-ńeech) v. do;
render ; act; amount;cause

czyrak (chí-rak) m. boil; furuncle; boil; anbury; rising
czynnik (chín-ńeek) m. factor
czysto (chý-sto) adv. clean
czysty (chís-ti) adj. m. clean
czyszczenie (chish-che-ńe) n. cleaning; brushing;diarrhoea
czyścić (chish-ćheećh) v. clean; scour; brush; rub;purge
czyściec (chish-ćhets) m. purgatory; woundwort
czytać (chi-táćh) v. read
czytelnia (chi-tel-ńa) f. reading room;lending library
czytelnik (chi-tel-ńeek) m. reader; reading individual
czytelny (chi-tel-ni) adj. m. legible; readable
czyż (chish) part. if; whether
ćma (ćhma) f. obscurity; swarm; night butterfly;night moth
ćmić (ćhmeećh) v. obscure; dim; darken; eclipse; smoke; sicken
ćwiartka (ćhvyart-ka) f. one quarter; one fourth of a liter
ćwierć (ćhwyerćh) f. one fourth (of a liter etc.)
ćwiczenie (chvee-che-ńe) n. exercise; instruction; drill
ćwiek (ćhvyek) m. nail; stud
ćwikła (ćhveek-wa) f. beetroot with horseradish (salad)
dach (dakh) m. roof; shelter
dać (daćh) v. give; pay;result
daktyl (dák-til) m. date
dal (dal) f. distance; remoteness; far away; aloof
dalece (da-lé-tse) adv. further by far; so far;(so)much so
dalej (dá-ley) adv. further; moreover; further on; so on
dalmierz (dal-myesh) m. range finder; telemeter
dalszy (dál-shi) adj. m. further farther; later; another
dama (dá-ma) f. lady; partner
dana (dá-na) adj.f.given (data)
danie (dá-ńe) m. serving; dish; course
danser (dan-ser) m. dancer
dane (dá-ne) pl. data
dar (dar) m. gift; present
daremnie (da-rém-ńe) adv. in vain; without success

daremny (da-rém-ni) adj. m. futile; vain; idle; ineffective
darmo (dár-mo) adv. free; gratuitously; to no avail
darować (da-ró-vaćh) v. give; forgive; overlook; spare
data (da-ta) f. date
datek (da-tek) n. small gift
dawać (da-vaćh) v. give (often)
dawno (dáv-no) adv. long ago
dąb (domp) m. oak tree (wood)
dąć (dowńćh) v. blow; resound
dąsać się (down-saćh śhań) v. sulk; be in the pouts; mump
dążyć (dówn-zhićh) v. aspire; tend; aim; be bound; trend
dbać (dbaćh) v. care;set store
dech (dekh) m. breath; gust
decydować (de-tsi-dó-vaćh) v. decide; resolve; determine
decyzja (de-tsis-ya) f. decision; ruling; resolve
delikatność (de-lee-kát-noshćh) f. delicacy; gentleness; tact
defekt (dé-fekt) m. defect
demaskować (de-mas-kó-vaćh) v. unmask; uncover; denounce
demokracja (de-mo-krats-ya) f. democracy,
denerwować (de-ner-vó-vaćh) v. bother; make nervous; irritate
dentysta (den-tis-ta) m. dentist
depesza (de-pe-sha) f. wire; telegram; cable; dispatch
deponować (de-po-nó-vaćh) v. deposit; put in safe keeping
depozyt (de-pó-zit) m. deposit
deptać (dép-taćh) v. trample; tread; pace up and down;stain
derka (dér-ka) f. rug; blanket
desen (dé-seń) m. pattern; design; decorative design
deska (dés-ka) f. plank; board
desperacja (des-pe-ráts-ya) f. desperation; despair
deszcz (deshch) m. rain
detal (dé-tal) m. retail; detail; trifling matter
determinacja (de-ter-mee-náts-ya) f. determination
dewiza (de-veé-za) f. foreign money; motto; slogan; device

dębina (dan-bee-na) f. oak wood; oak bark

dętka (dant-ka) f. pneumatic tire; tube; air chamber

diabeł (dyá-bew) m. devil

dieta (dye-ta) f. diet;regimen

dla (dla) prep. for; to;towards

dlaczego (dla—ché-go)prep. why; what for

dlatego (dla—té-go)prep. because; this is why; and so

dławić (dwa-veech) v. choke; squash; throttle; strangle

dłoń (dwoń) f. palm of the hand; metacarpus; quart

dłubać (dwoó-bach)v. groove; poke; tinker; pick one's teeth

dług (dwoog) m. debt; obligation

długi (dwoo-gee) adj. m. long

długo (dwoó-go) adv. a long time; a long way; long before

dłuto (dwoo-to) n. chisel

dłutować (dwoo-tó-vach) v. chisel; cut with chisel

dłuźnik (dwoozh-ńeek) m. debtor

dmuchać (dmoó-khach)v. blow

dniówka (dńoóv-ka) f. day's work; work by day; time work

dno (dno) n. bottom; utterness

do (do) prep. to; into; up;till

doba (dó-ba) f. 24 hours

dobić (dó-beech) v. deal a death blow; drive home

dobierać (do-byé-rach) v. match; take more; select

dobitny (do-beet-ni) adj. m. expressive; emphatic; distinct

doborowy (do-bo-ró-vi) adj. m. choice; select; picked

dobosz (dó-bosh) m. drummer

dobór (dó-boor) m. selection; assortment; choice;assortment

dobra (dób-ra) n. riches

dobranoc (do-bra-nots)(indecl.) good-night

dobrany (do-brá-ni) adj. m. matching; becoming;accordant

dobre (dób-re) adj. n. good

dobro (dób-ro) n. good; right

dobrobyt (do-bró-bit) m. well-being; prosperity; welfare

dobroczynnosc (do-bro-chin-noshch) f. charity; works of mercy; philanthropy

dobroc (dó—roch) f. kindness

dobroduszny (do-bro-doósh-ni) adj. m. kindhearted; kindly

dobrodziej (do-bró-dźhey) m. benefactor; his reverence

dobrotliwy (do-bro-tlee-vi) adj. m. kind; good natured

dobrowolny (do-bro-wól-ni) adj. m. voluntary; gratuitus

dobry (dób-ri) adj. m. good; kind; right; hearty; retentive

dobrze (dób-rze) adv. well; O K; rightly; properly;okay

dobudówka (do-boo-doóv-ka) f. building extension

dobyc (do-bićh) v. pullout

dobytek (do-bi-tek) m. be-longings; effects; livestock

doceniać (do-tse-ńach) v. duly appreciate; value

docent (do-tsent) m. associate professor ; lecturer

dochodzenie (do-kho-dze-ńe) n investigation; inquiry

dochodzić (do-kho-dźheech)v. draw near; investigate; reach

dochód (do-khoot) m. income; revenue; profit; returns

dociąc (do-chownch) c. sting; taunt; fit by cutting off

dociec (dó-chets) v. find out

dociekać (do-che'-kach) v. search; investigate; find out

docierać (do-chye-rach) v. draw near; reach; reduce friction ; rub up; get at

docinek (do-chee-nek) m. taunt

doczekać (do-che-kach) v. wait; live to see; wait 'til

doczepiac (do-chep-yach) v. fix append; attach; hitch; link

doczesny (do-chés-ni) adj. m. temporal; worldly; mundane

dodać (do-dach) v. add; sum up

dodatek (do-da-tek) m. supple-ment; addition; fixture; extra

dodatni (do-dat-ńee) adj. m. positive; advantageous; active

dodawanie (do-da-va-ńe) n. addition

dogadać się (do-ga-dach shan)v. come to terms;communicate well

dogadzać (do-gá-dzach) v. please; accommodate; satisfy

dogladać (do-glówn-dach) v.
supervise; tend; oversee

dogmat (dóg-mat) m. dogma

dogodny (do-gód-ni) adj. m.
convenient; suitable; handy

dogonić (do-go-ñeech) v. catch
up; overtake; be in hot pursuit

dogryzać (do-gri-zach) v. vex;
tease; finish munching; disturb

doić (do-eech) v. milk; fleece

dojarka (do-yár-ka) f. milk
maid; milking machine

dojazd (do-yazt) m. access; drive;
approach; means of transport

dojechać (do-ye-khach) v. reach;
arrive; approach; bang; hit

dojeżdżać (do-yezh-jach) v.
commute; be coming; pull in

dojmujący (doy-moo-yówn-tsi) adj.
m. acute; piercing; sharp: keen

dojrzały (doy-zha-wi) adj. m.
ripe; mellow; mature: adult

dojrzeć (doy-zhech) v. glimpse;
notice; ripen; be ripe; mellow

dojście (doy-shche) n. approach

dok (dok) m. dock

dokarmić (do-kár-meech) v.
nourish additionally

dokazać (do-ká-zach) v. prove;
achieve; accomplish; do the trick

dokazywać (do-ka-zí-vach) v.
frolic: gambol; romp and play

dokąd (do-kównt) adv. where; till
whither; where to ? how far? till

dokładać (do-kwa-dach) v. add;
throw in; pay more; give more

dokładny (do-kwad-ni) adj. m.
accurate; exact; precise

dokoła (do-ko-wa) adv. round;
round about; all round

dokonać (do-kó-nach) v. achieve;
accomplish; carry out; fulfil

dokończenie (do-koñ-che-ñe) n.
conclusion: completion; end

doktor (dók-tor) m. doctor

dokręcać (do-kráñ-tsach) v.
tighten; screw tight; turn off

dokuczać (do-koo-chach) v. vex;
annoy; nag; bully; sting; trouble

dola (do-la) f. fortune; lot

dolar (dó-lar) m. dollar

doliczyć (do-lée-chich) v.
count up ; add; charge more

dolina (do-lée-na) f. valley;
dale; glen; coomb; pocket

dolny (dol-ny) adj. m. lower

dołączyć (do-wówn-chich) v. add;
join; enclose; affix; tack on

dołek (do-wek) m. dimple; pit

dom (dom) m. house ∫ v. demand

domagać się (do-ma-gach shán)

domiar (do-myar) m. additional
assessment; surtax; on top of it

domniemany (do-mñe-ma-ni) adj.
m. supposed; assumed; alleged

domostwo (do-mós-tvo) n. household; homestead; farmstead

domownik (do-mow-ñeek) m.
inmate ; housemate

domowy (do-mó-vi) adj. m.
domestic; homemade; private

domysł (do-misw) m. guess

doniesienie (do-ñe-she-ñe) m.
denunciation; report; news

doniosły (do-ño-swi) adj. m.
significant; far reaching

donosiciel (do-no-shee-chel)
m. denunciator: informer

donośny (do-nósh-ni) adj. m.
resounding; renging; loud

dookoła(do-o-ko-wa) adv. round;
round about; all around; around

dopasć (do-pashch) v. catch up;
overtake: reach at a run; seize

dopalać (do-pa-lach) v. after-
burn; finish burning; burn up

dopasować (do-pa-so-vach) v.
fit; adapt; adjust; match; tone

dopatrywać (do-pa-tri-vach) v.
see to it; find out; keep an eye

dopełnić (do-péw-ñeech) v. fulfil;
fill up; complete ; make up

dopędzić (do-páñ-dźeech) v.
catch up with; overtake; gain on

dopiąć (do-pyównch) v. attain;
buckle up; button up; obtain

dopiero (do-pye-ro) adv. only;
just; hardly; barely ; not till

dopilnować (do-peel-no-vach) v.
see something done ; supervise

dopisek (do-pee-sek) m. postscript; foot note

dopłata (do-pwa-ta) f. extra
payment; surcharge; extra fare

dopływ (do-pwif) m. tributary

dopomagać (do-po-má-gach) v.
help; be of assistance

dopominać się (do-po-mee-nach
shan) v. put in claim; demand

dopóki (do-pooki) conj. as
long; as far; while; until; till

dopóty (do-poo-ti) conj. 'til ;
until ; so far; up to here

dopraszać się (do-pra-shach
shan) v. solicit; beg; insist

doprawdy (do-práv-di) adv.
truly; indeed; really

doprawiać (do-práv-yach) v.
add (to taste); replace

doprowadzić (do-pro-va-dźheech)
v. lead to; cause; provoke

dopust Boży (dó-poost Bo-zhi)
m. calamity; scourge; act of God

dopuszczać (do-poosh-chach) v.
admit; allow; permit; be open

dopytać się (do-pi-tach shan)
v. find out; inquire; question

dorabiać (do-ráb-yach) v. make
additionally; replace; finish

doradca (do-rad-tsa) m. adviser; counselor ; guide

dorastać (do-rás-tach) v.
mature; grow; grow up; reach

doraźnie (do-rázh-ńe) adv.
(immediately) on the spot

doręczyć (do-rán-chich) v.
hand in; deliver; transmit

dorobek (do-ró-bek) m. acquisition; rise to affluence

dorobkiewicz (do-rob-ḱe-veech)
m. upstart; parvenu

doroczny (do-róch-ni) adj. m.
yearly; annual; recurring yearly

dorodny (do-ród-ni) adj. m.
handsome; fine-looking; shapely

dorosły (do-rós-wy) adj. m.
adult; grown up; mature; grown

dorożka (do-rozh-ka) f. cab

dorównywać (do-roov-ni-vach) v.
match; equal; catch up with

dorsz (dorsh) m. cod (fish)

dorywczy (do-riv-chi) v.
occasional; improvised; fitful; off-and-on; hit-and-run

dorzecze (do-zhe-che) n.
river basin; drainage area

dorzeczny (do-zhech-ni) adj. m.
reasonable; sensible; efficient;
adequate; acceptable; logical

dorzucać (do-zhoo-tsach) v.
throw in; add; throw as far as

dosadny (do-sád-ni) adj. m.
forceful; expressive; crisp

dosiadać (do-sha-dach) v.
mount (horse); bestride

dosięgać (do-shan-gach) v.
reach; attain; catch up with

doskonalić (dos-ko-na-leech)
v. perfect; improve; cultivate

doskwierać (do-skvye-rach) v.
pinch; gripe; trouble; worry

dosłowny (do-swov-ni) adj. m.
literal ; verbal; textual

dosłyszeć (do-swi-shech) v.
hear well; catch a sound

dostać (dos-tach) v. get;
obtain; reach; take out

dostarczyć (dos-tar-chich) v.
provide; supply; deliver

dostateczny (do-sta-téch-ni)
adj. m. sufficient; adequate

dostatek (do-stá-tek) m. abundance; wealth; affluence

dostawca (do-staw-tsa) m.
supplier; provider

dostawa (do-stá-va) f. delivery

dostawać (do-stá-vach) v. reach;
receive ; be attended to

dostęp (do-stanp) m. access

dostojnik (do-stóy-ńeek) m.
dignitary; notable of high rank

dostosować (do-sto-so-vach) v.
accommodate; subordinate; fit

dostroić (do-stró-yeech) v.
tune up ; conform; adapt

dostrzec (do-stzhets) v. notice;
behold ; perceive; spot; spy; see

dostudzić (do-stoo-dźheech) v.
cool off ; plenty; sufficient

dosyć (do-sich) adv. enough;

dosztukować (do-shtoo-kó-vach)
v. piece on; eke out; sew on

dość (dośhch) adv. enough

dośrodkowy (do-śhrod-kó-vi)
adj. m. centripetal; concentric

doświadczyć (do-śhvyad-chich) v.
experience ; sustain; feel

dotarcie (do-tar-che) n. reaching; overcoming friction

dotąd (do-townt) adv. up till
now; here to fore ; hitherto;
thus far; so far; yet; by then;
till then; still; not...as yet

dotkliwy (dot-kleé-vi) adj. m.
 painful ; keen; intense; severe
dotknąć (dot-knównch) v. touch
dotknięcie (dot-kñán-che) n.
 touch; contact; feeling; stroke
dotrzeć (do-tzhech) v. reach;
 overcome friction; rub up
dotrzymać (do-tzhi-mach) v.
 keep; stick to one's
 commitment ; adhere; redeem
dotychczas (do-tíkh-chas) adv.
 up to now; hitherto; to date
dotyczyć (do-tí-chich) v.
 concern; relate; regard; affect
dotyk (do-tik) m. touch; feel
dowcip (dóv-cheep) m. wit;
 joke; jest; gag; quip; sally
dowiedzieć się (do-vye-dzhe-
 śhán) v. get to know; learn
dowidzenia (do-vee-dze-ña)
 good bye; see you later
dowierzać (do-vye-zhach) v.
 trust; have confidence in
dowieść (do-vyeshch) v. prove
dowieźć (do-vyeźhch) v.
 1. supply 2. drive to
dowodzić (do-vó-dźheech) v.
 conduct; keep proving
dowolnie (do-vól-ñe) adv. at
 will; optionally; freely
dowolny (do-vól-ni) adj. m.
 optional; any; whichever
dowód (dó-voot) m. proof;
 evidence; record; token
dowódca (do-vóod-tsa) m.
 commander ⌠delivery
dowóz (dó-voos) m. supply;
doza (dó-za) f. dose
dozbroić (do-zbro-eech) v.
 rearm; supplement weapons
dozgonny (do-zgón-ni) adj. m.
 lifelong; lasting til death
doznać (do-znach) v. go through;
 undergo; endure; feel; suffer
dozorca (do-zor-tsa) m. caretaker; watchman; overseer
dozorować (do-zo-ro-vach) v.
 oversee; supervise; attend
dozór (do-zoor) m. surveillance
dozwolić (do-zvó-leech) v.
 allow to happen; let happen
dożynki (do-zhín-kee) pl.
 harvest festivities

dożywocie (do-zhi-vó-che)n.
 life estate; life pension
dół (doow) m. pit; bottom part
drab (drap) m. ruffian; scamp
drabina (dra-bee-na) f. ladder
dramat (drá-mat) m. drama
drań (drań) m. scoundrel; crumb
drapacz (drá-pach) m. scraper
drapać (dra-pach) v. scratch
drapieżnik (dra-pyezh-ñeek) m.
 beast of prey; plunderer
drastyczny (dra-stich-ni) adj.
 m. drastic; rough; violent
dratwa (drát-va) f. pitched-
 thread; shoemaker's twine
draźliwy (drazh-leé-vi) adj.
 m. touchy; irritable; ticklish
drażnić (drazh-ñeech) v. tease;
 irritate; whet; vex; annoy; jar
drąg (drównk) m. pole; bar
drążyć (drówn-zhich) v. hollow
 out; bore; torment; fret; gnaw
drelich (dre-leekh) m. denim
dren (dren) n. drain (pipe)
dreptać (drép-tach) v. trip-
 trot; toddle; totter; patter
dreszcz (dreshch) m. chill;
 shudder; thrill; flutter; shiver
dreszczowiec (dresh-chó-vyets)
 m. thriller (novel or movie)
drewno (drév-no) n. piece of
 wood; timber ; log; xylem
dręczyć (dráñ-chich) v. torment
drętwieć (dráñ-tvyech) v. grow
 numb; grow stiff; stiffen
drgać (drgach) v. tremble;
 vibrate; quiver; throb; wobble
drobiazg (drób-yazk) m. trifle;
 detail; trinket; small fry
drobina (dro-bee-na) f. particle
drobne (drób-ne) n. small
 change; petty cash ; small coin
drobnica (drob-ñee-tsa) f.
 small goods; packages
drobnostka (drob-nóst-ka) f.
 trifle; small matter; trinket
drobny (dro-bni) adj. m. small;
 tiny; trivial; petty; slight
droga (dro-ga) f. 1. road;
 2. journey; 3. adj. f. dear
drogeria (dro-gér-ya) f. drugstore ; drysaltery

drogi (dró-gee) adj. m. dear;
expensive; costly; beloved
drogowskaz (dro-góv-skas) m.
road sign; signpost
drozd (drozt) m. thrush
drożdże (drozh-je) pl. yeast
drożeć (dro-zheċh) v. grow
dear; rise in price;appreciate
drożyzna (dro-zhiz-na) f. high
cost of living; high prices
drób (droop) pl. paltry
dróżka (droozh-ka) f. path
druciany (droo-ćha-ni) adj. m.
of wire; made out of wire
drugi (droó-gee) num. second;
other; the other one; latter
druh (drookh) m. buddy;
companion; friend; boy scout
druk (drook) m. print; printing
drut (droot) m. wire
druzgotać (drooz-go-tach) v.
smash; shatter; crush to pieces
drużba (droozh-ba) m. best man
drużyna (droo-zhi-na) f. team
drwal (drval) m. lumber jack
drwić (drveeċh) v. mock;deride
drwiny (drvee-ny) pl. mockery
dryg (drik) m.knack; flair for
drzazga (dzház-ga) f. splinter
drzeć (dzheċh) v. tear; pull
drzemka (dshem-ka) f. nap
drzewo (dshe-vo) n. tree
drzeworyt (dshe-vo-rit) m.
woodcut; wood engraving
drzwi (dzhvee) n. door
drżeć (drzheċh) v. shiver;shake
dubeltówka (doo-bel-toóv-ka) f.
double barrel gun; shotgun
duch (dookh) m. spirit; ghost;
state of mind; intent; life
duchowieństwo (doo-khov-yeń-stvo)
pl. clergy; priesthood
dudek (doo-dek) m. 1. hoopoe;
2. dupe; fool; dolt; booby
dudnić (dóod-ńeech) v. resound
dudy (doo-di) pl. bagpipe
dukat (doo-kat) m. ducat
dulka (dool-ka) f. oarlock
duma (doo-ma) f. pride ; epic
dumać (doo-mach) v. meditate
dumny (doom-ni) adj. m. proud
dupa (doo-pa) f. ass (vulg.)
dur (door) m. typhoid fever

dureń (doo-reń) m. fool; ass
durzyć (doo-zhich) v. fool;
infatuate; bewilder; dupe
dusić (doo-śheech) v. strangle
dusigrosz (doo-śhee-grosh) m.
penny pincher; niggard
dusza (doo-sha) f. soul;psyche
dużo (doo-zho) adv. much; many
duży (doo-zhi) adj. m. big;
large; great; fair-sized
dwa (dva) num. two
dwakroć (dvá-kroch) num. twice
dwanaście (dva-náśh-che) num.
twelve
dwieście (dvyésh-che) num. 200
dwoić (dvo-eeċh) v. double
dwojaczki (dvo-yach-kee) pl.
twins ; double pot the two;
dwoje (dvo-ye) num. two;in two;
couple ;two(fold);two(ways)
dwór (dvoor) m. country manor
dworski (dvór-skee) adj. m.
courtly; manorial; of court
dworzec (dvo-zhets) m. (railway) station ; depot
dwukrotnie (dvoo-krot-ńe) adv.
twice ; twice over
dwunastka (dvoo-nást-ka) f.
twelve ;(team)of twelve
dwustronny (dvoo-stron-ni)adj.
m. two-sided; bilateral
dyg (dik) m. curtsy; bob
dygnitarz (dig-ńee-tash) m.
dignitary; high ranking man
dygotać (di-go-tach) v. tremble
dykta (dík-ta) f. plywood
dyktator (dik-tá-tor) m.
dictator ;absolute ruler
dylemat (di-le-mat) m. dilem-
ma; perplexity; fix
dym (dim) m. smoke; fumes
dymić (di-meech) v. smoke
dynamit (di-na-meet) m. dynamite; W.W.II German ersatz bread
dyndać (din-dach) v. dangle
dynia (di-ńa) f. pumpkin
dyplom (di-plom) m. diploma
dyplomacja (di-plo-mats-ya) f.
diplomacy; policy; tact
dyrekcja (di-rek-tsya) f.
management ; headquarters
dyrygent (di-ri-gent) m.
orchestra conductor

dyscyplina (dis-tsi-plee-na) f.
  discipline; branch; line
dysk (disk) m. disc; discus
dyskrecja (dis-krets-ya) f.
  discretion; management
dyskusja (dis-koos-ya) f.
  discussion; debate
dysponować (dis-po-no-vach) v.
  dispose; control; order
dysputa (dis-poo-ta) f. dispute; debate; controversy
dystans (dis-tans) m. distance
dystyngowany (dis-tin-go-va-
  ni) adj. m. distinguished
dysza (di-sha) f. nozzle;
  blast pipe; snout; twyer
dyszeć (di-shech) v. gasp;pant
dywan (di-van) m. carpet; rug
dywidenda (di-vee-den-da) f.
  dividend
dywizja (di-veez-ya) f. division
dyżurny (di-zhoor-ny) adj. m.
  on call; on duty; orderly
dzban (dzban) m. jug; pitcher
dziać się (dzhach shan) v.
  occur; happen; take place
dziadek (dzha-dek) m. grandfather; nut cracer
dział (dzhaw) m. section
działacz (dzha-wach) m. acti-
  vist(in politics, religion etc)
działać (dzha-wach) v. act;
  work; be active; be effective
działka (dzhaw-ka) f. parcel
działo (dzha-wo) n. cannon
dziarski (dzhar-skee) adj. m.
  brisk; lively; swinging; rakish
dziąsło (dzhown-swo)n. gum
dzicz (dzheech)pl. savages
dzida (dzhee-da) f. spear ;pike
dzieci (dzhe-chee) pl. children
dzieciństwo (dzhe-cheen-stvo)
  n. childhood; boyhood;infancy
dziecko (dzhets-ko) n. child;
  baby; trot; brat; kiddie; kid
dziedziczyć (dzhe-dzhee-chich)
  v. inherit(property,features)
dziedzina (dzhe-dzhee-na)f.
  realm; area;sphere ; domain
dziedziniec (dzhe-dzhee-nets)m.
  yard; court; backyard

dziegieć (dzhe-gech) m. tar
dzieje (dzhe-ye) pl. history
dziejowy (dzhe-yo-vi) adj. m.
  historical; historic
dziekan (dzhe-kan) m. dean
dzielić (dzhe-leech) v. divide;
  share; split; distribute
dzielnica (dzhel-nee-tsa) f.
  province; quarter; section
dzielny (dzhel-ni) adj. m.
  brave; resourceful; efficient
dzieło (dzhe-wo) n. achievement; work; composition
dziennik (dzhen-neek)m. daily-
  news; daily; journal; diary
dzienny (dzhen-ni) adj. m.
  daily; diurnal; day's
dzień (dzhen)m. day; daylight
dzień dobry(dzhen dob-ri)good morn-
dzierżawa (dzher-zha-va) f. ing
  lease; rental; holding
dzierżyć (dzher-zhich) v.
  wield (power); hold ; grip
dziesiątka (dzhe-shownt-ka) f.
  ten;(team of)ten
dziesięć (dzhe-shanch) num.
  ten
dziewczyna (dzhev-chi-na) f.
  girl; lass; wench; maid
dziewica (dzhe-vee-tsa) f.
  virgin; maiden
dziewięć (dzhe-vyanch) num.
  nine
dziewiętnaście (dzhe-vyant-
  nashche) num. nineteen
dzięcioł (dzhan-chow) m.
  woodpecker
dziękczynienie (dzhank-chi-
  ne-ne)n. thanks-giving
dziękować (dzhan-ko-vach) v.
  thank ; give thanks
dzik (dzheek) m. boar; tusker
dziobać (dzho-bach)v. peck
dziób (dzh-oob) m. beak; bill
dzisiejszy (dzhee-shey-shi)
  adj. m. today's ; modern
dziś (dzheesh) adv. today
dziupla (dzhoop-la) f. (tree)
  hollow(in a trnk)
dziura (dzhoo-ra) f. hole
dziurawy (dzhoo-ra-vi) adj. m.
  leaky; full of holes
dziw (dzheef) m. wonder

dziwactwo (dżhee-vats-tvo) n.
crank; fad; craze; peculiarity
dziwić (dżhee-veech) v. astonish
dziwny (dżheev-ni) adj.m.strange;
dzwon (dzyon) m. bell; chime
dźwięczeć (dźhvyan-chech) v.
ring; sound; jingle; clang
dźwięk (dżhvyank) m. sound
dźwig (dżhveek) n. crane
dźwigać (dżhvee-gach) v. lift;
hoist; raise; heave; erect;carry
dżdżysty (j-jis-ti) adj. m. wet;
rainy ; drizzly (weather)
dżem (jem) m. jam; fruit jam
dżet (jet) m. jet
dżinsy (jeen-si) pl. blue
jeans (pants)
dżokey (jo-key) m. jockey
dżudo (joo-do) m. judo (sport)
dżuma (joo-ma) f. plague
dżungla (joon-gla) f. jungle
echo (ekho) n. echo; response
edukacja (e-doo-kats-ya) f.
education; schooling;instruction
efekt (e-fekt) m. effect
efektowny (e-fek-tov-ni) adj.
m. showy; striking; attractive
efektywny (e-fek-tiv-ni) adj.
m. efficient; effective; real
egida (e-gee-da) f. protection;
auspices; protectorate
egoista (e-go-ees-ta) m.egotist
egoistyczny (e-go-ees-tich-ni)
adj. m. selfish; self seeking
egzamin (eg-za-meen) m. examination; exam ; standing a test
egzekucja (eg-ze-koots-ya) f.
execution ; seizure; flogging
egzemplarz (eg-zem-plash) m.
copy (sample); specimen
egzystencja (eg-zis-ten-tsya)
f. existence; livelihood
ekierka (e-ker—ka) f. set
square ;draftsman's triangle
ekipa (e-kee-pa) f. team;crew
ekonomia (e-ko-nom-ya) f.
economics; thrift; economy
ekran (ek-ran) m. screen;shield
ekspedient (ex-pe-dyent) m.
salesperson ; clerk;salesman
ekspedycja (ex-pe-dits-ya) f.
1. dispatch 2. expedition

ekspert (ex-pert) m. expert
eksploatować (ex-plo-a-to-vach)
v. exploit; sweat; utilize
eksponat (ex-po-nat) m. exhibit
ekspozytura (ex-po-zy-too-ra)
f. agency; branch office
ekwipować (ek-vee-po-vach) v.
equip; fit out; provide with
elaborat (e-la-bo-rat) m. study (elaboration)
elastyczność (e-las-tich-noshch)
elasticity; resilience;flexibility
elegancja (e-le-gants-ya) f.
elegance; fashion; style
elektrociepłownia (e-lek-tro-
chep-wov-ña) f. steamplant
elektryczność (e-lek-trich-
noshch) f. electricity
element (e-le-ment) m. element
elementarny (e-le-men-tar-ni)
adj. m. fundamental; primary
elewator (e-le-va-tor) m.
elevator ; hoist
emalia (e-mal-ya) f. enamel
emeryt (e-me-rit) m. retired
person; pensioner; pensionary
emigracja (e-mee-grats-ya) f.
emigration; exile; emigrants
emisja (e-mees-ya) f. emission
emocja (e-mo-tsya) f. thrill
entuzjazm (en-tooz-yazm) m.
enthusiasm; rapture
energia (e-nerg-ya) f. energy
energiczny (e-ner-geech-ni)
adj. m. energetic; vigorous
epoka (e-po-ka) f. epoch
epitet (e-pee-tet) m. epithet
era (era) f. era; epoch
erotyczny (e-ro-tich-ni) adj.
m. erotic; sexual
eskadra (es-kad-ra) f. squadron; aerial fleet: flight
eskorta (es-kor-ta) f. escort
estetyczny (es-te-tich-ni)
adj. m.esthetic; in good taste
etap (e-tap) m. stage (of development) ; halting place
etatowy (e-ta-to-vi) adj. m.
permanent (job); full time
eter (e-ter) m. ether
etyczny (e-tich-ni) adj. m.
ethical; moral

etykieta (e-ti-k̕e---ta) f. label; etiquette; formality;ceremonial

ewakuacja (e-va-koo-a-tsya) f. evacuation

ewangielia (e-van-ǵel--ya) f. gospel; gospel truth

ewangielik (e-van-ǵe---leek) m. protestant,; Lutheran

ewentualnosc (e-ven-too-al̕-nośḥćh) f. possibility

ewentualnie (e-ven-too-al̕-n̕e) adv. possibly; if need be

ewidencja (e-vee-dén-tsya) f. records; list; files ; roll

ewolucja (e-vo-loo-tsya) f. evolution; development

fabryczny (fa-brích-ni) adj. m. manufactured

fabryka (fa-brí-ka) f. factory

fabuła (fa-boo-wa) f. fable; plot of a novel etc.; story

facet (fá-tset) m. guy

fachowiec (fa-kho-vyets) m. expert; specialist;connoisseur

fajdac (fáy-dáćh) v. shit (vulg.)

fajans (fáy-ans) m. earthenware

fajerka (fa-yér-ka) f.cook-top unit; stove lid

fajka (fáy-ka)f. pipe (for smoking) wild boar's tusk

fajtłapa (fayt-wá-pa) m. all thumbs guy(awkward,clumsy man)

fakt (fakt) m. fact

faktor (fák-tor) m. broker; agent; factor; intermediary

faktycznie (fak-tích-n̕e) adv. in fact;actually; indeed; truly

fala (fa-la) f. wave; tide;surge

falisty (fa-lees-ti) adj. m. wavy; rolling; corrugated

falochron (fa-ló-khron) m. breakwater : pier; jetty; mole

falsyfikat (fal-si-fée-kat) m. forgery; counterfeit; fake

fałd (fawt) m. fold (wrinkle)

fałsz (fawsh) m. falsehood

fałszowac (faw-shó-vaćh) v. falsify; fake; forge; sing flat

fama (fa-ma) f. fame; rumor

fanaberie (fa-na-bér-ye) pl. whims; fads; frills; ostentation

fanatyk (fa-ná-tik) m. fanatic; enthusiast; bigot; maniac

fanfaron (fan-fa-ron) m. braggart; coxcomb; swaggerer

fantastyczny (fan-tas-tich-ni) adj. m. fantastic; wild; odd

fantazja (fan-táz-ya) f. dash; imagination; fiction; whim

fara (fá-ra) f. parish church

farba (fár-ba) f. paint; dye color; dyeing; blood

farbowac (far-bó-vaćh) v. dye

farsa (far-sa) f. farce;mockery

farsz (farsh) m. stuffing

fartuch (fár-tookh)m. apron

fasola (fa-so-la) f. bean

fasonowac (fa-so-no-vaćh) v. fashion; shape; mold model

fatalny (fa-tal-ni) adj. m. fatal; ill-fated; awful;fateful

fastryga (fas-tri-ga) f. tack; basting; baste; tacks

faszyzm (fa-shizm) m. fascism

fatyga (fa-ti-ga) f. trouble; fatigue ; trouble; bother;pains

fatałaszki (fa-ta-wash-kee) pl. knik-knacks; frippery; trinkets

febra (féb-ra) fever;the shakes

faworyzowac (fa-vo-ri-zo-vaćh) v. favor; play favorites

felczer (fél-cher) m. male nurse : medical assistant

federacja (fe-de-rats-ya) f. federation ; union

feralny (fe-rál-ni) adj. m. unlucky; ill fated; hapless

ferie (fér-ye) pl. holidays

ferma (fér-ma) f. farm; ranch

ferment (fér-ment) m. ferment

festyn (fes-tin) m. festival

fetor (fé-tor) m. stench

figa (feé-ga) f. fig; nix

figiel (feé-gel) m. practical joke ; prank; trick; ill turn

figura (fee-góo-ra) f. figure; shape ; form; image; big wig

fikcja (feek-tsya) f. fiction

filar (fee-lar) m. pillar

filatelista (fee-la-te-lees-ta) m. stamp-collector

filc (feelts) m. felt

filia (fee-l̕ya) f. branch (store); branch-office

filiżanka (fee-lee-zhan-ka) f. cup ; cupful; coffee-cup

film (feelm) m. film

filolog (fee-lo-lok) m. philologist; linguist

filozof (fee-lo-zof) m. philosopher

filtr (feeltr) m. filter

filut (fee-loot) m. jester;
rogue; sly boots; joker

finanse (fee-nan-se) pl.
finances; finance; funds

finisz (fee-neesh) m. end (of
a run); the finish

fiołek (fyo-wek) m. violet

fiołkowy (fyow-ko-vi) adj. m.
purple; violet; of the violet

firanka (fee-ran-ka) f.
curtain; drapery

firma (feer-ma) f. business;
firm; name of a firm

fisharmonia (fees-har-mon-ya)
f. harmonium

fizjognomia (feez-yo-gnom-ya)
f. face; external aspect

fizjonomia (feez-yo-nom-ya) f.
face; physiognomy

fizjolog (feez-yo-lok) m.
physiologist

fizyczny (feez-ich-ni) adj. m.
physical; bodily; manual

fizyk (fee-zik) m. physicist

flaczki (flach-kee) pl. tripe

flaga (fla-ga) f. banner;
flag; ensign; standard

flaki (fla-kee) pl. bowels

flakon (fla-kon) m. vase

flanela (fla-ne-la) f. flannel

flaszka (flash-ka) bottle

flama (fla-ma) f, lady-love

flądra (flown-dra) f. flounder

flegma (fleg-ma) f. phlegm

flejtuch (fley-tookh) m. slut

flet (flet) m. flute

flirt (fleert) m. flirt

flisak (flee-sak) m. raftsman

flora (flo-ra) f. flora

floret (flo-ret) m. foil

flota (flo-ta) f. navy; fleet

fluksja (flooks-ya) f. tooth-
infection swelling

fluid (floo-eet) m. fluid

fochy (fo-khi) pl. blues;
whims; sulks; pouts

foka (fo-ka) f. seal

folgować (fol-go-vach) v.
slacken; relax; indulge; abate

folklor (folk-lor) m. folklore

folusz (fo-loosh)m.fulling mill

folwark (fol-vark) m. farm

fonetyczny (fo-ne-tich-ni) adj.
phonetic

fontanna (fon-tan-na) f.
fountain ; spurt; waterworks

foremny (fo-rem-ni) adj. m.
shapely;handsome; symmetrical

forma (for-ma) f. shape; mold

format (for-mat) m. size

formularz (for-moo-lash) m.
(application) form ; blank

formuła (for-moo-wa) f. formula

fornir (for-neer) m. veneer

forsa (for-sa) f. (money);
dough; bread; tin; chink

forsować (forso-vach) v. force;
strain ; urge; exhort;overcome

fort (fort) m. fort; stronghold

forteca (for-te-tsa) f. for —
tress; citadel ; stronghold

fortel (for-tel) m. stratagem;
trick ; ruse; subterfuge

fortepian (for-te-pyan) m.
grand piano; piano

fortuna (for-too-na) f. fortune

fosa (fo-sa) f. moat

fosfat (fos-fat) m. phosphate

fosfor (fos-foor) m. phosphorus

fotel (fo-tel) m. armchair

fotograf (fo-to-graf) m.
photographer

fotografia (fo-to-graf-ya) f.
photograph ; snap shot; picture

fracht (frakht) m. freight

fragment (frag-ment) m. fragment ; episode; excerpt;scrap

frak (frak) m. evening formal

framuga (fra-moo-ga) f. recess
(structure); bay; embrasure

frant (frant) m. sly dog; knave

frasunek (fra-soo-nek) m. worry;
grief; sorrow; care; trouble

fraszka (frash-ka) f. trifle

frazes (fra-zes) m. platitude

frekwencja (fre-kven-tsya) f.
attendance; turnout; frequency

fredzla (frandz-la) f. fringe

fresk (fresk) m. fresco
front (front) m. front ;face,etc
froterować (fro-te-ró-vach) v.
rub ; polish; wax (floors)
frunąć (froo-nownch) v. fly
away ; fly about; flee
frymarczyć (fri-mar-chich) v.
barter ; trade; traffic
fryzjer (friz-yer) m. barber;
hairdresser ; beautician
fujara (foo-ya-ra) m. & f. all-
thumbs; nincompoop; pan-pipe
fukać (foó-kach) v. scold
fundacja (foon-dáts-ya) f.
foundation ; endowment
fundament (foon-da-ment) m.
foundation; substructure
fundusz (foon-doosh) m. fund
funkcja (foonk-tsya) f.
function; office ; duties
funt (foont) m. pound
fura (foo-ra) f. cart; wagon
furgon (foor-gon) m. truck
furia (foor-ya) f. fury; rage
furiat (foor-yat) m. madman
furman (foor-man) m. carter
furora (foo-ró-ra) f. sensation
furtka (foort-ka) f. gate
fusy (foo-si) pl. grounds
fuszer (foo-sher) m. bungler
futerał (foo-te-raw) m.
(gun)case; holster
futro (foo-tro) n. fur
futryna (foo-tri-na) f. door-
frame ; window-frame
futrzarz (foot-zhash) m.furrier
fuzja (fooz-ya) f. fusion;
rifle ; shotgun
gabardyna (ga-bar-di-na) f.
gabardine
gabinet (ga-bée-net) m. study;
(ruling)cabinet; office
gablotka (ga-blot-ka)f.showcase
gad (gat) m. reptile;mean guy
gadać (ga-dach) v. talk; yak;
prattle ; talk nonsense
gaduła (ga-doo-wa) m. clapper
gaj (gay) m. grove
gala (gá-la) f. gala
galanteria (ga-lan-ter-ya) f.
haberdashery
galareta (ga-la-re-ta) f. jelly

galeria (ga-ler-ya) f. gallery
galimatias (ga-lee-mát-yas) m.
gibberish; hotchpotch; mess
galon (ga-lon) m. gallon
galop (ga-lop) m. gallop; run
galwaniczny (gal-va-neech-ni)
adj. m. galvanic ; voltaic
gałąź (ga-wownzh) f. branch
gałgan (gaw-gan) m. rag; rascal; good-for-nothing;scamp
gałganiarz (gaw-ga-nash) m.
ragtagman; ragpicker
gałka (gáw-ka) f. knob
gama (ga-ma) f. scale
gamoń (ga-moń) m. lout; oaf
ganek (ga-nek) m. balcony
gangrena (gan-gre-na) f.
gangrene; depravity; corruption
ganić (ga-neech) v. blame
gapa (ga-pa) f. sucker
gapic się (ga-peech shañ) v.
gape; star-gaze ; moon; stare
gapie (ga-pye) pl. gapers
garaż (ga-rash) m. garage
garb (garb) m. hunch; hump
garbarnia (gar-bar-ña) f.
tannery ; tan-yard
garbować (gar-bó-vach) v. tan
garbaty (gar-ba-ti) adj. m.
hunch-backed; humpy; uneven
garbus (gar-boos) m.=garbaty
garbić (gár-beech) v. stoop
garderoba (gar-de-ro-ba) f.
wardrobe; dressing-room
gardło (gard-wo) n. throat
gardłować (gard-wo-vach) v.
v. talk big; clamor; cry for
gardłowy (gard-wo-vi) adj. m.
guttural; punishable by death
gardzić (gár-dźheech)v. scorn;
despise; have in contempt
gardziel (gar-dźhel) f. throat;
fauces; choke; gorge; jaws
garnąć (gar-nownch) v. gather
garncarz (garn-tsash) m. potter
garnek (gar-nek) m. pot; potful
garnirować (gar-ñee-ro-vach) v.
garnish; trim (a dress etc.)
garnitur (gar-ñee-toor) m. set;
suit; suite; assortment
garnizon (gar-ñee-zon) m.
garrison

garnuszek (gar-noo-shek) m. cup
garstka (garst-ka) f. handful
garsć (garshch) f. handful
gasic (ga-sheech) v. extinguish; quench ; put out;eclipse
gasnąc (gas-nownch) v. die out
gaśnica (gash-nee-tsa) f.
 fire-extinguisher
gastronomiczny (gas-tro-no-
 meech-ni) adj. m. gastronomic
gastryczny (gas-trich-ni)
 adj. m. gastric
gatunek (ga-too-nek) m. kind;
 quality; sort; class; species
gawęda (ga-van-da) f. chat
gawiedz (ga-vyedzh) f. mob;
 rabble ; populace; gaping crowd
gawron (ga-vron) m. rook
gaz (gas) m. gas; open throttle
gaza (ga-za) f. gauze
gazeciarz (ga-ze-chash) m.
 newspaperboy ; newsstand
gazeta (ga-ze-ta) f. newspaper
gazolina (ga-zo-lee-na) f.
 gasoline; gasolene: petrol
gazomierz (ga-zo-myesh) m.
 gas-meter
gazownia (ga-zov-na) f. gas-
 plant; gas works
gaznik (gazh-neek) m. carburet-
 or
gaza (ga-zha) f. wage; salary
gąbczasty (gownb-cha-sti) adj.
 m. spongy; squashy; mushy
gąbka (gownb-ka) f. sponge
gąsienica (gown-she-nee-tsa)
 f. caterpillar; band; track
gąsior (gown-shor) m. gander;
 jar; demijohn; ridge tile
gąszcz (gownshch) m. thicket
gbur (gboor) m. rude; boor
gburowaty (gboo-ro-va-ti) adj.
 m. boorish; rude ; churlish
gdakac (gda-kach) v. cackle;
 yak
gderac (dge-rach) v. grumble
gdy (gdi) conj. when; as; that
gdyby (gdi-bi) conj. if
gdyż (gdish) conj. for; because
gdzie (gdzhe) adv. conj. where
gdzie indziej(gdzhe-een-dzhey)
 adv. elsewhere

gdziekolwiek (gdzhe-kol-vyek)
 adv. anywhere; wherever
gdzie niegdzie (gdzhe-neg-dzhe)
 adv. here and there; in places
gdzies (gdzhesh) adv. somewhere; somewhere round
gejzer (gey-zer) m. geyser
gen (gen) m. (biol) gene
genealogia (ge-ne-a-log-ya) f.
 genealogy; origin
generacja (ge-ne-rats-ya) f.
 generation
generalny (ge-ne-ral-ni) adj.
 m. general ; widespread
generał (ge-ne-raw) m. general
genetyczny (ge-ne-tich-ni)
 adj. m. genetic
geneza (ge-ne-za) f. origin;
 genesis ; birth
genialny (ge-nal-ni) adj. m.
 ingenious; genial ; great
geniusz (ge-nyoosh) m. genius
geodezja (ge-o-dez-ya) f.
 geodesy
geografia (ge-o-graf-ya) f.
 geography
geologia (ge-o-log-ya) f.
 geology
geometra (ge-o-met-ra) m.
 surveyor ; land surveyor
geometria (ge-o-metr-ya) f.
 geometry ; geometry book
georginia (ge-or-gee-na) f.
 dahlia
germanski (ger-man-skee) adj.
 m. Germanic
gest (gest) m. gesture ;motion
gestykulowac (ges-ti-koo-lo-
 vach) v. gesticulate
getto (get-to) n. ghetto
gęba (gan-ba) f. mug; mouth;
 puss ; snout; muzzle; face
gęgac (gan-gach) v. cackle
gęs (gansh) f. goose
gęsl (ganshl) f. lute
gęstosc (gan-stoshch) f. density; thickness; closeness
gęstwina (gan-stvee-na) f.
 thicket; array; accumulation
giąc (gyownch)v. bow; bend
gibki (geeb-kee) adj. m.
 pliant; flexible; limber

giełda (gew-da) f. stock-
exchange; money-market
giez (ges) m. gadfly; breeze
giętki (gánt-kee) adj. m.
flexible; nimble; elastic
gigant (gee-gant) m. giant
gilza (geel-za) f. (cartridge)
case; shell; cigarette tube
gimnastyczny (geem-nas-tich-
ni) adj. m. gymnastic
gimnazjum (geem-náz-yoom) n.
high-school; middle-school
ginąć (gee-nównch) v. perish
ginekolog (gee-ne-ko-log) m.
gynecologist
gips (geeps) m. gypsum
gitara (gee-tá-ra) f. guitar
glazura (gla-zoo-ra) f. glaze
gleba (glé-ba) f. soil
glejt (gleyt) m. safe-conduct
ględzić (glan-dżheech) v. talk-
through one's hat; talk-
nonsense; twaddle; blather
gliceryna (glee-ce-ri-na) f.
glycerin
glin (gleen) m. aluminum
glina (glee-na) f. clay; loam
glista (glees-ta) f. earthworm; ascaris; nema
glob (glop) m. globe; sphere
gładki (gwad-kee) adj. m. plain;
smooth; sleek; even; level; glib
gładzić (gwa-dżheech) v. smooth;
(put to death); mangle; stroke
głaskać (gwas-kach) v. caress;
fondle; stroke; pet; tickle
głaz (gwas) m. boulder; rock
głąb (gwównp) f, depth
głąb (gwównp) m. stalk
głębia (gwánb-ya) f. depth;
deep; interior; intensity
głęboki (gwan-bó-kee) adj. m.
deep; distant; remote; intense
głębokość (gwań-bó-koshch) f.
depth; profundity; keenness
głodny (gwod-ni) adj. m. hungry
głodować (gwo-do-vach) v.
starve; hunger; lay off food
głodzić (gwo-dżheech) v. starve
(somone); underfeed; deprive
głos (gwos) m. voice; sound; tone
głosować (gwo-so-vach) v. vote

głośnik (gwosh-ńeek) m. loudspeaker; public-address system
głośno (gwósh-no) adv. loud
głośny (gwósh-ni) adj. m. loud
głowa (gwo-va) f. head; chief
głowić się (gwo-veech shań) v.
beat one's brains out; puzzle
głód (gwoot) m. hunger; famine
głóg (gwook) m. hawthorn
główka (gwoo-vka) f. pinhead;
knob; tip; top; boss; heading
głównodowodzący (gwoov-no-do-
vo-dzówn-tsi) m. commander-
in-chief
główny (gwoov-ni) adj. m.
main; predominant; foremost
głuchy (gwoo-khi) adj. m. deaf
głupi (gwoo-pee) adj. m. silly;
stupid; foolish; asinine
głupiec (gwoop-yets) m. dumb-
head; fool; idiot; loony; goof
głupota (gwoo-pó-ta) f. stupidity; imbecility; foolishness
głupstwo (gwoop-stwo) n.
nonsense; trifle; blunder
głuszec (gwoo-shets) m. grouse
gmach (gmakh) m. large building
gmatwać (gma-tvach) v. tangle;
embroil; mix up; complicate
gmerać (gme-rach) v. rummage
gmin (gmeen) m. populace
gmina (gmeé-na) f. county
subdivision; parish
gnat (gnat) m. bone (slang)
gnębić (gnań-beech) v. oppress
gniady (gńa-di) adj. m. bay
(horse); dark brown horse
gniazdo (gńaz-do) n. nest
gnić (gńeech) v. rot; decay
gnida (gńeeda) f. nit
gnieść (gńeshch) v. squeeze
gniew (gńev) m. anger; wrath
gnieździć się (gńeźh-dżheech
shań) v. nestle; cluster
gnilny (gńeel-ni) adj. m.
putrid; of rot; septic
gnoić (gno-eech) v. putrefy
gnojówka (gno-yoov-ka) f.
liquid manure; manure pit
gnój (gnooy) m. manure; dung;
stinker (vulg.); lousy bum
gnuśny (gnoósh-ni) adj. m.
sluggish; lazy; idle; listless

godło (gód-wo) n. emblem

godność (gód-nośhćh) f. dignity; name; pride; self-esteem

godny (gód-ni) adj. m. worthy

gody (go-di) n. nuptials; mating

godzić (go-dźheećh) v. reconcile; hire; square; engage

godzien (go-dźhen) adj. m.
deserving ; worth; worthy

godzina (go-dźhee-na) f. hour

godziwy (go-dźhee-vi) adj. m.
proper; suitable; just; fair

goić (go-eećh) v. heal; cure

goleń (go-leń) m. shin-bone

golić (go-leećh) v. shave

golonka (go-lon-ka) f. pig's
feet dish ; knuckle

gołąb (go-wównp) m. pigeon

gołoledź (go-wo-ledźh) f.
glazed frost ;frozen dew

gołosłowny (go-wo-swov-ni) adj.
m. unfounded; proofless; vain

goły (go-wi) adj. m. naked

gonić (go-ńeećh) v. chase; hunt

goniec (go-ńets) m. messenger

gonitwa (go-ńeet-va) f. chase

gont (gont) m. shingle

gorąco (go-równ-tso) n. heat

gorący (go-równ-tsi) adj. m.
hot; sultry; warm; hearty;lively

gorączka (go-rownch-ka) f. fever; shakes; excitement; heat

gorczyca (gor-chi-tsa) f.
mustard; charlock

gorętszy (go-ránt-shi) adj.
m.hotter; fervent; intense

gorliwiec (gor-lee-vyets) m.
zealot; ardent supporter

gorliwy (gor-lee-vi) adj. m.
zealous; keen; eager; devout

gorset (gor-set) m. girdle

gorszy (gor-shi) adj. m. worse

gorszyć (gor-shićh) v. demoralize; scandalize; shock;deprave

gorycz (go-rich) f. bitterness

goryl (go-ril) m. gorilla

gorzałka (go-zhaw-ka) f. brandy spirits ; booze; spirit

gorzeć (go-zhećh) v. be ablaze

gorzej (go-zhey) adv. worse

gorzelnia (go-zhel-ńa) f.
distillery; still

gorzki (gózh-kee) adj. n.bitter

gospoda (gos-pó-da) f. inn

gospodarczy (gos-po-dar-chi)
adj. n. economic;farm; charring

gospodarka (gos-po-dar-ka) f.
economy;housekeeping; farming

gospodarny (gos-po-dar-ni) adj.
m. economical; thrifty

gospodarstwo (gos-po-dar-stvo)
n. household; farm; possessions

gospodarz (gos-po-dash) m.
landlord; host; farmer;manager

gospodyni (gos-po-di-ńee) f.
landlady; hostess; manageress

gosposia (gos-po-śha) f.
housekeeper; maid; servant

gościć (gośh-cheećh) v. receive; entertain; treat; stay at

gościna (gośh-chee-na) f.
visit; stay at sb house

gościnność (gośh-cheen-nośhćh)
f. hospitality

gość (gośhćh) m. guest;caller

gościec (gośh-chets) m. gout;
arthritis

gotować (go-to-vaćh) v. cook;
boil; get ready; prepare

gotowość (go-to-vośhćh) f.
readiness; willingness

gotowy (go-to-vi) adj. m.
ready; done; complete;willing

gotówka (go-toov-ka) f. cash

gotyk (go-tik) m. Gothic

goździk (gózh-dźheek)m. carnation ; clove; gilly-flower

góra (goo-ra) f. mountain

góral (goo-ral) m. mountaineer

górnictwo (goor-ńeets-tvo) n.
mining; mining industry

górnik (goor-ńeek) m. miner

górnolotny (goor-no-lot-ni)
adj. m. lofty; soaring;gaudy

górny (goor-ni) adj. m. upper

górować (goo-ro-vaćh) v. prevail; excel; dominate; rise

górski (goor-skee) adj. m.
mountainous; mountain

górzysty (goo-zhis-ti) adj.
m. hilly ; mountainous

gówniarz (goov-ńash) m.
(vulg): shitass; whipster

gówno (goov-no) m. shit (vulg.)

gra (gra) f. game;sham; acting

grab (grap) m. hornbeam; hardbeam

grabarz (gra-bash) m. grave-
digger;sexton; burying beetle
grabić (gra-beech) v. rake;
plunder ; rob; sack; rake up
grabie (gra-bye) n. rake
grabież (gra-byesh) f. plunder
graca (gra-tsa) f. scraper
gracja (grats-ya) f. grace
gracować (gra-tso-vach) v.
scrape; rake; mix mortar
gracz (grach) m. player; gambler; double-dealer; sly fox
grać (grach) v. play; act;
gamble ; pretend; pulsate
grad (grad) m. hail; volley
grafika (fra-fee-ka) f. graphic
art ; graphics; art of writing
gram (gram) m. gram
gramatyka (gra-ma-ti-ka) f.
grammar; grammar book
gramofon (gra-mo-fon) m. record player; phonograph
gramolić się (gra-mo-leech
shan) v. clamber;climb
granat (gra-nat) m. grenade
granatnik (gra-nat-neek) m.
mortar ; howitzer
granatowy (gra-na-to-vi) adj.
m. navy blue ; of grenades
granda (gran-da) f. swindle
graniastosłup (gra-na-sto-
swoop) m. prism
granica (gra-nee-tsa) f. boundary; limit; border; range
granit (gra-neet) m. granite
granulować (gra-noo-lo-vach)
v. granulate
grań (gran) f. (mountain) ridge;
crest; edge; razor's edge
grasować (gra-so-vach) v. roam
about; prowl; maraud; stalk
grat (grat) m. run down furniture (or man); crock; trash
gratis (gra-tees) adv. free of
charge; something given free
gratka (grat-ka) f. windfall
gratulacja (gra-too-lats-ya)
f. congratulations;felicitation
grawer (gra-ver) m. engraver
grawitacja (gra-vee-tats-ya)
f. gravitation
grdyka (grdi-ka) f. Adam's
apple

grecki (grets-kee) adj. m.
Greek
gremialnie (grem-yal-ne) adv.
in-a-mass; completely;altogether
grobla (grob-la) f. dike; dam
grobowiec (gro-bov-yets) m.
tomb ; sepulchre ;family vault
grobowy (gro-bo-vi) adj. m.
grave; deathly; gloomy;dismal
groch (grokh) m. pea; pea plant
grom (grom) m. thunderclap
gromada (gro-ma-da) f. crowd;
throng; community; team
gromadzić (gro-ma-dźheech) v.
amass; hoard; gather;attract
gromić (gro-meech) v. storm;
rout ; reprimand; defeat
grono (gro-no) n. bunch of
grapes ; cluster; group;body
gronostaj (gro-no-stay) m.
ermine
grosz (grosh) m. penny (copper)
groszek (gro-shek) m. green
pea(s) ; spotted pattern
grot (grot) m. dart; spike
grota (gro-ta) f. grotto; care
groza (gro-za) f. dread; horror
grozić (gro-źheech) v. threaten
groźba (groźh-ba) f. threat
grób (groop) m. grave : tomb
gród (groot) m. (fortified) town
gródz (groodźh) f. bulkhead
grubiański (groob-yan-skee)
adj. m. rude ; coarse; obscene
grubość (groo-boshch) f. thickness ; girth; size; grist
gruby (groo-by) adj. m. thick;
fat; stout; big;low-pitched
gruchotać (groo-kcho-tach) v.
shatter ; batter; rattle;crash
gruczoł (groo-chow) m. gland
gruda (groo-da) f. lump; clod
grudzień (groo-dźhen) m.
December
grunt (groont) m. ground; soil
grupa (groo-pa) f. group ; class
grusza (groo-sha) f. pear-tree
gruz (groos) m. rubble; ruins
gruzeł (groo-zew) m. clot
gruzy (groo-zi) pl. debris
gruźlica (groozh-lee-tsa) f.
tuberculosis; consumption

gryka (gri-ka) f. buckwheat
grymas (gri-mas) m. grimace
grypa (gri-pa) f. flu;influenza
grysik (gri-sheek) m. grits
gryzoń (gri-zoń) m. rodent
gryźć (griżhch) v. bite;torment
grzać (gzhach) v. warm;thrash
;fire;
grządka (gzhownd-ka) f. flower
bed ; patch ; (hen-)roost
grzaść (gzhownshch) v. wade
grząski (gzhown-skee) adj. m.
quaggy; slimy; slushy; miry
grzbiet (gzhbyet) m. back;
spine ; ridge; butt; edge;rib
grzebać (gzhe-bach) v. bury;
rummage; dig;rake up; fumble
grzebień (gzhe-byeń) m. comb;
crest of a wave; ridge;teaser
grzech (gzhekh) m. sin; fault
grzechotka (gzhe-khot-ka) f.
rattle; flapper; clapper
grzechotnik (gzhe-khot-ńeek)
m. rattlesnake
grzeczność (gzhech-noshch) f.
politeness; favor; attentions
grzęznąć (gzhanz-nownch) v.
get stuck;wade; flounder;sink
grzmiący (gzhmyown-tsi) adj. m.
thundering; booming;fulminatory
grzmot (gzhmot) m. thunder; hag
grzyb (gzhip) m. mushroom;
fungus; snuff
grzywa (gzhi-ya) f. mane
grzywna (gzhiv-na) f. fine
gubernator (goo-ber-na-tor) m.
governor(general)
gubić (goo-beech) v. loose;ruin
gula (goo-la) f. knob; bump
gulasz (goo-lash) m. meat soup
gulgotać (gool-go-tach) v.
gurgle; bubble; gobble
guma (goo-ma) f. rubber
gumno (goom-no) n. barn (yard)
gust (goost) m. taste; palate
guz (goos) m. bump; tumor
guzdrać się (gooz-drach shań) v.
dawdle; dally; waste time;lag
gwałcic (gvaw-cheech) v. rape;
violate; compel; coerce;force
gwałt (gvawt) m. rape; outrage
gwałtowny (gvaw-tov-ni) adj.
m. 1. outrageous 2. urgent

gwar (gvar) m. hum; noise
gwara (gva-ra) f. dialect;
slang; jargon; lingo; cant;
patter; colloquial language
gwarancja (gva-ran-tsya) f.
warranty; guarantee; pledge
gwardia (gvar-dya) f. guard
gwarny (gvar-ni) adj. m. noisy
gwarzyć (gva-zhich) v. chat
gwiazda (gvyaz-da) f. star
gwint (gveent)m.thread (mech.)
gwintować (gveen-to-vach) v.
cut thread ; tap; rifle
gwizd (gveezt) m. whistle
gwoli (gvo-lee) conj. for the
sake of ; because of;in order
gwóźdź (gwoożhdżh) m. nail to
gzyms (gzims) m. molding
cornice; mantelpiece
habit (kha-bit) m. monk's
frock ; habit ; nun's frock
haczyk (kha-chik) m. small
hook ; barb; snag; catch
hafciarka (haf-char-ka) f.
embroideress
haft (khaft) m. embroidery
haftka (kháft-ka) f. clasp
hak (khak) m. hook ; clamp
hala (kha-la) f. (sports) hall
halka (khál-ka) f. petticoat
halny wiatr (hal-ni vyatr)
Tatra wind (foehn)
halucynacja (kha-loo-tsi-nats-
ya) f. hallucination
hałas (kha-was) m. noise; din
hałasować (kha-wa-so-vach) v.
make noise ; be noisy
hałastra (kha-was-tra) f. mob;
rabble; riff-raff; ragtag mob
hałaśliwy (kha-wash-lee-vi)
adj. m. noisy ; loud; rowdy
hamak (kha-mak) m. hammock
hamować (kha-mo-vach) v.apply
brakes; restrain; hamper;curb
hamulec (kha-moo-lets) m. brake
hamulec ręczny (kha-moo-lets
rańch-ni) handbrake
handel (khandel) m. commerce
handlarz (khand-lash) m. merchant;shopkeeper; peddler
handlować (khan-dlo-vach) v.
trade; deal; be in business

hangar (khán-gar) m. hangar

haniebny (kha-ńéb-ni) adj. m. disgraceful; dirty; foul; vile

hańba (khań-ba) f. disgrace

hańbić (khań-beech) v. disgrace

haracz (khá-rach) m. tribute

harcerstwo (khar-tsér-stvo) n. scouting

harcerz (khar-tsesh) m. boy scout

hardy (kha-rdy) adj. m. haughty

harfa (khár-fa) f. harp

harmider (khar-mee-der) m. hullabaloo; clatter; din; row

harmonia (khar-món-ya) f. harmony; accordion; harmonics

harować (kha-ró-vach) v. toil

harpun (khár-poon) m. harpoon

hart (khart) m. fortitude; hardness; sternness; temper; grit

hartować (khar-to-vach) v. temper; harden; anneal; quench

hasać (kha-sach) v. frisk; frolic; romp; gambol; dance

hasło (kha-swo) n. password

haubica (khau-beé-tsa) f. howitzer

haust (khaust) m. gulp; swig

hazard (khá-zard) m. risk; hazard; the gaming table

heban (khe-ban) m. ebony

hebel (khé-bel) m. plane

hebrajski (kheb-ráy-skee) adj. m. Hebrew

heca (khé-tsa) f. fun; fuss

hegemonia (khe-ge-món-ya) f. hegemony

hej (khey) excl.: hey! ho!

hejnał (khéy-naw) m. trumpet-call; bugle-call; reveille

hektar (khék-tar) m. hectare

hełm (khewm) m. helmet; dome

hemoroidy (khe-mo-róy-di) pl. piles; hemorrhoids

hen (khen) adv. far; away

herb (kherp) m. coat-of-arms

herbaciarnia (kher-ba-chár-ńa) f. teahouse

herbata (kher-bá-ta) f. tea

herbatnik (kher-bát-ńeek) m. biscuit

heretyk (khe-ré-tik) m. heretic

herezja (khe-réz-ya) f. heresy

hermetyczny (kher-me-tích-ni) adj. m. air-tight; hermetic

heroiczny (khe-ro-eéch-ni) adj. m. heroic

heroizm (khe-ró-eezm) m. heroism

herszt (khersht) m. ringleader

het (khet) adv. far; away

hetman (khét-man) m. commander

hiacynt (khyá-tsint) m. hyacinth

hiena (khee-é-na) f. hyena

hierarchia (khye-rár-khya) f. hierarchy

hieroglif (khye-ró-gleef) m. hieroglyph; illegible writing

higiena (khee-ǵe-na) f. hygiene; sanitation; hygienics

hinduski (kheen-doos-kee) adj. m. Hindu

hiperbola (khee-per-bó-la) f. hyperbola; hyperbole

hipnotyczny (kheep-no-tích-ni) adj. m. hypnotic; mesmeric

hipochondryk (khee-po-khón-drik) m. hypochondriac

hipokryta (khee-po-krí-ta) m. hypocrite; pretender; dissembler

hipopotam (khee-po-pó-tam) m. hippopotamus

hipoteka (khee-po-téka) f. title; mortgage; records office

hipoteza (khee-po-té-za) f. hypothesis; assumption

histeria (khees-ter-ya) f. hysteria; hysterical fit

historia (khees-tór-ya) f. story; history; affair; show; fuss

hiszpański (kheesh-pań-skee) adj. m. Spanish

hitlerowiec (kheet-le-ró-vyets) m. hitlerite

hodować (kho-do-vach) v. breed

hodowca (kho-dóv-tsa) m. breeder; grower; farmer; cultivator

hojny (khóy-ni) adj. m. generous; lavish; liberal; profuse

hokej (khó-key) m. hockey

holenderski (kho-len-der-skee) adj. m. Dutch

holować (kho-ló-vach) v. tow; haul; drag; tug; haul; truck

hołd (khowd) m. tribute
hołota (kho-wo-ta) f. riffraff
honor (kho-nor) m. honor
honorarium (kho-no-rar-yoom)
n. fee; honorarium
horda (khor-da) f. horde; throng
horrendalny (kho-ren-dal-ni)
adj. m. awful; horrible
hormon (khor-mon) m. hormone
horoskop (kho-ros-kop) m.
horoscope ; prophesy ;prospect
horyzont (kho-ri-zont) m.hor-
izon; vistas; prospects
hotel (kho-tel) m. hotel
hoży (kho-zhi) adj. m. brisk;
handsome; comely; fresh
hrabia (khrab-ya) m. count
hrabina (khra-bee-na) f.
countess
hrabianka (khra-byan-ka) f.
countess (miss)
hrabstwo (khrab-stwo) n. county
hreczka (khrech-ka) f. buckwheat
hreczkosiej (khrech-ko-shey)
m.country bumpkin
hubka (khoob-ka) f. tinder
huczec (khoo-chech) v. roar
hufnal (khoof-nal) m. horseshoe nail
huk (khook) m. bang; roar
hulac (khoo-lach) v. carouse;
riot; make merry; run wild
hulajnoga (khoo-lay-no-ga) f.
scooter (without motor)
hulaka (khoo-la-ka) m. carous-
er; debaucher; rioter: rake
hulanka (khoo-lan-ka) f. riot;
debauch ; junket: carouse;revel
hultaj (khool-tay) m. libertine;
rascal; rogue
humanista (khoo-ma-nees-ta) m.
humanist ; classical scholar
humanitarny (khoo-ma-nee-tar-
ni) m. humane ; humanitarian
humor (khoo-mor) m. humor
hura (khoo-ra) f. hurrah !
cheers ! long live !
huragan (khoo-ra-gan) m. hurricane ; cyclone
hurmem (khoor-mem) adv. in
swarms ; in a mass; altogether

hurt (khoort) m. wholesale
humus (khoo-moos) m. humus
husarz (khoo-sash) m. Polish
winged-armor cavalryman (hist.)
hustać (khoosh-tach) v. swing;
rock; dandle; toss up and down
hustawka (khoosh-tav-ka) f.
swing ; seesaw ; swing boat
huta (khoo-ta) f. metal or
glass mill; smelting works
hutnik (khoot-neek) m. metal
or glass(man)worker ;metalurgist
hycel (khi-tsel) m. dogcatcher;
rascal; good for nothing
hydrant (khid-rant) m. hydrant
hydraulika (khi-drau-lee-ka)
f. hydraulics ; plumbing
hymn (himn) m.anthem; hymn
i (ee) conj. and; also; too
ichtiologia (eekh-tyo-log-ya)
f. ichthyology
idea (ee-de-a) f. idea; aim
idealista (ee-de-a-lees-ta) m.
idealist ; dreamer; visionary
idealny (ee-de-al-ni) adj. m.
ideal ; perfect; visionary
identyczny (ee-den-tich-ni)
adj. m. identical; similar
ideologia (ee-de-o-log-ya) f.
ideology ; world view
idiosynkrazja (ee-dyo-sin-kraz-
ya) f. idiosyncrasy
idiota (ee-d-yo-ta) m. idiot
idiotka (eed-yot-ka) f. idiot
iglaste drzewo (ee-glas-te
dzhe-vo) m. coniferous tree
iglica (eeg-lee-tsa) f. spire
igła (eeg-wa) f. needle
ignorancja (eeg-no-ran-tsya) f.
ignorance; lack of knowledge
igrac (eeg-rach) v. play; trifle
igrzysko (ee-gzhis-ko) n.
spectacle (games); contest
ikra (eek-ra) f. spawn; roe
ile (ee-le) adv. how much
ilekroc (ee-le-kroch) adv.
every time; whenever ; when
iloczas (ee-lo-chas) m. quantity (of a vowel or syllable)
iloczyn (ee-lo-chin) m. (multiplication) product
iloraz (ee-lo-raz) m. (division)
quotient

ilościowy (ee-losh-cho-vi)adj.
m. quantitative; numerical
ilość (ee-loshch) f. quantity
iluminacja (ee-loo-mee-nats-ya)
f. illumination; floodlight
ilustracja (ee-loos-trats-ya)
f. illustration; figure;picture
iluzja (ee-looz-ya) f. illusion
ił (eew) m. loam
im (eem) conj. the more...
imać (ee-mach) v. size upon
imadło (ee-mad-wo) n . (shop)
vice ; chuck; holder ; vise
imaginacja (ee-ma-gee-nats-ya)
f. imagination; empty fancy
imbir (eem-beer) m. ginger
imbryk (eem-brik) m. teapot
imieniny (ee-mye-nee-ni) n.
name-day; name-day party
imiennie (ee-myen-ne) adv. by
name; personally; individually
imiennik (ee-myen-neek) m.
namesake
imiesłów (ee-mye-swoov) m.
participle
imię (ee-myan) n. name (given)
imigracja (ee-mee-grats-ya) f.
immigration; the immigrants
imigrant (ee-mee-grant) m.
immigrant;foreign settler
imigrować (ee-mee-gro-vach) v.
immigrate;settle in a new land
imitacja (ee-mee-tats-ya) f.
imitation; counterfeit; fake
imitować (ee-mee-to-vach) v.
imitate; mimic; simulate
impas (eem-pas) m. deadlock
imperialista (eem-per-ya-lees-
ta) m. imperialist
imperium (eem-per-yoom) n.
empire
impertynent (eem-per-ti-nent) m.
arrogant; pert,impertinent man
impet (eem-pet) m. impetus
imponować (eem-po-no-vach) v.
impress; impose on sb; dazzle
import (eem-port) m. import
impregnować (eem-preg-no-vach)
v. impregnate; make waterproof
impreza (eem-pre-za) f. enterprise; spectacle; show; stunt
improwizować (eem-pro-vee-zo-
vach) v. improvise; extemporize

impuls (eem-pools) m. impulse
inaczej (ee-na-chey) adv. otherwise; differently; unlike
inauguracja (ee-na-goo-rats-ya)
f. inauguration; opening
inaugurować (ee-na-goo-ro-vach)
v. inaugurate; initiate
in blanko (een-blan-ko) adv.
in blank; blank check
incydent (een-tsi-dent) m.
incident; happening; event
indagacja (een-da-gats-ya) f.
investigation; questioning
indeks (een-deks) m. index
indemnizacja (een-dem-nee-
zats-ya) f. indemnity
indukcja (een-dook-tsya) f.
induction; generalized reasoning
indyk (een-dik) m. turkey
indyczka (een-dich-ka) f.
turkey-hen
indywidualny (een-di-vee-doo-
al-ni) adj. m. individual
inercja (een-erts-ya) f. inertia; inaction; inertness
infekcja (een-fekts-ya) f.
infection; contamination
infiltracja (een-feel-trats-ya)
f. infiltration
inflacja (een-flats-ya) f.
inflation
influenza (een-floo-en-za) f.
influenza; flu; grippe
informacja (een-for-mats-ya) f.
information ; intelligence;news
informacyjny (een-for-ma-tsiy-
ni) adj. m. information (office)
informować (een-for-mo-vach) v.
inform; instruct; post up
ingerencja (een-ge-ren-tsya) f.
interference; meddling
inhalacja (een-kha-lats-ya) f.
inhalation; breathing in
inicjał (ee-neets-yaw) m. initial (letter); ornate letter
inicjator (ee-neets-ya-tor) m.
originator ; mover ; founder
inicjatywa (ee-neets-ya-ti-va)
f. initiative; enterprise
inkasować (een-ka-so-vach) v.
collect (money); get a blow
inklinacja (een-klee-nats-ya)
f. inclination ; liking

inkwizycja (een-kvee-zits-ya)
f. inquisition; investigation

innowacja (een-no-vats-ya) f.
innovation; novelty

innowierca (een-no-vyer-tsa)
m. dissenter; heretic

inny (een-ni) adj. m. other;
different; another (one)

inscenizacja (een-stse-nee-zats-
ya) f. putting on stage

inspekcja (een-spek-tsya) f.
inspection; review; inspectorate

inspekty (een-spek-ti) n. hotbed; glass covered frame

inspiracja (een-spee-rats-ya)
f. inspiration; breathing in

instalacja (een-sta-lats-ya) f.
installation; plumbing, etc

instalator (een-sta-la-tor) m.
plumber; fitter; electrician

instrukcja (een-strook-tsya)
f. instruction; order; training

instrument (een-stroo-ment) m.
instrument; tool; deed; appliance

instynkt (een-stinkt) m. instinct; aptitude; knack

instytucja (een-sti-toots-ya) f.
institution; establishment

insynuacja (een-si-noo-ats-ya)
f. insinuation; innuendo

integralny (een-te-gral-ni)
adj. m. integral; whole; entire

intelekt (een-te-lekt) m. intellect; intelligence; mind

intelektualista (een-te-lek-
too-a-lees-ta) m. intellectual

inteligencja (een-te-lee-gen-
tsya) f. intelligensia; intelligence; (quick) understanding

inteligentny (een-te-lee-gen-
tni) adj. m. intelligent

intencja (een-ten-tsya) f. intention; purpose; view; finality

intensywny (een-ten-siv-ni)
adj. m. intensive; strenuous

interes (een-te-res) m. inte r-
est; business; store; matter

interesowny (een-te-re-sow-ni)
adj. m. selfish; greedy

interesujący (een-te-re-soo-
yown-tsi) adj. m. interesting

internat (een-ter-nat) m. boarding school

interpretacja (een-ter-pre-
tats-ya) f. interpretation

interwencja (een-ter-ven-tsya)
f. intervention; interference

intratny (een-trat-ni) adj. m.
lucrative; profitable; paying

introligator (een-tro-lee-ga-
tor) m. bookbinder

intruz (een-troos) m. intruder

intryga (een-tri-ga) f. plot;
intrigue; machination

intuicja (een-too-eets-ya) f.
intuition; insight; feeling

intuicyjny (een-too-ee-tsiy-ni)
adj. m. intuitive

inwalida (een-va-lee-da) m.
invalid; disabled (soldier)

inwazja (een-vaz-ya) f. invasion

inwencja (een-ven-tsya) f. in-
ventiveness; invention

inwentarz (een-ven-tash) m.
inventory; stock; list

inwestycja (een-ves-tits-ya)
f. investment; capital outlay

inżynier (een-zhi-ner) m.
engineer (with college degree)

inżynieria (een-zhi-ner-ya) f.
engineering

ircha (eer-kha) f. suede-
leather; chamois; shammy

irlandzki (eer-landz-kee) adj.
Irish

irys (ee-ris) m. iris

ironia (ee-ro-nya) f. irony

irygacja (ee-ri-gats-ya) f.
irrigation; watering

irytacja (ee-ri-tats-ya) f.
irritation; vexation; chafe

iskać (eesk-ach) v. v. seek
lice; cleanse of vermin

iskra (ees-kra) f. spark

istnieć (eest-nech) v. exist

istnienie (eest-ne-ne) n.
existence; being; entity

istny (eest-ni) adj. m. real;
veritable; downright; sheer

istota (ees-to-ta) f. being;
essence; gist; sum; entity

istotny (ees-tot-ni) adj. m.
real; substantial; vital

istotnie (ees-tot-ne) adv.
indeed; truly; really; in fact

iście (eesh-che) adv. indeed;
truly; really; in truth

iść (eeshch) v. go; walk

izba (eez-ba) f. room; chamber

izba handlowa (eez-ba khan-dló-va) f. Chamber of Commerce

izolacja (ee-zo-láts-ya) f. isolation; insulation; seal

izolator (ee-zo-lá-tor) m. insulator; non-conductor

izolacyjna taśma (ee-zo-la-tsiy-na táśh-ma) f. insulating tape

izoterma (ee-zo-ter-ma) f. isotherm:line of equal temperature

izotop (ee-zo-top) m. isotope

izraelicki (eez-ra-e-leets-kee) adj. m. Israeli; of Israel

izraelita (eez-ra-e-lee-ta) m. Israelite; citizen of Israel

iż (eezh) conj. that(literary)

iżby (eezh-bi) conj.m. in order that; in order to; lest

ja (ya) pron. I;(indecl.):self

jabłecznik (yab-wech-ñeek) m. apple cider; apple pie

jabłko (yáp-ko) n. apple

jabłoń (yá-bwoń) f. apple tree

jacht (yakht) m. yacht

jachtklub (yákht-kloob) m. yacht club

jad (yat) m. venom; poison

jadalnia (ya-dál-ña) f. dining-room; mess; mess-hall

jadalny (ya-dál-ni) adj. m. eatable; edible; dining-

jadło (yád-wo) n. food;edibles

jadłodajnia (ya-dwo-dáy-na) f. restaurant; eating house

jadłospis (yad-wo-spees) m. menu; bill of fare

jaglana kasza (yag-lá-na ká-sha) f. millet-groats

jaglica (yag-lee-tsa) f. trachoma; viral eye infection

jagnię (yag-ñáń) n. lamb

jagoda (ya-gó-da)f. berry

jajko (yáy-ko) n. egg(small)

jajo (yá-yo) n. egg; ovum

jajko na twardo(yáy-ko na twar-do) hard-boiled egg

jajko na miękko(yáy-ko na myáń-ko) soft-boiled egg

jajecznica (ya-yech-ñee-tsa) f. scrambled eggs

jajnik (yáy-ñeek) m. ovary

jak (yak) adv. how;as;if; than

jakby (yák-bi) adv. as if; if

jakgdyby (yak-gdi-bi) adv. as if; seemingly; sort of

jaka (ya-ka) pron. f. what; which; f. jacket

jaki (ya-kee) pron. m. what; which one? that;some; like

jakie (ya-ke) pron. n. what; which=jaki(fem.& neuter)

jakiś (yak-eesh) pron. some

jakkolwiek (yak-kol-vyek) conj. though: pron. somehow;anyhow

jakkolwiek (yak-kol-vyek) adv. somehow; anyhow; however

jako (yá-ko) adv. as;by way of

jako tako(ya-ko ta-ko) adv. so-so; tolerably well

jakoś (ya-kosh) adv. somehow

jakość (ya-kośhch) f. quality

jakościowo (ya-kosh-chó-vo) adv. m. qualitatively

jakże (yák-zhe) pron. how;sure

jałmużna (yaw-moozh-na) f. alms; charity; (hist.endowment)

jałowcówka (ya-wov-tsoov-ka) f. gin; juniper-flavored vodka

jałowiec (ya-wo-vyets) m. juniper(Juniperus)

jałowiec (ya-wo-vyech) v. grow-sterile; grow unproductive

jałowy (ya-wo-vi) adj. m. barren;sterile;arid;aseptic

jałówka (ya-woov-ka) f. heifer

jama (yá-ma) f. pit; hole; den; cavity; cave; burrow; hollow

jamnik (yam-ñeek) m. dachshund

jankes (yán-kes) m. Yankee

Japończyk (ya-poń-chik) m. Japanese

japoński (ya-poń-skee) adj. m. Japanese; of Japan

jar (yar) m. canyon; ravine

jarmark (yár-mark) m. fair

jarosz (yá-rosh) m. vegetarian

jarski (yár-skee) adj. m. vegetarian; meatless

jary (ya-ri) adj. robust; vig-orous; hale; spring-

jarzębiak (ya-zháń-byak) m. sorb brandy; rowan-berry vodka

jarzębina (ya-zhän-bee-na) f.
sorb tree; rowan;rowan berry
jarzmo (yazh-mo) n. yoke
jarzyć (ya-zhich) v. sparkle;
glitter; glow; shimmer
jarzyna (ya-shi-na) f. vegetable ; dish of vegetables
jasełka (ya-sew-ka) pl. crib;
Nativity play; créche
jasiek (ya-shek) m. little
pillow ; bean; beans
jaskinia (yas-kee-ña) f. cave
jaskiniowiec (yas-kee-ño-vyets)
m. cave dweller; cave man
jaskółka (yas-koow-ka) f.
swallow; martin; harbinger
jaskrawy (yas-kra-vi) adj. m.
glowing ; showy ; vivid;extreme
jasno (yas-no) adv. clearly;
brightly; cheerfully;plainly
jasny (yas-ny) adj. m. clear;
bright ; light; shining;noble
jasnowidz (yas-no-veets) m.
clairvoyant; cristal gazer;seer
jastrząb (yas-tzhöwnp) m. fal-
kon; hawk; goshawk
jaszczyk (yash-chik) m. muni-
tion box; ammunition trailer
jaśmin (yash-meen) m. jasmine
jaśnieć (yash-ñech) v. shine;
sparkle, radiate; gleam; pale
jatka (yat-ka) f. shambles;
butcher's shop ; massacre
jatki (yát-kee) pl. shambles
jaw (yav) m. reality;v.expose
jawić (ya-veech) v. appear;show
jawny (yav-ni) adj. m. evident;
public ; open; notorious;sheer
jawor (ya-vor) m. plane tree;
maple; sycamore;sycamore wood
jaz (yas) m. weir ; milldam
jazda (yaz-da) f. ride;driving
jaźń (yazhñ) f. ego; self;
the I ; the inner man ; psyche
jąć (yownch) v. seize; begin
jądro (yown-dro) n. nucleus;
testicle; kernel; core
jąkać (yown-kach) v. stutter
jątrzyć (yown-tzhich) v. irritate; fester ;vex; embitter
jechać (ye-khach) v. ride;drive
jeden (ye-den) num. one; some

jedenaście (ye-de-nash-che)
num. eleven
jedlina (yed-lee-na) f. fir
grove; fir and spruce branches
jednać (yed-nach) v. conciliate
jednak (yed-nak) conj. however;
yet; still;but; after all;though
jednaki (yed-na-kee) adj. m.
identical; similar; equal;alike
jedno (yed-no) n. num. one; one-
jednocześnie (yed-no-chesh-ñe)
adv. simultaneously; also
jednoczyć (yed-no-chich) v.
unify; merge; join; unite
jednogłośnie (yed-no-gwosh-ñe)
adv. unanimously; in chorus
jednokrotnie (yed-no-krot-ñe)
adv. one time; once
jednostka (yed-nost-ka)f. unit;
individual;entity;measure;digit
jedność (yed-noshch) f. unity
jedwab (yed-vab) m. silk
jedynaczka (ye-di-nach-ka) f.
only daughter
jedynak (ye-di-nak) m. only son
jedynie (ye-di-ñe) adv. only;
merely; solely; nothing but
jedyny (ye-di-ni) adj. m. the
only one ; the sole; unique
jedzenie (ye-dze-ñe) n. meat;
food; victuals; feed; eats
jemioła (ye-myo-wa) mistletoe
jeleń (ye-leñ) m. stag; deer
jelito (ye-lee-to) n. intestine;
bowel ; gut
jełczeć (yew-chech) v. grow-
rancid :become rancid
jeniec (ye-ñets)m. captive
jerzyna (ye-zhi-na) f. blackberry
jesień (ye-sheñ) f. autumn;
fall; the fall of the leaf
jesienny (ye-shen-ni) adj. m.
autumnal; of autumn
jesion (ye-shon) m. ash tree
jesionka (ye-shon-ka) f. fall
overcoat; light overcoat
jesiotr (ye-shotr) m. sturgeon
jestestwo (yes-tes-tvo) m.
being ; nature; creature
jeszcze (yesh-che) adv. still;
besides; more; yet; way back

jeść (yeshch) v. eat; feed sb
jeśli (yesh-lee) conj. if
jezdnia (yézd-ña), f. roadwav
jezuita (ye-zoo-ee-ta) m. Jesuit: member of Jesuit Order
jeździec (yeźh-dżhets) m.
horseman; rider; equestrian
jeż (yesh) m. porcupine
jeżdżenie (yezh-dzhé-ńe) n.
riding; driving; tyrannizing
jeżeli (ye-zhé-lee) conj. if
jeżyć się (yé-zhich shäñ) v.
bristle up; stand on end
jeżyna (ye-zhí-na) f. blackberry; blackberry bush;bramble
jęczeć (yäñ-chech) v. moan;
groan; wail; whine;complain
jęczmień (yänch-myeñ) m. barley
jędrny (yändr-ni) adj. m. firm;
robust; strong; terse; pithy
jędza (yäñ-dza) f. witch; shrew
jęk (yäñk) m. groan; moan; wail
jęknąć (yäñk-nownch) v. moan;
groan; whine; bellyache(once)
język (yäñ-zik) m. tongue
jod (yod) m. iodine
jodła (yód-wa)f.fir tree; spruce
jodyna (yo-dí-na) f. tincture
of iodine; iodine
jon (yon) m. ion
jowialny (yo-vyal-ni) adj. m.
jovial; debonair; genial
jubiler (yoo-bee-ler) m. jeweler (store or profession)
jubileusz (yoo-bee-lé-oosh) m.
jubilee; anniversary
jucht (yoo-kht) m. Russian
leather: water-proof leather
juczny koń (yooch-ni koñ) adj.
m. pack-horse: beast of burden
judzić (yoo-dżheech)v.instigate
juki (yoo-kee) pl. packsaddle
junak (yoo-nak) m. brave; swaggerer; dashing fellow,
jurysdykcja (yoo-ris-dík-tsya)
f. jurisdiction;legal authority
juta (yoo-ta) f. jute;jute plant
jutro (yoo-tro) adv. tomorrow
jutrzejszy (yoo-tshéy-shi) adj.
m. tomorrow's : future
jutrzenka (yoo-tzhén-ka) f.
day-break; morning star; dawn

już (yoozh) conj. already;
at any moment; by now;no more
jużci (yoozh-chee) conj. of
course; certainly;sure thing!
kabalarka (ka-ba-lar-ka) f.
fortune teller (by cards)
kabała (ka-bá-wa) f. cabbala
kabaret (ka-bá-ret) m. cabaret
kabel (ká-bel) m. cable
kabestan (ka-bé-stan) m. cap-
stan; winch; windlass
kabina (ka-bée-na) f. cabin
kabłąk (kab-wówñk) m. bow;hoop
kabotyn (ka-bó-tin) m. poser;
buffoon; second-rate actor
kabriolet (ka-bryó-let) m.
convertible car; gig
kabza (káb-za) m. purse
kac (kats) m. hangover
kacerz (ká-tsesh) m. heretic
kacet (ká-tset) m. Nazi con-
centration camp
kaczka (kách-ka) f. duck
kaczor (ká-chor) m. drake
kadłub (kád-woop) m. trunk;
hull; fuselage; framework
kadra (kád-ra) f. staff; cadre
kadzić (ká-dżheech)v. incense;
flatter; fart (vulg.)
kadzidło (ka-dżheéd-wo)n.
incense; fragrance;frankincense
kadź (kadżh) f. tub; tubful
kafar (ká-far) m. piledriver
kafel (ká-fel) m. tile (ceramic)
kaftan (káf-tan) m. jacket
kaftan bezpieczeństwa (káf-tan
bez-pye-cheñ-stva) m. straight
jacket ;"waistcoat"
kaftanik (kaf-tá-ñeek) m. bodice; vest;jacket; caftan
kaganiec (ka-gá-ñets) m. muzzle;
torch ; oil lamp; lamp; cresset
kajać się (káy-ach shäñ) v.
repent; confess with contrition
kajak (ka-yak) m. kayak;canoe
kajdany (kay-dá-ni) pl. hand-
cuffs;shackles; chains; bonds
kajuta (ka-yoo-ta) f. ship-
cabin; living qvarter at sea
kajzerka (kay-zér-ka) f. fancy
roll of bread ; kaiser roll
kakao (ka-ká-o) n. cacao

kaktus (kák-toos) m. cactus
kalać (ká-lać) v. pollute;
foul up; stain;befoul; sully
kalafior (ka-lá-fyor) m. cauliflower ; form of snow
kalarepa (ka-la-ré-pa) f.
turnip-cabbage; kohlrabi
kalectwo (ka-léts-tvo) n. disability; lameness; cripplehood
kaleczyć (ka-le-chích) v. wound;
mutilate; hurt; injure;cripple
kalejdoskop (ka-ley-dós-kop) m.
kaleidoscope; medley;miscellany
kaleka (ka-lé-ka) m; f. cripple
kalendarz (ka-lén-dash) m.
calendar; almanach
kalesony (ka-le-só-ni) pl.
underware;drawers;under pants
kalina (ka-lée-na) f. guelder-
rose; cranberry shrub (tree)
kalka (kál-ka) f. carbon paper
kalkulacja (kal-koo-láts-ya) f.
calculation; computation
kalkulować (kal-koo-ló-vach) v.
calculate; compute; work out
kaloria (ka-lór-ya) f. calorie
kaloryfer (ka-lo-rí-fer) m.
radiator; steam heater; heater
kalosz (ká-losh) m. rubber
overshoe; galosh; rubber boot
kalumnia (ka-loom-ńa) f.
calumny; slander; aspersion
kalwin (kál-veen) m. Calvinist
kał (káw) m. excrement; stool
kałamarz (ka-wá-mash) m. ink-
stand; ink bottle; ink pot
kałuża (ka-woo-zha) f. puddle
kamelia (ka-mél-ya) f. camellia
kameralna muzyka (ka-me-rál-na
moo-zi-ka) chamber music
kamerdyner (ka-mer-dí-ner) m.
butler ; valet (de chambre)
kamerton (ka-mér-ton) m.
tuning-fork"U", shaped
kamfora (kam-fó-ra) f. camphor
kamgarn (kám-garn) m. worsted
kamienica (ka-mye-ńée-tsa) f.
apartment house; tenants
kamienieć (ka-mye-ńéch) v.
petrify; turn into stone
kamieniołom (ka-mye-ńó-wom) f.
quarry; stone pit

kamień (ká-myeń) m. stone
kamizelka (ka-mee-zél-ka) f.
waistcoat; vest; camisole
kampania (kam-pá-ńa) f. campaign ; drive(promotional)
kamrat (kám-rat) m. chum
kamyk (kám-ik) m. pebble
kanadyjski (ka-na-díy-skee) adj.
m. Canadian ; of Canada
kanalia (ka-nál-ya) f. scoundrel
kanalizacja (ka-na-lee-záts-ya)
f. sewers ;sanitation; drainage
kanał (ká-naw) m. channel; dyke;
sewer; duct; ditch; conduit;tube
kanapa (ka-ná-pa) f. sofa
kanapka (ka-náp-ka) f. sandwich; small size sofa
kanarek (ka-ná-rek) m. canary
kancelaria (kan-tse-lár-ya) f,
office: chancellery; archives
kancerować (Kan-tse-ró-vach) v.
damage: mangle; lacerate; hack
kanciarz (kán-chash) m. swindler; trickster ; con man
kanciasty (kan-chá-sti) adj.
m. angular; awkward: stiff
kanclerz (kán-tslesh) m.
chancellor(chief of government)
kandelabr (kan-dé-labr) m.
chandelier; street lamp
kandydat (kan-di-dat) m. candidate; applicant; aspirant
kangur (kán-goor) m. kangaroo
kanon (ká-non) m. canon (priest)
kanonierka (ka-no-ńér-ka) f.
gunboat; patrol boat
kanonik (ka-nó-ńeek) m. canon
(priest); monsignor; prelate
kanonizować (ka-no-ńee-zó-vach)
v. canonize ; glorify
kant (kant) m. edge; crease;
swindle; trick; racket; chant
kantar (kán-tar) m. halter
kantor (kán-tor) m. office;
counter; counting office
kantyna (kan-ti-na) f. canteen
kanwa (kán-va) f. canvas
kapa (ká-pa) f. bedspread;cover
kapać (ká-pach) v. dribble;
trickle ; drip;fall drop by drop
kapela (ka-pé-la) f. (music)
band; choir

kapelan (ka-pé-lan) m. chap-
lain(in armed forces, hospital)
kapelusz (ka-pé-loosh) m. hat
kapilarny (ka-pee-lár-ni) adj.
m. capillary
kapiszon (ka-pée-shon) m. hood
kapitalista (ka-pee-ta-leés-
ta) m. capitalist
kapitalizm (ka-pee-tá-leezm) m.
capitalism
kapitał (ka-pée-taw) m. capital
kapitan (ka-pée-tan) m. captain
kapitulacja (ka-pee-too-lá-
tsya) f. surrender; capitula-
tion ; giving up
kapitulować (ka-pee-too-ló-
vać) v. surrender; give up
kaplica (kap-lée-tsa) f. chapel
kapliczka (kap-leéch-ka) f.
shrine; wayside shrine
kapłan (ka-pwan) m. priest
kapłon (ká-pwon) m. capon
kapota (ka-pó-ta) f. long coat
kapral (káp-ral) m. corporal
kaprys (káp-ris) m. caprice;
fad; whim; fency; freak;vagary
kaptować (kap-tó-vać) v.
win over; bring over; canvas
kaptur (káp-toor) m. hood
kapturowy sąd (kap-too-ro-vi
sownd) kangaroo court
kapusta (ka-poós-ta) f. cabbage ; a dish of cabbage
kapuś (ka-poóś) m. stool-
pigeon ; informer; police spy
kapuśniak (ka-poóś-ñak) m.
cabbage soup; drizzle;mizzle
kara (ká-ra) f. penalty; fine;
punishment; correction;nuisance
karabin (ka-rá-been) m. rifle
karać (ka-rać) v. punish
karafka (ka-ráf-ka) f. serving-
bottle; water bottle; flagon
karakuły (ka-ra-koó-wi) pl.
astrakhan sheep fur
karalny (ka-rál-ni) adj. m.
punishable ;deserving a fine
karaluch (ka-ra-lookh) m.
cockroach ; black beetle
karambol (ka-rám-bol) m. collision ; cannon; carom
karaś (ka-raśh) m. crucian

karat (ká-rat) m. carat
karawaniarz (ka-ra-vá-ñash) m.
undertaker: coffin bearer
karb (karb) m. notch; score;
crease; fold: nick; tally;curl
karbid (kár-beed) m. carbide
karbol (kár-bol) m. carbolic
acid ; phenol
karbować (kar-bó-vać) v.
notch; curl; tally; crimp;fold
karbunkuł (kar-boón-koow) m.
ulcer ; carbuncle
karburator (kar-boo-rá-tor) m.
carburetor
karcer (kár-tser) m. prison;
dark cell; detention
karciarz (kár-ćhash) m. (cards)
gambler; card player; gamester
karcić (kár-ćheeć) v. reproof;
admonish; scold; castigate
karczemny (kar-ćhém-ni) adj.
m. rude ; vulgar; coarse
karczma (kárćh-ma) f. tavern
karczoch (kár-chokh) m. arti-
choke (thistlelike plant)
karczować (kar-chóv-ać) v.
dig up (stumps); clear land
kardiografia (kar-dyo-gráf-ya)
f. cardiography
kardynalny (kar-di-nál-ni) adj.
m. fundamental; essential
kardynał (kar-di-naw) m. cardi-
nał; prince(Catholic Church)
karetka (ka-rét-ka) f. ambulance;
(prison or mail) van; chaise
kariera (kar-yé-ra) f. career
kark (kark) m. neck ; nape
karkołomny (kar-ko-wóm-ni) adj.
m. neckbreaking ; breakneck
karłowaty (kar-wo-vá-ti) adj.
m. dwarfish ; undersized
karamel (ka-rá-mel) m. caramel
karmić (kár-meećh) v. feed;
nourish ; nurse; suckle;nurture
karmin (kar-meen) m. carmine
karnawał (kar-ná-vaw) m. carnival   penally
karnie (kar-ñe) adv. in order;
karność (kár-nośhćh) f. discipline ; orderly conduct
karny (kar-ni) adj. m. disci-
plined; penal ; punitive

karo (ká-ro) n. diamonds (in cards); square cut, décolleré

karoseria (ka-ro-sér-ya) f. car body ; truck body

karp (karp) m. carp (fish)

karta (kár-ta) f. card; page; note; sheet; ticket; charter

kartel (kar-tel) m.(industrial) trust ; cartel; combine; pool

kartofel (kar-tó-fel) m. potato

kartoflanka (kar-to-flán-ka) f. potato soup; type of onion

kartograf (kar-tó-graf) m. cartographer ; map maker

karton (kár-ton) m. cardboard

kartoteka (kar-to-té-ka) f. card index ; file

karuzela (ka-roo-zé-la) f. merry-go-round ; carousel

kary koń (ká-ri koń)m.black horse; horse of black color

karygodny (ka-ri-gód-ni) adj. m. unpardonable ; guilty;gross

karykatura (ka-ri-ka-too-ra) f. cartoon ; caricature;parody

karykaturzysta (ka-ri-ka-too-zhís-ta) m. cartoonist

karzeł (ká-zhew) m. dwarf

kasa (ká-sa) f. cashier's desk; cash register; ticket office

kasjer (kás-yer) m. cashier

kask (kask) m. helmet ; tin hat

kaskada (kas-ká-da) f. cascade

kasować (ka-só-vach) v. cancel

kasta (kás-ta) f. caste

kastrować (kas-tro-vach) v. castrate; geld

kasyno (ka-sí-no) n. casino; club ; mess-hall; mess room

kasza (ká-sha) f. grits; groats; cereals ; gruel; porridge;mess

kaszel (ká-shel) m. cough

kaszkiet (kásh-ket) m. cap

kasztan (kásh-tan) m. chestnut

kat (kat) m. executioner

katafalk (ka-tá-falk) m. bier

kataklizm (ka-ták-leezm) m. cataclysm ; disaster; calamity

katalizator (ka-ta-lee-zá-tor) m. catalyst

katalog (ka-tá-lok) m. catalog

katar (ká-tar) m. headcold ; running nose ; catarrh

katarakta (ka-ta-rák-ta) f. cataract; opaque eye lens

kataryniarz (ka-ta-ri-ńash) m. organ grinder

katarynka (ka-ta-rín-ka) f. barrel organ; street organ

katastrofa (ka-tas-tró-fa) f. catastrophe ; disaster; crash

katecheta (ka-te-khé-ta) m. teacher of catechism

katedra (ka-té-dra) f. pulpit; univ. dept. chair; cathedral

kategoria (ka-te-gór-ya) f. category; division; class

kategoryczny (ka-te-go-rich-ni) adj. m. absolute; categorical

katoda (ka-tó-da) f, cathode

katolicki (ka-to-leets-kee) adj. m. Catholic

katować (ka-tó-vach) v. torture; beat cruelly; hack

kaucja (káw-tsya) f. bail; deposit; security; recognizance

kauczuk (káw-chook) f. India natural rubber; caoutchouc

kaukaski (kaw-kás-kee) adj. m. Caucasian; of Caucasus

kawa (ká-va) f. coffee

kawaler (ka-vá-ler) m. bachelor; suitor; beau; cavalier

kawaleria (ka-va-lér-ya) f. cavalry ; young folks

kawalkada (ka-val-ká-da) f. cavalcade

kawał (ká-vaw) m. piece; joke; cheat; lump; funny business

kawałek (ka-vá-wek) m. bit; morsel; scrap; chunk;1000zł.

kawiarnia (kav-yár-ńa) f. café

kawior (káv-yor) m. caviar

kawka (káv-ka) f. jackdaw

kawon (ká-von) m. watermelon

kawowy (ka-vó-vi) adj. m. (of) coffee; coffee-

kazać (ká-zach) v. order;tell; preach; make sb. do something

kazanie (ka-zá-ńe) n. sermon

kazić (ká-żheech)v. pollute; corrupt; blemish;contaminate

kazirodztwo (ka-żhee-ródz-tvo) n. incest

kaznodzieja (kaz-no-dżhe-ya) m. preacher; evangelist

kaźń (kaźhń) f. execution,
kazdorazowy (kazh-do-ra-zó-vi)
 adj.m.every;each;every single
każdy (kázh-di) pron. every;
 each; respective; any; all
kącik (koẃn-cheek) m. nook
kąkol (koẃn-kol) m. cockle-
 weed; corn cockle
kąpać (koẃn-pach) v. bathe;soak
kąpiel (koẃn-pyel) f. bath
kąpielisko (koẃn-pye-leés-ko)
 n. resort;spa; public bath
kąsać (koẃn-sach) v. bite
kąsek (koẃn-sek) m. bit; nip
kąt (koẃnt) m. corner; angle
kątomierz (koẃn-tó-myesh) m.
 protractor ; dial-sight
kciuk (kchook) m. thumb
kelner (kél-ner) m. waiter
kelnerka (kel-nér-ka) f.
 waitress; bar maid
keson (ke-son) m. caisson
kędzierzawy (kań-dzhe-zha-vi)
 adj. m. curly; curled; fuzzy
kędzior (kań-dzhor) m. curl;
 lock; ringlet
kępa (kań-pa) f. cluster;
 holm ; hurst; clump; tuft
kęs (kańs) m. bit; mouthful
kibic (kee-beets) m. kibitzer
kibić (kee-beech) f. figure;
 waist; middle
kichać (kee-khach) v. sneeze
kiecka (kéts-ka) f. frock;
 skirt; petticoat (inelegant)
kiedy (ke-di) conj. when; as;
 ever; how soon?;while; since
kiedy indziej (ke-di een-dzhey)
 adj. some other time
kiedykolwiek (ke-di-kól-vyek)
 adv. whenever; at any time
kiedyś (ke-dish) adv. someday; in the past; once;one day
kiedyż ? (ke-dish) adv. when-
 then ? when on earth?
kielich (ke-leekh) m. goblet;
 chalice; cup; cupful; glassful
kielnia (kel-ńa) f. trowel
kieł (kew) m. tusk; canine-
 tooth; fang;cutting bit
kiełbasa (kew-ba-sa) f. sausage

kiełek (ke-wek) m. sprout
kiełkować (kew-kó-vach) v.
 sprout; germinate; spring up
kiełzać (ke-ew-zach) v. bridle
kiep (kep) m. oaf; fool; gull
kiepski (kép-skee) adj. m.
 mean; bad; poor; second-rate
kier (ker) m. (cards) hearts
kierat (ke-rat) m. thrasher
kiermasz (ker-mash) m. fair
kierować (ke-ró-vach) v.steer;
 manage; run; show the way
kierownik (ke-rov-ńeek) m.
 manager; director ;supervisor
kierunek (ke-róo-nek) m.
 direction ; course; trend;line
kiesa (ke-sa) m. purse
kieszeń (ke-sheń) f. pocket
kij (keey) m. stick; cane; staff
kijanka (kee-yan-ka) f. tadpole
kikut (kee-koot) m. stump ;stub
kilim (kee-leem) m. rug ;carpet
kilka (keel-ka) num. a few;some
kilkakroć (keel-ká-kroch) adv.
 repeatedly ;again and again
kilkakrotny (keel-ka-krót-ni)
 adj. m. repeated ;recurring
kilkudniowy (keel-koo-dńó-vi)
 adj. m. of several days
kilkoro (keel-kó-ro) num. some;
 several ; one or two; a number
kilof (kee-lof) m. pick ; hack
kilogram (kee-ló-gram) m. kilogram ; 2.2 pounds
kilometr (kee-ló-metr) m. kilometer: 3,280.8 feet
kiła (kee-wa) f. syphilis
kinetyka (kee-ne-ti-ka) f.
 kinetics; science of motion
kino (kee-no) n. cinema;movies
kiosk (kyosk) m. kiosk; booth
kipieć (kee-pyech) v. boil
kisić (kee-sheech) v. ferment
kisnąć (kees-nóẃnch) v. turn
 sour ; ferment; pickle; fug
kiszka (keesh-ka) f. intestine
kiść (keeshch) f. bunch; wrist
kit (keet) m. putty; mastic
kiwać (kee-vach) v. rock; nod;
 wag; dangle;fool dodge; jink
klacz (klach) f. mare
klajster (kláy-ster) m. glue;
 paste ; water base glue

klakson (klák-son) m. car horn

klamka (klám-ka) f. door knob

klamra (klám-ra) f. buckle; clasp; bracket; fastener;staple

klapa (klá-pa) f. lapel: valve

klapsy (kláp-si) pl. spanking

klarować (kla-ró-vach) v. clarify; filter;clear; purify

klarnet (klár-net) m. clarinet

klasa (klá-sa) f. class; classroom; rank; order; division

klaskać (klás-kach) v. clap

klasowy (kla-só-vi) adj. m. class; of classes; class-

klasyczny (kla-sich-ni) adj. m. classic; standard;conventional

klasyfikować (kla-si-fee-kó-vach) v. classify;sort; grade

klasztor (klásh-tor) m. monastery; convent; cloister

klatka (klát-ka) f. cage; crate

klatka schodowa (klát-ka skhodó-va) staircase; stairway

klatka piersiowa (klát-ka pyer-shó-va) ribcage; chest

klauzula (klaw-zóo-la) f. clause; proviso; reservation

klawisz (klá-veesh) m. (piano) key;stool pigeon; jailer

kląć (klownch) v. curse; swear

klątwa (klównt-va) f. curse; ban; excommunication; anathema

klecić (kle-cheech) v. botch

kleić (kle--eech) v. glue; stick together; fudge; shape

kleik (klé—eek) m. gruel

klej (kley) m. glue; cement

klejnot (kley-not) m. jewel

klekotać (kle-kó-tach) v. clatter; rattle; chatter; prate

kleks (kleks) m. blot;ink-spot

klepać (klé-pach) v. hammer; flatten; prattle; pat;blab;clap

klepka (klép-ka) f. stave

klepsydra (klep-síd-ra) f. hourglass; obituary notice

kleptomania (klep-to-má-ña) f. kleptomania: impulse to steal

kler (kler) m. clergy;priesthood

kleszcz (kleshch) m. tick

kleszcze (klésh-che) n. pliers; tongs; claws; pincers; nippers

klękać (klán-kach) v. kneel down; bend the knee; kneel

klęska (kláns-ka) f. defeat; disaster; calamity

klęsnąć (kláns-nównch) v. shrink; subside; go down

klient (klee—ent) m. customer

klika (klee-ka) f. clique

klimat (klee-mat) m. climate

klin (kleén) m. wedge;cotter

klinga (kleén-ga) f. (sword) blade; sabre-blade

kliniczny (klee-ñeech-ni) adj. clinic; clinic-

klinika (klee-ñee-ka) f. clinic

klisza (klee-sha) f. (photo) plate; printing plate

klitka (kleet-ka) f. cell

kloc (klots) m. log; block

klomb (klomp) m. flower bed

klon (klon) m. maple

klops (klops) m. meat loaf

klosz (klosh) m. glass cover; lamp shade; dish cover

klozet (kló-zet) m. toilet

klub (kloob) m. club; union

klucz (klooch) m. key; wrench

kluska (kloós-ka) f. boiled dough strip; dumpling

kładka (kwád-ka) f. footbridge; gangway; brow

kłaki (kwá-kee) pl. oakum; shaggy hair; matted hair

kłam (kwam) m. lie; falsehood

kłamać (kwá-mach) v. lie

kłamca (kwám-tsa) m. liar

kłaniać się (kwá-nach śhan) v. salute; bow; greet; worship

kłaść (kwaśhch) v. lay; put dawn; place; set; deposit

kłąb (kwównp) m. clew; ball

kłąbek (kwówn-bek) m. ball (of thread); hunk of yarn

kłębic się (kwán-beech śhan) v. whirl; swirl; surge; billow

kłoda (kwo-da) f. log; clog

kłopot (kwo-pot) m. trouble

kłopotać (kwo-pó-tach) v. trouble; disturb; worry

kłopotliwy (kwo-pot-lee-vi) adj. troublesome; baffling

kłos (kwos) m. (corn) ear

kłócić (kwoó-ćheećh) v. quarrel
kłódka (kwoód-ka) f. padlock
kłótliwy (kwoot-lee-vi) adj.
m. quarrelsome; cantankerous
kłótnia (kwoo-tña) f. quarrel
kłuć (kwooćh) v. stab; prick
kłus (kwoos) m. trot;jog trot
klusownik (kwoo-sóv-ñeek) m.
poacher; trespassing hunter
kmieć (kmyećh) m. peasant
kminek (kmeé-nek) m. cumin
knajpa (knáy-pa) f. tavern
knebel (kné-bel) m. gag
knocić (knó-ćheećh) v. bungle
knot (knot) m. wick;fuse;bungle
knuć (knooćh) v. plot; scheme
koalicja (ko-a-leéts-ya) f.
coalition: temporary union
kobiałka (ko-byáw-ka) f.
wicker-basket; chip basket
kobieciarz (ko-byé-ćhash) m.
ladychaser; lady's man
kobiecość (ko-byé-tsoośhćh) f.
womanhood; femininity
kobiecy (ko-byé-tsi) adj. m.
female; womanish; feminine
kobierzec (ko-byé-zhets) m.
carpet; anything like a carpet
kobieta (ko-byé-ta) f. woman
kobyła (ko-bí-wa) f. mare
kobza (kób-za) f. bagpipe
koc (kóts) m. blanket; coverlet
kochać (kó-khaćh) v. love
kochanie (ko-kha-ñe) n. love;
darling; sweetheart; affection
kochany (ko-khá-ni) adj. m.
beloved; loving; affectionate
kochliwy (kokh-leé-vi) adj. m.
easily in love; amorous
koci (kó-ćhee) adj. m. catlike
kociak (kó-ćhak) m. kitty;
lassie; lass; pinup girl
kocioł (ko-ćhov) m. kettle;
boiler; pot; encirclement
kocur (ko-tsoor) m. tomcat
koczować (ko-chó-vaćh) v. nomad-
ize; wander about;be encamped
koczownik (ko-chóv-ñeek) m.
nomad; wanderer; vagrant
kodeks (kó-deks) m. (legal)code
koedukacja (ko-e-doo-káts-ya)
f. coeducation

koegzystencja (ko-eg-zis-tén-
tzya) f. coexistence
kofeina (ko-fɛ—eé-na) f.
caffeine; alkaloid in coffee
kogut (ko-goot) m. cock ;rooster
koić (kó—eećh) v. soothe
kojarzenie (ko-ya-zhé-ñe) n.
matching ; association; union
kojarzyć (ko-ya-zhićh) v. unite;
bind; join; link; connect
kojący (ko-yóẃn-tsi) adj. m.
soothing ; comforting; balmy
kojec (kó-yets) m. coop ; pen
kokaina (ko-ka-eé-na) f.́ co-
caine; an alkaloid drug
kokarda (ko-kár-da) f. rosette;
bow ; slip-knot; knot
kokietka (ko—k ét-ka), f. flirt
kokietować (ko—ke —tó-vaćh) v.
flirt ; court; woo; coquet
koklusz (kók-loosh) m.
whooping-cough
kokos (kó-kos) m. 1. coconut
2. good business ; a grand thing
kokoszka (ko-kósh-ka) f. brood-
hen; laying hen
koks (koks) m. coke; gas coke
koksownia (kok-sóv-ña) f. cok-
ing plant ; cokery
kolaboracja (ko-la-bo-ráts-ya)
f.collaboration ; collaborators
kolacja (ko-láts-ya) f. supper
kolano (ko-lá-no) m. knee
kolarstwo (ko-lár-stvo) n.
cycling ; bicycle sport
kolarz (kó-lash) m. cyclist
kolący (ko-lóẃn-tsi) adj. m.
prickly; thorny; spiked
kolba (kól-ba) f. (rifle) butt
kolczasty (kol-chás-ti) adj. m.
barbed ; thorny; spiny
kolczyk (kól-chik) m. earring;
earmark; ear tag; eardrop
kolebka (ko-léb-ka) f. cradle
kolec (kó-lets) m. thorn
kolega (ko-lé-ga) m. buddy;
colleague; fellow worker
koleina (ko-le-eé-na) f. truck;
rut; groove; wheel trace
kolej (ko-ley) f. railroad
kolejka (ko-léy-ka) f. (waiting)
line; narrow-gage railroad; turn

kolejno (ko-léy-no) adv. by turns; one after the other

kolejny (ko-léy-ni) adj. m. next; successive; following

kolekcja (ko-lék-tsya) f. collection ; things collected

kolektywizacja (ko-lek-ti-vee-záts-ya) f. collectivization

koleżeństwo (ko-le-zhéń-stvo) n. fellowship; comradeship

kolęda (ko-láń-da) f. Christmas carol; song of joy or praise

kolędować (ko-lań-dó-vach) v. sing carols; wait a long time

koliber (ko-lee-ber) m. hummingbird

kolia (kól-ya) f. necklace

kolidować (ko-lee-dó-vach) v. collide ; interfere

koligacja (ko-lee-gáts-ya) f. (family) relationship

kolisty (ko-lées-ti) adj. m. circular ; round

kolizja (ko-leéz-ya) f. collision; clash; interference

kolka (kól-ka) f. colic

kolokwium (ko-lók-vyoom) m. oral examination; test

kolonia (ko-lón-ya) f. colony

kolonista (ko-lo-ñees-ta) m. settler; colonist; colonial

kolońska woda (ko-lóń-ska vo-da) cologne water

kolor (kó-lor) m.color;tint;hue

koloryt (ko-ló-rit) m. coloring

kolosalny (ko-lo-sál-ni) adj. m. colossal; vast;tremendous

kolportaż (kol-pór-tash) m. (paper) distribution

kolumna (ko-loóm-na) f. column

kołatać (ko-wá-tach) v. knock; rattle; beg; throb; bang;

kołczan (ków-chan) m. quiver

kołdra (ków-dra) f. quiltercover; quilt; coverlet

kolek (kó-wek) m. peg ;stake

kolnierz (ków-ñesh) m. collar

koło (kó-wo) n. wheel; circle

koło (kó-wo) prep. around; near; about; by; in vicinity

kołodziej (ko-wo-dźhey) m. wheelwright

kołowacizna (ko-wo-va-chéez-na) f. dizziness

kołować (ko-wó-vach) v. revolve; confuse ; circle; stray; whirl

kołowrotek (ko-wo-vró-tek) m. spinning-wheel; reel; winch

kołowrót (ko-wo-vroot) m. windlass ; hoist; gin; whip;turnpike

kołowy ruch (ko-wo-vi rookh) vehicular traffic

kołpak (ków-pak) m. pointed fur cap ; calpack

kołtun (kow-toon) m. hair snarl; bigot; moron; obscurant

kołysać (ko-wí-sach) v. rock; sway ; toss to and fro; roll

kołysanka (ko-wi-sán-ka) f. lullaby ; cradle song;berceuse

kołyska (ko-wís-ka) f. cradle

komar (kó-mar) m. mosquito

kombajn (kóm-bayn) m. combine

kombinacja (kom-bee-náts-ya) f. combination ;union; scheme;slip

kombinować (kom-bee-nó-vach) v. combine; speculate ; scheme

komedia (ko-méd-ya) f. comedy

komenda (ko-mén-da) f. command ; headquarters ; an order

komentarz (ko-mén-tash) m. commentary ; glossary; remark

kometa (ko-mé-ta) f. comet

komfort (kom-fort) m. comfort

komiczny (ko-meéch-ni) adj. m. comic ; amusing; funny;droll

komin (ko-meen) m. chimney

kominek (ko-mee-nek) m. fireplace ; hearth; open fire

kominiarz (ko-mee-ñash) m. chimney-sweep

komis (ko-mees) m. (on) commission sale; commission shop

komisariat (ko-mee-sar-yat) m. police station: commissariat

komisja (ko-mees-ya) f. commission; board (of inquiry etc.)

komitet (ko-mee-tet) m. committee ; board

komitywa (ko-mee-ti-va) f. intimacy ; good friendly terms

komiwojażer (ko-mee-vo-ya-zher) m. traveling salesman

komnata (kom-ná-ta) f. chamber

komoda (ko-mó-da) f. chest of
drawers ; low-boy;commode

komora (ko-mó-ra) f. chamber

komora celna (ko-mó-ra tsél-na)
customs office; custom house

komorne (ko-mor-ne) n. (appartment) rent ; rental

komórka (ko-moo-rka) f. cell

kompan (kóm-pan) m. chum ;pal

kompania (kom-pán-ya) f. company ; stock company; society

kompas (kóm-pas) m. compass

kompensata (kom-pen-sá-ta) f.
compensation; indemnity

kompetentny (kom-pe-ten-tni)
adj. m. competent; qualified

kompleks (kóm-pleks) m. complex; group;(inferiority)complex

komplement (kom-ple-ment) m.
compliment ;complement

komplet (kóm-plet) m. set

kompozytor (kom-po-zi-tor) m.
composer (of music)

kompot (kóm-pot) m. compote

kompres (kóm-pres) m. compress

kompromis (kom-pro-mees) m.
compromise ;accomodation

kompromitacja (kom-pro-mee-tá-
tsya) f. disgrace; loss of face

komuna (ko-moo-na) f. commune

komunał (ko-moo-naw) m. platitude; banality; commonplace

komunia (ko-moón-ya) f. communion;part of Catholic mass

komunikacja (ko-moo-ñee-kats-
ya) f. communication ;contact

komunikat (ko-moo-ñee-kat) m.
bulletin ; communiqué; report

komunikować (ko-moo-ñee-ko-vach)
v. inform; give news; report

komunista (ko-moo-ñees-ta) m.
communist(advocate or supporter)

konać (ko-nach) v. agonize;
expire; be dying;die(with greed)

konar (ko-nar) m. limb; branch

koncentryczny (kon-tsen-trich-
ni) adj. m, concentric

koncept (kon-tsept) m. concept;
idea; joke; plan ;brain wave

koncert (kon-tsert) m. concert

koncesja (kon-tsés-ya) f. concession; license; license to do...

koncha (kón-kha) f. shell;
lobe

kondensator (kon-den-sá-or) m.
condenser ; capacitor

kondolencja (kon-do-lén-tsya)
f. condolence ;words of sympathy

kondukt (kón-dookt) m. funeral
procession ;funeral service

konduktor (kon-dook-tor) m.
conductor (train-ticket inspector in charge of passengers

kondycja (kon-dits-ya) f.
condition; form; status

konewka (ko-nev-ka) f.
(watering) can; pot:jug:pewter

konfederacja (kon-fe-de-ráts-
ya) f. confederation; confederacy

konfekcja (kon-fék-tsya) f.
ready-made clothes (pl.)

konferencja (kon-fe-rén-tsya)
f. conference ; meeting (official)

konferować (kon-fe-ró-vach) v.
confer ;hold a conference

konfesjonał (kon-fes-yo-naw)
m. confessional

konfiskata (kon-fees-ká-ta) f.
seizure ; confiscation

konfitura (kon-fee-too-ra) f.
jam ; preserve; candied fruits

konfrontować (kon-fron-tó-vach)
v. confront ;bring face to face

kongres (kón-gres) m. congress

koniak (kó-ñak) m. brandy;cognac

koniczyna (ko-ñee-chi-na) f.
clover ; trefoil; shamrock

koniec (kó-ñets) m. end;
conclusion; tip; point ;close

koniecznie (ko-ñech-ñe) adv.
absolutely; necessarily

konieczny (ko-ñech-ni) adj. m.
indispensable ;vital;necessary

konik (ko-ñeek) m. pony

konik polny (kó-ñeek pól-ni)
grasshopper; cricket (Locusta)

konina (ko-ñee-na) f. horse-
meat; horseflesh

koniunktura (kon-yoonk-too-ra)
f. market condition ;situation

konkluzja (kon-klooz-ya) f.
conclusion ; inference

konkretny (kon-kret-ni) adj. m.
concrete; definite ;real

konkurencja (kon-koo-rén-tsya)
f. competition; rivalry;contest
konkurs (kón-koors) m. contest
konnica (kon-ñee-tsa) f. cavalry ; cavalry unit; horse
konno (kón-no) adv. on horseback ; sit astraddle ;mounted
konny (kón-ni) adj. m. mounted
konopie (ko-nóp-ye) n. hemp
konował (ko-nó-vaw) m. farrier;
quack doctor ; sawbones
konserwa (kon-sér-va) f. preserve; conservatists
konserwatorium (kon-ser-va-tór-
yoom) n. conservatory
konsola (kon-só-la) f. console
konspirować (kon-spee-ró-vach)
v. plot ; conspire; keep secret
konstatować (kon-sta-tó-vách)
v. state; ascertain ; find
konsternacja (kon-ster-náts-ya)
f. consternation ; dismay
konstrukcja (kon-strook-tsya)
f. construction;design; plan
konstruować (kon-stroo-o-vách)
v. construct;build; make
konstytucja (kon-sti-toots-ya)
f. constitution; physique
konsulat (kon-sóo-lat) m. consulate (office or term of office)
konsumować (kon-soo-mó-vách) v.
consume ; eat; drink; use up
konsylium (kon-síl-yoom) n.
consultation (usually medical)
konszachty (kon-shakh-ti) pl.
collusion; scheming
kontakt (kón-takt) m. contact
kontaktować się (kon-tak-tó-
vach śhäñ) v. contact :touch
konto (kón-to) n. account
kontrabanda (kon-tra-bán-da)
f. smuggling ;contraband
kontrakt (kon-trakt) m. contract enforcable by law
kontraktować (kon-trak-tó-vách)
v. contract; hire; engage
kontrast (kon-trast) m. contrast (pointing the differences)
kontrastować (kon-tras-tó-vach)
v. contrast ;stand in contrast
kontratak (kontr-a-tak) m.
counter-attack

kontrola (kon-tró-la) f. control; checking; check up
kontrolny (kon-tról-ni) adj.
m. of control;of supervision
kontrolować (kon-tro-lo-vách)
v. control; check; verify
kontrpropozycja (kontr-pro-po-
zits-ya) f. counterproposal
kontrrewolucja (kontr-re-vo-
loots-ya)f.counterrevolution
kontrowersja(kon-tro-vérs-ya)
f. controversy; a quarrel
kontuar (kon-too-ar) m. counter
kontur (kón-toor) m. outline
kontusz (kon-toosh) m. split-
sleeve Polish overcoat (of old)
kontuzja (kon-tóoz-ya) f. shock
kontynent (kon-ti-nent) m.
continent; mainland ;land mass
konwalia (kon-vál-ya) f. lily
of the valley ; convallaria
konwikt (kón-veekt) m. boarding school (for boys or girls)
konwój (kón-vooy) m. convoy
konwulsja (kon-vóols-ya) f.
convulsion; a fit; a spasm
koń (kóñ) m. horse; steed
koń mechaniczny (kóñ me-kha-
ñeech-ni) mechanical horsepower; horsepower
końcowy (koñ-tso-vi) adj. m.
final; terminal; last; late
końcówka (koñ-tsoov-ka) f.
ending; remainder;tail-piece
kończyć (koñ-chich) v. end;
finish; quit; be dying; stop
kończyna (koñ-chi-na) f. extremity; limb; member; leg
kooperacja (ko-o-pe-rats-ya)
f. cooperation ; acting together
koordynacja (ko-or-di-náts-ya)
f. coordination (mental&phys.)
kopa (kó-pa) threescore (60);
pile; dozens; stack
kopa siana (ko-pa śha-na) haystack ; hayrick
kopać (ko-pach) v. dig; kick
kopalnia (ko-pál-ña) f. mine
koparka (ko-pár-ka) f. excava-
tor; mechanical shovel
kopcić (kop-ćheećh) v. soot;
smoke; blacken with smoke

kopciuszek (kop-choo-shek) m.
Cinderella; drudge
kopeć (ko-pech) m. soot
koper (ko-per) m. dill; fennel
koperta (ko-per-ta) f. envelope; quilt-case;(watch-)case
kopiasty (kop-yas-ti) adj. m.
heaped; piled up;heaped(plate)
kopiec (kop-yets) m. mound;
barrow ; mound;heap; knoll
kopiować (kop-yo-vach) v. copy
kopuła (ko-poo-wa) f. dome
kopyto (ko-pi-to) n. hoof
kora (ko-ra) f. bark; cortex
koral (ko-ral) m. coral (red)
korale (ko-ra-le) pl. bead
necklace; coral beads; gills
korba (kor-ba) f. crank; winch
kordon (kor-don) m. cordon
korek (ko-rek) m. cork; fuse;
stopper; traffic jam; tie-up
korekta (ko-rek-ta) f. proof
korepetycja (ko-re-pe-tits-ya)
f. tutoring; private lessons
korespondencja (ko-res-pon-den-
tsya) f. correspondence;letters
korespondent wojenny (ko-res-
pon-dent vo-yen-ni) war correspondent; war reporter
korkociąg (kor-ko-chownk) m.
cork-screw; tail-spin; twist
korniszon (kor-nee-shon) m.
pickled cucumber; gherkin
korny (kor-ni) adj. m. humble
korona (ko-ro-na) f. crown
koronacja (ko-ro-nats-ya) f.
coronation; crowning
koronka (ko-ron-ka) f. lace
koronować (ko-ro-no-vach) v.
crown ; be crowned
korowód (ko-ro-vood) m. procession; pageant; train;difficulty
korporacja (kor-po-rats-ya) f.
corporation ; association;guild
korpulentny (kor-poo-len-tni)
adj. m. fat; corpulent; obese
korpus (kor-poos) m. body;
staff, (army) corps, etc
korsarz (kor-sash) m. pirate
kort tenisowy (kort te-nee-so-
vi) tennis court
korupcja (ko-roop-tsya) f. corruption; venality; bribery

korygować (ko-ri-go-vach) v.
correct; rectify; put right
korytarz (ko-ri-tash) m. corridor; passage-way; lobby
koryto (ko-ri-to) n. through;
river-bed; channel; chute
korzec (ko-zhets) m. bushel
korzeń (ko-zheň) m. root; spice
korzyć (ko-zhich)v. humble;
humiliate ; prostrate
korzystać (ko-zhis-tach) v.
profit; gain;enjoy a right
korzystny (ko-zhist-ni) adj.
m. profitable; favorable
korzyść (ko-shishch) f. profit
kos (kos) m. blackbird
kosa (ko-sa) f. scythe; tress
kosiarka (ko-shar-ka) f. mower
kosić (ko-sheech) v. mow; scythe
kosmaty (kos-ma-ti) adj. m.
shaggy ; hairy; fleecy
kosmetyczka (kos-me-tich-ka) f.
vanity bag ; beautician
kosmetyk (kos-me-tik) m. cosmetic : makeup(skin and hair)
kosmiczny (kos-meech-ni) adj.
m. cosmic ; outer space
kosmopolita (kos-mo-po-lee-ta)
m. cosmopolite ;cosmopolitan
kosmyk (kos-mik) m. wisp ; strand
kosodrzewina (ko-so-dzhe-vee-
na) f. dwarf mountain pine
kosooki (ko-so-o-ki) adj. m.
with slanting eyes; with scowl-
ing eyes; cross-eyed
kostium (kos-tyoom) m. suit;dress
kostka (kost-ka) f. small bone;
ankle; knuckle; die; lump
kostnica (kost-nee-tsa) f.
morgue ; mortuary ;dead house
kostnieć (kost-nech) v. grow
stiff ; ossify; freeze
kosy (ko-si) adj. m. slanting
kosz (kosh) m. basket ;Tartar camp
koszary (ko-sha-ry) pl. barracks (military); caserns
koszenie (ko-she-ne) n. mowing
koszerny (ko-sher-ni) adj. m.
kosher (clean or fit to eat)
koszmar (kosh-mar) m. nightmare ; frightening experience
koszt (kosht) m. cost ; price;
expense; charge; economic costs

kosztorys (kosh-to-ris) m.
estimate (of cost),
kosztowny (kosh-tov-ni) adj.
m. expensive ; costly;precious
koszula (ko-shoo-la) f. shirt
koszyk (ko-shik) f. small
basket ; grab bag; hilt guard
koszykówka (ko-shi-koov-ka) f.
basketball
kościany (kosh-cha-ni) adj. m.
bone ; osseous;made out of bone
kościec (kosh-chets) m. skeleton ; framework ; frame
kościelny (kosh-chel-ni) adj.
m, of church ; ecclesiastical
kościotrup (kosh-cho-troop) m.
skeleton (vulg.)
kościół (kosh-choow), m. church
kościsty (kosh-chee-sti) adj.
m. bony; angular ; rawboned
kość (koshch) f. bone ; spine
koślawić (ko-shla-veech) v.
deform ; distort; crook
koślawy (ko-shla-vi) adj. m.
crooked; lame ; lopsided
kot (kot) m. cat; pussy cat;puss
kotara (ko-ta-ra) f. curtain
kotek (ko-tek) m. kitten ;puss
kotlet (kot-let) m. cutlet
kotlina (kot-lee-na) f. dale
kotłować (kot-wo-vach) v.whirl;
seethe; surge; drive crazy
kotłownia (kot-wov-ña) f.
boiler room ;boiler house
kotwica (kot-vee-tsa) f. anchor
kotwiczyć (kot-vee-chich) v.
anchor ; lie at anchor
kowadło (ko-vad-wo) m. anvil
kowal (ko-val), m. blacksmith
kowalny (ko-val-ni) adj. m.
malleable ; ductile; forgeable
koza (ko-za)f. goat; jail
kozioł (ko-zhow) m. buck;gambol
koźlę (kozh-añ) n. kid;goatling
kożuch (ko-zhoukh) m. sheepskin
furcoat ;coating on hot milk
kół (koow) m. stake; post
kółko (koow-ko) m. small wheel;
small circle: (soc.) circle
kpiarz (kpyash) m. scoffer
kpić (kpeech) v. jeer; sneer
kpiny (kpee-ni) n. mockery ;
this is preposterous ! (exp.)

kra (kra) f. ice floe
krach (krakh) m. crash
kraciasty (kra-chas-ti) adj.
m. chequered ; grated;checkered
kradzież (kra-dzhesh) f. theft
kradziony (kra-dzho-ni) adj.
m. stolen ; robbed
kraina (kra-ee-na) f. land;
region ; province ;country
kraj (kray) m. country; verge;
edge; hem of a garment; land
krajać (kra-yach) v. cut;slice;
carve; operate; hack; saw
krajobraz (kray-ob-ras) m.
landscape; scenery painting
krajowy (kra-yo-vi) adj. m.
native; nationally made,
krajoznawczy (kra-yo-znav-chi)
adj. m. hiking, touring
krakać (kra-kach) v. croak
kram (kram) m. booth; mess;
trouble; stall; odds and ends
kramarz (kra-mash) m. huckster
kran (kran) m. tap; faucet
kraniec (kra-ñets) m. border;
edge; end; extremity; margin
krańcowy (krań-tso-vi) adj. m.
extreme; marginal; excessive
krasa (kra-sa) f. grace;
beauty; loveliness; splendor
krasić (kra-sheech) v. decorate
krasomówca (kra-so-moov-tsa) m.
orator(very eloquent)
kraść (krashch) v. steal; rob
kraśnieć (krash-ñech) v. blush;
grow beautiful; redden
krata (kra-ta) f. grate
krater (kra-ter) m. crater
krawat (kra-vat) m. (neck) tie
krawcowa (krav-tso-va) f.
seamstress ;tailor's wife
krawędź (kra-vañdzh) f. edge
krawężnik (kra-vañzh-ñeek) m.
curb(stone); roof-hip
krawiec (krav-yets) m. tailor
krąg (krownk) m. ring ; ver-
tebre; disk; range; sphere
krążek (krown-zhek) m. small
disk; potter's wheel;pulley
krążyć (krown-zhich) v. circulate; rotate; wander; stray
kreacja (kre-ats-ya) f. (dress)
creation; theatre part

kreda (kré-da) f. chalk
kredens (kré-dens) m. china
cabinet ; cupboard; buffet
kredka (kred-ka) f.crayon;
lipstick; chalk for writing
kredowy (kre-dó-vi) adj. m.
cretaceous;chalky;made of chalk
kredyt (kré-dit) m. credit
krem (krém) m. cream;custard
krematorium (kre-ma-tór-yoom)
n. crematorium ; crematory
kremowy (kre-mó-vi) adj. m.
creamcolored; cream yellow
kreować (kre-o-vać) v. create;
act; set up; institute; appoint
krepa (kré-pa) f. crape
kres (krés) m. end; limit;term
kreska (kres-ka) f. dash(line);
stroke; hatch; scar; accent
kreślić (kresh-leech) v. draw;
trace; sketch; cross out
kret (kret) m. mole ; ochemer
kretowisko (kre-to-vees-ko) n.
molehill
krew (krev) f. blood
krewetka (kre-vet-ka) f. shrimp
krewki (krév-kee) adj. m. rash;
quick-tempered; impetuous
krewny (krév-ni) m. relative
kręcić (krań-cheech) v. twist;
turn; shoot film;fuss; boss
kręcony (krań-tso-ni) adj. m.
twisted; curled;winding;spiral
kręgle (kráng-le) n. bowling
(ninepin)game of bowles;tenpins
kręgosłup (krań-gós-woop) m.
spine; vertebral column
kręgowiec (kran-gó-vyets) m.
vertebrate ;animal with spine
krepować (krań-po-vać) v. bind;
embarass; hamper; hinder
krępy (krán-pi) adj. m. stocky;
thickset; sturdy; short
kretactwo (kran-tats-tvo) n.
cheat; foul dealing; shuffle
kretacz (krán-tach) m. double-
dealer; dodger; quibbler;cheat
kręty (kran-ti) adj. m. curved;
curly; winding; tortuous
krnąbrny (krnownbr-ni) adj. m.
stubborn; unruly; restive;balky
krochmal (krokh-mal) m. starch
krochmalić (krokh-má-leech) v.
starch ; beat up; stiffen

krocie (kró-che) pl. thousands
kroczyć (kró-chich) v. stride
kroić (kró-eech) v. cut; slice
krok (krók) m. step ;pace;march
krokiew (kró-kev) f. rafter
krokodyl (kro-kó-dil) m. crocodile ; split flap (aviation)
kromka (króm-ka) f. slice
kronika (kro-ñee-ka) f.chronicle
kropić (kró-peech) v. sprinkle
kropka (króp-ka) f. dot ; point
kropkować (krop-ko-vach) v. dot
kropla (króp-la) f. drop
krosno (krós-no) n. loom
krosta (krós-ta) f. pimple
krotochwila (kro-to-khvee-la)
f. joke; burlesque; farce
krowa (kró-va) f. cow; mine
krój (krooy) m. cut; fashion
król (krool) m. king; rabbit
królestwo (kroo-les-tvo) n.
kingdom; the realms; sphere
królewicz (kroo-le-veech) m.
crown prince ; king's son
królewski (kroo-lev-skee) adj.
m. royal; king's; queen's
królik (krool-eek) m. rabbit
królikarnia (kroo-lee-kár-ña)
f. warren ; rabbit warren
królowa (kroo-ló-va) f. queen
krótki (kroot-kee) adj. m.
short; brief ;terse; concise
krótko (kroo-tko) adv. briefly;
shortly; tersely;(hold) tightly
krtań (krtań) f. larynx
kruchy (kroó-khi) adj. m. brittle;
frail; tender; crisp; crusty
krucjata (kroots-ya-ta) f. crusade ; action for some cause
krucyfiks (kroo-tsi-feeks) m.
crucifix ; cross of Jesus
kruczek (kroó-chek) m. trick
kruczy (kroo-chi) adj. m. jet-
black; raven's (color)
kruk (krook) m. raven
krupy (kroó-pi) pl. groats
kruszec (kroo-shets) m. (metal)
ore ; metal; gold; silver
kruszeć (kroo-shech) v. crumble;
grow brittle; repent
kruszyć (kroo-shich) v. crush;
crumb; destroy; shatter;disrupt

kruszyna (kroo-shí-na) f. crumb

krużganek (kroozh-gán-ek) m.
portico ; gallery;ambulatory

krwawica (krva-vee-tsa) f. hard-
won money; toil ; labor

krwawić (krva-veech) v. bleed

krwawy (krva-vi) adj. m. bloody;
bloodthirsty; bloodstained

krwiobieg (krvee-ó-byeg) m.
blood circulation

krwisty (krvées-ti) adj. m.
sanguineous; blood-red

krwotok (krvó-tok) m. hemorrhage : bleeding

kryć (krich) v. hide; conceal;
cover ;roof over;shield; mask

kryjówka (kri-yoov-ka) f.
hiding-place ; hide-out

kryminalista (kri-mee-na-lees-
ta) m. criminal, crime;thriller

kryminał (kri-mée-naw) m. prison;

krynica (kri-ńée-tsa) f. spring

krystalizować (kris-ta-lee-zó-
vach) v. crystallize ; shape

kryształ (krish-taw) m. crystal

kryterium (kri-tér-yoom) n.
criterion; touchstone; test

kryty (kri-ti) adj. m. covered

krytyczny (kri-tích-ni) adj. m.
critical; decisive; crucial

krytyk (kri-tik) m. critic

krytyka (kri-ti-ka) f. criticism; review; censure

kryzys (kri-zis) m. crisis

krzaczasty (kzha-chás-ti) adj.
m. bushy; shaggy; beetle

krzak (kzhak) m. bush

krzątać (kzhówn-tach)v. bustle

krzątanina (kzhown-ta-ńée-na)
f. bustle ; comings and goings

krzem (kzhem) m. silicone

krzemień (kzhe-myeń) f. flint

krzepić (kzhe-peech) v. brace
up; refresh; invigorate;fortify

krzepki (kzhep-kee) adj. vigorous; lusty; robust; husky

krzepnąć (kzhep-nownch) v. coagulate; gather strength

krzesać (kzhe-sach) v. strike
fire ; strike sparks

krzesiwo (kzhe-shee-vo) n.
tinder-box ; flint

krzesło (kzhés-wo) n. chair

krzew (kzhev) m. shrub

krzewić (kzhe-veech) v. spread;
propagate; teach; graft

krzta (kzhta) f. whit; bit

krztusiec (kzhtoo-shets) m.
whooping-cough

krztusić się (kzhtoo-sheech
śhań) v. choke; stifle

krzyczeć (kzhi-chech) v. shout;
cry ; scream; yell; clamor

krzyk (kzhik) m. cry; scream;
shriek ; yell; outcry; call

krzykacz (kzhi-kach) m. bawler;
crier ; shouter; agitator

krzykliwy (kzhik-lee-vi) adj.
m. noisy; clamorous; loud

krzywa (kzhi-ya) f. curve

krzywda (kzhiv-da) f. harm;
wrong ; a sense of wrong

krzywdzący (kzhiv-dzówn-tsi)
adj. m. harmful; injurious

krzywdzić (kzhiw-dźheech)v.
harm; wrong ;damage;be unfair

krzywica (kzhi-vee-tsa) f.
rickets ;rachitis;sweep saw

krzywić (kzhi-veech) v. bend

krzywić się (kzhi-veech śhań)
v. make faces; bend ; warp

krzywo (kzhi-vo) adv. crooked

krzywy (kzhi-vi) adj. m. crooked; skew; distorted;slanting

krzyż (kzhish) m. cross

krzyżować (kzhi-zhó-vach) v.
cross; thwart; crucify

krzyżówka (kzhi-zhoov-ka) f.
crossword puzzle

ksiądz (kśhownts) m. priest

książę (kśhown-zhan) m. prince;
duke; ruler of a duchy

książka (kśhównzh-ka) f. book

księga (kśhan-ga) f. register;
large book; volume; tome

księgarnia (kśhan-gar-ńa) f.
bookstore ; bookshop

księgarz (kśhań-gash) m. bookseller; owner of a bookstore

księgować (kśhan-go-vach) v.
keep-books ;enter, in the books

księgowy (kśhań-gó-vi) m. bookkeeper ; accountant

księgozbiór (kśhań-go-zbyoor)
m. book collection; library

księstwo (kshan-stvo) n. duchy

księżna (kshanzh-na) f. princess ; wife of a prince

księży (kshan-zhi) adj. m. priestly ;belonging to a priest

księżyc (kshan-zhits) m. moon

kształcić (kshtaw-cheech) v. educate ; train; form;school

kształt (kshtawt) m. form; shape ; configuration; figure

kształtny (kshtawt-ni) adj. m. shapely ; neat; nicely made

kształtować (kshtaw-to-vach) v. shape ; form; mold ; fashion

kto (kto) pron. who ; all;those

kto inny (kto een-ni) pron. somebody else ; someone else

kto bądź (kto bowndch) pron. anybody ; nayone;just anyone

ktoś (ktosh) pron. somebody

którędy (ktoo-ran-di) adv. which way, how to get there?

który (ktoo-ri) pron. who; which; that ; any; whichever

któż (ktoosh) pron. whichever

ku (koo) prep. towards; to

kubatura (koo-ba-too-ra) f. (building) volume;cubature

kubek (koo-bek) m. cup; mug

kubeł (koo-bew) m. pail;bucket

kucharka (koo-khar-ka) f. cook

kucharz (koo-khash)m. cook

kuchenka gazowa (koo-khen-ka ga-zo-va)f.(gas) hotplate

kuchnia (kookh-na) f. kitchen stove; cooking range; kitchen

kucnąć (koots-nownch)v. squat

kucyk (koo-tsik) m. small pony

kuć (kooch) v. hammer; shoe a horse; cram lessons: peck;coin

kudłaty (kood-wa-ti) adj. m. shaggy; hairy ; hirsute

kudły (kood-wi) pl. shaggy hair

kufel (koo-fel) m. beer mug

kufer (koo-fer) m. trunk

kuglarz (koog-lash) m. juggler

kukiełkowy teatr (koo-kew-ko-vi teatr) puppet-show

kukła (kook-wa) f. puppet

kukułka (koo-koow-ka) f. cuckoo bird; cuckoo clock

kukurydza (koo-koo-ri-dza) f. maize; corn; Indian corn

kula (koo-la) f. sphere; bullet crutch; ball; globe; shot

kulawy (koo-la-vi) adj. m. lame

kulbaczyć (kool-ba-chich) v. saddle (a horse)

kuleć (koo-lech) v. limp

kulić się (koo-leech shan) v. snuggle ; crouch; cringe;nestle

kulinarny (koo-lee-nar-ni) adj. m. culinary; of cooking

kulisy (koo-lee-si) pl. theatre scenes ; the inner facts; links

kulisty (koo-lee-sti) adj. m. spherical; ball-shaped

kulminacyjny (kool-mee-na-tsiy-ni) adj. m. culminant; climactic

kult (koolt) m. cult ;worship

kultura (kool-too-ra) f. culture ; good manners;cultivation

kuluar (koo-loo-ar) m. lobby

kułak (koo-wak) m. fist;punch

kum (koom) m. godfather; crony

kumoterstwo (koo-mo-ter-stvo) n. favoritism; log rolling

kumulacja (koo-moo-lats-ya) f. cumulation; merger; fusion

kuna (koo-na) f. marten

kundel (koon-del) m. mongrel

kunszt (koonsht) m. art;skill

kunsztowny (koon-shtov-ni) adj. m. artistic; artful;ingenious

kupa (koo-pa) f. heep; pile; lot; excrement; assemblage

kupczyć (koop-chich) v. bargain; trade; influence peddling

kupić (koo-peech) v. buy

kupiec (koo-pyets) m. shop-keeper; merchant; dealer

kupno (koop-no) n. purchase

kupon (koo-pon) m. coupon

kur (koor) m. cock; cock crow

kura (koo-ra) f. hen; hen bird

kuracja (koo-rats-ya) f. cure

kuratorium (koo-ra-tor-yum) n. board of trustees (of schools)

kurcz (koorch) m. cramp;shrinking

kurczę (koor-chan) n. chicken

kurczyć (koor-chich) v. shrink

kurek (koo-rek) m. tap; cock

kurier (koor-yer) m. courier

kurnik (koor-neek) m. chicken house; hen house; hen roost poultry house; hen cote kuropatwa (koo-ro-pát-va) f. partridge (game bird)

kurowac (koo-ró-vach) v. heal; cure ; treat for an illness

kurs (koors) m. course;rate;fare

kursowac (koor-só-vach)v. circulate; ferry; run; ply

kurtka (koór-tka) f. jacket

kurtyna (koor-ti-na)f. curtain

kurwa (koór-va) f. whore (vulg.)

kurz (koosh) m. dust

kurza slepota (koózha shle-pó-ta) night blindness

kusic (koo-sheech) v. tempt

kustosz (koos-tosh) m. custodian; curator ; conservator

kusy (koosi) adj. m. short

kusza (koo-sha) f. crossbow

kusnierz (koósh-nesh) m. furrier

kuter (koo-ter) m. cutter

kutwa (koót-va) f. miser

kuty (koo-ti) adj. m. forged; shod; cunning; sly; shrewd

kuzyn (koo-zin) m. cousin

kuzynka (koo-zin-ka) f. cousin

kuznia (koózh-na) f. forge

kwadra (kvád-ra)f.quarter moon

kwadrans (kvád-rans) m. quarter of an hour; fiftee minutes

kwadrat (kvád-rat) m. square

kwakac (kvá-kach) v. quack

kwalifikacja (kva-lee-fee-káts-ya) f. qualification;evaluation

kwalifikowac (kva-lee-fee-kó-vach) qualify ; class;appraise

kwapic sie (kva-peech shan) v. be eager; be in a hurry

kwarantanna (kva-ran-tán-na) f, quarantine; period of isolation

kwarc (kvárts) m. quartz

kwarta (kvár-ta) f. quart

kwartalny (kvar-tál-ni) adj. m. quarterly;occuring quarterly

kwas (kvas) m.acid; pl.discord

kwasic (kvá-sheech) v. sour; ferment; pickle;embitter;be idle

kwaskowaty (kvas-ko-vá-ti) adj. m. sourish ; acidulous

kwasy (kvá-si) pl. fusses; bad-blood; ill humor; dissent

kwasny (kvásh-ni) adj. m. sour

kwatera (kva-té-ra) f. quarters; lodging; living accommodation

kwaterka (kva-tér-ka) f. quarter of a liter; quarter liter bottle

kwesta (kves-ta) f. collection (for); passing the hat around

kwestia (kvést-ya) f. question

kwestionariusz (kves-tio-nár-yoosh) m. questionnaire

kwekac (kván-kach) v. complain

kwiaciarka (kvya-chár-ka) f. florist; flower girl

kwiaciarnia (kvya-chár-na) f. flower shop; florist's

kwiat (kvyat) m. flower

kwiczec (kvee-chech) v. squeak

kwiczol (kvee-chow) m. field-fare (Turdus pilavis)

kwiecien (kvye-chen) m. April

kwiecisty (kvye-chees-ti) adj. m. flowery; colorful; ornate

kwietnik (kvyet-neek) m. flower-bed; carpet bed

kwik (kveek) m. squeal; squeak

kwit (kyeet) m. receipt

kwitnac (kveet-nownch)v. blossom ;grow moldy;look healthy

kwitowac (kvee-to-vach) v. give receipt; relinquish; forgo

kwoka (kvó-ka) f. sitting hen

kwota (kvó-ta) f. amount (of money); amount ; allocation

kynologiczny zwiazek (ki-no-lo-geech-ni zvyown-zek) kennel club ; kennel association

labirynt (la-bee-rint) m. labyrinth; maze

laborant (la-bó-rant) m. lab. technician; assistant chemist

laboratorium (la-bo-ra-tor-yoom) m. laboratory ; lab

lac (lach) v. pour; shed; (spill)

lada (lá-da) f. counter; chest

lada (lá-da) part. any; whatever; the least; paltry

lada kto (lá-da kto) anybody

ladacznica (la-dach-nee-tsa) f. harlot; prostitute; strumpet

laik (lá-eek) m. layman

lak (lak) m. sealing wax

lakier (la-ker) m. varnish

lakmus (lak-moos) m. litmus

lakoniczny (la-ko-neech-ni) adj. m. terse; brief; curt; laconic stating much in few words

lakowac (la-kó-vach) v. seal
lalka (lál-ka) f. doll ;puppet
laktoza (lak-to-za) f. lactose
lament (la-ment) m. lament
lamowac (la-mo-vach) v. laminate
lamówka (la-moóv-ka) f. trim;
border ; edge; trimming; piping
lampa (lám-pa) f. lamp
lampart (lám-part) m. leopard
lampas (lám-pas) m.stripe;lampas
lampion (lám-pyon) m. lampion
lamus (la-moos) m.storeroom
lanca (lan-tsa) f. lance; spear
lancet (lán-tset) m. lancet ;fleam
landara (lan-dá-ra) f. jalopy;
old crate ; rumble-tumble
lanie (la-ñe) n. pouring; cast-
ing; beating ;thrashing; licking
lanolina (la-no-lee-na) f. lanolin ; wool-fat (in ointments)
lansady (lan-sá-di) pl. pranc-
ing gait ; skips; leaps; bounds
lansowac (lan-so-vach) v. launch
lapidarny (la-pee-dár-ni) adj.
m. terse; concise ;curt; crisp
lapis (lá-pees) m. silver nitrate ; lunar caustic
lapsus (láp-soos) m. lapse(slip)
laryngologia (la-rin-go-lóg-ya)
f. laryngology
las (las) m. wood; forest ;thicket
lasek (lá-sek) m. grove
laska (lás-ka) f. cane ; stick
laskowy orzech (las-kó-vi
ó-zhekh)m. hazelnut
lasowac (la-só-vach) v. slake
lata (lá-ta) pl. years
latac (la-tach)v.fly;be running
latarka (la-tár-ka) f. flashlight ; torch ; small lamp
latarnia (la-tár-ña) f. street-
light ; lantern; beacon
latarnia morska (la-tar-ña mór-
ska) lighthouse
latarnik (la-tár-ñeek) m. lighthouse keeper
latawiec (la-táv-yets) m. kite
lato (lá-to) n. Summer
latorosl (la-to-roshl) f. shoot;
offspring: scion; sprig; sprout
laubzega (lawb-ze-ga) f. fret-
saw; jigsaw; scroll saw

laufer (law-fer) m. runner;
(chess) bishop
laury (law-ri) pl. laurels
laureat (law-ré-at) m. laure-
ate ; prize-winner
lawa (lá-va) f. vulcanic lava
lawenda (la-vén-da) f. lavender ; lavender water
laweta (la-ve-ta) f. gun-
carriage ; heavy gun base
lawina (la-vee-na) f. avalanche ; shower (of words)
lawirowac (la-vee-ró-vach) v.
veer; tack; intrigue
lazaret (la-zá-ret) m. field
hospital (for infections)
lazur (lá-zoor) m. azure; sky
blue; blue pigment
ląd (lownd) m. 1. land;
2. mainland; 3. continent
lądowac (lown-do-vach) v. land;
disembark; go ashore; alight
leciec (le-chech) v. fly; run;
hurry ;wing; drift; drop; fall
leciutko (le-choot-ko) adv.
bearly touching ;very lightly
leciwy (le-chee-vi) adj. m.
up in years ;advanced in years
lecz (lech) conj. but;however
leczenie (le-che-ñe) n. healing ; cure; treatment
lecznica (lech-ñee-tsa) f. hospital; clinic ;nursing home
leczyc (le-chich) v. heal;
treat; nurse;practice medicine
ledwie (led-vye) adv. hardly;
scarcely ; barely ;almost;nearly
ledwo że nie (le-dvo zhe ñe)
adv. almost; nearly; hardly
legacja (le-gáts-ya) f. legation; legacy; bequest
legalizowac (le-ga-lee-zó-vach)
legalize; certify; attest
legalny (le-gál-ni) adj. m.
legal; lawful;allowed by law
legat (le-gat) m. bequest;
papal muncio
legawiec (le-gá-vyets) m.
pointer ; setter
legenda (le-gén-da) f. legend
legendarny (le-gen-dár-ni) adj.
m. legendary ; fabulous;storied

legia (lég-ya) f. legion
legion (lég-yon) m. legion
legitymacja (le-gee-ti-máts-ya)
f. i-d card; identification
papers; membership card etc
legitymować się (le-gee-ti-mó-
vach shán) v. prove one's
identity; identify oneself
lęgnąć (lég-nównch) v. fall
in battle; perish; lie down
legowisko (le-go-vee-sko) n.
berth; bedding; encampment; den
legumina (le-goo-mée-na) f.
dessert; sweet dish; legumin
lej (ley) m. crater; funnel
lejce (léy-tse) pl. reins
lejek (lé-yek) m. small funnel
lek (lek) m. medicine; drug
lekarski (le-kár-skee) adj. m.
medical; medicinal
lekarz (le-kash) m. physician
lekceważący (lek-tse-va-zhówn-
tsi) adj. m. disrespectful
lekceważenie (lek-tse-va-zhe-
ñe) n. disdain; disrespect
lekceważyć (lek-tse-vá-zhich)
v. slight; scorn; neglect
lekcja (lék-tsya) f. lesson
lekki (lék-kee) adj. m. light;
light-hearted; graceful; slight
lekko (lék-ko) adv. easily
lekkoatleta (le-ko-at-le-ta) m.
field&track man
lekkomyślny (lek-ko-míshl-ni)
adi. m. careless; thoughtless;
reckless; rash; fickle
lektura (lek-too-ra) f. reading
matter; reading list; reading
lemiesz (lé-myesh) m. plough-
share; blade; vomer
lemoniada (le-mo-ńá-da) f. lemonade; lemon squash
len (len) m. flax; linen;
lenić się (le-ñeech shán) v.
be idle; be lazy; shed hair
leniec (le-ñech) v. shed hair
leninizm (le-ñee-neezm) m. Le-
ninism: Lenin's interpretation
lenistwo (le-ñees-tvo) n. laziness ; idleness; sluggishness
leniwy (le-ñee-vi) adj. m. lazy
lennik (lén-ñeek) m. vassal
pledging fealty to overlord

lenno (lén-no) n. fief
leń (leñ) m. lazy-bones; idler;
lazy bum ; sluggard
lep (lep) m. glue ; flypaper
lepianka (lep-yán-ka) f. adobe;
mud hut; mud cabin
lepić (le-peéch) v. stick; glue
lepiej (lép-yey) adv. better;
rather ;(feel) better
lepki (lép-kee) adj. m. sticky
lepszy (lép-shi) adj. m. better
lesbijka (les-beéy-ka) f. les-
bian : homosexual women
lesisty (le-shees-ti) adj. m.
wooded; woody; forest-
leszcz (leshch) m. bream
leszczyna (lesh-chí-na) f.
hazelnut tree; hazel grove
leśnictwo (lesh-ñeets-tvo) n.
forestry ; forest-range
leśniczówka (lesh-ñee-choov-ka)
f. ranger's house (forester's)
leśniczy (lesh-ñee-chi) m. ranger ; forest-ranger; forester
leśnik (lesh-ñeek) m. forester
leśny (lesh-ni) adj. m. of
forest; of forestry; forest-
letarg (lé-targ) m. lethargy
letni (let-ñee) adj. m. lukewarm; half-hearted; summer
letnik (let-ñeek) m. vacationer
letnisko (let-ñees-ko) n. summer
resort; summer vacation spot
lew (lev) m. lion; lady's man
lewa (le-ya) f. left (side)
lewar (le-var) m. lever; jack
lewatywa (le-ya-ti-va) f. enema
lewica (le-vee-tsa) f. the left
(polit.) ; left-hand side
lewo (lé-vo) adv. to the left
lewy (lé-vi) adj. m. left; false
lezć (lezhch) v. crawl; creep-
along; plod along; climb; jostle
leżak (le-zhak) m. folding
(canvas) chair; deck-chair
leżeć (le-zhech) v. lie; (fit)
lędźwie (láñdzh-vye) pl. loins
legnąć (láńg-nównch) v. hatch
lęk (láńk) m. fear; anxiety; dread
lękać się (lán-kach shán) v.
be afraid; dread; stand in awe
lękliwy (láñk-lee-vi) adj. m.
timid; faint-hearted; apprehensive

lgnąć (lgnownch) v. adhere;sink;
stick; be partial; feel attracted
libacja (lee-bats-ya) f. drinking party; drinking bout
liberalny (lee-be-ral-ni) adj.
m.liberal; broad-minded
liberał (lee-be-raw) m. liberal
libertyn (lee-ber-tin) m. libertine; free thinker
lice (lee-tse) n. face; cheek;
the right side; evidence
licencja (lee-tsen-tsya) f. license (ermission to practice)
licho (lee-kho) adv. poorly
licho (lee-kho) n. evil; devil
lichota (lee-kho-ta) f. rubbish
lichtarz (leekh-tash) m. candlestick ; candelabrum;candelabra
lichwa (leekh-va) f. usury
lichwiarz (leekh-vyash) m. usurer; loan shark; money lender
lichy (lee-khi) adj. m. shoddy;
shabby; poor; mean;rotten;petty
lico (lee-tsom.face; cheek; surface; front; outer part
licować (lee-tso-vach) v. fit
for... ; comport ;veneer; face
licytacja (lee-tsi-tats-ya) f.
auction ; bidding; the bid
licytować (lee-tsi-to-vach) v.
auction; bid; offer; call
liczba (leech-ba) f. number;
figure; integer; group; class
liczbowy (leech-bo-vi) adj. m.
numerical ;numeral
licznik (leech-neek) m. counter;
numerator; gasmeter; electro-
meter, etc;taximeter; register
liczny (leech-ni) adj. m.numer-
ous ; large; abundant;plentiful
liczyć (lee-chich) v. count;
reckon; compute; calculate
liczydło (lee-chid-wo) n. aba-
cus; counter; register
liga (lee-ga) f. league ;alliance
lik (leek) m. lot ;countless
lignina (leeg-nee-na) f. lignin
likier (lee-ker) m. liquor
likwidacja (leek-vee-dats-ya)
f. liquidation ;closing down
likwidować (leek-vee-do-vach) v.
liquidate ;do away with

lila (lee-la) adj. m. (color)
pale-violet; lily-
lilia (leel-ya) f. lily
liliowy (leel-yo-vi) adj. m.
lilac (color) ; lily-
liliput (lee-lee-poot) m.
little dwarf ; midget; pygmy
limfa (leem-fa) f. lymph
limit (lee-meet) m. limit
limuzyna (lee-moo-zi-na) f.
limousine; pilot's enclosure
lin (leen) m. tench
lina (lee-na) f. line; rope
lincz (leench) m. lynch
linczować (leen-cho-vach) v.
lynch; kill by mob action
lingwista (leen-gvees-ta) m.
linguist (specialist)
linia (leen-ya) f. line; lane
linijka (lee-neey-ka) f. ruler
liniować (lee-nyo-vach) v.
rule; line (paper)
liniowy okręt (leen-yo-vi ok-
 rant) liner (ship);battleship
linoleum (lee-no-le-oom) n.
linoleum (floor covering)
linoskoczek (lee-no-sko-chek)
m. tightrope artist
linotyp (lee-no-tip) m. lino-
type (typesetting machine)
lingwa kolejka (lee-no-va ko-
ley-ka) cable car
lipa (lee-pa) f.l.linden tree
2. fake; cheat; fraud
lipiec (leep-yets) m. July
lira (lee-ra) f. lyre
liryczny (lee-rich-ni) adj. m.
lyric; lyrical
liryk (lee-rik) m. lyrist;lyric
liryka (lee-ri-ka) f. lyric
poetry ; lyricism
lis (lees) m. fox; sly man
list (leest) m. letter;note
lista (lees-ta) f. list;roll
listonosz (lees-to-nosh) m.
postman
listopad (lees-to-pad) m. November
listownie (lees-tov-ne) adv.
by letter ; by mail
listwa (lees-tva) f. trim
liszaj (lee-shay) m. herpes

liszka (leesh-ka) f. caterpillar; vixen; sly fox
liściasty (leesh-chas-ti) odj.
m. leafy; leafed; foliaceous
liść (leeshch) m. leaf; frond
litania (lee-táń-ya) f. litany
litera (lee-té-ra) f. letter
literacki (lee-te-ráts-kee)
adj. m. literary; of letters
literat (lee-té-rat) m. writer
literatura (lee-te-ra-too-ra)
f. literature; writings
litewski (lee-tev-skee) adj. m.
Lithuanian;Lithuanian language
litograf (lee-to-graf) m.
lithographer
litościwy (lee-tosh-chee-vi)
adj. m. merciful; compassionate
litość (lee-toshch) f. pity;
mercy; compassion
litować się (lee-to-vach śhań)
v. have pity;feel pity
litr (leetr) m. liter
liturgia (lee-toor-gya) f.
liturgy; religious ritual
lity (lee-ti) adj. m. massive
solid; cast; pure
lizać (lee-zach) v. lick
lizol (lee-zol) m. lysol
lizus (lee-zoos) m. bootlicker
lniany (lńa-ni) adj. m. linen;
flaxen; linseed
loch (lokh) m. dungeon; cellar
lodołamacz (lo-do-wa-mach) m.
icebreaker : ice shield
lodowaty (lo-do-vá-ti) adj. m.
icy ; ice-cold; chilling;frigid
lodowiec (lo-do-vyets) m. glacier;mass of ice and snow
lodowisko (lo-do-vees-ko) n.
skating-rink ; ice rink
lodownia (lo-dov-ńa) f. ice-
chamber; ice-cellar; icy cold
lodowy (lo-do-yy) adj. m. of ice
lodówka (lo-dov-ka) f. refrigerator; ice box; ice chest
lody (lo-di) pl. ice cream
logarytm (lo-gá-ritm) m. loga-
rithm
logiczny (lo-geech-ni) adj. m.
logical ;consistent; sound
logik (ló-geek) m. logician;
expert in logic

logika (lo-gee-ka) f. logic
lojalność (lp-yál-nośhćh) f.
loyalty;straightforwardness
lojalny (lo-yál-ni) adj. m.
loyal; staunch; low-abiding
lok (lok) m. curl; coil
lokaj (lo-kay) m. lackey
lokal (ló-kal) m. premises
lokalizować (lo-ka-lee-zó-vach)
localize; locate; range
lokalny (lo-kál-ni) adj. m.
local; regional;of a place
lokata (lo-ka-ta) f. investment
lokator (lo-ká-tor) m. tenant
lokomocja (lo-ko-mots-ya) f.
locomotion; communication
lokomotywa (lo-ko-mo-ti-va) f.
train engine; locomotive
lokować (lo-ko-vach) v. place
lombard (lom-bard) m. pawnshop
lont (lont) m. fuse;slow-match
lornetka (lor-nét-ka) f. field
glasses; opera glasses
los (los) m. lot; fate; chance;
lottery-ticket; destiny;hazard
losować (lo-so-vach) v. draw
lots ; raffle ; draw cuts
lot (lot) m. flight ; speed
loteria (lo-ter-ya) f. lottery
lotnia (lot-ńa) f. hang glider
lotnictwo (lot-ńeets-tvo) n.
aviation; aeronautics;air force
lotnik (lot-ńeek) m. aviator
lotnisko (lot-ńees-ko) n. airport; airfield; aerodrome
lotniskowiec (lot-ńees-kov-
yets) m. aircraft carrier
lotny (lot-ni) adj. m. bright;
quick; swift;sharp; subtle
lotos (lo-tos) m. lotus
loża masońska (lo-zha ma-sońs-
ka) shriner's lodge
lód (loot) m. ice; pl.ice cream
lśniący (lshńówn-tsi)adj. m.
shining; bright;glossy; sleek
lśnić (lshńeech) v. glitter;
shine;gleam; glimmer; shimmer
lub (loop) conj. or;or else
luba (loo-ba) f. sweetheart
lubić (loo-beech) v. like;
be fond; enjoy; be partial
lubieżny (loo-byezh-ni) adj.
m. lustful; voluptuous; lewd

lubość (loo-boshch) f. delight
lubować się (loo-bó-vach śhań)
v. take delight ; find pleasure
lud (loot) m. people; nation
ludność (lood-noshch) f. population (of a given territory)
ludny (lood-ni) adj. m. populous ; teeming; crowded
ludobójstwo (loo-do-booy-stvo)
n. genocide;killing of a nation
ludowy (loo-do-vi) adj. m.pop-
ulist; popular; country
ludożerca (loo-do-zher-tsa) m.
cannibal ; man man-eater
ludzie (loo-dzhe) pl. people
ludzkość (loodz-koshch) f.
mankind; humaneness; humanity
lufa (loo-fa) f. gunbarrel
luk (look) m. hatch ;skylight
luka (loo-ka) f. gap;blank;break
lukier (loo—ker) m. sugar-
icing ; frosting
lukratywny (look-ra-tiv-ni) adj.
m. lucrative ; profitable
luksus (look-soos) m. luxury
lunatyk (loo-ná-tik) 1. sleepwalker; 2. loony
lunąć (loo-nownch) v. rain in
torrents;slap ;lash down;whack
luneta (loo-né-ta) f. field-
glass ;spy-glass; telescope
lupa (loo-pa) f. magnifying
glass ; jeweler's glass (loop)
lusterko (loos-ter-ko) n. hand-
glass ; rear-view mirror(in a car)
lustro (loos-tro) n. mirror
lustrować (loos-tro-vach) v.
inspect; review ; check; audit
lut (loot) m. solder
luteranin (loo-te-rá-ñeen) m.
Lutheran
lutnia (loot-ña) f. flute
lutować (loo-to-vach) v. solder
luty (loo-ti) m. February
luty (loo-ty) adj. m. bleak;
grim ; severe; bleak
luz (loos) m. clearance; play
luzak (loo-zak) m. loose (replacement) horse
luzować (loo-zo-vach) v. replace;
relieve ; loosen;slacken;ease off
luźny (loozh-ni) adj. m. loose

lwi (lvee) adj. m. lion's
lżej (lzhey) adv. lighter;
easier ; with less weight
lżenie (lzhe-ñe) n. abuse; in-
sults;vituperation
lżyć (lzhich) v. abuse; insult
Łabędz (wa-bandzh)m. swan
Łach (wakh) m. rag ; clout
Łacha (wa-kha) f. sandbank
Łachman (wakh-man) m. rag
Łachudra (wa-khood-ra) m.
ragtagman ; ragamuffin
Łaciarz (wa-chash) m. patcher
Łaciaty (wa-chá-ti) adj. m.
in patches ; pinto(horse)
Łacina (wa-chee-na) f. Latin
Łaciński (wa-cheeñ-skee) adj.
m. Latin; of Latin
Ład (wad) m. order;orderliness
Ładnie (wad-ñe) adv. nicely
Ładnieć (wad-ñech) v. grow
pretty; grow prettier
Ładny (wad-ny) adj. m. nice
Ładować (wa-do-vach) v. load;
charge; cram; fill
Ładownica (wa-dow-ñee-tsa) f.
cartridge pouch (or box)
Ładunek (wa-doo-nek) m. load;
cargo; charge; shipload;burden
Łagodność (wa-god-noshch) f.
gentleness; kindliness;suavity
Łagodny (wa-god-ni) adj. m.
gentle ;mild;soft;meek;easy
Łagodzący (wa-go-dzown-tsi) adj.
m. alleviating; extenuating
Łagodzic (wa-go-dźheech)v.
soothe; relieve; alleviate
attenuate; mitigate; smooth
Łajać (wá-yach) v. scold; chide
Łajdactwo (way-dats-tvo) n.
mean trick;scoundrels;rabble
Łajdak (wáy-dak) m. scoundrel
Łajno (wáy-no) n. dung; shit
Łaknąć (wak-nownch) v. hunger
for; thirst for ;crave for
Łakocie (wa-ko-che) pl. deli-
cacies; sweets;tidbits;candy
Łakomić się (wa-ko-meech śhań)
v. covet; lust;be tempted
Łakomy (wa-ko-mi) adj. m.
greedy; covetous; avid
Łakomstwo (wa-kom-stvo) n.
greed; gluttony;greediness

Łamać (wa-mach) v. break;crush; quarry;shatter; crack; snap
Łamigłówka (wa-mee-gwoow-ka) f. riddle; puzzle;jig-saw puzzle
Łamistrajk (wa-mee-strayk) m. scab; strikebreaker
Łamliwy (wam-lee-vi) adj. m. fragile;frail;brittle;breakable
Łan (wan) m. stand of wheat
Łania (wa-ña) f. hind; doe
Łańcuch (wań-tsookh) m. chain; range; series; train;succession
Łańcuchowa reakcja (wań-tsoo-khó-va re-ák-tsya) chain reaction
Łapa (wa-pa) f. paw ;claw;arm
Łapać (wá-pach) v. catch;snatch
Łapanka (wa-pan-ka) f. roundup
Łapcie (wáp-che) n. bast sandals: moccasins
Łapczywość (wap-chi-vośhch) f. greed; greediness; avidity
Łapczywy (wap-chi-vi) adj. m. greedy; money-grubbing
Łapka (wáp-ka) f. (mouse) trap
Łapówka (wa-poov-ka) f. bribe
Łapserdak (wap-sér-dak) m. rogue; ragamuffin;scoundrel
Łasica (wa-shee-tsa) f. weasel
Łasić się (wa-sheech shań) v. fawn;fawn on sb.; toady
Łaska (was-ka) f. grace ; clemency; favor; generosity;mercy
Łaskawy (was-ká-vi) adj. m. gracious; kind; generous
Łaskotać (was-ko-tach) v. tickle; titillate
Łaskotliwy (was-kot-lee-vi) adj. m. ticklish; titillating
Łasy (wa-si) adj. m. greedy
Łaszczyć się (wash-chich shań) v. covet; lust
Łata (wa-ta) f. patch
Łatać (wá-tach) v. patch up
Łatanina (wa-ta-nee-na) f. patch work; bungling
Łatwo (wát-vo) adv. easily
Łatwopalny (wat-vo-pál-ni) adj. m. inflammable ; combustible
Łatwość (wát-vośhch) f. ease; facility ;aptitude; fluency
Łatwowierny (wat-vo-vyér-ni) adj. m. credulous ;gullible

Łatwy (wát-vi) adj. m. easy
Ława (wa-va) f. bench ;footing
Ławica (wa-vée-tsa) f. (fish) shoal ; sandbank; shelf; layer
Ławka (wáf-ka) f. pew; bench
Ławnik (wáv-ñeek) m. juror; alderman ; assessor
Łazić (wá-źheech)v. crawl; loiter ; slouch about;creep
Łazienka (wa-źheń-ka) f. bath-room; toilet: bath
Łazik (wa-źheek) m. tramp; jeep
Łaźnia (waźh-ña) f. bath
Łażący (wa-zhówn-tsi) adj. m. dragging; crawling;scansorial
Łączący (wówn-chówn-tsy) adj. m. uniting; joining; unitive
Łącznica (wównch-ñée-tsa) f. junction ;switchboard
Łącznie (wówn-chñe) adv. together; including; inclusive of
Łącznik (wównch-ñeek) m. hyphen; liaisonman ;link; tie; bond
Łączność (wównch-nośhch) f. contact; communication; unity; signal service; connection
Łączny (wównch-ni) adj. m. joint; combined;total; global
Łączyć (wown-chich) v. join; unite ;merge;link;bind;weld
Łąka (wówn-ka) f. meadow
Łeb (wep) m. head; pate
Łechtać (wékh-tach) v. tickle; flatter ; titillate; lure
Łęk (wańk) m. saddlebow; syncline; arch; bow; pommel
Łgać (wgach) v. lie;brag;boast
Łgarstwo (wgár-stvo) n. lie
Łgarz (wgash) m. liar; braggart
Łkać (wkách) v. sob
Łobuz (wo-boos) m. rogue; rascal; scamp; scoundrel
Łodyga (wo-di-ga) f. stem
Łoić (wo-eech) v. tallow; beat up; wallop; curry
Łokieć (wo-kech) m. elbow
Łom (wom) m. crowbar;scrap;junk
Łomot (wo-mot) m. crash; crack
Łono (wo-no) n. lap; bosom;womb
Łopata (wo-pa-ta) f. spade
Łopot (wo-pot) m. (sail)flutter
Łoskot (wos-kot) n. clatter; bang; din; rumble;racket;boom

Łosoś (wo-sosh) m. salmon

Łoś (wosh) m. elk; moose

Łotewski (wo-tev-skee) adj. m.
Latvian ; Latvian language

Łotr (wotr) m, vicious scoun—
drel;knave; rascal; rogue

Łowczy (wov-chi) adj. m. hunting; huntsman's; hunter's

Łowić (wov-eech) v. trap;
fish; catch; hunt; chase

Łowiectwo (wov-yets-tvo) n.
hunting; game shooting

Łowy (wo-vi) pl. hunt; chase

Łozina (wo-zhee-na) f. wicker;
sallow; osier; osier-bed

Łoże (wo-zhe) n. bed; cradle

Łożyć (wo-zhich) v. spend

Łożysko (wo-zhis-ko) n.(river)
bed; (ball) bearing

Łódka (wood-ka) f. small boat

Łódż (woodzh) f. boat;craft

Łój (wooy) m. tallow;suet:sebum

Łów (woov) m. hunt; chase

Łóżeczko (woo-zhech-ko) n.
(child's) bed; small bed

Łóżko (woozh-ko) n. bed;bunk

Łubin (woo-been) m. lupin

Łucznik (wooch-ñeek) n. archer

Łuczywo (woo-chi-vo) n. resin-
ous kindling;resinous chips

Łudzący (woo-dzown-tsi) adj.
m. delusive; deceptive

Łudzić (woo-dżheech)v. delude;
deceive; give false hope

Ług (woog) m. lye

Ługować (woo-go-vach) v. leach;
lixiviate

Łuk (wook) m. bow; arch; bent;
vault

Łuna (woo-na) f. glow (of sun
or fire)

Łup (woop) m. booty; spoils

Łupać (woo-pach) v. cleave;
split; ache; give shooting pain

Łupek (woo-pek) m, slate

Łupić (woo-peech) v. plunder

Łupież (woo-pyezh) f. dandruff

Łupieżca (woo-pyezh-tsa) m.
plunderer; looter; pillager

Łupina (woo-pee-na) f. husk;
shell; peel; skin; hull;rind

Łuska (woos-ka) f. scale; husk;
shell; pod; flake; rind

Łuskać (woos-kach) v. scale;
husk; peel;;pod; hull (rice)

Łuszczyć (woosh-chich) v. peel;
pare; flake off; shell off

Łuza (woo-za) f. billiard
pocket

Łydka (wit-ka) f. calf(leg-shank)

Łyk (wik) m. gulp; sip; draft

Łykać (wi-kach) v. swallow;
gulp; sip; bolt; gorge; drink

Łyko (wi-ko) n. bast; phoem

Łykowaty (wi-ko-va-ti) adj. m.
wiry; tough; fibrous

Łypać (wi-pach) v. blink

Łysek (wi-sek) m. (boldhead)
boldy; bold-faced animal

Łysieć (wi-shech) v. become
bold; grow bold; lose hair

Łysina (wi-shee-na) f. pate

Łyskać (wis-kach) v. flash

Łysy (wi-si) adj. m. bold

Łyżeczka (wi-zhech-ka) f. tea-
spoon; dessert spoon; curette

Łyżka (wizh-ka) f. spoon;spoonful

Łyżwa (wizh-va) f. skate

Łyżwiarz (wizh-vyash) m.skater

Łyżwowy (wizh-vo-vi)adj.of skates

Łza (wza) f. tear

Łzawy (wza-vi) adj. m. tearful

Łzowy kanał (wzo-vi ka-naw)
tear canal; tear duct

maca (ma-tsa) f. matzos

macać (ma-tsach) v. feel; grope

machać (ma-khach) v. wave;whisk;
swing; wag; lash; flap;brandish

macher (ma-kher) m. trickster

machina (ma-khee-na) f. (large)
machine; bureaucratic machine

machinacja (ma-khee-nats-ya) f.
machination; dodge; intrigue

machlojka (ma-khloy-ka) f.
swindle; defraudation

macica (ma-chee-tsa) f. uterus;
womb; screw nut; tap root

macierz (ma-chesh) f. mother
country; matrix; mother

macierzanka (ma-che-zhan-ka) f.
thyme ; wild thyme

macierzyński (ma-che-zhiñ-ski)
adj. m. maternal; mother's

macierzyństwo (ma-che-zhiñ-stvo)
n. maternity; motherhood

macierzysty (ma-che-zhis-ti)
  adj. m. maternal; (parental)
maciora (ma-cho-ra) f. sow
macka (mats-ka) f. tentacle;
  feeler; antenna; horn
macocha (ma-tso-kha) f. stepmother; not as good as mother
maczac (ma-chach) v. dip; soak
maczuga (ma-choo-ga) f. bat;
  club; bludgeon; cudgel
magazyn (ma-ga-zin) m. store;
  warehouse; repository; store
magazynier (ma-ga-zi-ner) m.
  warehouseman; storekeeper
magia (mag-ya) f. sorcery
magiczny (ma-geech-ni) adj. m.
  magic; conjuring tricks
magiel (ma-gel) m. mangle
magik (ma-geek) m. magician
magister (ma-gees-ter) m. master (diplomat); chemist
magisterium (ma-gees-ter-yoom)
  n. master's degree
magistrat (ma-gees-trat) m.
  city hall; municipality
maglowac (mag-lo-vach) v, mangle; calender; bother; crush
magnat (mag-nat) m. magnate
magnes (mag-nes) m. magnet
magnetofon (mag-ne-to-fon) m.
  tape-recorder
magnetyczny (ma-gne-tich-ni)
  adj. m. magnetic; magnetical
magnetyzm (mag-ne-tizm) m.
  magnetism; personal charm
magnez (mag-nes) m. magnesium
magnezja (mag-nez-ya) f. mag-
  nesia; magnesium
magnolia (mag-nol-ya) f. magnolia (Magnolia)
mahometanin (ma-kho-me-ta-neen)
  m. Mohammedan; Moslem
mahon (ma-khon) m. mahogany
maic (ma-eech) v. decorate
  with green leaves
maj (may) m. May
majaczyc (ma-ya-chich) v. rave;
  loom; be delirious
majatek (ma-yown-tek) m. fortune; estate; property; wealth
majdan (may-dan) m. parade-
  ground; personal junk; traps

majeranek (ma-ye-ra-nek) m.
  marjoram; fragrant mint (cooking)
majestat (ma-yes-tat) m. majesty; kingship; stateliness
majetnosc (ma-yant-noshch) f.
  wealth; fortune; property
majetny (ma-yant-ni) adj. m.
  well to do; wealthy; affluent
majonez (ma-yo-nes) m. mayonnaise; egg yoke dressing
major (ma-yor) m. major
majowka (ma-yoov-ka) f. May-
  outing ; picnic; junket
majster (may-ster) m. qualified
  craftman; boss; master; foreman
majstersztyk (may-ster-shtik) m.
  masterpiece; greatest work
majstrowac (may-stro-vach) v.
  tinker ; make (an object)
majtek (may-tek) m. deckhand
majtki (mayt-kee) pl. panties
mak (mak) m. poppy seed
makaron (ma-ka-ron) m. macaroni
makata (ma-ka-ta) f. tapestry
makler (mak-ler) m. broker
makolagwa (ma-ko-lowng-va) f.
  linnet; lass; lassie
makrela (ma-kre-la) f. mackerel
maksyma (ma-ksi-ma) f. axiom;
  maxim ; adage : rule of conduct
maksymalny (ma-ksi-mal-ni) adj.
  m. maximum ; top-; peak-; most-
makulatura (ma-koo-la-too-ra) f.
  waste-paper; spoilage; rubbish
makuch (ma-kookh) m. oilcake
malaria (ma-lar-ya) f. malaria
malarstwo (ma-lar-stvo) m.
  painting (art); house painting
malarz (ma-lash) m. painter
malec (ma-lets) m. youngster
malec (ma-lech) v. shrink; dwindle
malenki (ma-len-kee) adj. m.
  very, small; tiny; insignificant
malenstwo (ma-len-stvo) n. tiny
  thing; little one; little mite
malina (ma-lee-na) f. raspberry
malowac (ma-lo-vach) v. paint;
  stain; color; make up; depict
malowidlo (ma-lo-veed-wo) n.
  painting; picture (painted)
malowniczy (ma-lov-nee-chi)
  adj. m. picturesque; vivid

maltretować (mal-tre-to-vach)
v. abuse; mistreat; il treat

malwersacja (mal-ver-sáts-ya)
f. embezzlement; peculation

mało (má-wo) adv. little; few;
seldom; lack; not enough

małoduszny (ma-wo-doósh-ni)
adj. m.small-minded; narrow-
minded; cheap;fainthearted

małoletni (ma-wo-lét-ñee)adj.
m. minor; under age;juvenile

małomowny (ma-wo-moóv-ni) adj.
m. reticent; laconic;taciturn

małostkowy (ma-wost-kó-vi) adj.
m. fussy; petty; mean

małpa (máw-pa) f, ape; monkey

małpować (maw-po-vach) v. ape

mały (má-wi) adj. m. little;
small size; low; modest;slight

małżenski (maw-zhen-skee) adj.
m. matrimonial ;conjugal

małżenstwo (maw-shen-stwo) n.
married couple; wedlock

małżonek (maw-zhó-nek) m. husband ; spouse; consort; mate

małżonka (maw-zhón-ka) f. wife

mama (má-ma) f. mamma ; mother

mamałyga (ma-ma-wí-ga) f.
maize gruel ; hominy

mamić (má-meech) v. deceive;
delude ;beguile; lure;tempt

mamidło (ma-meéd-wo) n. illusion ; delusion;lure;seduction

mamona (ma-mó-na) f. mammon

mamlać (mám-lach) v. mumble

mamrotać (mam-ró-tach) v. mutter ; mumble; gibber

mamut (má-moot) m. mammoth

manatki (ma-nát-kee) pl. personal belongings; traps

mandaryn (man-dá-rin) n. man-
darin; Chinese digninitary.

mandat (man-dat) m. mandate;
traffic ticket ; fine

mandolina (man-do-lee-na) f.
mandolin with 8 to 10 strings

manekin (ma-ne-keen)m.mannequin

manewr (má-nevr) m. maneuver

manewrować (ma-nev-ró-vach) v.
maneuver; steer;handle; switch

maneż (ma-nesh) m. riding-
school; horse-driven thrasher

mangan (mán-gan) m. manganese

mania (ma-ńya) f. mania ;fad

maniak (ma-ńyak) m. maniac;crank

manicure (ma-ñee-keer) m.
manicure;doing one's fingernails

manić (ma-ñeech) v. deceive;tempt

maniera (ma-ñe-ra) f. manner

manierka (ma-ñer-ka) f. canteen

manifest (ma-ñee-fest) m. man-
ifesto: a public declaration

manifestacja (ma-ñee-fes-tats-ya)
f. manifestation; demonstration

manifestować (ma-ñee-fes-tó-
vach) v. demonstrate; display

manipulacja (ma-ñee-poo-láts-ya)
f. manipulation; handling

manipulować (ma-ñee-poo-lo-vach)
v. manipulate;handle; tinker

mankiet (man-ket) m. cuff;turn-up

mankament (man-ka-ment) m. defect; shortcoming; fault

manko (man-ko) n. (acc.) shortage; allowance for cash errors

manna (mán-na) f. cream of
wheat; a godsend manna

manometr (ma-nó-metr) m. pressure gauge; steam gauge

manowce (ma-nóv-tse) pl. road-
less area; misguided direction

manufaktura (ma-noo-fak-too-ra)
f. fabrics; manufacture; shop

manuskrypt (ma-noós-kript) m.
manuscript(hand or typewritten)

mankuctwo (man-koóts-tvo) n.
left-handedness;

mapa (má-pa) f. map; chart

mara (má-ra) f. ghost; apparition; nightmare; dream; vision

marazm (ma-razm) m. sluggishness

marchew (mar-khev) f. carrot

marcepan (mar-tse-pan) m. mar-
zipan; marchpane

margaryna (mar-ga-ri-na) f.
margarine; marge (slang)

margines (mar-gee-nes) m. margin; edge; border;minor thing

mariaz (mar-yazh) m. marriage

marionetka (mar-yo-nét-ka) f.
puppet;dummy ; figurehead

marka (már-ka) f. mark; brand;
stamp; trade mark; reputation

markotno (mar-kót-no) adv. sad

markotny (mar-kót-ni) adj. m.
peevish; moody; sullen; sad,
marksistowski (mark-shees-tóvs-
kee) adj..m.. Marxist;..of Marx
marksizm (márk-sheezm) m.
Marxism; Marxist believes
marmolada (mar-mo-lá-da) f.
marmalade; jam; shambles
marmur (már-moor) m. marble
marniec (már-ńech) v. deteriorate;,waste; decline; perish
marnosc (már-noshch) f. futil-
ity; flimsiness; vanity
marnotrawny (mar-no-tráv-ni)
adj. m. wasteful; prodigal
marnowac (mar-no-vách) v. waste
marny (már-ni) adj. m. poor;
meagre; sorry; of no value
marsz(marsh) m. march; walk
marsz ! (marsh) excl.: (command)
forward march; split ! get
out !   off you go !
marszałek (mar-shá-wek) m.
marshal ; Polish Seym speaker
marszczyc (mársh-chích) v.
wrinkle; frown; crease; ripple
marszruta (marsh-róo-ta) f.
route ; itinerary
martwica (mart-vée-tsa) f.
necrosis ; sinter; travertine
martwic (márt-veech) v. distress;grieve; vex; worry;afflict
martwy (márt-vi) adj. m. dead
martyr (már-tir) m. martyr
maruder (ma-róo-der) m. maraud-
er; straggler; loiterer
marudzic (ma-roo-dżheech)v.
loiter; grumble; lag behind
mary (má-ri) pl. mar; bier
marynarka (ma-ri-nár-ka) f.
jacket; sportscoat; navy
marynarz (ma-ri-nash) m. mariner; sailor; seaman;jack(tar)
marynata (ma-ri-ná-ta) f. pickle
marynowac (ma-ri-nó-vach) v.
pickle; marinade; side-track
marzec (ma-zhets) m. March
marzenie (ma-zhé-ńe) n. dream;
reverie; day dream; pensiveness
marznąc (márzh-nównch) v. freeze
marzyciel (ma-zhi-chel) m.
dreamer; fantast; visionary

marzyc (má-zhich) v. dream
masa (ma-sa) f. bulk; mass,
masa perłowa (má-sa per-wó-va)
f. mother of pearl
masakra (ma-sák-ra) f. massacre; carnage; butchery
masakrowac (ma-sak-ro-vách) v.
massacre; slaughter;butcher;
masarnia (ma-sár-ńa) f. pork·
meat shop; pork butcher's shop
masarz (ma-sash) m. pork-
butcher; pork meat worler
masaż (má-sash) m. massage
masażysta (ma-sa-zhis-ta) m.
masseur ; rubber
maselniczka (ma-sel-ńeech-ka)
f. butter-dish; small churn
maska (más-ka) f. mask; hood
maskowac (mas-kó-vach) v.
disguise; mask;hide; screen
masło (más-wo) n. butter
masonski (ma-són-skee) adj. m.
masonic; freemason's
masowac (ma-só-vach) v. massage
masowo (ma-só-vo) adv. wholesale; in a mass; in masses
masywnosc (ma-siv-noshch) f.
massiveness ;,solidity
masywny (ma-siv-ni) adj. m.
massive ;,solid; bulky; massy
maszerowac (ma-she-ró-vach) v.
march ; march on; keep marching
maszkara (mash-ka-ra) f. monster; scarecrow; eyesore
maszt (masht) m. mast;flagstaff
maszyna (ma-shí-na) f. machine
maszynka do golenia (ma-shín-
ka do go-le-ńa) safety razor
maszyneria (ma-shi-nér-ya) f.
machinery ; mechanism
maszynista (ma-shi-ńees-ta) m.
railroad engineer
maszynistka (ma-shi-ńeest-ka)
f. typist
maszynopis (ma-shi-nó-pees) m.
typescript; typewritten copy
masc (mashch) f. ointment;
horse color; unguent
maslanka (ma-shlan-ka) f.
buttermilk; product of churning
mat (mat) m. flat color; check-
mate (one's opponent)

mata (má-ta) f. mat; matting

matactwo (ma-táts-tvo) n. legal trickery; fraudulence; deceit

matczyny (mat-chí-ni) adj. m. maternal ; mother's

matematyczny (ma-te-ma-tích-ni) adj. m. mathematical

matematyk (ma-te-má-tik) m. mathematician (also student)

matematyka (ma-te-má-ti-ka) f. mathematics : science of numbers

materac (ma-té-rats) m. mattress

materia (ma-tér-ya) f. matter; stuff; subject ;point;puss;cloth

materialista (ma-ter-ya-lees-ta) m. materialist

materialistyczny (ma-ter-ya-lees-tich-ni) adj. m. materialistic (opposite to spiritual)

materiał (ma-tér-yaw) m. material; substance; stuff ; cloth

matka (mát-ka) f. mother

matnia (mát-ña) f. snare; trap

matowy (ma-tó-vi) adj. m. flat color; dull; without luster

matrona (ma-tró-na) f. matron

matryca (ma-tri-tsa) f. matrix; die ; type;mold ; stencil;swage

matrykuła (ma-tri-koo-wa) f. register of university students

matrymonialny (ma-tri-mo-nál-ni) adj. m. matrimonial ;marital

matura (ma-too-ra) f. final highschool examination

mauretański (maw-re-tán-skee) adj. m. Moorish ; of Moors

mazać (ma-zách) v. smear; daub

mazgaj (máz-gay) m. crybaby

mazur (ma-zoor) m. mazurka rythm; Mazurian ; Mazovian

maź (maźh) f. grease;tallow

mącić (mown-cheećh) v. blur; ruffle; muddy; cloud;confuse

mączka (mownch-ka) f. fine flour;powder; dust; starch

mądrość (mown-droshćh) f. wisdom; intelligence; sagacity

mądry (mown-dri) adj. m. sage

mąka (mown-ka) f. flour; meal

mąż (mownsh) m. husband; man

mąż stanu (mównsh stá-noo) statesman ; outstanding politician; outstanding diplomat

mdleć (mdlećh) v. faint ;weaken

mdlić (mdleećh) v. nauseate

mdłość (mdwoshćh) f. nausea

mdło (mdwo) adv. dull; nauseating; sickening; faintly;dimly

meble (méb-le) pl. furniture

mecenas (me-tsé-nas) m. lawyer

mech (mekh) m. moss; down

mechaniczny (me-kha-ñeech-ni) adj. m. mechanical;automatic

mechanik (me-khá-ñeek) m. mechanic; Jack of all trades

mechanika (me-kha-ñee-ka) f. mechanics ;practical mechanics

mechanizm (me-kha-ñeesm) m. mechanism;gear ; device

mecz (mech) m. sport match

meczet (me-chet) m. mosque

medal (me-dal) m. medal

mediacja (med-yáts-ya) f. mediation: settling of differences

meduza (me-doo-za) f. jellyfish

medycyna (me-di-tsí-na) f. medicine: art of healing

medyczny (me-dích-ni) adj. m. medical; medicinal

medyk (me-dik) m. medical student; medic(hist. :physician)

medykament (me-di-ká-ment) m. drug; medicine (hist. expr.)

medytacja (me-di-táts-ya) f. meditation: thinking deeply

megafon (me-gá-fon) m. loudspeaker; megaphone

megaloman (me-ga-lo-man) m. megalomaniac;self appointed boss

melancholia (me-lan-khól-ya) f. melancholy; the blues;dejection

melasa (me-la-sa) f. molasses

meldować (mel-do-vách) v. report; register;announce

meldunek (mel-doo-nek) m. report; announcement; notification

melioracja (mel-yo-ráts-ya) f. reclamation of land; drainage

melodia (me-lód-ya) f. melody

meloman (me-ló-man) m. music lover: music enthusiast

melon (me-lon) m. melon

melonik (me-lo-ñeek) m. bowler hat; derby; bowler;billycock

memoriał (me-mor-yaw) m. memorial;minutes' journal (commercial)

menażeria (me-na-zhér-ya) f.
menagerie ;animal collection
menażka (me-nazh-ka) f. mess kit
mennica (men-née-tsa) f. mint
menstruacja (men-stroo-ats-ya)
f. menstruation ; menses
mentalność (men-tal-noshch) f.
mentality ; a way of thinking
menu (me-noo) m. menu ;bill of
mer (mer) m. mayor [fare
merdać (mer-dach) v. wag tail
merytoryczny (me-ri-to-rich-ni)
adj. m. of substance ;essential
meszek (mé-shek) m. down; nap
meta (me-ta) f. goal; hang-out
metafizyka (me-ta-feé-zi-ka) f.
metaphysics (speculative phil.)
metal (me-tal) m. metal
metalowy (me-ta-ló-vi) adj. m.
metallic[luster, sound etc)
metalurgia (me-ta-lur-gya) f.
metallurgy ; science of metals
metamorfoza (me-ta-mor-fo-za)
f. metamorphosis ;metamorphism
meteor (me-té-or) m. meteor
meteorologia (me-te-o-ro-lóg-
ya) f. meteorology [system
metoda (me-tó-da) f. method;
metodyczny (me-to-dich-ni) adj.
m. methodical ;systematic
metr (metr) m. meter : 39.37in.
metro (met-ro) n. subway
metropolia (me-tro-pól-ya) f.
metropolis ; main large city
metryczny (me-trich-ni) adj. m.
metric ; metrical
metryka (me-tri-ka) f. birth-
certificate;the public register
metys (mé-tis) m. metis
mewa (me-va) f. sea -gull
mezalians (me-zál-yans) m. mis-
alliance ; improper alliance
mezanin (me-za-ñeen) m. mezzanine
męczarnia (mań-chár-ña) f. torture; torment; anguish; agony
męczennik (mań-chen-ñeek) m.
martyr : sufferer for faith etc.
męczyć (man-chich) v. bother;
torment; oppress;tire; exhaust
mędrek (man-drek) m. smart
aleck;know-all; wiseacre
mędrzec (man-dzhets) m. sage

męka (mań-ka) f. fatigue; torment;pain;distress; nuisance
męski (mańs-kee) adj. m. masculine; manly; man's; virile;male
męskość (mańs-koshch) f. manhood ; virility; manliness
męstwo (mańs-tvo) n. bravery
mętny (mańt-ni) adj. m. turbid;
dull;dim; blurred;vague; fishy
męty (mań-ti) n. dregs; scum of
society; underworld; raffle
mężatka (mań-zhát-ka) f. married woman; femme covert (legal.)
mężczyzna (mánzh-chiz-na) m. man
mężnieć (mánzh-ñech) v. grow
manly; muster courage;take heart
mężny (manzh-ni) adj. m. brave
mglisty (mgleés-ti) adj. m.
foggy; misty; dim;nebulous;vague
mgła (mgwa) f. fog; mist; cloud
mgławica (mgwa-vee-tsa) f, neb-
ula ; cloud; hazy idea; haze
mgnienie (mgne-ñe) n. blink;
twinkle ; wink; flash;jiffy;trice
miał (myaw) m. dust; powder
miałki (myaw-kee) adj. m. fine
(sugar ; sand etc.) powdered
miano (mya-no) n. name ;designation
mianować (mya-no-vach) v. appoint ; promote; give a title
mianowicie (mya-no-vee-che)
adv. namely ; to wit : that is ...
mianownik (mya-nov-ñeek) m.
denominator; nominative
miara (mya-ra) f. measure; gauge
yard-stick;foot-rule;amount;limit
miarkować (myar-ko-vach) v.
guess; note; mitigate one's self
miarodajny (mya-ro-dáy-ni) adj.
m. authoritative; competent
miarowy (mya-ro-vi) adj. m.
rythmic ; steady; regular
miasteczko (myas-tech-ko) n.
borough ;country town
miasto (myas-to) n. town
miałczeć (myaw-chech) v. mew
miazga (myaz-ga) f. pulp ; squash
miażdżyć (myazh-dzhich) v. crush;
squash ; smash; grind;lacerate
miąć (myownch) v. crumple ;wrinkle
miąższ (myównzhsh) m. pulp;
flesh of fruit; pomace; squash

miech (myekh) m. bellows

miecz (myech) m. sword

miec (myećh) v. have;hold; run

miednica (myed-ńee-tsa) f. hand
washtub ; pelvis;wash basin

miedza (myé-dza) f. farm boundary
strip ; bounds; balk

miedź (myedzh) f. copper

miedziak (myé-dźhak) m. copper
penny; copper coin

miedziany (mye-dźha-ni) adj. m.
of copper; of brass

miedzioryt (mye-dźhó-rit) m.
copper engraving

miejsce (myejs-tse) n. place;
location; spot; room; space;
seat; employment;berth; scene

miejscowość (myey-stso-vośćh)
f. locality ; place;town;village

miejscowy (myeys-tso-vi) adj.
m. local; native; indigenous

miejski (myeys-kee) adj. m. of
town; of city ;urban

mielizna (mye-leez-na) f. shoal;
shallow water ; sandbank; shelf

mielenie (mye-lé-ńe) n. grinding;
milling; mincing; jabber;prattling

mielony (mye-lo-ni) adj. m.
ground ; milled; minced;chewed up

mieniać (mye-ńach) v. change;
swap; exchange; convert

mienić (mye-ńeećh) v. call; glitter;
shimmer; change color

mienić się (mye-ńeech śhań) v.
change one's color; glitter

mienie (mye-ńe) n. property;
belongings ;estate; effects

miernictwo (myer-ńeets-tvo) m.
surveying; land measuring

mierniczy (myer-ńee-chi) m. surveyor;
adj. m. geodetic

mierność (myer-nośćh)f.mediocrity
; average range

miernota (myer-no-ta) f. average
intelligence; mediocrity

mierny (myer-ny) adj. m. mediocre;
mean; moderate;indifferent

mierzeja (mye-zhe-ya) f. sand-bar

mierzić(myer-źheećh) v. be disgusting;
sicken;make unbearable

mierznąc (myezh-nówńch) v. become
disgusting; pall on sb

mierzwa (myesh-va) f. litter

mierzwić (myezh-veećh) v. tousle

mierzyć (mye-zhićh) v. measure;
judge; try on; aim;tend towards

miesiąc (mye-śhownts) m. month;
moon ; lunar month massage

miesić(mye-śheećh)v. knead;

miesięcznie (mye-śhańch-ńe)
adv. monthly ; every month

miesięcznik (mye-śhańch-ńeek)
m. monthly paper ; monthly

mieszać (mye-shaćh) v. mix;
mingle; shuffle; confuse

mieszać się (mye-shaćh śhań)
v. meddle; become confused

mieszanina (mye-sha-ńee-na) f.
mixture; compound ; medley

mieszanka (mye-shan-ka) f.
blend ;mix; mixture;miscellany

mieszczanin (myesh-cha-ńeen) m.
burgher ; townsman; citizen

mieszczaństwo (myesh-chań-stvo)
n. middle class ;narrow-minded

mieszek (mye-shek) m.small ness
bellows; bag ; money-bag

mieszkać (myesh-kaćh) v. dwell;
live; stay ;have a flat; lodge

mieszkalny (myesh-kál-ny) adj.
m. inhabitable; habitable

mieszkanie (myesh-ká-ńe) n.
apartment; rooms; lodgings

mieszkaniec (myesh-ká-ńets) m.
inhabitant; lodger; resident

mieść (myeśhćh) v. sweep; fling

mieścić (myeśh-ćheećh) v. contain;
fit ;hold; store; place

mieścina (myeśh-ćhee-na) f.
small town, out-of-the-way

miewać (mye-vaćh) v. have
occasionally; feel sometimes

mięczak (myań-chak) m. mollusk

międlić (myańd-leećh) v. bruise;
hackle; crush; hold forth

między (myań-dzi) prep. between;
among; in the midst

międzymorze (myań-dzi-mo-zhe) n.
isthmus : narrow strip between sea

międzynarodowy (myań-dzi-na-rodo-vi)
adj. m. international

międzyplanetarny (myań-dzi-planetár-ni)
adj. m. interplanetary
; of cosmic space

miękczyc (myáńk-chich) v. soft-
en; move; touch; palatalize
miękisz (myáń-keesh) m. pulp
miękki (myáńk-kee) adj. m.
soft ; flabby; limp; supple
miękko (myáńk-ko) adv. softly
miękkosc (myáńk-kośhch) f.
softness ; irresolution;pliancy
mięknąc (myáńk-nównch) v.
soften up ;relax; relent
mięsien (myáń-śheń) m. muscle
mięsisty (myáń-śhees-ti) adj.
m. fleshy ;meaty; pulpous
mięsiwo (myáń-śhee-vo) n. meat
mięso (myáń-so) n. flesh; meat
mięsozerny (myáń-so-zhér-ni)
adj. m. carnivorous;meat eating
mięta (myáń-ta) f. mint ;trifle
miętosic (myáń-to-śheech) v.
crumble; knead ; crush up
mig (meeg) m. split second;
twinkle; sign language
migac (mee-gách) v. twinkle
migawka (mee-gáv-ka) f. camera
shutter; news in brief
migdał (meeg-daw) m. almond;
tonsil ; good and tasty thing
migi (mee-gee) pl. sign language; speaking by signs
migotac (mee-go-tách) v. twinkle; flicker; waver;whisk;flit
nigracja (mee-gráts-ya) f. mi-
gration: migrating (of groups)
nigrena (mee-gre-na) f. mi-
graine; sick headache
mijac (mee-yách) v. go past;
pass by; pass away: go by
mijac się z prawdą (mee-yách
śhań z práv-dówn) swerve from
the truth; to be untrue
mika (mee-ka) f. mica
mikrob (mee-krob) m. microbe
mikrofon (mee-kró-fon) m. microphone ;transmitter
mikroskop (mee-krós-kop) m. microscope
mikroskopijny (m ee-kros-ko-
peey-ni) adj. m. microscopic
mikstura (meeks-too-ra) f. mixture; concoction; medicine
mila (mee-la) f. mile (1609,35m)
mila morska (mee-la mór-ska) f.
nautical mile (1853,2 meters)

milczący (meel-chówn-tsi) adj.
m. silent; reticent ; mum;tacit
milczec (meel-chech) v. be silent; quit talking; be quiet
milczenie (meel-che-ńe) n. silence; keeping still; stillness
milczkiem (meelch-kem) adv.
secretly; stealthily;on the sly
mile (mee-le) adv. pleasantly;
kindly ; warmly; courteously
miliard (meel-yard) m. thousand
million; billion
milicja (mee-leets-ya) f. mi-
litia; police; constabulary
milicjant (mee-leets-yant) m.
policeman; constable
miligram (mee-lee-gram) m. mil-
ligram ; 1/1,000 of a gram
milimetr (mee-lee-metr) m. mil-
limeter: 1/1,000 of a meter
milion (meel-yon) m. million
milioner (meel-yo-ner) m. mil-
lionaire; a very wealthy man
milionowe miasto (meel-yo-no-ve
mya-sto) city of million people
militarny (mee-lee-tár-ni) adj.
m. military; of soldiers
militaryzowac (mee-lee-ta-ri-
zo-vach) v. militarize
milknąc (meelk-nównch) v. abate;
quit talking; die away;subside
miło (mee-wo) adv. nicely;
pleasantly; agreeably,
miło poznac (mee-wo póz-nach)
glad to meet ; nice to meet
miłosierdzie (mee-wo-śher-dzhe)
m. charity; mercy;compassion
miłosierny (mee-wo-śhér-ni) adj.
m. merciful; charitable
miłosny list (mee-wós-ni leest)
love letter
miłostka (mee-wóst-ka) f. little
love affair
miłosc (mee-wośhch) f. love
miłosnik (mee-wósh-ńeek) m.
fancier; amateur ; fan
miłowac (mee-wo-vach) v. love
miły (mee-wy) adj. m. pleasant;
beloved; likable;nice;enjoyable
mimiczny (mee-meech-ni) adj. m.
mimic; imitative:make-believe
mimo (mee-mo) prep. in spite of;
notwithstanding ; (al)though

mimo (mee-mo) adv. past; by
mimochodem (mee-mo-khó-dem) adv.
by the way; incidentally
mimo woli (mee-mo vó-lee) adv.
involuntarily: unintentional
mimowolny (mee-mo-vól-ni) adj.
m. involuntary; unintentional
mimo wszystko (mee-mo vshist-ko)
after all; in spite of all
mina (mee-na) f. 1. facial
expression; 2. mine ; air
minaret (mee-na-ret) m. minaret
minąć (mee-nownch) v. pass by
mineralny (mee-ne-rál-ni) adj.
m. mineral;containing minerals
mineralogia (mee-ne-ra-lóg-ya)
f. mineralogy
minerał (mee-ne-raw) m. mineral
minia (meen-ya) f. minium; red
lead base; red lead
miniatura (meen-ya-too-ra) f.
miniature; miniature copy
minimalny (mee-nee-mál-ny) adj.
m. minimal;the least possible
minimum (mee-nee-moom) n. minimum;adv. at the very least
miniony (mee-ńo-ni) adj. m. bygone; of long ago; olden
minister (mee-ńees-ter) m. minister; cabinet member
ministerialny (mee-ńees-ter-
yál-ni) adj. m. ministerial
ministerstwo (mee-ńees-ter-stvo)
n. ministry;department of state
minorowy (mee-no-ró-vi) adj. m.
in minor key; low-spirited
minuta (mee-noo-ta) f. minute
minutowy (mee-noo-tó-vi) adj.
m. of one minute
miodownik (myo-dóv-ńeek) m.
gingerbread
miodowy miesiąc (myo-do-vi mye-
shównts) honeymoon
miodosytnia (myo-do-sit-ńa) f.
meadbar
miot (myot) m. throw; cast; lit-
ler; brood ;animal birth; fling
miotacz (myo-tach) m. thrower
miotacz ognia (myo-tach óg-ńa)
m. firethrower
miotać (myo-tach) v. throw; fling;
toss ;hurl; stir; rave; storm
miotła (myot-wa) f. broom

miód (myoot) m. honey ; mead
mir (meer) m. esteem ;respect
miriady (meer-yá-di) pl. myr-
iads : large numbers
mirra (meer-ra) f. myrrh
mirt (meert) m. myrtle
misa (mee-sa) f. platter; bowl
misja (mees-ya) f. mission
misjonarz (mees-yo-nash) m.
missionary
miska (mees-ka) f. dish; pan
misterny (mees-tér-ni) adj. m.
fine; delicate; subtle;clever
mistrz (meestsh) m. master;
maestro; champion; expert
mistrzostwo (mees-tzhos-tvo)
m. championship; mastery
mistrzowski ruch (mees-tzhóvs-
kee rookh) masterstroke
mistycyzm (mees-ti-cizm) m.
mysticism ;intuitive knowledge
mistyczny (mees-tich-ni) adj.
m. mystic ; mystical: occult
mistyfikacja (mees-ti-fee-
káts-ya) f mystification
mistyfikować (mees-ti-fee-kó-
vach) v. mystify; hoax;deceive
mistyk (mees-tik) m. mystic
misyjny (mee-siy-ni) adj. m.
missionary; mission-
miś (meesh) m. teddy bear;
nylon fur coat or jacket
mit (meet) m. myth; mythology
mitologia (mee-to-log-ya) f.
mythology : study of myths
mitologiczny (mee-to-lo-geéch-
ni) adj. m. mythologic
mitra (mee-tra) f. mitre
mitręga (mee-trán-ga) f. delay;
waste of time; delay; dawdler
mitrężyć (mee-trán-zhych) v.
loiter; waste time;dally; lag
mityczny (mee-tích-ni) adj. m.
mythical; mythic ; fictitious
mitygować (mee-ti-gó-vach) v.
quiet; appease;check;restrain
mityng (mee-ting) m. (mass)
meeting : a gathering of people
mizantrop (mee-zán-trop) m.
misanthrope ; hater of people
mizdrzyć się (meez-dzhich shań)
v. ogle; wheedle ;make eyes

mizerak (mee-zé-rak) m. poor
soul; weakling; poor devil

mizeria (mee-zer-ya) f. cucumber salad: shabby possessions

mizerny (mee-zér-ni) adj. m.
meager; ill-looking; mean;paltry

mknąć (mknównćh) v. fleet;rush

mlaskać (mlás-kaćh)v. lap; smack

mlecz (mlech) m. marrow ;milt

mleczarnia (mle-chár-ña) f.
dairy ; creamery : milk bar

mleczny (mlech-ni) adj. m. milk;
milky; dairy; lactic;milk-white

mleć (mlećh) v. grind; mill

mleko (mle-ko) n. milk

młocarnia (mwo-tsár-ña) f.
thresher ;threshing-machine

młocka (mwóts-ka) f. threshing

młoda (mwo-da) adj. f. young

młode (mwo-de) adj. pl. young
n.pl. the young; litter

młodociany (mwo-do-chá-ni) adj.
m. juvenile; youthful

młodość (mwo-dóshćh) f. youth

młody (mwo-di) adj. m. young

młodzian (mwo-dżhan) m. young
man ; lad ; youth

młodzieniaszek (mwo-dżhe-ña-
shek) m. sprig; stripling;lad

młodzieniec (mwo-dżhe-ñets) m.
young man ; lad: youth

młodzieńczy (mwo-dżheń-chi)
adj. m. youthful

młodzież (mwo-dżhesh) f. youth;
young generation

młodzik (mwo-dżheek)m. youngster; teenager; youngling

młokos (mwo-kos) m. kid

młot (mwot), m. sledge; hammer

młotek (mwo-tek) m. hammer;
tack-hammer ;clapper

młócić (mwoo-ćheech) v. thrash

młyn (mwin) m. mill; grinder

młynarz (mwi-nash) m. miller

młynek (mwi-nek) m. handgrinder

młyński (mwiń-skee) adj. m.
mill-; of a mill

mnich (mñeekh) m. monk; friar

mniej (mñey) adv., less; fewer

mniej wiecej (mñey vyań-tsey)
more or less ; about; round

mniejsza o to (mñey-sha o to)
never mind that (exp.)

mniejszość (mñey-shoshćh) f.
minority: the lesser part

mniejszy (mñey-shi) adj. m.
smaller; lesser ;less; minor

mniemać (mñe-mać) v. suppose;
deem; imagine;think; consider

mniemanie (mñe-ma-ñe) n. opinion ;notion;conviction

mniszka (mñeesh-ka) f. nun

mnoga (mno-ga) num. plural

mnogi (mno-gee) adj. m. nume-r-
ous ; of the plural

mnogość (mno-goshćh) f. abundance; plurality; multitude

mnożenie (mno-zhe-ñe) n. multiplication ;increase; breeding

mnożyć (mno-zhićh) v. multiply

mnóstwo (mnoos-tvo) n. very
many; multitude; swarm; loads

mobilizacja (mo-bee-lee-záts-
ya) f. mobilization ;call-up

mobilizować (mo-bee-lee-zó-
vaćh) v. mobilize; call up

moc (mots)f. might; great-
deal; power;vigor;strength

mocarstwo (mo-tsár-stvo) n.
strong country;(world)power

mocarz (mo-tsash) m. strong
man; potentate; powerful man

mocny (mots-ni) adj. m. strong

mocować się (mo-tsó-vaćh śhań)
v. wrestle; exert oneself

mocz (moch) m. urine

moczar (mo-char) m. bog; marsh

moczopędny (mo-cho-pańd-ni)
adj. m. diuretic

moczowy (mo-chó-vi) adj. m.
uric; urinary: of urine

moczyć (mo-chich) v. wet;
drench; steep; soak;urinate

moda (mo-da) f. fashion

model (mo-del) m. model

modelować (mo-de-ló-vaćh) v.
model; shape; mold; fashion

modernizować (mo-der-ni-zó-vaćh)
v. modernize;bring up to date

modlić się (mod-leećh śhań) v.
pray; say one's prayers

modlitewnik (mod-lee-tev-ñeek)
m. prayer-book

modlitwa (mod-leét-va) f.
prayer ; grace(at meal time)

modła (mód-wa) f. mold; standard; fashion; model; pattern

modniarka (mod-ńár-ka) f. milliner; modiste; hat maker

modny (mód-ni) adj. m. fashionable; in fashion;in vogue

modry (mód-ri) adj. m. azureblue; deep blue;cerulean blue

modrzew (mód-zhev) m. larch

modulacja (mo-doo-láts-ya) f. modulation;inflection

modulować (mo-doo-ló-vach) v. modulate; inflect; regulate

modyfikacja (mo-di-fee-káts-ya) f. modification; alteration

modyfikować (mo-di-fee-kó-vach) v. modify; alter; qualify

modystka (mo-dist-ka) f. modiste; milliner; hat maker

mogący (mo-gówn-tsi) adj. m. able; capable; competent

mogiła (mo-gee-wa) f. tomb

mojżeszowy (moy-zhe-shó-vi) adj. m. Mosaic : of Moses

mokka (mók-ka) f. natural coffee ; mocha: Mocha coffee

moknąć (mok-nownch) v. get wet; get soaked, drenched:be soaked

mokradło (mo-krád-wo) n. bog

mokry (mók-ri) adj. m. wet; moist; watery;rainy; sweaty

molekularny (mo-le-koo-lár-ni) adj. m. molecular; of molecule

molekuła (mo-le-koó-wa) f. molecule; smallest particle

molestować (mo-les-tó-vach) v. molest; annoy; vex; trouble

molo (mó-lo) n. pier; mole; jetty; breakwater; quay

moment (mo-ment) m. moment

momentalny (mo-men-tál-ni) adj. m. instantaneous ;immediate

monarcha (mo-nár-kha) m. monarch; sovereign: king

monarchista (mo-nar-khees-ta) m. monarchist; royalist

moneta (mo-né-ta) f. coin ;chink

moneta brzecząca (mo-ne-ta bzhán-chówn-tsa) cash; coins

mongolski (mon-gól-skee) adj. m. Mongol: of Mongolia

monitor (mo-ńee-tor) m. monitor

monitować (mo-ńee-tó-wach) v. admonish; monitor : check on

monogram (mo-nó-gram) m. monogram; initials in a design

monokl (mo-nokl) m. eye-glass

monolog (mo-nó-log) m. monologue; soliloquy of one actor

monopol (mo-nó-pol) m. monopoly

monoteizm (mo-no-té-eezm) m. monotheism; belief in one god

monotonia (mo-no-tóń-ya) f. monotony; sameness; no variety

monotonny (mo-no-tón-ni) adj. m. monotonous ;drab; dull

monstrualny (mon-stroo-ál-ni) adj. m. monstrous; horrible

monstrum (mon-stroom) n. monster; monstrosity

montaż (món-tazh) m. mounting; assembling;installation; set-up

monter (món-ter) m. installator

montować (mon-tó-vach) v. install; put together; put up

monumentalny (mo-noo-men-tál-ni) adj. m. monumental

mops (mops) m. pug-dog

moralizator (mo-ra-lee-zá-tor) m. moralizer

moralizować (mo-ra-lee-zó-vach) v. moralize; discuss morality

moralność (mo-rál-noshch) f. morals; morality; ethics

moralny (mo-rál-ni) adj. m. moral; ethical:of good conduct

morał (mó-raw) m. moral lesson

moratorium (mo-ra-tor-yoom) n. moratorium; legalized delay

mord (mord) m. murder; slaughter

morda (mór-da) f. snout; muzzle; vulg: mug; kisser; puss; phiz

morderca (mor-dér-tsa) m. murderer; assassin;cutthroat

morderczy (mor-dér-chi) adj. m. murderous; cutthroat; deadly

morderstwo (mor-dér-stvo) n. murder; assassination

mordęga (mor-dan-ga) f. toil; drudge; moil;fag; strain

mordować (mor-do-vach) v. kill; torment;harass;toil;sweat;worry

mordować się (mor-do-vach shań) v. toil; kill oneself with work morela (mo-ré-la) f. apricot

morena (mo-ré-na) f. moraine

morfina (mor-fée-na) f. morphine (derivative of opium)

morfologia (mor-fo-lóg-ya) f. morphology: science of forms

morga (mór-ga) f. acre

morowy (mo-ró-vi) adj. m. pestilential; clever; good buddy; fine fellow; first-rate

mors (mors) m. walrus

morska choroba (mórs-ka kho-ró-ba) seasickness; dizziness

morski (mórs-kee) adj. m. maritime; sea; nautical; naval

morwa (mór-va) f. mulberry

morze (mozhe) n. sea ; ocean

morzyć (mo-zhićh) v. starve

mosiądz (mo-śhównts) m. brass

moskit (mos-keet) m. mosquito

most (most) m. bridge

mościć (mósh-ćheećh) v. pad (nest); make a bed of straw

motać (mo-tać)v. reel; embroil; entangle; intrigue; spool

motek (mo-tek) m. reel ; ball

motłoch (mot-wokh) m. mob

motocykl (mo-to-tsikl) m. motorcycle (a two-wheeled vehicle)

motor (mo-tor) m. motor

motorówka (mo-to-róov-ka) f. motorboat

motoryzacja (mo-to-ri-záts-ya) f. motorization;mechanization

motoryzować (mo-to-ri-zo-vać) v. motorize; mechanize

motyka (mo-ti-ka) f. hoe

motyl (mo-til) m. butterfly

motyw (mo-tiv) m. motif; motive

motywować (mo-ti-vó-vać) v. give reasons; explain;justify

mowa (mo-va) f. speech; language

mozaika (mo-záy-ka) f. mosaic

mozolić (mo-zo-leećh) v. toil; take pains; exert oneself

mozolny (mo-zol-ni) adj. m. toilsome, ;strenuous arduous

mozół (mo-zoow) m. exertion

moździerz (móżh-dżhesh) m. mortar ; mine thrower

może (mo-zhe) adv. perhaps; maybe; very likely; how about?

możliwość (mozh-lee-vośhćh) f. possibility; chance; contigency

możliwości (mozh-lee-vosh-ćhee) pl. scope ;vistas; capabilities

możliwy (mozh-lee-vi) adj. possible ; fairly good; passable

można (mozh-na) v. imp. it is possible; one may; one can

możność (mozh-nośhćh) f. power; freedom to; free choice to

możny (mózh-ni) adj. m. potent; powerful; mighty

móc (moots) v. (potentially) to be able ; be capable

mój (mooy) pron. my; mine

mól (mool) m. moth

mól książkowy (mool kśhównzh-kó-vi) bookworm

mór (moor) m. pestilence; epidemic ;plague ; pest

mórg (moorg) m. acre

mówca (móov-tsa) m. speaker

mówić (moo-veećh) v. speak; talk; say; tell,;say things

mównica (moov-ńee-tsa) f. (pulpit); speaker's platform

mózg (moozk) m. brain

mózgowy (mooz-gó-vi) adj. m. cerebral ; of the brain

mroczny (mroch-ni) adj. m. dusky; gloomy ;obscure;dark

mrok (mrok) m. dusk; twilight

mrowić się (mró-veećh śhań) v. swarm; teem; be alive

mrowie (mrov-ye) n. swarm; tingle ;gooseflesh;creeps

mrowisko (mro-vées-ko) n. anthill ; ants'nest

mrozić (mro-żheećh) v. freeze; congeal; refrigerate ; chill

mroźny (mróżh-ni) adj. m.frosty; icy ; freezing

mrówka (mroov-ka) f. ant ;emmet

mróz (mroos) m. frost ;the cold

mruczeć (mroo-chećh) v. mumble; mutter ; purr; murmur; grumble

mrugać (mroo-gaćh) v. twinkle; blink; wink ; flicker; flinch

mruk (mrook) m. mumbler; grumbler; man of few words;growler

mrukliwy (mrook-lee-vi) adj. m. mumbling; sulky; gruff;taciturn

mrużyć (mroo-zhich) v. blink;
wink ; squint; half-shut(eyes)
mrzonka (mzhon-ka) f. illusion
msza (msha) f. mass (in church)
mszalny (mshal-ni) adj. m. for
mass; of mass (in the church)
mszał (mshaw) m. missal
mściciel (mshchee-chel) m.
avenger ; retaliator
mścić (mshcheech) v. avenge
mściwy (mshchee-vi) adj. m.
vindictive; vengeful
mszczenie (mshche-ne) n. vengeance ; retaliation
mszyca (mshi-tsa) f. mite
mszysty (mshis-ti) adj. m. mossy
mucha (moo-kha) f. fly
mufka (moof-ka) f. muff
mularz (moo-lash) m. mason
mulat (moo-lat) m. mulatto
mulisty (moo-lees-ty) adj. m.
muddy; oozy; slimy ; sludgy
muł (moow) m. ooze; slime
muł (moow) m. mule
mumia (moom-ya) f. mummy
mundur (moon-door) m. uniform
municypalny (moo-nee-tsi-pal-ni)
adj. m. municipal
munsztuk (moon-shtook) m. (bridle) bit; mouthpiece
mur (moor) m. brick wall
murarz (moo-rash) m. bricklayer
murawa (moo-ra-va) f. lawn
murować (moo-ro-vach) v. lay-
bricks ; build in brick(in stone)
murowany (moo-ro-va-ni) adj. m.
of bricks; of stone ; certain
murzyn (moo-zhin) m. negro
mus 1, (moos) m. necessity; compulsion ; constraint
mus 2, (moos) m. froth;mousse
musieć (moo-shech) v. be obliged
to; have to;be forced; must
muskać (moos-kach) v. touch
lightly ; skim; stroke
muskularny (moos-koo-lar-ni) adj.
m. muscular ; strong;hefty;beefy
muskuł (moos-koow) m. muscle
musować (moo-so-vach) v. foam;
froth; bubble; fizz; sparkle
muszka (moosh-ka) f. fly; gun-
bead; face skin-spot ;bow-tie;
midge; dry-fly; patch (on skin)

muszkat (moosh-kat) m. nutmeg
muszkiet (moosh-ket) m. musket ; smooth bore firearm
muszla (moosh-la) f. shell;conch
musztarda (moosh-tar-da) f.
mustard seasoning
musztra (moosh-tra) f. (drill)
training; exercise
muslin (moosh-leen) m. muslin
mutacja (moo-tats-ya) f. muta-
tion; change; variation
muterka (moo-ter-ka) f. (bolt)
nut; female screw
muza (moo-za) f. Muse
muzealny (moo-ze-al-ni) adj. m.
of museum
muzeum (moo-ze-oom) n. museum
muzułmanin (moo-zoow-ma-neen)
m. Moslem (Mussulman)
muzyczny (moo-zich-ni) adj. m.
musical; set to music
muzyk (moo-zik) m. musician
muzyka (moo-zi-ka) f. music
muzykalność (moo-zi-kal-noshch)
f. ear for music
muzykalny (moo-zi-kal-ni) adj.
m. having ear for music
muzykant (moo-zi-kant) m. low
class musician ; bandsman
my (mi) pron. we ; us
myć (mich) v. wash
mycka (mits-ka) f. skull-cap
mydlarnia (mid-lar-na) f. soap-
store; soap-works; perfumery
mydlarstwo (mid-lar-stvo) n.
soap-making; soap-boiling
mydlarz (mid-lash) m. soap-maker
mydlić (mid-leech) v. soap;
froth; dress someone down
mydlić oczy (mid-leech o-chi) v.
pull wool over eyes
mydliny (mid-lee-ni) pl. soap-
suds; lather
mydło (mid-wo) n. soap; soft soap
mylić (mi-leech) v. mislead;
misguide;confuse; deceive
mylny (mil-ni) adj. m. wrong
mysz (mish) f. mouse
myszkować (mish-ko-vach) v.
covertly explore; trace scent
myśl (mishl) f. thought; idea
myślący (mish-lown-tsi) adj. m.
thoughtful; reflective

myśleć (mish-lech) v. think

myśliciel (mish-lee-chel) m. thinker; one who thinks a lot

myśliwiec (mish-leev-yets) m. fighter plane: fighter pilot

myśliwy (mish-lee-vi) m. hunter

myślnik (mishl-ñeek) m. dash (mark); hyphen

myślowy (mish-ló-vi) adj. m. mental; reflective; intellectual

myto (mí-to) n. toll; tollgate

mżyć (mzhich) v. drizzle

na (na) prep. on; upon; at; for; by; in;
NOTE: verbs with prefix na NOT INCLUDED HERE: CHECK WITHOUT THE PREFIX na

nabawić się (na-bá-veech shañ) v. bring upon oneself; incur

nabawić strachu (na-bá-veech strá-khoo)v.frighten

nabiał (ná-byaw) m. dairy products including eggs

nabiegać się (na-bye-gach shañ)v. have run a lot; exert oneself

nabić (na-beech) v. load weapon; beat up (somebody); whack

nabiegły krwią (na-byeg-wi krvyówn) adj.m. bloodshot

nabierać (na-bye-rach) v. take; take in; tease; cheat; amass

nabijać (na-bee-yach) v. stud; (repeatedly) load gun

nabijać się (na-bee-yach shañ) v. make fun of (somebody)

nabożeństwo (na-bo-zheñ-stvo) n. church service

nabożny (na-bozh-ni) adj. m. pious; religious; godly;devoutly

nabrać (na-brach) v. take; take in; tease; cheat; gather;swell

nabój (ná-booy) m. charge; cartrige; round of ammunition

nabrzeże (na-bzhe-zhe) n. wharf; embankment; landing-pier

nabrzmiały (na-bzhmyá-wi) adj. m. swollen : distended

nabytek (na-bi-tek) m. acquisition; purchase;new recruit

nabrzmiewać (na-bzhmye-vach) v. swell ;plump up; plump out

nabywać (na-bi-vach) v. acquire; obtain; gain; buy; purchase

nabywca (na-bív-tsa) m. buyer

nacechowany (na-tse-kho-vá-ni) adj. m. marked; characterized

nachodzić (na-khó-dżheech)v. intrude; (abstr.) haunt

nachylać (na-khí-lach) v. stoop; bend; incline; lean ;tilt;slant

nachylenie (na-khi-lé-ñe) n.tilt slope; inclination;batter;slant

nacięcie (na-chan-che) n. incision; notch; cut :nick:score

naciągać (na-chówn-gach) v. streach; draw; strain; pull one's leg;;take sb in; infuse

naciek (ná-chek) m. infiltration; leak ; swelling

nacierać (na-ché-rach) v. rub; attack; harass ; demand

nacinać (na-chee-nach) v. notch; cut; score; nick;hoax;dupe

nacisk (na-cheesk) m. pressure; stress; accent;thrust; push

naciskać (na-chees-kach) v. press; urge ;bear on; push

nacjonalista (na-tsyo-na-leés-ta) m. nationalist

nacjonalizacja (na-tsyo-na-lee-záts-ya) f. nationalization

nacjonalizm (na-tsyo-ná-leezm) m. nationalism

nacjonalizować (na-tsyo-na-lee-zó-vach) v. nationalize

naczekać się (na-ché-kach shañ) v. wait too long;tire of waiting

na czczo (na chcho) adv. on an empty stomach : unfed; fasting

naczelnik (na-chél-ñeek) m. manager; chief; head; master

naczelny (na-chél-ni) adj. m. chief; head; paramount; primate; principal;main;paramount

naczerpać (na- cher-pach) v. dip up; draw (fluid);scoop up

naczynie (na-chí-ñe) n. vessel

nad (nad) prep. over; above; on upon; beyond; at; of;for

nadajnik (na-dáy-ñeek) m. transmitter; feeder

nadal (ná-dal) adv. still; in future; continue (to do)

nadaremnie (na-da-rém-ñe) adv. in vain; unsuccessfully; to no purpose; without result

nadaremny (na-da-rém-ni) adj.
m. fruitless; vain;unsuccessful

nadarzać się (na-da-zhach śhán)
v. happen; occur; turn up

nadawać (na-da-vach) v. confer
bestow ;grant; endow; christen

nadawca (na-dav-tsa) m. sender

nadąć (na-downch) v. puff up

nadąsany (na-down-sa-ni) adj.
m. sulky; sullen; stuffy

nadążać (na-down-zhach) v. keep
up with; cope with :keep pace

nadbałtycki (nad-baw-tits-kee)
adj. m. on the Baltic :Baltic

nadbiec (nad-byets) v. come
running up; hasten up :run up

nadbrzeże (nad-bzhe-zhe) n.
shore; coast; littoral

nadbrzeżny (nad-bzhezh-ni) adj.
m. coastal; sea-shore

nadbudowa (nad-boo-do-va) f.
superstructure :added floor

nadbudować (nad-boo-do-vach)
v. build on ;add an upper floor

nadchodzić (nad-khó-dzheech)v.
approach; arrive; come

nadciągać (nad-chown-gach) v.
draw near; be nearing; come

nadciśnienie (nad-cheesh-ne-ne)
n. excess pressure;hypertension

nadczłowiek (nad-chwo-vyek) m.
superman; superhuman man

nadejście (na-dey-śhche) v.
coming; arrival; oncoming

nadepnąć (na-dep-nownch) v.
step on; tread on (crushing)

nader (na-der) adv. greatly;
excessively; highly; most

nadesłać (na-de-swach) v. send
in; forward; remit

nade wszystko (na-de vshist-ko)
adv. above all (else)

nadęty (nad-an-ti) adj. m.
puffed up; inflated; superior

nadgraniczny (nad-gra-neech-ni)
adj. m. near-border;frontier-

nadjechać (nad-yé-khach) v.
drive up; come up; arrive

nadlecieć (nad-le-chech) v. fly
in; arrive in a hurry

nadleśniczy (nad-lesh-nee-chi)
m. chief ranger; forest inspector: head of rangers

nadliczbowy (nad-leech-bó-vi)
adj. m. overtime; additional

nadludzki (nad-loodz-ki) adj.
m. superhuman ; divine

nadmiar (nád-myar) m. excess

nadłamać (nad-wa-mach) v. break
slightly; cause a slight break

nadmienić (nad-mye-neech) v.
mention ; allude;hint; add

nadmierny (nad-myer-ni) adj.
m. excessive; extravagant;undue

nadmorski (nad-mor-skee) adj.
m. seaside-;maritime

nadmuchać (na-dmoo-khach) v.
inflate; blow up with air

nadobny (na-dob-ny) adj. m.
handsome; comely; pretty

nadobowiązkowy (nad-o-bo-vyowiz-
ko-vi) adj. m. optional

na dół (na doow) down; down
stairs; downwards

nadpić (nad-peech) v. take a
sip; start overfilled drink

nadpłynąć (nad-pwi-nownch) v.
sail in; swim in; arrive

nadprodukcja (nad-pro-dook-
tsya) f. excess production

nadprogramowy (nad-pro-gra-mo-
vi) adj. m. extra; additional

nadprzyrodzony (nad-pzhy-ro-dzo-
ni) adj. m. supernatural

nadpsuty (nad-psoo-ti) adj. m.
partly spoiled; impaired

nadrabiać (nad-rab-yach) v.
catch up with; make up; work
ahead of schedule:compensate for

nadruk (na-drook) m. overprint

nadrzędny (nad-zhand-ni) adj.
m. superior; primary;precedent

nadskakiwać (nad-ska-kee-vach)
v. try to ingratiate oneself

nadsłuchiwać (nad-swoo-khee-
vach) v. strain to listen

nadspodziewany (nad-spo-dżhe-vá-
ni) adj. m. unexpected

nadstawiać (nad-stáv-yach) v.
expose; risk; hold out; cock

nadto (nád-to) adv. moreover;
besides; too much; too many

nadużycie (nad-oo-zhi-che) n.
abuse; excess; misuse

nadużywać (nad-oo-zhi-vach) v.
abuse; take advantage ;strain

nadwaga (nad-vá-ga) f. overweight;allowed extra weight
nadwartość (nad-vár-tośhćh) f.
overvalue in economics
nadwątlić (nad-vównt-leećh) v.
weaken; impair; damage
nadwiślański (nad-veeśh-lań-
skee) adj. m. on the Vistula
nadwodny (nad-vód-ni) adj. m.
near water; riverside; aquatic
nadwozie (nad-vó-zhe) m. car-
body; body of a car or truck
nadwyrężać (nad-vi-rán-zhać)
v. impair; strain; weaken
nadwyżka (nad-vízh-ka) f. surplus; excess amount
nadymać (na-di-mać) v. puff up
nadymić (na-di-meećh) v. fill
with smoke;make a lot of smoke
nadzieja (na-dzhe-ya) f. hope
nadziemski (nad-źhem-skee) adj.
m. celestial; heavenly;divine
nadzienie (na-dźhe-ńe) n.
stuffing ; filling; forcemeat
nadziewać (na-dźhe-vać) v.
stuff;pierce with;put on; fill
nadzorca (nad-zór-tsa) m. overseer; superintendent;supervisor
nadzór (nád-zoor) m. supervision
nadzwyczaj (nad-zvi-chay) adv.
unusually; extremely; most
nadzwyczajny (nad-zvi-cháy-ni)
adj. m. extraordinary; extreme
nafta (náf-ta) f. petroleum
naftalina (naf-ta-lée-na) f,
naphthalene; naphthaline
nagabywać (na-ga-bi-vać) v.
annoy; accost; trouble;molest
nagana (na-gá-na) f. blame
nagi (ná-gi) adj. m. naked;
bare ; nude; bald; empty
naginać (na-geé-nać) v. bend
down; submit to; adapt; bow
nagle (nág-le) adv. suddenly
naglić (nág-leećh) v. urge
nagłość (nág-wośhćh) f. urgency
nagłówek (na-gwoó-vek) m. heading; caption; title; headline
nagły (nág-wi) adj. m. sudden;
urgent;instant;abrupt; pressing
nagminny (na-gmeen-ni) adj. m.
universal;usual;current;general

nagniotek (na-gńo-tek) m.
(skin) corn; callus on the skin
nagonka (na-gón-ka) f. campaign
against; hue and cry against
nagość (ná-gośhćh) f. nudity
nagradzać (na-gra-dzać) v.
reward; give prize;recompense
nagrobek (na-gró-bek) m. tomb
nagroda (na-gró-da) f. reward
nagrodzić (na-gró-dźheećh)v.
reward; requite; recompense
nagromadzić (na-gro-má-dźheećh)
v. accumulate; amass; heap up
nagrzewać (na-gzhe-vać) v.
warm up ; heat up; preheat
naigrawać (na-ee-gra-vać) v.
mock; scoff; deride;ridicule
naiwny (na-eev-ni) adj. m. naive
najazd (ná-yazt) m. invasion
najbardziej (nay-bár-dźhey)
adv. most(of all)
najechać (na-ye-khaćh)v.overrun;
invade; run into;ram; crowd
najedzony (na-ye-dzó-ni) adj.
m. full (of food): satiated
najem (ná-yem) m. hire
najemnik (na-yém-ńeek) m.
hireling; mercenary;free lance;
soldier of fortune;wage earner
najemny (na-yém-ni) adj. m.venal;
mercenary; hired labor
najeść się (ná-yeśhćh śháń) v.
eat plenty of; eat a lot
najeźdźca (na-yeźhdźh-tsa) m.
invader; assailant: violator
najeżdżać (na-yezh-dzhać) v.
invade; run into; attack; ram
najeżony (na-ye-zhó-ni) adj. m.
bristling; bristly; beset
najgorszy (nay-gor-shi) adj. m.
worst; the worst of all
najgorzej (nay-go-zhey) adv.
worst of all : worst possible
najlepiej (nay-lép-yey) adv.
best ; best of all
najlepszy (nay-lép-shi) adj. m.
best; best of all; best possible
najmniej (náy-mńey) adv. least
najmniejszy (nay-mńéy-shi) adj.
m. least; smallest; least of all
najmować (nay-mó-vać) v. rent;
hire; engage; lease

najpierw (náy-pyerv) adv. first of all ;in the first place

najście (naysh-che) n. intrusion; inroad; invasion;incursion

najść (nayshch) v. intrude

najwięcej (nay-vyáṅ-tsey) adv. most of all (worst of all)

największy (nay-vyáṅk-shi) adj. m. biggest; largest; extreme

najwyżej (nay-vi-zhey) adv. highest; at the very most

najwyższy (na-vizh-shi) adj. m. highest; top; utmost

nakarmić (na-kár-meech) v. feed

nakaz (ná-kas) m. order ;writ

nakazywać (na-ka-zi-vach) v. order; demand; command

nakleić (na-kle-eech) v. stick on ; paste up; mount; post

nakład (na-kwad) m. outlay

nakładać (na-kwa-dach) v. lay on; put on; place; set;spread

nakładca (na-kwád-tsa) m. publisher (of printed work)

nakłaniać (na-kwa-ñach) v. persuade ;induce; bring;get;urge

na koniec (na kó-ñets) adv. finally ; at the end

nakreślać (na-krésh-lach) v. delineate ; sketch;draft;write

nakręcać (na-kráṅ-tsach) v. wind up; shoot (movie);turn ;direct

nakrętka (na-kráṅt-ka) f.(screw) nut; female screw; jam nut

nakrycie (na-kri-che) n. cover

nakrywać (na-kri-vach) v. cover

nakrywka (na-kriv-ka) f. lid

na kształt (na kshtawt) in form of...;in shape of; a kind of...

nalać (na-lach) v. pour in; pour on (liquid only,no sand etc.)

nalegać (na-le-gach) v. insist

naleganie (na-le-gá-ñe) n. insistence ; urgent demand

nalepiać (na-lep-yach) v. stick on; paste on; mount; glue on

nalepka (na-lep-ka) f. label

naleśnik (na-lésh-ñeek) m. pancake wrap around stuffing

nalewać (na-le-vach) v. pour in

należeć (na-le-zhech) v. belong

należność (na-lézh-noshch) f. due; ration ; charge; fee

należny (na-lézh-ni) adj. m. due, owing; rightful; proper

należycie (na-le-zhi-che) adv. properly; duly; suitably

należyty (na-le-zhi-ti) adj. m. proper; right; appropriate

nalot (na-lot) m. air raid; (skin) rush ; coating

naładować (na-wa-do-vach) v. load; charge; cram

nałogowiec (na-wo-go-vyets) m. addict; chain-smoker

nałogowy (na-wo-go-vi) adj. m. addicted ; inveterate;habitual

nałogowy pijak (na-wo-go-vi pee-yak) alcoholic

nałóg (na-woog) m. addiction

namacalny (na-ma-tsál-ni) adj. m. tangible; substantial

namaszczać (na-másh-chach) v. anoint ; grease; smear

namaszczenie (na-mash-che-ñe) n. unction ;anointing

namawiać (na-máv-yach) v. persuade ; prompt; urge;egg on

namazać (na-ma-zach) v. daub-over; anoint ; scrawl(scribble)

namiastka (na-myást-ka) f. substitute; ersatz; stopgap

namiernik (na-myér-ñeek) m. direction finder ; pelorus

namiestnik (na-myest-ñeek) m. regent; governor; viceroy

namiętność (na-myáṅt-noshch) f. passion ; infatuation; fervor

namiętny (na-myáṅt-ni) adj. m. passionate; keen; ardent;lusty

namiot (ná-myot) m. tent

namoczyć (na-mo-chich) v. wet; soak ; soak; steep; drench

namoknąć (na-mok-nównch) v. get soaked ; become saturated

namowa (na-mó-va) f. persuasion

namulić (na-moo-leech) v. slime up ; silt up; mud up; ooze up

namydlić (na-mid-leech) v. soap up ; put soap lather on

namysł (ná-misw) m. reflection

namyślać się(na-mísh-lach śhan)v. ponder; reflect; think over

nanosić (na-nó-śheech) v. bring; deposit; plot; track (mud)

na nowo (na nó-vo) adv. anew

naocznie (na-och-ñe) adv. by
eye; visually ; clearly
naoczny świadek (na-och-ni
shvya-dek) eyewitness;bystander
na odwrót (na od-vroot) adv.
inversely:the other way round
na ogół (na o-goow) adv. (in
general) generally: on the whole
na około (na o-ko-wo) adv. all
around; about:right round
naokoło (na-o-ko-wo) prep. round
naoncznas (na-on-chas) adv. at
that time; then;in those days
naoliwić (na-o-lee-veech) v. oil;
lubricate ; grease;make slippery
na opak (na o-pak) adv. backward; perversely; the wrong way
na ostatek (na o-sta-tek) adv.
finally, in the end; at last
naostrzyć (na-os-tzhich) v.
sharpen up ; become sharp
na oścież (na osh-chesh) adv.
wide open; opened all the way
na oślep (na osh-lep) adv. blind-
ly; full tilt; headlong
na ówczas (na oov-chas) adv. at
that time ;then; in those days
napad (na-pad) m. assault:attempt
napadać (na-pa-dach) v. assail
napar (na-par) m. infusion;
brew ; a beverage brewed
naparstek (na-par-stek) m. thimble: dram; thimble full
naparzyć (na-pa-zhich) v. infuse
napaskudzić (na-pas-koo-dźheech)
v. soil up; make a mess; dirty
napastliwy (na-past-lee-vi) adj.
m. aggressive ;malicious;bitter
napastnik (na-past-ñeek) m. aggressor; forward center (sport)
napastować (na-pas-to-vach) v.
pester; attack; wax molest;worry
napaść (na-pashch) f. assault
napawać (na-pa-vach) v. fill up
(with feelings panic, wander)
napatrzyć się (na-pat-shich shan)
v, see enough;have a good look
napełniac (na-pew-ñach) v. fill
up ; inspire; imbue; pervade
napewno (na-pev-no) adv. surely;
certainly; for sure;without fail
naped (na-pand) m. propulsion;
drive:force; driving gear

napędowy (na-pan-do-vi) adj.
m. motive ;driving; impulsive
napędzać (na-pan-dzach) v. chase
in; propel ;round up;drift in
napić się (na-peech shan) v.
have a drink; quench one's thirst
napierać (na-pye-rach) v. press
forward; insist, ; advance
napięcie (na-pyan-che) n. tension; strain; voltage;intensity
napiętek (na-pyan-tek) m. heel
napiętnować (na-pyant-no-vach)
v. brand; stigmatize;censure
condemn as being very bad;stamp
napięty (na-pyan-ty) adj. m.
tense; taut; strained; tight
napinać (na-pee-nach) v. strain
napis (na-pees) m. inscription
napitek (na-pee-tek) m. drink
napiwek (na-pee-vek) m. tip
napluć (na-plooch) v. spit on
napływ (na-pwiv) m. influx
napływać (na-pwi-vach) v. inflow; flow in; flock:pour in
napływowy (na-pwi-vo-vi) adj.
m. alluvial; immigrant; allien
napoczynać (na-po-chi-nach) v.
start up; open; broach
napominać (na-po-mee-nach) v.
admonish; reprimand: rebuke
napomknąć (na-pom-known´ch) v.
mention; hint at; allude to
napomnienie (na-pom-ñe-ñe) n.
admonition; reprimand;rebuke
na pomoc ! (na po-mots) excl.
help ! give help! please,help!
napotny (na-pot-ni) adj. m.
sudatory; perspiratory
napotykać (na-po-ti-kach) v.
run in; come across:be faced with
napowietrzny (na-po-vyetzh-ni)
adj. m. aerial; overhead
na powrót (na pov-root) adv.
return; again; on the way back
na pozór (na po-zoor) adv. apparently; on the face of it
napój (na-pooy) m. drink
na pół (na poow) adv. in half
napór (na-poor) m. pressure
naprawa (na-pra-va) f. repair;
redress: renovation; reform
naprawdę (na-prav-dan) adv. indeed; really: truly; positively

naprawiać (na-praw-yach) v. repair; fix; mend; rectify;reform
naprędce (na-prand-tse) adv.
hastily; in a hurry;slapdash
naprężenie (na-pran-zhe-ne) n.
tension; strain; tautness
naprężyć (na-pran-zhich) v.
tauten; stretch;strain
naprowadzać (na-pro-va-dzach)
v. lead in; direct to;advise
na próżno (na proozh-no) adv.
in vain: uselessly;to no avail
naprzeciw (na-pzhe-cheev) adv.
opposite: vis-a-vis
naprzec (na-pzhech) v. press;
urge : press hard; insist on
na przekor (na pzhe-koor) adv.
in despite; just to spite
na przełaj (na pzhe-way) adv.
shortcut (across obstacles)
na przemian (na pzhe-myan) adv.
alternately ; by turns
naprzód (na-pzhoot) adv. forwards;first;in the first place
na przykład (na pzhik-wat) adv.
for instance; for example
naprzykrzać się(na-pshik-shach
shan)v bother;molest;pester
napuchnąc (na-pookh-nownch) v.
swell ; become swollen
napuchły (na-pookh-wi) adj. m.
swollen;bulging; distended
napuścić (na-poosh-cheech) v.
set up ; impregnate; let in
napuszony (na-poo-sho-ni) adj.
m. puffed up; bristling;ruffled
napychać (na-pi-khach) v. stuff;
cram ;cram;fill;pack:crowd,stow
narada (na-ra-da) f. consultation ; council;. conference
naradzać się (na-ra-dzach shan)v.
consult; confer with;deliberate
naramiennik (na-ra-myen-neek)
m. epaulet; shoulder-strap
narastać (na-ras-tach) v. grow
on ;increase; accumulate;accrue
naraz (na-ras) adv. suddenly
na razie (na ra-zhe) adv. for
the time being ;for the present
narażać (na-ra-zhach) v. expose
to endanger
narciarstwo (nar-char-stvo) n.
skiing

narciarz (nar-chash) m. skier
narcyz (nar-tsis) m. narcissus
nareszcie (na-resh-che) adv.
at last; finally;at long last
naręcze (na-ran-che) n. armful
narkotyczny (nar-ko-tich-ni)
adj. m. narcotic:causing numbness
narkotyk (nar-ko-tik) m.narcot-
ic :drug for sleep and relief
narkoza (nar-ko-za) f. anesthe-
sia ; anaesthetization
narobić (na-ro-beech) v.mess up;
cause nuisance; make a mess
narodowość (na-ro-do-voshch) f.
nationality:national status
narodowy (na-ro-do-vi) adj. m.
national;of national character
narodzenie (na-ro-dze-ne) n.
birth; a being born;the beginning
narodzić się (na-ro-dzheech shan)
v. be born; originate; arise
narodziny (na-ro-dzhee-ni) n.
birth; origin; the beginning
narosl (na-roshl) f. tumor;
growth;excrescence; wart;knar
narowisty (na-ro-vees-ti) adj.
m. restive;vicious:skittish
narożnik (na-rozh-neek) m. corner ;angle; cross-roads;gusset
narożny (na-rozh-ni) adj. m.
corner-; at the street corner
naród (na-root) m. nation;people
narów (na-roof) m. vice (res-
tivness); bad habit; fault
narta (nar-ta) f. ski; sleigh
naruszać (na-roo-shach) v. disturb; violate; injure; harm
naruszenie (na-roo-she-ne) n.
offense; disturbance; breach
narwany (na-rva-ni) adj. m.
hot-head; reckless; rash
narybek (na-ri-bek) m. small
fry; coming generation
narząd (na-zhownt) m. organ
narzecze (na-zhe-che) n. (primitive)dialect
narzeczona (na-zhe-cho-na) f.
fiancée: an engaged woman
narzeczony (na-zhe-cho-ni) m.
fiance
narzekać (na-zhe-kach) v. complain: grumble: lament

narzekanie (na-zhe-ká-ñe) n.
  complaints;kick; bitching
narzędzie (na-zhañ-dźhe) n.
  tool; utensil; implement
narzucać (na-zhoo-tsać) v.
  throw over; impose;shovel on
nasada (na-sá-da) f. base
nasenna pigułka (na-sén-na pi-
  goow-ka) sleeping-pill
nasiadówka (na-śha-doov-ka) f.
  sitzbath; hip-bath
nasiąkać (na-śhown-kach) v.
  soak up;become saturated;imbibe
nasienie (na-śhe-ñe) m. seed;
  sperm; semen: posterity
nasilenie (na-śhee-le-ñe) n.
  intensification; intensity
naskórek (na-skoo-rek) m. outer
  skin; epidermis;.cuticle
naskarżyć (na-skár-zhich) v.
  denounce; lodge a complain
nasłuchać się (na-swoo-khach
  śhań) v. hear plenty
nasłuchiwać (na-swoo-khee-vach)
  v. monitor (radio);listen
nasmarować (na-sma-ro-vach) v.
  smear over; grease; lubricate
nastać (ná-stach) v. set in;
  enter; occur; come about
nastanie (na-stá-ñe) n. arrival;
  setting-in; advent; coming
nastarczyć (na-stár-chich) v.
  supply enough; keep pace; cope
nastawać (na-stá-yach) v. insist
nastawiać (na-stáv-yach) v. set
  up; set right; tune in; point
nastawienie (na-sta-vyé-ñe) n.
  attitude; bias; disposition
następca (na-stanp-tsa) m. successor : heir
następnie (na-stanp-ñe) adv.
  next; then; subsequently
następny (na-stánp-ni) adj. m.
  next; the next: the following
następować (na-stán-po-vach) v.
  follow; tread; come after:ensue
następstwo (na-stanp-stvo) n.
  result; succession; upshot
następujacy (na-stán-poo-yown-
  tsi) adj. m. successive; following; the following
nastraszyć (na-stra-shich) v.
  frighten; intimidate

nastręczać (na-strań-chach) v.
  afford; present; offer; procure
nastroic (na-stró-eech) v. at-
  tune; tune up; dispose to
nastroszyć (na-stro-shich) v.
  bristle up; perk up; heap up
nastrój (na-strooy) m. mood
nasturcja (na-stoor-tsya) f.
  nasturtia; lark-heel
nasuwać (na-sóo-vach) v. shove
  up; draw over: afford;overthrust
nasycać (na-si-tsach) v. satiate; satisfy; sate; saturate
nasycenie (na-si-tse-ñe) n. sa-
  tiation; saturation;satisfaction
nasycony (na-si-tsó-ni) adj. m.
  satiate; saturated; replete
nasyłać (na-si-wach) v. send on
nasyp (ná-sip) m. embankment
nasypać (na-si-pach) v. pour in;
  spread up (dry powder etc)
nasz (nash) pron. our; ours
naszyć (na-shich) v. sew on;
  trim with; trim
naszkicować (na-shkee-tso-vach)
  v. sketch; make a sketch
naszyjnik (na-shiy-ñeek) m.
  necklace; neck jewelry
naśladować (na-śhla-do-vach) v.
  imitate; mimic; reproduce
naśladowanie (na-śhla-do-va-ñe)
  n. imitation; copy
naśladowca (na-śhla-dóv-tsa)
  m. imitator
naśmiewać się (na-śhmye-vach
  śhań) v. laugh at; deride
naświetlać (na-śhvyet-lach) v.
  explain; irradiate; expose
natarcie (na-tár-che) n.
  1. rubbing; 2. onslaught; attack; offensive; advance
natarczywość (na-tar-chi-voshch)
  n. insistency; obtrusiveness
natarczywy (na-tar-chí-vi) adj;
  n. insistent; pressing;urgent
natchnąć (nát-khnownch) v. inspire; infuse; penetrate
natchnienie (nat-khñe-ñe) n.
  inspiration; brain wave;impulse
natenczas (na-ten-chas) adv.
  then: at that time; as
natężać (na-tan-zhach) v. strain;
  intensify; strenghten; exert

natężenie (na-tań-zhe-ńe) n.
tension;strain: effort;pitch
natężony (na-tań-zho-ni) adj.
m. intense.: strained
natknąć (nát-knównch) v. come
across ;butt; stick; stud
natłoczony (na-two-chó-ni) adj.
m. crowded: packed; huddled
natłoczyć (na-two-chich) v.
cram: pack: crowd; huddle
natłok (ná-twok) m. crowd;
throng; pressure accumulation
natomiast (na-to-myast) adv.
however:, yet; on the contrary
natłuścić (na-twoósh-ćheećh) v.
oil; grease; lubricate
natrafić (na-tra-feećh) v. encounter;. come across
natręctwo (na-tráńts-tvo) n.
intrusiveness;importunity
natręt (ná-trańt) m. intruder
natrętny (na-tráńt-ni) adj. m.
intrusive:, bothersome
natrysk (na-trisk) m. shower-
bath: shower; sprying
natrząsać się (na-tzhown-sach
śhań)v.scoff at: sneer;poke fun
natrzeć (ná-tzhećh) v. rub;
attack; harass: scold; rate
natura (na-too-ra) f. nature
naturalizacja (na-too-ra-lee-
záts-ya) f. naturalization
naturalizować (na-too-ra-lee-zó-
vach) v. naturalize
naturalny (na-too-rál-ni) adj.
m. natural; true to life
natychmiast (na-tikh-myast) adv.
at once;instantly; right away
natychmiastowy (na-tikh-myas-
tó-vi), adj. m. instantaneous
nauczać (na-oo-chach) v. teach;
instruct: tutor; train
nauczanie (na-oo-cha-ńe) n.
teaching; instruction
nauczka (na-oóch-ka) f. (pointed) lesson (unpleasant)
nauczyciel (na-oo-chi-ćhel) m.
teacher; instructor
nauczyć się (na-oo-chich śhań)
v. learn: come to know
nauka (na-oo-ka) f. science;
learning; study; teaching

naukowiec (na-oo-kóv-yets) m.
scientist; scholar: researcher
naukowość (na-oo-kó-vośhćh) f.
erudition; scholarship;learning
naukowy (na-oo-kó-vi) adj. m.
scientific; scholarly;academic
naumyślnie (na-oo-míshl-ńe)
adv. on purpose; of set purpose
nawa (ná-va) f. nave; aisle
nawadniać (na-vád-ńach) v.
irrigate; saturate with water
nawalić (na-va-leećh) v. pile
up; fail; bungle;break down
nawał (ná-vaw) m. no end of
nawała (na-vá-wa)f. overwhelm-
ing mass; swarms; onslaught
nawałnica (na-vaw-ńee-tsa) f.
tempest; storm; hurricane
nawarstwienie (na-var-stvyé-ńe)
n. stratification
nawarzyć (na-vá-zhićh) v. brew;
cook; concoct; get in trouble
nawet (ná-vet) adv. even
nawet gdyby (na-vet gdí-bi)
adv. even if; even though
nawias (ná-vyas), m. parenthesis
nawiasem (na-vyá-sem) adv. incidentally; by way of digression
nawiasowy (na-vya-só-vi) adj.
m. parenthetical; incidental
nawiązać (na-vyown-zach) v.
tie to; refer to; enter in
nawiązanie (na-vyówn-zá-ńe) n.
connection; reference to
nawiedzać (na-vyé-dzach) v.
visit; haunt; afflict; obsess
nawierzchnia (na-vyezh-khña) f.
surface (finish); pavement
nawijać (na-veé-yach) v. wind
up;reel; roll up; spool: coil
nawlekać (na-vlé-kach) v. thread;
string; slip on
nawodnienie (na-vod-ńe-ńe) n.
irrigation, saturation with water
nawoływać (na-vo-wi-vach) v.
call; hail; exhort to; halloo
nawozić (na-vó-źheećh) v. fertilize; manure :truck;cart; fill
nawóz (ná-voos) m. manure :dung
na wpół (na vpoow) adv. half;
semi-: half-(finished, boiled)
nawracać (na-vra-tsach) v. turn
around; convert ; turn back

nawrócenie (na-vroo-tse-ñe) n.
conversion; being converted

nawrót (ná-vroot) m. return;
relapse; recurrence; set-back

na wskros (na vskrosh) adv.
throughout; from end to end

nawyk (ná-vik) m. habit; wont

nawykać (na-vi-kach) v. accustom; fall into a habit

nawykły (na-vik-wi) adj. m..
accustomed; get used to...

na wylot (na vi-lot) adv. through
and through; right through

nawymyślać (na-vi-mish-lach) v.
revile; abuse;insult; invent

na wyrywki (na vi-riv-kee) adv.
at random;at haphazard

nawzajem (na-vzá-yem) adv. mu-
tually; same to you

na wznak (ná vznak) adv. on
one's back; on one's supine

nazad (ná-zat) adv. back (wards)

nazajutrz (na-zá-jootsh) adv.
next morning; next day

nazbierać (na-zbyé-rach) v.
gather up; collect;assemble

nazbyt (ná-zbit) adv. too much

na zewnątrz (na zév-nówntsh)
adv. out; outwards; outside

naznaczyć (na-zna-chich) v.
mark;fix; appoint;outline;scar

nazwa (náz-va) f. designation;
name; appellation; title

nazwisko (naz-vee-sko) m. family name; surname;reputation

nazywać (na-zi-vach) v. call;
name;term; denominate; christen

nażarty (na-zhar-ti) adj. m.
gorged; stuffed(greedily)

nażreć się (ná-zhrech shán) v.
gorge; stuff oneself (vulg.)

negacja (ne-gáts-ya) f. negation; opposite of positive

negatyw (ne-gá-tiv) m. negative

negatywny (ne-ga-tiv-ni) adj.
m. negative; saying "no"

negliż (nég-leesh) m. undress;
morning dress; dishabille

negocjacje (ne-go-tsyáts-ye) pl.
negotiations;settling a treaty

negować (ne-gó-vach) v. deny

nekrolog (ne-kró-log) m. obituary notice : obituary

nektar (nék-tar) m. nectar

neofita (ne-o-fée-ta) m. convert; neophyte; proselyte

neologizm (ne-o-ló-geezm) m.
neologism; new word;new meanning

neon (né-on) m. neon light

nepotyzm (ne-pó-tizm) m. nepo-
tizm; favoritism to relatives

nerka (ner-ka) f. kidney

nerw (nerv) m. nerve;vigor;ardor

nerwica (ner-vee-tsa) f. neurosis; nervous disturbance

nerwoból (ner-vo-bool) m. neuralgia; severe pain along a nerve

nerwowość (ner-vo-voshch) f.
nervosity; irritability; fidgets

nerwowy (ner-vo-vi) adj. m. nervous;made up of nerves; fearful

neseser (ne-sé-ser) m. dressing
case; make-up case; toilet case

netto (nét-to) adv. net (cost)

neutralizować (ne-oo-tra-lee-
zó-vach) v. neutralize

neutralność (ne-oo-trál-noshch)
f. neutrality; neutral status

neutralny (ne-oo-trál-ni) adj.
m. neutral; indifferent

neutron (ne-oo-tron) m. neutron

newralgia (ne-vrál-gya) f.
neuralgia; pain along a nerve

newroza (ne-vró-za) f. neurosis

nęcić (náñ-cheech) v. entice;
court; allure; tempt;be seductive

nędza (náñ-dza) f. misery

nędzarz (náñ-dzash) m. destitute
wretch; beggar; pauper

nędznik (náñdz-ñeek) m. villain

nędzny (náñdz-ni) adj. m. wretched;miserable ; shabby; sorry

nękać (náñ-kach) v. molest; hurry;
torment; harass; annoy; worry

ni to ni owo (ñee to ñee ó-vo)
adv. neither this nor that

ni stąd ni zowąd (ñee stównt
ñee zo-vównt) without reason;
suddenly ; for no reason whatever

niania (ñá-ña) f. (baby's)
nurse ; nanny; dry nurse

niańczyć (ñáñ-cheech) v. nurse

nianka (ñáñ-ka) f. nurse

niby (ñee-bi) adv. as if; pre-
tending ;as it were; like

nic (ñeets) pron. nothing; nought

nic nie szkodzi (ńeets ńe shko-dźhee) expr.: does not matter

nic z tego (ńeets z té-go) expr.: no use: to no purpose; to no avail

nicość (ńee-tsoshch) f. nothingness; oblivion; nonentity

nicpoń (ńets-poń) m. good-for-nothing; "nogoodnik"; scamp

niczyj (ńee-chiy) adj. m. no-man's: nobody's; no one's

nici (ńee-ćhee) pl. 1. threads 2. nothing; nothing of it

nić (ńeećh) f. thread

nie (ńe) part. no; not (any)

nie jeszcze (ńe yesh-che) not-yet; not for a long time

nieagresja (ńe-a-gres-ya) f. nonaggression (treaty)

niebaczny (ńe-bach-ni) adj. m. imprudent; rush; inconsiderate

niebawem (ńe-ba-vem) adv. soon

niebezpieczeństwo (ńe-bez-pye-chéń-stvo) m. danger; peril

niebezpieczny (ńe-bez-pyech-ni) adj. m. dangerous; risky; tricky

niebiański (ńe-byan-skee) adj. m. heavenly; divine

niebieskawy (ńe-byes-ká-vi) adj. m. bluish

niebieski (ńe-byes-kee) adj. m. blue; heavenly; of the sky

niebieskooki (ńe-byes-ko-ó-kee) adj. m. blue-eyed

niebiosa (ńe-byó-sa) pl. Heavens: the visible sky

niebo (ńe-bo) ŋ. sky

nieborak (ńe-bo-rak) m. poor soul; poor soul; poor devil

nieboszczyk (ńe-bósh-chik) m. deceased; dead person

niebosiężny (ńe-bo-shäńzh-ni) adj. m. sky-high; towering

niebotyczny (ńe-bo-tich-ni) adj. m. sky-high; sky reaching

niebożę (ńe-bo-zhän) n. poor soul; poor thing; poor devil

nie byle jak (ńe bi-le yak) expr.: not just any way; not carelessly

niebyły (ńe-bi-vi) adj. m. null and void : unexisting

niebywale (ńe-bi-va-le) adv. unusually; exceptionally

niebywały (ńe-bi-va-wi) adj. m. unheard-of; unusual; uncommon

niecały (ńe-tsá-wi) adj. m. incomplete: defective; less than

niecenzuralny (ńe-tsen-zoo-rál-ni) adj. m. indecent; unprintable : obscene; suggestive

niech (ńekh) part. let; suppose

niechcący (ńe-khtsówn-tsi) adv. unintentionally; unawares

niechęć (ńe-khänćh) f. disinclination; aversion; ill-will

niechętny (ńe-khänt-ni) adj. m. unwilling; reluctant: averse

niechluj (ńe-khlooy) m. grub; sloppy; slut: dirty: sloven

niechybny (ńe-khib-ni) adj. m. without fail: certain: unerring

niechże (ńekh-zhe) part. let

niecić (ńe-ćheećh) v. kindle; stir up; light (a fire)

nieciekawy (ńe-ćhe-ka-vi) adj. m. blank; void of interest

niecierpliwić się (ńe-ćher-plee-veećh shän) v. be impatient

niecierpliwy (ńe-ćher-plee-vi) adj. m. impatient; restless

niecnota (ńe-tsno-ta) m. scamp; rogue; rascal: scoundrel

niecny (ńets-ni) adj. m. vile

nieco (ńe-tso) adv. somewhat; a little: a trifle; slightly

niecodzienny (ńe-tso-dźhén-ni) adj. m. uncommon; unusual

nieczesany (ńe-che-sá-ni) adj. m. unkempt : disorderly

nieczęsty (ńe-chäń-sti) adj. m. infrequent: not frequent

nieczuły (ńe-choo-wi) adj. m. callous: heartless: insensible

nieczynny (ńe-chin-ni) adj. m. inert; inactive: out of order

nieczysty (ńe-chis-ti) adj. m. unclean: polluted: dirty: shady

nieczytelny (ńe-chi-tel-ni) adj. m. illegible; cramped: crabbed

niedaleki (ńe-da-le-kee) adj. m. near; not distant; at hand

niedaleko (ńe-da-le-ko) adv. near; not far; a short way off

niedawno (ńe-dáv-no) adv. recently; not long ago; newly

niedbale (ńe-dba-le) adv. carelessly; casually: nonchalantly

niedbalstwo (ńe-dbal-stvo) n. negligence; laxity; carelessness

niedbały (ńe-dba-wi) adj. m.
negligent;untidy;lax;careless

niedługi (ńe-dwoo-gee) adj. m.
short; not long

niedługo (ńe-dwoo-go) adv. soon;
not long; before long;by and by

niedobitki (ńe-do-beet-kee) pl.
survivors; routed soldiers

niedobór (ńe-do-boor) m. deficit; shortage; scarcity; loss

niedobrany (ńe-do-bra-ni) adj.
m. ill-suited; ill-matched

niedobry (ńe-dob-ri) adj. m.
no-good; bad; wicked; nasty

niedobrze (ńe-dob-zhe) adv. not
well; badly;wrong;improperly

nie doceniać(ńe-do-tse-ńach) v.
underestimate; estimate too low

niedociągnięcie (ńe-do-chówn-
gnań-che) n. shortcoming

niedogodność (ńe-do-gód-noshch)
f. inconvenience; drawback

niedogodny (ńe-do-gód-ni) adj.
m. inconvenient; undesirable

nie dogotowany(ńe-do-go-to-va-
ni) adj. m. underdone; half-
cooked; half-raw: under done

nie dojadać(ńe-do-ya-dach) v.
not eat enough;starve

niedojda (ńe-dóy-da) m. nitwit;
bungler; fumbler; lout

niedojrzały (ńe-doy-zha-wi) adj.
m. unripe; immature ; under age

niedokładny (ńe-do-kwád-ni) adj.
m. inaccurate; inexact

niedokończony (ńe-do-koń-chó-ni)
adj. m. unfinished;incomplete

niedokrwisty (ńe-do-krvees-ti)
adj. m. anemic; anaemic

niedola (ńe-dó-la) f. adversity

niedołęga (ńe-do-wán-ga) m.
blunderer; cripple;duffer

niedołęstwo (ńe-do-wán-stvo) m.
inefficiency; clumsiness

niedomagać (ńe-do-má-gach) v.
be unwell; be ailing

nie domknięty(ńe-do-mkńań-ti)
adj. m. ajar; slightly open

niedomówienie (ńe-do-moo-vyé-ńe)
n. vague hint; insinuation

niedomyślny (ńe-do-miśhl-ni)
adj. m. slow thinking

niedopałek (ńe-do-pá-wek) m.
(cigarette) butt: stub;ember

niedopatrzenie (ńe-do-pa-tzhe-
ńe) n. oversight; neglect

niedopuszczalny (ńe-do-poosh-
chál-ni) adj. m. inadmissible

niedorozwinięty (ńe-do-roz-
vee-ńań-ti) adj. m. underdeveloped; mentally retarded

niedorzeczny (ńe-do-zhéch-ni)
adj. m. absurd; ridiculous

niedoskonały (ńe-dos-ko-ná-wi)
adj. m. imperfect:deficient

niedosłyszalny (ńe-do-swi-shál-
ni) adj. m. inaudible

niedosmażony (ńe-do-sma-zhó-ni)
adj. m. underdone : half-raw

nie dospać(ńe-dos-pach) v.
sleep too short time; not sleep
enough; not to have enough sleep

niedostateczny (ńe-dos-ta-tech-
ni) adj. m. insufficient

niedostatek (ńe-dos-tá-tek) m.
shortage; indigence; poverty

niedostępny (ńe-do-stánp-ni)
adj. m. inaccessible;out of reach

niedostosowanie (ńe-dos-to-so-
vá-ńe)n. maladjustment

niedostrzegalny (ńe-do-stzhe-
gál-ni) adj. m. imperceptible

niedościgły (ńe-do-śhcheeg-wi)
adj. m. matchless; inimitable

niedoświadczenie (ńe-do-śhvyad-
ché-ńe) n. inexperience

niedouczony (ńe-do-oo-chó-ni)
adj. n. half-educated

nie dowarzony (ńe do-va-zhó-ni)
adj. m. half-boiled; rough

niedowarzony (ńe-do-va-zhó-ni)
adj. m. immature ;undereducated

niedowiarek (ńe-do-vya-rek) m.
unbeliever; atheist; skeptic

niedowidzieć (ńe-do-vee-dźech)
v. be short-sighted

nie dowierzać(ńe-do-vyé-zhach)
v. distrust; disbelieve

niedowład (ńe-do-vwat) m. pare-
sis : partial paralysis

niedozwolony (ńe-do-zvo-ló-ni)
adj. m. not allowed ;illicit

niedrogi (ńe-dro-gee) adj. m.
cheap ; inexpensive

nieduży (ńe-doó-żhi) adj. m.
small; little;not big;not tall

niedwuznaczny (ńe-dvoo-znách-ni)
adj. m. unequivocal; clear

niedyskrecja (ńe-dis-krets-ya)
f. indiscretion;indelicacy.

niedyspozycja (ńe-dis-po-zits-
ya) f. indisposition

niedziela (ńe-dźhé-la)f. Sunday

niedźwiadek (ńe-dźhvya-dek) m.
bear cub; Teddy bear.

niedźwiedzica (ńe-dzhvye-dźhee-
tsa) f. female bear:she-bear

niedźwiedź (ńe-dźhvyedźh) m.
bear: bearskin; clumsy man

nieelastyczny (ńe-e-las-tích-
ni) adj. m. inelastic

nieestetyczny (ńe-es-te-tich-
ni) adj. m. unesthetic

nieetyczny (ńe-e-tich-ni) adj.
m. unethical; immoral

niefachowy (ńe-fa-khó-vi) adj.
m. incompetent; inexpert

nieforemny (ńe-fo-rém-ni) adj.
m. shapeless; deformed

nieformalnie (ńe-for-mál-ńe)
adv. informally; illegally

niefortunny (ńe-for-tóon-ni)
adj. m. unlucky; regrettable

niefrasobliwy (ńe-fra-sob-lee-
vi) adj. m. care-free;jaunty

niegdyś (ńég-diśh) adv. formerly; once; at one time

niegodny (ńe-gód-ni) adj. m.
unworthy;undignified;yile;base

niegodziwy (ńe-go-dźhee-vi)adj.
m. wicked;vile;base;mean;foul

niegościnny (ńe-gośh-cheen-ni)
adj. m. inhospitable;desolate

niegrzeczny (ńe-gzhéch-ni) adj.
m. rude; impolite;unkind: bad

niegustowny (ńe-goos-tóv-ni)
adj. m. tasteless:in bad taste

niehigieniczny (ńe-khee-ǵe-
ńeéch-ni) adj. m. unsanitary

niehonorowy (ńe-kho-no-ró-vi)
adj. m. dishonorable; unfair

nieistotny (ńe-ees-tó-tni) adj.
m. inessential; immaterial

niejaki (ńe-yá-kee) adj. m. a;
one; certain:some;slight

niejasno (ńe-yás-no) adv. dimly:
vaguely;ambiguously;obscurely

niejasny (ńe-yás-ni) adj. m.dim;
unclear;indistinct;vague;obscure

niejeden (ńe-yé-den) adj. m.
many a; quite a number

niejednokrotnie (ńe-yed-no-krót-
ńe) adv. repeatedly;recurrently

nie karany (ńe ka-rá-ni) adj. m.
with a clean record; not con-
victed before

niekiedy (ńe-kyé-di) adv. now
and then; sometimes; at times

niekonsekwentny (ńe-kon-se-kvént-
ni) adj. m. inconsistent

niekorzystny (ńe-ko-zhist-ni)
adj. m. disadvantageous

niekorzyść (ńe-kó-zhiśhch) f.
disadvantage; detriment

niekształtny (ńe-kshtáwt-ni)
adj. m. unshapely; formless

niektóry (ńe-ktoó-ry) adj. m.
some;one here and there

nieledwie (ńe-léd-vye) adv. all
but: almost;practically

nielegalny (ńe-le-gál-ni) adj.
m. illegal;unlawful:illicit

nieletni (ńe-lét-ńee) adj. m.
under age;juvenile; minor

nieliczny (ńe-leéch-ni) adj. m.
not numerous; scarce;rare;small

nielitościwy (ńe-lee-tośh-chee-
vi) adj. m. unmerciful

nielogiczny (ńe-lo-geéch-ni)
adj. m. illogical; nonsensical

nieludzki (ńe-loódz-kee) adj.
inhuman: atrocious;ruthless

nieład (ńe-wat) m. disorder;
disarray; confusion:mess

nieładnie (ńe-wád-ńe) adv. not
nicely: unattractively;wrongly

niełaska (ńe-wás-ka) f. disgrace;
disfavor;loss of respect

niemal (ńe-mal) adv. almost;
nearly;pretty nearly;well-nigh

niemało (ńe-má-wo) adv. not a
few; pretty much:not a little

niemały (ńe-má-wi) adj. m. pretty big;fair-sized;goodly;no mean

niemądry (ńe-mownd-ri) adj. unwise; ill-judged;silly;stupid

niemczyć (ńem-chích) v.Germanize

niemęski (ńe-mán-kee)adj.m.unmanly

niemiecki (ńem-yéts-kee) adj. m.
German ; German language

niemiły (ñe-mée-wi) adj. m. unpleasant;unsightly;harsh;surly
niemniej jednak (ñe-mney yed-
nak) nevertheless; all the
same;none the less; however
niemoc (ñe-mots) f. impotence
niemodny (ñe-mód-ni) adj. m.
outmoded; out of fashion
niemoralny (ñe-mo-rál-ni) adj.
m. immoral; dishonest
niemowa (ñe-mó-ya) m.∝ f. mute
niemowlę (ñe-mov-lań) n. baby
niemożliwy (ñe-mozh-leé-vi)
adj. m. impossible
niemrawy (ñe-mrá-vi) adj. m.
sluggish; tardy; indolent
niemy (ñie-mi) adj. m. dumb
nienaganny (ñe-na-gán-ni) adj.
m. blameless; faultless
nienaruszalny (ñe-na-roo-shál-
ni) adj. m. inviolable
nienaruszony (ñe-na-roo-shó-ni)
adj. m. intact·undisturbed
nienasycony (ñe-na-si-tso-ni)
adj. m. insatiable; (chem.
unsaturated); voracious
nienaturalny (ñe-na-too-rál-ni)
adj. m. unnatural; insincere
nienawistny (ñe-na-veest-ni)
adj. m. hateful;full of hatred
nienawiść (ñe-ná-veeshch) f.
hate; abomination;detestation
nie nazwany (ñe naz-vá-ni) adj.
m. unnamed; not maned
nienormalny (ñe nor-mál-ni)
adj. m. abnormal; insane
nieobecność (ñe-o-béts-noshch)
f. absence; non-attendance
nieobecny (ñe-o-béts-ni) adj.
m. absent; not present;not in
nieobeznany (ñe-o-bez-na-ni)
adj. m. uninformed; ignorant
nieobliczalny (ñe-o-blee-chál-
ni) adj. m. unreliable; incalculable;irresponsible
nieobyczajny (ñe-o-bi-cháy-ni)
adj. m. immoral;ill-manhered
nieoceniony (ñe-o-tse-ño-ni)
adj. m. inestimable
nieoczekiwany (ñe-oche-kee-vá-
ni) adj. m. unexpected
nieodłączny (ñe-od-wovnch-ni)
adj. m. inseparable

nieodmienny (ñe-od-myén-ni)
adj. m. invariable;undeclinable
nieodparty (ñe-od-pár-ti) adj.
m. irrefutable; compelling
nieodpowiedni (ñe-od-po-vyéd-nee)
adj. m. inadequate; wrong
nieodpowiedzialny (ñe-od-po-vye-
dżhál-ni) adj. m. irresponsible
nieodstępny (ñe-od-stáhp-ni)
adj. m. inseparable;ever present
nieodwołalny (ñe-od-vo-wál-ni)
adj. m. irrevocable; final
nieodzownie (ñe-od-zóv-ñe) adv.
inevitably; absolutely
nieodzowny (ñe-od-zóv-ni) adj.
m. indispensable;irrevocable
nieodżałowany (ñe-od-zha-wo-vá-
ni) adj. m. never enough regretted; much regretted
nieoględny (ñe-o-glánd-ni) adj.
m. inconsiderate;reckless;rash
nieograniczony (ñe-o-gra-nee-chó
ni) adj. m. infinite; boundless
nieokiełzany (ñe-o-kew-za-ni)
adj. m. unbridled; uncontrollable
nieokreślony (ñe-o-kresh-ló-ni)
adj. m. indefinite;undetermined
nieokrzesany (ñe-o-kzhe-sa-ni)
adj. m. rude;crude;ill-mannered
nieomal (ñe-o-mal) adv. almost;
nearly; pretty nearly;practically
nieomylny (ñe-o-mil-ni) adj. m.
infallible;unerring;sure
nieopatrzny (ñe-o-pátzh-ni) adj.
m. unguarded;inconsiderate
nieopisany (ñe-o-pee-sa-ni) adj.
m. indescribable;excessive;extreme
nieopłacalny (ñe-o-pwa-tsál-ni)
adj. m. unprofitable
nieopłacony (ñe-o-pwa-tso-ni)
adj. m. unpaid;not paid for
nieopodal (ñe-o-pó-dal) adv.
near by; close at hand;next door
nieorganiczny (ñe-or-ga-ñeech-
ni) adj. m. inorganic;inanimate
nieosobowy (ñe-o-so-bó-vi) adj.
m. inpersonal; not personal
nieostrożny (ñe-os-trozh-ni)
adj. m. careless; imprudent
nieoswojony (ñe-os-vo-yo-ni)
adj. m. untamed; unfamiliar
nieoświecony (ñe-oshh-vye-tso-
ni) adj. m. dark; ignorant

nieoznaczony (ňe-oz-na-chó-ni)
  adj. m. indefinite;unmarked
niepalący (ňe-pa-lówn-tsi) adj.
  m. not smoking; non smoking
niepalność(ňe-pál-nošch)f.in-
  combustibility;non-inflammability
niepalny (ňe-pal-ni) adj. m.
  incombustible;uninflammable
niepamięć (ňe-pá-myáňch) f.
  oblivion; forgetfulness
niepamiętny (ňe-pa-myáňt-ni)
  adj. m. forgetful; immemorial
nieparlamentarny (ňe-par-la-
  men-tár-ni) adj. unparliamen-
  tary rough (language)
nieparzysty (ňe-pa-zhis-ti)
  adj. m. odd;uneven; unpaired
niepełnoletni (ňe-pew-no-let-
  ňee) adj. m. minor; underage
niepewność (ňe-pév-nošch) f.
  uncertainty; incertitude
niepewny (ňe-pév-ni) adj. m.
  uncertain ;insecure; unsafe
niepisany (ňe-pee-sá-ni) adj.
  m. unwritten; not in writing
niepiśmienny (ňe-peesh-myen-ni)
  adj. m. illiterate;unlettered
niepłacący (ňe-pwa-tsówn-tsi)
  adj. m. non-paying
niepłodny (ňe-pwod-ni) adj. m.
  sterile; barren; infertile
niepłonny (ňe-pwon-ni) adj. m.
  well-founded ; motivated
niepochlebny (ňe-po-khléb-ni)
  adj. m. unfavorable
niepocieszony (ňe-po-che-shó-
  ni) adj. m. desolate
niepoczciwy (ňe-poch-chee-vi)
  adj. m. wicked; unkind
niepoczytalny (ňe-po-chi-tál-ni)
  adj. m. irresponsible ;insane
niepodejrzany (ňe-po-dey-zha-ni)
  adj. m. unsuspected
niepodległość (ňe-pod-lég-wošch)
  f. independence ;sovereignty
niepodległy (ňe-pod-lég-wi) adj.
  m. independent; sovereign
niepodobieństwo (ňe-po-do-byeň-
  stvo) n. impossibility
niepodobna (ňe-po-dób-na) adv.
  it's impossible ;there is no way
niepodobny (ňe-po-dób-ni) adj.
  m. unlike; unlikely ;dissimilar

niepodzielny (ňe-podzhél-ni)
  adj. m. indivisible;undivided
niepogoda (ňe-po-gó-da) f. bad
  weather; foul weather
niepogwałcony (ňe-po-gvaw-tso-
  ni) adj. m. inviolate
niepohamowany (ňe-po-ha-mo-
  vá-ni) adj. m. unrestrained
niepojętny (ňe-po-yáňt-ni)
  adj. m. dull(man);stupid
niepojęty (ňe-po-yáň-ti) adj.
  m. inconceivable; incomprehensible; unimaginable
niepokalany (ňe-po-ka-lá-ni)
  adj. m. immaculate;faultless
niepokaźny (ňe-po-káźh-ni) adj.
  m. inconspicuous;modest;shabby
niepokoić (ňe-po-ko-eech) v.
  disturb; trouble; annoy;pester
niepokonany (ňe-po-ko-ná-ni)
  adj. m. invincible;irresistible
niepokój (ňe pó kooy) m. anxiety; unrest;trouble;agitation
niepolityczny (ňe-po-lee-tich-
  ni) adj. m. impolitical; in-
  expedient; improper;impolitic
niepomierny (ňe-po-myer-ni)
  adj. m. excessive ; extreme
niepomny (ňe-póm-ni) adj. m.
  forgetful; oblivious
niepomyślny (ňe-po-mishl-ni)
  adj. m. adverse ; unlucky
niepopłatny (ňe-po-pwát-ni)
  adj. m. unprofitable
niepoprawny (ňe-po-práv-ni)
  adj. m. incorrigible
niepopularny (ňe-po-poo-lár-ni)
  adj. m. unpopular
nieporadny (ňe-po-rád-ni) adj.
  m. awkward ;helpless
nieporęczny (ňe-po-ráňch-ni)
  adj. m. cumbersome ;unhandy
nieporozumienie (ňe-po-ro-zoo-
  myé-ňe) n. misunderstanding
nieporównany (ňe-po-roov-ná-
  ni) adj. m. incomparable
nieporuszony (ňe-po-roo-shó-ni)
  adj. m. immovable; firm
nieporządek (ňe-po-zhówn-dek)
  adj. m. disorder; mess
nieporządny (ňe-po-zhównd-ni)
  adj. m. disorderly; untidy;
  messy;slipshod;chaotic

nieposłuszeństwo (ñe-po-swoo-
shéñ-stvo) n. disobedience
nieposłuszny (ñe-po-swoosh-ni)
adj. m. disobedient:unruly
niepospolity (ñe-pos-po-leé-ti)
adj. m. uncommon: rare
niepostrzeżenie(ñe-po-stshe-zhé-
ñe)adv.imperceptibly;unnoticeably
niepotrzebny (ñe-po-tzhéb-ni)
adj. m. unnecessary; useless
niepowetowany (ñe-po-ve-to-va-
ni) adj. m. irreparable
niepowodzenie (ñe-po-vo-dzhé-
ñe) n. failure; adversity
niepowołany (ñe-po-vo-wa-ni)
adj. m. uncalled for; incompetent; unfit; undesirable
niepowrotny (ñe-pov-rót-ni)
adj. m. irrevocable; irrecoverable; beyond recall
niepowstrzymany (ñe-pov-stzhi-
má-ni) adj. m. irresistible
niepowszedni (ñe-pov-shed-ñee)
adj. m. uncommon: exceptional
niepowściągliwy (ñe-pov-shchówng-
leé-vi) adj. m. intemperate
niepozorny (ñe-po-zór-ni) adj.
m. inconspicuous; modest
niepożądany (ñe-po-zhówn-da-ni)
adj. m. undesirable: undesired
niepożyteczny (ñe-po-zhi-tech-
ni) adj. m. useless;unprofitable
niepraktyczny (ñe-prak-tich-ni)
adj. m. impractical;unwieldy
niepraktykujący (ñe-prak-ti-koo-
yówn-tsi)adj. m. noncommuni-
cant ; retired (professional)
nieprawda (ñe-práv-da) f. untruth; falsehood; lie
nieprawdopodobny (ñe-prav-do-
po-dób-ni) adj. m. improbable
nieprawdziwy (ñe-prav-dzhee-vi)
adj. m. untrue; false ;faked
nieprawidłowość (ñe-pra-vee-dwo-
voshch) f. anomaly; irregula-
ity; falsity;incorrectness
nieprawidłowy (ñe-pra-vee-dwo-
vi) adj. m. anomalous; irregular; contrary to the rules
nieprawny (ñe-práv-ni) adj. m.
illegal: unlawful; invalid
nieprawomyślny (ñe-pra-vo-miśhl-
ni) adj. m. unorthodox:disloyal

nieprawy (ñe-pra-vi) adj. m.
unrighteous; adulterous; bastard; unlawful; illegitimate
nieproporcjonalny (ñe-pro-por-
tsyo-nál-ni) adj. m. dispro-
portional:out of proportion
nieproszony (ñe-pro-shó-ni)
adj. m. uncalled for; self-in-
vited; unwelcome (guest)
nieprzebaczalny (ñe-pzhe-ba-
chál-ni) adj. m. unpardonable
nieprzebłagany (ñe-pzhe-bwa-ga-
ni) adj. m. implacable
nieprzebrany (ñe-pzhe-brá-ni)
adj. m. inexhaustible; countless
nieprzebyty (ñe-pzhe-bi-ti)
adj. m. impassable; unfordable
nieprzejednany (ñe-pzhe-yed-
ná-ni) adj. m. irreconcilable
nieprzejrzysty (ñe-pzhey-zhis-
ti) adj. m. not clear
nieprzekupny (ñe-pzhe-koop-ni)
adj. m. unbribable;incorruptible
nieprzemakalny (ñe-pzhe-ma-kál-
ni) adj. m. waterproof
nieprzenikniony (ñe-pzhe-ñeek-
ñó-ni) adj. m. impenetrable
nieprzepuszczalny (ñe-pzhe-
poosh-chál-ni) adj. m. impervious ;impenetrable
nieprzerwany (ñe-pzher-vá-ni)
adj. m. continuous ;ceaseless
nieprześcigniony (ñe-pzhésh-
cheeg-ñó-ni) adj. m. unsur-
passable ; unexcelled
nieprzewidziany (ñe-pzhe-vee-
dżhá-ni) adj. m. unforeseen
nieprzezorny (ñe-pzhe-zór-ni)
adj. m. improvident; unfor-
seeing ;wanting of foresight
nieprzezroczysty (ñe-pzhezh-ro-
chís-ti) adj. m. opaque
nieprzezwyciężony (ñe-pzhez-vi-
chan-zhó-ni) adj. m. invincible ;insurmountable
nieprzychylny (ñe-pzhi-khil-ni)
adj. m. unfriendly ;prejudiced
nieprzydatny (ñe-pzhi-dat-ni)
adj. m. useless ; unserviceable
nieprzygotowany(ñe-pzhi-go-to-
va-ni) adj. m. unprepared
nieprzyjaciel (ñe-pzhi-ya-chel)
m. enemy; foe ;ill-wisher

nieprzyjacielski (ňe-pzhi-ya-chél-skee) adj. m. enemy; hostile: enemy's: enemy-

nieprzyjazny (ňe-pzhi-yáz-ni) adj. m.unfriendly; inimical

nieprzyjaźń (ňe-pzhi-yazň) f. hostility; unfriendliness

nieprzyjemność (ňe-pzhi-yém-nośhch) f. unpleasantness

nieprzyjemny (ňe-pzhi-yém-ni) adj. unpleasant; disagreeable

nie :.vmuszory (ňe-pzhi-moo-shó-ni) adj. m. free; unconstrained; voluntary

nieprzystępny (ňe-pzhis-tańp-ni) adj. m. inaccessible

nieprzytomność (ňe-pzhi-tóm-nośhch) f. unconsciousness; absentmindedness

nieprzytomny (ňe-pzhi-tóm-ni) adj. m. unconscious; absent-minded ;frantic:mad; wild

nieprzyzwoitość (ňe-pzhi-zvo-ee-tośhch) f. indecency

nieprzyzwoity (ňe-pzhiz-vo-eé-ti) adj. m. indecent; obscene

nieprzyzwyczajony (ňe-pzhi-zvi-cha-yó-ni) adj. m. unaccustomed: lacking of habit

niepunktualny (ňe-poon-ktoo-ál-ni) adj. m. unpunctual; late

nierad (ňe-rad) adj. m. unwilling; discontent; annoyed

nieraz (ňe-ras) adv. often; again and again ;many a time

nierdzewny (ňe-rdzév-ni) adj. m. rustproof ;stainless

nierealny (ňe-re-ál-ni) adj. m. imaginary; unreal; unrealizable

nieregularność (ňe-re-goo-lár-nośhch) f. irregularity

nieregularny (ňe-re-goo-lar-ni) adj. m. irregular; erratic

niereligijny (ňe-re-lee-geéy-ni) adj. m. irreligious

nierogacizna (ňe-ro-ga-cheez-na) f. pl. swines pl.

nierozdzielny (ňe-roz-dźhél-ni) adj. m. inseparable

nierozerwalny (ňe-ro-zer-vál-ni) adj. m. indissoluble

nierozgarnięty (ňe-roz-gar-ňań-ti) adj. m. dull; (dim-witted)

nierozłączny (ňe-roz-wównch-ni) adj. m. inseparable

nierozmyślny (ňe-roz-mishl-ni) adj. m. unintentional

nierozpuszczalny (ňe-roz-poosh-chál-ni) adj. m. indissoluble

nierozsądny (ňe-roz-sównd-ni) adj. m. unwise; unreasonable

nierozwaga (ňe-roz-vá-ga) f. inconsideration; rashness

nierozważny (ňe-roz-vázh-ni) adj. m. imprudent; inconsiderate; thoughtless; rush: hasty

nierówność (ňe-roov-nośhch) f. inequality;unevenness

nierówny (ňe-roov-ni) adj. m. unequal; crooked; uneven

nieruchliwy (ňe-rookh-lee-vi) adj. m. slow ; unwieldy

nieruchomość (ňe-roo-kho-mośhch) f. real estate: immobility

nieruchomy (ňe-roo-khó-mi) adj. m. immobile; fixed;still:at rest

nierychło (ňe-rikh-wo) adv. not soon: slowly: not forthcoming

nierzadko ňe-zhád-ko) adv. often: now and then: not seldom

nierzad (ňe-zhównt) m. prostitution; anarchy; debauchery

nierzeczowy (ňe-zhe-chó-vi) adj. m. pointless; futile

nierzeczywisty (ňe-zhe-chi-veés-ti) adj. m. unreal ;fictitious

nierzetelny (ňe-zhe-tél-ni) adj. m. dishonest: unreliable

niesamowity (ňe-sa-mo-veé-ti) adj. m. weird; uncanny : unearthy

niesforny (ňe-sfór-ni) adj. m. unruly; disorderly ;turbulent

nieskalany (ňe-ska-lá-ni) adj. m. immaculate : spotless: pure

nieskazitelny (ňe-ska-źhee-tél-ni) adj. m. unblemished; upright: spotless: moral

nieskładny (ňe-skwad-ni) adj. m. awkward ;discordant;clumsy

nieskończoność (ňe-skoń-cho-nośhch) f. infinity

nieskończony (ňe-skoń-chó-ni) adj. m. unfinished; infinite

nieskromny (ňe-skrom-ni) adj. m. indecent: immodest;morally offensive: improper

nieskuteczny (ńe-skoo-téch-ni)
adj. m. ineffective: futile
niesłabnący (ńe-swab-nówn-tsi)
adj. m. unabated;unflagging
niesława (ńe-swá-va) f. infamy
niesławny (ńeswáv-ni) adj. m.
infamous ;inglorious;disgraceful
niesłowny (ńe-swóv-ni) adj. m.
unreliable; undependable
niesłusznosć (ńe-swoosh-noshch)
f. injustice ;groundlessness
niesłuszny (ńe-swoosh-ni) adj.
m. unjust; wrong ;groundless
niesłychany (ńe-swi-khá-ni) adj.
m. unheard of; unprecedented
niesmaczny (ńe-smach-ni)adj. m.
tasteless; unsavory: unseemly
niesmak (ńes-mak) m. bad taste;
disgust: repugnance;nasty taste
niesnaski (ńes-nás-kee) pl. dissension ;discord; quarrels
niespełna (ńes-pew-na) adv. nearly; not all;not quite: about
niespodzianka (ńe-spo-dżán-ka)
f. surprise : surprise gift
niespodziewany (ńe-spo-dżhe-vá-ni)
adj. m. unexpected ;unlooked for
niespokojny (ńe-spo-koy-ni) adj.
m. restless; fussy ;upset;fretful
niesporo (ńe-spo-ro) adv. slowly
nie sposób (ńe spo-soop) adv.
it's impossible ;by no means
niespożyty (ńe-spo-zhi-ti) adj.
m. durable; indefatigable
niesprawiedliwość (ńe-spra-vyed-
lee-vośhch) f. injustice
niesprawiedliwy (ńe-spra-vyed-
lee-vi) adj. m. unjust;unfair
niesprawny (ńe-správ-ni) adj. m.
ineffective; inefficient
nie sprzyjający (ńe spzhi-ya-
yówn-tsi) adj. m. adverse
niestały (ńe-stá-wi) adj. m. unsteady; inconsistent ;variable
niestaranny (ńe-sta-ran-ni) adj.
m. careless ;sloppy: dowdy
niestateczny (ńe-sta-tech-ni) adj.
m. unstable; fickle; flighty
niestety (ńe-sté-ti) adv. alas;
unfortunately: I am sorry
niestosowny (ńe-sto-sóv-ni) adj.
m. improper; unsuitable;unfit:
inappropriate: out of place

niestrawność (ńe-strav-nośhch)
f. indigestion: dyspepsia
niestrawny (ńe-stráv-ni) adj.
m. indigestible: stodgy; dull
niestrudzony (ńe-stroo-dzo-ni)
adj. m. indefatigable; untiring
niestworzony (ńe-stvo-zhó-ni)
adj. m. unreal; nonsense
niesumienny (ńe-soo-myen-ni)
adj. m. unscrupulous ;unreliable
nieswojo (ńe-svo-yo) adv. un-
easily;strangely; qualmishly
nieswój (ńe-svooy) adj. m. ill
at ease; uncomfortable;seedy;
strange : off color
niesymetryczny (ńe-si-me-trich-
ni) adj. m. asymmetrical
niesympatyczny (ńe-sim-pa-tich-
ni) adj. m. unpleasant
nieszczególny (ńe-shche-góol-ni)
adj. m. mediocre: so-so
nieszczelny (ńe-shchel-ni) adj.
m. leaky ; not shut tight
nieszczery (ńe-shché-ri) adj.
m. insincere; double-dealing
nieszczęsny (ńe-shcháns-ni) adj.
m. miserable; ill-fated
nieszczęście (ńe-shchan-śhche)
n. misfortune; disaster
nieszczęśliwy (ńe-shchan-shlee-
vi) adj. m. unhappy;ill-starred
nieszkodliwy (ńe-shkod-lee-vi)
adj. m. harmless; not grave
nieszlachcic (ńe-shlakh-tseets)
m. commoner: man not of gentry
nieszpetny (ńe-shpet-ni) adj.
m. fairly good-looking
nieszpory (ńe-shpó-ri) pl. ves-
pers; evening prayers
nieścisły (ńe-śhchees-wi) adj.
m. inexact: inaccurate; faulty
nieścisliwy (ńe-śhcheesh-lee-vi)
adj. m. incompressible
nieść (ńeśhch) v. carry; bring;
bear; lay; afford; drive;waft
nieślubny (ńe-shloob-ni) adj. m.
illegitimate: out of wedlock
nieśmiały (ńe-shmyá-wi) adj. m.
coy; shy; timid; bashful
nieśmiertelny (ńe-shmyer-tél-ni)
adj. m. immortal: everlasting
nieświadomy (ńe-shvya-dó-mi) adj.
m. ignorant; unaware :involuntary

nietakt (ñe-takt) m. lack of
tact; slip: tactlessness

nietaktowny (ñe-tak-tóv-ni) adj.
m. tactless: indelicate

nietknięty (ñe-tknañ-ti) adj. m.
intact;virgin;untouched

nietolerancja (ñe-to-le-ránts-ya)
f. intolerance

nietoperz (ñe-to-pesh) m. bat

nietowarzystki (ñe-to-va-zhis-
kee) adj. n. unsociable

nietrafny (ñe-tráf-ni) adj. m.
wrong; missing the mark

nietrzeźwy (ñe-tzhezh-vi) adj.
m. drank; tipsy;unsound

nietutejszy (ñe-too-téy-shi) adj.
m. stranger; non-resident

nietykalny (ñe-ti-kál-ni) adj.
m. immune; inviolable

nie tyle (ñe ti-le) adv.not so
much: not exactly; but;rather

nie tylko (ñe til-ko) adv. not
only; anything but

nieubłagalny (ñe-oo-bwa-gál-ni)
adj. m. implacable:irrevocable

nieuchronny (ñe-oo-khron-ni) adj.
inevitable; inescapable

nieuchwytny (ñe-oo-khvit-ni) adj.
m. elusive;evasive;inaudible

nieuctwo (ñe-oóts-tvo) n. lack
of education: ignorance

nieuczciwy (ñe-ooch-chee-vi) adj.
m. dishonest; foul;unfair

nieuczynny (ñe-oo-chin-ni) adj.
m. unobliging: disobliging

nieudolny (ñe-oo-dól-ni) adj. m.
awkward; clumsy; decrepit

nieufny (ñe-oóf-ni) adj. m. distrustful; suspicious

nieugaszony (ñe-oo-ga-shó-ni)
adj. m. unextinguished; un-
quenchable; unsuppressible

nieugięty (ñe-oo-gyáñ-ti) adj.
m. inflexible ;unyielding

nieuk (ñe-ook) m. know-nothing

nieukojony (ñe-oo-ko-yó-ni) adj.
m. inconsolable

nieuleczalny (ñe-oo-le-chál-ni)
adj. m. incurable

nieumiarkowany (ñe-oo-myar-ko-
vá-ni) adj. m. intemperate

nieumiejętny (ñe-oo-mee-yáñt-
ni) adj. m. inexpert; unskilled

nieumyślny (ñe-oo-miśhl-ni)
adj. m. unintentional

nieunikniony (ñe-oo-ñeek-ñó-ni)
adj. m. unavoidable:inevitable

nieuprzedzony (ñe-oo-pzhe-dzo-
ni) adj. m. unbiased; not
forwarned; not prejudiced

nieuprzejmy (ñe-oo-pzhey-mi)
adj. m. impolite; discourteous

nieurodzaj (ñe-oo-ró-dzay) m.
bad harvest; bad crops;scarcity

nie usprawiedliwiony (ñe-oos-pra-
vyed-lee-vyó-ni) adj. m. un-
excused;unjustified; wantom

nieustanny (ñe-oos-tán-ni) adj.
m. constant: perpetual;unceasing

nieustraszony (ñe-oos-tra-sho-
ni) adj. m. fearless; intrepid

nieusuwalny (ñe-oo-soo-vál-ni)
adj. m. immovable: irremovable

nie uszkodzony (ñe oosh-ko-dzo-
ni) adj. m. unhurt; undamaged

nieuwaga (ñe-oo-vá-ga) f. inat-
tention; absentmindedness

nieuważny (ñe-oo-vazh-ni) adj.
m. inattentive;careless

nieuzasadniony (ñe-oo-za-sad-ñó-
ni) adj. m. unfounded;unjustified

nieuzbrojony (ñe-ooz-bro-yó-ni)
adj. m. unarmed: disarmed

nieużyteczny (ñe-oo-zhi-tech-
ni) adj. m. useless: superfluous

nieużyty (ñe-oozhi-ti) adj. m.
unused; uncooperative;disobliging

niewart (ñe-vart) adj. m. not
worth; unworthy; not deserving

nie warto (ñe vár-to) adv. not
worth (talking):not worth while

nieważny (ñe-vázh-ni) adj. m.
invalid; trivial;null and void

niewątpliwy (ñe-vównt-plee-vi)
adj. m. sure; doubtless

niewczesny (ñe-vches-ni) adj.
m. untimely; late; inopportune

niewdzięczny (ñe-vdzháñch-ni)
adj. m. ungrateful; thankless

niewesoły (ñe-ve-so-wi) adj.
m. sad; joyless; pretty bad

niewiadomy (ñe-vya-dó-mi) adj.
m. unknown(direction, origin etc.)

niewiara (ñe-vyá-ra) f. disbelief; mistrust; unbelief

niewiasta (ñe-vyás-ta) f. woman

niewidomy (ńe-vee-do-mi) adj.
m. blind;lacking insight
niewidzialny (ńe-vee-dżhal-ni)
adj. m. invisible
niewiedza(ńe-vye-dza) adj. m.
ignorance: unawarness
niewiele (ńe-vye-le) adv. not
much; not many: little: few
niewielki (ńe-vyel-kee) adj. m.
small; little: unimportant
niewierny (ńe-vyer-ni) adj. m.
disloyal; infidel; unfaithful
niewieści (ńe-vyeśh-chee) adj.
m. womanly: feminine
niewinność (ńe-veen-nośhch) f.
innocence: puritv: chastitv
niewinny (ńe-veen-ni) adj. m.
not guilty: innocent:harmless
niewłaściwy (ńe-vwaśh-chee-vi)
adj. m. improper: unsuitable
niewola (ńe-vo-la) f. captivity;
slavery; bondage:servitude
niewolić (ńe-vo-leech) v. enslave; compel: oppress
niewolnica (ńe-vol-ńee-tsa) f.
slave: serf: prisoner of war
niewolnik (ńe-vol-ńeek) m. slave
nie wolno (ńe vól-no) v. not
allowed · not permitted
niewod (ńe-voot) m. dragnet
niewprawny (ńe-vprav-ni) adj.
m. unversed; unskilled; inexpert: incompetent: inefficient
niewspółmierny (ńe-wspoow-myer-
ni) adj. m. incommensurable
nie wtajemniczony(ńe-vta-yem-
nee-chó-ni) adj. m. uninitiat-
ed; outsider: not privy
niewyczerpany (ńe-vi-cher-pa-ni)
adj. m. inexhaustible
niewygoda (ńe-vi-gó-da) f. discomfort: trouble: hardshin
niewygodny (ńe-vi-gód-ni) adj.
m. uncomfortable· awkward
niewykonalny (ńe-vi-ko-nál-ni)
adj. m. unfeasible· unworkable
niewykształcony (ńe-vi-kshtaw-
tsó-ni) adj. m. uneducated
niewymierny (ńe-vi-myer-ni) adj.
m. irrational; surd
niewymowny (ńe-vi-móv-ni) adj.
m. unspeakable:inexpressible

niewymuszony (ńe-vi-moo-shó-ni)
adj. m. free (and easy)
niewymyślny (ńe-vi-miśhl-ni)
adj. m. unsophisticated
niewypał (ńe-vi-paw) m. dud
niewypłacalny (ńe-vi-pwa-tsal-
ni) adj. m. insolvent
niewypowiedziany (ńe-vi-po-vye-
dżhá—ni) adj. m. untold
niewyraźnie (ńe-vi-ráżh-ńe) adv.
indistinctly: seedily
niewyraźny (ńe-vi-rażh-ni) adj.
m. queer; indistinct
niewyrobiony (ńe-vi-ro-byo-ni)
adj. m. raw; inexperienced
niewyrozumiały (ńe-vi-ro-zoo-
myá-wi) adj. m. intolerant
niewysłowiony (ńe-vi-swo-vyo-
ni) adj. m. ineffable
niewyspany (ńe-vis-pa-ni) adj.
m. sleepy; not slept enough
niewystarczający (ńe-vis-tar-
cha-yówn-tsi) adj. m. insufficient: inadequate
niewystawny (ńe-vis-tav-ni) adj.
m. frugal; modest; simple
niewytłumaczony (ńe-vi-twoo-ma-
chó-ni) adj. m. inexplicable
niewytrwały (ńe-vi-trva-wi)
adj. m. not persistent
niewytrzymały (ńe-vi-tzhi-má-wi)
adj. m. not enduring
niewzruszony (ńe-vzroo-shó-ni)
adj. m. unmoved: rigid
niezachwiany (ńe-za-khvya-ni)
adj. m. unshaken ·undeterred
niezadowolenie (ńe-za-do-vo-le-
ńe) n . discontent:displeasure
niezadowolony (ńe-za-do-vo-ló-ni)
adj. m. dissatisfied:displeased
niezakłócony (ńe-za-kwoo-tsó-ni)
adj. m. undisturbed:unmarred
niezależność (ńe-za-lezh-nośhch)
f. independence :self-sufficiency
niezależny (ńe-za-lezh-ni) adj.
m. independent: self contained
niezamężna (ńe-za-mążh-na) adj.
f. unmarried :single woman
niezamożny (ńe-za-mozh-ni) adj.
m. rather poor· indigent
niezapominajka (ńe-za-po-mee-
náy-ka) f. forget-me-not

niezapomniany (ně-za-pom-ňa-ni) adj. m. not-to-be-forgotten

niezaprzeczalny (ňe-za-pzhe-chál-ni) adj. m. undeniable

niezaradny (ně-za-rád-ni) adj. m. helpless; resourceless

niezasłużony (ňe-za-swoo-zhó-ni) adj. m. undeserved

niezawisły (ně-za-vées-wi) adj. m. independent; self-dependent

niezawodnie (ňe-za-vód-ňe) adv. surely; without fail; infallibly

niezawodny (ně-za-vód-ni) adj. m. sure; never failing; safe

niezbadany (ňe-zba-da-ni) adj. m. unexplorable; inscrutable

niezbędny (ňe-zbánd-ni) adj. m, indispensable; essential

niezbity (ňe-zbée-ti) adj. m. irrefutable; uncontrovertible

niezbyt (ňe-zbit) adv. not very (much); none too; not too

niezdarny (ňe-zdar-ni) adj. m. clumsy; awkward; bungled

niezdatny (ňe-zdat-ni) adj. m. unfit; unqulified; unserviceable

niezdecydowany (ňe-zde-tsi-do-vá-ni) adj. m. undecided

niezdolność (ňe-zdol-noshch) f. inability; unfitness

niezdolny (ňe-zdol-ni) adj. m. incapable; unable; unfit: dull

niezdrowy (ňe-zdro-vi) adj. m. unhealthy; unwell; ill; sickly

niezdyscyplinowany (ňe-zdis-tsi-plee-no-vá-ni) adj. m. undisciplined; unruly

niezgłębiony (ňe-zgwanb-yó-ni) adj. m. inscrutable; abyssal

niezgoda (ňe-zgó-da) f. discord; disagreement; dissension

niezgodność (ňe-zgod-noshch) f. inconsistency; clash

niezgodny (ňe-zgod-ni) adj. m. discordant; incompatible

niezgrabny (ňe-zgráb-ni) adj. m. unhandy; clumsy; shapeless

nieziszczalny (ňe-zeesh-chál-ni) adj. m. unattainable

niezliczony (ňe-zlee-chó-ni) adj. m. uncountable; countless

niezłomny (ňe-zwom-ni) adj. m. inflexible; firm; steadfast

niezmącony (ňe-zmwon-tsó-ni) adj. m. unruffled; undisturbed

niezmienny (ňe-zmyen-ni) adj. m. invariable; constant; fixed

niezmierny (ňe-zmyer-ni) adj. m. immense; vast; boundless

niezmordowany (ňe-zmor-do-vá-ni) adj. m. indefatigable; tireless

nieznaczny (ňe-znach-ni) adj. m. trivial; insignificant

nieznajomość (ňe-zna-yó-moshch) f. ignorance; unawareness

nieznajomy (ňe-zna-yó-mi) adj. m. unknown; strange (faces etc.)

nieznany (ňe-zna-ni) adj. m. unknown; unfamiliar; obscure

nieznośny (ňe-znosh-ni) adj. m. unbearable; annoying; nasty; pesky

niezręczny (ňe-zrǎnch-ni) adj. m. awkward; clumsy; tactless

niezrozumiały (ňe-zro-zoo-mya-wi) adj. m. unintelligible

niezrównany (ňe-zroov-ná-ni) adj. m. matchless; incomparable; peerless; unique; grand

niezwłoczny (ňe-zvwoch-ni) adj. m. instant; prompt; immediate

niezwyciężony (ňe-zvi-chán-zho-ni) adj. m. invincible

niezwykły (ňe-zvik-wi) adj. m. unusual; extreme; rare; odd

nieżonaty (ňe-zho-ná-ti) adj. m. unmarried; single; bachelor

nieżyczliwy (ňe-zhich-lee-vi) adj. m. unfriendly; ill-disposed

nieżyt (ňe-zhit) m. inflammation; catarrh; hay fever; colitis

nieżywy (ňe-zhi-vi) adj. m. dead; lifeless; inanimate

nigdy (ňeeg-di) adv. never

nigdzie (ňeeg-dzhe) adv. no-where; anywhere (after negation)

nijaki (ňee-ya-kee) adj. m. none; neuter (gender)

nikczemnik (ňeek-chém-ňeek) m. villain; scoundrel; wretch

nikczemny (ňeek-chém-ni) adj. m. vile; abject; despicable; base

nikel (ňee-kel) m. nickel

nikły (ňeek-wi) adj. m. scanty

niknąć (ňeek-nównch) v. vanish

nikotyna (ňee-ko-tí-na) f. nisotine; poisonous tabacco extract nikt (ñeekt) pron. nobody

nim (ñeem) conj. before:till

nimb (ñeemp) m. halo:aureole

niniejszy (ñee-ñey-shi) adj. m. this; present: the present

niski (ñees-kee) adj. m. low

nisko (ñees-ko) adv. low

nisza (ñee-sha) f. niche:recess

niszczący (ñeesh-chówn-tsi) adj. m. destructive: disruptive

niszczeć (ñeesh-chećh) v. waste away: deteriorate: decay:waste

niszczyciel (ñeesh-chi-ćhel) m. devastator: destroyer:waster

niszczyć (ñeesh-chićh) v. destroy;spoil:ruin: wreck;damage

nit (ñeet) m. rivet

nitka (ñeet-ka) f. thread

nitować (ñee-tó-vach) v. rivet

niwa (ñee-va) f. field:soil

niweczyć (ñee-vé-chićh) v. destroy: annihilate: lay waste

niwelacja (ñee-ve-láts-ya) f. leveling; survey: surveying

niwelować (ñee-ve-ló-vach) v. level: survey

nizina (ñee-zhee-na) f. lowland

niż (ñeezh) m. lowland;atmospher ic low

niż (ñeesh) conj. than |

niżej (ñee-zhey) adv. lower; below; down: further down

niższość (ñeesh-shośhćh) f. inferiority

niższy (ñeezh-shi) adj. m. lower; inferior: shorter

no (no) part. why; well; now; then: just: there: there now!

noc (nots) f. night

nocleg (nots-leg) m. place to sleep : night's lodging

nocny (nots-ni) adj. m. nocturnal; night-

nocować (no-tsó-vach) v. spend night: stay overnight: sleep

noga (no-ga) f. leg : foot

nogawica (no-ga-vee-tsa) f. legging : trouser leg

nomenklatura (no-men-kla-too-ra) f. nomenclature

nominacja (no-mee-náts-ya) f. appointment : nomination

nominalny (no-mee-nál-ni) adj. m. nominal : face(value)

nonsens (nón-sens) m. nonsense

nora (nó-ra) f. burrow

norma (nór-ma) f. standard; norm: rule: general principle

normalizacja (nor-ma-lee-záts-ya) f. normalization:standard

normalizować (nor-ma-lee-zó-vach) v. normalize: standardize

normalny (nor-mál-ni) adj. m. normal: standard: ordinary

normować (nor-mo-vach) v. regulate: standardize:normalize

nos (nos) m. nose : snout

nosić (nó-śheećh) v. carry; wear: bear :have about one

nosorożec (no-so-ro-shets) m. rhinoceros (with horn)

nostalgia (nos-tál-gya) f. nostalgia: homesickness

nosze (nó-she) pl. stretchers

nota (nó-ta) f. note; grade

notariusz (no-tár-yoosh) m. notary public

notatka (no-tát-ka) f. note

notatnik (no-tát-ñeek) m. notebook: diary: notes

notes (nó-tes) m. pocket notebook: notebook

notoryczny (no-to-rích-ni) adj. m. notorious : flagrant:arrant

notować (no-to-vach) v. make notes; take notes: write down

notowanie (no-to-vá-ñe) n. quotation : record

nowela (no-vé-la) f. short story : amendment

nowelista (no-ve-lees-ta) f. short story writer

nowicjat (no-veéts-yat) m. novitiate : novitiate

nowicjusz (no-veéts-yoosh) m. novice : beginner: tiro

nowina (no-vee-na) f. news

nowinka (no-veén-ka) f. fad

nowiutki (no-vyóot-kee) adj. m. brand-new; spick-and-span

nowoczesny (no-vo-chés-ni) adj. m. modern :up to date:newest

noworoczny (no-vo-róch-ni) adj. m. New Year's : of New Year

nowość (nó-voshćh) f. novelty

nowotwór (no-vo-tvoor) m. tumor : new coined word

nowożytny (nu-vo-zhít-n¹) adj.
  m. (of) modern (peric
nowy (nó-vi) adj. m. new
nozdrze (nóz-dzhę) n. nostril
nożownik (no-zhov-ńeek) m.
  knifer; knife-fighter
nożyce (no-zhí-tse) pl. shears;
  clippers : large shears
nożyczki (no-zhích-kee) pl.
  scissors : small scissors
nożyk (no-zhik) m. pocketknife
nów (noov) m. new moon
nóż (noosh) m. knife : cutter
nucić (noo-ćheech) v. hum
nuda (nóo-da) f. boredom
nudności (nood-nósh-chee) pl.
  nausea : impulse to vomit
nudny (nood-ni) adj. m. boring;
  nauseating : dull: sickening
nudysta (noo-dis-ta) m. nudist
nudziarz (noo-dźhash) m. bore
nudzić (noo-dźheech) v. bore
numer (noo-mer) m. number
numerować (noo-me-ró-vach) v.
  number : give a number to
numerowy (noo-me-ro-vi) adj. m.
  porter; bell-boy: hotel waiter
numizmatyka (noo-meez-ma-ti-ka)
  f. numismatics : study of coins
nuncjusz (noon-tsyoosh) m. nun-
  cio ; papal ambassador
nurek (noo-rek) m. diver
nurkować (noor-ko-vach) v. dive
nurt (noort) m. current (flowing): stream: trend: wake
nurtować (noor-tó-vach) v. fret;
  penetrate : pervade: ferment
nurzać (noo-zhach) v. dip; welter in; plunge : immerse: steep
nuta (nóo-ta) f. (sound) note
nuty (nóo-ti) pl. written music: printed music: score
nuż (noozh) adv. if; and if
nużący (noo-zhówn-tsi) adj. m.
  tiring : tiresome: wearisome
nużyć (noo-zhich) v. tire : weary
nygus (ni-goos) m. lazybones
nygusować (ni-goo-só-vach) v.
  lounge about; loiter : loaf
nylon (ne-lon) m. nylon
nyża (ni-zha) f. niche; alcove

o (o) prep. of; for; at; by;
  about; against; with : to: over
oaza (o-á-za) f. oasis
oba (o-ba) pron. both
obabrać (o-ba-brach) v. besmear
obaj (o-bay) pron. both
obalenie (o-ba-le-ńe) n. overthrow: subversion; abolition
obalić (o-ba-leech) v. overthrow: knock down: fell: refute
obarczyć (o-bar-chich) v. encumber; saddle: load: burden
obarzanek (o-ba-zha-nek) m.
  round cracknel torus shaped
obawa (o-bá-va) f. fear; apprehension : phobia; anxiety
obawiać się (o-báv-yach śhäń) v.
  be anxious ; fear: dread
obcas (ób-tsac) m. heel
obcążki (ob-tsównzh-kee) pl.
  (small) tongs : pincers: pliers
obcesowo (ob-tse-so-vo) adv.
  headlong; outright: abruptly
obcęgi (ob-tsáń-gee) pl. tongs
obchodzić (ob-kho-dźheech) v.
  go around; evade; elude;
  celebrate: inspect: by-pass
obchód (ob-khoot) m. (daily)
  beat; celebration circuit
obciągać (ob-chówn-gach) v.
  pull down; cover; pull tight
obciążać (ob-chówn-zhach) v.
  burden; charge (account)
obcierać (o-ćhe-rach) v. wipe
obcinać (ob-chee-nach) v. cut
  off; clip: crop: chop off
obcisły (ob-chees-wi) adj. m.
  tight : close fitting: clinging
obcokrajowiec (ob-tso-kra-yó-
  vyets) m. foreigner: alien
obcokrajowy (ob-tso-kra-yo-vi)
  adj. m. foreign: alien
obcować (ob-tsó-vach) v. associate: have an intercourse
obcowanie (ob-tso-va-ńe) n. intercourse; association
obcy (ób-tsi) adj. m. strange;
  foreign: unfamiliar: unrelated
obczyzna (ob-chiz-na) f. foreign
  country : exile: foreign land
obdarować (ob-da-ro-vach) v.
  bestow : lavish gifts on ...

obdarty (ob-dár-ti) adj. m. ragged in rags: tattered

obdarzyć (ob-dá-zhich) v. bestow: lavish gifts on ...

obdzielić (ob-dzhe-leech) v. divide; distribute :deal:endow

obdzierać (ob-dzhé-rach) v. rip off; skin off ;strip; fleece

obecnie (o-béts-ñe) adv. at present :just now:to-day

obecnosc (o-béts-noshch) f. presence: attendance

obejmować (o-bey-mo-vach) v. embrace; enfold; span; include; take over; take in; grasp

obejrzeć (o-bey-zhech) v. inspect; glance at; see

obejście (o-béy-shche) n. bypass; farmyard : manner

obejsć (o-béyshch) v. go around

obelga (o-bél-ga) f. insult; outrage; abuse affront

obelżywy (o-bel-zhi-vi) adj. m. insulting; abusive opprobrious

oberwać (o-bér-vach) v. tear off; cop it; pluck get a knock

oberża (o-bér-zha) f. inn

oberżysta (o-ber-zhis-ta) m. innkeeper owner of an inn

oberznąć (o-ber-zhnównch) v. cut off; trim; clip

obeschnąć (o-bes-khnownch) v. dry up: get dry: dry

obetrzeć (o-be-tzhech) v. wipe out: dust: rub sore: skin

obezwładnić (o-bez-vwad-ñeech) v. overpower subdue: disable

obeznany (o-bez-ná-ni) adj. m. familiar: acquainted;conversant

obfitosć (ob-fee-toshch) f. plenty: abundance profusion

obfity (ob-feé-ti) adj. m. abundant: ample: profuse:liberal

obgadywac (ob-ga-di-vach) v. talk ill; talk over: crab

obgryzać (ob-gri-zach) v. nibble bare: gnaw: pick a bone: bite

obiad (ob-yat) m. dinner

obicie (o-bee-che) n. upholstery; padding; chip; beating :drubbing

obiecywać (o-bye-tsi-vach) v. promise look forward to

obieg (o-byek) m. circulation

obiegać (o-bye-gach) v. runaround; circulate ;revolve

obiekcja (o-byek-tsya) f. objection: demur

obiekt (ob-yekt) m. object; target: subject: building

obiektyw (o-byek-tiv) m.object-lens : object-glass; objective

obiektywny (o-byek-tiv-ni) adj. m. objective ;impartial

obierać (o-bye-rach) v. choose; elect; peel: pick: strip

obierzyny (o-bye-zhi-ni) pl. peelings; parings

obieralny (o-bye-rál-ni) adj. m. elective: eligible

obietnica (o-byet-ñee-tsa) f. promise: engagement

obijać (o-bee-yach) v. chip; hoop; loaf :hurt: injure

objadać się (ob-ya-dach śhań) v. gorge; overeat : cram

objaśniać (ob-yásh-ñach) v. explain : make clear: gloss

objaw (ób-yav) m. symptom

objawić (ob-ya-veech) v. reveal

objazd (ób-yazt) m. tour; circuit :detour:diversion by-pass

objąć (ob-yównch) v. embrace; assume: grasp: encompass:span

objeżdżać (ob-yezh-dzhach) v. ride; around;break in a horse

objętosć (ob-yañ-toshch) f. volume; bulk:capacity: content

obkładać (ob-kwa-dach) v. wrap; cover: line: impose hit:buffet

oblegać (ob-le-gach) v. besiege

oblac (ób-lach) v. pour on(water)

oblekać (ob-le-kach) v. clothe; put on; cover; encase: don

oblepiać (o-le-pyach) v. paste over: stick: post:plaster over

oblewać (ob-le-vach) v. pour on: drench: bathe: sprinkle:wash

oblężenie (ob-lań-zhe-ñe) m. siege: state of siege

obliczać (ob-lee-chach) v. count: reckon; figure out: mean

oblicze (ob-lee-che) n. face

obliczenie (ob-lee-ché-ñe) n. calculation: evaluation: count

obligacja (ob-lee-gáts-ya) f.
obligation; bond; share

oblizać (ob-leé-zach) v. lick

obładować (ob-wa-dó-vach) v.
load down; heap; burden

obława (ob-wá-va) f. roundup;
posse; man hunt: chase: raid

obłąkany (ob-wówn-ká-ni) adj.
m. insane; loony; madman

obłęd (ób-wańt) m. insanity

obłędny (ob-wánd-ni) adj. m.
mad; wild; insane: crazy

obłok (ób-wok) m. cloud

obłowić się (ob-wó-veech śhań)
v. pick up a lot·make a pile

obłożnie (ob-wózh-ńe) adv. bedridden; severely (ill)

obłożyc (ob-wo-zhich) v. cover;
wrap: line:impose: hit:buffet

obłuda (ob-woo-da) f. hypocrisy

obłudnik (ob-wood-ńeek) m.hyp-
ocrite:snuffler:dissembler

obłudny (ob-wood-ni) adj. m.
hypocritical:false: canting

obłupać (ob-woó-pach) v. shell;
peel:bark: flay: skin

obłuszczac (ob-woosh-chach) v.
scale; shell: husk; flay: skin

obły (ob-wi) adj.oval;tapering;
terete; cylindrical: oval

obmacac (ob-ma-tsach) v. feel
about; explore with fingers

obmawiać (ob-máv-yach) v. slander; backbite; gossip:speak ill

obmierznąć (ob-myerzh-nównch) v.
get sick of (something)

obmowa (ob-mó-va) f. slander;
detraction: backbiting

obmurowac (ob-moo-ró-vach) v.
brick in; brick veneer

obmyślac (ob-mish-lach) v. design; contrive; reflect

obmywać (ob-mí-vach) v. wash-
up:sponge down:give a wash

obnażać (ob-na-zhach) v. denude;
bare; unclothe:strip:uncover

obniżać (ob-ńee-zhach) v. lower;
sink; drop; abate; level down

obniżenie (ob-ńee-zhé-ńe) n.
decrease; reduction; lowering

obniżka (ob-ńeezh-ka) f. reduction; depreciation:drop:fall

obojczyk (o-bóy-chik) m. collar
bone;clavicle: amice:gorget

obnosić (ob-nó-śheech) v. take
around; flaunt; parade

obojętnie (o-bo-yáńt-ńe) adv.
indifferently:slang:no matter

obojętność (o-bo-yáńt-nośhch)
f. indifference;:neutrality

obojętny (o-bo-yáńt-ni) adj. m.
indifferent; neutral

obok (ó-bok) adv. prep. beside;
next; about:close by:by:close

obopólny (o-bo-pool-ni) adj. m.
common; mutual:reciprocal

obora (o-bó-ra) f. cowbarn

obosieczny (o-bo-śhéch-ni) adj.
m.two-edged: double edged

obowiązek (o-bo-vyówn-zek) m.
duty; obligation: responsibility

obowiązkowy (o-bo-vyównz-ko-vi)
adj. m. dutiful; compulsory

obowiązany (o-bo-wyówn-za-ni)
adj. m. obligated;compelled

obowiązujący (o-bo-vyówn-zoo-
yówn-tsi) adj. m. obligatory

obowiązywac (o-bo-vyówn-zi-vach)
v. be in force (law etc)

obozować (o-bo-zó-vach) v. camp;
camp out: tent·encamp:bivouac

oboj (o-booy) m. oboe, (horn)

oboz (o-boos) m, camp

obrabiać (ob-ra-byach) v. machine (metal, wood etc.); work-
over; fashion; shape;till:hem

obrabiarka (ob-rab-yar-ka) f.
machine tool: lathe

obrabowac (ob-ra-bo-vach) v. rob

obracać (ob-ra-tsach) v. turnover; rotate: crank

obrachować (ob-ra-kho-vach) v.
compute· figure out: calculate

obrachunek (ob-ra-khoo-nek) m.
settlement; bill;"day of reckoning":count: reckoning

obrada (ob-ra-da) f, conference

obradować (ob-ra-do-vach) v.
confer; deliberate: debate; sit

obradzać (ob-ra-dzach) v. bear
crops; yield a crop:be plentiful

obramowac (ob-ra-mó-vach) v.
frame:encircle: encase:hem:edge

obrastac (ob-ras-tach) v. overgrow: grow .:grow all over

obraz (ob-raz) m. picture;
image : painting:drawing

obraza (ob-ra-za) f. affront;
offense :insult:outrage:offence

obrazek (ob-ra-zek) m. illustration; small picture

obrazić (ob-ra-źheech) v. offend: affront: insult:sting

obrazowy (ob-ra-zó-vi) adj. m.
pictorial : picturesque:vivd

obrażenie (ob-ra-zhe-ńe) n.
offense; injury: insults

obraźliwy (ob-raźh-lee-vi) adj.
m. offensive;touchy:resentful

obrażać (ob-ra-zhach) v. offend;
(repeatedly) insult: affront

obrąb (ob-równb) m. cutoff

obrąbek (ob-równ-bek) m. hem

obrączka (ob-równch-ka) f. ring

obręb (ob-rańb) m. compass;
area:reach:extent:precincts

obrębiać (ob-ranb-yach) v. hem

obręcz (ob-rańch) f. hoop; tire;
rim: band: gridle: ring:circle

obrobić (ob-ro-beech) v. machine

obrok (ob-rok) m. feed;fodder

obrona (ob-ro-na) f. defense

obronność (ob-ron-noshch) f.
defense capability:defences

obronny (ob-ron-ni) adj. m. de-
fensive:fortified:protective

obrońca (ob-roń-tsa) m. defender
guard; barrister:advocate

obrośnięty (ob-rośh-ńań-ti) adj.
m. overgrown;, unshaven

obrotny (ob-rot-ni) adj. m.
active; skillful;,nimble:agile

obrotowy (ob-ro-to-vi) adj. m.
turnover (tax);rotary;revolving

obroża (ob-ro-zha) f. (dog) collar: neck band

obrócić (ob-roo-cheech) v. rotate ;revolve :turn; go

obrót (ob-root) m. turn; turnover: revolution: slew: sales

obrus (ob-roos) m. tablecloth

obruszać (ob-roo-shach) v. loos-
en up: irritate: bring down

obrywać (ob-ri-vach) v. tear
off: tear away:pluck:wrench off

obryzgiwać (ob-riz-gee-vach) v.
splash; spatter

obrzęd (ob-zhańd) m. rite; ceremony , custom

obrzęk (ob-zhańk) m. swelling

obrzękły (ob-zhańk-wi) adj. m.
swollen: oedemous: tumid

obrzmiały (obzh-mya-wi) adj.
m. swollen: oedemous: tumid

obrzucać (ob-zhoo-tsach) v.
throw upon: hurl:pelt; fell

obrzydliwy (ob-zhid-lee-vi)
adj. m. revolting; disgusting

obrzydzenie (ob-zhi-dze-ńe) n.
aversion: nausea: disgust

obrzynać (ob-zhi-nach) v. clip;
cut: cut off; edge: trim;cheat

obsada (ob-sá-da) f. cast; crew;
garrison; staff: mounting

obsadka (on-sád-ka) f. penholder: small mounting

obsadzać (ob-sá-dzach) v. plant;
staff: set: fix: occupy;stock

obserwacja (ob-ser-váts-ya) f.
observation: remark

obserwator (ob-ser-vá-tor) m.
observer: look out man:witness

obserwatorium (ob-ser-va-tor-
yoom) m. observatory

obserwować (ob-ser-vo-vach) v.
watch; observe; take stock

obsługa (ob-swoo-ga) f. attendance; service: staff

obsługiwać (ob-swoo-gee-vach)
v. wait-upon; service

obstalować (ob-sta-lo-vach) v.
order (a suit of clothes etc.)

obstalunek (ob-sta-loo-nek) m.
order: a request to supply

obstawać (ob-sta-vach) v. insist on; hold to; stand by;
persist in; abide by

obstąpić (ob-stown-peech) v.
surround: form a circle;cluster

obstrzał (ob-stzhaw) m. gunfire; scope of fire: firing

obstrukcja (ob-strook-tsya) f.
obstruction; constipation

obsuwać (ob-soo-vach) v. slide
down; creep: lower:bring down

obsuwisko (ob-soo-vees-ko) n.
landslide : landslip

obsychać (ob-si-khach) v. dry
up : get parched: run dry:go dry

obsyłać (ob-si-wach) v. send around (messengers,etc.)

obsypywać (ob-si-pi-vach) v. strew: sprinkle: shower:heap

obszar (ob-shar) m. area; range

obszarnik (ob-shár-ñeek) m. landowner:large,scale farmer

obszerny (ob-sher-ni) adj. m. spacious: extensive:vast:broad

obsztorcować (ob-shtor-tso-vach) v. snub; give hard time

obszukać (ob-shoo-kach) v. search : ransack:make a search

obszyć (ob-shich) v. sew around

obuch (o-bookh) m. back of axe; sledge; head,of an axe

obudzić (o-boo-dzheech)v. wake up:awaken: excite; stir up

obumarły (o-boo-mar-wi) adj. m. deadened; half dead:decaying

obumierać (o-boo-myé-rach)v. wither; atrophy:decay: shrink

oburącz (o-boo-rówñch) adv. with both hands:with both arms

oburzać (o-boo-zhach) v. revolt; shock: provoke indignation

oburzony (o-boo-zhó-ni) adj. m. indignant; resentful

obustronny (o-boo-strón-ni) adj. m. bilateral;mutual:reciprocal

obuwie (o-boo-vye) n. footwear

obwarowywać (ob-va-ro-vi-vach) v. fortify; entrench: secure

obwąchiwać (ob-vówñ-khee-vach) v. sniff around:smell around

obowiązywać (ob-vyówñ-zi-vach) v. bind up; bandage; tie

obwieszczać (ob-vyesh-chach) v. announce; proclaim: notify

obwieszczenie (ob-vyesh-ché-ñe) n. proclamation· notice

obwiniać (ob-vee-ñach) v. accuse

obwisać (ob-vee-sach) v. sag; droop: hang loosely: flag

obwodowy (ob-vo-do-vi) adj. m. circumferential; district

obwoluta (ob-vo-loo-ta) f. wrapper: book-jacket: file cover

obwołać (ob-vó-wach) v. acclaim; proclaim· call names

obwód (ób-voot) f. perimeter

oby (obi) part. may...may you

obycie (o-bi-che) n. good manners: experience:familiarity

obyczaj (o-bi-chay) m. custom

obyczajność (o-bi-chay-noshch) f. decency; morality: morals

obyczajny (o-bi-chay-ni) adj. m. decent; moral

obydwaj (o-bi-dvay) num. both

obyty (o-bi-ti) adj. m. familiar; easy mannered:polished

obywać się (o-bi-vach śhañ) v. do without: dispense with

obywatel (o-bi-va-tel) m. citizen; squire:inhabitant

obywatelka (o-bi-va-tél-ka) f. citizen: inhabitant: citizeness

obywatelstwo (o-bi-va-tél-stvo) m. citizenship;nationality

obznajomić (ob-zna-yo-meech)v. familiarize: acquaint:inform

obżarstwo (ob-zhar-stvo) n. gluttony: stuffing oneself

ocalać (o-tsa-lech) v.survive (danger)·rescue: save

ocalenie (o-tsa-lé-ñe) n. rescue: salvation: escape

ocalić (o-tsa-leech) v. rescue

ocean (o-tsé-an) m. ocean

ocena (o-tse-na) f. grade; estimate; appraisal

ocet (o-tset) m. vinegar

och!(okh !) excl.: oh !

ochędożyć (o-kháñ-do-zhich) v. clean; put in order

ochlapać (o-khla-pach) v. splash: splatter(with mud)

ochładzać (o-khwa-dzach) v. cool; chill: refresh

ochłap (o-khwap) m. offal; trash ; scrap of meat

ochłonąć (o-khwo-nówñch) v. calm down: get cooler: cool

ochoczo (o-kho-cho) adv.eagerly; cheerfully: gladly:gaily

ochota (o-khó-ta) f. eagerness; forwardness; willingness

ochotnik (o-khót-ñeek) n. volunteer: serving of free will

ochraniać (o-khra-ñach) v. protect; preserve: shield

ochrona (o-khró-na) f. (shelter) protection; conservation

ochronny (o-khrón-ni) adj. m.
protective ; preventive

ochrypły (o-khríp-wi) adj. m.
hoarse; husky; raucous

ochrypnąć (o-khríp-nównch) v.
hoarsen; grow hoarse

ochrzcić (okh-zhcheéch) v. baptize; christen; name: dub

ociągać się(o-chówn-gach śhán)
v. linger: delay:put off

ociec (o-chets) v. drain; drip

ociekać (o-che-kach) v. drain;
drip: stream: overflow: drv

ociemniały (o-chem-ña-wi) adj.
m. blind man

ocieniać (o-che-ñach) v. shade
over: protect from the sun

ocieplać (o-chép-lach) v. warm
up: make warmer: get warm

ocierać (o-che-rach) v. wipe
off: rub sore: gall; abrade

ociężały (o-chán-zha-wi) adj.
m. inert; (lazy) heavy; tardy;
dull: ponderous: languid·bovine

ociosać (o-cho-sach) v. hew

ocknąć się (óts-knównch śhán)
v. wake up (from a nap) awake

oclić (óts-leéch) v. assess custom duty; levy duty;pay duty

oczarować (o-cha-ro-vach) v.
charm; enchant;fascinate:ravish

oczekiwać (o-che-kee-vach) v.
wait for; await; expect;hope

oczekiwanie (o-che-kee-vá-ñe)
n. expectation: prospect

oczerniać (o-cher-ñach) v.
slander; malign; defame; vilify

oczko (óch-ko) n. (needle) eyelet; little eye:mesh:stitch

oczny (óch-ni) adj. m. optic

oczyszczać (o-chish-chach) v.
clean; purify; dust: clear

oczytany (o-chi-ta-ni) adj. m.
well-read : of wide reading

oczywisty (o-chi-veés-ti) adj.
m. obvious; self-evident;plain

oczywiście (o-chi-veéśh-che)
adv. obviously; of course

od (od) prep. from; off; of;
for; since; out of; with; per;
by; then (idiomatic)

odbarwić (od-bár-veech) v.
bleach; decolorize

odbicie (od-bee-che) n. reflection; bounce; ricochet; beating
back: deflection: repercussion

odbic (od-beech) v. bounce back;
rescue; recover; reflect:print

odbiegać (od-byé-gach) v. desert; deviate; stray; digress

odbijać (od-bee-yach) v. reflect; print; put off; fend
off; recapture: leave a trace

odbiorca (od-byór-tsa) m. receiver; customer; addressee

odbiornik (od-byór-neek) m.
(radio) receiver: collector

odbior (od-byoor) m. receipt;
reception; collection

odbitka (od-beét-ka) f. copy;
reprint: impression: proof:slip

odblask (od-blask) m. reflection
of light: gleam: irradiation

odbudowa (od-boo-dó-va) f. reconstruction: restoration

odbudować (od-boo-do-vach) v.
rebuild: restore: reconstruct

odbyt (od-bit) m. 1. sale
2. anus: end of alimentary tract

odbywać (od-bi-vach) v. do;
perform; be in progress

odcedzić (od-tsé-dzeech) v.
strain: strain out: drain away

odchodzić (od-kho-dżhaech)v.
go away; leave; walk off;
split;sail; retire; withdraw

odchudzać (od-khoo-dzach) v.
reduce (weight); slim:slenderize

odchylać (od-khi-lach) v. deflect; slant; slope:bend back

odchylenie (od-khi-le-ñe) n.
deviation· declination:variation

odciągać (od-chówn-gach) v.
draw aside : retract:divert:delay

odciążać (od-chówn-zhach) v.
relieve;unburden; lighten:ease

odcień (od-chen) m. shade; tint;
undertone: tinge:hue:cast: tone

odcierpieć (od-cher-pyech) v.
suffer for; expiate; atone

odcinać (od-chee-nach) v. cut
off; sever; amputate; detach

odcinek (od-chee-nek) m. sector;
segment; space; period; receipt

odcisk (od-cheesk) m. imprint;
skin-corn: stamp:trace: squeeze

odcyfrować (od-tsi-fró-vać) v. decipher; make out

odczekać (od-che-kać) v. wait out · wait for the right moment

odczepić (od-che-peech) v. detach; unhook; get rid·clear out

odczuć (od-chooć) v. feel; notice; resent; smart from

odczyn (ód-chin) m. (chem) reaction· chemical change

odczynnik (od-chin-ńeek) m. reagent·; reacting substance

odczyt (ód-chit) m. lecture

odczytać (od-chi-tać) v. read over; take the reading; call

oddać (od-dać) v. give back; pay back; render; deliver

oddalać (od-da-lać) v. remove; send away; drive away

oddalony (od-da-ló-ni) adj. m. distant; remote; far away

oddany (od-dá-ni) adj. m. given up; devoted ·loving; intent

oddawać (od-dá-vać) v. give back; pay back; return·repay

od dawna (od dáv-na) since a long time ·long since

oddech (ód-dekh) m. breath

oddychać (od-di-khać) v. breathe; take breath; respire

oddział (ód-dźaw) m. division; section; ward; branch; detail

oddziaływać (od-dźha-wi-vać) v. influence; affect

oddzielać (od-dźhé-lać) v. separate; divorce; split

oddzielny (od-dźhél-ni) adj. m. separate ·individual·discrete

oddzierać (od-dźhe-rać) v. tear off; pull off·pull away

oddźwięk (od-dźhvyáhk) m. echo; resonance; repercussion

odebrać (o-dé-brać) v. take away; receive; withdraw·regain

odechcieć się (o-dekh-chech shan) v. ·lose interest·cease liking

odegnać (o-dég-nać) v. chase away· drive away; drive off

odegrać się (o-dé-grać shań) v. win back; recover;take place

odejmować (o-dey-mo-vać) v. subtract; deduct; take away diminish·withdraw; deprive

odejście (o-dey-shche) n. departure·; withdrawal·deviation

odejść (o-deyshch) v. depart; go away; leave; abandon

odemknąć (o-dem-knównch) v. open; half open·set ajar·unbolt

odepchnąć (o-dep-khnównch) v. shove away; beat back·reject

odeprzeć (o-dep-zhech) v. repel; repulse; fight off; retort

oderwać (o-dér-vać) v. tear off; break off; detach; sever

odesłać (o-dés-wać) v. send back· return·refer; direct

odetchnąć (o-dét-knównch) v. breathe (freely); respire

odetkać (o-dét-kać) v. unstop; open; uncork· unchoke· fall out

odezwa (o-déz-va) f. proclamation; appeal·urgent request

odgadywać (od-ga-di-vać) v. guess· surmise; solve a riddle

odgałęziać (od-ga-wáń-źhać) v. branch away; fork off; ramify

odganiać (od-ga-ńać) v. chase away· drive off; dismiss

odgarniać (od-gar-ńać) v. shove away·rake aside· push aside

odginać (od-gée-nać) v. unbend; fold back; straighten· curve

odgłos (ód-gwos) m. echo; resonance· sound; noise; thud

odgniatać (od-gńa-tać) v. bruise; wrinkle; crease (the skin)

odgrażać się (od-gra-zhach shań) v.talk big; threaten

odgradzać (od-gra-dzać) v. fence off; separate; shut out

odgrodzić (od-gro-dźheech) v. divide off; fence off; shut off

odgruzować (od-groo-zo-vać) v. clear off rubbish from a space

odgrywać (od-gri-vać) v. play off; perform; act; make believe

odgryzać (od-gri-zać) v. bite off; snap off; gnaw off

odgrzebywać (od-gzhe-bí-vać) v. dig up; rake up·unearth· turn up

odgrzewać (od-gzhe-vać) v. rewarm; rehash; warm up (food)

odjazd (ód-yazt) m. departure

odjeżdżać (od-yézh-dźhać) v. depart; be off; abandon·start

odjęcie (od-yañ-che) n. deduction; amputation; weaning

odkazic (od-ka-żheeć) v. disinfect; sterilize

odkażać (od-ka-zhać) v. disinfect (repeatedly); sterilize

odkażenie (od-ka-zhe-ńe) n. disinfection: sterilization

odkąd (od-kownt) adv. since; since when ? ever since; from

odkleic (od-kle-eeć) v. unglue; unstick; detach; ungum

odkładac (od-kwa-dać) v. put aside; save; put back; put off

odkłonic się (od-kwo-ńeech śhań) v. greet back

odkopac (od-ko-pać) v. dig up

odkorkowac (od-kor-ko-wać) v. uncork; unjam (the traffic)

odkręcic (od-krań-cheeć) v. unscrew; turn around

odkroic (od-kro-yeeć) v. cut off; carve off; slice off

odkryc (od-krich) v. discover; uncover: lay bare; expose; notice

odkrycie (od-kri-che) n. discovery; exploration; exposure

odkupic (od-koo-peech) v. repurchase; redeem; buy ; replace

odkupienie (od-koo-pye-ńe) n. redemption ; repurchase

odkurzacz (od-koo-zhach) m. vacuum cleaner; carpet sweeper

odkuwac się (od-koo-vach śhań) v. recoup losses; forge; knock off

odlac (od-lać) v. pour off; cast

odlatywac (od-la-ti-vach) v. fly away; fly off; take off

odległość (od-leg-wośhćh) f. distance: remotness; interval

odległy (od-leg-wi) adj. m. distant; remote; far away; long ago

odlepiac (od-lep-yach) v. unglue; unstick; detach; ungum

odlew (od-lev) m. cast; pour

odlewac (od-le-vach) v. pour off; cast; mould; pour out

odlewacz (od-le-vach) m. founder

odlewnia (od-lev-ña) f. foundry

odliczac (od-lee-chach) v. deduct; count; reckon off; allow

odliczenie (od-lee-che-ńe) n. deduction; allowance

odlot (od-lot) m. departure (by plane): take-off; start

odludek (od-loo-dek) m. recluse

odludny (od-lood-ni) adj. m. solitary; lonely; secluded

odłam (od-wam) m. fraction

odłamac (od-wa-mać) v. break off; sever; snap off

odłamek (od-wa-mek) m. chip; splinter; fragment; chip; stub

odłazic (od-wa-żheech) v. crawl away; get unstuck; come off

odłączyc (od-wown-chich) v. sever; disconnect; separate

odłożyc (od-wo-zhich) v. set aside; put off; put back

odłog (od-wook) m. fallow

odłupac (od-woo-pach) v. split off; chip off; break off

odma płucna (od-ma pwoots-na) f. pneumothorax; pneumatosis

odmarznąc (od-mar-znowńch) v. thaw; melt; get warm; unfreeze

odmawiac (od-mav-yach) v. refuse; say prayers; decline; recite

odmeldowac (od-mel-do-vach) v. take a formal leave

odmęt (od-mańt) m. chaotic whirlpool; confusion; depths

odmiana (od-mya-na) f. change; alteration; modification

odmieniac (od-mye-ńach) v. change; alter; decline ; conjugate

odmienny (od-myen-ni) adj. m. mutable; different; unlike

odmierzac (od-mye-zhach) v. measure off ; mark off

odmłodzic (od-mwo-dźheech) v. rejuvenate; make (look) younger

odmowa (od-mo-va) f. refusal; denial; saving "no"

odmowic (od-moo-veech) v. refuse; say prayers ; say "no"

odmrozic (od-mro-żheech) v. get frostbite ; get frozen; thaw

odmrożenie (od-mro-zhe-ńe) n. frostbite ; kibe

odmruknąc (od-mrook-nowńch) v. mutter back; grunt out

odnajac (od-na-yowńch) v. sublet

odnawiac (od-nav-yach) v. renew; renovate ; restore; reform

odnajdywać (od-nay-di-vach) v.
recover; find; discover
od niechcenia (od ñe-khtse-ña)
adv. carelessly; willy-nilly
odniemczać (od-ñem-chach) v.
de-Germanize (language etc.)
odniesienie (od-ñe-she-ñe) n.
carrying back; reference (line)
odnieść (od-ñeshch) v. bring
back; take back;sustain
odnoga (od-no-ga) f. spur;
branch; offshoot; river pass
odnosić (od-no-sheech) v. take
back; carry back (repeatedly)
odnośnie (od-nósh-ñe) prep.
concerning; in comparison
odnośnik (od-nosh-ñeek) m. reference; footnote(in a text)
odnośny (od-nosh-ni) adj. m.
relative; respective;proper
odnotować (od-no-to-vach) v.
check off; note down; state
odnowa (od-no-va) f. renewal;
restoration; regeneration
odnowić (od-no-veech) v. renew; renovate;reform;revive
odosobnić (od-o-sób-ñeech) v.
isolate; confine;stand alone
odosobnienie (od-o-sob-ñe-ñe)
n. isolation;privacy;seclusion
odor (o-door) m. reek; smell
odpad (ód-pat) m. refuse; dropout; waste; muck; scraps
odpadać (od-pa-dach)v. drop off;
fall off; peel off; come off
odpadki (od-pad-kee) pl. waste
odparcie (od-pár-che) n. repulsion; rejection; refutation
odparować (od-pa-ro-vach) v.
parry; repel; evaporate
odparzenie (od-pa-zhé-ñe) n.
gall; scald ; chafe (skin)
odparzyć (od-pa-zhich) v. blister; chafe one's skin
odpędzać (od-pán-dzach) v.chase-
away; repel; expel;banish
odpiąć (od-pyoñch) v. unfasten;
unbutton ;unbuckle; unclasp
odpieczętować (od-pye-chán-to-
vach) v. unseal ;open(a letter)
odpinać (od-pée-nach) v. unbutton; disconnect; undo;unclasp

odpierać (od-pye-rach) v. repel;
refute; force back; disprove
odpiłować (od-pee-wo-vach) v.
saw off; file off; cut off
odpis (od-pees) m. copy
odpisać (odpee-sach) v. copy;
write back; answer· deduct
odpłacić (od-pwa-cheech) v.
repay; reciprocate;get back at
odpłata (od-pwa-ta) f. retribution; repayment; retaliation
odpłynąć (od-pwi-nownch) v.
float away; sail away; swim
away; put to sea low tide
odpływ (od-pwif) m. ebb; outflow;
odpoczynek (od-po-chi-nek) m.
rest; repose; relax from work
odpoczywać (od-po-chi-vach) v.
rest; have a rest;take a rest
odpokutować (od-po-koo-to-vach)
v. expiate; atone; pay dearly
odporność (od-pór-noshch) f.
immunity;resistance; hardiness
odpowiadać (od-po-vya-dach) v.
answer to; correspond to
odpowiedni (od-po-vyed-ñee) adj.
m. respective; adequate; suitable; fit; right;due;opportune
odpowiedzialność (od-po-vye-
dzhal-noshch) f. responsibility;
liability· civil liability
odpowiedzialny (od-po-vye-dzhal-
ni) adj. m. responsible; liable;
accountable; trustworthy
odpór (od-poor) m. opposition;
resistance; opposition
odprasować (od-pra-so-vach) v.
press; iron; press out;express
odprawa (od-pra-va) f. dispatch;
rebuff;briefing; debriefing
odprawiać (od-práv-yach) v.dis-
patch; dismiss; celebrate
(mass); order away; send away
odprężać (od-prán-zhach) v. relax; slacken; let down;recoil
odprężenie (od-prán-zhe-ñe) m.
relax; easing of tension;détente
odprowadzać (od-pro-va-dzach)
v. divert; drain off; escort
odpruwać (od-proo-vach) v.
rip off (buttons);rip away
odprzedać (od-pzhe-dach)v. resell

odprzedaż (od-pzhe-dash) f. re-
sale;sale at second hand

odpust (od-poost) m. indulgence

odpuszczenie (od-poosh-che-ñe)
n.foregiveness;remission

odpychać (od-pi-khach) v. repel

odpychanie (od-pi-kha-ñe) n.
repulsion; repelling

odra (od-ra) f. measles pl. ru-
beola(high fever&skin eruption)

odrabiać (od-rab-yach) v. work
off; work out; get done;undo

odraczać (od-ra-chach) v. put
off; postpone; defer: delay

odradzać (od-ra-dzach) v. advise
against; regenerate; revive

odrapać (o-dra-pach) v. scratch
up; dilapidate; scrape off

odrastać (od-ras-tach) v. grow
back; sprout again; shoot again

odraza (od-ra-za) f. aversion

odrazu (od-ra-zoo) adv. at once

odrażający (od-ra-zha-yówn-tsi)
adj. m. repulsive; hideus

odrąbać (od-równ-bach) v. chop
off; hew away; cut off

odrębność (od-ránb-noshch) n.
distinction; individuality

odrębny (od-ránb-ni) adj. m.
distinct; individual:separate

odręczny (od-ránch-ni) adj. m.
freehand; personal; longhand

odrętwiały (od-ránt-vya-wi) adj.
m. numbed; torpid : stiff

odrobić (od-ro-beech) v. work
off; work out; get done· do

odrobina (od-ro-bee-na) f. small
bit; particle· shred; a dash

odroczenie (od-ro-che-ñe) n.
adjournment; postponment

odroczyć (od-ro-chich) v. put
off; delay; defer; postpone

odrodzenie (od-ro-dze-ñe) m.
rebirth; renaissance

odrodzić (od-ro-dźheech) v.
regenerate :renew; revive

odróżniać (od-roozh-ñach) v. distinguish; differentiate

odróżniać się (od-roozh-ñach
shań) v. differ :be different

odruch (od-rookh) m. reflex

odrywać (od-ri-vach) v. tear
off; sever;separate;break off

odrzec (od-zhech) v. reply

odrzucać (od-zhoo-tsach) v.
reject; repulse; cast away

odrzutowiec (od-zhoo-tov-yets)
m. jet (plane)

odrzwia (od-zhvya) pl. door-
frame: mine prop set

odrzynać (od-zhi-nach) v. cut
off; cut away; detach; sever

odsądzać (od-sówn-dzach) v.
deny; infamize;deprive of merit

odsetka (od-set-ka) f. interest
point; percentage; proportion

odsiadywać (od-sha-di-vach) v.
sit out; serve (sentence)

odsiecz (od-shech) f. rescue

odskoczyć (od-sko-chich) v.
jump off; spring back;dart away

odsłonić (od-swo-ñeech) v. un-
veil;expose; display: show

odsprzedać (od-spzhe-dach) v.
resell; sale at second hand

odstawać (od-sta-vach) v. hang-
loose; not fit; come off

odstawić (od-sta-veech) v. put
aside; deliver; play(dumb)

odstąpić (od-stówn-peech) v.
step back; secede; cede

odstęp (od-stámp) m. margin;
space; interval; lapse (of time)

odstępca (od-stámp-tsa) m.ren-
egade; deserter; turncoat

odstępne (od-stámp-ne) n. payment for giving up a lease

odstraszyć (od-stra-shich) v.
deter; frighten away;scare

odstręczyć (od-strán-chich) v.
dissuade; turn away;repel;deter

odstrzał (od-stzhaw) m. shooting
off; firing (game, mine)

odsunąć (od-soo-nównch) v. push
away; shove away; brush aside

odsyłacz (od-si-wach) m. reference mark; footnote mark

odsyłać (od-si-wach) v. send
back; refer ;return; direct

odsypać (od-si-pach) v. pour
off (not liquid);alluviate

odsypiać (od-sip-yach) v. catch
up on sleep; sleep off

odszkodowanie (od-shko-do-va-ñe)
n. indemnity : compensation

odszukać (od-shoo-kach) v. retrieve; run down; seek out; find
odśrodkowy (od-śhrod-ko-vi)
adj. m. centrifugal
odświeżyć (od-śhvye-zhich) v.
refresh; recondition; restore
odświętny (od-śhvyańt-ni) adj.
m. festive; ceremonial; showy
odtąd (od-tównt) adv. henceforth; from now on; from here
odtłuścić (od-twoosh-ćheech)
v. degrease; reduce weight
odtrącać (od-trown-tsach) v.
repel; jostle; knock off; deduct (charges); thrust aside
odtrutka (od-troot-ka) f. antidote! counterpoison
odtwarzać (od-tva-zhach) v.
reproduce; reconstitute
odtwórca (od-tvoor-tsa) m. re-
producer; performer
oduczać (od-oo-chach) v. un-
teach; unlearn; break a habit
odurzać (o-doo-zhach) v. stun;
make dopey; stupefy; daze; dizzy
odurzenie (o-doo-zhe-ńe) n.
stupor; giddiness; intoxication
odwadniać (od-vad-ńach) v.
drain; dehydrate; dewater
odwaga (od-va-ga) f. courage
odwalić (od-va-leech) v. push
away; beat it; copy; get over
with; roll aside; remove; sham
odwar (od-var) m. decoction
odważnik (od-vazh-ńeek) n.
scale-weight
odważny (od-vazh-ni) adj. m.
brave; courageous; bold; daring
odważyć (od-va-zhich) v. weigh
odważyć się (od-va-zhich śhań)
v. dare; have the courage; risk
odwdzięczyć się (od-vdźhan-chich
śhań) v. repay (with gratitude; return; requite; repay
odwet (od-vet) m. retaliation;
retort; revenge; requital
odwiazać (od-vyown-zach) v.
untie; unfasten; unbuckle; undo
odwieczny (od-vyech-ni) adj. m.
eternal; immemorial; age long
odwiedzać (odvye-dzach) v. visit; call on; pay a visit;
pay a call; come to see

odwiedziny (od-vye-dźhee-ni) n.
visit; call; coming to see
odwijać (od-vee-yach) v. unwrap
odwilż (od-veelzh) f. thaw
odwlekać (od-vle-kach) v. put
off; postpone; delay; drag away
odwodnić (od-vod-ńeech) v. drain
odwodzić (od-vo-dźheech) v. draw
off; draw aside; dissuade
odwołać (od-vo-wach) v. take
back; appeal; refer; recall
odwołanie (od-vo-wa-ńe) n. recall; appeal; repeal; cancellation
odwozić (od-vo-źheech) v. take
back (by car); drive back
odwód (od-voot) m. reserve
odwracać (od-vra-tsach) v. reverse; turn around; invert
odwrotny (od-vrót-ni) adj. m.
reverse; opposite; converse
odwrót (od-vroot) m. retreat;
reverse; withdrawal
odwykać (od-vi-kach) v. break
a habit; loose the habit
odwzajemniać (od-vza-yem-ńach)
v. reciprocate; repay; return
odyniec (o-di-ńets) m. boar
odzew (od-zev) m. echo; reply
odziedziczyć (o-dźhe-dźhee-chich)
v. inherit; succeed (to a title)
odzienie (o-dźhe-ńe) n. clothing
odzież (o-dźhezh) f. clothes
odznaczać (od-zna-chach) v.
distinguish; decorate; mark off
odznaczenie (od-zna-che-ńe) n.
distinction; award; decoration
odznaka (od-zna-ka) f. badge
odzwierciadlać (od-zvyer-ćhad-
lach) v. reflect (something)
odzwyczajać (od-zvi-ćha-yach)
v. break a habit; make loose a
                  habit
odzyskać (od-zis-kach) v. retrieve; regain; recover; win back
odzywać się (od-zi-vach śhań) v.
speak up; drop a line; respond
odźwierny (od-dźhvyer-ni) m.
doorman; janitor; caretaker
odżyć (od-zhich) v. come back to
life; revive; be reborn; reappear
odżywczy (od-zhiv-chi) adj. m.
nutritious; nourishing; alimentary
odżywiać (od-zhiv-yach) v. nourish; feed; supply with food

odżywienie (od-zhiv-yé-ñe) n.
food; nourishment; diet

ofensywa (o-fen-sí-va) f. offensive; push; attack

oferma (o-fér-ma) f. sad sack

oferta (o-fér-ta) f. offer

ofiara (o-fyá-ra) f. victim;
offering;sacrifice; dupe

oficer (o-fée-tser) m. (military) officer

oficjalny (o-feets-yál-ni) adj.
m. official;formal;reserved

oficyna (o-fee-tsí-na) f. back-
house; printing shop;annex

ofuknąć (o-fook-nówñch) v. rebuke; reprimand;trounce;rate

ogar (ó-gar) m. bloodhound

ogarek (o-ga-rek) m. candle-
end; stump; stub:cigarette end

ogarniać (o-gár-ñach) v. seize;
comprehend;take in;grasp

ogień (o-ğeñ) m. fire; flame

ogier (o-ğer) m. stallion

oglądać (o-glówn-dach) v. inspect; consider; see

oględny (o-glánd-ni) adj. cir-
cumspect;moderate;cautious

ogłada (o-gwá-da) f. good manners;refinement;urbanity:polish

ogłaszać (o-gwa-shach)v. ad-
vertize; declare; publish

ogłuchnąć (o-gwookh-nówñch) v.
become deaf; be hushed

ogłupieć (o-gwoop-yech) v.
become stupid;grow silly

ognie sztuczne (óg-ñe shtooch-
ne) pl. fireworks

ogniotrwały (o-ğño-trvá-wi) adj.
fireproof;incombustible

ognisko (od-ñees-ko) n. hearth;
focus; camp fire·fire place

ognisty (og-ñees-ti) adj. m.
fiery;flaming; passionate

ogniwo (og-ñee-vo) n. link

ogolić (o-gó-leech) v. shave

ogon (ó-gon) m. tail;trail;scut

ogonek (o-gó-nek) m. waiting
line;queue;diacritical mark

ogorzały (o-go-zhá-wi) adj. m.
sunburnt;tanned;weather beaten

ogólnie (o-gól-ñe) adv. generally;as a rule;universally

ogólny (o-gól-ni) adj. m. general;prevailing; global; total

ogół (ó-goow) m. people; public

ogółem (o-goo-wem) adv. on the
whole; as a whole; altogether

ogórek (o-goó-rek) m. cucumber

ogórkowy sezon (o-goor-kó-vi
se-zon) slack time(season)

ograbić (o-grá-beech) v. rob

ograniczony (o-gra-ñee-chó-ni)
adj. m. narrow-minded; limited

ogrodnik (o-gród-ñeek) m. gardener; horticulturist

ogrodzic (o-gró-dźheech)v. fence
in; enclose;wall in; rail in

ogromny (o-grom-ni) adj. m. huge

ogród (ó-good) m. garden

ogryzać (o-grí-zach) v. gnaw
away; nimble at; pick(a bone)

ogrzewać (o-gzhe-vách) v. heat

ohydny (o-khid-ni) adj. m.
hideous; gastly;abominable:vile

o ile (o ée-le) conj. as far as

ojciec (óy-chets) m. father

ojciec chrzestny (oy-chyets
khzhést-ni) godfather

ojczym (óy-chim) m. stepfather

ojczysty język (oy-chís-ti yan-
zik) native tongue

ojczyzna (oy-chíz-na) f. native
country; motherland;homeland

okaleczyć (o-ka-le-chích) v.
maim;cripple·lame;mutilate

oka mgnienie (o-ka mgñe-ñe) n.
eye blink; split second

okap (ó-kap) m. eaves;overlap

okaz (ó-kas) m. specimen;type

okazać (o-ka-zach) v. show; demonstrate; evidence;exhibit

okazały (o-ka-zá-wi) adj. m.
magnificent;stately;grand

okaziciel (o-ka-żhee-chel) m.
bearer (of a check etc.)

okazja (o-kaz-ya) f. opportunity

okazyjny (o-ka-zíy-ni) adj. m.
occasional; chance(acquaintance)

okazywać (o-ka-zí-vach) v. demonstrate; show;manifest;display

oklaski (o-klas-kee) pl. applause;clapping; acclamations

oklaskiwać (o-klas-kee-vach) v.
applaud ; clap(one's hands)

okleić (o-kle-eech) v. paste-
over;stick over; smear over

oklepany (o-kle-pá-ni) adj. m.
commonplace; (well) worn

okład (ó-kwat) m. compress;
hotpad ; lining;wrapping

okładka (o-kwád-ka) f. (book)
cover; book binding

okłamać (o-kwa-mach) v. deceive; tell a lie; delude

okno (ók-no) n. window

oko (ó-ko) n. eye; eve sight

okolica (o-ko-lee-tsa) f. region; surroundings;vicinity

okolicznosc (o-ko-leech-noshch)
f. circumstance; fact;occasion

około (o-ko-wo) prep. near;
about; more or less;at;on;or so

okon (ó-koń) m. perch; bass

okop (ó-kop) m. trench

okopcic (o-kop-cheech) v. soot

okostna (o-kóst-na) f. perios-
teum; lining of the bones

okólnik (o-kool-ñeek) m. circular; corral;poultry yard

okpic (o-kpeech) v. pool wool
over eyes; deceive;cheat;gull

okradać (o-kra-dach) v. pickpocket; burglarize; rob

okrakiem (o-kra-kem) adv.
astraddle;with legs wide apart

okrasa (o-kra-sa) f. fat; ornament ; seasoning ;gravy;lard

okrasić (o-kra-sheech) v. adorn;
season ;add a condiment

okratować (o-kra-to-vach) v.
grate; bar (a window)

okratowanie (o-kra-to-vá-ñe)
m. grating; railings; bars

okrąg (o-krownk) m. district

okrągły (o-krówng-wi) adj. m.
round; spherical full(month etc)

okrążać (o-krown-zhach) v. encircle; circle;revolve;detour

okres (ó-kres) m. period;phase

okreslać (o-kresh-lach) v.
define; qualify;fix;appoint

okręcać (o-krań-tsach) v. coil
around;wrap; turn around

okręt (o-krańt) m. ship;boat

okrężny (o-kranzh-ni) adj. m.
roundabout;indirect;devious
circuitous; circular;travelling
pedlar's(trade etc.)

okropnosc (o-krop-noshch) f.
horror; atrocity;outrage

okropny (o-krop-ni) adj. m.
horrible;fearful;awful;extreme

okruch (o-krookh) m. crumb

okrucienstwo (o-kroo-chyeń-
stvo) n. cruelty;atrocities

okrutny (o-kroot-ni) adj. m.
cruel;savage;excessive; sore

okrycie (o-kri-che) n. covering; wrap;garment;overcoat

okrywac (o-kri-vach) v. cover

okrzyczany (o-kzhi-cha-ni) adj.
m. notorious;famous;renowned

okrzyk (ó-kzhik) m. outcry

okrzyknąć (o-kzhik-nownch) v.
proclaim;declare; brand

oktawa (ok-ta-va) f. octave

okucie (o-koo-che) n. hardware; ferrule; fitting

okuć (o-kooch) v. shoe a horse;
shackle; fit a lock and hinges

okular (o-koo-lar) m. eyeglass

okularnik (o-koo-lar-ñeek) m.
cobra;poisonous snake of Asia

okulista (o-koo-lees-ta) m.
eye doctor;eye surgeon;oculist

okultyzm (o-kool-tizm) m. oc-
cultism; hidden knowledge

okup (ó-koop) m. ransom

okupacja (o-koo-páts-ya) f.
occupation; occupancy

okupować (o-koo-po-vach) v.
occupy;invade a territory

okupywać (o-koo-pi-vach) v. pay
ransom; compensate;redeem;atone

olbrzym (ol-bzhim) m. giant

olbrzymi (ol-bzhi-mee) adj. m.
gigantic;huge;cllossal;excessive

olcha (ól-kha) f. alder tree

oleander (o-le-án-der) m. oleander (an evergreen shrub)

olej (ó-ley) m. oil; oil paint

olej lniany (ó-ley lña-ni) adj.
m. linseed-oil

oligarchia (o-lee-gár-khya) m.
oligarchy;the ruling persons

oliwa (o-lee-va) f. olive; oil

oliwić (o-lee-veech) v. oil

oliwka (o-leev-ka) f. olive-tree

olszyna (ol-shi-na) f. alder-
tree stand; alder wood

olśniewać (ol-shñe-vach) v.
dazzle; ravish;enchant·

ołów (owoof) m. lead;lead shot
ołówek (o-woo-vek) m. lead
pencil;drawing in pencil
ołtarz (ow-tash) m. altar
omackiem (o-mats-'kem) adv.
gropingly ; blindfold
omal (o-mal) adv. nearly
omamić (o-ma-meech) v. deceive
omaścić (o-mash-cheech) v. add
fat; add butter(on bread etc.)
omawiać (o-mav-yach) v. discuss
omdlały (om-dla-wi) adj. m.
fainted; faint; languid
omdleć (om-dlech) v. faint
omen (o-men) m. omen
omieszkać (o-myesh-kach) v.
fail;omit;neglect·
omijać (o-mee-yach) v. pass
omlet (om-let) m. omelet
omłócić (o-mwoo-cheech) v.
thresh out; give a thrashing
omotać (o-mo-tach) v. entangle
omówić (o-moo-veech) v. discuss
omylić (o-mi-leech) v. mislead
omylny (o-mil-ni) adj. m. fal-
lible;misleading;deceitful
omyłka (o-miw-ka) f. error
on; ona; ono (on; o-na; o-no)
pron. he; she; it
oni (o-ñee) m. pl. they;
one (o-ne) f. pl. they
ondulacja (on-doo-lats-ya) f.
(hair) wave;permanent wave
ondulacja trwała (on-doo-lats-
ya trva-wa) permanent (wave)
onegdaj (o-neg-day) adv. the
other day;two days ago
ongiś (on-geesh) adv. (arch)
at one time;once upon a time
oniemiały (o-ñe-mya-wi) adj.
m. mute; dumb; speechless
oniesmielać (o-ñe-shmye-lach)
v. intimidate;browbeat; cow
opactwo (o-pats-tvo) n. abbey
opaczny (o-pach-ni) adj. m.
wrong; mistaken;improper
opad (o-pat) m. (rain) fall
opadać(o-pa-dach) v. subside
(na)opak (na o-pak) adv. up-
side down; reverse;wrong way
opakowanie (o-pa-ko-va-ñe) n.
wrapping ; packing

opal (o-pal) m. opal
opalać się (o-pa-lach shañ) v.
suntan; tan;bronze;lie on the sun
opalanie (o-pa-la-ñe) n. heating (house etc.);fire marking
opalenizna (o-pa-le-ñeez-na) f.
suntan; tan; scorched remains
opał (o-paw) m. fuel for heating
opamiętać (o-pa-myan-tach) v.
sober down; bring to reason
opanować (o-pa-no-vach) v.
master;conquer;seize; learn
opanowany (o-pa-no-va-ni) adj.
m. cool-headed;composed;calm
opary (o-pa-ri) pl. fumes
oparcie (o-par-che) n. support
oparzyć (o-pa-zhich) v. scald
opasać (o-pa-sach) v. belt;
girdle;grid;encircle;surround
opaska (o-pas-ka) f. band
opasły (o-pas-wi) adj. m. obese
opaść (o-pashch) v. drop; sink;
hang loose;settle;collapse;slope
opatentować (o-pa-ten-to-vach)
v. patent ;take out a patent
opatrunek (o-pa-troo-nek) m.
dressing; bandage; field dressing
opatrywać (o-pa-tri-vach) v.
fix; dress; provide;prepare
opera (o-pe-ra) f. opera; opera
house; no end of a joke
operacja (o-pe-rats-ya) f. surgery; operation; action;process
operować (o-pe-ro-vach) v.oper-
ate; manipulate; act; handle
opętanie (o-pan-ta-ñe) n. obsession;demonical possession
opieczętować (o-pye-chan-to-
vach) v. seal up; seal
opieka (o-pye-ka) f. care
opiekować (o-pye-ko-vach) v.
take care; care for;have charge
opiekun (o-pye-koon) m. guardian; curator; foster-parent
opierać się (o-pye-rach shañ)
v. lean; base; relay;rest;defy
opieszały (o-pye-sha-wi) adj.
m. slow; tardy; lazy; inert
opinia (o-peeñ-ya) f. opinion;
view; reputation; sentiment
opis (o-pees) m. description
oplątać (o-plown-tach) v. ensnare; entangle; entwine

opluwać (o-ploo-vach) v. spit on; spit at; slander; defame

opłacać (o-pwa-tsach) v. pay; bribe; cover the cost; reward

opłakany (o-pwa-ka-ni) adj. m. deplorable; sad; pitiful

opłakiwać (o-pwa-kee-vach) v. lament; deplore; mourn

opłata (o-pwa-ta) f. fee

opłatek (o-pwa-tek) m. wafer

opłucna (o-pwoots-na) f. pleura; membrane around the lungs

opłukiwać (o-pwoo-kee-vach) v. rinse; wash with water

opływać (o-pwi-vach) v. sail around; abound; encircle; roll

opływowy (o-pwi-vo-vi) adj. m. streamlined; streamline

opodal (o-po-dal) adv. near by

opodatkować (o-po-dat-ko-vach) v. tax; impose a tax

opona (o-po-na) f. tire

oponować (o-po-no-vach) v. oppose; take exception

opornie (o-por-ne) adv. with difficulty; arduosly

oporny (o-por-ni) adj. m. balky; recalcitrant; refractory

opowiadać (o-pov-ya-dach) v. tell - tale; relate; record

opozycja (o-po-zits-ya) f. opposition; resistance

opór (o-poor) m. resistance

opóźniać (o-poozh-nach) v. delay; retard; slow down; defer

opóźnienie (o-poozh-ne-ne) n. delay; deferment; tardiness

opracować (o-pra-tso-vach) v. work up; elaborate; compile

oprawa (o-pra-va) f. frame; binding; framework; handle

oprawca (o-prav-tsa) m. skinner; executioner; torturer; assassin

opresja (o-pres-ya) f. oppression

oprocentowanie (o-pro-tsen-to-wa-ne) n. interest (on money)

oprowadzać (o-pro-va-dzach) v. show around; act as a guide

oprócz (o-prooch) prep.: except; besides; apart from; but; save

opróżniać (o-proozh-nach) v. empty; clear; evacuate; unload

opryskliwy (o-prisk-lee-vi) adj. m. peevish; gruff; harsh

opryszek (o-pri-shek) m. hoodlum; hooligan; rowdy; rough-neck

oprzec (op-zhech) v. lean; base; resist; become inffamed; inflame

oprzytomnieć (o-pzhi-tom-nech) v. recover; collect oneself

optyk (op-tik) m. optician

optymista (op-ti-mees-ta) m. optimist; one of cheerful views

opublikować (o-poo-blee-ko-vach) v. publish; make public

opuchły (o-pookh-wi) adj. m. swollen; dilated

opuchlina (o-pookh-lee-na) f. swelling; dilatation

opuszczać (o-poosh-chach) v. leave; omit; abandon; lower

opustoszały (o-poos-to-sha-vi) adj. m. deserted; desolate; empty

opuszczenie (o-poosh-che-ne) n. omission; lowering; reduction

orać (o-rach) v. till; plough

oranżeria (o-ran-zher-ya) f. greenhouse; hothouse; orangery

oraz (o-raz) conj. as well as

orbita (or-bee-ta) f. orbit

order (or-der) m. decoration; order (for service rendered etc.)

ordynarny (or-di-nar-ni) adj. m. gross; coarse; vulgar; trashy

oredzie (o-ran-dzhe) n. (official) message; proclamation

oręż (o-ranzh) m. weapon

organiczny (or-ga-neech-ni) adj. m. organic; constitutional

organista (or-ga-nees-ta) m. organist; organ player

organizacja (or-ga-nee-zats-ya) f. organization; organized group

organizm (or-ga-neezm) m. organism; any living thing

orgia (org-ya) f. orgy

orka (or-ka) f. tillage

orkiestra (or-kes-tra) f. orchestra; orchestra pit

orny (or-ni) adj. m. arable

orszak (or-shak) m. retinue

ortodoksja (or-to-doks-ya) f. orthodoxy; conventionality

ortografia (or-to-gra-fya) f.
orthography;correct spelling
oryginalny (o-ri-gee-nal-ni)
adj. m. original;inventive;new
orzech (o-zhekh) m. nut;walnut
orzeczenie (o-zhe-che-ne) m.
decision; sentence; ruling
orzeł (o-zhew) m, eagle;genius
orzeźwiać (o-zheźh-vyach) v.
refresh; brace up; invigorate
osa (o-sa) f. wasp; vixen;shrew
osad (o-sat) m. sediment; dregs
osada (o-sa-da) f. settlement
osadnik (o-sad-neek) m. settler
osadzać (o-sa-dzach) v. plant;
seat; settle; place;fix;steadv
osamotnienie (o-sa-mot-ne-ne)
n. isolation;loneliness
osądzać (o-sown-dzach) v.
sentence ; judge ;preiudge
oschły (oskh-wi) adj. m. arid;
dry; cold: stiff; stand-offish
oselka (o-sew-ka) f. whetstone
oset (o-set) m. thistle,teasel
osiadać (o-sha-dach) v. settle;
subside; make a settlement
osiągnąć (o-showng-nownch) v.
attain;achieve;gain;reach
osiedlać (o-shed-lach) v.
settle;make a settlement
osiem (o-shem) num. eight
osiemdziesiąt (o-shem-dzhe-
shownt) num. eighty
osiemnaście (o-shem-nash-che)
num. eighteen
osiemset (o-shem-set) num.
eight hundred
osierocić (o-she-ro-cheech)
v. be orphaned
osika (o-shee-ka) f. aspen
osikać (o-shee-kach) v. sprinkle; piss on (vulg.)
osiodłać (o-shod-wach) v. saddle ; reduce to subiugation
osioł (o-shyow) m. donkey; ass
oskarżać (o-skar-zhach) v.
accuse ;charge with;indict
oskrzela (o-skzhe-la) pl. n.
bronchia ;main part of windpipe
oskrzydlać (o-skzhid-lach) v.
outflank ;go bevond; cut off
oskubać (o-skoo-bach) v. fleece;
feather ;pluck;skin: soak
osłabiać (o-swab-yach) v. weak-
en ;reduce; lessen;diminish

osłabienie (o-swa-bye-ne) n.
weakness ; diminuation;debilitation
osłona (o-swo-na) f. shield;
cover ; protection: defense
osładzać (o-swa-dzach) v. sweet-
en; put sugar; cheer up
osłupiały (o-swoo-pya-wi) adj.
m. amazed; aghast ; astounded
osmarować (o-sma-ro-vach) v.
besmear; libel ; run down; soil
osoba (o-so-ba) f. person
osobisty (o-so-bees-ti) adj.
m. personal; private ;narticular
osobiście (o-so-beesh-che) adv.
personally ; in person
osobnik (o-sob-neek) m. individual; specimen; person
osobny (o-sob-ni) adj. m.sep-
arate; private ; individual
osobowość (o-so-bo-voshch) f.
personality ; individuality
osowiały (o-so-vya-wi) adj. m.
depressed; dejected ·plum:monish
ospa (os-pa) f. smallpox
ospały (os-pa-wy) adj. m.
drowsy; sleepy; sluggish; dull
ostatecznie (o-sta-tech-ne) adv.
finally; after all; at last
ostateczny (o-sta-tech-ni) adj.
m. final ;ultimate; eventual
ostatek (o-sta-tek) m. reminder; rest; remains; scran
ostatni (o-stat-nee) adj. m.
last; late; end;closing; parting
ostatnio (o-stat-no) adv.of late;
lately; not long ago ; recently
ostoja (o-sto-ya) f. mainstay
ostroga (o-stro-ga) f. spur
ostrokątny (o-stro-kownt-ni)
adj. m. sharp-angled
ostrożność (o-strozh-noshch)
f. caution; prudence; care
ostrożny (o-strozh-ni) adj. m.
careful; prudent;cautious; warv
ostry (o-stri) adj. m. sharp
ostryga (o-stri-ga) f. oyster
ostrze (o-stzhe) n. cutting
edge; spike ;blade; point;prong
ostrzegać (o-stzhe-gach) v.
warn of: warn against;admonish

ostrzeliwać (o-stzhe-lee-vach)
v. shoot at; strafe; fire at;
accustom to gun fire

ostrzeżenie (o-stzhe-zhé-ńe)
n. warning ;danger sign·notice

ostrzyć (o-stzhíć) v. sharp-
en : whet;grind;put an edge

ostrzygać (o-stzhi-gaćh) v.
cut (hair) ; shear sheep;trim

ostudzać (o-stoo-dzaćh) v. cool

ostygać (o-stí-gaćh) v. cool
down ; chill; cool off: abate

osuszać (o-soo-shaćh) v. dry;
drain: dehumidify;wipe; mop

oswobodzić (o-svo-bo-dźheećh)
v. free; liberate:rescue:rid

oswoić (o-svo-eećh) v. tame;
familiarize; tame;domesticate

oszacować (o-sha-tso-vaćh) v.
evaluate; estimate;appraise

oszczep (osh-chep) m. javelin

oszczerstwo (osh-chér-stvo) n.
calumny; libel; defamation

oszczędności (osh-chánd-nosh-
ćhee) pl. savings(money)

oszklenie (o-shkle-ńe) n. glaz-
ing (of windows)

oszołomić (o-sho-wó-meećh) v.
stun: daze:stupefy:bewilder

oszpecić (o-shpe-ćheećh) v. deface; disfigure:deform; mar

oszukać (o-shoo-kaćh) v. cheat

oszust (o-shoost) m. cheater

oś (osh) f. axle (axis)

ościenny (o-shćhén-ni) adj. m.
bordering: adjoining: adjacent

ość (oshćh) f. (fish) bone

oślepiać (o-shle-pyaćh) v.
blind; dazzle; strike blind

ośmieszać (o-shmye-shaćh) v.
ridicule;deride:make fun of

ośrodek (o-shro-dek) m. center

oświadczenie (o-shviad-ché-ńe)
n. declaration; pronouncement

oświadczyny (o-shvyad-chi-ni)
pl. marriage proposal

oświata (o-shvya-ta) f. education; learning

oświecać (o-shvye-tsaćh) v.
light up; enlighten; educate

oświetlenie (o-shvyet-lé-ńe) n.
lighting ;light: illumination

otaczać (o-tá-chaćh) v. sur-
round:enclose:turn on a lathe

otchłań (ot-khwań) f. abyss

otępienie (o-tań-pye-ńe) n.
dullness ;stupor:stupefaction

oto (ó-to) part. here; there

otoczenie (o-to-ché-ńe) n. environment;setting; associates

otoczyć (o-to-chíćh) v. surround: enclose;turn on a lathe

otomana (o-to-ma-na) f. couch

otóż (o-toosh) conj. now

otruć (o-trooćh) v. poison

otrucie (o-troo-ćhe) n. poisoning

otrzaskać (o-tshás-kaćh)v.acquaint

otrząsać (o-tzhówn-saćh) v.
shake loose; shudder; strew

otrzewna (o-tzhév-na) f. peri-
toneum; lining of abdomen

otrzeźwieć (o-tzhezh-vyećh) v.
sober up;be disillusioned:brisk up

otrzymać (o-tzhi-maćh) v. receive; get; be given;acquire

otulić (o-too-leećh) v. tuck in;
wrap;wrap up: shroud:enfold: lap

otwarcie (o-tvar-ćhe) adv.openly;
frankly; in plain words;outright

otwarty (o-tvar-ti) adj. m.
open; frank:overt;professed

otwierać (ot-vye-raćh) v. open

otwór (ót-voor) m. opening

otyły (o-tí-wi) adj. m. obese

owacja (o-váts-ya) f. ovation

owad (ó-vad) m. insect

owal (ó-val) m. oval

owca (óv-tsa) f. sheep

owczarek (ov-chá-rek) m. sheep-dog

owczarnia(ov-chár-ńa)f. sheep-fold

owdowiały (ov-do-vyá-wi) adj.
m. widowed : one who lost wife

owies (ó-vyes) m. oats

owiewać (o-vye-vaćh) v. blow
upon;sweep over: encompass:inspire

owijać (o-vee-yaćh) v. wrap up

owłosiony (o-vwo-sho-ni) adj.
m. hairy; hirsute: shaggy; pilose

owo (ó-vo) pron. that : that thing

owoc (ó-vots) m. fruit ;fruitage

owrzodzenie (o-vzho-dze-ńe) n.
ulceration : sore: sores

owsianka (ov-shan-ka) f. oatmeal; kasha; porridge

owszem (óv-shem) part. yes;
certainly; on the contrary

ozdabiać (o-zdáb-yaćh) v. dec-
:orate; adorn :trim: garnish

ozdoba (oz-dó-ba) f. decoration
oziębiać (o-żhań-byach) v. cool
off; chill; cool down; damp
oziębły (o-żhanb-wi) adj. m.
frigid; cold; reserved; dry
oznaczać (o-zna-chach) v. mark;
signify ; indicate; fix; spell
oznajmiać (o-znay-myach) v.
announce ;inform; notify;state
oznaka (o-zna-ka) f. sign;
symptom; badge; mark
ozor (o-zoor) m. (bull's)
tongue; gossiping tongue
ożenić (o-zhe-ńeech) v. marry
ożywiać (o-zhiv-yach) v. bring
to life; animate;brisk up
ożywienie (o-zhi-vye-ńe) n.
animation ;liveliness; stir
ożywiony (o-zhiv-yo-ni) adj. m.
animated; lively; brisk;
osemka (oo-sém-ka) f. eight
ósma godzina (oós-ma go-dżhée-
na) eight o'clock
ósmak (oós-mak) m. eighth grad-
er; eighth grade pupil
ow (oof) m. pron. that
owa (ó-va)f. pron. that
owo (ó-vo)n. pron. that
owi (ó-vee)pl. m. pron. that
owe (ó-ve)pl. f. pron. that
owczesny (oov-chés-ni) adj. m.
the then;of those days
ówdzie (oóv-dżhe) adv. elsewhere; there
pa ! (pa) excl.: bye-bye !
pacha (pá-kha) f. armpit
pachnąć (pákh-nównch) v. smell
(good) ;have a fragrance
pachołek (pa-kho-wek) m. boy;
page;servant;menial; flunkey
pachwina (pakh-vee-na) f. groin
pacierz (pá-chesh) m. prayer
pacierzowy stos (pa-che-zhó-vi
stos) spinal column; spine
paciorki (pa-chór-kee) pl.
string of beads ;short prayer
pacjent (páts-yent) m. patient
pacyfista (pa-tsi-fées-ta) m.
pacifist ;believer in peace
pacyfizm (pa-tsi-feezm) m.
pacifism; ideology of peace
paczka (pách-ka) f. parcel

paczyć (pa-chich) v. warp
padać (pá-dach) v. fall down
padalec (pa-dá-lets) m. blind-
worm; slow warm
padlina (pad-lée-na) f. carrion
pagórek (pa-goo-rek) m. hill
pająk (pa-yównk) m. spider
pajęczyna (pa-yáń-chi-na) f.
cobweb ; spider web;gossamer
paka (pá-ka) f. crate;lock-up
pakować (pa-kó-vach) v. pack;
cram; wrap ; pack off; pack up
pakunek (pa-koo-nek) m. baggage
pal (pál) m. pile ; stake;picket
palący (pa-lówn-tsi) m. smoker
palec (pá-lets) m. finger: toe
palenie (pa-le-ńe) n. smoking
palenisko (pa-le-ńees-ko) n.
hearth ; fireplace; grate
paleta (pa-lé-ta) f. palette
palić (pá-leech) v. burn; smoke
cigarette; heat;scorch;shoot
paliwo (pa-lée-vo) n. fuel
palma (pál-ma) f. palm-tree
palnik (pál-ńeek) m. burner
palto (pál-to) n. overcoat
pałac (pá-wats) m. palace
pałka (páw-ka) f. stick; club
pamflet (pám-flet) m. pamphlet
pamiątka (pa-myównt-ka) f.
souvenir; token of remembrance
pamięć (pa-myánch) f. memory
pamiętać (pa-myáń-tach) v. remember; recall;be careful
pamiętnik (pa-myánt-ńeek) m.
diary; memoirs; album
pan (pan) m. lord; master;
mister; you;gentleman; squire
pan młody (pan mwo-di) m. bridegroom; man about to be married
pani (pa-ńee) f. lady; you;
madam ; mistress(in school etc.)
panika (pa-ńee-ka) f. panic; scare
panna (pán-na) f. miss; girl;lass
panna młoda (pán-na mwo-da) f,
bride; woman about to be married
panoszyć się (pa-nó-shich śhań)
v. domineer ;.boss : run the show
panować (pa-no-vach) v. rule;
reign; be master of; command;rife
panteizm (pan-te-eezm) m. pan-
theism

pantera (pan-té-ra) f. panther
pantoflarz (pan-to-flash) m.
henpecked husband
pantofel (pan-to-fel) m. slipper;
shoe; light low shoe
pantomima (pan-to-mee-ma) f.
pantomime; gestures no words
panujący (pa-noo-yówn-tsi) adj.
m. prevailing; ruling
pański (pań-skee) adj. m.
lord's; your's
państwo (pań-stvo) n. state;
married, couple
papa (pá-pa) f. feltpaper
papier (pá-pyer) m. paper
papieros (pa-pyé-ros) m. cigarette;tabacco rolled in paper
papieski (pa-pyés-kee) adj. m.
papal; of the Pope
papież (pá-pyesh) m. pope
papka (páp-ka) f. pulp; mash;
pap; gruel; paste; slurry
paplać (páp-lach) v. prattle
paproć (pá-proch) f. fern
papryka (pa-pri-ka) f. red-
pepper; paprica; paprika
papuga (pa-poo-ga) f. parrot
para 1. (pá-ra) f. couple
para 2. (pá-ra) f. steam
parabola (pa-ra-bó-la) f. parabola
parada (pa-rá-da) f. parade
paradoks (pa-rá-doks) m. para-
dox; apparent, contradiction
parafia (pa-ráf-ya) f. parish
parafina (pa-ra-fee-na) f.
paraffin(waxy petroleum)
paragraf (pa-ra-graf) m. para-
graph(a distinct section)
paraliż (pa-rá-leesh) m. paralysis;crippling of activities
parametr (pa-rá-metr) m. para-
meter;element of an orbit
parapet (pa-ra-pet) m. window-
sill; stool; rail; breastwork
parasol (pa-rá-sol) m. umbrella
parawan (pa-rá-van) n. screen
parcelować (par-tse-ló-vach) v.
parcel out(land);cut up
parcie (pár-che) n. thrust
park (párk) m. park
parkan (pár-kan) m. fence; net;
hoarding

parlament (par-lá-ment) m.
parliament; national legislature
parny (pár-ni) adj. m. sultry
parobek (pa-ró-bek) m. farmhand; plough man; rustic
parodia (pa-ród-ya) f. parody
parokrotnie (pa-ro-krót-ńe) adv.
repeatedly; a couple of times
parostatek (pa-ro-stá-tek) m.
steamboat; steamer; steamship
parować (pa-ro-vach) v. evaporate; vaporize; cook by steam
parowiec (pa-ró-vyets) m. steamboat; steamer; steamship
parowóz (pa-ro-voos) m. steam
locomotive · railroad engine
parów (pa-roov) m. ravine
parowki (pa-roov-kee) pl. hot
dogs; sausages; frankfurters
parszywy (par-shi-vi) adj. m.
mangy; scabby; lousy; horrid
partacki (par-táts-kee) adj. m.
bungled up; botched;fudged
partacz (pár-tach) m. bungler
parter (par-ter) m. ground
floor; first floor; parterre
partia (párt-ya) f. party; card
game; political party; game
partner (pár-tner) m. partner
partyjny (par-tíy-ni) adj. m.
party(member); party member
partykuła (par-ti-koo-wa) f.
particle;
partyzantka (par-ti-zánt-ka)
f. guerrilla; partisan war
parytet (pa-ri-tet) m. parity
parzyć (pá-zhich) v. scald;
steam; burn; percolate; couple
parzysty numer (pa-zhis-ti noo-
mer) even number
pas (pas) m. belt; traffic lane
pasat (pá-sat) m. trade wind
pasażer (pa-sá-zher) m. passenger : chap; fellow; liner
pasek (pá-sek) m. belt; band
pasieka (pa-śhe-ka) f. apiary
pasierb (pa-śherb) m. stepson
pasierbica (pa-śher-bee-tsa) f.
stepdaughter
pasja (pás-ya) f. passion
paskarz (pás-kash) m. profiteer
pasmo (pás-mo) n. streak; tract;
range; traffic lane

pasożyt (pa-só-zhit) m. parasite ; sponger

pasta (pás-ta) f. paste

pasterka (pas-tér-ka) f. midnight mass; shepherdess

pasterz (pás-tesh) m. shepherd

pastwa (pás-tva) f. prey

pastwisko (pas-tvées-ko) n.
pasture ; grass land

pastylka (pas-til-ka) f. tablet

pasywny (pa-sív-ni) adj. m.
passive acted upon

pasza (pá-sha) f. fodder

paszcza (pásh-cha) f. jaw

paszport (pásh-port) m. passport ; certificate

paść (pashch) v. fall down;
graze ; tend cattle; feed

patelnia (pa-tél-ña) f. frying-
pan with a handle

patent (pá-tent) m. patent

patetyczny (pa-te-tích-ni) adj.
m. pathetic ; pompous; turgid

patolog (pa-to-lok) m. patholo-
gist ; specialist in pathology

patriarcha (pa-tree-ár-kha) m.
patriarch

patriota (pa-tree-ó-ta) m.
patriot

patron (pá-tron) m. sponsor;
stencil; pattern ; protector

patronat (pa-tró-nat) m.patron-
age power to grant favors

patroszyć (pa-tró-shich) v.
disembowel; gut ; draw (a fowl)

patrzeć (pá-tzhech) v. look

patyk (pá-tik) m. stick

patyna (pa-tí-na) f. patina

pauza (páw-za) f. pause

paw (pav) m. peacock

paznokieć (paz-nó-kyech) m.
(finger) nail ; toe nail

pazur (pá-zoor) m. claw

paź (pash) m. page

październik (pazh-dzhér-ñeek)m.
October

pączek (pówn-chek) m. bud

pąsowy (pówn-so-vi) adj. m. red;
crimson : bright red poppy red

pchać (pkhach) v. push; thrust

pchła (pkhwa) f. flea

pchnięcie (pkhñań-che) n. push;
thrust; jostle : shove lunge

pech (pekh) m. bad luck

pechowiec (pe-khó-vyets) m.
unlucky fellow; lackless chap

pedagog (pe-dá-gok) m. peda-
gogue educator: educationist

pedał (pé-daw) m. 1. pedal;
2. gay; homosexual; pansy boy

pedant (pé-dant) m. pedant

pejcz (peych) m. horsewhip

pejzaż (péy-zash) m. landscape

peleryna (pe-le-rí-na) f. cape

pelikan (pe-leé-kan) m. pelican

pełnia (péw-ña) f. fullness

pełnić (péw-ñeech) v. fulfill

pełno (péw-no) adv. plenty

pełnoletni (pew-no-lét-ñee) adj.
m. adult; of age

pełnomocnictwo (pew-no-mots-
ñeets-tvo) n. power of attorney; full powers (legal)

pełny (péw-ni) adj. m. full

pełzać (péw-zach) v. creep;
crawl; fawn; drag: cringe

penicylina (pe-ñee-tsi-leé-na)
f. penicillin

pensja (pén-sya) f. salary;
pension; allowance; wages

pensjonat (pen-syó-nat) m.
boarding house

perfidny (per-feéd-ni) adj. m.
perfidious; double dealing

perfumy (per-foó-mi) pl. scent;
perfume ; perfumes

pergamin (per-gá-meen) m.
parchment : sheep skin

period (pér-yod) m. period

perkal (pér-kal) m. calico

perła (pér-wa) f. pearl

peron (pe-ron) m. train- platform at railroad station

perski (pér-skee) adj. m. Per-
sian; Iranian; of Iran

personalny (per-so-nál-ni) adj.
m. personal; personnel officer

personel (per-só-nel) m. staff;
personnel; employees

perspektywa (per-spek-tí-va) f.
perspective;sense of proportion

perswazja (per-svaz-ya) f. persuasion; power of persuading

pertraktacja (per-trak-táts-ya)
f. negotiation; parley

peruka (pe-roó-ka) f. wig

peruwiański (pe-roo-vyań-skee)
adj. m. Peruvian; of Peru

peryskop (pe-ris-kop) m. peri-
scope

pestka (pest-ka) f. kernel;pip;
drupe; stone; trifle

pesymista (pe-si-mees-ta) m.
pessimist

petent (pé-tent) m. petitioner

pewien (pé-vyen) adj. m. certain; one; a; an; some; sure

pewnik (pév-ńeek) m. axiom

pewniak (pév-ńak) m. cinch;
surefooted man; certainty

pewny (pév-ni) adj. m. sure;
secure; dependable; safe

pęcak (pań-tsak) m. peeled
barley; hulled barley

pęcherz (pań-khesh) m. bladder

pęczniec (pańch-ńech) v. swell

pęd (pańd) m. rush; dash; run;
speed;impetus;urge;shoot;sprout

pędzel (pań-dzel) m. (paint)
brush; tuft of hair

pędzić (pań-dżeech) v. drive;
run; lead; distill;hurry

pęk (pańk) m. bunch

pękać (pań-kach) v. burst;split;
crack;go off; burst; snap

pępek (pań-pek) m. navel

pętać (pań-tach) v. shackle;
hobble;knock about

pętak (pań-tak) m. squirt

pętelka (pań-tél-ka) f. loop;
noose; knot

piać (pyach) v. crow; sing

piana (pya-na) f. foam

pianino (pya-ńee-no) n. piano

piasek (pya-sek) m. sand

piasta (pyás-ta) f. hub; nave

piastować (pyas-to-vach) v.
nurse; tend; hold

piąć się(pyovńch shań)v.climb

piątek (pyown-tek) m. Friday

piątka (pyown-ka) f. five

piąty (pyown-ti) num. fifth

picie (pee-che) n. drinking

pić (peech) v. drink; booze

picuś (pee-tsoosh) m. dandy

piec (pyets) m. stove; oven;
furnace; kitchen stove; kiln

piec (pyets) v. bake; roast;
burn; scorch; sting; smart

piechota (pye-kho-ta) m. infantry ;a variety of beans

piechotą (pye-kho-town) adv.
on foot; (go) on foot

piecza (pye-cha) f. care; charge

pieczarka (pye-chár-ka) f. meadow mushroom

pieczątka (pye-chownt-ka) f.
seal; stamp; signet

pieczeń wołowa (pye-cheń vo-wó-
va) f. roast beef

pieczyste (pye-chis-te) n. roast
meat; meat course; joint; roast

pieczywo (pye-chi-vo) n. bakery-
goods; bread; baking

pieg (pyeg) m. freckle ;ephelis

piegowaty (pye-go-vá-ti) adj.
m. freckled

piekarnia (pye-kár-ńa) f. bakery; baker's shop

piekarz (pyé-kash) m. baker

piekielny (pye-kél-ni) adj.
m. infernal; of hell; hellish

piekło (pyék-wo) n. hell

pielęgniarka (pye-lang-ńár-ka)
f. nurse; hospital nurse

pielęgnować (pye-lang-no-vach)
v. nurse; tend; care;cultivate

pielgrzym (pyél-gzhim) m. pilgrim ;wanderer to holy place

pielucha (pye-loo-kha) f. diaper; baby's napkin

pieniądz (pye-ńownts) m. money;
coin; currency; funds

pienić (pye-ńeech) v. foam;
sparkle; cover with foam

pieniężny (pye-ńanzh-ni) adj.
m. monetary; pecuniary;moneyed

pień (pyeń) m. trunk; stem;
stump; snag; stock; root

pieprz (pyepsh) m. pepper

pierdzieć (pyér-dżech) v. fart
(vulg.); stink up

pierdzioch (pyér-dżokh)m. old
fart (vulg.); old stinker

piernat (pyer-nat) m. featherbed; bedding

piernik (pyer-ńeek) m. gingerbread; duffer

pierś (pyersh) f. breast; chest

pierścień (pyersh-cheń) m. ring

pierścionek (pyersh-chó-nek) m.
ring (small)

pierwej (pyer-vey) adv. of
first; sooner; before; first

pierwiastek (pyer-vyas-tek) m.
root; element; radical;

pierworodny (pyer-vo-rod-ni)
adj. m. firstborn,

pierwotny (pyer-vot-ni) adj.
m. primitive; primary;original

pierwszenstwo (pyerv-shen-stvo)
n. priority; precedence

pierwszy (pyer-vshi) num. first

pierzchac (pyezh-khach) v. run
away;flv;flee; disperse;scutter

pierze (pye-zhe) n. feathers

pierzyna (pye-zhi-na) f.feather-
bed; eider down; quilt

pies (pyes) m. dog

pieszczota (pyesh-cho-ta) f.
caress; endearment

pieszo (pye-sho) adv. on foot

piescic (pyesh-cheech) v. fondle;caress;pet;hug; babble

piesn (pyeshn) f. song

pietruszka (pyet-roosh-ka) f.
parsley,

piecioboj (pyan-cho-booy) m.
pentathlon

piecioletni (pyan-cho-let-nee)
adj. m. five year old

piec (pyanch) num. five

piedz (pyandzh) m. palm; span

piecdziesiat (pyan-dzhe-shownt)
num. fifty

piecset (pyanch-set) num. five-
hundred

pieknosc (pyank-noshch) f.
beauty; good looks; loveliness

piekny (pyan-kni) adj. m.beau-
tiful; lovely; fine:handsome

piesciarz (pyansh-chash) m.
boxer ; pugilist

piesc (pyanshch) f. fist,

piesciarstwo (pyansh-char-stvo)
m. box; boxing; pugilism

pieta (pyan-ta) f. heel

pietnastoletni (pyant-nas-to-
let-ni) adj. m. fifteen years
old

pietnasty (pyant-nasti) num.
fifteenth

pietnascie (pyant-nash-che) num.
fifteen

pietno (pyant-no) n. mark;stig-
ma; brand; stamp; impress

pietro (pyant-ro) n. story;
floor ;storey

pietrzyc (pyant-zhich) v. pile
up ; bank up;heap; accumulate

pigulka (pee-goow-ka) f. pill

pijak (pee-yak) m. drunk

pijany (pee-ya-ni) adj. m.
drunk ; tipsy; intoxicated;elated

pijawka (pee-yav-ka) f. leech

pikantny (pee-kant-ni) adj. m.
spicy; niquant; pungent; sharp

piknik (pee-nnek) m. picnic

pilnik (peel-neek) m. file

pilnosc (peel-noshch) f. diligence; urgency;industry; care

pilny (peel-ni) adj. m. diligent; urgent; industrious:careful

pilot (pee-lot) m. pilot

pilsn (peelshn) f. felt

pila (pee-wa) f. saw; bore

pilka (peew-ka) f. ball; hand-
saw : football; socker; shot

pilowac (pee-wo-vach) v. file;
saw : bore; rasp

pingwin (peen-gveen) m. penguin

piolunowka (pyo-woo-noov-ka) f.
absinth flavored liqueur

pion (pyon) m. plumb (line)

pionek (pyo-nek) m. pawn

pionier (pyo-ner) m. pioneer

pionowy (pyo-no-vi) adj. m.
vertical; upright; plumb

piorun (pyo-roon) m. thunder-
bolt; lightning shaft

piorunochron (pyo-roo-no-khron)
m. lightning-rod

piosenka (pyo-sen-ka) f. song

piorko (pyoor-ko) n. (small)
feather; pen ; plumelet

pioro (pyoo-ro) n. feather; pen

piramida (pee-ra-mee-da) f.
pyramid

pirat (pee-rat) m. pirate

pirotechnika (pee-ro-tekh-nee-
ka) f. pyrotechnics

pisac (pee-sach) v. write

pisarz (pee-sash) m. writer

pisemnie (pee-sem-ne) adv. in
writing; in black and white

pisk (peesk) m. squeal

piskliwy (peesk-lee-vi) adj. m.
shrill; squeaky; thin; strident;
piping; reedy

pisklę (peesk-láň) n. chicken; nestling; squealer

piskorz (pees-kosh) m.loach;eel

pismo (pees-mo) n. writing; letter; newspaper; scripture; alphabet; type; print

pisownia (pee-sóv-ňa) f. spelling; orthography

pistolet (pees-tó-let) m. pistol; handgun : gun ; spray gun

pisuar (pee-soo-ar) m. urinal

piszczeć (peesh-chech) v.creak: squeak; screech; squeal;peep

piszczel (peesh-chel) m. shinbone; tibia; blow pipe

piśmiennictwo (peesh-myen-ňeets-tvo) n. literature

piśmiennie (peesh-myén-ňe) adv. in writing;in black and white

piwiarnia (pee-vyár-ňa) f. beer hall;beer house;saloon

piwnica (peev-nee-tsa) f. cellar; basement; coal cellar

piwny (peev-ni) adj. m. brown (color); hazel; beer-

piwo (pee-vo) n. beer

piwonia (pee-vó-ňa) f. peony

piwowar (pee-vó-var) m. brewer

piżama (pee-zhá-ma) f. pyjamas

plac (plats) m. square; area; ground;building site; field

plac boju (plats bo-yoo) battle field; field of battle

placek (plá-tsek) m. cake; pie

placówka (pla-tsoov-ka) f. sentry; post; outpost:agency

plaga (plá-ga) f. plague

plagiator (plag-ya-tor) m. plagiarist

plakat (plá-kat) m. poster

plama (plá-ma) f. blot; stain

plamić (pla-meech) v. blot; stain; soil; tarnish; defile

plan (plan) m. plan; design:map

planeta (pla-né-ta) f. planet

planować (pla-nó-vach) v. plan

planowo (pla-nó-vo) adv. according to plan; systematically

plantacja (plan-táts-ya) f. plantation

plaster (plás-ter) m. plaster; patch; tape; adhesive; slice

plastyczne sztuki (plas-tích-ne shtoo-kee) fine arts

plastyczny (plas-tích-ni) adj. m. plastic; artistic; vivid

plastyk (plás-tik) m. artist; plastic (substance)

platerować (pla-te-ró-vach) v. plate (with an other metal)

platforma (plat-fór-ma) f. platform :truck; lorry; shelf

platoniczny (pla-to-ňeech-ni) adj. m. Platonic;unsubstantial

platyna (pla-tí-na) f. platinum

plazma (pláz-ma) f. plasma

plaża (plá-zha) f. beach

plażować (pla-zho-vach)v.sun-bathe

plądrować (plown-dró-vach) v. plunder; ransack

pląsy (plown-si) pl. dance

plątać (plówn-tach) v. entangle

plebania (ple-bá-ňa) f. rectory

plebiscyt (ple-bees-cit) m. plebiscite; people's direct vote

plecak (ple-tsak) m. rucksack

plecionka (ple-chón-ka) f. plaid braid; wattle; basket work

plecy (ple-tsi) pl. back;backing

pleć (plech) v. weed (a garden)

plemienny (ple-myen-ni) adj. m. tribal; of a trbe

plemię (ple-myeň) n. tribe

plemnik (plém-neek) m. sperm

plenum (ple-noom) n. plenary session; plenary assembly

pleść (pleshch) v. twist; blab; weave;interlace; talk nonsense

pleśnieć (plesh-ňech) v. mold

płetwa (plet-va) f. fin;dovetail

plewić (ple-veech) v. weed

plik (pleek) m. bundle; sheaf

plisa (plee-sa) f. pleat

plomba (plom-ba) f. lead seal; tooth filling; stopping

plon (plon) m. crop;yield

plotka (plót-ka) f. gossip; rumor; piece of gossip

pluć (plooch) v. spit; abuse

plugawy (ploo-gá-vi) adj. m. filthy; squalid:foul;obscene

plus (ploos) m. plus; asset

plusk (ploosk) m. splash

pluskać (ploos-kach) v. splash

pluskiewka (ploos-kév-ka) f.
thumbtack;drawing pin
pluskwa (ploos-kva) f. bedbug
plusz (ploosh) m. plush
plutokracja (ploo-to-kráts-ya)
f. plutocracy
pluton (ploo-ton) m. platoon
plwocina (plvo-chée-na) f.
spittle;expectoration; spit
płaca (pwa-tsa) f. wage;salary
płachta (pwákh-ta) f. sheet
płacić (pwá-cheech) v. pay
płacz (pwach) m. cry; weep
płakać (pwá-kach) v. cry; weep
płaski (pwás-kee) adj. m. flat
płaskorzeźba (pwas-ko-zhéźh-ba)
f. (bas) relief; bas-relief
płaskowyż (pwas-kóvish) m. pla-
teau; table land
płaszcz (pwashch) m. overcoat
płaszczyć (pwásh-chich) v. flatten; become flat;fall,flat
płaszczyzna (pwash-chíz-na) f.
plane;surface;area;sheet;plain
płat (pwat) m. slice; lobe
płatać (pwá-tach) v. cut; play
(tricks);slice;split;fell
płatek (pwa-tek) m. flake
płatność (pwát-noshch) f. payment ; remittance
pławić (pwa-veech) v. float;
wallow : duck; drown;soak
płaz (pwas) m. reptile
płaz (pwas) m. flat of sabre
płciowy (pwchó-vi) adj. m.
sexual; genital; sex-(urge etc.)
płeć (pwech) f. sex; complexion
płetwa (pwet-va) f. fin
płochliwy (pwo-khlée-vi) adj.
m. timid ;shy; skittish
płochy (pwo-khi) adj. m. fri-
volous ;shy;timid;fickle
płodny (pwod-ni) adj. m. fertile :productive; prolific
płodzić (pwo-dźheech)v. beget
płomień (pwo-myeń) m. flame
płonąć (pwo-nównch) v.be on
fire :blaze:be inflamed;glow
płonny (pwon-ni) adj. m. sterile ;useless:vain;of no avail
płoszyć (pwo-shich) v. frighten
płot (pwot) m. fence ;hoarding

płowieć (pwo-vyech) v. fade
płowy (pwó-vi) adj. m. flaxen;
fair; buff; fallow; fawn
płód (pwoot) m. fetus; fruit
płócienny (pwoo-chén-ni) adj.
m. linen; canvas-(sail,shoes etc.)
płótno (pwoot-no) n. linen;canvas
płuco (pwoo-tso) n. lung
płucny (pwoots-ni) adj. m. pul-
monary
pług (pwook) m. plough; plow
płukać (pwoo-kach) v. rinse;
wash; gargle
płyn (pwin) m. liquid: fluid
płynąć (pwi-nównch) v. flow;
swim; sail; drift; go by;come
płynny (pwin-ni) adj. m. liquid;
fluent; fluid;smooth;graceful
płyta (pwi-ta) f, plate; slab;
disk; sheet; board;record
płyta gramofonowa (pwi-ta gra-
mofo-nó-va) f. (musical) record ; disk
płytki (pwit-kee) adj. m. shallow; flat;trivial; poinless
pływać (pwi-vach) v. swim; float;
navigate; be afloat; be evasive
pływak (pwi-vak) m. swimmer;
float; quibler; buoy
pniak (pñak) m. stump; trunk
po (po) prep. after; to; up to;
till; upon; for; at; in; up;
of; next; along; about; over;
past; behind ; as far as
pobicie (po-bee-che) n. battery
pobić (po-beech) v. beat up;
defeat ; beat in; thrash; spank
pobielać (po-bye-lach) v. whiten;
tin : make white; paint white
pobierać (po-bye-rach) v. take;
collect ; receive;get;draw:charge
pobliski (pob-lees-kee) adj. m.
nearby ; neighboring
pobłażać (po-bwa-zhach) v. indulge; forbear ; be tolerant
pobłażliwy (po-bwazh-lee-vi)
adj. m. lenient; forgiving
poboczny (po-boch-ni) adj. m.
lateral; secondary ; accessory
poborca (po-bór-tsa) m. (tax)
collector : tax gatherer
poborowy (po-bo-ró-vi) m. recruit; recruiting

pobory (po-bó-ri) pl. salary

pobrać (po-brać) v. receive; collect; get: draw: gather

pobudka (po-bood-ka) f. incentive: motive; reveille

pobudliwy (po-bood-lee-vi) adj. m. excitable: ebullient

pobyt (pó-bit) m. stay: visit

pocałować (po-tsa-wo-vach) v. kiss: give a kiss

pocałunek (po-tsa-woo-nek) m. kiss: caress with the lips

pochlebiać (po-khle-byach) v. flatter: adulate:, expect:fawn

pochlebny (po-khleb-ni) adj. m. flattering: complimentary

pochłaniać (po-khwa-ñach) v. absorb: swallow up:engulf

pochmurny (po-khmoor-ni) adj. m. gloomy; cloudy: overcast

pochodnia (po-khod-ña) f. torch

pochodny (po-khod-ni) adj. m. derivative: derived

pochodzenie (po-kho-dze-ñe) n. origin; descent; source

pochopny (po-khop-ni) adj. m. hasty; eager; rush: ready

pochować (po-kho-vach) v. bury

pochód (pó-khoot) m. march; procession: parade

pochwa (pókh-va) f. sheath; vagina

pochwała (po-khva-wa) f. praise: eulogy; approval: applouse

pochylić (po-khi-leech) v. incline; slope: slant: droop

pochyły (po-khi-wi) adj. m. inclined; stooped: sloping:oblique

pociąć (pó-chówñch) v. cut up; slash; sting; saw up:intersect

pociąg (póch-ówñk) m. train; affinity: inclination

pociągać (po-chówñ-gach) v.pull: draw: attract:tug: attract:coat

pociągnięcie (po-chówñg-ñán-che) n. pull; move; stroke: pluck

po cichu (po chee-khoo) adv. secretly; silently; softly

pocić (pó-cheech) v. sweat

pociecha (po-che-kha) f. comfort; joy:solace: satisfaction

po ciemku (po chem-koo) adv. in the dark:while in the dark

pocierać (po-che-rach) v. rub

pocieszać (po-che-shach) v. console; comfort;cheer up;, solace

pocieszenie (po-che-she-ñe) n. consolation; comfort; solace

pocieszny (po-chesh-ni) adj. m. funny; amusing;droll; comic

pocisk (po-cheesk) m. missile; bullet: projectile

po co ? (po tso) what for ?

począć (po-chówñch) v. begin; conceive: become pregnant

początek (po-chówñ-tek) m. beginning; start:outset:fore-part

początkujący (po-chowñt-koo-yówñ-tsi) m. beginner

poczciwy (poch-chee-vi) adj. m. good-hearted ; friendly ;kindly

poczekać (po-che-kach), v. wait

poczekalnia (po-che-kal-ña) f. waiting room

poczęstować (po-chán-sto-vach) v. treat: entertain; serve

poczęstunek (po-chán-stoo-nek) m. treat; drinks; entertainment

poczta (póch-ta) f. post; mail

pocztówka (poch-toov-ka) f. postcard; picture postcard

poczucie (po-choo-che) n. feeling; sense: consciousness

poczwórny (po-chvoor-ni) adj. m. fourfold;four times as large, as tall:as long,as strong,as big

poczynać (po-chi-nach) v. begin (aggressively); conceive

poczytalny (po-chi-tál-ni) adj. m. accountable; sane

poczytny (po-chit-ni) adj. m. popular (book):widely read

pod (pod) prep. under; below; towards; on; in ; underneath

podać (po-dach) v. give; hand; pass :serve: shake (hand)

podanie (po-da-ñe) n. application : request; legend

podarek (po-da-rek) m. gift

podarty (po-dár-ti) adj. m. torn

podatek (po-dá-tek) m. tax :duty

podatnik (po-dát-ñeek) m. tax-payer; rate payer

podaż (pó-dazh) f. supply

podążać (po-down-zhach) v. make for; draw to: make ons's way

podbicie (pod-bee-che) n. conquest; instep; lining ;ceiling

podbiec (pod-byets) v. run up

podbiegunowy (pod-bye-goo-nó-vi) adj. m. polar; near pole

podbój (pod-booy) m. conquest

podbudowa (pod-boo-dó-va) f. substructure; base course

podbródek (pod-broo-dek) m. chin; bib; feeder

podburzać (pod-boo-zhach) v. stir up; incite to revolt

podchmielony (pod-khmye-ló-ni) adj. m. tipsy; in drink

podchodzić (pod-khó-dzheech)v. approach; assume an attitude

podchwycić (pod-khvi-cheech) v. catch up; snatch up; spot

podchwytliwy (pod-khvit-lee-vi) adj. m. captious (question etc.)

podciągać (pod-chówn-gach) v. draw up; pull up; improve; class

podczas (pod-chas) prep. during; while; when; whereas

podczerwony (pod-cher-vó-ni) adj. m. infrared

poddać (pod-dach) v. surrender; suggest; submit; expose

pod dostatkiem (pod dos-tat-kyem) adv. plenty; enough

podejmować (po-dey-mo-vach) v. take up; entertain; pick up

podejrzany (po-dey-zha-ni) adj. m. suspect; suspicious; shady

podejrzliwy (po-dey-zhlee-vi) adj. m. suspicious; distrustful

podeptać (po-dep-tach) v. tramp (under foot); bustle about

poderwać (po-der-vach) v. jerk up; pick up; weaken; rouse

podeszwa (po-desh-va) f. sole

podginać (pod-gée-nach) v. tuck up; cock; turn up; bend (a knee)

podglądać (pod-glown-dach) v. spy; peep; pry; snoop

podgórski (pod-goor-skee) adj. m. foot-hill; piedmont

podjechać (pod-ye-khach) v. drive up; ride uphill; come up

podgrzewać (pod-gzhe-vach) v. warm up; heat up

podjudzać (pod-yoo-dzach) v. stir up; incite (to evil)

podkasać (pod-ká-sach) v. tuck up; turn up; rise

podkład (pod-kwat) m. base; railroad tie; undercurrent; bedding

podkładać (pod-kwá-dach) v. lay under; put under; plant as evidence

podkop (pod-kop) m. mine; sap

podkowa (pod-kó-va) f. horseshoe; semicircle

podkradać (pod-krá-dach) v. thieve; pilfer; creep up

podkreślać (pod-kresh-lach) v. stress underline; emphasize; accentuate

podkuwać (pod-koo-vach) v. shoe(horse); hoppail a shoe; cram

podlegać (pod-le-gach) v. be subject; be liable; succomb; undergo

podległość (pod-leg-woshch) f. dependence; subjection; subordination

podlewać (pod-le-vach) v. water

podlizywać się (pod-lee-zi-vach shan) v. suck up to; make up to

podlotek (pod-ló-tek) f. fledgling; flapper; girl in her teens

podłoga (pod-wó-ga) f. floor

podłość (pod-woshch) f. meanness

podług (pod-wook) prep. : according to; in conformity with

podłużny (pod-woozh-ni) adj. m. oblong; longitudinal; elongated

podły (pod-wi) adj. m. mean

podmiejski (pod-myey-skee) adj. m. suburban

podminować (pod-mee-nó-vach) v. undermine; sap

podmiot (pod-myot) m. subject

podmuch (pod-mookh) m. gust; blow; puff; waft; breath; blast

podmywać (pod-mi-vach) v. wash under; sap; undermine; wash away

podniebienie (pod-ne-bye-ne) n. palate; roof of the mouth

podniecać (pod-ne-tsach) v. flurry excite; agitate; rouse; egg on

podnieść (pod-neshch) v. lift; hoist; rise; elevate; rear; increase

podnieta (pod-ne-ta) f. stimulus; impulse; spur; stimulant

podniosły (pod-nos-wi) adj. m. sublime; elevated; lofty

podnosić (pod-nó-sheech) v. hoist; raise; lift; take up; elevate

podnóżek (pod-noo-zhek) m. footstool; ottoman; leg rest

podobać się (po-dó-bach shän)
v. please; be attractive;like
podobny (po-dób-ni) adj. m.
similar; like; congenial
podoficer (pod-o-fee-tser) m.
noncommissioned officer
podołać (po-dó-wach) v. be up
to;be equal to;cope;manage
podomka (po-dóm-ka) f. house-
robe; dressing gown
podówczas (pod-oov-chas) adv.
at that time;at the time;then
podpadać (pod-pá-dach) v. be
spotted; fall under a category
podpalenie (pod-pa-le-ńe) n.
arson; setting of fire
podpatrzyc (pod-pa-tzhich) v.
spy; peep; find out; pry
podpierać (pod-pye-rach) v.
prop up ; support; bolster
podpinać (pod-pee-nach) v.pin;
buckle up; strap;fasten;gird
podpis (pód-pees) m. signature
podpływać (pod-pwi-vach) v.
swim up; sail up; row up
podpora (pod-pó-ra) f. prop
podporucznik (pod-po-roóch-
ńeek) m. second lieutenant
podporządkować (pod-po-zhównt-
ko-vach) v. subordinate,
podprowadzić (pod-pro-va-
dźheech) v. bring near
podpułkownik (pod-poow-kov-
ńeek) m. lieutenant colonel
podrażnić (pod-rázh-ńeech) v.
displease; irritate;vex;gall
podręcznik (pod-rańch-ńeek) m.
handbook; textbook; manual
podrożeć (pod-ró-zhech) v. go
up; grow dear; rise in price
podróż (pód-roozh) f. travel;
voyage; journey; passage
podróżnik (pod-roozh-ńeek) m.
traveler; voyager; wayfarer
po drugie (po droo-ge) adv.
in the second place; second
podrzeć (pód-zhech) v. tear up
podrzędny (pod-zhánd-ni) adj.
m. subordinate; secondary
podsądny (pod-sownd-ni) m. defendant; the person sued
podskakiwać (pod-ska-kee-vach)
v. leap; jump up;hop;skip

podsłuch (pód-swookh) m. eavesdropping; wire tapping;listen in
podstawa (pod-stá-va) f. base;
basis;footing;mount;principle
podstawić (pod-stá-veech) v.
substitute;put under;bring round
podstęp (pod-stánp) m.trick;ruse;
guile; deceit;piece of deceit
podstępny (pod-stánp-ni) adj. m.
deceitful; tricky; crafty;insidious
podstrzygać (pod-stzhi-gach) v.
trim the hair; shorten the hair
podsuwać (pod-soó-vach) v. push
near; plant; suggest; slip under
podsycać (pod-sí-tsach) v. foment; feed; fan (a quarrel etc.)
podsypywać (pod-si-pi-vach) v.
pour (sand etc.);strew; sprinkle
podszept (pod-shept) m. suggestion: prompting; insinuation
podszeptywać (pod-shep-ti-vach)
v. prompt; suggest;hint;insinuate
podszewka (pod-shév-ka) f.lin-
ing ; inside information
podswiadomy (pod-shvya-do-mi)
adj. m. subconscious(mental process)
podupadać (pod-oo-pá-dach) v.
decline; deteriorate;fall into decay
poduszka (po-doósh-ka) f. pillow;
pad; cushion; ball (of the thumb)
podwajać (pod-va-yach) v. double;
duplicate; increase twofold
podważyć (pod-va-zhich) v. lever
up; pry up; shake(an opinion)
podwiązka (pod-vyowns-ka) f.
garter; suspender; ligature
podwieczorek (pod-vye-cho-rek) m.
afternoon tea; afternoon snack
podwieźć (pod-vyeżch) v. give
a ride; give a lift(in one's car)
podwładny (pod-vwad-ni) adj. m.
subordinate (to somebody);inferior
podwodna łódz (pod-vod-na woodżh)
f. submarine (under water warship)
podwoic (pod-vo-eech)v. double
podwozie (pod-vo-zhe) n. chassis
podworko (pod-voor-ko) n. backyard ;farmyard;court;courtyard
podwyżka (pod-vizh-ka) f. raise
podzelować (pod-ze-ló-vach) v.
resole (shoes, boots, foot ware)
podziać (po-dźhach) v. loose
podział (po-dźhaw) m. division

podziałka (po-dżhaw-ka) f.
scale; graduation; division
podzielać (po-dżhe-lаćh) v.
share; participate; concur
podzielić (po-dżhe-leećh) v.
divide (into parts)
podzielny (po-dżhel-ni) adj. m.
adj. m. divisible(easily)
podziemie (pod-żhem-ye) n.base-
ment; underworld
podziemny (pod-żhem-ni) adj. m.
underground; secret
podziękować (po-dżhań-ko-vaćh)
v. thank; decline with thanks
podziewać (po-dżhe-vaćh) v.
loose; mislay;leave somewhere
podziw (po-dżheef) m. admiration; wander
podzwrotnikowy (pod-zvrot-nee-
ko-vi) adj. m. tropical
podżegacz (pod-zhe-gach) m. instigator; warmonger; abettor
poemat (po-e-mat) m. poem
poeta (po-e-ta) m. poet
poetka (po-et-ka) f. poet
poezja (po-ez-ya) f. poetry
pogadanka (po-ga-dán-ka) f.
talk; chat; chatty lecture
poganiać (po-ga-naćh) v. drive;
egg on; urge on; prod on;hustle
poganin (po-ga-neen) m. pagan
pogarda (po-gár-da) f. contempt
pogarszać (po-gár-shaćh) v.
make worse; aggravate;worsen
pogawędka (po-ga-vánd-ka) f.
chat; chit-chat
pogląd (po-glównd) m. opinion
pogłębiać (po-gwánb-yaćh) v.
deepen; dig deeper; dredge
pogłoska (po-gwos-ka) f. rumor
pogniewać się (po-gne-vaćh shań)
v. get angry; be angry
pogoda (po-gó-da) f. weather;
cheerfulness; fine weather
pogodny (po-gód-ni) adj. m.
serene; cheerful; sunny
pogodzić (po-dzheećh) v.
reconcile; square (things)
pogoń (pó-goń) f. pursuit;
chase; hunt; quest; pursuers
pogorszenie (po-gor-she-ne) n.
worsening; deterioration

pogorszyć (po-gór-shićh) v.
make worse; aggravate
pogorzelisko (po-go-zhe-lees-
ko) n. after fire ruins
pogotowie (po-go-tó-vye) n.
ambulance service; readiness
pogranicze (po-gra-nee-che) n.
borderland; border line
pogrom (pó-grom) m. rout
pogromca (po-gróm-tsa) m.tam-
er; conqueror
pogróżka (po-groozh-ka) f.
threat;threatening expression
pogrzeb (pó-gzhep) m. funeral
pogrzebacz (po-gzhe-bach) m.
poker (for stirring a fire)
pogwałcić (po-gvaw-ćheećh) v.
violate; outrage;transgress
poić (pó-eećh) v. water; ply
pojawić się (po-ya-veećh shań)
v. appear; emerge; occur;arise
pojazd (pó-yazt) m. car;vehicle
pojąć (po-yównch) v. grasp;
marry; comprehend;understand
pojechać (po-ye-khaćh) v. go;
leave; take (train, boat etc.)
pojednać (po-yéd-nach) v. reconcile (two or more parties)
pojednawczy (po-yed-náv-chi)
adj. m. conciliatory
pojedynczy (po-ye-dín-chi) adj.
m. single; individual; onefold
pojedynek (po-ye-di-nek) m.
duel; encounter; single combat
pojemnik (po-yém-neek) m. container; vessel; receptacle
pojemność (po-yem-noshćh) f.
capacity; cubic content
pojezierze (po-ye-żhe-zhe) n.
lake land ; lake district
pojęcie (po-yán-će) n. notion;
idea; concept; comprehension
pojętny (po-yánt-ni) adj. m.
intelligent; sharp; teachable
pojmować (poy-mó-vaćh) v.grasp;
comprehend; conceive;imagine
pojutrze (po-joot-zhe) adv. day
after tomorrow
pokarm (pó-karm) m. food; feed
pokaz (pó-kas) m. display; shaw
pokazywać (po-ka-zi-vaćh) v.
show; point; exhibit; let see

pokaźny (po-kaźh-ni) adj. m.
  respectable; appreciable
pokład (pók-wad) m. deck; layer
pokątny (po-kównt-ni) adj. m.
  underhanded; secret; illegal
pokłon (pók-won) m. bow; homage
pokłócic się (po-kwoo-cheech
  śhań) v. fall out with quarrel
pokochać (po-ko-khach) v. fall
  in love; become fond of
pokoik (po-kó-eek) m. little
  room; little cozy room
pokojówka (po-ko-yoov-ka) f.
  maid; housemaid; chamber maid
pokolenie (po-kole-ńe) n. generation; about 30 years
pokonać (po-ko-nach) v. defeat
pokorny (po-kor-ni) adj. m.
  humble; meek; submissive
pokost (po-kost) m. varnish
pokrajać (po-kra-yach) v. cut
  up; carve up; slice; slash
pokój (po-kooy) m. room; peace
pokrapiać (po-krá-pyach) v.
  sprinkle; wash down (a meal)
pokrewieństwo (po-krev-yeń-stvo)
  n. kinship; kindred; relation
pokrewny (po-krév-ni) m. related; akin; kindred; cognate
pokrótce (po-kroot-tse) adv.
  in short; in brief; concisely
pokrycie (po-kri-che) n. cover
pokryć (po-krich) v. cover
po kryjomu (po-kri-yó-moo) adv.
  secretly; on the sly; in secret
pokrywa (po-kri-va) f. lid
pokrywać (pokri-vach) v. cover;
  upholster; serve (mare)
pokrzepić (po-kzhe-peech) v.
  invigorate; refresh; fortify
pokrzywa (po-kzhee-va) f. nettle
pokrzyżować (po-kzhi-zho-vach)
  v. cross up; confound; tangle
pokup (po-koop) m. demand
pokupny (po-koop-ni) adj. m.
  in demand; selable
pokusa (po-koo-sa) f. temptation
pokuta (po-koo-ta) f. penance
pokwitować (po-kvee-to-vach) v.
  receipt; acknowledge receipt
pokwitowanie (po-kvee-to-va-ńe)
  n. receipt   (liquid)
polać (po-lach) v. pour over

Polak (pó-lak) m. Polonian;
  Pole; Polonius; vulg.: polack
polana (po-lá-na) f. glade
polano (po-lá-no) n. billet; log
polarny (po-lár-ni) adj. m. polar ; of the polar axis
pole (po-le) n. field
polec (pó-lets) v. fall; be
  killed (in battle)
polecać (po-le-tsach) v. recommend; commend; instruct; order
polegać (po-le-gach) v. rely
polemika (po-le-mee-ka) f. po-
  lemics; controversy
polepszać (po-lep-shach) v. improve; ameliorate; mend; better
polerować (po-le-ro-vach) v.
  polish; furbish; burnish; refine
polewać (po-le-vach) v. water;
  glaze; glaze; enamel; ice
polewka (po-lév-ka) f. broth
polędwica (po-land-vee-tsa) f.
  sirloin; loin; fillet (of beef)
policja (po-leets-ya) f. police
policzek (po-lee-chek) m. cheek
politechnika (po-lee-tekh-ńee-
  ka) f. polytechnic college
politowanie (po-lee-to-va-ńe)
  n. pity; compassion
polityk (po-lee-tik) m. politician; statesman
polka (pol-ka) f. polka; Polish
  girl; Polish woman; Pole
polny (pol-ni) adj. m. field
polon (pó-lon) m. polonium
  (chem.)
polonez (po-ló-nez) m. polonaise
  (dance)
Polonia (po-loń-ya) f. Polish
  colony ; Polish emigrants
Polonus (po-ló-noos) m. Pole of
  old ; typical Pole of the past
polot (pó-lot) m. elan ; imagination
polować (po-ló-vach) v. hunt
polski (pól-skee) adj. m. Polish ; Polish language
polszczyć (polsh-chich) v. Polo-
  nize ; invest with Polish traits
polszczyzna (pol-shchiz-na) f.
  Polish language ; Polish traits
polubić (po-loo-beech) v. get to
  like ; become fond; take a fancy

polubownie (po-loo-bov-ñe) adv. amicably; by compromise

połamać (po-wa-mach) v. break

połączenie (po-wown-che-ñe) n. connection; linkage; contact

połknać (pow-known´ch) v. swallow; gulp down; drink down

połowa (po-wo-va) f. half

położenie (po-wo-zhe-ñe) n. position; situation; site

położna (po-wozh-na) f. midwife

położnica (po-wozh-ñee-tsa) f, woman in childbed

położyć (po-wo-zhich) v. lay down; place; deposit; fell; ruin

połóg (po-wook) m. childbirth

połów ryb (po-woov rib) fish catch; fishing; fish haul

południe (po-wood-ñe) n. noon; south; midday; the South

południk (po-wood-ñeek) m. meridian; the line of longitude

południowo-wschodni (po-wood-ño-vo wskhod-ñee) south-east

południowo-zachodni (po-wood-ño-vo za-khod-ñee) south-west

południowy (po-wood-ño-vi) adj. m. south; midday; southerly

połykać (po-wi-kach) v. swallow

połysk (po-wisk) m. glitter; gloss; luster; sheen; sparkle

pomadka (po-mad-ka) f. lipstick

pomagać (po-ma-gach) v. help

pomalenku (po-ma-len-koo) adv. little by little; very slowly

pomału (po-ma-woo) adv. little by little; slowly; leisurely

pomarańcza (po-ma-rań-cha) f. orange; orange tree

pomarszczony (po-marsh-cho-ni) adj. m. wrinkled; creased

pomazać (po-ma-zach) v. smear-over; anoint; soil; scrawl

pomawiać (po-mav-yach) v. accuse; impute; charge with

pomiar (po-myar) m. measurement; survey; surveying; mensuration

pomiatać (po-mya-tach) v. push around; spurn; hold in contempt

pomidor (po-mee-dor) m. tomato

pomieszać (po-myé-shach) v. mix up; mingle; blend; stir; tangle; muddle up; embroil; mistake

pomieszanie zmysłów (po-mye-sha-ñe zmis-woov) insanity; madness

pomieszczać (po-myesh-chach) v. admit; contain; accomodate

pomiędzy (po-myán-dzi) prep. between; among; in the midst

pomijać (po-mee-yach) v. pass over; omit; overlook; leave out

pomimo (po-mee-mo) prep. in spite of; notwithstanding

pomnażać (po-mna-zhach) v. multiply; increase; intensify

pomniejszać (po-mñey-shach) v. diminish; lessen; reduce; belittle

pomnik (pom-ñeek) m. monument

pomoc (po-mots) f. help; aid

pomocnik (po-mots-ñeek) m. helper; assistant; helpmate; aid

pomocny (po-mots-ni) adj. m. helpful; instrumental

pomorski (po-mor-skee) adj. m. Pomeranian; of Pomerania

pomost (po-most) m. platform

pomóc (po-moots) v. help; assist

pompa (pom-pa) f. pump; pomp

pompować (pom-po-vach) v. pump

pomsta (po-msta) f. vengeance

pomruk (pom-rook) m. murmur; grumble; growl; purr; rumble

pomstować (pom-sto-vach) v. curse; swear; revile; vituperate

pomyje (po-mi-ye) pl. dishwater; hog-wash; swill; lap

pomylić (po-mi-leech) v. confound; be mistaken; mislead

pomyłka (po-miw-ka) f. error

pomysł (po-misw) m. idea

pomyślność (po-mishl-noshch) f. prosperity; success; happiness

pomyślny (po-mishl-ni) adj. m. successful; favorable; good

pomywaczka (po-mi-vach-ka) f. dishwasher; scullery maid

ponad (po-na‹) prep. above; over; beyond; upwards of; super-; more than; over and above; besides

ponadto (po-nad-to) prep. moreover; besides; furthermore; also

ponaglać (po-nág-lach) v. rush; urge; remind; press; urge on

ponaglenie (po-nag-le-ñe) n. reminder; pressure

ponawiać (po-nav-yach) v. renew

ponętny (po-naht-ni) adj. m.
seductive; attractive; alluring
poniechać (po-ńe-khach) v.give
up ;relinquish; renounce;desist
poniedziałek (po-ńe-dzha-wek)
m. Monday
poniekąd (po-ńe-kownt) adv.
partly;in a way; in a sense
ponieść (po-ńeshch) v. sustain;
carry ;bear; suffer;incur;push
ponieważ (po-ńe-vash) conj. because; as; since; for
poniewczasie (po-ńev-cha-she)
adv. too late ;after the event
poniewierać (po-ńe-vye-rach) v.
kick around;slight ;mishandle
poniżej (po-ńee-zhey) adv. below; beneath ;hereunder;under
poniżyć (po-ńee-zhich) v. degrade; humble ;tread down
ponosić (po-no-sheech) v. bear;
carry (away) ;suffer;incur
ponowić (po-no-veech) v. renew
ponownie (po-nov-ńe) adv. anew;
again ; afresh; a second time
ponowny (po-nov-ni) adj. m. repeated; renewed;reiterated
ponton (pon-ton) m. pontoon
ponury (po-noo-ri) adj m.gloomy
dismal; sullen; dreary; sullen
pończocha (pon-cho-kha) f.
stocking
popadać (po-pa-dach) v. fall in
poparcie (po-par-che) n. support; backing; promotion;push
popaść (po-pa-shch) v. fall in
popatrzeć (po-pa-tzhech) v. look
popelina (po-pe-lee-na) f.
poplin; a ribbed cloth
popchnąć (pop-khnownch) v. push;
shove ;hustle; jostle;steer
popełniać (po-pew-ńach) v. commit ;perpetrate
popęd (po-pant) m. impulse
popędliwy (po-pand-lee-vi) adj.
impetuous; rush ;hot headed
popędzać (po-pan-dzach) v. drive
on; urge; push on; prod;spur
popielaty (po-pye-la-ti) adj. m.
charcoal-grey; ashen; gray
popielec (po-pye-lets) m. Ash
Wednesday

popielniczka (po-pyel-ńeech-
ka) f. ash-tray ; ash pan
popierać (po-pye-rach) v. support; back ;promote;favor;uphold
popiersie (po-pyer-she) n. bust
popić (po-peech) v. rinse down
popiół (po-pyoow) m. ashes;ash;
cinders ; slag
popis (po-pees) m. show; parade
popisywać się (po-pee-si-vach
shan)v.show off;flaunt;parade
poplecznik (po-plech-ńeek) m.
backer; upholder; partisan
popłatny (po-pwat-ni) adj. m.
profitable; lucrative
popłoch (po-pwokh) m. panic
popołudnie (po-po-wood-ńe) n.
afternoon
po południu (po po-wood-ńoo) in
the afternoon
poprawa (po-pra-va) f.improve-
ment;change for the better
poprawka (po-prav-ka) f. correction;amendment; alteration
poprawny (po-prav-ni) adj. m.
correct;faultless;proper
po prostu (po pros-too) adv.
simply;openly;uncremoniously
poprzeczka (po-pzhech-ka) f.
crossbar; crossbeam;the bar
poprzedni (po-pzhed-ńee) adj.
m. previous; preceding;former
poprzedzać (po-pzhe-dzach) v.
precede;orelude;go before
poprzestać (po-pzhes-tach) v.
settle for; be satisfied

popularny (po-poo-lar-ni) adj.
m. popular; prevalent
popychać (po-pi-khach) v. push;
shove; ill treat; hustle; jostle
popychadło (po-pi-khad-wo) n.
drudge; scapegrace
popyt (po-pit) m. demand
pora (po-ra) f. time; season
porachunek (po-ra-khoo-nek) m.
reckoning; a bone to pick
porada (po-ra-da) f. advice
poradnia (po-rad-ńa) f. information bureau;dispensary;clinic
poradnik (po-rad-ńeek) m. guide;
handbook; reference book
poradzić (po-ra-dzhech) v. advise

poranek (po-ra-nek) m. morning
porastać (po-ras-tach) v. overgrow; grow; become overgrown
poratować (po-ra-to-vach) v.
help in distress; recuperate
porażenie (po-ra-zhe-ne) n.
stroke; shock; paralysis
porażka (po-razh-ka) f. defeat; set back; reverse
porcelana (por-tse-la-na) f.
china; porcelain
porcja (por-tsya) f. portion
poręcz (por-anch) f. banister
poręczenie (po-ran-che-ne) n.
guarantee; bail;warranty;pledge
poręka (po-ran-ka) f. guaranty;
pledge;sponsorship; surety
poronić (po-ro-neech) v. abort;
miscarry; have a miscarriage
porost (po-rost) m. growth
porowaty (po-ro-va-ti) adj. m.
porous; full of pores
porozdawać (po-roz-da-vach) v.
give away; pass around
porozumienie (po-ro-zoo-mye-ne)
m. understanding;agreement
poród (po-root) m. child delivery; childbirth; partitution
porównać (po-roov-nach) v. compare; draw a comparison; liken
porównanie (po-roov-na-ne) n.
comparison;equalization
poróżnić (po-roozh-neech) v.
disunite; divide; embroil
port (port) m. port; harbor
portfel (port-fel) m. wallet
portier (port-yer) m. doorman
portki (port-kee) pl. pants
(vulg.);breeches; trousers
portmonetka (port-mo-net-ka) f.
purse; billfold; wallet
porto (por-to) n. postage
portret (por-tret) m. portrait
portugalski (por-too-gal-skee)
adj. m. Portuguese
poruczać (po-roo-chach) v. entrust; charge with
porucznik (po-rooch-neek) m.
lieutenant
poruszać (po-roo-shach) v. move:
touch; sway; set in motion
poruszenie (po-roo-she-ne) n.
agitation;movement; stir;touch

poryw (po-riv) m. impulse; rapture; gust; onrush; elation
porywać (po-ri-vach) v. snatch;
carry off; whisk away;grab;thrill
porywacz (po-ri-vach) m. kid-
naper; abductor; ravisher
porywczy (po-riv-chi) adj. m.
rash;irritable;impetuous;hasty
porządek (po-zhown-dek) n.
order;tidiness;regularity;system
porządny (po-zhownd-ni) adj. m.
neat; decent; accurate;reliable
porzucać (po-zhoo-tsach) v.
abandon; desert;forsake; leave
porzucić (po-zhoo-cheech) v.
abandon; give up; cast away
posada (po-sa-da) f. employment
posadzka (po-sadz-ka) f. parquet floor; tile floor
posąg (po-sownk) m. statue
poselstwo (po-sel-stvo) n. legation; deputation; envoys
poseł (po-sew) m. envoy; con-
gressman; deputy; legate
posępny (po-sanp-ni) adj. m.
gloomy; dismal; dreary; dark
posiadacz (po-sha-dach) m. bearer; holder; possessor;owner
posiadać (po-sha-dach) v. hold;
own; possess; acquire;dominate
posiadłość (po-shad-woshch) f.
estate; property; dominion
posiedzenie (po-she-dze-ne) n.
session; conference; meeting
posilać (po-shee-lach) v. refresh; nourish; feed
posiłek (po-shee-wek) m. meal;
refreshment; reinforcement
posłać (po-swach) f. send; make a
bed; dispatch,somewhere
posłanie (po-swa-ne) n. bed;
bedding; message;dispatch
posłaniec (po-swa-nets) m. messenger; commissionaire
posłuchać (po-swoo-khach) v.
listen; obey; take advice
posługa (po-swoo-ga) f. service
posługacz (po-swoo-gach) m. servant; attendant; commissionaire
posłuszny (po-swoosh-ni) adj. m.
obedient; submissive;docile
pospolity (pos-po-lee-ti) adj. m.
vulgar; common;commonplace

posrebrzać (po-sreb-zhach) v.
silver (plate);silver foil
post (post) m. fast; fast day
postać (po-stach) f. form;shape;
figure;human shape;personage
postanowić (po-sta-no-veech) v.
decide; enact;resolve;determine
postanowienie (po-sta-no-vye-ńe)
n. decision; resolve; provision
postarać się (po-sta-rach shań)
v. procure; obtain;get;try;find
postawa (po-sta-va) f. attitude;
posture; pose;bearing; position
postawny (po-staw-ni) adj. m.
portly;handsome;well made
postawić (po-sta-veech) v. set
up; put up;set on;put on;raise
postąpić (po-stown-peech) v.
proceed; act; deal;follow;treat
posterunek (po-ste-roo-nek) m.
outpost; sentry; police station
postęp (po-stańp) m. progress;
advance;march;headway
postępowanie (postań-po-va-ńe)
n. behavior; advance;procedure
postojowe (po-sto-yo-ve) n.
demurrage;adj.n.parking
postój (po-stooy) m. halt;stop;
stand; parking;stopping place
postrach (po-strakh) m. terror;
dread;scare;fright;bugaboo
postrzał (po-stzhaw) m. gunshot;
wound;shot;rifle shot;lumbago
postrzelony (po-stzhe-lo-ni)
adj. m. wounded; crazy;cracked
postulat (po-stoo-lat) m. demand; claim; requirement
postument (po-stoo-ment) m.
pedestal; socle
posucha (po-soo-kha) f. drought
posuw (po-soov) m. feed (of a
drill); feed of a lathe
posuwać (po-soo-vach) v. move;
shove; push on;carry;dash;speed
posyłać (po-si-wach) v.send over
posyłka (po-siw-ka) f. errand
posypywać (po-si-pi-vach) v.
dust; pour; sprinkle (dry)
poszanowanie (po-sha-no-va-ńe)
n. respect; observance(of a law)
poszarpać (po-shar-pach) v.maul;
tear up; jag up;mangle;rend

poszczególny (po-shche-gool-
ni) adj. m. individual
poszerzać (po-she-zhach) v.
widen;broaden;extend;ream;spread
poszewka (po-shev-ka) f. pil-
low-case ; pillow slip
poszkodowany (po-shko-do-va-
ni) adj. m. victim ;sufferer
poszlaka (po-shla-ka) f.trace;
circumstantial evidence; sign
poszukiwać (po-shoo-kee-vach)
v. search;look for;inquire;claim
poszukiwanie (po-shoo-kee-va-
ńe) n. search;quest;research
pościć (posh-cheech) v. fast
pościel (posh-chel) f. bedclothes sheets and blankets
pościg (posh-cheeg) m. chase
pośladek (po-shla-dek) m. but-
tock; rump; bum
pośliznać się (po-shleez-nownch
shań) v. slip ;make a slip
poślubić (po-shloo-beech) v.
marry; take in marriage
pośmiertny (po-shmyert-ni) adj.
m. posthumous (child, works etc.)
pośmiewisko (po-shmye-vees-ko)
n.laughingstock;butt of ridicule
pośpiech (posh-pyekh) m. haste;
hurry; dispatch
pośredni (po-shred-nee) adj.
m. intermediate; indirect
pośrednik (po-shred-neek) m.
go-between; intermediary
pośredniczyć (po-shred-nee-
chich) v. mediate;be a go-between
pośród (posh-rood) prep. among
poświadczać (po-shvyad-chach)
v. attest; certify;testify;witness
poświadczenie (po-shvyad-che-
ńe) n. certificate;attestation
poświęcać (po-shvyań-tsach) v.
sacrifice; sanctify
poświęcenie (po-shvyań-tse-ńe)
n. devotion; sacrifice
pot (pot) m. sweat; prespiration
potajemny (po-ta-yem-ni) adj.
m. secret; clandestine;underhand
potakiwać (po-ta-kee-vach) v.
assent; agree; acquiesce
potas (po-tas) m. potassium
potaż (po-tash) m. potash

potąd (po-townt) adv. up to
here ;up to this place

potem (po-tem) adv. after ;
afterwards; then; later on

potencjalny (po-ten-tsyal-ni)
adj. m. potential ;virtual

potęga (po-tań-ga) f. power;
might ;force;impressiveness

potęgowac (po-tań-go-vach) v.
intensify ;raise to a power

potepiac (po-tań-pyach) v.
damn; run down;condemn

potępienie (po-tań-pye-ńe) n.
damnation ;disapproval;blame

potężny (po-tanzh-ni) adj. m.
mighty; tremendous;powerful

potknąc sie (pot-knownch shan)v.
slip ;trip; stumble;make a slip

potknięcie (pot-kńan-che) n.
slip; stumble; trip ; a lapse

potoczny (po-toch-ni) adj. m.
current; common ;everyday;daily

potok (po-tok), m. stream;brook

potomek (po-tó-mek) m. descendant ; offspring; scion

potomnosc (po-tom-noshch) f.
posterity ;future generations

potomstwo (po-tom-stvo) pl.is-
sue; progeny; offspring;breed

potop (po-top) m, deluge; flood

potrafic (po-tra-feech) v. know
how to do ;manage;be able to do

potrawa (po-tra-ya) f. dish

potrawka (po-trav-ka) f. fricassee ;ragout

potracic (po-trown-cheech) v.
knock; deduct ;poke;push;jostle

po trochu (po-tro-khoo) adv.
little by little ;gradually

potrojny (po-trooy-ni) adj. m.
triple ;triplicate;treble

potrzask (pot-shask) m. trap

potrzasac (po-tzhown-sach) v.
shake ; brandish; agitate;strew

potrzeba (po-tzhé-ba) f. need;
want;call;emergency;extremity

potrzebny (po-tzhéb-ni) adj. m.
necessary ;needed;wanted

potulny (po-tool-ni) adj. m.
docile ;submissive;humble;meek

poturbowac (po-toor-bó-vach) v.
manhandle; rough up ;beat;maul
batter;knock about;ill-treat;
give a rough handling; hurt

potwarz (po-tvash) f, slander

potwierdzac (po-tyyer-dzach) v.
confirm; attest;corroborate

potwor (po-tvoor) m. monster

potykac się (po-ti-kach shan)
v. stumble; skirmish;joust

potylica (po-ti-lee-tsa) f.
occiput; back part of skull

pouczac (po-oo-chach) v. instruct; teach ;give instructions

pouczenie (po-oo-che-ńe) n.
instruction;giving instructions

poufalic się(po-oo-fá-lich shan)v
take liberties; familiarize

poufały (po-oo-fá-wi) adj. m.
intimate;unceremonious;free with
too familiar; maty;hob-nobbing

poufny (po-oof-ni) adj. m. confidential ;private;secret

powab (po-vap) m. charm;attrac-
tion ;lure;seduction; loveliness

powabny (po-váb-ni) adj. m. attractive; charming;alluring

powaga (po-va-ga) f. gravity;
seriousness;dignity;prestige

powalac (po-va-lach) v. soil;
dirty ; overthrow;kill;slay

powalic (po-va-leech) v. knock
down;overthrow;kill;slay;fell

powała (po-va-wa) f. ceiling

poważac (po-va-zhach) v. respect;esteem;have regard

poważny (po-vazh-ni) adj. m.
earnest; grave;dignified;serious

powątpiewac (po-vownt-pye-vach)
v. doubt;have doubts; be dubious

powetowac (po-ve-to-vach) v.
make up ;idemnify oneself;retrieve

powiadac (po-vyá-dach) v. say;
tell; speak ;(the legend)has it

powiadomic (po-vya-do-meech) v.
inform; notify; let know

powiastka (po-vyast-ka) f. tale

powiat (po-vyat) m. county;
district; district authorities

powicie (po-vee-che) n. swad-
dling clothes; child delivery

powidła (po-veed-wa) pl. jam;
marmalade; jam

powiedziec (po-vye-dżhech) v.
say; tell; declare

powieka (po-vye-ka) f. eyelid

powielacz (po-vye-lach) m.
mimeograph

powiernica (po-vyer-nee-tsa) f.
confidante; trusted friend
powierzać (po-vye-zhach) v.
confide; charge with a task
powierzchnia (po-vyezhkh-na) f.
surface; plane; area; acreage
powiesić (po-vye-sheech) v.
hang; suspend; hung up; ring off
powieść (po-vyeshch) f. novel
powieść się (po-vyeshch shan)
v. succeed; be successful
powietrze (po-vyet-zhe) n. air
powiew (po-vyev) m. breeze
powiększać (po-vyank-shach) v.
enlarge; augment; extend; add
powiększenie (po-vyank-she-ne)
n. enlargement; magnification
powijaki (po-vee-ja-kee) pl.
swathings; initial stage
powikłać (po-veek-wach) v.
complicate; embroil
powinność (po-veen-noshch) f.
duty; obligation
powinowaty (po-vee-no-va-ti)
adj. m. related; akin
powitać (po-vee-tach) v. welcome; salute; bid welcome
powlekać (po-vle-kach) v. cover; drag; coat; smear; spread
powłoczka (po-vwoch-ka) f. pillowcase; envelope; covering
powłoka (po-vwo-ka) f. (paint)
coat; covering; envelope; shell
powłoczysty (po-vwoo-chis-ti)
adj. m. trailing; enticing
powodować (po-vo-do-vach) v.
cause; bring about; touch off;
effect; induce; give occasion
powodzenie (po-vo-dze-ne) n.
success; well-being; prosperity
powodzić się (po-vo-dzhech shan)
v. fare (well; ill); be well off
powojenny (po-vo-yen-ni) adj.
m. post-war; after-war
powoli (po-vo-lee) adv. slow
powolny (po-vol-ni) adj. m.
slow; tardy; leisurely; gradual
powołanie (po-vo-wa-ne) n. vocation; call; appointment; quot.
powonienie (po-vo-ne-ne) n.
sense of smell; smell
powód (po-voot) m. cause: reason; ground; motive; plaintiff

powódź (po-voodzh) f. flood
powój (po-vooy) m. bindweed
powóz (po-woos) m. carriage
powracać (po-vra-tsach) v. return; come back; resume; recover
powrotny (po-vrot-ni) adj. m.
return; return(ticket)
powrót (po-vroot) m. return
powróz (po-vroos) m. rope
powstanie (po-vsta-ne) n. rising; uprising; insurrection
powstaniec (po-vsta-nets) m.
insurgent(against a government)
powstawać (po-vsta-vach) v.
rise up; stand up; revolt
powstrzymać (po-vstzhi-mach) v.
restrain; refrain; hold back
powszechny (po-vshekh-ni) adj.
m. universal; general; public
powszedni (po-vshed-nee) adj.
m. everyday; commonplace; daily
powściągliwość (povshchowng-
lee-voshch) f. abstinence;
temperance; moderation; restraint
powściągliwy (povshchowng-lee-
vi) adj. m. reserved; absti-
nent; moderate; temperate
powtarzać (pov-ta-zhach) v. say
again; go over; repeat; reproduce
po wtóre (po vtoo-re) adv. secondly; in the second place; then
powtórnie (pov-toor-ne) adv.
anew; again; a second time
powtórny (pov-toor-ni) adj. m.
repeated; renewed; second-
powyżej (po-vi-zhey) adv. above;
here in before; higher up; over
powziąć (pov-zhownch) v. take
up; form; decide; conceive(a plan)
poza (po-za) f. pose; attitude;
sham;
poza (po-za) prep. beyond; besides; except; apart; outside; extra-
pozagrobowy (po-za-gro-bo-vi)
adj. m. beyond the grave;
hereafter; from beyond the grave
pozbawiać (po-zbav-yach) v.
deprive; dispossess; take away
pozbyć się (poz-bich shan) v.
rid oneself; get rid; shake off
pozdrawiać (po-zdra-vyach) v.
greet; send one's greetings
pozew (po-zef) m. summons; writ;
citation

poziom (po-żhom) m. level

poziomka (po-żhom-ka) f. wild strawberry(fruit or plant)

poziomy (po-żho-mi) adj. m. horizontal;level;uninspired

pozłota (po-zwo-ta) f. gilding

poznać (po-znać) v. get to know; recognize;taste;acquaint

poznajomic (po-zna-yo-meech) v. acquaint; introduce

poznanie (po-zna-ñe) n. cognition; acquaintance; learning

pozornie (po-zor-ñe) adv. apparently; on the surface

pozostać (po-zos-tać) v. remain; stay behind;continue

pozostały (po-zos-ta-wi) adj. m. remaining; residual;left

pozostawiac (po-zos-tav-yach) v. leave (behind);bequeath

pozór (po-zoor) m. appearance; pretext; sham;look;mask;cloak

pozwac (póz-vach) v. summon

pozwalać (po-zva-lach) v. let; allow; permit; tolerate;suffer

pozwany (po-zva-ni) m. defendant; person sued or accused

pozwolenie (po-zvo-le-ñe) n. permission;consent; permit

pozycja (po-zyts-ya) f. position; item; status;posture

pozyskać (po-zis-kach) v. gain; win over ; conciliate

pozytywny (po-zi-tiv-ni) adj. m. positive; affirmative

pozywać (po-zi-vach) v. sue; cite; summon; cite(to court)

pożałować (po-zha-wo-vach) v. repent; regret; take pity

pożar (po-zhar) m. fire (woods, buildings);conflagration

pożądać (po-zhown-dach) v. desire; covet; lust after

pożądany (po-zhown-da-ni) adj. m. desirable; welcome;desired

pożądliwy (po-zhownd-lee-vi) adj. m. greedy;covetus;lewd

pożegnac (po-zheg-nach) v. bid goodbye; see off; dismiss

pożerać (po-zhe-rach) v. devour

pożoga (po-zhó-ga) f. fire; conflagration; ravages (of war)

pożółknąc (po-zhoówk-nownch) v. grow yellow;turn yellow

pożycie (po-zhi-che) v. intercourse; conjugal life

pożyczka (po-zhich-ka) f. loan

pożyteczny (po-zhi-tech-ni) adj. m. useful;profitable

pożytek (po-zhi-tek) m. use; advantage;usefulness; benefit

pożywic (pozhi-veech) v. feed; nourish; refresh;give food

pożywny (po-zhiv-ni) adj. m. nutritious; nourishing

pójsc (pooyshch) v. go; go away; go up..;leave;fly;drift;pan out

poki (poo-kee) conj. till; until; as long as;while; when

pół (poow) num. half;semi- ; demi-;one half; mid(way);hemi-

półbucik (poow-boo-cheek) m. half boot; low shoe

półgłosem (poow-gwo-sem) adv. in a low voice;in an undertone

półgłowek (poow-gwoo-vek) m. half-wit; fool; simpleton; dolt

półka (poow-ka) f. shelf;ledge

półkole (poow-ko-le) n. semicircle; half-circle;hemicycle

półksiężyc (poow-kshan-zhits)m. half-moon; crescent;the Crescent

półkula (poow-koo-la)f. hemisphere ;half of a sphere

półmisek (poow-mee-sek) m. charger dish; dish

połnagi (poow-na-gee) adj. m. half naked ; half dressed

północ (poow-nots) f. midnight; north; North; the North

północno-wschodni (poow-nots-no wskhód-ñee) north-east

północno-zachodni (poow-nóts-no zakhód-ñee) north-west

północny (poow-nóts-ni) adj. north ; Northern; Northerly

półroczny(poow-róch-ni) half-yearly; semi-annual

półświatek (poow-shvyá-tek) m. love industry;demimonde

półtora (poow-tó-ra) num. one and half; a (day etc.) and half

połurzędowy (poow-oo-zhań-dó-vi) adj. m. semi-official

półwysep (poow-vi-sep) m. peninsula; almost an island

póty (poo-ti) conj. as long

później (poozh-ney) adv. later on; afterwards; at a later date

późno (poozh-no) adv. late; latepóźny (poozh-ni) adj. m. late

prababka (pra-báb-ka) f. great grandmother

praca (pra-tsa) f. work; job

pracodawca (pra-tso-dáv-tsa) m. employer (employing for wages)

pracowity (pra-tso-vee-ti) adj. m. industrious; hard-working

pracownik (pra-tsóv-ñeek) m. worker; emploee; clerk; official

praczka (prách-ka) f. washwoman; laundress; washerwoman

prać (prach) v. wash; beat up

pradziad (pra-dzhad) m. great grandfather; ancestor

pragnąć (prag-nównch) v. be thirsty; desire; wish; long for

pragnienie (prag-ñe-ñe) n. wish; thirst; desire; lust for

praktyczny (prak-tich-ni) adj. m. practical; sensible; expedient

praktyka (prak-ti-ka) f. practice; usage; apprenticeship

praktykować (prak-ti-kó-vach) v. practice; be in training

pralka (prál-ka) f. washing machine; washer; wash board

pralnia (prál-ña) f. laundry

pranie (pra-ñe) n. washing

praojciec (pra-oy-chets) m. forefather; ancestor

prasa (pra-sa) f. press; print

prasować (pra-só-vach) v. iron (linen etc.); press; print

prawda (práv-da) f. truth

prawdomówność (prav-do-moóv-noshch) f. truthfulness

prawdopodobny (prav-do-po-dob-ni) adj. m. probable; likely

prawdziwie (prav-dźhéev-ye) adv. truly; genuinely; indeed

prawdziwy (prav-dźhee-vi) adj. m. true; real; authentic

prawica (pra-vee-tsa) f. the Right; right hand; right wing

prawić (prá-veech) v. talk; say

prawidło (pra-veed-wo) n. rule; boot tree; law; centering

prawidłowy (pra-veed-wó-vi) adj. m. regular; correct; proper

prawie (práv-ye) adv. almost; nearly; practically; all but

prawnik (prav-ñeek) m. lawyer

prawnuczka (prav-noóch-ka) f. great granddaughter

prawnuk (práv-nook) m. great grandson

prawny (práw-ni) adj. m. legal; lawful; legitimate; rightful

prawo (pra-vo) adv. right; law

prawo (prá-vo) n. law; (driving) license; statute; claim

prawodawca (pra-vo-dáv-tsa) m. legislator; lawmaker; lawgiver

prawodawstwo (pra-vo-dav-stvo) n. legislation; legislature

prawomocny (pra-vo-móts-ni) adj. m. legal; valid

prawosławny (pra-vo-swáv-ni) adj. m. orthodox

prawosć (pra-voshch) f. honesty; integrity; righteousness

prawować się (pra-vo-vach shán) v. litigate; sue; be engaged in a lawsuit; be at law with...

prawowity (pra-vo-vee-ti) adj. m. legal (heir etc.)

prawy (prá-vi) adj. m. honest; right; rigth hand; upright; lawful

prażyć (pra-zhich) v. grill; roast burn; keep heavy gunfire on

prąd (prównd) m. current; flow stream; air flow; tendency; trend

prądnica (prownd-ñee-tsa) f. generator; dynamo

prąd stały (prównd sta-wi) m. direct current

prąd zmienny (prównd zmyen-ni) alternating current

prążek (prówn-zhek) m. stripe

precyzja (pre-tsíz-ya) f. precision; accuracy; exactness

precyzować (pre-tsi-zó-vach) v. define; state precisely; define

precz ! (prech) adv. go away; do away with; down with

prefabrykować (pre-fa-bri-ko-vach) v. prefabricate

prefiks (pre-feeks) m. prefix

prelegent (pre-le-gent) m. lecturer (presenting a lecture)

prelekcja (pre-lek-tsya) f. lecture (informative talk)

preliminarz (pre-lee-mee-nash) m. estimate of a budget

premedytacja (pre-me-di-tats-ya) f. premeditation

premia (prem-ya) f. premium; bonus;bounty; prize; gift

premier (pre-myer) m. prime minister ; premier

premiera (pre-mye-ra) f. first night show;first night

prenumerata (pre-noo-me-ra-ta) f. subscription(to a paper etc.)

preparat (pre-pa-rat) m. preparation;concoction;specimen

prerogatywa (pre-ro-ga-ti-va) f. privilege; prerogative

presja (pres-ya) f. pressure

prestiż (pres-teesh) m. prestige; high esteem

pretekst (pre-tekst) m. pretext; excuse; false reason or motive

pretensja (pre-tens-ya) f. claim; grudge;debt;pretentiousness

prezerwatywa (pre-zer-va-ti-va) f. contraceptive sheath

prezent (pre-zent) m. gift

prezes (pre-zes) m. chairman

prezydent (pre-zi-dent) m. president; mayor; Lord Mayor

pręcik (pran-cheek) m. (small) stick; stamen ;rod; graphite

prędki (prand-kee) adj. m. swift; quick; rapid; fast; prompt;hasty

prędko (prand-ko) adv. quickly; fast; 2. soon;at once

prędkość (prand-koshch) f. speed; swiftness; velocity;impetuosity

prędzej (pran-dzey) adv. quicker sooner; rather; with all haste

pręga (pran-ga) f. stripe; wale

pręgierz (pran-gesh) m. pillory

pręgowaty (pran-go-va-ti) adj. m. striped ;with stripes

pręt (prant) m. rod; bar; pole; switch;stick;wand;twig;perch

prężność (pranzh-noshch) f. resilience; elasticity;energy

prężny (pranzh-ni) adj. m. elastic; resilient;supple

prężyć (pran-zhich) v. strain

probierczy kamień (pro-byer-chi kam-yen) m. touch-stone

problem (prob-lem) m. problem

probostwo (pro-bos-tvo) n. parsonage; parish; rectory

proboszcz (pro-boshch) m.pastor; parish priest;parson

probówka (pro-boov-ka) f. test-tube; test glass

proca (pro-tsa) f. sling

proceder (pro-tse-der) m.trade; (shady)dealings; a plot

procedura (pro-tse-doo-ra) f. procedure; legal practice

procent (pro-tsent) m. percentage; interest on money

procentować się (pro-tsen-to-vach shan) v. bring interest

proces (pro-tses) m. lawsuit

procesja (pro-tses-ya) f. procession; moving as in parade

procesować (pro-tse-so-vach) v. sue; be engaged in a litigation ;litigate a cause

proch (prokh) m. powder; dust

proch strzelniczy (prokh stzhel-nee-chi) m. gunpowder

producent (pro-doo-tsent) m. producer; manufacturer; maker

produkcja (pro-dook-tsya) f. production ;output;performance

produkować (pro-doo-ko-vach) v. produce; grow;generate;stage

produkt (pro-dookt) m. product

profanować (pro-fa-no-vach) v. profane; desecrate :despoil

profesor (pro-fe-sor) m. professor ; teacher

profil (pro-feel) m. profile

profilaktyczny (pro-fee-lak-tich-ni) adj. m. prophylactic

prognoza (prog-no-za) f. prognosis ; forcast(of weather etc.)

program (prog-ram) m. program

progresja (pro-gres-ya) f. progression ; sequence

prohibicja (pro-hee-beets-ya) f. prohibition ;forbidding

projekcja (pro-yek-tsya) f. projection (on a screen etc.)

projekt (pró-yekt) m. project
projektować (pro-yek-tó-vach)
v. design ;plan;lay out;draft
proklamować (pro-kla-mo-vach)
v. proclaim;announce officially
prokurator (pro-koo-ra-tor) m.
public prosecutor
proletariat (pro-le-tar-yat) m.
proletariat ;working class
prolog (pró-lok) m. prologue
prolongować (pro-lon-gó-vach)
v. prolong; extend
prom (prom) m. ferry (boat)
promieniec (pro-mye-ńech) v.
radiate; beam(with joy etc.)
promieniotwórczy (pro-mye-ño-
tvoór-chi) adj. m. radio-
active(matter, isotopes, etc.)
promieniować (pro-mye-ño-vach)
v. radiate;beam;glow;brim over
promienisty (pro-mye-ńees-ti)
adj. m. radial;radiant;radiate
promienny (pro-myen-ni) adj.
m. radiant; beaming;bright
promień (pro-myen) m. beam;
ray; gleam;radius; fin ray
promocja (pro-móts-ya) f. promotion;conferment of a degree
propaganda (pro-pa-gán-da) f.
propaganda;publicity;boosting
propagować (pro-pa-go-vach) v.
propagate; publicize;boost
proponować (pro-po-no-vach) v.
propose;put forwards;suggest
proporcja (pro-ports-ya) f.
proportion;ratio; relation
proporcjonalny (pro-por-tsyo-
nál-ni) adj. m. proportional
proporzec (pro-pó-zhets) m.
pennon; banner;streamer;jack
propozycja (pro-po-zíts-ya) f.
proposal; offer; suggestion
proroctwo (pro-rots-tvo) n.
prophecy; prediction
prorok (pro-rok) m. prophet
prosić (pro-sheech) v. beg;
pray; ask; invite; request
prosię (pro-shan) n. young pig
proso (pro-so) n. millet
prospekt (prós-pekt) m. prospect;folder;view;panorama
prosperować (pros-pe-ró-vach)
v. prosper;be prosperous;thrive

prostacki (pros-táts-kee) adj.
m. boorish; rude ;vulgar;coarse
prostak (prós-tak) m. boor; gull
prostata (pros-tá-ta) f. prostate (gland at the of male bladder)
prosto (prós-to) adv. straight;
right; upright;simply;candidly
prostoduszny (pros-to-doosh-ni)
adj. m. simple-hearted ;naive
prostokąt (pros-tó-kównt) m.
rectangle(with four right angles)
prostolinijny (pros-to-lee-ñeey-
ni) adj. m. straightforward
prostopadła (pros-to-pád-wa) f.
perpendicular ;normal; sheer
prostota (pros-tó-ta) f. simplicity ; neatness; boorishness
prostować (pros-to-vach) v.
straighten; correct;revise
prosty (prós-ti) adj. m. straight;
right; direct simple;vulgar;plain
prostytucja (pros-ti-too-tsya) f.
prostitution; streetwalking
prostytutka (pros-ti-toot-ka) f.
prostitute; streetwalker
proszek (pro-shek) m. powder
(for baking etc.); wafer
proszę (pró-shan) please
prośba (prósh-ba) f. request;
demand; petition; application
proszkować (prosh-kó-vach) v.
pulverize; grind to powder
protegowany (pro-te-go-vá-ni)
adj. m. protégé
protekcja (pro-ték-tsya) f. pull;
patronage; backing;influence;push
protest (pro-test) m. protest
protestant (pro-tés- tant) m.
Protestant ; evangelical
protestantyzm (pro-tes-tán-tizm)
m. Protestantism
proteza (pro-té-za) f. artificial limb or denture
protokół (pro-tó-koow) m. record;
protocol;minutes; official record
prototyp (pro-tó-tip) m. proto-
type; archetype; protoplast
prowadzenie (pro-va-dzé-ńe) n.
management; conduct;leadership
prowadzić (pro-va-dzheech) v. steer;
lead;conduct; guide; keep; live;
carry on ;show the way;escort;run;
manage (an institution)

prowadzić auto (pro-va-dźheech) áu-to) drive a car

prowiant (pro-vyant) m. provisions;eatables; rations

prowincjonalny (pro-veen-tsyo-nál-ni) adj. m. provincial

prowizja (pro-veéz-ya) f. commission; percentage; brokerage

prowizoryczny (pro-vee-zo-rich-ni) adj. m. provisional

prowodyr (pro-vó-dir) m. ringleader; gang leader

prowokacja (pro-vo-káts-ya) f. provocation; stirring trouble

proza (pró-za) f. prose;dullness

próba (proo-ba) f. trial; test; proof; ordeal;acid test;try;go

próbka (proob-ka) f. sample

próbny (proob-ni) adj. m. experimental; tentative ;test-

próbować (proo-bo-vach) v. try; test; taste;put to test;offer

próchnica (prookh-ńee-tsa) f. moulder; (tooth) decay;humus

próchno (prookh-no) n. rotten wood; mould;rot; wood dust

prócz (prooch) prep. save; except;besides;apart from

próg (prook) m. threshold

prószyć (proo-shich) v. sift; flake; make dust;sprinkle;spray

próżnia (proozh-ńa) f. vacuum

próżniaczy (proozh-ńa-chi) adj. m. lazy; idle;inactive;leisured

próżniak (proozh-ńak) m. idler

próżno (proozh-no) adv. vainly; empty ;in vain; to no avail

próżność (proozh-noshch) f. vanity; false pride;futility

próżny (proozh-ni) adj. m. 1. empty; void; 2. vain

pruć (prooch) v. rip; unsew

pruski (proos-kee) adj. m. Prussian ; of Prussia

prychać (pri-khach) v. snort

prycza (pri-cha) f. plank-bed

pryk stary (prik sta-ri) adj. m. old goat; old duffer

prym (prim) m. lead; first place; superiority;the lead

prymas (pri-mas) m. primate

prymka (prim-ka) f. chewing tobacco;plug of chewing tobacco

pryskać (pris-kach) v. splash; spray; fly;clear out;bolt;burst

pryszcz (prishch) m. pimple

prysznic (prish-ńeets) m. shower bath; shower

prywatny (pri-vat-ni) adj. m. private; personal;confidential

pryzmat (priz-mat) m. prism

prządka (pzhównd-ka) f. spinner

prząść (pzhównshch) v. spin

przebaczać (pzhe-bá-chach) v. forgive; pardon; condone

przebaczenie (pzhe-ba-ché-ńe) n. pardon; forgiveness;remittal

przebąkiwać (pzhe-bówn-kee-vach) v. mutter ;hint;allude;mention

przebić (pzhe-beech) v. pierce; perforate; puncture;stab;recoin

przebieg (pzhé-byeg) m. curse; run ;progress;process; milage

przebiegać (pzhe-bye-gách) v. run cross ;take place;proceed

przebiegły (pzhe-byeg-wi) adj. m. cunning; sly ;wily;crafty

przebierać (pzhe-bye-rach) v. choose; sort;change clothes;sift

przebijać (pzhe-bee-yach) v. pierce; puncture;show through

przebłysk (pzhé-bwisk)m.glimpse; ray; flash; sparkle;glimmer

przebłyskiwać (pzhe-bwis-kee-vach) v. gleam ;shine;flash

przebolec (pzhe-bo-lech) v. get over; put up with ;get over it

przeboj (pzhe-booy) m. hit; success; breakthrough; clou

przebranie (pzhe-brá-ńe) m. disguise ;being disguised

przebrnąć (pzhe-brnownch) v. muddle through; wade through

przebrzmiały (pzhe-bzhmyá-wi) adj. m. overblown; has-been

przebudowa (pzhe-boo-dó-va) f. remodeling; rebuilding

przebudzić (pzhe-boo-dźheech)v. wake up; awake ;rouse;revive

przebyć (pzhe-bich) v. be over through; surmount; ride out storm ;travel;cross;pass;dwell

przebywać (pzhe-bi-vach) v. stay; reside ;dwell;inhabit

przecedzać (pzhe-tse-dzach) v. filter;strain through a sieve przeceniać (pzhe-tse-ńach) v. overrate; lower the price

przechadzka (pzhe-chádz-ka) f. walk; stroll; tour; airing

przechadzać się (pzhe-kha-dzách śhań) v. take a walk; stroll; go for a walk; saunter

przechodzić (pzhe-kho-dżheech) v. pass (through)

przechodzień (pzhe-kho-dżheń) m. passerby; pedestrian

przechowanie (pzhe-kho-va-ńe) n. safekeeping; storage

przechowywać (pzhe-kho-vi-vach) v. store; preserve; harbor; keep

przechrzcić (pzhekh-zhcheech) v. convert; change name

przechwalać (pzhe-khva-lach) v. talk big; overpraise; extol; puff

przechwycić (pzhe-khvi-cheech) v. intercept; seize

przechylić (pzhe-khi-leech) v. tilt; lean; tip; incline

przechytrzyć (pzhe-khit-zhich) v. outwit; overreach; outsmart

przeciąg (pzhe-chównk) m. draught; span; spell; time lapse

przeciąć (pzhe-chównch) v. cut; cross; intersect; slice; cleave

przeciągać (pzhe-chówn-gach) v. draw; drag; delay; stretch

przeciążać (pzhe-chówn-zhach) v. overload; overburden

przecie (pzhe-che) conj. yet; still; of course but; after all

przeciekać (pzhe-che-kach) v. leak; ooze; drain; percolate

przecierać (pzhe-che-rach) v. rub; wipe clear; threadbare; fret; polish (shoes); clear up

przecierpieć (pzhe-cher-pyech) v. endure; bear; suffer

przecież (pzhe-chezh) conj. yet; still; after all; now; though

przeciętny (pzhe-chánt-ni) adj. m. average; ordinary; mediocre

przecinać (pzhe-chee-nach) v. cut; intersect; slice; cleave

przecinek (pzhe-chee-nek) m. comma; point (in mathematics)

przeciskać się (pzhe-chees-kach śhań) v. squeeze through; push through; elbow one's way

przeciw (pzhe-cheev) prep. against; versus; contrary to

przeciwko (pzhe-cheev-ko) prep. against; contrary; versus

przeciwdziałać (pzhe-cheev-dżha-wach) v. counteract

przeciwległy (pzhe-cheev-leg-wi) adj. m. opposite; contrary

przeciwlotniczy (pzhe-cheev-lot-nee-chi) adj. m. antiaircraft (artillery, defence etc.)

przeciwnie (pzhe-cheev-ńe) adv. on the contrary; reverse

przeciwnik (pzhe-cheev-ńeek) m. opponent; adversary; enemy; foe

przeciwność (pzhe-cheev-nośhch) f. adversity; set-back; reverse

przeciwstawiać (pzhe-cheev-stav-yach) v. oppose; set against

przeciwwaga (pzhe-cheev-va-ga) f. counterweight; balance weight

przecudny (pzhe-tsood-ni) adj. m. most wonderful; just marvellous

przeczący (pzhe-chown-tsi) adj. m. negative; contradictory

przeczenie (pzhe-che-ńe) n. negation; negative; denial

przecznica (pzhech-nee-tsa) f. side-street; cross street

przeczucie (pzhe-choo-che) n. foreboding; presentiment

przeczulony (pzhe-choo-ló-ni) adj. m. high-strung; over-sensitive; touchy; irritable

przeczyć (pzhe-chich) v. deny; belie; negate; contradict

przeczyszczać (pzhe-chish-chach) v. purge; cleanse; scour; wipe

przeczytać (pzhe-chi-tach) v. read through; peruse; read over

przeć (pzhech) v. insist on; urge; press on; push; exert pressure. impel; drive; insist; bear down; strive

przed (pzhet) prep. before; in front of; ahead of; previous to; from; since; ago; against

przedajny (pzhe-day-ni) adj. m. venal; open to bribery

przedawnienie (pzhe-dav-ńe-ńe) n. expiration of validity

przedawniony (pzhe-dav-ńó-ni) adj. m. of expired validity

przeddzień (pzhéd-dżheń) m. eve

przede wszystkim (pzhe-de
vshíst-keem) adv. above all;
first; first of all; in the
first place; to begin with
przedhistoryczny (pzhed-hees-
to-rích-ni) adj. m. pre-
historic;before recorded hist.
przedimek (pzhed-ée-mek) m.
article (in grammar)
przedkładać (pzhed-kwá-dach) v.
submit; refer; propose; present; prefer;give priority
przedłużać (pzhed-woo-zhách)
v. lengthen; prolong;extend
przedmieście (pzhed-myésh-che)
n, suburb;outskirts of a city
przedmiot (pzhéd-myot) m. object; subject; subject matter
przedmiotowy (pzhed-myo-tó-vi)
adj. m. objective; at issue
przedmowa (pzhed-mó-va) f. preface; foreword;introduction
przedmówca (pzhed-moóv-tsa) m.
previous speaker
przedni (pzhéd-ńee) adj. m.
leading; front; forward;
choice; fine ;foremost;superior
przedostać się (pzhe-dós-tach
sháń) v. penetrate;pass through
przedostatni (pzhed-os-tát-ńee)
adj. m. last but one
przedpłata (pzhed-pwá-ta) f.
advance payment;subscription
przedpokój (pzhed-po-kooy) m.
(waiting-room) lobby; ante-
chamber; anteroom; hall
przedpole (pzhed-pó-le) n. foreground; foreland
przedpołudnie (pzhed-po-woód-ńe)
n. morning; forenoon
przedpotopowy (pzhed-po-to-pó-
vi) adj. m. fossil; antedilu-
vian; fossilized; obsolete
przedramię (pzhed-ram-yáń) n.
forearm; antebrachium
przedrostek (pzhed-ros-tek) m.
prefix (in grammar)
przedruk (pzhed-rook) m. reprint; reimpression;impression
przedrzeć (pzhed-zhech) v. tear
up; tear through; rend;
break through;penetrate;burst

przedrzeźniać (pzhed-zhéźh-
ńach) v. ape; mimic; mock;
take off; immitate like an ape
przedsiębiorca (pzhed-shań-byor-
tsa) m. contractor;businessman
przedsiębiorstwo (pzhed-shań-
byor-stvo) n. business; concern; enterprise; firm
przedsiębrać (pzhed-sháń-brach)
v. undertake;embark upon
przedsionek (pzhed-shó-nek) m.
lobby; vestibule; porch;auricle
przedsmak (pzhéd-smak) m. foretaste;earnest(of future events)
przedstawić (pzhed-stá-veech)
v. present; represent;recommend
przedstawiciel (pzhed-sta-vee-
chel) m. representative
przedstawicielstwo (pzhed-sta-
vee-chel-stvo) n. agency
przedstawienie (pzhed-sta-vyé-
ńe) n. performance;show;version
przedszkole (pzhed-shko-le) n.
kindergarten; nursery school
przedświt(pzhed-shveet)m. pre-
dawn; daybreak;dawn; harbinger
przedtem (pzhed-tem) adv. before; formerly;in advance;earlier
przedterminowy (pzhed-ter-mee-
nó-vi) adj. m. advance;
premature; done ahead of time
przedwczesny (pzhed-vches-ni)
adj. m. premature; untimely
przedwczoraj (pzhed-vcho-ray)
adv. the day before yesterday
przedwieczny (pzhed-vyéch-ni)
adj. m. eternal;primeval;ancient
przedwiośnie (pzhed-vyosh-ńe)
n. early spring
przedwojenny (pzhed-vo-yén-ni)
adj. m. prewar; before the war
przedział (pzhe-dźaw) m. partition; compartment; section
przedzielić (pzhe-dźe-leech)
v. divide; part;separate
przedzierać (pzhe-dźhe-rach) v.
tear down; tear up; rend
przedziurawić (pzhe-dźhoo-ra-
veech) v. perforate; puncture;
riddle; pierce ;make a hole
przedziwny (pzhe-dźheev-ni) adj.
m. prodigious; admirable; odd

przeforsować (pzhe-for-so-vach)
v. ram through;force through

przegapić (pzhe-ga-peech) v.
let slip; over look;miss

przeginać (pzhe-gee-nach) v.
bend (over) turn up;turn down

przegląd (pzhe-glownt) m. review; inspection; survey

przegłosować (pzhe-gwo-so-vach)
v. outvote; take a vote

przegonić (pzhe-go-neech) v.
overtake; drive out; drive
through; drive away;rush past

przegotować (pzhe-go-to-vach)
v. boil; overcook;overboil

przegrać (pzhe-grach) v.lose
(war; game etc.);gamble away

przegradzać (pzhe-gra-dzach) v.
partition;divide;separate

przegrana (pzhe-gra-na) f. defeat; loss;beating; licking

przegryzać (pzhe-gri-zach) v.
bite through;bite in two

przegroda (pzhe-gro-da) f. partition;division;stall;cell

przegub (pzhe-goop) m. wrist;
ball -and-socket joint

przeholować (pzhe-kho-lo-vach)
v. overshoot; rush into excess

przeistoczyć (pzhe-ees-to-chich)
v. transform; remould;convert

przejaśnienie (pzhe-yash-ne-ne)
n. clearing up;bright interval

przejaw (pzhe-yav) m. symptom;
sign; indication;manifestation

przejawiać (pzhe-ya-veeach) v.
reveal; display; manifest;show

przejazd (pzhe-yazt) m. crossing; passage ;thoroughfare

przejąć (pzhe-yownch) v. take
over; seize;adopt;master;thrill

przejechać (pzhe-ye-khach) v.
pass; ride; cross; run over

przejęty (pzhe-yan-ti) adj. m.
impressed; upset; deeply
stirred ;perturbed;wrapped up

przejmować (pzhe-mo-vach) v.
take over ;seize;penetrate

przejrzeć (pzhey-zhech) v. see
through; recover sight ;revise

przejrzysty (pzhey-zhis-ti) adj.
m. transparent; clear ;sheer

przejście (pzhey-shche) n. pass;
transition;conversion;roadway

przejściowo (pzhey-shcho-vo)
adv. temporarily;provisionally

przejść (pzheyshch) v. pass;
cross; experience; go across

przekaz (pzhe-kas) m. transfer;
money order;remittance

przekazywać (przhe-ka-zi-vach)
v. transfer; pass on; send on;
transmit:deliver; direct

przekaźnik (pzhe-kazh-neek) m.
relay; repeater; transmitter

przekąsem (pzhe-kown-sem)adv.iro-
nically; mockingly; spitefully

przekąska (pzhe-kowns-ka) f.
snack; refreshment

przekątna (pzhe-kownt-na) f.
diagonal(line)

przekleństwo (pzhe-klen-stvo)
n. curse; profanity;damnation

przekład (pzhe-kwat) m. translation; rendering;rearrangement

przekładać (pzhe-kwa-dach) v.
shift; transfer; prefer; move;
translate;reach;put between

przekładnia (przek-wad-na) f.
gearbox; clutch ;transposition

przekłuć (pzhe-kwooch) v. prick;
pierce; puncture;perforate

przekonać (pzhe-ko-nach) v.
convince; persuade ;bring round

przekonanie (pzhe-ko-na-ne) n.
conviction; persuasion;opinion

przekop (pzhe-kop) m. trench;
ditch; tunnel;cutting;piercing

przekopać (pzhe-ko-pach) v. dig-
through ;turn over; excavate;cut

przekora (pzhe-ko-ra) f. spite

przekraczać (pzhe-kra-chach) v.
overstep; cross ;surpass

przekradać się (pzhe-kra-dach
shan) v. steal through

przekreślić (pzhe-kresh-leech)
v. cross out; delete; annul

przekręcić (pzhe-kran-cheech) v.
twist; distort(a statement)

przekroczenie (pzhe-kro-che-ne)
n. trespass;offence;transgression

przekroczyć (pzhe-kro-chich) v.
cross; trespass; exceed; offend; violate;transgress(the law)

przekroić (pzhe-kró-eech) v. cut
przekrój (pzhé-krooy) v. cross
section; profile; review
przekrwienie (pzhe-krvye-ńe) n.
hyperemia; congestion
przekształcić (pzhe-kshtaw-
cheech) v. transform
przekupić (pzhe-koo-peech) v.
bribe; buy over; corrupt
przekupka (pzhe-koop-ka) f.
huckstress; vendor; wrangler
przekupny (pzhe-koop-ni) adj.
m. venal; bribable
przekupstwo (pzhe-koop-stvo) n.
bribery; graft; corruption
przekwitać (pzhe-kvee-tach) v.
wither; fade; decay; shed blossom
przelatywać (pzhe-la-ti-vach)
v. fly through; cross; run; pass
przelew (pzhe-lef) m. transfusion; transfer; over flow
przelewać (pzhe-le-vach) v.
overfill; transfer; shed
przelękły (pzhe-lan-kwi) adj.
m. frightened; intimidated
przelęknąć (pzhe-lank-nownch)v.
frighten; scare; terrify
przelicytować (pzhe-lee-tsi-
to-vach) v. outbid
przeliczyć (pzhe-lee-chich) v.
miscalculate; count over
przelot (pzhe-lot) m. over-
flight; flight; passage
przelotny (pzhe-lot-ni) adj. m.
fleeting; passing; transient
przeludnienie (pzhe-lood-ńe-ńe)
n. overpopulation; congestion
przeładować (pzhe-wa-do-vach)
v. overload; transship; reload
przeładunek (pzhe-wa-doo-nek)
m. load, transfer; reloading
przełamać (pzhe-wa-mach) v.
break through; break in two
przełazić (pzhe-wa-żheech) v.
climb over; creep across
przełącznik (pzhe-wównch-ńeek)
m. switch; shift; commutator
przełęcz (pzhe-wańch) v. (mountain) pass; saddle; col
przełknąć (pzhew-knównch) v.
swallow; swollow down
przełom (pzhe-wom) m. breakthrough; turning point; gorge

przełożony (pzhe-wo-zhó-ni)
adj. m. principal; superior
przełożyć (pzhe-wo-zhich) v.
transfer; prefer; shift; reach
przełyk (pzhé-wik) m. gullet;
esophagus
przemakać (pzhe-má-kach) v.
ooze; get wet; be permeable
przemarsz (pzhe-marsh) m.
marching past; march of troops
przemarznąć (pzhe-mar-znowńch)
v. be chilled; freeze stiff
przemawiać (pzhe-má-vyach) v.
speak; harangue; address
przemądrzały (pzhe-mównd-zhá-
wi) adj. m. smart aleck
przemęczać (pzhe-man-chach) v.
overstrain; overwork; spend
przemęczenie (pzhe-man-che-ńe)
n. strain; overwork; tiredness
przemiał (pzhe-myaw) m. grinding; milling; meal; grist; shoal
przemiana (pzhe-mya-na) f.change;
transformation; alteration
przemianować (pzhe-mya-no-vach)
v. rename; change name
przemienić (pzhe-mye-ńeech) v.
change; transform; alter; turn
przemieścić (pzhe-myésh-cheech)
v. displace; dislocate; shift
przemijać (pzhe-mee-yach) v.
go by; be over; pass; cease
przemilczeć (pzhe-meel-chech)
v. keep secret; leave unsaid
przemoc (pzhe-mots) f. force;
violence; constraint; compulsion
przemoczyć (pzhe-mo-chich) v.
soak; drench; wet; seep; sop
przemoknąć (pzhe-mok-nownch) v.
be soaked; be permeable; get wet
przemowa (pzhe-mo-va) f. speech;
oration; address: harangue
przemóc (pzhe-moots) v. overcome; conquer; defeat; master; prevail
przemówić (pzhe-moo-veech) v.
speak up; make a mistake (speaking)
przemówienie (pzhe-moov-ye-ńe)
n. speech; address; oration
przemycać (pzhe-mi-tsach) v.
smuggle (into a country, a room etc.)
przemyć (pzhe-mich) v. rinse; scrub;
wash; give a wash; lavage; flush
przemysł (pzhe-misw) m.industry

przemysłowy (pzhe-mis-wo-vi) adj.
m. industrial;manufacturing
przemyśliwać (pzhe-miśh-lee-
vach) v. ponder; think over
przemyślny (pzhe-miśhl-ni) adj.
m. ingenious;clever;cunning
przemyt (pzhe-mit) m. smuggling
przemytnik (pzhe-mit-ńeek) m.
smuggler; contrabandist
przemywać (pzhe-mi-vach) v.
rinse; wash; scrub;lavage;flush
przenieść (pzhe-ńeshch) v.
transfer; surpass; carry over;
remove;convey; move; retrace
przenigdy (pzhe-ńeeg-di) adv.
nevermore; never, never
przenikać (pzhe-ńee-kach) v.
penetrate; pierce; permeate
przenikliwy (pzhe-ńeek-lee-vi)
adj. m. penetrating; acute;
sharp; piercing;keen;shrewd
przenocować (pzhe-no-tso-vach)
v. pass the night;put up
przenośnia (pzhe-nosh-ńa) f.
metaphor; figure of speach
przenośny (pzhe-nosh-ni) adj. m.
portable; mobile;metaphorical
przeobrażać (pzhe-o-bra-zhach)
v. transform; modify;change
przeoczenie (pzhe-o-che-ńe) m.
oversight; omission
przeoczyć (pzhe-o-chich) v.
overlook; leave out;omit
przepadać (pzhe-pa-dach) v. be
lost; be extremely fond;vanish
przepalić (pzhe-pa-leech) v.
burn through;overheat;scorch
przepasać (pzhe-pa-sach) v.
gird ;belt;tie;overfeed
przepaska (pzhe-pás-ka) f. band
przepaść (pzhe-pashch) f. abyss
przepchać (pzhep-khach) v. push
through; pass through;clean out
przepełniać (pzhe-pew-ńach) v.
overfill; cram ; over cram
przepełnienie (pzhe-pew-ńe-ńe) n.
overfill; crowd;excess
przepędzać (pzhe-pan-dzach) v.
drive away; spend ;distil;stay
przepić (pzhe-peech) v. spend
on drinking; drink away;waste
przepierać (pzhe-pye-rach) v.
launder; wash clothes

przepierzenie (pzhe-pye-zhe-ńe)
n. partition (wall etc.)
przepiękny (pzhe-pyáń -kni)
adj. , very beautiful; gorgeous
przepiłować (pzhe-pee-wo-vach)
v. saw,through; file through
przepiórka (pzhe-pyoor-ka) f.
quail(migratory game bird)
przepis (pzhe-pees) m. 1. regulation; 2. recipe
przepisać (pzhe-pee-sach) v.
1. prescribe; 2. copy
przepłacać (pzhe-pwa-tsach) v.
overpay; pay too much; bribe
przepłukać (pzhe-pwoo-kach) v.
rinse; gargle ;scoup; wash
przepłynąć (pzhe-pwi-nównch) v.
swim across ;row across
przepływać (pzhe-pwi-vach) v.
flow; float across; swim
across; row across;sail across
przepocić (pzhe-po-cheech) v.
sweat through ;sweat (a shirt)
przepoić (pzhe-po-eech) v. impregnate ;saturate; fill
przepona (pzhe-po-na) f. diaphragm ;midriff; stiffener
przepowiadać (pzhe-po-vya-dach)
v. predict ;foretell;repeat
przepracować się (pzhe-pra-tso-
vach śhąń) v. overwork (oneself) ;overstrain oneself
przepraszać (pzhe-pra-shach) v.
apologize; excuse oneself
przeprawa (pzhe-pra-va) f.
1. passage; crossing ;journey
2. fight ;incident;scene; row
przeprawiać (pzhe-práv-yach) v.
cross over ;carry across
przeproszenie (pzhe-pro-shé-ńe)
n. apology; apologies
przeprowadzać (pzhe-pro-vá-dzach)
v. convey; lead; move ;pass
przeprowadzka (pzhe-pro-vadz-ka)
f. moving (form a house etc.)
przepuklina (pzhe-poo-klee-na)
f. hernia ; rupture
przepustka (pzhe-poost-ka) f.
pass; permit ; liberty; sluice
przepuszczać (pzhe-poosh-chach)
v. let pass ;promote;leak;miss;
let slip;waste;squander away

przepuszczalność (pzhe-poosh-
chál-noshch) f. permeability
przepych (pzhe-pikh) m. luxury;
pageantry;splendor;ostentation
przepychać (pzhe-pi-khach) v.
push through; force through
przepytywać (pzhe-pi-ti-vach) v.
examine; inquire;question
przerabiać (pzhe-ra-byach) v.
do over; revise;remodel;alter
przerachować (pzhe-ra-kho-vach)
v. miscalculate; count over
przeradzać się (pzhe-ra-dzach
shań) v. change (into)
przerastać (pzhe-ras-tach) v.
outgrow; rise above;surpass
przerazić (pzhe-ra-zheech) v.
terrify; appal; consternation
przeraźliwy (pzhe-razh-lee-vi)
adj. m. appalling; terrifying
shrill; awesome; acute;sharp
przerażenie (pzhe-ra-zhe-ńe) n.
terror;horror;dread;dismay
przerażony (pzhe-ra-zho-ni)
adj. m. horror stricken
przeróbka (pzhe-roob-ka) f.
revision;reshaping; alteration
przerwa (pzher-va) f. pause;
break; recess; interval
przerys (pzhe-ris) m. tracing
przerysować (pzhe-ri-so-vach)
v. trace; copy;retrace
przerwać (pzher-vach) v. interrupt; pause; cut-off
przerzedzić(pzhe-zhe-dzheech)v.
thin out; decimate(a population)
przerzucać (pzhe-zhoo-tsach) v.
throw over; shift; move; flip;
browse;transfer; ransack
przerzynać (pzhe-zhi-nach) v.
cut through;cut in two
przesada (pzhe-sá-da) f. exaggeration;overstatement
przesadzać (pzhe-sa-dzach) v.
1. exaggerate; 2. transplant
przesalać (pzhe-sa-lach) v.
oversalt;put too much salt
przesąd (pzhe-sownt) m. prejudice; superstition;fallacy
przesądny (pzhe-sownd-ni) adj.
m. superstitious;prejudiced
przesiadać się (pzhe-sha-dach
shań) v. change(places; seats)

przesiedlać (pzhe-shed-lach)
v. displace; migrate;transplant
przesiewać (pzhe-she-vach) v.
sift; sieve;screen out;riddle
przesilać się (pzhe-shee-lach
shań) v. subside;get over;
culminate;overcome;overstrain
przesilenie (pzhe-shee-le-ńe)
n. crisis;turning point
przeskoczyć (pzhe-sko-chich) v.
jump over;vault;outstrip;skip
przesłać (pzhe-swach) v. 1.send;
2. make bed over;rearrange a bed
przesłaniać (pzhe-swa-nach) v.
screen off;veil;cover;hide;shade
przesłanka (pzhe-swan-ka) f.
premise;prerequisite;condition
przesłuchiwać (pzhe-swoo-khee-
vach) v. interrogate;question
przesmyk (pzhes-mik) m. strait
przesolony (pzhe-so-lo-ni) adj.
m. oversalted;with excess salt
przespać (pzhes-pach) v. sleep
over;fail to wake up for...
przestać (pzhes-tach) v. cease
przestanek (pzhes-ta-nek) m.
pause; rest; stop
przestankować (pzhe-stan-ko-
vach) v. punctuate (written
matter)
przestarzały (pzhe-sta-zha-vi)
adj. m. obsolete;time worn
przestawać (pzhe-sta-vach) v.
1.cut out; break off; 2. associate; hobnob;keep company
przestawiać (pzhe-stav-yach) v.
displace; transpose;shift
przestąpić (pzhe-stown-peech)
v. step over;transgress;cross
przestępca (pzhe-stanp-tsa) m.
criminal;felon;law beaker
przestępny (pzhe-stanp-ni) adj.
m. leap (year);felonious
przestępstwo (pzhe-stanp-stvo)
n. offense; crime;transgression
przestrach (pzhe-strakh) m.
fright; alarm; fear; terror
przestraszyć (pzhe-stra-shich)
v. scare; startle;alarm
przestroga (pzhe-stro-ga) f.
warning; admonition;caution
przestronny (pzhe-stron-ni) adj.
m. spacious; roomy

przestrzegać (pzhe-stzhe-gach)
v. observe (rules); caution
przestrzelić (pzhe-stzhe-leech)
v. shoot through;shoot down
przestrzenny (pzhe-stzhen-ni)
adj. m. spatial; roomy
przestrzeń (pzhe-stzheń) f.
space ; outer space; room
przestworze (pzhe-stvo-zhe) n.
expanse; infinity ; space,
przesunięcie (pzhe-soo-nań-che)
n. shift ; transfer;displacement
przesuwać (pzhe-soo-vach) v.
move; shift ; shove; transfer
przesycać (pzhe-si-tsach) v.
saturate; glut; impregnate
przesyłać (pzhe-si-wach) v.
send ; dispatch; forward
przesyłka (pzhe-siw-ka) f.
shipment ; mail; parcel
przesypiać (pzhe-sip-yach) v.
oversleep; sleep away
przesyt (pzhe-sit) m. glut
przeszczep (pzhe-shchep) m.
transplant; graft; grafting
przeszkadzać (pzhe-shka-dzach)
v. hinder; trouble ;prevent
przeszkoda (pzhesh-ko-da) f.
obstacle ; hitch; obstruction
przeszkolenie (pzhe-shko-le-
ńe) n. training ; course
przeszło (pzhesh-wo) adv.
more than ; over (an amount)
przeszłość (pzhesh-wośhch) f.
past ; record;antecedents
przeszukać (pzhe-shoo-kach) v.
search over ; ransack
przeszyć (pzhe-shich) v. sew-
through; pierce; gore;quilt,
prześcieradło (pzhesh-che-rad-
wo) n. bedsheet; sheet,
prześcignąć (pzhe-shcheeg-
nownch) v. outdistance; outdo; outstrip;overtake;excel
prześladować (pzhe-shla-do-
vach) v. persecute;harass;haunt
prześladowanie (pzhe-shla-do-
va-ńe) n. persecution;obsession
prześliczny (pzhe-shleech-ni)
adj. m. most beautiful;lovely
prześliznąć (pzhe-shleez-nownch)
v. slip through;glide past
przeświadczenie (pzhe-shvyad-
che-ńe) n. conviction;certitude

prześwietlać (pzhe-shvyet-lach)
v. shine through; fluoroscope
przetak (pzhe-tak) m. riddle
przetaczać (pzhe-ta-chach) v.
1. rollover; 2. transfuse
przetapiać (pzhe-tap-yach) v.
recast; smelt(metals); melt
przetarg (pzhe-tark) m. auction
przetarty (pzhe-tar-ti) adj. m.
threadbare; rubbed through,
przetłumaczyć (pzhe-twoo-ma-
chich) v. translate; explain
przeto (pzhe-to) conj. therefore;accordingly;consequently
przetrawić (pzhe-tra-veech) v.
digest;ruminate;etch;corrode
przetrwać (pzhe-trvach) v.
survive; outlast;remain;keep
przetrwonić (pzhe-trvo-ńeech)
v. squander,;waste;fritter away
przetrząsnąć (pzhe-tzhowns-
nownch) v. search (shake
through);ransack;comb out
przetrzymać (pzhe-tzhi-mach) v.
endure; outdo; keep waiting
przetwarzać (pzhe-tva-zhach)
v. remake; manufacture
przetwórnia (pzhe-tvoor-ńa) f.
factory; processing plant
przewaga (pzhe-va-ga) f. predominance ; overbalance ;lead
przeważać (pzhe-va-zhach) v.
outweigh; prevail; overbalance
przeważający (pzhe-va-zha-yown-
tsi) adj. m. prevailing; superior; predominant,
przeważnie (pzhe-vazh-ńe) adv.
mainly; mostly; chiefly;largely
przewiązać (pzhe-vyown-zach) v.
bind up; change dressing
przewidywać (pzhe-vee-di-vach)
v. anticipate; foresee
przewiercić (pzhe-vyer-cheech)
v. drill through (pierce)
przewiesić (pzhe-vye-sheech) v.
sling over;hang over;rehang
przewietrzyć (pzhe-vyet-zhich)
v. ventilate;
przewiew (pzhe-vyev) m. draught;
breeze; breath of air;whiff
przewiezienie (pzhe-vye-zhe-ńe)
n. transport ;transportation;
carriage; conveyance

przewijać (pzhe-vee-yach) v.
wrap up; change dressing
przewinienie (pzhe-vee-ńe-ńe)
n. offense; delinquency
przewlekły (pzhe-vlek-wi) adj.
m. protracted; lingering;lasting
przewodni (pzhe-vod-ńee) adj.
m. leading ;guiding(principle)
przewodniczący (pzhe-vod-ńee-
chówn-tsi) m. chairman
przewodnik (pzhe-vod-ńeek) m.
guide; conductor; leader
przewodzić (pzhe-vo-dżheech) v.
head; command ;lead;conduct
przewozić (pzhe-vo-żheech) v.
convey; transport;cart across
przewoźnik (pzhe-vożh-ńeek) m.
ferryman;carter; carrier
przewód (pzhe-voot) m. conduit;
channel; wire;procedure
przewóz (pzhe-voos) m. transport; freight ; cartage
przewracać (pzhe-vra-tsach) v.
overturn; turn over; upset;
toss ; topple; invert;reverse
przewrotność (pzhe-vrót-noshch)
f. perversity; perfidy;deceit
przewrót (pzhe-vroot) m. revolution;upheaval;coup d'état
przewyższać (pzhe-vizh-shach)
v. out do; exceed; surpass
przez (pzhes) prep. ; across;
over; through; during; within; in; on;on the other side
przeziębić się (pzhe-żhań-beech
shań) v. catch cold;grow cold
przezimować (pzhe-żhee-mo-vach)
v. winter; hibernate
przeznaczać (pzhe-zna-chach) v.
intend; earmark ; mean; destine; assign; allocate;design
przeznaczenie (pzhe-zna-che-ńe)
n. destiny; destination
przezorność (pzhe-zór-noshch) f.
caution; prudence;foresight
przeźrocze (pzhe-żhró-che) n.
transparency; slide;open work
przeźroczysty (pzhe-żhro-chis-
ti) adj. m. transparent
przezwisko (pzhes-vees-ko) n.
1. nickname; 2. abusive name
przezwyciężać (pzhez-vee-chań-
zhach) v.overcome; conquer

przezywać (pzhe-zi-vach) v. revile; abuse; call names,
przeżegnać się (pzhe-zheg-nach
shań) v. cross oneself
przeżuwać (pzhe-zhoo-vach) v.
chew;masticate; ponder over
przeżycie (pzhe-zhi-che) n.
experience; survival
przeżyc (pzhe-zhich)v.survive;
live through;outlive
przeżytek (pzhe-zhi-tek) m.
relic of the passd;old timer
przędza (pzhań-dza) f. yarn
przędzalnia (pzhań-dzal-ńa) f.
spinning mill;spinning room
przęsło (pzhańs-wo) n. (bridge)
bay; (stair) flight; span
przodek (pzho-dek) m. 1. ancestor; 2. front;heading;end;top
przodować (pzho-do-vach) v.
lead; excel; be the best
przodownictwo (pzho-dov-ńeets-
tvo) n. leadership; hegemony
przodownik (pzho-dov-ńeek) m.
leader;foreman;police inspector
przód (pzhoot) m. front; ahead
przy (pzhi) prep. by; at; near
by; with; on; about; close to
przybić (pzhi-beech)v. nail down
przybiec (pzhi-byets) v. run
up ; hasten;come up,running
przybierać (pzhi-bye-rach) v.
dress up; put on; adopt;adorn
przybliżać (pzhi-blee-zhach) v.
bring near;draw near;magnify
przybliżony (pzhi-blee-zhó-ni)
adj. m. approximate;very near
przyboczny (pzhi-bóch-ni) adj.
m. side(kick) ; personal (aide);
body (guard); adjutant (officer)
przybory (pzhi-bo-ri) pl. accessories;outfit; tools;tackle
przybór (pzhi-boor) m. rise
(of flood);rise (of a river)
przybrać (pzhi-brach) v. adorn;
put on; assume; adopt;rise;grow
przybrzeżny (pzhi-bzhézh-ni)
adj. m. coastal; riverside
przybudówka (pzhi-boo-doóv-ka)
f. annex;addition(to a building)
przybycie (pzhi-bi-che) n. arrival;gain;growth; accession
przybysz (pzhi-bish) m. newcomer

przybytek (pzhi-bi-tek) m. increase; sanctuary;repository

przybywać (pzhi-bi-vach) v. 1. arrive 2. increase;rise

przychodnia (pzhi-khod-na) f. outpatient clinic;ambulatory

przychodzić (pzhi-kho-dźheech) v. come over, around, along, to, again; turn up; arrive

przychód (pzhi-khoot) m. income;profit; takings;proceeds

przychylać (pzhi-khi-lach) v. incline: comply; bend

przychylny (pzhi-khil-ni) adj. m. favorable; kind;friendly

przyciągać (pzhi-ćhown-gach) v. attract; draw near;appeal;lure

przyciąganie ziemskie (pzhi-ćhown-ga-ne zhem-ske) gravitation; gravitational pull

przyciemniać (pzhi-ćhem-ñach) v. dim; darken;shade;black out

przycinać (pzhi-ćhi-nach) v. 1. cut; slip; 2. make fun of

przycisk (pzhi-ćheesk) m. 1. pressure; 2. accent; 3. paper-weight; weight;emphasis

przyciskać (pzhi-ćhis-kach) v. press; keep down;squeeze

przycupnąć (pzhi-tsoop-nownch) v. squat down;crouch;lie in wait

przyczaić się (pzhi-cha-eech shañ) v. lurk; sulk; ambush;hide

przyczepić (pzhi-che-peech) v. attach; fasten;link;fix;pin;hook

przyczepić się (pzhi-che-peech shañ) v. cling; pick a quarrel; find fault; hold tight; attach

przyczepka (pzhi-chep-ka) f. trailer

przyczółek (pzhi-choo-wek) m. abutment; bridgehead; beachhead;fronton;frontal;pediment

przyczyna (pzhi-chi-na) f.cause; reason; ground; intercession

przyczynek (pzhi-chi-nek) m. contribution(to science etc.)

przyczyniać (pzhi-chi-ñach) v. add; add to; contribute

przyczynowość (pzhi-chi-no-vośhćh) f. causation;causality

przyćmiewać (pzhi-chmye-vach) v. dim; tarnish; obscure; outshine; overshadow;darken; eclipse

przydać (pzhi-dach) v. add; apend; lend; add weight

przydatny (pzhi-dat-ni) adj. m. useful;helpful;serviceable

przydawka (pzhi-dáv-ka) f. attribute (gram.);gulifier

przydeptać (pzhi-dep-tach) v. thread upon; step on

przydługi (pzhi-dwoo-gee) adj. m. lengthy;somewhat too long

przydomek (pzhi-do-mek) m. by-name; surname;nickname

przydreptać (pzhi-drep-tach) v. trip along; come tripping

przydrożny (pzhi-drozh-ni) adj. m. roadside(shrine etc.)

przydusić (pzhi-doo-śheech) v. throttle; smother;press down

przydybać (pzhi-di-bach) v. overtake; take unawares;nab

przydymać (pzhi-dimach) v. foot it along; run up(slang)

przydymiony (pzhi-dim-yó-ni) adj. m. smoky; tinted

przydział (pzhi-dźhaw) m. allotment; ration;allowance

przydzielać (pzhi-dzhe-lach) v. assign; allocate;allot

przyganiać (pzhi-ga-ñach) v. blame; find fault with; criticize;rebuke;reprimand

przygarnąć (pzhi-gár-nównch) v. take up; adopt;hug;grasp;shelter

przygasać (pzhi-ga-sach) v. dim; subside; abate;go out;die down

przyglądać się (pzhi-glówn-dach shañ) v. observe;look on;scan;see

przygnać (pzhi-gnach) v. drive near; bring; run up; hasten

przygnębiać (pzhi-gnań-byach) v. depress; deject;dishearten

przygnębienie (pzhi-gnań-bye-ñe) n. depression; low spirits

przygniatać (pzhi-gña-tach) v. crush;overwhelm; oppress; burden; press down;squeeze; pinch

przygoda (pzhi-go-da) f. adventure; accident; experience

przygodny (pzhi-gód-ni) adj. m. occasional; casual; accidental

przygotować (pzhi-go-tó-vach) v. prepare; get ready; worn ; fit; coach; train; make ready; pack up; turn on (the bath) przygotowanie (pzhi-go-to-va-ne) n. preparation;getting ready

przygotowawczy (pzhi-go-to-vav-chi) adj.,m. preparatory;initial

przygrywac (pzhi-gri-vach) v. 1. accompany; 2. play(music)

przygrzewac (pzhi-gzhe-vach) v. warm up; heat up;swelter

przygwozdzic (pzhi-gvozh-dzheech) v. nail down;pin down

przyimek (pzhi-eé-mek) m. preposition(relation word)

przyjaciel (pzhi-ya-chel) m. friend;good friend;close friend

przyjaciołka (pzhi-ya-choow-ka) f. girl friend;close friend

przyjazd (pzhi-yazt) m. arrival; time of arrival

przyjazny (pzhi-yaz-ni) adj. m. friendly; amicable; kindly

przyjazn (pzhi-yazhn) f. friendship; friendly relations;amity

przyjaznic sie (pzhi-yazh-ňeech shaň) v. be friends;pal;chum

przyjechac (pzhi-ye-khach) v. come (over); arrive; come

przyjemnosc (pzhi-yém-noshch) f. pleasure; enjoyment; gusto;zest

przyjemny (pzhi-yém-ni) adj. m. pleasant;attractive;nice;cosy

przyjezdny (pzhi-yezd-ni) m. stranger; sightseer;visitor

przyjeżdżac (pzhi-yezh-dżhach) v. arrive (by transportation)

przyjęcie (pzhi-yan-che) n. admission; adoption; reception

przyjęty (pzhi-yan-ti) adj. m. customary; acceptable

przyjmowac (pzhiy-mo-vach) v. receive; accept; entertain

przyjscie (pzhiysh-che) n. arrival; coming; advent

przyjsc (pzhiyshch) v. come-over; come along; come around

przykazac (pzhi-ka-zach) v. order; tell; enjoin to do

przykazanie (pzhi-ka-za-ňe) n. commandment; injunction

przyklasnac (pzhi-klas-nownch) v. applaud;commend;praise

przykleic (pzhi-kle-eech) v. stick; glue; paste; stick on (stamp etc.)

przyklękac (pzhi-klan-kach) v. genuflect; bend the knee

przykład (pzhi-kwat) m. example; instance; pattern; sample

przykładac (pzhi-kwa-dach) v. 1. apply;affix; lend a hand; 2. beat up with;.apply a force

przykładny (pzhi-kwad-ni) adj. m. exemplary; model(husband)

przykrajac (pzhi-kra-yach) v. cut off; cut out(garments etc.)

przykrawac (pzhi-kra-vach) v. cut out(garments etc.);cut off

przykręcac (pzhi-kraň-tsach) v. screw on; 2. turn tight

przykrosc (pzhi-kroshch) f. annoyance;irritation;vexation

przykry (pzhi-kri) adj. m. disagreeable;painful;nasty;bad

przykrywac (pzhi-kri-vach) v. cover; roof over

przykrywka (pzhi-kriv-ka) f. lid; cover (of friendship etc.)

przykrzyc się (pzhi-kzhich shaň) v. be bored; have nothing to do;pall on;weary;long

przykucnąc (pzhi-koots-nownch) v. squat down;crouch; squat

przykuc (pzhi-kooch) v. 1. hammer; 2. arrest(attention);chain;grip;rivet;fascinate

przylatywac (pzhi-la-ti-vach) v. fly in; fly into (a room)

przylądek (pzhi-lown-dek) m. cape ; tip of land; headland

przyleciec (pzhi-le-chech) v. fly in; arrive;come running

przylegac (pzhi-le-gach) v. 1. fit; cling; 2. adjoin

przyległy (pzhi-leg-wi) adj. m. adjacent;adjoining;contiguous

przylepic (pzhi-le-peech) v. stick; glue on;stick to;post

przylepiec (pzhi-le-pyets) m. adhesive; tape; court plaster

przylgnąc (pzhil-gnownch) v. stick; cling; adhere;nestle up

przylot (pzhi-lot) m. plane arrival(of an airplane)

przylutowac (pzhi-loo-to-vach) v. solder on; sweat on

przyłączac (pzhi-wown-chach) v. annex; join; add;connect;attach przyłączenie (pzhi-wown-ché-ne) n. annexation;incorporation

przyłbica (pzhiw-bee-tsa) f. visor; beaver;welder's helmet

przymawiać (pzhi-máv-yach) v. criticize;rebuke;pinprick;nettle

przymawiać się (pzhi-máv-yach śháń) v. hint around for

przymiarka (pzhi-myár-ka) f. fitting on; trying on clothes

przymierać (pzhi-mye-rach) v. starve;be half dead;be dying

przymierzać (pzhi-mye-zhach) v. try on;set to; apply to

przymierze (pzhi-mye-zhe) n. alliance; covenant; Testament

przymierzyć (pzhi-mye-zhich) v. try on; set on; apply to

przymieszka (pzhi-myésh-ka) f. admixture;addition;modicum;dash

przymiot (pzhi-myot) m. (man's) quality; trait; attribute

przymiotnik (pzhi-myót-ńeek) m. adjective (grammar)

przymknięty (pzhim-knáń-ti) adj. m. half-closed; shut up

przymocować (pzhi-mo-tso-vach) v. fasten; fix; secure;attach

przymówka (pzhi-móov-ka) f.gibe; hint; allusion;scoff;jeer

przymrozek (pzhi-mró-zek) m. slight frost;ground frost

przymrużyć oczy (pzhi-mroo-zhich o-chi) blink; narrow one's eyes; wink

przymus (pzhi-moos) m. compulsion; constraint; coersion

przymusić (pzhi-moo-śheech) v. compel;force;oblige;coerce

przymusowy (pzhi-moo-so-vi) adj. m. obligatory;coercive;forced

przynaglać (pzhi-nag-lach) v. urge; haste; push on;hustle;spur

przynajmniej (pzhi-náy-mńey) adv. at least;at any rate;anyway

przynależeć (pzhi-na-lé-zhech) v. belong; be member(of a party)

przynależność (pzhi-na-lezh-nośhćh) f.(nationality) membership;affiliation;(national)status

przynależny (pzhi-na-lézh-ni) adj. m. belonging; appurtenant

przynęta (pzhi-náń-ta) f. bait; lure; enticement; lure; decoy

przynosić (pzhi-no-śheech) v. 1. bring; fetch; 2. bear; yield; bring(profit);afford

przyobiecać (pzhi-obye-tsach) v. promise; give a promise

przyobiecywać (pzhi-ob-ye-tsí-vach) v. promise;give a promise

przypadać (pzhi-pá-dach) v. be due; fall; come ; happen

przypadek (pzhi-pá-dek) m. event; chance; case; incident

przypadkiem (pzhi-pád-ḱem) adv. by chance; accidentally

przypadkowo (pzhi-pad-kó-vo) adv. accidentally;unintentionally

przypadłość (pzhi-pád-wośhćh) f. affliction; ailment; disease

przypalić (pzhi-pa-leech) v. singe; burn; smoke;scorch;sear

przypasać (pzhi-pá-sach) v. attach (to belt); grid on

przypatrywać się (pzhi-pa-trí-vach śháń) v. observe; look at; contemplate;have a look at

przypatrzyć się (pzhi-pá-tzhich śháń) v. observe;contemplate

przypędzać (pzhi-páń-dzach) v. 1. come in haste; 2. drive (to)

przypiąć (pzhi-pyówńch) v. pin; fasten;attach;buckle; pin on

przypieczętować (pzhi-pye-cháń-tó-vach) v. seal up; confirm

przypisek (pzhi-pee-sek) m. note; postscript; added note

przypisywać (pzhi-pee-sí-vach) v. ascribe; attribute; credit

przypłacać (pzhi-pwa-tsach) v. pay (with life; health; property etc.); pay (dearly)

przypłynąć (pzhi-pwi-nówńch) v. arrive sailing or swimming; come to shore; swim up;sail up

przypływ (pzhi-pwif) m. high tide; inflow;influx; high water

przypodobać się(pshi-po-dó-bach śháń)v.get into good graces

przypominać (pzhi-po-mee-nach) v. remind; recollect;resemble

przypomnienie (pzhi-pom-ńé-ńe) n. reminder; memento;souvenir

przypowieść (pzhi-póv-yeshch)
f. tale; parable; allegory

przyprawa (pzhi-prá-va) f. seasoning; spice;relish;sause

przyprawiać (pzhi-práv-yach)
v. 1. season; 2. cause a loss

przyprowadzać (pzhi-pro-va-
dzach) v. bring along; fetch

przypuszczać (pzhi-poosh-chach)
v. suppose;let approach;admit

przypuszczalnie (pzhi-poosh-
chál-ñe) adv. supposedly

przypuszczalny (pzhi-poosh-
chál-ni) adj. m. supposed

przypuszczenie (pzhi-poosh-che-
ñe) n. guess; supposition

przyroda (pzhi-ro-da) f. nature

przyrodni brat (pzhi-ród-ñee
brát) half brother

przyrodnia siostra (pzhi-ród-ña
shos-tra) half sister

przyrodnik (pzhi-ród-ñeek) m.
naturalist;natural historian

przyrodzony (pzhi-ro-dzó-ni)
adj. m. innate;natural;inborn

przyrost naturalny (pzhi-rost
na-too-rál-ni) birthrate

przyrostek (pzhi-rós-tek) m.
suffix (grammar)

przyrząd (pzhi-zhównd) m. instrument;tool; appliance;device

przyrządzać (pzhi-zhówn-dzach)
v. make ready; prepare;cook

przyrzeczenie (pzhi-zhe-che-ñe)
n. promise; plighted word

przyrzekać (pzhi-zhe-kach) v.
promise to do(something)

przysadka (pzhi-sád-ka) f. pi-
tuitary gland; stipule

przysądzać (pzhi-sówn-dzach) v.
award; adjudge; allocate

przysiad (pzhi-shad) m. squat

przysiadać (pzhi-sha-dach) v.
sit down; crouch; sit up

przysięga (pzhi-shan-ga) f.
oath; sworn attestation

przysięgać (pzhy-shan-gach) v.
swear to do; take an oath

przysięgły (pzhy-shang-wi)adj.
m. sworn (jury man)

przysłać (pzhi-swach) v. send in

przysłaniać (pzhi-swa-ñach) v.
shade; vail;cover up;screen

przysłona (pzhi-swo-na) f. veil;
shade; screen; diaphragm; stop

przysłowie (pzhi-swov-ye) n.
proverb; by word

przysłówek (pzhi-swoo-vek) m.
adverb (grammar)

przysłuchiwać się (pzhi-swoo-
khee-vach shań) v. listen to

przysługa (pzhi-swoo-ga) f.
service;good turn;favor;kindness

przysługiwać (pzhi-swoo-gee-
vach) v. to have right;be vested

przysłużyć się (pzhi-swoo-shich
shań) v. render service

przysmak (pzhis-mak) m. delicacy

przysmażyć (pzhi-sma-zhich) v.
roast; fry a little; brown;devil

przysparzać (pzhi-spa-zhach) v.
1. increase; add to 2. cause
(trouble);bring unpleasantness

przyśpieszać (pzhish-pye-shach)
v. accelerate; urge;speed up

przyśpieszenie (pzhish-pye-she-
ñe) n. acceleration;speeding up

przysposabiać (pzhis-po-sab-yach)
prepare; adapt; adopt;fit;qualify

przystać (pzhis-tach) v. join;
comply;cohere;fit together;befit

przystanąć (pzhi-sta-nównch) v.
stop; pause; halt

przystanek (pzhi-sta-nek) m.
stop; station; bus stop etc.

przystań (pzhi-stań) f. small
(boat) harbor(inland); port

przystawać (pzhi-sta-vach) v.
fit; enlist; coincide; halt

przystawiać (pzhi-stav-yach) v.
place near; set against; put

przystawka (pzhi-stav-ka) f.
side dish; hors-doeuvre

przystęp (pzhi-stańp) m. access

przystępny (pzhi-stańp-ni) adj.
m. 1. accessible; 2. moderate

przystojny (pzhi-stóy-ni) adj.
m. handsome; decent; suitable

przystosować (pzhi-sto-so-vach)
v. adjust; fit;accomodate;adapt

przystrajać (pzhi-stra-yach) v.
decorate; adorn; dress; trim

przysunąć (pzhi-soo-nównch) v.
move near; push nearer

przyswajać (pzhi-sva-yach) v.
acquire; assimilate; adopt(ways)

przysyłać (pzhi-si-wach) v.
send; send along; send up

przysypać (pzhi-si-pach) v. cover (with earth; snow etc.)

przyszłość (pzhish-woshch) f.
future; days to come; the future

przyszyć (pzhi-shich) v. sew on

przyszykować (pzhi-shi-ko-vach)
v. prepare; make ready

przyśnić się (pzhish-ñeech shañ)
v. appear in a dream

przyśrubować (pzhi-shroo-bo-vach)
v. screw on; screw down

przyświadczyć (pzhi-shviad-chich) v. agree with; attest

przytaczać (pzhi-ta-chach) v.
quote; cite; wheel up; bring up

przytakiwać (pzhi-ta-kee-vach)
v. say yes; assent; acquiesce

przytępić (pzhi-tañ-peech) v.
dull; blunt somewhat; dim; befog

przytępienie (pzhi-tañ-pye-ñe)
n. dullness; bluntness

przytknąć (pzhit-knownch) v.
place touching; set to; apply to

przytłaczać (pzhi-twa-chach) v.
overwhelm; press to earth; crush

przytłumić (pzhi-twoo-meech) v.
damp; deaden; stifle; subdue; dim

przytoczyć (pzhi-to-chich) v.
quote; cite; roll up; bring up

przytomnie (pzhi-tom-ñe) adv.
with presence of mind; lucidly

przytomność (pzhi-tom-noshch)
f. consciousness; (one's) senses

przytomny (pzhi-tom-ni) adj.m.
conscious; quickwitted

przytrafiać się (pzhi-traf-yach
shañ) v. happen; occur; befall

przytrzymać (pzhi-tzhi-mach) v.
hold; detain; keep in place; arrest

przytulić (pzhi-too-leech) v.
snuggle; cuddle; hug; cuddle; fold

przytułek (pzhi-too-wek) n.
shelter; alms house; poor house

przytwierdzić (pzhi-tvyerdżheech)
v. fasten; fix; attach; assent

przytyk (pzhi-tik) m. dig; allusion; tilt; reference; junction

przytykać (pzhi-ti-kach) v.
1. adjoin; 2. set; apply; border

przy tym (pzhi-tim) adv. besides

przyuczać (pzhi-oo-chach) v.
train; accustom an animal

przywabiać (pzhi-vab-yach) v.
decoy; allure; lure

przywara (pzhi-va-ra) f. vice;
fault; defect; shortcoming

przywiązać (pzhi-vyown-zach) v.
bind; tie; attach; hitch; lash; fasten

przywdziewać (pzhi-vdźhe-vach)
v. put on (clothes)

przywidzenie (pzhi-vee-dze-ñe)
n. illusion; delusion; phantasm

przywieźć (pzhi-vyeżhch) v.
import; bring; drive up; recall

przywilej (pzhi-vee-ley) m.
privilege; prerogative; charter

przywitać (pzhi-vee-tach) v.
welcome; greet; bid good morning

przywłaszczać (pzhi-vwash-chach) v. usurp; appropriate

przywodzić (pzhi-vo-dźheech) v.
lead; bring about; remind; drive

przywłaszczenie (pzhi-vwash-che-ñe) n. appropriation;
usurpation (of rights etc.)

przywołać (pzhi-vo-wach) v.
summon; call in; signal; sign

przywozić (pzhi-vo-żheech) v.
bring (by car); import; deliver

przywódca (pzhi-vood-tsa) m.
leader; ringleader; chieftain

przywóz (pzhi-voos) m. import;
delivery; transport; carriage

przywracać (pzhi-vra-tsach) v.
restore; bring back; reappoint

przywrócenie (pzhi-vroo-tse-ñe)
n. restoration; reinstatement

przywyknąć (pzhi-vik-nownch) v.
get accustomed; get used

przyznać (pzhi-znach) v. award;
admit; allow; acknowledge; grant

przyzwalać (pzhi-zva-lach) v.
consent; approve; agree; concede

przyzwoitość (pzhi-zvo-ee-toshch) f. decency; propriety

przyzwoity (pzhi-zvo-ee-ti) adj.
m. decent; proper; seemly; suitable

przyzwolenie (pzhi-zvo-le-ñe)
n. consent; acquiescence

przyzwyczajać (pzhi-zvi-cha-yach) v. accustom; habituate

przyzwyczajenie (pzhi-zvi-cha-ye-ne) n. habit; custom

przyzywać (pzhi-zi-vach) v. call in ; call sb;beckon;sign

psalm (psalm) m. psalm

pseudonim (psew-do-ñeem) m. pseudonym; pen name

psiarnia (pshar-ña) f. kennel

psie pieniądze (pshe pye-nown-dze) dirt cheap; dog cheap

psikus (pshee-koos) m. prank

psota (pso-ta) f. prank; mischief; practical joke; trick

psotnik (psot-ñeek) m. prankster; practical joker;scamp

pstrąg (pstrowng) m. trout; kelt

pstry (pstri) adj. m. 1. mottled; speckled; 2. uncertain;freaked

psuć (psooch) v. spoil; decay; waste; corrupt; deprave; damage;put out of order;mess up

psychiatra (psi-khyat-ra) m. psychiatrist; shrink; alienist

psychiczny (psi-kheech-ni) adj. m. mental(state,disease etc.)

psycholog (psi-kho-lok) m. psychologist; behaviorist

pszczelarstwo (pzhche-lar-stvo) n. beekeeping ; apiculture

pszczelarz (pshche-lash) m. beekeeper; apiarist

pszczoła (pshcho-wa) f. bee

pszenica (pshe-ñee-tsa) f. wheat

ptactwo (ptats-tvo) pl. fowl; birds; the species of birds

ptak (ptak) m. bird;fowl

ptaszek (pta-shek) m. little bird; small bird; rogue

publicysta (poo-blee-tsis-ta) m. columnist; journalist

publiczność (poo-bleech-noshch) pl. public;community; audience

publikacja (poo-blee-kats-ya) f. publication;something published

puch (pookh) m. down;fluff

puchacz (poo-khach) m. eagle owl(night bird of prey)

puchar (poo-khar) m. cup; bowl

puchlina wodna (poo-khlee-na wod-na)f.dropsy ;hydropsy

puchnąć (pookh-nownch) v. swell

puchowy (poo-kho-vi) adj. m. downy;fluffy;eiderdown

pucołowaty (poo-tso-wo-va-ti) adj. m. chubby cheeked

pucz (pooch) m. Putsch

pudełko (poo-dew-ko) n. box (small); tin ; can;hand box

puder (poo-der) m. powder

puderniczka (poo-der-ñeech-ka) f. powder box; compact;puff box

pukać (poo-kach)v. knock ;rap

pugilares (poo-gee-la-res) m. billfold; pocket book;wallet

pukiel (poo-kel) m. curl;lock

pula (poo-la) f. pool;kitty

pularda (poo-lar-da) f. poularde; fowl

pulchny (pool-khni) adj. m. plump;mellow;loose;spongy

pulower (poo-lo-ver) m. pullover (sweater)

pulpit (pool-peet) m. desk; lectern; shelf;book rest

puls (pools) m. pulse;vibration

pulsować (pool-so-vach) v. pulsate;palpitate;throb;vibrate

pułap (poo-wap) m. ceiling

pułapka (poo-wap-ka) f. trap

pułk (poowk) m. regiment;group

pułkownik (poow-kov-ñeek) m. colonel; group captain

pumeks (poo-meks) m. pumice

punkt (poonkt) m. point; mark

punktualny (poonk-too-al-ni) adj. m. punctual;exact;prompt

pupa (poo-pa) f. behind; buttocks; bottom

pupil (poo-peel) m. ward; pupil; favorite

purchawka (poor-khav-ka) f. 1. puff-ball; 2. grumpy fellow

purpura (poor-poo-ra) f. purple

purytanin (poo-ri-ta-ñeen) m. Puritan;man of strict religion

pustelnia (poos-tel-ña) f. hermitage;solitary secluded place

pustelnik (poos-tel-ñeek) m. hermit; recluse

pustka (poost-ka) f. solitude; empty (place);emptiness;void

pustkowie (poost-kov-ye) n. deserted place;desert;solitude

pustoszyć (poos-to-shich) v. devastate;ravage;lay waste;ruin

pusty (poos-ti) adj.m. empty

pustynia (poos-ti-ña) f. desert

puszcza (poosh-cha) f. primeval forest; wilderness

puszczac (poosh-chach) v. let go; let fall; set afloat; free; fade; drop; let out; emit; start

puszczac się (poosh-chach shan) v. draw apart; let go; be a permissive girl; go to bed with

puszek (poo-shek) m. down

puszka blaszana (poosh-ka blasha-na) tin can; tin box

puszysty (poo-shis-ti) adj. m. downy; fluffy; flossy; flaky; nappy

puscic (poosh-cheech) v. let go; let free; release; let fall

puzon (poo-zon) m. trombone (one octave lower than trumpet)

pycha (pi-kha) f. 1. pride; 2. excellent tidbit; fine stuff

pykac (pi-kach) v. puff; pop

pylic (pi-leech) v. dust; be dusty

pył (piw) m. dust; powder

pyskowac (pis-ko-vach) v. be saucy; bark; bawl

pysk (pisk) m. muffle; snout; mug; muzzle; phiz; rowdyism

pyskaty (pis-ka-ti) adj. m. foulmouthed; saucy; pert; bawling

pyszałek (pi-sha-wek) m. boaster; braggart; coxcomb

pysznic się (pish-ñeech shan) v. swagger; prance; swank; strut

pysznie (pish-ñe) adv. proudly; admirably; in grand fashion

pytac (pi-tach) v. ask; inquire; question; interrogate

pytanie (pi-ta-ñe) n. question; inquiry; query; interrogation

pytel (pi-tel) m. bolter

pytlowac (pi-tlo-vach) v. sift; bolt (flour); be a chatterbox

pyton (pi-ton) m. python

pyza (pi-za) f. dumpling

pyzaty (pi-za-ti) adj. m. chubby

rab (rab) m. slave; servant

rabarbar (ra-bar-bar) m. rhubarb

rabat (ra-bat) m. discount; rebate; reduction (in price)

rabin (ra-been) m. rabbi

rabowac (ra-bo-vach) v. rob; maraud; plunder; pirate; take by force; steal

rabunek (ra-boo-nek) m. robbery; plunder; holdup; spoliation

rabus (ra-boosh) m. robber; plunderer; pillager

rachityczny (ra-khee-tich-ni) adj. m. rickety; rachitic

rachmistrz (rakh-meestsh) m. accountant; calculator; reckoner

rachowac (ra-kho-vach) v. calculate; count; reckon; compute; rely

rachunek (ra-khoo-nek) m. bill; account; count; calculation; sum

rachunkowosc (ra-khoon-ko-voshch) f. bookkeeping

racica (ra-chee-tsa) f. cloven hoof; cow hoof

racja (rats-ya) f. reason; right; ration; propriety; correctness

racjonalizowac (ra-tsyo-na-lee-zo-vach) v. rationalize; improve

racjonalny (ra-tsyo-nal-ni) adj. m. rational; reasonable

raczej (ra-chey) adv. rather; sooner; rather than

raczkowac (rach-ko-vach) v. go on all fours; crawl on all four

raczyc (ra-chich) v. deign; be pleased; treat; condescend; stoop

rad (rad) adj. m. 1. pleased; glad 2. m. radium

rada (ra-da) f. advice; counsel

radar (ra-dar) m. radar

radca (rad-tsa) m. advisor; counselor; legal advisor

radcostwo (rad-tsos-tvo) n. councillorship; post of advisor

radio (rad-yo) n. radio; wireless; broadcasting (system)

radiofonia (ra-dyo-fo-ña) f. broadcasting; radiotelephony

radioaktywny (rad-yo-ak-tiv-ni) adj. m. radioactive

radiostacja (rad-yi-stats-ya) f. radio station

radiodepesza (rad-yo-de-pe-sha) f. radiotelegram

radioterapia (rad-yo-te-rap-ya) f. radiotherapy; X-ray therapy

radny (rad-ni) m. alderman

radosny (ra-dos-ni) adj. m. gay; glad; festive (day etc.)

radosc (ra-doshch) f. joy; gladness; delight; merriment; glee

radykalny (ra-di-kal-ni) adj. m.
  radical;man of radical views
radykał (ra-di-kaw) m. radical
radzić (ra-dźheech) v. deliberate; suggest; advice;counsel
radziecki (ra-dźhets-kee) adj.
  m. Soviet;of Soviet Union
rafa (ra-fa) f. reef;rim;ripple
rafineria (ra-fee-ner-ya) f.
  refinery; refining works
rafinować (ra-fee-no-vach) f.
  refine; purify; distil
raid (rayd) m.sport rally (race)
raj (ray) m. paradise; heaven
rak (rak) m. crayfish; cancer
rakieta (ra-ke-ta) f. 1. rocket; flare; 2. (tennis) racket
rama (ra-ma) f. frame;scheme;case
ramię (ra-myań) n. shoulder
ramowy (ra-mo-vi) adj. m. frame
rampa (ram-pa) f. ramp; loading
  platform;bar;barier; float
rana (ra-na) f. wound;injury;sore
randka (rand-ka) f. date
ranek (ra-nek) m. morning; day-
  break; break of day
ranga (ran-ga) f. rank; standing
ranic (ra-ńeech) v. wound; hurt
ranny (ran-ni) adj. m. 1. wounded; injured; 2. morning; early
rano (ra-no) adv. 1. early;
  2. morning; forenoon;too early
rapier (ra-pyer) m. rapier
raport (ra-port) m. report; account; statement; log
raptem (rap-tem) adv. suddenly;
  abruptly;no more than;all in all
raptowny (rap-tov-ni) adj. m.
  abrupt; sudden;impulsive;heady
rasa (ra-sa) f. race; stock;
  breed ;(plant)variety; blood
rasizm (ra-sheezm) m. racism
rasowy (ra-so-vi) adj. m. racial;
  thoroughbred;purebred;racy
raszpla (rash-pla) f. rasp
rata (ra-ta) f. instalment (payment);part payment(system)
ratować (ra-to-vach) v. rescue;
  save; deliver(from danger)
ratownictwo (ra-tov-ńeets-tvo) n.
  life saving (system)
ratownik (ra-tov-ńeek) m. lifeguard; rescuer; life saver

ratunek (ra-too-nek) m. rescue;
  salvation;help;assistance;resort
ratunkowy pas (ra-toon-ko-vi
  pas) m. life belt; life jacket
ratusz (ra-toosh) m. city hall
ratyfikacja (ra-ti-fee-kats-
  ya) f. ratification
raut (rawt) m. evening party
raz (ras) m. 1. one time;
  2. blow; stroke; buffet
raz (ras) adv. once; at one
  time; at last; time being
razem (ra-zem) adv. together
razić (ra-źheech) v. 1. strike;
  2. offend; 3. dazzle; shock;hit
razowy (ra-zo-vi) adj. m. brown
  (bread); whole meal (bread)
razowiec (ra-zo-vyets) m. whole
  meal bread; brown bread
rażący (ra-zhown-tsy) adj. m.
  1. glaring; 2. flagrant; rank
raźnie (raźh-ńe) adv. cheerfully; briskly; at a lively pace
rąb (rownb) m. rim;pane;clearing
rąbać (rown-bach) v. 1. chop;hew;
  2. say truth to face ; slash
rączka (rownch-ka) f. handle;
  small hand; handgrip;holder
rączy (rown-chi) adj. m. swift
rdza (rdza) f. rust;mildew;blight
rdzenny (rdzen-ni) adj. m.
  essential; original;specific
rdzeń (rdzeń) m. core; pith;
  marrow; gist; essence; log
rdzoodporny (rdzo-od-por-ni)
  adj. rust-proof;stainless
reagować (re-a-go-vach) v.
  react; respond;be suscrptible
rdzewieć (rdze-vyech) v. corrode;
  rust; get rusty; gather rust
reakcja (re-ak-tsya) f. reaction
reakcjonista (re-ak-tsyo-ńees-
  ta) m. reactionary ;
reakcyjny (re-ak-tsiy-ni) adj.
  m. reactionary;retrograde
reaktywować (re-ak-ti-vo-vach)
  v. 1. start again; 2. reacti-
  vate;bring back to life;recall
realia (re-al-ya) pl. realia;
  realities
realista (re-a-lees-ta) m. re-
  alist; advocate of realism
realizm (re-a-leezm) m. realism

realizować (re-a-lee-zó-vach) v.
actualize; realize;cash(assets)

realność (re-al-nośhch) f. 1.
real estate;2. reality;the real

realny (re-ál-ni) adj. m. real;
concrete; actual;genuine;true

rebelia (re-bél-ya) f. rebellion;uprising against government

recenzent (re-tsen-zent) m.critic
reviewer (of books, plays, etc.)

recenzja (re-tsen-zya) f. review (of books, plays, etc.)

recepcja (re-tsep-tzya) f. reception;formal social function

recepis (re-tse-pees) m. receipt; recipe;written receipt

recepta (re-tsep-ta) f. pre-
scription; doctor's order

rechot (re-khot) m. shrieking
laughter; croak(of forgs)

recydywista (re-tsi-di-vees-ta)
m. recidivist;old offender

recytować (re-tsi-to-vach) v.
recite;give a recitation

redagować (re-da-go-vach) v.
edit;draw up;formulate;draft

redakcja (re-dak-tsya) f. 1.
editing; 2. editors office

redaktor (re-dak-tor) m. editor

redukcja (re-dook-tsya) f. re-
duction(in size,price etc.)

redukować (re-doo-kó-vach) v.
reduce; lay off;cut down

referat (re-fé-rat) m. report

referencja (re-fe-rén-tsya) f.
reference; testimonial

referent (re-fe-rent) m. clerk

refleks (re-fleks) m. reflex

refleksja (re-fleks-ya) f. reflection; thought; cogitation

reflektor (re-flek-tor) m. re-
flector; searchlight;headlight

reflektować (re-flek-to-vach)
v. 1. apply for; want; 2. reflect;bring to reason;moderate

reforma (re-for-ma) f. reform

reformacja (re-for-máts-ya) f.
reformation; Reformation

reformować (re-for-mo-vach) v.
reform; reorganize

regaty (re-gá-ti) pl. boat race

regencja (re-gén-tsya) f. regency; regency style

regionalny (re-gyo-nál-ni)
adj. regional; local

regulacja (re-goo-láts-ya) f.
regulation;control;regulator

regularny (re-goo-lár-ni) adj.
m. regular; even;systematic

regulować (re-goo-lo-vach) v.
1. regulate control 2. settle

reguła (re-góo-wa) f. rule

rehabilitować (re-kha-bee-lee-
to-vach) v. rehabilitate

reja (re-ya) f. yardarm

rejent (re-yent) m. notary
public; notary; regent

rejestr (re-yestr) m. register;
file; index;roll;register mark

rejestracja (re-yes-tráts-ya)
f. registration; licensing

rejestrować (re-yes-tro-vach)
v. register; enroll;record

rejon (re-yon) m. region

rejwach (rey-vakh) m. uproar;
hullabaloo;row;hurly-burly

rekin (re-keen) m. shark

reklama (rek-lá-ma) f. advertising; commercial publicity

reklamacja (re-kla-máts-ya) f.
complaint;demand for compensation

reklamować (re-kla-mo-vach) v.
1. complain; 2. advertise

rekolekcje (re-ko-lék-tsye) pl.
retreat;period of contemplation

rekomendacja (re-ko-men-dáts-
ya) f. recommendation;reference

rekompensata (re-kom-pen-sá-ta)
f. compensation;recompense

rekonvalescent (re-kon-va-lés-
cent) m. convalescent

rekord (re-kord) m. (sports)
record; (world) record

rekordzista (re-kor-dżhees-ta)
m. record holder;champion

rekreacja (re-kre-áts-ya) f.
recreation;opposing action

rekrut (rék-root) m. recruit;
conscript;recently enlisted man

rekrutować (re-kroo-to-vach)
v. recruit; enlist(new people)

rektor (rék-tor) m. university
president;university head

rektyfikować (rek-ti-fee-kó-
vach)v. rectify;correct; put
right; purify

rekwizycja (rek-vee-zits-ya) f.
  requisition;seizure
relacja (re-lats-ya) f. 1. report; 2. rate; relation
relatywizm (re-la-ti-veezm) m.
  relativity; relativism
relegacja (re-le-gats-ya) f.
  expulsion; relegation
religia (re-leeg-ya), f. religion
religijny (re-lee-geey-ni) adj.
  m. religious; godly
relikwia (re-leek-vya) f. relic
remanent (re-ma-nent) m. remainder; inventiry;stock
remis (re-mees) m. (sport)draw
remiza (re-mee-za) f. engine-
  shed ; engine-house; depot;barn
remont (re-mont) m. 1. repair;
  2. (horse) remount
remontować (re-mon-to-vaćh) v.
  repair; recondition;overhaul
renumeracja (re-noo-me-rats-ya)
  f. renumeration;recount
ren (ren) m. reindeer; caribou
renegat (re-ne-gat) m. renegade
renifer (re-nee-fer) m. reindeer ;(domesticated)arctic deer
renoma (re-no-ma) f. renown
renta (ren-ta) f. rent ; fixed
  income; annuity; pension
rentowność (ren-tov-nośhćh) f.
  profitability;earning capacity
rentgenolog (rent-ge-no-lok) m.
  radiologist; roentgenologist
rentowny (ren-tov-ni) adj. m.
  profitable;renumerative
reorganizacja (re-or-ga-nee-
  zats-ya) f. reorganization
reparacja (re-pa-rats-ya) f.
  1. repair; 2. reparation
repatriacja (re-pa-tree-ats-ya)
  f. repatriation
reperować (re-pe-ro-vaćh) v.
  mend; repair;fix; set right
repertuar (re-per-too-ar) m.
  repertory; repertoire
repetycja (re-pe-tits-ya) f.
  repetition(of a lesson etc.)
replika (rep-lee-ka) f. 1, re-
  plica; 2. rebuttal; 3. (theatre)cue; retort;rejoinder
replikować (re-plee-ko-vaćh) v.
  answer back; rejoin; retort

reportaż (re-por-tash) m. 1.
  account; 2. reporting; commentary;coverage (of event etc.)
represja (re-pres-ya) f.
  reprisal;repressive measures
reprezentacja (re-pre-zen-tats-
  ya) f. representation
reprezentant (re-pre-zen-tant)
  m. representative
reprezentować (re-pre-zen-to-
  vaćh) v. represent; display
reprodukcja (re-pro-dook-tsya)
  f. reproduction;copy;replica
republika (re-poob-lee-ka) f.
  republic
republikański (re-poob-lee-kań-
  skee) adj. m. republican
reputacja (re-poo-táts-ya) f.
  reputation; (character)
resor (re-sor) m. (car) spring
resort (re-sort) m. 1. agency;
  2. competence;scope;province
respekt (res-pekt) m. respect
restauracja (res-taw-rats-ya)
  f. 1. restaurant; 2. restoration (of objects of art etc.)
restrykcja (res-trik-tsya) f.
  restriction; reservation
restytucja (res-ti-toots-ya)
  f. restitution; restoration
reszta (resh-ta) f. rest; reminder; change; residue
retoryka (re-to-ri-ka) f. rhetoric;manual of rhetoric
retusz (re-toosh) m. retouch
retuszować (re-too-sho-vaćh)
  v. touch up; retouch
reumatyczny (re-oo-ma-tich-ni)
  adj. m. rheumatic
reumatyzm (re-oo-ma-tizm) m.
  rheumatism(pain in joint etc.)
rewanż (re-vansh) m. 1. rematch;
  2. revenge; get back at
rewelacja (re-ve-lats-ya) f.
  revelation;striking disclosure
rewers (re-vers) m. 1. receipt;
  2. reverse (side etc.)
rewia (rev-ya) f. 1. parade;
  2. (theatre) revue
rewidować (re-vee-do-vaćh) v.
  1. revise; 2. search; 3. audit
rewizja (re-veez-ya) f. revision
  search;audit;inspection;retrial

rewizjonizm (re-veez-yo-ñeezm)
m. revisionism

rewizyta (re-vee-zi-ta) f. return visit

rewolucja (re-vo-loots-ya) f.
revolution;complete change

rewolucyjny (re-vo-loo-tsiy-ni)
adj. m. revolutionary

rewolwer (re-vol-ver) m. revolv-
er; gun (with revolv.cylinder)

rezerva (re-zer-va) f. reserve

rezerwat (re-zer-vat) m. reservation;game preserve

rezerwować (re-zer-vo-vach) v.
reserve; set aside; book

rezerwuar (re-zer-voo-ar) m.
reservoir;(storage)tank

rezolutny (re-zo-loot-ni) adj.
m. resolute;determined; game

rezonans (re-zo-nans) m. reso-
nance(intesifying vibrations)

rezultat (re-zool-tat) m. result; effect; numerical answer

rezydencja (re-zi-den-tsya) f.
residence;dwelling place

rezydent (re-zi-dent) m. resi-
dent(not a transient)

rezygnacja (re-zig-nats-ya) f.
resignation;patient submission

reżim (re-zheem) m. regime

reżyser (re-zhi-ser) m. stage
manager; (film) director

ręcznie (rañch-ñe) adv. by hand

ręcznik (rañch-ñeek) m. towel

ręczny (rañch-ni) adj. m. manual;
hand made; wrist(watch)

ręczyć (rañ-chich) v. guarantee

ręka (rañ-ka) f. hand; arm;touch

rękaw (rañ-kav) m. sleeve

rękawica (rañ-ka-vee-tsa) f.
mitten; gauntlet;mitt;glove

rękawiczka (rañ-ka-veech-ka) f.
glove(fur lined,velvet, etc.)

rękodzielnik (rañ-ko-dzhel-ñeek)
m. craftsman;handicraftsman

rękojeść (rañ-ko-yeshch) f. hilt;
handle; handgrip; helve

rękojmia (rañ-koy-mya) f. guaranty; pledge; gage;warranty

rękopis (rañ-ko-pees) m. manuscript; script; MS

robactwo (ro-bats-tvo) n.vermin·

robak (ro-bak) m. worm;beetle;grub

rober (ro-ber) m. (bridge) rubber (in card game)

robić (ro-beech) v. make; do;act;
work; become; get;feel;turn;knit

robociarz (ro-bo-chash) m. common laborer (slang); mechanic

robocizna (ro-bo-cheez-na) f.
wages;cost of labor; labor

roboczogodzina (ro-bo-cho-go-
dżhee-na)f. man-hour

robot (ro-bot) m. robot

robota (ro-bo-ta) f. work; job

robotnica (ro-bot-ñee-tsa) f.
worker (bee) ; operative;mechanic

robotnik (ro-bot-ñeek) m. worker; worker;operative;mechanic

robótki (ro-boot-kee) pl.
needlework; fancy work

rocznica (roch-ñee-tsa) f.
anniversary

rocznie (roch-ñe) adv. yearly

rocznik (roch-ñeek) m. annual;
yearbook; annual set; age group

roczny (roch-ni) adj. m. annual; one year's (duration etc.)

rodak (ro-dak) m. compatriot

rodowity (ro-do-vee-ti) adj.
m. native; by birth; trueborn

rodowód (ro-do-voot) m. genealogy; origin;pedigree;descent

rodzaj (ro-dzay) m. kind; sort;
gender;type; race; manner;aspect

rodzajnik (ro-dzay-ñeek) m. article (definite or indefinite)

rodzeństwo (ro-dzeñ-stvo) n.
brothers and sisters

rodzice (ro-dzhee-tse)pl. par-
ents;father and mother

rodzić (ro-dzheech)v. bear;
procreate breed; yield (crops)

rodzina (ro-dżhee-na)f. family

rodzinny (ro-dzheñ-ni)adj. m.
family; native; home(life etc.)

rodzynek (ro-dzi-nek) m. raisin;
currant

rogacz (ro-gach) m. 1. stag;
2. cuckold;deceived husband

rogatka (ro-gat-ka) f. tollgate; toll bar; turnpike

rogaty (ro-ga-ti) adj. m..
horned; haughty; deceived
(husband)

rogatywka (ro-ga-tiv-ka) f.
four-cornered cap(Polish style)
rogowacieć (ro-go-va-chech) v.
grow horny;become corneous
rogowaty (ro-go-va-ti) adj.
corneous ; horny
rogówka (ro-goov-ka) f. cornea
rogóżka (ro-goozh-ka) f. (door)
mat (flat,woven of straw etc.)
roić (ro-yeech) v. 1. dream;
imagine; 2. swarm; teem; run
rojalista (ro-ya-lees-ta) m.
royalist; supporter of the king
rojny (roy-ni) adj. m. teeming;
swarming(crowds etc.)
rojowisko (ro-yo-vees-ko) n.
hive; swarm;gathering place
rok (rok) m. year;a twelvemonth
rok przestępny (rok pzhe-stahp-
ni) leap year
rokować (ro-ko-vach) v. 1. negotiate 2. expect; promise
rokowania (ro-ko-va-ña) pl. 1.
negotiations; 2. prognosis
rola (ró-la) f. 1. arable land
2. (theatre) part;scroll;weight
rolka (ról-ka) f. roll; spool;
reel;runner;pulley;castor
rolnictwo (rol-ñeets-tvo) v.
agriculture;farming;husbandry
rolnik (rol-ñeek) m. farmer
romans (ró-mans) m. 1. novel;
2. love affair; laison
romantyczny (ro-man-tich-ni) adj.
m. romantic;full of romance
romantyk (ro-man-tik) m. romantic
romantyzm (ro-man-tizm) m. ro-
manticism(literary style etc.)
romański (ro-mań-skee) adj. m.
Romance; Romanesque
romb (romb) m. rhomb;diamond
rondel (ron-del) m. stewpan
rondo (ron-do) n. brim; circular
plaza; traffic circle;circus
ronić (ro-ñeech) v. 1. shed;
2. miscarry;drop;cast;emit;moult
ropa (ró-pa) f. puss; 2. crude
oil;rock oil; naphta;petroleum
ropieć (rop-yech) v. fester;have
oozing sore; suppurate
ropień (rop-yeń) m. abscess
ropny (róp-ni) adj. m. purulent;
oil fired; oil-(derrick etc.)

ropucha (ro-poo-kha) f. toad
rosa (ró-sa) f. dew
rosły (ros-wi) adj. m. tall;
big frame; stalwart
rosnąć (ros-nownch) v. grow
rosół (ró-soow) m. broth;
bouillion; clear soup;pickle
rostbef (rost-bef) m. roast-
beef; baked beef
rosyjski (ro-siy-skee) adj. m.
Russian; of Russia
roszczenie (rosh-che-ñe) n.
claim; pretension; pretence
rościć (rosh-cheech) v. claim
roślina (rosh-lee-na) f. plant;
vegetable; living plant
roślinność (rosh-leen-noshch)
f. flora, ; vegetation
rowek (ro-vek) m. (small) channel; groove; gutter; rut;furrow
rower (ró-ver) n. bike; cycle
rowerzysta (ro-ve-zhis-ta) m.
cyclist
rozbawiony (roz-ba-vyó-ni) adj.
m. merry; amused;in high spirits
rozbestwić (roz-best-veech) v.
enrage;turn into a wild beast
rozbicie (roz-bee-che) n. break;
wreck;jumble;defeat;rout; hurt
rozbić (roz-beech) v. smash;
defeat; wreck;shatter;disrupt
rozbiegać się (roz-bye-gach śhań)
v. scatter; run; swarm (through)

rozbierać (roz-bye-rach) v. undress; strip; dismount; analyze
rozbieżny (roz-byezh-ni) adj. m.
divergent;different;discordant
rozbijać (roz-bee-yach) v. break
up; rout; crush;bluster;storm
rozbiór (róz-byoor) m. 1. analysis; 2. dismemberment;partition
rozbiórka (roz-byoor-ka) f. de-
molition;taking to pieces
rozbitek (roz-bee-tek) m. shipwreck person; castaway; wreck
rozbój (roz-booy) m. robbery;
piracy; banditry;highjacking
rozbójnik (roz-booy-neek) m.
bandit;robber;cutthroat;brigand
rozbrajać (roz-bra-yach) v.
disarm(a person etc.);dismantle
(a ship);appease; pacify

rozbrat (róz-brat) m. split;
disunion;break with somebody

rozbrojenie (roz-bro-ye-ne) n.
disarmament;reduction of arms

rozbrojeniowy (roz-bro-ye-ńo-vi)
adj. m. disarmament

rozbrzmiewać (roz-bzhmyé-vach)
v. resound;ring out; (re)echo

rozbudowa (roz-boo-dó-va) f.
build up; extension;expansion

rozbudować (roz-boo-do-vach) v.
extend;enlarge;expand;develop

rozbudzić (roz-boo-dźheech) v.
rouse up; wake up ;excite;stir

rozchmurzyć (roz-khmoo-zhich)
v. clear up; brighten up

rozchodzić (roz-kho-dźheech) v.
1. stretch (shoes); 2. spread;
3. come apart

rozchód (róz-khoot) m. expendi-
ture; expenses; outgoings

rozchwytać (roz-khvi-tach) v.
snatch up;scramble for;sweep off

rozchylać (roz-khi-lach) v.
open; force apart;spread

rozciągać (roz-chówn-gach) v.
stretch; extend;widen;expand

rozcieńczyć (roz-cheń-chich) v.
thin; dilute; rarefy;attenuate

rozcierać (roz-che-rach) v. rub;
grind;crush;spread (ointment)

rozcinać (roz-chee-nach) v.
cut up; dissect; rip open

rozczarować (roz-cha-ró-vach) v.
disappoint;disenchant

rozczesać (roz-che-sach) v. comb
down;brush out (one's hair)

rozczłonkować (roz-chwon-ko-vach)
v. dismember;divide;break up

rozczulić (roz-choo-leech) v.
move; touch;affect;stir(feelings)

rozczyn (róz-chin) m. solution
(chem.); leaven (yeast)

rozdać (róz-dach) v. distribute

rozdarcie (roz-dár-che) n.
1. tear; 2. disruption

rozdeptać (roz-dep-tach) v.
trample out under foot;tread on

rozdęcie (roz-dáń-che) n. swelling; inflation;expansion

rozdmuchać (roz-dmoo-khach) v.
fan; inflate;blow about;amplify

rozdrapać (roz-dra-pach) v.
1. scratch; 2. snatch up

rozdrażnić (roz-drázh-ńeech)
v. irritate; exaspreate; vex

rozdrobnić (roz-drób-ńeech) v.
split up; divide;crumble;morsel

rozdroże (roz-dro-zhe) n.
crossroads; parting of the ways

rozdwoić (roz-dvo-eech) v.
split; cleave; divide in two

rozdymać (roz-di-mach) v. inflate; swell;expand;puff out

rozdział (róz-dźhaw) m. distribution; disunion; parting
(hair);dispensation;chapter

rozdzielać (roz-dźhe-lach) v.
divide; distribute;set at odds

rozdzierać (roz-dźhe-rach) v.
tear up;tear asunder;rend;pierce

rozdźwięk (róz-dźhvyánk) m.
discord ;dissonance; clash

rozebrać (ro-zéb-rach) v. undress; analyze; take apart

rozedma (ro-zéd-ma) f. emphy-
sema(swelling produced by gas)

rozejm (ro-zeym) m. truce

rozejrzeć się (ro-zéy-zhech
śhań) v. look around

rozejść się (ro-zeyśhch śhań)
v. split; part; separate

rozerwać się (ro-zér-vach śhań)
v. divert oneself;get torn

rozgałęzić (roz-ga-wáń-źheech)
v. branch out; fork off

rozgałęzienie (roz-ga-wáń-źhe-
ńe) n. branching;ramification

rozgardiasz (roz-gard-yash) m.
bustle; chaos; confusion

rozgarnąć (roz-gar-nównch) v.
rake aside; part;brush apart

rozgarnięty (roz-gar-ńáń-ti)
adj. m. bright; clever; sharp

rozglądać się (roz-glówn-dach
śhań) v. look around;look for

rozgłaszać (roz-gwa-shach) v.
make known; broadcast

rozgłos (róz-gwos) m. publicity;
fame; renown;repute;notoriety

rozgłośnia (roz-gwosh-ńa) f.
broadcasting station

rozgmatwać (roz-gmát-vach) v.
disentangle; extricate

rozgnieść (roz-gńeśhćh) v.
flatten; squash (once)
rozgniatać (roz-gńa-taćh) v.
squash; flatten (often)
rozgniewać (roz-gńe-vaćh) v.
anger; vex; irritate
rozgoryczenie (roz-go-ri-che-ńe)
n. bitterness; exasperation
rozgoryczyć (roz-go-ri-chićh) v.
embitter; exacerbate;disgust
rozgotować (roz-go-to-vaćh) v.
cook to a pulp;cook to rags
rozgraniczyć (roz-gra-ńee-chićh)
v. delimit; mark boundaries
rozgromić (roz-gro-meećh) v.
rout(the enemy);crush(an army)
rozgrywać (roz-gri-vaćh) v. play
one's game ;put through;carry out
rozgryźć (roz-griźhćh) v. bite
through;bite in two;crack(nuts)
rozgrzać (roz-gzhaćh) v. warm up
rozgrzebać (roz-gzhe-baćh) v.
dig up; rake up; scatter
rozgrzeszyć (roz-gzhe-shićh) v.
absolve(of sins); forgive
rozgrzewać (roz-gzhe-vaćh) v.
warm up; rouse; stimulate
rozhukany (roz-khoo-ka-ni) adj.
m. wild; unruly;riotus
rozhustać (roz-khoośh-taćh) v.
set swinging; set rocking
roziskrzyć (roz-eéśk-zhićh) v.
start sparkle; make sparkle
rozjaśnić (roz-yaśh-ńeećh) v.
brighten; clear up; clarify
rozjątrzyć (roz-yównt-zhićh) v.
exasperate; irritate; chafe
rozjemca (roz-yém-tsa) m. referee; arbiter; umpire
rozjeżdżać się (roz-yézh-dzhaćh
śhań) v. disperse; part
rozjuszyć (roz-yoo-shićh) v.
enrage;infuriate; exasperate
rozkapryszony (roz-ka-pri-sho-
ni) adj. m. whimsical; fitful
rozkaz (roz-kas) m. order
rozkiełznąć (roz-kéwz-naćh) v.
unbridle; unchain; let loose
rozkleić (roz-kle-eećh) v. 1.
unglue; weaken; 2. post up
rozkład (roz-kvat) m. dissolution;
decay; disposition; timetable ;
train schedule;breakdown

rozkładać (roz-kva-daćh) v. de-
compose; spread; display; stagger (hours);lay out; distribute
rozkołysać (roz-ko-wi-saćh) v.
set rocking; set swinging;agitate
rozkopywać (roz-ko-pi-vaćh) v.
dig up; rip up; make excavations
rozkosz (roz-kosh) f. delight
rozkrajać (roz-kra-yaćh) v.
cut up; carve; slice; divide
rozkręcić (roz-krań-ćheećh) v.
unscrew; unreel;take to pieces
rozkruszyć (roz-kroo-shićh)
v. crush up; grind;disintegrate
rozkrzewić (roz-kzhe-veećh) v.
propagate; increase; diffuse
rozkuć (roz-koóćh) v. unshackle;
unshoe (horse);unchain;hammer out
rozkulbaczyć (roz-kool-ba-chićh)
v. unsaddle; take the saddle off
rozkupić (roz-koó-peećh) v. buy
up; buy everything;buy all
rozkwit (roz-kveet) m. bloom
rozkwitać (roz-kvee-taćh) v.
flower; burst into flower;beam
rozlatywać się (roz-la-ti-vaćh
śhań) v. fly away; break up;
scatter;disperse;run away;burst
rozlaźły (roz-láz-wi) adj. m.
slack; loose;spread out;sloppy
rozległy (roz-lég-wi) adj. m.
spacious; vast; wide;extensive
rozleniwiać (roz-le-ńeev-yaćh)
v. make lazy;induce to laziness
rozlepić (roz-le-peećh) v. post;
put up;paste up;stick;unstick
rozlew (roz-lev) m. flood
rozlew krwi (roz-lev krvee) m.
bloodshed;killing; slaughter
rozlewać (roz-le-vaćh) v. spill;
shed; pour(out);ladle out(soup)
rozliczenie (roz-lee-che-ńe) n.
settling; reckoning;settlement
rozliczny (roz-leech-ni) adj.
m. manifold; diverse;numerous
rozliczyć (roz-lee-chićh) v.
settle up (accounts);calculate
rozlokować (roz-lo-ko-vaćh) v.
put up; make at home; quarter
rozlosować (roz-lo-so-vaćh) v.
allot; distribute by lot
rozluźnić (roz-loóźh-ńeećh) v.
slacken; relax;unfasten

rozluźnienie (roz-loozh-ńe-ńe)
n. loosening;laxity;slackness

rozładować (roz-wa-do-vać) v.
unload; discharge(a battery)

rozłam (róz-wam) m. breach;
split;break;division;dissent

rozłamać (roz-wa-mać) v.
break (in two); split

rozłazić się (roz-wa-zheech
śhań) v. fall apart; disperse

rozłączenie (roz-wown-che-ńe)
n. separation; disjunction

rozłączyć (roz-wown-chich) v.
disconnect;sever;uncouple

rozłąka (roz-wown-ka) f. separation (of people)

rozłożyć (roz-wó-zhich) v.
spread;lay out;disassemble

rozłupać (roz-woo-pać) v.
split; cleave; rift; slit;
crack(nuts,etc.); rive

rozmach (roz-makh) m. impetus;
dash; grand style;force;swing

rozmaitości (roz-ma-ee-tosh-
chee) pl. miscellanea; vaude-
ville theater;variety theater

rozmaity (roz-ma-ee-ti) adj.
m. various; miscellaneous

rozmaryn (roz-ma-rin) m. rose-
mary (Rosmarinus)

rozmarzenie (roz-ma-zhe-ńe) n.
daydream;dreaminess;reverie

rozmawiać (roz-mav-yach) v.
converse; talk; speak with

rozmazać (roz-ma-zach) v. blur;
smear;daub; let out (a secret)

rozmiar (róz-myar) m. dimension;
extent;size;proportion;scale

rozmienić (roz-mye-ńeech) v.
change (money);get the change

rozmieszczać (roz-myesh-chach)
v. arrange; dispose;place;put

rozmieszczenie (roz-myesh-che-
ńe) n. distribution; layout

rozmiękczyć (roz-myank-chich) v.
soften; soak;steep;make soft

rozmięknąć (roz-myank-nownch)
v. become soft ;get soaked;sop

rozmijać się (roz-mee-yach śhań)
v. miss; swerve from;fail to meet

rozmiłować się (roz-mee-wo-vach
śhań) v. take a liking to

rozminąć się(roz-mee-nownch śhań)v.
miss (on road):pass each other

rozmnażać (roz-mna-zhach) v.breed;
multiply; propagate; imcrease

rozmoczyć (roz-mo-chich) v.soak.
steep; wet thoroughly; sodden

rozmoknąć (roz-mok-nownch) v.
become soaked; get soggy

rozmowa (roz-mo-va) f. conversation; talk ;discourse

rozmowny (roz-mov-ni) adj. m.
communicative; talkative

rozmówca (roz-moov-tsa) m.
interlocutor (in conversation)

rozmówić się (roz-moo-veech
śhań) v. talk over;get understood

rozmysł (róz-misw) m. premeditation; consideration; intention

rozmyślać (roz-miśh-lach) v.
meditate; ponder how to do

rozmyślanie (roz-mish-la-ńe) n.
meditation; contemplation

rozmyślić się (roz-miśh-leech
śhań) v. change one's mind

rozmyślny (roz-miśhl-ni) adj.
m. deliberate;intentional;wilful

roznamiętnic (roz-na-myant-
ńeech) v. impassion; excite

rozniecic (roz-ńe-cheech) v.
inflame; enkindle a fire;inspire

roznosić (roz-no-śheech) v.
carry around; serve;rout;cut up

rozochocić (roz-o-kho-cheech)
v. make merry;enliven; animate

rozogniać się (roz-og-nach
śhań) n. inflame; excite;flare up

rozpacz (róz-pach) f. despair

rozpad (róz-pat) m. decay;break up

rozpakować (roz-pa-ko-vać) v.
unpack(one's luggage) ;unwrap

rozpalić (roz-pa-leech) v.fire up;
ignite; start a fire; set ablaze

rozpamiętywać (roz-pa-myan-ti-
vach) v. contemplate ;reflect upon

rozpaplać (roz-pa-plach) v.
blab out;divulge ; babble out

rozpasany (roz-pa-sa-ni) adj. m.
unbridled; dissolute; licentious

rozpatrywać (roz-pa-tri-vach)
v. consider; act upon ;examine

rozpęd (róz-pańt) m. impetus;
dash ;momentum; taking a run

rozpędzać (roz-páń-dzać) v. pick up speed; scatter;disperse

rozpętać (roz-pán-tać) v. unshackle; unleash;let loose

rozpiąć (roz-pyówńch) v. unbuckle; undo; stretch; set (sail)

rozpieczętować (roz-pye-cháńto-vać) v. unseal;open

rozpierać (roz-pye-rać) v. expand; extend; push aside

rozpierzchnać się (roz-pyezh-khówńch śhań) v. scatter

rozpieszczać (roz-pyésh-chać) v. pamper; spoil;coddle up

rozpiętość (roz-pyán-tośhch) f. span; spread; range;strech

rozpinać (roz-pee-nać) v. unbutton; stretch; spread (sails etc.)

rozplątać (roz-plówn-tać) v. untangle;untie(a knot);unravel

rozpleść (roz-leśhch) v. unbraid; untwine; unplait(hair);unravel

rozpłakać się (roz-pwa-kać śhań) v. burst into tears;start weeping

rozpłaszczyć (roz-pwash-chich) v. flatten out; flat (metal)

rozpłatać (roz-pwa-tać) v.slit; split; cleave; split in two

rozpłodowy (roz-pwo-do-vi) adj. m. (for) breeding; breeding-

rozpłodzić (roz-pwó-dźheech) v. propagate;cause reproduction

rozpłód (roz-pwoot) m. propagation; reproduction

rozpływać się(roz-pwi-vać śhań)v. melt away;dissolve; flow;spread

rozpoczęcie (roz-po-cháń-che) n. start; outbreak;beginning;start

rozpoczynać (roz-po-chi-nać) v. begin; start going; open;initiate

rozpogodzić się (roz-po-go-dźheech śhań) v. clear up brighten up;cheer up;rise spirit

rozporek (roz-po-rek) m. fly; slit

rozporządzać (roz-po-zhówn-dzać) v. dispose; decree; order;control

rozpościerać (roz-pośh-che-rać) v. unfurl; spread out;expand

rozpowiadać (roz-po-vya-dać) v. tell tales;divulge; talk about

rozpowszechniać (roz-pov-shekh-ńach) v. widespread; diffuse disseminte;propagate; spread

rozpowszechnienie (roz-pov-shekh-ńe-ńe) n. propagation; spread;diffusion;prevalence

rozpoznać (roz-poz-nać) v. recognize; spot; diagnose

rozpoznanie (roz-po-zna-ńe) n. diagnosis; identification; reconnaissance;recognition

rozpoznawczy (roz-poz-nav-chi) adj. m. diagnostic;distinctive

rozpraszać (roz-prá-shać) v. scatter; dispel; distract;disperse

rozprawa (roz-pra-va) f. trial; showdown; dissertation; debate

rozprawiać (roz-prav-yach) v. debate: argue; dispute; reason; talk at length;discuss

rozprawić się (roz-pra-veech śhań) v. settle matters; fight out;dispose of; floor

rozprężyć (roz-práń-zhich) v. distend; expand; dilate; resile;deprive of elasticity

rozprostować (roz-pros-to-vać) v. straighten;unbend;stretch(legs)

rozproszyć (roz-pró-shich) v. disperse;scatter;dispel;distract

rozprowadzić (roz-pro-va-dźheech) v. spread; retail; distribute; dilute; convey;smear

rozpruć (roz-prooch) v. rip up; open; unsew;unravel;rip open

rozprzedać (roz-pzhe-dach) v. sell out;sell(successively)

rozprzedaż (roz-pzhe-dash) f. sale;complete sale;retailing

rozprzestrzenic (roz-pzhe-stzhe-ńeech) v. spread;propagate

rozprzęgać (roz-pzháń-gać) v. 1. unhitch; 2. disorganize

rozprzężenie (roz-pzhan-zhé-ńe) n. anarchy; demoralization

rozpusta (roz-poós-ta) f. debauch; riot; libertinism

rozpustnica (roz-poost-ńee-tsa) f. rake; rip; libertine; debauchee; profligate; libertine

rozpustnik (roz-poost-ńeek) m. libertine; debauchee; rake; profligate;rip; reprobate

rozpuszczać (roz-poosh-chach) v. dissolve; dismiss; let go; disband;thaw;melt;defrost;unfreeze

rozpuszczalnik (roz-poos-chál-
neek) m. solvent;pain thinner
rozpuszczalny (roz-poos-chál-
ni) adj. m. soluble;dissolvable
rozpychać się (roz-pi-khách
shán) v.shove aside; jostle;
elbow one's way;push one's way
rozpylacz (roz-pí-lach) m.
sprayer; nozzle; atomizer
rozpylać (roz-pí-lach) v. spray;
pulverize; atomize
rozpytywać (roz-pi-ti-vach) v.
ask for;inquire for;ask questions
rozrachować (roz-ra-kho-vach) v.
settle accounts; calculate
rozrachunek (roz-ra-khoo-nek)
m. squaring up accounts
rozradzać się (roz-ra-dzách
shán) v. breed;propagate
rozrastać się (roz-ras-tách
shan) v. grow larger; in-
crease; develop; expand
rozrąbać (roz-równ-bach) v. cut
asunder; hew apart;chop up
rozrobić (roz-ro-beech) v. stir
up; dilute;scheme;intrigue;brawl
rozrodczość (roz-rod-choshch)
f. reproduction;reproductiveness
rozróżniać (roz-roozh-nach) v.
distinguish; tell apart;discern
rozruchy (roz-roo-khy) pl.
riots; disturbances
rozruszać (roz-roo-shach) v.
start up; stir up; put in motion;set in motion;animate
rozrywać (roz-ri-vach) v. burst;
disrupt;tear open;entertain
rozrywka (roz-riv-ka) f. amusement; recreation; pastime
rozrządnica (roz-zhownd-nee-
tsa) f. control panel
rozrzedzić (roz-zhe-dżheech) v.
dilute; rarefy;thin down;weaken
rozrzewnić (roz-zhev-neech) v.
move; touch;affect;stir(the soul)
rozrzucać (roz-zhoo-tsach) v.
scatter; squander;distribute
rozrzutność (roz-zhoot-noshch)
f. extravagance;lavishness
rozrzutny (roz-zhoot-ni) adj.
m. wasteful; extravagant;
thriftless;squandering;prodigal;
spendthrift; lavish

rozsada (roz-sa-da) f. seedling; seedlings
rozsadzać (roz-sa-dzach) v.
space-out;place; seat sepa-
rately; blow up;explode;split
rozsądek (roz-sówn-dek) m.
good sense; discretion;reason
rozsądny (roz-sownd-ni) adj.
m. sensible; reasonable;
advisable;sound;judicious
rozsiadać się(roz-sha-dach shan)v.
sit stretched; sprawl round
rozsiekać (roz-she-kach) v.
cut up; slash asunder; hack up
rozsiewać (roz-she-vach) v.
saw; disseminate;spread;shed
rozsiodłać (roz-shod-wach) v.
unsaddle;take the saddle off
rozsławiać (roz-swav-yach) v.
glorify; make famous; extol
rozstać się (roz-stach shán)
v. part; give up; part with
rozstanie (roz-sta-ne) n.
parting; separation
rozstawać się (roz-sta-vach
shán) v. part with; give up
rozstawiać (roz-stav-yach) v.
disperse; place apart; space;
spread;put at intervals
rozstąpić się(roz-stówn-peech shán)
v. step aside;come apart;split
rozstęp (roz-stanp) m. gap;
space; slit;interval;heave
rozstroić (roz-stro-eech) v.
put out of tune; upset; disarray;derange;disorder; untune
rozstrój (roz-strooy) m. upset;
disorder;confusion;derangement
rozstrzelać (roz-stzhe-lach) v.
1. scatter; 2. execute by
shooting;put before a firing squad
rozstrzygać (roz-stzhi-gach) v.
try out; decide; fight out; judge
rozstrzygnięcie (roz-stzhig-
nan-che) v. decision; settlement
rozsuwać (roz-soo-vach) v. part;
draw aside;separate;expand(a compas)
rozsyłać (roz-si-wach) v. distribute; circulate; send out
rozsypać (roz-si-pach) v. dis-
perse(a granular substance);spill
rozszarpać (roz-shar-pach) v.
tear up; claw; disjoin;mangle

rozszczepiać (roz-shchep-yach)
v. split; cleave; fissure
rozszczepienie (roz-shche-pye-
ne) n. split; diffraction
rozszerzać (roz-she-zhach) v.
widen; broaden; enlarge; expand;spread out;extend;open
rozszerzenie (roz-she-zhe-ne)
n. enlargement; dilation
rozsznurować (roz-shnoo-ro-
vach) v. unlace;loosen the lace
rozszyfrować (roz-shif-ro-vach)
v. decode; break the code
rozścielać (roz-shche-lach) v.
spread; make the bed
rozśmieszać (roz-shmye-shach) v.
amuse; make laugh;be amusing
rozświecić (roz-shvye-cheech) v.
light up;throw light on;shine on
roztaczać (roz-ta-chach) v. roll
out; spread;unfold;display;bore
roztajać (roz-ta-yach) v. thaw
roztapiać (roz-tap-yach) v.
melt; smelt(metal);thaw (ice)
roztargać (roz-tar-gach) v.
tear to pieces;ruffle;dishevel
roztargniony (roz-targ-no-ni)
adj. m. absentminded ; distracted; scatterbrained ; far-away
rozterka (roz-ter-ka) f. tearing
between; dissension;suspense
roztkliwiać (roz-tklee-vyach) v.
feel for; touch; move;stir
roztłuc (roz-twoots) v. smash up
roztopy (roz-to-pi) pl. thaw
roztratować (roz-tra-to-vach)
v.run over; trample; tread
under foot;trample to death
roztrąbić (roz-trown-beech) v.
broadcast; blaze abroad
roztrącić (roz-trown-cheech) v.
push aside;elbow;part;jostle
roztropność (roz-trop-noshch) f.
prudence; thoughtfulness
roztropny (roz-trop-ni) adj. m.
wise;cautious;circumspect;politic
roztrwonić (roz-trvo-neech) v.
squander(a fortune,money etc.)
roztrzaskać (roz-tzhas-kach) v.
smash; shatter; crash to pieces
roztrzepanie (roz-tzhe-pa-ne) n.
scatterbrain; fickleness

roztrzepany (roz-tzhe-pa-ni)
adj. m. scatterbrain; giddy
roztwór (roz-tvoor) m.(chem.)
solution(colloidal,molal etc.)
roztyć się (roz-tich shan) v.
grow fat; become fat
rozum (ro-zoom) m. mind; reason; intellect; understanding;
wit;senses; judgment; brains
rozumieć (ro-zoom-yech) v.
understand; get; perceive
rozumny (ro-zoom-ni) adj. m.
rational;reasonable; wise
rozumować (ro-zoo-mo-vach) v.
reason; argue
rozwaga (roz-va-ga) f. thoughtfulness; prudence; reflection;
deliberation; consideration
rozwalać (roz-va-lach) v. shatter; demolish; smash; sprawl
rozwarty kąt (roz-var-ti kownt)
m. obtuse angle
rozważać (roz-va-zhach) v.
1. weigh out; 2. consider
rozweselić (roz-ve-se-leech) v.
cheer up; put in good humor
rozwiać (roz-vyach) v. blow
away; blow to and fro;scatter
rozwiązać (roz-vyown-zach) v.
untie; solve; undo; dissolve;
loosen; unbind; unravel; undo
rozwiązanie (roz-vyown-za-ne)
n. solution; way out; (child)
delivery; realization;execution
rozwiązły (roz-vyown-zwi) adj.
m. fast; dissolute;debauched
rozwidniać (roz-veed-nach) v.
dawn; be lit up;become lit up
rozwiedziony (roz-vye-dzho-ni)
adj. m. divorced(f.divorcee)
rozwierać (roz-vye-rach) v.
open wide; fling open
rozwieszać (roz-vye-shach) v.
hang about;stretch; spread out
rozwieść się (roz-vyeshch shan)
v. divorce; dwell upon
rozwijać (roz-vee-yach) v. unwrap; unfold; develop; spread
rozwikłać (roz-veek-wach) v.
disentangle; unravel; clear up
rozwikłanie (roz-veek-wa-ne) n.
unraveling; disentanglement

rozwlekać (roz-vle-kaćh) v.
drag out; protract; spread
rozwlekły (roz-vlek-wi) adj. m.
verbose; lengthy; long-spun
rozwodnić (roz-vod-ńeećh) v.
dilute;water down; weaken
rozwodnik (roz-vod-ńeek) m. divorced man; divorcee
rozwodowy (roz-vo-do-vi) adj. m.
divorce-(proceedings etc.)
rozwodzić (roz-vo-dźheećh) v.
divorce(a married couple)
rozwojowy (roz-vo-yo-vi) adj.
evolutional; developmental
rozwolnienie (roz-vol-ńe-ńe) n.
diarrhea;lax bowels;open bowels
rozwozić (roz-vo-źheećh) v.
transport; deliver (mail etc.)
rozwód (roz-vood) m. divorce
rozwódka (roz-vood-ka) f. divorcee ; divorced woman
rozwój (roz-vooy) m. development; evolution; growth
rozwścieczony (roz-vśhćhe-cho-
ni) adj. m. enraged; furious
rozwydrzony (roz-vid-zho-ni)
adj. m. rampant; wild;lawless
rozzłościć (roz-zwośh-ćheećh)
v. irritate; make angry;provoke
rozżalenie (roz-zha-le-ńe) n.
grudge; resentment;bitterness
rozżarzyć (roz-zha-zhićh) v.
inflame; set on fire; fire
rożek (ro-zhek) m. small horn;
croissant;small corner
rożen (ro-zhen) m. roasting spit
ród (rood) m. clan; breed; family; stock;race;origin; line
róg (roog) m. horn; corner; bugle;antler; corner kick(sport)
rój (rooy) m. swarm;hive;cluster
rość (roośhćh) v. grow;age;go up
rów (roov) m. ditch;trench;trough
rówieśnik (roo-vyeśh-ńeek) m.
peer of same age;contemporary
równać (roov-naćh) v. equalize;
level; make even; smooth out
równanie (roov-na-ńe) n. equation ;equalization;comparison
równia (roov-ńa) f. plane; level
równie (roov-ńe) adv. equally
również (roov-ńesh) conj. also;
too; likewise; as well

równik (roov-ńeek) m. equator
równina (roov-ńee-na) f.plain;
flat country; level landscape
równo (roov-no) adv. even;(equi-)
równoboczny (roov-no-boch-ni)
adj. m. equilateral
równoczesny (roov-no-chés-ni)
adj. m. simultaneous
równoległobok (roov-no-leg-wó-
bok) m. parallelogram
równoległy (roov-no-leg-wi) adj.
m. parallel to;collateral
równoleżnik (roov-no-leżh-ńeek)
m. parallel(of latitude)
równomierny (roov-no-myer-ni)
adj. m. even; uniform;steady
równoramienny (roov-no-ra-myen-
ni) adj. m. isosceles(triangle)
równorzędny (roov-no-zhánd-ni)
adj. m.equal rank;equivalent
równość (roov-nośhćh) f. equality ; parity; identity
równouprawnienie (roov-no-oo-
prav-ńe-ńe) n. equality of
rights(of women,men etc.)
równowaga (roov-no-va-ga) f.
equilibrium; balance ; poise
równowartościowy (roov-no-var-
tosh-ćho-vi) adj. m. equivalent; equipollent
równoważny (roov-no-vazh-ni)
adj. m. equivalent;equiponderant
równoważyć (roov-no-vazhićh)
v. balance; equalize; even up
równoznaczny (roov-no-znach-ni)
adj. m. synonymous;tantamount
rozga (rozg-ga) f. switch; cane
róż (roozh) m. rouge ; pink
róża (roo-zha) f. rose(flower etc.)
różaniec (roo-zha-ńets) m. ro-
sary;beads;telling one's beads
różdżka (roozhdzh-ka) f. dowsing
rod ; twig;divining rod(or wand)
różnica (roozh-ńee-tsa) f. difference ; disparity; dissent
różniczka (roozh-ńeech-ka) f.
differential;small difference
różnić się (roozh-ńeećh śhań) v.
differ ; be at variance
różnobarwny (roozh-no-barv-ni)
adj. m.many colored ; motley
różnojęzyczny (roozh-no-yáń-
zich-ni) adj. m. many-tongued

różnolity (roozh-no-lee-ti) adj. m. diverse; varied

różnorodny (roozh-no-ród-ni) adj. m. heterogeneous; varied

różnoznaczny (roozh-no-znach-ni) adj. m. ambiguous

różny (roozh-ni) adj. m. different miscellaneous; sundry

różowy (roo-zho-vi) adj. m. pink; rosy; ruddy; rose color

rtęciowy (rtān-cho-vi) adj. m. mercuric (compounds etc.)

rtęć (rtānch) f. mercury

rubaszny (roo-bash-ni) adj. m. coarse; ill-mannered

rubin (roo-been) m. ruby (red)

rubryka (roo-bri-ka) f. space; column; blank space; rubric

ruch (rookh) m. move; movement; traffic; motion; gesture stir

ruchawka (roo-kháv-ka) f. riot

ruchliwy (rookh-lee-vi) adj. m. busy; mobile; agile; active

ruchomości (roo-kho-mósh-chee) pl. movables (personal property); belongings; (one's things)

ruchomy (roo-kho-mi) adj. m. mobile; moving; shifting flexible

ruczaj (roo-chay) m. brook

ruda (roo-da) f. ore (metallic)

rudera (roo-dé-ra) f. run-down house; shanty; ruin; hovel

rudy (roo-di) adj. m. red (haired); russet; ginger; foxy; ruddy

rufa (roo-fa) f. stern; poop

rugować (roo-go-vach) v. eject; oust; evict; eliminate; displace

ruina (roo-ee-na) f. ruin; wreck

ruja (roo-ya) f. heat; rut

rujnować (rooy-no-vach) v. ruin; undo; destroy; wreck

ruleta (roo-lé-ta) f. roulette

rulon (roo-lon) m. roll; rouleau

rum (room) m. rum (drink)

rumak (roo-mak) m. charger; steed; palfrey; courser

rumianek (roo-mya-nek) m. camomile; chamonile (tea)

rumiany (roo-mya-ni) adj. m. rosy; ruddy; browned; florid

rumienić (roo-mye-neech) v. blush; brown; redden; color

rumieniec (roo-mye-nets) m. blush; ruddiness; floridity

rumor (roo-mor) m. racket; uproar; rumble; clatter; din

rumowisko (roo-mo-vees-ko) n. debris; rubble; brash

rumuński (roo-moon-skee) adj. m. Rumanian; of Rumania

runąć (roo-nownch) v. fall down; collapse; crash; swoop; resound

runda (roon-da) f. bout; round; lap; fall (in wrestling)

runo (roo-no) n. fleece; nap

rupiecie (roo-pyé-che) n. rubbish; trash; junk; stuff; oddments

ruptura (roop-too-ra) f. hernia

rura (roo-ra) f. tube; pipe

rurka (roor-ka) f. small pipe

rurociąg (roo-ro-chówng) m. pipeline; run of pipes; piping

rusałka (roo-saw-ka) f. undine; naiad; water nymph; vanessa

ruszać (roo-shach) v. move; stir; touch; start; take away; withdraw

rusznikarz (roosh-nee-kash) m. gunsmith (man or shop)

rusztowanie (roosh-to-va-ńe) n. scaffold; cradle (hanging)

rutyna (roo-ti-na) f. routine

rutynowany (roo-ti-no-vá-ni) adj. m. experienced; competent

rwać (rvach) v. pluck; tear; pull out; pull up; rush; burst

rwący (rvówn-tsy) adj. m. rapid; racking (pain); swift flowing

rwetes (rvé-tes) m. bustle; ado; racket; turmoil; agitation; stir

ryba (ri-ba) f. fish; the Fish

rybak (rí-bak) m. fisherman

rybny staw (rib-ni stav) fish pond (artificially made)

rybołóstwo (ri-bo-woós-tvo) n. fishery; fishing

rycerski (ri-tser-skee) adj. m. chivalrous; courteous

rycerz (ri-tsesh) m. knight

rychło (rikh-wo) adv. soon; quickly; early; soon after

rychły (rikh-wi) adj. m. speedy; quick; early; prompt; approaching

rycina (ri-chee-na) f. engraving; illustration; cartoon; drawing; plate

rycynus (ri-tsi-noos) m. castor oil; castor oil plant

ryczałt (ri-chawt) m. lump sum; global sum

ryczeć (ri-chech) v. roar; moo;
bellow;low;growl;bray;hoot;yell
ryć (rich) v. dig; root: engrave;
carve;excavate;burrow;plough
rydel (ri-del) m. spade; spud
rydwan (rid-van) m. chariot
rygiel (ri-gel) m. bolt;bar;lock
rygor (ri-gor) m. rigor;severity
ryj (riy) m. snout;phiz;mug;(vulg.)
ryk (rik) m. roar;moo;low;yell
rylec (ri-lets) m. burin; graver;
chisel; etching· needle;dry point
rym (rim) m. rhyme;rhyme word
rymarz (ri-mash) m. saddler
rymować (ri-mó-vach) v. rhyme
rynek (ri-nek) m. market(square)
rynna (rin-na) f. gutter; chute
rynsztok (rin-shtok) m. sewer
rynsztunek (rin-shtoo-nek) m.
armor; armature; outfit ; kit
rys (ris) m. feature; trait
rysa (ri-sa) f.crack; flow; fissure;scratch;rift;crevice;chink
rysopis (ri-só-pees) m. descrip-
tion(of a person for a passport)
rysować (ri-so-vach) v. draw;
design; sketch;draft;trace;show
rysownica (ri-sov-nee-tsa) f.
drawing board;drafting table
rysownik (ri-sov-neek) m. draftsman; illustrator; designer
rysunek (ri-soo-nek) m. sketch;
drawing ; draft; outline;cartoon
rysunkowy (ri-soon-kó-vi) adj.m.
tracing; drawing; cartoon;drawn
ryś (rish) m . lynx
rytm (ritm) m. rhythm ;cadence
rytmiczny (rit-meech-ni) adj. m.
rhythmic;regular; measured
rytownictwo (ri-tov-neets-tvo)
n. engraving; die sinking
rytownik (ri-tóv-neek) m. engraver; die sinker
rytuał (ri-too-aw) m. ritual
rywal (ri-val) m. rival;contestant
rywalizacja (ri-va-lee-záts-ya)
f. rivalry;competition;emulation
ryza (ri-za) f. ream; restraint
ryzyko (ri-zi-ko) n. risk;venture
ryzykować (ri-zi-ko-vach) v.
risk; venture; gamble; hazard
ryzykowny (ri-zi-kóv-ni) adj.m.
risky; hazardous;venturesome

ryż (rizh) m. rice
ryży (ri-zhi) adj. m. red (haired);russet;ginger;foxy;red-brown
rzadki (zhad-kee) adj. m. rare;thin
rzadko (zhad-ko) adv. seldom;thinly
rarely;far apart;exceptionally
rzadkość (zhad-koshch) f. rar-
ity:sparseness;curiosity; curio
rząd (zhownt) m. row; rank;
file; line up; government
rządca (zhownd-tsa) f. administrator; ruler;land steward
rządowy (zhówn-do-vi) adj. m.
governmental;government;state-
rządzić (zhówn-dzheech) v. rule;
govern; control; direct;be in power
rzec (zhets) v. say; utter
rzecz (zhech) f. thing; matter; act;
stuff; deal; work; subject;theme
rzeczka (zhech-ka) f. small river;
river; brook; stream
rzecznik (zhech-neek) m. spokesman; attorney ; patent agent
rzeczownik (zhech-ov-neek) m.
noun; substantive (grammar)
rzeczowo (zhe-chó-vo) adv.
factually; terse; business
like ; to the point;objectively
rzeczoznawca (zhe-cho-znáv-tsa)
m. expert;specialist(authority)
rzeczpospolita (zhech-pos-po-
lee-ta) f. republik; commonwealth
rzeczywistość (zhe-chi-vées-
toshch) f. reality;actuality
rzeczywisty (zhe-chi-vees-ti)
adj. m. real; actual; virtual
rzednieć (zhed-ńech) v. grow
thin; become rare;scatter;thin
rzeka (zhe-ka) f. river; stream
rzekomo (zhe-kó-mo) adv. would
be; allegedly ; supposedly;ostensibly
rzekomy (zhe-kó-mi) adj.m.make
believe; reputed; supposed;
sham; alleged; immaginary;so called
rzemień (zhe-myeń) m. leather
strap; leather band; leather belt
rzemieślniczy (zhe-myeshl-ńee-
chi) adj. m. trade; craft-
rzemieślnik (zhe-myeshl-neek)
m. artisan; craftsman;tradesman
rzemiosło (zhe-myós-vo) n. (handi)
craft;trade;job;business

rzemyk (zhe-mik) m. small leather
  strap;chin strap; thong
rzepa (zhe-pa) f. turnip
rzepak (zhe-pak) m. rapeseed;cole
rzesza (zhe-sha) f. crowd; Reich
rzeszoto (zhe-sho-to) n. sieve
rzeski (zhesh-kee) adj. m. lively; brisk; spry; fresh;brisk
rzeskosc (zhesh-koshch) f. vigor
rzetelny (zhe-tel-ni) adj. m.
  honest; upright; fair; real
rzewny (zhev-ni) adj. m. wistful
rzezac (zhe-zach) v. slaughter;
  castrate ; circumcise
rzezimieszek (zhe-zhee-mye-shek)
  m. cutpurse; thief; pickpocket
rzez (zhezh) f. carnage; massacre;slaughter ; shambles;carnage
rzezba (zhezh-ba) f. sculpture
rzezbiarstwo (zhezh-byar-stvo)
  n. sculpture; sculpturing
rzezbiarz (zhezh-byash) m. sculptor;artist creating sculptures
rzezbic (zhezh-beech) v. carve;
  cut;sculpture;weather(the earth)
rzeznia (zhezh-na) f. slaughter-
  house
rzeznik (zhezh-neek) m. butcher
rzezwic (zhezh-veech) v. refresh
rzezwosc (zhezh-voshch) f. agil-
  ity; briskness;sprightliness
rzezwy (zhezh-vi) adj. m. agile;
  brisk; smart;spry;lively;bracing
rzezaczka (zhe-zhovnch-ka) f.
  gonorrhea
rzedem (zhan-dem) adv. in a row
rzedna (zhand-na) f. ordinate
rzepolic (zhan-po-leech) v.
  scrape (on fiddle);rasp(the fiddle)
rzesa (zhan-sa) f. eyelash
rzesisty (zhan-shees-ti) adj. m.
  profuse; heavy; abundant;copious
rzezic (zhan-zheech) v. death
  rattle ; ruckle (in sickness)
rznac (zhnovnch) v. cut,carve;
  butcher; vulg.:screw;have sex
rzodkiew (zhod-kev) f. radish
rzodkiewka (zhod-kev-ka) f. rad-
  ish(the pungent root eaten raw)
rzucac (zhoo-tsach) v. throw;
  fling; pitch; dash;hurl; toss
rzucic (zhoo-cheech) v. throw;
  cast; plunge; dash; pitch; fling

rzut (zhoot) m. throw; cast;
  projection; view; sketch
rzutki (zhoot-kee) adj. m.
  brisk;lively; enterprising
rzutkosc (zhoot-koshch) f.
  briskness; initiative
rzyc (zhich) f. (vulg.) ass
rzygac (zhi-gach) v. vomit;
  belch; spew; eject;emit
rzymski (zhim-skee) adj. m.
  Roman; of Rome(church;rite)
rzec (rzhech) v. whinny; neigh
rznac (rzhnovnch) v. cut; saw;
  engrave; carve; butcher; bang;
  play cards; (vulg.): screw
rzniecie (rzhnan-che) n. colic;
  bellyache; (slang): beating
rzysko (rzhis-ko) n. stubble-
  field; rye field
sabat (sa-bat) m, Sabbath
sabotaz (sa-bo-tash) m. sabotage; act of sabotage
sacharyna (sa-kha-ri-na) f.
  saccharine
sad (sad) m. orchard
sadlo (sad-wo) n. leaflard
sadowic (sa-do-veech) v. place;
  show to a seat; seat
sadownik (sa-dov-neek) m. fruit-
  grower;fruit farmer; orchardist
sadyba (sa-di-ba) f. dwelling ;
  house; human habitation; home
sadysta (sa-dis-ta) m. sadist
sadza (sa-dza) f. soot; black
sadzac (sa-dzach) v. show to
  a seat; seat;make sit down
sadzawka (sa-dzav-ka) f. pool
sadzic (sa-dzheech) v. plant;
  set; run; speed;stud(decorate)
sadzonka (sa-dzon-ka) f. seedling; quickset; cutting
sadzonejajka (sa-dzo-ne yay-ka)
  s. fried eggs sunny side up
safandula (sa-fan-doo-wa) f.
  bungler; yes-man; oaf;muff;duffer
safian (sa-fyan) m. morocco
  (lather); saffian
sagan (sa-gan) m. kettle ;pot
sak (sak) m. dipnet; sack
sakrament (sa-kra-ment) m. sacrament (of matrimony etc.)
sakwa (sak-va) f. wallet;purse
  money-bag; feed-bag ;nose bag

sala (sá-la) f. 1. hall; 2. audience (in a hall)

salaterka (sa-la-tér-ka) f. salad bowl; vegetable dish

salceson (sal-tse-son) m. headcheese; (mock)brawn

saletra (sa-let-ra) f. niter; saltpeter;potassium nitrate

salina (sa-lee-na) f. saltworks; saline; salt mine

salmiak (sal-myak) m. ammoniumchloride; sal-ammoniac

salon (sa-lon) m. drawing-room

salonka (sa-lón-ka) f. club car (railroad);parlor car

salutować (sa-loo-to-vach) v. salute; dip the flag

salwa (sál-va) f. volley;salvo

sałata (sa-wá-ta) f. 1. lettuce; salad; 2. cabman(slang)

sam (sam) adj. m. alone; oneself; myself; yourself; nothing but

samica (sa-mée-tsa) f. female

samiec (sam-yets) m. male

samobójca (sa-mo-bóoy-tsa) m. suicide; suicidal man

samobójczy (sa-mo-bóoy-chi) adj. m. suicidal;leading to suicide

samobójstwo (sa-mo-bóoy-stvo) n. suicide;act of killing oneself

samochód (sa-mo-khood) m. automobile; car;motor car

samochwał (sa-mó-khvaw) m. braggart; boaster; blow hard

samodział (sa-mó-dżhaw) m. homespun (cloth)

samodzielność (sa-mo-dżhél-noshch) f. independence

samodzielny (sa-mo-dżhél-ni) adj. m.self-reliant; independent; self-contained

samogłoska (sa-mo-gwos-ka) f. vowel; vocal

samogon (sa-mó-gon) m. moonshine

samoistny (sa-mo-eést-ni) adj. m. independent;autonomous

samokrytyka (sa-mo-kri-tí-ka) f. self-criticism;self-accusation

samokształcenie (sa-mo-kshtaw-tse-ńe) n. self-education

samolot (sa-mó-lot) m. airplane

samolub (sa-mó-loob) m. egoist

samolubstwo (sa-mo-loób-stvo) n . selfishness ; egoism

samolubny (sa-mo-loob-ni) adj. m. selfish; self-seeking;egoistic

samoobrona (sa-mo-o-bró-na) f. f. self-defense

samopas (sa-mó-pas) adv. alone; by oneself; loosely; unheeded

samopoczucie (sa-mo-po-choo-ćhe) n. frame of mind; feeling

samopomoc (sa-mo-pó-mots) f. self-help; mutual aid (society)

samorodek (sa-mo-ró-dek) m. (gold) nugget

samorodny (sa-mo-ród-ni) adj. m. autogenous; natural; virgin

samorząd (sa-mó-zhownt) m. autonomy; self-government

samotnik (sa-mót-ńeek) m. recluse; hermit;solitary;rogue

samostanowienie (sa-mo-sta-no-vyé-ńe) n. self-determination

samotność (sa-mót-noshćh) f. solitude; loneliness

samouctwo (sa-mo-oóts-tvo) n. self-education;self instruction

samouczek (sa-moo-oó-tchek) m. handbook (for self-instruction)

samouk (sa-mo--ook) m. self-taught (man);self taught person

samowładczy (sa-mo-vwád-chi) adj. m. autocratic; arbitrary

samowola (sa-mo-vó-la) f. license (arbitrariness);lawlessness

samowystarczalny (sa-mo-vis-tar-chál-ni) adj. m. self-sufficient; self contained;unsubsidized

samozachowawczy instynkt (sa-mo-za-kho-váv-chi eén-stinkt) m. self-preservation instinct

samozapalenie się (sa-mo-za-pa-lé-ńe shań) n. spontaneous combustion; self ignition

samozwaniec (sa-mo-zva-ńets) m. usurper; pretender

sanatorium (sa-na-tór-yoom) m. sanitorium; sanatorium

sandacz (sán-dach) m. perch-pike

sandał (sán-daw) m. sandal

sanie (sá-ńe) pl. sleigh; sledge

sanitariuszka(sa-ńee-tar-yoosh-ka) f. nurse(emergency, military)

sanitarny (sa-ñee-tár-ni) adj.
  m. sanitary; health-
sankcja (sánk-tsya) f. sanction
sankcjonować (sank-tsyo-no-
  vać) v. sanction;authorize
sanki (sán-kee) pl. sled
sanskryt (san-skrit) m. San-
  skrit; Sanscrit
sapać (sa-pać) v. gasp; pant;
  heave; snort;puff and blow;chug
saper (sa-per) m. combat engineer;army engineer; sapper
sardynka (sar-dín-ka) f. sardine
sarkać (sar-kać) v. grumble
sarkastyczny (sar-kas-tích-ni)
  adj. m. sarcastic(smile etc.)
sarna (sár-na) f. roe deer
sarnia skóra (sár-ña skoo-ra)
  f. buckskin;roe-deer's hide
satelita (sa-telée-ta) m. satellite; attendant
satyna (sa-ti-na) f. satin
satyra (sa-ti-ra) f. satire
satysfakcja (sa-tis-fák-tsya)
  f. satisfaction; compensation
sączyć się (sóẃn-chich śhãn)
  v. drip; trickle; distill;
  sift ; ooze out; seep;percolate
sąd (sóẃnd) m. judgment ; court
sądownictwo (sóẃn-dov-ñeets-tvo)
  n. judicature ;jurisdiction
sądowy (sóẃn-do-vi) adj. m. judicial; of court;judiciary
sądzić (sóẃn-dźheech) v. judge;
  think; believe; expect; guess
sąg (sóẃng) m. cord (of wood)
sąsiad (sóẃn-śhad) m. neighbor
sąsiadka (sóẃn-śhad-ka) f.
  neighbor; lady next door
sąsiedni (sóẃn-śhed-ñee) adj.
  m. adjacent;neighboring
sąsiedztwo (sóẃn-śhedz-tvo) n.
  neighborhood; nearness;proximity
sążeń (sóẃn-zheñ) m. fathom;
  cord;approximately six feet
scalić (stsa-leech) v. integrate
scedzić (stse-dźheech) v. strain
  off;decant; pour off(a liquid)
scena (stse-na) f. scene; stage
scenariusz (stse-nár-yoosh) m.
  scenario; script; screenplay
sceneria (stse-nér-ya) f. scenery;stage decorations;backdrops

sceptyczny (stsep-tích-ni) adj.
  m. sceptic; skeptical(smile etc.)
sceptyk (stsep-tik) m. skeptic
schab (skhab) m. pork chop
schadzka (skhádz-ka) f. date
scheda (skhé-da) f. inheritance; inheritance; heirloom
schemat (skhé-mat) m. scheme;
  plan;draft;outline; diagram
schematyczny (skhe-ma-tích-ni)
  adj. m. schematic (drafting...)
schizma (skhéez-ma) f. schism
schlebiać (skhléb-yać) v.
  flatter;wheedle;adulate;gratify
schludny (skhlood-ni) adj. m.
  neat; clean;trim;slick;tidy
schnąć (skhnóẃnćh) v. dry; dry
  up; wane; waste;parch;wither
schodki (skhód-kee) pl. steps
  (small);small stairs
schodowa klatka (skho-dó-va
  klat-ka) staircase
schody (skho-di) pl. stairs
schodzic (skho-dźheech) v. get
  down; go down stairs;step down
scholastyka (zkho-las-ti-ka) f.
  scholasticism; Scholasticism
schorowany (skho-ro-va-ni) adj.
  m. invalid;ailing;ill;sick
schować (skho-vać) v. hide;
  pocket;conceal;put away; save
schowek (skho-vek) m. closet;
  safe; hiding place; cubby;recess
schód (skhood) m. stair; step
schron (skhron) m. shelter;
  pillbox; air raid shelter etc.
schronić się (skhro-ñeech śhãn)
  v. take refuge;take cover
schronisko (skhro-ñees-ko) n.
  shelter;hiding place;refuge
schudnięcie (skhood-ñán-che) n.
  loss of fat (weight);slimming
schwycić (skhvi-cheech) v.
  seize; catch; get hold of
schylać (skhi-lać) v. bend;
  bow; incline; stoop down
schyłek (skhi-wek) m. decline
scyzoryk (stsi-zó-rik) m. pocketknife; clasp knife;pen knife
seans (sé-ans) m. seance; sitting;showing;performance
secesja (se-tses-ya) f. secession;Secession style(architecture)

sedes (se-des) m. toilet seat

sedno (sed-no) n. crux; core;
gist; essence (of the matter)

sejm (seym) m. Polish parliament (600 years old)

sekcja (sek-tsya) f. dissection;
section; cross-section; division

sekret (sek-ret) m. secret

sekretarz (se-kre-tash) m. secretary; reporter; minuter

seksualny (se-ksoo-al-ni) adj.
m. sexual; sex-(appeal, urge etc)

sekta (sek-ta) f. sect

sektor (sek-tor) m. sector

sekunda (se-koon-da) f. second

sekundnik (se-koond-neek) m.
second-hand (of a watch)

sekutnica (se-koot-nee-tsa) f.
shrew; scold; vixen

seledynowy (se-le-di-no-vi) adj.
m. aquamarine; willow green

selekcja (se-lek-tsya) f. selection (by elimination, natural etc)

seler (se-ler) m. celery

semafor (se-ma-for) m. semaphore

semicki (se-meets-kee) adj. m.
Semitic (character etc.)

seminarium (se-mee-nar-yoom) n.
seminar; seminary; trainning school

sen (sen) m. sleep; dream

senat (se-nat) m. senate (in Poland evolved from royal council
in XV c.); Upper House

senator (se-na-tor) m. senator

senior (sen-yor) m. senior

senny (sen-ni) adj. m. sleepy

sens (sens) m. sense; significance; gist; drift; meaning; point

sensacja (sen-sats-ya) f. sensation; a hit; making a hit

sensacyjny (sen-sa-tsiy-ni) adj.
m. sensational; exciting

sentencja (sen-tents-ya) f.
maxim; dictum; pronouncement

sentyment (sen-ti-ment) m. sentiment; partiality; fondness; feeling

separacja (se-pa-rats-ya) f.
separation (from bed and board)

separatka (se-pa-rat-ka) f. private-room; solitary cell

separować (se-pa-ro-vać) v.
separate; isolate

seplenić (se-ple-ńeech) v.
lisp; have a lisp; speak with lisp

ser (ser) m. cheese

serce (ser-tse) n. heart; kindness

sercowy (ser-tso-vi) adj. m.
cardiac; love-(affair, secret etc.)

serdak (ser-dak) m. sleeveless
(furred) waistcoat

serdeczność (ser-dech-nośćch)
f. cordiality; heartiness; caresses

serdeczny (ser-dech-ni) adj.
m. hearty; cordial; sincere

serdelek (ser-de-lek) m. small
sausage (specially smoked)

serenada (se-re-na-da) f. serenade (music and song at night)

seria (ser-ya) f. series;
chain; set; train (of events etc.)

serio (ser-yo) adv. seriously

sernik (ser-neek) m. cheesecake; casein

serwatka (ser-vat-ka) f. whey

serweta (ser-ve-ta) f. (small)
table cloth; doily; serviette

serwetka (ser-vet-ka) f. napkin

serwilizm (ser-vee-leezm) m.
servility; humbly submission

serwis (ser-vees) m. dinner set;
service; (tennis), turn of serving

serwować (ser-vo-vać) v. (tennis) serve; do services; aid; help

seryjny (se-riy-ni) adj. m.
serial; consecutive

sesja (ses-ya) f. session

setka (set-ka) f. hundred

setny (set-ni) num. hundredth

sezon (se-zon) m. season

sędzia (san-dzha) m. judge; umpire; referee; magistrate

sędziwy (san-dzhee-vi) adj. m.
aged; old; grey headed; ancient

sęk (sank) m. knot; knag; knar

sękaty (san-ka-ti) adj. m. knotty; knaggy; gnarly; nodose; rugged

sęp (samp) m. vulture

sfera (sfe-ra) f. sphere; zone

sferyczny (sfe-rich-ni) adj. m.
spherical (geometry, triangle etc.)

sfinks (sfeenks) m. sphinx

sfora (sfo-ra) f. pack of dogs

siać (shach) v. sow (corn, terror...)

siadać (sha-dach) v. sit down;
take a seat; get stranded; go flat

siano (śha-no) n. hay

sianokosy (śha-no-kó-si) pl.
haymaking; hay cutting

siarczan (śhar-chan) m. sulfate

siarka (śhár-ka) f. sulfur

siarkowy (śhar-kó-vi) adj. m.
sulfuric(acid etc.)

siatka (śhat-ka) f. net; screen

siatkówka (śhat-koóv-ka) f. ret-
ina; volley-ball

siąść (śhanśhch) v. sit down

sidło (śhid-wo) n. snare; trap

siebie (śhe-bye) pron. (for)
self; oneself;one;each other

siec (śhets) v. cut; mow; whip

sieczka (śhech-ka)f.chop straw;
chaff; empty head(slang)

sieczna (śhech-na) f. secant

sieczna broń (śhech-na broń) f.
cutting weapons

sieć (śhech) f. net; network;
grid;fishing net;trap;snare;web

siedem (śhe-dem) num. seven

siedemdziesiąt (śhe-dem-dźhe-
shownt) num. seventy

siedemdziesiąty (śhe-dem-dźhe-
shówn-ti) num. seventieth

siedemnasty (śhe-dem-nás-ti)
num. seventeenth

siedemnaście (śhe-dem-naśh-che)
num. seventeen

siedemset (śhe-dém-set) num.
seven hundred

siedlisko (śhed-lees-ko) n, seat;
abode;habitation;hotbed;nest

siedmiokrotny (śhed-myo-krót-ni)
adj. m. sevenfold

siedmioletni (śhed-myo-lét-ńee)
adj. m. seven year (old; lasting)

siedzący (śhe-dzówn-tsi) adj. m.
sitting(posture);sedentary

siedzenie (śhe-dze-ńe) n. seat;
bottom; behind

siedziba (śhe-dzhee-ba) f. seat;
abode;habitat(of an animal)

siedzieć (śhe-dźhech) v. sit
(stay);be perched;be settled

siejba (śhey-ba) f. sowing; sowing time

siekacz (śhe-kach) m. incisor;
chopping knife; chopper

siekanina (śhe-ka-ńee-na) f.
hash;chopping up;cutting up

siekiera (śhe-ké-ra) f. axe

siekierka (śhe-ḱer-ka) f.
hatchet; small axe

sielanka (śhe-lán-ka) f. idyll

sielankowy (śhe-lan-kó-vi) adj.
m. idyllic; pastoral;bucolic

sielski (śhel-skee) adj. m.
rural;idyllic; pastoral

siemię (śhe-myáń) n. bird seed

siennik (śhen-ńeek) m. straw-
mattress;pallet;paillasse

sień (śheń) f. hallway; corridor;vestibule;entrance hall

siepacz (śhe-pach) m. (rough)
henchman;hired assassin

sierota (śhe-ro-ta) m. f. orphan;lonsome person;poor fellow

sierp (śherp) m. sickle

sierpień (śher-pyeń) m. August

siersć (śherśhch) f. hair (coat)

sierżant (śher-zhant) m. sergeant (military rank)

siew (śhev) m. sowing; seeds

siewca (śhev-tsa) m. sower

siewnik (śhev-ńeek) m. seeder;
sowing-machine

się (śhań) pron. self (oneself;
myself etc.;of itself)each other

sięgać (śhań-gach) v. reach

sikać (śhe-kach) v. squirt;
spout; gush; piss (vulg.)

sikawka (śhee-kav-ka) f. fire
hose; squirt; fire engine

sikora (śhee-ko-ra) f. titmouse

siksa (śheek-sa) f. hussy; small
girl piddler

silnik (śhil-ńeek) m. motor

silnik spalinowy (śhil-ńeek spa-
lee-no-vi) combustion engine

silny (śhil-ni) adj. m. strong;
powerful;mighty;hefty;lusty;stiff

silos (see-los) m. silo;(store)pit

siła (śhee-wa) f. 1. force; might;
strength; power; 2. many; much

siłacz (śhee-wach) m. strongman

siłownia (shee-wóv-ńa) f. power
plant;power station;power house

sinawy (shee-ná-vi) adj. m.
bluish; somewhat blue

siniak (shee-ńak) m. bruise

sinus (see-noos) m. sine (of
an angle)

siny (shee-ni) adj. m. livid;
blue; purple; blue in the face

siodełko (sho-dew-ko) n. bicycle seat; small saddle

siodlarz (shod-lash) m. saddler

siodłać (shod-wach) v. saddle

siodło (shod-wo) n. saddle

sioło (sho-wo) m. hamlet; village

siostra (shos-tra) f. sister

siostrzenica (shos-tshe-nee-
tsa) f. niece

siostrzeniec (shos-tshe-nets)
m. nephew

siostrzyczka (shos-tzhich-ka)
f. little sister

siódemka (shoo-dem-ka) f. seven

siódmy (shood-mi) num. seventh

sito (shee-to) n. sieve; strainer

sitowie (shee-tov-ye) n. bulrush

siusiać (shoo-shach) v. tinkle;
urinate ; piss; pee; piddle

siwek (shee-vek) m. grey horse

siwieć (shee-vyech) v. grow gray

siwucha (shee-voo-kha) f. low
grade vodka; rot gut

siwy (shee-vi) adj. m. gray;
blue; grizzly; grey haired; hoary

skafander (ska-fan-der) m. diving
suit ; pressure suit; wind jacket

skakać (ska-kach) v. jump; spring;
bounce; leap; pop; skip ; dive

skakanka (ska-kan-ka) f. jumping
rope; skipping rope

skala (ska-la) f. scale; extent

skaleczenie (ska-le-che-ne) n.
cut; injury; hurt; wound

skaleczyć (ska-le-chich) v. hurt;
injure; cut; prick; wound

skalisty (ska-lees-ti) adj. rocky

skalp (skalp) m. scalp

skała (ska-wa) f. rock

skamieniały (ska-mye-na-wi) adj.
m. petrified ; fossil-; stone-

skamieniec (ska-mye-nech) v. become petrified ; turn into stone

skandal (skan-dal) m. scandal

skarb (skarb) m. treasure; treasury; riches; beloved person; hoard

skarbiec (skar-byets) m. treasury;
strong room; safe deposit

skarbnik (skarb-neek) m. treasurer; cashier; paymaster

skarbonka (skar-bon-ka) f.
piggy bank; money box; poor box

skarcić (skar-cheech) v. admonish; rebuke; reprimand; scold

skarga (skar-ga) f. complaint;
suit; claim; charge; grievance

skarłowaciały (skar-wo-va-
cha-wi) adj. m. stunted;
dwarfish

skarpa (skar-pa) f. scarp; buttress; slope; escarpment

skarpetka (skar-pet-ka) f.
sock; a short stocking

skarżyć (skar-zhich) v. sue;
denounce; complain; tell tales

skarżypyta (skar-zhi-pi-ta) m.
squealer; informer; telltale

skaza (ska-za) f. tarnish; brab;
blot; flaw; defect; spot; speck

skazać (ska-zach) v. condemn;
sentence; pass judgement; doom

skazaniec (ska-za-nets) m.
condemned man (to death)

skazić (ska-zheech) v. spoil;
corrupt; adulterate; pollute

skąd (skownt) adv. from where;
since when; where from?

skądinąd (skownd-ee-nownt) adv.
otherwise; on the other hand

skąpić (skown-peech) v. skimp;
stint; begrudge (food, money...)

skąpiec (skownp-yets) m. miser

skąpstwo (skownp-stvo) n. par-
simony; avarice; stinginess

skąpy (skown-pi) adj. m. stingy; scanty; meager; scant

skiba (skee-ba) f. clod

skinać (skee-nownch) v. signal;
motion; nod; bow (one's head)

skinienie (skee-ne-ne) m. nod;
bow; sign ; call; gesture; motion

sklejać (skle-yach) v. glue
together; stick; paste; patch

sklejka (skley-ka) f. plywood

sklep (sklep) m. store; shop

sklepienie (skle-pye-ne) n.
vault ; vaulting; dome

sklepikarz (skle-pee-kash) m.
shopkeeper; tradesman

sklepowa (skle-po-va) f. saleslady; saleswoman

skleroza (skle-ró-za) f. scle-
rosis;hardening of body

skład (skwat) m. composition;
warehouse; store;framework

składać (skwa-dać) v. make up;
compose; piece;fold;set together

składacz (skwa-dach) m. type-
setter; compositor

składany (skwa-da-ni) adj. m.
compound; folding;miscellaneous

składka(skwad-ka) f. contribution;collection;membership fee

składnia (skwad-na) f. syntax

składnica (skwad-nee-tsa) f.
depository; warehouse;depot

składnik (skwad-neek) m. ingredient; component;element

składowe (skwa-do-ve) n. warehouse fee; storage charges

skłamać (skwa-mać) v. tell
a lie;tell an untruth; lie

skłaniać (skwa-nach) v. bend;
lean; incline;induce;impel;rest

skłon (skwon) m. slope; bow

skłonność (skwon-nośhćh) f.
inclination;tendency;disposition

skłonny (skwon-ni) adj. m. disposed; inclined;prone;apt

skłócić (skwoó-ćheećh) v. stir
up; agitate; cause to disagree

sknera (skne-ra) m.& f. miser

skobel (skó-bel) m. staple

skoczek (sko-chek) m. jumper

skocznia (skóch-na) f. ski-
jump (ramp);take off ramp

skoczny (skóch-ni) adj. m. brisk;
lively; vivacious;saltary

skoczyć (sko-chich) v. leap;
jump; spring;make a dash;hurry

skojarzenie (sko-ya-zhé-ne) n.
association; union;conjunction

skok (skok) m. jump; leap; hop

skok tłoka (skok two-ka) m. piston stroke

skołatany (sko-wa-tá-ni) adj. m.
worn; battered; shattered

skołować (sko-wo-vach) v. confound; muddle; exhaust

skomleć (skom-lech) v. whine

skomplikowany (skom-plee-ko-va-
ni) adj. m. complex; intricate

skonać (skó-nach) v. expire; die

skończyć (skoń-chićh) v. finish; end;stop;have done

skoro (sko-ro) conj. after;at;
since; as;quickly;soon;if;once
adv. very soon; by and by

skoroszyt (sko-ro-shit) m.
folder ;letter file

skorowidz (sko-ro-veets) m.
index; indexed note book

skorpion (skor-pyon) m. scor-
pion; Scorpio

skorupa (sko-roo-pa) f. crust;
shell;hull;incrustation;carapace

skory (sko-ri) adj. m. quick;
eager;prompt(to act); swift

skostniały (skost-na-wi) adj.
m. ossified;numb;stiff;fossilized

skosny (skóśh-ni) adj. m. slanting; oblique; inclined

skotłować (skot-wo-vach) v. whirl;
bewilder;agitate;swirl; seethe

skowronek (sko-vro-nek) m.
lark; skylark

skowyczeć (sko-vi-chech) v.
yelp; whipe;squeal;whimper;whine

skowyt (sko-vit) m. yelp;squeal

skóra (skoo-ra) f. skin; hide;
leather; hide;skin;coat;pelt;derm

skórka (skoor-ka) f. skin; peel;
crust; cuticle;agnail;pelt;fur

skórny (skoor-ni) adj. m. cuta-
neous; dermal;skin-(disease etc.)

skórzany (skoo-zha-ni) adj. m.
leather made; leathery;leather-

skra (skra) f. spark (poetic)

skracać (skra-tsach) v. short-
en; cut down;lessen;abridge

skradać się (skra-dach śhań) v.
steal; creep up;advance stealthily

skraj (skray) m. border; edge;
brink; margin;fringe;rand;outskirts

skrajać (skrá-yach) v. cut off;cut
(cloth);cut up;(to pieces)

skrajność (skray-nośhćh) f.
extremism; extreme

skrajny (skray-ni) adj. m.
extreme;intense;utmost;ultra;utter

skrapiać (skrap-yach) v.damp;
sprinkle ;moisten; water

skraplać (skrap-lach) v. liquefy; condense;precipitate

skrawek (skra-vek) m. shred;snip;
strip; patch; chip;fragment;patch
box;hutch;case;crate;coffer
skreślić (skresh-leech) v.
sketch; cancel; jot down;delete
skręcać (skrān-tsach) v. twist;
turn off; break (neck);strand
skrępować (skrān-po-vach) v. tie
up; restrict;embarrass;impede
skręt (skrānt) m. twist; twist-
ing; coil; turn; torsion
skrobaczka (skro-bach-ka) f.rasp;
scraper; foot scraper(for mud)
skrobać (skro-bach) v. scrape;
rasp; scratch; scale (fish)
skromny (skrom-ni) adj. m.coy;
modest;unassuming;simple;lowly
skroń (skroń) f. temple
skropić (skro-peech) v. liquefy;
sprinkle;water;moisten;damp
skrócić (skroo-cheech) v. abbreviate; shorten ;cut down;curtail
skrót (skroot) m. abbreviation
skrucha (skroo-kha) f. contrition; repentance;compunction
skrupulatny (skroo-poo-lát-ni)
adj. m. scrupulous;precise,exact
skrupuł (skroo-poow) m. scruple
skruszyć (skroo-shich) v. crumble;crush;bring to repentance
skrycie (skri-che) adv. secretly
skryć (skrich) v. hide;obscure
skrypt (skript) m. script; mi-
meographed lecture; I.O.U.
skrytka pocztowa (skrit-ka poch-
to-va) post office box
skrytość (skri-toshch) f. secrecy; secretiveness
skryty (skri-ti) adj. m. underhanded; secret; reticent
skrzek (skzhek) m. scream; croak
skrzep (skzhep) m. clot; coagu-
lation(of blood);grume;thrombus
skrzepnąć (skzhep-nownch) v. clot;
coagulate;set;freeze;solidify
skrzętnie (skzhant-ñe) adv. sed-
ulously ; diligently;busily
skrzętny (skzhant-ni) adj. m.
industrious; busy; diligent
skrzydlaty (skzhid-la-ti) adj.
m. winged;wing-shaped;winglike
skrzydło (skzhid-wo) n. wing;
leaf; brim; (fan) arm;extension

skrzynia (skzhi-ña) f. chest;bin;
box;hutch;case;crate;coffer
skrzynka (skzhin-ka) f. box;chest
skrzynka biegów (skzhin-ka
bye-goov) f. gearbox;gear case
skrzypce (skzhip-tse) n. violin; fiddle;person playing fiddle
skrzypek (skzhi-pek) m. violinist; fiddler
skrzypiec (skzhi-pyech) v. crunch;
creak; screech; grind;squeak;gride
skrzywiać (skzhi-vyach) v. bend;
distort; twist;contort;put awry
skrzyżowanie dróg (skzhi-zho-
vá-ñe droog) pl. f. cross-
roads;crossing;intersection
skrzyżowany (skzhi-zho-vá-ni)
adj. m. crossbred; cross-
legged
skubać (skoo-bach) v. nibble;
pluck; pick; fleece;graze;tease
skuć (skooch) v. shackle; chain
skulić (skoo-leech) v. curl up;
cuddle up; squat; lie low;crouch
skup (skoop) m. purchasing center
skupiać (skoo-pyach) v. concentrate; bring together; gather
skupienie (skoop-yé-ñe) n. con-
centration;focussing;compression
skupiony (skoop-yo-ni) adj. m.
collected; concentrated ;dense
skupować (skoo-po-vach) v. buy;
buy up ;keep buying; buy out
skurcz (skoorch) m. cramp; shrinking;
spasm; twitch; systole;contraction
skurczyć (skoor-chich) v. draw in;
shrink; contract; lessen;diminish
skuteczność (skoo-tech-noshch)
f. efficiency; efficacy;good trsult
skutecznie(skoo-tech-ñe) adv.
with good result;effectively
skuteczny(skoo-téch-ni) adj. m.
effective;efficient; operative
skutek (skoo-tek) m. effect;
result; outcome; consequence
skuter (skoo-ter) m. motor-
scooter
skutkować (skoot-ko-vach) v.
have effect; work; operate
skwapliwy (skwap-lee-vi) adj.
m. eager; willing;ready
skwar (skvar) m. scorching heat

skwarek (skva-rek) m. crackling
skwaśniały (skvash-ña-wi) adj.
m. sour;turned sour; glum
skwer (skver) m. square
słabiutki (swa-byoot-kee) adj.
m. very weak(in diminutive)
słabnąć (swab-nownch) v. weaken;
grow feeble;decline;diminish
słabość (swa-boshch) f. weakness;
illness;debility;fragility
słabowity (swa-bo-vee-ti) adj.
m. weakly; feeble;fragile;puny
słaby (swa-bi) adj. m. weak;frail;
feeble;infirm;faint;flimsy;poor
słać (swach) v. send; make bed;
spread(a table cloth etc.);strew
słaniać się(swa-ñach śhañ) v.
totter; stagger;lurch; reel
sława (swa-va) f. glory; renown;
fame; celebrity;reputation;repute
sławetny (swa-vet-ni) adj. m.
notorious;famous;ill famous
sławić (swa-veech) v. praise;
celebrate; glorify;laud;blazon
sławny (swav-ni) adj. m. famous;
glorious;celebrated;illustrious
słodkawy (swod-ka-vi) adj. m.
sweetish; slightly sweet
słodki (swod-kee) adj. m. sweet
słodycze (swo-di-che) pl. sweets
słodzić (swo-dżheech) v. sweeten
słoik (swo-eek) m. jar; gallipot;
glass;pot ;small jar;little jar
słojowaty (swo-yo-va-ti) adj. m.
grained;veined ;shownig grain
słoma (swo-ma) f. straw
słomianka (swo-myan-ka) f. straw
mat;doormat;straw plaited basket
słomiany wdowiec (swo-mya-ni
vdo-vyets) m. grass widower
słomka (swom-ka) f. small straw
słonecznik (swo-nech-ñeek) m.
sunflower
słoneczny (swo-nech-ni) adj. m.
sunny;solar(system,year etc.)
słonina (swo-ñee-na) f. lard
słoniowa kość (swo-ño-va kośhch)
f. ivory
słonka (swon-ka) f. wood-cock
słony (swo-ni) adj. m. salty
słoń (swoñ) m. elephant
słońce (swoń-tse) n. sun;sunlight

słota (swo-ta) f.foul weather
słotny dzień (swot-ni dżheñ) m.
rainy day; bad weather day
słowacki (swo-vats-kee) adj.
m. Slovak; Slovakian
słowianin (swo-vya-ñeen) m.
Slav
słowiański (swo-vyan-skee) adj.
m. Slav; Slavonic
słowik (swo-veek) m. nightingale; good singer
słownictwo (swov-ñeets-tvo) n.
vocabulary; list of words
słownik (swov-ñeek) m. dictionary; vocabulary; language
słowny (swov-ni) adj. m. verbal; reliable; dependable
słowo (swo-vo) n. word; verb
słoworód (swo-vo-rood) m. etymology; origin of words
słowotwórstwo (swo-vo-tvoor-
stvo) n. word formation
słód (swood) m. malt
słój (swooy) m. jar; (tree)
ring;pot;vain;grain
słówko (swoov-ko) n. (little
or sweet) word;nice word
słuch (swookh) m. hearing
słuchacz (swoo-khach) m. listener; student ;hearer;auditor
słuchać (swoo-khach) v. hear;
obey;listen;obey orders
słuchawka (swoo-khav-ka) f.
(tel.) receiver; earphone
słuchowisko (swoo-kho-vees-ko)
m. radio drama;broadcast drama
słuchy (swoo-khy) pl. rumors;
(animal) ears;uncertain news
sługa (swoo-ga) f. servant
słup (swoop) m. pillar; column;
post; pole; pylon; landmark
słupek (swoo-pek) m. pillaret;
small post;stake;stud; rail
słuszność (swoosh-noshch) f.
rightness; equity; rightful-
ness; legitimacy;aptness;justice
słuszny (swoosh-ni) adj. m.
just; fair; right;pertinent;apt
służalczy (swoo-zhal-chi) adj.
m. servile ;cringing;subservient
służąca (swoo-zhown-tsa) f.
maid ;servant; cleaning woman

służący (swoo-zhówn-tsi) m.
  servant;manservant;domestic
służba (swoozh-ba) f. service
służbowy (swoozh-bo-vi) adj. m.
  official;business(trip etc.)
służyć (swoo-zhich) v. serve
słychać (swi-khach) v. people
  say; one hears;be heard
słynąć (swi-nównch) v. be famed
słynny (swin-ni) adj. m. famous
słyszalny (swi-shál-ni) adj. m.
  audible;within hearing range
słyszeć (swi-shech) v. hear
smacznego ! (smach-né-go) exp.
  good appetite
smaczny (smach-ni) adj. m. tasty
smagać (smá-gach) v. lash; whip
smagły (smág-wi) adj. m. swarthy
smak (smak) m. taste; relish;
  savor;palate;liking;appetite
smakołyk (sma-ko-wik) m. tidbit;
  delicacy;dainty;choice morsel
smakować (sma-ko-vach) v. taste
smakowity (sma-ko-vee-ti) adj.
  m. savory;appetizing;tasty
smalec (sma-lets) m. lard; fat
smar (smar) m. grease; lubricant
smarkać (smár-kach) v. blow nose
smarkacz (smar-kach) m. squirt;
  snot; whippersnapper;raw lad
smarkaty (smar-ká-ti) adj. m.
  snotty; callow;raw
smarować (sma-ro-vach) v. smear
smarowidło (sma-ro-víd-wo) n.
  grease; lubricant; ointment
smażyć (sma-zhich) v. fry
smętny (smán-tni) adj. m. melancholy; blue;doleful; dolorous
smoczek (smó-chek) m. nipple;
  pacifier;dummy;comforter
smok (smok) m. dragon
smoking (smo-king) m. dinner
  jacket; tuxedo;formal jacket
smolny (smól-ni) adj. m. resi-
  nous; pitchy;tarry
smoła (smó-wa) f. pitch; tar
smrodliwy (smrod-lee-vi) adj. m.
  rank; stinky; smelly; foul
smród (smroot) m. stench; fetor
smucić (smoó-cheech) v. sadden
smukły (smoók-wi) adj. m. slender; slim; willowy; gracile
smutek (smoo-tek) m. sorrow;
  sadness ; grief; mournfulness

smutny (smoot-ni) adj. m. sad
smycz (smich) f. leash;dog lead
smyczek (smi-chek) m. (violin)
  bow; fiddle stick
smyk (smik) m.whippersnapper;
  brat; kid; small boy
snop (snop) m. sheaf; bunch
snop światła (snop shvyat-wa)
  light beam;light shaft
snuć (snooch) v. spin;reel off
snycerz (sni-tsesh) m. sculptor
sobek (so-bek) m. egoist
sobota (so-bo-ta) f. Saturday
sobowtór (so-bóv-toor) m. double
sobol (so-bool) m. sable (fur)
sobór (só-boor) m. synod
socjalista (so-tsya-lees-ta)
  m. socialist
socjalizacja (so-tsya-lee-zá-
  tsya) f. socialization
socjalizm (so-tsya-leezm) m.
  socialism
socjologia (so-tsyo-lóg-ya) f.
  sociology ; social science
soczewica (so-che-vee-tsa) f.
  lentil; lentils
soczewka (so-chev-ka) f. lens
soczysty (so-chís-ti) adj. m.
  juicy ; sappy; mellow; coarse
soda (so-da) f. soda
sodowa woda (so-dó-va vo-da) f.
  soda water
sofa (só-fa) f. lounge; sofa
sofistyczny (so-fees-tích-ni)
  adj. m. sophistical; captious
sojusz (so-yoosh) m. alliance
sojusznik (so-yoosh-neek) m.
  ally;associate joined for a
                   common purpose
sok (sok) m. sap; juice
sokół (so-koow) m. falcon
solanka (so-lan-ka) f. salt
  spring; solted bread roll:brine
solić (so-leéch)v.salt;add salt
Solidarność (so-lee-dár-noshch)s.
  Solidarity Labor Union;solidarity
solidarny (so-lee-dár-ni) adj.
  m. solidary; sympathetic
solidny (so-leéd-ni) adj. m.
  solid; firm;sound:reliable;safe
solista (so-lees-ta) m. soloist
soliter (so-leé-ter) m. tapeworm; solitary tree; solitaire
  (gem stone)

solniczka (sol-neech-ka) f.
saltshaker; saltcellar
solo (so-lo) adv. solo
solny (sol-ni) adj. m. saline
solony (so-lo-ni) adj. m. salt-
ed ; corned(beef);salt cured
sołtys (sow-tis) m. village
head(officer below wójt)
sonata (so-na-ta) f. sonata
sonda (son-da) f. probe; feeler;
lead;plummet;sounding ballon
sonet (so-net) m. sonnet
sopel (so-pel) m. icicle
sopran (sop-ran) m. soprano
sortowac (sor-to-vach) v. sort
sos (sos) m. gravy; sauce
sosna (sos-na) f. pine
sosnina (sosh-nee-na) f. pine-
wood;pine tree;pine branches
sowa (so-va) f. owl
sowity (so-vee-ti) adj. m. lav
ish;ample;abundant;rich
sód (sood) m. sodium
sól (sool) f. salt
spacerowac (spa-tse-ro-vach) v.
walk; stroll; walk about
spacja (spa-tsya) f. (print)
space
spaczac (spa-chach) v. warp;
pervert; twist;distort
spaczenie (spa-che-ne) n. distortion; perversion; warp
spac (spach) v. sleep;slumber
spad (spat) m. slope; drop
spadac (spa-dach) v. fall; drop
spadek (spa-dek) m. fall; inheritance; downfall;slope;dip
spadkobierca (spad-ko-byer-tsa)
m. heir;inheritor;successor
spadochron (spa-do-khron) m.
parachute
spadzisty (spa-dzhees-ti) adj.
m. steep;sloping;precipitous
spajac (spa-yach) v. weld; solder; link;join;unite;bond
spalenizna (spa-le-neez-na) f.
(smell of) burning (smoke)
spalic (spa-leech) v. burn out
spalony (spa-lo-ni) adj. m.
adust; (sport) offside
sparzyc (spa-zhich) v. burn;
sting ; scald;blister;scorch

spasły (spas-wi) adj. m. fat
spasc (spashch) v. fall; fatten
spawacz (spa-vach) m. welder
spawac (spa-vach) v. weld; solder; weld metal
spawanie (spa-va-ne) n. weld-
ing(of metals etc.)
spazm (spazm) m. spasm;convulsion
spec (spets) m. specialist;expert;
craftsman; dab hand; dab
specjalizacja (spe-tsya-lee-
zats-ya) f. specialization
specjalnosc (spe-tsyal-noshch)
f. specialty;peculiarity
specjalny (spe-tsyal-ni) adj.
m. special;express;particular
specificzny (spe-tsi-feech-ni)
adj. m. specific;peculiar
spedytor (spe-di-tor) m. shipp-
ping agent; forwarding agent
spekulacja (spe-koo-lats-ya) f.
speculation; venture
spekulant (spe-koo-lant) m.
profiteer; speculator;gambler
spekulowac (spe-koo-lo-vach) v.
speculate; profiteer; gamble
spelunka (spe-loon-ka) f. joint
spełniac (spew-nach) v. perform;
fulfill;comply with;accomplish
spędzac (span-dzach) v. round
up (cattle); spend (time);
abort;drive away;gather;pass time
spichlerz (spee-khlesh) m. gran-
ary
spiczasty (spee-chas-ti) adj. m.
pointed;peaked;tapering;sharp
spiec (spyets) v. burn;scorch;
sunblister;blush; parch;sinter
spieniężyc (spye-nan-zhich) v.
cash(checks);sell(property)
spieniony (spye-no-ni) adj. m.
foamy;foaming;covered with foam
spierac się (spye-rach shan) v.
argue;contend;quarrel;dispute
spieszny (spyesh-ni) adj. m.
hasty; quick; hurried
spieszyc się (spye-shich shan)
v. hurry; dismount;be eager
spięcie (spyan-che) n. buckle;
short circuit;collision; clash
spiętrzyc (spyan-tzhich) v.
pile up; heap up;bank up;dam up

spiker (spee-ker) m. (radio) announcer; disc jokey;Speaker

spinacz (spee-nach) m. fastener

spinać (spee-nać) v. fasten;
pin up; clasp; spur (horse)

spinka (speen-ka) f. clasp

spirala (spee-ra-la) f. spiral;
coil;volute;helix;spiral glide

spiralny (spee-ral-ni) adj. m.
spiral;helical;involuted

spirytus (spee-ri-toos) m. spirit; alcohol; spirits

spis (spees) m. list; register;
inventory;record;roll;census

spis rzeczy (spees zhe-chi)
table of contents

spisać (spee-sać) v. record;
write down;acquit oneself(well...

spisek (spee-sek) f. plot; conspiracy; hatching a plot

spiskowiec (spees-ko-vyets) m.
conspirator; plotter

spiż (speezh) m. brass; bronze

spiżarnia (spee-zhar-ña) f.
pantry; buttery; cupboard

spiżowy (spee-zhó-vi) adj. m.
brass ; bronze; booming(voice)

splatać (spla-tać) v. braid;
interlace;interlock;plait

splątać (splown-tać) v. snarl
up; mat;ravel;confuse;muddle up

spleśniały (spleśñ-ña-wi) adj.
m. moldy; musty ;mildewy

splot (splot) m. twine; twist;
coil;tangle;plaitcoincidence

splunąć (sploo-nównch) v. spit

spluwaczka (sploo-vách-ka) f.
spittoon ;cuspidor

spłacić (spwa-ćheećh) v. pay off

spłaszczyć (spwash-chich) v.
flatten out; humble (another)

spłata (spwa-ta) f. refund; instalment payment; repayment

spłatać figla (spwa-tać feeg-la)
v. play a trick;play a joke

spław (spwav) m. rafting;floating

spławiać (spwav-yać) v. float;
get rid;shunt; raft (timber etc.)

spławik (spwa-veek) m. (fishing)
float(dipping when fish bites)

spławny (spwav-ni) adj. m. navigable (river, waterway etc.)

spłodzić (spwo-dżheećh)v. beget; generate;put out;produce

spłonąć (spwo-nównch) v. burn
down;go up in flames; redden

spłonka (spwon-ka) f. percussion cap; primer;detonator

spłoszyć (spwo-shich) v. scare
away; frighten;startle; flush

spłowiały (spwo-vya-wi) adj.
m. faded (appearance)

spłukać (spwoo-kach) v. rinse;
flush;swill out;wash away

spływać (spwi-vach) v. flow
(down);drift;float(down stream)

spochmurnieć (spo-khmoor-ñećh)
v. grow cloudy; gloomy

spocić się (spo-ćheećh śhán) v.
sweat; become sweaty;prespire

spoczynek (spo-chi-nek) m. rest

spoczywać (spo-chi-vach) v. sit;
rest; lie down;be at rest;rest on

spod (spot) prep. form under

spodek (spo-dek) m. saucer

spodenki (spo-den-ki) pl.
(knee) pants; shorts

spodlić (spod-leećh) v. debase;
degrade; disgrace; demean

spodnie (spod-ñe) n. trousers;
pants; slacks; breeches

spodobać się (spo-do-bach śhán)
v. take a liking; take a fancy

spodziewać się (spo-dżhe-vach
śhán)v.expect; hope for

spoglądać (spo-glown-dach) v.
look out; look at; contemplate

spoić (spo-eećh) v. make drunk;
weld; ply with liquor

spoistość (spo-ees-toshćh) f.
cohesion; compactness; density

spoisty (spo-ees-ti) adj. m.
compact;cohesive;dense;tenacious

spojenie (spo-yé-ne) n. weld;
joint; pubic symphysis

spojówka (spo-yoov-ka) f. con-
junctiva

spojrzeć (spoy-zhech) v. look;
glance at; gaze at;view

spojrzenie (spoy-zhe-ñe) n.
glance; look; gaze;peep

spokojny (spo-koy-ni) adj. m.
quiet; calm; peaceful;still

spokój (spó-kooy) m. peace; calm ;quiet;serenity;placidity

spokrewniony (spo-krev-ño-ni) adj. m. related to; related

spoliczkować (spo-leech-ko-vaćh) v. slap face

społeczeństwo (spo-we-cheń-stvo) n. society; public;community

społeczny (spo-wéch-ni) adj. m. social (evil etc.);public;welfare

społem (spó-wem) adv, together in common ;jointly; unitedly

spomiędzy (spo-myáń-dzi) prep. from among;from the midst

sponad (spó-nat) prep. from above ; from over(the top of...)

sponiewierać (spo-ne-vye-raćh) v. abuse; ill-treat; maltreat

spontaniczny (spon-ta-ńeech-ni) adj. m. spontaneous; voluntary

sporadyczny (spo-ra-dich-ni) adj. m. sporadic; occasional

sporny (spor-ni) adj. m. controversial;debatable;questionable

sporo (spo-ro) adv. good deal; a lot of; briskly;quite a few

sport (sport) m. sport;athletics

sportowiec (spor-tó-vyets) m. sportsman;athlete;sporting man

spory (spó-ri) adj. m. pretty big; fast; useful; lasting

sporządzać (spo-zhówn-dzaćh) v. make up;draw up; make out

sposobić (spo-só-beećh) v. prepare; make ready(colloquial exp.)

sposobność (spo-sob-noshćh) v. opportunity;occasion;chance

sposobny (spo-sób-ni) adj. m. convenient; capable; able

sposób (spó-soop) m. means; way

spostrzegać (spo-stzhe-gaćh) v. notice; perceive;observe;spot

spostrzegawczy (spo-stzhe-gav-chi) adj. m. quick to notice; keen;observant;perceptive

spostrzeżenie (spo-stzhe-zhe-ńe) n. observation ;awareness;notice

spośród (spó-shrood) prep. from amongst;from the midst

spotęgować (spo-tán-gó-vaćh) v. intensify; increase ;strengthen

spotkać (spot-kaćh) v. come across; meet ;run across;befall

spotkanie (spot-ka-ńe) n. meeting; date; encounter

spotwarzać (spo-tva-zhaćh) v. calumniate;defame; slander

spoufalać się (spo-oo-fa-laćh śhán) v. become intimate

spowiadać (spo-vya-daćh) v. confess; listen to confession

spowiednik (spo-vyed-ñeek) m. confessor (priest)

spowiedź (spo-vyedzh) f. confession; confided secrets

spowijać (spo-vee-yaćh) v. swathe; wrap;shroud; cover

spowodować (spo-vo-do-vaćh) v. cause ; induce; set off

spoza (spó-za) prep. from behind;from beyond;from outside

spozierać (spo-zhe-raćh) v. glance at;look;gaze at

spożycie (spo-zhi-ćhe) n. consumption;intake (food,calories)

spożywać (spo-zhi-vaćh) v. consume; eat; drink; have a meal

spożywca (spo-zhiv-tsa) m. consumer

spożywcze artykuły (spo-zhiv-che ar-ti-koo-wi) pl, n. groceries;food products

spód (spoot) m. bottom; foot

spódnica (spod-ñee-tsa) f. skirt ; petticoat;apron strings

spójnia (spooy-ña) f. bond; union; tie; bond; link

spójnik (spooy-ñeek) m. conjunction

spółdzielczość (spoow-dżhel-choshćh) f. cooperation

spółdzielnia (spoow-dżhel-ña) f. coop; cooperative

spółgłoska (spoow-gwos-ka) f. consonant (grammar)

spółka (spoow-ka) f. partnership; company ;society

spór (spoor) m. strife; dispute

spóźniać się (spoozh-ñaćh śhán) v. be late; be slow;come late

spóźnienie (spoozh-ñe-ńe) n. delay; late coming;late arrival

spóźniony (spoozh-ño-ni) adj. m. late ;delayed;belated;tardy

spracować się (spra-tso-vaćh śhán) v. be tired; be exhausted ; have worked hard

spracowany (spra-tso-va-ni) adj.
m. overworked;exhausted; tired

spragniony (sprag-no-ni) adj.
m. thirsty;thirsting for

sprawa (spra-va) f. affair; matter; cause; case;question;job

sprawca (sprav-tsa) m. doer;
author; culprit;originator

sprawdzic (správ-dźheeć) v.
verify;examine; test; check

sprawdzian (sprav-dżhan) n.
test; gauge; criterion;template

sprawiac (sprav-yaćh) v. cause;
bring to pass;occasion;afford

sprawiedliwosc (spra-vyed-lee-
vośhćh) f. justice; equity

sprawiedliwy (spra-vyed-lee-vi)
adj. m. just;righteous;fair

sprawka (sprav-ka) f. doing;
trick; small offense; prank

sprawnosc (správ-nośhćh) f. efficiency; dispatch; skill

sprawny (sprav-ni) adj. m. able;
efficient; deft; dexterous

sprawowac (sprav-vo-vaćh) v. perform;discharge; hold; exercise

sprawowanie (spra-vo-vá-ňe) n.
conduct; behavior;performance

sprawozdanie (spra-voz-dá-ňe) n.
report; account;statement

sprawozdawca (spra-voz-dáv-tsa)
m. reviewer; reporter

sprawunek (spra-voo-nek) m.
purchase(made while shopping)

spręzać (spran-żáćh) v. compress; tense;prestress

spręzarka (spran-zhár-ka) f.
compressor; air compressor

spręzenie (sprán-zhe-ňe) n.
compression;prestress;pretension

spręzyna (sprań-zhi-na) f.
spring; mainspring; impulse

spręzystość (sprań-zhis-tośhćh)
f. elasticity; energy;resilience

spręzysty (sprań-zhis-ti) adj.
m. elastic; springy; energetic

sprostowac (spros-to-vaćh) v.
rectify; correct; right

sprostowanie (spros-to-vá-ňe)
v. rectification;correction

sproszkowac (sprosh-ko-vaćh) v.
pulverize; levigate;triturate

sprosny (sprośh-ni) adj. m.
obscene; lewd ;foul(language)

sprowadzac (spro-va-dzaćh) v.
bring; import; fetch; call in

sprochniały (sprookh-ňá-wi)
adj. m. rotten;decayed

sprochniec (sprookh-ňećh) v.
rot; decay; moulder;grow carious

spryciarz (spri-ćhash) m. dodger; trickster; slyboots

spryskac (spriśh-kaćh) v. splash

spryt (sprit) m. shrewdness;
cunning; gumption; knack

sprytny (sprit-ni) adj. m.
tricky; clever;cunning; cute

sprzączka (spzhówńch-ka) f.
buckle ;clasp

sprzątaczka (spzhówn-tách-ka)
f. cleaning woman;charwoman

sprzątac (spzhówn-taćh) v.
tidy up; clean up; clear up;
pich up; take away;snatch away

sprzątanie (spzhówn-tá-ňe) n.
clearing; tidying up;housework

sprzeciw (spzhe-ćheev) m. objection; opposition; resistance

sprzeciwiac się (spzhe-ćheev-
yaćh śhań) v. object; oppose

sprzeczac sie (spzhe-chaćh
śhań) v. fight; argue; dispute;
squabble; quarrel;contend about

sprzeczka (spzhéch-ka) f. quarrel; squable;altercation; tiff

sprzecznosc (spzhéch-nośhćh) f.
contradiction; discrepancy

sprzeczny (spzhéch-ni) adj. m.
contradictory;incompatible

sprzedac (spzhe-daćh) v. dispose of; sell; trade away

sprzedajny(spzhe-day-ni) adj.
m. venal;corrupt; corruptible

sprzedawca (spzhe-dav-tsa) m.
salesman; shop keeper;dealer

sprzedawczyni (spzhe-dav-chi-
ňee) f. saleslady;saleswoman

sprzedaż (spzhe-dash) f. sale

sprzedaż detaliczna (spzhe-
dash de-ta-leećh-na) f. retail;sale at retail prices

sprzedaż hurtowa (spzhe-dash
khoor-tó-va) f. wholesale

sprzeniewierzenie (spzhe-ňe-
vye-zhe-ňe) n. embezzlement

sprzęgać (spzhán-gach) v. couple; tie; link, team up; connect

sprzęgło (spzhán-gwo) n. clutch; coupling; coupler;attachment

sprzęt (spzhánt) m. implement; furniture; accessories; utensils; tackle; outfit; chattels

sprzyjać (spzhi-yach) v. favor

sprzykrzyć (spzhik-zhich) v. get sick of; get fed up with

sprzymierzeniec(spzhi-mye-zhe-nets) m. ally; confederate

sprzymierzony (spzhi-mye-zhó-ni) adj. m. allied;confederated

sprzysięgać się (spzhi-shán-gach shan) v. conspire; plot

sprzysiężenie (spzhi-shán-zhe-ne) n. plot; conspiracy

spuchnąć (spookh-nównch) v. swell

spulchniać (spoolkh-nach) v. fluff up;loosen;cultivate(soil)

spust (spoost) m. release; catch; slip; trigger; appetite; drain

spustoszenie (spoos-to-she-ne) n. devastation; ravage;ruin

spustoszyć (spoos-to-shich) v. devastate; ravage; make havoc

spuszczać (spoosh-chach) v. let down; drop; droop; lower; drain

spuścizna (spoosh-cheez-na) f. inheritance; legacy;heritage

spychacz (spi-khach) m. bulldozer; stripper

spychać (spi-khach) v. push down; relegate; drive away

spytać się (spi-tach shan) v. ask; ask a question

srać (srach) v. shit (vulg.)

srebrnik (srebr-neek) m. silver-coin; silversmith

srebrny (srebr-ni) adj. m. silver; of silver

srebro (sreb-ro) n. silver

srebrzyć (sreb-zhich) v. silver-plate;silver;wash with silver

srebrzysty (sreb-zhis-ti) adj. m. silvery (glow,color etc.)

srogi (sró-gee) adj. m. fierce; cruel; severe; srict; grim

sroka (sró-ka) f. magpie

srokaty (sro-ká-ti) adj. m. piebald (horse);with patches

srom (srom) m. disgrace; vulva

sromota(sro-mo-ta)f.shame;ignomity;disgrace

sromotny (sro-mót-ni) adj. m. shameful; disgraceful;infamous

srożyć (sro-zhich) v. rage; torment; storm;oppress;be severe

ssać (ssach) v. suck; exploit

ssak (ssak) m. mammal;mammalian

ssawka (ssav-ka) f. sucker

ssąca pompa (ssówn-tsa póm-pa) f. suction pump

stabilizować (sta-bee-lee-zó-vach) v. stabilize; fix

stacja (státs-ya) f. station

stacja benzynowa (státs-ya ben-zi-nó-va) f. filling or service station

stacjonować (sta-tsyo-no-vach) v. be stationed;be in garrison

staczać (sta-chach) v. roll down; fight (battle)

staczać się (sta-chach shan) v. roll down; go from bad to worse;be on the down grade

stać (stach) v. stand; be stopped; farewell; ill-afford;rise

stać się (stach shan) v.become; grow; occur; happen

stadion (sta-dyon) m. stadium

stadło (sta-dwo) n. couple

stadnina (stad-nee-na) f. stud

stado (sta-do) n. flock; herd

stagnacja (stag-nats-ya) f. stagnation;recession;stagnancy

stajnia (stay-na) f. stable

stal (stal) f. steel

stale (sta-le) adv. constantly; always; for ever;incessantly

stalownia (sta-lóv-na) f. steel-mill; steel plant; steel works

stalowy (sta-ló-vi) adj. m. steel; steely; steel gray

stała (sta-wa) f. constant

stałość (sta-wośhch) f. stability; firmness; steadiness

stały (sta-wi) adj. m. stable; permanent; solid; fixed;firm

stamtąd (stam-tównd) adv. from there; from over there;out of it

stan (stan) m. state; status; condition;order; estate; class

stanąć (sta-nównch) v. stand up; stop at; put up; rise; set foot standaryzować (stan-da-ri-zo-vach) v. standardize

stanik (sta-ńeek) m. bodice; bra; brassière;waste; corsage

staniol (stań-yol) m. tin foil

stanowczość (sta-nov-choshch) f. determination; finality

stanowczy (sta-nov-chi) adj. m. final; positive; decided;firm

stanowić (sta-no-veech) v. establish; determine; constitute;; decide; proclaim

stanowisko (sta-no-vees-ko) n. position; post; status; stand

starać się (sta-rach shań) v. take care; try one's best

staranie (sta-ra-ńe) n.care; endeavor; exertion; pains

staranny (sta-rán-ni) adj. m. careful; accurate; nice;exact

starcie (star-che) n. clash; collision; friction ; squabble

starczy (star-chi) adj. m. senile; v.:it is enough (exp.)

starczyć (star-chich) v. suffice

starodawny (sta-ro-dav-ni) adj. m. old time; ancient;antique

staromodny (sta-ro-mod-ni) adj. m. old fashioned;outmoded

starosta (sta-ros-ta) m. county-head; wedding host; foreman

starość (sta-roshch) f. old age

staroświecki (sta-rosh-vyets-kee) adj. m. old fashioned

starożytność (sta-ro-zhit-noshch) f. antiquity; ancient times

starożytny (sta-ro-zhit-ni) adj. m. ancient; antique ;old world

starszeństwo (star-sheń-stvo) n. seniority ; superiority

starszy (star-shi) adj. m. older; elder; superior(officer)

starszyzna (star-shiz-na) f. the elders; the seniors;the chiefs

start (start) m. take-off; start

startować (star-to-vach) v. start; take off; make a start

staruszek (sta-roo-shek) m. old fellow;old man;old gentleman

stary (sta-ri) adj. m. old

starzec (sta-zhets) m. old man

starzec się (sta-zhech shań) v. grow old ;age;grow stale;go bad

stateczny (sta-tech-ni) adj. m. stable; bouyant; staid

statek (sta-tek) m. ship; craft; vessel;boat;steamship

statki (stat-kee) pl. kitchen pots & pans

statua (sta-too-a) f. statue

statut (sta-toot) m. statute

statyka (sta-ti-ka) f. statics

statysta (sta-tis-ta) m. supernumerary (actor);dummy;mute

statystyczny (sta-tis-tich-ni) adj. m. statistical; statistic

statystyka (sta-tis-ti-ka) f. statistics ;returns

staw (stav) m. pond; joint

stawać się (sta-vach shań) v. become; grow (scarce,big etc.)

stawiać (sta-vyach) v. place; erect; put; stand; offer; lay down ;post; station;put upright

stawka (stav-ka) f. stake

stąd (stownd) adv. from here; away;therefore;that is why

stągiew (stown-gyev) f. vat

stąpać (stown-pach) v. pace; tramp;tread;plod along;lumber

stchórzyć (stkhoo-zhich) v. show fear; shrink with fright

stearyna (ste-a-ri-na) f. stearin (glyceryl tristearate)

stek (stek) m. steak; pile of... (lies; insults etc.); pack of...

stelmach (stel-makh) m. cartwright;wheelwright

stempel (stem-pel) m. stamp; prop; ramrod; punch; die

stemplowany (stem-plo-va-ni) adj. m. cancelled; used

stenograf (ste-no-graph) m. stenographer;sorthand writer

stenografia (ste-no-graph-ya) f. shorthand ;stenography

stenotypistka (ste-no-ti-peest-ka) f. stenotypist ; steno

step (step) m. steppe

ster (ster) m. helm; rudder

sterczeć (ster-chech) v. stand out; stick out; tower; bulge

stereoskop (ste-re-os-kop) m. stereoscope

stereotypowy (ste-re-o-ti-po-
vi) adj. m. stereotyped
sternik (ster-ńeek) m. pilot
sterować (ste-ro-vaćh) v. steer
sterta (ster-ta) f. stack
stebnować (stań-bno-vaćh) v.
stitch; quilt
stęchlizna (stań-khleez-na) f.
fusty smell; musty smell
stęchły (stańkh-wi) adj. m.
musty; stałe; foul;fusty;frowsty
stękać (stań-kaćh) v. moan;
groan; utter a groan;complain
stępić (stań-peećh) v. blunt;
dull; take the edge off
stępienie (stań-pye-ńe) n. dullness (of knife; mind etc.)
stęskniony (stań-skńo-ni) adj.
m. sick for; yearning for;
hankering for;nostalgic
stężały (stań-zhá-vi) adj. m.
hardened; stiff; concentrated ; solidified;coagulated
stężec (stań-zhećh) v. harden;
stiffen ; coagulate;concentrate
stężenie (stań-zhe-ńe) n. con-
centration; strength(solutions)
stłoczyć (stwo-chićh) v. cram;
compress;jam;squize;pack;pile up
stłuc (stwoots) v. smash; break;
bruise;shatter;injure;beat up
stłuczenie (stwoo-che-ńe) n.
bruise; break;contusion;injury
stłumiać (stwoom-yaćh)v. dampen;
muffle;deaden;suppress;stifle
sto (sto) num. hundred
stocznia (stoch-ńa) f. shipyard
stodoła (sto-do-wa) f. barn
stoik (sto-eek) m. Stoic
stoisko (sto-ees-ko) n. stand
stojak (sto-yak) m. stand
stojący (sto-yown-tsi) adj. m.
standing; stagnant;erect;upright
stok (stok) m. slope;hillside
stokroć (sto-kroćh)adv.hundred
times;a hundred times;hundredfold
stokrotka (sto-krot-ka) f. daisy
stokrotny (sto-krot-ni) adj.
m. hundredfold repeated
stolarnia (sto-lár-ńa) f. joiner's shop ;carpinter's shop
stolarz (sto-lash) m. cabinetmaker; joiner; carpenter

stolec (sto-lets) m. stool
(large); bowel movement
stolica (sto-lee-tsa) f. capi-
tal(of a country)
stolik (sto-leek) m. small
table ;nice little table
stolnica (stol-ńee-tsa) f. molding board ; paste board
stołeczny (sto-wech-ni) adj. m.
metropolitan (taxes);capital(city)
stołek (sto-wek) m. stool
stołować (sto-wo-vaćh) v. board
stołownik (sto-wov-ńeek) m.
boarder
stołówka (sto-woov-ka) f. mess
hall; mess; cantine
stonka (ston-ka) f. potato
beetle ;potato bug;Colorado beetle
stonoga (sto-no-ga) f. centi-
pede ; wood louse
stop (stop) m. (metal) alloy;
melt;traffic sign :stop; halt
stopa (sto-pa) f. foot;standard
stopa procentowa (sto-pa pro-
tsen-to-va) f. interest rate
stopa życiowa (sto-pa zhi-cho-
va) f. living standard
stoper (sto-per) m. stopwatch
stopić (sto-peećh) v. melt
stopień (sto-pyeń) m. (stair)
step; degree; grade;extent
stopniały (stop-ńa-wi) adj.m.
molten away; dwindled;shrunk
stopnieć (stop-ńech) v. melt
down ;melt away;srink;dwindle
stopniowo (sto-ño-vo) adv.
gradually;little by little
stopniowy (stop-ńo-vi) adj. m.
gradual ;progressive
stora (sto-ra) f. shade; blind
storczyk (stor-chik) m. orchid
stos (stos) m. (wood) pile
stos atomowy (stos a-to-mo-vi)
m. atomic pile
stosować (sto-so-vaćh) v. use
stosownie (sto-sov-ńe) adv.
accordingly; properly
stosowny (sto-sov-ni) adj. m.
proper; convenient;opportune
stosunek (sto-soo-nek) m. rate;
relation; proportion;attitude
stosunek płciowy (sto-soo-nek
pwćho-vi) m. sexual intercourse

stosunki handlowe (sto-soon-kee khand-lo-ve) pl. trade relations ;commercial relations

stosunkowy (sto-soon-ko-vi) adj. m. relative; proportional

stowarzyszenie (sto-va-zhi-she-ńe) n. association; club

stożek (sto-zhek) m. cone

stożkowaty (stozh-ko-va-ti) adj. m. conical; cone shaped

stog (stoog) m. stack (rick)

stoł (stoow) m. table

stracenie (stra-tse-ńe) n. execution; loss ; doom

straceniec (stra-tse-ńets) m. desperado; madcap

strach (strakh) m. fear; fright

stracić (stra-cheech) v. lose; execute(a man);shed(teeth etc.)

stragan (stra-gan) m. booth; stand; (market) stall

straganiarz (stra-ga-nash) m. stand owner; stall holder

strajkować (stray-ko-vach) v. go on strike; strike

strapienie (stra-pye-ńe) n. worry; distress; heartbreak

strapiony (stra-pyo-ni) adj. m. worried; dejected; distressed

straszak (stra-shak) m. noisy toy pistol; scarecrow; bugaboo

straszliwy (strash-lee-vi) adj. m. horrible; fearsome;awful

straszny (strash-ni) adj. m. awful; terrible;awesome;frightful

straszyć (stra-shich) v. frighten; haunt; threaten; bluff

straszydło (stra-shid-wo) n. scarecrow; fright

strata (stra-ta) f. loss

strategia (stra-teg-ya) f. strategy ;generalship

strategiczny (stra-te-geech-ni) adj. m. strategic

stratny (strat-ni) adj. m. one that lost;being the looser

strawa (stra-va) f. food ; meal

strawić (stra-veech) v. digest; consume; bear;stomach; stand

strawne (strav-ne) n. food ration (in the army etc.)

straż (strash) f. guard; watch ; safe custody;strict guard;escort

straż pożarna (strash po-zhar-na) f. fire brigade

straż przednia (strash pzhed-ńa) f. vanguard ;advance guard

straż tylna (strash til-na) f. rearguard ; rear guard

strażak (stra-zhak) m. fireman

strażnica (strazh-ńee-tsa) f. guardhouse; watchtower

strażnik (strazh-ńeek) m. guard; watchman ;sentry

strącić (stroun-cheech) v. knock off (apples); throw down

strączek (stroun-chek) m. (small) pod ;hull;husk;legume

strąk (strounk) m. pod;hull;husk

strefa (stre-fa) f. zone ;area

streszczać (stresh-chach) v. sum up; summarize;abbreviate

streszczenie (stresh-che-ńe) n. resume; summary ;digest

stręczyciel (stran-chi-chel) m. pimp; procurer ; broker

stręczyć (stran-chich) v. procure (women) ; recommend

strofa (stro-fa) f. strophe

strofować (stro-fo-vach) v. reprimand ;admonish;scold;chide

stroić (stro-eech) v. dress up; tune up; make fun ;add beauty

strojny (stroy-ni) adj. m. dressed up ; elegant; smart

stromy (stro-mi) adj. m. steep

strona (stro-na) f. side; page; region ; aspect; part; party

stronnictwo (stron-ńeets-tvo) n. party (political)

stronniczy (stron-ńee-chi) adj. m. partial; biased;unfair

stronnik (stron-ńeek) m. partisan; supporter;follower;henchman

strop (strop) m. ceiling ;roof

stropić (stro-peech) v. discourage ; confound; abash;disconcert

stroskany (stros-ka-ni) adj.m. worried; sorrowful; dejected

strój (strooy) m. attire ;dress

stróż (stroosh) m. watchman

strudzony (stroo-dzo-ni) adj. m. weary ; tired;exhausted

strug (stroog) m. plane (tool)

struga (stroo-ga) f. stream; creek ; trickle;flow in streams strugać (stroo-gach) v. whittle

struktura (strook-too-ra) f. structure; flow; flux; jet; torrents

strumień (stroo-myeń) m. stream; syringe; hypodermic syringe

struna (stroo-na) f. string; chord; wire; (metal) wire

struna głosowa (stroo-na gwo-so-va) vocal cord

strup (stroop) m. scab; crust

struś (stroosh) m. ostrich

strych (strikh) m. attic

strychnina (strikh-ńee-na) f. strychnine

stryczek (stri-chek) m. (hanging) rope; noose; the halter

stryj (striy) m. uncle

stryjeczny brat (stri-yech-ni brat) m. cousin

strzał (stzhaw) m. shot

strzała (stzha-wa) f. arrow

strzaskać (stzhas-kach) v. smash to pieces; shatter

strząsać (stzhown-sach) v. shake off: shake down; flick off

strzec (stzhets) v. guard; protect; watch; keep an eye on

strzelać (stzhe-lach) v. shoot; fire; slap; score; blunder

strzelanie (stzhe-la-ńe) n. shooting (practice); gunfire

strzelanina (stzhe-la-ńee-na) f. gunfire; shots; gunplay

strzelba (stzhel-ba) f. shotgun

strzelec (stzhe-lets) m. shooter; rifleman; sniper; gunner; scorer

strzelnica (stzhel-ńee-tsa) f. shooting range; rifle range

strzelniczy proch (stzhel-ńee-chi prokh) m. gunpowder

strzemienne (stzhe-myen-ne) n. parting drink; stirrup cup

strzemię (stzhe-myeń) n. stirrup

strzepać (stzhe-pach) v. brush off; flick off; shake off (away)

strzęp (stzhanp) m. shred; tatter

strzępić (stzhań-peech) v. shred

strzępić język (stzhań-peech yań-zik) v. wag one's tongue; waste breath; talk nonsense

strzyc (stzhits) v. cut; clip; shear; cut (hair); mow; trim; graze

strzyc uszami (stzhits oo-sha-mee) v. prick up ears

strzykać (stzhi-kach) v. squirt; spray; inject; ache

strzykawka (stzhi-kav-ka) f. syringe; hypodermic syringe

strzyżenie (stzhi-zhe-ńe) n. (hair) cut; sheep shearing

strzyżony (stzhi-zho-ni) adj. m. cropped; cut clipped

student (stoo-dent) m. student

studenteria (stoo-den-tér-ya) pl. students; student folks

studiować (stoo-dyo-vach) v. study; investigate; peer

studnia (stood-ńa) f. well

studzić (stoo-dzheech) v. cool down (one's tea etc.)

studzienny (stoo-dźhen-ni) adj. m. well (shaft; water etc.)

stuk (stook) m. knock; clutter

stukać (stoo-kach) v. knock; tap; hit; rap; patter; rattle; drum

stulecie (stoo-le-chè) n. century; an age; hundred years

stuletni (stoo-lét-ńee) adj. m. hundred years old; age old

stulić (stoo-leech) v. press tight; close up; coil up

stwardnieć (stvard-ńech) v. harden; stiffen; grow callous

stwardniały (stvard-ńa-wi) adj. m. hardened; hard; sclerotic

stwardnienie (stvard-ńe-ńe) n. hardening; callosity

stwierdzać (stvyer-dzach) v. state; find out; confirm

stwierdzenie (stvyer-dze-ńe) n. statement; ascertainment

stworzenie (stvo-zhe-ńe) n. creature; formation; creation

stworzyciel (stvo-zhi-chel) m. creator; maker (of the world)

stworzyć (stvo-zhich) v. create; produce; set up; compose

Stwórca (Stvoor-tsa) m. Creator; Maker

styczeń (sti-cheń) m. January

styczna (stich-na) f. tangent

styczność (stich-nośhch) f. contact; tangency; adjacency

stygmat (stig-mat) m. stigma

stygnąć (stig-nównch) v. cool down; cool off; cool

styk (stik) m. contact; butt

stykać się (sti-kach shan) v.
contact; touch;adjoin;meet

styl (stil) m. style; fashion

stylista (sti-lees-ta) m. styl-
ist

stylistyka (sti-lees-ti-ka) f.
art of composition ;syntax

stylowy (sti-lo-vi) adj. m. stylish; of style;in a given style

stypa (sti-pa) f. wake; funny
confusion; funeral banquet

stypendium (sti-pend-yoom) n.
scholarship; stipend; grant

subiektywny (soo-byek-tiv-ni)
adj. m. subjective

sublokator (soob-lo-ka-tor) m.
lodger ;subtenant

subordynacja (soob-or-di-nats-
ya) f. subordination

subskrypcja (soob-skrip-tsya) f.
subscription

substancja (soob-stan-tsya) f.
substance; matter

subsydiować (soob-sid-yo-vach)
v. subsidize

subtelność (sub-tel-noshch) f.
subtlety; niceness; delicacy

subtelny (soob-tel-ni) adj. m.
subtle;nice;fine;refined

subwencja (soob-ven-tsya) f.
subsidy; grant in aid

suchar (soo-khar) m. dry-bread
ration; cracker; biscuit

sucharek (soo-kha-rek) m. cracker ; biscuit

suchość (soo-khoshch) f. dryness

suchotnik (soo-khot-neek) m. con-
sumptive

suchoty (soo-kho-ti) pl. consumption; phthisis

suchy (soo-khi) adj. m. dry

sufit (soo-feet) m. ceiling

sugerować (soo-ge-ro-vach) v.
suggest;allude;hint

sugestia (soo-ges-tya) f. suggestion; motion; proposal

sugestywny (soo-ges-tiv-ni) adj.
m. suggestive(speech etc.)

suka (soo-ka) f. bitch

sukces (sook-tses) m. success

sukcesja (sook-tses-ya) f. succession; inheritance; devolution

sukienka (soo-ken-ka) f. dress

sukiennice (soo-ken-nee-tse)
n. weaver's or draper's market
hall ; cloth hall

sukiennik (soo-ken-neek) m.
draper; clothier

suknia (sook-na) f. gown

sukno (sook-no) n. cloth

sultan (soow-tan) m. sultan

sum (soom) m. sheatfish

suma (soo-ma) f. sum; total;
high mass ;entirety;whole

sumaryczny (soo-ma-rich-ni)
adj. m. summary; total;global

sumienie (soo-mye-ne) n. conscience

sumienny (soo-myen-ni) adj. m.
conscientious;scrupulous

sumować (soo-mo-vach) v. sum up

sunąć (soo-nownch) v. glide;
slide; push; move; skim along

supeł (soo-pew) m. knot

surdut (soor-doot) m. frock
coat; overcoat

surogat (soo-ro-gat) m. surro-
gate; substitute for

surowica (soo-ro-vee-tsa) f.
serum

surowiec (soo-ro-vyets) m.
raw material;staple; rawhide

surowość (soo-ro-voshch) f.
severity; crudeness ;rigor

surowy (soo-ro-vi) adj. m.
severe; raw; coarse; harsh

surówka (soo-roov-ka) f. pig
iron;fruit salad;raw hide

susza (soo-sha) f. drought;
dryness ;dry weather

suszarka (soo-shar-ka) f. (hair)
dryer ; desciccator

suszarnia (soo-shar-na) f. dry-
ing shed ;drying plant;kiln

suszka (soosh-ka) f. blotter

suszyć (soo-shich) v. dry

sutanna (soo-tan-na) f. cassock

sutener (soo-te-ner) m. cadet;
souteneur ; bully ;ponce

suterena (soo-te-re-na) f.base-
ment

sutka (soot-ka) f. nipple

suty (soo-ti) adj. m. copious;
abundant ; lavish ;plentiful;rich

suwać (soo-vach) v. shove
suwak (soo-vak) m. slide rule
swada (sva-da) f. eloquence
swar (svar) m. squabble; quarrel;rife;dissension
swarliwy (svar-lee-vi) adj. m.
quarrelsome;cantankerous
swastyka (svas-ti-ka) f. swas-
tica; swastika.
swat (svat) m. matchmaker
swatać (sva-tach) v. matchmake
swaty (sva-ti) n. matchmaking
swawola (sva-vo-la) f. anarchy
swawolny (sva-vol-ni) adj. m.
unruly;playful;frolicsome;wilful
swąd (svownd) m. reek; stench
sweter (sve-ter) m. sweater
swędzenie (svan-dzhe-ne) n.
itch; an itch; tingle
swędzić (svan-dzheech) v. itch
swoboda (svo-bo-da) f. freedom;
ease; latitude;liberty
swoboda działania (svo-bo-da
dzha-wa-na) v. freedom to act
swobodny (svo-bod-ni) adj. m.
free; easy;at liberty;loose;lax
swoisty (svo-ees-ti) adj. m.
specific;characteristic
swojski (svoy-skee) adj. m.
homely;familiar;friendly;tame
sworzeń (svo-zhen) m. carriage
bolt; lug bolt;cotter;pin
swój (svooy) pron. his; hers;my;
its;our;your;their;one's own
swój człowiek (svooy chwo-vyek)
m. trustworthy man
sybaryta (si-ba-ri-ta) m. Sy-
barite;sybarite; voluptuary
syberyjski (si-be-riy-skee) adj.
m. Siberian; of Siberia
sycić (si-cheech)v. satiate
syczec (si-chech) v. hiss
syfon (si-fon) m. siphon
sygnalizować (sig-na-lee-zo-
vach) v. signalize; signal
sygnał (sig-naw) m. signal
sygnatura (sig-na-too-ra) f.
(official) signature
sygnet (sig-net) m. signet;
seal ring; imprint;colophon
syk (sik) m. hiss;sizzle;fizzle
sylaba (si-la-ba) f. syllable

sylogizm (si-lo-geezm)m. syllo-
gism;rozumowanie dedukcyjne
sylweta (sil-ve-ta) f. silhou-.
ette; outline;profile;figure
symbioza (sim-byo-za) f. symbio-
sis:living together
symbol (sim-bol) m. symbol
symboliczny (sim-bo-leech-ni)
adj. m. symbolic ;symbolical
symbolizować (sim-bo-lee-zo-
vach) v. symbolize
symetria (si-metr-ya) f. symmetry
symetryczny (si-me-trich-ni)
adj. m. symmetrical
symfonia (sim-fon-ya) f. symphony
symfoniczny (sim-fo-neech-ni)
adj. m. symphonic
sympatia (sim-pat-ya) f. liking
sympatyczny (sim-pa-tich-ni)
adj. m. congenial;attractive
sympatyk (sim-pa-tik) m. well-
wisher; sympathizer
sympatyzować (sim-pa-ti-zo-vach)
v. like; go along; feel with
symptom (simp-tom) m. symptom
symulacja (si-moo-lats-ya) f.
simulation;make believe;sham
symulować (si-moo-lo-vach) v.
simulate ;feign;pretend;affect
syn (sin) m. son
synagoga (si-na-go-ga) f. synagogue
syndykat (sin-di-kat) m. syndi-
cate;syndicat;labor union
synek (si-nek) m. sonny
synekura (si-ne-koo-ra) f.
sinecure; cosy job;fat job
synod (si-nod) m. synod
synonim (si-no-heem) m. synonym
synowa (si-no-va) f. daughter
in law
synowiec (si-no-vyets) m. nephew
syntetyczny (sin-te-tich-ni)
adj. m. synthetic
synteza (sin-te-za) f. synthesis
sypać (si-pach) v. strew; pour;
scatter (dry matter);betray secrets
sypialnia (si-pyal-na) f. bedroom ;bedroom furniture suite
sypki (sip-kee) adj. m. loose
(dry);granular(substance);friable

sypki towar (sýp-kee tó-var) m.
granular goods; dry goods
syrena (si-re-na) f. siren;
mermaid;hooter;Warsaw's emblem
syrop (si-rop) m. syrup
syryjski (si-riý-skee) adj. m.
Syrian; of Syria
system (sís-tem) m. system
systematyczny (sys-te-ma-tich-
ni) adj. m. systematic; neat
syt (sit) adj. m. satiate; full
sytny (sit-ni) adj. m. filling
up; nourishing; satiating
sytuacja (si-too-ats-ya) f.
situation;circumstances;things
sytuować (si-too-o-vách) v. sit-
uate ; locate; position
sytuowany (si-too-o-vá-ni) adj.
m. situated ; placed;located
syty (si-ti) adj. m. satiate;
dilled up; well-fed;nourishing
szabla (sháb-la) f. sabre
szablon (sháb-lon) m. stencil;
pattern; model; stereotype
szablonowy (sha-blo-nó-vi) adj.
m. routine; stereotype
szach-mat (shakh-mat) m. check-
mate (in a chess game etc.)
szachista (sha-khees-ta) m.
chess player
szachować (sha-kho-vách) v.
check (in chess); check
szachownica (sha-khov-ñee-tsa)
f. chessboard ;checker board
szachraj (shákh-ray) m. cheat
szachrować (zhakh-ro-vách) v.
cheat; swindle; jockey
szachy (sha-khi) pl. chess
szacować (sha-tso-vách) v.
evaluate; estimate ;size up
szacunek (sha-tsóo-nek) m.
1. valuation; 2. respect
szafa (sha-fa) f. chest; wardrobe; bookcase ; cupboard
szafir (shá-feer) m. sapphire
szafka nocna (shaf-ka nóts-na)
f. night table;bedside table
szafot (sha-fot) m. (execution)
scaffold
szafować (sha-fó-vach) v. lavish ; squander;be liberal
szafran (shaf-ran) m. saffron

szajka (sháy-ka) f. gang
szakal (shá-kal) m. jackal
szal (shal) m. shawl ;scarf
szala (shá-la) f. scale
szalbierstwo (shal-byer-stvo)
n. swindle ; fraud;imposition
szalbierz (shál-byesh) m. fraud;
swindler ; quack ;impostor
szaleć (shá-lech) v. rage ;rave
szalenie (sha-lé-ñe) adv. mad-
ly; terribly;awfully;like mad
szaleniec (sha-lé-ñets) m. madman; daredevil ; desperado
szaleńczy (sha-leń-chi) adj. m.
frantic;mad;insane;reckless
szaleństwo (sha-leń-stvo) n.
fury; madness ; craze;frenzy
szalik (sha-leek) m. scarf
szalony (sha-ló-ni) adj. m. mad
szał (shaw) m. rage;fury;frenzy
szałas (sha-was) m. tent; shanty ; shed; shelter; chalet;hut
szamotac się (sha-mo-tach shán)
v. scuffle;, struggle; tussle
szampan (sham-pan) m. champagne
szaniec (shá-ñets) m. bastion
szanować (sha-nó-vach) v. respect; honor; have regard;esteem
szanowny (sha-nov-ni) adj. m.
honorable;worthy; dear(sir)
szansa (shán-sa) f. chance
szantaż (shán-tazh) m. blackmail ; extortion
szantażować (shan-ta-zhó-vach)
v. blackmail ;make squeal
szantażysta (shan-ta-zhis-ta)
m. blackmailer ;extortioner
szarak (shá-rak) m. hare; average man of the street ;yeoman
szarańcza (sha-rań-cha) v. locust ;swarm of locust;swarm
szarfa (shár-fa) f. scarf; sash
szargać (shár-gach) v. besmear;
foul up; slander;tarnish;slur
szarlatan (shar-lá-tan) m. confidence man; charlatan
szarotka (shar-ót-ka) f. edelweiss
szarość (sha-rośhch) f. greyness;
drabness ;dullness; duskiness
szarpać (shár-pach) v. jerk; pull;
tear; tousle ; knock about;assail

szaruga (sha-roo-ga) f. gray,
foul weather; gray skies

szary (sha-ri) adj. m. gray;drab

szarzec (sha-zhech) v. loom;
gray; grow dusky; show grey

szarzyzna (sha-zhiz-na) f.
grayness; drabness; duskiness

szarża (shar-zha) f. (cavalry)
charge;(military)rank; officer

szarżować (shar-zho-vach) v.
charge (recklessly);overact

szastać (shas-tach) v. squander

szata (sha-ta) f. garment;gown

szatan (sha-tan) m. satan; devil; very strong coffee

szatański (sha-tań-skee) adj.
m. devilish; infernal;satanic

szatkować (shat-ko-vach) v.
cut; chop; shred;slice

szatnia (shat-ńa) f. locker
room; coat room

szatynka (sha-tin-ka) f. dark-
blond girl;auburn haired woman

szczać (shchach) v. piss (vulg.)

szczapa (shcha-pa) f. split log;
splint; chip; sliver;thin man

szczaw (shchav) m. sorrel

szczątek (shchown-tek) m. remnant; vestige;fragment

szczebel (shche-bel) m.(ladder)
rung; spoke; grade ;round

szczebiot (shche-byot) m. chatter; chirp;babble;prattle;warble

szczebiotać (shche-byo-tach) v.
chirrup ; chirp; chatter;bable

szczebiotanie (shche-byo-ta-ńe)
n. chatter; prattle;chirp;warble

szczecina (shche-chee-na) f.
bristle (of hogs);stubble beard

szczególność (shche-gool-nośch)
f. peculiarity;singularity

szczególny (shche-gool-ni) adj.
m. peculiar; special; specific

szczegół (shche-goow) m. detail

szczegółowy (shche-goo-wo-vi)
adj. m. detailed; minute

szczekać (shche-kach) v. bark

szczekanie (shche-ka-ńe) n. bark

szczelina (shche-lee-na) f. slot;
crevice; cleft ;slit; rift;crack

szczelny (shchel-ni) adj. m.
(water) tight; (air) tight etc.

szczeniak (shche-ńak) m. puppy ; kid ; pup

szczep (shchep) m. graft; tribe;
seedling

szczepić (shche-peech) v. graft;
vaccinate; inoculate

szczepienie (shche-pye-ńe) n.
grafting; vaccination

szczepionka (shche-pyon-ka) f.
vaccine

szczerba (shcher-ba) f. jag;
notch; gap ;nick; chip; dent

szczerbaty (shcher-ba-ti) adj.
m.gap-toothed; jagged

szczerbić (shcher-beech) v. jag

szczerość (shche-rośch) f.
sincerity ; open-heartedness

szczerozłoty (shche-ro-zwo-ti)
adj. m. pure golden

szczery (shche-ri) adj. m.
sincere ;frank; candid

szczędzić (shchan-dźheech) v.
spare; economize ;grudge;stint

szczęk (shchank) m. clink;clash;
clang ;jangle; rattle

szczęka (shchan-ka) f. jaw

szczękać (shchan-kach) v.
clink; clang ;jangle;rattle

szczęścić się (shchańsh-cheech
śhań) v. have good luck

szczęście (shchańśh-che) n.
happiness; good luck success

szczęśliwy (shchań-shlee-vi)
adj. m. happy; lucky;successful

szczodrość (shchod-rośch) f.
generosity ;open-handedness

szczodry (shchod-ri) adj. m.
generous ;abundant; ample

szczoteczka (shcho-tech-ka) f.
small brush; toothbrush

szczotka (shchot-ka) f. brush

szczotkarski (shchot-kar-skee)
adj. m. brush ;brush maker's

szczotkować (shchot-ko-vach) v.
brush down; bursh;polish(a floor)

szczuć (shchooch) v. hiss; bait;
embitter against ;set dogs on

szczudło (shchood-wo) n. stilt ;
crutch

szczupak (shchoo-pak) m. pike

szczuplec (shchoop-lech) v.
slim down; reduce; diminish

szczupłość (shchoop-woshch) f. slimness; scarcity;scantiness

szczupły (shchoop-wi) adj. m. slim; slender; thin; lean

szczur (shchoor) m. rat

szczycic się (shchi-cheech shän) v. boast; take pride; be proud

szczypać (shchi-pach) v. pinch

szczypce (shchip-tse) pl. tongs; pliers; pincers; clippers

szczypczyki (shchip-chi-kee) pl. tweezers; forceps

szczypiorek (shchi-pyo-rek) m. chive

szczypta (shchip-ta) f. pinch

szczyt (shchit) m. top; summit

szczytny (shchit-ni) adj. m. lofty; sublime ;commendable

szczytowy (shchi-to-vi) adj.m. pick; culminant ; uppermost;top

szef (shef) m. boss; chief

szelest (she-lest) m. rustle

szeleścic (she-lesh-cheech) v. rustle; whisper(in the wind)

szelki (shel-kee) pl. suspenders; straps; belts; braces

szelma (shel-ma) f. rogue; scoundrel; wretch; knave

szelmostwo (shel-most-vo) n. roguery;rascally trick

szemrać (shem-rach) v. murmur; grumble;prattle;repine against

szept (shept) m. whisper

szeptać (shep-tach) v. whisper

szepnąć (shep-nownch) v. whisper; murmur; conspire; scheme

szereg (she-reg) m. row; file; series;range;chain(of events)

szeregować (she-re-go-vach) v. rank; classify; arrange

szeregowy (she-re-go-vi) adj.m. series; soldier in the ranks

szermierka (sher-myér-ka) f. fencing

szermierz (sher-myesh) m. fencer

szeroki (she-ro-kee) adj. m. wide;broad; ample; extensive

szerokość (she-ro-koshch) f. width; latitude; breath

szerokotorowa kolej (she-ro-ko-to-ro-va ko-ley) f. wide gauge railroad (Russian)

szerszeń (sher-sheń) m. hornet; wasp

szerzenie (she-zhe-ne) n. spread

szerzyć (she-zhich) v. spread

szesnasty (shes-nás-ti) num. sixteenth

szesnaście (shes-násh-che) num. sixteen

sześcian (shesh-chan) m. cube

sześcienny (shesh-chen-ni) adj. m. cubic

sześciokrotny (shesh-cho-krot-ni) adj. m. sixfold

sześcioro (shesh-cho-ro) num. six

sześć (sheshch) num. six

sześćdziesiąt (sheshch-dzhe-shownt) num. sixty

sześćdziesiąty (sheshch-dzhe-shown-ti) adj. m. sixtieth

sześćset (sheshch-set) num. six hundred

szew (shev) m. seam ;stitch

szewc (shevts) m. shoemaker

szewstwo (shev-stvo) n. shoemaking;shoemaking,trade

szkalować (shka-lo-vach) v. slander;defame; calumniate

szkapa (shka-pa) f. jade

szkaradny (shka-rad-ni) adj.m. hideous; ugly; abominable;nasty

szkarlatyna (shkar-la-ti-na) f. scarlet fever;scarlatina

szkarłat (shkar-wat) m. scarlet

szkarłatny (shkar-wat-ni) adj. m. scarlet;crimson; purple

szkatuła (shka-too-wa) f. casket

szkic (shkeets) m. outline; sketch; essay; study;draught

szkicować (shkee-tso-vach) v. sketch; outline; draw up;design

szkicownik (shkee-tsov-neek) m. sketch pad; sketchbook

szkielet (shke-let) m. skeleton; framework; shell; carcass

szkiełko (shkew-ko) n. small glass; pane;slide

szklanka (shklan-ka) f. (drinking) glass; glassful (of water etc.)

szklany (shkla-ni) adj. m. glass; glassy(eyes); vitreous

szklarz (shklash) m. glazier

szklić (shkleech) v. glaze;brag
szklisty (shklees-ti) adj. m.
glassy;glazy;vitreous;hyaline
szkliwo (shklee-vo) n. enamel;
glaze;(desert)varnish
szkło (shkwo) n. glass;pane
szkocki (shkots-kee) adj.m.
Scottish; of Scotland
szkoda (shko-da) f. damage;
harm;detriment;mischief
szkodliwy (shkod-lee-vi) adj.m.
harmful;detrimental;damaging
szkodnik (shkod-neek) m. wrongdoer;pest;nuisance
szkodzić (shko-dzheech) v. harm;
injure;be harmful;cause damage
szkolenie (shko-le-ne) n. training;instruction; schooling
szkolić (shko-leech) v. school;
train;give instruction;instruct
szkolnictwo (shkol-neets-tvo) n.
school system; education
szkolny (shkol-ni) adj. m.
school; scholastic; school-
szkoła (shko-wa) f. school
szkop (shkop) m. Kraut; Hun(vulg.)
szkopuł (shko-poow) m. obstacle
szkorbut (shkor-boot) m. scurvy
szkuner (shkoo-ner) m. schooner
szkwał (shkvaw) m. squall;flaw
szlaban (shla-ban) m. tollgate ;
barrier;train crossing barrier
szlachcic (shlakh-cheets) m.
squire ; nobleman; gentleman
szlachecki (shla-khets-kee) adj.
m. noble; gentle; gentleman's
szlachetny (shla-khet-ni) adj.
m. noble ; noble-minded;elegant
szlachta (shlakh-ta) f. gentry
szlafrok (shlaf-rok) m. house-
robe ; wrapper; dressing gown
szlak (shlak) m. trail; track;
border;route;band;selvage;scent
szlam (shlam) m. slime;ooze;slit
szlem (shlem) m. big slam
(bridge)(card game)
szlemik (shle-meek) m. little
slam (card game,bridge)
szlifa (shlee-fa) f. epaulette
szlifierka (shlee-fyer-ka) f.
grinding machine;grinder
szlifierz (shlee-fyesh) m. pol-
isher; cutter;grinder

szlifować (shlee-fo-vach) v.
polish; burnish;cut(diamonds)
szlochać (shlo-khach) v. sob
szmaciany (shma-cha-ni) adj.
m. rag; made out of rags
szmaragd (shma-ragd) m. emerald; emerald green
szmat (shmat) m. large piece;
long way;a good bit;expanse
szmata (shma-ta) f. clout; rag
szmatławiec (shma-twa-vyets)
m. shabby newspaper; smear
sheet;rag
szmelc (shmelts) m. scrap
szmer (shmer) m. murmur;rustle
szmergiel(shmer-gel)m. emery
szminka (shmeen-ka) f. lipstick; paint;rouge;make up
szmugiel (shmoo-gel) m. smuggle;smuggling;contraband
szmuglować (shmoo-glo-vach) v.
smuggle(goods)
szmonces (shmon-tses) m. Jewish
quip or joke; nonsense(slang)
szmuklerstwo (shmook-ler-stvo)
n. haberdashery
szmuklerz (shmook-lesh) m.
haberdasher
sznur (shnoor) m. rope; cord
sznurek (shnoo-rek) m. string
sznurować (shnoo-ro-vach) v.
lace up; lace; tie
sznurowadło (shnoo-ro-vad-wo)
n. shoe lace;lace;shoe string
sznurowany (shnoo-ro-va-ni) adj.
m. laced
sznycel po wiedeńsku (shni-tsel
po vye-den-skoo) m. Wiener
cutlet
szofer (sho-fer) m. chauffeur;
driver;(bus)driver;truck driver
szopa (sho-pa) f. shed;lark;fun
szopka (shop-ka) f. puppet show
szorować (sho-ro-vach) v. rub;
scour; scrub; wash;grate;run
szorstki(shorst-kee) adj. m.
coarse; rough; crude; harsh
szorstkość (shorst-koshch) f.
roughness; harshness;bluntness
szosa (sho-sa) f. highway;road
szowinizm (sho-vee-neezm) m.
chauvinism
szósty (shoos-ti) adj.m. num.
sixth

szpada (shpá-da) f. sword

szpagat (shpa-gat) m. string; (ballet) split;cord;twine;twist

szpaler (shpa-ler) m. double (tree) row; lane; hedge

szpalta (shpál-ta) f. (newspaper) column;(printer's)slip

szpara (shpa-ra) f. gap; slot; rift;chink;crack;slit;crevice

szparag (shpa-rak) m. asparagus

szpargał (shpar-gaw) m. scrap-paper;scrap of paper

szpecić (shpe-cheech) v. disfigure; make ugly;mar beauty

szperacz (shpe-rach) v. ferreter; scout;sniper;searcher

szperać (shpe-rach) v. forage; burrow;poke about;search books

szpetny (shpet-ni) adj. m. ugly

szpic (shpeets) m. spike;peak; (sharp) point;Pomeranian dog

szpicel (shpee-tsel) m. stool pigeon; informer;plainclotheman

szpiczasty (shpee-chás-ti) adj. m. pointed; tapering

szpieg (shpyeg) m. spy; sleuth

szpiegostwo (shpye-gós-tvo) n. espionage ; spying

szpiegować (shpye-go-vach) v. spy upon;shadow;watch;eavesdrop

szpik (shpeek) m. marrow

szpikować (shpee-ko-vach) v. stuff (meat);lard(meat etc.)

szpilka (speel-ka) f. pin(small)

szpilkowy (shpeel-kó-vi) adj.m. conifer; pegged (soles)

szpinak (shpee-nak) m. spinach

szpital (shpee-tal) m. hospital

szpon (shpon) m. claw; talon

szponder (shpon-der) m. flank (meat); sirloin

szprotka (shprot-ka) f. sprat

szpryca (shpri-tsa)f. syringe

szprycha (shpri-kha) f. spoke

szprycować (shpri-tso-vach) v. sprinkle ; syringe

szpulka (shpool-ka) f. bobbin

szpunt (shpoont) m. plug; stopper; bung.;peg; tongue;feather

szpuntować (shpoon-to-vach) v. bung (barrel); plug;peg

szrama (shra-ma) f. scar

szranki (shrán-kee) pl. lists; bounds; reins;tilt yard;barriers

szczreń (shreń) f. neve ; frost

szron (shron) m. hoar-frost; rime; coat of rime

sztab (shtab) m. staff;headquarters

sztaba (shtá-ba) f. bar;(gold) ingot ;ingot(of silver)

sztabowy (shta-bó-vi) adj. m. staff (officer)

sztachety (shta-khe-ti) pl.(picket) fence; railing

sztafeta (shta-fe-ta) f. relay (race); relay race

sztaluga (shta-loo-ga) f. easel

sztanca (shtan-tsa) f. die; stamp ; punch

sztandar (shtan-dar) m. banner

sztokfisz (shtok-fish) m. stockfish; cod; codfish

sztolnia (shtól-ńa) f. gallery

sztucer (shtoo-tser) m. rifle (gun); sporting rifle

sztuciec (shtoo-chets) m. fork

sztuczka (shtooch-ka) f. trick; small piece; dodge;manoeuvre

sztuczne tworzywo (shtooch-ne tvo-zhi-vo) n. plastic

sztuczny (shtooch-ni) adj. m. artificial;sham;false;immitation-

sztućce (shtooch-tse) pl. (table) silver;knife,fork and spoons

sztuka (shtoo-ka) f. art; piece; cattlehead; (stage) play;stunt

sztukateria (shtoo-ka-tér-ya) f. stucco work; stucco

sztukować (shtoo-ko-vach) v.piece; patch up; eke out; lengthen

szturchać (shtoor-khach) v. poke; dig; prod; jab; push; jostle

szturm (shtoorm) m. attack; storm; assault ;onslaught

szturmować (shtoor-mo-vach) v. storm; attack assault; harass

sztych (shtikh) m. stab; engraving ; etching;woodcut; spade

sztyft (shtift) m. tag; pin; peg

sztylet (shti-let) m. stiletto; dagger; poniard; bodkin; spike

sztywnieć (shtiv-nech) v. stiffen ;grow stiff;become stiff

sztywny (shtiv-ni) adj. m. stiff

szubienica (shoo-bye-ńee-tsa)
f. gallows; hanging matter

szubrawiec (shoo-bra-vyets) m.
scoundrel; rascal; rogue

szubrawstwo (shoob-rav-stvo) n.
villainy; rascally trick; rabble

szufla (shoof-la) f. shovel

szuflada (shoof-lá-da) f. drawer; shunting; shelving

szuja (shoo-ya) f. scoundrel

szukać (shoo-kać) v. look for;
seek; search; cast about for

szukanie (shoo-ka-ńe) n. search

szuler (shoo-ler) m. gambler

szum (shoom) m. (wind) noise; hum;
roar; uproar; scum; frost

szumieć (shoom-yeć) v. buzz;
roar; froth; hum; rustle; fizz

szumny (shoom-ni) adj. m. roaring; boistrous; noisy; frothy

szumowiny (shoo-mo-vee-ni) pl.
scum; scum of the society

szurgać (shoor-gać) v. shuffle
noisily; scrape foot on the floor

szuter (shoo-ter) m. gravel

szwaczka (shvách-ka) f. seamstress; needlewoman

szwadron (shvad-ron) m. squadron; (cavalry) squadron; troop

szwagier (shva-ger) m. brother-in-law

szwagierka (shva-ger-ka) f.
sister-in-law

szwajcar (shvay-tsar) m. doorman; (Szwajcar = Swiss)

szwajcarski (shvay-tsar-skee)
adj. m. Swiss; of Switzerland

szwalnia (shval-ńa) f. underwear
factory; tailoring shop

szwargot (shvar-got) m. gibberish; jabber; lingo

szwedzki (shvedz-kee) adj. m.
Swedish; of Sweden

szyb (shib) m. shaft; (oil) well

szyba (shi-ba) f. (glass) pane

szybki (shib-kee) adj. m. quick;
fast; prompt; rapid; sharp; smart

szybko (shib-ko) adv. quickly;
fast; promptly; swiftly; apace

szybkość (shib-kośhć) f. speed;
velocity; rate; fastness

szybować (shi-bo-vać) v. glide;
soar; tower; sail; plane

szybowiec (shi-bo-vyets) m.
glider (motorless)

szychta nocna (shikh-ta nots-na) v. night shift

szycie (shi-će) n. sewing

szyć (shić) v. sew; sew up

szydełko (shi-dew-ko) n. crochet needle; crochet hook

szydełkować (shi-dew-ko-vać)
v. crochet

szyderca (shi-der-tsa) m.
scoffer; giber; railer

szyderczy (shi-der-chi) adj.
m. scoffing; sarcastic

szyderstwo (shi-der-stvo) n.
scoff; jeer; sneer; gibe; derision

szydło (shid-wo) n. awl; pricker

szydzić (shi-dżheeć) v. scoff

szyfr (shifr) m. code; cipher

szyja (shi-ya) f. neck; bottleneck

szyk (shik) m. order; elegance;
(battle) array; order; formation

szykana (shi-ka-na) f. chicanery; vexation; difficulties; style

szykanować (shi-ka-no-vać) v.
vex; chicane; annoy; nag; pick at

szykować (shi-ko-vać) v. make
ready; prepare; get ready

szykować się (shi-ko-vać śhań)
v. get ready; be in prospect

szykowność (shi-kov-nośhć) f.
elegance; smartness; style; chic

szykowny (shi-kóv-ni) adj. m.
smart; elegant; fashionable; chic

szyld (shild) m. sign-board

szyldwach (shild-vakh) m. sentry; military guard

szyling (shi-ling) m. shilling

szympans (shim-pans) m. chimpanzee

szyna (shi-na) f. rail

szynk (shink) m. bar; saloon; pub

szynka (shin-ka) f. ham

szynkarz (shin-kash) m. barman

szyszak (shi-shak) m. helmet

szyszka (shish-ka) f. (tree)
cone; trobile; bigwig; topdog

ściana (śhćha-na) f. wall

ścianka (śhćhán-ka) f. partition; bulkhead; small wall

ściągać (śhćhówn-gać) v. draw
down or together; cheat in class;
assemble; collect (taxes)

ściągaczka (śhćhówn-gach-ka)
f. cheat note; crib
ścieg (śhćheg) m. stitch
ściec (śhćhets) v. drain off;
run off;trickle down; drip
ściek (śhćhek) m. sewer; gutter;
sink; sewage;drain;sewer;gully
ściekać (śhćhe-kaćh) v. drain
off; flow down;trickle down
ściemniać (śhćhem-ńaćh) v. dark-
en; dim; obscure;dim the lights
ścienny (śhćhen-ni) adj. m. mu-
ral(painting);wall (map etc.)
ścierać (śhćhe-raćh) v. rub off;
dust off;grind down;wear off
ścierka (śhćher-ka) f. duster;
rug; kitchen towel;clout
ściernisko (śhćher-ńees-ko) n.
stubble field; stubble
ścierń (śhćherń) m. stubble
ścierpły (śhćherp-wi) adj. m.
numb; gone to sleep
ścierwo (śhćher-vo) n. carrion
ścieśniać (śhćheśh-ńaćh) v.cramp;
tighten;narrow;restrict;close
ścieżka (śhćhezh-ka) f. trail;
pass ;(foot) pass; alley
ścięcie (śhćhań-che) n. behead-
ing; cutting off;truncation
ścięgno (śhćhäng-no) n. tendon
ścięty (śhćhań-ti) adj. m.
truncated;cut off; beheaded
ścigacz (śhćhee-gach) m. torpedo boat;motor gun boat
ścigać (śhćhee-gaćh) v. chase;
pursue;run after;hunt;procecute
ścinać (śhćhee-naćh) v. cut off;
cut down; fell (tree);clip;clot
ścinać się (śhćhee-naćh śhäń) v.
coagulate; congeal;fix;clot;fail
ściółka (śhćhóow-ka) f. litter
bed; litter,bedding;barn litter
ścisk (śhćheesk) m. throng;press;
crowd; squeeze ;crush;clamp
ściskać (śhćhees-kaćh) v. compress; shake (hand); squeeze;
embrace;clasp;harass;hamper;hug
ścisłość (śhćhees-wośhćh) f.
exactness; accuracy; compactness; density; reliability
ścisły (śhćhees-wi) adj. m.
exact; precise; compact;dense

ściśle (śhćheeśh-le) adv. exactly;tightly; compactly
ślad (śhlat) m. trace; track;
(foot) print; footstep
ślamazara (śhla-ma-za-ra) f.
sluggard; slowheaded person
ślamazarny (śhla-ma-zár-ni)
adj. m. sluggish
śląski (śhlówns-kee) adj. m.
Silesian ;of Silesia
śledczy (śhled-chi) adj. m.
inquisitional ; of inquiry
śledzić (śhle-dźheećh) v. spy;
watch; investigate; observe
śledziona (śhle-dźhó-na) f.
spleen; milt
śledziowy (śhle-dźhó-vi) adj.
m. herring (oil,salad etc.)
śledztwo (śhledz-tvo) n.
investigation ;inquest;inquiry
śledź (śhledźh) m. herring
ślepie (śhlep-ye) n. (animal's)
eye ; eye; lights
ślepnąć (śhlep-nównćh) v. go
blind ;loose one's eyesight
ślepa ulica (śhle-pa oo-lee-
tsa) s. dead end street
ślepota (śhle-pó-ta) f. blindness ;cecity;lack of foresight
ślepy (śhle-pi) adj. m. blind
ślęczeć (śhlań-chećh) v. drag
study or reading; drudge;
pore; plod; slog away; boggle
śliczny (śhleech-ni) adj. m.
pretty; lovely; dandy
ślimacznica (śhlee-mach-ńee-
tsa) s. road access ramp;helix
ślimak (śhlee-mak) m. snail
ślina (śhlee-na) f. saliva
śliniak (śhlee-ńak) m. bib
śliski (śhlees-kee) adj. m.
slippery ; slimy;scabrous
śliwa (śhlee-va) f. plum tree
śliwka (śhleev-ka) f. plum
śliwowica (śhlee-vo-vee-tsa)
f. plum brandy;plum vodka
ślizgacz (śhleez-gach) m.speed-
boat; gliding boat
ślizgać się (śhleez-gaćh śhäń)
v. slide; glide; slip; skate
ślizgawka (śhleez-gáv-ka) f.
skating rink ;kid's slide

ślizgowiec (śhleez-go-vyets)
m. hydrofoil; gliding boat;
speed boat

ślub (śhloob) m. wedding; vow

ślubna obrączka (śhloob-na ob-
rownch-ka) f. wedding ring

ślubny (śhloob-ni) adj. m. nup-
tial; wedding-(ring);legitimate

ślubować (śhloo-bo-vach) v. vow

ślusarz (śhloo-sash) m. locksmith; ironworker;metal worker

śluz (śhloos) m. slime; phlegm

śluza (śhloo-za) f. sluice

śmiać się (śhmyach śhan) v.
laugh;chuckle;scoff;make sport

śmiałek (śhmya-wek) m. daredevil; mad cap

śmiałość (śhmya-woshch) f. bold-
ness;courage;bravery;daring;guts

śmiały (śhmya-wi) adj. m. bold

śmiech (śhmyekh) m. laughter

śmieci (śhmye-chee) pl. rubbish;
garbage;rag;shred;scrap;refuse

śmiecić (śhmye-cheech) v. litter; throw litter about

śmiecie (śhmye-che) pl. rubbish;
garbage;refuse;litter;scrap

śmieć (śhmyech) m. litter; rag

śmiercionosny (śhmyer-cho-nosh-
ni) adj. m. lethal; deadly

śmierć (śhmyerch) f. death

śmierdzieć (śhmyer-dźhech) v.
stink; smell; reek(of nicotine)

śmiertelnik (śhmyer-tel-neek)
m. mortal man

śmiertelność (śhmyer-tel-noshch)
f. mortality; deadliness

śmiertelny (śhmyer-tel-ni) adj.
m. mortal;deadly;death(throes)

śmieszność (śhmyesh-noshch) f.
comic trait; the ridiculous

śmieszny (śhmyesh-ni) adj. m.
funny; ridiculous;comic;absurd

śmieszyć (śhmye-shich) v. make
laugh; cause laughter;amuse

śmietana (śhmye-ta-na) f. sour-
cream; clotted cream

śmietanka (śhmye-tan-ka) f.
cream; flower(of society etc.)

śmietnik (śhmyet-neek) m. garbage can; garbage dump

śmiga (śhmee-ga) f. (wind mill)
sail

śmigło (śhmeeg-wo) n. propeller

śmigłowiec (śhmeeg-wov-yets)
m. helicopter

śniadanie (śhna-da-ne) n. breakfast ; luncheon

śniady (śhna-di) adj. swarthy;
sun-tanned;dusky;tawny

śnić (śhneech) v. dream (about
something);have a dream

śniedź (śhnedźh) f. verdigris

śnieg (śhneg) m. snow;snowscape

śniegowce (śhne-gov-tse) pl.
snowboots;overshoes; galishes

śnieg pada (śhneg pa-da) exp.:
it snows

śnieżka (śhnezh-ka) f. snowball

śnieżnobiały (śhnezh-no-bya-
wi) adj. m. snow-white

śnieżny (śhnezh-ni) adh. m.
snowy;snow white; snow-

śnieżyca (śhne-zhi-tsa) f.
snow-storm; blizzard

śpiący (śhpyown-tsi) adj. m.
sleepy;drowsy;slumberous

śpiączka (śhpyownch-ka) f.
sleeping sickness

śpieszyć się (śhpye-shich śhan)
v. hurry;hasten;be in a hurry

śpiew (śhpyev) m. song;singing

śpiewaczka (śhpye-vach-ka) f.
singer (girl or woman)

śpiewać (śhpye-vach) v. sing

śpiewak (śhpye-yak) m. singer

śpiewnik (śhpyev-neek) m.
songbook; hymn-book

śpiewny (śhpyev-ni) adj. m.
melodious; singsong-(accent)

śpioch (śhpyokh) m. sleepy
head; lie-abed; slug-abed

śpiwór (śhpee-voor) m. sleeping
bag

średni (śhred-nee) adj. m. average; medium; mean(temperature)

średnica (śhred-nee-tsa) f. diameter; bore; middle register

średnik (śhred-neek) m. semicolon

średnio (śhred-no) adv. average; medium- ;fairly well

średniowiecze (śhred-no-vye-
che) n. Middle Ages

średniowieczny (śhred-no-vyech-
ni) adj. m. medieval

środa (śhró-da) f. Wednesday

środek (śhró-dek) m. center;
middle; measures; means; remedy;midst;inside;agent;medium

środkowy (śhrod-ko-vi) adj. m.
central; center-(line);middle

środowisko (śhro-do-vees-ko) n.
surroundings; environment;circle

śródmieście (śhrood-myesh-che)
n. city center; center of town

Śródziemne morze (śhrood-źhem-
ne mó-zhe) n. Mediterranean
sea; Mediterranean

śruba(śhroo-ba) f. screw

śrubokręt (śhroo-bo-kránt) m.
screwdriver; turn-screw

śrut (śhroot) m. (lead) shot

świadczenie (śhvyad-ché-ne) n.
benefit; charge; testimony

świadczyć (śhvyad-chich) v.
witness;attest;bear,witness

świadectwo (śhvya-dets-tvo) n.
certificate; bill of health

świadek naoczny (śhvya-dek na-
óch-ni) exp.: eyewitness

świadomość (śhvya-do-moshch) f.
consciousness; awareness

świadomy (śhvya-do-mi) adj.m.
conscious; aware; wilful

świat (śhvyat) m. world

światło (śhvyat-wo) n. light

światłomierz (śhvyat-wó-myezh)
m. lightmeter ; photometer

światopogląd (śhvya-to-pog-lównd)
m. ideology ;outlook on life

światowy (śhvya-to-vi) adj. m.
world; worldly;global;society-

świąteczny (śhvyown-tech-ni)
adj. m. festive;holiday(mood...)

świątynia (śhvyown-ti-ña) f.
temple;place of worship

świder (śhvee-der) m. drill;
auger; bore; borer;perforator

świdrować (śhvid-ro-vach) v.
drill;bore;perforate;pierce

świeca (śhvye-tsa) f. candle

świecić (śhvye-cheech) v. light
up; shine; glitter; sparkle

świecki (śhvyets-kee) adj. m.
secular;mundane;laic;lay

świecki ksiądz (śhvyets-kee
kshównts) m. secular priest

świeczka (śhvyéch-ka) f. (small)
candle

świecznik (śhvyech-ñeek) m.
chandelier; candlestick

świergot (śhvyer-got) m. twitter;
chirp; warble; chirrup; tweet

świergotać (śhvyer-go-tach) v.
chirp;chirrup;warble; tweet

świerk (śhvyerk) m. fir tree

świerkowy (śhvyer-ko-vi) adj.
m. fir;spruce; of spruce

świerszcz (śhvyershch) m. cricket; grasshopper

świerzb (śhvyezhb) m. scabies

świerzbiec (śhvyezh-byech) v.
itch; be itching

świetlica(śhvyet-lee-tsa) f.
reading hall;community center

świetlik (śhvyet-leek) m. firebug ;glow worm; skylight;fire fly

świetlny(śhvyetl-ni)adj.m.
lighting (gas etc.)

świetność (śhvyet-noshch) f.
splendor; magnificence;glamor

świetny (śhvyet-ni) adj. m.
splendid; excellent;first rate

świeżo (śhvye-zho) adv. fresh

świeży (śhvye-zhi) adj. m. fresh;
new; recent; fresh;raw;ruddy

świecenie (śhvyan-tse-ñe) n. celebration; blessing ;observance

świecić (śhvyań-cheech) v. celebrate ;keep a holiday; bless

świecone (śhvyan-tso-ne) n. Easter blessed food (Polish style)

święta (śhvyań-ta) pl. holidays

święto (śhvyań-to) n. holiday

świętokradztwo (śhvyan-to-krads-
tvo) n. sacrilege

świętoszek (śhvyan-to-shek) m.
bigot;sanctimonious hypocrite

świętość (śhvyan-toshch) f. sanc-
tity; holiness; sainthood

świety (śhvyan-ti) adj. m. saint;
holy; saintly; pious;sacred

świnia (śhvee-ña) f. swine;hog;pig

świnić (śhvee-ñeech) v. make
a mess; litter up; play dirty

świnka morska (śhveen-ka mor-ska)
f. guinea-pig ;cavy

świństwo (śhveeń-stvo) n. dirty
deed ;meanness;nasty stuff;dross

świsnąć (śhvees-nównch) v.
whistle; pilfer; bolt

świst (śhveest) m. whistle
sound; bullet sound

świstak (śhvees-tak) m. marmot

świstawka (śhvees-tav-ka) f.
whistle

świstek (śhvees-tek) m. scrap
of paper; slip of paper

świt (śhveet) m. daybreak; dawn

świtać (śhvee-tach) v. dawn
(upon) ; rise (of sun or moon)

świtezianka (śhvee-te-źhan-ka)
f. water-nymph

tabaka (ta-bá-ka) f. snuff

tabakierka (ta-ba-kér-ka) f.
snuffbox

tabela (ta-bé-la) f. table;
index; list

tabletka (tab-lét-ka) f. tablet;
pill;blackboard;switchboard;slab

tablica (tab-lee-tsa) f. board;

tablica rozdzielcza (tab-lee-
tsa roz-dźhel-cha) switchboard

tabliczka mnożenia (tab-leech-ka
mno-zhe-ńa) f. multiplication
table

tabor kolejowy (tá-bor ko-le-
yó-vi) m. rolling stock (r.r.)

taboret (ta-bo-ret) m. taboret

tabu (tá-boo) n. taboo

tabun (tá-boon) m. horse herd

taca (tá-tsa) f. tray; salver

taczki (tách-kee) m. wheelbarrow

tafla (taf-la) f. plate; slab

taić (ta-eech) v. hide; conceal

tajać (tá-yach) v. thaw; melt

tajemnica (ta-yem-nee-tsa) f.
secret; mystery;secrecy

tajemniczy (ta-yem-nee-chi) adj.
m. mysterious;inscrutable'weird

tajny (táy-ni) adj. m. secret

tak (tak) part. yes; adv. thus;
as;indecl.:like this;so

tak czy tak (tak chi tak) exp.
anyhow ; either way;in any case

taki (tá-kee) adj. m. such

taki sam (tá-kee sam) adj. m.
identical ; similar

takielunek (ta-ke-lóo-nek) m.
rig; rigging; tackle

taksa (tak-sa) f. tariff; rate

taksacja (tak-sáts-ya) f. tax-
appraisal

taksować (tak-so-vach) v. estimate; rate; appraise;value

taksówka (tak-sóov-ka) f. taxi

takt (takt) m. tact

taktowny (tak-tóv-ni) adj. m.
tactful;cosiderate

taktyczny (tak-tích-ni) adj.m.
tactical; political

taktyka (tak-tí-ka) f. tactics

także (ták-zhe) adv. also; too;
as well; likewise; alike

talent (tá-lent) m. talent

talerz (tá-lesh) m. (food)plate;
plateful; disk ;planting scalp

talerzyk (ta-lé-zhik) m. small
plate; ski-stick disk; scale

talia (tál-ya) f. waist; card
deck; tackle; middle

talk (tá-lk) m. talcum ;talc

talon (tá-lon) m. coupon

tam (tam) adv. there; yonder

tama (tá-ma) f. dam; dike

tamować (ta-mó-vach) v. dam up;
block ; check; stem; clog

tamtejszy (tam-téy-shi) adj. m.
from there; living there

tamten (tám-ten) pron. that

tamtędy (tam-tán-di) adv. that
way; the other way

tamże (tam-zhe) adv. there in;
in the same place;ay which place

tancerka (tan-tser-ka) f. dancer ; ballet-dancer; partner

tancerz (tán-tsesh) m. dancer

tandeta (tan-dé-ta) f. trashy
products; shoddy goods

taneczny (ta-nech-ni) adj. m.
dancing ;dance-(step;music etc.)

tangens (tan-gens) m. tangent

tani (tá-ńee) adj. m. cheap

taniec (tá-ńets) m. dance

tanieć (tá-ńech) v. get cheaper; cheapen; grow cheaper

taniość (ta-ńóśhch) f. cheap-
ness; low prices

tańczyć (tań-chích) v. dance

tankowiec (tan-ko-vyets) m.
tanker

tapczan (táp-chan) m. couch;
convertible bed

tapeta (ta-pé-ta) f. wallpaper

tapicer (ta-peé-tser) m. upholsterer ;upholsterer's shop

taran (ta-ran) m. battering ram

tarapaty (ta-ra-pá-ti) pl. trouble; predicament;sad fix

taras (tá-ras) m. terrace

tarasować (ta-ra-so-vach) v. block;stand in the way

tarcica (tar-chee-tsa) f. deal; plank

tarcie (tár-che) n. friction; frictional resistance

tarcza (tár-cha) f. shield;disk

tarczowa piła (tar-chó-va peewa) circular saw

tarczyca (tar-chi-tsa) f. thyroid gland

targ (targ) m. country market

targać (tar-gach) v. tear;jerk

targować (tar-gó-vach) v. sell; bargain; trade; haggle ;deal

tarka (tár-ka) f. rasp; grater

tartak (tár-tak) m. sawmill

taryfa (ta-rí-fa) f. tariff

tarzać się (ta-zhach shan) v. wallow; welter; roll(in mud)

tasak (ta-sak) m. chopper; cleaver

tasiemiec (ta-she-myets) m. tapeworm; cestoid; taenia

tasiemka (ta-shem-ka) f. ribbon; tape

tasować (ta-so-vach) v. shuffle

taśma (tásh-ma) f. band; tape;

taśma ruchoma (tásh-ma roo-khoma) f. belt conveyor

tatarka (ta-tár-ka) f. buckwheat

taternik (ta-tér-neek) m. mountain climber;alpinist

tatuować (ta-too-o-vach) v. tattoo; make a tattoo mark

tatuś (ta-toosh) m. daddy;dad

tchawica (tkha-vee-tsa) f. trachea; windpipe

tchnąć (tkhnownch) v. inspire

tchnienie (tkhńe-ńe) n. breath

tchórz (tkhoosh) m. skunk; coward;craven;poltroon; funk

tchórzliwy (tkhoo-zhleé-vi) adj. m. cowardly;chicken-hearted

tchórzostwo (tkhoo-zhoost-vo) n. cowardice

teatr (te-atr) m. theatre;the stage

teatralny (te-a-tral-ni) adj. m. theatrical; scenic; stage-

techniczny (tekh-ńeech-ni) adj. m. technical(terms,school,staff...)

technik (tekh-ńeek) m. technician; engineer; mechanic

technika (tekh-ńee-ka) f. technique; engineering;technology

technologia (tekh-no-log-ya) f. technology;production engineering

teczka (tech-ka) f. briefcase; folder;portfolio;jacket;binder

tegoroczny (te-go-roch-ni)adj.m. this year's

teka (té-ka) f. (large) briefcase; portfolio;file;folder

tekst (té-kst) m. text;wording

tekstylny (teks-til-ni) adj.m. textile;textile-;draper-;clothier-

tektura (tek-too-ra) f. cardboard; pasteboard(corrugated)

telefon (te-le-fon) m. telephone;phone;phone receiver

telefonistka (te-le-fo-ńeest-ka) f. telephone operator

telefonować (te-le-fo-nó-vach) v. ring up; telephone;call up

telegraf (te-le-graph) m. telegraph;telegraph office

telegraficzny (te-le-gra-feéch-ni) adj. m. telegraphic

telegrafować (te-le-gra-fo-vach) v. cable; wire; telegraph

telegram (te-le-gram) m. telegram; cable; wire;cablegram

telepatia (te-le-pát-ya) f. telepathy;thought transference

teleskop (te-les-kop)m. telescope; telescopic spring

teleskopowy (te-les-ko-po-vi) adj. m. telescopic

telewizja (te-le-veéz-ya) f. television; TV

telewizor (te-le-vee-zor) m. television set;TV set

temat (te-mat) m. subject

temblak (tem-blak) m. sling

temperament (tem-pe-rá-ment) m. temper;nature;mettle

temperatura (tem-pe-ra-too-ra) f. temperature; fever

temperować (tem-pe-ro-vach) v.
temper; sharpen; mitigate
temperówka (tem-pe-roov-ka) f.
pencil sharpener
tempo (tém-po) n. rate; tempo
temu (te-mu) adv. ago
ten; ta, to (ten, ta, to) m.f.n.
pron. this
ten sam (ten sam) pron. the
same (man, pencil etc.)
tendencja (ten-den-tsya) f. tendency; inclination; proclivity
tendencyjny (ten-den-tsiy-ni)
adj. m. biased; tedentious
tenis (té-nees) m. tennis
tenor (té-nor) m. tenor (voice)
tenuta (te-noo-ta) f. land holding; rent; tenure; lease
tenże (tén-zhe) m. pron. the
same (individual etc.)
teolog (te-o-lok) m. theologian
teologia (the-o-log-ya) f. theology; Faculty of Theology
teoretyczny (te-o-re-tich-ni)
adj. m. theoretical; speculative
teoretyk (te-o-ré-tik) m. theo-
retician; theorist
teoria (te-or-ya) f. theory
terapia (te-ráp-ya) f. therapeut-
ics; therapy
teraz (te-ras) adv. now; nowadays
teraźniejszość (te-rażh-ńey-
shośhćh) f. present (time)
teraźniejszy kurs (te-rażh-ńey-
shi koors) m. present rate
teren (té-ren) m. terrain
terenowy samochód (te-re-no-vi
sa-mó-khood) m. cross-country
car (four wheel drive)
terkotać (ter-ko-tach) v. rattle; clatter; chatter (away)
termin (tér-meen) m. term; apprenticeship; time limit (fixed)
termin ostateczny (tér-meen os-
ta-tech-ni) m. deadline
terminator (ter-mee-ná-tor) m.
apprentice; terminator
terminarz (ter-mee-nash) m. appointment calendar; agenda
terminologia (ter-mee-no-log-
ya) f. terminology; nomenclature
terminowo (ter-mee-nó-vo) adv.
on time; in due time; punctually

termit (tér-meet) m. termite
termometr (ter-mó-metr) m.
thermometer
termos (tér-mos) m. thermos-
bottle; vacuum bottle (flask)
terpentyna (ter-penti-na) f.
turpentine (oil)
terror (tér-ror) m. terror
terroryzować (ter-ro-ri-zó-
vach) v. terrorize; bully
terytorialny (te-ri-tor-yal-
ni) adj. m. territorial
terytorium (te-ri-tór-yoom) n.
territory
testament (tes-ta-ment) m.
testament; (last) will
teściowa (teśh-chó-va) f.
mother-in-law
teść (teśhch) m. father-in-law
teza (te-za) f. thesis; argument
też (tesh) adv. also; too; likewise
tęchnąc (tánkh-nównćh) v. get
musty; grow mouldy; reduce swelling
tęcza (tán-cha) f. rainbow
tęczówka (tań-choov-ka) f. iris
tędy (tań-di) adv. this way
tęgi (tań-gee) adj. m. stout;
strong; solid; fat; big; portly
tego (tań-go) adv. stoutly; ably;
amply; mightly; powerfully
tepak (tań-pak) m. dullard
tepić (tań-peech) v. dull;
blunt; destroy; combat; exterminate; oppose; persecute
tępota (tan-pó-ta) f. dullness;
stupidity; obtuseness; stolidity
tępy (tań-pi) adj. m. dull;
point less; slow-witted
tęsknić (tańsk-ńeech) v. long
(for); yearn; be nostalgic
tęsknota (tańsk-nó-ta) f. longing; hankering; nostalgia
tęskny (tańsk-ni) adj. m. melancholy; wietful; longing; yearning
tętent (tań-tént) m. hoof beat
tętnica (tań-tńee-tsa) f. artery
tętnic (tań-ńeech) v. pulsate
tętno (tań-no) n. pulse; vibrations
tężec (tań-zhets) m. tetanus
tężeć (tań-zhećh) v. stiffen;
solidify; set; clot; curdle; coagulate;
grow stronger; acquire vigor

tężyzna (tán-zhíz-na) f. vigor

tkacki (tkáts-kee) adj. m. textile; weaver's;of textiles

tkactwo (tkáts-tvo) n. weaving

tkacz (tkách) m. weaver (man)

tkać (tkáćh) v. weave; poke

tkanina (tka-ńee-na) f. fabric

tkanka (tkan-ka) f. tissue

tkliwość (tklee-voshćh) f. tenderness;love;affection

tkliwy (tklee-vi) adj. m. tender;loving;affectionate;sensitive

tknąć (tknówńćh) v. touch;size

tkwić (tkveećh) v. stick;stay

tlec (tlećh) v. smoulder

tlen (tlen) m. oxygen

tlenek (tlé-nek) m. oxide

tlić się (tleećh śhań) v. smoulder; glow; burn lightly

tło (two) n. background

tłocznia (twóćh-ńa) f. press

tłoczyć (two-chíćh) v. press; crowd; print; stamp; crush

tłok (twók) m. piston; crowd

tłuc (twoots) v. pound; hammer; batter; smash; shatter

tłuczek (twoo-chek) m. pestle

tłuczeń (twoo-cheń) m. macadam; broken stone; road gravel

tłum (twoom) m. crowd;mob;host

tłumacz (twoo-mach)m. interpreter ; translator

tłumaczenie (twoo-ma-che-ńe) n. translation;explanation;excuse

tłumaczyć (twoo-ma-chíćh) v. translate; interpret;justify

tłumić (twoo-meećh) v. muffle; put down; dampen;suppress;stifle

tłumik (twoo-meek) m. muffler

tłumny (twoom-ni) adj. m. crowded ; numerous ;populous

tłumok (twoo-mok) m. bundle

tłusty (twoos-ti) adj. m. obese; fat(meat,pig etc.);podgy; oily

tłuszcz (twooshch) m. fat ; grease

tłuszcza (twoósh-cha) f. mob

tłuścić (twoósh-ćheećh) v. grease; smear with grease

to (to) pron. it; this; that;so

toaleta (to-a-le-ta) f. toilet

toaletowe przybory (to-a-le-tó-ve pzhi-bó-ri) pl. toilet-articles; cosmetics

toast (to-ast) m. toast

tobół (to-boow) m. pack; bundle

toczony (to-chó-ni) adj. m. turned; shaped;rounded

toczyć (to-chíćh) v. roll; machine; wage (war);wheel;carry on

toga (to-ga) f. gown;Roman toga

tok (tok) m. course; progress

tokarka (to-kár-ka) f. lathe

tokarnia (to-kár-ńa) f. lathe

tokarz (to-kash) m. machinist; turner; lathe operator

tokować (to-ko-vać) v. toot

tolerancja (to-le-ran-tsya) f. tolerance;broad-mindedness

tolerować (to-le-ro-vać) v. tolerate;suffer;stand for

tom (tom) m. volume

ton (ton) m. sound; tone;note

tona (to-na) f. ton(metric etc.)

tonacja (to-nats-ya) f. pitch ; key ; mode; tone

tonaż (to-nash) m. tonnage

tonąć (to-nówńćh) v. drown

toń (ton) f. deep (water); flood;deep sea;depth of water

topaz (tó-pas) m. topaz

topić (tó-peećh) v. drown;thaw; melt down; smelt (metals);sink

topiel (to-pyel) f. abyss;gulf

topliwy (top-lee-vi) adj. m. meltable;fusible;liquescent

topnieć (top-ńećh) v. melt

topografia (to-po-gráf-ya) f. topography;lay of the land

topola (to-pó-la) f. poplar

toporek (to-pó-rek) m. hatchet

topór (to-poor) m. (big) hatchet; axe; battle axe

tor (tor) m. track;lane;path

tor kolejowy (tor ko-le-yó-vi) m. rail-track;railroad track

torba (tor-ba) f. bag; bagful

torcik (tor-ćheek) m. small layer cake

torebka (to-reb-ka) f. (hand) bag; purse; small bag(or pouch)

torf (torf) m. peat

torfowisko (tor-fo-vees-ko) n. peat bog; turbary

torować (to-ro-vać) v. clear; pave; clear a path;show the way

torpeda (tor-pé-da) f. torpedo;motor driven rail car

torpedować (tor-pe-do-vach) v.
torpedo; scuttle;obstruct
torpedowiec (tor-pe-do-vyets)
m. torpedo boat
tors (tors) m. torso
tort (tort) m. tort (multi-layer) fancy cake
tortura (tor-too-ra) f. torture
torturować (tor-too-ro-vach) v.
torture;torment;put to torture
totalny (to-tal-ni) adj. m. totalitarian; total;entire
towar (to-var) m. merchandise
towarowy dom (to-va-ro-vi dom)
m. department store
towarzystki (to-va-zhis-kee)
adj- m. sociable; social
towarzystwo (to-va-zhist-vo) n.
company;society;companionship
towarzysz (to-va-zhish) m. companion;pal;associate;camerade
towarzyszka (to-va-zhish-ka) f.
companion (female);associate
towarzyszyć (to-va-zhi-shich) v.
accompany;escort;keep company
tożsamość (tozh-sa-moshch) f.
identity; sameness
tracić (tra-cheech) v. lose;
waste;shed(leaves); execute
tradycja (tra-dits-ya) f. tradition;handing down customs etc
tradycyjny (tra-di-tsiy-ni) adj.
m. traditional
traf (traf) m. happenstance;
chance;luck; coincidence
trafem (tra-fem) adv. by chance
trafiać (tra-fyach) v. hit
(target);guess right; home
trafność (traf-noshch) f. accuracy ; rightness; soundness
trafny (traf-ni) adj. m. exact;
correct; right; fit; apt
tragarz (tra-gash) m. porter
tragedia (tra-ged-ya) f. tragedy;very sad or tragic event
tragiczny (tra-geech-ni) adj. m.
tragic; disastrous;very sad
tragikomedia (tra-gee-ko-med-
ya) f. tragicomedy
trajkotać (tray-ko-tach) v.
chatter; jabber;rattle;gabble
trak (trak) m. square saw;frame
saw

trakcja (trak-tsya) f. traction
trakt (trakt) m. highway; course
traktat (trak-tat) m. treaty
traktor (trak-tor) m. tractor
traktować (trak-to-vach) v.deal;
treat; negotiate ; discuss
trampolina (tram-po-lee-na) f.
spring board; diving board
tramwaj (tram-vay) m. tramway
tramwajarz (tram-va-yash) m.
tramway worker
tran (tran) m. (cod or whale)
oil; cod liver oil
trans (trans) m. trance ;ectasy
transakcja (trans-akts-ya) f.
transaction; deal
transatlantycki (trans-at-lan-
tits-kee) adj. m. transatlantic
transformator (trans-for-ma-tor)
m. transformer;converter
transfuzja (trans-fooz-ya) f.
transfusion(of blood etc.)
transmisja (trans-mees-ya) f.
transmission; broadcast
transmitować (trans-mee-to-vach)
v. transmit; broadcast
transparent (trans-pa-rent) m.
(marching) slogans; banner
transport (trans-port) m. transport; haulage; consignment
tranzyt (tran-zit) m. transit
tranzytowy (tran-zi-to-vi) adj.
m. transit-;through(traffic etc.)
trapez (tra-pes) m. trapeze
trapić (tra-peech) v. molest;
pester; worry; annoy; bother
trasa (tra-sa) f. route;(bus)line
trasa podróży (tra-sa pod-roo-
zhi) f. itinerary
tratować (tra-to-vach) v. trample; tred down
tratwa (trat-va) f. raft;float
trawa (tra-va) f. grass
trawić (tra-veech) v. digest
trawienie (tra-vye-ne) n. digestion;consumption
trawnik (trav-neek) m. lawn
trąba (trown-ba) f. trumpet;
trunk (elephant); tornado;
twister;horn;whiflwind; ninny
trąba wodna (trown-ba vod-na) f.
waterspout; wind spout

trąbić (trown-beech) v. bugle;
 toot;hoot;, roar; proclaim
trąbka (trownb-ka) f. horn;bugle
trącać (trown-tsach) v. jostle;
 elbow; tip; knock; nudge;strike
trącić (trown-cheech) v. jostle;
 smell;be,fusty;be out of date
trąd (trownd) m. leprosy
trel (trel) m. trill
trelować (tre-lo-vach) v. trill
trema (tre-ma) f. stage fright
trener (tre-ner) m. coach;trainer
trening (tre-neeng) m. training
trenować (tre-no-vach) v. train;
 coach; practise(shooting)
trepanacja (tre-pa-nats-ya) f.
 trepanation
trepki (trep-kee) pl. sandals
tresować (tre-so-vach) v. train;
 tame; drill; break in(horses)
tresura (tre-soo-ra) f. taming;
 training(of animals)
treściwy (tresh-chee-vi) adj.m.
 concise ;,substantial;meaty;pithy
treść (treshch) f. content;jist;
 substance; essence;pith;marrow
trębacz (tran-bach) m. trumpeter
trędowaty (tran-do-va-ti) adj.m.
 leprous;, leper
triumfować (tree-oom-fo-vach) v.
 triumph;achieve triumphs;prevail
trochę (tro-khan) adv. a little
 bit; a few ;some;awhile;a spell
trociny (tro-chee-ni) pl. sawdust; scraps (of writings etc.)
trofea (tro-fe-a) pl. trophies
trojaki (tro-ya-kee) adj. m.
 threefold; triple;treble;triplex
troje (tro-ye) num. three
troki (tro-kee) pl. straps
trolejbus (tro-ley-boos) m.
 trolleybus
tron (tron) m. throne;the throne
trop (trop) m. track; trace
tropić (tro-peech) v. track
tropikalny (tro-pee-kal-ni) adj.
 m. tropical;of the tropics
troska (tros-ka) f. care; anxiety; worry; concern;solicitude
troskać się (tros-kach shan) v.
 care and worry about;be cocerned
troskliwość (tros-klee-voshch)
 f. thoughtfulness; care; heed

troskliwy (tros-klee-vi) adj.m.
 careful; attentive;thoughtful
troszczyc się (trosh-chich
 shan) v. care; be anxious
 about ; take care; look after
trotuar (tro-too-ar) m. sidewalk; pavement(for,pedestrians)
trójbarwny (trooy-barv-ni) adj.
 m., tricolor ;three-colored
trójca (trooy-tsa) f. trinity
trójka (trooy-ka) f. three
trójkąt (trooy-kownt) m.
 triangle; set square
trójnasób (trooy-na-soob)
 three times,as much
trójnik (trooy-neek) m. three-
 way (pipe) connection;"T"(-tee)
 joint; "Y" joint; wye ; tee
truchtem (trookh-tem) adv. by
 jogging ; by trot;at a trot
trucizna (troo-cheez-na) f.
 poison; venom
truć (trooch) v. poison; bother
 (slang); molest; worry
trud (troot) m. pains; toil
trudnić się (trood-neech shan)
 v. occupy oneself;be engaged
trudno (trood-no) adv.with
 difficulty; too bad;hard
trudność (trood-noshch) f.
 difficulty; hardshiphandicap
trudny (trood-ni) adj. m.
 difficult;hard;tough;laborious
trudzić (troo-dźheech)v. trouble; disturb; cause trouble
trujący (troo-yown-tsi) adj. m.
 poisonous; toxic; poison-
trumna (troom-na) f. coffin
trunek (troo-nek) m. drink
trup (troop) m. corpse;cadaver
trupiarnia (troop-yar-ña) f.
 mortuary; morgue
truskawka (troos-kav-ka) f.
 strawberry
truteń (troo-teñ) m. drone
trwać (trvach) v. last; persist; stay; remain;linger on
trwały (trva-wi) adj. m. durable
trwanie (trva-ñe) n. duration
trwoga (trvo-ga) f. awe; fright
trwonić (trvo-ñeech) v. waste;
 squander; trifle away; fritter
 away (money,time, energy etc.)

trwoźliwy (trvozh-leé-vi) adj.
m. timid; fearful; shy

trwoźny (trvozh-ni) adj. m.
anxious; fearful; timid ;shy

trwożyć (trvo-zhich) v. startle;
frighten; scare ;be frightening

tryb (trib) m. manner; mode;
mood; gear; procedure ;course

trybuna (tri-boo-na) f. tribune;
stand; speaker's platform

trybunał(tri-boo-naw) m.tribunal

trychina (tri-khee-na) f. trichina; trichinosis

trygonometria (tri-go-no-metr-ya)
f. trigonometry(spherical etc.)

tryk (trik) m. 1.ram(ing);2.trik

trykot (tri-kot) m. tricot

trykotowy (tri-ko-to-vi) adj.m.
tricot; made of tricot

trykotaże (tri-ko-tá-zhe) pl.
hosiery; knittings

trykotowy (tri-ko-to-vi) adj.m.
knitted(goods,fabric,wear etc.)

trylion (tril-yon) num. trillion

tryskać (tris-kach) v. spurt;
spout; gush ;jet;squirt;flow

trywialny (tri-vyal-ni) adj.m.
trivial; vulgar; coarse; trite

trzask (tzhask) m. crack; bang

trzaska (tzhás-ka) f. chip(wood)

trzaskać (tzhás-kach) v. crack;
bang ; smash; shatter;knock;hit

trząść (tzhownshch) v. shake

trzcina (tzhchee-na) f. cane;
reed(of bamboo etc.)

trzcina cukrowa (tzhchee-na
coo-kró-va) f. sugar cane

trzcinowy (tzhchee-no-vi) adj.
m. cane(chair);made out of cane

trzeba (tzhe-ba) v. imp. ought
to; one should ____ gut;geld

trzebić (tzhe-beech) v. clear;

trzeci (tzhe-chee) num. third

trzeć (tzhech) v. rub; grate

trzepaczka (tzhe-pach-ka) f.
whisk; beater;carpet beater

trzepać (tzhe-pach) v. hit
dust out ; beat(carpet); slap

trzepnąć (tzhep-nownch) v. hit;
crump; strike;spank;slap;wag

trzepotać (tzhe-po-tach) v.
flap; flutter;flicker; toss

trzeszczeć (tzhésh-chech) v.crack;
crackle;creak;crunch:rustle

trzewia (tzhev-ya) pl. bowels;guts

trzewik (tzhe-veek) m. shoe;slipper

trzeźwić (tzhéżh-veech) v. sober up;bring back to consciousness

trzeźwość (tzheżh-voshch) f.
sobriety;level-headedness

trzeźwy (tzheżh-vi) adj. m.
sober;clear headed;wide awake

trzęsawisko (tzhán-sa-vees-ko)
n. bog;swamp;quagmire;slough

trzęsienie ziemi (tzhán-she-ñe
żhe-mee) n. earthquake

trzmiel (tzhmyel) m. bumblebee

trznadel (tzhna-del) m. yellow
bunting;yellow hammer;bunting

trzoda (tzho-da) f. herd;
flock; heard(of swine,pigs etc.)

trzon (tzhon) m. handle; hilt;core

trzonek (tzho-nek) m. shaft;shank;
handle(of a hammer, axe etc.)

trzonowy ząb (tzho-no-vi zównb)
m. molar; grinder

trzpień (tzhpyeń) m. pin

trzpiot (tzhpyot) m. giddy; gay

trzustka (tzhoost-ka) f. pan-
creas; sweetbread

trzy (tzhi) num. three

trzydziestokrotny (tzhi-dźhes-
to-krót-ni) adj. m. thirtyfold

trzydziestoletni (tzhi-dźhes-to-
lét-ñee) adj. m. thirty year
old(man,oak,house,horse etc.)

trzydziesty (tzhi-dźhes-ti) num.
thirtieth

trzydzieści (tzhi-dźhésh-chee)
num. thirty

trzykrotny (tzhi-krót-ni) adj.
m. threefold

trzylampowy (tzhi-lam-pó-vi)
adj. m. three-lamp

trzyletni (tzhi-lét-ñee) adj.
m. three year old(boy,car etc.)

trzymać (tzhi-mach) v. hold;
keep;cling;clutch;hold on to

trzynasty (tzhi-nás-ti) num.
thirteenth

trzynaście (tzhi-náshche) num.
thirteen

trzypietrowy (tzhi-pyáñ-tro-vi)
adj. m. three-story high(house)

trzysta (tzhís-ta) num.
three hundred
tu (too) adv. here;in here
tuba (too-ba) f. tube;horn
tubka (toob-ka) f. small tube
tuberkuliczny (too-ber-koo-
leéch-ni) adj. m. tuberculous
tubylczy (too-bíl-chi) adj. m.
native;indigenous; local
tubylec (too-bí-lets) m. native;
aboriginal; local inhabitant
tucznik (tooch-neek) m. porker
tuczyć (too-chích) v. fatten
tulejka (too-léy-ka) f. socket
tulić (too-leéch) v. hug; fondle
tulipan (too-leé-pan) m. tulip
tułacz (too-wach) m. wanderer;
vagrant ;exile;homeless wanderer
tułaczka (too-wach-ka) f. homeless wandering;wandering life
tułać się (too-wach shán) v.
wander;be homeless;be in exile
tułów (too-woov) m. torso
tum (toom) m. cathedral;minster
tuman (too-man) m. 1. dust-cloud;
2. dummie;nitwit;duffer
tunel (too-nel) m. tunnel
tupać (too-pach) v. stamp;tramp
tupet (too-pet) m. nerve;chutz-
pah; self-assurance;impudence
tur (toor) m. bison; aurochs
turbina (toor-beé-na) f. turbine
turecki (too-réts-kee) adj. m.
Turkish(saddle,fashion etc.)
turkawka (toor-káv-ka) f. turtledove;wild dove
turkot (toor-kot) m. rumble;rattle
turkotać (toor-ko-tach) v.
rumble ;bump along; rattle
turkus (toor-koos) m. turquoise
turniej (toor-ney) m. tournament
turysta (too-ris-ta) m. tourist
turystyczny (too-ris-tich-ni)
adj. m. tourist; touring-
tusz (toosh) m. 1. shower; hit;
2. India ink;mascara
tusza (too-sha) f. corpulence
tuszować (too-sho-vach) v.
1. draw with ink; 2. cover up;
hush up; stifle (a scandal etc.)
tutaj (too-tay) adv. here
tutejszy (too-téy-shi) adj. m.
local;of this place;of our place

tuzin (too-zheen) m. dozen
tuż (toosh) adv. near by;
close by; just before;just after
tuż obok (toosh o-bok) adv.
next too; near by: close by
twardnieć (tvárd-nech) v. hard-
en; stiffen; fix; bind
twardość (tvar-doshch) f. hardness ; stiffness; severity
twardy (tvar-di) adj. m. hard
twarożek (tva-ró-zhek) m. cottage cheese;small cottage cheese
twaróg (tvá-roog) m. cottage
cheese curds; cottage cheese
twarz (tvash) f. face;physionomy
twarzowy (tva-zhó-vi) adj. m.
becoming; facial(bone etc.)
twierdza (tvyér-dza) f. fortress ; stronghold;citadel
twierdzący (tvyer-dzown-tsi)
adj. m. affirmative(answer etc.)
twierdzenie (tvyer-dze-ne) n.
affirmation; theorem;assertion
twierdzić (tvyer-dźheech) v.
assert; maintain;affirm; say
twornik (tvor-neek) m. armature
tworzyć (tvo-zhich) v. create;
form; compose; produce; make
tworzywo sztuczne (tvo-zhi-vo
shtooch-ne) n. plastic
twój (tvooy) pron. yours; your
twór (tvoor) m. creation; piece
of work; origination;outgrowth
twórca (tvoor-tsa) m. creator;
author; maker;originator
twórczość (tvoor-choshch) f.
creation;output ;production
twórczy (tvoor-chi) adj. m.
creative ; originative;formative
ty (ti) pron. you(familiar form)
tyczka (tich-ka) f. pole; perch
tyczyć się (ti-chich shán) v.
concern; regard;refer to
tyć (tich) v. grow fat
tydzień (ti-dźhen) m. week
tyfus (ti-foos) typhus
tygiel (ti-gel) m. crucible
tygodnik (ti-god-neek) m.
weekly (magazine etc.)
tygodniowy (ti-god-no-vi) adj.
m. weekly (pay etc.)
tygrys (tig-ris) m. tiger ;type
of German tank in World War II

tygrysica (tig-ri-shee-tsa) f. tigeress

tyka (ti-ka) f. perch: pole

tyka miernicza (ti-ka myer-nee-cha) f. surveyor's rod ;affect-

tykać (ti-kach) v. touch; tick; strike

tykwa (tik-va) f. pumpkin

tyle (ti-le) adv. so much; as many;as, much;so many:that much

tylekroc (ti-le-kroch) adv. so many times: that many times

tylko (til-ko) adv. only:but:just

tylko co (til-ko tso) adv. just now:a moment ago; this instant

tylna straż (til-na strash) f. rear guard

tylny (til-ni) adj. m. back; hind(leg etc.);rear (light etc)

tył (tiw) m. back; rear; stern

tym lepiej (tim le-pyey) adv. so much better

tymczasem (tim-cha-sem) adv. meantime:during ; at the time

tymczasowo (tim-cha-so-vo) adv. provisionally:temporarily

tymczasowy (tim-cha-so-vi) adj. m. temporary; provisional

tynk (tink) m. plaster(work)

tynkować (tin-ko-vach) v. plaster· rough cast (a wall)

tynktura (tink-too-ra) f. tinc-ture: tinge; light color

typ (tip) m. type ;model; guy

typowy (ti-po-vi) adj. m. typi-cal; standard(article etc.)

tyrada (ti-ra-da) f. tirade

tyran (ti-ran) m. tyrant; bully

tyrania (ti-ran-ya) f. tyranny

tyrański (ti-ran-skee) adj.m. tyrannical;tyrannous; bullying

tysiąc (ti-shownts) num. thou-sand

tysiąclecie (ti-shownts-le-che) n. millennium

tysiącletni (ti-shownts-let-ni) adj. m. millenary

tysięczny (ti-shanch-ni) num. thousandth

tytan (ti-tan) m. titan; tita-nium ;demon(of work etc.)

tytaniczny (ti-ta-neech-ni) adj. m. titanic ; huge

tytoniowy (ti-to-no-vi) adj.m. tobacco ;of tobacco leaves

tytoń (ti-toń) m. tobacco

tytularny (ti-too-lar-ni) adj. m. titular; nominal

tytuł (ti-toow) m. title

tytułowa strona (ti-too-wo-va stro-na)f. title page

tytułować (ti-too-wo-vach) v. entitle; address;style as a...

u (oo) prep. beside; at; with;

u boku (oo bo-koo) exp.:at one's side (to have a helper,a sabre...)

ubarwić (oo-bar-veech) v. color

ubawić się (oo-ba-veech śhań) v. have fun; have a good laugh

ubezpieczać (oo-bez-pye-chach) v. insure; secure; protect

ubezpieczalnia (oo-bez-pye-chal-na) f. health insurance cen-ter; insurence company

ubezpieczenie (oo-bez-pye-che-ne) n. insurance;protection

ubezpieczenie życia (oo-bez-pye-che-ne zhi-cha) n. life insu-rance: life assurance

ubezpieczenie społeczne (oo-bez-pye-che-ne spo-wech-ne) n. social security insurance

ubiec (oo-byets) v. run; pass

ubiegac się (oo-bye-gach śhań) v. solicit; compete for

ubiegły (oo-byeg-wi) adj. m. past; last (year,week etc.)

ubierać (oo-bye-rach) v. dress

ubijaczka (oo-bee-yach-ka) f. stamper; compactor;kitchen whisk

ubijać (oo-bee-yach) v. stamp; churn; chip; kill ;pack; ram

ubijać interes (oo-bee-yach een-te-res) v. strike a bar-gain; strike a deal

ubikacja (oo-bee-kats-ya) f. toilet; rest room;powder room;W.C.

ubiór (oob-yoor) m. attire ;grab

ubliżać (oo-blee-zhach) v. in-sult ; offend; affront

ubliżający (oo-blee-zha-yown-tsi) adj. m. offensive insulting; disparaging

uboczny produkt (oo-boch-ni pro-dookt) m. byproduct

ubogi (oo-bó-gee) adj. m. poor
ubolewać (oo-bo-lé-vach) v.
deplore; feel sympathy for...
ubolewanie (oo-bo-le-vá-ñe) n,
regret; lamentation;sympathy
ubożeć (oo-bó-zhech) v. become
poor; become impoverished
ubój (oo-booy)m. slaughter
ubóstwiać (oo-boost-vyach) v.
idolize; love;be crazy about
ubóstwo (oo-boost-vo) n. poverty;destitution;meagerness
ubość (oó-booshch) v. gore
ubrać (oob-rach) v. dress
ubranie (oob-rá-ñe) n. clothes;
decoration:putting in a fix
ubytek (oo-bi-tek) m. decrease
ubytek krwi (oo-bí-tek krvee)
blood loss
ubywać (oo-bi-vach) v. retire;
go; lessen; reduce; decrease
ucałować (oo-tsa-wo-vach) v.
kiss (good night,good bye etc.)
ucho (oo-kho) n. ear; handle;
(needle) eye;ring(of anchors)
uchodzić (oo-kho-dźheech)v. go
away; flee; pass (for)
uchodźca (oo-khódźh-tsa) m.
refugee;displaced person
uchować (oo-kho-vach) v. save;
preserve;save;retain;keep;rear
uchronić (oo-khro-ñeech) v.
guard; preserve;protect;keep
uchwalać (oo-khva-lach) v.
pass a law ; resolve; decide
uchwała (oo-khvá-wa) f. resolution; vote; law
uchwycić (oo-khvi-chich) v.
grasp; catch; seize; see ;get
uchwyt (ookh-vit) m. handle
uchwytny (oo-khvit-ni) adj.m.
graspable; palpable;audible
uchybiać (oo-khib-yach) v.
fail; offend ; transgress
uchybienie (oo-khi-byé-ñe) n.
offense ; transgression ;insult
uchylać (oo-khi-lach) v. put
aside ; half-open; set ajar
uciążliwy (oo-chówn-zhlee-vi)
adj. m. burdensome ; heavy
ucichać (oo-chee-khach) v.
calm down ; be hushed;abate
uciecha (oo-che-kha) f. joy

ucieczka (oo-chech-ka) f. escape ; flight; desertion;recourse
ucieleśnić (oo-che-leśh-ñeech)
v. embody ; personify
uciekać (oo-che-kach) v. flee
uciemiężać (oo-che-myan-zhach)
v. oppress ; burden;tread down
ucierać (oo-che-rach) v. wipe
off; grind; grate; level;pound
ucierpieć (oo-cher-pyech) v.
suffer ; be hard hit;sustain a loss
ucieszny (oo-chesh-ni) adj. m.
funny ; comical; droll;amusing
ucieszyć (oo-che-shich) v. gladden ; please; gratify; delight
uciąć (oo-chee-nach) v. cut off
ucisk (oo-cheesk) m. oppression
uciskać (oo-chees-kach) v. press;
pinch; opress ; hurt;compress
uciszyć (oo-chee-shich) v. silence ; quiet; still; soothe;lull
uciułać (oo-choo-wach) v. scrape
together ; save ;put aside
uczcić (ooch-cheech) v. honor;
dignify ; celebrate ;commemorate
uczciwy (ooch-chee-vi) adj. m.
honest ; upright; straight
uczelnia (oo-chel-ña) f. school;
college ; academy ;university
uczenie (oo-che-ñe) adv. learned-
ly ; n. learning ; teaching
uczennica (oo-chen-ñee-tsa) f.
schoolgirl;(girl) pupil
uczeń (oó-chen) m. schoolboy
uczepić (oo-che-peech) v. hang
on; hitch; hook; attach;fasten
uczesać (oo-che-sach) v. comb
(hair);brush hair;dress hair
uczesanie (oo-che-sa-ñe) n.
hairdo ; hairstyle; coiffure
uczestniczyć (oo-chest-ñee-chich)
v. take part; share in;participate
uczestnik (oo-chest-ñeek) m.
participant ;(sport)competitor
uczęszczać (oo-chansh-chach) v.
frequent; attend(concerts,school…)
uczony (oo-cho-ni) m. scientist;
learned; erudite; scholarly man
uczta (ooch-ta) f. feast;banquet
uczucie (oo-choo-che) n. feeling
uczuciowy (oo-choo-cho-vi)adj.
m. sensitive ; emotional;sentimental
uczuć (oo-chooch) v. feel;realize

uczyć (oo-chich) v. teach; train
uczyć się (oo-chich shān) v.
learn; study; take lessons
uczynek (oo-chi-nek) m. deed
uczynić (oo-chi-ñeech) v. make
uczynność (oo-chin-noshch) f.
kindness ; helpfulness
uczynny (oo-chin-ni) adj. m.
obliging ; helpful ; cooperative
udany (oo-da-ni) adj. m. successful; put on; sham
udar słoneczny (oo-dar swo-
nech-ni) m. sunstroke
udaremnić (oo-da-rém-ñeech) v.
frustrate; foil; upset; defeat
udawać (oo-da-vach) v. pretend
udawać się(oo-da-vach shān)v.go;
succeed;manage;pan out;make for
udeptać (oo-dép-tach) v. tread
down; beat a path ; tread on
uderzać (oo-dé-zhach) v. hit
uderzenie (oo-de-zhe-ñe) n.
blow; stroke; hit; bump ;impact
udo (oo-do) n. thigh
udobruchać (oo-do-broo-khach)
v. appease; win over; coax
udogodnić (oo-do-god-ñeech) v.
facilitate; improve
udoskonalenie (oo-dos-ko-na-le-
ñe) n. perfection;improvement
udoskonalić (oo-dos-ko-na-leech)
v. perfect; improve
udostępnic (oo-dos-tānp-ñeech)
v. give access;put within reach
udowodni∻ (oo-do-vod-ñeech) v.
prove; demonstrate;substantiate
udowodnienie (oo-do-vod-ñe-ñe)
n. evidence; proof;demonstration
udręka (ood-rān-ka) f. anguish;
torment; distress; worry
udusić (oo-doo-sheech) v. strangle; smother; stifle; throttle
udział (oo-dzhaw) m. share;
part; quota;participation
udziałowiec (oo-dzha-wo-vyets)
m. shareholder; partner
udzielać (oo-dzhe-lach) v.
give; grant; furnish; apply
udzielenie (oo-dzhe-le-ñe) n.
giving; granting;dispensing
ufać (oo-fach) v. trust;confide
ufność (oof-noshch) f. confidence; trust; reliance

ufny (oof-ni) adj. confident;
trustful;hopeful;reliant;sanguine
ufundować (oo-foon-do-vach) v.
found; set up ;endow;establish
uganiać się (oo-ga-ñach shān)
v. chase after;seek(graces,job...)
ugaszczać (oo-gash-chach) v.
entertain ; treat; feast;treat to
uginać (oo-gee-nach) v. bend-
down; deflect, inflect;bow before
ugłaskać(oog-was-kach) v. tame
ugniatać (oog-ña-tach) v. press-
down; exert pressure; pinch
ugoda (oo-go-da) f. agreement
ugodowiec (oo-go-do-vyets) m.
compromiser;advocate of conciliation
ugodowy (oo-go-do-vi) adj.m.
conciliatory ; amicable
ugodzić (oo-go-dzheech)v.hit;hire
ugór (oo-goor) m. fallow
ugryźć (oog-rishch) v. bite off
ugrzęznać (oo-gzhānz-nownch)
v. stick; be stuck; get bogged
uiszczenie (oo-eesh-che-ñe) n.
payment(of a bill,rent etc.)
uiścić (oo-eesh-cheech) v. pay
up ; remit(a sum); acquit(a debt)
ujadać (oo-ya-dach) v. yelp;quarrel
ujarzmić (oo-yazh-meech) v.
subdue; enslave; enthrall
subjugate
ujawniać (oo-yav-ñach) v. reveal ; disclose;expose;unmask;show
ująć (oo-yownch) v. conceive;
deduct ; seize; grasp; lessen;win
ujednolicić (oo-yed-no-lee-
cheech) v. standardize ;unify
ujemny (oo-yém-ni) adj. m.
negative(value, etc.);unfavorable
ujeżdżać (oo-yezh-dzhach) v.
break in (a horse);smooth(a road)
ujeżdżalnia (oo-yezh-dzhal-ña)
f. riding school ;manege
ujęcie (oo-yan-che) n. grasp
ujma (ooy-ma) f. detraction
ujmować (ooy-mo-vach) v. seize
restrain;embrace;apprehend;express
ujmujący (ooy-moo-yown-tsi) adj.
m. winsome;egaging;prepossessing
ujrzeć (ooy-zhech) v. see;glimpse
ujście (ooysh-che) n. escape;
(river) mouth;withdrawal;retreat;
outlet;issue;vent (to indignation)

ukamienowac (oo-ka-mye-no-vach) v. stone to death; lapidate

ukazac (oo-ka-zach) v. show (appear) ; exhibit; reveal

ukasic (oo-kown-sheech) v. bite

ukaszenie (oo-kown-she-ne) n. bite ; sting

uklęknąc (oo-klank-nownch) v. genuflect; kneel down

uklad (oo-kwat) m. scheme; agreement; disposition ;system

ukladac się (ook-wa-dach shan) v. lay down; negotiate;pan out

ukladanka (oo-kwa-dan-ka) f. jigsaw puzzle;building blocks

ukladny (ook-wad-ni) adj. m. polite ; urbane; affable;mannerly

uklon (ook-won) m. bow (greeting)

uklonic się (oo-kwo-neech shan) v. bow; tip one's hat ; greet

ukłucie (oo-kwoo-che) n. prick; sting ; sharp pain; prod;twinge

ukochac (oo-ko-khach) v. take a fancy ; grow fond ; hug

ukochana (oo-ko-kha-na) adj. f. beloved ; darling; pet (female)

ukochany (oo-ko-kha-ni) adj. m. beloved ; darling; pet (male)

ukoic (oo-ko-eech) v. soothe

ukojenie (oo-ko-ye-ne) n. relief ; consolation;allevivtion

ukonczyc (oo-kon-chich) v. complete; finish ; end (school etc)

ukos (oo-kos) m. slant ; incline

ukosny (oo-kosh-ni) adj. m. oblique ; sloping; skew; diagonal

ukracac (oo-kra-tsach) v. curb; subdue ; reform; check;put an end

ukradkiem (oo-krad-kem) adv. stealthily ; by stealth;furtively

ukrainski (ook-ra-een-skee) adj. m. Ukrainian; pf Ukraine

ukrajac (oo-kra-yach) v. cut off

ukręcic (ook-ran-cheech) v. twist off ; roll up; wrench off

ukrop (ook-rop) m. boiling water ; feverish bustle

ukrocic (oo-kroo-cheech) v. repress; curb; reform;put an end to

ukrycie (ook-ri-che) n. hiding place ; hideaway; hideout;cover

ukrywac (oo-kri-vach) v. hide; cover up ; conceal; hold back

ukryty (ook-ri-ti) adj. m. hidden; concealed;put out of sight

ukrywac (ook-ri-vach) v. hide

uksztaltowac (ook-shtaw-to-vach) v. shape; fashion; cast

uksztaltowanie (oo-kshtaw-to-va-ne) n. configuration; formulation; form; shape

ukuc (oo-kooch) v. hammer out

ul (ool) m. beehive ; hive

ulac (oo-lach) v. pour off; cast(metal);pour off water

ulatac (oo-la-tach) v. fly off

ulatniac się (oo-lat-nach shan) v. evaporate; volatize; vanish ; melt away; leak; escape

ulatywac (oo-la-ti-vach) v. fly away; leak (vapors; odors, smells) ; rise in the air

uleczalny (oo-le-chal-ni) adj. m. curable; remediable; medicable

uleczenie (oo-le-che-ne) n. cure; successful recovery

uleczyc (oo-le-chich) v. heal

ulegac (oo-le-gach) v. yield

ulegly (oo-leg wi) adj. m. submissive; docile; compliant

ulepszac (oo-lep-shach) v. improve; better; ameliorate

ulepszenie (oo-lep-she-ne) n. improvement ; amelioration

ulewa (oo-le-va) f. rainstorm

ulewac (oo-le-vach) v. pour off; cast (metals);pour(water)

ulga (ool-ga) f. relief;solace

uleżec się (oo-le-zhech shan) v. mellow; settle;lie quiet

ulica (oo-lee-tsa) f. street

uliczka (oo-lech-ka) f. lane

ulicznica (oo-leech-nee-tsa) f. prostitute; streetwalker

ulicznik (oo-leech-neek) m. gamin; guttersnipe ;nipper

ulitowac się (oo-lee-to-vach shan) v. have pity;take pity

ulotka (oo-lot-ka) f. hand - bill; leaflet;throwaway

ultimatum (ool-tee-ma-toom) n. ultimatum;final offer(demand)

ultrafioletowy (ool-tra-fyo-le-to-vi) adj. m. ultraviolet

ulubieniec (oo-loo-bye-nets) n. favorite ; darling; pet

ulubiony (oo-loo-byo-ni) adj.
m. beloved;favorite; pet
ulżyć (ool-zhích) v. relieve
ułamać (oo-wa-mach) v. break
off ; be broken off;come off
ułamek (oo-wa-mek) m. fraction;
fragment;mathematical fraction
ułamkowy (oo-wam-ko-vi) adj.m.
fractional(number,report etc.)
ułan (oo-wan) m. uhlan (Polish
light cavalryman (lancer)
ułaskawić (oo-was-ká-veech) v.
pardon(a condemned person)
ułaskawienie (oo-was-ka-vyé-ñe)
n. pardon; reprieve
ułatwić (oo-wat-veech) v. facilitate; simplify,make easier
ułatwienie (oo-wat-vyé-ñe) n.
facilitation; simplification
ułomność (oo-wóm-noshch) f. de-
formity; defect ; frailty
ułomny (oo-wóm-ni) adj. m. disabled; defective; lame;faulty
ułożony (oo-wo-zhó-ni) adj.m.
arranged; well-mannered; set
umacniać (oo-máts-ñach) v.
strengthen; fortify; secure
umaczać (oo-ma-chách) v. dip;
wet; soak; sop;have hand in;
umarły (oo-mar-wi) adj. m. deceased; dead
umartwiać (oo-mart-vyach) v.
mortify(a person)
umarzać (oo-ma-zhách) v. amortize; discontinue ; remit
umawiać się (oo-mav-yach shañ)
v. make a date (or plan)
umeblować (oo-meb-lo-vách) v.
furnish; fit out; fit up
umeblowanie (oo-meb-lo-va-ñe)
n. furniture ;furnishings
umiar (oóm-yar) m. moderation
umiarkowany (oo-myar-ko-va-ni)
adj.,m. moderate; temperate
umieć (oó-myech) v. know how
umiejętność (oo-mye-yáñt-noshch)
f. science; skill; know how
umiejscowić (oo-myey-stso-veech)
v. locate; assign a place;place
umierać (oo-myé-rach) v. die
umieszczać (oo-myésh-chach) v.
place; put; set;insert;seat

umilać (oo-mee-lach) v. make
pleasant; add charm:give charm
umilknąć (oo-meelk-nównch) v.
fall silent ; cease, talking
umiłowany (oo-mee-wo-va-ni) adj.
m. beloved ; favorite; dear
umizgać się (oo-meez-gach shañ)
v. flirt; woo; court; ogle
umizgi (oo-meez-gee) pl. flirt-
ing ; courtship; love making
umniejszać (oo-mney-shach) v.
diminish; lessen belittle;abate
umocnić (oo-móts-ñeech) v.
strengthen; fortify; beef up
umocnienie (oo-mots-ñe-ñe) n .
consolidation; fortification
umocować (oo-mo-tso-vach) v.
fasten; hitch; fix; secure
umorzyć (oo-mó-zhich) v. absolve;
amortize; extinguish
umowa (oo-mó-ya) f. contract
umowny (oo-móv-ni) adj. m.
contractual; conventional
umożliwić (oo-mozh-leé-veech)
v. make possible; enable
umówić ≈ umawiać
umundurowanie (oo-moon-doo-ro-
va-ñe) n. uniforms; uniform
umyć (oó-mich) v. wash up
umykać (oo-mi-kách) v. run away
umysł (oó-misw) m. mind; intellect
umysłowy (oo-mis-wo-vi) adj.m.
mental; intellectual; brain-
umyślnie (oo-mishl-ñe) adv. on
purpose ; specially; purposely
umyślny (oo-mishl-ni) adj. m.
intentional; deliberate;special
umywać się (oo-mi-vach shan) v.
wash up; be fit for comparison
umywalnia (oo-mi-wal-ña) f.
washbasin ; washroom;washstand
unaocznić (oo-na-óch-ñeech) v.
make evident; visualize
unarodowić (oo-na-ro-dó-veech)
v. nationalize;put to state control;
unarodowienie (oo-na-ro-do-vye-
ñe) nationalization
uncja (oón-tsya) f. ounce
unia (oóñ-ya) f. union
unicestwić (oo-ñee-tses-tveech)
v. annihilate ; frustrate

unicestwienie (oo-ñee-tses-tvye-
ñe) n. annihilation;frustration
uniemożliwić (oo-ñe-mozh-lee-
veech) v. make impossible
unieruchomić (oo-ñe-roo-khó-
meech) v. immobilize ; tie up
unieszkodliwić (oo-ñe-shkod-
leé-veech) v. render harmless
unieść (oó-ñeshćh) v. lift up
unieważnić (oo-ñe-vazh-ñeech)
v. annul ; void; cancel; repeal
unieważnienie (oo-ñe-vazh-ñe-
ñe) n. annulment; invalidation
uniewinnić (oo-ñe-veen-ñeech)
v. acquit;exculpate; excuse
uniewinnienie (oo-ñe-veen-ñe-ñe)
n. acquittal
uniezależnić (oo-ñe-za-lezh-
ñeech) v. make independent
uniform (oo-ñee-form) m. uniform
unikać (oo-ñee-kach) v. avoid;
shun; steer clear;abstain from
unikat (oo-ñee-kat) m. unique
item ; rare specimen;curiosity
uniwersalny (oo-ñee-ver-sal-
ni) adj. m. universal;versatile
uniwersytet (oo-ñee-ver-si-tet)
m. university
uniżać się (oo-ñee-zhach shañ)
v. humble oneself;be servile
uniżony (oo-ñee-zho-ni) adj.m.
humble ; servile; cringing
unormować (oo-nor-mo-vach) v.
normalize; regulate:regularize
unosić (oo-no-sheech) v. carry
up; lift off;bear (a weight)
unowocześnić (oo-no-vo-chesh-
ñeech) v. modernize
uodpornić (oo-od-pór-ñeech) v.
immunize; harden; inure
uogólnić (oo-o-gool-ñeech) v.
generalize (rules,observations)
uogólnienie (oo-o-gool-ñe-ñe)
n. generalization
uosabiać (oo-o-sa-byach) v.
personify;embody;typify
uosobienie (oo-o-so-bye-ñe) n.
personification;embodiment
upadać (oo-pa-dach) v. fall
down; collapse; topple over
upadek (oo-pa-dek) m. fall;drop
upadłość (oo-pad-wośhćh) f.
bankruptcy ; insolvency

upadły (oo-pad-wi) adj. m. fall-
en; bankrupt; insolvent
upajać (oo-pa-yach) v. intoxicate; elate; fuddle ; make drunk
upalny dzień (oo-pal-ni dźheń)
m. hot day :very hot day
upał (oo-paw) m. (intense) heat
upaństwowić (oo-pań-stvo-veech)
v. nationalize; socialize
upaństwowienie (oo-pań-stvo-vye-
ñe) n. nationalization
uparty (oo-pár-ti) adj. m.
stubborn; obstinate;pigheaded
upatrywać (oo-pa-tri-vach) v.
look for; suspect; perceive
upełnomocnić (oo-pew-no-mots-
ñeech) v. give powers (of attorney); empower; commission
upewnić (oo-pév-ñeech) v. assure ; reassure ; make sure
upić się (oo-peech shañ) v.
get drunk; be intoxicated
upierać się (oo-pye-rach shañ)
v. persist; insist; stick to
upinać (oo-pee-nach) v. fasten
on; pin up; tie(one's hair)
upiór (oóp-yoor) m. ghost
upiorny (oo-pyor-ni) adj. m.
ghostly;weird;nightmarish;ghastly
upłynnienie (oo-pwin-ñe-ñe) n.
make fluid;flux; liquefaction
upływ (oóp-wiv) m. run off;
(blood) loss; lapse; expiration
upływać (oo-pwi-vach) v. flow
away; pass; lapse; go by;flow
upłynąć (oo-pwi-nównch) v.
elapse; pass; expire ;sail away
upodobać (oo-po-dó-bach) v.
take a liking ; take to; fancy
upodobanie (oo-po-do-ba-ñe) n.
liking; fancy; predilection for
upodobnić się (oo-po-dób-ñeech
shañ) v. assimilate; conform to
upoić (oo-po-eech) v. intoxicate; make drunk; elate
upojenie (oo-po-ye-ñe) n. ine-
briation; rapture ;intoxication
upokorzenie (oo-po-kozhe-ñe)
n. humiliation; abasement
upokorzyć (oo-po-kó-zhich) v.
humiliate ;make eat crow:abase
upominać (oo-po-meé-nach) v.
admonish; warn; scold;rebuke

upominek (oo-po-mee-nek) m.
gift; souvenir;present;token

uporać się (oo-po-rach shan)
v. get over;cope with;negotiate

uporczywy (oo-por-chi-vi) adj.
m. stubborn;obstinate;severe

uporządkować (oo-po-zhownd-ko-
vach) v. put in order;tidy up

uposażenie (oo-po-sa-zhe-ne)
n. pay; allowance;salary;wages

uposażyć (oo-po-sa-zhich) v.
endow; give allowance

upośledzenie (oo-poshle-dze-ne)
n. handicap(mental,physical etc.)

upośledzony (oo-po-shle-dzo-ni)
adj. m. feebleminded;deprived

upoważnić (oo-po-vazh-neech) v.
authorize;commission;entitle

upoważnienie (oo-po-vazh-ne-ne)
n. authorization;full powers

upowszechniać (oo-pov-shekh-
nach) v. put into general use

upór (oo-poor) m. obstinacy

upragniony (oo-prag-no-ni) adj.
m. desired; longed for

upraszać (oo-pra-shach) v. request; beg; beseech

uprawa (oo-pra-va) f. culture;
cultivation;agriculture;tillage

uprawiać (oo-prav-yach) v.
cultivate;till(the soil)

uprawnić (oo-prav-neech) v. entitle; qualify; legalize

uprawniony (oo-prav-no-ni)
adj. m. entitled

uprosić (oo-pro-sheech) v. get
by begging; persuade;ask to do

uprościć (oo-prosh-cheech) v.
simplify; reduce; cancel

uprowadzić (oo-pro-va-dzheech)
v. abduct; kidnap;lead away

uprzątać (oo-pzhown-tach) v.
clean up; tidy up;put away;kill

uprząż (oop-zhownsh) f. harness;
(horse);gear of draught animals

uprzedni (oo-pzhed-nee) adj.
m. previous;prior;foregoing

uprzedzać (oo-pzhe-dzach) v.
anticipate; warn; have bias

uprzedzenie (oo-pzhe-dze-ne) n.
anticipation; prejudice;notice

uprzedzony (oo-pzhe-dzo-ni) adj.
m. prejudiced; forewarned

uprzejmość (oo-pzhey-moshch) f.
polite kindness;courtesy

uprzejmy (oo-pzhey-mi) adj.m.
kind ; polite; nice; suave;affable

uprzemysłowić (oo-pzhe-mi-swo-
veech) v. industrialize

uprzemysłowienie (oo-pzhe-mi-
swo-vye-ne) n. industrializa-
tion;development of industry

uprzykrzyć się (oo-pzhik-zhich
shan) v. get fed up with

uprzystępnić (oo-pzhis--tanp-
neech) v. facilitate; make
available; make accessible

uprzytomnić (oo-pzhi-tom-neech)
v. realize; impress upon (sb)

uprzywilejowany (oo-pzhi-vee-le-
yo-va-ni) adj. m. privileged

upuścić (oo-poosh-cheech) v.
let fall;let drop; bleed

upychać (oo-pi-khach) v. staff;
pack tight; cram;ram; fill

urabiać (oo-rab-yach) v. fashion

uraczyć (oo-ra-chich) v. treat

uradować (oo-ra-do-vach) v.
gladden ; delight; rejoice

uradzić (oo-ra-dzheech) v. agree
decide; resolve; contrive

uran (oo-ran) m. uranium

urastać (oo-ras-tach) v. grow

uratować (oo-ra-to-vach) v.
save ; salvage; rescue

uraz (oo-ras) m. injury; complex; resentment; grudge

uraza (oo-ra-za) f. grudge;
rancor; soreness; ill feeling

urazić (oo-ra-zheech) v. hurt;
offend ; wound sb's feelings

urągać (oo-rown-gach) v. insult

uregulować (oo-re-goo-lo-vach)
v. stettle; put in order; pay

urlop (oor-lop) m. leave; fur-
lough ; vacation; holiday

urna (oor-na) f. urn;ballot box

uroczy (oo-ro-chi) adj. m.
charming;enchanting ;delightful

uroczystość (oo-ro-chis-toshch)
f. celebration; festivity

uroczysty (oo-ro-chis-ti) adj.
m. solemn ; ceremonial;festive

uroda (oo-ro-da) f. beauty;
loveliness; attraction; charm

urodzaj (oo-ró-dzay) m. good
harvest;abundance; harvest;crop
urodzajny (oo-ro-dzay-ni) adj.
m. fertile; fecund
urodzenie (oo-ro-dze-ńe) n.
birth
urodzić (oo-ró-dźheeć)v. give
birth; breed; bear; yield
urodziny (oo-ro-dźhee-ni) n.
birthday; birth
urodzony (oo-ro-dzó-ni) adj.
m. born; born and bred
uroić (oo-ró-eeć), v. imagine
urojenie (oo-ro-ye-ńe) n.
fiction; fancy; illusion
urojony (oo-ro-yo-ni) adj.m.
imaginary; abstract; fictitious
urok (oo-rok), m. charm; spell
uronić (oo-ró-ńeeć) v. shed;
drop; let fall; lose;shed;miss
urozmaicenie (oo-roz-ma-ee-tse-
ńe) n. variety; diversity;change
urozmaicić (oo-roz-ma-ee-ćheeć)
v. diversify; vary ;while away
uruchomić (oo-roo-khó-meeć) v.
start; put in motion;set going
urwać (oor-vać) v. tear off;
pull off; wrench away; deduct
urwis (oor-vees) m. urchin
urwisko (oor-vees-ko) n. precipice; crag; cliff ; steep rock
urwisty (oor-vees-ti) adj. m.
steep; precipitous; abrupt
urywek (oo-ri-vek) m. fragment
urząd (oózh-ownt) m. office
urzadzać (oozh-own-dzać) v.
arrange; settle; set up
urządzenie (oo-zhówn-dze-ńe) n.
furniture; installation;gear
urzec (oo-zhets) v. enchant;
bewitch; fascinate;cast a spell
urzeczywistnić (oo-zhe-chi-
veest-ńeeć) v. make real;fulfil
urzeczywistnienie (oo-zhe-chi-
veest-ńe-ńe) n. realization
urzędnik (oo-zhánd-ńeek) m.
official; white-collar worker
urzędowanie (oo-zhán-do-va-ńe)
n. office hours;clerical duties
urzędowy (oo-zhán-do-vi) adj.
m. official(document,capacity...)
urzynać (oo-zhi-nać) v. cut off

usadowić się (oo-sa-dó-veeć
śhań) v. sit or settle down
uschły (oos-khwi) adj. m.
dried up; withered;wasted away
usiąść (oo-śhównśhch) v. sit
down; take a seat;perch;alight
usidłać (oo-śheed-wać) v.
entrap; ensnare ;enmesh; inveigle
usilny (oo-śheel-ni) adj.m.
strenuous; intense; pressing
usiłować (oo-śhee-wó-vać) v.
strive; try hard; attempt
usiłowanie (oo-śhee-wo-vá-ńe)
n. attempt; efford; endeavor
uskarżać się(oos-kár-zhać śhań)
v.complain; grumble (about...)
uskutecznić (oo-skoo-tech-
ńeeć) v. bring about;effect
usłuchać (oo-swoo-khać) v.
follow order (advice);obey
usługa (oo-swoo-ga) f. service;
favor; good turn; help
usługiwać (oo-swoo-gee-vać)
v. wait on; serve;attend
usłużyć (oo-swoo-zhić) v.
do a service; do a good turn
usnąć (oo-snównch) v. fall
asleep; go to sleep
uspokoić(oo-spo-kó-eeć) v.
calm down; soothe; set at ease
uspołecznić (oos-po-wech-ńeeć)
v. socialize; civilize;collectivize
usposobić (oos-po-so-beeć) v.
dispose; predispose; incline
usposobienie (oos-po-so-bye-
ńe) n. disposition;temper;mood
usprawiedliwić (oos-pra-vyed-
lee-veeć) v. justify;explain
usprawiedliwienie (oos-pra-
vyed-lee-vye-ńe) n. excuse;
apology; plea; reason;justification
usprawnić (oos-práv-ńeeć) v.
rationalize; make efficient
usta (oós-ta) n. mouth; lips
ustalenie (oo-sta-lé-ńe) n.
determination; settlement
ustalić (oo-stá-leeć) v. determine; settle; fix; set
ustały (oo-sta-wi) adj. m.
settled (fluid)
ustanawiać (oo-sta-ná-vyać)
v. constitute; enact; set up

ustanowienie (oo-sta-no-vye-ńe)
n. instituting; establishing

ustatkować się (oo-stat-ko-
vach shan) v. settle down

ustawa (oo-sta-ya) f. law; rule

ustawać (oo-sta-vach) v. cease;
be weary; hardly stand

ustawiać (oo-stav-yach) v. arrange; place; put; set up

ustawiczny (oo-sta-veech-ni)
adj. m. constant; continual

ustawienie (oo-sta-vye-ńe) n.
dispositon; installation

ustawodawca (oo-sta-vo-dav-tsa)
m. legislator

ustawodawstwo (oo-sta-vo-dav-
stvo) n. legislation

usterka (oo-stér-ka) f. defect

ustęp (oos-tanp) m. restroom;
paragraph; passage

ustępliwy (oos-tan-plee-vi) adj.
m. yielding; compliant

ustępować (oos-tan-po-vach) v.
yield ;withdraw; recede;cease

ustępstwo (oos-tanp-stvo) n.
concession;meeting half way

ustnik (oost-neek) m. mouthpiece

ustny (oost-ni) adj. m. oral;
verbal; spoken

ustosunkowany (oo-sto-soon-ko-
va-ni) adj. m. influential

ustrój (oos-trooy) m. structure;
government system; organism

ustrzec (oos-tzhets) v. guard;
avoid; safeguard;protect from

usunięcie (oo-soo-nań-che) n.
removal; withdrawal

usuwać (oo-soo-vach) v. remove

usychać (oo-si-khach) v. wither

usypać (oo-si-pach) v. pile up;
pour out; pour off (sand etc.)

usypiać (oo-sip-yach) v. put to
sleep;lull to sleep;send to sleep

uszanować (oo-sha-no-vach) v.
respect; spare(life etc)

uszanowanie (oo-sha-no-va-ńe)
n. respect; respects

uszczelka (oosh-chel-ka) f.
gasket;seal; packing

uszczelniać (oosh-chel-ńach) v.
pack; caulk; stop(a leak etc.)

uszczęśliwić (oosh-chan-shlee-
veech) v. make happy ;delight

uszczerbek (oosh-cher-bek) m.
harm; damage; loss

uszczuplić(oosh-choop-leech)
v. curtail; reduce ;lessen

uszczypliwy (oosh-chip-lee-vi)
adj. m. sarcastic; biting

uszko (oosh-ko) m. (small) ear;
(needle) eye; ravioli

uszkodzenie (oosh-ko-dze-ńe)
n. damage; injury ;imperment

uszkodzić (oosh-ko-dźheech) v.
damage ;injure; impair; spoil

uszny (oosh-ni) adj. m. ear

uścisk dłoni (oosh-cheesk dwo-
ńee)m.handshake

uścisnąć (oosh-chees-nownch) v.
embrace; grasp;hug;squeeze(hand)

uśmiać się (oosh-myach shan) v.
laugh heartily;have a good lough

uśmiech (oosh-myekh) m. smile

uśmiechać się (oosh-mye-khach
shan) v. smile; give a smile

uśmiercić (oosh-myer-cheech)
v. kill; put to death

uśmierzyć (oosh-mye-zhich)
v. calm down;mitigate;alleviate

uśpić (oosh-peech) v. put to
sleep; anesthetize ;etherize

uświadomić (oosh-vya-do-meech)
v. instruct; initiate;realize

uświadomienie (oosh-vya-do-mye-
ńe) n. consciousness;information

uświetnić (oosh-vyet-ńeech) v.
give prestige; add splendor

utaić (oo-tá-eech) v. conceal

utajony (oo-ta-yo-ni) adj.m.
secret; latent; potential

utalentowany (oo-ta-len-to-va-
ni) adj. m. talented; gifted

utarczka (oo-tarch-ka) f. skirmish; encounter; squabble

utarg (oo-tark) m. receipts;
take; takings

utargować (oo-tar-go-vach) v.
make a bargain; realize

utarty (oo-tar-ti) adj. m.
usual; well-worn;wide spread

utęsknienie (oo-tans-khe-ńe-ńe) n.
longing; earnest desire

utknąć (oot-knownch) v. get stuck
stall; stick fast; get to a stop

utlenić (oo-tle-ńeech) v. oxi-
dize(metals);peroxidize(hair)

utłuc (oot-woots) v. pound;
 bruise; crush; pestle; mash; grind
utonąć (oo-to-nownch) v. be
 drowned ; sink; be lost
utopia (oo-top-ya) f. Utopia
utopić (oo-to-peech) v. sink;
 drown (an animal etc.)
utorować (oo-to-ro-vach) v.
 clear a path; show the way
utożsamić (oo-tozh-sa-meech) v.
 identify with
utracić (oo-tra-cheech) v. loose;
 waste ; forfeit a right (etc)
utracjusz (oo-trats-yoosh) m.
 spendthrift; squanderer
utrapienie (oo-trap-ye-ne) n.
 worry; torment ; nuisance
utrata (oo-tra-ta) f. loss
utrącać (oo-trown-tsach) v.
 chip; knock of; blackball
utrudniać (oo-trood-nach) v.
 make difficult; hinder
utrudnienie (oo-trood-ne-ne) n.
 difficulty ; hindrance
utrwalić (oo-trva-leech) v.
 make permanent; fix; record
utrzymanie (oo-tzhi-ma-ne) n.
 living; upkeep; board; support
utuczyć (oo-too-chich) v.
 fatten; grow fat; fatten up
utulić (oo-too-leech) v. comfort; console; nestle (face...)
utwierdzić (oo-tvyer-dźheech) v.
 confirm; fix; set; consolidate
utworzenie (oo-tvo-zhe-ne) n.
 formation ; initiation; creation
utworzyć (oo-tvo-zhich) v.
 create; form; compose; initiate
utwór (oot-voor) m. work; composition; production; creation
utyć (oo-tich) v. become fat
utykać (oo-ti-kach) v. limp
utylitarny (oo-ti-lee-tar-ni)
 adj. m. utilitarian; useful
utyskiwać (oo-tis-kee-vach) v.
 complain ; grumble (at, about)
uwaga (oo-va-ga) f. attention;
 remark; notice; exp.: Caution!
uwalniać (oo-val-nach) v. set
 free ; rid; let off; dismiss
uważać (oo-va-zhach) v. pay
 attention ; be careful; mind;
 take care; look after ;
 watch out; consider; reckon

uważny (oo-vazh-ni) adj. m.
 careful; attentive; watchful
uwiąd (oov-yownt) m. atrophy
uwiązać (oo-vyown-zach) v.
 attach; bind; tie; fasten
uwidocznić (oo-vee-doch-neech)
 v. make evident; show; expose
uwiecznić (oo-vyech-neech) v.
 perpetuate; immortalize
uwielbiać (oo-vyel-byach) v.
 adore; worship; admire
uwielbienie (oo-vyel-bye-ne) n.
 adoration; admiration; worship
uwierać (oo-vye-rach) v. (shoe)
 pinch; rub; hurt
uwierzytelnic (oo-vye-zhi-tel-
 neech) v. legalize; certify; attest
uwierzytelnienie (oo-vye-zhi-
 tel-ne-ne) n. certification;
 accreditation; authentication
uwięzić (oo-vyan-źheech) v.
 imprison; throw into prison
uwijać się (oo-vee-yach shan)
 v. be busy; bustle about
uwikłać (oo-veek-wach) v. entangle; involve; get entangled
uwłaczać (oov-wa-chach) v. belittle ; insult; outrage; affront
uwłosiony (oo-vwo-sho-ni) adj.
 m. hairy; hirsute; pilose
uwodziciel (oo-vo-dźhee-chel)
 m. seducer (of women); inveigler
uwodzić (oo-vo-dźheech) v. seduce (men or women)
uwolnić (oo-vol-neech) v. free
uwolnienie (oo-vol-ne-ne) n.
 liberation; rescue; acquittal
uwydatnic (oo-vi-dat-neech) v.
 accentuate; set off; bring out
uwypuklić (oo-vi-pook-leech) v.
 accentuate; set off; protrude
uwzględnić (oovz-gland-neech)
 v. consider; comply; acquiesce
uwzględnienie (oovz-gland-ne-ne)
 n. allowance for; compliance
uzależnić (oo-za-lezh-neech) v.
 make dependent; subordinate
uzasadnić (oo-za-sad-neech) v.
 substantiate; justify; motivate
uzasadnienie (oo-za-sad-ne-ne)
 n. justification; motive
uzbrajać się (ooz-bra-yach shan)
 v. arm oneself; equip oneself

uzbrojenie (ooz-bro-ye-ńe) n.
arming; armament; weapons

uzda (ooz-da) f. bridle

uzdolnić (ooz-dol-ńeech) v.
enable; qualify; capacitate

uzdolnienie (ooz-dol-ńe-ńe) n.
talent; gift; aptitude

uzdolniony (ooz-dol-no-ni) adj.
m. gifted; talented; capable; apt

uzdrawiać (ooz-dra-vyach) v.
heal; cure; bring back to health

uzdrowisko (ooz-dro-vees-ko)
n. health resort

uzębienie (oo-zań-bye-ńe) n.
dentition; toothing (of gears..)

uzgadniać (ooz-gad-ńach) v.
reconcile; coordinate; adjust

uziemienie (oo-żhe-mye-ńe) n.
grounding; earth

uzmysłowić (ooz-mi-swo-veech)
v. visualize; convey (meaning)

uznawać (ooz-na-vach) v. acknowledge; do justice; confess

uznanie (ooz-na-ńe) n. recognition; admission; approval

uzupełniać (oo-zoo-pew-ńach) v.
complete; fill up; make up

uzurpator (oo-zoor-pa-tor) m.
usurper (who takes without right)

uzyskać (oo-zis-kach) v. obtain;
gain; win; get; acquire; secure

użerać się (oo-żhe-rach śhań)
v. fight over; quarrel; wrangle

użyczać (oo-zhi-chach) v.
grant; give; lend; spare; impart

użyć (oo-zhich) v. use; exert;
take (medicine); profit; employ

użyteczny (oo-zhi-tech-ni) adj.
m. useful; serviceable; helpful

użytek (oo-zhi-tek) m. use

użytkownik (oo-zhit-kov-ńeek)
m. user (of appartment etc.)

używać (oo-zhi-vach) v. use;
enjoy; exercise right; make use

używalność (oo-zhi-val-nośhch)
f. use; enjoyment; utilization

używalny (oo-zhi-val-ni) adj. m.
usable; in working order

używany (oo-zhi-va-ni) adj. m.
used; second-hand; worn

użyźniać (oo-zhiżh-ńach) v.
fertilize; enrich (the soil)

w (v) prep. in; into; at

we (ve) prep. in; into; at

wabić (va-beech) v. lure

wabik (va-beek) m. decoy; lure

wachlarz (vakh-lash) m. fan;
range(of questions, subjects..)

wada (va-da) f. fault; defect; flaw

wadliwy (wad-lee-vi) adj. m.
faulty; defective; imperfect

wafel (va-fel) m. wafer; cornet

waga (va-ga) f. weight; balance;
pair of scales; importance

wagary (va-ga-ri) pl. skipping
school; playing truant; the wag

wagon (va-gon) m. car; wagon

wagon restauracyjny (va-gon res-
taw-ra-tsiy-ni) dining car

wahać się (va-khach śhań) v.
hesitate; sway; rock; swing

wahadło (va-kha-dwo) n. pendu-
lum (swinging backwards and forwards)

wahadłowy (va-khad-wo-vi) adj.
m. rocking; swinging; oscilatory

wakacje (va-kats-ye) pl. vacation; holidays; taking a holiday

walać (va-lach) v. soil; stain; dirty

walc (valts) m. waltz

walcować (val-tso-vach) v. roll;
flatten; mill; laminate

walczyć (val-chich) v. fight; vie;
straggle; be in conflict; contend

walec (va-lets) m. cylinder; roller

waleczność (va-lech-nośhch) f.
bravery; valor; gallantry; courage

waleczny (va-lech-ni) adj. m.
valiant; brave; gallant; courageous

walić (va-leech) v. demolish; hit; pile

walijski (va-leey-skee) adj. m.
Welsh; of Wales

walizka (va-leez-ka) f. suitcase; valise; portmanteau

walka (val-ka) f. struggle;
fight; war; battle; wrestling

walny (val-ni) adj. m. general;
complete; decisive; outstanding

walor (va-lor) m. value; quality

waluta (va-loo-ta) f. currency

wał (vaw) m. 1. rampart; dike; bank:
2. shaft; arbor; billow

wałach (va-wakh) m. gelding

wałek (va-wek) m. roller; shaft;
cylinder; rolling pin; wad; roll

wałęsać się (va-wan-sach shan)
v. rove; loaf; idle about

wałkoń (vaw-koń) m. loafer;
do-nothing; idler

wałkować (vaw-kó-vach) v. roll;
mangle; debate; thresh out

wampir (vam-peer) m. vampire

wandal (van-dal) m. vandal

wanienka (va-ńen-ka) f. little
tub ; bathtub; laboratory dish

wanna (van-na) f. bath tub

wapienny (va-pyen-ni) adj.m.
limy; limestone;calcareus

wapień (va-pyeń) m. limestone

wapno (vap-no) n. lime

wapń (vapń) m. calcium

warcaby (var-tsá-bi) pl. check-
ers; draughts (game)

warchlak (varkh-lak) m. boar-
cub;young wilde boar; piglet

warchoł (var-khow) m.brawler ;
discord sower; squabbler

warczeć (var-chech) v. growl

warga (var-ga) f. lip; labium

wariant (vár-yant) m. variant

wariactwo (var-yáts-tvo) n.
madness;piece of folly; folly

wariat (var-yat) m. lunatic;
insane; madman; fool;crazy man

wariować (var-yó-vach) v. go
insane ; rave ;go mad; be mad

warkocz (var-koch) m. braid

warkot (vár-kot) m. growl;
whirr; throb; rattle; drone

warowny (va-rov-ni) adj. m.
fortified;made into fortress

warować (va-ró-vach) v. fortify

warstwa (várs-tva) f. layer;
stratum; coat;coating; class

warstwowy (var-stvo-vi) adj.
m. laminar; stratal;foliated

warsztat (varsh-tat) m. workshop; workbench;(weaver's)loom

warsztatowy (var-shta-tó-vi)
adj. m. workshop-(equipment etc.)

warta (vár-ta) f. watch; guard

wartki (várt-kee) adj. m. rapid; fast(current);animated

wartko (várt-ko) adv. fast; rap-
idly ; impetuously

warto (vár-to) adv. it's
worth (while); it's proper; it's
worth one's while; it pays

wartościowy (var-tosh-chó-vi)
adj. m. valuable; precious

wartość (var-toshch) f. value;
worth (quality;power;magnitude

wartownik (var-tov-ńeek) m.
guard; sentry; sentinel

warunek (va-roo-nek) m. condition; requirement; term;stipulation

warunkowy (va-roon-kó-vi) adj.
m. conditional;contingent;provisory

warząchew (va-zhówn-khev) v.
ladle

warzyć (va-zhich) v. cook; brew

warzywa (va-zhí-va) pl. vegetables: pot herbs;truk garden produce

warzywny (va-zhiv-ni) adj. m.
vegetable ; vegetable-

wasz (vash) pron. your; yours

waśnić (vash-ńeech) v. saw
discord (among men or women)

waśń (vashń) f. quarrel

wata (vá-ta) f. cotton wool

watować (va-tó-vach) v. pad;
quilt ;wad (a jacket etc.)

wawrzyn (vav-zhin) m. laurel

waza (vá-za) f. vase;soup tureen

wazelina (va-ze-lee-na) f.
vaseline

wazon (va-zon) m. flower pot

ważki (vazh-kee) adj. m. grave;
weighty ; ponderable

ważny (vazh-ni) adj. m. important;valid; significant

ważyć (vá-zhich) v. weigh

ważyć się (va-zhich shan) v.
dare; weigh oneself;poise;venture

wąchać (vown-khach) v. smell

wągr (vowngr) m. blackhead;
scolex; comedo; tapeworm larva

wąs (vowns) m. moustache;whisker

wąski (vown-skee) adj. m. narrow; tight(fitting);narrow-(gage)

wąskotorowa kolej (vówns-ko-to-
ro-va ko-ley) f. narrow gauge
railroad

wątek (vown-tek) m. weft; plot

wątły (vowmt-wi) adj. m. frail

wątpić (vownt-peech) v. doubt

wątpliwy (vownt-plee-vi) adj.
m. doubtful;open to doubt;toss-up

wątroba (vown-tro-ba) f. liver

wątróbka (vown-troob-ka) f.
liver (dish);(calf's) liver

wąwoz (vów̃-voos) m. ravine; gorge; gully ; canyon ; defile

wąż (vówñsh) m. snake; hose

wbiec (vbyets) v. run in; run up

wbijać (vbeé-yach)v.hammer in

wbrew (vbrev) prep. in spite of ; in defiance; against

wbudować (vboo-do-vach) v. build in; incorporate

w bród (v broot) adv. 1. in abundance; 2. fording (river)

wcale (vtsa-le) adv. quite

wcale nie (vtsa-le ñe) not at all (exp,);not in the least

wchłaniac (vkhwa-ñach) v. absorb; soak up; take in;soak in

wchodzic (wkho-dźheech) v. enter; get in; set in; climb

w ciągu (v chown-goo) adv. during ;while; in time of

wciągać (vchown-gach) v. pull in; drag in; inhale;implicate

wciaż (vchówñsh) adv. continually; constantly;persistently

wcielać (vche-lach) v. incorporate; embody; merge; realize

wcielenie (vche-le-ñe) n. incarnation ; embodiment;merger

wcierac (vche-rach) v. rub in

wcięcie (vchań-che) n. incision notch.narrow waist;low cut neck

wciskać (vchees-kach) v. press in; squeeze in;wedge; cram

w czas (v chas) on time

wczasy (vcha-si) pl. vacations

wczesny (vches-ni) adj. m. early;in the small hours

wcześnie (vcheśh-ñe) adv. early

wczoraj (vcho-ray) adv. yesterday; during yesterday

wczoraj wieczorem (vcho-ray vye-cho-rem) adv. last night

wczuwać się (vchoo-vach śhañ) v. sympathize; get in spirit

wdarcie (vdar-che) n. invasion

wdawać się (vda-vach śhañ) v. 1. intervene; 2. associate

wdech (vdekh) m. aspiration

wdowa (vdo-va) f. widow

wdowiec (vdo-vyets) m. widower

w dół (v doow) adv. down; downwards ; downstairs; (go)lower

wdrapać się (vdra-pach śhañ) v. climb up ; shin up(a tree)

wdrażać (vdra-zhach) v. train; implant ; accustom to;enter upon

wdychać (vdi-khach) v. breathe; inhale ; breathe in; imbibe

wdzierać się (vdźhe-rach śhañ) v. break in; struggle up hill

wdziewać (vdźhe-vach) v. put on (clothes); slip on;take(the veil)

wdzięcznosc (vdźhanch-nośhch) f. gratitude ; thankfulness

wdzięczny (vdźhanch-ni) adj. m. grateful; thankful;graceful;cute

wdzięk (vdźhañk) m. grace;charm

według (ved-wook) prep. according to; after; along;near;next

wegetacja (ve-ge-táts-ya) f. vegetation; bare existence

wegetarianin (ve-ge-tar-ya-ñeen) m. vegetarian(on meatless diet)

wegetować (ve-ge-to-vach) v. exist barely; vegetate

wejrzec (véy-zhech) v. glance in;look in;get an insight;inspect

wejrzenie (vey-zhe-ñe) n.glance in; (eye)expression; insight

wejscie (véysh-che) n . entrance; way in; admission;entry

wejsciowy (veysh-cho-vi) adj. m. entrance-(door;gate,etc.)

wejsc (veyshch) v. enter;get in

weksel (vék-sel) m. loan note

welon (vé-lon) m. veil

wełna (vew-na) f. wool

wełniany (vew-ña-ni) adj. m. woolen; worsted; wool-(fabric...)

wełnisty (vew-ñees-ti) adj.m. wooly; fleecy;wool bearing

weneryczna,choroba (ve-ne-rich-na kho-ro-ba) f. venereal disease

wenezuelski (ve-ne-zoo-él-skee) adj. m. Venezuelan;of Venezuela

wentyl (ven-til) m. vent;valve

wentylacja (ven-ti-láts-ya) f. ventilation;ventilation system

wentylator (ven-ti-la-tor) m. ventilator ; ventilating-fan

weranda (ve-ran-da) f. porch

werbel (ver-bel) m. ruffle; drum-call; drumbeat ;drum

werbować (ver-bo-vach) v. enlist; recruit; canvas
werbunek (ver-boo-nek) m. draft;
recruitment;enlisting;recruiting
wersja (vee-sya) f. version
werwa (ver-ya) f. verve;zip;pep
weryfikować (ve-ri-fee-ko-vach)
v. verify;confirm
wesele (ve-se-le) n. wedding
wesołość (ve-so-woshch) f.joy
gaiety; glee; hilarity
wesoły (ve-so-wi) adj. merry;
gay; jolly; gleeful; funny
wespół (ves-poow) adv. together;
jointly; all together
westchnienie (vest-khne-ne) n.
sigh(of relief etc.)
wesz (vesh) f. louse
wet za wet (vet za vet) exp.:
tit for tat; retaliate
weteran (ve-te-ran) m. veteran
weterynarz (ve-te-ri-nash) m.
vet; veterinary; farrier
wetknąć (vet-known'ch) v. stick
in;slip in;tuck away; stuff
wewnątrz (vev-nown'tsh) prep.,
adv. inside; within; intra-
wewnętrzny (vev-nan'tzh-ni) adj.
m. inner;internal; inward
wezbrać (vez-brach) v. swell
wezbrany (vez-bra-ni) adj. m.
flush; overflowing; swollen
wezwać (vez-vach) v. call in
wezwanie (vez-va-ne) n. call
węch (vankh) m. smell; nose
wędka (vand-ka) f. fishing rod
wędkarz (vand-kash) m. angler
wędlina (vand-lee-na) f. meat
products; pork products
wędliniarnia (vand-lee-nar-na)
f. pork-butcher's shop
wedrować (van-dro-vach) v.
wander; roam; rove; hike
wędrowiec (van-dro-vyets) m.
wanderer; tramp; rover
wędrówka (van-droov-ka) f. mi-
gration; roam; tramp;wandering
wędzić (van-dżeech) v. smoke;
cure; meat; bloat fish
wędzidło (van-dżeed-wo) n.
(horse) bit;bridle;curb
wędzonka (van-dzon-ka) f. bacon

węgiel (van-gel) m. coal;crayon
węgielny kamień (van-gel-ni ka-
myen) m. corner stone;corner stone
węgieł (van-gew) m. corner; quoin
węgierski (van-ger-skee) adj.
m. Hungarian; of Hungary
węglan (van-glan) m. carbonate
węglowodan (van-glo-vo-dan) m.
carbohydrate (chemical compound)
węglowodór (van-glo-vo-door) m.
hydrocarbon;rock oil etc.
węglowy (van-glo-vi) adj. m.
carbonic; coal; carboniferous;
carbon-
węgorz (van-gosh) m. eel
węzeł (van-zew) m. knot; junction; noose; loop; snarl;hitch
węższy (vanzh-shi) adj. m. nar-
rower(than)
wgląd (vglown't) m. insight; view
wglądać (vglown'-dach) v. look
into; get an insight;inquire
wgłębić się (vgwan-beech shan')
v. sink; study;go into (matter)
wgryźć się (vgriżhch shan') v.
penetrate; get teeth into...
wiać (vyach) v. blow; beat it
wiadomo (vya-do-mo) v. (imp.)
it is known;everybody knows
wiadomość (vya-do-moshch) f.
news; information; message
wiadomy (vya-do-mi) adj. m.
known; a certain;well known
wiadro (vya-dro) n. bucket;pail
wiadukt (vya-dookt) m. viaduct
wianek (vya-nek) m. flower
crown; wreath; maidenhead
wiara (vya-ra) f. faith;belief
wiarogodny (vya-ro-god-ni) adj.
m. reliable; credible;veracious
wiarołomny (vya-ro-wom-ni) adj.
m. unfaithful; treacherous
wiarus (vya-roos) m. veteran
(old guard)   breeze
wiatr (vyatr) m. wind;gale;
wiatrak (vyat-rak) m. windmill
wiatrówka (vya-troov-ka) f.
air gun; wind breaker (jacket)
wiąz (vyowns) m. elm (Ulmus)
wiązać (vyown-zach) v. tie; bind
wiązanie (vyown-za-ne) n. tie;
truss; bond; link;fixation;weave

wiązanka (vyǒwn-zán-ka) f. garland; bunch; banquet;cluster

wiązka (vyówńz-ka) f. bundle;
bunch; cluster; beam(of rays)

wibracja (vee-brá-tsya) f.
vibration; jarring; jar

wichrować się (vee-khro-vách
śhań) v. warp; curl

wicher (veé-kher) m. windstorm;
gale;strong wind

wichrzyciel (veekh-zhi-chel) m.
warmonger; firebrand;instigator

wichrzyć (veékh-zhich) v. make
trouble; create discord;tousle

wichura (vee-khoo-ra) f. windstorm; gale; strong wind

wichura śnieżna (vi-khoo-ra-
śhnezh-na) snowstorm;blizzard

wić (veech) v. wind; meander;
build nest; curl;m.twig;osier

widelec (vee-dé-lets) m. fork

widełki (vee-dew-kee) pl.
fork (small);forked branch

widełkowaty (vee-dew-ko-vá-ti)
adj. m. forked;fork shaped

widły (veéd-wi) pl. pitch fork

widmo (veéd-mo) n . ghost;
phantom ;spectrum;specter

widno (ved-no) adv. 1. evidently; 2. in daylight ;in light

widnokrąg (veed-no-krównk) m.
horizon; sea-line ;true horizon

widocznie (vee-dóch-ńe) adv.
evidently ;apparently; clearly

widoczność (vee-doch-noshch)
f. visibility;field of vision

widoczny (vee-dóch-ni) adj. m.
visible; evident; noticeable

widok (veé-dok) m. view; sight

widokówka (vee-do-koóv-ka) f.
picture postcard

widowisko (vee-do-vees-ko) n.
show; spectacle; pageant

widownia (vee-dov-ńa) f. audience; theatre house ;scene

widz (veets) m. spectator

widzenie (vee-dze-ńe) n. sight;
vision ; visit; hallucination

widzialny (vee-dźhál-ni) adj.
m. visible (to the naked eye...)

widzieć (veé-dźhech) v. see

wiec (vyets) m. meeting;rally

wieczerza (vye-zhé-zha) f. supper ;Lord's Supper

wieczność (vyéch-noshch) f.
eternity; ages ;eternal life

wieczny (vyéch-ni) adj. m.
eternal; perpetual; endless

wieczorek (vye-chó-rek) m. evening (party); nice evening

wieczorem (vye-cho-rem) exp.: in
the evening ;during the evening

wieczorny (vye-chór-ni) adj. m.
evening -(dress,newspaper,etc.)

wieczorowy (vye-cho-ró-vi) adj.
m. nightly; evening (performance)

wieczór(vye-choor), m. evening

wieczysty (vye-chís-ti) adj. m.
eternal; perpetual;imperishable

wiedza (vyé-dza) f. knowledge;
learning;erudition; science

wiedzieć (vyé-dźhech) v. know

wiedzma (vyedźh-ma) f. witch

wiejska droga (vyey-ska dró-ga)
f. village road; country road

wiejski (vyey-skee) adj. m.
village; rural; rustic;country

wiek (vyek) m. age; century

wiekowy (vye-kó-vi) adj. m.
secular; ancient; aged;very old

wiekuistość (vye-koo-ees-toshch)
f. eternity ; all time

wiekuisty (vye-koo-ees-ti) adj.
m. eternal; everlasting

wielbiciel (vyel-bee-chel) m.
devotee; admirer; idolator (man)

wielbicielka (vyel-bee-chél-ka)
f. devotee; idolatress (woman)

wielbłąd (vyél-bwównd) m. camel

wielce (vyél-tse) adv. very;
greatly; extremely ;very much

wiele (vyé-le) adj. m. many;
a lot;much; far out;a great deal

wielebny (vye-leb-ni) adj. m.
reverend (Father etc.)

Wielkanoc (vyel-ka-nots) f.
Easter

wielkanocny (vyel-ka-nóts-ni)
adj. m. Easter; of Easter

wielki (vyél-kee) adj. m. big;
large; great; vast; keen;mighty

wielkoduszny (vyel-ko-doósh-ni)
adj. m. magnanimous ;generous

wielkolud (vyel-kó-lood) m.giant

wielkomiejski (vyel-ko-myey-skee) adj. m. metropolitan; urban ; of a large city

wielkość (vyel-koshch) f. greatness; size; dimension

wielobarwny (vye-lo-barv-ni) adj. m. multicolor (ed)

wieloboczny (vye-lo-boch-ni) adj. m. multilateral ;polygonal

wielokrążek (vye-lo-krown-zhek) m. set of pulleys ; pulley-block

wielokrotny (vye-lo-krot-ni) adj. m. repeated ; multiple

wieloletni (vye-lo-let-ni) adj. m. long; years long;many years'

wielopiętrowy (vye-lo-pyan-tro-vi) adj. m. multistory

wieloraki (vye-lo-ra-kee) adj. m. manifold ; varied ;multiple

wieloryb (vye-lo-rib) m. whale

wielorybnik (vye-lo-rib-neek) m. whaler;whaleman;whaling ship

wielostronny (vye-lo-stron-ni) adj. m. multilateral; many-sided ; versatile; various

wielozgłoskowy (vye-lo-zgwos-ko-vi) adj. m. polysyllabic

wieloznaczny (vye-lo-znach-ni) adj. m. multivocal; ambiguous

wielożeństwo (vye-lo-zhen-stvo) n. polygamy,

wieniec (vye-nets) m. wreath; garland; crown ; chaplet

wieńczyć (vyen-chich) v. crown

wieprz (vyepsh) m. hog; pig

wieprzowina (vyep-zho-vee-na) f. pork (meat)

wieprzowy (vyep-zho-vi) adj.m. pork ;pork's;pig's;hog's;porcine

wiercenie (vyer-tse-ne) n. drilling ; perforation;boring

wiercić (vyer-chich) v. bore; drill ; pester; bother

wierność (vyer-noshch) f. fidelity; loyalty; faith; truth

wierny (vyer-ni) adj. m. faithful ; true;loyal;exact

wiersz (vyersh) m. verse; poem

wiertarka (vyer-tar-ka) f. drill

wiertnictwo (vyert-neets-tvo) n. drilling(activity)

wierutny (vye-root-ni) adj.m. stark(liar); notorious; through-and-through ; rank; arrant;born

wierzacy (vye-zhown-tsi) adj. m. believer; believing Christian

wierzba (vyezh-ba) f. willow

wierzch (vyezhkh) m. top; brim head; surface; cover; lid

wierzchni (vyezh-khnee) adj. m. upper ; top; outer;outside

wierzchołek (vyezh-kho-wek) m. top; peak; summit; apex;vertex

wierzyciel (vye-zhi-chel) m. creditor; mortgagee; obligee

wierzycielka (vye-zhi-chel-ka) f. creditor (woman)

wierzyć (vye-zhich) v. believe; trust;rely; believe in God

wierzytelność (vye-shi-tel-noshch) f. debt; claim

wieszać (vye-shach) v. hang

wieszadło (vye-shad-wo) v. hanger; peg; ;coat-stand

wieszak (vye-shak) v. rack

wieszcz (vyeshch) m. bard; seer; poet (leading,national)

wieszczy (vyesh-chi) adj. m. prophetic ;visionary

wieś (vyesh) f. village; country-side; hamlet;the villagers

wieść (vyeshch) l. f. news 2. v. lead; conduct; draw; succeed ;stand at the head

wieśniaczka (vyesh-nach-ka) f. countrywoman ;peasant woman

wieśniak (vyesh-nak) m. country-man; villager; yokel ;rustic

wietrzeć (vyet-zhech) v. decay

wietrzyć (vyet-zhich) v. ventilate; smell; nose; aerate

wietrzenie (vyet-zhe-ne) n. ventilation; decay (of rocks)

wiewiórka (vye-vyoor-ka) f. squirrel; squirrel fur

wieźć (vyezhch) v. carry (on wheels) ;transport;convey;drive

wieża (vye-zha) f. tower; rook

wieżowiec (vye-zho-vyets) m. skyscraper;high-rise(building)

wieżyczka (vye-zhich-ka) f. turret; pinnacle;small tower

więc (vyants) conj. now; well; therefore ; so;consequently

więcej (vyan-tsey) adv. more

więdnąć (vyand-nownch) v. wither; fade; wilt

więcierz (vyáń-chezh) m. fishing net (set taut on hoops)
większość (vyánk-shoshch) f. majority; the bulk; most
większy (vyáńk-shi) adj. m. bigger; larger; greater
więzić (vyáń-zheech) v. imprison ;confine; detain;restrain
więzienie (vyáń-zhe-ńe) n. prison; confinement; jail;restraint
więzień (vyáń-zheń) m. prisoner
więzy (vyáń-zi) pl. fetters; restrains; chains; bonds
wigilia (vee-geél-ya) f. Xmas Eve; eve
wiklina (vee-kleé-na) f. osier
wikłać (veek-wach) v. entangle
wikt (veekt) m. board; keep
wilczur (veel-choor) m.wolf dog
wilgoć (veel-goch) f. humidity
wilgotny (veel-gót-ni) adj. m. moist; humid ; damp; wet
wilia (veel-ya) f. eve
wilk (veelk) m. wolf;wolfskin
wilżyć (veel-zhich) v. moisten
wina (vee-na) f. guilt; fault
winda (veén-da) f. elevator
winiarnia (vee-ńar-ńa) f. wine-shop ;vine vault; winery
winić (vee-ńeech) v. accuse; blame for ;fix the blame on
winien (vee-ńen) adj. m. indebted; owing; guilty; at fault
winnica (veen-ńee-tsa) f. vine yard; vine growing plantation
winny (veen-ni) adj. m. guilty
winny (veén-ni) adj. m. of wine; vineous ; vine-; winy
wino (vee-no) n. wine ;grapevine
winogrono (vee-no-gró-no) n. grape
winorośl (vee-no-roshl) f. vine
winowajca (vee-no-vay-tsa) m. culprit; evildoer;the guilty one
winszować (veen-sho-vach) v. congratulate (on having success)
wiosenny (vyo-sén-ni) adj. m. spring -(flowers,month etc.)
wioska (vyós-ka) f. hamlet
wiosło (vyós-wo) n. oar;paddle
wiosłować (vyos-wó-vach) v. row
wiosna (vyós-na) f. Spring (time)

wioślarz (vyósh-lash) m. oarsman ; rower
wiotki (vyót-kee) adj. m. limp
wiór (vyoor) m. shaving ; chip
wir (veer) m. whirl; eddy ;vortex
wiraż (vee-rash) m. curve; bend
wirować (vee-ro-vach) v. whirl
wirówka (vee-roóv-ka) f. centrifuge ;hydro-extractor
wirtuoz (veer-too-os) m. virtuoso ;maestro; great musician etc.
wirus (vee-roos) m. virus
wisieć (vee-shech) v.hang; sag
wisiorek (vee-shó-rek) m. pendant
wiśnia (veésh-ńa) f. cherry (tree)
wiśniak (veésh-ńak) m. cherry-brandy; cherry liqueur
witać (vee-tach) v. greet; welcome; meet to welcome;bid welcome
witamina (vee-ta-mée-na) f. vitamin (A,B,C,D,E etc.)
witryna (vee-tri-na) f. shopwindow ; glass case
wiza (vee-za) f. visa
wizerunek (vee-ze-roo-nek) m. likeness; image;picture; effigy
wizja (veéz-ya) f. vision ;view
wizyta (vee-zí-ta) f. call; visit; be on a visit
wizytówka (vee-zi-toóv-ka) f. calling card; visiting card
wjazd (vyazt) m. (car) entrance
wjeżdżać (vyézh-dzhach) v. drive in ;ride to the top
wkleić (vkle-eech) v. stick in
wklęsłodruk (vklań-swo-drook) m. copper plate print
wklęsły (vklańs-wi) adj. m. concave; hollow; sunken
wkład (vkwat) m. input; deposit; investment; outlay; inset
wkładać (vkwa-dach) v. put in
w koło (vkó-wo) adv. round;in circles; over and over again
wkoło (vkó-wo) prep. round; about; in circles [appear;
wkraczać (vkrá-chach) v. step in; invade; intervene; enter; stalk
wkradać się (vkra-dach shań) v. steal in; slip in; creep in
wkrapiać (vkráp-yach) v. put drops in; beat up

wkręcać (vkrań-tsach) v. screw
in ; drive in; push into a job
wkroczyć (vkro-chich)v. enter
(formally) ; appear ; invade
wkrótce (vkroot-tse) adv. soon
wkupić się (vkoo-peech shań) v.
buy way in;pay one's footing
wlac (vlach) v. pour in
wlatywać (vla-ti-vach) v. fly
in ; rush in; dart in;run in
wlec (ylets) v. drag ; tow
wlepić (vle-peech) v. 1. paste
in; 2, glare at; stare at
wlewać (vle-vach) v. pour in
wleźć (vleżhch) v. crawl in ;
climb up; barge in; step in
wliczenie (vlee-che-ne) n. inclusion; counting in
wliczyć (vlee-chich) v. count
in ; reckon in ;include
w lot (v lot) adv. in a flash;
quickly; in a hurry
wlot (vlot) m. inlet ; intake
wlot kuli (vlot koo-lee) m.
bullet entry
władać (vwa-dach) v. rule ;wield
władca (vwad-tsa) m. ruler
władny (vwad-ni) adj. m. sovereign ; having the authority
władza (vwa-dza) f. authority
włamać się (vwa-mach shań) v.
break in; burglarize
włamanie (vwa-ma-ne) n. burglary ; house breaking
włamywacz (vwa-mi-vach) m. burglar; housebreaker; picklock
własnoręcznie (vwa-sno-rańch-ne)
adv. personally; with one's
hand ; with one's own hand
własnosc (vwas-noshch) f. property ; characteristic feature
własnowolny (vwas-no-vol-ni)
adj. m. spontaneous;voluntary
własny (vwas-ni) adj. m. own;very
właściciel (vwash-chee-chel) m.
proprietor ; holder;owner
właściwy (vwash-chee-vi) adj.m.
proper ; right; suitable; due
właściwość (vwash-chee-voshch) f.
propriety ; characteristic
właśnie (vwash-ne) adv. exactly;
just so; precisely; very;just
as;just now;just then;only just

właz (vwas) m. manhole ;hatch
włazić (vwa-żheech) v. crawl
in ; barge in; step in;go deep
włączać (vwown-chach) v. include; switch on; plug in
włącznie (vwownch-ne) adv. in-
clusively; inclusive;including
włączenie (vwown-che-ne) n.
inclusion ; merger ;incorporation
włochaty (vwo-kha-ti) adj. m.
hairy ; shaggy; hirsute;nappy
włos (vwos) m. hair ; fur
włosień (vwo-sheń) m. trichina
włoski (vwos-kee) adj.m. Italian; of Italy
włoskowaty (vwos-ko-va-ti) adj.
m. capillary ; hairlike (tubes)
włoszczyzna (vwozh-chiz-na) pl.
vegetables ; Italian studies
włościanin (vwosh-cha-ñeen) m.
farmer ; peasant ; country man
włożyć (vwo-zhich) v. put in
włóczęga (vwoo-chań-ga) m.
tramp ;rover; vagrant;roam
włóczka (vwooch-ka) f. yarn
włócznia (vwooch-ña) f. spear
włóczyć (vwoo-chich) v. drag
włókienniczy (vwo-kyen-ñee-chi)
adj. m. textile (trade,fiber etc.)
włókniarz (vwook-ñash) m.
weaver; textile worker
włóknisty (vwook-ñees-ti) adj.
m. fibrous; stringy;thready
włókno (vwook-no) n. fibre
wmawiać (vmav-yach) v. talk
into; persuade; make believe
wmieszać się (vmye-shach shań)
v. interfere ; join; mix;mingle
wmuszać (vmoo-shach) v. force
(upon) ; press upon ;directly
wnet (vnet) adv. soon; shortly;
wnęka (vnań-ka) f. niche ;recess
wnętrze (vnań-tzhe) n. interior
wnętrzności (vnantzh-nosh-chee)
pl. bowels ; intestines ;entrails
Wniebowzięcie (vñe-bo-vzhań-che)
n. Assumption ;put in; infer;
wnieść (vñeshch) v. carry in ;
gather;conclude
wnikać (vñee-kach) v. penetrate
wnikliwy (vñee-klee-vi) adj. m.
penetrating;discerning; piercing
wniosek (vño-sek) m. conclusion;
proposition; suggestion;motion

wnioskodawca (vnos-ko-dav-tsa)
m. mover; giver of a motion

wnioskować (vnos-ko-vach) v.
conclude; deduct; infer; gather

wnioskowanie (vnos-ko-va-ne)
n. conclusion; inference

wnosić (vno-sheech) v. carry in;
conclude; infer; gather

wnuczka (vnooch-ka) f. granddaughter

wnuk (vnook) m. grandson

wnyk (vnik) m. snare

woalka (vo-al-ka) f. veil(hat)

wobec (vo-bets) prep. in the
face of; before; towards

woda (vo-da) f. water; froth; bull

wodnisty (vod-nees-ti) adj. m.
watery; wishy-washy; aqueous

wodno-płatowiec (vod-no-pwa-to-
vyets) m. hydroplane; water plane

wodny (vod-ni) adj. m. water-

wodociąg (vo-do-chownk) m. waterworks ; water tap

wodolecznictwo (vo-do-lech-neets-
tvo); n. hydrotherapy; water cure

wodopój (vo-do-pooy) m. watering spot ; cow-pond; water hole

wodorost (vo-do-rost) m. seaweed; alga

wodorowa bomba (vo-do-ro-va
bom-ba) f. H-bomb

wodospad (vo-do-spat) m. waterfall; cascade

wodotrysk (vo-do-trisk) m. fountain; waterspout

wodować (vo-do-vach) v. launch
on water ; splash down(on water)

wodowstręt (vo-do-vstrant) m.
hydrophobia; rabies

wodór (vo-door)m. hydrogen

wodza (vo-dza) f. rein; hold; sway

wodzić (vo-dzheech) v. lead; run

wodzirej (vo-dzhee-rey) m. dance
leader; ringleader; bell wether

w ogóle (vo-goo-le) adv. generally; on the whole; in the main

wojak (vo-yak) m. warrior; soldier

wojenny (vo-yen-ni) adj. m. military; war; wartime; of war

województwo (vo-ye-voodz-tvo) n.
province; voivodeship

wojłok (voy-wok) m. felt (thick)

wojna (voy-na) f. war ; warfare

wojna domowa (voy-na do-mo-va)
f. civil war

wojować (vo-yo-vach) v. wage
war ; combat; contend

wojowniczy (vo-yov-nee-chi)
adj. m. warlike; aggresive

wojownik (vo-yov-neek) m.
(tribal) warrior

wojsko (voy-sko) n. army; troops

wojskowość (voy-sko-voshch) f.
military science; the army

wojskowy (voy-sko-vi) adj.m.
military ; army(post etc.)

wokalny (vo-kal-ni) adj. m.
vocal ⎰all around

wokoło (vo-ko-wo) adv. round;

wola (vo-la) f. will; volition

woleć (vo-lech) v. prefer

wolno (vol-no) adv. slowly

wolnomyśliciel (vol-no-mi-
shlee-chel) m. freethinker

wolność (vol-noshch) f. liberty; freedom ; independence

wolnościowy (vol-nosh-cho-vi)
adj. m. for liberation

wolny (vol-ni) adj. m. free

wolt (volt) m. volt

woltomierz (vol-to-myesh) m.
voltmeter

wołać (vo-wach) v. call; cry

wołanie (vo-wa-ne) n. call; cry

wołowina (vo-wo-vee-na) f.
beef

wonny (von-ni) adj. m. fragrant; aromatic; sweet-smelling

woniec (vo-nech) v. scent;
smell ; be fragrant

woń (von) f. fragrance

woreczek (vo-re-chek) m. small
bag ; pouch; cyst

worek (vo-rek) m. bag ; sack

wosk (vosk) m. wax

woskować (vos-ko-vach) v. wax

wozić (vo-zheech) v. carry (on
wheels); transport; drive; cart

wozownia (vo-zov-na) f. coach
house

woźnica (vozh-nee-tsa) m. coach-
man ; driver; waggoner

wożenie (vo-zhe-ne) n. transport; transportation; carriage

wodka (vood-ka) f. vodka
wódz (voots) m. commander;chief
wójt (vooyt) m. village mayor
wół (voow) m. ox ;steer;bullock
wór (voor) m. (big) sack(ful)
wówczas (voov-chas) adv. then;
that time; at the time
wóz (voos) m. car; cart;wagon
wózek (voo-zek) m. (small) car
wpadać (vpa-dach) v. fall in;
rush in; drop in;run into
wpajać (vpa-yach) v. put in
(head); implant; instill
wpatrywać się (vpa-tri-vach
shan) v. stare;look intently
wpełzać (vpew-zach) v.crawl in;
creep in(into a cave etc.)
wpędzać (vpan-dzach) v. drive
sb in;bring on sb...(death etc)
wpić się (vpeech shan) v. sink
into; penetrate; bury(teeth)
wpierw (vpyerv) adv. first
wpis (vpees) m. enrollment
wpisać (vpee-sach) v. write in
wpisowe (vpee-so-ve) n. registration fee;inscription fee
wplatać (vpla-tach) v. twine
in; weave; braid ;intersperse
wplątać (vplown-tach) v. entangle;implicate;involve
wpłacać (vpwa-tsach) v. pay in
wpłata (vpwa-ta) f. payment
wpław (vpwaf) adv. (swim)across
wpływ (vpwif) m. influence; income ; effect; impact of
wpływać (vpwi-vach) v. flow in;
influence; have effect
wpływowy (vpwi-vo-vi) adj. m.
influential
w pobliżu (v po-blee-zhoo) adv.
near ;in the vicinity;close by
w poprzek (v po-pzhek) prep.
adv. across; crosswise
wpół (vpoow) adv. in half; halfway ; half past;half-;semi-
w pośród (v posh-rood) adv.
among;in the midst of
wprawa (vpra-va) f. skill;
practice ; proficiency
wprawdzie (vprav-dzhe) adv. in
truth ; to be sure; indeed
wprawić (vpra-veech) v. set in;
train in ; insert; put in

wprawny (vprav-ni) adj. m.
skillful ;trained; experienced
wprost (vprost) adv. directly;
straight ahead; outright;simply
wprowadzenie (vpro-va-dze-ne) n.
introduction; initiation
wprowadzać (vpro-va-dzach) v.
usher; introduce; lead in;put in
wprzęgać (vpzhan-gach) v. harness, (horse, river etc)
wprzód (vpshoot) adv. ahead; before; first; in the first place
wpuszczać (vpoosh-chach) v. let
in; admit; insert;allow to enter
wpychać (vpi-khach) v. push in
wracać (vra-tsach) v. return
wrastać (vras-tach) v grow in
wraz (vras) prep. together
wrażenie (vra-zhe-ne) n. impression;sensation;feeling;thrill
wrażliwość (vrazh-lee-voshch) f.
sensitivity; susceptibility
wrażliwy (vrazh-lee-vi) adj. m.
sensitive; thin-skinned;tender
wreszcie (vresh-che) adv. at
last;finally; after all;eventually
wręcz (vranch) adv. down right
wręczać (vran-chach) v. hand in
wrodzony (vro-dzo-ni) adj. m.
innate; inborn; inbred;congenital
wrogi (vro-gee) adj. m. hostile
wrogość (vro-goshch) f. hostility; ill-will; enmity;malevolence
wrona (vro-na) f. crow
wrota (vro-ta) n. gate
wrotki (vrot-kee) pl. roller
skates
wróbel (vroo-bel) m. sparrow
wrócić (vroo-cheech) v. return
wróg (vrook) m. foe; enemy
wróżba (vroozh-ba) f. omen
wróżbiarz (vroozh-byash) m.
fortune-teller; soothsayer
wróżka (vroozh-ka) f. fortune-
teller;palmist; fairy
wróżyć (vroo-zhich) v. tell
fortunes; foretell; predict
wryć się (vrich shan) v. dig in;
sink in; imbed
wrzask (vzhask) m. scream;yell
wrzaskliwy (vzhas-klee-vi) adj.
m. shrill;piercing; clamorous

wrzawa (vzha-va) f. noise

wrzący (vzhówn-tsi) adj. m. boiling ; scalding(hot)

wrzątek (vzhówn-tek) m. boiling water

wrzeciono (vzhe-chó-no) n. spindle ; verge

wrzec (vzhech) v. boil ; rage

wrzesien (vzhe-śheń) m. September

wrzeszczec (vzhesh-chech) v. shriek ; yell; scream; cry

wrzos (vzhos) m. heather

wrzosowisko (vzho-so-veés-ko) n. heath; moor

wrzód (vzhoot) m. abscess

wrzucac (vzhóo-tsach) v. throw in; drop in; put in; cast

wsadzac (vsa-dzach) v. put in; plant ; stick; lock sb up

wschodni (vskhód-nee) adj. m. east; easterly; eastern

wschodzic (vskho-dźheech) v. shoot up; rise; sprout

wschod słonca (vskhóod swoń-tsa) m. sunrise

wsiadac (vśha-dach) v. get in; mount; get on board; take seat

wsiąkac (vshówn-kach) v. sink in; infiltrate ;percolate

wskazany (vska-za-ni) adj. m. advisable;indicated;desirable

wskazówka (vska-zoóv-ka) f. hint; direction; (clock) hand

wskazujący palec (vska-zoo-yówn-tsi pa-lets) m. forefinger

wskazywac (vska-zí-vach) v. point out;show; indicate

wskaźnik (vskaźh-neek) m. index; pointer; indicator;signal

w skos (v skos) adv. slant

wskros (vskrosh) prep. through

wskutek (vskoó-tek) prep. as a result; due to; thanks to

wskrzesic (vskzhe-śheech) v. resuscitate; revive;wake;recall

wspaniałomyslny (vspa-na-wo-miśhl-ni) adj. m. magnanimous

wspaniałosc (vspa-na-woshch) f. splendor; grandeur;lordliness

wspaniały (vspa-ńa-wi) adj. m. superb; glorious; grand;great; smashing; magnificient;splendid

wsparcie (vspar-che) n. support

wspierac (vspye-rach) v. support; prop up; assist; help

wspinac się (vspee-nach śhań) v. climb up;toil up hill;rear

wspomagac (vspo-má-gach) v. help

wspominac (vspo-mee-nach) v. remember ; recall; mention

wspornik (vspor-neek) m. cantilever (beam);bracket; support

wspólnik (vspool-neek) m. partner; accomplice ; associate

wspólny (vspool-ni) adj. m. common; joint; combined ;collective

współczesnosc (vspoow-ches-noshch) f. the present time (day,age)

współczesny (vspoow-ches-ni) adj. m. contemporary ; modern ;present

współczucie (vspoow-choo-che) n. sympathy ; compassion ;pity

współczynnik (vspoow-chin-neek) m. coefficient; factor

współdziałac (vspoow-dźha-wach) v. cooperate ; act jointly

współistniec (vspoow-eest-nech) v. coexist

współistnienie (vspoow-eest-ńe-ńe) n. coexistence

współpraca (vspoow-pra-tsa) f. cooperation ; team-work

współrzędna (vspoow-zhánd-na) f. coordinate axis

współudział (vspoow-oó-dżhaw) m. participation; share

współwłasciciel (vspoow-vwaśh-chee-chel) m. joint owner

współzawodnictwo (vspoow-za-vod-neets-tvo) m. competition

współzawodnik (vspoow-za-vod-neek) m. competitor; rival

współżyc (vspoow-zhich) v. get along; live together; coexist

wstawac (vsta-vach) v. get up

wstawiac (vsta-vyach) v. set in

wstawiac się (vsta-vyach śhań) v. get tipsy; plead for sb

wstąpic (vstown-peech) v. step in; drop in; step up; enter

wstążka (vstównzh-ka) f. ribbon

wstecz (vstech) adv. backwards

wsteczny (vstech-ni) adj. m. reactionary; reverse;backward

wstęga (vstáň-ga) f. (large)
ribbon ; band;sash:wreath;wisp
wstęp (vstánp) m. entrance;
admission ; preface; opening
wstępny (vstánp-ni) adj. m.in-
troductory ; initial;preliminary
wstręt (vstráňt) m. aversion
wstrętny (vstránt-ni) adj. m.
hideous ; foul;vile; nasty
wstrząs (vstzhówns) m. shock,
wstrząsający (vstzhówn-sa-yowń-
tsi) adj. m. shocking; thrilling
wstrzemięźliwość (vstzhe-myáń-
żhleé-vośhćh) f. moderation
wstrzemięźliwy (vstzhe-myáń-
żhleé-vi) adj. m. moderate
wstrzykiwać (vstzhi-keé-vach)
v. inject; give a shot
wstrzymać (vstzhi-mach) v. stop;
abstain; put off; hold back
wstyd (vstid) m. shame; dis -
grace;dishonor;indecency
wstydliwy (vstid-leé-vi) adj.m.
shy; bashful; timid;embarassing
wstydzić się (vsti-dżheech śhań)
v. be ashamed; blush for sb
wsunąć (vsoo-nówńch) v. slip in;
put in; insert into;tuck in
wsypa (vsí-pa) f.a bad break;
gaffe; give-away of a plot
wsypać (vsi-pach) v. pour in;
tell on somebody; pour (grain)
wszakże (vshák-zhe) conj. adv.
yet; however; nevertheless
wszcząć (vshówńch) v. start; begin; institute; enter(talks)
wszechmocny (vshekh-móts-ni) adj.
m. omnipotent; almighty
wszechnica (vshekh-ńee-tsa) f.
university
wszechstronny (vshekh-stróń-ni)
adj. m. universal; versatile
wszechświat (vshékh-śhvyat) m.
universe; cosmos : macrocosm
wszelki (vshel-kee) adj. m.
every; all; any; whatever
wszerz (vshesh) adv. broadside
wszędzie (vshàń-dźhe) adv. everywhere; on all sides :all over
wszystek (vshís-tek) adj. m.
whole; all; ever; the whole
wszywać (vshi-vach) v. sew in

wścibski (vśhćheeb-skee) m.
busybody; meddler; snooper
wściekać się (vśhćhé-kach śhàń)
v. rage; rave; be furious
wścieklizna (vśhćhe-kleéz-na) f.
rabies ; madness;hydrophobia
wściekłość (vśhćhek-wóśhćh) f.
fury; rage; tantrums;madness
wślad (vśhlad) adv. following
in tracks; following closely
wślizgnąć się (vśhleéz-nówńch
śhàń) v. sneak in; slip in
wśród (vśhrood) prep. among
wtaczać (vta-chach) v. roll in
wtajemniczyć (vta-yem-ńee-chićh)
v. initiate; acquaint;instruct
wtargnąć (vtarg-nówńch) v. invade; break into; interrupt
wtedy (vte-di) adv. then
wtem (vtem) adv. suddenly
wtenczas (vtéń-chas) adv. then;
at that time; at this junction
wtoczyć (vtó-chićh) v. roll in
wtorek (vtó-rek) m. Tuesday
wtórny (vtoor-ni) adj. m. secondary ; incidental;repeated
wtrącać się (vtrówn-tsach śhàń)
v. meddle; cut into; butt in
wtyczka (vtích-ka) f. plug
wtykać (vti-kach) v. insert
w tył (vtiw) adv. back
wuj (vooy) m. uncle
wujenka (voo-yéń-ka) f. aunt
wulgarny (vool-gár-ni) adj. m.
vulgar; coarse; low
wulkan (vool-kan) m. volcano
wulkanizować (vool-ka-ńee-zó-
vach) v. vulcanize ;cure(rubber)
wwozić (v-vó-żheećh) v. import
wwóz (v-voos) m. import importation
wy (vi) pron. you; you people
wybaczać (vi-ba-chach) v. forgive; pardon; buckle out of line
wybawca (vi-báv-tsa) m. savior;
rescuer; liberator ;redeemer
wybawić (vi-bá-veećh) v. save;
deliver ; free;rescue; rid
wybebeszyć (vi-be-bé-shićh) v.
gut (chicken etc.)
wybić (vi-beećh) v. knock out
(something); strike; cover;kill
wybiec (vi-byets) v. run out

wybieg (vi-byek) m. evasion;
runway; playground; fowl run

wybielić (vi-bye-leech) v. whitewash; bleach; coat with tin

wybierać (vi-bye-rach) v. choose
elect; select; pick out ; mine

wybierak (vi-bye-rak) m. selec-
tor (technical term)

wybieralny (vi-bye-rál-ni) adj.
m. elective; eligible ; electable

wybitny (vi-beet-ni) adj. m.
prominent; eminent ; marked

wybladły (vi-blad-wi) adj. m.
pale; dim; faded; colorless

wybłagać (vi-bwa-gach) v. get by
entreaty; impetrate

wyblakły (vi-blak-wi) adj. m.
faded; dim; dilute; weathered

wyboisty (vi-bo-ees-ti) adj. m.
rough; full of holes; bumpy

wyborca (vi-bór-tsa) m. voter

wyborczy (vi-bór-chi) adj. m.
electoral; election-(precinct...)

wyborny (vi-bór-ni) adj. m. excellent; prime; choice; splendid

wyborowy (vi-bo-ro-vi) adj. m.
choice; select; first rate

wybory (vi-bo-ri) pl. election

wybór (vi-boor), m. choice; option

wybrany (vi-bra-ni) adj. m.
elected; chosen; selected

wybredny (vi-bréd-ni) adj. m.
fastidious; particular; exacting

wybrnąć (vibr-nownch) v. get out;
pull through; wade; clear out of

wybrukować (vi-broo-kó-vach) v.
pave (the road, the street etc.)

wybryk (vi-brik) m. prank; freak;
antic; whim; frolic; caprice

wybrzeże (vi-bzhe-zhe) n. coast;
beach; sea-shore; sea-coast

wybrzuszenie (vi-bzhoo-she-ńe)
n. bulge; swelling; knob; belly

wybuch (vi-bookh) m. explosion;
eruption; outbreak; outburst

wybudować (vi-boo-do-vach) v.
build; erect; raise; construct

wycelować (vi-tse-lo-vach) v.
take aim; level a gun at

wychodek (vi-khó-dek) m. privy

wychodzić (vi-khó-dzheech) v.
get out; walk out; climb out

wychodźca (vi-khodźh-tsa) m.
emigrant; émigré

wychować (vi-khó-vach) v. bring
up; rear; rise; train; educate

wychowanek (vi-kho-vá-nek) m.
pupil; alumnus; ward; foster child

wychowanie (vi-kho-vá-ńe) n.
upbringing; manners; education

wychowawca (vi-kho-váv-tsa) m.
tutor; educator; foster father

wychudły (vi-khóod-wi) adj. m.
gaunt; skinny; haggard; emaciated

wychwalać (vi-khvá-lach) v.
praise; exalt; extol; speak highly

wychylać (vi-khi-lach) v. stick
out; empty (glass); bend; incline

wychylać się (vi-khi-lach śhań)
v. lean out; stick one's neck
out; hang out; appear; be visible

wyciąg (vi-chownk) m. extract;
elevator; hoist; winch; excerpt

wyciągać (vi-chown-gach) v.
pull out; stretch out; derive;

wycie (vi-che) n. howl; scream

wycieczka (vi-chéch-ka) f. trip;
excursion; outing; ramble; hike

wyciekać (vi-ché-kach) v. leak
out; flow out; ooze out; scamper

wycieńczać (vi-cheń-chach) exhaust

wycieńczenie (vi-cheń-che-ńe) n.
exhaustion; weakness; debility

wycieraczka (vi-che-rách-ka) f.
wiper; doormat

wycierać (vi-che-rach) v. wipe;
erase; efface; dust; wear out

wycięcie (vi-chán-che) n. opening; cut; décolleté; notch; jag

wycinać (vi-chee-nach) v. cut
out ; carve out; fell; cut down

wycisk (vi-cheesk) m. press;
squeeze; beating (slang)

wyciskać (vi-chees-kach) v.
squeeze out; impress; wring

wycofać (vi-tsó-fach) v. withdraw; remove; retract; call off

wycofanie (vi-tso-fá-ńe) n .
withdrawal; recall; retirement

wyczerpać (vi-cher-pach) v.
exhaust; drain; deplete; scoop

wyczerpanie (vi-cher-pa-ńe) n.
exhaustion; depletion; prostration

wyczesywać (vi-che-si-vach) v.
comb out; dress hair (beard etc.)

wyczuwać (vi-choo-vaćh) v. sense;
feel; scent; ascertain; perceive

wyczyn (vi-chin) m. feat; stunt

wyczyszczać (vi-chish-chaćh) v.
clean; brush; clean out; polish

wyć (vić) v. howl; roar; shriek

wycwiczony (vich-vee-cho-ni)
adj. m. trained; skilled

wydajność (vi-day-noshćh) f.
yield; productivity; output

wydajny (vi-day-ni) adj. m.
productive; effective

wydalać (vi-da-laćh) v. dismiss;
sack; expel; eliminate; excrete

wydalenie (vi-da-le-ne) n. expulsion; dismissal; excretion

wydanie (vi-da-ne) n. edition

wydarty (vi-dar-ti) adj. m.
torn out; plucked out; snached out

wydarzać się (vi-da-zhaćh śhäń)
v. happen; turn out well; occur

wydarzenie (vi-da-zhe-ne) n.
event; happening; circumstance

wydatek (vi-da-tek) m. expense

wydatkować (vi-dat-ko-vaćh) v.
spend; lay out funds; expend

wydatny (vi-dat-ni) adj. m.
prominent; salient; distinct

wydawać (vi-da-vaćh) v. spend;
give the change; publish

wydawca (vi-dav-tsa) m. publisher; editor; publishing house

wydawnictwo (vi-dav-neets-tvo)
n. publication; publishing
house; publishing firm

wydąć (vi-downćh) v. expand;
puff up; inflate; blow up

wydech (vi-dekh) m. exhalation

wydeptać ścieżkę (vi-dep-taćh
śhćhezh-käń) beat a path (exp.)

wydłubywać (vi-dwoo-bi-vaćh) v.
scrape out; poke; hollow out

wydłużać (vi-dwoo-zhaćh) v. prolong; lengthen; elongate

wydma (vid-ma) f. dune; snowdrift

wydobrzeć (vi-dob-zhećh) v. recover; get better; improve

wydobycie (vi-do-bi-će) n. output; yield; production

wydobywać (vi-do-bi-vaćh) v. extract; mine; wring; get; obtain

wydostać (vi-dos-taćh) v. bring
out; extricate; obtain; pull out

wydra (vi-dra) f. otter; vulg.:
bitch; hussy; minx; vixen

wydrapać (vi-dra-paćh) v.
scratch out; erase a stain

wydrapać się (vi-dra-paćh śhäń)
v. climp up; scramble up (out)

wydrążać (vi-drown-zhaćh) v.
hollow out; drill; excavate

wydrwić (vi-drveećh) v. jeer;
mock; cheat; gibe; deride

wydrwigrosz (vi-drvee-grosh)
m. swindler; fraud; take-in

wydusić (vi-doo-śheećh) v.
squeeze out; extort; strangle

wydychać (vi-di-khaćh) v.
breathe out; exhale; emit

wydymać (vi-di-maćh) v. puff out;
inflate; belly out; blow up; bulge

wydział (vi-dżhaw) m. department

wydziedziczać (vi-dżhe-dżhee-
chaćh) v. disinherit

wydzielać (vi-dżhe-laćh) v. emit;
detach; distribute; secrete

wydzielenie (vi-dżhe-le-ne) n.
secretion; assignment; elimination; emanation; issue

wydzieliny (vi-dżhe-lee-ni) pl.
sercreta; excretions; discharge

wydzielony (vi-dżhe-lo-ni) adj.
m. emited; segregated; alloted

wydzierać (vi-dżhe-raćh) v. tear
out; roar out; blare out; scramble

wydzierżawić (vi-dżher-zha-veećh)
v. lease; farm out; rent; let out

wydzierżawienie (vi-dżher-zha-
vye-ne) n. leasing; renting

wyegzekwować (vi-eg-zek-vo-vaćh)
v. exact; enforce; carry out

wyekwipowanie (vi-ek-vee-po-va-
ne) n. outfit; equipment

wyeleganciec (vi-e-le-gan-ćhećh)
v. acquire elegance; become elegant

wyeliminowanie (vi-e-lee-mee-no-
va-ne) n. elimination; exclusion

wyga (vi-ga) m. old experienced
hand; sly fox; old stager

wygadać (vi-ga-daćh) v. blab out

wygadany (vi-ga-da-ni) adj. m.
glib; eloquent; wordy; talkative

wyganiać (vi-ga-naćh) v. expel;
chase out; turn out (cattle)

wygarniać (vi-gar-naćh) v. rake
out; tell off; say openly; shoot

wygasać (vi-ga-sač) v. extinguish; expire; go out; die out

wyginać (vi-gee-nač) v. bend

wygląd (vig-lównd) m. appearance;aspect; air;looks;semblance

wyglądać (vig-lówn-dač) v. look out; appear;appear;look

wygładzać (vi-gwa-dzač) v. smooth;level;even; sleek

wygłodzić (vi-gwo-dźheeč) v. starve out; underfeed; famish

wygłosić (vi-gwo-śheeč) v. pronounce; utter;deliver(speech)

wygnać (vig-nač) v.expel;banish

wygnanie (vig-ńa-ńe) n. exile

wygniatać (vi-gńa-tač) v. press out; squeeze out; extort; kill

wygoda (vi-go-da) f. comfort

wygodny (vi-god-ni) adj. m. comfortable; cozy; handy

wygolony (vi-go-lo-ni) adj. m. clean-shaven; well shaven

wygotować (vi-go-to-vač) v. boil away; distill; prepare

wygórowany (vi-goo-ro-va-ni) adj. m. excessive; stiff(price)

wygrać (vi-grač) v. win; score

wygramolić się (vi-gra-mo-leeč śhań) v. scramble up (out)

wygrana (vi-gra-na) f. winning; victory; prize; a win

wygryzać (vi-gri-zač) v. 1.bite out; corrode; 2. drive out by harassment;oust;bore a hole

wygrzebywać (vi-gzhe-bi-vač) v. dig out; unearth; rake out

wygrzewać się (vi-gzhe-vač śhań) v. bask; warm oneself

wygwizdać (vi-gveez-dač) v. hiss off (stage); whistle away

wyjałowić (vi-ya-wo-veeč) v. sterilize; exhaust(brain,soil...)

wyjaśnić (vi-yaśh-ńeeč) v. explain; clear up; elucidate

wyjaśnienie (vi-yaśh-ńe-ńe) n. explanation; interpretation

wyjawić (vi-ya-veeč) v. disclose;reveal; bring to light

wyjazd (vi-yazt) m. departure

wyjąkać (vi-yówn-kač) v. stammer out;stutter out; falter out

wyjątek (vi-yown-tek) m. exception; excerpt; extract

wyjątkowy (vi-yówn-ko-vi) adj. m. exceptional;unusual;unique

wyjechać (vi-ye-khač) v. drive away; leave ;come out with

wyjeżdżać (vi-yezh-dzhač) v. leave; drive away; set out

wyjmować (viy-mo-vač) v. take out; remove; extract; excerpt

wyjście (viyśh-če) n. exit; way out; departure;egress

wyka (vi-ka) f. vetch ; tare

wykadzić (vi-ka-dźheeč) v. smoke out; fumigate; perfume

wykałaczka (vi-ka-wač-ka) f. toothpick

wykarczować (vi-kar-cho-vač) v. grub out; clear;dig up(trees)

wykaz (vi-kas) m. list; register; roll; schedule;docket

wykąpać (vi-kówn-pač) v. bathe

wykipieć (vi-kee-p-yeeč) v. boil over (milk,water,soup etc.)

wyklęty (vi-klań-ti) adj. m. cursed; excommunicated

wykluczyć (vi-kloo-chiče) v. exclude;expel; shut out;except

wykład (vik-wat) m. lecture

wykładać (vi-kwa-dač) v. lecture; lay out ; display; cover

wykładnik (vi-kwad-ńeek) m. exponent; expression; ratio

wykładowca (vi-kwa-dov-tsa) m. lecturer; instructor

wykłuwać (vi-kwoo-vač) v. stab out; put out; tattoo;prick out

wykoleic (vi-ko-le-eeč) v. derail; lead astray;ditch(a train)

wykombinować (vi-kom-bee-no-vač) v. contrive; think out

wykonać (vi-ko-nač) v. execute; do; fulfil ; carry out; perform

wykonalny (viy-ko-nál-ni) adj.m. feasible; workable;realizable

wykonanie (vi-ko-ná-ńe) n. execution;realization;fulfilment

wykonawczy (vi-ko-nav-chi) adj. m. executive ;executory(details...)

wykończenie (vi-kon-che-ńe) n. finish; trimming;last touch

wykończyc (vi-kon-chich) v. finish off ; dress; do sb in

wykop (vi-kop) m. excavation ; potato lifting; flying kick

wykopać (vi-ko-pach) v. dig out
wykopalisko (vi-ko-pa-lees-ko)
n. find (archaeological)
wykorzenić (vi-ko-zhe-neech) v.
root out ; uproot; eradicate
wykorzystać (vi-ko-zhis-tach) v.
take advantage; exploit:use up
wykpić (vik-peech) v. deride
wykraczać (vi-kra-chach) v. step
over; break law,; transgress
wykradać (vi-kra-dach) v. steal;
kidnap ;purloin;pilfer;abduct
wykrajać (vi-kra-yach) v. cut
out ; carve out;make a low cut
wykres (vi-kres) m. graph; chart
wykreslić (vi-kresh-leech) v.
trace; cross out; draw ;erase
wykręcać (vi-kran-tsach) v. screw
out; distort; elude; twist
wykręt (vi-krant) m. shift;
excuse ; dodge ;guibble
wykrętny (vi-krant-ni) adj. m.
shifty ;evasive; sophistical
wykroczenie (vi-kro-che-ne) n.of-
fense; misdemeanor;delinquency
wykroić (yi-kro-eech) v. cut out
wykruszyć (vi-kroo-shich) v.
crumble out ; shell(corn etc.)
wykryć (vi-krich) v. discover;
detect; reveal(the truth etc.)
wykrztusić (vi-kzhtoo-sheech) v.
cough up; choke out ;hawk up
wykrzyknać (vi-kzhik-nownch) v.
call out ; shout; cry out
wykształcić (vi-kzhtaw-cheech) v.
educate ; train; shape; form
wykup (yi-koop) m. ransom
wykupić (vi-koo-peech) v. buy up
wykurzać (vi-koo-zhach) v. smoke
out (foxes,bees, etc.)
wykwintny (vi-kveent-ni) adj.m.
elegant; exquisite; urbane
wyleczalny (vi-le-chal-ni) adj.
m. curable;possible to cure
wyleczyć (vi-le-chich) v. cure
wylew krwi (vi-lev krvee)
hemorrhage; blood effusion
wylewać (vi-le-vach) v. pour out;
overflow;spill;bail out water
wylęgać (vi-lan-gach) v. hatch
wylękły (vi-lank-wi) adj. m.
frightened ; scared ;terrified

wyliczać (vi-lee-chach) v.
count up; count out; recite
wylosować (vi-lo-so-vach) adj.
m. draw out by lots ;toss for
wylot (vi-lot) m.flight departure; nozzle; exhaust; exit
wyludniać (vi-lood-nach) v.
depopulate;desolate;devastate
wyładować (vi-wa-do-vach) v.
unload; discharge; cram pack
wyładowanie (vi-wa-do-va-ne)
n. unloading;discharge
wyłamać (vi-wa-mach) v. break
out;break loose;break away
wyławiać (vi-wav-yach) v. fish
out; spot out; catch (a sound)
wyłaniać (vi-wa-nach) v. evolve;
emerge; show; appoint;form
wyłączać (vi-wown-chach) v.
exclude; switch off;disconnect
wyłącznik (vi-wownch-neek) m.
switch; circuit-breaker;cut off
wyłączny (vi-wownch-ni) adj.
m. exclusive; sole; only;entire
wyłudzić (vi-woo-dzheech) v.
coax; beguile; trick; fool
wyłom (vi-wom) m. breach; gap
wyłuskać (vi-woos-kach) v. husk;
scale; fleece; shell; hull; pod
wymaczać (vi-ma-chach) v. soak
wymagać (vi-ma-gach) v. require;
expect; demand; need; exact
wymaganie (vi-ma-ga-ne) n. requirement; demand;requisite;need;
want
wymawiać (vi-mav-yach) v. pronounce; reproach; cancel;express
wymazać (vi-ma-zach) v. erase;
efface; blot out; smear; use up
wymiana (vi-mya-na) f. exchange
wymiar (vi-myar) m. dimension
wymiatać (vi-mya-tach) v.
sweep out; clean out; sweep
wymieniać (vi-mye-nach) v.
exchange; convert; replace
wymierać (vi-mye-rach) v. die
out; become extinct(gradually)
wymierzać (vi-mye-zhach) v. aim;
measure; assess; survey;mete out
wymię (yi-myan) n. udder ;evade
wymijać (vi-mee-yach) v. pass by;
wymiotować (vi-myo-to-vach) v.
vomit; be sick;spew up(one's food)

wymogi (vi-mo-gee) pl. require-
ments; exigencies;needs

wymowa (vi-mo-va) f. pronunciation; significance(of facts...)

wymowny (vi-mov-ni) adj. m.
eloquent; telltale; telling

wymoc (vi-moots) v. extort;
compel; wring; force;prevail

wymówienie (vi-moov-ye-ńe) n.
notice (to quit or dismiss)

wymówka (vi-moov-ka) f. reproach;
pretext; excuse; put-off;evasion

wymusić (vi-moo-śhich) v. extort

wymuszenie (vi-moo-she-ńe) n.
extortion;blackmail;shakedown

wymykać się (vi-mi-kach śhań)
v. escape;slip away;sneak out

wymysł (vi-misw) m. fiction;
invention ;fiction; abuse

wymyślać (vi-miśh-lach) v. think
up; call names; invent; abuse

wymyślny (vi-miśhl-ni) adj. m.
clever; ingenious;sophisticated

wymywać (vi-mi-vach) v. wash out

wynagradzać (vi-na-gra-dzach) v.
reward; pay; indemnify;make up

wynagrodzenie (vi-na-gro-dze-ńe)
n. reward; pay; fee; reparation

wynajdywać (vi-nay-di-vach) v.
find (out); invent; devise

wynajmować (vi-nay-mo-vach) v.
hire ; rent   ;rent; hire

wynajem (vi-na-yem) m. lease;

wynalazca (vi-na-laz-tsa) m.
inventor; contriver

wynalazek (vi-na-la-zek) m. invention ; device;contrivance

wynaleźć (vi-na-leżhch) v. invent

wynaradawiać (vi-na-ra-dav-yach)
v. denationalize ; divest

wynik (vi-neek) m. result; score

wyniosłość (vi-ńos-wośhch) f.
eminence; haughtiness ; prance

wyniosły (vi-ńos-wi) adj. m.
lofty; high-handed ;insolent

wyniszczać (vi-ńeesh-chach) v.
ruin ; exhaust; weaken;devastate

wynosić (vi-no-śheech) v. carry
out; elevate; amount ;wear out

wynudzać (vi-noo-dzach) v. get
by bothering; bore stiff

wynurzenie (vi-noo-zhe-ńe) n.
emergence; (personal) outpouring

wyobraźnia (vi-o-brażh-ńa) f.
imagination ; fancy;empty fancy

wyobrażać (vi-o-bra-zhach) v.
imagine; picture; fancy;suppose

wyobrażenie(vi-o-bra-zhe-ńe) n.
notion; idea ; image;representation

wyodrębniać (vi-od-rańb-ńach)
v. single out; separate; isolate

wyodrębnienie (vi-od-rańb-ńe-
ńe) n. separation; isolation

wyolbrzymiać (vi-ol-bzhi-myach)
v. magnify; exaggerate(very much)

wypaczyć (vi-pa-chich) v. warp

wypad (vi-pat) m. sally; attack

wypadać (vi-pa-dach) v. fall
out; rash out; become; turn
out; happen; occur; work out

wypadek (vi-pa-dek) m. accident;
case ;event; chance;instance

wypadkowa (vi-pad-ko-va) f. resultant (force, effect etc.)

wypakować (vi-pa-ko-vach) v.
unpack; cram ; pack tight

wypalać (vi-pa-lach) v. burn out

wypaplać (vi-pap-lach) v. babble
out ; blurt out(the truth,secret)

wyparcie się (vi-par-che śhań)
n. disclaimer; repudiation

wyparować (vi-pa-ro-vach) v.
evaporate; vanish into thin air

wypatrywać (vi-pa-tri-vach) v.
watch (for) ; look out;espy;descry

wypełniać (vi-pew-ńach) v. fulfil; fill up ; while away;fill in

wypełnienie (vi-pew-ńe-ńe) n.
fulfilment ; order execution;filler

wypędzać (vi-pań-dzach) v. drive
out; expel ; discharge;dislodge

wypiekać (vi-pye-kach) v. bake;

wypierać (vipye-rach) v. oust;
push out;force out;supplant

wypierać sie (vi-pye-rach śhań)
v. deny ; repudiate;disown;abjure

wypijać (vi-pee-yach) v. drink
(empty); drink to; drink off

wypinać (vi-pee-nach) v. extend;
strech out ; show one's back side

wypis (vi-pees) m. extract;passage

wypisywać (vi-pee-si-vach) v.
(write) extract;make out(a check)

wyplątać (vi-plown-tach) v.
extricate ; disentangle;disengage;
free from tangles

wyplątany (vi-plown-tá-ni) adj.
m. disembroiled;extricated

wyplenić (vi-ple-ńeech) v. weed
out; root out; eradicate

wypluć (vi-plooch) v. spit out

wypłacać (vi-pwa-tsach) v. pay
out; pay up; pay off; repay

wypłacalny (vi-pwa-tsál-ni) adj.
m. solvent; sound(financially)

wypłata (yi-pwa-ta) f. pay (day)

wypłoszyc (vi-pwo-shich) v.
scare away; drive away(cats...)

wypłowieć (vi-pwo-vyech) v. fade

wypłukać (vi-pwoo-kach) v. rinse;
wash out; swill out ;give a rinse

wypływ (vi-pwiv) m. outflow;
discharge; efflux; leakage

wypływać (vi-pwi-vach) v. flow
out; sail out; swim out; rise

wypocić (vi-po-cheech) v. sweat
out; perspire ;be soaked in sweat

wypoczynek (vi-po-chí-nek) m.
rest; repose

wypoczywac (vi-po-chí-vach) v.
rest;have a rest;take a rest

wypogadzać sie (vi-po-ga-dzach
shán) v. clear up; cheer up

wypomnieć (vi-pom-ńech) v. reproach; remind ;keep reminding

wyporność (vi-por-noshch) f.
displacement; draught ;buoyancy

wyposażać (vi-po-sa-zhach) v.
equip; endow; fit out; stock

wyposażenie (vi-po-sa-zhe-ńe) n.
equipment; outfit; wages ;dowry

wyposażyć (vi-po-sa-zhich) v.
endow; equip; fit out;stock

wypowiadać (vi-po-vya-dach) v.
pronounce; declare ; express

wypowiedzenie (vi-po-vye-dze-ńe)
n.(discharge) notice; (war) declaration; renunciation;utterance

wypożyczać (vi-po-zhi-chach) v.
lend out ;borrow from;hire to

wypożyczalnia (vi-po-zhi-chál-na)
f. rental business ;rental agency

wypracowanie (vi-pra-tso-va-ńe)
n. (school) composition; elaboration ; essay; exercice

wyprać (vi-prach) v. wash out

wypraszać (vi-pra-shach) v.
1. plead; 2. show (the door) ;
give somebody the gate;turn out

wyprawa (vi-pra-va) f. expedition; outfit; tanning;dowry

wyprawiac (vi-pra-vyach) v.
send; tan;plaster;give(a party)

wyprężać (vi-pran-zhach) v.
stretch out; tense(a muscle etc.)

wyprostować (vi-pros-to-vach)
v. straighten;set streight

wyprowadzać (vi-pro-va-dzach)
v. lead out; move out; trace

wypróbować (vi-proo-bo-vach)
v. test; try out;put to test

wypróżniać (vi-proozh-ńach) v.
empty; clear out; evacuate

wyprzedawać (vi-pzhe-da-vach)
v. sell out; clear out(stock)

wyprzedaż (vi-pzhe-dash) v.
(clearance) sale

wyprzedzać (vi-pzhe-dzach) v.
pull ahead;outpace;overtake

wyprzęgać (vi-pzhan-gach) v.
unharness; unhitch (a horse)

wypukły (vi-pook-wi) adj. m.
convex; bulging; cambered

wypuścić (vi-poosh-cheech) v.
let out; set free; let go;
omit;release;launch;lease out

wypychac (vi-pi-khach) v. oust;
push out; stuff;pack; fill;cram

wypytywać (vi-pi-ti-vach) v.
question;ask questions;inquire

wyrabiac (vi-ra-byach) v.
1. make; form; 2. play pranks

wyrachowany (vi-ra-kho-va-ni)
adj. m. scheming; thrifty

wyratować (vi-ra-to-vach) v.
rescue; save (a life etc.)

wyraz (vi-ras) m. word; expression; look; term (in vocabulary)

wyraźny (vi-rázh-ni) adj. m.
explicit; clear; distinct

wyrażać (vi-ra-zhach) v. express

wyrażenie (vi-ra-zhe-ńe) n.
expression; utterance; phrase
                              statement

wyrąb (vi-rownp) m. clearing;
felling; cutting; slash;fell

wyrąbać (vi-rown-bach) v. cut
out (with axe); clear; hack out

wyręczać (vi-ran-chach) v. help
out; replace; relieve of tasks

wyrobnik (vi-rób-neek) m. laborer; day-laborer ; navvy

wyrocznia (vi-roch-ña) f. oracle

wyrodny (vi-ród-ni) adj. m. degenerate;unnatural(son);base

wyrodzic się (vi-ró-dżheech śhãn) v. degenerate;deteriorate

wyrok (vi-rok) m. sentence; verdict; judgment; pronouncement

wyrostek (vi-ros-tek) m. outgrowth; stripling; teenager

wyrosnięty (vi-rosh-nãn-ti)adj. m. grown up ; overgrown

wyrozumiały (vi-ro-zoo-myá-wi) adj. m. indulgent; lenient

wyrozumienie (vi-ro-zoo-myé-ñe) n. sympathetic understanding

wyrób (vi-roob) m. manufacture

wyrownac (vi-roov-nach) v. equalize; pay up; smooth

wyrownanie (vi-roov-ná-ñe) m. leveling;balancing(accounts)offset

wyrózniac (vi-roozh-ñach) v. distinguish ; favor; single out

wyruszyc (vi-roo-shich) v. start out;set out;march out;sail away

wyrwac (vir-vach) v. extract; tear out; pull out; run away

wyrywki (vi-riv-kee) pl. random

wyryc (vi-rich) v. engrave; root up; dig out;gully;furrow;incise

wyrzec się (vi-zhets śhãn) v. renounce;give up; forgo;repudiate

wyrzucac (vi-zhoo-tsach) v. expel; throw out; dump; reproach

wyrzut (vi-zhoot) m. reproach

wyrzutnia (vi-zhoot-ña) f. launch (ing)pad; chute; launcher

wyrzutek (vi-zhoo-tek) m. outcast

wyrzynac (vi-zhi-nach) v. cut out; carve; slaughter; bang; slap

wysadzic (vi-sá-dżheech) v. set out;land; blow up ; eject;plant

wyschnac (vis-khnonch) v. dry up

wysepka (vi-sép-ka) f. islet

wysiadac (vi-śha-dach) v. get out (from car etc.); go bust;get off

wysiadywac (vi-śha-di-vach) v. sit out; hatch out; sit late

wysiedlac (vi-śhed-lach) v. expel (from home); resettle;eject

wysilac (vi-śhee-lach) v. exert

wysiłek (vi-śhee-wek) m. effort

wyskoczyc (vi-sko-chich) v. jump out; pop up;run out;bale out

wyskok (vis-kok) m. 1. fling; freak; 2. cam;ledge;run out

wyskokowy (vis-ko-ko-vi) adj. m. alcoholic; intoxicating

wyskrobac (vi-skro-bach) v. scratch out; erase ;scratch

wyskubac (vi-skoo-bach) v. pluck out; pull out(hair etc.)

wysłac (vi-swach) v. send off; dispatch ;emit; let fly

wysłaniec (vi-swa-ñets) m. messenger; envoy ; deputy

wysłowic (vi-swo-veech) v. express ;say; utter; speak

wysłuchac (vi-swoo-khach) v. hear out ;give a hearing

wysługiwac się (vi-swoo-gee-vach śhãn) v. lackey; use s.o.

wysmarowac (vi-sma-ro-vach) v. smear ;lubricate; soil;stain

wysmażony (vi-sma-zho-ni) adj. m. well done (meat);cooked

wysmukły (vi-smook-wi) adj.m. slender ; slim and tall

wysoce (vi-só-tse) adv. highly

wysoki (vi-só-kee) m. tall; high ; soaring; lofty;towering

wysokosc (vi-só-kośhch) f. height; altitude;level;extent

wysokosciomierz (vi-so-kośh-cho-myesh) m. altimeter

wyspa (vís-pa) f. island; isle

wyspac się (vis-pach śhãn) v. sleep enough; sleep off

wyspowiadac się (vis-po-vya-dach śhãn) v. confess

wyssac (vis-sach) v. suck out ; suck dry

wystarac się (vi-sta-rach śhãn) v. procure ;obtain; secure

wystarczyc (vi-stár-chich) v. suffice ; do enough;be enough

wystawa (vi-stá-va) f. exhibition; display (window dressing)

wystawac (vi-sta-vach) v. stand out; stand long time ;stick out

wystawca (vi-stáv-tsa) m. exhibitor; signer (of check)

wystawiac (vi-stáv-yach) v. put out; stick out; sign (check) ; exhibit ;expose

wystawienie (vi-sta-vyé-ñe) n. exposition; exposure ;display

wystąpić (vi-stown-peech) v.
step forward;perform;resign
wystąpienie (vi-stown-pye-ne)
n. withdrawal; appearance
występ (vi-stanp) m. protrusion;
(stage) appearance; utteramce
występek (vi-stan-pek) m. felony; crime; vice; offense
występny (vi-stanp-ni) adj. m.
criminal; immoral; illicit
wystraszyc (vi-stra-shich) v.
frighten away; terrify; scare
wystroic (vi-stro-eech) v. dress
up ; trig out; deck out; adorn
wystrzał (vi-stzhaw) m. shot
wystrzegac się (vi-stzhe-gach
shan) v. avoid ; beware; shun
wystrzelic (vi-stzhe-leech) v.
fire a gun;shoot out; go off
wystrzępic (vi-stzhan-peech) v.
ravel out ; fray; unravel
wystygac (vi-sti-gach) v. cool
off ; grow cold;get cold
wysuszyc (vi-soo-shich) v. dry
up ; wither ;parch; shrivel
wysuwac (vi-soo-vach) v. shove
forward ; protrude; put out
wyswobodzic (vi-svo-bo-dźheech)
v. liberate; deliver; free
wysychać (vi-si-khach) v. dry out
wysypac (vi-si-pach) v. pour out
wysypka (vi-sip-ka) f. (skin)
rash ; eruption ;exanthema
wysysac (vi-si-sach) v. suck
wyszczególnic (vi-shche-gool-
neech) v. specify;detail out
wyszeptac (vi-sheptach) v. whis-
per(not vibrating the vocal
rchords)
wyszkolic (vi-shko-leech) v.
train ;school; educate ;instruct
wyszpiegowac (vi-shpye-go-vach)
v. spy out; spy out that...
wyszukac (vi-shoo-kach) v. find
out ; hunt up; search out
wyszukany (vi-shoo-ka-ni) adj.m.
choice; unusual ; elaborate
wyszydzac (vi-shi-dzach) v.
scoff at ; jeer; deride
wyszynk (vi-shink) m. liquor
store; liquor retail on licence
wyszywac (vi-shi-vach) v. embroider;desing with needlework

wyscielac (vi-shche-lach) v.
pad; line; strew;cushion
wyscig (vish-cheek) m. race;
contest ; rivalry ;(horse)race
wyśledzic (vi-shle-dźheech) v.
spy out; track out;detect
wyśliznąc się (vi-shleez-nownch
shan) v. slip out;slide out
wyśmiac (vish-myach) v. laugh
at; deride ;mock;ridicule
wyśmienity (vish-mye-nee-ti)
adj. m. choice; excellent
wyspiewac (vi-shpye-vach) v.
squeal; sing; say ;sound praises
wyswiadczyc (vish-vyad-chich)
v. do (favor); do (good);do (wrong)
wyswiechtany (vi-shvyekh-ta-ni)
adj. m. well worn; beat up
wyswietlac (vish-vyet-lach) v.
clear up; project (film)
wytaczać (vi-ta-chach) v. roll
out ; set forth; draw;turn
wytargowac (vi-tar-go-vach) v.
buy by haggling; haggle a lot
wytarty (vi-tar-ti) adj.m.
worn out; thread bare;shabby
wytchnąc (vi-tkhnownch) v. rest
up ; relax ;take a rest;breathe
wytchnienie (vi-tkhne-ne) n.
rest ; break; relax; truce
wytępic (vi-tan-peech) v.extermi-
nate; eradicate; wipe out
wytężac (vi-tan-zhach) v. strain
wytknąc (vit-knownch) v. put out;
point out; reproach; trace
wytłuc (vi-twoots) v. kill off;
break up ; ruin; beat up
wytłumaczenie (vi-two-ma-che-
ne) n. explanation; excuse
wytłumaczyc (vi-twoo-ma-chich)
v. explain; excuse; justify
wytrawny (vi-trav-ni) adj. m.
experienced; dry (wine) ;seasoned
wytrącac (vi-trown-tsach) v.
knock of; deduct; snatch
wytrwały (vi-trva-wi) adj. m.
enduring; persevering; dogged
wytrwanie (vi-trva-ne) n. endurance; persistence ;lasting
wytrwac (vi-trvach) v. persevere
wytrych (vi-trikh) m. pick-a-
·lock; pass-key; skeleton-key

wytrząść (vi-tzhównśhch) v.
shake out ; empty ; jolt

wytrzebić (vi-tzhe-beech) v.
devastate; exterminate ; clear

wytrzeźwieć (vi-tzheźh-vyech) v.
sober up; get sober; sober down

wytrzymać (vi-tzhi-mach) v. endure; stand; hold out; keep

wytrzymałość (vi-tzhi-ma-wośhch)
f. endurance ; stamina; strength

wytrzymały (vi-tzhi-ma-wi) adj.
m. enduring ; tough; durable

wytworny (vi-tvor-ni) adj. m.
exquisite ; elegant; stylish

wytwórca (vi-tvoor-tsa) m. producer; manufacturer; maker

wytwórczość (vi-tvoor-choshch)
v. productivity ; output ; product

wytwórnia (vi-tvoor-ña) f. manufacture; factory; plant; works

wytyczna (vi-tich-na) f. direc-
tive; guideline: guiding rule

wyuzdanie (vi-ooz-da-ne) n. unbridled license ; adv. dissolutely

wywiad (vi-vyat) m. interview;
reconnaissance ; espionage

wywiązać się (vi-wyówn-zach śhan)
v. develop; arise; discharge
(duty); result; set in; evolve

wywierać (vi-vye-rach) v. exert

wywiercać (vi-vyer-tsach) v. bore
out; sink a well; drill a hole

wywlekać (vi-vle-kach) v. drag
out ; tug; bring out ; pull out

wywietrzać (vi-vyet-zhach) v.
ventilate ; air; nose out

wywłaszczać (vi-vwash-chach) v.
expropriate ; dispossess

wywłaszczenie (vi-vwash-che-ne)
n. expropriation; dispossession

wywnioskować (vi-vnos-ko-vach)
v. infer; draw a conclusion

wywodzić (vi-vo-dźheech) v. lead
out; derive ; deduce ; lead nowhere

wywojować (vi-vo-yo-vach) v.
fight out ; gain by force

wywołać (vi-vo-wach) v. call;
cause; develop (film); recall

wywozić (vi-vo-źheech) v. export

wywód (vi-voot) m. deduction

wywóz (vi-voos) m. export ; removal

wywracać (vi-vra-tsach) v. overturn; overthrow; reverse ; upset

wywyższać (vi-vizh-shach) v.
exalt; elevate ;extol; rise

wyzbyć się (viz-bich śhan) v.
get rid ; sell out; get over

wyzdrowieć (vi-zdro-vyech) v.
recover; get well; recuperate

wyziębić (vi-zhán-beech) v.
chill ; let get cold ; cool

wyzionąć (vi-żho-nównch) v.
expire; give up (the ghost)

wyznaczać (vi-zna-chach) v.
mark out; appoint; point out

wyznanie (vi-zna-ne) n. denomination; declaration; creed

wyznawać (vi-zna-vach) v. profess;
declare; hold a belief; confess

wyznawca (vi-znav-tsa) m. believer; follower; advocate

wyzuć (vi-zooch) v. deprive;
take off (shoe); strip; divest;
bereave

wyzywać (vi-zi-vach) v. challenge ; call names; abuse; revile

wyzwalać (vi-zva-lach) v. liberate; free; let loose; exempt

wyzwolenie (vi-zvo-le-ne) n .
liberation; release; exemption

wyzwolić (vi-zvo-leech) v. liberate; free; release; set free

wyzysk (vi-zisk) m. exploita-
tion; sweating (of labor)

wyzyskiwacz (vi-zis-kee-vach) m.
exploiter; slave driver

wyż (vizh) m. hight; highland;
high pressure; peak; atm. high

wyżarty (vi-zhar-ti) adj. m.
over-fed; corroded; bloated

wyżej (vi-zhey) adv. higher;
above; mentioned above; higher up

wyżeł (vi-zhew) m. pointer

wyżerać (vi-zhe-rach) v. eat
away; corrode; erode; eat up

wyżłobić (vi-zhwo-beech) v.
hollow out; gully; erode; groove

wyżłobienie (vi-zhwo-byé-ne) n.
groove; gully; erosion; channel

wyższość (vizh-shoshch) f. superiority; excellence; predominance

wyższy (vizh-shi) adj. m. higher
(up) ; taller; superior; top (floor)

wyżyć (vi-zhich) v. use up;
hardly live ; make ends meet;
pull through; survive; pull through;
find an outlet for...

wyżyć się (vi-zhich shan) v.
live up; fulfill oneself
wyżymaczka (vi-zhi-mach-ka) f.
wringer (also machine)
wyżymać (vi-zhi-mach) v. wring
wyżyna (vi-zhi-na) f. high
ground; upland;summit(of glory)
wyżywić (vi-zhi-veech) v. feed
wyżywienie (vi-zhi-vye-ne) m.
food; board; subsistence;diet
wzajemny (vza-yem-ni) adj. m.
mutual; reciprocal; inter-
w zamian (vza-myan) adv. in
exchange; instead; in return
wzbić się (vzbeech shan) v.
soar (up); shoot up; rise
wzbogacić (vzbo-ga-cheech) v.
enrich; add to; dress;make rich
wzbraniać (vzbra-nach) v. forbid; prohibit
wzbroniony (vzbro-no-ni) adj.m.
forbidden; prohibited
wzbudzać (vzboo-dzach) v. excite; inspire;arouse; stir
wzburzenie (vzboo-zhe-ne) n.
agitation; unrest; tumult
wzburzyć (vzboo-zhich) v. stir
up; agitate;dishevel;covulse
wzdąć (vzdownch) v. puff up;fan
wzdłuż (vzdwoosh) prep. along
wzdrygać się (vzdri-gach shan)
v. flinch; object; shudder
wzdychać (vzdi-khach) v. sigh
wzgarda (vzgar-da) f. contempt
wzgardliwy (vzgard-lee-vi) adj.
m. disdainful; scornful
względność (vzgland-noshch) f.
relativity (of understanding...)
względny (vzgland-ni) adj. m.
relative; indulgent; kind of
względy (vzglan-di) pl. favors
wzgórze (vzgoo-zhe) n. hill
wziąć (vzhownch) v. take;possess
wziernik (vzher-neek) m. peep-
hole; scope;view-finder;spy-hole
wzięty (vzhan-ti) adj. m. popular;in demand; in vogue
wzlot (vzlot) m. ascend; rise
wzmacniać (vzmats-nach) v. reinforce; brace up; fortify
wzmagać (vzma-gach) v. intensify
wzmianka (vzmyan-ka) v. mention

wzniesienie (vzne-she-ne) n.
elevation; height;erection
wznieść (vzneshch) v. raise;
elevate; erect; lift; rear
wzniosły (vznos-wi) adj. m.
lofty; noble; elevated;sublime
wznowić (vzno-veech) v. renew
wznowienie (vzno-vye-ne) n.
resumption; come back;reissue
wzorowy (vzo-ro-vi) adj. m.
exemplary ;model; perfect
wzór (vzoor) m. pattern; model;
formula; fashion; standard
wzrok (vzrok) m. sight; vision
wzrost (vzrost) m. growth;size;
height; increase; rise;stature
wzruszać (vzroo-shach) v. move;
touch; affect; thrill; stir
wzruszający (vzroo-sha-yown-tsi)
adj. m. touching; moving;pathetic
wzuć (vzooch) v. put on (shoe)
wzuwacz (vzoo-vach) m. shoe
horn(for pulling boots,shoes on)
wzwyż (vzvizh) adv. up; upwards
skok wzwyż (skok vzvizh) m.
high jump
wzywać (vzi-vach) v. call; call
in; summon; cite; ask in
z (z) prep. with; off; together
ze (ze) prep. with; off; together;from(the ceiling etc.)
za (za) prep. behind; for; at;
by; beyond; over(a wall)
zabarwić (za-bar-veech) v. stain;
dye ; tint; color;tinge;tincture
zabarwienie (za-bar-vye-ne) n.
color(ing); pigmentation; tinge
zabawa (za-ba-va) f. play; fun;
party; game; recreation;amusement
zabawiać (za-bav-yach) v. entertain ;amuse;dwell;stay; last
zabawka (za-bav-ka) f. toy;trife
zabawny (za-bav-ni) adj. m.
funny; comical; ridiculous
zabezpieczenie (za-bez-pye-che-
ne) n. protection ; safety
zabezpieczyć (za-bez-pye-chich)
v. safeguard; secure ;protect
zabić (za-beech) v. kill; slay;
plug up; nail down;beat(a card)
zabieg (za-byek) m. measure;
procedure; exertions; fuss

zabiegać (za-bye-gach) v. strive;
try hard; court; woo; fuss over
zabierać (za-bye-rach) v. take
away; take along;take on (up)
zabierać się (za-bye-rach śhań)
v. clear out; get ready for
zabijać (za-bee-yach) v. kill;
deaden; wear out; exhaust
zabijaka (za-bee-ya-ka) m. bully;
blusterer; swaggerer; hector
zabity (za-bee-ti) adj. m. killed; dead; out-and-out;thorough
zabliźniać (za-bleezh-nach) v.
form cicatrize; scar up
zabłądzić (za-bwown-dżheech) v.
go astray; get lost; stray
zabłąkany (za-bwown-ka-ni) adj.
m. stray (bullet, man,steer,etc)
zabłocić (za-bwo-cheech) v. get
muddy; muddy (shoes etc)
zabobon (za-bo-bon) m. superstition;belief in omens,stars etc.
zaboleć (za-bo-lech) v. ache
zaborca (za-bor-tsa) m. invader
zabójca (za-booy-tsa) m. killer
zabójczy (za-booy-chi) adj. m.
murderous; seductive ;lethal
zabójstwo (za-booy-stvo) n. killing; murder; homicide
zabór (za-boor) m. annexed territory; annexation;rape(of Peru..)
zabraniać (za-bra-nach) v. forbid
zabrudzać (za-broo-dzach) v.dirty;
soil; make a mess (of something)
zabudować (za-boo-do-vach) v.
build over; build upon; close
zabudowania (za-boo-do-va-na) pl.
buildings (on farm,factory etc.)
zaburzenie (za-boo-zhe-ne) n.
disorder; rout; agitation
zabytek (za-bi-tek) m. relic;
monument(of art,nature etc.)
zachcianka (zakh-chan-ka) f. fad;
fancy; caprice; whim;megrim
zachęta (za-khan-ta) f. encouragement; stimulus;incentive;spur
zachłanność (za-khwan-noshch) f.
greed; rapacity ;cupidity
zachłysnąć się (za-khwis-nownch
śhan) v. choke;swallow a bad way
zachmurzyć (za-khmoo-zhich) v.
cloud; become gloomy;overcloud

zachmurzenie (za-khmoo-zhe-ne)
n. cloudiness; gloom;gloominess
zachodzić (za-kho-dżheech) v.
call on; occur; arise; become;
set; creep from behind;drop in
zachodni (za-khod-nee) adj. m.
western; westerly
zachorować (za-kho-ro-vach) v.
get sick; fall ill;be taken ill
zachowanie (za-kho-va-ne) n.
behavior; maintainance;manners
zachowawczy (za-kho-vav-chi)
adj. m. conservative
zachowywać (za-kho-vi-vach) v.
preserve; maintain;keep(calm)
zachowywać się (za-kho-vi-vach
śhan) v. behave; survive;go on
zachód (za-khoot) m. west;sunset;
pains; trouble; endeavor
zachód słońca (za-khoot swon-
tsa) m. sunset
zachrypnięty (za-khrip-nan-ti)
adj. m. hoarse;of a hoarse voice
zachwalać (za-khva-lach) v.
praise; crack up;boost;cry up
zachwiać (zakh-vyach) v. rock;
shake; unsettle (balance etc.)
zachwycać (za-khvi-tsach) v.
fascinate; charm ;delight;enchant
zachwyt (zakh-vit) m. fascination; rapture ;enchantment
zaciąg (za-chowng) m. recruitment; levy; draft ;conscription
zaciągać (za-chown-gach) v.
recruit; drag to; run in debt
zaciekać (za-che-kach) v. leak;
stain; run down; fill(up)
zaciekawić (za-che-ka-veech) v.
interest; puzzle; intrigue
zaciekawienie (za-che-ka-vye-ne)
n. interest; curiosity
zaciekły (za-chek-wi) adj. m.
stubborn; bitter; rabid;stiff
zaciemnić (za-chem-neech) v.
obscure; dim; darken ;black out
zacieniać (za-che-nach) v.
shade; darken ;throw shade
zacierać (za-che-rach) v. efface; erase; hush up ;cover up
zaciesniać (za-chesh-nach) v.
tighten up; narrow; limit
zacięty (za-chan-ti) adj. m.
obstinate; stubborn ;dogged

zacinac (za-chee-nach) v. notch;
cut; lash; hack; taper;set(teeth)

zaciskac (za-chees-kach) v.
tighten; clench; squeeze;clasp

zacisze (za-chee-she) n. retreat

zacny (zats-ni) adj. m. worthy;
good; upright;respectable

zacofany (za-tso-fa-ni) adj.m.
backward;old fashioned

zaczaic sie (za-cha-eech shan)
v. lie in ambush; lurk; hide

zaczarowac (za-cha-ro-vach) v.
enchant; bewitch; cast a spell

zaczac (za-chownch) v. start;
begin; fire away; go ahead

zaczepiac (za-chep-yach) v.
hook on; accost; touch upon

zaczepny (za-chep-ni) adj. m.
aggressive; offensive;provocative

zaczerpac (za-cher-pach) v.
scoop up; dip up; draw; lade

zaczerwienic (za-cher-vye-neech)
v. redden; blush; flush;paint red

zaczynac (za-chi-nach) v. start;
begin; cut (into a new loaf)

zacmienie (zach-mye-ne) n. e-
clipse ; obfuscation

zad (zad) m. posterior; rump

zadac (za-dach) v. give; put;
deal; associate; treat with

zadanie (za-da-ne) n. task; charge; assignment; problem;job;stint

zadatek (za-da-tek) m. earnest
money; down payment;installment

zadławic (za-dwa-veech) v. choke

zadłużyc sie (za-dwoo-zhich shan)v.
get in debt;debit; take mortgage

zadłużenie (za-dwoo-zhe-ne) n.
debts; indebtedness; liabilities

zadowalający (za-do-va-la-yown-
tsi) adj. m. satisfactory; fair

zadowolic (za-do-vo-leech) v.
satisfy; gratify; please;suffice

zadowolony (za-do-vo-lo-ni) adj.
m. satisfied; content;pleased

zadra (za-dra) f. sliver; splinter (in one's finger etc.)

zadrapac (za-dra-pach) v. scratch
open; make a scratch; scratch

zadrasnac (za-dras-nownch) v.
scratch ; wound (pride etc)

zadraznic (za-drazh-neech) v.
irritate; embitter; inflame

zadrgac (zadr-gach) v. twitch;
vibrate ; tremble; flicker

zadrwic (za-drveech) v. sneer

zaduch (za-dookh) m. bad air;
stuffy air; stink;fustiness;fug

zaduma (za-doo-ma) f. meditation; reverie;musing;wistfulness

zadusic(za-doo-sheech) v.throttle;
smother; choke ;strangle;suffocate

Zaduszki (za-doosh-kee) n.
All Souls Day

zadymka (za-dim-ka) f. snow-
storm; blizzard

zadyszany (za-di-sha-ni) adj.
m. breathless; panting

zadzierac (za-dzhe-rach) v.
tear open; turn up; quarrel

zadzierzysty (za-dzher-zhis-
ti) adj. m. defiant; perky

zadziwiac (za-dzheev-yach) v.
astonish; amaze; astound

zadzwonic (za-dzvo-neech) v.
ring; ring up ; ring for

zagadka (za-gad-ka) f. puzzle;
riddle ;crux; problem;quizz

zagadnienie (za-gad-ne-ne) n.
problem ; question; issue

zagajnik (za-gay-neek) m. grove
shubbery ; scrub ; coppice;copse

zagiac (za-gyownch) v. bend

zaginiony (za-gee-no-ni) adj.
m. lost ; missing (person)

zagladac (za-glown-dach) v.
peep; look up; look into

zagłada (za-gwa-da) f. extinc-
tion ; extermination;annihilation

zagłebic (za-gwan-beech) v.
plunge; sink; dip;immerse

zagłodzic (za-gwo-dzheech) v.
starve to death; starve out

zagłuszac (za-gwoo-shach) v.
silence; jam; drown out; stifle

zagmatwac (za-gmat-vach) v.
entangle; confuse; embroil

zagniewany (za-gne-va-ni) adj.
m. angry; cross; sore;in a huff

zagospodarowywac (za-gos-po-da-
ro-vi-vach) v. make property
productive ; manage (an estate)

zagotowac (za-go-to-vach) v.
boil; start boiling; flare up

zagrabic (za-gra-beech) v. rake
over; grab; seize;carve out

zagradzac (za-gra-dzach) v. bar;
fence; obstruct; intercept

zagranica (za-gra-nee-tsa) f.
foreign countries; ouside world

zagraniczny (za-gra-neech-ni)
adj. m. foreign; external(trde...)

zagrazac (za-gra-zhach) v.
threaten; impend; be imminent

zagroda (za-gro-da) f. farm
house with yard; enclosure

zagrodzic (za-gro-dzeech) v.
fence in; bar; enclose; obstruct

zagrozony (za-gro-zho-ni) adj.
m. threatened; endangered

zagrzebac (za-gzhe-bach) v.
bury (in the grave, in the past..)

zagrzewac (za-gzhe-vach) v. heat;
warm up; animate; inspire; spur

zahaczac (za-kha-chach) v. hook;
question; accost; find fault

zahamowac (za-kha-mo-vach) v.
restrain; put brakes on; stop

zaimek (za-ee-mek) m. pronoun

zainteresowanie (za-een-te-re-
so-va-ne) n. interest; concern

zaiste (za-ees-te) adv. truly;
indeed; very true; verily; yea

zajadac (za-ya-dach) v. enjoy
eating ; gorge; eat heartily

zajadly (za-yad-wi) adj. m.
fierce; rabid; bitter driveway

zajazd (za-yazt) m. motel; inn;

zajac (za-yownts) m. hare

zajac (za-yownch) v. occupy

zajechac (za-ye-khach) v. drive
up; block; stump; pull in; stink

zajecie (za-yan-che) v. occupation; work; trade; interest

zajmowac (zay-mo-vach) v. occupy

zajmujacy (zay-moo-yown-tsi) adj.
m. interesting; absorbing

zajscie (zaysh-che) n. incident

zakalec (za-ka-lets) m. slack
baked bread (or cake)

zakatarzony (za-ka-ta-zho-ni)
adj. m. having a cold

zakatowac (za-ka-to-vach) v.
flog to death; torture to death

zakaz (za-kas) m. prohibition

zakazic (za-ka-zheech) v. infect

zakazywac (za-ka-zi-vach) v.
forbid; ban; suppress; prohibit;
forbid to do; suppress(activity..)

zakazny (za-kazh-ni) adj. m.
infectious ; contagious

zakaska (za-kowns-ka) f. snack

zaklecie (za-klan-che) n. spell;
curse; incantation; charm; entreaty

zaklad pogrzebowy (za-kwat po-
gzhe-bo-vi) m. funeral parlor

zaklad (za-kwat) m. plant; shop;
institute; bet; wager; fold

zakladac (za-kwa-dach) v.
found; initiate; put on; lay

zakladka (za-kwad-ka) f. fold;
book- mark; tuck; pleat; splice

zakladnik (za-kwad-neek) m.
hostage (for ransom etc.)

zaklamanie (za-kwa-ma-ne) n.
hypocrisy ; mendacity; distortion

zaklopotanie (za-kwo-po-ta-ne)
n. embarrassment; confusion

zaklocac (za-kwoo-tsach) v.
disturb; unsettle; ruffle

zakluwac (za-kwoo-vach) v. stab
to death ; prick ; stick (a pig)

zakochac sie (za-ko-khach shan)
v. fall in love ; become infatuated

zakochany (za-ko-kha-ni) adj. m.
in love ; infatuated; enamorated

zakomunikowac (za-ko-moo-nee-ko-
vach) v. communicate; let
know; convey a message; notify

zakon (za-kon) m. monastic
order ; convent; sisterhood

zakonnica (za-kon-nee-tsa) f.
nun ; religious (woman)

zakonnik (za-kon-neek) m. monk

zakonczenie (za-kon-che-ne) n.
end; ending; termination; tip

zakopac (za-ko-pach) v. bury

zakorkowac (za-kor-ko-vach) v.
plug up; cork up; jam(the traffic)

zakorzenic sie (za-ko-zhe-neech
shan) v. get roots in; take roots

zakorzeniony (za-ko-zhe-no-ni)
adj. m. rooted; deep rooted

zakradac sie (za-kra-dach shan)
v. creep; steal; sneak(into)

zakrapiac (za-krap-yach) v.
put drops in; sprinkle; have
a drink; instil(in one's eyes)

zakres (za-kres) m. range; field;
scope; domain; sphere; realm

zakreslic (za-kresh-leech) v.
outline; mark off; encircle

zakręcić (za-kran-cheech) v.
turn; twist; turn off; curl

zakręt (za-krant) m. curve;bend
turn   turnbuckle ; cap; nut;

zakretka (za-krant-ka) f. latch;

zakrwawić (za-krva-veech) v.
stain with blood;draw blood

zakryć (za-krich) v. cover; hide

zakrzatnąć się (za-kzhównt-
nównch shan) v.get busy ;bustle

zakrztusić (za-kzhtoo-sheech)v.
choke (on food,fish bone etc.)

zakrzywić (za-kzhi-veech) v.
bend; bend down; bend back

zaksięgować (za-kzhán-go-vach)
v. post; enter in the books

zakup (za-koop) m. purchase

zakurzony (za-koo-zho-ni) adj.
m. dusty ;covered with dust

zakuty (za-koo-ti) adj. m.
shackled; chained; dull (witted)

zakwitnąć (za-kveet-nównch) v.
blossom out; go moldy

zalażek (za-lown-zhek) m. germ;
ovule;seed; origin;embryo

zalecać (za-letsach) v. recommend; advise; enjoin; court; woo

zaledwie (za-led-vye) adv. barely;
scarcely; merely; but; only just

zalegać (za-le-gach) v. be behind (in paying);lie useless;fill

zaległy (za-leg-wi) adj. m. unpaid; overdue;unaccomplished

zalepić (za-le-peech) v. glue (up)
over; gum up; paste over;seal up

zalesienie (za-le-she-ne) n.
forestation; afforestation

zaleta (za-le-ta) f. virtue;
advantage; quality; good point

zalew (za-lev) m. flood; bay;
invasion; deluge;lagoon

zalewać (za-le-vach) v. pour
over; flood;submerge;swarm;spill

zależeć (za-le-zhech) v. depend

zależny (za-lezh-ni) adj.m.
dependent; contingent;subordinate

zaliczać (za-lee-chach) v. include; count in; credit;rate;accept

zaliczka (za-leech-ka) f. earnest
money; down payment;installment

zalotnica (za-lot-nee-tsa) f.
flirt; coquette; kitten(slang)

zalotnik (za-lot-neek) m. suit-
or ; wooer; wheedler

zaloty (za-lo-ti) adj. m.
courtship;wooing;love making

zaludniać (za-lood-nach) v.
populate ;bring in population

zaludnienie (za-lood-ne-ne) n.
population;population density

załadować (za-wa-do-vach) v.
load up; embark;ship(goods)

załagodzić (za-wa-go-dźheech)
v. mitigate; alleviate; soothe

załamać (za-wa-mach) v. break
down; collapse; crash; slump

załamanie (za-wa-ma-ne) n.
break down; (light) refraction

załatwiać (za-wat-vyach) v.
settle; transact; deal;dispose

załączać (za-wown-chach) v.
enclose ; connect;annex;plug in

załącznik (za-wównch-neek) m.
enclosure; attachment; annex

załoga (za-wo-ga) f. crew;
garrison; staff; personnel

założenie (za-wo-zhe-ne) n.
layout; foundation; assumption

założyciel (za-wo-zhi-chel) m.
founder; initiator;promotor

zamach (za-makh) m. attempt;
swing; sweep; coupd'état;spar

zamaczać (za-ma-chach) v. steep;
dip; wet; soak; drench

zamarzły (za-mar-zwi) adj.m.
frozen; frezen over;frozen stiff

zamarznąć (za-mar-znównch) v.
freeze up;freeze over;congeal

zamaskować (za-mas-ko-vach) v.
mask; conceal; hide; disguise

zamaszysty (za-ma-shis-ti) adj.
m. brisk; vigorous;dashing;heavy

zamawiać (za-ma-vyach) v. reserve; order ;book; engage(workers)

zamazać (za-ma-zach) v. smear
over; soil up; daub;blur(a picture)

zamącić (za-mown-cheech) v.ruffle;
disturb; make turbid; stir a liquid

zamążpójście (za-mównzh-pooy-
shche) n. marriage

zamek (za-mek) m. lock; castle

zamek błyskawiczny (za-mek
bwis-ka-veech-ni) m. zipper

zamęt (za-mánt) m. confusion;welter

zamężna (za-mánzh-na) adj. f.
married(woman in married state)

zamiana (za-myá-na) f. exchange

zamianować (za-mya-no-vach) v.
nominate ; appoint;design

zamiar (za-myar) m. purpose ;

zamiast (za-myast) prep. instead of;in place;in lieu

zamiatać (za-mya-tach) v. sweep

zamieć (za-myech) f. snowstorm;
blizzard;snow in a windstorm

zamiejscowy (za-myeys-tso-vi)
adj. m. out of town;long distance

zamienić (za-mye-ñeech)v. change;
convert; replace;swap;turn into

zamienny (za-myen-ni) adj. m.
exchangeable;interchangeable

zamierać (za-mye-rach) v. die
out; fade out ; wither;die away

zamierzać (za-mye-zhach) v. intend; mean;propose;plan;think

zamierzenie (za-mye-zhe-ñe) n.
aim; purpose ; plan; project

zamieszać (za-mye-shach) v. stir
up; blend; mix up ; involve

zamieszanie (za-mye-shá-ñe) n.
confusion ; disarray;turmoil;stir

zamieszkać (za-myesh-kach) v.
take up residence ;put up;live

zamieszkiwać (za-myesh-kee-vach)
v. inhabit ; reside;occupy;live

zamilknąć (za-meel-known'ch) v.
became silent ; be hushed

zamiłowanie (za-mee-wo-vá-ñe) n.
predilection ; fondness ;liking

zamknąć (zám-known'ch) v. close;
shut; lock ;wind up; fence in

zamoczyć (za-mo-chich) v. wet;
soak; steep; drench ;submerge

zamorski (za-mor-skee) adj. m.
overseas; from overseas

zamożny (za-mozh-ni) adj. m.rich;
wealthy; affluent ;well to do

zamówić (za-moo-veech) v. order;
reserve ; commission ;book;engage

zamówienie (za-moo-vye-ñe) n.
order ; commission ;custom order

zamrażać (za-mra-zhach) v. freeze

zamroczyć (za-mró-chich) v. dim;
gloom; confuse; darken ;bewilder

zamsz (zamsh) m. chamois ; suede

zamulić (za-moo-leech) v. fill
with slime ; silt up (a harbor)

zamurować (za-moo-ro-vach) v.
brick over ; brick up ;wall up

zamydlić (za-mid-leech) v.
soap over ;pull wool over eyes

zamykać (za-mi-kach) v. shut;
conclude ; close (the view etc.)

zamysł (za-misw) m. design

zamyślać się (za-mish-lach sháñ)
v. contemplate; muse; ponder

zamyślenie (za-mi-shle-ñe) n.
reverie; pondering; meditation

zanadto (za-nad-to) adv. too
much ; excess ;beyond measure

zaniechać (za-ñe-khach) v.
give up ; wave; desist from

zanieczyścić (za-ñe-chish-cheech)
v. soil ; dirty; litter;grime

zaniedbanie (za-ñed-bá-ñe) n.
neglect; negligence ;sloppiness

zaniemóc (za-ñe-moots) v. become ill ; fall ill ;get sick

zaniemówić (za-ñe-moo-veech)
v. become speechless (dumb)

zaniepokoić (za-ñe-po-ko-eech)
v. alarm; up set; disturb

zaniepokojenie (za-ñe-po-ko-ye-ñe) n. anxiety ; alarm; concern

zanieść (za-ñeshch) v. carry

zanik (za-ñeek) m. disappearance

zanikać (za-ñee-kach) v. disappear ;vanish; decay; wither

zanim (za-ñeem) conj. before ;

zanocować (za-no-tso-vach) v.
stay over night ; put up at

zanotować (za-no-to-vach) v.
note; write down ;take down

zanurzyć (za-noo-zhich) v. dip

zaocznie (za-och-ñe) adv. in
absence;(judgement)by default

zaognić (za-og-ñeech) v. inflame ; irritate ;excite;kindle

zaokrąglić (za-o-krowng-leech)
v. round off ; make even

zaopatrzenie (za-o-pa-tzhe-ñe)
n. supplies;equipment;provision

zaopatrzyć (za-o-pa-tzhich) v.
provide ; equip; supply ;fit out;
furnish;stock;

zaorać (za-o-rach) v. plough
over(a field etc.);plough up

zaostrzyć(za-os-tzhich) v. sharpen; whet; tighten (restrictions);
stimulate(the appetite);intensify

zaoszczędzić (za-osh-chan-
dźheech) v. save ; spare(trouble)
zapach (za-pakh) m. smell;aroma
zapadać (za-pa-dać) v. fall in;
sink ; set in; drop; settle
zapakować (za-pa-kó-vać) v.
pack up ; stow away; pack off
zapalczywy (za-pal-chi-vi) adj.
m. hotheaded; impetuous
zapalenie (za-pa-lé-ńe) n. ignition ; inflammation(of the skin..)
zapaleniec (za-pa-le-ńets) m.
fanatic ; enthusiastic;hot head
zapalić (za-pa-leech) v. switch
on light; set fire ; animate
zapalniczka (za-pal-ńeech-ka)
f. (cigarette) lighter
zapalnik (za-pál-ńeek) m. fuse
zapalny (za-pál-ni) adj. m.
inflammable ; ardent;impetuous
zapał (za-paw) m. enthusiasm
zapałka (za-páw-ka) f. match
zapamiętać (za-pa-myán-tać) v.
remember ; memorize;keep in mind
zaparcie (za-pár-che) n. constipation; denial
zaparzać (za-pá-zhać) v. draw
(tea) ;brew; gall ;make(tea) ;heat
zapas (za-pas) m. stock; store;
reserve ; supply ;fund;refill
zapasowy (za-pa-só-vi) adj. m.
spare ; emergency(door,part,etc)
zapaść (za-pashch) v. collapse
zapaśnik (za-pásh-ńeek) m.
wrestler
zapatrywać się (za-pa-tri-vać
shán) v. have opinion; consider; stare ; take example
zapatrywanie (za-pa-tri-va-ńe)
n. opinion; view ;slant
zapełnić (za-péw-ńeech) v. fill
up ; stop a gap ;fill(a space etc.)
zaperzyć się (za-pé-zhich shán)
v. flare up ;be testy ;get mad
zapewne (za-pev-ne) adv. certainly ; surely; doubtless ;I daresay
zapewnić (za-pév-ńeech) v. assure
zapewnienie (za-pev-ńe-ńe) n. assurance ; protestation ;assertion
zapieczętować (za-pye-chan-to-
vać) v. seal up;seal with wax
zapierać się (za-pye-rać shán)
deny; disavow ;resist;repudiate

zapinać (za-pee-nać) v. button up; fasten;buckle up
zapis (za-pees) m. registration;
bequest; record; notation
zapisać (za-pee-sać) v. note
down; prescribe; enroll; bequeath; record; write down
zapisek (za-pee-sek) m. note
zaplątać (za-plown-tać) v.
entangle ;snarl;involve
zaplecze (za-plé-che) n. hinterland; base(of supplies etc.)
zapłacić (za-pwa-cheech) v. pay
zapłakany (za-pwa-ka-ni) adj.
m. in tears; tearful;tear stained
zapłata (za-pwa-ta) f. payment
zapłodnić (za-pwód-ńeech) v.
fertilize ; inseminate;fecundate
zapłon (za-pwon) m. ignition
zapobiegać (za-po-bye-gać) v.
prevent;avert; ward off;stave off
zapobiegliwy (za-po-bye-glee-
vi) adj. m. anticipating;thrifty
industrious;thrifty;provident
zapodziać (za-pó-dźhach) v.
misplace;mislay; get lost
zapominać (za-po-mee-nać) v.
forget;neglect; unlearn
zapomnienie (za-pom-ńe-ńe) n.
oblivion; forgetfulness
za pomocą (za-po-mó-tsówn) adv.
by means; with help(of a tool...)
zapomoga (za-po-mó-ga) f. hand
out; relief; benefit; grant
zapora (za-pó-ra) f. dam; obstacle; barrier;check;barrage
zapotrzebowanie (za-po-tzhe-bo-
vá-ńe)n.(demand) requisition
zapowiadać (za-po-vyá-dać) v.
announce; forecast; pretend
zapoznać (za-poz-nać) v. acquaint;introduce;instruct
zapożyczać (za-po-zhi-chać) v.
borrow; adopt from ;take from
zapracować (za-pra-tsó-vać) v.
earn; get by hard work
zapracowany (za-pra-tso-vá-ni)
adj. m. earned; overworked
zapraszać (za-pra-shać) v.
invite(to dinner etc.);offer
zaprawa (za-pra-va) f. mortar;v.
seasoning; training ;work out

zaprawdę (za-praw-dáń) adv. in
  deed ; to tell you the truth...
zaprawic (za-pra-veech) v. season ;train; learn;dress;spice
zaproszenie (za-pro-she-ńe) n.
  invitation (to dinner etc.)
zaprowadzic (za-pro-va-dżheech)
  v. lead in; establish ;initiate
zaprzag (za-zhówng) m. team
zaprzeczac (za-pzhe-chach) v.
  deny ; contest ; dispute
zaprzeczenie (za-pzhe-che-ńe) n.
  denial ; negation;contradiction
zaprzepascic (za-pzhe-paśh-
  ćheech) v. loose; waste ; miss
zaprzestac (za-pzhés-tach) v.
  discontinue; stop ; cease;quit
zaprzeg (za-pzhäng) m. team; cart;
  harness ; yoke; carriage;turn out
zaprzyjaznic się (za-pzhi-yáźh-
  ńeech śhań) v. make friends
zaprzysiąc (za-pzhi-śhownts) v.
  swear by oath ;vow; pledge
zaprzysiężony (za-pzhi-śhäń-zho-
  ni) adj. m. sworn in ;pledged
zapusty (za-poós-ti) pl.carni-
  val; Shrovetide
zapuszczac (za-poósh-chach) v.
  let in (dye); grow (hair);
  neglect; let down;sink into
zapychac (za-pi-khach) v. stuff;
  cram;fill;block ;choke;crowd
zapytanie (za-pi-ta-ńe) n. question; inquiry ; query; asking
zapytywac (za-pi-ti-vach) v. ask
zarabiac (za-ráb-yach) v. earn
zaradczy (za-rád-chi) adj. m.
  preventive ; remedial(measure)
zaradny (za-rád-ni) adj. m. resourceful (man, boy etc.)
zaranie (za-ra-ńe) n. downing
zarastac (za-rás-tach) v. overgrow; cicatrize (a wound)
zaraz (za-ras) adv. at once;
  directly;right away; soon
zaraza (za-rá-za) f. infection;
  plague ; epidemic ;pestilence
zarazek (za-ra-zek) m. virus;
  germ ; microbe ;(disease)bacteria
zarazem (za-rá-zem) adv. at the
  same time ; as well; also
zarazic (za-ra-żheech) v. infect

zarażenie (za-ra-żhe-ńe) n.
  infection (with a disease etc.)
zardzewiec (zar-dze-vyech) v.
  rust ; get rusty;corrode
zaręczyny (za-ráń-chi-ni) n.
  betrothal; engagement;engagement-
zarobek (za-ro-bek) m. gain;bread;
  earnings; wages;livelihood;living
zarobkowac (za-rob-ko-vach) v.
  earn working ; earn a living
zarodek (za-ro-dek) m. embryo
zarosły (za-rós-wi) adj. m.
  overgrown (with vegetation etc.)
zarost (za-rost) m. beard; hair
zarosla (za-rósh-la) n. thicket
zarozumiały (za-ro-zoo-mya-wi)
  adj. m. conceited ; uppish
zarówno (za-roóv-no) adv. equally; as well ; alike ; both
zarumienic się (za-roo-mye-ńeech
  śhań) v. blush ;flush; brown
zaryglowac (za-rig-lo-vach) v.
  bolt a door; bar an entrance
zarys (za-ris) m. sketch; outline ; broad lines;design;draft
zarzad (za-zhównd) m. management ; administration; board
zarządca (za-zhównd-tsa) m.
  administrator; manager
zarządzenie (za-zhówn-dze-ńe)
  n. administrative order
zarzucac (za-zhoo-tsach) v. fill;
  give up; reproach ; fling ;cast
zarzut (za-zhoot) m. reproach;
  objection ; accusation; blame
zasada (za-sá-da) f. principle;
  alkali; base ; law ;rule;tenet
zasadniczy (za-sad-ńee-chi) adj.
  m. fundamental;essential; basic
zasadzka (za-sádz-ka) f. ambush
zasądzic (za-sówn-dżheech) v.
  sentence ; adjudge to(somebody)
zasępiony (za-sań-pyo-ni) adj.
  m. gloomy; despondent;dejected
zasiadac (za-śha-dach) v. take
  a seat ; sit down; settle down
zasięg (za-śhańk) m. reach ;scope
zasięgac rady (za-śhań-gach ra-
  di) v. consult; seek advice
zasiłek (za-śhee-wek) m. hand-
  out; grant ;relief;subvention
zaskarżyc (za-skár-zhich) v. sue

zasklepić się (za-skle-peech śhań) v. scab; shut oneself up (in); seal up; vault;wall up

zaskoczyć (za-sko-chich) v. surprise; attack unawares;click;lock

zaskórny (za-skoor-ni) adj. m. subcutaneous;underground(water)

zasłabnąć (za-swab-nownch) v. faint; get sick;grow faint;swoon

zasłać (za-swach) v. cover (bed)

zasłona (za-swo-na) f. blind; veil; screen; curtain;shield

zasłonić (za-swo-neech) v. curtain; shade ; shield;cover up

zasługa (za-swoo-ga) f. merit

zasługiwać (za-swoo-gee-vach) v. deserve ; be worthy;merit

zasłużony (za-swoo-zho-ni) adj. m. man of merit ;just; fair

zasmucić (za-smoo-cheech) v. sadden ; pain; distress;grieve

zasmucony(za-smoo-tso-ni) adj. m. sad; grieved;distressed

zasnąć (za-snownch) v. fall asleep; sleep;drop off to sleep

zasobnik(za-sob-neek) m. container; tank;storage tank

zasób (za-soop) m. store; resource ; stock; supply

zaspa (zas-pa) f. snowdrift; dune; drifted sand;drifted snow

zaspać (zas-pach) v. oversleep

zaspokoić (za-spo-ko-eech) v. satisfy; quench; appease;provide

zastanowić się (za-sta-no-veech śhań) v. reflect; puzzle;ponder

zastaw (za-stav) m. pawn; deposit; security;pledge;forfeit;lien

zastawić (za-sta-veech) v. 1. bar; 2. pledge; 3. set a table ; cram a room;lay(snares)

zastąpić (za-stown-peech) v. replace; bar passage;do duty for

zastępca (za-stanp-tsa) adj.m. proxy; substitute; deputy

zastępczo (za-stanp-cho) adv. replacing; temporary; in lieu

zastępstwo (za-stanp-stvo) n. replacement;proxy; agency

zastosować (za-sto-so-vach) v. adopt; apply; employ;make use

zastosować się (za-sto-so-vach śhań) v. comply ; toe the line

zastosowanie (za-sto-so-va-ńe) n. application; use compliance

zastój (za-stooy) m. stagnation

zastraszyć (za-stra-shich) v. intimidate ;cow;bully;bulldoze

zastrzał (za-stzhaw) m. (knee) brace; strut; boom; cramp

zastrzec (za-stzhets) v. reserve ; stipulate;condition

zastrzeżenie (za-stzhe-zhe-ńe) n. reservation; proviso

zastrzyk (za-stzhik) m. injection ; shot(in the arm)

zastygnąć (za-stig-nownch) v. congeal ; set; harden;petrify

zasuszyć (za-soo-shich) v. dry up ; wither ; shrivel(the skin)

zasuwa (za-soo-va) f. bar; (door) bolt;valve ;shutter

zasuwka (za-soov-ka) f. small bolt ;damper; valve

zasypać (za-si-pach) v. bury; cover; add (to soup);fill up

zasypiać (za-sip-yach) v. cat nap; doze off; fall asleep

zaszczepiać (za-shche-pyach) v. inoculate; graft;instill

zaszczycać (za-shchi-tsach) v. honor; dignify; favor; grace

zaszczyt (zash-chit) m. honor; distinction; privilege;dignity

zaszkodzić (za-shko-dźheech) v. harm; hurt; damage; injure

zasznurować (za-shnoo-ro-vach) v. tie up; lace(shoes);tighten

zaszyć (za-shich) v. sew up

zaszyć się (za-shich śhań) v. hide; burrow ; conceal oneself

zaś (zaśh) conj. but; whereas; and ; while; specially

zaślepić (za-shle-peech) v. blind; infatuate;blind to facts

zaślepiony (za-shle-pyo-ni) adj. m. infatuated; fanatic ;blind

zaślubić (za-shloo-beech)v. marry ; get married

zaślubiny (za-shloo-bee-ni) pl. wedding ; marriage ;nuptials

zaśmiecić (za-shmye-cheech) v. litter ; clutter up (a room etc.)

zaśniedziały (za-śhńe-dźha-wi) adj. m. rusty; stagnant

zasrubować (za-shroo-bo-vach)
v. screw tight ; screw on (a lid)
zaswiadczenie (za-shvyad-che-
ńe) n. certificate ;affidavit
zaswiadczyć (za-shvyad-chich)v.
certify; attest; witness
zaswiecić (za-zhvye-cheech) v.
put light on ; light up ;turn on
zataczać (za-ta-chach) v. roll in;
describe(a circle); stagger;wheel
zataić (za-ta-eech) v. conceal;
suppress; keep secret ;hold back
zatamować (za-ta-mo-vach) v.
dam up; stop ; block ;impede
zatańczyć (za-tań-chich) v.
dance; perform a dance
zatapiac (sa-tap-yach) v.flood;
sink ; penetrate ;inundate;scuttle
zatarasować (za-ta-ra-so-vach)
v. obstruct; block up; bolt
zatarg (za-tark) m. conflict
zatem (za-tem) adv. then; consequently; therefore ; and so
zatemperować (za-tem-pe-ro-vach)
v. sharpen a pencil etc.
zatkać (za-tkach) v. stop up
zatlic się (za-tleech shań) v.
catch fire ; smoulder
zatłoczony (za-two-cho-ni) adj.
m. crowded ; crammed; cluttered
zatoka (za-to-ka) f. bay; gulf
zatonać (za-to-nownch) v. sink
zator (za-tor) m. (traffic) jam
zatracić (za-tra-cheech) v. lose;
waste ; lose all sense of
zatroskać(za-tros-kach) v. grieve
zatrucie (za-troo-che) n. poisoning ; intoxication; toxaemia
zatruć (za-trooch) v. poison
zatrudniać (za-trood-ńach) v.
employ ; engage ;take on(workers)
zatrzask (za-tzhask) m. (door)
latch; (snap) fastener lock
zatrzymać (za-tzhi-mach) v. stop;
retain; detain ;arrest; hold
zatwardzenie (za-tvar-dze-ńe) n.
constipation; costiveness
zatwierdzać (za-tvyer-dzach) v.
approve ;confirm; ratify;affirm
zatwierdzenie (za-tvyer-dze-ńe)
n. ratification; approval;assent
zatwierdzić (za-tvyer-dżheech) v.
ratify; approve ;confirm;validate

zatyczka (za-tich-ka) f. plug
zatykać (za-ti-kach) v. stop
up ; plug up; insert a plug
zaufać (za-oo-fach) v. confide
zaufanie (za-oo-fá-ńe) n. confidence ; trust ;faith; reliance
zaufany (za-oo-fá-ni) adj. m.
reliable; confidential;trusted
zaułek (za-oo-wek) m. alley;
back street; lane ;recess; nook
zauważyć (za-oo-vá-zhich) v.
notice; catch sight;remark
zawada (za-vá-da) f. obstruction; nuisance; hindrance
zawadiaka (za-vad-yá-ka) m.
bully; blusterer;swashbuckler
zawadzać (za-vá-dzach) v. hinder; scrape; touch ;be a drag
zawalać (za-vá-lach) v. soil
zawalić (za-vá-leech) v. collapse; obstruct; bury;bungle
zawartość (za-vár-toshch) f.
contents ; subject (of a book)
zawczasu (za-vchá-soo) adv.
in good time ; in advance
zawczoraj (za-vcho-ray) adv.
the day before yesterday
zawdzięczać (za-vdzhań-chach)
v. owe (gratitude) ; be indebted
zawezwać (za-vez-vach) v. call;
summon ; call in (a doctor etc)
zawiadomić (za-vya-do-meech)
v. inform; give notice ;let know
zawiadomienie (za-vya-do-mye-
ńe) n. notification ;information
zawiadowca stacji (za-vya-dóv-
tsa státs-yee) m. stationmaster ;superintendent
zawiasa (za-vyá-sa) f. hinge
zawiązać (za-vyown-zach) v.
tie up ; bind; set up (a club)
zawieja (za-vyé-ya) f. blizzard
za wiele (za vye-le) adv. too
much ; too many(expenses etc.)
za widna (za veed-na) adv. in
day light; in light;before dark
zawierać (za-vyé-rach) v. contain; conclude; shut;strike up
zawierucha (za-vye-roo-kha) f.
wind storm ; gale; (war)clouds
zawieszenie broni (za-vye-shé-
ńe bro-ńee) n. armistice ;truce;
cessation of hostilities

zawietrzna (za-vyetzh-na) f.
lee side(sheltered from the wind)

zawijać (za-vee-yach) v. wrap
up; tuck in; put in at a port

zawikłać (za-veek-wach) v. complicate; entangle;embroil;tangle

zawiły (za-vee-wi) adj. m. intricate; baffling;knotty(problem)

zawinąć (za-vee-nównch) v. wrap

zawinić (za-vee-ńeech) v. be
guilty;commit an offense

zawisły (za-vees-wi) adj. m.
dependent(on somebody etc.)

zawistny (za-veest-ni) adj. m.
envious;jealous (of something...)

zawiść (za-veeshch) f. envy

zawitać (za-vee-tach) v. call
on; come and see   wrap

zawlec (za-vlets) v. drag;tug;

zawodnik (za-vod-neek) m. competitor (in sport);contestant

zawodowiec (za-vo-do-vyets) m.
professional; specialist

zawody (za-vo-di) pl. (sport)
competition;match;race;game;event

zawodzić (za-vo-dźheech) v.
1. lead; 2. disillusion;lament

zawołać (za-vo-wach) v. call out;
exclaim; shout; cry out; summon

zawołany (za-vo-wa-ni) adj. m.
excellent; perfect;born(poet etc.)

zawozić (za-vo-źheech) v. convey;
take to; cart; deliver;give rides

zawód (za-vood) m. 1. profession;
2. disappointment; deception

zawór (za-voor) m. valve; vent

zawrót głowy (za-vroot gwo-vi) m.
dizziness; vertigo;giddiness

zawstydzić (za-vsti-dźheech) v.
shame; embarrass ;overwhelm

zawsze (zav-she) adv. always;
evermore;(for)ever;at all times

zawszyc (zav-shich) v. louse up

zawziąć się (zav-źhównch śhan) v.
be obstinate; persist ; set on

zawziętość (zav-źhán-toshch) f.
persistence; obstinacy; keenness

zazdrosny (zaz-dros-ni) adj. m.
jealous; envious;resentful

zazdrość (záz-droshch) f. envy

zaziębić się (za-źhán-beech śhan)
v. catch a cold

zaznaczyć (za-zna-chich) v.
mark ; make a note; state;

zaznać (zaz-nach) v. experience;
taste ; enjoy; undergo

zaznajomić (za-zna-yo-meech)
v. acquaint ; introduce to

zazwyczaj (za-zvi-chay) adv.
usually ; generally; ordinarily

zażalenie (za-zha-lé-ńe) n.
complaint; grievance

zażarty (za-zhár-ti) adj. m.
fierce; bitter ;vehement

zażądać (za-zhówn-dach) v.
demand ; require; order

zażenować (za-zhe-nó-vach) v.
shame ;embarrass;confuse;abash

zażyły (za-zhi-wi) adj. m. familiar; intimate ;close; chummy

zażywać pigułki (za-zhi-vach
pee-gów-kee) v. take pills

ząb (zównp) m. tooth; fang;
prong; cog;notch;indentation

ząb mleczny (zównp mlech-ni)
m. milk tooth (of a child etc.)

ząb trzonowy (zównp tzho-nó-vi)
adj. m. molar

ząbkować (zównb-ko-vach) v.
teethe; jag;cut one's teeth

zbaczać (zba-chach) v. deviate

zbankrutowany (zban-kroo-to-vá-
ni) adj. m. bankrupt; insolvent

zbawca (zbáv-tsa) m. savior

zbawiciel (zba-vee-ćhel) m.
savior; redeemer; Saviour

zbawicielka (zba-vee-ćhel-ka)
f. savior; redeemer

zbawić (zbá-veech) v. save;
redeem ; rescue;take(time)

zbawienie (zba-vyé-ńe) n. salvation;deliverance;rescue;redemption

zbesztać (zbésh-tach) v. scold

zbezcześcić (zbez-chéśh-ćheech)
v. desecrate; defile;profane

zbędny (zbánd-ni) m. superfluous ; redundant; needless;useless

zbieg(zbyek) m. fugitive ;runaway

zbieg okoliczności (zbyek o-ko-
leech-nóśh-chee) m. coincidence ;occurrence at the same time

zbiegać (zbye-gach) v. run down

zbiegowisko (zbye-go-vees-ko)
n. concourse; throng; crowd

zbieracz (zbye-rach) m. collector; gatherer ; picker

zbierać (zbye-rach) v. gather;
pick; summon; clear; take in

zbieżny (zbyezh-ni) adj. m.
convergent; tapering;concurrent

zbijać (zbee-yach) v. knock
together; refute;beat down

zbiornik (zbyor-ñeek) m. tank;
reservoir; container;receptacle

zbiór (zbyoor) m. harvest; collection; set; crop;class;series

zbiórka (zbyoor-ka) f. rally;
assembly ;meeting;gathering

zbir (zbeer) m. thug; ruffian

zbity (zbee-ti) adj. m.close;
1 beaten up; 2. compact;dense

zblednąc (zbléd-nownch) v.pale;
grow pale; fade;turn pale

z bliska (zblees-ka) adv. from
near ; close up ;from near

zbliżać (zblee-zhach) v. nearby

zbliżyć sie (zblee-zhich shañ)
v. become close; approach;be near

zbliżenie (zblee-zhe-ñe) n. rap-
prochement; close-up

zbliżony (zblee-zho-ni) adj. m.
approximate; nearing;congenial

zbłądzic (zbwown-dżheech) v.
go astray; make mistake; lose
trail ;err; wander off;err;blunder

zbocze (zbo-che) n. (hill) slope

zboczenie (zbo-che-ñe) n. de-
viation; aberration;drift;sag

zbolaly (zbo-lá-wi) adj. m. aching ; sore; woeful; wretched

zboże (zbo-zhe) n. corn; grain

zbój (zbooy) m. bandit; robber

zbór ewangielicki (zboor e-van-
ge-leets-kee)m. Protestant
Church; Evangelical Church

zbratać sie (zbrá-tach shañ) v.
fraternize; chum up (with)

zbroczony krwią (zbro-cho-ni
krvyown) adj. m. blood-stained

zbrodnia (zbród-ña) f. crime

zbrodniarz (zbród-ñash) m. criminal; felon; malefactor

zbroic (zbro-eech) v. arm

zbroja (zbro-ya) f. armor

zbrojony beton (zbro-yo-ni bé-
ton) m. reinforced concrete

zbrojownia (zbro-yov-ña) f.
arsenal; armory ; gunroom

zbryzgac (zbriz-gach) v. spatter ; bespatter; splash

zbrzydnąc (zbzhid-nownch) v.
grow ugly; lose good looks

zbudować (zboo-do-vach) v. build

zbudzic sie (zboo-dżheech shañ)
v. wake up ; awake; be roused

zbujac (zboo-yach) v. fool;
hoax ; pull one's leg

zburzyć (zboo-zhich) v. demolish

zbutwiec (zboo-tvyech) v. mold-
er. ; rot;decompose;decay;spoil

zbydlęcic (zbi-dlan-cheech) v.
imbrute;turn into a brute

zbyt (zbit) adv. too, (much)

zbyt wiele (zbit vye-le) adv.
too much ; excessively;over-

zbyt (zbit) m. sale; market

zbyteczny (zbi-tech-ni) adj. m.
superfluous ;needless; redundant

zbytek (zbi-tek) m. frills;
luxury ;pl ;pranks;follies

zbytni (zbit-ñee) adj. m. excessive; undue;more than needed

zbytnik (zbit-ñeek) m. rogue

zbywac (zbi-vach) v. dispose;
dismiss; put off;sell;lack;want

z czasem (z chá-sem) adv.
with time ;eventually; later

z dala (z dá-la) adv. from far

z daleka (z da-le-ka) adv. from
far; from afar; away from

zdalnie (zdál-ñe) adv. remote;
from afar; by remote control

zdanie (zda-ñe) n. opinion;
judgment; sentence; proposition

zdanie sprawy (zda-ñe spra-vi)
n. report; account;giving account

zdarzac sie (zda-zhach shañ) v.
happen; take place;occur

zdarzenie (zda-zhe-ñe) n. happening; event; incident

zdatnosc (zdát-noshch) f. fitness; capability;suitability

zdatny (zdát-ni) adj. m. able;
fit; apt;suitable (for the purpose)

zdawac (zda-vach) v. entrust;
submit;turn over;give up;pass(tests)

zdawac sie (zda-vach shañ)
1. seem; 2. surrender; 3.rely

z dawien dawna (zda-vyen dáv-na) adv. from way back

z dawna (zdáv-na) adv. since a long time; from way back

zdążyć (zhówn-zhich) v. come on time; keep pace; tend

zdechlak (zdékh-lak) m. weakling

zdechły (zdékh-wi) adj. m. peaky; dead (animal); weakly; sickly

zdecydować się (zde-tsi-dó-vach śhań) v. decide ; determine

zdejmować (zdey-mó-vach) v. take off ; strip(clothes); snap(photo)

zdenerwowany (zde-ner-vo-va-ni) adj. m. nervous ; excited

zderzak (zde-zhak) m. bumper

zderzenie (zde-zhe-ńe) n. collision; clash; crash, smash-up

zderzyć się (zde-zhich śhań) v. collide ; clash; run into

zdjęcie (zdyań-che) n. snapshot

zdjęcie rentgenowskie (zdyań-che rent-ge-nóv-skye) n. X-ray picture; X-ray phtograph

zdmuchiwać (zdmoo-khee-vach) v. blow off ; blow out; blow away

zdobić (zdo-beech) v. decorate

zdobycz (zdo-bich) f. booty; spoils; prey; prize; trophy

zdobyć (zdo-bich) v. conquer

zdolność (zdól-nośhch) f. ability; capacity ; talent, aptitude

zdolny (zdól-ni) adj. m. clever; able ; capable; fit ;competent

zdołać (zdo-wach) v. be able

zdrada (zdra-da) f. treason

zdradliwy (zdrad-lee-vi) adj.m. treacherous; tricky; unsafe

zdradzać (zdra-dzach) v. betray

zdrajca (zdráy-tsa) adj. m. traitor ; informer; turncoat

zdrapać (zdra-pach) v. scratch off ; scrape off; loosen up

zdrętwieć (zdrănt-vyech) v. grow numb ; stiffen ;grow torpid

zdrętwienie (zdrănt-vye-ńe) n. numbness; stiffnes; torpidity

zdrobniały (zdrob-ńa-wi) adj.m. diminutive; grown smaller

zdrojowisko (zdro-yo-vees-ko) n. spa ; health resort ;baths

zdrowie (zdrov-ye) n. health ; good constitution; being well

zdrowotne jedzenie (zdro-vót-ne ye-dzé-ńe) n. health food

zdrowy (zdro-vi) adj. m. healthy; sound ; mighty ;in good health

zdrożny (zdrozh-ni) adj. m. vicious ; wicked; wrong ; fatigued

zdrój (zdrooy) m. spring; spa

zdrów i cały (zdroóv ee tsa-wi) m. safe and sound

zdrzemnąć się (zdzhém-nownch śhań) v. doze off; sleep light; catnap; take a nap

zdumienie (zdoo-mye-ńe) n. astonishment; amazement

zdumiony (zdoo-myo-ni) adj.m. astonished; flabbergasted

zdun (zdoon) m. stove fitter

zdwajać (zdvá-yach) v. double

zdychać (zdi-khach) v. die

zdyszany (zdi-shá-ni) adj.m. breathless; panting out of breath

zdziałać (zdzha-wach) v. accomplish; achieve ;manage to do

zdziczeć (zdzhee-chech) v. grow wild; become savage; turn wild

zdziecinnieć (zdzhe-cheen-ńech) v. grow childish(in the old age)

zdzierać (zdzhe-rach) v. strip off; fleece; tear down; peel

zdzierstwo (zdzhér-stvo) n. extortion; exorbitance

zdziwaczeć (zdzhee-va-chech) v. become odd; grow whimsical

zdziwić (zdzhee-veech) v. surprise; astonish; make wonder

zdziwienie (zdzhee-vyé-ńe) n. surprise; wonderment; astonishment

zebra (ze-bra) f. zebra

zebrać (ze-brach) v. gather; clear

zebranie (ze-bra-ńe) n. meeting

zecer (ze-tser) m. type setter

zechcieć (zékh-chech) v. be willing; feel inclined; choose

zegar (zé-gar) m. clock ;meter

zegar słoneczny (zé-gar swo-nech-ni) sundial

zegarek (ze-ga-rek) m. watch

zegarmistrz (ze-gar-mees tsh) m. watchmaker; watchmaker's shop

zejście (zéysh-che) n. descent

zejść (zeyśhch) v. descend

zejść się (zeyśhth śhań) v. meet; rendez vous; have a date

zelówka (ze-loov-ka) f.(shoe)sole
zelżec (zél-zhech) v. lighten
up ;ease; let up;diminish;abate
zemdlec (zem-dlech) v. faint;
pan out ; swoon;feel weak
zemsta (zem-sta) f. revenge
zepchnąc (zép-khnownch)v. push
down; drive out ;shove down
zepsuc (zép-sooch) v. damage;
spoil; worsen; pervert;harm;injure
zepsuty (zep-soo-ti) adj. m.
damaged; spoiled ; corrupt;bad
zerkac (zér-kach) v. squint;peep
zero (zé-ro) n. zero; nought; nil
zerwac (zér-vach) v. pick off;
snap loose; break off; sprain
zerwanie (zer-va-ńe) n. rupture
zeskakiwac (ze-ska-kee-vach) v.
jump down ; dismount ;jump off
zeskrobywac (se-skro-bi-vach) v.
scrape off ; erase ;srcape clean
zesłac (ze-swach) v. deport;
send down ; send into exile
zesłanie (ze-swa-ńe) n. deportation ; exile ; penal colony
zespolic (ze-spo-leech) v. unite
zespół (ze-spoow) m. team; group;
gang ; crew; set; troupe;complex
zestarzec się (ze-sta-zhech shań)
v. grow old ; age; stale;get old
zestawienie (ze-sta-vye-ńe) n.
comparison ; balance sheet; list
zestrzelenie (ze-stzhe-le-ńe) n.
shotting down; downing(a plane)
zeszłoroczny (ze-shwo-rocz-ni)
adj. m. last year's (crop etc.)
zeszpecic (ze-shpe-cheech) v.
disfigure ; make look ugly;deface
zeszyt (ze-shit) m. notebook
zeslizgiwac się (ze-shleez-gee-
vach shań) v. glide down; slip
zetknąc się (zét-knownch shań)
v. meet face-to-face; get in
touch; contact; meet;put in touch
zew (zef) n. call ; appeal;slogan
zewnątrz (zév-nowntsh) adv.& prep.
out; outside; outwards;outdoors
zewnętrzny (zev-nántzh-ni) adj.
m. exterior;external; outward
zewsząd (ze-vshownt) adv. from
everywhere; from all points
zez (zez) m. squint; crosseye

zeznawac (zez-na-vach) v. declare; testify ;give evidence
zezowac (ze-zo-vach) v. squint
zezwalac (zez-va-lach) v. allow ; give permission;permit
zezwolenie (zez-vo-le-ńe) n.
permission ; leave;license
zębaty (zán-ba-ti) adj. m.
toothed ; cogged; indented
zębate koło (zán-ba-te ko-wo)
n. cog wheel; gear (wheel)
zęby (zán-bi) pl, teeth; cogs
zgadywac (zga-di-vach) v.
guess ; anticipate ;give a guess
zgadzac się (zga-dzach shań)
v. agree ;fit in;see eye-to-eye
zgaga (zga-ga) f. heartburn
zganic (zga-ńeech) v. blame
zgarnąc (zgar-nownch) v. rake
together ;gather; brush aside
zgasic (zga-sheech) v. put out;
extinguish; switch off; dim
zgęszczenie (zgán-shche-ńe) n.
condensation ; compression
zgiełk (zgyewk) m. uproar;
clamor ; turmoil; tumult
zgięcie (zgyan-che) n. bend;
fold ; inflection ;inflexion
zginac (zgee-nach) v. bend
(over); fold; stoop; bow
zgliszcza (zgleesh-cha) pl.
cinders ; ashes ;site of fire
zgłaszac (zgwa-shach) v. notify; call for; tender ;submit
zgłębic (zgwán-beech) v. probe;
sound out ; deepen ;go deeply
zgłodniały (zgwod-ná-wi) adj.
m. hungry ; starving ;hungering
zgłosic (zgwo-sheech) v. notify
zgłoska (zgwos-ka) f. syllable
zgłupiec (zgwoo-pyech) v. grow
silly ; grow stupid ;be astounded
zgnębic (zgnán-beech) v. depress ; deject; oppress ;dishearten
zgnic (zgńeech) v. rot ;decay;ret
zgniesc (zgńeshch) v. crush;stub;
squash ; suppress; quell ;squeeze
zgnilizna (zgńee-leez-na) f.
rot; corruption; foul smell
zgniły (zgńee-wi) adj. rotten;foul
zgoda .zgo-da) f. concord; assent;
consent ;unity; approval ;harmony

zgodnie (zgod-ne) adv. according; in concert ; peaceably ;in unison

zgodnosc (zgod-noshch) f. accord ; agreement ; unanimity ;consistence

zgodny (zgod-ni) adj. m. compat- ible ; good-natured ;unanimous

zgoic sie (zgo-eech shan) v. heal up; heal over ;heal a wound

zgon (zgon) m. death; decease

zgorszyc (zgor-shich) v. horrify; scandalize ; shock; arouse

zgorzkniały (zgozh-kna-wi) adj. m. sour; embittered;acrimonious

zgotowac (zgo-to-vach) v. pre- pare;cook; give (an ovation)

z góry (zgoo-ri) adv. in advance

zgrabny (zgrab-ni) adj. m.skill - ful; clever; deft; smart;neat; shapely ; slick; deft;well-built

zgraja (zgra-ya) f. gang; mob

zgromadzenie (zgro-ma-dze-ne) n. assembly ; congress ; meeting

zgromadzac sie (zgro-ma-dzach shan) v. assemble ; gather

zgroza (zgro-za) f. horror

z grubsza (zgroob-sha) adv. roughly; approximatively

zgryzota (zgri-zo-ta) f. grief

zgryźliwy (zgrizh-lee-vi) adj. m. sarcastic; peevish; harsh

zgrzac sie (zgzhach shan) v. get hot; sweat; become hot

zgrzebło (zgzheb-wo) n. horse- comb ; harrow;curry comb;comb

zgrzyt (zgzhit) m. screech; jar

zguba (zgoo-ba) f. loss; doom; undoing ; ruin; destruction

zgubic (zgoo-beech) v. lose; undo;drop;bring to ruin;destroy

zgubic sie (zgoo-beech shan) v. get lost; get mixed up ;be mislaid

zgubny (zgoob-ni) adj. m. disas- trous; fatal; ruinous ;calamitous

zgwałcic (zgvaw-cheech) v. rape

ziarnisty (zhar-nees-ti) adj.m. granular ; grainy;whole grain-

ziarno (zhar-no) n. grain; corn

ziele (zhe-le) n. weed; herb

zielen (zhe-len) f. greenery

zielonawy (zhe-lo-na-vi) adj. m. greenish;of greenish color

zielony (zhe-lo-ni) adj. m.green; young and inexperienced (man)

ziemia (zhem-ya) f. earth; land ground; soil ;native land;district

ziemianin (zhe-mya-neen) m. squire; landowner; mortal

ziemianka (zhe-myan-ka) f. 1. dugout; 2. landowner's wife

ziemniak (zhem-nak) m. potato

ziemski (zhem-skee) adj. m. earthly; worldly; landed ;land-

ziewac (zhe-vach) v. yawn; gape

zięba (zhan-ba) f. finch;chaffinch

ziębic (zhan-beech) v. cool; chill;expose to the cold

ziec (zhanch) m. son-in-law

zima (zhee-ma) f. winter

zimno (zheem-no) n. cold;chill

zimno (zheem-no) adv. coldly

zimny (zheem-ni) adj. m. cold

zimowac (zhee-mo-vach) v. hibernate; winter;pass the winter

zioło (zho-wo) n. herb(mint,sage…)

ziszczac (zeesh-chach) v. real- ize; fulfill ; carry out (a plan)

zjadac (zya-dach) v. eat; eat up ; have food; ruin ; drain

zjadliwy (zya-dlee-vi) adj.m. biting; caustic ; spiteful ;vicious

zjawa (zya-va) f. apparition: ghost ; vision ;specter; phantom

zjawisko (zya-vees-ko) n. fact; event; phenomenon ;vision ;occurence

zjazd (zyast) m. meeting; co- ming; descent ; downhill drive ;slide

zjednoczenie (zyed-no-che-ne) n. union ; unification ;association

zjesc (zyeshch) v. eat up ;outdo

zjeżdżac (zyezh-dzhach) v. ride down; slide down ;make way;slate

zlecac (zle-tsach) v. commission; order ;entrust; instruct;charge with

zlecenie (zle-tse-ne) n. commis- sion; order ; errand; message

z ledwoscia (zled-vosh-chown) adv. hardly; with difficulty

z lekka (zlek-ka) adv. lightly; softly ; slightly; gently

zlepek (zle-pek) m. agglomerate

zlew (zlef) m. sink;kitchen sink

zlewac (zle-vach) v. pour off; pour together ; mix ;flunk;whip

zliczyc (zlee-chich) v. count up; total; add up ; reckon;tot up

zlikwidować (zlee-kvee-do-vačh)
v. liquidate; wind up;destroy
zlodowacenie (zlo-do-va-tse-ne)
n. freezing; glaciation
zlot (zlot) m. rally;flocking in
złagodzenie (zwa-go-dze-ne) n.
mitigation; softening
złagodzić (zwa-go-dźheećh) v.
mitigate;soothe;lessen;soften
złamać (zwa-maćh) v. break;smash
złamanie (zwa-ma-ne) n. fracture
złazić (zwa-żheećh) v. climb
down ; get off; come off;peel off
złączenie (zwown-che-ne) n. connection; junction ;weld link;fuse
złączyć (zwown-chićh) v. join;
złe (zwe) n. evil; wrong; ill
zło (zwo) n. evil; devil;harm
złocenie (zyo-tse-ne) n. gilding
złocić (zwo-ćheećh) v. gild
złoczyńca (zwo-chiń-tsa) n.
evildoer; criminal;malefactor
złodziej (zwo-dżhey) m. thief
złodziejka (zwo-dżhey-ka) f.
thief; electrical adapter
złom (zwom) m. scrap; waste
złość (zwoshćh) f. anger; malice;
spite; soreness; resentment
złośliwy (zwosh-lee-vi) adj.m.
malignant; spiteful ;malicious
złotnik (zwot-ñeek) m. goldsmith
złoto (zwo-to) n . gold;gold work
złoty (zwo-ti) adj. m. 1, golden
m. 2. Polish money unit
złowić (zwo-veećh) v. catch;net;
hook (a fish,a husband etc)
złowrogi (zwo-vro-gee) adj.m.
ominous ; sinister;protentous
złoże (zwo-zhe) n. stratum; bed
złożony (zwo-zho-ni) adj. m.
complex; multiple; intricate
złuda (zwoo-da) f. illusion
złudny (zwood-ni) adj. m. illusory; deceptive; illusive
zły (zwi) adj. m. bad; evil;ill;
vicious ; cross; poor;rotten
zmagać się (zma-gaćh shañ) v.
struggle with; grapple with
zmaganie (zma-ga-ne) n. struggle
zmarły (zmar-wi) adj. m. deceased; dead; defunct; the late
zmarszczka (zmarshch-ka) f.
wrinkle; crease; fold; pucker

zmartwienie (zmar-tvye-ne) n.
worry; sorrow; grief;trouble
zmartwychwstać (zmar-tvikh-
vstaćh) v. rise form the dead
zmartwychwstanie (zmar-tvikh-
vsta-ñe) n. resurrection
zmarznąć (zmar-znownćh) v.
freeze ; freeze over; be cold
zmawiać się (zma-vyaćh shañ) v.
conspire ; plot; arrange;collude
zmaza (zmá-za) f. stain; blemish; blot; wet dream; slur
zmazywać (zma-zi-vaćh) v. wipe
out; efface ; erase; expiate
zmęczenie (zmań-che-ne) n. fatigue ; weariness;lassitude
zmiana (zmya-na) f. change ;
variation; shift; relay;exchange
zmiatać (zmya-taćh) v. sweep up
zmiażdżyć (zmyázh-dzhićh) v.
crush ; overwhelm(the enemy etc.)
zmienić (zmye-ńeećh) v. change
zmierzać (zmye-zhaćh) v. aim;
tend; make one's way;drive at
zmierzch (zmyezhkh) m. dusk;
twilight; decline; fall; dark;
at dark
zmierzyć (zmye-zhićh) v. measure; gauge ; take aim;make for
zmieszanie (zmye-sha-ñe) n.
mix up; confusion, embarrassment
zmiłowanie (zmee-wo-vá-ñe) n.
mercy; pity;disposition to forgive
zmniejszenie (zmñey-she-ñe) n.
reduction; decrease; relief
zmniejszyć (zmñey-shićh) v.
diminish; lessen; abate; reduce
zmoczyć (zmo-chićh) v. wet; soak
zmora (zmó-ra) f. nightmare;bane
zmorzyć (zmó-zhićh) v. overpower
zmordować (zmor-do-vaćh) v.tire
wear; do in; tire out; exhaust
zmowa (zmó-va) f. conspiracy;
collusion; plot;secret deal
zmrok (zmrok) m. dusk; twilight
zmursza ły (zmoor-sha-wi) adj.m.
mouldy decaying; rotten;musty
zmuszać (zmoo-shaćh) v. coerce;
compel; force; oblige;constrain
zmykać (zmi-kaćh) v. cut and run;
bolt; scoot off; scurry away
zmylić (zmi-leećh) v. fool; mislead; deceive; lose way;outwit

zmysł (zmłsw) m. sense; instinct;knack;aptitude;reason

zmysłowy (zmis-wo-wi) adj. m. sensual;sensory;sense-; lewd

zmyślać (zmish-lach) v. invent; trump up ; fake up; bluff;cook up

zmyślony (zmish-lo-ni) adj.m. fictitious; invented ; unreal

znaczący (zna-chown-tsi) adj. m. significant ; emphatic;telling

znaczek (zna-chek) m. sign;stamp

ziarzny(znach-ni)adj.m. notable; goodly

znać (znach) v. know;know how

znajdować (znay-do-vach) v. find ; see; meet; experience

znajomość (zna-yo-moshch) f. acquaintance ; knowledge

znajomy (zna-yo-mi) adj. m.well acquainted;well known;familiar

znak (znak) m. mark; sign; stamp

znakomity (zna-ko-mee-ti) adj. m. excellent ; illustrious

znalazca (zna-laz-tsa) m. finder

znaleźne (zna-lezh-ne) n.finder's reward;finder's share

znamienny (zna-myen-ni) adj.m. significant ; characteristic

znamię (zna-myań) n. stigma; mole ; trait; birthmark

znany (zna-ni) adj. m. noted; known ; famed; familiar;well known

znawca (znav-tsa) m. expert

znęcać się (znań-tsach shań) v. torment; harass; ill-treat

znękany (znań-ka-ni) adj. m. dejected; harassed ; wasted

znicz (zneech) m. (holy) fire; fireside ; pilot-light

zniechęcać (zne-khań-tsach) v. discourage ; sicken; indispose

zniecierpliwić się (zne-cher-plee-veech shań) v. grow impatient ; get vexed;lose patience

znieczulić (zne-choo-leech) v. anesthetize ; deaden; harden

zniedołężniały (zne-do-wań-zhna-wi) adj. m. impotent; decrepit; infirm; disable; feeble(old man)

zniekształcać (zne-ksztaw-tsach) v. deform; disfigure ;distort

zniemczać (znem-chach) v.Germanize; make into a German;force to accept German identity

znienacka (zne-nats-ka) adv. all of a sudden ;unawares

znienawidzieć (zne-na-vee-dżheech) v. grow to hate;loathe

znieprawić (zne-pra-veech) v. deprave ; demoralize; debauch

zniesienie (zne-she-ne) n. abrogation; abolition;repeal

zniesławienie (zne-swa-vye-ne) n. defamation ; slander

zniewaga (zne-va-ga) f. insult

zniewalać (zne-va-lach) v. coerce; rape; captivate; win

znikać (znee-kach) v. vanish

zniewieściały (zne-vyesh-cha-wi) adj. m. effeminate;sissy

znikąd (znee-kownt) adv. from nowhere; out of nowhere

znikomy (znee-ko-mi) adj. m. perishable;negligible;minute

zniszczeć (zneesh-chech) v. decay; go to ruin; be worn out

zniszczenie (zneesh-che-ne) n. destruction; ravage;ruin;havoc

zniszczyć (zheesh-chich) v. destroy; ruin; ware out;ravage

zniweczyć (znee-ve-chich) v. annihilate; wreck; lay waste

zniżać (znee-zhach) v. lower

zniżka (zneezh-ka) f. reduction; decline; slump; drop; fall

znosić (zno-sheech) v. annul; endure; carry down;ware out

znośny (znosh-ni) adj. m. tolerable; bearable; so-so; fair

znowu (zno-voo) adv. again;anew

znój (znooy) m. toil; sweat

znów (znoof) adv. again; anew

znudzenie (znoo-dze-ne) n.boredom; till one is sick and tired

znużenie (znoo-zhe-ne) n. weariness; fatigue (people,metals etc.)

zobaczyć (zo-ba-chich) v. see

zobojętnić (zo-bo-yant-neech) v. neutralize;make indifferent

zobojętnieć (zo-bo-yant-nech) v. grow indifferent;grow listless

zobowiązać (zo-bo-vyown-zach) v. oblige ;obligate to do

zobowiązanie (zo-bov-yown-za-ne) n. obligation;commitment

zobrazować (zob-ra-zo-vach) v. illustrate; describe ;depict

zogniskować (zog-nees-ko-vach)
v. focus ; concentrate

zohydzać (zo-khi-dzach) v. defame; make loathsome; sicken of

zoolog(zo-ó-log) m. zoologist

zorza północna (zo-zha poow-
nóts-na) f. aurora borealis

zostać (zós-tach) v. remain;stay;
become; get to be; be left

zostawiać (zos-táv-yach) v.
leave;abandon; put aside

z powodu (zpo-vó-doo) prep.
because of; owing to;due to

z powrotem (zpov-ró-tem) adv.
back; backwards;on the way back

zrabować (zra-bó-vach) v. rob

z rana (zrá-na) adv. in the
morning;during the morning

zranić (zra-neech) v. wound;
injure; hurt(feelings);mangle

zrastać (zrás-tach) v. grow
into one; fuse; heal up;blend

zrazu (zrá-zu) adv. at first

zrażać (zrá-zhach) v. discourage; set against; alienate

zrąb (zrownp) m. frame (work);
clearing ; trunk; shell

zrąbać (zrówn-bach) v. hew; cut
down; hack; chop; pick to pieces

zrealizować (zre-a-lee-zó-vach)
v. realize; actualize; execute

zredagować (zre-da-gó-vach) v.
draw up; compose; edit; draft

zresztą (zresh-tówn) adv.
1. moreover; besides; 2.after
all; though; any way;in the end

zręczność (zránch-noshch) f.
cleverness; dexterity; skill

zrobić (zro-beech) v. make; do;
turn; execute; perform

zrodzić (zro-dźheech) v. give
birth; beget; originate

zrosnąć się (zros-nównch shán)
v. grow into one; fuse;blend

zrozpaczony (zros-pa-chó-ni) adj.
m. desperate; brokenhearted

zrozumiały (zro-zoo-mya-wi) adj.
m. intelligible; understandable

zrozumieć (zro-zoo-myech) v.
understand;grasp;see;make out

zrozumienie (zro-zoo-myé-ne) n.
understanding;sympathy; sense;
grasp; comprehension; spirit

zrównać (zroóv-nach) v. level;
make even; align;equalize

zrównoważyć (zroov-no-va-zhich)
v. balance; equalize;equilibrate

zróżniczkować (zroozh-neech-kó-
vach) v. differentiate

zryć (zrich) v. dig up; furrow

zrywać (zri-vach) v. rip; tear
off; tear down; pick; quarrel

z rzadka (zzhád-ka) adv. rarely

zrządzenie losu (zzhówn-dze-ne
ló-soo) n. fate ;decree of fate

zrzeczenie się (zzhe-ché-ne
shán) n. resignation; renunciation ; renouncement;abdication

zrzeszenie (zzhe-shé-ne) n.
association; union

zrzęda (zzhán-da) m. grumbler

zrzucać (zzhoó-tsach) v. throw
(down); buck off; drop; shed

zrzut lotniczy (zzhoót lot-nee-
chi) m. drop (from plane)

zsiadać (zshá-dach) v. dismount

zstąpić (zstówn-peech) v. descend;step down (one time)

zstępować (zstán-po-vach) v.
descent; step down

zsyłać (zsí-wach) v. deport;exile

zsyłka (zsíw-ka) f. deportation

zsypywać (zsi-pí-vach) v. heap
up; pour off;shoot into

zszyć (zshich) v. sew together

zubożeć (zoo-bó-zhech) v. im-
poverish; grow poor;pauperize

zuch (zookh) m. brave fellow

zuchwalstwo (zookh-vál-stvo) n.
insolence; audacity; impudence

zuchwały (zookh-va-wi) adj. m.
insolent; impudent; bold

zupa (zoo-pa) f. soup

zupełny (zoo-péw-ni) adj. m.
entire;whole;total;out and out

zużycie (zoo-zhí-che) n. consumption; wear and tear; waste

zużytkować (zoo-zhit-ko-vach) v.
utilize ; use up; exploit

zużyty (zoo-zhi-ti) adj.m. worn
out; used up; wasted; trite

zwać (zvach) v. call; name

zwalczyć (zval-chich) v. overpow
er; overcome; cope; strive

zwalić (zva-leech) v. demolish;
fell; collapse; pile up;knock down

zwalniac (zval-nach) v. release;
loosen; let go; slow dawn;vacate
zwal (zvaw) m. heap; bank ; pile
zwapnienie (zvap-ne-ne) n. cal-
cification ;adv.densely;closely
zwarcie (zvar-che) n. short
(cirquit); contraction;infighting
zwariowac (zvar-yo-vach) v. go
mad ; go crazy; alter (a score...)
zwarzyc (zva-zhich) v. boil; nip;
frost damage ; turn sour ;blight
zwazac (zva-zhach) v. pay attention ; weigh (words);consider
zwazyc (zva-zhich) v. weigh;
consider ; give heed ;regard
zwachac (zvown-khach) v. smell
out; get wind; sniff ;scent
zwatpic (zvownt-peech) v. despair of ; lose hope ;give up
zwedzic (zvan-dzheech) v. swipe
zweglic (zvang-leech) v. carbon-
ize ; char; get charred
zwezic (zvan-zheech) v. narrow
down ; contract; restrict ;confine
zwiady (zvya-di) pl. reconnaissance ; scouting ;reconnoitring
zwiastowac (zvyas-to-vach) v.
announce ; herald ;foreshadow
zwiastowanie (zvyas-to-va-ne) n.
Annunciation
zwiastun (zvyas-toon) m. harbinger ; herald; omen ;forerunner
zwiazac (zvyown-zach) v. bind;
fasten; join; tie up;strap;frame
zwiazek (zvyown-zek) m. alliance;
connection; bond· compound ;tie
zwichnac (zveekh-nownch)v. strain;
dislocate; disjoin; luxate ;warp
zwichniecie (zveekh-nan-che) n.
dislocation ; luxation; sprain
zwiedzac (zvye-dzach) v. visit;
see the sights ; tour; see ;inspect
zwiedzanie (zvye-dza-ne) n.
sightseeing ;touring
zwierciadlo (zvyer-chad-wo) n.
mirror ; reflection ;looking glass
zwierz (zvyesh) n. beast of prey
zwierzac sie (zvye-zhach shan) v.
disclose a secret; confide in...
zwierzchnik (zvyezh-khneek) m.
boss; superior ; chief; lord;
master; suzerain;feudal lord

zwierzchnictwo (svyezh-khneets-
tvo) n. sovereignty; superior
authority; supremacy; control
zwierze (zvye-zhan) n. animal
zwierzyna (zvye-zhi-na) f.
game (animals); game
zwierzyniec (zvye-zhi-nets) m.
zoo; zoological garden ;zodiac
zwieszac (zvye-shach) v. hang
low;droop; dangle ; hang down
zwietrzec (zvye-tzhech) v. de-
compose; go stale; spoil
zwiewac (zvye-vach) v. cut and
run; blow away; run away
zwiedly (zvyand-wi) adj. m.
withered; wilted ;faded
zwiednac (zvyand-nownch) v.
wither; wilt; fade
zwiekszyc (zvyank-zhich) v. increase; magnify; heighten
zwiezly (zvyanz-wi) adj. m.
concise; brief; terse;compact
zwijac (zvee-yach) v. roll up;
wind up;coil; twist up ;furl
zwilzac (zveel-zhach) v. moist-
en; wet; dampen(often)
zwilzyc (zveel-zhich) v. moist-
en; wet; dampen(one time)
zwinac (zvee-nownch) v. roll
up; wind up; coil up; twist up
zwinny (zveen-ni) adj. m. agile;
nimble; deft; dexterous ;lissome
zwisac (zvee-sach) v. hang
down; droop; dangle ;sag;beetle
zwlekac (zvle-kach) v. delay
zwlaszcza (zvwash-cha) adv.
particularly; chiefly; especially; most of all;specially
zwloka (zvwo-ka) f. delay;respite
zwloki (zvwo-kee) n. corpse
zwodzic (zvo-dzheech) v. delude;
deceive; let down; lower
zwolenniczka (zvo-len-neech-ka)
f. adherent; follower;advocate
zwolennik (zvo-len-neek) m. adherent; follower; advocate
zwolna (zvol-na) adv. slowly
zwolniec (zvol-nech) v. slow
down; slack off; relax ;slacken
zwolnienie (zvol-ne-ne) n.
1. dismissal; release; acquittal; sack;exemption;2.slowing

zwoływać (zvo-wi-vach) v. call
together: assemble; convene
zwój (zvooy) m. roll;reel;coil
zwracać (zvra-tsach) v. return;
give back; pay(attention)
zwrot (zvrot) m. 1; turn; 2. restitution 3.revulsion;4.phrase
zwrotka (zvrot-ka) f. stanza
zwrotnica (zvrot-nee-tsa) f.
switch (large); steering
zwrotnik (zvrot-neek) m. tropic
zwrotny (zvrot-ni) adj. m. flexible; returnable;repayable
zwrócić się (zvroo-cheech shań)
v. turn (to); give back
zwycięski (zvi-chans-kee) adj.
m. victorious;triumphant;winning
zwycięstwo (zvi-chans-tvo) n.
victory; triumph; win
zwyciężać (zvi-chan-zhach) v.
conquer; win; prevail;overcome
zwyczaj (zvi-chay) m. custom;
habit; fashion; usage;practice
zwyczajny (zvi-chay-ni) adj. m.
usual; ordinary; common;simple
zwyczajowy (zvi-cha-yo-vi) adj.
m. customary; regular; usual
zwykły (zvik-wi) adj. m. common
zwyrodniały (zvi-rod-ńa-wi) adj.
m. degenerate; degenerated
zwyrodnienie (zvi-rod-ńe-ńe) n.
degeneration; degradation
zwyżka (zvizh-ka) f. rise;advance
zwyżka cen (zvizh-ka tsen) f.
price rise;price increase
zygzak (zig-zak) m. zigzag
zysk (zisk) m. gain; profit
zyskać (zis-kach) v. gain;earn
zyskowność (zis-kov-nośhch) f.
profitability;remunerativeness
zyskowny (zis-kov-ni) adj. m.
profitable; lucrative
zza (z-za) prep. from behind
zziajać się (zzha-yach shań) v.
get out of breath;tire oneself
zzieleniec (zzhe-le-ńech) v.
turn green; become green
zziębnąć (zzhańb-nownch) v. feel
cold;be chilled to the bone
zziębnięty (zzhańb-nań-ti) adj.
m. chilled (to the bone)
zżyć się(zzhich shań) v. grow
familiar;grow accustomed

żymać (zzhi-mach) v. wring
żżynać (zzhi-nach) v. cut
down; reap; mow (the grass etc.)
zżywać się (zzhi-vach shań) v.
grow familiar; reconcile
ździbło (żhdżhbwo) n. stalk;
blade;trifle; a bit; a little
źle (żhle) adj. n,& adv. ill;
wrong; badly; falsely;mistakenly
źrebak (żhre-bak) m. colt
źrebie (żhre-byań) n. foal;colt
źrenica (żhre-ńee-tsa) f. pupil
źródlany (żhrood-lá-ni) adj.m.
spring (water); of spring
źródło (żhrood-wo) n. spring;
source; well;fountainhead
źródłosłów (żhrood-wó-swoof) m.
root word; etymology; radical
źródłowy (żhrood-wó-vi) adj.m.
original; spring (water)
żaba (zha-ba) f. frog
żaden (zhá-den) pron. none;
neither; not any; no one; no-
żagiel (zhá-gel) m. sail
żakiet (zhá-ket) m. jacket
żal (zhal) m. regret; grief;
sorrow; remorse;grudge; rancor
żalić się (zhá-leech shań) v.
complain; lament;find fault
żaluzja (zha-looz-ya) f. blind
żałoba (zha-wo-ba) f. mourning
żałobny marsz (zha-wób-ni marsh)
m. funeral march
żałosny (zha-wos-ni) adj. m.
lamentable; wretched;plaintive
żałość (zha-wośhch) f. grief;
desolation; sorrow ;deep sorrow
żałować (zha-wó-vach) v. regret
żar (zhar) m. heat; glow; ardor
żarcie (zhár-che) n. swill;dub
żargon (zhár-gon) m. jargon
żarliwość (zhar-lee-vośhch) f.
ardor; zeal; earnestness
żarliwy (zhar-lee-vi) adj. m.
ardent; zealous;fervent
żarłoczny (zhar-woch-ni) adj.m.
greedy;voracious; gluttonous
żarłok (zhár-wok) m. glutton
żarówka (zha-roov-ka) f. light
bulb; electric bulb; bulb
żart (zhart) m. joke; jest;quip;
żartować (zhar-to-vach) v. joke
make fun; poke fun; trifle ;jest

żarzyć (zha-zhich) v. glow;anneal

żąć (zhownch) v. mow; cut; reap

żądać (zhown-dach) v. demand; require; exact; stipulate

żądanie (zhown-da-ne) n. demand; claim;requirement;stipulation

żądło (zhownd-wo) n . sting;fang

żądny (zhownd-ni) adj. m. eager; anxious; greedy;avid (of fame etc)

żądny przygód (zhownd-ni pzhi-goot) adventurous (man)

że (zhe) conj. that; then; as

żebrać (zhe-brach) v. beg

żebraczka (zhe-brach-ka) f. beg-gar; pauper (girl, woman)

żebrak (zhe-brak) m. beggar (man)

żebranina (zhe-bra-nee-na) f. beggary; begging; alms

żebro (zhe-bro) n. rib;fin

żeby (zhe-bi) conj. so as; in order that;if;may;if only

żeglarski (zhe-glar-skee) adj.m. nautical; seaman's (life etc.)

żeglarstwo (zhe-glar-stvo) n. sailing;navigation;seamanship

żeglarz (zhe-glash) m. seaman; sailor ; mariner; seafarer

żeglować (zhe-glo-vach) v. sail; navigate (the seas,the ocean)

żeglowny (zhe-glow-ni) adj. m. navigable (river, canal etc.)

żegluga (zhe-gloo-ga) f. naviga-tion ; shipping; sailing

żegnać (zheg-nach) v. bid fare-well; bless;bid good-bye;see off

żelatyna (zhe-la-ti-na) f.jelly

żelazko (zhe-laz-ko) n. press-iron ; cutting iron; edger

żelazny (zhe-laz-ni) adj. m. iron

żelazo (zhe-la-zo) n. iron;armor

żelazobeton (zhe-la-zo-be-ton) m. reinforced concrete

żelaztwo (zhe-laz-tvo) n. scrap iron; hardware;iron junk

żelbet (zhel-bet) m. reinforced concrete

żeliwo (zhe-lee-vo) n. cast iron

żenić (zhe-neech) v. marry

żenować (zhe-no-vach) v. embarrass

żeński (zhen-skee) adj. m. female

żer (zher) m. food; prey; feeding

żerdka (zherd-ka) f. (small)perch

żerdź (zherdzh) f. perch

żłobek (zhwo-bek) m. crib

żłobić (zhwo-beech) v. chan-nel; erode; furrow; groove

żłob (zhwoop) m. trough; crib

żmija (zhmee-ya) f. viper; adder; poisonous snake

żmudny (zhmood-ni) adj. m. uphill; toilsome; strenuous

żniwiarka (zhnee-vyar-ka) f. harvester; reaper

żniwo (zhnee-vo) n. harvest

żołądek (zho-wown-dek) m. stomach

żołądź (zho-wowndzh) f. acorn

żołd (zhowd) m. (soldier's) pay

żołdactwo (zhow-dats-tvo) n. soldiery ;the soldiery

żołnierz (zhow-nesh) m. soldier

żona (zho-na) f. wife

żonaty (zho-na-ti) adj. m. married; family man

żółć (zhoowch) f. bile

żółciowy (zhoow-cho-vi) adj.m. gall; peevish; harsh; biting

żółknąć (zhoow-knownch) v. turn yellow; become yellow

żółtaczka (zhow-tach-ka) f. jaundice; the yellows

żółtawy (zhow-ta-vi) adj. m. yellowish;nankeen; sallow

żółtko (zhoowt-ko) n. yolk

żółty (zhoow-ti) adj. m. yellow

żółto-blady (zhoow-to-bla-di) adj. yellow-pale; sallow

żółw (zhoowf) m. turtle;tortoise

żółwi krok (zhoow-vee krok) m. snail's pace; turtle's gait

żrący (zhrown-tsi) adj. m. corrosive; caustic ; biting

żubr (zhoobr) m. (European-Po-lish) bison; aurochs

żuchwa (zhookh-va) f. jawbone

żuć (zhooch) v. chew;masticate

żucie (zhoo-che) n. chewing; mastication; chew;munducation

żuk (zhook) m. beetle;dung beetle

żulik (zhoo-leek) m. swindler; rogue; cheat; street urchin

żuławy (zhoo-wa-vi) pl. marsh-land ; lowlands;fertile lowlands żupa (zhoo-pa) f. saltworks

żupan (zhoo-pan) m. old Polish costume; (hist.) district chief

żur (zhoor) m. soup of fermented meal; sour soup

żuraw (zhoo-rav) m. crane;gantry

żurawina (zhoo-ra-vee-na) f. cranberry

żurnal (zhoor-nal) m. fashion magazine

żużel (zhoo-zhel) m. slag; cinder; scoria;clinker;cinder track

żużlobeton (zhoo-zhlo-be-ton) m. slag concrete

żwawo (zhva-vo) adj. m. briskly; alertly; apace; jauntily

żwawy (zhva-vi) adj. m. brisk; quick; lively; spry;sprightly

żwir (zhveer) m. gravel upkeep

życie (zhi-che) n. life ;pep;

życiodajny (zhi-cho-day-ni) adj. m. life-giving ; vivifying

życiorys (zhi-cho-ris) m. biography; life history

życzenie (zhi-che-ne) n. wish; desire ; request ; greeting

życzliwy (zhich-lee-vi) adj.m. favorable; friendly; kindly

żyć (zhich) v. be alive; live; exist; subsist; get along

Żyd (zhid) m. Jew

żydowski (zhi-dov-skee) adj.m. Jewish; Judaic; Yiddish

żydostwo (zhi-dos-tvo) n. Jewry

Żydówka (zhi-doov-ka) f. Jewess

żyjący (zhi-yown-tsi) adj.m. living ; pl. the living

żyjątko (zhi-yownt-ko) n. animalcule ; tiny animal

żylak (zhi-lak) m. varix

żylakowy (zhi-la-ko-vi) adj.m. varicose; of varicose vein

żylasty (zhi-las-ti) adj. m. venous; stringy; sinewy

żyletka (zhi-let-ka) f. (razor) blade; safety razor blade

żyła (zhi-wa) f. vein; seam; core; strand; streak; string

żyłka (zhiw-ka) f. veinlet; thread

żyrafa (zhi-ra-fa) f. giraffe

żyrant (zhi-rant) m. endorser

żyrować (zhi-ro-vach) v. endorse

żytni (zhit-nee) adj. m. rye

żytniówka (zhit-noov-ka) f. corn vodka ; gin; rye vodka

żyto (zhi-to) n. rye

żywcem (zhiv-tsem) adv. alive

żywe srebro (zhi-ve sreb-ro) n. mercury; restless person

żywica (zhi-vee-tsa) f. resin

żywiec (zhi-vyets) m. cattle for slaughter; live bait

żywić (zhi-veech) v. feed; nourish; cherish ; feel

żywioł (zhi-vyow) m. element

żywiołowy (zhi-vyo-wo-vi) adj. m. elemental; spontaneous; impulsive; impetuous

żywność (zhiv-noshch) f. food; provisions; eatables; fodder

żywo (zhi-vo) adv. quickly; briskly ;exp.: make it snappy!

żywopłot (zhi-vo-pwot) m. hedge

żywość (zhi-voshch) f. animation; liveliness; vivacity; vitality; vigor; esprit

żywot (zhi-vot) m. life; womb; belly ;life (of a saint)

żywotnie (zhi-vot-ne) adv. vitally; exuberantly;luxuriantly

żywotność (zhi-vot-noshch) f. vitality ; liveliness ;vivacity

żywotny (zhi-vot-ni) m. vital

żywy (zhi-vi) adj. m. alive; lively; vivid; intense; gay; brisk; live;acute; keen; bright

żyzność (zhiz-noshch) f. fertility ; fruitfulness;richness

żyzny (zhiz-ni) adj. m. fertile; generous (soil) fruitful; fat; fecund; rich

ENGLISH-POLISH

a (ej) art.jeden; pewien;
pierwsza litera angielskiego
alfabetu; pierwszej kategorii
A-O'k (ej okej) zupełnie gotów
aback (e'baek) adv. wstecz;
w tył: do tylu; nazad
abandon (e'baendon) v. opuszczać ; porzucić ; zarzucić
abandonment (e'baendonment) s.
opuszczenie:brak pohamowania
abashed (e'baeszt) adj. speszony; zmieszany (czymś)
abate ('ebejt) v. osłabiać;
zmniejszać: mityǵować:uciszyć
abbey ('aebi) s. opactwo
abbreviate (e'bry:wjejt) v.
skrócić; skracać
abbreviation (e'bry:wjejszyn)
s. skrót: skrócenie; skracanie
ABC ('ej'bi:'si) alfabet
abdicate ('aebdykejt) v. zrzekać się ; abdykować
abdomen ('aebdemen) s. brzuch
abduct (aeb'dakt) v. uprowadzić: porwać: porywać
abhor (eb'ho:r) v. mieć odrazę
abide, abode, abode (e'bajd,
e'boud, e'boud)
abide (e'bajd) v. znosić; obstawać; dotrzymywać; trwać
ability (e'bylyty) s. zdolność
abject ('aebdżekt) adj. podły;
nędzny: nikczemny: skrajny
abjure (eb'dżuer) v. poprzysiąc
able ('ejbl) adj. zdolny; zdatny: utalentowany; poczytalny
abnormal (aeb'no:rmel) adj.
anormalny: nieprawidłowy
aboard (e'bo:rd) adv. na pokła-
dzie; na statku: w pociągu
abode (e'boud) v. był posłuszny
abode (e'boud) s. mieszkanie;
v. zob. abide
abolish (e'bolysz) v. obalić;
znieść: znosić; obalać
abolition (aebe'lyszyn) n. obalenie; zniesienie(zwyczaju etc.)
A-bomb ('ejbom) s. bomba atomowa: bomba jądrowa
abominable (e'bomynebl) adj.
ohydny; wstrętny: obrzydliwy

abortion (e'bo:rszyn) s.przerwa-
nie ciąży; poronienie
abound (e'baund) v. obfitować
about (e'baut) adv. naokoło;
około:dookoła; po; o; wobec;przy
about (e'baut) prep. o; przy;
odnośnie: naokoło; wokoło
about to (e'baut tu) gotów do
above (e'baw) adv. powyżej;
w górze; wyżej: na górze
above (e'baw) prep. nad; ponad
above (e'baw) adj. powyższy
abreast (e'brest) adv. obok;
rzędem: ramię przy ramieniu
abridge (e'brydż) v. skrócić
abroad (e'bro:d) adv. zewnątrz;
za granicą: za granicę; w dal
abrogate ('aebrogejt) v. obalić:
unicestwić; odwoływać; znosić
abrupt (e'brapt) adj. nagły;
szorstki: urwany; ostry; oschły
abscess ('aebses) s. wrzód:ropień
absence ('aebsens) s. brak;
nieobecność: niestawiennictwo
absent ('aebsent) adj. nieobecny;v. być nieobecnym
absent-minded ('aebsent'majndyd)
adj. roztargniony
absolute ('aebselu:t) adj. abso-
lutny; zupełny: nieodwołalny
absolutely ('aebselu:tly) adv.
absolutnie; oczywiście
absolve (eb'zolw) v. rozgrzeszyć;
darować: uwolnić; oczyścić
absorb (eb'zo:rb) v. chłonąć;
tłumić; absorbować: łagodzić
abstain (eb'stejn) v. powstrzymywać się; być abstynentem
abstention (eb'stenszyn) s.
wstrzymanie się(od jedzenia...)
abstinence ('aebstynens) s.
wstrzemięźliwość: abstynencja
abstract ('aebstraekt) adj.
oderwany; abstrakcyjny;
s. abstrakcja; streszczenie;
v. streszczać; abstrahować;
odrywać: ukrasc: sprzątnąć
absurd (eb'se:rd) adj. absurdalny: bezsensowny: niedorzeczny
abundance (e'bandens) s. obfitość: znaczna ilość; dostatek

abundant (e'bandent) adj. obfity;liczny;bogaty; zasobny;płodny

abuse (e'bju:s) s. nadużycie;
obelga; (e'bju:z) v. obrażać;
nadużywać;lżyć;obrzucać obelgami

abyss (e'bys) n. otchłań; przepaść; głębia;pierwotny chaos

acacia (e'kejsze) s. akacja

academic (,aeke'demyk) adj.
akademicki;jałowy; s.uczony

academy (e'kaedemy) s. akademia

accelerate (aek'selerejt) v.
przyśpieszać; przyśpieszyć

accelerator (aek'selerejter) s.
przyśpieszacz; gaźnik; akcele-
rator; katalizator

accent ('aeksent) s. wymowa;
akcent; (aek'sent) v. akcento-
wać; uwydatniać; znakować

accept (ek'sept) v. akceptować;
zgadzać się na;zechcieć wziasć

acceptable (ek'septebl) adj.
do przyjęcia; znośny; zadawalający; mile widziany

access ('aekses) s. dostęp

accessible (aek'sesybl) adj.
dostępny; przystępny

accession (aek'seszyn) s.,
wstąpienie; dostęp; dojście;
przystąpienie;objęcie(urzędu)

accessory (aek'sesery) s. dodatek; adj. dodatkowy; pomocniczy

access road ('aekses roud)
droga dojazdowa

accident ('aeksydent) s. traf;
wypadek; katastrofa;awaria

accidental (,aeksy'dentl) adj.
przypadkowy; nieważny;uboczny

acclimatize (e'klajmetajz) v.
aklimatyzować

accommodate (e'komedejt) v. przystosować; zakwaterować; wy-
świadczyć; załagodzić(spór)

accommodation (e,kome'dejszyn)
s. wygoda; dostosowanie; kwatera; pogodzenie się; ugoda

accompaniment (e'kampenyment) s.
towarzyszenie; akompaniament

accompany (e'kampeny) v. towarzyszyć;odprowadzać;akompaniować

accomplice (e'komplys) s. współ-
sprawca; współwinny

accomplish (e'kamplysz) v. dokonać; spełnić; zrealizować

accomplished (e'kamplyszt) adj.
utalentowany; znakomity; wy-
kończony; z ogładą;skończony

accomplishment (e'kamplyszment)
s. osiągnięcie; realizacja;
dokonanie;wykonanie: ogłada

accord (e'ko:rd) s. zgoda;
v. uzgadniać; dać; licować

according (e'ko:rdyng) prep.
według; zależnie od

accordingly (e'ko:rdyngly) adv.
odpowiednio; więc; zatem

accost (e'kost) v. zaczepić
(kogoś);zagadnąć;przystąpić do

account (e'kaunt) s. rachunek;
sprawozdanie; v. wyliczać;
wytłumaczyć; uważać; oceniać

account for (e'kaunt fo:r) v.
dać powód; wytłumaczyć

accountant (e'kauntent) s.
księgowy

accounting (e'kauntyng)s. księgowość

accumulate (e'kju:mju,lejt) v.
gromadzic;zbierać;piętrzyć

accuracy ('aekjuresy) s. ścisłość; dokładność; celność

accusation (aekju:zejszyn) s.
oskarżenie;winienie;posądzenie

accuse (e'kju:z) v. oskarżać

accused (e'kju:zd) adj. oskar-
żony; oskarżona

accustom (e'kastem) v. przyzwy-
czajac; przyzwyczaić

accustomed (e'kastemd) adj.
przyzwyczajony; zwykły;zwyczajny

ace (ejs) s. as; oczko(in cards)

ache (ejk) s. ból; v.bolec

achieve (e'czi:w) v. dokonać;
osiągnąć(cel);zdobywać(sławę)

achievement(e'czi:wment) s.
osiągnięcie; wyczyn;zdobycz

aching ('ejkyng) adj. bolący

acid ('aesyd) adj. kwaśny;
s. kwas; kwaśna substancja

acid trip ('aesyd tryp) halu-
cynacje po narkotyku

acknowledge (ek'noßlydż) v.
uznać; potwierdzić; przyznać

acknowledgement (ek'noʁlydžment)
s. przyznanie; potwierdzenie;
uznanie; dowód uznania

acoustics (e'ku:styks) pl. akustyka

acquaint (e'kłejnt) v. zaznajomić; zapoznać; zapoznawać(kogoś)

acquaintance (e'kłejntens) s.
znajomość; znajomy

acquiesce (,aekły'es), v. zgadzać się; przyzwalać (bez oporu); przychylić się(do prośby)

acquire (e'kłajer) v. nabywać

acquisition (,aekły'zyszyn) s.
nabytek; nabycie; zdobycz

acquit (e'kłyt) v. zwolnić; wywiązać się; spłacić; uniewinnić

acquittal (e'kłytl) s. zwolnienie; uiszczenie; wywiązanie się

acre (ejker) s. akr; morga;
4047 m²

acrid ('aekryd) adj. żrący;
ostry; cierpki; kwaskowaty

acrimonious (,aekry'mounjes)
adj. szorstki; zjadliwy;
cierpki; zgorzkniały

acrobat ('aekrebaet) s. akrobata

across (e'kros) adv. w poprzek;
na krzyż; prep. przez; na przełaj; po drugiej stronie (czegoś)

act (aekt) v. czynić; działać;
postępować; s. czyn; akt; uczynek; akt sztuki; uchwła; ustawa

action ('aekszyn) s. działanie;
czyn; akcja; ruch; poces

active ('aektyw) adj. czynny;
obrotny; rzutki; ożywiony; żywy

activity (aek'tywyty) s..działalność; czynność; ożywienie; ruch

actor ('aekter) s. aktor

actress ('aektrys) s. aktorka

actual ('aekczuel) adj. istotny;
faktyczny; bieżący; obecny

actually ('aekczuely) adv. rzeczywiście; obecnie; istotnie; nawet

acute (e'kju:t) adj. ostry;
przenikliwy; bystry; przenikliwy

ad (aed) s. ogłoszenie (reklama)
(slang)

adapt (e'daept) v. dostosować;
przerobić; przystosować; dostrajać

adaptation (,aedaep'tejszyn)
s. przystosowanie; dostrojenie

add (aed) v. dodać; doliczyć

addict (aedykt) s. nałogowiec;
v. oddawać; poświęcać się

addicted (e'dyktyd) adj. nałogowy; nałogowo poświęcający się

addition (e'dyszyn) s. dodawanie; dodatek; (ponadto)

additional (e'dyszynl) adj.
dodatkowy; dalszy

address (e'dres) s. adres; mowa; odezwa; v. zwracać się;
adresować; skierować(prośbę)

addressee (,aedre'si:) s. adresat; adresatka

adequate ('aedykłyt) s. stosowny; dostateczny; właściwy

adhere (ed'hjer) v. lgnąć; należeć; trzymać; przylegać

adhesion (ed'hi:żyn) s. lepkość; zrost; przynależność

adhesive (ed'hi:syw) adj. lepki; przylegający; s. plaster

adjacent (e' dzejsent) adj.
przyległy; sąsiedni

adjective ('aeddżyktyw) s.
przymiotnik; adj. dodatkowy

adjoin (e'ddżoyn) v. stykać się;
sąsiadować; dołączać

adjourn (e'ddże:rn) v. odraczać;
przerywać; zakończyć (obrady)

adjust (e'ddżast) v. dostosowywać; uregulować; nastawić

administer (ed'mynyster) v. dawać; sprawować; administrować

administration (ed,myny'strejszyn) s. zarząd; rząd; administracja; ministerstwo; wymiar

administrative (ed'mynystrejtyw) adj. administracyjny

administrator (ed'mynystrejtor)
s. zarządca; administrator

admirable ('aedmerebl) adj.
godny podziwu; zachwycający

admiral ('aedmyrel) s. admirał

admiration (aedmy'rejszyn) s.
podziw; zachwyt; przedmiot podziwu

admire (ed'majer) v. podziwiać

admirer (ed'majrer) s. wielbiciel; wielbicielka

admissible (ed'mysybl) adj. do-
puszczalny; do przyjęcia
admission (ed'myszyn) s. wstęp:
dostęp; przyznanie; uznanie;
(dopływ); bilet wstępu
admission ticket (ed'myszyn'tykyt) bilet wstępu
admit (ed'myt) v. wpuszczać;
uznać; przyjmować; przyznać
admittance (ed'mytens) s. dostęp; przyjęcie;przyznanie się
admonish (ed'monysz) v. upominać; ostrzegać; pouczać
ado (e'du) s. wrzawa; kłopot;
trudności; grymasy; narzekania
adolescence (,aede'lesns) s.
młodość(pokwitanie-dojrzałość)
adolescent (,aede'lesnt) adj.
młodociany; dorastający
adopt (e'dopt) adoptować; przyjmować; akceptować; wybierać
adoption (e'dopszyn) s. adopcja;
adaptacja; przyjęcie; przyspo-
sobienie;akceptacja; wybór
adorable (e'do:rebl) adj. godny
uwielbienia; bardzo miły
adoration (,aede:rejszyn) s.
uwielbienie; wielka miłość
adore (e'do:r) v. czcić; uwielbiać; bardzo lubieć; kochać
adorn (e'do:rn) v. zdobić;
upiększać; być ozdobą
adrift (e'dryft) adv. na fali;
na wodzie bez steru zdany na los
adult ('aedalt) adj. dorosły;
dojrzały; s. osoba dorosła
adulterate (e'dalterejt) v.
fałszować; podrabiać;zatruwać
adultery (e'daltery) s. cudzo-
łóstwo
advance (ed'waens) v. iść naprzód; pospieszać; awansować;
przedkładać; popierać; pożyczać; adj. wysunięty; wczes-
niejszy; w przodzie
advanced (ed'waenst) adj. postępowy; światły; wysunięty
naprzód; stary; przedwczesny
advanced reservation (ed'waenst,
rezeł'wejszyn) rezerwacja
z góry zamówiona

advantage (ed'waentydż) s. korzyść; pożytek; przewaga
advantageous (,aedwaen'tejdżes)
adj. korzystny; zyskowny
adverb ('aedwe:rb) s. przy-
słówek(oznaczający czas,sposób..)
adversary ('aedwersery) s.
przeciwnik; wróg; oponent
adverse ('aedwe:rs) adj. wrogi;
przeciwny; szkodliwy;niekorzystny
advertise ('aedwertajz) v.
ogłaszać; reklamować
advertisement ('edwertysment)
s. ogłoszenie; reklama
advertising ('aedwertajzyng)s.
reklama; ogłoszenia handlowe
advice (ed'wajs) s. rada; in-
formacje;porada;pouczenie
advisable (ed'wajzebl) adj.
wskazany; rozsądny;ostrożny
advise (ed'wajz) v. radzić; po-
wiadamiać; pouczać
adviser (ed'wajzer) s. doradca;
radca(prawny etc.)
advocate ('aedwekejt) v. zalecać; bronić;s.rzecznik;orędownik
aerial ('eerjel) adj. powietrzny; s. antena (radiowa etc.)
aeronautics (eere'no:tyks) s.
aeronautyka; lotnictwo
aeroplane ('eereplejn) s. samolot
aesthetic (i:stetyk) adj.
estetyczny;wrażliwy na piękno
afar (e'fa:r) adv. daleko;z daleka
affair (e'feer) s. sprawa; interes; romans; przedsięwzięcie
affect (e'fekt) v. wpływać; oddziaływać;wzruszać;dotyczyć;udawać
affected (e'fektyd) adj. dotknięty;przejęty; sztuczny
affection (e'fekszyn) s. uczucie;
przywiązanie; choroba; miłość
affectionate (e'fekszynyt) adj.
czuły; kochający;tkliwy;przywiązany
affidavit (aef'ydejwyt) s. poręczenie pod przysięgą
affinity (e'fynyty) s. pokrewieństwo;przyciąganie;powinowactwo
affirm (e'fe:rm) v. potwierdzać; zapewniać;zaręczać

affirmation (,aefe:r'mejszyn) s.
twierdzenie; oświadczenie; zapewnienie;zatwierdzenie(wyroku)
affirmative (e'fe:rmetyw) adj.
pozytywny; twierdzący
afflict (e'flykt) v. gnębić
affliction (e'flykszyn) s. przygnębienie; choroba;ból;cierpienie
affluence ('aefluens) s. dostatek; bogactwo;obfitosc;natłok
affluent ('aefluent) adj. zamożny; s. dopływ (rzeki)
afford (e'fo:rd) v. zdobyć się;
dostarczyć; stać na coś
affront (e'frant) v. znieważać
afficionado (éfisienado) s.
entuzjasta (walki byków etc.)
aflame (e'flejm) adv. w ogniu;
w podnieceniu
afraid (e'frejd) adj. przestra-
szony;wyrażający rezerwę
African ('aefryken) adj. afrykański
Afro ('aefro) s. (niby) styl
afrykański (uczesania,ubioru)
after ('a:fte:r) prep. po; za;
odnośnie; według;poniekąd
after all ('a:fte: o:l) prep.
jednak; przecież;mimo wszystko
after that ('a:fte: daet)
następnie ; potem
afternoon ('a:fte:rnu:n) s. popołudnie; adj. popołudniowy
afterwards ('aftełerdz) adv.
później; potem; następnie
again (e'gen) adv. ponownie;
znowu;na nowo;więcej;ponadto
again and again (e'gen end
e'gen) wciąż; ciągle
against (e'genst) prep. przeciw;
wbrew; na; pod;na wypadek
age (ejdż) s. wiek;stulecie;czasy
aged ('ejdżyd) adj. stary; sędziwy;wiekowy;w podeszłym wieku
age ten (ejdż ten) w wieku lat
dziesięciu
agency ('ejdżensy) s. ajencja;
działanie;pośrednictwo
agenda (e'dżende) s. agenda;
lista;porządek dzienny
agent ('ejdżent) s. pośrednik;
ajent; czynnik;przedstawiciel

aggravate ('aegrewejt) v. pogarszać; rozjątrzać;denerwować
aggression (e'greszyn) s. napaść; agresja;napastliwość
aggressive (e'gresyw) adj. napastliwy; zaczepny;napastniczy
aggressor (e'grese:r) s. napastnik; agresor
aghast (e'gaest) adj. przerażony; osłupiały;skonsternowany
agile ('aedżyl) adj. zwinny;
obrotny;zręczny;ruchliwy
agitate ('aedżytejt) v. poruszać; miotać; agitować
agitation (,aedżytejszyn) s.
poruszenie; agitacja;podniecenie
agitator ('aedżytejter) s. agitator; mieszadło; trzęsarka
agnostic (áegnostyk) s. agno-
styk; adj. agnostyczny
ago (e'gou) adv. przed; ...temu
agonize ('aegenajz) v. męczyć
się; dręczyć się
agony ('aegeny) s. śmiertelna
męka; agonia;katusze; spazm
agree (e'gri:) v. godzić się;
zgadzać się; uzgadniać
agree about (e'gri: e'baut) v.
zgadzać się co do...
agree to (e'gri: tu) v. zgadzać się na...
agreeable (e'gri:ebl) adj.
zgodny; miły; chętny;sympatyczny
agreement (e'gri:ment) s. zgoda; umowa;porozumienie;układ
agricultural(,aegry'kalczerel)
adj. rolniczy; rolny
agriculture (,aegry'kalczer) s,
rolnictwo; uprawa ziemi
agriculturist (,aegry'kalcze-
ryst) s. rolnik
ague ('ejgju:) s. febra; dreszcze;malaria; zimnica
ahead (e'hed) adv. naprzód; dalej; na przedzie;z przodu
aid (ejd) s. pomoc; pomocnik;
v. pomagać; subwencjonować
aide (ejd) s. asystent;pomocnik
ailing ('ejlyng)s. choroba
aim (ejm) s. zamiar; cel;
v. celować; mierzyć; zamierzać;skierować;dążyć

aimless (éjmlys) adj. bezcelowy
air (eer) s. 1. powietrze;
  2. mina; postawa;wygląd;nastrój
air ('eer) v. 1. wietrzyć;
  2. obnosić się; nadawać
air base ('eerbejs) s. baza lotnicza (wojskowa)
air brake ('eer,brejk) s. hamulec na sprężone powietrze
air-conditioning (,eer-ken'dy-
  szynyn) s. klimatyzacja
air compressor (,eer-kem'presor)
  s. sprężarka
aircraft ('eer-kra:ft) s. samolot;lotnictwo(wiedza,flota etc.)
aircraft carrier ('eer-kra:ft'
  kaerje:r) s. lotniskowiec
airfield ('eer-fi:ld) s. lotnisko (do startowania i lądowania)
air force ('eer fo:rs) s. lotnictwo (wojskowe)
airline ('eerlajn) s. linia lotnicza (system transportu)
airmail ('eermejl) s. poczta
  lotnicza
airplane ('eerplejn) s. samolot
airport ('eerpo:rt) s. lotnisko
air raid ('eerejd) atak lotniczy
air show ('eerszou) pokaz lotniczy
airsickness ('eersyknys) s.cho-
  roba powietrzna
airtight ('eertajt) adj. hermetyczny
air traffic ('eer-traefyk) ruch
  lotniczy(samolotów, pasażerów)
airway ('eerłej) linia lotnicza
airy ('eery) adj. przewiewny
aisle (ajl) s. przejście; nawa
  boczna(kościoła)
ajar (e'dża:r) adv. uchylony;
  pół otwarty;nieco otwarty
akin (e'kyn) adj. pokrewny
alacrity (e'laekryty) s. ochota;
  gotowość; żwawość; skwapliwość
alarm (e'la:rm) s. popłoch;
  strach; sygnał alarmowy;trwoga;
  v. alarmować; trwożyć;płoszyć
alarm clock (e'la:rm,klok) s.
  budzik
alas ! (e'laes)excl. niestety
alcohol ('aelkehol) s. alkohol;
  spirytus

alcoholic (,aelke'holyk) s.
  alkoholik; adj.alkoholowy
alcove ('aelkouw) s. altanka;
  alkowa; nisza
alder ('o:lder) s. olcha; ol-
  sza
ale (ejl) s, piwo (gorzkie,
  angielskie)
alert (e'le:t) adj. czujny;
  raźny; żwawy; s.alarm
algae ('aeldży:) pl. glony;
  algi
alias ('ejliaes) adv. inaczej;
  alias; vel; s. pseudonim
alibi ('aelybaj) s. alibi; wymówka; v.usprawiedliwiać się
alien ('ejljen) adj. obcy
alienate ('ejljenejt) v. od-
  stręczać; odrywać; zrażać
alike (e'lajk) adj. jednakowy;
  podobny; adv. tak samo; jedna-
  ko; podobnie; zarówno; także
alimony ('aelimeny) s. alimenty
alive (e'lajw) adj. żywy; żyjący; ożywiony;pełen życia
all (o:l) adj.& pron. cały;
  wszystek; każdy; adv. całkowicie; w pełni; s. wszystko
all of us (o:l ow as) my
  wszyscy; my wszyscy razem
all at once (o:l et łans)wszys-
  cy na raz; wszyscy jednocześnie
all the better (o:l dy beter)
  tym lepiej
all told (o:l told) wszystkiego
  razem ; razem wziąwszy
alleged(e'ledżd) adj. rzekomy
alleviate (e'li:wjejt) v. łagodzić; zmniejszać
alley ('aely)s. aleja; przejście; zaułek; boczna ulica ;tor
alliance (e'lajens) s. związek;
  sojusz; powinowactwo;skoligacenie
allot (e'lot) v. przydzielać;
  losować; wyznaczać;wyasygnować
allotment (e'lotment) s. przydział; działka; asygnata
allow (e'lau) v. pozwalać; użyczać; uznawać; uwzględniać
allow for (e'lau fo:r) v.
  uwzględniać; dawać (czas)
allowance (e'lauens) s. przydział; pozwolenie; kieszonkowe

alloy ('aeloj) s. stop; próba; domieszka;stop kilku metali

all—round (o:l-raund) adj. wszechstronny; universalny

allude (e'lu:d) v. robić aluzje

allure (e'lju:) v. wabić; kusić; oczarować;nęcić;znęcić;zwabić

allusion (e'lu:żyn) s. aluzja; przymówka;przytyk;napomknienie

ally (e'laj) v. sprzymierzać się; łączyć;połączyć;skoligacić

ally ('aelaj) s. sprzymierze- niec; sojusznik

almighty (o:l'majty) adj. wszechmogący;ogromny;straszliwy

almond (am 'end) s. migdał

almost ('o:lmoust) adv. prawie; niemal;jak gdyby;o mało;ledwo

almost never ('o:lmoust'newer) prawie nigdy; rzadko kiedy

alms (a:mz) s, jałmużna

aloft (e'loft) adv. wysoko;hen; w górze; w górę; do góry

alone (e'loun) adj. sam; samot- ny;w pojedynkę;sam jeden;jedyny

along (e'lo:ng) adv. naprzód; wzdłuż; z sobą

alongside (e'lo:ngsajd) adv. obok; wzdłuż ;przy(molu,burcie...)

aloof (e'lu:f) adv. z dala; na uboczu; z daleka

aloud (e'laud) adv. głośno

alphabet ('aelfebyt) s. alfabet

already (o:l'redy) adv. już; wcześniej;poprzednio:uprzednio

also (o:lsou) adv. także;również

altar ('o:lter) s, ołtarz

alter ('o:lter) v. zmieniać; poprawiać:odmieniać;przemienić

alteration (o:lte'rejszyn) s. zmiana; poprawka;przemiana

alternate ('o:lternejt) v. zmie- niać się (kolejno);brać kolejno

alternate ('o:lternyt) adj. co drugi; na zmianę;kolejny

alternating current (o:lternej- tyngkarent) prąd zmienny

alternative (ol-ter'netyw) s. alternatywa; adj.alternatywny

although (o:lzou) conj. chociaż

altitude ('aeltytju:d) s. wy- sokość(nad poziomem morza)

altogether (o:lte'gedze:r) adv. zupełnie; całkowicie

aluminum (e'lumynem) s. aluminium

alumnus (e'lamnes) s. były student uczelni

always ('o:lłejz) adv. stale; zawsze;ciągle;wciąż

am (aem) v. jestem

amass (e'maes) v. gromadzić

amateur ('aemecze:r)s, miłos- nik; amator;dyletant

amaze (e'mejz) v. zdumiewać; zadziwiać;wprawić w zdumienie

amazement (e'mejzment) s. zdu- mienie; osłupienie

amazing (e'mejzyng)adj. zdumie- wający; zadziwiający

ambassador (aem'baesede:r)s. ambasador; poseł

amber ('aembe:r)s. bursztyn

ambient ('aembient) adj. ota- czający

ambiguous (aem'bygjues) adj. dwuznaczny;mętny;zagadkowy

ambition (aem'byszyn) s. ambi- cja;chęć wybicia się

ambitious (aem'byszes) adj. ambitny; żądny

ambulance ('aembjulens) s. ambulans

ambush ('aembusz) s. zasadzka

amen (ej'men) amen

amend (e'mend) v. poprawiać

amendment (e'mendment) s. po- prawa; ulepszenie; uzupełnienie

amends (e'mendz) s. odszkodowa- nie; zadośćuczynienie

American (e'meryken) s. Amery- kanin; adj. amerykański

amiable ('ejmjebel) adj. miły; uprzejmy: sympatyczny

amicable ('aemykebl) adj. po- lubowny; przyjacielski

amid (e'myd) prep. wśród; po- śród; między; pomiędzy

amidst (e'mydst) prep. wśród; pośród; między; pomiędzy

amiss (e'mys) adv. na opak; błędnie; źle;niefortunnie

ammo ('aemou) s. amunicja

ammunition (,aemju'nyszyn) s. amunicja

amnesty (aemnysty) s. ułaskawienie; amnestia
among (e'mang) prep. wśród; pomiędzy; miedzy; pośrod
amongst (e'mangst) prep. wśród;
pomiędzy; miedzy; pośrod
amount (e'maunt) v. wynosic;
s. suma; kwota; wynik
amount to (e'maunt tu) v. wynosic (w sumie)
ample ('aempl) adj. rozległy;
dostatni:hojny:suty;obfity
amplifier ('aemplyfajer) v.
wzmacniacz; amplifikator
amplify ('aemplyfy) v. rozszerzać; wzmacniac; przesadzać
amplitude ('aemplytju:d) s.
amplituda; wielkość; obfitość
amply ('aemply) adv. obszernie;
szeroko;zupełnie wystarczajaco
amulet ('aemjulyt) s. amulet
amuse (e'mju:z) v. bawic;ubawić;
smieszyc: zabawic;rozśmieszać
amusement (e'mju:zment) s. rozrywka; zabawa
amusing (e'mju:zyng)adj. zabawny: smieszny
an (aen; en) art. jeden ;jakiś
anemia (e'ni:mja) s. anemia
anesthetic (e'nystetyk) s.
środek znieczulający
analogous (e'naeleges) adj.
analogiczny; zbieżny
analogy (e'naeledży) s. podobieństwo; analogia
analysis (e'naelysys) s. analiza
analyze (e'naelajz) v. analizować; rozpatrywać; zanalizować
anathema (e'naetyma) s, klątwa
anatomize (e'naetemajz) v. rozbierać; anatomizować
anatomy (e'naetemy) s. anatomia
ancestor ('aensester) s. przodek
ancestry ('aensestry) s. przod-
kowie; starożytność rodu
anchor ('aenker) s. kotwica
anchovy ('aenchewy) s. sardela
ancient ('ejnszent) adj. starodawny; stary;sędziwy;wiekowy
and (aend; end) conj. i; coraz
anecdote ('aenyk,dout)s. dykte-
ryjka ; anegdota

anew (e'nju:) adv. na nowo
angel ('ejndźl) s. anioł
anger ('eanger) s. gniew;
złość;v.gniewac;irytować
angina (aendżajna) s. angina
angle ('aengl) s. kąt; narożnik; kątówka v. kluczyc
Anglican ('aenglyken) adj.
anglikanski
Anglo-Saxon (aenglou'saeksen)
adj. anglo-saski
angry (aengry) adj. zagniewany
anguish (aengłysz) s. udręka;
mękac;udręczenie;boleśc;ból
angular ('aengjuler) adj. kanciasty; narożny; kątowy; gra-
niasty
animal ('aenyml) s. zwierzę;
stworzenie;adj.zwierzęcy
animate ('aenymejt) v. ożywiac;
adj. ożywiony; żywy
animated cartoon ('aenymejtyd
'ka:rtu:n) film rysunkowy;kres-
ówka
animation (,aeny'mejszyn) s.
ożywianie; ożywienie; żywość
animosity (,aeny'mosyty) s.
uraza; niechęć; animozja
ankle ('aenkl) s. kostka u sto-
py:staw między stopą i łydką
annex ('aeneks) v. przyłączac;
wcielac;s.przybudówka;załącznik
annihilate (e'najlejt) v. unicestwić; niszczyć;niweczyć
anniversary (,aeny've:rsery) s.
rocznica adj. doroczny(obchód)
annotation (,aene'tejszyn) s.
uwaga; komentarz;przypis
announce (e'nauns) v. zapowiadać; ogłaszać;oznajmiać
announcement (e'naunsment) s.
zapowiedź; zawiadomienie
announcer (e'naunser) s.
1. zapowiadacz; 2. (radio)
speaker; konferansjer
annoy (e'noj) v. dokuczać;
draznić; nękać;trapić;martwić
annoyance (e'nojens) s. udręka;
przykrość;irytacja ; kłopot
annoyed (e'nojd) adj. rozgnie-
wany; rozdrażniony;strapiony
annual (e'aenjuel) adj. coroczny; s. rocznik;jednorocznik

annuity (e'njuyty) s. renta
roczna; renta dożywotnia
annul (e'nal) v. unieważniac;
anulowac; skasowac; kasować
anodyne ('aenedajn) s. anodyna;
środek od bólu,łagodzący
anomalous (e'nomeles) adj. nienormalny; nietypowy
anonym ('aenenym) s. anonim
anonymous (e'nonymes) adj. bez-
imienny; anonimowy
another (e'nadzer) adj.& pron.
drugi;inny; jeszcze jeden
another time (e'nadzer,tajm)
kiedy indziej;innym razem
answer ('aenser) s. odpowiedż;
v. odpowiadac; spełnic(prośbę)
answer for ('aenser fo:r) v.
odpowiadac za(przed kimś)
ant (aent) s. mrówka
antagonist (aen'taegenyst) s.
przeciwnik; przeciwniczka
antagonize (aen'taege'najz) v.
zrażac; narażac; zwalczać
antelope ('aentyloup) s. anty-
lopa
anterior (aen'tierjer) adj. po-
poprzedni;uprzedni;wcześniejszy
anthem ('aentem) s. hymn narodowy
anti ('aenty) pre . przeciw-
anti-aircraft ('aentaj'e:r-
kra:ft) adj. przeciwlotniczy
antibiotic ('aentybajotyk) s.
antybiotyk
antic ('aentyk) adj. dziwaczny;
groteskowy; s. figiel; dzi-
wactwa; błazeństwo
anticipate (aen'tysypejt) v.
przewidywać; uprzedzac
anticipation (aen'tysypejszyn)
s. uprzedzenie; przewidywanie;
przyspieszenie;oczekiwanie
anticlimax ('aenty'klajmaeks)
s. rozczarowanie; zawod
anticyclone (,aenty'sajkloun)
s. antycyklon; wyż(atmosf.)
antidote ('aentydout) s. odtrutka ; antidotum
antifreeze('aentyfri:z) s. mieszanka niemarznąca
antiknock ('aentynok) s. mieszanka przeciwstukowa

antipathy (aen'typety) s. odraza; niechęc (do kogoś)
antiquated ('aentykłejtyd) adj.
przestarzały; staroswiecki
antique (aen'ti:k)adj.stary;
starożytny; staromodny
antiquity (aen'tykłyty) s. sta-
rożytnosc; zabytki
antiseptic (aenty'septyk) adj.
antysyptyk; przeciwgnilny
antlers ('aentlerz) pl. rogi
(np. jelenia)
anvil ('aenvyl) s. kowadło
anxiety (aeng'zajety) s. niepokój; troska; pożądanie
anxious ('aenkszes) adj. zaniepokojony; zabiegający;pragnący
anxious about ('aenkszes e'baut)
trosliwy o...;niepokojący się o...
anxious for ('aenkszes fo:r)
pragnący bardzo czegoś
anxious to ('aenkszes tu) pragnący żeby;mający ochotę na
any ('eny) pron. jakikolwiek;
któryś; jakis;żaden;lada;byle
any farther ('eny fa:rdzer) trochę dalej;nieco dalej
any more ('eny mo:r) trochę
więcej; teraz; obecnie
anybody ('eny'body) pron. ktos;
ktokolwiek; każdy; nikt
anyhow ('enyhau) adv. jakkolwiek
anyone ('enyłan) pron. ktokolwiek; każdy; ktos; nikt
anything ('enytyng)pron. coś;
cokolwiek; wszystko(oprócz);nic
anything else ('enytyngels)
jeszcze cos; cos więcej
anyway ('enyłej) adv. w każdym
razie; jakkolwiek;byle jak
anywhere ('enyhłeer) adv.gdzie-
kolwiek;byle gdzie; nigdzie
apart (e'pa:rt) adv. osobno;
niezależnie;na boku;od siebie
apart from (e'pa:rt, from) niezależnie od...;poza;oprócz;prócz
apartment (e'pa:rtment) s.
mieszkanie; izba; pokój
apartment house (e'pa:rtment,
haus) blok mieszkalny;kamienica
apathetic (aepe'tetyk) adj.
apatyczny;obojętny;bez uczuć

ape (ejp) s. małpa (bezogonowa)
v. małpować;naśladować;błaznować
apex ('ejpeks) s. szczyt; czu-
bek; wierzchołek
apiary ('ejpjery) s. pasieka
apiece (e'pi:s) adv. na osobę;
od sztuki;za sztukę; każdy
aplomb (e'plom) s. pewność siebie; opanowanie; zimna krew
apologize (e'poledżajz) v.
usprawiedliwiać; przepraszać
apology (e'poledży) s. usprawiedliwienie; obrona;przeprosiny
apoplexy ('aepepleksy) s. apo-
pleksja ; udar
apostle (e'posl) s. apostoł
apostolic (,aepe'stolyk) adj.
apostolski
apostrophe (e'postrefy) s.
apostrof; apostrofa
appal (e'po:l) v. przerażać
apparatus (aepe'rejtes) s. aparat; urządzenie;przyrząd;organ
apparent (e'paerent) adj. jawny; pozorny; oczywisty;widoczny
appeal (e'pi:l) v. apelować;
odwoływać się;uciekać się do
appeal to (e'pi:l tu) v. zwracać się do...;zwracać się z apelem
appear (e'pier) v. ukazywać się;
zjawiać się;pokazywać się
appearance (e'pierens) s. wygląd;
pozór; wystąpienie;zjawienie się
appease (e'pi:z) v. łagodzić;
uśmierzać; zaspakajać;ugłaskać
append (e'pend) v. dołączać; do-
czepiać;dodawać;zawieszać
appendicitis (ependy'sajtys) s.
zapalenie wyrostka robaczkowego
appendix (e'pendyks) s. dodatek;
uzupełnienie;ślepa kiszka
appetite ('aepitajt) s. apetyt
appetizing ('aepitajzing) adj.
apetyczny; smakowity
applaud (e'plo:d) v. oklaskiwać;
klaskać;bić brawo;przyklasnąć
applause (e'plo:z) s. aplauz;
oklaski;poklask;pochwała;aprobata
apple ('aepl) s. jabłko
apple-pie('aeplpaj) s. placek
jabłkowy ; szarlotka

applesauce ('aepl so:s) s.
purée z jabłek
apple tree ('aepltri:) s. jabłoń
appliance (e'plajens) s. przyrząd; urządzenie;akcesoria
applicant ('aeplykent) s. petent; zgłaszający się;kandydat
application (,aeply'kejszyn)
s. podanie; użycie; zastosowanie;przykładanie:pilność
apply (e'plaj) v. używać; stosować; odnosić się;naciskać
apply for (e'plaj fo:r) v. starać się o...;wnosić podanie o
apply to (e'plaj tu) v. zwracać
się do..;zgłaszać się do(o coś)
appoint (e'point) v. mianować;
wyznaczać; ustanawiać;ustalić
appointment (e'pointment) s.
nominacja; oznaczenie czasu
i miejsca; umówione spotkanie
apportion (e'po:rszyn) v. wyznaczać; wydzielać;przydzielać
appreciate (e'pri:szjejt) v.
cenić wysoko; zyskiwać na war-
tości;ocenić; oszacować;docenić
appreciation (e'pri:szjejszyn)
s. ocena; uznanie; wzrost war-
tości;zrozumienie czegoś
apprehend (,aepry'hend) v. ująć;
pojmać; rozumieć
apprehension (,aepry'henszyn) s.
obawa; pojęcie; aresztowanie;lęk
apprehensive (,aepry'hensyw)
adj.obawiający się; pojętny
apprentice (e'prentys) s. czeladnik; uczeń; terminator
apprenticeship (e'prentysszyp)
s. termin;nauka rzemiosła
approach (e'proucz) v. zbliżać
się; podchodzić;s. dostęp
approach road (e'proucz,roud)
droga dojazdowa
appropriate (e'prouprjejt) adj.
właściwy; odpowiedni;stosowny
appropriation (e'prouprejszyn)
s. asygnowanie; przywłaszczenie;przeznaczenie; kredyty
approval (e'pru:wel) s. aproba-
ta; uznanie; zatwierdzenie

approximate (e'proksymyt) adj.
zbliżony; przybliżony; mniej
więcej;v.zbliżać(się);być około

apricot ('ejprykot) s. morela

April ('ejprel) s. kwiecień

apron ('ejpren) s. fartuch;
płyta przednia;przedpole

apropos (aepre'pou) adv. do tego celu; w związku z tym ,,

apt (aept) v. mieć skłonność

apt to (aept tu) v. być skłon-
nym do..;często coś robić

aquarium (e'kłerjem) s. akwarium

aquatic (e'kłaetyk) adj. wodny

aquatic sports (e'kłaetyk
spo:rts) sport wodny

aqueduct ('aekłydakt) s. wodociąg; akwedukty rzymskie

aquiline ('aekłylajn) adj. orli

Arabic (ae'rebyk) adj. arabski

arable ('aerebl) adj. orny

arbitrary ('a:rbytrery) adj. dowolny; samowolny

arbor ('a:rber) s. altanka; wał
napędowy; oś maszyny; drzewo

arc (a:rk) s. łuk

arc lamp (a:rk lemp) lampa łu-
kowa

arcade (a:r'kejd) s. arkada;
podcienie

arch (a:rcz) s. łuk; sklepienie;
podbicie;v. tworzyć łuk

arch (a:rcz) adj.chytry; wierutny;
arcy...;figlarny

archaeologist (a:rky'oledżyst)
s. archeolog

archeology (a:rky'oledży) s.
archeologia

archaic (a:rkejyk) adj. archai-
czny; przestarzały; staroświecki

archangel ('a:rkejndżel) s.
archanioł

archbishop ('a:rczbyszep) s.
arcybiskup

archer ('a:rczer) s. łucznik

archery ('a:rczery) s. łucznic-
two; łuki i strzały

architect ('a:rkytekt) s. architekt;twórca;budowniczy

architecture ('a:rkytekczer) s.
architektura;styl budowy

archives ('a:rkajwz) pl. archi-
wa ; archiwum

archway ('a:rczłej) s. skle-
pione przejście ᐧ brama

arctic ('a:rktyk) adj. arktycz-
ny ; polarny

ardent ('a:rdent) adj. rozpalo-
ny; prażący ;płonący;gorliwy

ardor ('a:rder) s. żar; żarliwość; gorliwość; zapał

arduous ('a:rdżues) adj. mozolny; wytrwały; stromy;żmudny

are (a:r) v. są ;jesteś;jesteście

area ('e:rje) s. obszar; zakres;
powierzchnia;teren;okolica;strefa

Argentine ('a:rdżentajn) adj.
argentyński

argot ('a:rgou) s. żargon
(złodziejski)

argue ('a:rgju:) v. wykazywać;
rozumować; spierać się; rozpatrywać; dowodzić ;udowadniać

argument ('a:rgjument) s. argument; dowód; sprzeczka ;spór

argumentation (,a:rgjumen'tejszyn) s. roztrząsanie; argu-
mentacja; rozumowanie

arid ('aeryd) adj. suchy; jałowy; oschły;wypalony;spieczony

arise, arose, arisen (e'rajz;
e'rouz; e'rɪzn)

arise (e'rajz) v. powstawać;
wstawać; wynikać;nadarzyć się

arithmetic (,aeryt'metyk) s.
rachunki; adj. arytmetyczny;
rachunkowy

ark (a:rk) s. arka; skrzynia

arm (a:rm) s. ramię; odnoga;
konar; rękaw; poręcz

arm (a:rm) v. broń (rodzaj);
uzbrojenie; v. uzbroić; opan-
cerzyć; nastawiać (zapłon)

armament ('a:rmement) s. uzbrojenie; zbrojenia; siły zbrojne

armament race ('a:rmement, rejs)
wyścig zbrojeń

armchair (,a:rm'cze:r) s. fotel

armistice ('a:rmystys) s. zawieszenie broni;rozejm

armor ('a:rmer) s. zbroja;
opancerzenie ;v.zbroić w płyty
pancerne;opancerzać

armored car ('a:rmerd,ca:r)
samochód pancerny

arm-twisting ('a:rm,tłysty∩)
napór na (kogoś); (wykręcanie
ręki);nagabywanie kogoś

arms ('a:rmz) pl. broń; uzbrojenie; herby; herb

army ('a:rmy) s. wojsko; armia

aroma (e'roume) s. aromat

arose (e'rouz) v. powstał;
wstał; wynikł; zob. arise

around (e'raund) prep. dokoła;
naokoło; wokoło; adv. wokół;
tu i tam; około; wszędzie

arousal (e'rauzel) s. pobudze-
nie do czynu (działania)

arouse (e'rauz) v. pobudzić;
budzić; wzniecać(uczucia)

arraign(e'rejn) v. pozwać;
oskarżyć;atakować pogląd

arrange (e'rejndż) v. układać;
szykować; porządkować;ustalać

arrangement (e'rejndżment) s.
układ; ułożenie się; urządzenie; zaaranżowanie;porządek;szyk

array (e'rej) v. szykować; przybrać; rozmieszczać; s. szyk;
szereg; uszeregowanie;wystawa

arrears (e'rierz) pl. zaległości;
długi;zaległe prace(płatności)

arrest (e'rest) s. areszt;
aresztowanie; zatrzymanie;
v. aresztować; zatrzymywać;
wstrzymywać;przyciągać(uwagę)

arrival (e'rajwel) s. przyjazd;
przybysz; rzecz nadeszła

arrive (e'rajw) v. przybyć;
dojść; osiągnąć;wspólnie ustalać

arrive at (e'rajw,aet) v. dojsć
do...;wspólnie ustalać

arrogance ('aeregens) s. zarozumiałość; buta; arogancja

arrogant ('aeregent) adj. butny; arogancki; wyniosły

arrow ('aerou) s. strzała;
strzałka (kierunkowa)

arrow head ('aerou hed) s. grot

arse (a:rs) s. vulg. rzyć; zadek; dupa ; dupsko

arsenal ('a:rsynl) s. arsenał

arsenic ('a:rsnyk) s. arszenik;
arsen; ('a:rsenyk) adj. arse-
nowy

arson ('a:rsen)s. podpalenie
(zbrodnia); podpalanie

art (a:rt) s. sztuka; chytrość;
zręczność; rzemiosło;fortel

arterial (a:r'tyerjal) adj.
tętniczy; magistralny

arterial road(a:r'tyerjal,roud)
magistrala;główna szosa

artery (a:rtery) s. arteria;
tętnica; arteria ruchu

artful ('a:rtful) adj. chytry;
zręczny; pomysłowy;dowcipny

article ('a:rtykl) s. rodzajnik;
artykuł; warunek;paragraf;temat

articulate (a:rtykjulejt) v.
wyrażać jasno; adj. artykuło-
wany; wyraźny;stawowy

artifact (,a:rty'faekt) s. wytwór ludzkiej ręki

artificial(,a:rty'fyszel) adj.
sztuczny;udany;symulowany

artillery (a:r'tylery) s. artyleria

artisan ('a:rtyzaen) s. rzemieślnik

artist ('a:rtist) s. artysta;
artystka

artiste (a:r'ty:st) s. artysta;
odtwórca; artysta estradowy

artless ('artlys) adj. niewinny; niedołężny;szczery;otwarty

as (aez; ez) adv. pron. conj;
jak; tak; co; jako; jaki; skoro; żeby; choć; z (dniem)

as... as (ez...ez) tak jak

as far as (ez fa:r ez) co do

as many (ez meny) tak wiele

as well (ez łel) również

as well as (ez łel ez) jak także ; tak jak; jak również

as for (ez fo:r) co się tyczy

asbestos (aez'bestes) s. azbest

ascend (e'send) v. piąć się;
iść w górę; wznosić się; wracać w przeszłość; wstępować

ascension (e'senszyn) s. wznoszenie się; Wniebowstąpienie

ascent (e'sent) s. wzlot;
wzrost;stok; postęp;wchodzenie

ascertain (aeser'tejn) v.
stwierdzać; ustalać;konstatować

ascetic (e'setyk) s. asceta;
adj. ascetyczny;odmawiający sobie

ascribe (e'skrajb) v. przypisywać; przypisać(coś komuś)
aseptic ('eseptyk) adj. jałowy;
wyjałowiony; aseptyczny
ash (aesz) s. popiół ;jesion
ashamed (e'szejmd) adj. zawstydzony ;zażenowany
ashamed of (e'szejmd ow)adj.
wstydzący się czegoś
ash can (aesz kaen) wiadro na
śmieci; wiadro na popiół
ashen ('aeszen) adj. popielaty
ashes ('aeszyz) s. popioły
ashore (e'szo:r) adv. na brzeg;
na brzegu ; na ląd; na lądzie
ashtray ('aesztrej) s. popielniczka
Ash Wednesday (,aesz'łenzdy) -
Środa Popielcowa
Asiatic (,ej ży'atyk) adj. azja-
tycki
aside (e'sajd) adv. na stronę;
na stronie; na boku;na uboczu
aside, from (e'sajd,from) adv.
oprócz; z wyjątkiem; poza:prócz
asinine ('aesynajn) adj. ośli;
głupi; idiotyczny
ask (aesk) v. pytać ;zapytywać
ask a question ('aesk ej'kłesz-
czyn) stawiać pytanie; pytać
ask to dinner ('aesk tu'dyner)
zapraszać na obiad
ask for ('aesk fo:r) prosić o...
askance (es'kaens) adv. z ukosa
zezem ; niepewnie; podejrzliwie
askew (es'kju:) adv. krzywo;
skośnie ; z ukosa
aslant (e'sla:nt) adv. ukośnie;
skośnie ; na ukos; w poprzek
asleep (e'sli:p) adv. we śnie;
adj. śpiący;zdrętwiały;ścierpły
asparagus (es'paereges) s. szparag
aspect ('aespekt) s. aspekt; wygląd; wyraz; faza; postać;
strona;mina;przejaw;wystawa domu
aspen ('aespen) s. osika; osina
asphalt ('aesfo:lt) s. asfalt
aspire (es'pajer) v. dążyć; marzyć; wzdychać do...
aspire after (es'pajer'a:fter)
aspirować; dążyć do (czegoś);
mieć aspiracje żeby...

ass (aes) s. osioł;wulg.: dupa
assail (e'sejl) v. napadać;
przystępować;atakować;uderzać
assailant (e'sejlent) s. napastnik
assassin (e'saesyn) s. morderca (najęty); zamachowiec
assassinate (e'saesynejt) v.
zamordować; dokonać zamachu
assassination (e,saesy'nejszyn)
s. morderstwo;zabójstwo;zamach
assault (e'sa:lt) s. napad;
atak; zgwałcenie;v.atakować;bić
assemblage (e'semblydż) s. zebranie; zbiór; zmontowanie
assemble (e'sembl) v. zbierać;
montować;nagromadzać;złożyć
assembly (e'sembly) s. zebranie; zbiórka; montaż
assembly line (e'sembly,lajn)
taśma montażowa;linia montażowa
assent (e'sent) s. zgoda; pogodzenie się;v.zgadzać się;uznawać
assent to (e'sent tu) v. zgadzać się na coś;zatwierdzać coś
assert (e'se:rt) v. twierdzić;
upominać się;dowieść;stawiać się
assess (e'ses) v. szacować;
oceniać; wymierzać; opodatkować;nałożyć podatek
assets ('aesets) pl. własność;
aktywa; wartościowi pracownicy
assign (e'sajn) v. przydzielać;
ustalać; odnosić; przekazywać
assignment (e'sajnment) s. przy-
dzielenie; przypisanie; przekazanie;przydział;podział
assimilate (e'symylejt) v. upodabniać; wcielać; wchłaniać;
asymilować;przyswajać sobie
assist (e'syst) v. pomagać;
brać udział; być przy
assistance (e'systens) s. pomoc;
asysta; wsparcie
assistant (e'systent) s. asystent; pomocnik;adj.pomocniczy
assizes (e'sajzyz) pl. okresowe
sesje sądu (wyjazdowe)w Anglii
associate (e'souszjejt) s. towarzysz; wspólnik-sprzymierze-
niec; rzecz związana z czyms
v. łączyć;obcować ; kojarzyć;
brać do spółki;adj.towarzyszący

association (e,soušzy'ejszyn) s.
łączenie; współpraca; kojarzenie; przyłączanie sie ;związek

assort (e'so:rt) v. sortowac;
dobierać; obcować klasyfikować

assorted (e'so:rtyd) adj. dobrany; posortowany; mieszany

assortment (e'so:rtment) s.
asortyment; wybór; sortowanie

assume (e'sju:m) v. zakładać;
obejmować; przybierać; przypuszczać ;wdziewać;udawać

assurance (e'szu: rens) s. zapewnienie; pewność; ubezpieczenie

assure (e'szu: r) v. zapewniać;
ubezpieczać zabezpieczać

assured (e'szu: rd) adj. pewny
(siebie); s. ubezpieczony

asthma (aesma) s. dusznica;
astma ; dychawica

astigmatic (,aestyg'maetyk) adj.
astygmatyczny

astir (e'ste:r) adv. poruszony;
w ruchu; na nogach ;ożywiony

astonish (es'tonysz) v. zadziwiać; zdumiewać ;zdziwić

astonished (es'tonyszt) adj.
zdumiony ; bardzo zdziwiony

astonishment (es'tonyszment) s.
zdumienie ; zdziwienie

astray (es'trej) adv. na błędną
drogę; na bezdrożu ;na manowce

astride (es'trajd) adv. okrakiem;
rozstawionymi nogami

astringent (es'tr: ndżent) adj.
ściągający; surowy ;wstrzymujący

astrodome('aestre,doum)s. astro-
kopuła (nad stadionem sportowym)

astrologer (es'troledżer) s.
astrolog

astronaut ('aestreno:t) s. astro-
nauta

astute (es'tu:t) adj. bystry;
przebiegły ;wnikliwy

asunder (e'sander) adv. oddziel-
nie; na boki; na strony

asylum (e'sajlem) s. azyl; schronisko ; przytułek; schronienie

at (aet; et) prep. w; na; u;
przy; pod; z ;za; do; o; po

ate (ejt) v. jadłem; jadłes; jadl
etc; zob. eat

athlete ('aeŧli:t) s. atleta;
siłacz; sportowiec

athletic ('aeŧ'letyk) adj.
atletyczny; sportowy

athletics (aeŧ'letyks) pl.atle-
tyka; sport;wychowanie fizyczne

Atlantic (et'laentyk) adj.
atlantycki

atlas ('aetles) s. atlas

atmosphere('aetmesfier) s.
atmosfera ;otoczenie;nastrój

atoll ('aetol) s, atol

atom ('aetem) s. atom

atom bomb ('aetem bom) s. bomba atomowa

atomic (e'tomyk) adj. atomowy

atomic age (e'tomyk ejdż)
epoka atomowa

atomic pile (e'tomyk pajl)
stos atomowy

atomic weight (e'tomyk łejt)
ciężar atomowy

atomize ('aetemajz) v. rozbijać
na atomy ; rozpylać

atomizer ('aetemajzer) s. rozpylacz (cieczy)

atone (e'toun) v. odpokutować;
okupić; załagodzić

atrocious (e'trousze) adj.
potworny; okropny ;skandaliczny

atrocity (e'trosyty) s. okrucieństwo ;okrutny czyn;ohyda

attach (e'taecz) v. przywiązywać; przyczepiać; przydzielać;
łączyć ;przymocowywać;nalepiać

attachment (e'taeczment) s. załącznik; przymocowanie ;więź

attack (e'taek) v. napadać;
atakować; s. atak; uderzenie

attempt (e'tempt) v. usiłować;
czynić zamach; próbować
s. próba; usiłowanie; zamach

attend (e'tend) v. uczęszczać;
leczyć; obsługiwać ;towarzyszyć

attendance (e'tendens) s. obsługa; opieka; uczęszczanie

attendant (e'tendent) s. obecny; służący ;adj.towarzyszący

attention (e'tenszyn) s. uwaga;
uprzejmość ;troska;opieka

attentive (e'tentyw) adj. uważny; gorliwy; uprzejmy ;pilny

attest (e'test) v. poświadczyć;
stwierdzać;zalegalizować

attic ('aetyk) s. poddasze;
attyka; strych

attitude ('aetitu:d) s. postawa; ustosunkowanie się;poza

attorney (e'te:rny) s. pełnomocnik; adwokat;prawnik

attract (e'traekt) v. przyciągać;zwabić; być pociągającym

attraction (e'traekszyn) s.
przyciąganie;powab;urok;atrakcja

attractive (e'traektyw) adj. pociągający;przyciągajacy; miły

attribute ('aetrybju:t) s, przymiot; cecha;właściwość

attribute (e'trybju:t) v. przypisywać komuś; odnosić do czegos

attrition (e'tryszyn) s. wy-
niszczenie; ścieranie; skrucha

auburn ('o:bern) adj. (barwa)
kasztanowa; złotobrązowa

auction ('o:kszyn) s. licytacja;
aukcja

auction off ('o:kszyn of) v.
licytować; sprzedawać na licytacji;wystawiać na licytację

audacious (o:'dejszes) adj. odważny; śmiały; zuchwały

audacity (o:'daesyty) s. śmiałość; odwaga; zuchwałość

audible ('o:dybel) adj. słyszal-
ny:odbierany słuchem

audience ('o:djens) s. publiczność; audiencja

audit ('o:dyt) s. sprawdzenie
rachunków; rozliczenie;
v. kontrolować rachunki

aught (a:t) s. cos; nic; zero

August ('o:gest) s, sierpień

august ('o:gast) adj. wyniosły;
dostojny;majestatyczny

aunt (aent) s. ciotka; wujenka;
stryjenka

aurora (o:'ro:re) s. brzask;
jutrznia; jutrzenka; zorza po-
larna

austere (o:s'tier) adj. surowy;
poważny; prosty;czysto użytkowy

austerity (o:s'teryty) s. surowość; powaga; prostota;srogość;
charakter czysto użytkowy

Australian (o:s'trejljen) adj.
australijski

Austrian ('o:strjen) adj.
austriacki;s. Austryjak

authentic (o:'tentyk) adj.
autentyczny; prawdziwy

author ('o:ter) s. autor; pisarz; sprawca

authoritative (o:'torytejtyw)
adj. stanowczy; miarodajny

authority (o:'toryty) s. władza; autorytet; znaczenie;
powaga;moc rozkazywania

authorize ('o:terajz) v. upoważniać; zatwierdzać;aprobować

authorship ('o:terszyp) s.
autorstwo;zawod pisarza

autobiography ('o:tebaj'ogrefy)
s. autobiografia

autograph ('o:tegraef) s. podpis; autograf

automat ('o:temaet) n . restauracja z automatem na monety

automatic (,o:te'maetyk) adj.
automatyczny; machinalny

automation (,o:te'mejszyn) s.
automatyzacja

automobile ('o:temeby:l) s. samochód; auto

autumn ('o:tem) s. jesień

auxiliary (o:g'zyljery) adj.
pomocniczy

avail (e'wejl) v. pomagać;
znaczyć; być przydatny

available (e'wejlebl) adj.
dostępny; osiągalny

avalanche ('aewelaencz) s. lawina; v. spadać lawiną

avarice ('aewerys) s. chciwość;
skąpstwo

avaricious (,aewe'ryszes) adj.
chciwy; skąpy

avenue ('aewynju:)s. bulwar;
aleja;ulica;dojazd;dojście

average ('aewerydż) adj. przeciętny; średni; s. średnia;
przeciętna; v. osiągać średnio; obliczać średnią; wy-
posrodkowywać;pracować średnio..

averse (e'we:rs) adj. niechętny; czujący odrazę;przeciwny

aversion (e'weržyn) s. odraza;
niechęc

avert (e'we:rt) v. odwracać
(np. myśli; oczy); oddalić(cios)
aviation (,ejwy'ejszyn) s. lotnictwo
aviator ('ejwejter) s.lotnik
avid ('ewyd) adj. chciwy; zachłanny
avoid (e'woyd) v. unikać; uchylać się; stronić
avow (e'wau) v. wyznawać
avowal (e'wauel) s. wyznanie;
przyznanie się; zeznanie
await (e'łejt) v. czekać; oczekiwać;być a oczekiwaniu
awake; awoke; awoke (e'łejk;
e'łouk; e'łouk)
awake (e'łejk) v. budzić się;
otwierać oczy na...; adj. czujny; przebudzony; na jawie
awaken (e'łejkn) v. budzić;
uświadamiać komus (kogoś)
award (e'ło:rd) v. przysądzać;
wyznaczać; s. nagroda; zapłata; grzywna sądowa
aware (e'łeer) adj. świadomy
away (e'łej) adv. precz; z dala
awe (o:) s. lęk; nabożna częsc
awful ('o:ful) adj. straszny;
budzący lęk i szacunek
awhile (e'hłajl) adv. na krótko;
przez chwilę;chwilę; króciutko
awkward ('o:kłerd) adj. niezgrabny; niezdarny; kłopotliwy;
nieporęczny;zaklopotany;trudny
awning ('o:nyng)s. dach z płótna; markiza; zasłona; stora
awoke (e'łouk) v. zbudzony;
zob. awake
awry (e'raj) adv. skosnie; krzywo; na opak; adj. krzywy; błędny; opaczny; wypaczony
ax (aeks) s. siekiera; topór;
v. obcinać siekierą;redukować
axe (aeks) = ax
axes (aeksyz) pl. osie;siekiery
axis ('aeksys) s. oś ;ośka
axle ('aeksel) s. oś (koła);
ośka(łącząca tylnie koła wozu)
azimuth ('aezymet) s. azymut
azure ('aeżer) s. błękit; lazur;
adj. błękitny; lazurowy

b (bi) b; druga litera alfabetu angielskiego
babble ('baebl) v. paplać; gadać; s. paplanina; gadanina
babe (bejb) s. niemowlę
baboon (be'bu:n) s. pawian
baby ('bejby) s. niemowlę
baby carriage ('bejby kaerydź)
s. wózek dziecinny
babyhood ('bejbyhud) s. nie-
mowlęctwo
bachelor ('baecheler) s. niezamężna; nieżonaty; stopien
uniwersytecki (najniższy)
back (baek) s. tył; grzbiet;
v. cofać się; wycofać się
backbone ('baekboun) s. kręgosłup; stos pacierzowy
back door ('baek'do:r) s. tylne
drzwi;adj.zakulisowy;potajemny
backfire ('baek'fajer) s,, wybuch odwrotny;   zawiść; v.
spalić na panewce
background ('baekgraund) s. tło;
dalszy plan; przeszłość czyjaś
back number('baeknamber)s. zaległy numer;stare wydanie pisma
backseat ('baek'si:t) s. tylne
siedzenie;wycofanie się z akcji
backstairs ('baeksteerz) s.
tylne schody;adj.zakulisowy
backstroke ('baek'strouk) s.
pływanie na plecach; rzut
odbity od lewa w tenisie
back tire ('baek'tajer) s. tylna
opona samochodowa (slang)
backward ('baekłerd) adj. tylny; zacofany;zapóźniony
backwards ('baekłerds) adv.
w tyle; odwrotnie; do tyłu
back wheel ('baekhłil) s. tylne
koło (samochodu,ciężarówki)
bacon ('bejkn) s. słonina; boczek; bekon
bacon and eggs ('bejkn end egz)
jajka z boczkiem
bacterium (baek'tierjem) s.
bakteria
bacteria (baek'tierje) pl.
bakterie
bad (baed) adj. zły; niedobry;
przykry;sfałszowany;słaby;zdrożny

bade (baed) v. proponował; oferował cenę; kazał; zob.: bid

badge (baedź) s. odznaka; oznaka (członkostwa, rangi etc.)

badger ('baedżer) s. borsuk; v. zadręczać (narzekaniem)

badly ('baedly) adv. źle; bardzo

badly wounded ('baedl 'Źu:ndyd) ciężko ranny ;ciężko zraniony

badminton ('baedmynten) s. rodzaj tenisa (piłka z piórkiem)

bad mouth('baedmaus) v. oczerniać; obgadywać obmawiać

baffle ('baefl) v. udaremniać; łudzić ;niweczyć;s.przegroda

bag (baeg) s. torba; worek; babsztyl; v. pakować; zwędzić

baggage ('baegydż) s. bagaż

baggage check ('baegydż,czek) kwit bagażowy

baggy ('baegy) adj. workowaty

bag-pipe ('baegpajp) s. kobza

bail (bejl) s. kaucja; poręka

bail out (bejl'ałt) v. zwolnić za kaucją ;wywinąć się z opresji

bailiff ('bejlyf) s. wozny sądowy; komornik ;rządca majątku

bait (bejt) s. przynęta; pokusa

bake (bejk) v. piec; wypalać

baker ('bejker) s. piekarz

bakery (bejkery) s. piekarnia

baking powder ('bejkyŋ,pałder) proszek do pieczenia

balance ('baelens) s. waga; bilans; równowaga; v. równoważyć; bilansować; wahać się

bald (bo:ld) adj. łysy ;jawny

bale (bejl) s. zwój płótna; bela; v. zob. bail

balk (bo:k) v. opierać się; przeszkadzać; zniechęcać; s. belka ;miedza; zawada

ball (bo:l) s. 1. piłka; pocisk; kłębek; 2. bal;zabawa taneczna

ballad ('baeled) s. ballada; pieśń (sentymentalna opisowa)

ballast ('baelest) s. balast; v. obciążać balastem

ball bearing ('bo:l'bearyŋ) łożysko kulkowe

ballet ('baelej) s. balet ; zespół baletowy(tancerzy)

ball game('bo:lgejm) s. rozgrywka; gra w piłkę

ballistic (be'lystyk)adj. balistyczny

balloon (be'lu:n) s. balon

ballot ('bealet) s. (tajne) głosowanie; kartka; v. tajnie głosować

ballot box ('baeletboks) s. urna wyborcza

ball-point pen ('bo:l-point-pen) s. kulkowy pisak;długopis

balm (ba:m) s. balsam

balmy ('ba:my) adj. błogi; balsamiczny

balustrade (,baeles'trejd) s. poręcz; balustrada

bamboo (baem'bu:) s. bambus

ban (baen) s. zakaz; klątwa; v. zabraniać;wyjąć spod prawa

banana (be'na:ne) s. banan

band (baend) s. szajka; kapela; taśma; v. wiązać się; przepasywać opaską ;zrzeszać

bandage ('baendydż) s. bandaż; v. bandażować ; obandażować

bandmaster ('baend,ma:ster) s. kapelmistrz

bandstand ('baendstaend) s. estrada

bang (baeŋ) s. huk; zryw; uciecha; bęc; v. trzaskać ;walnąć

banish ('baenysz) v. wygnac; usunąć; wykluczać ;wypędzać

banishment ('baenyszment) s. wygnanie ; banicja

banisters ('baenystez) pl. banistry (schodów); poręcze

banjo ('baendżou) s. rodzaj gitary okrągłej pokrytej skórą

bank ('baeŋk) s.1.brzeg;Żacha;nasyp; szkarpa; 2. bank; 3. stoł roboczy; 4. rząd 5.nachylenie toru v. 1. prowadzić bank; 2. składać w banku; 3. piętrzyć; pochylać; 4. polegać 5.obwałować

bank bill ('baeŋk,byl) s. banknot

banker ('baeŋker) s. bankier

banking ('baeŋkyŋ)s. bankowość

bank note('baeŋknout) s. banknot ; papierowy pieniądz

bankrate ('baeŋkrejt) s. stopa
dyskontowa;stopa procentowa
bankrupt ('baeŋkrept) s. bankrut
banner ('baener) s. chorągiew;
transparent; tytuł (czołowy)
banns (baenz) pl. zapowiedzi
banquet ('baenkłyt) s. bankiet
baptism ('baeptyzem) s. chrzest
baptize ('baeptajz) s. chrzcic
bar (ba:r) s. belka; drąg; rogatka; krata; v. zagradzac;
hamowac; prep.: oprócz
bar (ba:r) s. 1. izba adwokacka,
sądowa; 2. bar; bufet z wy-
szynkiem ;szynkwas
barb (ba:rb) s. haczyk; docinek;
kolec; skaza (na odlewie);szew
barbarian (ba:r'bearjen) s. barbarzyńca; adj. barbarzyński
barbed wire ('ba:rbd,łajer)
drut kolczasty
barber ('ba:rber) s. fryzjer
(męski); golibroda
barbiturate (ba:r'byczeret) s.
lek uspakajający ;nasenny lek
bare (beer) adj. nagi; goły; łysy; v. obnażac ;odkrywać
barefoot ('beerfut) adj.& adv.
boso; bosy
bareheaded ('beerhedyd) adj.
z gołą głową
barely ('beerly) adv. ledwie;
otwarcie; ubogo; zaledwie
bargain ('ba:rgyn) s. ubicie
targu; dobre kupno; v. targo-
wac się; spodziewac się
barge (ba:rdż) s. barka; v. pakowac się; trynic się
bark (ba:rk) s. 1. kora; 2.
szczeknięcie; v. zdzierac korę;
garbowac korę; szczekac; pyskowac; kaszlec;warkliwie mówic;
wyszczekac; zakaszleć
barley ('ba:rly) s. jęczmień
barmaid ('ba:rmejd) f. bufetowa;
kelnerka; szynkarka
barn (ba:rn) s. stodoła; stajnia; obora; wozownia ;remiza
barometer(be'romyter) s. barometr
barracks ('baereks) pl. koszary;
baraki; budyn'.i koszarowe etc.;
wygwizdywanie (zawodników,graczy)

barrel ('baerel) s. beczka;
lufa; rura;cylinder;walec;bęben
barren ('baeren) adj. jałowy;
wyczerpany;nieurodzajny
barricade (,baery'kejd) s. barykada; v. barykadowac się
barrier ('baerjer) s. zapora;
zastawa; rogatka;ogrodzenie
barrister ('baeryster) s. adwokat;adwokatka;obrońca;obrończyni
barrow ('baerou) s. taczki
bartender ('ba:rtender) s. barman; bufetowy;bufetowa;barmanka
barter ('ba:rter) v. wymieniac;
handlowac; s. handel wymienny
base (bejs) n. podstawa; nasada; adj. podły; nędzny; niski
baseball ('bejsbo:l) s. palant
amerykański(grany piłką i maczugą)
baseless ('bejslys) adj. bezpodstawny;nieuzasadniony
basement ('bejsment) s. suterena; piwnica ;podziemie
bashful ('baeszful) a. wstydliwy;nieśmiały;trwożliwy;lękliwy
basic ('bejsyk) a. podstawowy;
zasadniczy ;zasadowy
basin ('bejsn) s. miednica;
zbiornik; dorzecze; zagłębie
basis ('bejsys) pl. fundamenty;
podstawy;podłoże;grunt;zasada
bask (baesk) v. wygrzewac się
na słońcu;wylegiwac się;pławic się
basket ('ba:skyt) s. kosz; koszyk;v. wrzucac do kosza
basketball ('ba:skytbo:l) s.
koszykówka; piłka do koszykówki
bass (bejs) s. bas (głos,śpiewak)
bass (baes) s. okoń; łyko lipo-
we ; okoń morski lub rzeczny
bastard ('baesterd) s. bękart;
bastard;adj. nieślubny;nędzny
baste (bejst) v. fastrygowac;
polewac tłuszczem pieczeń
bat (baet) s. nietoperz; maczuga; kij;v. mrugac; hulac(slang)
bath (ba:s) s. łazienka
bathe (bejz) v. kąpac; moczyc;
bathing (bejzyŋg)s. kąpanie
bathing cap ('bejzyŋgkaep)
czapka kąpielowa

bathing suit ('bejżyŋg sju:t)
stroj kąpielowy;kostium kąpielowy
bathing trunks ('bejżyŋg traŋks)
spodenki kąpielowe
bathrobe ('ba:żroub) s. płaszcz
kąpielowy
bathroom ('ba:żru:m) s. łazienka;ubikacja;ustęp;klozet
bath towel ('ba:ż tałel) ręcznik kąpielowy
bathtub ('ba:żtab) s. wanna
baton ('baeton) s. buława; pałka;batuta;paleczka dyrygenta
battalion (be'taeljen) s. batalion ;pododdział pułku
batter ('baeter) v. tłuc; walić
battered ('baeterd) adj. pobity
battery ('baetery) s. bateria;
komplet; pobicie;zestaw armat
battle ('baetl) s. bitwa;walka
battleship ('baetlszyp) s. okręt
wojenny
baulk (bo:k) s. przeszkoda;
rozczarowanie;v.przeszkadzać
bawl (bo:l) v. wrzeszczec; drzeć
się; krzyczeć; zwymyślać
bay (bej) adj. czerwono-brązowy;
gniady (koń); wawrzyn;laur
bay (bej) s. zatoka; wnęka;
prześło; v. ujadać; wyć
bay window ('bej'łyndoł) okno
we wnęce
bazaar(be'za:r) s. bazar
be; was; been (bi:; łoz; bi:n)
be (bi:) v. być; żyć; trwać;
dziać się ;istnieć;stawać się
beatnik (bi:tnyk) s. nonkonfor-
mista; (-tka)
be reading (bi:'ry:dyŋ) czytać
właśnie;być w trakcie czytania
beach (bi:cz) s. brzeg; plaża
beachhead ('bi:czhed) s. przyczółek (nad wodą)
beachwear ('bi:człe:r) s.odzież
plażowa ;kostiumy,plaszcze etc.
beacon ('bi:ken) s. sygnał (og-
niowy); latarnia morska
bead (bi:d) s. paciorek; kora-
lik; v. nawlekać korale; per-
lić się ;ozdabiać paciorkami
beak (bi:k) s. dziób ; belfer

beam (bi:m) s. belka; dźwigar;
promień; radosny uśmiech
v.promieniować; nadawać sygnał; rozpromieniać się
bean (bi:n) s. fasola; bób;
ziarnko; łeb; animusz
bear; bore; borne (beer; bo:r;
bo:rn)
bear (beer) s. niedźwiedź;
v. dźwigać; ponosić; znosić;
trzymać się ; rodzić;mieć(podpis)
beard (bierd) s. broda (zarost)
bearer ('beerer) s. nosiciel;
okaziciel; zwiastun;karawaniarz
bearing ('beeryŋg)s. zachowanie;
wzgląd; wspornik; rodzenie;łożysko
beast (bi:st) s. bestia; bydle
beastly ('bistly) adj. bydlęcy;
potworny;adv.strasliwie;okrutnie
beast of prey ('bi:st ow prej)
s. drapieżnik
beat; beat; beaten (bi:t; bi:t;
bi:tn)
beat (bi:t) v. bić; bić się;
ubijać ;tłuc;trzepotać;zbić;kuć
beat it ! ('bi:t,yt) excl.:
precz !wynoś się! wynoście się !
beaten ('bi:tn) adj. ubity; wy-
deptany; wyczerpany; znany
beautiful ('bju:teful) adj.
piękny,cudny;wspaniały;swietny
beautify ('bju:tyfaj) v.upięk-
szać; upiększyć
beauty ('bju:ty) s. piękność;
piękno ;uroda;piękna kobieta
beauty parlor ('bju:ty'pa:rler)
salon kosmetyczny
beaver ('bi:wer) s. bóbr;
przedsiębiorczy człowiek
because (bi'ko:z) conj. dlatego; że; gdyż; adv. z powodu
beckon('beken) v. skinąć; nęcić; s. skinienie
become; became; become (bi'kam;
bi'kejm; bi'kam)
become (bi'kam) v. stawać się;
nadawać się;zostawać kimś(czymś)
becoming ('bikamyŋg)adj. stosowny; odpowiedni;twarzowy
bed (bed) s. łoże; łożysko; klomb;
grządka; ławica ;podkład;nocleg

bedclothes ('bedklouz) s. pos-
ciel; przescieradła,kołdry etc.
bedding ('bedyng)s. pościel
bed linen ('bed,lynyn) s. pos-
ciel ;bielizna pościelowa
bedridden ('bed,rydn) adj. obłożnie chory ;złożony chorobą
bedroom ('bedrum) s. sypialnia
bedside ('bedsajd) przy łożu
bedsore ('bedso:r) s. odleżyna
bedtime ('bedtajm) s. pora do
spania ;pora snu
bee (bi:) s. pszczoła
beech (bi:cz) s. buk ;adj.bukowy
beef (bi:f) s. wołowina; siła;
narzekanie ;wyrzekanie(slang)
beefsteak ('be:f'stejk) s. befsztyk (do smażenia lub pieczenia)
beefy ('bi:fy) adj. krzepki;
flegmatyczny ;muskulary
beehive ('bi:hajw) s. ul
beekeeper ('bi:kiper) s. pszczelarz
beeline ('bi:lajn) s. najkrótsza
droga ;linia powietrzna
been (bi:n) v. były, zob. be
beer (bier) s. piwo
beet (bi:t) s. burak
beetle ('bi:tl) s. tłuczek; ubijak;v.ubijać;wystawać;zwisać
beetroot ('bi:tru:t) s. burak
befall (by'fo:l) v. zdarzać się;
przydarzać się; przytrafiać się
before (by'fo:r) adv. przedtem;
dawniej; z przodu;na przedzie
beforehand (by'fo:rhend) adv.
uprzednio; przedtem; z góry
befriend (by'frend) v. zaprzy-
jaźniać się; wspomagać
beg (beg) v. prosić; żebrać
began (b 'gaen) v. zaczęty;
zob. begin
beget; begot; begotten (by'get;
by'got; by'gotn)
beget (by'get) v. płodzić; rodzić; powodować ;wywoływać
beggar ('beger) s. żebrak
begin; began; begun (by'gyn;
by'gaen; by'gan)
begin (by'gyn) v. zaczynać
beginner (by'gyner) s. początkujący ;nowy(człowiek)

beginning (by'gynyŋ)s. początek ;rozpoczęcie
begun (by'gan) v. p.p. zob.
begin
behalf (by'hae:f) s. w imie-
niu kogoś ; poparcie
behave (by'hejw) v. zachowywać się; prowadzić się
behavior (by'hejwjer) v. postępowanie; zachowanie się
behind (by'hajnd) adv. w tyle;
z tyłu; do tyłu; prep. za; poza;
being ('by:yŋ)s. byt; s.tyłek
istnienie; istota
belated (by'lejtyd) adj. spóz-
niony ;zapoźniony;późny
belch (belcz) v. zionąć; odbijać się; s. bekanie; bucha-
nie; huk ;odbijanie się
belfry ('belfry) s. dzwonnica
Belgian ('beldżen) adj. bel-
gijski
belief (by'li:f) s. wiara;
wierzenie zaufanie;przekonanie
believe (by'li:w) v. wierzyć;
sądzić;mieć przekonanie;zakładać
believer (by'li:wer) s. wyznawca; wierzący ;zwolennik
bell (bel) s. dzwon; dzwonek
belligerent (by'lydżerent) adj.
wojujący; wojowniczy;wojenny
bellow (by'belou) v. ryczeć;
s. ryk ;ryczenie;porykiwanie
bellows ('belouz) s. miech;
płuca;przedmiot podobny do miecha
belly ('bely) s. brzuch;żołądek
belong (byloŋg) v. należeć
belongings (byloŋgyŋz) pl.
rzeczy; bagaż; przynależności
beloved (by'lawd) adj. ukochany; drogi;s.kochana osoba
below (by'lou) adv. niżej; w
dole; na dół; pod spodem;
prep. poniżej; pod ;w piekle
belt (belt) s. pas; pasek;
strefa; v. bić pasem ;opasywać
bench (bencz) s. ława; ławka;
stół; terasa;miejsce sędziego
bend; bent; bent (bend; bent;
bent)
bend (bend) s. zgięcie; krzywa;
v. giąć;wyginać;przeginać;zginać

beneath (by'ni:s) prep. pod; poniżej; pod spodem; na dół
benediction (,beny'dykszyn) s.
błogosławieństwo
benefactor (,beny'faekter) s.
dobroczyńca; dobrodziej
beneficient(bi'nefyszent)adj.
dobroczynny
beneficial (,beny'fyszel) adj.
pożywny;korzystny;dobroczynny
benefit ('benyfyt) s. korzyść;
dobrodziejstwo;pożytek;zasiłek
benevolent (by'newelent) adj.
dobroczynny;życzliwy;łaskawy
bent (bent) s. sitowie; skłonność; zgięcie; adj. skłonny;
zgięty; zdecydowany;uparty
benzene ('benzi:n) s. benzen
benzine (benzi:n) s. (lekka)
benzyna (do czyszczenia)
bequeath (by'kłys) v. zostawiać
w spadku;przekazać potomności
bequest (by'kłest) s. zapis;
spadek;spuścizna; legat
bereave; bereft; bereaved
(by'ri:w, by'reft; by'ri:wd)
bereave (by'ri:w) v. pozbawiać;
odzierać;wyzuwać; osierocić
bereft (by'reft) adj. osierocony; pozbawiony;wyzuty
beret ('berej) s. beret
berry ('bery) s. jagoda;ikra
berth (be:rs) s. koja; łóżko;
stoisko;miejsce postoju statku
beseech; besought; besought
(by'si:cz; by'so:t; by'so:t)
beseech (by'si:cz) v. błagać;
upraszać; zaklinać
beside (by'sajd) adv. poza tym;
ponadto; inaczej; prep. obok;
przy; w pobliżu; w porównaniu
besides (by'sajdz) adv. prócz
tego; poza tym; prep.: oprócz;
poza;ponadto w dodatku
besiege (by'si:dż) v. oblegać
best (best) adj.& adv. najlepszy; najlepiej;v.okpiwać
best wishes (best'łyszys) naj-
lepsze życzenia
best of all (best,ow o:l) najlepszy; najlepiej ;a najlepiej...

bestow (by'stou) v. podarować;
składać ;nadawać;użyczać;darzyć
bet (bet) s. zakład; v. zakładać się ;iść o zakład
betray (by'trej) v. zdradzić;
mylić; zawodzić dawać dowód
betrayal (by'trejel) s. zdrada
betrayer (by'trejer) s. zdrajca
better ('beter) adv. lepiej;
lepszy; v. poprawić; przewyż-
szyć ;prześcignąć;prześcigać
better than ('beter dzaen) exp.
więcej (slang) ; ponad ; lepiej
between (by'tłi:n) prep. między
adv. w pośrodku; tymczasem
beverage ('bewerydż) s. napój
beware (by'łe:r) v. strzec się
beware of the dog (by'łe:r ow
dy dog) strzeż się psa; zły
pies
bewilder (by'łylder) v. zmieszać (kogoś);oszołamiać
bewilderment (by'łylderment) s.
zaczarowanie ;oszołomienie;chaos
bewitch (by'łycz) v. zaczarować;oczarować;ująć(kogoś czymś)
beyond (by'jond) adv.& prep.
za; poza; dalej niż; nad; ponad ;dalej(położony etc.)
bias ('bajes) s. uprzedzenie;
fałsz; kierunek; v. skłonić;
nachylić; uprzedzić;usposabiać
biased ('bajest) adj. stronniczy; uprzedzony ;nastawiony
bib (byb) s. śliniak ;v.popijać
Bible ('bajbl) s. Biblia
bicycle ('bajsykl) s. rower
bid (byd) v. oferować cenę; licytować; kazać; s. oferta na
licytacji ;stawka; zaproszenie
bid farewell (byd fa:rłel)
żegnać się ;pożegnać kogoś
bier (bjer) s. mary (pod trumną)
big (byg) adj. & adv. duży;
wielki; ważny ;głośny;godny
big business (byg'byznys) wielkie interesy;wielkie korporacje
big wig (byg łyg) s. wielka
szyszka ; ważniak;gruba ryba
bike (bajk) s. rower
bilateral (baj'laeterel) adj.
dwustronny; obustronny

bile (bajl) s. żółć;zgorzkniałość
bilious ('byljes) adj. żółciowy;zrzedny;popędliwy;tetryczny
bill (byl) s. dziób;pika;cypel
bill (byl) s. rachunek; kwit;
afisz; plakat; v. ogłaszać;
afiszować;oblepiać afiszami
billboard ('byl,bo:rd) s. tablica ogłoszeniowa
billfold ('byl,fould) s. port-
fel(na dokumenty i pieniadze)
billiards ('byljerdz) s. bilard
billion ('byljen) s. tysiąc
milionów (USA); miliard
bill of exchange ('byl,ow'
eksczendż) weksel
billow ('bylou) s. bałwan; kłąb;
v. piętrzyc; falowac;balwanic
bin (byn) s. skrzynia; paka;
v. pakować; chować do skrzyni
bind (bajnd) v. wiązać; zobowiązywać; opatrywac; oprawiac
binding ('bajndyng)adj. wiążący;
s. połączenie; oprawa;wiązanie
binoculars (bajnokjulez) pl.
lornetka(polowa,teatralna etc.)
biography (baj'ogrefy) s. bio-
grafia;opis życia i działalności
biology (baj'oledży) s. biologia
birch (be:rcz) s. brzoza
bird (be:rd) s. ptak ;dziwak
bird of passage ('be:rd ow
paesydż) przelotny ptak
bird of prey ('de:rd ow prej)
drapieżny ptak
bird's eye view ('be:rds aj,wju)
widok z lotu ptaka
birth (be:rt) s. urodzenie
birth control ('be:rt kon,troul)
kontrola urodzin
birthday ('be:rtdej) s. urodziny; poczatek czegos
birthday party ('be:rtdej'
pa:rty) przyjęcie urodzinowe
birthplace ('be:rt-plejs)
miejsce urodzenia
biscuit ('byskyt) s. bułka;
sucharek lekko strawny
bishop ('byszep) s. biskup
bison ('bajsn) s. bizon
bit (byt) s. wędzidło; ostrze;
wiertło; ząb; szczypta;odrobina;
12½centów;moment;krótki czas

bitch (bycz) s. suka;wulg.kurwa
bite; bit; bitten (bajt; byt;
bitn)
bite (bajt) v. gryźć; kąsać;
docinać; s. pokarm; przynęta;
ukąszenie;cietość;lekki posiłek
bitter ('byter) adj. gorzki;
ostry; zły;zgorzkniały;przykry
blab (blaeb) v. paplać; gadać;
s. plotkarz; gaduła;plotkarka
black (blaek) adj. czarny; ponury; s, murzyn;v.czernić
blackberry ('blaekbery) s. jeżyna
blackbird ('blackbe:rd) s. kos
blackboard ('blackbo:d) s. tablica
blacken ('blaekn) v. czernić
black eye ('blaekaj) s. pod-
bite oko
blackhead ('blaekhed) s. wągier
blackmail ('blaemejl) s. szantaż; wymuszenie
black-market ('black ma:rkyt)
s. czarny rynek
blackout ('blaekaut) s. za-
ciemnienie (miasta, okien)
black pudding ('blaek'pudyng)
s. kaszanka; kiszka
blacksmith ('blaeksmys) s. ko-
wal(wiejski)
bladder ('blaeder) s. pęcherz
blade (blejd) s. zdźbło; liść;
ostrze;płetwa;klinga;wesołek
blame (blejm) s. wina; nagana;
v. tajać; ganić ;winić
blame for ('blejm fo:r) v. winić za (coś)
blameless ('blejmlys) adj. bez
winy; niewinny
blank (blaenk) adj. biały;
pusty; s. puste miejsce; nie-
wypełniony formularz;ślepak
blanket ('blaenkyt) s. koc wełniany ;ciepły koc
blasphemy ('blaesfymy) s. bluź-
nierstwo;pogarda dla Boga
blast (bla:st) s. wybuch; podmuch; odgłos eksplozji;
v. wysadzić w powietrze; de-
tonować; niszczyć
blast furnace ('bla:st,fe:rnys)
s. wielki piec hutniczy

blatant ('blejtent) adj. krzykliwy; ryczący; przesądny
blaze (blejz) s. błysk; płomień; wybuch; v. płonąc
bleach (bli:cz) v. wybielać
bleak (bli:k) adj. ponury;
smutny;wystawiony do wiatru
blear (blier) adj. metny; zamglony; niewyraźny
bleat (bli:t) v. beczeć
bleed; bled; bled (bli:d; bled;
bled)
bleed (bli:d) v. krwawić
blemish ('blemysz) s. plama;
wada; v. zniekształcić; splamić;poplamić;pobrudzić
blend; blent; blent (blend;
blent; blent)
blend (blend) v. mieszać się;
łączyć się; s, mieszanina
bless (bles) v. błogosławić
bless my soul ('bles,maj'so:l)
excl.: o Boże !
blessed ('blesyd) adj. błogosła-
wiony;święty; kojący
blessing ('blesyŋg)s. błogosławieństwo ;aprobata;dobra rzecz
blew (blu:) v. zob.: blow
blight (blajt) s. zniszczenie;
zaraza ;v.niszczyć
blind (blajnd) adj. ślepy;
v. oślepić; s. zasłona
blind alley ('blajnd,alej)
ślepa ulica
blindfold ('blajnd,fould)
adj.& adv. na ślepo; z zawiąza-
nymi oczami; v. zawiązywać
oczy ;s. zasłona oczu
blink (blyŋk) v. mrugać;
s. błysk oka ;mignięcie
bliss (blys) s. radość; błogość
blithe ('blajz) adj. wesoły
blizzard ('blyzerd) s. śnieżyca;
zawieja ;zadymka;zamieć
bloat (blout) v. nadymać; nabrzmiewać ;uwędzić;wędzić
bloater ('blouter) s. śledź wędzony ; pikling
block (blok) s. blok; kloc; zeszyt; przeszkoda; v. tamować;
wstrzymywać;tarasować;zatykać;
zablokować;blokować;zatamować

block up ('blokap) v. zablokować ;zablokowywać;zamurować
blockade (blo'kejd) s. blokada;
v. blokować ;robić zator
blonde (blond) s. blondynka
blood (blad) s. krew ;pokrewieństwo
bloodshed ('bladszed) s. krwi
rozlew ; rozlew krwi
bloodshot ('bladszot) adj. nabrzmiały krwią ;zaszły krwią
blood vessel ('blad,wesl) s.
naczynie krwionośne
bloody ('blady) adj. krwawy
bloom (blu:m) s. kwiecie;
v. kwitnąć ;rozkwitać
blooming (blu:myŋg) adj. kwitnący; przeklęty (slang)
blossom ('blosem) v. kwitnąć;
s. kwiecie ; kwiat
blot (blot) s. plama; v. plamić
blot out ('blot aut)v.wymazać;
usunąć ;wykreślać;zamazywać
blotter (bloter) s. bibularz;
rejestr aresztowań;suszka
blotting paper ('blotyŋg,pejper)
bibuła ;suszka
blouse (blauz) s. bluza
blow; blew; blown (blou; blu;
blołn)
blow (blou) s. cios; rzut; rozkwit; v. zakwitać; rozkwitać
blue (blu:) adj. niebieski;
smutny; v. farbować na niebiesko ;pomalować na niebiesko
bluebell ('blu:bell) s. dzwonek
(kwiat)
blues (blu:s) pl. smutek; przygnębienie ;smutne piosenki
bluff (blaf) s. oszustwo; nabieranie; adj. szorstki; stromy; v. wprowadzać w błąd
bluish ('blu:ysh) adj. niebieskawy
blunder ('blander) s. ciężki
błąd ;v.popełniać błąd (gafę)
blunt (blant) adj. tępy; nieczuły; v. stępić ;przytępić
blur (ble:r) s. plama v. zatrzeć; splamić; zamazać
boar (bo:r) s. dzik; odyniec
board (bo:rd) s. deska; władza
naczelna ;tablica;rada;pokład

boarder ('bo:rder) s. pensjo-
nariusz; pasażer;stołownik

boardinghouse ('bo:rdyŋghaus)
s. pensjonat

boarding school ('bo:rdyŋ,sku:l)
s. szkoła z internatem

boardwalk ('bo:rd łok) chodnik z desek

boast (boust) v. chwalić się;
s. samochwalstwo;przechwałki

boat (bout) s. łódź; statek

boat race('bout rejs) s. regaty; wyścigi łodzi

bob (bob) v. kiwać się; krótko
strzyc; szturchnąć; s. wisiorek; kłąb włosów; szturchnięcie

bobby ('boby) s. angielski policjant

bobsled ('bob sled) s. bob-
slej; sanki z kierownicą etc.

bodice ('bodys) s. stanik

bodily ('bodyly) adj.& adv.
osobiście; fizycznie; całkowicie;gremialnie; cielesnie

body ('body) s. ciało; karoser-
ja; korpus;grupa;gromada;ogół

bodyguard ('bodyga:rd) s. straż
przyboczna;ochrona osobista

bog (bog) s. bagno

boil (bojl) v. wrzeć; kipieć;
gotować; s. wrzenie; czyrak

boil over ('bojl,ouwer) v. wygotować; wygotować się

boiled eggs ('bojld egs) gotowane jajka

boiler ('bojler) s. kocioł

boisterous ('bojsteres) adj.
hałaśliwy;niesforny;burzliwy

bold (bould) adj. śmiały; zuchwały; zauważalny;wyrazny

bolster ('boulster) s. miękka
podkładka; v. miękko podeprzeć

bolt (boult) s. zasuwa; bolec;
piorun; wypad; v. zasuwać;
rzucić się; wypaść;czmychać

bomb (bom) s. bomba; v. bombar-
dować;atakować bombami

bombard (bom'ba:rd) v. bombardo-
wać(artylerią lub bombami)

bond (bond) s. więz; obligacja

bone (boun) s. kość;osc

bonfire ('bonfajer) s. płonący
stos ;ognisko (obozowe etc.)

bonnet ('bonyt) s. czapka
(damska) ; czepek

bonny ('bony) adj. piękny; ładny

bonus ('bounes) s. premia

bony ('bouny) adj. kościsty

book (buk) s. książka; v. księgować; rezerwować; aresztować

booked up ('bukt ap) adj. wyprzedany; pełny

bookcase ('bukkejs) s. półka
na książki

booking clerk ('bukyŋ,klerk)
s. kasjer kolejowy

booking office ('bukyŋ,ofys)
biuro biletowe-rezerwacyjne

bookkeeper ('buk,ki:per) s.
księgowy; ksiegowa

bookkeeping ('buk,ki:pyŋg)s.
księgowość

booklet ('buklyt) s. książeczka

bookseller ('buk,seler) s. księgarz

book shop('bukszop) s. księgarnia

bookstore ('buksto:r) s. księgarnia

boom (bu:m) s. huk; nagła zwyżka; v. zwyżkować; podbijać ceny

boomerang ('bu:meraeŋg) s. bumerang;v.działać jak bumerang

boor (bu:r) s. prostak; gbur;
chłop; prostaczka

boost (bu:st) v. forsować; podnosić znaczenie; zachwalać;
wzmacniać;rozreklamować

boot (bu:t) s. but; cholewa

booth (bu:s) s. budka; stragan

booty ('bu:ty)s.łup. zdobycz

booze ('bu:z)s. alkohol pitny

border ('bo:rder) s. granica;
brzeg; rąbek; v. obrębiać;
graniczyć;oblamować;obszyć

bore (bo:r) v. wiercić; drążyć;
nudzić; s. otwor; nudy; nudziarz;natret;rzecz nieznosna

bore (bo:r) v. zob. bear

born (bo:rn) adj. urodzony

borough ('be:rou) s. miasteczko

borrow ('borou) v.(za)pożyczać

bosom ('busem) s.(łono) piers

boss (bo:s) s. szef; v. rządzić

botany ('botenv) s. botanika

botch (bocz) s. fuszerka; lata-
nina; v. partaczyć; fuszerować

both (bous) pron.& adj. obaj;
obydwaj ;obie;obydwie;oboje
bother (bodzer) s. kłopot;
v. niepokoić; dokuczać;dręczyć
bother about (,bodzer e'baut)
v. kłopotać się czyms
bottle ('botl) s. butelka
bottom ('botem) s. dno; spód;
dolina; głąb; adj. dolny;
spodni; podstawowy; v. sięgać
dna; wstawiać dno ;osiągać dno
bough (bau) s. konar ;gałąź
bought (bo:t) v. kupiony; zob.:
buy (zakupiony,przekupiony...)
boulder ('boulder) s. głaz
bounce (bauns) v. odbijać się;
podskakiwać; s. gwałtowne odbicie ;odskok;samochwalstwo
bound (baund) s. granica; adj.
będący w drodze; v. graniczyć
boundary (baundry) s. linia
graniczna ;adj. graniczny
boundless (baundlys) adj. bezgraniczny ; niezmierzony
bouquet (bu:'kej) s. bukiet
kwiatów; zapach (wina)
bout (baut) s. okres; runda;
próba sil ;atak(choroby)
bow (bau) s. łuk; kabłąk; smyczek; ukłon; v. zginać się;
kłaniać się ;wygiąć w kabłąk
bowels ('bauelz) pl. trzewia;
wnętrzności
bower ('bauer) s. altana; chat-
ka; kotwica przednia
bowl (boul) s. miska; czerpak;
stadion; szala; v. grać kulami (w kręgle); toczyć koło
box (boks) s. skrzynka; pudełko;
loża; boks; v. pakować; oddzielać; uderzać pieścią
boxer ('bokser) s. pieściarz;
bokser
boxing ('boksyng)s. pięściarst-
wo; boks
box office('boks,ofys) s. kasa
w teatrze ;kasa biletów wstępu
bov (boj) s. chłopak; służący
boycott ('bojkot) s. bojkot;
v. bojkotować
boyfriend ('boy-frend) przyjaciel (dziewczyny);kochanek

boyhood('bojhud) s. wiek chłopięcy ;dzieciństwo chłopca
boyish ('bojysz) adj. chłopięcy
boy-scout ('boj-skaut) harcerz
bra (bra:) s. biustnik; stanik;
biustonosz
brace (brejs) s. klamra; korba;
podpora; v. wzmacniać; krzepić;
podpierać :spiąć klamrą;związać
brace up (brejs ap) v. wytężyć
się; zebrać siły; orzeźwić
bracelet ('brejslyt) s. bransoletka; kajdanek
bracket ('braekyt) s. wspornik;
ramię; nawias; grupa; klamra;
v. brać w nawiasy; grupować
brag (braeg) v. chełpić się
braggart('braegert) s. samochwał; pyszałek ;bufon;fanfaron
braid (brejd) s. warkocz; plecionka; v. pleść; opasywać
brain (brejn) s. mózg; rozum
brain wave(brejnkejw) s. swietny pomysł :świetna myśl
brake (brejk) s. hamulec
bramble ('braembel) s. krzak ja-
gody ;krzak jeżyny; jeżyna
branch (bra:ncz) s. gałąź; odnoga; filja; v. odgałęziać się;
zbaczać ;rozwidlać się
brand-new (,braen'nju) adj. nowiutki;nowiusieńki;jak z igły
brass (braes) s. mosiądz; spiż;
ranga; starszyzna; instrumenty
dęte :forsa;pieniądze;czelność:
śmiałość;przedmioty z mosiądzu
brass band(,braes'baend) s. kapela dęta ;orkiestra dęta
brassiere (bre'zier) s. biustnik;
stanik; biustonosz
brat (braet) s. brzdąc; bachor
brave (brejw) adj. dzielny zuch;
v. stawiać czoło ;odważyć się
Brazilian (Bre'zyljen) a. bra-
zylijski ;s.Brazylijczyk
breach (bry:cz) s.naruszenie;
wyłom; zerwanie; v. przełamać
(się); zrobić wyłom;przerwać się
bread (bred) s. chleb; forsa
(slang);środki utrzymania
bread and butter (bred-en-bater)
chleb z masłem ;środki utrzymania

breadth (bredą) s. szerokość;
rozmach; szerokość poglądów
break; broke; broken (brejk;
brouk; brouken)
break (brejk) v. łamać; rujnować; przerywać; s. załamanie;
wyłom; nagła zmiana; wada
break away ('brejk ełej) v.
oderwać (się);uciekać
break down ('brejk dałn) v. za-
łamać(się); s. zepsucie się;
upadek; rozbiór;awaria
break in ('brejkyn) v. włamać
(się);wtargnąć;wtrącić się
break off ('brejkof) v. urwać;
odłamać;zerwać stosunki
break out ('brejkaut) v. wyrwać
(się);pokryć się pryszczami
break up ('brejkap) v. połamać
(się);rozpadać się;rozejść się
breakable('brejkebel) adj. kruchy; łamliwy;łatwy do zbicia
breakfast ('brekfest) s. śniadanie; v. jeść śniadanie
breast (brest) s. piers
breaststroke ('brest,strouk)
pływanie żabką
breath (breš) s. oddech; tchnienie;dech;oddychanie;powiew
breathe (bri:z) v. oddychać;
tchnąć; żyć; dać wytchnać; powiewać;natchnąć;wionąć;szepnąć
breathing ('bri:zyng) s. oddech; wytchnienie;adj.żywy
breathless (breslys) adj. bez
tchu ;zasapany;zadyszany;zziajany
bred (bred) zob.: breed;wychowany
breeches ('bry:czyz) pl. spodnie do konnej jazdy; bryczesy
breed; bred; bred; (bri:d; bred;
bred)
breed (bri:d) v. rodzić; rozmnażać; hodować; s. chów; rasa;
ród ;plemię; ród ludzki
breeder ('bri:der) s. hodowca;
rozsadnik (choroby);rozpłodnik
breeding (bri:dyng) s. hodowla;
obejście; dobre wychowanie
breeze (bri:z) s, wietrzyk;zwada;
v. wiać; śmigać;odejść;oszukać
brevity ('brewyty) s. zwięzłość;
krótkość ; krótkotrwałość

brew (bru:) v. warzyć (piwo);
knuć; s. napój uwarzony; preparat;warzenie;parzenie;odwar
brewery (bru:ery) s. browar
bribe (brajb) v. dawać łapówkę;
przekupywać; s. łapówka
bribery ('brajbery) s. przekupstwo; łapownictwo;korupcja
brick (bryk) s. cegła; kostka;
adj. ceglany; v. obmurować;
zamurować(okno;drzwi,etc.)
bricklayer ('bryk,lejer) s.
murarz
brickwork ('brykłork) s. muro-
wanie;wykonana robota murarska
brickyard ('brykja:rd) s. cegielnia
bridal ('brajdel) adj. ślubny;
weselny;s.ślub;wesele
bride (brajd) s. panna młoda
bridegroom ('brajdgru:m) s, pan
młody; nowożeniec
bridesmaid ('brajdzmejd) s.
druhna;drużka
bridge (brydż) s. most; mostek;
v. łączyć mostem;zapełnić lukę
bridgehead ('brydžhed) s. przyczółek mostowy;przyczółek
bridle ('brajdl) s. uździenica;
uzda; cuma; v. kiełzać; powściągać;opanowywać;okiełzać
bridle path ('brajdl,pas) s.
ścieżka do konnej jazdy
brief (bri:f) s. streszczenie;
odprawa; krótkie majtki;
v. zwięźle streścić; pouczyć
informować; adj. krótkotrwały;
treściwy; zwięzły;krótki
briefcase ('bri:f,kejs) s.
teczka
brigade (bry'gejd) s. brygada
bright (brajt) adj. jasny;
świetny; bystry; adv. jasno
brighten ('brajtn) v. rozjas-
nić; błyszczeć; promieniować
brightness (brajtnys) s. jasność;światło;blask;żywość
brilliance ('bryljens) s.blask;
wielkie zdolności ;świetność
brilliancy ('bryljensy) s.
świetność ; blichtr; połysk
jasne światło;blask;jasność

brilliant ('bryljent) adj. błyszczący; świetny; wybitny
brim (brym) s. brzeg (naczynia); rondo (kapelusza);v.napełniać
brimful ('brym'ful) adj. pełen po brzegi;przepełniony
bring; brought; brought (bryng; bro:t; bro:t)
bring (bryng)v. przynosić; przyprowadzać;powodować;zmusić (się)
bring an action ('bryngen'aekszyn) v. wszczynać działanie, akcje
bring about ('brynge'baut) v. uskutecznić;wywoływać;dokonać
bring forth ('bryng,fo:rs) v. ujawniać; wywoływać;urodzić
bring in (bryngyn)v. wprowadzać; przynosić;wydawać(wyrok etc.)
bring up (bryngap) v. poruszyć; przynieść na górę; przysunąć
brink (brynk) s. skraj; brzeg
brisk (brysk) adj. żywy; raźny; rześki;trzaskający;wesoły
bristle ('brysl) s. szczecina
British ('brytysz) adj. brytyjski; Anglik
brittle ('brytl) a. kruchy
broach (broucz) v. żłobić; zaczynać; poruszać;s.szydło;rożen
broad (bro:d) adj. szeroki; z rozmachem; wyraźny; obszerny s. szeroka płaszczyzna; wulg.: kobieta; adv. szeroko;z akcentem
broadcast ('bro:dka:st) v. transmitować; rozsiewać; szerzyć
broadminded ('bro:d'majndyt) adj. pobłażliwy; z otwartą głową
brochure ('brouszjuer) s. broszura
broke (brouk) adj. złamany; bez grosza; zob. break
broken (brouken) adj. połamany; zepsuty; zob. break
broker (brouker) s. pośrednik; ajent;makler;handlarz narkotyków
bronchia ('bronkje) pl. oskrzela
bronze (bronz) s. brąz; adj.brązowy; v. brązować; brązowiec
brooch (broucz) s. brosza; spinka
brood (bru:d) s. wyląg; potomstwo; v. wysiadywać; tkwić; rozmyślać ponuro;być pogrążonym w myślach

brook (bruk) s. potok ;v.ścierpieć
broom (bru:m) s. miotła; v. zamiatać;wymiatać;obmiatać
broth (bros) s. rosół;bulion
brothel ('brodzel) s. burdel
brother ('bradzer)s. brat
brothers and sisters ('bradzers, en'systers) rodzeństwo
brotherly ('bradzerly) adj. braterski
brought (bro:t) adj. przyniesiony; zob. bring
brow (brau) s. brew; czoło; nawias ;szczyt;pomost;kładka
brown (braun) adj. brunatny; brązowy; opalony; v. brązowieć; opalać się;przyrumieniać (mięso)
brown paper ('braun,pejpe:r)s. papier pakunkowy
bruise (bru:z) s. siniak; stłuczenie; v. tłuc; otłuc; połamać kości; ranić;zgnieść;wyklepać
brush (brasz) s. szczotka; pędzel; draśnięcie; v. szczotkować; otrzepać; pędzlować
brush up ('brasz ap) v. wygładzić; odświeżyć;zgarnąć szczotką
brutal ('bru:tl) a. brutalny; zmysłowy;zwierzęcy
brutality (bru:'taelyty) s. brutalstwo ; brutalność
brute (bru:t) s. bydlę; zwierzę ludzkie; adj. tępy; brutalny; bezduszny; bydlęcy;nieokrzesany
bubble ('babl) s. bąbel; bańka; kipienie; v. kipieć; burzyć się; wydzielać bańki;musować
buck (bak) s. kozioł; fircyk; dolar adj. rogowy; męski; zwykły (szeregowy); v. skakać narowiscie; opierać się;ługować
bucket ('bakyt) s. wiadro; czerpak (koparki);tłok;miska
buckle ('bakl) v. spinać; łączyć; wichrować; s. spinka; sprzączka
buckle on ('bakl on) v. pozapinać się ; zapiąć pas ;przypiąć
buckskin ('bakskyn) s. wyprawiona kozla skóra (też sarnia)
bud (bad) s. pączek; v. pączkować; wyrastać;być w zarodku;rozwijać się;dobrze zapowiadać się

buddy ('bady) s. bliski kolega
budget ('badżyt) s. budżet;
v. budżetować ;asygnować
buffalo ('bafelou) s. bawół
buffer ('bafer) s. bufor;
zderzak ;odbój
buffet ('bafyt) s. bufet; kułak; cios ;raz;uderzenie
buffet ('befej) s. niski kredens ;dania barowe
bug (bag) s. owad; pluskwa;
defekt; amator ;insekt;robak
bugle ('bju:gl) s. róg (do
trąbienia) ;v.trąbić;zatrąbić
build; built; built (byld;bylt;
bylt)
build (byld) v. budować; rozbu-
dowywać ;stworzyć;wznosić
builder ('bylder) s. budowniczy
building ('byldyŋg)s. budowla
built (bylt) adj. zbudowany;
zob. build
bulb (balb) s. cebula; żarówka
bulge ('baldż) v. wzdymać; wybrzu-
szać; wydymać; wytrzeszczać;
s. wypukłość; wzdęcie; wzdyma-
nie się;wybrzuszenie;przewaga
bulk (balk) s. masa; kolos;
większość;v.gromadzić;komasować
bulky ('balky) adj. wielki;otyły;
ciężki; masywny ;nieporęczny
bull (bul) s. byk; duży samiec;
głupstwo;nonsens=bull-shit(bul-
szyt)
bullet ('bulyt) s. kula (nabój)
bulletin ('buletyn) s. komunikat; biuletyn
bulletin board ('buletyn,bo:rd)
s. tablica na ogłoszenia
bullion ('bulijen) s. złoto i
srebro w sztabach
bully ('buly) v. dręczyć; tyranizować; s. awanturnik; kłot-
nik; najęty drab; adj. byczy;
żywy; wesoły;świetny;kapitalny
bum (bam) s. włóczęga; nierób;
popijawa; zadek; v. włóczyć
się; cyganić; pić; adj. marny
bumblebee ('bambl-bi:) s.
trzmiel
bump, (bamp) v. zderzyć się; łup-
nąć; odbić się z łomotem; nabić guza: s. zderzenie; grzmotnięcie; guz;wybój;wstrząs; uderzenie; wypukłość; zdolności

bumper ('bamper) s. zderzak;
pełny kielich ;rekord
bun (ban) s. ciastko drożdżowe;
kok(włosów)
bunch (bancz) s. pęk; banda;
zgraja; guz; v. składać w pęki; skupiać się; kulić się
bunch of grapes ('bancz,ow
grejps) kiść (gałązka) winogron ; pęk winogron
bundle ('bandl) s. tłumok;
wiązka ;v.pakować(w tobół)
bundle up ('bandl,ap) v. zawinąć się;zebrać;zbierać
bungalow ('baŋgelou) s. domek
letni parterowy
bungle ('baŋgl) s. partactwo;
v. partaczyć; bałaganić
bunion ('banjen) s. zapalenie
stawu w stopie(bolesny guz)
bunk ('baŋk) s. koja;banialuki
bunk bed ('baŋk,bed) s. łóżko
piętrowe; łóżko do podnoszenia
bunny ('bani) s. królik; trus
buoy (boj) s. boja; znak pływający ;pława;v.znaczyć bojami
burden ('be:rdn) s. brzemię;
ciężar; obowiązek; v. obciążać;
przygniatać; obładowywać
bureau ('bjurou) s. komoda;
biuro ;sekretarzyk; urząd
bureaucracy (bju'rokresy) s.
biurokacja
burglar (be:rgler) s. włamywacz
burglary ('be:rlery) s. włama-
nie(zwłaszcza w nocy)
burial ('berjel) s. pogrzeb
burly ('be:rly) adj. krzepki;
tęgi;duży i silny
burn; burnt; burnt (be:rn;
be:rnt; be:rnt)
burn (be:rn) v. palić; płonąć;
zapalić; s, oparzelizna;
dziura wypalona;oparzenie
burner ('be:rner) s. palnik
burning ('be:rnyŋg) s. palenie
burnt (be:rnt) v. spalony;
zob. burn(przypalony,opalony...)
burst; burst; burst (be:rst;
be:rst; be:rst)
burst (be:rst) v. rozsądzać;
rozrywać; s. wybuch;pęknięcie;
salwa; zryw;szał;grzmot;hulanka

burst of laughter ('be:rst,ow
'lafter) wybuch śmiechu
burst into flames ('be:rst,
yntu'flejms) buchać ogniem
burst into tears ('be:rst,
yntu'tiers) wybuchnąć płaczem ;zalać się łzami
bury ('bery) v. pochować; zagrzebać; chować ;zakopywać
bus (bas) s. autobus
bush (busz) s. krzak; gąszcz
bushel ('buszel) s. korzec
(8 galonów);v.przerabiać
bushy ('buszy) adj. nastroszony;
krzaczasty ;gęsty
business ('byznys) s. interes;
zajęcie ;sprawa;przedsiębiorstwo
business hours ('byznys,aurs)
godziny urzędowe
business letter ('byznys,leter)
oficjalny list
businesslike ('byznys,lajk)
adj. rzeczowy ;solidny;poważny
businessman ('byznysman) s.
przedsiębiorca; człowiek interesów ;handlowiec
business trip ('byznys,tryp)
podróż służbowa
bus stop ('bas-stop)s.przystanek autobusowy
bust (bast) s. popiersie; biust;
v. rujnować; psuć; rozwalić;
niszczyć ;bankrutować;wybuchnąć
bustle ('basl) v. krzątać się;
zapędzać do pracy; s. rozgardiasz; krzątanina ;bieganina
busy ('byzy) adj. zajęty;
skrzętny; wścibski;ruchliwy
busybody ('byzy,body) wścibski;
złośliwy ;plotkarz;intrygant
but (bat) adv. conj.prep. lecz;
ale; jednak; natomiast; tylko;
inaczej niż; z wyjątkiem
but for ('bat fo:r) exp. oprócz;
bez ; gdyby nie
but now ('bat nau) exp. dopiero
teraz ;dopiero w tej chwili
but once ('bat łans) exp. tylko
raz ;chociaż tylko raz
butcher ('buczer) s. rzeźnik ;kat;
v.zarzynać; mordować; masakrować;brutalnie zabijać;partaczyć

butt (bat) 1. s. drzewce; kolba; nasada; niedopałek papierosa; pośladki; cel; przedmiot
kpin; ofiara; tarcza; v. bość;
trącać; przytykać; 2. s. styk;
zetknięcie: uderzenie głową
butt in ('bat yn) v. wtrącać
się;przerywać rozmowę
butter ('bater) s. masło; v.
smarować masłem ;przychlebiać
buttercup ('baterkap) s. jaskier
butterfly ('baterflaj) s. motyl;
adj. motyli
buttocks ('bateks) pl. pośladki
button ('batn) s. guzik;v.zapinać
button up ('batn ap) v. zapinać
się ; zapinać na guziki
buttonhole ('batnhoul) s. dziurka od guzika;v.zmuszać do słuchania
buttress ('batrus) s. podpora
buxom ('baksem) adj. dorodny;
okazały;pełny(biust) ;ładna(babka)
buy; bought; bought (baj; bo:t;
bo:t)
buy (baj) v. kupować ;przekupić
buyer (bajer) s. nabywca
buzz (baz) s. brzęczenie;
v. brzęczeć ;przelotywać nisko
buzzard ('bazed) s. myszołów
by (baj) prep. przy; koło; co(dzień);
przez; z; po;w(nocy);o;według
by myself ('baj majself) ja sam
by and large ('baj end'la:rdż)adv.
ogólnie mówiąc; ogólnie biorąc
by twos ('baj,tuz) dwójkami
by the dozen('baj dy 'dazn) tuzinami
by the end ('baj dy,end) przy
końcu ;ku końcowi;z końcem
by land ('baj,laend) lądem
by bus ('baj,bas) autobusem
by day ('baj,dej) za dnia
by-and-by ('baj-end-baj) s.
przyszłość; adv. wnet ;po chwili
bye-bye ! ('baj'baj) excl.: pa !
by-election (,baj-e'lekszyn) s.
wybory uzupełniające
bygone ('bajgon) adj. miniony;
przestarzały ;s.zdarzenia minione
bygones ('bajgonz) pl. przeszłość; dawne urazy ;dawne zatargi

bylaw ('bajlo:) s. przepis;
zarządzenie(miejscowe etc.)
byname ('bajnejm) s. przydomek
bypass ('baj-pas) s. droga dojazdowa; objazd ;v.objeżdżać
by-product (,baj-'prodakt) s.
produkt uboczny
byroad (,baj-'roud) s. boczna
droga ;droga drugorzędna
bystander (,baj-'stander) s.
przygodny widz
bystreet (,baj-'stri:t) s.
boczna ulica(drugorzędna)
byway ('baj-łej) s. boczna
droga ;boczne przejście
byword ('baj-,łe:rd) s. przysłowie; przydomek(pogardliwy)
by work ('baj,-łe:rk) s. praca
uboczna poza zajęciem głównym
c (si:) litera "c"; trzecia litera alfabetu angielskiego
cab (kaeb) s. taksówka; dorożka-
szoferka ;budka maszynisty
cabaret (,kaebe'rej) s. lokal
taneczny ; kabaret;serwis na tacy
cabbage ('kaebydż) s. kapusta
cabin ('kaebyn) s. kabina; chat-
ka ;prymitywnie zbudowany domek
cabinet ('kaebynyt) s. szafka;
rada ministrów adj.tajny
cabinetmaker ('kaebynyt,mejke:r)
s. stolarz meblowy
cable ('kejbl) s. przewód; lina;
depesza; v. depeszować; umocowywać liną ;przesyłać kablem
cable-car ('kejbl,ka:r) s. wóz
linowy; kolejka; linowa
cabman ('kaebmen) s. taksówkarz
cabstand ('kaeb staend) s. postój taksówek
cackle ('kaekl) v. gdakać; gę-
gać; chichotać; s. gdakanie;
gęganie; chichot
cacti ('kaektaj) pl. kaktusy
:actus ('kaektes) s. kaktus
cad (kaed) s. ordynus; cham
café ('kaefej) s. kawiarnia;
kawa ;restauracja; bar
cafeteria (,kaefy'tierja) s.
restauracja samoobsługowa
cage (kejdż) s. klatka; kosz;
v. zamykać w klatce

cake (kejk) s. ciastko; kostka
(mydła) smażony placek(z ryby)
cake tin ('kejk,tyn) s. forma
na ciastko
calamity (ke'laemyty) s. nieszczęście; klęska ;niedola
calculate ('kaelkjulejt) v,
rachować; sądzić; oceniać
calculation (,kaelju'lejszyn)
s. liczenie ;ostrożność
calendar ('kaelynder) s, kalendarz ;terminarz
calf (kaef) s. cielak; łydka
caliber ('kael yber) s. średnica wewnętrzna; kaliber;
wzorzec; sprawdzian
call (ko:l) y. wołać; wzywać;
telefonować; odwiedzać; zawijać do portu; wyzywać;
s. krzyk; wezwanie; apel; powołanie; wizyta ;nazwanie;rządanie
call for help ('ko:l,fo:r help)
wołanie o pomoc ;wzywanie pomocy
call names ('ko:l,nejmz) przezywać; wyzywać ;ubliżać
call back ('ko:l,baek) odtele-
fonować; odwołać z powrotem
call at ('ko:l,aet) odwiedzać
call for ('ko:l,fo:r) żądać;
chodzić po coś(żeby otrzymać)
call on ('ko:l,on) odwiedzać
(kogoś);prosić o wypowiedź
call up ('ko:l,ap) telefonować
caller ('ko:ler) s. gość; od-
wiedzający ;adj.rześki;świerzy
calling ('ko:lyng) s. zawód;
powołanie ;zatrudnienie;fach
callous ('kaeles) adj. stwardniały; nieczuły ;zrogowaciały
calm (ka:m) adj. spokojny; cichy; s. spokój; cisza; opanowanie;
v. uspokajać; uciszać ;uciszyć się
calm down ('ka:m,dałn) v. uciszyć się ;uspokoić się
calorie ('kaelery) s. kaloria
calves (ka:wz) pl. cielaki;
łydki
camber ('kaember) v. wyginać;
s. wygięcie ;wypukłość (jezdni)
came (kejm) v. przyszedł; zob.
come

camel ('kaemel) s. wielbłąd

camera ('kaemere) s. aparat fotograficzny; prywatna izba

camomile ('kaemoumajl) s. rumianek

camouflage ('kaemufla:ż) s. maskowanie; v. maskować (wojsk.)

camp, (kaemp) s. obóz; v. obozować: rozlokowywać w namiotach

camp, out (kaemp aut) v. obozować w namiocie

campaign (kaem'pejn) s, kampania; akcja; v, odbywać kampanię; agitować

camp bed ('kaemp,bed) s. łóżko polowe;łóżko składane

camper ('kaemper) adj.obozujący;s. wóz lub przyczepa do obozowania; mieszkalny wóz(turystyczny)

camping ('kaempyŋg) s. obozowanie; życie obozowe

camping ground ('kaempyŋg,graund) obozowisko; miejsce do obozowania

campus ('kaempes) s. teren uniwersytecki lub szkolny

can (kaen) s., puszka blaszana; ustęp; v, móc; konserwować; wyrzucać;umieć;zdołać;potrafić

Canadian (ke'nejdjen) adj. kanadyjski

canal (ke'nael) s. kanał ;kanalik

canard (kae'na:rd) s. kaczka dziennikarska; plotka

canary (ke'nery) s. kanarek

cancel ('kaensel) v. znosić; kasować;odwoływać;skreślać

cancer ('kaenser) s. rak (choroba); nowotwór

candid ('kaendyd) adj. szczery; bezstronny;otwarty

candidate ('kaendydyt) s. kandydat;kandydatka

candied ('kaendyd) adj. pocukrzony; lukrowany

candle ('kaendl) s. świeca

candlestick ('kaendlstyk) s. świecznik; lichtarz

candy ('kaendy) s. cukierki; lukier;cukier lodowaty

cane (kejn) s. trzcina; laska; pałka; v. chłostać ;wyplatać trzciną; ukarać trzciną

canned (kaend) adj. zakonserwowany w puszce

cannery (kaenery) s. fabryka konserw

cannibal ('kaenybel) s. ludożerca; adj. ludożerczy

cannon ('kaenen) s. działo

cannot ('kaenot) v. nie móc (od cannot);nie potrafić

canoe (ke'nu:) s. czółno; kajak; v. jeździć kajakiem; wiosłować

canopy ('kaenepy) s. baldachim; okap;firmament; sklepienie

cant ('kaent) s. żargon; frazes

can't (ka:nt) v. nie móc (od can);nie potrafić

canteen (kaen'ti:n) s. manierka; menażka; kantyna

canvas ('kaenves) s. płótno impregnowane

canvass ('kaenves) s. badanie; zabieganie; v.zabiegać; badać; starać się o głosy

cap (kaep) s. czapka; pokrywa; wieko; kapiszon;beret

cap (kaep) v. wkładać czapkę lub nakrywkę; wieńczyć; zakładać spłonkę; zakasować

capability (,kaepe'bylyty) s. zdolność;zdatność; możliwość

capable (,kejpebl) adj. zdolny

capacity (ke'paesyty) s. zdolność; kompetencja; pojemność; właściwość;nośność;objętość

cape (kejp) s. 1. peleryna; 2. przylądek

caper (kejper) v. wywijać kozły; s. hołubiec; sus; skok

capital ('kaepytl) s. stolica; kapitał; adj. główny; zasadniczy; stołeczny; fatalny

capital crime ('kaepytlkrajm) s. morderstwo

capitalism ('kaepytlyzemys. kapitalizm

capital letter ('kaepytl,leter) duża litera

capital punishment ('kaepytl 'panyszment) kara śmierci

capricious (ke'pryszes) adj. kapryśny

capsize (kaep'sajz) v. wywracać
(statek) dnem do góry

capsule ('kaepsju:l) s. kapsuł-
ka;torebka;pochewka;kabinka

captain ('kaeptyn) s. kapitan;
naczelnik;v.dowodzić

caption ('kaepszyn) s. nagłówek;
napis ;poświadczenie;aresztowanie

captivate ('kaeptywejt) v. ująć;
czarować; urzekać;zniewalać

captive ('kaeptyw) adj. jeniec

captivity ('kaeptyvyty) s. niewola

capture ('kaepczer) s. owładnię-
cie; łup; v. pojmać; owładnąć

car (ka:r) s. samochód; wóz

caravan('kaerevaen) s. karawana;
wóz kryty;przyczepka mieszkalna

carbohydrate ('ka:rbe'hajdrejt)
s. węglowodan

carbon ('ka:rben) s. węgiel;
kopia (kalka)

carbon dioxide ('ka:rben
daj'oksajd) s. CO_2 dwutlenek
węgla

carbon paper ('ka:rben,pejper)
s. kalka

carburetor ('ka:rbjureter) s.
gaźnik

car carrier (ka:r-'kaerjer) s.
wóz do przewozu aut

carcass ('ka:r-kes) s. ścierwo;
padlina; szkielet

card ('ka:rd) s. karta; bilet;
pocztówka;legitymacja; atut

cardboard ('ka:rdbo:rd) s. tektura;adj.tekturowy

card box('ka:rdboks) s. karton

cardigan ('ka:rdygen) s. wełniana kurta (kamizelka)

cardinal ('ka:rdynl) adj. główny; kardynał

card index ('ka:rd yndeks) s.
kartoteka

car papers (ka:r pejpers) s. dokumenty samochodowe

care (keer) s. opieka; troska;
ostrożność:zgryzota;dozór;uwaga

care of (keer ow) c/o: adres
(u kogoś)

care for (keer fo:r) v. dbać
o kogoś:lubić;kochać;mieć ochotę

career (ke'rier) s. kariera;
zawód;tok;pęd;bieg;v. cwałować

carefree (keerfri:) adj. beztroski

careful (keerful) adj. ostrożny;
troskliwy;dbały;pieczołowity

careless (keerles) adj. niedbały; nieuważny;nieostrożny

caress (ke'res) s. pieszczota;
v. pieścić; popieścić

caretaker ('keertejker) s.
dozorca; stróż

careworn ('keerło:rn) s.zgnę-
biony kłopotami

carfare ('ka:rfeer) s. opłata
za jazdę

cargo ('ka:rgou) s. ładunek

caricature (,kaeryke'czjuer)
s. karykatura;v.karykaturować

car mechanic (ka:r-my'kaenyk)
s. mechanik samochodowy

carnation ('ka:r'nejszyn) 1.
s.& adj. ciemno-czerwony;cielis-
ty;2. goździk ogrodowy

carnival ('ka:rnywel) s. karnawał;zapusty

carnivorous (ka:r'nyweres) adj.
mięsożerny

carol ('kaerel) s. kolenda;
v. kolendować

carp (ka:rp) s. karp; v. czepiać się;ganić;przycinać

car parking ('ka:r-pa:rkyŋg)
s. parking samochodowy

carpenter ('ka:rpynter) s.
cieśla; stolarz

carpet ('ka:rpyt) s. dywan;
v. wyściełać dywanem

carriage ('kaerydż) s. wagon;
powóz; postawa;kareta;chód

carrier ('kaerjer) s. firma
przewozowa; nośnik; tragarz;
rozsadnik (zakażenia); lotniskowiec;okaziciel

carrion ('kaerjen) s. padlina

carrot ('kaeret) s. marchewka

carry ('kaery) v. nosić; wozić; zanieść; unosić

carry off ('kaery,of) v. uprowadzić; zabrać;zdobywać(nagrodę)

carry on ('kaery,on) v. kontynuować;wytrwać;awanturować się

carry out ('kaery,aut) v. wykonać; przeprowadzić;spełnić

cart ('ka:rt) s. woz

cartel ('ka:rtel) s. kartel

carter ('ka:rter) s. woźnica

cart horse ('ka:rţhors) s.
koń pociągowy

carton (ka:rten) s. karton

cartoon (ka:r'tun) s. karykatura;v. rysować karykatury

cartoonist (ka:r'tunyst) s.
karykaturzysta

cartridge ('ka:rtrydż) s. nabój

cartwheel ('ka:rt-hłi:l) s.
kołodziej

carve ('ka:rw) v. rzeźbić; krajać;cyzelować;pociać an części

carver ('ka:rwer) s. snycerz

carving ('ka:rwyng) s. rzeźba

cascade (kaes'kejd) s. wodospad;v.spadać jak wodospad

case (kejs) s. 1. wypadek; sprawa; dowod; 2. skrzynia; pochwa;
torba; 3. sprawa sądowa;
v. zamykać w pochwie; otaczać
czymś ;oszalować; oprawić

casement ('kejsment) s. rama
okienna; okno z kwaterami

cash (kaesz) s. gotówka; pieniądze; v. spieniężać; inkasować; płacić (gotówką)

cash on delivery (kaesz on
dy'lywery) zapłata przy od-
biorze; C.O.D.

cashier (kae'szjer) s. kasjer

cash register(kaesz'redżyster)
s. kasa (zmechanizowana)

casing ('kejsyng)s. 1. powłoka;
pochwa; 2. obudowa; oprawa;
3. łuska; 4. opancerzenie

cask (kaesk) s. beczułka

casket (kaeskyt) s. trumna; urna; szkatuła

cassock ('kaesek) s. sutanna

cast; cast; cast (ka:st; ka:st;
ka:st)

cast (ka:st) s. rzut; odlew;
gips; odcien: v, rzucać; łowić; odlewać; powalić; dzielić
role teatralne

castaway ('ka:st,e'łej) s. wyrzutek ;rozbitek

cast down (ka:st dałn) adj.
przygnębiony;.v.deprymować

caste (ka:st) s. kasta

cast iron(ka:stajren) s. żeliwo

castle ('ka:sl) s. zamek

castor oil ('ka:ster,ojl) s.
olej rycynowy

cast steel ('ka:st,sti:l) s.
lana stal

casual ('kaeżuel) adj. przypadkowy; niedbały;dorywczy

casualty ('kaeżuelty) s. wypadek; ofiara wypadku; lista
strat;nieszczęście

cat (kaet) s. kot;jędza

catalog ('kaetelog) s. katalog

catamaran (,kaeteme'raen) s.
dwu-czółnowa łódż

cataract ('kaeteraekt) s. katarakta; ulewa;wodospad

catarrh (ke'ta:r) s. katar

catastrophe (ke'taestrefy) s.
katastrofa

catch; caught; caught (kaecz;
ko:t; ko:t)

catch (kaecz) v. łapać; łowić;
ujmować; słyszeć; wybuchać;
nabawić się; s. łup; połów

catch cold (kaecz kold) v. za-
ziębiać się

catch fire (kaecz fajer) v. zapalać się

catch up (kaecz ap) v. dogonić

catching (kaeczyng)adj. zaraźliwy;s.tryby;uchwyt;zazębienie

category ('kaetygery) s. kategoria

cater ('kejter) v. dostarczać
żywności; obsługiwać

caterpillar ('kaetepyler) s.
gąsienica (traktora.czołgu etc.)

cathedral (ke'ţi:drel) s. katedra

Catholic ('kaeţelyk) adj. katolicki; s. katolik

cattle (kaetl) s. bydło rogate

caucus ('ko:kes) s. tajne na-
rady partyjne; klika

caught (ko:t) złapany; zob.
catch

cauldron ('ko:ldren) s,kocioł

cauliflower ('kalyflauer) s. kalafior

cause (ko:z) s. przyczyna; sprawa;racja;motywacja;proces

causeless(ko:zles) adj. przypadkowy ; bezpodstawny

caution ('ko:szyn) s. ostrożność; uwaga;v.ostrzegać

cautious ('ko:szes) adj. ostrożny;rozważny;roztropny;uważny

cavalry ('kaevelry) s. kawaleria

cave (kejw) s. pieczara; jaskinia; v. zapadać się; drążyć

cavern ('kaewen) s. jama; jaskinia; grota; pieczara

cavity ('kaewyty) s. wklęsłość;
dziura(w zębie);dół;wydrążenie

cease (sy:s) v. ustawać; przestawać; położyć kres

ceaseless (sy:slys) adj. bezustanny;ciągły; nieprzerwany

cede (si:d) v. ustąpić; cedować

ceiling ('sy:lyng)s. sufit; pułap; górna granica

celebrate ('selybrejt) v. świę-
cić ;uczcić;sławićobchodzić

celebrated ('selybrejtyd) adj.
sławny; słynny; głośny

celebration ('selybrejszyn) s.
obchód; odprawianie; święcenie

celebrity ('sylebryty) s. sławna
osoba;sława;znakomita osobowość

celery ('selery) s. seler (jarzyna)

celibacy ('selybesy) s. bez-
żeństwo; celibat

cell (sel) s. cela; komórka

cellar ('seler) s. piwnica

Celtic (keltyk) adj. celtycki

cement (sy'ment) s. cement;
v. cementować; kleić; utwierdzać ;spoić; złączyć

cemetery ('semytry) s. cmentarz

censor ('sensor) s. cenzor

censorship ('senserszyp) s. cenzura

censure ('senszer) s. nagana;
krytyka; v. krytykować

cent (sent) s. cent

centenary (sentynery) adj. stuletni; s. stulecie; setna rocznica

centennial ('sen'tenjel) s.
stulecie; adj. stuletni

center ('senter) s. ośrodek;
v. ześrodkowywać

centigrade ('sentygrejd) adj.
stustopniowy(termometr)

centimeter ('sentymi:ter) s.
centymetr

central ('sentral) adj. środkowy; czołowy ; s. centrala

Central Europe ('sentral
juerop) Europa Środkowa

central heating ('sentrel
hi:tyng)centralne ogrzewanie

centralize ('sentrelajz) v.
centralizować;ześrodkowywać

center ('senter) s. ośrodek

centrum; v. ześrodkowywać;
centrować ;skupiać się

century ('senczury) s.stulecie

cereals ('syerjelz) pl, zboża

cerebral ('serybrel) adj. mózgowy

ceremonial (,sery'mounjel) adj.
ceremonialny; s. rytuał;ce-
remonial; ceremonialność

ceremonious (,sery'mounjes)
adj. drobiazgowy; ceremonialny

ceremony ('serymeny) s. ceremonia;v.sztywno się zachowywać

certain ('se:rtyn) adj. niejaki; pewien;pewny;ustalony;jakiś

certainly ('se:rtnly) adv. napewno; oczywiście;bezwzględnie

certainty ('se:rtynty) s. pewność; pewnik; rzecz pewna

certificate (se'rtyfykyt) s.
świadectwo; poświadczenie;
v. zaświadczać ;dyplomować

certify ('se:rtyfaj) v. zaświadczać; zapewniać; uznawać za

certitude ('se:rtytju:d) s.
pewność; przeświadczenie

chafe (czejf) v. trzeć; otrzeć;
irytować; s. tarcie; otarcie;
irytacja; rozdrażnienie; złość

chaff(cza:f) s. 1. sieczka;
2. żart; naciąganie; wyśmiewać żartobliwie; naciągać

chagrin ('szaegryn) s. smutek; rozczarowanie; v.upo-
karzać;rozczarowywać boleśnie

chain (czejn) s. łańcuch; syndykat; trust; v, wiązać na łańcuchu; mierzyc;uwiązać; zakuć

chair (czeer) s. krzesło; stołek; fotel; katedra; v. przewodniczyc; sadzac na krzesle

chair lift ('czeerlyft)s. wyciąg linowy

chairman ('czeermen) s. przewodniczący; prezes ___[kredą

chalk (czo:k) s. kreda;v.pisić

challenge ('czaelyndż) s. wyzwanie; zadanie; v. wyzywać; zarzucać; wzywać;korcić;prowokować

chamber ('czejmber) s. izba; komora;sala;pokój:v.wydrążyć

chambermaid ('czejmbermejd) s. pokojowa

chamois ('szaemła:) s. giemza; ircha; zamsz

champagne ('szaem'pejn) s. szampan

champion ('czaempjen) s. mistrz; obrońca; v. bronić; walczyc o...

championship ('czaempjenszyp) s. mistrzostwo

chance (cza:ns) s. okazja; przypadek; szczęście; szansa;ryzyko; adj. przypadkowy; przygodny; v. zdarzac się; ryzykować; próbować;przytrafić się;natknąć się

chancellor (cza:seler) s. kanclerz; pierwszy sekretarz (ambasady):najwyższy sędzia

chandelier (szaendy'lyer) s. żyrandol; świecznik

change (czejndż) s, zmiana; wymiana; drobne; v. zmienić; przebierać (się); wymieniac

change one's mind ('czejndż, łans'majnd) zmienic czyjeś zdanie (przekonania etc.)

change trains ('czejndż,trejns) v. przesiąść sie (na kolei)

changeable('czejndżebl) adj. zmienny;podlegający zmianom

channel ('czaenl) s. kanał; koryto; łożysko; v, żłobić; przesyłać drogą (urzędową)

chaos ('kejos) s. chaos

chap (czaep) s. chłop; chłopiec; człek; v.pękać; powodować pęknięcia (warg);zarysowywać

chapel ('czaepel) s. kaplica

chaplain ('czaeplyn) s. kapelan

chaps (cza:ps)pl. skórzane nogawice (kowboja);ochraniacze

chapter ('czaepter) s. rozdział; oddział; v. dzielić na rozdziały

character ('kaerykter) s. charakter; typ; cecha; reputacja; moralność; facet; znak

characteristic ('kaerykterystyk) adj. charakterystyczny; typowy; s. cecha; własność; właściwość

characterize ('kaerykterajz) v. charakteryzować (opisywać)

charge (cza:rdż) s. ciężar; ładunek; obowiązek; piecza; podopieczny; zarzut; opłata; należność; szarża; godło; v. ładować; nasycac; obciążać; zadać; liczyc sobie; oskarżać; atakować; szarżować

charge account (cza:rdż e'kaunt) s. otwarty kredyt (w banku)

charge card (cza:rdż'ka:rd) s. karta kredytowa do zakupów

chariot ('czaerjet) s. wóz; rydwan

charitable ('czaerytebl) adj. litościwy; dobroczynny

charity ('czaeryty), s. miłosierdzie; dobroczynność

charm (cza:rm) s, czar; urok; amulet; v. czarować; oczarować

charming (cza:rmyŋg)adj. czarujący

chart (cza:rt) s. wykres; mapa morska; v. robić wykres; wytyczać; pokazywać (jak)

charmless (cza:rmlys) adj. bez wdzięku

charter (cza:rter)s. statut; przywilej; dyplom; akt nadania prawa do... v. nadawać; zakładać na statutach; wynajmować statek lub samolot

charter plane (cza:rter plejn) s. wynajęty grupowo samolot

charwoman ('cza:rłumen) s. sprzątaczka; dochodząca sprzataczka;posługaczka

chase 1. (czejs) s. pościg; pogoń; polowanie; v. gonić; ścigać; polować; wyganiać
chase 2. (czejs) s. łożysko; wgłębienie; wykop; v. żłobić
chasm ('kaezem) s. otchłań
chaste (czejst) adj. czysty; niewinny;nieskażony;cnotliwy
chastity ('czaestyty) s. niewinność; prostota;dziewictwo
chat (czaet) s. pogawędka; v. gawędzić; gadać;rozmawiać
chatter (czaeter) v. szczebiotać; klapać; s.szczebiot; klapanie; klekot;paplanie;terkot
chatterbox (czaeterboks) s. trajkotka;gaduła;pleciuga
chauffer ('szoufer) s. zawodowy kierowca; przenośny piecyk
cheap (czi:p) adj. tani; marny
cheapen (czi:pen) v. taniec; obniżać wartość;spadać w cenie
cheat (czi:t) s. oszust; oszustwo; v. oszukiwać; zdradzać (w małżeństwie);okpiwać
check (czek) s. wstrzymanie ; przerwa; sprawdzenie; czek; kwit; szach; a. szachownicowy; kontrolny; pokreślony; v. hamować; sprawdzać; zakreślać; nadawać; zgadzać się; szachować;ganić;krytykować;opanowywać
check in (czek yn) v. wmeldowywać się (w pracy,w wojsku etc.)
check out (czek aut) v. wymeldowywać się;zapłacić za hotel
checked (czekt) adj, w kratkę
checkroom (czekrum) s. przechowalnia (bagażu);szatnia
cheek (czi:k) s. policzek; bezczelne gadanie; v. mówić bezczelnie do kogoś; stawiać się
cheeky ('czi:ky) adj. bezczelny; zuchwały;pełen tupetu;z tupetem
cheer (czier) s. brawo; hurra; radość; jadło; v. krzyczeć; rozweselać;dodawać otuchy
cheer on ('czier on) v. zachęcać ;zagrzewać;dodawać otuchy
cheer up ('czier ap) v. pocieszać; nabrać otuchy;rozpogodzić
cheerful ('czierful) adj. pogodny; wesoły; ochoczy;rozweselający

cheerless ('czierlys) adj. ponury; smutny; przybity
cheery ('cziery) adj. wesoły; radosny; pogodny
cheese ('czi:z) s. ser
chef (czef) s. kuchmistrz
chemical ('kemykel) adj. chemiczny;s.substancja chemiczna
chemicals ('kemykels) pl. chemikalia;leki;lekarstwa
chemise (sze'mi:z) s. damska koszula luźna i długa
chemist ('kemyst) s. chemik; aptekarz
chemistry ('kemystry) s. chemia
cheque (czek) s. czek (poza USA)
chequered ('czekerd) adj. kratkowany; urozmaicony; burzliwy
cherish ('czerysz) v. lubić; tulić; żywić (uczucie);miłować
cherry ('czery) s. czereśnia; wiśniowy kolor; vulg.:prawiczka; adj. wiśniowy; vulg.: prawiczy; czerwony
chess (czes) s. szachy
chess-board (czes-bo:rd) s. szachownica
chess man(czesmen) s. figurka szachowa
chest (czest) s. skrzynia; komoda; piers ;płuca;kufer;skrzynka
chestnut ('czesnat) s. kasztan
chest of drawers (czest ow dro:ers) komoda
chew (czu:) v. żuć; przeżuwać; besztać; gderać; s. żucie; tytoń do żucia; prymka
chewing gum('czu:yŋgam) s. guma do żucia
chicken ('czykyn) s. kurcze; adj.tchórzliwy; bojący się
chicken out ('czykyn aut) v. stchórzyć;ustąpić ze strachu
chide; chid; chidden (czajd; czyd; czydn)
chide (czajd) v. łajać; droczyć się; skarżyć;besztać; łajać
chicken pox('czykyn poks) s. ospa wietrzna
chief (czy:f) s. wódz; szef; adj. główny; naczelny
chilblain ('czylblejn) s, odmrożenie

child (czajld) s. dziecko
childish ('czajldysz) adj.
dziecinny
childless ('czajldlys) adj. bezdzietny
childlike ('czajldlajk) adj.
dziecięcy; jak dziecko
children('czyldren) pl. dzieci
chill (czyl) s. chłod; dreszcz;
v. studzić; mrozic ;oziębiać
chilly (czyly) adj. chłodny;
adv. chłodno; zimno
chime ('czajm) s. dzwony grające;
rytm; kurant; v. bić w dzwony;
wydzwaniać; rymować;zabrzmieć
chimney ('czymny) s. komin; wylot; szkło lampy naftowej
chimney sweeper ('czymny,sli:per)
s. kominiarz;adj. kominiarski
chin (czyn) s. broda; v. podciąg-
gać brodę do drążka;s.podbródek
china ('czajna) s. porcelana
chinese ('czaj'ni:z) adj. chiński;Chinese s. chińczyk
chink('czynk) 1. s. brzęk; v.po-
brzękiwać; brzęczeć; 2. szpara;
szczelina; v. zapychać szpary
chip (czyp) s. drzazga; odłamek;
skrawek; v. otłuc; obijać; dokuczać; nabierać; ciosać;
ćwierkać; piszczeć; nogę podstawiać; złuszczać się;odłupać
chirp (czy:rp) s. świergot;
v. ćwierkać; szczebiotać
chisel ('czyzl) s. dłuto; przecinek; v. ciąć; rzeźbić;oszukać
chivalrous ('czywelres) adj.
rycerski
chivalry ('czywelry) s. rycer-
stwo; rycerskość
chive (czajw) s. szczypiorek
chlorine ('klo:ry:n) s. chlor
chloroform ('klo:refo:rm) s.
chloroform; v. maczać w chlo-
roformie;usypiać chloroformem
chock (czok) s. klin; v. osadzać na klinach; adv. szczelnie; ciasno; mocno ; w pełni
chocolate ('czoklyt) s. czekolada;adj. czokoladowy(kolor etc.)
choice (czoys) s. wybór; wybran-
ka; adj.wyborowy;doborowy

choir ('kłajer) s. chór
choke (czouk) v. dusić; zadusić; tłumić; dławić; s. durze-
nie; dławik; gardziel; prze-
wężenie;odgłosy duszenia;zawór
choke down (czouk dałn) v. dławić;zmniejszać gardziel
choke up (czouk ap) v. zatykać
(rurę); zadławić(motor etc.)
choose; chose; chosen (czu:z;
czouz; czouzn)
choose (czu:z) v. wybierać; woleć; postanowić;zadecydować
chop (czop) v. rąbać; obcinać;
s. rąbnięcie; kotlet;krótka fala
chop down (czop dałn) v. powalić (drzewo etc.); ściać;zrąbać
chord (ko:rd) s. struna; cięciwa;struna głosowa
chorus ('ko:res) s. chór;
v. mówić chórem;śpiewać chórem
chose (czouz) v. wybrał;zob.
choose
chow (czau) s. jadło (slang)
Christ (krajst) Chrystus
christen ('krisn) v. ochrzcić
Christian ('krystjen) adj.
chrześcijański; s. chrześci-
janin(slang:cywilizowany)
Christianity (krys'czaenyty) v.
chrześcijaństwo
Christian name ('krystjen,nejm)
s. imię(inne niż nazwisko)
Christmas ('krysmas) s. Boże
Narodzenie
Christmas Day ('krysmas dej)
Dzień Bożego Narodzenia
Christmas Eve ('krysmas 1:w)
wilia, wigilia Bożego Narodzenia
chromium ('kroumjem) s. chrom
chronic ('kronyk) adj. chroniczny;strawszliwy (ból)
chronicle ('kronykl) s. kronika
chronological (krone'lodżykel)
adj. chronologiczny
chubby ('czaby) adj. pucołowaty; pyzaty;mały i gruby
chuck (czak) v. rzucać; gdakać;
cmokać; s. kurczątko; dzieci-
na; kochanie;gdakanie;cmokanie

chuckle (czakl) v. chichotać;
s. chichot; zduszony śmiech
chum (czam) v. przyjaźnić się
blisko; s. serdeczny kolega;
współlokator;v.przyjaźnić sie
church (cze:rcz) s. kościół
churchyard (cze:rczja:rd) s.
cmentarz; dziedziniec kościelny; adj. cmentarny
churn (cze:rn) v. robić masło;
kłócić się; burzyć się; kotłować się; pienić się; s. maślni-
ca; maślniczka;bańka na mleko
chute (szu:t) s. koryto zrzuto-
we; spadek; wodospad; spadochron; tor zjeżdżalni dla dzieci
chutzpah (hucpa) s. nachalność;
śmiałość;tupet(po nowohebrajsku)
cider ('sajder) s. wino z jabłek
cigar (sy'ga:r) s. cygaro
cigaret(te) (sige'ret) s. papieros
cinder ('synder) s. popiół; żużel; v. spalać na żużel
cinderella (,synde'rele) s. kopciuszek; Kopciuszek
cinder track ('synder-traek) s.
bieżnia żużlowa;tor żużlowy
cine camera ('syni:'kaemere) s.
aparat filmowy
cinema ('syneme) s. kino
cinema projector ('syneme-
prodżekter) s. rzutnik filmowy
cipher ('sajfer) s. cyfra; szyfr;
zero; v. szyfrować; rachować
circle ('se:rkl) s. koło; krąg;
obwód; v. otaczać; kręcić się
w koło; opasywać; krążyć;okrążać
circuit ('se:rkyt) s. obwód;
okrężna; okólna (podróż)
circular ('se:rkjuler) s. okólnik; adj. okrągły; kolisty
circulate ('se:rkjulejt) v.
krążyć; cyrkulować; puszczać
w obieg; być w obiegu
circulation ('se:rkjulejszyn)
s. krążenie; obrót; nakład
circumference (se'rkamfyrens)
s. obwód (koła etc.)
circumcision   (se:rkem'syżyn)s.
obrzezanie;obcięcie napletka

circumscribe (,se:rkem'skrajb)
v. opisywać; zakreślać
circumstance ('se:rkemstaens)
s. okoliczności; szczegóły
circus ('se:rkes) s. cyrk;
okrągły plac;rondo; desant(sl.)
cistern ('systern) s. zbiornik
na wodę; cysterna
cite (sajt) v. cytować; przytaczać; pozywać; wymieniać
w komunikacie;wzywać do sądu
citizen ('sytyzn) s. obywatel
citizenship ('sytyzenszyp) s.
obywatelstwo;cnoty obywatelskie
city ('syty) s. (wielkie) miasto; centrum finansowe;ośrodek
city center ('syty,senter) s.
centrum miasta
city guide ('syty'gajd) s. plan
miasta;przewodnik po mieście
city hall('syty,ho:l) s. zarząd
miasta; magistrat
civics ('sywyks) s. nauka praw
i obowiązków obywatela[uprzejmy;
civil ('sywl) adj. społeczny;
obywatelski;cywilny(kodeks);
civilian (sy'wyljen) adj. cywilny; s. cywil; obywatel
civility (sy'wylyty) s. uprzejmość; grzeczność
civilization (,sywylaj'sejszyn)
s. cywilizacja;całość kultury
civilize ('sywylajz) v. cywili-
zować; ucywilizować
civil marriage ('sywl'maerydż)
s. ślub cywilny
civil rights ('sywl,rajts) s.
prawa obywatelskie
civil service ('sywl'se:rwys)
s. służba państwowa
civil war ('sywl,ło:r) s. wojna domowa
clack (klaek) v. klekotać; gdakać; s. klekot; wieko
clad (klaed) adj. odziany; zob.
clothe
claim (klejm) v. żądać; twierdzić; s. żądanie; twierdzenie;
działka;skarga;zażalenie;dług
claimant (klejment) s. rości-
ciel; pretendent;adj.pilny;rażący

clammy ('klaemy) adj. mokro-
lepki;wilgotny i zimny
clamor ('klaemer) s. zgiełk;
krzyk; v. krzyczeć; robić
wrzawę; wymuszać krzykiem
clamorous ('klaemeres) adj.
zgiełkliwy; krzykliwy
clamp (klaemp) s. klamra; zacisk;v.zaciskać (jak)klamrą
clan (klaen) s. klan; szczep
szkocki;v.tworzyć klikę
clandestine (klaen'destyn) adj.
potajemny; skryty; tajny
clang (klaeng) s.dźwięk: szczęk;
klekot; v. dzwięczeć; szczękać;
klekotać;rozbrzmiewać;dzwonić
clank (klaenk) s. chrzęst;
brzęk; v. brzękać; chrzęscić
clap (klaep) s. huk; klaskanie;
v. łopotać; oklaskiwać; klepać
claret ('klaeret) s. czerwone
wino; bordo; slang:krew
clarify ('klaeryfaj) v. wyjas-
niać; rozjaśniać; oczyszczać
clarity ('klaeryty) s. czystość;
jasność; przejystość;klarowność
clash (klaesz) s. brzęk; starcie;
v. brzęczeć; ścierać się; kolidować; uderzać w coś
clasp (klaesp) s. klamra; uchwyt; okucie; v. spinać; ściskać
clasp knife ('klaesp-najf) s.
scyzoryk;kozik, nóż składany
class (klaes) s. klasa; lekcja;
rocznik; grupa; v. klasyfikować ;segregować; sortować
classmate ('kla:s,mejt) s. kolega szkolny
classroom ('kla:s,rum) s. klasa
(w szkole); sala szkolna
class struggle (,kla:s'stragl)
s. walka klas w społeczeństwie
classic ('klaesyk) s. klasyk;
studia klasyczne; adj. klasyczny; uznany autotytet;klasyk
classical ('klaesykel) adj. typowy; klasyczny;humanistyczny
classification (klaesyfy'kejszyn)
s. klasyfikacja;klasyfikowanie
classify ('klaesyfaj) v. klasyfikować; sortować; zaklasyfikować
clatter ('klaeter) v. brzęczeć;
klapać; s. brzęk;łoskot;gwar

clause (klo:z) s. klauzula;
zdanie; punkt umowy
claw (klo:) s. pazur; szpon;
łapa; kleszcze; v. drapać; wydrapać; łapać w szpony
clay (klej) s. glina; sl.trup
clean (kli:n) adj. czysty; wyraźny; zgrabny; adv. całkiem;
zupełnie; poprostu; v, oczys-
cić; opróżniać; ogołocić; wygrać; uprzątnąć;dużo zyskać(sl,)
clean out ('kli:n aut) v. oczys-
cić; opróżniać;wyczyścić
clean up ('kli:n ap) v. po-
sprzątać; wygrać; zrobić na
czysto;robić porządek
cleaner ('kli:ner) s. czyści-
ciel; oczyszczalnik; właściciel pralni;pralnia chemiczna
cleaning ('kli:nyng) s. czyszczenie; sprzątanie;porządki
cleanliness ('klenlynys) s.
czystość;zamiłowanie do czystości
cleanly ('klenly) adj. czysty;
adv. czysto; schludnie
cleanness ('kli:nnys) s. czystość;zamiłowanie do czystości
cleanse (klenz) v. czyścić;
zmywać (grzechy);oczyszczać
clear (klier) adj. jasny; czysty; bystry; adv. jasno; wyraźnie; z dala; zupełnie; dokładnie; s. wolna przestrzeń
clear away('klier,ełej) v. usunąć (przeszkodę etc.)
clear up ('klier,ap) v. wyjaśnić
clear-cut ('klier,kat) adj. wyraźny; czysty ; poprawny
clearing ('klieryng) s. karczo-
wisko; rozrachunek;obrachunek
clearly ('klierly) adv. wyraźnie; jasno; oczywiście
cleave (kli:w) s. cleft; cleft (kli:w;
kleft; kleft)
cleave (kli:w) v. 1. łupać; pe-
kać; rozdwajać; 2. trzymać się
wiernie ; nie odstępować
clef (klef) s. klucz (muzyczny)
cleft (kleft) s. szczelina;
pęknięcie; zob. cleave
clemency ('klemensy) s. miłosierdzie;łagodność (klimatu etc.)

clench (klencz) v. ściskać; zaciskać; zewrzeć się; s. uścisk;
zaciśnięcie; zagięcie;ubić(targu
clergy ('kle:rdży) s. duchowieństwo ;kler
clergyman ('kle:rdżymen) s.
duchowny; ksiądz; pastor
clerical ('klerykel) adj. urzęd-
niczy; duchowny; biurowy
clerk (kla:rk) s. subjekt;
urzędnik; pisarz; ekspedient
clever ('klewer) adj. zdolny;
sprytny; zręczny;pomysłowy;uprzejmy
click (klyk) v. szczękać; cmokać; trzaskać; dopiąć swego;
wygrać; s. trzask; zatrzask;
klamka;mlaśniecie;klekot;brzęk
client ('klajent) s. klient
cliff (klyf) s. urwisko; stroma
ściana; sciana skalna
climate ('klajmyt) s. klimat
climax ('klajmaeks) s. szczyt;
zakończenie; v. stopniować;
szczytować; kuliminować
climb (klajm) s.wspinaczka;
miejsce wspinania; v. piąć się;
wspinać; wzbijać się;wdrapać się
climb up (klajm ap) v. wspinać
sie w górę; wdrapywać się
climber (klajmer) s.taternik;
karierowicz; pnącz (roślina)
clinch (klyncz) v. zaciskać;
zaginać; zanitować;zakończyć
cling; clung; clung (klyng;klang;
klang)
cling (klyng)v. trzymać sie;
chwytać się; czepiać się;trwać
clinic ('klynyk) s. klinika; poradnia; adj. kliniczny
clink (klynk) s. dzwonienie;
ciupa ; v. dzwonic (kluczami etc.)
clip 1. (klyp) s. sprzączka
v. spinać; 2. s. strzyżenie;
nożyce; v. strzyc; orżnąć
clippings ('klypyns) pl. wycinki (z gazet);okrawki;obrzynki
cloak (klouk) s. płaszcz;maska;
v. okryć płaszczem;wdziewać
clock (klok) s. zegar scienny
clockwise ('klokłajz) adj. (obrót) w prawo wg. zegarka

clod (klod) s. gruda; ziemia;
gamoń.v.obrzucać grudkami ziemi
clog (klog) s. kłoda; chodak;
v. zatykać; zapychać;zawadzać
cloister ('klojster) s. krużganek; klasztor
close (klouz) v. zamykać; zatykać; zakończyć; zwierać; zgodzić się; s. zakończenie; koniec; miejsce ogrodzone;
adv. szczelnie; blisko; prawie
adj. zamknięty; skąpy; gęsty;
bliski; ścisły:ekskluzywny:skąpy
close to ('klous tu) przy;tuż o-
close by ('klous baj) obok bok
close down ('klouz dałn) v. zamykać;kończyć (działalność etc.)
close in (klouz yn) v. nadchodzić; ogarniać; okrążyć;otoczyć
closet ('klozyt) s. pokoik;
klozet; kredens
close-up ('klousap) s. zdjęcie
zbliżone; zbliżenie
closing time ('klouzyng,tajm)
s. koniec pracy; zamknięcie
(sklepu);koniec urzędowania
clot (klot) s. skrzep; v. ścinać się; skrzepnąć;zsiadać się
cloth (kloz) s. materiał; szmata; szafa; obrus;sukno;żagiel
cloth-bound (kloz baumd) s.
oprawny w płótno
clothe (klouz) s. materiał; sukno;v.przywdziewać; zamaskować
clothes (klouz) pl. ubranie;
pościel; pranie; odzierz;ubiór
clothes brush ('klouz,brasz) s.
szczotka do ubrań
clothes hanger ('klouz,hanger)
s. wieszak do ubrań
clothesline ('klous,lajn) s.
sznur na bieliznę do suszenia
clothespin ('klouz,pyn) s.
spinacz do bielizny
clothing (klouzyng) s. odzież;
osłona; bielizna;odzienie
cloud (klaud) s. chmura; obłok;
zasępienie; v. chmurzyć; sę-
pić; rzucać cień ;ufarbować
cloudy ('klaudy) adj. chmurny;
posępny; zamglony; mętny

clove (klouw) s. goździk; ząbek
czosnku: zob. cleave

clover (klouwer) s. koniczyna

clown (klaun) s. błazen; prostak; v. błaznować; wygłupiać się

club (klab) s. klub; pałka; kij; v. bić pałką; zbijać; łączyć; zrzeszać;stowarzyszać się

clue (klu:) s. klucz; ślad; wątek; v. informować(o wątku)

clumsy ('klamzy) adj. niezgrabny; nietaktowny;niekształtny

clung (klang)v.przywarty; zob. cling

cluster ('klaster) s. grono; kiść; pęk; kupka; v. tworzyć pęki; skupiać się; zbierać się

clutch (klacz) s. chwyt; szpon; sprzęgło;v.trzymać się kurczowo

clutch pedal ('klacz,pedl) s. pedał sprzęgła

coach (koucz) s. wóz pasażerski; trener; v. jechać wozem; trenować; uświadamiać;pouczać

coagulate (kou'aegjulejt) v. stężać; skrzepnąc;koagulować

coal (koul) s. węgiel

coalfield ('koul'fi:ld) s. zagłębie węglowe

coalition (,koue'lyszyn) s. związek; koalicja;przymierze

coal mine(koul-majn) s. kopalnia węgla

coal pit ('koul-pyt) s. kopalnia węgla ;szyb kopalniany

coarse (ko:rs) adj. pospolity; gruboziarnisty; szorstki

coast (koust) s. brzeg; v. jechać bez napędu;płynąć brzegiem

coastguard ('koustga:rd) s. straż przybrzeżna

coat (kout) s. marynarka; surdut; powłoka; v. okrywac; pokrywać warstwa;powlekać(farbą)

coat hanger('kouthaenger) s. wieszak (do ubrania)

coating (koutyng) s. powłoka; warstwa ;pokrycie

coat of arms('kout ow,a:rms) s. herb; godło

coax (kouks) v. namówić pochlebstwem; udobruchać;przymilać się; wycyganiać; wyczrowywać(z butelki)

cob (kob) s. głąb; kucyk; łabędź samiec;kaczan;kutwa;bochenek

cobra ('koubre) s. kobra

cobweb ('kobłeb) s. pajęczyna

cock (kok) s. kogut; kurek; kran; kutas (vulg.) v. postawić; nastroszyć; napiąć; odwodzić; podnieść; zadzierać;wznieść

cock-and-bull ('koken'bul) exp.: o żelaznym wilku

cockchafer ('kok,chejfer) s. chrząszcz

cockle ('kokl) s. kąkol;piecyk

cockpit ('kokpyt) s. kokpit; kabina;arena do walki kogutów

cockroach('kokroucz) s. karaluch

cocksure ('kokszuer) adj. pewny siebie; zarozumiały

cocktail ('koktejl) s. cocktail

coco ('koukou) s. palma kokosowa; kokos

cocoa ('koukou) s. kakao

coconut ('koukenat) s. orzech kokosowy

cocoon (ke'ku:n) s. kokon; oprzęd

cod(kod)s.dorsz;sztokfisz;wątłusz;v.wystrychnąć na dudka

coddle ('kodl) v. podgotować; pieścić; tuczyć; zepsuć

code (koud) s. kodeks; szyfr; v. szyfrować ;pisać szyfrem

cod-liver oil ('kod,lywer ojl) s. tran (lekarski)

coexist ('kougz'zyst) v. współistnieć ;koegzystować

coexistence ('kougz'zystens) s. współistnienie;współżycie

coffee('kofy) s. kawa

coffee bean ('kofy-bi:n) s. ziarno kawy

coffee mill ('kofy-myl) s. młynek do kawy

coffeepot ('kofy-pot) s. maszynka do kawy

coffin ('kofyn) s. trumna

cogwheel ('kog-hłil) s. koło zębate; tryb

coherence ('kou'hierens) s. sens; spoistość ;związek logiczny

coherency (kou'hierensy) s. sens; zwartość ;spójność

coherent (kou'hierent) adj. logiczny; zwarty; spoisty

cohesive (kou'hi:syw) adj. spoisty; zwarty ; kleisty

coiffure (kŕa:'fjuer) s. fryzura; styl uczesania

coil (kojl) s. zwój; cewka; lok;
v. zwijać; skręcać; wić się

coin (koyn) s. moneta; v. bić
monety; spieniężać; ukuć (nowe pojęcie) ;tłoczyć

coinage (koynydź) s. bicie monety; monety; system monetar-
ny; wymyśl nowe słowo

coincide (kouyn'sajd) v. zbiegać się; pokrywać się; przystawać do siebie; pasować

coincidence (kou'ynsydens) s.
zbieg okoliczności; zgodność;
przystawanie; zgodność faktów

coke (kouk) s. koks; kokaina;
Coca-Cola; v. koksować

cold (kould) s. zimno; przezię-
bienie; adj.zimny;chłodny;mroźny

cold storage room(kould-
storedźru:m) chłodnia

colic ('kolyk) s. kolka (w
brzuchu);ostry ból w brzuchu

collaborate (ke'laeberejt) v.
współpracować;kolaborować

collaboration (ke'laeberejszyn)
s. współpraca; kolaboracja

collapse (ke'laeps) s. załamanie się; v. załamać się; upaść;
opaść; zawalić się;załamywać

collapsible (ke'laepsebl) adj.
składany (mebel,,stół,łóżko etc.)

collar ('koler) s. kołnierz;
szyjka; pierścień; obroża; cho-
mąto; piana (na piwie) v.wkła-
dać obrożę; pojmać; ująć

collarbone ('koler-boun) s.
obojczyk

colleague ('koli:g) s. kolega
(po fachu);współpracownik

collect ('ke'lekt) v. zbierać;
odbierać; inkasować

collected ('ke'lektyd) adj.
skupiony; opanowany ;spokojny

collection (ke'lekszyn) s.
zbiór; kolekcja; inkaso ;zain-
kasowane pieniadze

collective ('ke'lektyw) adj.
zbiorowy; wspólny;s. kolektyw

collector ('ke'lektor) s. in-
kasent; poborca; zbieracz

college ('kolydż) s. uczelnia;
kolegium;zrzeszenie;akademia

collide (ke'lajd) v. zderzyć
się; kolidować;wejść w kolizję

colliery ('koljery) s. kopalnia węgla

collision (ke'lyżen) s. zderzenie; kolizja

colloquial (ke'loukŕjel) adj.
potoczny (język);familiarny

colon ('koulen) s. grube jelito; dwukropek

colonel('ke:nl) s. pułkownik

colonial (ke'lounjel) a. kolo-
nialny;s. mieszkaniec kolonii

colonialism (ke'lounjelyzem)s.
kolonializm

colonist ('kolenyst) s. osadnik ;mieszkaniec kolonii

colonize ('kolenajz) v. osiedlać; kolonizować

colony ('koleny) s. kolonia

color ('kaler) s. barwa; farba;
koloryt; v. barwić; farbować;
koloryzować; rumienić się

color bar ('kaler ba:r) s. oddzielenie ras

colored ('kaleret) s. murzyn;
kolorowy;adj.przekręcony

colored man ('kaleret men)
s. murzyn

colored people ('kaleret'pi:pl)
s. murzyni

colorful ('kalerful) adj.
pstry; barwny ;żywy;kolorowy

coloring ('kaleryng) s. koloryt; kolorowanie; rumieńce

colorless ('kalerlys) adj.
bezbarwny; nudny;monotonny

colorline ('kalerlajn) s.
przedział rasowy

color print ('kaler,prynt) s.
chromodruk

colt (koult) s. źrebak

column ('kolem) s. kolumna;
stos; trzon; szpalta;formacja

coma ('koume) s. omdlenie; ko-
ma; śpiączka;ogon(komety)

comb (koum) s. grzebień; grzbiet
(fali); v. czesać; kłębić się
combat ('kombet) s. walka;
v. zwalczać; walczyć
combatant ('kombetent) adj.
walczący; s. kombatant;bojownik
combination (komby'nejszyn)s.
kombinacja; zespół;związek
combine-harvester (kembajn-
ha:rwyster) s. kombajn
combustible (kem'bastebl) adj.
palny; s. paliwo; materiały
palne;opał;adj;popędliwy
combustion (kem'bastszyn) s.
spalanie; zapłon
come; came; come (kam; kejm;
kam)
come (kam) v. przybyć; pochodzić; wynosić;dziać się;być
come about ('kam,e'baut) v. zdarzyć się;stać się;odwracać się
come across ('kam,e'cros) v.
natknąć się;dać się przekonać
come along ('kam,e'long) v.
pospieszyć się; nadejść
come around ('kam,e'raund) v.
zmienić zdanie; odwiedzić
come at ('kam,et) v. podejść;
dotrzeć; przyjść o (czwartej...)
come by ('kam,baj) v. dojść do
czegoś; minąć; nabyć
come for ('kam,for) v. przyjść
po coś
come loose ('kam,luz) v. ob-
luźniać się
come off ('kam,of) v. odpaść;
odlecieć;puszczać;mieć miejsce
come on ('kam,on) v. chodź-że;
przestań; daj spokój!
come round ('kam,raund) v. zmienić zdanie;przechytrzyć;obejść
come to see ('kam tu si:) v. odwiedzić;przyjść z wizytą
come up to ('kam ap tu) v. podejść do..;wejść na sam(szczyt)
come-and-go ('kam-en'-go) s.
bieganina;ruch tam i z powrotem
comeback ('kam-'baek) s. powrót ; bystra odpowiedź;poprawa
comedian (ke'mi:djen) s. komik;

comedy ('komydy) s.komedia

comer ('kamer) s. przybysz
comet ('komyt) s. kometa
comfort ('kamfert) s. wygoda;
pociecha; v. pocieszać; czynić wygodnym;dodawać otuchy
comfortable ('kamfertebl) adj.
wygodny; zadowolony;spokojny
comforter ('kamferter) s. po-
cieszyciel; kołdra;smoczek
comical ('komykel) adj. zabawny; śmieszny;komiczny
comic strips ('komyk,stryps) s.
seryjne obrazkówki;kreskówki
comma ('kome) s. przecinek
command (ke'maend) v. rozkazywać; kazać; rozporządzać; panować nad; dowodzić; s. rozkaz;
nakaz; komenda;dowództwo
commander (ke'maender) s. dowódca; komendant;kapitan(fregaty)
commander-in-chief (ke'maender
yn'czi:f) głównodowodzący
commandment (ke'maendment) s.
przykazanie (boskie)
commend (ke'mend) v. chwalić;
zalecać; polecać opiece
comment ('koment) s. objaśnie-
nie; v. robić uwagi krytyczne
lub złośliwe;wypowiadać zdanie
comment on ('koment on) v. ko-
mentować; oceniać (utwór etc.)
commentary ('komentery) s. komentarz;uwaga; notatka
commentator ('komentejter) s.
komentator; sprawozdawca
commerce ('kome:rs) s. handel
commercial (ke'ke:rszel) adj.
handlowy;s.ogłoszenie(w radiu...)
commissar (,komy'sa:r) s. komisarz w ZSRR
commission (ke'myszyn) s. zlecenie; misja; urząd; v. delegować; powierzać; objąć; zlecać;zamianować;upoważniać
commissioner (ke'myszener) s.
delegat; pełnomocnik; komisarz
rządowy;członek komisji rządowej
commit (ke'myt) v. powierzać;
przekazywać; odsyłać; popełniać; wciągać; zobowiązywać
się;oddawać w opiekę;zamykć w
(domu wariatów);obiecywać

commitment (ke'mytment) s. zobowiązanie; dopuszczenie się;
przekazanie ;zaangażowanie się
committee (ke'mytji) s. komitet;
komisja;opiekun(umysłowo chrego)
commodity (ke'modyty) s. towar;
rzecz przydatna ;artykuł handlu
common ('komen) adj. wspólny;
publiczny; ogólny; pospolity;
zwyczajny ;prosty;publiczny
commoner ('komener) s. człowiek
z gminu ; nie szlachcic
common law marriage ('komen,lo:
'maerydż) pożycie na wiarę
common market ('komen'ma:rkyt)
wspólny rynek (Zach.Eur.)
commonplace ('komen-plejs) s.
banał; adj. banalny ;oklepany
common sense ('komen,sens)
zdrowy rozsądek
commonwealth ('komen,łels) s.
wspólnota; rzeczpospolita
commotion (ke'mouszyn) s. zamieszki; tumult; poruszenie
commune ('komju:n) s. gmina;
komuna; v. obcować; rozmawiać
communicate (ke'mju:ny,kejt) v.
dzielić się; komunikować; łączyć się ;przenosić (ciepło etc.)
communication (ke,mju:ny'kejszyn)
s. łączność; komunikacja; po-
rozumiewanie się;zakomunikowanie
communicative (ke'mju:nykejtyw)
adj. otwarty; rozmowny; towarzyski; przystępny
communion (ke'mju:njen) s. obcowanie; uczestnictwo; wspólnota; komunia;wyznanie wiary
communism ('komju,nyzem) s. komunizm ;ruch komunistyczny
communist ('komjunyst) s. komunista ;adj. komunistyczny
community (ke'mju:nyty) s. środowisko; społeczność; gmina;
kolektyw; wspólnota ;koło;zakon
commute (ke'mju:t) v. zamieniać;
zastępować; łagodzić; dojeżdżać
do pracy;brać bilet okresowy
comose ('koumous) adj. włochaty;
puszysty ;włóknisty
compact (kem'paekt) adj. gęsty;
zbity; zwarty; v. ubijać; zbijać; zagęszczać ;s.puderniczka

compact ('kempaekt) s. 1. ugoda;
porozumienie; 2. puderniczka
samochód średniej wielkości(USA)
companion (kem'paenjen) s. towarzysz; (coś) do pary
companionship (kem'paenjenszyp)
s. koleżeństwo; towarzystwo
company ('kempeny) s. towarzystwo; załoga; goście; partnerzy;
spółka; kompania ;trupa teatralna
comparable ('komperebl) adj.
porównywalny ;wytrzymujący porów-
comparative (kem'paeretyw) adj.
porównawczy; względny; stosunkowy ;s, stopień wyższy(przymiot-
compare (kem'peer) v. porówny-
wać; dawać się porównać; stopniować (gram)
comparison (kem'paeryson) s. porównanie ;zestawienie
compartment (kem'pa:rtment) s.
przedział; przegroda; komora
wodoszczelna
compass ('kempes) s. kompas;
busola; obwód; obręb;cyrkiel
zasięg v. obchodzić; otaczać;
ogarniać;osiągać;dopiąć
compassion (kem'paeszyn) s;
litość; współczucie
compassionate (kem'paeszynyt)
adj. litościwy ;v.litować się
compatible (kem'paetebl) adj.
zgodny ;licujący; do pogodzenia
compatriot (kem'paetryet) s.
rodak; ziomek ;rodaczka
compel (kem'pel) v. zmuszać;
wymuszać (coś) ;wzbudzać
compensate ('kompen,sejt) v.
wyrównywać; nagradzać; wypłacić
odszkodowanie; kompensować
compensation (kompen'sejszyn)
s. rekompensata; wynagrodzenie;
odszkodowanie ;wyrównanie
compete (kem'pi:t) v. konkuro-
wać; rywalizować; ubiegać się
compete for (kem'pi:t,fo:r) v.
(o coś) współzawodniczyć;
współubiegać sie ;prześcigać się
competence ('kompytens) s. fa-
chowość; kwalifikacja; uzdolnienie; zasobność; dobrobyt
competent ('kompytent) adj. własciwy;kwalifikowany;odpowiedni;
kompetentny

competition (,kompy'tyszyn) s.
konkurencja; konkurs; zawody;
współzawodnictwo;turniej
competitor (kem'petyter) s.
rywal; konkurent; współzawodnik;współzawodniczka;rywalka
compile (kem'pajl) v. zbierać;
zestawiać; kompilować
complacent (kem'plejsnt) adj.
zadowolony (z siebie; ze świata);błogi
complain (kem'plejn) v. żalić
się; narzekać; skarżyć; wnosić
zażalenie;wnosić skargę
complaint (kem'plejnt) s. skarga; zażalenie; dolegliwość
complete (kem'pli:t) adj. całkowity; zupełny; kompletny;
v. uzupełniać; udoskonalić;
ukończyć;wypełniać (formularz)
completion (kem'pli:szyn) s.
ukończenie; uzupełnienie;
udoskonalenie;spełnienie(woli)
complexion (kem'plekszyn) s.ce-
ra; płeć; postać; aspekt (charakter);wygląd
complicate ('komply,kejt) v.
wikłać; splatać; komplikować
compliment ('komplyment) s.
komplement; gratulacje; ukło-
ny; uszanowanie; v. mówić
komplementy; gratulować
comply (kem'plaj) v. zastosować
się; spełnić; podporządkować
się;uczynić zadość;przestrzegać
comply with (kem'plaj,łys) v.
spełniać;przestrzegać czegoś
component (kem'pounent) s.
składnik; część składowa; siła
składowa;adj.składowy
compose (kem'pouz) v. składać;
układać; tworzyć; komponować;
skupiać (myśli); uspokoić; załagodzić;uspokajać się
composed (kem'pouzd) adj. opanowany; spokojny;stateczny
composer (kem'pouzer) s. kompozytor;kompozytorka
composition (,kempe'zyszyn) s.
skład; układ; ugoda; wypracowanie; budowa;usposobienie
composure (kem'poużer) s. spokój; opanowanie;zimna krew

compote ('kompout) s. kompot
(z puszki);kompotiera
compound (kom'paund) adj. złożony; sprężony; s. związek(chem.)
mieszanka; złożenie; v. mieszać; składać; powiększać;
łączyć;zawrzeć;załatwić
comprehend (,kompry'hend) v.
pojmować; rozumieć; zawierać
comprehensible (,kompry'hensebl)
adj. zrozumiały;pojętny
comprehensive (,kompry'hensyw)
adj. obszerny; szeroki;rozumo-
wy; wyczerpujący;ogólny;wszech-
stronny
compress (kem'pres) v. ściskać;
s. kompres; okład;v.streszczać
comprise (kem'prajz) v. włączać; obejmować;składać się
compromise ('kompre,majz) s.
kompromis; ugoda; kompromitacja; narażenie; v. załatwiać
ugodowo; kompromitować
compulsion (kem'palszyn) s.
przymus; siła przymusu
compulsory (kem'palsery) adj.
przymusowy;przymuszający
compunction (kem'pankszyn) s.
skrucha;żal za grzechy
computation (,kompju'tejszyn) s.
obliczenie; kalkulcja
computer (kem'pju:ter) s. kalku-
lator; komputer; przelicznik
comrade ('komread) s. kolega;
druh; współpracownik
comradeship ('komraedszyp) s.
koleżeństwo; braterstwo
conceal (ken'si:l) v. taić;
ukrywać;przemilczać;zataić
concede (ken'si:d) v. przyznawać; ustępować; poddawać się
conceit (ken'si:t) s. próżność;
zarozumiałość;mniemanie;koncept
conceited (ken'si:tyd) adj.
próżny; zarozumiały
conceivable (ken'si:webl) adj.
wyobrażalny; zrozumiały
conceive (ken'si:w) v. wymyślić;
wyobrażać; rozumieć; ujmować;
zajść w ciążę;pojąć;redagować
concentrate ('konsentrejt) v.
skupiać się; stężać;s.roztwór
conception (ken'sepszyn) s. pomysł; poczęcie (dziecka)początek

concern (ken'se:rn) s. interes;
troska; związek; v. tyczyć się;
dotyczyć; obchodzić; niepokoić
się o...;wchodzić w grę
concerned (ken'se:rnd) adj. zainteresowany; zaaferowany;
strapiony; niespokojny
concert ('konsert) s. koncert;
porozumienie; v. ułożyć; ukar-
tować;porozumieć się
concession (ken'se szyn) s.
koncesja; ustępstwo;przyzwolenie
conciliate (ken'syly,ejt) v.
zjednywać; jednać; godzić; łagodzić; pogodzić;udobruchać
conciliatory (ken'syljeto:ry)
adj. pojednawczy
concise (ken'sajs) adj. zwięzły;
treściwy ;krotki i węzłowaty
conclude (ken'klu:d) v. zakończyć; zawierać; wnioskować;
postanawiać ;kończyć się
conclusion (ken'klu:żyn) s. zakończenie; wynik; postanowienie; wniosek; konkluzja; zawar-
cie układu ;wynik ostateczny
conclusive (ken'klu:syw) adj.
rozstrzygający; dowodny
concord ('konko:rd) s. zgoda;
jedność; harmonia;v. zgadzać się
concrete ('konkri:t) s. beton;
konkret; adj. rzeczywisty;
realny; zwarty; stały; konkretny; specyficzny; betonowy
concur (ken'ke:r) v. zgadzać
się; schodzić się;współdziałać
concurrence (ken'ke:rens) s.
zgodność; zbieżność ; zgoda
concussion (ken'kaszyn) s.
wstrząs (mózgu); uderzenie
condemn (ken'dem) v. potępiać;
skazywać ;krytykować;wybrakować
condemnation (,kendem'nejszyn)
s. potępienie; skazanie
condense (ken'dens) v. kondenso-
wać; zgęszczać;streszczać
condenser (ken'denser) s. kondensator; skraplacz
condescend (,kondy'send) v.
zniżać się; raczyć; zezwalać;
zachowywać się z wyższością

condition (ken'dyszyn) s. stan;
warunek; zastrzeżenie; poprawa-
ka; v.uwarunkowywać; zastrzegać; naprawiać; przygotowywać; przyzwyczajać;klimatyzować
conditional (ken'dyszynl) adj.
warunkowy;uzależniony;zależny
condole (ken'doul) v. składać
kondolencje;współczuć;ubolewać
condolence (ken'doulens) s.
wyrazy współczucia;kondolencje
conduct (kon'dakt) s. prowadzenie; sprawowanie; prowadzenie
się; sprawowanie się; kierownictwo; v. prowadzić; wieść;
przewodzić;dyrygować;dowodzić
conduction (kon'dakszyn) s.
przewodzenie (fiz.)
conductor (kon'dakter) s. kierownik; przewodnik; dyrygent;
przewód;odgromnik;piorunochron
cone (koun) s. stożek; szyszka;
v. nadawać kształt stożka
confection (ken'fekszyn) s.
sporządzanie; konfitura; słodycze; konfekcja (damska)
confectioner (ken'fekszyner) s.
cukiernik;właściciel cukierni
confectionery (ken'fekszynery)
s. cukiernia; wyroby cukier-
nicze
confederacy (ken'federesy) s.
konfederacja; sojusz; związek; spisek; sprzysiężenie
confederate (ken'federyt) adj.
sprzysiężony; v. jednoczyć;
spiskować; knuć;sprzymierzać
confederation (ken,fede'rejszyn)
s. sprzymierzenie; skonfedero-
wanie; konfederacja
confer (ken'fe:r) v. naradzać
się; nadawać ;przyznawać
conferee (,konfe'ri:) s. uczestnik konferencji; nagrodzony
conference ('konferens) s. narada; liga;zebranie;zjazd
confess (ken'fes) v. wyznać;
przyznać się; spowiadać się
confession (ken'feszen) s. wyznanie; spowiedź; przyznanie
się ; religia

confessor (ken'feser) s. spowiednik; ksiądz spowiednik
confide (ken'fajd) s. ufać (komuś); zwierzać się; powierzać
confidence ('konfydens) s. zaufanie; bezczelność; pewność; ufność; zwierzenie;śmiałość
confident ('konfydent) adj. dufny; bezczelny ;przekonany
confidential (,konfy'denczel) adj. tajny; poufny; zaufany; poufały;intymny
confine ('konfajn) v. ograniczać; odsabniać;s,kres;granica
confinement (kon'fajnment) s. uwięzienie; ograniczenie; odosobnienie; połóg; poród
confirm (ken'fe:rm) v. potwierdzać; zatwierdzać; umacniać; bierzmować;utwierdzać;pokrzepić
confirmation (,konfer'mejszyn) s. potwierdzenie; zatwierdzenie; bierzmowanie;pokrzepienie
confiscate ('konfyskejt) v. konfiskować; skonfiskować
conflagration (,konfle'grejszyn) s. pożar; pożoga
conflict ('konflykt) s. zatarg; starcie; konflikt; kolizja
conform (kon'fo:rm) v. dostosować; upodabniać;dostrajać
conformity (kon'fo:rmyty) s. zgodność; dostosowanie się
confound (kon'faund) v. mieszać; zawieść; pokrzyżować;poplątać
confound it ! (kon'faund,yt) exp. do licha ! niech to diabli wezmą!
confront (ken'frant) v. stawiać czoło; konfrontować;unaocznić
confuse (ken'fju:z) v. zmieszać (kogoś; siebie); wikłać;gmatwać
confusion (ken'fju:żyn) s. nieład; zamieszanie;bałagan;chaos
congeal (ken'dżi:l) v. mrozić; ścinać; marznąć;zakrzepnąć
congestion (ken'dżestczyn)s. przeludnienie; przeciążenie (ruchu); przekrwienie
conglomerate (ken'glomerejt) v. skupiać; zlewać w jedną masę
congratulate (ken'graetju,lejt) v. gratulować ;składać(komuś) gratulacje;pogratulować

congratulation (ken,graetju'lejszyn) s. gratulacje; gratulowanie; gratulacja
congregate ('kongry,gejt) adj. zbiorowy; v. skupiać; zbierać (się); gromadzić (się)
congregation (,kongry'gejszyn) s. zbieranie; zgromadzenie
congress ('kongres) s. zjazd; zebranie; parlament USA
conjecture (ken'dżekczer) s. domysł; przypuszczenie; v. przypuszczać; mniemać
conjugal ('kondżugel) adj. małżeński
conjugate ('kondżu,gejt) v. odmieniać się; kopulować; parzyć się;adj.połączony
conjugation (,kondżu'gejszyn) s. koniugacja; zespalanie się; kopulacja;odmiana czasownika
conjunction (ken'dżankszyn) s. zbieg; związek; skojarzenie; spójnik; połączenie
conjunctive mood (ken'dżanktyw, mu:d) s. tryb łączący
conjure (kan'dżur) v. zaklinać; błagać;robić sztuczki
conjure ('kandżer) v. czarować
conjurer ('kandżerer) s. czarownik; magik;kuglarz
connect (ke'nekt) v. łączyć; wiązać;mieć połączenie
connected (ke'nektyd) a. zwarty (logiczny); ustosunkowany
connection(xion) (ke'nekszyn) s. połączenie; pokrewieństwo
conquer ('konker) v. zdobyć; zwyciężyć; pokonać
conqueror ('konkerer) s. zdobywca; zwycięzca
conquest ('konkłest) s. podbój; zdobycie;zawojowanie
conscience ('konszyns) s. sumienie;świadomość zła i dobra
conscientious (,konszy'enszes) adj. sumienny;skrupulatny
conscious ('konszes) adj. przytomny; świadomy;naumyślny
consciousness ('konszesnys) s. świadomość;całość myśli i uczuć
conscript ('konskrypt) s.& adj. poborowy ;s.rekrut;v.rekwirować; brać do wojska

consecrate ('konsy,krejt) v.
poświęcać;adj.poświęcony
consecutive (ken'sekjutyw)
adj. kolejny;nieprzerwany;skut-
consent (ken'sent) s. zgoda; kowy
v. zgadzać się;przyzwalać
consequence ('konsykŁens) s.wy-
nik; znaczenie; konsekwencja
consequently ('konsykŁently)
adv. a zatem; przeto; tym samym;w skutek tego; więc
conservative (ken'se:rwatyw)
adj. ostrożny; zachowawczy;
konserwatywny; s. konserwatys-
ta; środek konserwujący
conserve (ken'se:rw) v. konserwować; zachowywać; zabezpieczać; s. konserwa owocowa
consider (ken'syder) v. rozważać; rozpatrywać; uważać; szanować; mieć wzgląd;sądzić
considerable (ken'syderebl)
adj. znaczny;adv.znacznie
considerate (ken'syderyt) adj.
myślacy; uważający; troskliwy
consideration (ken,syde'rejszyn)
s. wzgląd; rozważanie; warunek;
uprzejmość; rekompensata
consign (ken'sajn) v. przekazać;
powierzać;złożyć do(banku,grobu..)
consignment(ken'sajnment) s.
przesyłka ; powierzenie
consist (ken'syst) v. składać
się; polegać;zgadzać się
consistency (ken'systensy) s.
konsystencja; solidność; stałość; zgodność;logiczność
consistent (ken'systent) adj.
zgodny; stały; konsekwentny
consolation (,konse'lejszyn) s.
pocieszenie; pociecha;ukojenie
console (ken'soul) v. pocieszać;
s. konsola; wspornik;podpora
consolidate (ken'solydejt) v.
utwierdzać; scalać; jednoczyć
consonant ('konsenent) s. spółgłoska; adj. spółgłoskowy;
zgodny; harmonijny
conspicuous ('ken'spykjues) adj.
widoczny; zwracający uwagę
conspiracy (ken'spyresy) s. spisek; konspiracja; zmowa; umowa

conspirator (ken'spyreter) s.
spiskowiec; konspirator
conspire (ken'spajer) v. konspirować;spiskować;uknuć
constable ('kanstebl) s. policjant; posterunkowy
constant ('konstent) adj. stały; trwały;s. liczba stała
consternation (,konste:rnejszyn)
s. przerażenie;osłupienie
constipation (,konsty'pejszyn)
s. zatwardzenie ; zaparcie
constituency (ken'stytjuensy)
s. okręg wyborczy; wyborcy
constituent (ken'stytjuent)
adj. składowy; s. wyborca;
część składowa; element
constitute ('konsty,tju:t) v.
stanowić; ustanawiać; wyznaczać
constitution (,konsty'tju:szyn)
s. statut; konstytucja; struktura; założenie;układ psychiczny
constitutional (,konsty'tu:szenl)
adj. zasadniczy; istotny; zdrowotny;s.przechadzka dla zdrowia
constrain (ken'strejn) v. wymuszać; zmuszać; ograniczać;
więzić; zniewalać;przymuszać
constraint (ken'strejnt) s.
przymus; skrępowanie; ograniczenie swobody(ruchów etc.)
construct (ken'strakt) v. budować; tworzyć; rysować(figury geom.)
construction (ken'strakszyn)
s. budowa; konstrukcja;układ:
konstruowanie;ujęcie;interpretacja
constructive (ken'straktyw)
adj. twórczy; konstruktywny
consul ('konsel) s. konsul
consular ('konsjuler) adj.
konsularny
consulate ('konsjulyt) s. konsulat;uprawnienia konsula
consulate general ('konsjulyt'
'dżenerel) s. konsulat generalny
consult (ken'salt) v. radzić
się; informować się
consultation (,konsel'tejszyn)
s. porada; konsultacja
consultative (ken'saltetyw) a.
doradczy; konsultatywny

consume (ken'sju:m) v, spożywać; zużywać; trawić; niszczeć; marnieć;uschnąć

consumer (ken'sju:mer) s. konsumer; spożywca;odbiorca

consummate(ken'samyt) a. doskonały;wielkiej miary;skończony

consummate('kensemejt) v. spełniać małżeństwo

consumption (ken'sampszyn) s. zużycie; suchoty; pylica

contact ('kontaekt) s. styczność; stosunki; znajomości v. kontaktować; porozumiewać się;stykać się;zetknąć się

contact lenses ('kontaekt,lenzys) pl. szkła kontaktowe

contagious (ken'tejdżes) a. zaraźliwy ; zakaźny;udzielający się

contain (ken'tejn) v. zawierać; opanowywać się; wiązać;hamować

container (ken'tejner) s. zasobnik; zbiornik; naczynie

contaminate (ken'taemynejt) v. zakazić;skalać;deprawować

contamination (ken'taemynejszyn) s. kontaminacja; zakażenie; skażenie; ujemny wpływ

contemplate ('kontemplejt) v. oglądać; rozważać; liczyć się z (czyms); medytować;planować

contemplation ('kontemplejszyn) s. oglądanie; kontemplacja; rozważanie;planowanie;medytacja

contemplative ('kontemplejtyw) adj. kontemplacyjny; zamyślony

contemporary (ken'temperery), adj.& s. współczesny (rówiesnik)

contempt (ken'temt) s. pogarda; lekceważenie;obraza (sądu etc.)

contemptible (ken'temtebl) adj. godny pogardy, lekceważenia

contemptuous (ken'temtjues) adj. pogardliwy;nadęty;lekceważący

contend (ken'tend) v. spierać się; walczyć;rywalizować;upierać się

content 1. (ken'tent) adj. zadowolony; s. zadowolenie; v. zadowalać

content 2. ('kontent) s. zawartość; treść; objętość; pojemność;powierzchnia;kubatura;istota

contented (ken'tentyd) adj. zadowolony; zaspokojony

contents ('kontents) s. zawartość(pojemnika,treści

contest ('kontest) s. rywalizacja; spór; v. walczyć; spierać się; ubiegać; kwestionować

context ('kontekst) s. kontekst

continent ('kontynent) s. kontynent; część świata

continental ('kontynentl) adj. kontynentalny; s. mieszkaniec kontynentu

continual (ken'tynjuel) adj. ciągły; powtarzający się;stały

continuance (ken'tynjuens) s. ciągłość; trwanie; przebieg; ciąg dalszy;odroczenie;pobyt

continuation (ken,tynju'ejszyn) s. kontynuacja; ciąg dalszy

continue (ken'tynju:) v. kontynuować; ciągnąć dalej; trwać; ciągnąć się ;odroczyć;upierać

continuous (ken'tynjues) adj. nieprzerwany;stały;ciągły

contort (ken'to:rt) v. skręcać; wykrzywiać ;zwichnąć;przekrzywić

contour ('kontuer) s. zarys; kontur,warstwica;v.konturować

contraceptive (,kontre'septyw) s. środek zapobiegający zapłodnieniu ;adj.antykoncepcyjny

contract ('kontraekt) s. umowa; układ; kontract ;obietnica

contract (ken'traekt) v. ściągać; kurczyć; zobowiązywać

contractor (ken'traekter) s. przedsiębiorca (budowlany etc.)

contradict (,kontre'dykt) v. zaprzeczać ;posprzeczać się

contradiction (,kontre'dykszyn) s. sprzeczność ;zaprzeczenie

contradictory (,kontre'dyktery) adj. sprzeczny,przekorny;kłótliwy

contrary ('kontrery) adj. przeciwny; s. przeciwieństwo; adv. w przeciwieństwie

contrariwise ('kontrery,łajz) adv. odwrotnie; natomiast

contrast (ken'traest) v.przeciwstawiać; kontrastować; s.kontrast; przeciwieństwo

contribute (ken'trybjut) v.,
przyczynić się; dostarczyć;
współdziałać;zasłużyć się
contribution (,kontry'bju:szyn)
s. przyczynek; wkład; ofiara;
kontrybucja;datek;wsparcie
contributor (ken'trybjuter) s.
ofiarodawca; współpracownik
(pisarz);współpracowniczka
contrite (ken'trajt) adj. skruszony ;pełen skruchy
contrivance (ken'trajwens) s.
pomysł; sztuczka; fortel; wynalazek;wynalazczość;pomysłowość
contrive (ken'trajw) v. wymys-
lić; wynaleźć; doprowadzić do
czegoś; zaplanować;wykombinować
control (ken'troul) v. sprawdzać; rządzić; kontrolować;
opanować, s. kontrola; sterowanie; regulowanie; ster;władza
controller (ken'trouler) s.
kontroler;regulator;zarządca
controversial (,kentre'we:rżel)
adj. sporny; sprzeczający się
controversy ('kontre,we:rsy)
s. spór;kłótnia;polemika;dysputa
contuse (ken'tju:z) v. stłuc;
kontuzjować
convalesce (,konwe'les) v. wyzdrowieć i odzyskać siły
convalescence (,konwe'lesens)
s. wyzdrowienie
convalescent (,konwe'lesnt) s.
rekonwalescent; ozdrowieniec
convenience (ken'wi:njens) s.
wygoda; korzyść;dogoność
convenient (ken'wi:njent) adj.
wygodny;łatwy do osiągnięcia
convent ('konwent) s. zakon
convention (ken'wenszyn) s.
zjazd; zgromadzenie; układ;
umowa; konwent;zebranie
conventional (ken'wenszynl)
adj. zwyczajowy; konwencjonal-
ny; umowny;powszechnie stosowany
conversation (,konwer'sejszyn)
s. rozmowa; konwersacja
converse (ken'we:rs) v. rozmawiać;obcować;prowadzić rozmowę
converse ('konwe:rs) s. rozmowa;
adj. odwrotny; s.rzecz odwrotna

conversion (ken'we:rżyn) s.od-
wrócenie; przemiana; nawrócenie;przeistoczenie
convert (ken'we:rt) v. zmie-,
niać; nawracać; przekształcać;
odwracać;przemieniać;przystosować
convert ('konwert) s. neofita
convertible (ken'we:rtybl) adj.
wymienialny; s. otwarty samochód z podnoszonym dachem
convey (ken'wej) v. przewozić;
przenosić; przesyłać; przekazywać; komunikować;zapisywać
conveyance (ken'wejens) s. przewóz; przenoszenie; uzmysławia-
nie; pojazd; przekazanie
conveyor belt (ken'wejer,belt)
s. przenośnik taśmowy
convict ('konwykt) s. skazaniec;
więzień; v. udowadniać; przekonywać; uznać winnym
conviction (ken'wykszyn) s.
przeświadczenie; przekonanie;
zasądzenie;skazanie
convince (ken'wyns) v. przekonać;przekonywać
convoy ('konwoj) s. konwój;
eskorta; straż
convoy (kon'woj) v. konwojować
convulsion (ken'walszyn) s.
drgawki; wstrząs; konwulsje
convulsive (ken'walsyw) adj.
konwulsyjny;niepohamowany
cook (kuk) s. kucharz; kucharka; v. gotować; preparować
cooking (kukyng) s. gotowanie
cool (ku:l) adj. chłodny;
oziębły; spokojny; v. chłodzić;
studzić; ochłonąć; s. chłód
cooler ('ku:ler) s. chłodnica;
element chłodzący;więzienie
coolness ('ku:lnys) s. chłód;
zimna krew;opanowanie;spokój
co-op (kou'op) s. spółdzielnia
cooperate (kou'operejt) v.,
współpracować; współdziałać
cooperation (kou,ope'rejszyn)
s. współpraca; współdziałanie
kooperacja; spółdzielczość
cooperative (kou,ope'rejtyw)
adj. spółdzielczy; uspołecznio-
ny; uczynny; współpracujący

cooperator (kou'ope,rejter) s.
współpracownik; współdzielca
coordinate (kou'o:rdynejt) adj.
współrzędny; współrzędna
cop (kop) s. policjant (slang)
v. złapać; wygrać; buchnąć;
nakryć ;porwać; ukraść(slang)
coPartner (kou'pa:rtner) s.
uczestnik; wspólnik; udziało-
wiec(we wspólnym interesie)
cope ('koup) v. uporać; dawać
sobie radę; pokrywać; zwień-
czać; s. kapa;peleryna(duża)
copilot ('kou'pajlot) s. ko-
pilot:zastępca pilota
copious ('koupjes) adj. obfity;
suty; bogaty;płodny;obfitujący
copper ('koper) s. miedź; v.mie-
dziować; slang: glina; policjant;miedziak;kocioł z miedzi
copy ('kopv) v. kopiować; prze-
pisywać; naśladować; s. kopia;
odpis; odbitka; egzemplarz;
wzór; model;rękopis do druku
copybook ('kopy,buk) s. zeszyt
copyright ('kopy,rajt) s. prawo
autorskie.v.chronić prawem autor-
skim
coral ('korel) s. koral
cord (ko:rd) s. sznur; lina;
v. wiązać; ustawiać w sągi
cordial ('ko:rdżel) adj. serdeczny; nasercowy;s.lek nasercowy
cordiality (,ko:rdy'aelyty) s.
serdeczność; kordialność
corduroys ('ko:rde,rojz) pl.
sztruksowe spodnie
core (ko:r) s. rdzeń v. usuwać
rdzeń; wycinać rdzeń
cork (ko:rk) s, korek;v.korkować
corkscrew ('ko:rk,skru:) s. korkociąg;adj.w kształcie korkociąga
corn (ko:rn) s. 1. ziarno; zboże; kukurydza; 2. nagniotek
corner ('ko:rner) s. róg; narożnik; kąt; zakręt; zapędzać do
kąta; zmuszać; monopolizować
cornered ('ko:rnerd) adj. rogaty;
schwytany;zapędzony w ślepą uli-
cę
cornet ('ko:rnyt) s. kornet;
trąbka (mosiężna)
cornflakes ('ko:rn,flejks) pl.
płatki z kukurydzy

coronary disease('korenery dy
'zi:z)s.choroba wieńcowa
coronation (,kore'nejszyn)s.koro-
nacja
coroner('korener)s. sędzia śledczy, lekarz sądowy(oględziny zwłok)
corporal ('ko:rperel) adj. cielesny; osobisty; s. kapral
corporation (,ko:rpe'rejszyn)
s. korporacja; zrzeszenie;
osoba prawna zbiorowa
corpse (ko:rps) s. trup;zwłoki
corpulent ('ko:rpjulent) adj.
tęgi; otyły; gruby;tłusty
corral (ke'rael) s. ogrodzenie
dla bydła; tabór; v. zamykać
w ogrodzeniu; łapać; ustawiać
tabor;wpędzać do ogrodzenia
correct (ke'rekt) adj, poprawny;
v. korygować; karcić; prostować;leczyć;naprawiać
correction (ke'rekszyn) s. poprawka; korektura ;kara
correspond (,korys'pond) v.
odpowiadać; korespondować
correspondence (,korys'pondens)
s. zgodność; korespondencja
correspondent (,korys'pondent)
s. korespondent; adj. odpowiedni; zgodny z; odpowiadający
corridor ('korydo:r) s. korytarz
corrigible ('korydżybl) adj.
dający się poprawić;uległy
corroborate (ke'robe,rejt) v.
potwierdzić ;potwierdzać
corrode (ke'roud) v. zżerać;
rdzewieć; niszczeć; niszczyć
corrosion (ke'roużyn) s. koroz-
ja; zżeranie; niszczenie
corrugate ('korugejt) v.
marszczyć; fałdować;karbować
corrugated iron('korugejtyd'
ajron) s. pofałdowana blacha
corrupt (ke'rapt) adj. zepsuty;
sprzedajny;v.korumpować;psuć się
corruption (ke'rapszyn) s. zepsucie; korupcja;rozkład;fałszowanie
corset ('ko:rsyt) s. gorset;
sznurówka; v.wkładać gorset
cosmetic (koz'metyk) s. kosmetyk; adj. kosmetyczny
cosmetician (koz'metyszyn) s.
kosmetyczka

cosmonaut ('kozme,no:t) s. kos-
monauta ;astronauta (w USA)
cost; cost; cost (kost; kost;
kost)
cost (kost) v. kosztowac;
s. koszt; strata; cena
costly ('kostly) adj. kosztowny; wspaniały;drogi;cenny
costume ('kostju:m) s. kostium;
strój; v. przystroic w kostium
cosy ('kouzy) adj. przytulny;
v. przytulić się
cot (kot) s. łóżko składane;
szałas; schronienie
cottage ('kotydż) s. chata; dwo-
rek;domek letniskowy
cottage cheese ('kotydż, czi:z)
s. biały ser krowi z kwaśnego mle-
cotton ('kotn) s. bawełna; v.po-
lubić; kapować;adj.bawełniany
cotton wool ('kotn,żul) s. wata
couch (kaucz) s. tapczan; posłanie; łóżko;v.rozsiadać się;mó-
cougar ('ku:ger) s. puma; kuguar
cough (kof) s. kaszel; v. kaszleć ; wykaszleć;,zakaszleć
could (kud) v. mógłby; zob.:cań;
council ('kaunsyl) s. rada; konsylium; sobór;zarząd (miejski etc.)
councilor ('kaunsyler) s. radny;
radca; członek zarządu)
counsel ('kaunsel) s. rada; zamysł; radca prawny; v. radzić;
doradzać; przyjmować radę
count (kaunt) v. liczyć; sądzić;
liczyć się; znaczyć; s. rachuba;
liczenie; suma; zarzut; hrabia
countdown (kaunt-dałn) s. liczenie do startu (rakiety)
count in (kaunt yn) v. brać w rachubę; wliczać; włączyć
count out (kaunt aut) v. wyli-
czyć; nie brać w rachubę
countenance ('kauntynens) s. mina; wyraz twarzy; śmiałość;
pewność siebie; animusz; fantazja; v. zachęcać; popierać;
zatwierdzać;usankcjonować
counter ('kaunter) s. 1. kantor;
lada; licznik; żeton; 2. przeciwieństwo; cios odbijający;
napiętek; adj. przeciwny; prze-

ciwległy; podwójny; v. sprzeciwiać się; reagować; uderzać;
adv. przeciwnie; na przekór;
wbrew (instrukcjom,poleceniom..)
counteract (,kaunter'aekt) v.
przeciwdziałać;neutralizować
counterbalance ('kaunter,-
,baelens) s. przeciwwaga
counterespionage ('kaunter'-
'espje,na:ż) s. kontrwywiad
counterfeit ('kaunterfyt) adj.
fałszywy; podrobiony:v.udawać;
counterintelligence
('kaunteryn'tylydżens) s.
kontrwywiad
counterpart ('kaunter,pa:rt)
s. odpowiednik; duplikat
countess ('kauntys) s. hrabina; hrabianka
countless ('kauntlys) adj. niezliczony; nie do zliczenia
country ('kantry) s. kraj;
ojczyzna; wieś; prowincja
country house ('kantry-'haus)
s. dom wiejski;dom na wsi
countryman ('kantrymen) s.
rodak; wieśniak;człowiek ze wsi
countryside ('kantry,sajd) s.
okolica; krajobraz;ludzie ze wsi
country town ('kantry,tałn)
s. miasteczko: duża wieś
county ('kaunty) s. powiat;
hrabstwo ;adj.powiatowy
couple ('kapl) s. para; v. łączyć; parzyć się; żenić
coupling ('kaplyng) s. złącze;
skojarzenie; sprzęgło
coupon ('ku:pon) s. odcinek;
kupon wymienny(w sklepie,banku...)
courage ('karydż) s. odwaga
courageous (ke'rejdżes) adj.
odważny; śmiały;dzielny;waleczny
courier ('kurjer) s, posłaniec;
goniec;kurier; agent turystyczny
course (ko:rs) s. bieg; kierunek; ruch naprzód; droga; danie; kolejność; bieżnia;
warstwa; kurs; ciąg; v. gnać;
pędzić; ścigać; uganiać się
court (ko:rt) s. podworze; hala; dwór; hotel; sąd; v.zale-
cać się; wabić; zabiegać;

courteous ('ke:rczjes) adj.
grzeczny; uprzejmy i miły
courtesy ('ke:rtysy) s. grzeczność; uprzejmość; kurtuazja;
(darmowa) usługa; gest przez
grzeczność; adj.grzecznościowy
courtly ('ko:rtly) adj. układny;wytworny: dworski;dostojny
courtmartial ('ko:rt'ma:rszel) s.
sąd wojenny;v.sądzić sadem wojskowym
court of justice ('ko:rt,ow
'dżastys) s. sad
courtroom ('ko:rt.ru:m) s. sala sądowa (rozpraw)
courtship ('ko:rtszyp) s. zaloty; umizgi do kobiety
courtyard ('ko:rt,ja:rd) s. podwórze; dziedziniec
cousin ('kazyn) s. kuzyn; kuzynka; krewny;cioteczny brat(siostra)
cover ('kawer) s. koc; wieko;
oprawa; osłona; koperta; nakrycie (stołu); pokrycie; v. kryć;
pokryć (klacz);ubezpieczać; dać
opis;nakrywać;rozlać;chowac;przejechać
coverage ('kawerydż) s. pokrycie ubezpieczeniem; zasięg radiowy; omówienie w prasie
covering ('kaweryng) s. osłona;
pokrycie (dachu);przykrycie
covert ('kawert) s. schronienie;
adj. ukryty; potajemny;przebrany
covet ('kawyt) v. pożądać (cu-
dzego);patrzyć z zawiścią
covetous (kawytes) adj. chciwy;
pożądliwy; łapczywy;zawistny
cow (kał) s. krowa; v. zastraszyć się; przestraszyć się
coward ('kauerd) s. tchórz;
adj. tchórzliwy; bojaźliwy
cowardice ('kauerdys) s.
tchórzostwo ;tchorzliwość
cowardly ('kauerdly) adj.
tchórzliwy; adv. tchórzliwie
cowboy ('kałboj) s. konny pastuch;pastuch bydła;krowiarz
cower ('kauer) v. skulić się;
kucnąć; przykucać do ziemi
cowherd ('kał,he:rd) s. pasterz
bydła; pastuszka
cowhide ('kał,hajd) s. krowia
skóra; skóra wołowa

cowshed ('kał,szed) s. krowia
szopa; obora
cowslip ('kał,slyp) s. pier-
wiosnek(kwiat bagienny)
coxcomb ('koks,koum) s. błazen;
fircyk; pajac;głupi zarozumialec
coxswain ('kok,słejn) s. sternik na regatach
coy (koj) adj. skromny; nieśmiały; ostrożny; cichy;udający
cozy (kouzy) adj. wygodny;
przytulny;s.okrycie czajnika
crab (kraeb) s. krab; rak;
(wulg.) menda; v. łowić kraby;
krytykować; rujnować;narzekać
crab louse ('kraeb,laus) s.
wesz łonowa
crack (kraek) s. trzask; rysa;
szpara; próba; dowcip;
v. trzaskać; żartować; łupać;
uderzyć; rujnować; adj. wyso-
kiej jakości; doskonały
crack a joke (kraek e dżok) v.
palnąć żart;palnąć kawał
crack a smile('kraek,e smajl)
v. (slang) uśmiechnąć się
cracker ('kraeker) s. sucharek; petarda; łupacz;kłamstwo
crackpot ('kraekpot) s. wariat;
bez piątej klepki (slang)
crackle ('kraekl) v. trzeszczeć; s. trzeszczenie; pajęczyna; porcelana zdobiona
cradle ('krejdl) s. kołyska;
kolebka; wywrotka; v. kraść
w kołysce; kołysać; kosić
(kosa z ramą);płukać złoto
craft (kraeft) s. rzemiosło;
branża; sztuka; cech; podstęp;
chytrość; biegłość; pojazd
craftsman ('kraftsmen) s. rzemieślnik;mistrz w swoim zawodzie
crafty ('kra-fty) adj. sprytny;
zręczny; podstępny;przebiegły
crag (kraeg) s. skała (stroma);
turnia;nawis skalny
cram (kraem) v. tłoczyć; napychać; opychać; wytłaczać; wkuwać (się); s. tłok; ciżba;
wkuwanie się do egzaminu;ścisk;
kłamstwo; uczenie się do egzaminu
intensywnie i w pośpiechu

cramp (kraemp) s.skurcz; klamra; zwornik; v. ściskać; krępować; ograniczać; adj. ściśnięty; stłoczony; nieczytelny; sztuczny;uchwycony w imadło

cranberry ('kraenbery) s. żurawina; brusznica błotna

crane (krejn) s. żuraw; dźwig; v. podnosić; wyciągać szyję

crank (kraenk) s. korba; dziwak; bzik; v. puszczać w ruch (korba); kręcić; wydębić

crank up ('kraenk,ap) v. zapuszczać (motor);uruchomić(motor)

crape (kraep) s. gra w kości; brednie; bzdury;nonsens

crape (krejp) s. krepa

crash (kraesz) s. huk; łomot; upadek; katastrofa; ruina; krach; samodział; v. trzaskać; huczeć; roztrzaskiwać; wpaść na...; adv. z hukiem;z trzaskiem ;z łomotem;z hałasem

crash helmet ('kraesz,helmyt) s. kask ochronny (motocyklisty)

crash landing ('kraesz;laendyng) s. rozbicie się przy lądowaniu

crate (krejt) s. stare pudło; skrzynia; paka; v. pakować w skrzynie;wkładać do pak

crater ('krejter) s. krater

crave (krejw) v. pożądać; pragnąć; prosić usilnie; błagać

crawfish ('kro:fysz) s. rak; v. wycofywać się(rakiem)

crawl (kro:l) v. pełzać; czołgać się; wlec; roić się; s. czołganie; pływanie kraulem; ciarki;basen do hodowli raków

crayfish ('krejfysz) s. rak (rzeczny);rak morski bez kleszczy

crayon ('krejen) s. kredka; rysunek kredką; v. rysować kredką; szkicować;narysować węglem

crazy ('krejzy) adj. zwariowany; pomylony; walący się (np.dom)

crazy about ('krejzy,e'baut) zwariowany na punkcie czegoś

creak (kri:k) v. skrzypieć; trzeszczeć; s. skrzypienie; pisk; zgrzyt; trzask; trzeszczenie;pisknięcie; zgrzytnięcie

cream (kri:m) s. śmietana; śmietanka; krem; v. ustać się; zbierać śmietankę; zabielać

cream cheese(kri:m,czi:z) s. ser śmietankowy(biały i miękki)

creamy ('kri:my) adj. śmietankowy ; jak śmietana

crease ('kri:s) s. fałda; kant (spodni); v. fałdować; plisować; prasować; zmiąć;pomiąć

create (kry:'ejt) v. tworzyć; wywoływać ;zapoczątkować;powodować

creation (kry'ejszyn) s. stworzenie; kreacja; świat ;wszechświat

creative (kry'ejtyw) adj. twórczy;wynalazczy;tworzący

creator (kry'ejter) s. twórca

creature ('kri:czer) s. stwór; istota; kreatura (dominowana)

credentials (kry'denszelz) pl. dokumenty; listy uwierzytelniające (tożsamość posła etc.)

credibility gap (,kredy'bylyty gaep) s. niedowierzanie; luka w zaufaniu ;brak zaufania

credible ('kredybl) adj. wiarogodny ; wiarygodny

credit ('kredyt) s. kredyt; wiara; autorytet; powaga; uznanie; chluba; v. dawać wiarę; zapisywać na rachunek; zaliczać ;przypisywać(coś komuś)

creditable ('kredytebl) adj. zaszczytny; chlubny;godny pochwały

credit card ('kredyt ka:rd) karta kredytowa do zakupów

creditor ('kredyter) s. wierzyciel(handlowy,prywatny etc.)

credulous ('kredjules) adj. łatwowierny;zbyt łatwowierny

creed (kri:d) s. wiara; wierzenia; głębokie przekonania

creek (kri:k) s. potok; zatoka

creep; crept; crept (kri:p; krept; krept)

creep (kri:p) v. pełzać; wkradać sie; mieć ciarki; s. pełzanie; ciarki; obsuwanie; poślizg; nędzny typ;pełzanie się

creeper ('kri:per) s. pnącz

cremate (krymejt) v. spalać zwłoki na popiół

crept (krept) v.podpełzał; zob.:
creep
crescent ('kresnt) s. półksiężyc; adj. półksiężycowy; rosnący; przybywający;a.rogalik
cress (kres) s. rzeżucha
crest (krest) s. czub; grzebień; grzywa; pióropusz; kita;
hełm; klejnot; grzbiet; v.for-
mować grzbiet; osiągnąć szczyt
crestfallen (krest-folen) adj.
z opadnietym czubem; speszony;
zawstydzony; przygnębiony
crevasse (kry'waes) s. szczelina; pęknięcie (w lodowcu etc.)
crevice ('krewys) s. szczelina; rysa; pęknięcie; szpara
crew (kru:)s. załoga; drużyna;
zgraja; zob. crow
crib (kryb) s. żłob z pętami;
stajnia; obora; ciupka; pokoik;
domek; kojec; plagiat; v. stła-
czać; wyposażać w żłoby; ocemb-
rować; zwędzić;używać ściągaczki
cricket ('krykyt) s. świerszcz;
krykiet; v. grać w krykieta
crime (krajm) s. zbrodnia
criminal ('krymynl) s. zbrodniarz; kryminalista; adj. :
zbrodniczy; kryminalny
crimson ('krymzn) s. & adj. kar-
mazyn(owy); v. zabarwiać na
karmazynowo; zaczerwieniać się
cringe (kryndż) s. uniżonosc;
v. kulić; kurczyć się; kłaniać
sie; płaszczyć sie (usłużnie)
cripple ('krypl) kulawy; kaleka
v. okulawić; osłabiać; kuleć;
utykać; okaleczyć;przeszkadzać
crisis ('krajsys) s. przesilenie; kryzys:krytyczna sytuacja
crises ('krajsi:z) pl. prze-
silenia; kryzysy; opały
crisp (krysp) adj. rześki;
chrupki; energiczny; v.robić
kruchym;marszczyć; kędzierza-
wić;fryzować; ufryzować
critic ('krytyk) s. krytyk
critical ('krytykel) adj. kryty-
kujący; krytyczny; trudny do
nabycia; ważny(moment etc.)

criticism ('krytysyzem) s. krytyka; krytycyzm;znajdowanie błędów
criticize ('krytysajz) s. krytykować; ganić; znajdywać błędy
croak (krouk) v. rechotać; krakać;s. rechot;rechotanie;krąkanie
crochet ('krouszej) v. robić
na szydełku ; szydełkować
crockery ('krokery) s. naczynia gliniane(dzbany, słoje etc.)
crocodile ('krokedajl) s. krokodyl; adj.krokodylowy
crocus ('kroukes) s. krokus;
szafran(z rodziny irysów)
crook (kruk) s. hak; zagięcie;
krzywizna; kanciarz; krzywić;
wyginać; krasć; kantować
crooked (krukyd) adj. zakrzy-
wiony; krzywy; wypaczony;
zgarbiony; cygański; szachraj-
ski; oszukańczy;zgięty;wygięty
crop (krop) s. plon; biczysko:
bacik; całość; przycinanie;
krótko strzyżone włosy; ucinek;
v. strzyc; skubać; zbierać;
zasiewać; obrodzić; wyłaniać
się; uprawiać ziemię; obradzać
crop up (krop ap) v. nagle
zjawiać się; wyskoczyć nagle
cross (kros) s. krzyż; skrzyżowanie; mieszaniec; kant;
cygaństwo; v. żegnać się;
krzyżować; przecinać coś; iść
w poprzek; przekreślać;
udaremnić; adj. poprzeczny;
skośny; krzyżujący; przeciwny; gniewny; opryskliwy
cross out ('kros,aut) v. wy-
kreślać;skreślać;przekreślać
cross-examination ('kros -
ig'zaemynejszyn) s. przesłuchanie; badanie (w śledztwie)
crossing ('krosyng) s. skrzyżowanie; przejście lub przejazd na druga stronę (rzeki...)
crossroads ('krosroudz) pl.
rozstaje; skrzyżowanie dróg
crossword puzzle ('krosłord-
'pazl) s. krzyżówka
crouch (kraucz) v. kulić się;
kurczyć; przysiąść;gotować się
do skoku

crow (krou) s. kruk; wrona;
pianie; wesoły pisk; v. piac;
piszczec wesoło;krzyczec z radosci
crowbar ('krouba:r) s. drąg;
lewar; łom(do podważania etc.)
crowd (kraud) s. tłum; tłok;
banda; mnóstwo; v. tłoczyc;
natłoczyc; napierac; wypchac;
spieszyc; przepełniac
crowded ('kraudyd) adj. zatłoczony; zapchany;przeludniony
crown (kraun) s. korona; wieniec; v. wienczyc; koronowac
crucial ('kru:szel) adj. decydujący; przełomowy; krytyczny
crucifixion (,kru:sy'fykszyn)
s. ukrzyżowanie; krucyfiks
crucify (kru:syfaj) v. ukrzyżo-
wac;torturowac;znęcac się
crude (kru:d) adj. surowy;
szorstki; niepożyty;obskórny
cruel (kruel) adj. okrutny
cruelty ('kuelty) s. okrucieństwo; znęcanie się(nad kims)
cruet ('kru:yt) v. flaszeczka;
ampułka;buteleczka(na ocet etc.)
cruise (kru:z) v. krążyc; leciec; podróżowac; s. wycieczka
morska; przejażdżka; rejs
crumb (kram) s. okruch; (slang)
drań; v. kruszyc; drobic; do-
dawac okruszyn;obtoczyc(w bułce)
crumble ('kramb) v. kruszyc; (się)
crumple ('krampl) v. zmiąc;
zmarszczyc;załamywac się
crumple up ('krampl,ap) v. po-
miąc; zawalic się;załamac się
crunch (krancz) v. miażdżyc;
chrupac; s, chrupanie; chrzęst
crusade (kru:'sejd) s. wyprawa
krzyżowa ;v.isc z krucjatą
crusader (kru:'sejder) s. krzy-
żowiec;aktywny działacz
crush (krasz) v. kruszyc; miażdżyc; miąc; s, miażdżenie;
tłok; ciżba; zadurzenie się
crusher (kraszer) s. łamacz;
miażdżarka;druzgocący cios
crust (krast) s. skorupa; skóra;
v. zaskorupiac (się)
crutch (kracz) s. kula; podpórka ;laska;v.podpierac się

cry (kraj) s. krzyk; płacz;
wrzask; okrzyk; hasło; v.krzy-
czec; płakac; urągac; ujadac
cry-baby ('kraj,bejby) s. mazgaj; beksa; płaksa(dziecinna)
crying ('krajyng) s. wołanie;
płacz adj. płaczący;skandalicz-
ny
cry of rage ('kraj,ow'rejdż)
s. krzyk szału (wściekłości)
crypt (krypt) s. krypta
crystal ('krystl) s. kryształ;
szkiełko od zegarka;adj.kryszta-
łowy
crystalline ('krystelajn) adj.
krystaliczny;kryształowy
crystallize ('krystelajz) v.
krystalizowac się
cub (kab) s. szczenię (dzikie-
go zwierza); zuch;młodzik
cube (kju:b) s. sześcian; kostka; (slang) facet; v. podnosic do sześcianu; obliczac
kubaturę;formowac w sześciany
cube root ('kju:b,ru:t) s.
pierwiastek sześcienny
cubicle ('kju:bykl) s. pokoik;
mała sypialnia;małe mieszkanie
cuckoo ('kuku) s. kukułka;
głuptas;kukanie;dureń
cucumber ('kju:kamber) s. ogórek
cuddle ('kadl) s. tulic;
pieścic; kulic się;gnieździc
cudgel ('kadżel) s. pałka;
v. bic pałką
cue (kju:) s. wskazówka; nastrój; ogonek (do sklepu); kij
bilardowy; warkocz;v.dac wska-
zówkę
cuff (kaf) s. mankiet; kajdan-
ki; v. bic pięścią; uderzac;
kułakowac;potarmosic;szturchac
cuff links ('kaf,lynks) pl.
spinki do mankietów
culminate ('kalmynejt) y.
szczytowac; kulminowac
culmination (,kalmy'nejszyn) s.
kulminacja; punkt szczytowy
culprit ('kalpryt) s. oskarżo-
ny; winowajca;winowajczyni
cultivate ('kaltywejt) s. uprawiac; rozwijac; kultywowac;
pielęgnowac; spulchniac

cultivation (,kaltu'wejszyn)
s. uprawa; kultura; kultywo-
wanie;kultura duchowa

cultivator ('kaltyvejter) s.
plantator; kultywator;rolnik

cultural ('kalczerel) adj.
kulturalny;kulturowy

culture ('kalczer) s. kultura;
uprawa; v. uprawiac; hodowac;
kształcic;hodować bakterie

cultured ('kalczerd) adj.
kulturalny;oczytany;wykształcony

cumulative ('kju:mjulejtyw)
adj. łączny; kumulacyjny;
skumulowany; kumulujący się

cunning ('kanyng) s. chytrosc;
przebiegłosc; adj. chytry;
przebiegły; miły; ładny

cup (kap) s. kubek; kielich;
czasza; filiżanka; v. wgłę-
biac; stawiac bańki

cupboard ('kaberd) s. kredens;
szafka;pó̷łka na kubki

cupola ('kju:pele) s. kopuła;
piec kopułowy; żeliwiak

cur (ke:r) s. kundel; szelma

curable ('kjuerebl) adj. uleczalny; wyleczalny

curate ('kjueryt) s. wikary

curb (ke:rb) s. krawężnik;
łancuszek; wędzidło; oszczep;
twarda spuchlizna; v. okiełzać; hamowac; ograniczać

curd (ke:rd) s. twaróg; tłuszcz

curdle (ke:rdl) v. ścinac;
zsiadac się;formować w gródki

cure (kjuer) s. kuracja; lek;
lekarstwo; v. uleczyc; wyle-
czyc; zaradzic; wykurować

cure-all ('kjuero:l) s. pana-
ceum;lek na wszystkie dolegliwoᵕ

curfew ('ke:rfju:) s. godzina
policyjna: capstrzyk

curio ('kjuerjou) s. okaz;
osobliwość ;unikat; rzadkość

curiosity ,(,kjurj'osyty) n.
ciekawosc; osobliwość

curl (ke:rl) s. kędzior; lok;
pukiel; skręt; spirala; wir
v. kręcic; skręcać; zwijac;
marszczyc; złościc;skulic się

curl up ('ke:rl ap) v.zwinac (się)

curly ('ke:rly) adj. kędzierzawy; kręty ;falujący;kręcony

currant ('karent) s. porzeczka;
rodzynek bez pestki

currency ('karensy) s. waluta;
obieg; potocznosc; popularnosc

current ('karent) adj. bieżący; obiegowy; obiegający; powszechnie znany; panujący (pogląd);.s. prąd; bieg; nurt;
tok ;strumień;natężenie prądu

curriculum (ke'rykjulem) s.
plan studiów ;program nauki

curriculum vitae (ke'rykjulem,
wajti:) s. życiorys

curse (ke:rs) s. przekleństwo;
klątwa; v. przeklinac; wykli-
nac; kląc; bluznic;złorzeczyć

cursed (ke:rsyd) adj. przeklęty; cholerny; adv. paskudnie;
cholernie ;po diable

curt (ke:rt) adj. krotki; zwięzły;lakoniczny;szorstki;suchy

curtail (ke:r'tejl) v. obcinac;
skracac; zmniejszac ;uczszuplać

curtain ('ke:rtn) s. zasłona;
firanka; kurtuna; v. zasłaniać

curtsy ('ke:rtsy) s. dyg; v. dy-
gać;złożyć głęboki ukłon

curve (ke:rw) s. krzywa; krzywizna; krzywka; v. wyginać
(się); wykrzywiac (się);zakręcać

cushion ('kuszyn) s. poduszka

custody ('kastedy) s. opieka;
nadzor; areszt ;przetrzymanie

custom ('kastem) s. zwyczaj;
klientela; zrobiony na zamówienie ;nawyk;stałe zaopatrywanie się

customary ('kastemery) adj. zwyczajny; zwyczajowy,s.zbior praw

customer ('kastemer) s. klient

customhouse ('kastem-haus) s.
komora celna ;urząd celny

custom-made ('kastem-mejd) adj.
zrobiony na zamówienie

customs ('kastemz) pl. cło

customs clearance ('kastemz;
klierens) s. odprawa celna

customs declaration('kastemz,
decle'rejszyn) s. deklaracja
celna (przy przekraczaniu gra-
nicy etc.)

customs examination ('kastemz
ig,zamy'nejszyn) s. rewizja
celna (bagażu,towarów etc.)
cut; cut; cut; (kat; kat; kat)
cut (kat) s. cięcie; przecięcie; wycięcie; ścięcie; odrzy-
nek; krój; styl (krawiecki);
wykop; drzeworyt; v. ciąć;
zaciąć; skaleczyć; ranić; krajać; kroić; przycinać; kosić;
rznąc; rzeźbić; szlifować; wycinać; obcinać; uciąć; ścinać
cut down ('kat,dałn) v. obniżać;
redukować;wyciąć w pień(wroga)
cut in ('kat,yn) v. wtrącać się
cut off ('kat,of) v. odcinać;
przerwać(dopływ);wydziedziczać
cut out ('kat,aut) v. wykroić;
przestać;zaprzestać (palić etc.)
cut up ('kat,ap) v. posiekać;
skrytykować;wypatroszyć;siec
cute (kju:t) adj. miły; ładny;
chytry; sprytny;ciekawy;bystry
cuticle ('kju:tykl) s. naskórek
cuticle scissers 'kju:tykl'-
syzez) s. nożyczki od naskórka
cutlery ('katlery) s. wyroby
nożownicze; sztućce
cutlet ('katlyt) s. kotlet (bity);kotlet mielony(mięsny,rybi)
cut-off ('katof) s. odcięcie;
skrót; wyłącznik; wycinek; za-
wór(wodny,parowy,gazowy etc.)
cutout ('kat aut) = cut-off
cutpurse ('kat pe:rs) s. rzezimieszek; kieszonkowiec;opryszek
cutter ('kater) s. kuter; przecinek; przykrawacz; odcinacz
cutting ('katyŋg) adj. bolesny;
przenikliwy; cięty;s.sadzonka
cycle (sajkl) s. cykl; rower;
v. jechać na rowerze; obiegać
cyklicznie(tam i nazad,w koło...)
cyclist ('sajklyst) s. rowerzysta;
rowerzystka ; cyklista;cykilstka
cyclone ('sajkloun) s. cyklon
cylinder ('sylynder) s. walec;
cylinder;bęben(rewolweru etc.)
cynic ('synyk) s. cynik
cynical ('synykel) adj. cynicz-
ny(pomysł,programczłowiek etc.)
cynicism('syny,syzem)s.cynizm

cypress ('sajprys) s. cyprys
cyst (syst) s. cysta; torbiel
czar (za:r) s. car; (od nafty;
sportu;komisarz generalny USA)
Czech (czek) adj. czeski
Czechoslovak ('czekou,slouwaek)
adj. czechosłowacki
d (di) czwarta litera alfabetu
angielskiego; oznaczenie centa
dab (daeb) v. musnąć; klepać;
dotknąc; dziobnać; s. muśnięcie; klaps; stuknięcie; dziob-
niecie;plama;bryzg;odrobina
dachshund ('daekshund) s. jamnik ;a.jamniczy;jamnika
dad (daed) s. tato; tatuś
daddy ('daedy) s. tatuś
daffodil ('daefedyl) s. żółty
narcyz ;żonkil;adj.bladożółty
daffy ('daefy) adj. zwariowany
daft ('daeft) adj. pomylony;
głupkowaty; zwariowany
dagger ('daeger) s. sztylet;
v. sztyletować ;s. odsyłacz
daily ('dejly) adj. codzienny;
adv. codziennie; s. dziennik
dainty ('dejnty) adj. wyszukany; wyborowy; delikatny;
gustowny; miły; wybredny
daiquiri ('daikery) s. rum z
sokiem cytrynowym, cukrem
i lodem (po amerykańsku)
dairy ('deery) s, mleczarnia
dairyman ('deerymen) s. mleczarz;właściciel mleczarni
daisy (dejzy) s. stokrotka;
ładny okaz(człowieka)
dale (dejl) s. dolina
dally ('daely) v. marudzić;
igrać; flirtować;tracić czas
dam (daem) s. tama; zapora
damage ('daemydż) v. szkoda;
uszkodzenie; odszkodowanie;
(slang) koszt; v. uszkodzić;
ponieść szkody; uwłaczać
dame (dejm) s. dziewczyna;
kobieta; pani(starsza)
damn (daem) v. potępiać; prze-
klinać; adj. przeklęty
damnation (daem'nejszyn) s. potępienie; excl.: psiakrew; cholera;a niech to piorun trzaśnie!

damp (daemp) v. zwilżyć; skropić; tłumić; ostudzić; amortyzować; butwieć; s. wilgoć; przygnębienie; zwątpienie
dampen ('daempen) v. wilgotnieć; zwilgotnieć;zwilżyć
dance (da:ns) s. taniec; zabawa taneczna; v. tańczyć; skakać; kazać tańczyć; hustać
dancer ('da:nser) s. tancerz; tancerka; baletnica
dancing ('da:nsyŋg) s. taniec; adj. tańczący;do tańca
dandelion ('daendylajon) s. mniszek lekarski; mlecz
dandruff ('daendref) s. łupież
danger ('dejndżer) s. niebezpieczeństwo; groźba
dangerous ('dejndżeres) adj. niebezpieczny;niepewny(grunt...)
dangle ('daeŋgl) v. dyndać; bujać; kręcić się;nadskakiwać
Danish (dejnysz) adj. duński
dapper ('daeper) adj. wytworny; elegancki;dobrze ubrany;zwinny
dare (deer) v. śmieć; ważyć się; wyzywać; s. wyzwanie
daring ('deeryŋg) adj. śmiały; s. śmiałość; odwaga
dark (da:rk) adj. ciemny; ponury; s. ciemność; mrok; cień; murzyn;tajemniczość;niewiedza
dark-brown ('da:rk braŁn) adj. ciemno-brazowy
darken (da:rkn) v. zaciemniać
darkness ('da:rknys) s. ciemność; ciemnota; śniadość
darling ('da:rlyŋg) s. kochanie; ulubieniec; adj. kochany; ulubiony; ukochany
darn (da:rn) v. cerować; s.cera; adj. (slang) przeklęty
dart (da:rt) s. żądło; szybki ruch; oszczep; zryw; v. pędzić; rzucać; wybuchać;strzelać
dash (daesz) v. roztrzaskać; rzucać się; pędzić; popisywać się; zakropić; opryskać; niweczyć; mieszać; oniesmielać; odbić; naszkicować; s. uderzenie; zderzenie; plusk; barwna plama; szczypta; przy-

mieszka;myślnik; kreska; pęd; skok; rozmach; rozpęd; popis
dash-board ('daeszbo:rd) tablica rozdzielcza; zestaw zegarów (lotniczych, samochodowych, etc,) ; błotnik
dashing (daeszyŋg) adj. dziarski; z werwą; z rozmachem
data ('dejte) pl. dane; podstawa odniesienia ;dane liczbowe
data processing ('dejte'prousesyŋg) s. przetwarzanie danych
date (dejt) v. datować; nosić datę; chodzić z kimś; s. data; spotkanie; randka; umówienie się; palma daktylowa; daktyl
date from ('dejt,from) data z... (dnia, miejsce)
dative case('dejtyw,kejs) trzeci przypadek ;celownik
datum ('dejtem) s, dana (fakt; szczegół);punkt wyjściowy
daub (do:b) v. babrać; mazać; oblepiać; s. tynk; polepa; plama; kicz sknocony ;gips
daughter ('do:ter) s. córka
daughter-in-law ('do:ter,yn lo:) s. synowa
dawdle ('do:dl) v. próżniaczyć; mitrężyć ;wałkonić się
dawdle away ('do:dl,a'Łej)v. marnować czas;trcić czas
dawn (do:n) v. świtać; zaświtać; dnieć; jasnieć; s. świt; brzask; zaranie;zdanie sobie sprawy
day (dej) s. dzień; doba
daybreak('dejbrejk)s.świt;brzask
day by day('dej,baj dej)exp.: dzień w dzień :dzień po dniu
daydream('dejdri:m)s. marzenie;v. marzyć;budować zamki na lodzie
day in day out(dej,yn'dej aut)exp. codziennie; dzień w dzień
daylight('dejlajt)s.swiatŁo dzienne: biały dzień ┌(dzienny)
day nursery('dej,ne:rsery)s.żŁobek
day off('dej of)s.dzień wolny
days to come('dejs,tu kam) exp.: przyszłość
day's work(dejz,Łe:rk)s. dniówka
daytime ('dejtajm)s. dzień od świtu do zmroku

daze (dejz) v. oszałamiac;
otumaniac; oslepiac; s. oszołomienie; otumanienie
dazzle (daezl) v. oslepiac;
olsniewac; zamaskowac;
s. oslepiający blask
dead (ded) adj.& s. zmarły;
martwy; wymarły; matowy
dead body (ded'body) s. zwłoki
dead center ('ded'senter) s.
punkt martwy, zwrotny
deaden ('deden) v. zabijać siły, uczucia etc.: tłumic;
osłabiac; stępiac; zmartwiec;
obumrzec; pozbawiac blasku,
połysku, zapachu;znieczulac
dead end('dedend)s.slepa(ulica)
deadline('dedlajn)s.nieprzekra-
czalny termin;ostateczna granica
deadlock ('dedlok) s. impas;
martwy punkt;v. powodować impas
deadly (dedly) adj. smiertelny;
adv. smiertelnie;nieludzko
deadweight ('dedłejt) s. ciężar własny (urządzenia); kula
u nogi;kamień u szyi
deaf (def) adj. głuchy
deafen (defn) v. ogłuszac
deafening (defnyng) adj. ogłu-
szający
deal; dealt; dealt (di:l; delt;
delt)
deal (di:l) v. zajmowac się;
traktowac o: załatwiac; prze-
stawac z; postępowac; handlowac; rozdzielac (karty)
s. ilosc; sprawa;sporo;wiele
deal with ('di:l łyt) v. postępowac z...;miec do czynienia
dealer ('di:ler) s. kupiec;
handlarz;rozdający karty
dealing ('di:lyng)s. postępowanie z; stosunki; transakcje
dealt (delt) zob. deal
dean (di:n) s. dziekan
dear (kier) adj. kochany; drogi
dear Sir ('dier,se:r) exp.:sza-
nowny panie;Drogi Panie
dear me ! (kier mi) exp.:ojej !
moj Boże ! czyżby! ależ nie!
death (des) s. smierc; zgon
deathly (desly) adj. smiertelny;
adv. smiertelnie;grobowo;trupio

debar ('dyba:r) v. wykluczac;
zabraniac (komuś);zakazywać
debase (dy'bejs) v. obniżac;
poniżac; fałszowac;upadlac
debate (dy'bejt) v. roztrząsac;
rozważac; debatowac;s.debata
debauchery ('dy'bo:czery) s.
rozpusta;wyuzdanie;rozwiązłość
debit ('debyt) s. debet; obciążenie rachunku
debrief (dy'bri:f) s. przesłu-
chania po (akcji); v. prze-
słuchiwac po (akcji)
debris ('dejbri:) pl. gruzy
debt (det) s. dług
debtor ('deter) s. dłużnik;
dłużniczka
decade ('dekejd) s. dziesięcio-
letni okres
decadence ('dekejdens) s. de-
kadencja; chylenie się ku
upadkowi; schyłek; upadek
decapitate (dy'kaepytejt) v.
scinac głowę;pozbawić wodza
decay (dy'kej) v. gnic; rozpadac się; psuc się; s. upadek;
ruina; zanik; rozkład; gnicie
decease (dy'si:s) v. umierac;
s. zgon ; smierc
deceased (dy'si:st) adj. zmarły; s. nieboszczyk
deceit (dy'si:t) s. oszukanst-
wo; podstęp; złuda ; fałsz
deceitful (dy'si:tfel) adj.
kłamliwy; zwodniczy;podstępny,
deceive (dy'si:w) v. okłamywac;
zwodzic; łudzic; zawodzic
deceiver (dy'si:wer) s. oszu-
kaniec; zwodziciel; kłamca
decelerate (dy:'selerejt) v.
zwalniac;zmniejszac szybkość
December (dy'sember) s. grudzień
decency ('di:snsy) s. przyzwoi-
tosc; obyczajnosc;dobre obyczaje
decent ('di:sent) adj. przyzwoity; porządny; znosny
deception (dy'sepszyn) s. łu-
dzenie; okłamywanie; podstęp;
zawod; szachrajstwo;oszukanie
decide (dy'sajd) v. rozstrzygac;
postanawiac; decydować się;
zadecydowac; skłaniac się

decided (dy'sajdyd) adj. zdecydowany; stanowczy;definitywny

decimal('desymel) adj. dzie-
siętny;s. ułamek dzisiętny

decipher (dy'sajfer) v. odcyfrować; rozszyfrować;rozwiazać

decision (dy'syżyn) s. rozstrzygnięcie; postanowienie;
decyzja; zdecydowanie; sta-
nowczosc; wygrana na punkty
(sport);ustalenie;rezolutnosc

decisive (dy'sajsyw) adj. decydujący; rozstrzygający;
zdecydowany; stanowczy

deck (dek) s. pokład; pomost;
podłoga; talia; v. pokrywac
pokładem; przystrajać

deck chair (dek chzeer) s. leżak (do opalania się na statku)

declaration (dekle'rejszyn) s.
deklaracja; zapowiedź; oświadczenie (oficjalne)

declare (dy'kle:r) v. deklaro-
wać; oświadczac; zeznawac;
ogłaszac; uznawac za; stwier-
dzac;wykazac;dawac do oclenia

declension (dy'klenszyn) s. de-
klinacja (gram.); przypadkowa-
nie; odchylenie; upadek

decline (dy'klajn) v. uchylac
(się); pochylac (się);skłaniac
(się); isc ku schyłkowi; opadac; obniżac; podupadac; marniec; słabnąc; zanikac; przy-
padkowac;s.schyłek;utrata;spadek

declivity (dy'klywyty) s. po-
chyłosc; spadzistosc;stok;skłon

decode (, dy'koud)v.rozszyfrowac

decorate('dekerejt)v.ozdabiac;od-
znaczac; udekorowac; upiększac

decompose(,dy:kem'pouz)v.rozkła-
dac się; rozłożyć się;gnic

decoration (,deke'rejszyn) s.
ozdoba; odznaczenie;medal etc.

decorative (,deke'rejtyw) adj.
ozdobny; dekoracyjny

decorator (dekerejter) s. dekorator; architekt wnętrz

decoy ('dy:koj) s. wabik; przynęta; v. wabic; usidlac; zwa-
biac; wciągac w pułapkę;zacia-
gac sidła;wabic w pułapkę

decrease ('dy:kri:s) v. zmniejszac; słabnąc; obniżac;
s. zmniejszenie; spadek(cen)

decree (dy'kri:) s. dekret;
rozporządzenie; wyrok rozwodowy; postanowienie o sepera-
cji; v. zarządzac; dekretowac;
rozporządzać;nakazywac dekretem

decrepit (dy'krepyt) adj.
zgrzybiały; wyniszczony

decry (dy'kraj) v. potępic;
okrzyczec;zohydzic;obgadac

dedicate ('dedykejt) v. dedyko-
wac; poswięcac; inaugurowac

dedication ('dedykejszyn) s.
dedykacja; poswięcenie;otwarcie

deduce (dy'du:s) v. wnioskowac;
dedukowac; wywodzic (rodowod)

deduct (dy'dakt) v. potrącac;
odciągac;odejmowac;odtrącac

deduction (dy'dakszyn) s. potrącenie; odciągnięcie; wnioskowanie; wniosek;wywód

deed (di:d) s. czyn; wyczyn;
akt; v. przekazywać aktem
(własność);przelewać pieniadze

deep (di:p) adj. głęboki;
s. głębia; adv. głęboko

deepen('di:pn) v. pogłębiac

deep-freeze ('di:p,fri:z) s.
(głębokie) zamrożenie

deeply ('di:ply) adv. głęboko

deep-rooted ('di:p'ru:tyd)
adj. głęboko zakorzeniony

deer (dier) s. jelen; sarna;
łos; łania ;daniel;renifer

deface (dy'fejs) v. szpecic;
zniekształcac; zacierac

defame (dy'fejm) v. zniesławic

defeat (dy'fi:t) v. pokonac;
pobic; unicestwic; udaremnic;
uniemożliwic; unieważnic
prawnie;s.klęska;udaremnienie

defect (dy'fekt) s. brak; wada; błąd; defekt; v. odpasc;
skłonic do odstępstwa;odstąpic

defective (dy'fektyw) adj. wadliwy; wybrakowany; niepełny

defence (dy'fens) = defense

defend (dy'fend) v. bronic

defendant (dy'fendent) s. pozwany;oskarżony; obrońca

defender (dy'fender) s. obrona (prawo i sport)

defensive (dy'fensyw) adj. obronny; defensywny; s. defensywa; być w defensywie

defense (dy'fens) s. obrona

defenseless (dy'fenslys) adj. bezbronny

defer (dy'fe:r) v. odraczać; ustępować; ulegać; mieć wzgląd

defiant (dy'fajent) adj. zbuntowany; nieufny; buntowniczy

deficiency (dy'fyszynsy) s. brak; niedobór; należność niezapłacona; niedostatek; słabość

deficit ('defysyt) s. deficyt; niedobór; nadwyżka rozchodu

defile ('dy:fail) v. kalać; plugawić; brukać; bezcześcić; iść szeregami; defilować

define (dy'fajn) v. określać; definiować; zakreślać (granice); zarysowac; określać

definite ('defynyt) adj. określony; wyraźny; pewny; prostolinijny; określający(rodzajnik)

definition (,drfy'nyszyn) s. określenie; definicja; ostrość; czystość;oznaczenie

definitive (dy'fynytyw) adj. ostateczny; definitywny; stanowczy; konkluzywny;definiujący

deflate (dy'flejt) v. wypuszczać powietrze (z dętki); zmniejszać(obieg,znaczenie etc.)

deform (dy'fo,rm) v. szpecić; znieksztalcać;oszpecać

deformed (dy'fo:rmd) adj. ułomny; szpetny;zniekształcony

defrost (dy'frost) v. odmrozić

defunct (dy'fankt) adj. zmarły; zlikwidowany;już nie istniejący

defy (dy'faj) v. stawiać czoło; rzucać wyzwania (by zrobić,wykazać)

degenerate (dy'dżeneryt) adj. zwyrodniały; s. degenerat

degrade (dy'grejd) v. poniżać; obniżać; wyrodnieć;znieważać

degree (dy'gri:) s. stopień (np. naukowy, ciepła etc.)

dejected (dy'dżektyd) adj. przygnębiony ;zgaszony(człowiek) zdeprymowany;strapiony

dejectedly (dy'dżektydly) adv. z przygnębieniem;z niechęcią

delay (dy'lej) v. odraczać; opóźniać; zwlekać; s. odroczenie; zwłoka; opóźnienie

delegate ('delegejt) s. zastępca; wysłannik; v. delegować; udzielać delegacji; zlecać (władzę);udzielać(władzy)

delegation (,dely'gejszyn) s. delegacja;grupa delegatów

deliberate (dy'lyberejt) adj. rozmyślny; spokojny; v. rozmyślać; rozważać; obradować; naradzać się (dy,ly'berejt)v.

delicacy ('delykesy) s. delikatność; smakołyk;takt

delicate ('delykyt) adj. delikatny; wyśmienity;taktowny

delicatessen (,delyka'tesn) s. sklep z delikatesami

delicious (dy'lyszes) adj. rozkoszny;bardzo smaczny etc.

delight (dy'lajt) s. rozkosz; v. zachwycać się; rozkoszować się; lubować się

delightful (dy'lajtful) adj. zachwycający; czarujący

delinquency (dy'lynkłensy) s. zaniedbanie; wina; przestępstwo;nie płacenie należności

delinquent (dy'lynkłent) a. winny; zaniedbany; zalegający z zapłatą (podatkiem); s. winowajca; przestępca (nieletni)osoba zalegająca etc.

deliver (dy'lywer) v. doręczać; zdawać; wydawać; wygłaszać; zadawać; uwalniać;podawać

deliverance (dy'lywerens) s. uwolnienie;wygłoszenie(opinii)

deliverer (dy'lywerer) s. zbawca;oswobodziciel;wybawca

delivery (dy'lywery) s. dostawa; wydawanie; wygłaszanie; podanie; poród; przekazanie

deluge ('delju:dż) s. potop

delusion (dy'lu:żyn) s. urojenie; zwodzenie;ułuda:iluzja

delusive (dy'lu:syw) adj. złudny;oszukańczy;bałamutny;zwodniczy

demand (dy'ma:nd) s. zadanie;popyt; v.żadać; dopytywać się

demeanor (dy'mi:ner) s. zachowanie się;postepowanie: postawa
demented (dy'mentyd) adj. obłąkany;oszalały;umysłowo chory
demi-('demy) pref. pół-
demilitarized ('dy:mylyterajzd)
adj. zdemilitaryzowany
demise (dy'majz) s. zgon; przekazanie spadku; v. przekazywać
testamentem lub zgonem
demobilize (dy;,moubylajz) v.
demobilizować;zdemobilizować
democracy (dy'mokresy) s. demokracja
democrat ('demokreat) s. demo-
krata; demokratka
democratic (,deme'kraetyk) adj.
demokratyczny
demolish (dy'molysz) v. burzyć;
niszczyć; obalać; demolować
demon ('di:men) s. diabeł; demon;doskonały zawodnik sportowy
demonstrate ('demenstrejt) v.
wykazywać; udowadniać; demon-
strować;urządzać manifestację
demonstration (,demen'strejszyn)
s. wykazywanie; okazywanie;
demonstracja;adj.wzorcowy;poglą-
demonstrative (dy'menstrejtyw)dowy
adj. wylewny; dowodowy; wskazujący;dowodzący;ekspansywny
demurrage (dy'me:rydż) s. prze-
stój; opłata za postojowe
den (den) s. nora; jaskinia;
ustronie; cicha pracownia
denial (dy'najel) s. zaprzeczenie; odmowa;wyparcie się
denomination (dynomy'nejszyn)
s. nazwa; miano; określenie;
wyznanie (rel.):kategoria
denounce (dy'nauns) v. oskarżać;
donosić; wypowiadać;denuncjować
dense (dens) adj. gęsty; zwarty;
tępy (człowiek);niepojętny
density ('densyty) s. gęstość;
zwartość; głupota;spoistość
dent (dent) s. wgłębienie; wrąb;
znaczenie;v.szczerbić;wyginać
dental ('dentl) adj. zębowy;
dentystyczny;stomatologiczny
dentist ('dentyst) s. dentysta;
dentystka; stomatolog

denture (denczer) s. (sztuczne) uzębienie; szczęka
deny (dy'naj) v. zaprzeczyć;
odrzucić; odmawiać; wypierać
się;zdementować: przeczyć
depart (dy'pa:rt) v. odjeżdżać;
odbiegać ;robić dygresje;odejść
department (dy'pa:rtment) s.
wydział; ministerstwo; dział
department store (dy'pa:rtment,
sto:r) s. dom towarowy
departure (dy'pa:rczer) s. odjazd; rozstanie; odchylenie
depend on (dy'pend on) v. polegać na...;zależeć od
depend upon (dy'pend,apon) v.
być zależnym od..;być na utrzy-
depends (dy'pends)v zależy maniu..
deplorable (dy'plo:rebl) adj.
godny pożałowania;opłakany
deplore (dy'plo:r) v. ubolewać;
boleć nad...;wyrażać ubolewanie
depolarize (dy'poulerajz) v.
depolaryzować;rozwiać złudzenia
depopulate (dy'popjulejt) v.
wyludniać;pustoszyć;opustoszyć
deport (dy'po:rt) v. zsyłać;
deportować; zachowywać się
depose (dy'pouz) s. składać;
zeznawać;usunąć(z tronu etc.)
deposit (dy'pozyt) s. osad;
warstwa; kaucja; depozyt;
v. składać; osadzać; deponować; nawarstwiać;złożyć (jaja...)
depositor (dy'pozyter) s. de-
ponent; osadnik
depot (depou) s. stacja kole-
jowa; skład;remiza; kadra
depraved (dy'prejwd) adj. zde-
prawowany;zepsuty moralnie
depress (dy'pres) v. przygnębiać; deprymować; spychać
w dół(ceny);deprymować;martwić
depression (dy'preszyn) s.
przygnębienie; depresja
deprive (dy'prajw) v. odzierać;
wykluczać; umartwiać się; pozbawiać;odwołać (z urzędu etc.)
depth (deps) s. głębokość;
głębia; głębina;dno(nędzy etc.)
deputy ('depjuty) s. zastępca;
deputowany; poseł; wice-

derail (dy'rejl) v. wykoleic
(się)(czyjś plan,zamiar etc.)
derange (dy'rejndż) v. pomie-
szac; rozstrajac; psuc; zakło-
cac; powodowac obłęd
deride (dy'rajd) v. wysmiewac
derision (dy'ryżyn) s. szyderstwo; pośmiewisko; drwina
derisive (dy'rajsyw) adj.kpią-
cy; ironiczny;wart śmiechu
derive (dy'rajw) v. uzyskiwac;
czerpac; wywodzic; pochodzic
derogatory (dy'rogeto:ry) v.
pomniejszający; uszczuplający;
uwłaczający ; szkodliwy;
descend (dy'send) v. zejsc;spasc
zniżac się;pochodzic; opadac
descendant (dy'sendent) s. po-
tomek(przedka;rodziny;grupy etc.)
descent (dy'sent) s. zejscie;
spadek; pochodzenie;nagły atak
describe (dys'krajb) v. opisywac; okreslac;przerysowywac
description (dy'skrypszyn)
s. opis;sposob opisywania
desegregate (dy'segrygejt) v.
(Am.) zniesc podział rasowy
desert ('desert) adj. pustynny;
pusty; s. pustynia;pustkowie
desert (dy'ze:rt) v. porzucac;
opuszczac; dezerterowac; s.za-
służenie; zasługa;nagroda;kara
deserted (dy'ze:rted) adj.
opuszczony;bezludny
deserter (dy'ze:rter) s. dezer-
ter;dezerterka;zbieg;zbiegła
desertion (dy'ze:rszyn) s.
opuszczenie; dezercja;porzucenie
deserve (dy'ze:rw) v. zasługiwac na...;miec zasługi wobec...
design (dy'zajn) s. zamiar;
plan; szkic; v. pomyslec; za-
mierzac; przeznaczac; projekto-
wac;zamyslac;uplanowac;kreslic
designate ('dezygnejt) v. wyznaczac; okreslac; desygnowac
designer (dy'zajner) s. projek-
tant; konstruktor; rysownik;
intrygant;projektodawca;autor
desirable (dy'zajerebl) adj. pożądany;pociągający;atrakcyjny
celowy;mile widziany;wskazany

desire (dy'zajer) v. pożądac;
pragnąc; życzyc sobie
desirous (dy'zajeres) adj. żądny;pragnący;spragniony
desk (desk) s. biuro; referat;
pulpit; ambona ;ławka szkolna
desk set ('desk set) s. zestaw
przyborów do pisania
desolate ('deselyt) adj.
opuszczony; posępny;wyludniony
desolate (deselejt) v. pusto-
szyc; wyludniac; opuszczac
desolation (,dese'lejszyn) s.
wyludnienie; spustoszenie;
pustka; żałość; strapienie
despair (dys'peer) s. rozpacz
despairingly (dys'peeryngly)
adv. rozpaczliwie;beznadziejnie
desperate ('desperyt) adj.
rozpaczliwy;beznadziejny;zacie-
desperation (,despe'rejszyn)
s. rozpacz; desperacja
despise (dys'pajz) v. pogar-
dzac;gardzic;lekceważyć
despite (dys'pajt) s. przekora; złość; prep. pomimo;
wbrew;na przekór(komuś,czemuś)
despond (dys'pond) v. przygnę-
biac się;s.przygnębienie
despondent (dys'pondent) adj.
przygnębiony; zniechęcony
dessert (dy'ze:rt) s. deser;
legumina; ciastka
destination (desty'nejszyn) s.
miejsce przeznaczenia
destine ('destyn) v. przezna-
czac(z góry);przeznaczyć
destiny ('destyny) s. przezna-
czenie(wypadków,ludzi...);los
destitute ('destytju:t) adj.
bez środków;pozbawiony;w nędzy
destroy (dy'stroj) v. burzyc;
niweczyc;zabijac;zagładzac
destroyer (dy'strojer) s.kontr-
torpedowiec; niszczyciel
destruction (dys'trakszyn) s.
zniszczenie;ruina;zguba;zagłada
destructive (dy'straktyw) adj.
niszczycielski;s.niszczyciel
detach (dy'taecz) v. odczepic;
odłączyc; odpiąc; odwiazac;
odkomenderowac;odlepiac;urwac

detached (dy'taeczt) adj. odosobniony; obojętny;niezależny
detail ('di:tejl) s. szczegół;
wyszczególnienie; v. wyłuszczać; przydzielać do zadań
detain (dy'tejn) v. wstrzymywać; więzić; przeszkadzać
detect (dy'tekt) v. wykrywać;
wysledzić;wypatrzyć;przychwycić
detection (dy'tekszyn) s. wy-
krywanie; wyśledzenie
detective (dy'tektyw) s. detek-
tyw; adj. detektywistyczny
detention (dy'tenszyn) s. więzienie; zatrzymanie;przetrzymanie
deter (dy'te:r) v. odstraszać
od...;pohamować;onieśmielać
detergent (dy'te:rdżent) s.&
adj. czyszczący (środek)
deteriorate (dy'tierjerejt) s.
psuć; marnieć;tracić na wartość
determination (dyte:rmy'nejszyn)
s. określenie; postanowienie;
ustalenie; orzeczenie;wygaśnięcie
determine (dy'te:rmyn) v. rozstrzygać; określać; postanawiać; ustalać;zdefiniować
deterrent (dy'terent) adj. od-
straszający; s.(czynnik) od-
straszający;środek zaradczy
detest (dy'test) v. nienawidzić;
czuć wstręt;nie cierpieć
detestable (dy'testebl) adj.
wstrętny; nienawistny;obmierzły
detonate ('detounejt) v. wybuchać; powodować wybuch
detour ('dy:tuer) s. objazd
devaluation (,dy:vaelju'ejszyn)
s. dewaluacja;zdewaluowanie
devaluate (dy:waelju:ejt)v,dewalu-
ować;obniżać wartość;zdewaluować
devastate ('devestejt) v. pustoszyć;niweczyć;dewastować
develop (dy'velop) v. rozwijać
(się); wywoływać (zdjęcia)
development (dy'velepment) s.
rozwój; rozbudowa; osiedle;
wywołanie(filmu);ewolucja
deviate (,'di:wyejt) v. zbaczać;
odchylać;schodzić z drogi
device (dy'wajs) s. plan; pomysł;
urządzenie; dewiza; hasło;środek

devil ('dewl) s. chart; diabeł
devilish ('dewlysh) adj. szatański; diabelski;adv.diabelsko
devise (dy'wajz) v. zapisać
(komuś); wymyślać; obmyślać
devoid (dy'woyd) adj. pozbawiony;próżny;czczy;wolny od..,.
devote (dy'wout) v. poświęcać;
ofiarować;oddawać się
devoted (dy'vouted) adj. oddany;przywiązany (do kogoś,,)
dew (dju:) s. rosa; świeżość;
powiew; v. rosić; zraszać
dew point ('dju:point)
s.temperatura powstawania rosy
dexter ('dekster) a. prawy
dexterity (deks'teryty) s.
zręczność; bystrość;sprawność
diabetes (,daje'by:ty:z) s.
cukrzyca;choroba cukrowa
diagram ('dajegraem) s. wykres;
schemat; diagram
dial ('dajel) s. tarcza nume-
rowa (zwł. zegarowa);
v. mierzyć; nakręcać (numer)
dial tone ('dajel,toun) s.
sygnał połączenia (tel.)
dialect ('dajelekt) s. gwara;
narzecze; dialekt
dialog(ue) ('dajelog) s. rozmowa; dialog(na scenie etc,)
diameter (daj'aemyter) s. średnica; długość średnicy
diamond ('dajemend) s. diament;
romb; a. diamentowy; romboidalny;s.boisko do gry w palanta
diaper ('dajeper) s. pielusz-
ka; wzór romboidalny;
v. przewijać; ozdabiać w romby
diaphragm ('dajefraem) s. przepona; membrana;przesłona
diarrhea (daje'rye) s. biegunka
diary ('daiery) s. dziennik
dice (dajs) v. grać w kości;
kratkować; pl. od die=kostka do
dictate (dyk'tejt) s. nakaz; gry
v. dyktować;narzucać(wolę etc.)
dictation (dyk'tejszyn) s.
dyktat; dyktowanie ;nakaz
dictator (dyk'tejter) s. dyktator;dyktujący dyktando;dyk-
tujący na głos (tekst;list etc.)

dictatorship (dyk'tejterszyp)
s. dyktatura;władza nieograniczo-
na;rów; v. osuszać rowem; otamować
dictionary ('dykszeneryjs.słow-
nik;mała encyklopedia
did (dyd) v. zrobić; zob.: do
die (daj) v. umierać; zdech-
nąć; zginąć; s. matryca;
sztanca; pl. zob,: dice
die-hard ('daj-ha:rd) adj.
twardy; nieustępliwy; s. zagorzały bojownik(szermierz etc.)
diet ('dajet) s. dieta; zjazd;
sejm; v. trzymać na diecie
differ ('dyfer) v. różnić się;
nie zgadzać się(z opinią etc.)
difference ('dyferens) s. różnica; sprzeczka; nieporozumienie
different ('dyferent) adj. różny; odmienny; niezwykły
difficult ('dyfykelt) adj.
trudny;ciężki; niełatwy
difficulty ('dyfykelty) s.
trudność; przeszkoda
diffident ('dyfydent) adj. nieśmiały; bez wiary we własne
siły;bez zaufania do siebie
diffuse (dy'fju:z) adj. rozwlekły; rozproszony; v. rozlewać; szerzyć; rozpraszać
dig; dug; dug (dyg; dag; dag)
dig (dyg) v. kopać; ryć; rozumieć; ocenić; bawić się; kuć
się; s. szarpnięcie; przytyk;
kujon;szturchnięcie;docinek
digest (dy'dżest) v. trawić;
przetrawiać; s. streszczenie;
skrót; przegląd;zbiór praw
digestible (dy'dżestebl) adj.
strawny;łatwy do przyswojenia
digestion (dy'dżestszyn) s.
trawienie; wygotowanie
diggings ('dygynz) s. kopalnia
(złota); mieszkanie
dignified ('dygnyfajd) adj. dostojny;godny;pełen godności
dignity ('dygnyty) s. godność;
dostojeństwo;powaga;zaszczyt
digress ('daj'gres) v. zbaczać;
odbiegać od rzeczy (tematu etc.)
digs (dygz) s, mieszkanie; pokój; buda; melina
dihedral (daj'hi:drel)adj.(kąt)
między dwoma ścianami

dike (dajk) s. tama; grobla;
rów; v. osuszać rowem; otamować
dilapidated (dy'laepydejtyd)
adj. zniszczony;walący się
dilate (daj'lejt) v. rozszerzać; rozwodzić się;rozciągać
diligence ('dylydżens) n. pilność;przykładanie się do pracy
diligent ('dylydżent) adj. pilny;przykładający się do pracy
dill (dyl) s. koper ogrodowy
dill-pickle ('dyl,pykl) s. kiszony ogórek
dilute (daj'lju:t) v. rozpuszczać; rozcieńczać; rozrzedzać;
adj. rozpuszczony; rozcieńczo-
ny; rozrzedzony; rozwodniony;
wypłukany; wyblady;spłowiały
dim (dym) v. przyćmić; zaciemnić; zamglić; adj. przyćmiony;
blady zamazany; niewyraźny
dime (dajm) s. dziesięcio-
centowa moneta U.SA.
dimension (dy'menszyn) s. wymiar; rozmiar; wielkość
diminish (dy'mynysz) v. zmniejszać; zwężać;uszczuplać;niknąć
diminutive (dy'mynjutyw) adj.&
s. drobniutki; zdrobniały;
zdrobnienie;malutka kobieta
dimple ('dympl) s. dołek (w
twarzy) ; v. robić dołki; mieć
dołki (w twarzy etc.)
dine (dajn) v. jeść obiad;
jeść; mieć na obiedzie
diner (dajner) s. stołówka
wagon restauracyjny; osoba
jedząca;restauracja
dining car ('dajnyŋg,ka:r) s.
wagon restauracyjny
dining room ('dajnyŋg,ru:m)
s. jadalnia;pokój jadalny
dinner ('dyner) s. obiad
dinner-jacket ('dyner,dżaekyt)
s. smoking
dinner-party ('dyner,pa:rty)
s. przyjęcie; obiad proszony
dip (dyp) v. zanurzać; czerpać;
farbować; pogrążać; płukać;
nachylać się; opadać; s. zanurzenie; zamoczenie; rozczyn;
nachylenie; obniżenie; łojówka;
sos do maczania;skok do wody

diphtheria (dyfteria) s. dyfteryt; błonica
diploma (dy'plouma) s. dyplom
diplomacy (dy'ploumesy) s. dyplomacja;takt
diplomat ('dyplemaet) s. dyplomata;człowiek taktowny
diplomatic(,dyple'maetyk) adj. dyplomatyczny; taktowny
direct (dy'rekt) v. kierować; kazać; zarządzić; dowodzić; zaadresować;nakierowywać; wymierzać polecić; dyrygować;adj. prosty; bezpośredni; otwarty; szczery; wyraźny; adv. wprost; prosto; bezpośrednio
direct current (dy'rekt'karent) s. prąd stały
direction (dy'rekszyn) s. kierunek; kierowanie; kierownictwo; zarząd; wskazówka; adres
directions (dy'rekszyns) pl. instrukcje; przepisy; przepis
directly (dy'rektly) adv. bezpośrednio; wprost; od razu; zaraz;natychmiast;dokładnie
director (dy'rektor) s. dyrektor; reżyser; celownik; kierownik;zarządzający
directory (dy'rektery) s. książka adresowa; telefoniczna(lub przepisów);skorowidz
dirigible ('dyrydżebl) adj.& s. sterowy; sterowiec
dirt (de:rt) s. brud; błoto; świnstwo; ziemia; język plugawy; mówienie oszczrstw;plotki
dirt-cheap (de:rt'czi:p) adv. za bezcen; adj, bardzo tani; tani jak barszcz;śmiesznie tani
dirty (de:rty) adj. brudny; sprosny; podły; wstrętny
disability (,dyse'dylyty) s. inwalidztwo; niemoc;niemożność
disabled (dyzejbld) s. kaleka; inwalida wojenny
disadvantage (dysed'wa:ntydż) s. niekorzysc; wada; strata; szkoda; niekorzystne położenie;v.szkodzić;zaszkodzić(komu)
disadvantageous (dysaedwa:ntejdżes) adj. niekorzystny; szkodliwy;ujemny

disagree (dyse'gri:) v. nie zgudzać się; rożnić się; nie służyć (jedzenie; klimat)
disagreeable (,dyse'gri:ebl) adj. nieprzyjemny; niemiły
disagreement (,dyse'gri:ment) s. niezgoda; różnica
disallow (,dyse'lau) v. niepozwalać; nie dopuszczać
disappear (,dyse'pier) v. znikać;zapodziewać się; przepaść
disappearance (,dyse'pierens) s. zniknięcie;zanik;zginięcie
disappoint (dyse'point) v. zawieść;rozczarować;nie spełnić
disappointment (dyse'pointment) s. zawod; rozczarowanie
disapproval (dyse'pru:wel) s. potępienie; niechęć;desaprobata
disapprove (dyse'pru:w) v. potępiać; ganić;źle widzieć(kogoś)
disarm (dys'a:rm) v. rozbroić; unieszkodliwić;odebrać broń
disarmament (dys'a:rmement) s. rozbrojenie;a.rozbrojeniowy
disarrange (,dyse'rejndż) v. rozstrajać; dezorganizować
disarray (,dyse'rej) v. wprowadzać nieład; rozstrajać; s. nieład; zamieszanie; bałagan;niekompletny stroj
disaster (dy'za:ster) s. nieszczęście; klęska(żywiołowa etc.)
disastrous (dy'za:stres) adj. katastrofalny; zgubny;fatalny
disbelief ('dysby'li:f) s. niewiara; niedowierzanie:nieufność
disbelieve (,'dysby'li:w) v. niewierzyc; niedowierzać
disc (dysk) s. krążek; tarcza; płyta; dysk;płyta gramofonowa
discard (dys'ka:rd) v. wyrzucać; odrzucać;zarzucać;zaniechać
discard ('dyska:rd) s. odrzucenie; odrzucona (rzecz lub osoba);odpadek;rzecz wybrakowana
discern (dy'se:rn) v. rozróżniać;odrożniać;rozpoznawać
discharge (dys'cza:rdż) v. rozładowoać; odciążać; zwalniać; wypuścić; wystrzelić; s. rozładowanie;wystrzał; zwolnienie; wydzielina;odpływ;odchody;ropa

disciple (dy'sajpl) s. uczeń;
wyznawca;jeden z apostołów
discipline ('dyscyplyn) s.
dyscyplina; karność; v. karać; ćwiczyć; musztrować
disc-jockey (dysk'dżoki) s.
nadający muzykę z płyt ;
(disk jockey)
disclaim (dys'klejm) v. wypierać się;rezygnować;zrzekać się
disclose (dys'k-ouz) v. odsłaniać; ujawniać;wyjawiać;odkryć
discolor (dys'kaler) v. odbarwiać
discomfort (dys'kamfert) s. niewygoda; niepokój; v. sprawiać
niewygody lub złe samopoczucie;krępować;żenować;dolegać
discompose (,dyskem'pouz) v.
niepokoić; mieszać;zmieszać
disconcert (,dysken'ser:t) v.
żenować; krzyżować plany
disconnect ('dyske'nekt) v. odłączyć; oderwać; odhaczyć
disconnected ('dyske'nektyd)
adj. bez związku; bezładny;
rozłączony; chaotyczny
disconsolate (dys'konselyt) adj.
niepocieszony; posępny
dicontent. ('dysken'tent) s. niezadowolenie; adj. niezadowol-
ny; v. wywoływać niezadowolenie ;wywoływać rozgoryczenie
discontented ('dysken'tentyd)
adj. niezadowolony; rozgory-
czony; zniecierpliwiony
discontinue (,dysken'tynju:) v.
zaprzestawać; przerywać; ustawać ;zakończyć; zaniechać
discord ('dysko:rd) s. niezgoda; różnica; dysonans;niesnaski
discordance,('dysko:rdens) s.
niezgodność ;dysonans
discotheque ('dyskoutek) s.
dyskoteka; nocny lokal z muzy-
ką z płyt do tańca
discount ('dyskaunt) s. dyskont;
rabat; odjęcie; v. potrącać;
odliczać; nie dawać wiary
discourage (dys'karydż) v. zniechęcać; odstraszać;być przeciwnym
discover (dys'kawer) v. wynaleźć; odkryć; odsłaniać;zobaczyć

discoverer (dys'kawerer) s.
odkrywca; wynalazca
discredit (dys'kredyt) v. dys-
kredytować; przynosić ujmę;
pozbawiać zaufania; s. utrata zaufania i dobrego imienia;
niewiara;zła opinia(kogo ,czego)
discreet (dys'kri:t) a. rozsądny; dyskretny; z rezerwą
discrepancy (dys'krepensy) s.
sprzeczność;rozbieżność
discretion (dys'kreszyn) s.
swoboda decyzji; rozwaga;
powściągliwość; dyskrecja
discriminate (dys'krymynejt),
v. odróżniać; dyskryminować;
robić różnicę;wyróżniać
discriminate against (dys'krymynejt e'genst) wprowadzać
dyskryminację w stosunku do..
discuss (dys'kas) v. dyskutować; roztrząsać ;debatować
discussion (dys'kaszyn) s.
dyskusja; debata ;debaty
disdain (dys'dejn) s. pogarda;
wzgarda;v.gardzić;lekceważyć
disease (dy'zi:z) s. choroba
diseased (dy'zi:zd) adj. chory; schorzały;cierpiący na...
disembark ('dysym'ba:rk) v.wy-
ładować; wysiadać; lądować
disengage ('dysen'gejdż) v.
odczepiać; wyłączać;odwikłać
disengaged ('dysyn'gejdżd) adj.
wolny; nie zajęty;zwolniony
disentangle ('dysyntaengl) v.
wyplątać; rozplątać;wywikłać
disfavor ('dys'fejwer) s. niełaska; dezaprobata; v. odnosić się nieprzychylnie; z niechęcią traktować;dezaprobować
disfigure (dys'fyger) v. zniekształcić ;zeszpecić
disgrace (dys'grejs) s. hańba;
niełaska; v. hańbić; zniesła-
wić; pozbawiać łaski;narobić wsty-
disgraceful (dys'grejsfel) adj.
haniebny; hańbiący;sromotny;niecny
disguise (dys'gajz) v. przebierać; ukrywać; maskować; z..taić;
s. charakteryzacja; udawanie;
pozory ;zamaskowanie; maska

disgust (dys'gast) s. odraza;
wstręt; obrzydzenie; v. budzic odrazę, wstręt, obrzydzenie, rozgoryczenie,oburzenie
disgusting (dvs'gastyng)adj.
wstrętny; obrzydliwy;oburzający
dish (dysz) s. półmisek; naczynie;potrawa; danie; v. nakładac; podawac; drążyc;okpiwac
dishes ('dyszyz) pl. statki;
naczynia;smaczne potrawy
dish-cloth ('dysz,klos) s.
scierka do wycierania talerzy
disheveled (dy'szeweld) adj.
rozczochrany; zaniedbany
dishonest (dys'onyst) adj. nieuczciwy; nie godny zaufania
dishonesty (dys'onysty) s. nie-
uczciwosc;nieuczciwy postępek
dishonor (dys'oner) s. hanba;
dyshonor; niehonorowanie;v.lżyc
dishonorable (dys'onerebl) adj.
haniebny; podły;bez czci i wiary
dishwasher ('dysh,łoszer) s.
pomywacz(ka)
dish-water (dysz,ło:ter) s. pomyje
disillusion (,dysylu:żyn) s.
rozczarowanie;otrzeźwienie
disincline (,dysyn'klajn) v.
zniechęcac; miec niechęc
disinclined (,dysyn'klajnd) adj.
zniechęcony;źle usposobiony
disinfect (,dysyn'fekt) v. od-
każac ;zdyzenfekowac
disinfectant (,dysyn'fektent)
s. srodek odkażający
disinherit ('dysyn'heryt) v.
wydziedziczyc; wydziedziczac
disintegrate (dys'yntegrejt) v.
rozpadac (się); rozkładac (się)
disinterested (dys'yntrystyd)
adj. bezinteresowny; nie zainteresowany;obiektywny
disjoint (dys'dżoint)v. rozłączac;
rozdzielac;zwichnąc;rozerwac
disk (dysk) s. krążek; tarcza;
płyta gramofonowa; dysk
dislike (dys'lajk) v. nie lubic;
miec odrazę; s. odraza; niechęc;awersja; wstręt

dislocate ('dyslekejt) v.
zwichnąc; przesunąc;zatrącic
disloyal (,dys'lojel) adj. niewierny; nielojalny; zdradziecki
dismal ('dyzmel) adj. nieszczęsny; ponury; posępny
dismantle (dys'maentl) v. roz-
montowywac; ogołacac; odzie-
rac;rozbroic;pozbawiac
dismay (dys'mej) s. trwoga;
przestrach; v. przerażac;
konsternowac;skonsternowac
dismember (dys'member) v. roz-
członowac; rozebrac na części
dismiss (dys'mys) v. odprawiac;
zwalniac; odsuwac od siebie
dismissal (dys'mysel) s. zwolnienie; dymisja;rozejście się
dismount ('dys'maunt) v. zsiadac z konia; wyjmowac z opra-
wy; wysadzac z siodła
disobedience (dyse'bi:djens)
s. nieposłuszenstwo; opór
disobedient (dyse'bi:djent)
adj. nieposłuszny; oporny
disobey (,dyse'bej) v. nie-
słuchac; byc nieposłusznym
disoblige (,dyse'blajdż) v.
lekceważyc; bagatelizowac
disorder (dys'o:rder) s. nieporządek; zamieszki;zaburzenie
disorderly (dys'o:rderly)adj.
nieporządny; niesforny; gorszący; burzliwy;bezładny
disown (dys'oun) v. wypierac
się; zaprzeczac; nie uznawac
disparage (dys'paerydż) v.
poniżac; ubliżac; dyskredyto-
wac;uwiaszczac;lekceważyc
dispassion (dys'paeszyn) s.
beznamiętnosc; odiektywizm
dispassionate (dys'paeszynyt)
adj. beznamiętny;obiektywny
dispatch (dys'paecz) s. wysył-
ka; wysłanie; sprawnosc; szybkosc; szybkie załatwienie;
v. wysyłac; załatwiac
dispel (dys'pel) v. rozwiewac
(obawy);rozpędzac(chmury)
dispensable (dys'pensebl) adj.
zbędny; niekonieczny;do uchyle-
nia

dispense (dys'pens) v. wydzie-
lac; wymierzac; wydawac;
udzielac;sporządzac'(lekarstwo)
dispense with (dys pens łys)
v. pomijac; obyc się
disperse (dys'pe:rs) v. roz-
praszac; rozpądzac; rozjeż-
dżac się; rozsiewac;płoszyc'
displace (dys'plejs) v. prze-
mieszczac; wypierac; usuwac'
display (dys'plej) v. wystawiac; popisywac się; s. wystawa; popis; pokaz;parada
displease (dys'pli:z) v. ura-
żac; drażnic; gniewac; dotykac; oburzac; irytowac'
displeased (dys'pli:zd) adj.
urażony; zirytowany; niezadowolony;obrażony;poirytowany
displeasure (dys'pleżer) s.
niezadowolenie; gniew;irytacja
disposal (dys'pouzel) s. rozkład; zbyt; sprzedaż; przekazanie; rozporządzenie;niszczenie
dispose (dys'pouz) v. rozmiesz-
czac; rozporządzic; pozbyc'
się; sprzedac;usunac;niszczyc'
disposed (dys'pouzd) adj. skłonny; usposobiony(dobrze,źle etc.)
disposition (dys'pouzyszyn) s.
skłonnosc; pociąg; zarządzenie; dyspozycje;rozporządzanie
disproportionate (,dyspre'po:r-
sznyt) adj. nieproporcjonalny
dispute (dys'pju:t) s. spór;
kłótnia; v. sprzeczac się;
kłócic się; kwestionowac'
disqualify (dys'kłolyfaj) v.
dyskwalifikowac'
disquiet (dys'kłajet) v. niepokoic; s. niepokój; adj. niespokojny;zaniepokojony
disregard (,dysry'ga:rd) v. pomijac; lekceważyc;s.lekceważe-
disrepute (,dysry'pju:t) s.   nie
niesława;hańba; zła reputacja
disrespectful (,dysry'spektfel)
adj. niegrzeczny; niedelikatny
disrupt (dys'rapt) v. rozrywac;
rozdzierac;przerwac; obalic'
dissatisfaction ('dysseatys'-
faekszyn) s. niezadowolenie

dissatisfied (dys,satys'fajd)
adj. niezadowolony
dissension (dy'senszyn) s. waśn;
niezgoda; swary
dissent (dy'sent) s. różnica;
rozbieżnosc zdań; v. różnic
się w zapatrywaniach;odstępstwo
dissimilar ('dy'symyler) adj.
niepodobny; różny
dissipate (dy'sypejt) v. roz-
praszac; marnowac; trwonic;
marnotrawic;rozgonic;hulac'
dissociate (dy'sousjejt) v.
rozłączac; zrywac(z kimś,czymś)
dissolute ('dyselu:t) adj. rozwiązły; rozpustny
dissolution (,dyse'elu:szyn) s.
rozkład; zanik; rozpuszczenie;
rozwiązanie;smierc;zgon;rozpad
dissolve (dy'zolw) v. rozpuszczac; rozkładac; niszczyc;
rozwiązywac; zanikac;skasowac'
dissuade (dy'słejd) v. odradzac;
odwodzic (kogos);wyperswadowac'
distance (dystens) s. odległosc;
odstęp; oddalenie;v.zdystansowac
distant ('dystent) adj. daleki;
odległy; powsciągliwy;z rezerwą
distaste (,dys'tejst) s. niesmak;
niechęc; odraza; awersja
distasteful (,dys'tejstful) adj.
odstręczający;wstrętny;przykry
distend (dys'tend) v. rozdymac;
rozszerzac;nabrzmiewac;nadąc'
distill (dy'styl) v. przekrap-
lac; destylowac;przesączac;kapac
distinct (dys'tynkt) adj. odmienny; odrębny; wyrazny; dobitny
distinction (dys'tynkszyn) s.
rozróżnienie; wyróżnienie;
wytwornosc; podział;wyrazistosc
distinctive (dys'tynktyw) adj.
odróżniający się;charakterystyczny
distinguish (dys'tyngłysz) v.
rozróżniac; klasyfikowac;odznaczyc
distinguished (dystyngłyszt)
adj. wybitny; znakomity;
dystyngowany;odznaczający się
distort (dys'to:rt) v. wykrzywiac; wykręcac; przekręcac
distract (dys'traekt) v. odry-
wac; rozproszyc; oszołomic'

distracted (dys'traektyd) adj.
oszalały; w rozterce; skłopotany:roztargniony;rozproszony
distraction (dys'traekszyn) s.
dystrakcja; roztargnienie;
rozrywka; rozterka; szaleństwo:zamieszanie;odwrócenie uwagi
distress (dys'tres) s. męka;
strapienie; niedostatek; potrzeba; niebezpieczeństwo
distressed (dys'trest) adj.
umęczony; udręczony;w niedoli
distribute (dys'trybju:t) v.
udzielać; rozmieszczać;rozdać
distribution (dys'tryju;szyn)
s. rozdział; podział; dystrybucja;roznoszenie;a.rozdzielczy
district ('dystrykt) s. okręg;
powiat; dystrykt;dzielnica;rejon
distrust (dys'trast) s. nieufność; niedowierzanie; v.nieufać; niedowierzać;podejrzewac
disturb (dys'te:rb) v. przeszkadzać; niepokoic; zakłocać;
mącić; zaburzyć;denerwowac
disturbance (dys'te:rbens) s.
zakłocenie; zaburzenie; naruszenie;burda;awantura;rozruchy
disuse (dys'ju:z) v. zarzucenie; nieużywanie;s.nieużywanie
ditch (dycz),s. rów; v. kopac;
drenować; utknąć w rowie; rzucać do rowu(:amolot w morze)
dive (dajw) v. nurkować; zanurzac się; skakać z trampoliny;
s. nurkowanie; zanurzenie; melina;lot nurkowy;pikowanie;knajpa
diver ('dajwer) s. nurek;skoczek
z trampoliny;ptak nurkujący
diverge (daj'we:rdż) v. rozchodzic się; odchylać się; zbaczać;
odbiegać;rozbiegać się
diverse (daj'we:rs) adj. odmienny; rozmaity;inny;zmienny
diversion (daj'we:rżyn) s.odchylenie;objazd;rozrywka;dywersja
diversion (dy'we:rżyn) s. zboczenie; dywersja; rozrywka;odwrócenie uwagi;oderwanie uwagi
diversity (daj'we:rsyty) s. rozmaitość różnorodność;urozmaicenie

diversity (dy'we:rsyty) s. odmienność;rozmorodność;rozmaitość
divert (daj'we:rt) v. odwracać (uwagę); odrywać; rozerwac; rozbawić;bawić(kogoś)
divide (dy'wajd) v. dzielić;
rozdzielać; oddzielać; różnić
divide by (dy'wajd,baj) v.
dzielić przez...(liczbę)
divine (dy'wajn) adj. boski;
boży; v. wróżyc; przepowiadac
diving ('dajwyŋg) s. skakanie
z trampoliny;pikować samolotem
divinity (dy'wynyty) s. bóstwo;
boskość; teologia
divisible (dy'wyzebl) adj. podzielny (przez,na etc.)
division (dy'wyżyn) s. podział;
rozdział; dzielenie; dział;
wydział; oddział; dywizja
divorce (dy'wo:rs) s. rozwód;
rozdzielenie; v. rozwodzić
się; oddzielać;a.rozwodowy
dizzy ('dyzy) adj. wirujący;
oszołomiony;v.oszałamiac
do (du:) v. czynic; robić; wykonac; zwiedzać;przyrządzać
do away ('du,ełej) v. znieść;
pozbyc się; zabic;skasować
do not ('du not) = don't (dont)
nie(rób);nie(idź);nie(stój,etc.)
do in ('du,yn) v.uwięzic; zlikwidować; zabic;wsadzic do paki
do up ('du,ap) v. przerobic;
odnowic; zmęczyc;upudrować etc.
do well (,du'łel) v. miec się
dobrze; powodzic się
do without (,du'łysout) v.obywac się bez (kogoś,czegoś)
do you know? (du: ju nou) expr.
czy pan wie (zna) ? czy pan słyszał?
docile ('dousajl) adj. uległy;
posłuszny;pojętny;giętki;łagodny
dock (dok) s. dok; basen; molo;
miejsce oskarżonego; v. umiescić w doku; cumować przy molu
dockyard (dokja:rd) s. stocznia
doctor ('dakter) s. lekarz;
doktor (medycyny;filozofii etc.)
doctrine ('daktryn) s. doktryna

document ('dokjument) s. dokument;v. udokumentować

documentary (,dokju'mentery)s. adj. dokumentarny (film etc.)

dodge (dodż) v. uchylić; uniknąć; zwodzić; s, unik; kruczek; sztuczka;odskok;kiwanie

doe (dou) s. łania ;pl.does (douz)

does (daz) v. on czyni; robi; zob.: do

dog (dog) s. pies;uchwyt;klamra

dog-catcher (dog'kaeczer) s. rakarz; oprawca; hycel

dogged ('dogyd) adj. uparty; zawzięty;wytrwały

doggie ('dogi) s. psina

dogma ('dogme) s. dogmat

dog-tired ('dog'tajerd) adj. skonany; ledwo żywy;zmęczony

doings ('du:yngs) pl. sprawki; uczynki; wyprawiania;psoty

dole (doul) s. zasiłek; zapomoga; smutek;v.mało dawać

doll (dol) s. lalka; (slang) dziewczyna;v.wystroić się

dollar ('doler) s. dolar

dollish ('dolysz) adj. lalkowaty(a);lalusiowaty

dolorous ('douleres) adj. smętny; żałosny; zbolały

dolphin ('dolfyn) s. delfin

dome (doum) s. kopuła; sklepienie;v.nakrywać kopułą

domestic (de'mestyk) adj. domowy; krajowy; domatorski; s. służący; służąca

domesticate (de'mestykejt) v. oswajać; zadomowić

domicile ('domysajl) s, miejsce zamieszkania; v. osiedlać; zamieszkać na stałe

dominate ('domynejt) v. dominować; górować; przeważać; panować;mieć zwierzchnictwo

domination ('domynejszyn) s. władza; panowanie; przewaga

domineer (,domy'nier) v. dominować; rządzić się; rozkazywać;tyranizować;panoszyć się

domineering (,domy'nieryng) adj. tyranizujący; apodyktyczny; despotyczny; władczy

donate (dou'nejt) v. podarować

donation (dou'nejszyn) s. darowizna, donacja; dar

done (dan) adj. zrobiony; uczyniony; zob.: do

donkey ('doŋky) s. osioł

donor ('douner) s. donator; dawca (krwi etc.);darujący

doom (du:m) s. zguba; zły los; śmierć; potępienie; v. potępiać; skazać na zgubę;przesądzać

Doomsday ('du:mzdej) s. dzień sądu ostatecznego

door (do:r) s. drzwi;brama

door handle ('do:r,haendl) s. klamka

doorkeeper ('do:r,ki:per) s. dozorca;portier; oddźwierny

doorknob ('do:r,nob) s. klamka

doormat ('do:r,maet) s, wycieraczka (przy drzwiach)

doorway ('do:r,łej) s. wejście

dope (doup) s. maź; lakier; narkotyk; informacja (poufna); głupiec (slang) v. narkotyzować; zaprawiać;fałszować

dormitory ('do:rmytry) s. dom studencki; sypialnia

dose (dous) s. dawka; dodatek; dawkowanie; v. dawkować (lekarstwo); mieszać; fałszować (wino);leczyć;dozować

dot (dot) s. kropka; punkt; v. kropkować; rozsiewać

dote (dout) v. wariować; kochać przesadnie; dziecinnieć

double ('dabl) adj. podwójny; dwukrotny; fałszywy; v. podwajać; adv. podwójnie;w dwójnasób

double up ('dabl,ap) v. składać się we dwoje! zsuwać się (razem);przybiegać;dzielić pokój

double bed ('dabl,bed) podwójne łóżko

double-breasted ('dabl,brestyd) adj. dwurzędowy(płaszcz,marynarka)

double-decker ('dabl-'deker) s. dwupokładowiec; dwupiętrowiec

double-park ('dabl-'pa:rk) v. parkować podwójnie (na jezdni)

double-room ('dabl,ru:m) s. pokój dwuosobowy(w hotelu etc.)

doubt (daut) s. wątpliwość; niedowierzanie; v. wątpić; powąt-
piewać; niedowierzać
doubtful ('dautful) adj. wątpliwy; niepewny;niezdecydowany
doubtless ('dautlys) adv. nie-
wątpliwie, bez wątpienia
douche (du'sz) s. natrysk
dough (dou) s. ciasto; (slang)
forsa; pieniądze
doughnut ('dounat) s. pączek
(z dziurą)
dove (daw) s. gołąb(ica)
down (dałn) s. wydma; puch;
meszek ;puszek;piórka
down (dałn) adv. na dół; niżej;
nisko; v. obniżać; poniżać;
przewrócić; strącić; przełknąć
downcast ('dałnka:st) adj.
przybity; przygnębiony; ze
spuszczonymi oczyma
downfall ('dałnfo:l) s. upadek;
klęska; ruina ; zguba
downhill ('dałn'hyl) adj. opa-
dający; s. spadek ;adv.na dół
downpour ('dałnpo:r) s. ulewa
downright ('dałnrajt) adv. zupełnie; wprost; adj. zupełny;
szczery; otwarty; uczciwy
downstairs ('dałn'steerz) adv.
na dół; w dole ;na dole;pod nami
downtown ('dałntałn) s. centrum
miasta; adv. w srodmieściu;
adj. srodmiejski
downwards ('dałnłodz) adv.
w dół; ku dołowi ;na dół;z góry
downy ('dałny) adj. puszysty;
(slang):chytry ;falisty;puchaty
dowry ('dałry) s. posag; wiano;
dar wrodzony; talent
doze (douz) s. drzemka; v. drzemać; zdrzemnąć się; zasnąć
dozen ('dazn) s. tuzin
drab (draeb) s.& adj. brudno-
brunatny; nudny; szary; brudas;
prostytutka; v. puszczać się
draft (dra:ft) s. szkic; brulion
zarys; przekaz; pobór; rysunek;
v. szkicować; projektować; rysować; odkomenderować ;wyżłobić
draftsman ('dra:ftsmen) s. kres-
larz; rysownik; projektodawca

drag (draeg) v. wlec; ciągnąć;
s. pogłębiarka; pojazd; wleczenie; opór czołowy
dragon ('draegen) s. smok
dragonfly ('draegenflaj) s.
ważka
drain (drejn) v. odwadniać;
wysączać; ociekać; s. dren;
spust; ściek;rów odwadniający
drainage ('drejnydż) s. odwad-
nianie; wody ściekowe; obszar odpływowy (rzeki)
drainpipe ('drejnpajp) s.dren
drake (drejk) s. kaczor
drama ('dra:ma) s. dramat
dramatic (dre'maetyk) adj.
dramatyczny;jak w sztuce;żywy
drank (draenk) s. pijak; pijany; zob.: drink
drape (drejp) v. upinać; spadać fałdami; drapować;s.kotara
drastic ('draestyk) adj. drastyczny ;gwałtowny; surowy
draught (draeft) s. przeciąg;
ciąg; łyk; dawka; zanurzenie
statku ;wyporność;a.pociągowy
draw; drew; drawn (dro:; dru:;
dro:n)
draw, (dro:) v. ciągnąć; wyciągać; przyciągać; czerpać; wdychać; ściągać (wodze); spuszczać (wodę); napinać (łuk);
wlec ;rysować; kreślić
draw near(dro:nier) v. zbliżać
się;przybliżać się
drawback (dro:baek) s. strona
ujemna; v. cofać się(draw back)
draw up (dro:,sp) v. podciągać
(się); redagować; zbliżać się;
zrównać się; ustawiać (wojska)
drawer ('dro:er) s. szuflada;
kreślarz; rysownik ;bufetowy
drawers ('dro:ers) pl. kalesony; majtki (damskie,dziecięce…)
drawing ('dro:yng) s. rysunek
drawing pen ('dro:yng,pen) s.
grafion ;piórko kreślarskie
drawing room ('dro:yng,ru:m)
s. salon ;wagon salonowy
drawn (dro:n) adj. nierozstrzygnięty; ciągniony; wychudzony;
zob.: draw(wyciągnięta:szabla)

drawn-out (dro:n aut) adj.
przewlekły ;wyciągniety(z pochwy)
dread (dred) s. strach; postrach; lęk; v. bać się bardzo; lękac się; adj. straszny
dreadful (dredful) adj. przeraźliwy; okropny ;straszny
dream; dreamt; dreamt (dri:m;
dremt; dremt)
dream (dri:m) v. śnic; marzyc;
s. sen; marzenie;mrzonka;uroje-
dreamt (dremt) v. miec sen, nie
marzenie; zob.: dream
dreamy ('dri:my) adj. marzycielski; mglisty;niewyrazny
dreary ('dryery) adj. posępny;
ponury;smątny;melancholijny
dregs (dregz) pl. osady; męty
drench (drencz) v. zmoczyc;
przemoczyc ;s. ulewa
dress (dres) s. ubiór; strój;
szata; suknia; v. ubierac;
stroic; opatrywac; czyscic;
czesac; przyrządzac; wykanczac; wyprawiac ;wygarbować
dress down ('dres dałn) v.
besztac ; czyscic (konia)
dress up ('dres,ap) v. stroic
dressing ('dresyŋg) s. przyprawa; opatrunek; nawóz ;ubiór
dressing-case ('dresyŋg,kejs)
s. neseser
dressing-gown('dresyŋ,gołn) s.
podomka; szlafrok
dressing-room ('dresyŋg,ru:m) s.
garderoba ;ubieralnia;umywalnia
dressing-table ('dresyŋg,tejbl)
s. toaleta (mebel)
dressmaker ('dresmejker) s.
krawiec damski; krawcowa
drew (dru:) zob.: draw
drift (dryft) s. dryf; znoszenie; biernosc; prąd; dążnosc;
tresc; zamiec; zaspa; nanos
v. dryfowac; znosic; plątac
się; nanosic;płynąc z prądem
drill 1. (dryl) s. swider; wiertarka; dryl; musztra; v. wiercic; swidrowac; cwiczyc; musztrowac;drążyc;sortowac(wagony)
drill 2. (dryl) s. rowek do sia-
nia; siewnik rzędowy; v. siac;
obsadzac w rowkach

drink; drank; drunk ('dryŋk;
draenk; draŋk)
drink ('dryŋk) v. pic; przepi-
jac; s, napój; woda (morze)
drip (dryp) v. kapac; ociekac;
ciec; s. kapanie; okap; piła(sl);
nudziara ;kapka;kropla(wody etc.)
drip-dry ('dryp,draj) s. bielizna niewymagająca prasowa-
nia (schnąca na wieszaku etc.)
dripping ('drypyŋg) s. tłuszcz
spod pieczeni; adj. kapiący;
ociekający ; przemoczony
drive; drove; driven (drajw;
drouw; drywn)
drive (drajw) v. pędzic; gnac;
wiezc; powozic; prowadzic; na-
pędzac; jechac; wbijac ;drążyc
s. przejażdżka; obława; napęd;
droga; dojazd ;energia;pościg
drive at (drajw et) v. kierowac (rozmowę ku...)
drive out (drajw,aut) v. wy-
jeżdżac (z garażu);wypędzac
drive-in (drajw,yn) s. obsługa
w samochodzie :bank; jadłodajnia; kino; sklep;poczta
drive-in movies (drajw,yn
mu:wiz) kino do oglądania
z samochodu
driven (drywn) v. napędzany;
zob.: drive
driver (drajwer) s. kierowca
driving license ('drajwyŋg-
,lajsens) s. prawo jazdy
drizzle ('dryzl) s. mżący
deszcz; v. mżyc; adj. mżący;
drobny (deszcz)
drone (droun) s. truten; bucze-
nie; dudniący mówca; v. zbijac
bąki; buczec; dudnic(monotonnie)
droop (dru:p) v. opadac; zwisac;
zwieszac (głowę); s. zwis;
spadek (tonu); utrata (otuchy)
drop (drop) v. kapac; ciec;
upuszczac; spadac; opadac;
s. kropla; cukierek; spadek
(temperatury);łyk;kieliszek;zniż-
ka;kotara;upadek;obniżenie
drop in ('drop,yn) v. wpasc (do
kogoś);wejsc na chwilę
dropout (dropaut) s. osoba prze-
rywająca (studia lub szkołę)

drove (drouw) zob.: drive

drown (draun) v. tonąć; topić;
tłumić; głuszyć; zagłuszać

drowsy ('drauzy) adj. senny;
śpiący; ospały;na pół śpiący

drudge (dradż) s. niewolnik;
popychadło; v. harować

drug (drag) s. lek; lekarstwo;
v. narkotyzować; przesycać

drug-addict ('drag,aedykt) s.
narkoman

drugstore ('drag,stor) s. apteka; drogeria

drum (dram) s. bęben; v. bębnić;zwoływać bębnieniem;zjedny-
wać

drummer ('dramer) s. dobosz

drunk (drank) adj. pijany;
zob.: drink

drunken driving (dranken
drajwyng) s. kierowanie po
pijanemu (samochodem etc.)

dry (draj) adj. suchy;wytrawny
(wino) v. osuszać; suszyć;(łzy)
zeschnąć;wyjaławiać;wycierać

dry up (draj,ap) v. wycierać;
wysychać;zapomnieć;zaniemówić

dry-clean ('draj kli:n) v.
oczyścić chemicznie (sucho)

dry goods('drajgudz) pl. materiały do szycia;konfekcja

dual ('dju:el) adj. podwójny;
dwoisty;dwudzielny;wspólny

duchess ('daczys) s. księżna

duck (dak) s. kaczka; unik; v.
zanurzyć; zrobić unik;nurkować

duct (dakt) s. przewód; kanał

dud (dad) s. poroniony pomysł;
safanduła; nieuk; niewypał;
strach na wróble;adj.niezdolny

dude (d(j)u:d) s. elegancik;
luluś; turysta;goguś;wycieczko-
wicz

dude ranch ('du:d,ra:nch) ran-
czo wakacyjne(dla mieszczuchów)

due (dju:) adj. należny; płatny;
należyty; adv. w kierunku na
(wschód); s. to co się należy;
należność; opłata;składka

due to ('dju:,tu) exp. z powodu

duel ('dju(;)el) s. pojedynek

dug (dag) s. cycek; wymię; zob.:
dig

dug2.(dag)s. dójka

dugout ('dagaut) s. ziemianka;
łódź drążona; okop; schron

duke (dju:k) s. książę

dull (dal) adj. tępy; głuchy;
ospały; niemrawy; nudny; ponury; ciemny;v.tępić;tłumić

duly ('dju:ly) adv. właściwie;
należycie; punktualnie;słusznie

dumb (dam) adj. niemy; milczący; głupi;v.odbierać mowę

dumbfounded (dam'faundyd) adj.
osłupiony;osłupiały;oniemiały

dummy ('damy) s, imitacja; bałwan; manekin; (wulg.) niemowa;
adj. udany; podstawiony; imito-
wany; na niby; niby to

dump (damp) s. śmietnisko; hałda;
magazyn; v. zwalać; rzucać; zarzucać (towarem obcym)

dun (dan) s. wierzyciel; inka-
sent długów; v. napastować
o zapłatę długu;a.ciemnobrązowy

dune (dju:n) s. wydma;diuna

dung (dang)s. nawóz; gnój; bagno moralne; v. nawozić; użyźniać
ziemię; gnoić

dungeon ('dandżen) s. loch;baszta
v. więzić w lochu lub baszcie

dupe (du:p) s. ofiara; wystrych-
nięty na dudka ;v. okpić;nabrać

duplicate ('dju:plykyt) adj.
podwójny; s. duplikat; w dwu
egzemplarzach; v. podwajać;
duplikować (niepotrzebnie)

duplicity (dju:'plysyty) s. dwu-
licowość; podstęp;fałsz;obłuda

durable ('djuerebl) adj. trwały

duration (dju'rejszyn) s. trwanie; czas trwania

duress (dju'res) s. przymus

during ('djueryng) prep. podczas; w czasie ;w ciągu;przez;za

dusk (dask) s. zmierzch; mrok;
cień; adj. ciemny; mroczny;
v. zaćmić; zamroczyć

dust (dast) s. pył; kurz; pro-
chy; pyłek; v. odkurzać; trzepać; kurzyć się; posypywać

dust bowl (dast,boul) s. kraj
suszy i burz(zamieci)piaskowych

dustcover ('dast, kawer) s.
obwoluta; pokrowiec od kurzu

duster ('daster) s. odkurzacz;
wiatr z kurzem;zmiotka
dust-pan ('dast,paen) s. śmiet-
niczka;łopatka na śmieci
dust-storm ('dast,sto:rm) s.
wicher z tumanami kurzu
dusty ('dasty) adj. zakurzony;
pokryty kurzem; suchy; nudny
Dutch (dacz) adj. holenderski;
w niełasce; lichy
duty ('dju:ty) s. powinność;
obowiązek; szacunek; służba;
uległość; cło; podatek od
sprzedaży;funkcja;obowiązki
dwarf (dło:rf) s. karzeł;
krasnoludek; adj. karłowaty;
v. pomniejszać; karleć; skar-
leć;skarłowacieć;zmniejszać
dwell (dłel; wzrost
dłelt; dłelt)
dwell (dłel) v. mieszkać; zatrzymywać się; rozwodzić się
(o czyms); zwlekać;przystanąć
dwelling (dłelyng) s. mieszkanie;pomieszczenie mieszkalne
dwelt (dłelt) v. mieszkał...
zob.: dwell
dwindle (dłyndl) v. maleć; topnieć; marnieć; kurczyć się;
tracić znaczenie;zwyrodnieć
dye (daj) v. barwić; farbować;
s. barwa; barwik;farba
dying (dajyng) v. umierający;
zanikający; zob.: die
dyke (dajk) s. grobla; rów;
tama;v.ogroblić;ochronić tamą
dynamic (daj'naemyk) adj. dyna-
miczny;energiczny;z wigorem
dynamics (daj'naemyks) s. dyna-
mika (sił działających razem)
dynamite ('dajne,majt) s. dynamit;v.wysadzać dynamitem
dynamo ('dajne,mou) s. dynamo
dynasty ('dajnesty) s. dynastia
dysentery ('dysnetry) s. czer-
wonka; dyzenteria(krwawa)
e (i:) piąta litera angielskiego
alfabetu
each (i:cz) pron. każdy;za(sztukę)
each other ('i:cz, odzer)siebie;
nawzajem (dwie osoby);sobie

eager ('i:ger) adj. gorliwy;ostry;
żądny;ożywiony pragnieniem;żywy
eagerness('i:gernyss) s. gorliwość;skwapliwość;pochopność
eagle ('i:gl) s. orzeł;a.orli
ear (ier) s. ucho; słuch; kłos
(zboża);a.uszny;dotyczący uszu
eardrum ('ierdram) s. bębenek
ucha; błona bębenkowa(ucha)
early ('e:rly) adj. wczesny;
adv. wcześnie;przedwcześnie
earn (e:rn) v. zarabiać; zasługiwać;zapracowć;zdobywać(sławę)
earnest ('e:rnyst) adj. poważny;
gorliwy; s. powaga;zadatek;dowód
earnings ('e:rnynz) pl. zarobki
earphone ('ierfoun) s. słuchawka;loki ułożone na uszach
earring ('ieryng) s. kolczyk
earshot ('ier,szot) w zasięgu głosu ;w zasięgu słuchu
earth (e:rs) s. ziemia;świat;gle-
ba
earthen ('e:rsen) adj. ziemis-
ty; gliniany;wypiekany z gliny
earthenware ('e:rsen,łe:r) s.
wyroby garncarskie(wypiekane)
earthly ('e:rsly) adj. ziemski
earthquake('e:rs,kłejk) s.
trzęsienie ziemi
earthworm ('e:rs,łe:rm) s.
(glista);dżdżownica
ease (i:z) v. łagodzić; uspokoić;
odciążyć; s. spokoj; wygoda;
beztroska;ulga;łatwość;bezczynność
easel ('i:zl) s. sztaluga
easily ('i:zyly) adv. łatwo;
lekko; swobodnie;bez trudności
east (i:st) s. wschod; adj.
wschodni; adv. na wschod
Easter ('i:ster) s. Wielkanoc
eastern ('i:stern) adj. wschodni;człowiek wschodu;prawosławny
eastwards ('i:stłerdz) adv. ku
wschodowi;na wschód;adj.wschodni
easy (i:zy) adj. łatwy; beztroski; wygodny; adv. łatwo
swobodnie; lekko;s.odpoczynek
easy chair ('i:zy,czeer) s.
fotel (klubowy) miękki
eat; ate; eaten (i:t; ejt; i:tn)
eat (i:t) v. jeść (posiłek)

eat up ('i:t,ap) v. wyjeść
eaten (i:tn) adj. zjedzony;
zob. eat
eaves (i:wz) pl. okap(dachu)
eavesdropping ('i:wzdropyng)
s. podsłuchiwanie(rozmowy)
ebbtide ('ebtajd) s. odpływ
w morze;v.odpływać(jak morze)
ebony ('ebeny) s. heban
eccentric (ik:sentryk) adj.
dziwaczny; s., ekscentryk;
dziwak; mimośród;dziwaczka
ecclesiastic (ik,ly:zi'eastyk)
adj. kościelny; s. duchowny
echo ('ekou) s. echo; v. odbijać się echem; powtarzać za
kims; odbijać głos
eclipse (i'klyps) s. zacmienie;
v. zaciemniac;zacmiewać
ecology (i'koledży) s. ekologia;
związek między srodowiskiem
a organizmem(część biologii)
economic (,i:ke'nomyk) adj;
ekonomiczny;gospodarczy
economical (,i:ke:nomykel) adj.
oszczędny; ekonomiczny
economics (,i:ke'nomyks) pl.
nauka o ekonomii (gospodarce)
economist (i'konemyst) s. ekono-
mista;specjalista od gospodarki
economize (i:kone,majz) v.
oszczędzać;zmniejszać wydatki
economy (i,konemy) s. ekonomia;
gospodarka;oszczędność
economy class (i'konemy,kla:s)
s. druga klasa (w pociągu;
samolocie);klasa turystyczna
ecstasy ('ekstesy) s. zachwyt;
ekstaza; uniesienie;siódme niebo
eddy ('edy) s. wir; v. wirować
edelweiss ('ejdl,wajs) s. szarotka (kwiat górski)
edge (edż) s. ostrze; krawędź;
kraj; v. ostrzyc; obszywać;
wyslizgiwać się;przysuwać po trochu
edging ('edżyng) s. brzeg; ob-
szywka; lamówka;skraj
edgy ('edży) adj. nerwowy;
podniecony;o ostrych kantach
edible('edybl) adj. jadalny
edict ('i:dykt) s. edykt; dekret

edifice ('dyfys) s. budowla;
gmach (duży i imponujący)
edifying ('edyfajyng) adj. po-
uczający(zwłaszcza moralnie)
edit ('edyt) v. redagować; wydawać;zarządzać gazetą etc.
edition (i'dyszyn) s. wydanie;
nakład (książki,gazety etc.)
editor (e'dyter) s. redaktor;
wydawca;pisarz"od redakcji"
editorial (,edy'to:rjel) s.
artykuł od redakcji; adj.
redakcyjny; redaktorski
educate ('edju:kejt) v. kształcić; wychowywać;płacić za szkołę
education (,edju'kejszyn) s.
wykształcenie; nauka; oświata;
wychowanie; tresura;wiedza
educational (,edju'kejszenl)
adj. kształcący; wychowawczy
educator ('edju,kejter) s.
wychowawca; wychowawczyni
eel (i:l) s. węgorz
effect (i'fekt) s. skutek; wrażenie; v. wykonywać; dokonywać
effects (i'fekts) pl. ruchomos-
ci; dobytek;manatki
effective (i'fektyw) adj. skuteczny; wydajny; rzeczywisty;
efektowny;wchodzący w życie
effeminate (i'femynyt) adj.
zniewieściały;nie męski;słaby
effervescent (,efer'wesnt) adj.
musujący; kipiący;tryskający życiem
efficacy ('efykesy) s. skuteczność;dawanie porządanych wyników
efficiency (i'fyszensy) s. wydajność; skuteczność; spraw-
ność(przy minimum nakładów)
efficient(i'fyszent) adj. skuteczny; wydajny; sprawny
effigy ('efydży) s, wizerunek;
podobizna; czyjaś kukła
effort ('efert) s. wysiłek;
usiłowanie;wyczyn; próba;popis
effusive (i'fju:syw) adj. wylewny;wylany;ekspansywny;wulka-
niczny
egg (eg) s. jajko; v. zachęcać;
namawiac;podbechtać;podniecać
eggcup ('eg,kap) s. kieliszek
na jajko;kieliszek do jaj

egghead ('eg,hed) s. intelektualista (nieżyciowy)

egoism ('egou,zyem) s. egoizm

egress ('i:gres) s. wyjście; wyjazd; uchodzenie;wypływ

Egyptian (i'dżypszen) adj. egipski

eiderdown ('ajder,dain) s. kaczy puch; kołdra;pierzyna

eight (ejt)num.osiem; s. ósemka; ośmioro;ośmiu wioślarzy

eighteen('ejt'i:n) num. osiemnaście; osiemnaścioro;osiemnaście

eightfold ('ejt,fould) num. ośmiokrotny; adv. ośmiokrotnie ;osiem razy

eighty ('ejty) num. osiemdziesiąt; s. osiemdziesiątka

either ('ajdzer) pron. każdy (z dwu); obaj; obie; oboje; jeden lub drugi;adv.także;też

either... or ('ajdzer..o:r) albo... albo

ejaculate (i'dżaekju,lejt) v. zawołać; krzyknąć;wytrysnąć

eject (i'dżekt) v. wyrzucać (się); eksmitować;usuwać

elaborate (i'laebe,rejt) v. opracować; adj. wypracowany, staranny;skomplikowany

elapse (i'laeps) v. minąć; przeminąć ;przemijać

elastic (i'laestyk) adj. sprężysty; rozciągliwy; elastyczny; s. guma; gumka(do majtek...)

elated (i'lejtyd) adj. podniecony; uniesiony; dumny

elbow ('elboł) s. łokieć; zakręt; kolanko; v. szturchać; przepychać się; zakręcać

elbow grease ('elboł,gri:s) s. ciężka praca; wysiłek

elder ('elder) s. człowiek starszy; adj. starszy (z dwoch);należący do starszyzny

elderly ('elderly) adj. podstarzały; starszy;starszawy

eldest ('eldyst) adj. najstarszy (syn)(w rodzinie)

elect (i'lekt) v. wybrać; postanawiać; decydować; adj.wybrany; wyborny; wyborowy

election (i'lekszyn) s. wybór; wybory (głosowaniem)

elector (i'lekter) s. wyborca; elektor;członek kolegium wyborczego

electric (i'lektryk) adj. elektryczny;bursztynowy;elektryzujący

electrical engineer (e'lektrykel,endży'nier) s. inżynier elektryk

electric chair (i'lektryk,cze:r) s. krzesło elektryczne (do egzekucji) (w USA)

electrician (ilek'tryszen) s. elektryk (monter) (instalator)

electricity (ilek'trysyty) s. elektryczność;prąd elektryczny

electrify (i'lektryfaj) v. elektryfikować; elektryzować

electrocute (i'lektrekju:t) v. uśmiercić prądem elektrycznym

electron (i'lektron) s. elektron

elegance ('elygens) s. elegancja

elegant ('elygent) adj. elegancki;dostojny;doskonały

element ('elyment) s. żywioł; pierwiastek; część składowa; ogniwo; część podstawowa

elemental (,ely'mentl) adj. żywiołowy; zasadniczy; elementarny; podstawowy;konieczny

elementary (,ely'mentery) adj. elementarny; zasadniczy; niepodzielny; pierwiastkowy

elementary school (,ely'mentery sku:l) s. szkoła powszechna

elephant ('elyfent) s. słoń

elevate ('ely,wejt) v. podnosić; unosić; wynosić (wzwyż)

elevation (ely'wejszyn) s. wysokość; godność; fasada; podwyższenie

elevator ('ely,wejter) s. winda; dźwig; wyciąg; spichlerz

eleven (i'lewn) num. jedenaście; s. jedenastka; jedenaścioro

eleventh (i'lewnt) num. jedenasty; jedenastka

eligible ('elydżebl) adj. nadający się; odpowiedni na wybór

eliminate (i'lymy,nejt) v. usuwać; wydzielać;pozbywać się;nie brać pod uwagę;opuszczać

elimination (i,lymy'nejszyn)
s. eliminacja ;pozbycie się

elk (elk) s. łoś

ell (ell) s. łokieć (miara)

ellipse (i'lyps) s. elipsa

elm (elm) s. wiąz

elongate (i'longejt) v. wydłużać się,adj.wydłużony

elope (i'loup) v. uciekać
z ukochanym (potajemnie)

eloquence ('eloukłens) s. elo-
kwencja; krasomówstwo

eloquent ('elokłent) adj. elo-
kwentny; wymowny(też w piśmie)

else (els) adv.inaczej; bo
inaczej; w przeciwnym razie;
poza tym; jeszcze;adj.różny in-
elsewhere (els'hłer) adv. gdzie
indziej;w innym miejscu

elude (i'lu:d) v. ujść; wymknąć
się;obejść prawo;uchylić się

elusive (ilu:syw) adj. nieuchwytny; wymykający się

emanate ('eme,nejt) v. wydobywać; pochodzić;wydzielać się

emancipate (i'maens,ypejt) v.
wyzwolić; wyemancypować

embalm (im'ba:lm) v. zabalsamo-
wać; napełnić aromatem

embankment (im'baenkment) s.
nasyp; grobla; nabrzeże

embargo (em'ba:rgou) s. zakaz
handlowania, wjazdu, wyjazdu

embark (im'ba:rk) v. ładować
(się); wsiadać (na statek);
rozpoczynać (przedsięwzięcie)

embark upon (im'ba:rk e'pon) v.
rozpoczynać ;przedsięwziąć

embarrass (im'baeres) v. zakłopotanie; wikłać; przeszkadzać;powodować zadłużenie

embarrassing (im'baeresyng)
adj. żenujący; kłopotliwy;
krępujący;zawstydzający

embarrassment (im'baeresment)s.
zakłopotanie; powikłanie;
skrępowanie;zaaferowanie

embassy ('embesy) s. ambasada

embed (im'bed) v. osadzić; sadzić;wmurować;wryć;wkopać

embedded (im'bedyd) adj. osadzo-
ny; wsadzony;wryty;wmurowany

embellish (im'belysz) v. upiększać;ozdabiać;podkolorowywać

embers ('emberz) pl. niewygas-
łe węgle; żar palące się polana

embezzle (ym'bezl) v. sprzeniewierzać (pieniądze,własność etc.)

embitter (im'byter) v. rozgoryczać; zatruwać; pogarszać

emblem ('emblem) s. godło; wzór

embody (im'body) v. wcielać;
uosabiać; zawierać włączać

embolden (im'boulden) v. ośmielać; rozzuchwalać ;dodać śmiałości

embolism (embelyzem) s. zator

embrace (im'brejs) v. uścisnąć
się; obejmować; przystępować;
imać się; korzystać; s. uścisk;
objęcie ;włączenie(do kategorii)

embroider (im'brojder) v. hafto-
wać;wyszywać;upiększać opowiadanie

embroidery (im'brojdery) s. haft;
hafciarstwo,upiększanie opowiadania

emerald ('emereld) s. szmaragd

emerge (i'me:rdż) v. wynurzać
się; wyłaniać,wynikać;nasunąć się

emergency (y'me:rdżensy) s.
nagła potrzeba; stan wyjątkowy

emergency brake (y'me:rdżensy,
,brejk) s. ręczny hamulec
w samochodzie;hamulec zapasowy

emergency call (y'me:rdżensy,kol)
s. wzywanie pogotowia (nagłe)

emergency exit (y'me:rdżensy,
,eksyt) s. wyjście zapasowe

emergency landing (y'merdżensy,
, laendyng)s. przymusowe lądowanie (samolotu)

emigrant ('emygrent) s. wychodźca; emigrant;adj.wychodźczy

emigrate ('emygrejt) v. emigro-
wać; wywędrować;przeprowadzać się

emigration (,emy'grejszyn) s.
emigracja; wychodźstwo

emigré ('emygrej) s. emigrant
(polityczny);a.emigracyjny(rząd)

eminent ('emynent) adj. dostojny; wybitny; wyniosły; wysoki

eminently ('emynently) adv.
szczególnie; wybitnie;wysoce

emit (y'myt) v. wydawać; wysyłać (światło; fale radiowe;
ciepło; opinie); wypuszczać
(banknoty);nadawać(audycje)

emotion (y'mouszyn) s. wzruszenie; emocja; uczucie(miłości,stra-
chu,gniewu,oburzenia,współczucia)

emotional (y'mouszynel) adj.
emocjonalny;poruszający uczucia
emperor ('emperer) s. cesarz
emphasis ('emfesys) s. nacisk;
emfaza;uwypuklenie;uwydatnienie
emphasize ('emfesajz) v. podkreślać; kłaść nacisk;uwypuklać
emphatic (ym'faetyk) adj. dobitny; wyraźny; stanowczy;
emfatyczny;mówiący z naciskiem
empire ('empajer) s. cesarstwo;
imperium ;adj.empirowy
emplacement (yn'plejsment) s.
umiejscowienie; stanowisko
employ (ym'ploj) v. zatrudniać;
używać; zajmować się; poświęcać (czas);posługiwać się
employee (,emploj'i:) s. pracownik;siła (robocza,biurowa...)
employer (em'plojer) s. pracodawca;pracodawczyni;szef
employment (ym'plojment) s. za-
trudnienie; używanie; zajęcie
employment agency (ym'plojment
'ejdżensy) agencja pośrednic-
twa pracy;biuro zatrudnienia
empower (ym'pałer) v. upełnomocnić; upoważniać;umożliwiać
empress ('emprys) s. cesarzowa
emptiness ('emptynys) s. pustka
empty ('empty) adj. pusty; próżny; v. wypróżniać; wysypywać;
wylewać;wpływać(do morza)
emulate ('emjulejt) v. rywalizować; współzawodniczyć
enable ('nejbl) v. umożliwiać;
upoważniać;dawać możność
enact (y'naekt) v. postanawiać;
uchwalać; grać (rolę); odgrywać (sztukę); uprawomocnić
enamel (y'naemel) s. emalia;
szkliwo(na zębach etc.)
encase (yn'kejs) v. wsadzać do
pochwy; oprawiać;wpakowywać
enchant (yn'czaent) v. zaczarować; oczarować; zachwycać
encircle (yn'se:rkl) v. otaczać;
okalać;okrążać;okrążyć;otoczyć
enclose (yn'klouz) v. ogradzać;
zamykać; dołączać; załączać;
zawierać;okrążyć(wroga)

enclosure (yn'kloużer) s. ogrodzenie; załącznik;ogradzanie
encounter (yn'kaunter) s. spotkanie; potyczka; pojedynek;
v. natknąć się; spotykać się;
potykać się; mieć utarczkę
encourage (yn'ka:rydż) v. zachęcać; ośmielać; popierać;
dodawać odwagi;pomagać
encouragement (yn'ka:rydżment)
s. zachęta; ośmielenie; po-
pieranie;dodanie odwagi
encroach (yn'kroucz) v. wdzierać się; naruszać; wkraczać
na cudze;targnąć się na cudze
encumber (yn'kamber) v. krępować; tarasować; obarczać; zawadzać;obciążać(długami etc.)
end (end) s. koniec; cel;
skrzydłowy w nożnej piłce;
v. kończyć (się); skończyć;
dokończyć;położyć kres
endanger (yn'dejndżer) v. narażać na niebezpieczeństwo
endear (yn'dier) v. czynić
drogim; lubianym;przymilać się
endeavor (yn'dewer) v. starać
się; usiłować; s. usiłowanie;
wysiłek; dążenie;zabiegi;próba
ending ('endyng) s. zakończenie; końcówka (wyrazu etc.)
endless ('endlys) adj. niekończący się; nieskończony;
ustawiczny;wieczny;ciągły
endorse (yn'do:rs) v. potwierdzać; popierać; podżyrować;
notować na odwrocie
endow (yn'dał) v. uposażyć;
wyposażyć;ufundować;zapisywać
endurance (yn'djuerens) s. wytrzymałość; cierpliwość
endure (yn'djuer) v. znosić
(ból); cierpieć; wytrzymać;
przetrwać; ostać się
enema ('enyme) s. lewatywa
enemy ('enymy) s. wróg; przeciwnik; adj. wrogi; nieprzyjacielski;przeciwny
energetic (,ene:r'dżetyk) adj.
energiczny; z wigorem
energy ('enerdży) s. energia

enervate ('ene:rwejt) v. osłabiać (nerwowo,na zdrowiu)wyczer-
pywać
enervate (y'ne:rwyt) adj. słaby; bez energii;wyczerpany
enfold (yn'fould) v. zawijać;
obejmować;zapakowywać
enfranchise (un'fraenczajz) v.
wyzwalać; nadawać prawo wyborcze; uwalniać;uwłaszczać
engage (yn'gejdż) v. zajmować;
angażować; skłaniać; ścierać
się;zaręczyć;zobowiązywać się
engaged (yn'gejdżd) adj. zajęty; zaręczony; włączony
engagement (yn'gejdżment) s.
zobowiazanie; zaręczyny
engine ('endżyn) s. silnik;
parowóz; maszyna; motor
engine-driver ('endżyn,drajwer)
s. maszynista (kolejowy)
engineer (,endży'nier) s. inżynier;v.planować;zręcznie prowadzić
engineering (,endży'nieryng)s.
technika; mechanika; inżynieria;zarząd dróg,maszyn etc.
engine trouble ('endżyn'trabl)
s. zepsucie silnika (samocho-
dowego);kłopot z silnikiem
English ('ynglysz) adj. angielski (język)
english ('ynglysz) v. uderzyć
piłkę fałszem; s. fałsz; pod-
kręcona piłka;v.zangielszczyć
engorge (yn'go:rdż) v. pożerać
engrave (yn'grejw) v. rytować;
ryć; grawerować;wyryć;wyrytować
engraving (yn'grejwyng) s.
sztych;rytownictwo;grawiura
engross (yn'grous) v. pochłaniać; monopolizować (rozmowę)
enigma (y'nygme) s. zagadka
enjoin (yn'dżoyn) v. nakazywać;
zarządzać; zakazywać;zalecać
enjoy (yn'dżoj) v. cieszyć się;
rozkoszować;mieć;posiadać
enjoyment (yn'dżojment) s. uciecha; korzystanie z uprawnie-
nia; rozkosz; przyjemność
enlarge (yn'la:rdż) v. powiększać; poszerzać;zwalniać z ciupy
enlargement (yn'la: rdżment) s.
powiększenie; poszerzenie

enlighten (yn'lajtn) v. oświecać; oświetlać;objaśniać
enlist (yn'lyst) v. zaciągać
(się); werbować;wstępować
enliven (yn'lajwn) v. ożywiać
enmesh (yn'mesz) v. wplatać
(w sieć); usidlać;usidlić
enmity ('enmyty) s. wrogość;
nieprzyjaźń;nienawiść
enormous (y'no:rmes) adj. olbrzymi; ogromny; kolosalny
enough (y'naf) adj.,s.& adv.
dosyć; dość;na tyle;nie więcej
enounce (y'nauns) v. ogłaszać;
wymawiać;wypowiadać;wymówić
enquire (yn'kłajer) v. pytać;
dowiadywać się;rozpytywać się
enquiry (yn'kłajry) s, pytanie;
śledztwo;badania;pytanie
enrage (yn'rejdż) v. rozwścieczać;doprowadzać do wściekłości
enraged (yn'rejdżd) adj. rozwścieczony; rozwścieczona
enrapt (yn'raept) adj. zachwycony;pogrążony w zachwycie
enrapture (yn'reapczer) v. zachwycać;oczarowywać;porywać
enrich (yn'rycz) v. wzbogacać;
użyźniać;ozdobić;ozdabiać
enrol(l) (yn'roul) v. zaciągać
(się); zapisywać (się)
ensue (yn'su:) v. wynikać; następować;wypływać (z czegoś)
ensure (yn'szuer) v. zabezpieczać; zapewniać;asekurować
entangle (yn'taengel) v. gmatwać; wplatać;zmieszać;kompliko-
wać
enter ('enter) v. wchodzić; wpi-
sywać;penetrować;wkładać;wpisywać
enter into ('enter,yntu) v. wdawać się; brać udział;zawierać
enter upon ('enter,apon) v.
wchodzić w posiadanie; przystępować do tematu; zaczynać
enterprise ('enterprajz) s.
przedsięwzięcie; przedsiębiorstwo; przedsiębiorczość
enterprising ('enterprajzyng)
adj. przedsiębiorczy;ryzykujący
entertain (,enter'tejn) v. zabawiać; przyjmować; żywić;
nosić się;brać pod uwagę

entertainer (,enter'tejner) s.
artysta (kabaretowy)
entertainment (,enter'tejnment)
s. rozrywka; zabawa; uciecha
enthusiasm (yn'tju:zjaezem)
s. zapał; entuzjazm
enthusiast (yn'tju:zaest) s.
entuzjasta;zapaleniec
enthusiastic (yn'tu:zy'aestyk)
adj. entuzjastyczny;zapalony
entice (yn'tajs) v. znęcic;
zwabic(nagrodą,przyjemnością)
entire (yn'tajer) adj. cały;
całkowity;nietknięty
entirely (yn'tajerly) adv.
całkowicie; jedynie; wyłącznie;kompletnie;niepodzielnie
entitle (yn'tajtl) v. uprawniac;
tytułowac; zatytułowac;nadawac
entity ('entyty) s. byt; istnienie; jednostka;istota
entrails ('entrejlz) pl. jelita
wnętrzności;wnętrze ziemi
entrance ('entrens) s. wejscie;
wstęp (za opłatą);dostęp;wjazd
entrance (,entraens) v. przejmowac; wprawiac w trans
entrance fee ('entrens,fi:)
opłata za wstęp;bilet wstępu
entreat (yn'tri:t) v. błagac
entreaty (yn'tri:ty) s. błaganie; usilna prośba
entrust(yn'trast) v. powierzać
entry ('entry) s. wejscie; wpis;
hasło (słownika);uczestnik wys-
entry permit (,entry,per'myt) s.
pozwolenie wejscia; wjazdu
enumerate (y'nju:merejt) v.
wliczac; sporządząc wykaz
envelop (yn'welep) v. owijac;
otaczac; ogarniac;okryc(całkiem)
envelope ('enweloup) s. koperta; otoczka;teczka(papierowa)
envenom (yn'wenem) v. zatruwac
enviable ('enwjebl) adj. godzien zazdrości;godny pożądania
envious (enwjes) adj. zazdrosny; zawistny;pełen zazdrości
environment (yn'wajerenment)
s. otoczenie; srodowisko
environmental pollution (yn'wa-
jerenmentel pel'u:szyn) za-
nieczyszczanie srodowiska

environs (yn'wajerenz) s. okolice podmiejskie;przedmieścia
envoy ('enwoj) s. wysłannik
envy ('enwy) s. zawisc; zaz-
drosc; przedmiot zazdrości
epic ('epyk) adj. epicki;
s. epos (o bohaterstwie)
epidemic (,epy'demyk) s. epi-
demia; adj. epidemiczny
epidermis (,epy'de:rmys) s. na-
skorek; skora (powierzchnia)
epilepsy ('epylepsy) s. epileps-
ja ; padaczka
epilog(ue) ('epylog) s. epilog
episode ('epysoud) s. epizod
epitaph ('epytaef) s. napis
na grobie(ku pamięci zmarłego)
epoch (i:'pok) s. epoka
equal ('i:kłel) adj. rowny;
jednaki; jednakowy; jednostajny; zrównoważony; s. rowny
(stanem); v. rownac się; do-
rownywac; wyrownywac;wyrównywać
equality (i'kłolyty) s. rowność
equalize (i'kłelajz) v. wyrów-
nywac; rownac;zrownywac(się)
equanimity (,i:kłe'nymyty) s.
opanowanie; spokój; równowaga
equate (i'kłejt) v. rownac;
przyrównywac;stawiac na rowni
equation (i'kłejżyn) s. rowna-
nie; równoważenie;bilansowanie
equator (i'kłejter) s. rownik
equilibrium (,i:kły'lybrjem) s.
rownowaga
equip (i'kłyp) v. wyposażac;
zaopatrywac;uzbrajac;ekwipowac
equipment (i'kłypment) s. wyposażenie; ekwipunek;sprzęt
equitable ('ekłytebl) adj.
słuszny; sprawiedliwy
equivalent (i'kływelent) adj.
rownowartosciowy; rownoznacz-
ny; rownej wielkości;s.rowno-
era ('yere) s. era
erase (y'rejz) v. wycierac;
wymazywac;zatrzec;zacierac
erect (y'rekt) adj. prosty; wy-
prężony; najeżony;v.budowac;sta-
wiac
erection (y'rekszyn) s. podniesienie; wyprostowanie; najeże-
nie; erekcja; budowla; montaż

erosion (y'roużyn) s. wyżera-
nie; żłobienie; erozja
ermine ('e:rmyn) s. gronostaj
erotic (y'rotyk) adj. erotyczny; miłosny; s. erotyk; ero-
toman; wiersz erotyczny
err (e:r) v. błądzić; być
w błędzie;grzeszyć; zgrzeszyć
errand ('erand) s. posyłka;
zlecenie; cel;sprawunek
erratic (y'raetyk) adj. błędny;
nieobliczalny;dziwny;s.dziwak
erroneous (y'rounjes) adj.
błędny;mylny;fałszywy
error ('erer) s. błąd
erudite ('erudajt) adj. uczony; s. erudyta (b.oczytany etc.)
erupt (y'rapt) v. wybuchać;
wyrzucać; przerzynać (się);
wysypywać się;wybuchać lawą
eruption (y'rapszyn) s. wybuch;
przerzynanie się; wysypka
escalation (,eske'lejszyn) s.
wzmożenie;rozszerzenie się
escalator ('eskelejter) s. ru-
chome schody; ruchoma skala
płac(wg. kosztów utrzymania etc.)
escape (ys'kejp) s. ucieczka;
wyciekanie; wchodzenie;ocalenie
v. wymknąć się; zbiec; wyjść
cało; uchodzić;ratować się uciec
ką
escort ('esko:rt) s. eskorta;
konwój; mężczyzna towarzyszą-
cy kobiecie; kawaler;v.eskorto-
wać
escort (i'sko:rt) v. eskortować
especial (ys'peszel) adj.
szczególny; wyjątkowy; specjalny; szczególny; główny
especially (ys'peszely) adv.
szczególnie; zwłaszcza
espionage (,espje'na:dż) s. wywiad; szpiegostwo;szpiegowanie
esprit (es'pri:) s. żywość; życie; dowcip;silne poczucie humoru
espy (ys'paj) v. spostrzegać;
wyśledzić;wykombinować
essay ('esej) s. esej; szkic
literacki; próba; v. próbować;
wypróbować;poddać próbie
essence ('esens) s. esencja;
istota czegoś; wyciąg; treść
istotna treść;sedno sprawy;olej

essential (y'senszel) adj. niezbędny; istotny; zasadniczy;
zupełny; etetyczny; s. cecha
istotna, nieodzowna, zasadni-
cza;rzecz podstawowa,konieczna
establish (ys'taeblysz) v. zakładać; osadzać; ustalać;
wprowadzac;udowodnić;ufundować
establishment (yz'taeblyszment)
s. założenie; osadzenie; ustalenie; ustanowienie; zakład;
gospodarstwo;koła rządzące;
organizacja państwowa lub wojskowa;firma;przedsiębiorstwo
estate (ys'tejt) s. majątek;
stan majątkowy;położenie w życiu
estate tax (ys'tejt,taeks) s.
podatek spadkowy (majątkowy)
esteem (ys'ti:m) v. cenić;
szanować; poważać; s. poważanie; szacunek;dobra opinia
estimate ('estymejt) v. oceniać;
szacować; s. szacunek; kosztorys; ocena;opinia;oszacowanie
estimation (,esty'mejszyn) s.
szacowanie; poważanie; szacunek;zdanie;mniemanie;sąd
estrange (ys'trejndż) v. od-
stręczać; zrażać;zniechęcać
estray (ys'trej) s. stworzenie
bezpańskie, zgubione
estuary ('estjuery) s. ujście
(rzeki) do morza (oceanu)
eternal (y'ternl) adj. wieczny;
odwieczny;bez początku i końca
eternity (y'ternyty) s. wieczność;trwnie bez końca i odpoczyn-
ku
ether ('i:ter) s. eter
ethics ('etyks) pl. etyka
ethnic ('etnyk) adj. etniczny;
pogański;odrębny zwyczajami i je-
etymology (,ety'moledży) s. ety-
mologia;pochodzenie i rozwój słów
eulogy ('ju:ledży) s. mowa
pochwała (pogrzebowa)
eunuch ('ju:nek) n. eunuch;
rzezaniec;człowiek wykastrowany
European (,ju:re'pi:en) adj.
europejski; s. Europejczyk
evacuate (y'waekjuejt) v. ewa-
kuować; opróżniać; wypróżniać;
wydalać;usuwać; wycofywać się

evacuation (y,waekju'ejszyn) s.
ewakuacja; wypróżnienie (się)
evade (y'wejd) v. ujść; uniknąć; obchodzić; wymykać się;
wykręcać się; pomijać
evaluate (y'waeljujet) v. obliczać; oceniać; analizować
evaporate (y'waeperejt) v. parować; ulatniać się; poddawać
parowaniu;wyparowywać;umrzeć
evasion (y'wejżyn) v. uniknięcie; wymknięcie się; obejście;
wykręt;oszustwo(podatkowe);wykręt
evasive (y'wejsyw) adj. wykrętny; wymijający; nieuchwytny
eve (i:w) s. wilia; wigilia
even ('i:wen) adj. równy;
jednolity; parzysty; adv. nawet; v. równać; wyrównać;
zemścić się;wygładzać;ujednostajević
even-handed ('i:wen,haendyd) adj.
sprawiedliwy; bezstronny
evening ('i:wnyng) s. wieczór
evening dress ('i:wnyn, dres)s.
strój wieczorowy
evening paper ('i:wnyn'pejper)
gazeta wieczorna
evensong ('i:wensong) s. nieszpory; pieśń wieczorna
event (y'went) s. wydarzenie;
możliwość; wynik; rezultat; zawody (sportowe);konkurencja
eventful(y'wentful) adj. burzliwy; pamiętny; pełen wydarzeń
eventual (y'wenczuel) adj.
w końcu pewny
eventually (y'wenczuely) adv.
w końcu napewno
ever ('ewer) adv. w ogóle; niegdyś;kiedyś; jak tylko; ile tylko; kiedykolwiek;jeszcze wciąż
ever after (,ewer'after) do tego czasu;już od tego czasu
ever since (,ewer'syns) od tego
czasu ; od kiedy (był etc.)
everlasting (,ewer'lastyng)adj.
wieczny; ciągły; nieustanny
evermore ('ewer'mi:re) adv.
zawsze; na zawsze; na wieki
every ('ewry) adj. każdy; wszelki; co(dzień, noc, rano etc.)
every other day (,ewry,odzer'dej)
co drugi dzień

everybody ('ewrybody) pron.
każdy; wszyscy(ludzie)
everyday ('ewrydej) adj. codzienny; powszedni; zwykły
everyone ('ewryłan) pron.
każdy; wszyscy;każda rzecz
everything ('ewrytyng) pron.
wszystko (co jest, etc.)
everywhere ('ewryhłer) adv.
wszędzie; gdziekolwiek
evidence ('ewidens) s. znak;
dowód; świadectwo; oczywistość;
jasność; v. świadczyć; dowodzić (czegoś);manifestować
evident ('ewydent) adj. oczywisty; widoczny;jawny;jasny
evil ('i:wl) adj. zły;fatalny
evildoer ('i:wl-duer) s.
złoczyńca
evince (y'wyns) v, wykazywać;
okazywać (życzenie);przejawiać
evoke (y'włouk) v. wywoływać;
wydobywać; zdobywać (odpowiedź)
evolution (,ewe'lu:szyn) s.
rozwój; ewolucja; rozwinięcie
(się); pierwiastkowanie
evolve (y'wolw) v. rozwijać;
wypracowywać; wytwarzać (ciepło etc.);rozwijać się stopniowo
ewe (ju:) s. owca
ex-(eks) pref. były; była;
prep. bez; ze; s. (litera)"x"
exacerbate (eks'aeserbejt) v.
drażnić; pogorszyć; irytować
exact (yg'zaekt) adj. dokładny;
ścisły; v. wymagać; ściągać;
egzekwować ;wymuszać
exactitude (yg'zaektytju:d)s.
ścisłość; dokładność;punktualność
exactly (yg'zaektly) adv. dokładnie; ściśle; właśnie;
zgadza się ;punktualnie; ostro
exactness (yg'zaektnys) s. dokładność; precyzja
exaggerate (yg'zaedżerejt) v.
przesadzać; wyolbrzymiać
exaggeration (yg'zaedże'rejszyn)
s. przesada; wyolbrzymienie
exalt (yg'zo:lt) v. wywyższać;
podnosić ;wychwalać;chwalić
exam (yg'zaem) s. egzamin
(slang); klasówka; egzamin w
szkole lub na uniwersytecie

examination (yg,zaemy'nejszyn)
s. egzamin; badanie;rewizja
examine (yg'zaemyn) v. badać;
sprawdzać; egzaminować; rozpatrywać; rewidować; przesłuchiwać;przeprowadzać śledztwo
example (yg'za:mpl) s. przykład; wzór; precedens
exasperate (yg'za:sperejt) v.
rozjątrzać; rozgoryczać; pogarszać; powodować rozpacz
excavate ('ekskewejt) v. kopać; odkopać; wykopać; drążyć;pogłębiać;wybierać(ziemię)
exceed (yk'si:d) v. przewyższać; celować; przekraczać
exceedingly (ek'si:dyŋly) adv.
niezmiernie; nadzwyczajnie
excel (yk'sel) v. przewyższać;
wybijać się; celować(w czyms)
excellence (yk'selens) s. wyższość; doskonałość; zaleta
excellent (yk'selent) adj. doskonały; wyborny;świetny;celuja-
except (yk'sept) conj. chyba
że...; żeby;oprucz;poza;wyjąwszy
except (yk'sept) v. wykluczać;
wyłączać; prep. z wyjątkiem;
pominąwszy; wyjąwszy;chyba że
exception (yk'sepszyn) s. wyjątek; wyłączenie; zarzut;objekcja
exceptional(yk'sepszenl) adj.
nadzwyczajny; wyjątkowy
excess (yk'ses) s. nadmiar;
nadwyżka;a.nadmierny;nad-
excess fare(yk'ses,fe:r) s. dopłata do biletu
excessive (yk'sesyw) adj. nadmierny;zbytni;nieumiarkowany
excess luggage (yk'ses,lagydż)
nadwyżka bagażu
exchange (yks'czendż) s. wymiana; zamiana; giełda; centrala
telefoniczna; v. wymienić;(towy
zamienić (się);a.wymienny;walu-
excitable (yk'sajtebl) adj. pobudliwy;pobudzajacy;podniecaja-
excite (yk'sajt) v. pobudzać;
podniecać;prowokować
excited (yk'sajtyd) adj. podniecony; zdenerwowany

excitement (yk'sajtment)
podniecenie; zdenerwowanie
exciting (yk'sajtyŋg) adj.
emocjonujący; pasjonujący
exclaim (yks'klejm) v. zawołać;
wykrzyknąć; zaprotestować
exclamation (,ekskla'mejszyn)
s. okrzyk; krzyk; wykrzyknik
exclamation mark (,ekskla'mejszyn,ma:rk) wykrzyknik
exclude (yks'klu:d) v. wykluczać; wydalać; usuwać
exclusion (yks'klu:żyn) n.
wykluczenie; wydalenie; usunięcie; wyłączenie
exclusive (yks'klu:syw) adj.
modny; wykluczający; wyłączny;
jedyny; ekskluzywny
excursion (yks'ker:żyn) s. wycieczka;dygresje;a.wycieczkowy
excuse (yks'kju:z) v. usprawiedliwiać; przepraszać; darować; zwalniać; s. usprawiedliwienie; wymówka ;pretekst
excuse me (yks'kju:z,mi)
przepraszam; przepraszam pana
excusable (iks'kju:zebl) adj.
usprawiedliwiony;wybaczalny
execute ('eksykju:t) v. wykonać (wyrok, plan); stracić
(skazańca);nadawać ważność
execution (,eksy'kju;szyn) s.
wykonanie; egzekucja;stracenie
executive (yg'zekjutyw) adj.
wykonawczy; s. władza wykonaw-
cza; stanowisko kierownicze
exemplary (yg'zemplery) adj.
wzorowy; przykładny; przykła-
dowy;wymierzony dla odstraszenia
exempt (yg'zempt) v. zwalniać;
adj. wolny; zwolniony; s. osoba zwolniona;człowiek zwolniony
exercise ('eksersajz) s. ćwiczenie; wykonywanie (zawodu);
korzystanie; v, ćwiczyć; używać;
wykonywać;spełniać;pełnić
exercise book ('eksersajs,buk)
s. zeszyt (szkolny)
exert (yg'ze:rt) v. wytężać
(się); wysilać (się); wywierać
(nacisk, wpływ, etc);zabiegać

exertion (yg'ze:rszyn) s. wy-
tężenie; wysiłek; wywieranie,
exhale (eks'hejl) v. wyziewać;
wydychać; zionąć; parować
exhaust (yg'zo:st) v. wydychać;
wyczerpywać; wyciągać; wypróżniać; odgazować; s. wydech; wydmuch; rura wydechowa; opróżnianie (z powietrza);
aspirator;rura wydechowa(auta)
exhaust fumes (yg'zo:st,fjums)
gazy wydechowe(z motoru)
exhaustion (yg'zo:stszyn) s.
wyczerpanie; opróżnienie; zużycie; pochłonięcie;zmęczenie
exhaust-pipe (yg'zo:st,pajp)
s. rura wydechowa (w aucie)
exhibit(yg'zybyt) s. wystawa;
pokaz; eksponaty; v. wystawiać; okazywać; pokazywać;
wykazywać; popisywać się
czyms;przedkładać;mieć wystawę
exhibition(,eksy'byszyn) s.
wystawa; wystawianie; pokazy-
wanie;pokaz; widowisko;popis
exhibitor(yg'zybyter) s. wystawca; wystawczyni
exile ('eksajl) s. wygnanie;
tułaczka; emigracja; wygnaniec; v. wygnać na banicję
exist (yg'zyst) v. istnieć;być;
żyć; egzystować ;zdarzać się
existence (yg'zystens) s. istnienie; byt; egzystencja
existent (yg'zystent) a. istniejący;będący;znajdujący się
exit ('eksyt) s. wyjście; odejście; ujście; wylot; swobodne
wyjście; v. wychodzić; kończyć
(slang);schodzić ze sceny
exit visa ('eksyt,wyza) s. wiza wyjazdowa
expand (yks'paend) v. rozszerzać; powiększać; wzrastać;
rozprężać; rozwijać; rozruszać;rozpościerać;powiększać
expanse (yks'paens) s. bezmiar;
rozległa przestrzeń; ekspansja
expansion (yks'paenszyn) s.
rozszerzanie; rozprężanie się;
ekspansja; rozposcieranie;
rozwijanie (się);ilość ekspansji

expansive (yks'paensyw) adj.
rozszerzalny; rozległy; roz-
prężalny; obszerny; wylewny
expect (yks'pekt) v. spodziewać się; przypuszczać;zgadywać
expectation (,ekspek'tejszyn)
s. oczekiwanie; nadzieja;
widoki;prospekt;przewidywanie
expedient (yks'pi:djent) adj.
celowy; wygodny; oportunistycz-
ny; korzystny; s. środek; zabieg; sposób;wybieg;fortel
expedition (,ekspy'dyszyn) s.
wyprawa; ekspedycja; sprawnosć;
szybkość;pospiech;marsz do,akcji
expel (yks'pel) v. wypędzać;
wydalać; usuwać; wyrzucać
expend (yks'pend) v. wydawać;
zużywać;poświęcać czas etc.
expense (yks'pens) s. koszt;
wydatek;rachunek;strata;ofiara
expensive (yks'pensyw) adj.
drogi; kosztowny;wysoko wycenio-
experience (yks'pierjens) s. ny
doświadczenie; przeżycie;
v. doświadczać; doznawać;
poznać (coś);przeżywać;przecho-
experienced (yks'pierjenst) dzić
adj. doświadczony;doznany
experiment (yks'peryment) s.
próba; eksperyment; doświadczenie; v. eksperymentować;
robić doświadczenia
expert ('ekspe:rt) s. biegły;
ekspert; znawca; adj. biegły;
światły;mistrzowski;wykonany
expiration (,ekspi'rejszyn) s. przez eksperta
wygaśnięcie: upłynięcie; wy-
dech; wzioniecie ducha;smierć
expire (yks'pajer) v. wygasać;
upływać; wydychać; wyzionąć
ducha;umierać;kończyć się
explain (yks'plejn) v. wyjaśnić; objaśnić; wytłumaczyć
explanation (,eks'plaenejszyn)
s. wyjaśnienie; wytłumaczenie
explicable ('eksplykebl) adj.
dający się wyjaśnić
explicit (yks'plysyt) adj. jasny; wyraźny; szczery; otwarty;definitywny;wygadany

explode (yks'ploud) v. wybu-
chac; explodowac; demaskowac
(fałsz) ;obalic(teorie etc.)
exploit (yks'ploit) v. użytko-
wac; exploatowac; wyzyskiwac
exploit ('eksploit) s. wyczyn
exploration (,eksplo:rejszyn)
s. poszukiwanie; badanie
explore (yks'plo:r) v. badac;
sondowac ;wybadac;przebadac
explorer (yks'plo:rer) s. badacz; sonda ;odkrywca;odkrywczyni
explosion (yks'ploużyn) s.
explozja; wybuch (kłotni etc.)
explosive (yks'plousyw) s, materiał wybuchowy; adj. wybuchowy;mogący wybuchnąc
exponent (yks'pounent) adj.
interpretujący; s. eksponent;
wyraziciel; interpretator;
wykładnik (potęgi);przedstawiciel
export (yks'po:rt) v. wywozic;
eksportowac; s. wywoz; eksport;
towar wywozowy;wywożenie
expose (yks'pouz) v. wystawiac
(na wpływ); poddawac (czemus);
odsłaniac; demaskowac; ekspo-
nowac; naswietlac; porzucac
(dziecko);zrobic zdjęcie
exposé (,ekspou'zej) s. zdemaskowanie; odsłonięcie skandalu
exposition (,ekspe'zyszyn) s.
wystawa; wykład; przedstawienie; wyjasnienie; opis; na-
swietlenie; ekspozycja; po-
rzucenie (dziecka)
exposure (yks'poużer) s. wystawienie (na zimę. etc); ujawnienie; zdemaskowanie; naswiet-
lenie;jedno zdjęcie na filmie
exposuremeter (yks'poużer'mi:ter)
s. swiatłomierz
expound (yks'paund) v. wykładac;
wyjasnic szczegółowo;przedstawic
express (yks'pres) s. ekspres ;
przesyłka pospieszna; adj. wyraźny; umyslny; dokładny;
adv. pospiesznie;expresem
expression (yks'preszyn) s. wyrażenie; wyraz; ekspresja; ton;
wydawanie; wytłoczenie;zwrot
wyciśnięcie;wyżymanie

expressive (yks'presyw) adj.
wyrażający; wyrazisty:
ekspresyjny;pełen wyrazu
expressly (yks'presly) adv.wy-
raźnie; kategorycznie; naumyslnie;specjalnie;formalnie
express way (yks'pres,łej) s.
droga przelotova (bez skrzy-
żowan jednopoziomowych)
expulsion (yks'palszyn) s. wydalenie; wyrzucenie; wypędze-
nie;wygnanie;wyparcie
exquisite ('ekskłyzyt) adj.
wyborowy; wyborny; wysmienity;
nadzwyczajny; ostry; przeszywający;s.lalus;goguś;pięknis
extent ('ekstent) adj. pozostały; jeszcze istniejący
extemporaneous (eks,tempe'rejn-
jes) adj. zaimprowizowany
extend (yks'tend),v wyciągac
(się); rozciągac (się);prze-
ciągac (się); rozszerzac (się);
dawac i udzielac; przedłużac;
powiększac ;rozposcierac się
extendible (yks'tendybl) adj.
rozszerzalny; rozciągalny
extension (yks'tenszyn) s. rozciąganie; wyciąganie; rozwinięcie; przedłużenie; zasięg;
rozmiar; zakres ;skrzydło(domu)
extensive (yks'tensyw) adj.
obszerny; rozległy;ekstensywny
extent (yks'tent) s. obszar;
rozmiar; zasięg; miara; stopien; wysokosc ;oszacowanie
extenuate (yks'tenjnejt) v.
zmniejszac; łagodzic
exterior (eks'tierjer) s. po-
wierzchownosc; wygląd zewnętrzny; strona zewnętrzna ;fasada
exterminate (yks'te:rmynejt) v.
tępic (np; pogląd);wyniszczyc
external (eks'te:rnal) adj.
zewnętrzny; zagraniczny
extinct (yks'tynkt) adj. wy-
gasły; zgasły;zanikły;wymarły
extinguish (yks'tyngłysz) y.
zgasic; zagasic; niszczyc;
unicestwic; umierac;tępic
extirpate ('ekster,pejt)v. wy-
korzeniac;plewic; tępic

extol (yks'tol) v. wysławiać;
wynosić pod niebiosa
extort (yks'tort) v. wymuszać;
zdzierać(pieniadze);wydrzeć
extra ('ekstre) adj. specjalny; dodatkowy; luksusowy;
nadzwyczajny; ponad normę;
adv. nadzwyczajnie; dodatkowo;
s. dodatek; dopłata; rzecz
szczególnie dobra;statysta
extra charge ('ekstre,cha:rdż)
s. dopłata;nadpłata
extract ('ekstraekt) s. wyciąg;
ekstrat;wyjątek;wypis
extract (yks'traekt) v. wyciągać; wydobywać; wypisywać
extraction (eks'traekszyn) s.
wyciągnięcie; wydobycie; wyr-
wanie (zęba); pochodzenie;ród
extradite ('ekstredajt) v.
wydawać (przestępcę przez granicę)do miejsca zbrodni
extraordinary (yks'tro:rdnery)
adj. niezwykły; nadzwyczajny
extravagance (yks'traewygens)
s. przesada; rozrzutność;
nieumiarkowanie; głupstwo;
niedorzeczność; ekstrawagancja
extravagant (yks'traewegent)
adj. rozrzutny; przesądny;
zwariowany;wygórowany;szalony
extravaganza (yks,traewe'gaenze)
s. ekstrawagancja;fantazja
extreme (yks'tri:m) adj. skrajny; krańcowy; najdalszy; ostatni; s. kraniec; ostateczna
granica; ostateczność;skrajność
extremity (yks'tremyty) s. koniec; kraniec; skrajność; kran-
cowość; kończyna; krytyczne
położenie;potrzeba;ostateczność
extrude (yks'tru:d) v. wypierać; wyrzucać; przeciągać lub
ciągnąć odlew;wytłoczyć
exuberant (yg'zju:berent) adj.
wybujały; pełen życia; kwitnący; wylewny; płodny; obfity
exult (yg'zalt) v. triumfować;
unosić się radością
eye (aj) s. oko;wzrok;v.patrzeć
eyeball ('ajbo:l) s. gałka oczna
w oczodołach za powiekami

eyeball to eyeball ('ajbo:l,tu
'ajbo:l) oko w oko
eyebrow ('ajbrau) s. brew
eyeglasses ('ajgla:sys) pl.
okulary;lupy;monokle
eyelash ('ajlaesz) s. rzęsa
eyelid ('ajlyd) s. powieka
eyesight ('aj-sajt) s. wzrok
eyewash ('ajłosz) s. woda do
oczu; mydlenie oczu (slang)
eyewitness ('aj'łytnes) s.
świadek naoczny
f (ef) szósta litera angielskiego alfabetu; stopień "f"
failure = niedostatecznie
fable (fejbl) s. bajka
fabric ('faebryk) s. tkanina;
materiał; osnowa; szkielet;
budowa; wytwór;a.sukienny
fabricate ('faebrykejt) v. tworzyć; wymyślać; zmyślać; montować;wyssać z palca;sfałszować
fabulous ('faebjules) adj. ba-
jeczny;legendarny;fantastyczny
facade (fe'sa:d) s. fasada
face (fejs) s. twarz; oblicze;
mina; grymas; czelność; śmiałość; powierzchnia lica; prawa strona; obuch; v. stawiać
czoła; stanąć wobec; napotykać; stać frontem do..; wykładać powierzchnię;oblicować
face-lifting ('fejs-lyftyng) v.
operacyjnie usuwać zmarszczki
facetious (fe'si:szes) adj.
żartobliwy;krotochwilny
facilitate (fe'sylytejt) v.
ułatwiać ; udogadniać;uprzy-
stępniać
facility (fe'sylyty) s. łatwość;
zręczność; udogodnienia; układ-
ność; swada;zgodność
fact (faekt) s. fakt; stan
rzeczywisty;podstawa twierdzenia
factor ('faekter) s. czynnik;
współczynnik; część;okoliczność
faculty ('faekelty) s. zdolność;
władza; wydział; fakultet; gro-
no profesorskie;dar; zmysł
fad (faed) s. moda; kaprys;konik;
bzik;chwilowa moda;dziwactwo
fade (fejd) v. więdnąć; bled-
nąć; zanikać;płowieć;pełznąć

fail (fejl) v. chybic; zawodzic;
nie udac sie; brakowac; bankru-
towac; omieszkac; slabnac;
zalamac sie; zamierac;zepsuc sie
failure ('fejljer) s. niepowodzenie; brak; upadek; zawal
(serca); niezdara; stopien
niedostateczny; pechowiec
faint (fejnt) adj. slaby; omdla-
ly; bojazliwy; s. omdlenie;
v. mdlec; slabnac;zaslabnac
fair (feer) adj. piekny; jasny;
uczciwy; honorowy; czysty;
pomyslny; niezly; adv. prosto;
honorowo; pomyslnie; pieknie;
v. wypogadzac sie; wygladzac;
przepisywac na czysto; s. targ;
targi; jarmark;targowisko
fairly ('feerly) adv. sluszie;
uczciwie; calkowicie; zupelnie;
dosc;rzetelnie;wrecz;poprostu
fairplay ('feer'plej) szlachetne
postepowanie;czysta gra
fairness ('feernys) s. pieknosc;
jasnosc; sprawiedliwosc; bezstronnosc; uczciwosc;uroda
fairy ('feery) s. czarodziejka;
adj. zaczarowany;czarodziejski
fairy-tale ('ferrytejl) s. bajka
faith (fejs) s. wiara; zaufanie;
wiernosc; wyznanie;slownosc
faithful ('fejsful) adj. wierny;
uczciwy;sumienny;skrupulatny
faithless ('fejslys) adj. niewierny; wiarolomny;zdradziecki
fake (fejk) v. falszowac; oszukiwac; podrabiac; s. falszerstwo
oszustwo;kant;lipa;szwindel
falcon ('fo:lken) s. sokol
fall; fell; fallen (fo:l; fel:
fo:len)
fall (fo:l) v. padac; opadac;
wpadac; marniec; zdarzac sie;
przypadac; s. upadek; spadek;
jesien;opad;schylek;obnizka
fall back ('fo:l, baek) v. cofac sie
fall ill ('fo:l,yl) v. zachoro-
wac;rozchorowac sie
fall in love ('fo:l,yn'law) v.
zakochac sie

fallout ('fo:lalt) s. skutek
uboczny; pyl radioaktywny;
wrazenie na publicznosci i
prasie(z wypowiedzi,planow)
fall out ('fo:l,alt) v. poroz-
nic sie; rozejsc sie! (komenda)
fall short ('fo:l,szo:rt) v.
nieosiagnac; niewywiazac sie
fallen ('fo:len) upadly; zob.
fall
false (fo:ls) adj. falszywy;
klamliwy;adv.zdradliwie;falszy-
wie
falsehood ('fo:lshud) s. falsz;
klamstwo;nieprawda;klamliwosc
falsify ('fo:lsyfaj) v. falszowac; przekrecac; klamac; zawodzic;podrabiac;oszukac
falter ('fo:lter) v. chwiac sie;
wahac sie; potykac sie; jakac
sie; s. chwiejnosc; jakanie
fame (fejm) s. slawa; wiesc;fa-
ma
famed (fejmd) adj. slawny; znany; glosny; slynacy z
familiar (fe'myljer) adj. za-
zyly; poufaly; znany; obeznany
familiarity (fe,myly'aeryty)
s. zazylosc; poufalosc; obez-
nanie;znajomosc;zazylosc
familiarize (fe'myljerajz) v,
obeznac; obznajomic; oswoic;
spoufalic;spopularyzowac
family ('faemyly) s. rodzina;
adj. rodzinny
family name ('faemyly,nejm) s.
nazwisko
family tree ('faemyly,tri:) s.
drzewo genealogiczne
famine ('faemyn) s. glod; kles-
ka glodu; ogolne braki wszystkiego
famish ('faemysz) v. glodzic;
wyglodniec; glodowac;morzyc glo-
dem
famous ('fejmes) adj. znany;
slawny;znakomity;swietny;nie byle
jaki
fan (faen) v. wachlowac; roz-
dmuchiwac; wiac; rozposcierac;
wywiewac; s. wachlarz; wentylator; wialnia; zagiel i
smiglo (wiatraka); entuzjasta;
milosnik,kibic;a.wachlarzowaty
fanatic (fe'naetyk) adj. zago-
rzaly; fanatyczny; s, fanatyk

fanciful ('faensyful) adj. dziwaczny; kaprysny; fantastyczny;zmyslony;wyszukany;fantazyjny

fancy ('faensy) s. urojenie;
zludzenie; fantazja; kaprys;
humor; pomysł; chetka;a.pstry..

fancy dress ball('faensy'fres,
,bo:l) s. bal kostiumowy

fancy-free ('faensy,fri:) adj.
wolny od trosk; niezakochany

fancywork ('faensy,łe:rk) s.
robotki reczne

fang (faeng) s. ząb jadowity;
kieł;sztyft;korzen;v.dławic pom-
fantastic (faen'taestyk) adj.
fantastyczny;s.fantastyk

far (fa:r) adv. daleko

far away ('fa:r,ełej) adv.
hen; daleko;adj.daleki;odległy

far from ('fa:r,from) adv. bynajmniej; daleko od

fare (feer) s. pasażer; bilet
pasażerski; pożywienie; potrawa; v. być w położeniu. miec
sie; wieść sie; czuc sie; od-
żywiac się; jadać; podróżowac

farewell (,feer'lel) s. pożegnanie; adj. pożegnalny;
v. żegnaj; do widzenia

farfetched (,fa:r'feczt) adj.
przesadny; naciągany; wyszukany;nierozsadny

far-flung (,fa:r'flang) adj.
szeroko rozrzucony; rozgałę-
ziony;zakrojony na szeroka skale

farm (fa:rm) s. ferma; gospodarstwo rolne; kolonia hodowlana;
v. uprawiac; dzierżawic; wy-
dzierżawiac; wynajmowac; pod-
dzierżawiac;prowadzic gospodar-stwo

farmer ('fa:rmer) s. rolnik;
farmer; dzierżawca;hodowca

farmhand ('fa:rm,haend) s. parobek;robotnik rolny

farmhouse ('fa:rm,haus) s. dwo-
rek; gospodarski dom mieszkalny

farming ('fa:rmyng)s. rolnictwo;
gospodarka rolna; dzierżawa

farm worker (,fa:rm'łe:rker) s.
robotnik rolny; parobek

farmyard ('fa:rm,ja:rd) s. podworze fermy;podworze gospodar-
skie na fermie

farsighted ('fa:r'sajtyd) adj.
przewidujący; dalekowidz;
dalekowzroczny;dalekowidz

farther ('fa:rdzer) adj. dalszy;
adv. dalej;ponadto;poza tym; prócz tego

farthest ('fa:rdzest) adj. najdalszy; adv. najdalej;najpóźniej

fascinate ('faesynejt) v. urze-
kac; czarowac; fascynowac;
hipnotyzowac;zachwycic

fascination (,faesy'nejszyn) s.
urok; czar;oczarowanie;olśnienie

fascist ('faeszyst) s. faszysta;
adj. faszystowski;faszystowska

fashion ('faeszyn) s. moda; fason; kształt; wzor; sposób;
v. kształtowac; fasonowac;
modelowac; urabiac

fashionable ('faesznebl) adj.
modny; s. człowiek wytworny

fast (faest) adj. szybki; przy-
twierdzony; mocny; twardy;
zwodniczy; adv. mocno; pewnie;
trwale; v. poscic; s. post

fasten ('faesn) v. umocowac;
zamykac;przymocowac

fastener ('faesner) s. przymocowanie (np. gwozdz); spinacz
zatrzask; zasuwka

fastidious (fes'tydjes) adj.
wybredny; grymasny; wymagający

fat (faet) s. tłuszcz; tusza;
adj. tłusty; tuczny; głupi;
tępy;urodzajny;zyskowny

fatal ('fejtl) adj. fatalny;
smiertelny; nieuchronny

fate ('fejt) s. los; przeznaczenie; zguba;fatum;v.los rzadzi...

father ('fa:dzer) s. ojciec

fatherhood ('fa:dzerhud) s.
ojcostwo;starszenstwo(w służbie)

father-in-law ('fa:dzerynlo:) s.
tesc;ojciec meza lub żony

fatherland ('fa:dzerlaend) s.
ojczyzna; ojczysty kraj

fatherly ('fa:dzerly) adj. oj-
cowski;jak ojciec;dobrotliwy

fathom ('faedzem) s. sążeń

fathomless ('faedzemlys) s. bez-
denny; niezgłębiony

fatigue (fe'ti:g) s. zmeczenie
(człowieka lub materiału);służ-
ba porzadkowa;v.trudzic;meczyć

fatten ('faetn) v. tuczyć; tyć;
urzyźniać ziemie; utyć;utuczyć
faucet ('fo:syt) s. kurek (od
wody; czop; tuleja
fault ('fo:lt) s. błąd; wada;
wina; uskok; usterka;brak;defekt
faultless ('fo:ltlys) adj. bezbłędny; nienaganny;doskonały
faulty ('fo:lty) adj. wadliwy;
nieprawidłowy;niescisły;błędny
favor ('fejwer) s. łaska;uprzej-
mość; upominek; v. sprzyjać;
zaszczycać; faworyzować
favorable ('fejwerebl) adj. życzliwy; łaskawy; sprzyjający;
korzystny(dla kagoś,czegoś)
favorite ('fejweryt) s. ulubieniec; faworyt; adj. ulubiony
fawn (fo:n) v. ocielić; łasić
się; przymilać (się); s. je-
lonek; sarenka; adj. brunatny;
płowy;płaszczyć się(przed kimś)
fear (fier) s. strach; obawa;
v. bać się; obawiać się
fearful ('fierful) adj. okropny;
straszny; wystraszony; bojaźliwy; bojący się;pełen strachu
fearless ('fierlys) adj. nieustraszony;bardzo odważny
feast (fi:st) s. swięto; odpust;
biesiada; v. ucztować; sycić
się; ugaszczać pragnienie
feat (fi:t) s. wyczyn; czyn
(bohaterski);(dokazana)sztuka
feather ('fedzer) s. pioro;
v. zdobić piorami
featherbed ('fedzerbed) s. piernat;pierzyna;lekka praca
feathered ('fedzerd) adj. upie-
rzony; pokryty piorami
feathery ('fedzery) adj. pucho-
waty; miękki jak puch;leciutki
feature ('fi:czer) s. cecha;
rys; atrakcja; film długo-
metrażowy;v.cechować;odgrywać
February ('februery) s. luty
fed (fed) adj. karmiony; zob.
feed
federal ('federel) adj. związkowy; federalny
federation (,fede'rejszyn) s.
federacja; konferencja

fee (fi:) s. opłata; wpisowe;
należność; honorarium; v. płacić honorarium;płacić wpisowe
feeble ('fi:bl) adj. słaby
feed: fed; fed (fi:d; fed; fed)
feed (fi:d) v. karmić; paść;
zasilać; s. pasza; obrok; za-
silacz; posuw
feeder (fi:der) s. boczna (droga); dopływ; przewód zasila-
jący
feel; felt; felt (fi:l; felt;
felt)
feel (fi:l) v. czuć (się); odczuwać; macać; dotykać
feel well ('fi:l,łel) v. czuć
się dobrze; być zdrowym
feel bed('fi:l,baed) v. czuć
się źle
feeler ('fi:ler) s. macka; sonda; próbny balon; szperacz
feeling ('fi:lyng) s. dotyk;
uczucie; odczucie; poczucie;
takt; wrażliwość; adj. wrażliwy; czuły; współczujący; szczery; wzruszony; szczery
feet (fi:t) pl. stopy; nogi
fell (fel) v. ścinać (drzewo);
zob. fall
felloe ('felou) s. dzwono(koła)
fellow ('felou) s. towarzysz;
człowiek; chłop; gość; facet;
odpowiednik;wykładowca;adjunkt
fellow being ('felou bi:yng) s.
bliźni
fellow citizen ('felou'sytyzen)
s. współobywatel
fellowship ('felouszyp) s.
udział; wspólnota; związek;
towarzystwo; przyjaźń; cech
felon ('felen) s. przestępca;
adj. okrutny; zły;zbrodniczy
felony ('feleny) s. przestępstwo;
zbrodnia
felt (felt) czuły; zob.; feel
felt (felt) s. wojłok; filc
female ('fi:mejl) s. kobieta;
niewiasta; samica; adj. żeński;
kobiecy; wewnętrzny (gwint)
feminine ('femynyn) adj. żeński;
kobiecy; zniewieściały; s. rodzaj żeński;a.rodzaju żeńskiego

fen (fen) s. bagno; trzęsawisko;nizina bagienna

fence (fens) s. płot; ogrodzenie; szermierka; v. ogrodzić;
fechtować się;odpowiadac wykrętie

fencing ('fencyng) s. szermierka;płot;ogrodzenie;paserstwo

fend for ('fend,fo:r) v. zaspo-
kajać potrzeby;utrzymywać

fend off ('fend,of) v. odbijac;
odparowywać;chronic;ochraniac

fender ('fender) s. błotnik;
(zderzak);zasłona;zderzak

fennel ('fenel) s. koper

ferment ('fe:rment) s. ferment;
fermentacja; v. wywoływać ferment; podniecac; fermentować

fermentation (,fe:rmen'tejszyn)
s. fermentacja; ferment

fern (fe:rn) s. paproć

ferocity (fe'rosyty) s. dzikość;
okrucieństwo; srogość

ferry ('fery) v. przeprawiac
promem; kursować; s. prom

ferryboat ('ferybout) s. prom

fertile ('fe:rtajl) adj. żyzny;
płodny;zapłodniony;obfitujący

fertility (fer'tylyty) z. żyz-
nosć; płodnosć;urodzjnosć

fertilize ('fe:rtylajz) v. użyźniac;nawozic;zapładniać;zapylac

fertilizer ('fe:rtylajzer) s.
nawóz sztuczny

fervent ('fe:rwent) adj. żarliwy; gorący;płomienny;gorliwy

fester ('fester) v. jątrzyc (sie)
ropieć; gnic; s. ropiejąca rana; mały wrzód;ropniak;zajad

festival ('festewel) adj. świąteczny;odswiętny;s.święto

festive ('festyw) adj. uroczysty;
wesoły; radosny;biesiadny

festivity (fes'tywyty) s. weso-
łosć; zabawa; uroczystosc

fetch (fecz) v. isc po cos;
przyniesć; przywiezć;s.odległosc

fetter ('feter) v. skuc; spętac

feud (fju:d) s. lenno; wasn ro-
dowa;wojna między klanami

feudal ('fju:dl) adj. feudalny

fever ('fy:wer) s. gorączka

feverish ('fy:werysz) adj. go-
rączkowy;rozgorączkowany

few (fju:) adj.& pron. mało;kilka;
niewielu ; nieliczni;kilku;kilko-
ro

fiance (fi'a:nsej) s. narzeczo-
ny(a)

fib (fyb) s. kłamstwo; v. cy-
ganic:okładać;s. cios;uderzenie

fiber ('fajber) s. włókno; siła ducha;charakter;łyko;budowa

fibrous ('fajberes) adj.
włóknisty; łykowaty

fickle ('fykl) adj. zmienny;
niestały;płochy; wietrzny

fiction ('fykszyn) s. fikcja;
urojenie; beltrystyka;wymysł

fictitious (fyk'tyszes) a.
fikcyjny; urojony; fałszywy

fiddle ('fydl) v. grać na
skrzypcach; baraszkować;
s. skrzypce

fiddler ('fydler) s. skrzypek;
skrzypaczka

fidelity (fy'delyty) s. wier-
nosć; dokładnosć; ścisłosc

fidget ('fydżyt) v. wiercic
się; niepokoic się; s. niepokój; człowiek niespokojny

fidgety ('fydżyty) adj. wiercą-
cy sie; niespokojny;niecirpliwy

field (fi:ld) s. pole; boisko;
drużyna; dziedzina; v. ustawiac na boisku; zatrzymac
(piłkę);poprowadzić do akcji

field-events ('fi:ld,y wents) pl.
lekkoatletyka

field-glasses('fi:ld,glasy) pl.
lornetka polowa

field-gun ('fi:ld,gan) s. działo
polowe

fiend (fy:nd) s. zły duch;
szatan; demon; nałogowiec;
zagorzalec

fierce (fiers) adj. dziki; srogi; zażarty; wsciekły; zaw-
ziety;nieopanowany;gwałtowny

fiery ('fajery) adj. ognisty;
płomienny; palący; zapalny;
burzliwy;popedliwy;choleryczny

fife (fajf) s. piszczałka; v.
grać na piszczałce (na fujarce)

fifteen ('fyf'ti:n) num. piet-
naście;piętnascioro;piętnastka

fifteenth ('fyf'ti:nt) num.
piętnasty;jedna piętnasta czesc

fiftieth ('fyftjet) num. pięć-
dziesiąty;jedna pięćdziesiąta
fifty ('fyfty) num. pięćdziesiąt
fig (fyg) s. figa; strój
fight; fought; fought (fajt;
fo:t; fo:t)
fight (fajt) s. walka; bitwa;
zapasy; bój; duch do walki;
mecz bokserski; v. walczyć
(przeciw lub o coś);bić się
fighter ('fajter) s. bojownik;
zapaśnik; samolot myśliwski
figurative ('fygjurejtyw) adj.
obrazowy; przenośny;symboliczny
figure ('fyg'er) s. kształt;
postać; wizerunek; cyfra;
wzór; v. figurować; liczyć;
rachować; oznaczać cenami;
wyobrażać; przedstawiać
figure out ('fyger,aut) v.obli-
czać; wynosić;składać się na
figure skating ('fyger, skejtyng)
s, jazda figurowa na łyżwach
file (fajl) s. rejestr; archiwum; seria; pilnik; v. archi-
wować; defilować; piłować pil-
nikiem; wnosić (podanie; skargę);iść rzędem(rzedami);maszero-
wać
fill (fyl) v. napełniać; plom-
bować ząb; obsadzać; s. wypełnienie; napicie i najedzenie do
syta; nasyp ;ładunek;porcja
fill in ('ful,yn) v. zapełniać;
wypełniać (formularze,blankiety)
fill up ('fyl,ap) v. wypełniać;
zapełniać ;nabierać benzyny
fillet ('fylyt) s. wstążki;
zraz zawijany; dzwonko; v.prze-
pasywać ;wycinać filety
fillet ('fylej) v. dzielić na
dzwonka ;wycinać dzwonka
filling ('fylyng) s. nadziewka;
plomba; wątek ;zapas benzyny
filling station ('fylyng,st'ejszyn) s. stacja benzynowa
filly ('fyly) s. źrebica; koza;
młoda dziewczyna ;dzierlatka
film (fylm) s. powłoka; błona;
warstwa; film; mgiełka; bielmo;
v. pokrywać błoną; filmować
filter ('fylter) s. filter; sączek; v. filtrować; przeciekać

filth (fyls) s. brud; plugastwo
filthy (fylsy) adj. brudny; plugawy;niegodziwy;sprośny
fin (fyn) s. płetwa; v. obcinać płetwy; ruszać płetwami
finagle ('fy'nejgl) v. oszukiwać; wyłudzać;nabierać
final ('fajnl) adj. koncowy;
ostateczny; s. finał (sport;
egzamin etc)coś ostatecznego
finally ('fajnly) adv. w końcu;
wreszcie; na końcu;ostatecznie
finance (faj'naens) s. finanse;
skarbowość; v. finansować;
udzielać pożyczki
financial (faj'naenszel) adj.
pieniężny; finansowy
financier (,fynaen'sjer) s. fi-
nansista; v. spekulować;
sprzeniewierzać pieniądze
finch (fynch) s. łuszczak;ptak
z krótkim dziobem
find; found; found (fajnd;
faund; faund)
find (fajnd) v. znajdować;
konstatować;dowiedzieć się
find out ('fajnd, aut) v. wykryć;
wynaleźć; dowiedzieć się
finder ('fajnder) s. znalazca;
odkrywca;wizier;dalekomierz
finding ('fajndyng) s. odkrycie; stwierdzenie;dane;wniosek
fine (fajn) adj. piękny; misterny; czysty; przedni; wyszukany;
świetny; dckładny; adv. świet-
nie; wspaniale; s. grzywna;
kara; v. ukarać grzywną
finery ('fajnry) s. szyk; elegancja; strojny ubiór
finger ('fynger) s. palec;
kciuk; v. przebierać w palcach;
wskazywać palcem;brać palcami
finger nail ('fynger,nejl) s.
paznokieć
finger print ('fynger,prynt)
odcisk palca
finish ('fynysz) s. koniec; wykończenie; v. kończyć; skon-
czyć; wykończyć ;dokończyć
finite ('fajnajt) adj. skończony; ograniczony;końcowy
Finnish ('fynusz) adj. fiński

fir (fe:r) s. jodła ; jedlina

fire ('fajer) s. ogień; pożar

fire alarm ('fajer,e'la:rm) s. sygnał pożarowy ; alarm pożaro-wy

firearm ('fajera:rm) s. broń palna (armaty.strzelby etc.)

firebug ('fajer,bag) s. swietlik ; robaczek swietojanski

fire brigade ('fajerbry,gejd) s. straż pożarna

fire department ('fajer,dy'-pa:rtment) s. miejska straż pożarna;straż ogniowa

fire engine ('fajer'endżyn) s. wóz straży ogniowej(pompa)

fire escape ('fajerys,kejp) s,we wyjście zapasowe;schody zapasowe

fire extinguisher ('fajeryks,-,tynglyszer) s. gaśnica

fireman ('fajermen) s. strażak

fireplace ('fajer-plejs) s. kominek; palenisko

fireproof ('fajerpru:f) adj. ogniotrwały; ognioodporny

fireside ('fajersajd) s. przy kominku;kominek;ognisko domowe

firewood ('fajerłud) s. drzewo opałowe; drewno opałowe

fireworks ('fajerłe:rks) pl. ognie sztucznie;hałasliwe sceny

firm (fe:rm) s. firma; adv. mocno; adj. pewny; stanowczy; trwały; v. ubijac ; osadzać (mocno);umacniac sie

firmness ('fe:rmnys) s. stałość; trwałość; stanowczosć; jędrność;moc;energia

first ('fe:rst) adj. pierwszy; adv. najpierw; po raz pierwszy; początkowo; na początku

first of all ('fe:rst,ow'o:l) przede wszystkim;najpierw

first aid ('fe:rst,ejd) pierwsza pomoc;doraźna pomoc;opatrunek

first aid kit ('fe:rst,ejd kyt) podreczna apteczka; zestaw pierwszej pomocy(opatrunkow etc.

firstborn ('fe:rstbo:rn) adj. pierworodny(syn, dziecko etc.)

first class ('fe:rst'klas) s. pierwsza klasa;a.najlepszej jakości

first-class ('fe:rst'klas) adj. pierwszorzedny; wspaniały

first floor ('fe:rst flo:r) s. parter(w Anglii pierwsze piętro)

first hand ('fe:rst,haend) adj. bezpośredni; z pierwszej ręki

firstly ('fe:rstly) adv. po pierwsze; najpierw

first name ('fe:rst,nejm) s. imię (chrzestne)

first-rate ('fe:rst,rejt) adj. pierwszorzędny; adv. pierwszorzędnie ;bardzo dobrze

firth (fe:rs) n. odnoga morska; zatoka (zwłaszcza w Szkocji)

fish (fysz) s. ryba;v.łowic ryby

fishbone ('fyszboun) s. ość

fisherman ('fyszemen) s. rybak

fishery ('fyszery) s. rybołostwo; teren połowu lub hodowli

fishing ('fyszyng) s, wędkarstwo; rybołostwo; połów

fishing line ('fyszyng,lajn) s. linka; żyłka (od wędki)

fishing rod ('fyszyng,rod)s. wędka

fishing tackle ('fyszyng,taekl) s. sprzęt rybacki

fishmonger ('fyszmanger) s. handlarz ryb;sklep z rybami

fission ('fyszyn) s. dzielenie; rozbicie (atomu);rozszczepienie; rozerwanie

fissure ('fyszer) s. szczelina; pęknięcie; v. rozszczepiac; pękać; łupać (sie)

fist (fyst) s. pieść ;v.uderzac

fit (fyt) s. atak (choroby; gniewu etc.); krój; dopasowanie; adj. dostosowany; odpowiedni; nadajacy się; gotów; zdatny; dobrze leżący; v. sprostać; dobrze leżeć;przygotowac sie

fit on (fyt on) v. przymierzac

fit out (fyt aut) v. zaopatrywać; s. wyposażenie; umeblowanie

fitness ('fytnys) s. stosownosc; kondycja;trafnosc (uwagi);przywoitosć

fitter ('fyter) s,. monter; krawiec dokonywujacy przymiarek;slusarz

fitting ('fytyng) s. okucie; oprawa; przymiarka; adj. odpowiedni; wlasciwy;trafny;stosowny

five (fajw) num. pięc ;pięcioro; piata(godzina);piątka (numer oougwia)

fix (fyks) v. umocować; przyczepiać; ustalać; utkwić;
ustalać; zgęszczać; tężeć;
krzepnąć; urządzic kogos(źle);
usytuowac; zaaranżować wynik (zapasów); s. kłopot;
dylemat; położenie nawigacyj-
ne (statku,samolotu etc.)
fix up (fyks,ap) v. naprawić;
uporządkować;ulokować(kogoś)
fixed (fykst) adj. trwały;
stały;nieruchomy;niezmienny
fixedly ('fyksydly) adv. stale; trwale; uporczywie
fixture ('fyksczer) s. urządzenie przymocowane
fizz (fyz) s. syk; napój musujący; v. syczeć; musować
flabbergast ('flaebergaest) v.
zdumieć; odebrać mowę (ze
zdumienia);oszołamiać
flabby ('flaeby) adj. zwiotcza-
ły; obwisły; miękki; słaby;
niedbały;bez charakteru
flag (flaeg) s. flaga; chorągiew; lotka; v. wywieszać
flagę; sygnalizować
flagstone ('flaeg,stoun) s. płyta brukowa; płyta chodnikowa
flak (flaek) s. artyleria prze-
ciwlotnicza (niemiecka)
flake (flejk) s. płatek; łuska;
iskra; v. proszyć; odpryskiwać;
łuszczyć;padać płatkami
flake off ('flejk;of) v. złuszczać (się);odpadać płatkami
flame (flejm) s. płomień;miłość;
v. zionąć; błyszczeć; płonąć;
opalać; migotać;być podnieconym
flank (flaenk) s. bok; flanka;
v. flankować; strzec flanki
flannel ('flaenl) s. flanela;
v. wycierać flanelą; ubierać
we flanelę (lekka wełnę)
flap (flaep) s. trzepot; klap-
nięcie; klapa; poła; płat; pokrywa; v. trzepotać; zwisać;
klapnąć;uderzyć czymś płaskim
flare (fleer) v. błyszczeć;
sygnalizować; popisywać się;
rozszerzać się;s.jasny płomień
flare up (fleer ap) s. wybuch;
błysk; v.wybuchnąć (gniewem;
płomieniem)reagować gwałtownie

flash (flaesz) s. błysk; blask;
adj. błyskotliwy; fałszywy;
gwarowy; v. zabłysnąć; sygnalizować; pędzić; mknąć; wysyłać
(natychmiastowo wiadomości etc.)
flashbulb ('flaeszbalb) s. żarówka (do zdjęc);flesz
flashlight ('flaeszlajt) s.
latarka (elektryczna)
flashy ('flaeszy) adj. błyskot-
liwy(chwilowo);jaskrawy;krzykliwy
flask (flaesk) s. flaszka; fla-
kon; kolba;opleciona flaszka wina
flat (flaet) adj. płaski; płytki;
nudny; równy; stanowczy; oczywisty; matowy; bezbarwny;
adv. płasko; stanowczo; dokładnie;
nie; s. płaszczyzna; równina;
mieszkanie; przedziurawiona
dętka ;v.rozpłaszczyc;matować
flatten ('flaetn) v. spłaszczyć
(się);matowieć;wietrzeć;równać
flatter ('flaeter) v. pochlebiać
flattery ('flaetery) s. pochleb-
stwo; schlebianie komuś
flavor ('flejwer) s. smak; zapach; v. dawać smak;mieć posmak
flaw (flo:) s. skaza; rysa; pęknięcie; v. psuć; pękać
flawless ('flo:les) adj. bez
skazy;(przedstawienie)bez usterek
flax (flaeks) s. len
flaxen(fkak'sn)adj.płowy;lniany
flea (fli:) s. pchła
fled (fled) zob. flee
fledgling ('fledżlyng) s. świeżo opierzony ptak;żółtodziób
flee; fled; fled (fli:; fled;
fled)
flee (fli:) v. uciekać;pierzchać
fleece (fli:s) s. runo; wełna;
czupryna; puch; v. strzyc;
skubać; pokrywać puchem
fleet (fli:t) s. flota; park po-
jazdów; v. mknąć; przemknąć;
mijać; adv. płytko; adj. płytki
flesh (flesz) s. ciało; miąższ
fleshy ('fleszy) adj. mięsisty;
tłusty;cielesny;zmysłowy
flew (flu:) zob. fly
flexible (fl'eksybl) adj. giętki; gibki; układny; obrotny;
elastyczny;łatwo przystosowywu-
jący się; ustępliwy;poddający się

flick (flyk) s. przytyk; śmignięcie; smuga; v. smignąć;
trzepnąć; rzucać się; trzepotać się;zapalać zapalniczkę
flicker ('flyker) s. mig; mi-
ganie; drganie; trzepot;
v. migać; drgać; trzepotać;
machać;lekko się poruszać
flier ('flajer) s. lotnik;
ulotka;pospieszny pociąg etc.
flight (flajt) s. lot; przelot; ucieczka;kondygnacja scho-
flight engineer ('flajt,endży'-
nier) s. mechanik pokładowy
flimsy ('flymzy) adj. cienki;
wątły; słaby(papier,wymówka..)
flinch (flyncz) v. uchylać się;
cofać się; drgać;s.unik
fling; flung; flung (flyng;
flang; flang)
fling (flyng) v. rzucać (się);
powalić; wypaść; wierzgać
fling open('flyn,oupen) v.
rozewrzec (gwałtownie)
flint (flynt) s. krzemień;
krzesiwo;kamyk do zapalniczki
flip (flyp) v. przytykać ; rzucać;wyprztykiwać;s.prztyk
flippant ('flypent) adj. nie-
poważny; impertynencki
flipper ('flyper) s. płetwa
nożna; graba;łapa;błona pławna
flirt (fle:rt) v. flirtować;
machać; s. flirciarz; flir-
ciarka; machnięcie(raptowne)
flirtation (,fle:r'tejszyn) s.
flirt;powierzchowny romans
flit (flyt) v. biegać; fruwać;
wyjechać;poruszać się zwinnie
float (flout) v. unosić się;
pływać na powierzchni; spławiać; puszczać w obieg; lan-
sować; s. pływak; tratwa;
platforma na kołach; gładzik
do tynku;niezdecydowany ruch
flock (flok) s. trzoda; stado;
tłum; v. tłoczyć się; iść
tłumem; gromadzić się
floe (flou) s. kra (lodowa)
flog (flog) v. chłostać; smagać; bić;biczować się
flood (flad) s. powód; wylew;
potok; v. zalewać; nawadniać

floodlights ('flad,lajts) pl.
reflektory (szeroko-stożkowe)
flood tide ('fladtajd) s. przypływ (morza);fala powodziowa
floor (flo:r) s. podłoga;dno
floor cloth ('flo:rklo:s) s.
szmata do podłogi;linoleum
floor lamp ('flo:r,laemp) s.
lampa stojąca na podłodze
floor show ('flo:r,szou) s.
przedstawienie kabaretowe
flop (flop) s. klapanie; klapa;
fiasco; v. klapnąć; załamać
się; zrobić klapę;a.dziadowski
florist ('floryst) s. kwiaciarz;
kwiaciarka;hodowca kwiatów
flounder ('flaunder) s. flądra;
brnięcie; v. brnąć; brodzić;
błądzić; występać (mowę)
flour (flauer) s. mąka; v. mleć
na mąkę;dodawać mąki(posypywać)
flourish ('flarysz) s. fanfara;
wymachiwanie; v. kwitnąć; zdobić kwiatami; wymachiwać
flow (flou) s. strumień; prąd;
przepływ; dopływ; v. płynąć;
lać się; zalewać;ruszać się płyn-
nie
flower (flauer) s. kwiat;
v. kwitnąć;być w rozkwicie
flown (floun) zob. fly
fluctuate ('flaktjuejt) v.
falować; wahać się;być niezdecydowanym
flu (flu:) s. grypa;influenca
fluent ('fluent) adj. płynny;
biegły i wymowny(mówca;pisarz..)
fluff (flaf) s. puch;v.trzepać;kno-
cić
fluffy (flafy) adj. puszysty;lekki
fluid ('flu:yd) s. płyn; adj.
płynny;płynnie poruszający się
flung (flang) zob. fling
flunk (flank) v. oblać (egzamin)
spalić (ucznia); nie zdać;zawalić
flurry ('fle:ry) s. wichura;
ulewa; śnieżyca; podniecenie;
rozgardiasz; v. oszałamiać;
denerwować;wprowadzać zamieszanie
flush (flasz) v. rumienić się;
napełniać; spłukiwać; s. rumieniec; rozkwit; blask; adj.
wylewający się; krzepki; rumiany; równy; etc.; adv. równo;
prosto;gładko;pełno;poziomo;sowi-
cie(wyposażać w pieniądze)

fluster ('flaster) s. podniecenie; niepokój; v. podniecać; oszałamiać; kręcić się
flute (flu:t) s. flet;rowkowa-nie
flutter ('flater) s. trzepotanie; dygotanie; niepokój;
v. trzepotać; drzeć; dygotać;
płoszyć;powodować trzepotanie
flux (flaks) s. prąd; przepływ;
potok; płynność; krwotok;
przypływ;pasta do lutowania
fly (flaj) s, mucha;klapka
fly; flew; flown(flaj; flu;
floun), v. latać; lecieć; powiewać; uciekać; przewozić
samolotem; puszczać (latawca)
fly across (,flaj e'kros) v.
przelatywać (przez)
flyblown ('flaj-bloun) adj.
popstrzony przez muchy
fly into a rage ('flaj,yntu
ej'rejdż) v. wpaść w pasję
flyer ('flajer) s. lotnik
flying ('flajyŋg)adj. latają-
cy; lotny; lotniczy; krótkotrwały;samolotowy;pośpieszny
flying boat ('flajyŋbout) s.
hydroplan (do wodowania)
flying buttress ('flajyŋ,ba-
trys) s. łuk przyporowy
flying machine ('flajyŋg
,meszi:n) s. samolot
flying time ('flajyŋg,tajm) s.
czas przelotu;czas lotu
fly weight ('flaj,łejt) s. waga musza (112 funtów lub mniej)
flywheel ('flajłi:l) s. koło
zamachowe (do regulowania szyb-kości)
foal (foul) s. źrebię
foam (foum) s, piana; v. pienić się ;a.pianowy;piankowy
foamy ('foumy) adj. pieniący
się ;pienisty;spieniony
focus ('foukes) s. ognisko;
ogniskowa; v. skupiać; ognis-
kować; koncentrować;zesrodkowy-wać
fodder ('foder) s. pasza
foe (fou) s. wróg ;przeciwnik
fog (fog) s. mgła;v.otumaniać
foggy ('fogy) adj. mglisty
foible ('fojbl) s. słabostkę;lek-
ka słabość charakteru;
stałość; wątłość

foil (fojl) s. folia; tło; flo-
ret; trop; ślad; v. udaremnić;
zacierać (ślad) :niweczyć
fold (fould) s. fałda; zagięcie;
zagroda (owiec) v. składać;
zaginać (się); splatać; zamykać owce (w owczarni);fałdować
folder ('foulder) s. składana
teczka; broszura;falcownik
folding ('fouldyŋg) adj. składany; rozsuwany;s.fałd;fałda
folding boat ('fouldyŋg bout)
składana łódz(turystyczna etc.)
folding chair ('fouldyŋg, czeer)
składane krzesło(kampingowe etc.)
foliage ('fouljydż) s. listowie;
liście (rosnące);ulistnienie
folk (fouk) s. ludzie; krewni;
lud; rasa; adj. ludowy;folkłorys-tyczny
folklore ('fouklo:r) s. folklor
folksy ('fouksy) adj. towarzyski; prosty;ludzki
folk song ('fouksoŋg) s. pieśń
ludowa (regionalna etc.)
follow ('folou) v. iść za; następować za; śledzić; rozumieć
(kogoś) wnikać;gonić;wynikać
follower ('folouer) s. stronnik;
zwolennik; uczeń; pomocnik
following ('folouyŋg) s. zwolen-
nicy; adj. następujący; nastep-
ny;s.orszak;świta;posłuch;autory-tet
folly ('foly) s. szaleństwo
foment (fou'ment) s. podżegać;
podsycać;nagrzewać;pobudzać
fond (fond) adj. kochający; czuły; łatwowierny;głupio czuły
fondle ('fondl) v. pieścić
fondness ('fondnys) s. czułość;
miłość; zamiłowanie;pociąg
food (fu:d) s. żywność; strawa;
pokarm; jedzenie;a.żywnościowy;
fool (fu:l) s. głupiec; głuptas;odżywczy;
błazen; v. błaznować; wyśmiewać;
oszukiwać;okpiwać;partaczyć
foolhardy ('fu:l,ha:rdy) adj.
szaleńczy; wariacki; lekkomyślny ;nieroztropny;gwałtowny
foolish ('fu:lysz) adj. głupi
foolishness ('fu-lysznys) s.
głupota ; głupstwo;bzdura;nonsens
foolproof ('fu:l,pru:f) adj.
niezawodny ;nie do zepsucia

foot (fut) s. stopa; dół; spód;
miara (30,5 cm);piechota;v.płacić
foot the bill ('fut,ty'byl) v.
zapłacić rachunek
football ('fut,bo:l) s. piłka
nożna; futbol;piłka do nożnej
foot brake ('fut,brejk) s. hamulec nożny(w samochodzie)
foothills ('futhylz) pl. pod-
górze(przy łancuchu górskim)
foothold ('futhold) s. oparcie (dla nóg); miejsce gdzie
można stanąć;pewna pozycja
footing ('futyŋg) s. fundament;
ostoja; podstawa; położenie
footpath ('futpas) s. ścieżka
dla pieszych; chodnik
footprint ('futprynt) s. ślad
stopy
footstep ('fut,step) s. odgłos
kroku; ślad;długość kroku
for (fo:r) prep. dla; zamiast;
z; do; na; żeby; że; za; po;
co do; co się tyczy; jak na;
mimo; wbrew; po coś; z powodu; conj. ponieważ; bowiem;
gdyż; albowiem; dlatego że
for two years ('fo:-tu-je:rs)
przez dwa lata
forbade (fe:r'bejd) zob. forbid
forbear ; forbore ; forborne
(fo:'beer; fe'bo:r; fe'bo:rn)
forbear ('fo:r'beer) v. znosić
cierpliwie; powstrzymywać(się)
s. wyrozumiałość; przodek
forbid; forbade; forbidden
(fer'byd; fe:r'bejd; fer'bydn)
forbid (fe'rbyd) s. zakazywać;
zabraniać; niedopuszczać;
uniemożliwiać;nie pozwalać
forbidding (fe'rbydyŋg) adj.
odpychający; posępny; ponury
forbore (fer'bo:r) zob. forbear
forborne (fer'bo:rn) zob. forbear
force (fo:rs) s. siła; moc; potęga; sens; v. zmuszać; pędzić; wpychać; forsować
forced landing ('fo:rst,laendyŋg)
przymusowe lądowanie
forceps ('fo:rsyps) pl. kleszcze; szczypce;szczypczyki

forcible ('fo:rsybl) adj. gwałtowny; przymusowy; przekonywujący;mocny;dosadny;bezprawny
ford (fo:rd) v.przeprawiać się
brodem; s. bród (płytkie miejsce)
fore (fo:r) adj. przedni; adv.
na przedzie; s. przednia część
foreboding (fo:r'boudyŋg) s.
przeczucie (złego) ;źle przeczucie
forecast ('fo:r-ka:st) v. przewidywać; s. przewidywanie
forefather ('fo:r,fa:dzer) s.
przodek ; antenat
forefinger ('fo:rfyŋger) s. palec wskazujący
forefoot ('fo:r-fut) s. przednia noga (zwierzęcia)
foregone (fo:r'gon) adj. prze-
sądzony ;miniony
foreground ('fo:rgraund) s.
pierwszy plan (obrazu)
forehead ('fo:ryd) s. czoło
foreign ('foryn) adj. obcy;
obcokrajowy ;cudzozieski
foreign currency (,foryn'karensy)
s. obca waluta
foreigner ('foryner) s. cudzoziemiec; cudzoziemka;obcokrajo-
wiec
foreign policy ('foryn,polysy)
polityka zagraniczna
foreign trade ('foryn,trejd)
handel zagraniczny
foreleg ('fo:rleg) s. przednia
noga (zwierzęcia)
foreman ('fo:rmen) s. majster;
sztygar; starszy przysięgły
foremost ('fo:r,maust) adj.
główny; przedni; adv. przede
wszystkim ;w pierwszym rzędzie
forenoon ('fo:rnu:n) s. przedpołudnie ;s.przedpołudniowy
foresee ('fo:rsi:) v. przewidywać ;przewidzieć;wiedzieć z góry
foresight ('fo:rsajt) s. przezorność; przewidywanie; muszka
celownika (przy strzelbie etc.)
forest ('foryst) s. las; v. za-
lesiać ;a. leśny; w lesie
forester ('foryster) s. leśniczy; leśnik;ptak leśny;ćma leśna
forestry ('forystry) s. leśnictwo; lasy ;wiedza o lesie

foretaste ('fo:rtejst) s. przedsmak;zapowiedź tego co ma nasta-
pić
foretell; foretold; foretold
(fo:rtel; fo:'rtould; fo:'r-
tould)
foretell (fo:r'tel) v. przepowiadać; zapowiadać ;wróżyć
forever (fe'rewer) adv. wiecz-
nie; na zawsze; ustawicznie
foreword ('fo:rře-rd) v. przedmowa; przedsłowie;słowo wstępne
forfeit ('fo:rfyt) s. grzywna;
fant; zastaw; utrata; v. stra-
cić(w skutek konfiskaty);utracić
forge ('fo:rdż) s. kuźnia; huta;
v. kuć; fałszować; posuwać się
z trudem;wykuwać sobie przyszłość
forgery ('fo:rdżery) s. fałszer-
stwo;podrobiony dokument
forget; forgot; forgotten
(fer'get; fer'got; fer'gotn)
forget (fer'get) v. zapominać;
pomijać; przeoczyć;zaniedbać
forgetful (fer'getful) adj. za-
pominający;zapominalski;niepomny
forget-me-not (fer'getmyna:t) s.
niezapominajka
forgive; forgave; forgiven
(fer'gyw; fer'gejw; fer'gywn)
forgive (fer'gyw) v. przebaczać; darować ;odpuszczać
forgiveness (fer'gywnys) s. przebaczenie; darowanie; wybaczenie
forgiving (fer'gywyŋg)adj. wyrozumiały; pobłażliwy
forgo (fo:r'gou) v. powstrzymywać się; obchodzić się bez
czegoś ;zrzekać się czegoś
forgot (fer'got) zob. forget
fork (fo:rk) s. widły; widelec;
widełki; v. rozwidlać (się);
brać na widły;spulchniać(ziemię)
forlorn (fer'lo:rn) adj. zapuszczony; opuszczony; beznadziejny; rozpaczliwy;niepocieszony
form (fo:rm) v. formować (się);
kształtować (się); utworzyć
(się); organizować (się); wy-
tworzyć; s, forma; kształt;
postać; formuła; formułka; formularz;.blankiet;styl;układ
formal ('fo:rmel) adj. formalny;
urzędowy; oficjalny;s.strój wieczorowy

formation ('fo:rmejszyn) s. for-
macja; szyk; układ; tworzenie
(się); kształtowanie; formowa-
nie (się); powstawanie;budowa
formative ('fo:rmetyw) adj. for-
mujący; kształtujący; tworzą-
cy (się);słowotwórczy
former ('fo:rmer) adj. & pron.
poprzedni; były; miniony; dawny;s. formierz;giser;wzornik
formerly ('fo:rmerly) adv. dawniej; przedtem; poprzednio
formidable ('fo:rmydebl) adj.
straszny;strszny;potężny;ogrom-
ny
formulate ('fo:rmjulejt) v.
formułować;wyrażać;redagować
fornicate ('fo:rnykejt) v.
cudzołożyć ;spółkować bez ślubu
forsake; forsook; forsaken
(fer'sejk; fer'suk; fer'sejken)
forsake (fer'sejk) v. opuszczać;
porzucać;poniechać;zaprzeć się
fort (fo:rt) s. fort
forth (fo:rs) adv. naprzód; dalej;wobec;na zewnątrz etc.
forthcoming (fo:rs'kamyŋg) adj.
zbliżający się;nadchodzący
forthwith ('fo:rs'žys) adv.
bezzwłocznie;natychmiast
fortieth ('fo:rtyjes) num.
czterdziesty;czterdziesta(część)
fortify ('fo:rtyfaj) s. wzmacniać; fortyfikować;umacniać
fortnight ('fo:rtnajt) s. dwa
tygodnie (czternaście nocy)
fortran ('fo:rtraen) = formula
translation, język dla progra-
mów na komputery
fortress ('fo:rtrys) s. twierdza; forteca;warownia
fortunate ('fo:rcznat) adj.
szczęśliwy;pomyślny;udany
fortunately ('fo:rcznytly) adv.
na szczęście; szczęśliwie
fortune ('fo:rczen) s. szczęście; los; majątek;traf;ślepy los
forty ('fo:rty) num. czterdzies-
ci;czterdziestka;czterdzieścioro
forward ('fo:rřerd) adj. przedni; naprzód; postępowy; wczesny; chętny; gotowy; v. przyspieszać; ekspediować; s. napastnik (w sporcie);gracz w ataku

forwards ('fo:rłerds) adv. naprzod; dalej;adj.frontowy;śmiały
foster-child ('foster.czajld)
s. wychowanek; wychowanka
fought (fo:t) zob. fight
foul (faul) adj. zgniły;plugawy;
wstrętny; adv. nieuczciwie;
wbrew regułom; s, nieuczci-
wosc; v. zawalac (się); zabrudzic (się);plugawic się;kalac
found (faund) v. 1. uzasadniac;
zakładac; odlewac; 2. zob.
find
foundation (faun'dejszyn) s.
podstawa; założenie; fundament; fundacja;podwalina
founder ('faunder) s. odlew-
nik; założyciel; v. zatonąc;
przepasc;okulawic;zatopic
foundling ('faundlyng) s.
podrzutek ; znajda
fountain ('fauntyn) s. fontanna; źrodło;wodotrysk;poijalnia
fountainpen ('fauntyn,pen) s.
wieczne pióro
four (fo:r) num; cztery;czworo;
fourscore ('fo:rskor) num.
osiemdziesiąt
four-stroke engine ('fo:r,strok-
'endżyn) motor cztero-taktowy
fourteen ('fo:rti:n) num. czternaście;czternaścioro;czternastka
fourth ('fo:rθ) num. czwarty
fourthly (fo:rsly) adv. po
czwarte;na czwartym miejscu
fowl (faul) s. drob; ptaki
fox (foks) s. lis; v.przechytrzyc
fraction ('fraekszyn) s. ułamek;częsc;odłam;frakcja
fracture ('fraekczer) s. złamanie; v. złamac;łamac się
fragile ('fraedżajl) adj. kruchy; łamliwy;słabowity;watły
fragment ('fraegment) s. fragment;urywek;odłamek;okruch
fragrance ('frejgrens) s. zapach; woń; aromat
fragrant ('frejgrent) adj. pachnący;aromatyczny;wonny
frail (frejl) adj. kruchy; wątły;lekkomyslny;s.kosz;plecionka
frailty ('frejlty) s. słabosc;
wątłosc ;chwila słabosci

frame ('frejm) s. oprawa; rama;
struktura; szkielet; v. oprawiac; kształtowac; wrabiac
frame of mind ('frejm,ow'majnd)
s. nastroj; nastawienie psychiczne;usposobienie do czegos
frame-house ('frejm,haus) s.
drewniany dom (typowy w USA)
framework ('frejm,łe:rk) s.
struktura; zrąb;szkielet;wiąza-
nie
franchise ('fraenczajz) s.
przywilej; prawo do prowadzenia filii lub firmy,do głosowania
frank (fraenk) adj. szczery;
otwarty;v.wysyłac bez opłaty
frankness ('fraenknys) s.
szczerosc; otwartosc
frantic ('fraentyk) adj.
wariacki; szalony;zapamiętały
fraternal (fre'te:rnl) adj.
braterski;bratni;bracki
fraternity (fre'te:rnyty) s.
braterstwo;korporacja studencka
fraud (fro:d) s. oszustwo;oszust
fray (frej) v. strzępic; wycierac; s. bójka; burda
freak (fri:k) s. kaprys; wybryk; potwor;a.fantazyjny
freckle ('frekl) s. pieg; v.po-
krywac piegami;powodowac piegi
free (fri:) adj. wolny; bezpłatny; nie zajęty; v. uwolnic;
wyzwolic; oswobodzic; adv.wol-
no; swobodnie; bezpłatnie
free and easy ('fri:,end'i:zy)
adj. beztroski;bez ceremonii
freedom ('fri:dem) s. wolnosc;
swoboda;nieskrępowanie;prawo do
freemason ('fri:,mejsn) s.
mason; wolnomularz
free port ('fri:, port) s.
wolnocłowy port
freethinker ('fri:tynker) s.
wolnomysliciel;wolnomyslicielka
freeway ('fri:łej) s. szosa
przelotowa wieloliniowa
freewheel ('fri:hłi:l) s. wolne koło (np, od roweru)
freeze; froze; frozen (fri:z;
frouz; frouzn)
freeze (fri:z) v. marznąc; za-
marzac;krzepnąc;przymarznąc;
mrozic;wyrugowac(konkurenta)

freezing point ('fri:zyŋ,point) s. punkt zamarzania

freight (frejt) s. przewóz; fracht; v. przewozić; frachtować statek;a.towarowy(pociag etc)

freighter ('frejter) s. frachtowiec; statek towarowy

French (frencz) adj. francuski

frenzy ('frenzy) s. szał; szaleństwo;v.doprowadzać do szału

frequency ('fri:kłensy) s. częstość; częstotliwość

frequent ('fri:kłent) adj. częsty; rozpowszechniony; v. uczęszczać; odwiedzać; bywać

fresh (fresz) adj. świeży; nowy; zuchwały; niedoświadczony; adv. świeżo; niedawno;dopiero co

freshman ('freszmen) s. student pierwszego roku

freshness ('fresznys) s. świeżość; zuchwałość;zuchwalstwo

freshwater ('fresz;ło:ter) adj. słodkowodny; s. woda słodka

fret (fret) v. gryźć się: niepokoić się; s. rozdrażnienie; niepokój;zdenerwowanie;irytacja

fretful ('fretful) adj. rozdrażniony; drażliwy;nerwowy;wzburzony

friar ('frajer) s. mnich; zakonnik ; biała plamka

friction ('frykszyn) s. tarcie; ścieranie się; ucieranie

Friday ('frajdy) s. piątek

fridge (frydż) s. lodówka (slang)

fried (frajd) adj. smażony

friend (frend) s. znajomy; znajoma; przyjaciel;kolega;klient

friendly ('frendly) adj. przyjazny; przychylny ;życzliwy

friendship ('frendszyp) s. przyjaźń osobista; dobra znajomość; znajomość powierzchowna; stosunki koleżeńskie lub handlowe

fright (frajt) s. strach;przerażenie;strach na wróble

frighten ('frajtn) v. straszyć

frightened ('frajtnd) adj.przestraszony ;zastraszony;wylękniony

frightful ('frajtful) adj. straszny; przerażający;strszliwy; alarmujący;nieprzyjemny;wstrętny

frigid ('frydżyd) adj. zimny; lodowaty; oziębły;zimna(kobieta)

frill (fryl) v. plisować; s. falbanka; pl. fochy; fanaberie;niepotrzebne ozdóbki

fringe (fryndż) s. frędzla; obrębek; v. obrębiać; obramowywać; ograniczać;wystrzepić

frisk (frysk) v. brykać; s.sus; podskok; skok;v.rewidować

frisky ('frysky) adj. rozbrykany; ożywiony; swawolny

fro (frou) exp.: to and fro; tu i tam; tam i z powrotem

frock (frok) s. sukienka; habit;mundur;surdut;anglez

frog (frog) s. żaba; strzałka (w kopycie konia);vulg.Francuz

frolic ('frolyk) s. wybryk;figiel swawola; v. dokazywać; swawolić; figlować; adj. rozbawiony; swawolny; figlarny

frolicsome ('frolyksem) adj. figlarny; swawolny;rozbawiony

from (from) prep. od; z; przed (zimnem); ze;(ponieważ; żeby)

from under (from ander) prep; spod (czegos)

from... to (from... tu) exp. stąd... dotąd ;od ..,do

front (frant) s. przód; front; czoło; adj. przedni; frontowy; czołowy; v. stawiać czoło; stać frontem; konfrontować

front-door ('frant,do:r) s. główne drzwi wejściowe

frontier ('frantjer) s. granica ; a. pograniczny

front-page ('frant,pejdż) s. strona tytułowa;a.sensacyjny

front tire ('frant,tajer) s. przednia opona (samochodu)

front-wheel ('frant,hłi:1) s. przednie koło (wozu)

front wheel drive ('frant, hłi:l'drajw) s. napęd na przednie koła (auta,etc.)

frost (frost) s. mróz; przymrozek; oziębłość;v.zmrozic';oszronic

frostbite ('frost,bajt) s. odmrożenie(nosa,reki,stopy etc.)

frosted ('frostyd) adj. matowy; oszroniony; matowy odcień

frosty ('frosty) adj. mroźny;
oszroniony; lodowaty
froth (froŋ) s. piana; szumowiny; v. pienić się;ubijać białko
frothy (froŋy) adj. spieniony
frown (fraun) v. marszczyć brwi;
s. zachmurzone czoło; wyraz
dezaprobaty;niezadowolona mina
froze (frouz) zob. freeze
frozen food ('frouzn, fu:d) s.
mrożonki:mrożona żywność
frugal ('fru:gel) adj. oszczędny;tani; skromny(posiłek etc.)
fruit (fru:t) s. owoc; v. owo-
cować;a. owocowy
fruitcake ('fru:t,kejk) s.
świąteczne ciasto z kandyzowa-
nymi owocami i orzechami
fruitful ('fru:tful) adj.
owocny;owocujący;zyskowny;wydaj-
fruitless ('fru:tlys) adj. bezowocny; bezpłodny;nieudany
frustrate (fra'strejt) v. udaremnić; zniechęcić; zawieść
fry (fraj) v. smażyć :s.narybek
frying pan (frajyŋ,paen) s.
patelnia
fuel (fjuel) s. paliwo; opał
fugitive ('fju:dżytyw) s. zbieg;
adj. zbiegły; przelotny
fulfill (ful'fyl) v. spełnić;
wykonać; dokonać; skończyć
fulfilment (ful'fylment) s.
spełnienie; wykonanie; dokonanie;wypełnienie;wysłuchanie
full(ful) adj. pełny; pełen; za-
pełniony; całkowity; kompletny;
cały; adv. w pełni; całkowicie
full board ('ful'bo:rd) s. pełne
utrzymanie;wikt i opierunek
full moon ('ful'mu:n) s. pełnia
księżyca
fullness (ful'nys) s. pełność;
dokładność;drobiazgowość
full-time ('ful'tajm) adj. pełno-
etatowy; całkowicie zajęty
fumble ('fambl) v. szperać; partaczyć; s. gmeranie; partactwo;
niezdarność;niezdarnę zagranie
fume (fju:m) v. dymić; kopcić;
s. dym (ostry); wyziew(przykry)
gazy spalinowe;zapach;won;na-
pad gniewu;wybuch gniewu

fun (fan) s. uciecha; zabawa;
wesołość; śmiech;powód do wesołoś-
in fun (yn,fan) adv. żartem;
make fun (mejk fan) v. dokuczać; kpić,wyśmiewać się
function ('fankszyn) v. działać; funkcjonować; s. działanie; funkcja; praca; obowiązek;
impreza; uroczystość;czynność
functionary ('fanksznery) s.
urzędnik; funkcjonariusz
fund (fand) s. fundusz
fundamental (,fande'mentel) adj.
podstawowy; s. zasada; podstawa zasada;nakaz:podstawa
funeral ('fju:nerel) s. pogrzeb;
adj. pogrzebowy;żałosny
funereal (fju'njerjel) adj. żałobny;pogrzegowny
funicular railway (fju'nykju-
ler'rejlłej) kolejka linowa
funnel ('fanl) s. lej; lejek;
komin (maszyny parowej etc.)
funny ('fany) adj. zabawny;
śmieszny; dziwny;humorystyczny
fur (fe:r) s. futro;v.okładać
furious ('fjuerjes) adj. wściekły; rozjuszony;gwałtowny;zaciek-
furl (fe:r) v. składać (się); ły
złożyć (się) ;s.zwitek;zawinięcie
furnace ('fe:rnys) s. piec
(centralny);palenisko;piekło
furnish ('fe:rnysz) v. zaopa-
rzyć; dostarczyć; umeblować;
wyposażyć;uzbrajać;meblować
furniture ('fe:rnyczer) s.
umeblowanie; urządzenie
furrier ('farjer) s. kuśnierz
furrow ('farou) s. bruzda;
zmarszczka; koleina; v. orać;
przeorać; zryć;ryć;pruć;żłobić
further ('fe:rdzer) adv. dalej;
dodatkowo; adj. dalszy; dodatkowy; v, pomagać; ułatwiać;
posuwać naprzód sprzyjać;popierać
further more (,fe:rdzermo:r) adv.
ponadto; oprócz tego; w dodatku
furtive ('fe:rtyw) adj. skryty;
potajemny ;ukradkowy;skradającej
furuncle ('fjuerankl) s. czyrak
fury ('fjuery) s. szał; furja;
pasja; gwałtowna siła; jędza;
megiera;siła burzy;siła wiatru

fuse (fju:z) v. stopić; s. zapalnik; bezpiecznik; korek

fuselage ('fju:zyla:ż) s. kadłub (samolotu)bez skrzydeł i ogona

fusion ('fju:żen) s. stopienie; spawanie; zlewanie się

fuss (fas) v. niepokoic; denerwowac; krzątac się; s. wrzawa; zamieszanie; krzątanina

fussy ('fasy) adj. grymaśny; hałaśliwy; nieznośny;zrzędny

futile ('fju:tajl) adj. daremny; bezskuteczny; próżny

future ('fju:tczer) s. przyszłość; adj. przyszły(czas...)

fuzzy ('fazy) adj. kędzierzawy; kręty; puszysty; niewyraźny; zamazany(obraz,pojęcie etc.)

g (dźi:) siodma litera angielskiego alfabetu

gab (gaeb) s. gadanie (slang)

gable ('gejbl) s. szczyt (dachu)trójkąt płaszczyzn dachu

gad-fly ('gaedflaj) s. giez; bąk;osoba zaczepna jak giez

gag (gaeg) s. knebel; v. kneblowac; nałożyc kaganiec; zamknąc debate;oszukiwac

gage (gejdż) s. wskaźnik; miara; rękojmia; v, mierzyc; oceniac; zastawiac;sadzic

gaiety (gejety) s. wesołość

gaily ('gejly) adv. wesoło

gain (gejn) s. zysk; zarobek; korzyśc; v. zyskiwac; zdobywac; pozyskiwac; wygrywac; osiągac;miec korzyśc;wyprzedzac

gait (gejt) s. chód;bieg(konia)

gaiter ('gejter) s. kamasz; getr

gale (gejl) s. poryw wiatru; sztorm;wybuch śmiechu;zefir

gall (go:l) s. żółc; złośc; gorycz;tupet;otarcie;v.urazic...

gallant ('gaelent) s. bawidamek; galant; adj. piękny; dzielny; waleczny; szarmancki

gallery ('gaelery) s. arkady; galeria; krużganek;balkon;chór

galley ('gaely) s. galera; kuchnia na statku;szufelka

galley proof ('gaely,pru:f) s. odbitka na korektcwa (szczotkowa)

gallon ('gaelen) s. miara płynu (ok. 4,5 litra)(am.gal.=3,78 1.)

gallop ('gaelep) v. galopowac; s. galop; cwał:galopada

gallows ('gaelouz) s. szubienica;kobylica;szelki;a.szbieniczny

galore (gr'lo:r) s. mnóstwo; adv. w bród;bardzo wiele

gamble ('gaembl) s. hazard; ryzyko; v, uprawiac hazard; ryzykowac;igrac;spekulowac

gambler ('gaembler) s. gracz-hazardzista; ryzykant

gambol (gaembel) v. podskakiwac; s. podskok; skok

game (gejm) s. gra; zabawa; zawody; sztuczki; machinacje; adj. dzielny; odważny; kulawy; v. uprawiac hazard

gamekeeper ('gejm,ki:per) s. gajowy; leśnik

gander ('gaender) s. gąsior

gang (gaeng) s. banda; szajka; grupa;v.łączyc się w bandę

gangster ('gaengster) s. gangster; bandyta

gangway ('gangłej) s. przejście; kładka;chodnik w kopalni

gaol = jail (dżejl) s. więzienie; ciupa;v.uwięzic;wsadzac do więzienia

gaoler = jailer ('dżejler) s. dozorca więzienny;strażnik więzienny

gap (gaep) s. szpara; luka;otwór; przerwa;odstęp;wyrwa;przełęcz;wyłom

gape (gejp) v. gapic się; ziewac; s. ziewanie; gapienie się

garage (gaera:dż) s. garaż; v. garażowac; zagarażowac

garbage ('ga:rbydż) s. odpadki; śmieci;bezwartościowe publikacje

garden ('ga:rdn) s. ogród;uprawiac ogród

gardener ('ga:rdner) s. ogrodnik

gardening ('ga:rdenyng) s. ogrodnictwo(warzywne,kwiatowe etc.)

gargle ('ga:rgl) v. płukac gardło;v.płyn do płukania gardła

garland ('ga:rlend) s. girlanda

garlic ('ga:rlik) s. czosnek

garment ('ga:rment) s. częśc ubrania;szaty;v.odziewac

garnish ('ga:rnusz) v. ozdabiac; s. ozdoba; przybranie (potraw) upiększenia literackie

garret ('gaeret) s. poddasze;
strych; mansarda;sl.:łeb
garrison ('gaerysn) s. załoga;
garnizon; v. garnizonować
garter ('ga:rter) s. podwiązka
gas (gaes) s. gaz; benzyna
gaseous ('gejzjes) adj. gazowy
gash (gaesz) s. skaleczyć się;
s. szrama; skaleczenie;blizna
gasket ('gaeskyt) s. uszczelka
gas-meter ('gaes,mi:ter) s.
gazomierz;zegar gazowy
gasoline ('gaesely:n) s. gazolina; benzyna
gasp (ga:sp) v. ciężko dyszeć;
sapać; s. ciężki oddech
gas station ('gaes,stejszyn)
s. stacja benzynowa
gas-stove ('gaes'stouw) s. kuchenka gazowa;kuchnia gazowa
gate (gejt) s. brama; furtka;
wrota; szlaban; ilość publiczność;wpływy kasowe ze wstępu
gateway ('gejtłej) s. przejście; wjazd; brama wjazdowa
gather ('gaedzer) v. zbierać;
wnioskować;wzbierać;narastać
gather speed ('gaedzer spi:d)
nabierać szybkości;rozpędzać się
gathering ('gaedzeryng) s. zebranie;nagromadzenie; ropień
gaudy (go:dy) adj. jaskrawy;
krzykliwy; s. obchód(uroczysty)
gauge (gejdż) s. wskaźnik; miara; skala; v. kalibrować; oceniać;szacować; oszacować
gaunt (go:nt) adj. chudy; nędzny;wycieńczony;ponury;posępny
gauze ('go:z) s. gaza; siatecz-
ka;mgiełka;gaza metalowa
gave (gejw) zob. give
gay (gej) adj. wesoły; jaskrawy; pstry; rozpustny; s. pederasta;pedzio;pedał
gaze (gejz) s. spojrzenie;
v. przyglądać się;przypatrywać
gaze at (gejz aet) v. wpatrywać
(się)w kogoś, w coś
gear (gier) v. włączyć (napęd)
s. przybory; bieg; układ
gear change ('gier,czeindż)
zmiana biegów

gearbox ('gier,boks) s. skrzynka biegów;skrzynia biegów
gearing ('gieryng) s. przekładnia;mechanizm napędowy
gear wheel ('gier-hłi:l) s.
tryb; koło zębate
geese (gi:s) pl. gęsi
gem (dżem) s. klejnot;perła
gender ('dżender) s. rodzaj;
płeć; wytwór; potomstwo
general ('dżenerel) adj. ogólny;
powszechny; generalny; naczelny; główny; nieścisły; ogólni-
kowy; s. generał; wódz
generalize ('dżenerelajz) v.
uogólniać; mówić ogólnikami
generally ('dżenerely) adv.
ogólnie; zazwyczaj; powszechnie; najczęściej; w ogóle
generate ('dżenerejt) v. rodzić;
wytwarzać;płodzić; wywoływać
generation ('dżenerejszyn) s.
powstawanie; pokolenie
generator ('dżenerejter) s.
prądnica; sprawca;generator
generosity (,dżene'rosyty) s.
szczodrość; wspaniałomyślność
generous ('dżeneres) adj. hojny;
wielkoduszny; suty; obfity; bogaty; żyzny;mocny; krzepiący
genial ('dżi:njel) adj. wesoły;
łagodny; miły;jowialny;ożywczy
genitive ('dżenityw) s. (gram.)
dopełniacz;adj.wesoły;łagodny
genius (dżi:njes) s. geniusz;
duch; talent;duch epoki etc.
genocide ('dżenousajd) s. ludo-
bójstwo(stematyczne mordowanie)
gentle ('dżentl) adj. łagodny;
delikatny; subtelny.stopniowy
gentleman ('dżentlmen) s. pan;
człowiek honorowy; dżentelmen
gentlemanly ('dżentlmenly) adj.
dżentelmeński; honorowy
gentleness ('dżentlnys) s. łagodność; delikatność
gentlewomen ('dżentl,łumen) s.
szlachcianka; dama;dama dworu
gentry ('dżentry) s. ziemiańst-
wo; szlachta; światek
genuine ('dżenjuyn) adj. prawdziwy; autentyczny; szczery

geography (dży'ogrefy) s. geografia; fizyczne cechy rejonu

geologist (dży'oledżyst) s. geolog

geology (dży'oledży) s. geologia

geometry (dży'omytry) s. geometria

germ (dże:rm) s. zarodek; zarazek; nasienie; pączek

German ('dże:rmen) adj. niemiecki(język,człowiek)s.Niemiec

germinate ('dże:rmynejt) v. kiełkować; rozwijać się

gerund (dżerend) s. rzeczownik odsłowny(z końcówką:"ing")

gestation ('dżes'tejszyn) s. ciąża

gesticulate ('dżes'tykjulejt) v. gestykulować; mówić na migi

gesture ('dżeszczer) s. gest

get; got; got (get; got; got) get (get) v. dostać; otrzymać; nabyć; zawołać; łupać; przynieść; zmusić; musić; mieć; dostać się; wpływać;wsiadać

get about (,get e'baut) v. poruszać się;rozchodzić się

get along (,get e'long) v. dawać sobie radę; współpracować

get away (,get e'łej) v. uciec; odejść;wyjeżdżać;oderwać się

get in (,get'yn) v. wejść; wsiąść

get off (,get'of) v. wysiąść

get on (,get'on) v. wdziewać; posuwać się; robić dalej

get out (,get'aut) v. wysiąść; wyjmować; wyciągać;wynosić się

get to (,get'tu) v. dotrzeć; przyjść; musieć;być zamuszonym

get together (,get te'gedzer) v. zebrać się; s. zebranie

get up (,get'ap) v. wstać;zbudzić się

get-up ('getap) s.wygląd;ubiór

get ready (,get'redy) v. przygotować(się);przygotowywać się

get to know ('get,tu'nou) v. zapoznać się (bliżej)

geyser ('gajzer) s. gejzer

ghastly ('ga:stly) adj. ohydny; upiorny; blady;adv.okropnie

gherkin ('ge:rkyn) s, korniszon

ghost (goust) s. duch; cień;widmo

ghostly ('goustly) adj. upiorny

giant ('dżajent) s. olbrzym

gibbet ('dżybyt) s. szubienica

gibe ('dżajb) s. kpina; drwina; v. kpić; szydzić; wyśmiewać

giblets ('dżyblyts) pl. podróbki (np. kurze);podroby

giddy ('gydy) adj. zawrotny; mający zawrót głowy; roztrzepany; v. przyprawiać o zawrót głowy

gift (gyft) s. dar; upominek; talent; uzdolnienie;a.darowany

gifted ('gyftyd) adj. utalentowany;mający naturalne zdolności

gigantic (dżaj'gantyk) adj. olbrzymi; gigantyczny;kolosalny

giggle ('gygl) s. chichot; v. chichotać;głupio śmiać się

gild (gyld) v. złocić; pozłocić;nadać lepszego wyglądu

gill (gyl) s. skrzela; wąwóz; potok;jedna czwarta galona

gilt (gylt) adj. pozłacany; s. złocenie; pozłocenie

gin (dżyn) s. jałowcówka

ginger ('dżyndżer) s. imbir

ginger bread ('dżyndżer,bred) s. piernik;przesadne dekoracje

gingerly ('dżyndżerly) adj. ostrożny; delikatny; adv. ostrożnie; delikatnie; nieśmiało

gipsy ('dżypsy)s. cygan

giraffe (dży'ra:f) s. żyrafa

gird; girt; girt (ge:rd; ge:rt; ge:rt) na

gird (ge:rd) v. opasać;kpić.s.kpina

girder ('ge:rder) s. dźwigar; belka; wzdłużnik

girdle ('ge:rdl) s. pas; v. opasać; okrążyć;opasywać gorsetem lekkim

girl (ge:rl) s. dziewczyna;ukochana

girlhood ('ge:rlhud) s. wiek dziewczęcy; dziewczęta (kraju etc.)

girl scout ('ge:rl skaut) s. harcerka

girl's name ('ge:rls,nejm) s. panieńskie nazwisko

girt (ge:rt) zob. gird

girth (ge:rt) s. popręg; obwód

gist (dżyst) s. treść; istota; sedno; esencja; osnowa;sens; główna treść give; gave; given (gyw; gejw; gywn)

give (gyw) v. dać; dawać; być elastycznym; zawalić się; ustąpić; s. elastyczność; ustępstwo pod naciskiem

give away (,gyw e'łej) v. wydawać; zdradzać;wydawać córkę

give in (,gyw'yn) v. ustępować; podawać(nazwisko);uznawać w końcu

give up (,gyw'ap) v. poddać się; ustąpić; zaniechać;dać za wygraną

give way (,gyw'łej) v. zrobić miejsce; ustąpić;obsunąć się

glacier ('glaesjer) s. lodowiec

glad (glaed) adj. rad; wesoły; radosny;dający radość;ochoczy

gladly ('glaedly) adv. z przyjemnością; chętnie;właściwie

gladness ('glaednys) s. wesołość; pogoda ducha; przyjemność

glamorous ('glaemeres) adj. czarujący; wspaniały; fascynujący

glance (gla:ns) v. spojrzeć; ześliznąć się; błyszczeć; połyskiwać; s. rzut oka; błysk; połysk;rekoszet;odbicie się

glance at ('gla:ns et) v. spojrzeć na (coś);rzucić spojrzenie

gland (glaend) s. gruczoł

glare (gleer) v. błyskać; razić; wlepiać wzrok; s.błysk; blask

glass (gla:s) s. szkło; szklanka;lampka;kieliszek;szyba etc.

glasses ('gla:sys) pl. okulary; szkła

glassy ('gla:sy) adj. szklisty; szklany;przeźroczysty;bez wyrazu

glaze (glejz) v. szklić; oszklić

glazier ('glejzjer) s. szklarz

gleam (gli:m) s. połysk; v. połyskiwać;zjawić się nagle

glee (gli:) s. wesele; radość

glen (glen) s. dolina(zacisza)

glib (glyb) adj. gładki; żwawy; płynny; wygadany(zanadto)

glide ('glajd) v. poślizg; szybowanie; v. ślizgać się; szybować; powodować poślizg

glider ('glajder) s. szybowiec

glimmer ('glymer) v. migotać; słabo świecić; s. słabe światło; migotanie;słabe postrzeganie

glimpse (glymps) s. mignięcie; przelotne spojrzenie; v. ujrzeć w przelocie;zerknąć

glint (glynt) s. błysk; odblask; v. błysnąć; zamigotać

glisten ('glysn) s. połysk; v. połyskiwać;lśnić;iskrzyć się

glitter ('glyter) v. świecić się; błyszczeć; s. połysk; blask; pretensjonalność

gloat ('glout) v. napawać się; złe patrzeć;pożerać oczami

gloat over ('glout,ower) v. napawać się (cudzym nieszczęściem);unosić się

globe (gloub) s. globus; kula ziemska;jabłko królewskie;gałka

gloom (glu:m) s. smutek; mrok; przygnębienie; v. zasmucać (się); zaciemniać (się);posępnieć

gloomy ('glu:my) adj. ponury; mroczny;posępny;przygnębiony

glorify ('glo:ryfaj) v. chwalić; wychwalać; gloryfikować

glorious ('glo:rjes) adj. sławny; wspaniały;przepiękny;chlubny

glory ('glo:ry) s. chwała; sława; v. szczycić się; chlubić się;chwalić się;chełpić się

gloss (glos) s. połysk; v. polerować;interpretować(błędnie)

glossary ('glosery) s. słownik (przy tekscie);glosarjusz

glossy ('glosy) adj. lśniący

glove (glaw) s. rękawiczka

glow (glou) v. żarzyć się; pałać; s. jarzenie; zapał; żarliwość;łuna;rumieniec;jasność

glowworm ('glou,łe:rm) s. robaczek świętojański

glue (glu:) s. klej; v. kleić; zalepiać;wlepiać(oczy);zlepić

glutton ('glatn) s. żarłok

gluttonous ('glatnes) adj. żarłoczny;jedzący zbyt dużo

gluttony ('glatny) s. żarłoczność;zwyczaj jedzenia za dużo

glycerine (,glyse'ry:n) s. gliceryna

gnarled ('na:rld) adj. sękaty; wykrzywiony; węzłowaty

gnash (naesz) v. zgrzytać zębami jak w złości

gnat (naet) s. komar;owad

gnaw (no:) v. gryźć; wgryzać;
ogryzać; nękać(stałym bólem)

go; went; gone (gou; lent; gon)

go (gou) v. iść; chodzić; jechać; stać się;być na chodzie

go about (,gou e'baut) v. zając się (czymś);afiszować się

go along (,gou e'long) v. to-
warzyszyc; zgadzac się;isc sobie

go away (,go e'łej) v. isc
precz; odchodzic;wyjeżdżać

go back (,gou'bek) v. wracać;
cofać się;siegać wstecz

go by (,gou'baj) v. mijać

go on (,gou'on) v. isc naprzód;
ciagnąc dalej; kontynuowac

go out (,gou'aut) v. wychodzic
(z kims); gasnąc;bywac(u ludzi)

go through (,gou'tru) v. przechodzic; brnąc przez;przebrnąc

go under (,gou'ander) v. to-
nąc; ulegac; zniknąc;umrzec

goad (goud) s. kolec; bodziec;
v. popędzać; drażnic; prowoko-
wac;doprowadzać do zrobienia

goal (goul) s. cel; meta; bramka

goalie (gouli) s. bramkarz

go-between (,gouby'tły:n) s.
pośrednik; stręczyciel

goblet ('goblyt) s. kieliszek;
czara;puchar;kielich na nóżce

goblin ('goblyn) s. chochlik

god (god) s. Bog; bożek;bóstwo

godchild ('godczajld) s. chrzes-
niak; chrześniaczka

goddess ('godys) s. bogini

godfather ('god,fa:dzer) s.
ojciec chrzestny;v.trzymać do chrztu

godless ('godlys) adj. bezboż-
ny;grzeszny;niegodziwy;nikczemny

godmother ('god,madzer) s.
matka chrzestna

goggles ('goglz) pl. okulary
ochronne; gogle;okrągłe okulary

going ('gouyng)s. chodzenie;
jazda;tempo;adj.ruchliwy;istnie-
jacy

going rate ('gouyn,rejt) bieżący kurs (dolara,oprocentowania)

gold (gould) s. złoto;adj.złoty

gold digger ('gould,dyger)
poszukiwacz złota ; naciagaczka

golden ('gouldn) adj. złoty

gold-plated ('gould,plejtyd)
s. plater złoty ;platerowany

goldsmith ('gould,smys) s.
złotnik   golfa

golf (golf) s. golf ;v.grać w

golf course ('golf,ko:rs) s.
pole golfowe

gondola ('gondele) s. gondola
(np. balonu);otwarty,niski wagon
towarowy

gone (gon) v. zob. go

good (gud) adj. dobry; s. dobro; pożytek; zaleta;wartość
better ('beter) lepszy;
best (best) najlepszy

good at it ('gud,et'yt) dobry
w tym; dobrze to robi

good-bye (,gud'baj) s. do widzenia; pożegnanie

good-for-nothing ('gudfe:r,na-
syng) s. nicpoń ;hultaj;łobuziak

good-looking ('gud'lukyng)adj.
przystojny; ładny

good-natured ('gud'nejczerd)
adj. dobroduszny;poczciwy

goodness ('gudnys) s. dobroc

good will ('gud'łyl) s. dobra
wola;wartość reputacji firmy

goose(gu:s) s. gęs; pl. geese
(gi:s) gęsi;gęsie mięso;duren

gooseberry ('gusbery) s. agrest

gooseflesh ('gu:sflesz) s. gęsia skórka (z zimna,strachu etc.)

gopher ('goufer) s. suseł; darke
v. grzebac;ryc;plądrowac gospo-

gore (go:r) v. bość; klinowac
s, klin w krawiectwie;posoka

gorge ('go:rdż) s. wąwóz; żarłoczność; treść żołądka; prze-
jedzenie; gardziel; v, obżerac
się; pożerac; połykac;opychac się

gorgeous ('go:rdżes) adj. wspaniały; okazały; suty; ozdobny;
wystawny;wspaniały;cudowny

gospel ('gospel) s. ewangielia

gossip ('gosyp) s. plotka;
plotkarz; plotkarka; v. plot-
kowac;pisac popularne artykuły

got (got) zob. get

Gothic ('gotyk) adj. gotycki

gotten ('gotn) = got; zob. get

gourd (go:rd) s. bania; tykwa

gourmet ('guermej) n. smakosz

gout (gaut) s. gościec;podagra

govern ('gawern) v. rządzić; kierować; dowodzić;trzymać w ryzach

governess ('gawernys) s. guwernantka;nauczycielka;instruktorka

government ('gawernment) s. rząd; ustrój;okręg;a.rządowy

governor ('gawerner) s. gubernator; zarządca;naczelnik;szef

gown (gaun) s. suknia; toga; v. układać togę;ubierać suknię

grab (graeb) v. łapać; zagarniać; grabić; s. łapanie; chwyt; zagarnięcie;porwanie

grace (grejs) s. łaska; wdzięk; przyzwoitość; v. czcić; ozdabiać; dodawać wdzięku;zaszczycić

graceful ('grejsful) adj. pełen wdzięku; wdzięczny;łaskawy

gracious ('grejszes) adj. łaskawy; miłosierny;exp. goodness gracious.('gudnys'grejszes) Boże miłosierny!

grade (grejd) s. stopień; klasa; nachylenie; v. stopniować; dzielić na stopnie; cieniować; równać teren;niwelować;profilować

grade crossing ('grejd'krosyng) s. skrzyżowanie dróg; przejazd przez tory(jedno poziomowe)

grade school('grejd'sku:l) s. szkoła podstawowa

gradient ('grejdjent) s. nachylenie; stopień nachylenia

gradual ('graedżuel) adj. stopniowy;po trochu

graduate ('graedżuejt) s. absolwent; v. stopniować; ukończyć studia;adj. podyplomowy(kurs)

graduation ('graedżu'ejszyn) s. ukończenie wyższych studiów; stopniowanie;cechowanie;podział

graft (gra:ft) v. szczepić; dawać łapówkę; przeszczepiać; s. szczepienie; łapówka; przeszczep;szufla(pełna ziemi)

grain (grejn) s. ziarno; zboże; odrobina; grań; włókno; słój; v. granulować; ziarnować

gram (graem) s. gram ;1/28uncji

grammar ('graemer) s. gramatyka

grammar school ('graemer,sku:l) s. szkoła podstawowa

grammatical (gre'maetykel) adj. gramatyczny (poprawny)

gramme (graem) s. gram (ang.)

gramophone ('graemefoun) s. patefon; gramofon

grand (graend) adj. wielki; główny; wspaniały; świetny; okazały; (slang):1000 dolarów;całkowity

grandchild ('graen,chajld) s. wnuk

granddaughter ('graen,do:ter) s. wnuczka

grandeur ('graendżer) s. wielkość; dostojność; okazałość; wspaniałość;majestat;blask;pompa

grandfather ('graend,fa:dzer)s. dziadek

grandma ('graenma:) s. babcia

grandmother ('graen,madzer) s. babka

grandpa ('graenpa:) s. dziadzio

grandparents ('graen,pearents) pl. dziadkowie

grandson ('graensan) s. wnuk

grandstand ('graenstaend) s. główna trybuna;popisywać się

granny ('graeny) s. babunia

grant (gra:nt) v. nadawać; udzielać; uznawać; zgadzać się na; przekazywać; s.pomoc; przekazanie tytułu własności;darowizna

granulated ('graenjulejtyd) adj. ziarnisty;rozdrobniony;granulowany

grape (grejp) s. winogrona

grapefruit ('grejp-fru:t) s. greipfrut(owoc lub drzewo)

grape-sugar ('grejp,szuger) s. cukier gronowy

grapevine ('grejp-wajn) s. winorośl; poczta pantoflowa; szeptanka; źródło kaczek prasowych

graph (fraef) s. wykres; krzywa

graphic ('graefyk) adj. graficzny; plastyczny; obrazowy(dosadny)

grasp (gra:sp) v. łapać; chwytać; pojmać; pojmować; dzierżyć; s. chwyt; uchwyt; pojęcie; panowanie;zrozumienie;kontrola

grass (gra:s) s. trawa; (slang): marijuana; "pot";haszysz

grasshopper ('gra:s,hoper) s.
konik polny(z czterema skrzydłami)
grass widower ('gra:s,łydouer)
s. słomiany wdowiec

grate (grejt) s. krata; ruszt;
v. trzec; ucierac; zgrzytac;
skrzypiec;irytowac;byc irytujacym

grateful ('grejtful) adj.
wdzięczny:dobrze widziany

grater ('grejter) s. tarko;
tarło;raszpla;tarnik do drzewa

gratification (,graetyfy'kejszyn)
s. zaspokojenie; wynagrodzenie; gratyfikacja;łapówka

gratify ('graetyfaj) v. dogadzac; uprzyjemniac; zadawalac;
przekupywac·wynagradzac

grating ('grejtyŋg) s. krata;
adj. zgrzytliwy; ochrypły

gratis ('grejtys) adv. gratis;
bezpłatnie; adj. bezpłatny;
gratisowy ;darmowy

gratitude ('graetytju:d) s.
wdzięcznosc(za pomoc etc.)

gratuitous (gre'tjuites) adj.
bezpłatny; niepotrzebny

gratuity (gre'tjuity) s. napiwek: zasiłek przy zwolnieniu

grave ('grejw) s. grob; adj.
poważny; v. wyryc; wryc;wykopac

gravel ('grawel) s. żwir; piasek;v.psypywac żwirem: kłopotac

graveyard ('grejwja:rd) s. cmentarz; nocna zmiana w pracy

gravitation (,graewy'tejszyn)
s. ciążenie(ciał);grawitacja

gravity ('graewyty) s. siła
ciężkosci; ciężkosc; powaga
(np. sytuacji);ciężar(gatunkowy)

gravy ('grejwy) s. sos mięsny;
sok;dodatkowy zysk;osobista ko-
gray (grej) adj. szary; zob.
grey ;v.szarzec;s.szary kolor

graze (grejz) v. pasc; drasnac;
s. drasnięcie muśnięcie;odarcie

grazing land ('grejzyŋg,laend)
s. pastwisko; pastwiska

grease (gri:s) s. tłuszcz; smar;
v. brudzic; smarowac; nasmaro-
wac smarem(samochod etc.)

grease gun ('gri:s,gan) s. sma-
rownica wyciskowa ;towotnica

greasy('gri:sy)adj.tłusty;śliski

great (grjet) adj. wielki; duży; swietny; znakomity; wspaniały;zamiłowany;doniosły;pra-

greatcoat ('grejt'kout) s.
palto; płaszcz;opoŕcza

great grandchild ('grejt'graend-
czajld) s. prawnuk

great grandfather ('grejt'-
graendfa:dzer) s. pradziadek

great grandmother ('grejt'-
grand,madzer) s. prababka

greatness ('grejtnys) s. wielkosc; ogrom;wielkodusznosc;powaga

greed (gri:d) s. chciwosc; za-
chłannosc;żądza(władzy etc)

greedy (gri:dy) adj. chciwy;
zachłanny; łakomy; łapczywy;
żądny:zarłoczny;spragniony

Greek adj. grecki; (niezrozumiały):s.język grecki;Grek

green (gri:n) adj. zielony;
naiwny; młody; niedoswiadczo-
ny; świeży; s. zielen; zieleni-
na; trawnik;v.zielenic;naciągac

greenback ('gri:nbaek) s.
(slang) dolar(banknot)

greenhorn ('gri:nhorn) s. nowicjusz ;zołtodziub

greenhouse ('gri:nhaus) s.
cieplarnia

greenish ('gri:nysh) adj. zie-
lonkawy

greet ('gri:t) v. kłaniac się;
pozdrawiac; ukazac się; dojsc
do (uszu);zaprezentowac się

greeting ('gri:tyŋg)s. pozdrowienie; powitanie;pozdrowienia

grew (gru:) zob. grow

grey (grej) adj. szary; siwy;
s. szarosc; v. szarzec; si-
wiec(ortografia brytyjska)

greyhound ('grejhaund) s.
chart(wysoki;chudy,szybki,pies)

grid (gryd) s. krata; siec;
siatka;siec wysokiego napięcia

grief (gri:f) s. zmartwienie;
zgryzota ;smutek;żal

grievance ('gri:wens) s. uraza;
krzywda; skarga; zażalenie

grieve (gri:w) v. martwic;
krzywdzic; smucic ;zasmucic

grievious ('gri:wes) adj. dre-
czący; przykry ;ciężki;smutny

grill (gryl) s. rożen; krata;
potrawa z rusztu; v. smażyć
na różnie; przesłuchiwać
grim (grym) adj. srogi; ponury;
okrutny;groźny;odrażający
grimace (gri'mejs) s. grymas;
v. grymasić
grime (grajm) s. brud; v. bru-
dzić(sadzą, smarem etc.)
grimy ('grajmy) adj. brudny;
wysmarowany; zatłuszczony
grin (gryn) v. szczerzyć zęby;
uśmiechać się; s. uśmiech
grind; ground; ground (grajnd;
graund; graund)
grind (grajnd) v. ostrzyć; toczyć; mleć; zgrzytać; trzeć;
harować; s. mlenie; harówka;
kujon;ciężka rutyna;kucie się
grindstone ('grajnd,stoun) s.
kamień szlifierski:harówka
grip (gryp) s. uchwyt; trzonek;
rękojeść; uścisk dłoni;walizka;
v. chwycić; złapać; trzymać
gripes (grajps) pl. kolka
gristle ('grysl) s. chrząstka
grit (gryt) s. żwir; piasek;
odwaga; wytrzymałość;charakter;
v. zgrzytać; skrzypieć;posypy-
wać
groan (groun) s. jęk; v. jęczeć
grocer ('grouser) s. właściciel
sklepu spożywczego
groceries ('grouserys) pl. towary spożywcze
grocery ('grousery) s. sklep
spożywczy;artykuł spożywczy
groin (grain) s. pachwina
groom (grum) s, parobek; pan
młody; v. obrządzać: przygotowywać do objęcia stanowiska
groove (gru:w) s. bruzda; rowek; rutyna; v. żłobić; rowkować;nacinać zwojnik;gwintować
grope (group) v. szukać po omacku; iść po omacku;iść na ślepo
gross (grous) adj. gruby; ordynarny; prostacki; całkowity;
hurtowy; tłusty; niesmaczny;
spasły;wybujały; s. 12 tuzi-
nów; v. uzyskać brutto...
ground (graund) s. grunt;zie-
mia; podstawa; podłoże; teren;
dno(morza);osad;powod:przyczyna

dno; v. l. osiąść na mieliźnie;
uziemiać; gruntować; zagrunto-
wać; v. 2. zob. grind
ground control ('graund,ken'troul)
kontrolna stacja (lotów)
ground crew ('graund.kru:) s.
załoga, ekipa na ziemi
ground floor ('graund,flo:r) s.
parter(bliski poziomu gruntu)
ground glass ('graund,glas) s.
tłuczone szkło
groundhog ('graundhog) s. świstak (amerykański)
groundless ('graundlys) adj.
bezpodstawny;gołosłowny
groundnut ('graundnat) s. orzeszek ziemny
ground staff ('graund,staf) s.
personel naziemny(lotnictwa etc.)
groundwork ('graundłerk) s. podstawa; podłoże; zasada; fundament;tło;osnowa;kanwa(utworu)
group (gru:p) s. grupa; v. grupować;rozsegregowywać na grupy
grove (grouw) s. gaj
grow; grew; grown(grou; gru:
groun)
grow (grou) v. rosnąć; stawać
się; dojrzewać; hodować; sadzić
growl (graul) s. ryk; pomruk;
warczenie; v. mruknąć; warknąć;
burczeć; warczeć; odburknąć;
gderać;mrukliwie odpowiadać
grown (groun) v. zob. grow
grown-up ('groun,ap) adj. dorosły; s. dorosły człowiek
growth (grouq) s. rozwój; wzrost;
uprawa; narośl;porost;przyrost
grub (grab) .v karczować; dłubać: harować; wcinać (jedzenie)
grubby (graby) adj. brudny;
niechlujny;robaczywy
grudge (gradż) v. żałować; skąpić; zazdrościć; mieć niechęć;
s. żal; uraza; niechęć
gruel (gruel) s. kaszka; kleik;
v. wymęczyć ;zadawać bobu(komuś)
gruesome ('gru:sem) adj. okropny
gruff (graf) adj. burkliwy;
gburowaty; ochrypły;gruby(głos)
grumble ('grambl) v. narzekać;
utyskiwać;gderać;skarżyć się;
s.narzekanie; pomruk;szemranie

grumbler (grambler) s. zrzęda
grunt (grant) s. kwik; v. kwi-
czeć;chrząkać;wymruczeć
guarantee (,gaeren'ti:) v.
gwarantować; poręczać; s. poręczyciel;poręka;rękojmia
guarantor (,gaeren'to:r) s.
poręczyciel; poręczycielka
guaranty (,gaerenty) s. gwarancja; poręka;rękojmia;poręczenie
guard (ga:rd) v. pilnować;chro-
nić; s. strażnik; opiekun;
obrońca; bezpiecznik
guard against ('ga:rd.e'genst)
v. zabezpieczać się przed...
guardhouse ('ga:rdhaus) s.
wartownia;tymczasowy areszt
guardian ('ga:rdjen) s. opiekun; kustosz;adj.opiekuńczy
guardianship ('ga:rdjenshyp)s.
opieka; opiekuństwo; kuratela
guess (ges) v. zgadywać; przypuszczać; myśleć; s. zgadywa-
nie; przypuszczenie;zgadnięcie
guest (gest) s. gość
guest house ('gesthaus) s. pensjonat; osobny domek dla gości
guest room ('gestru:m) s. pokój gościnny;gościnna sypialnia
guidance ('gajdens) s. kierownictwo; poradnictwo;kierowanie
guide (gajd) s. przewodnik;
doradca;v.wskazywać drogę;prowa-
dzić
guidebook ('gajdbuk) s. przewodnik (książka)dla turystów
guild (gyld) s. cech; związek
guildhall('gyld'ho:l) s. dom
cechowy; ratusz;dom związkowy
guile (gajl) s. oszustwo
guileless ('gajllys) adj.
szczery; otwarty(w postępowaniu)
guilt (gylt) s. wina;przestęp-
stwo
guiltless ('gyltlys) adj. niewinny;wolny od zarzutu
guilty ('gylty) adj. winny
guinea pig ('gynypyg) s. świnka morska;przedmiot experymen-
tów
guitar (gy'ta:r) s. gitara
gulf (galf) s. zatoka; przepaść; wir; v. pochłaniać
gull (gal) s. mewa;v.oszukiwać
gullet (galyt) s. przełyk; gardło; gardziel

gully ('galy) s. wąwóz; ściek;
kanał; v. żłobić;wyżłobić;poryć
gulp (galp) s. łyk; duży kęs
gulp down (galpdałn) v. łykać;
dławić się; hamować łzy
gum (gam) s. dziąsło; guma;
v. kleić;wydzielać żywicę
gun (gan) s. strzelba; armata;
pistolet;działo;wystrzał armatni
gunpowder ('gan,pałder) s. proch
strzelniczy;proch armatni
gurgle ('ge:rgle) v. bulgotać;
bełkotać;sbulgotanie;szemranie
gush (gasz) s. ulewa; wylew;
v. tryskać; lać się;wytrysnąć
gust (gast) s. podmuch; wybuch
gut (gat) s. kiszka; v. patroszyć ;wypalić wnętrze (domu)
guts (gats) pl. wnętrzności
gutter ('gater) v. wyżłobić;
okapywać; s. rynna; rynsztok;
rów; wyżłobienie; adj. ryn-
sztokowy; brukowy(dziennik)
guy (gaj) s. facet; człek; cuma; v. cumować; uwiązać
gym (dżym) s. sala gimnastyczna;
gimnastyka(przedmiot w szkole)
gymnasium (dżym'nejzjem) s. sala gimnastyczna;hala sportowa
gymnastics (dżym'naestyks) s.
gimnastyka;ćwiczenia fizyczne
gynecologist (,gajny'koledżyst)
s. ginekolog
gypsy ('dżypsy) s. cygan; cy-
ganka;cyganeria;język cygański
gyrate (,dżaje'rejt) v. wirować;
kręcić się(wg.koła lub spirali)
h (ejcz) ósma litera angielskiego alfabetu (prawie niema)
haberdasher ('haeberdaeszer) s.
kupiec galanteryjny;szmuklerz
habit ('haebyt) s. zwyczaj; nałóg; usposobienie; przyzwyczajenie; habit; v. odziewać się
habitation (,haeby'tejszyn) s.
miejsce zamieszkania;zamieszkiwa-
nie
habitual (he'bytjual) adj.
zwykły; nałogowy; zwyczajny
hack (haek) v. siekać; rąbać;
kopać; kaszleć; s. szrama; motyka; szkapa; najemnik; taksówka; adj. wynajęty; spowszednia-
ły; banalny;oklepany;szablonowy

hacksaw ('haekso:) s. piła do
metalu (z drobnymi zębami)

had (haed) zob. have

haddock ('haedek) s. łupacz

h(a)emorrhage ('hemerydż) s.
krwotok;v. mieć krwotok

hag (haeg) s. wiedźma; czarownica;brzydka zła kobieta

haggard ('haegerd) adj. wynędz-
niały; strapiony; wychudły

hail (hejl) s. grad;,powitanie;
v. grad pada; witać; pozdrawiać; zawołać;walić jak gradem

hair (heer) s. włos; włosy

hairbrush ('heerbrasz) s.
szczotka do włosów

haircut ('heerkat) s. ostrzyże-
nie;styl strzyżenia włosów

hairdo ('heerdu:) s. uczesanie;
fryzura;styl uczesania

hairdresser ('heer,dreser) s.
fryzjer damski

hairdryer ('heer,drajer) s. suszarka do włosów(elektryczna)

hairless ('h-erlys) adj. bez-
włosy; łysy;wyłysiały

hairpin ('heerpyn) s. szpilka
do włosów

hairy (heery) adj. włochaty

half (ha:f) s. połowa; adj.pół;
adv. na pół; po połowie

half an hour ('ha:f,en'aur) s.
pół godziny

half brother ('ha:f,bradzer)
s. przyrodni brat

half-breed ('ha:f,bri:d) s.
mieszaniec

halftime ('ha:f'tajm) s. przerwa; pół etatu;a.pół-etatowy

halfway ('ha:f'łej) adv. w pół
drogi; w połowie drogi

hall, (ho:l) s. sień; sala; hala;
dwór; gmach publiczny;westybul

hallo ! (he'lou) excl.;czesc !
halo ! czolem! dzień dobry!

halo ('hejlou) s. nimb; aureola

halt (ho:lt) v. zatrzymać; utykać; kulec; wahać się; s.po-
stój; przystanek;utykanie

halter ('ho:lter) s. kantar pa-
stewny; stryczek;v.nakładać kan-

halve (ha:w) v. przepołowić;po
dzielić się po połowie

ham (haem) s. szynka

hamburger ('haembe:rger) s. sie-
kany kotlet wołowy; bułka z
siekanym kotletem wołowym

hamlet ('haemlyt) s. wioska;
sioło; malutka wieś

hammer ('haemer) s. młotek;
v. bić młotkiem; walić

hammock ('haemok) s. hamak

hamper ('haemper) v. zawadzać;
krępować; s. kosz z wiekiem

hamster ('haemster) s. chomik

hand (haend) s. ręka; dłoń;
pismo; v. podać; zwijać; pomagać;a.podręczny;przenośny

hand back ('haend,baek) v. oddać; podać do tyłu

hand down ('haend,dałn) v. przekazać; dać w spadku;podać w dół

hand in ('haend,yn) v. wręczyc

hand over ('haend,ouwer) v.,
wręczyć; podać; dostarczyć

handbag ('haendbaeg) s. damska
torebka

handbill ('haendbyl) s. ulotka

handbook ('haend-buk) s. podręcznik; poradnik

hand brake ('haend,brejk) s.
hamulec ręczny

handcuff ('haendka:f) s. kajdany; v. zakuwać w kajdany

handful ('haendful) s. garść;
garstka; kłopotliwa osoba

handicap ('haendykaep) s. przeszkoda; upośledzenie; trudność

handicraft ('haendykra:ft) s.
rzemiosło; rękodzieło (tkactwo
etc.)

handkerchief ('henkerczy:f) s.
apaszka; chustka do nosa

handle ('haendl) s. trzonek;
rękojeść; uchwyt; sposób;
v. dotykać; manipulować; traktować; załatwiać; dać radę;
handlować;zarządzać;kontrolować

handlebar ('haendlba:r) s. kie-
rownica(od roweru)

hand luggage ('haend,lagydż) s.
bagaż ręczny

handmade ('haend'mejd) adj.
ręcznie zrobiony

handrail ('haend,rejl) s. poręcz; bariera;balustrada

handshake ('haend,shejk) s. uścisk dłoni(w pozdrowieniu,także) laky) adj. beztroski

handsome ('haensem) s. przystojny; szczodry;znaczny(datek)

handwork ('haend,że:rk) s. robota ręczna;praca fizyczna

handwriting ('haend,rajtyŋg) s. pismo; charakter pisma

handy ('haendy) adj. zręczny; wygodny; bliski;pod ręką

hang; hung; hung (haeŋg; haŋg; haŋg)

hang (haeŋg) s. wieszać; powiesić; rozwiesić; wywiesić; zwisać; s. nachylenie; pochyłość;powiązanie;orientacja

hang around ('haeŋg e'raund) v. wałęsać się;obijać się

hang out ('haeŋg'aut) v. wywieszać; wychylać się

hang up ('haeŋg,ap) v. zaczepić się; powiesić słuchawkę; opóźniać (pracę);wstrzymywać

hangar ('haeŋger) s. hangar

hang-glider ('haeŋg'glajder) s. lotnia; skrzydło Rogali

hangings ('haeŋyŋz) s. kotary, portiery;draperie;obicia;firanki

hang loose ('haeŋ,lu:z) v. być rozluźniony w akcji (sportowej); zwisać swobodnie

hangover ('haeŋg,ouwer) s. (slang) kac; przeżytek

hanky-panky ('haeŋky²paenky) s. hokus-pokus;też rozwiązłość

haphazard ('haep'haezerd) s. los szczęścia; przypadek; adj. przypadkowy; doryczwy; adv. przypadkowo;na chybił,trafił

happen ('haepen) v. zdarzać się; trafić się; przypadkowo być (gdzieś);mieć(nie)szczęście

happen on ('haepen,on) v. przypadkiem spotkać;natknąć się na

happening ('haepenyŋg) s. wydarzenie; wypadek;zdarzenie

happily ('haepyly) adv. szczęśliwie;na szczęście;trafnie

happiness ('haepynys) s. szczęście; zadowolenie; radość

happy ('haepy) adj. szczęśliwy; zadowolony;właściwy (wybór); mądra (rada); radosny

happy-go-lucky ('haepy,gou²laky) adj. beztroski

harass ('haeres) v. niepokoić; trapić; dręczyć; nękać

harbor ('ha:rber) s. przystań; port; v. gościć; dawać schronienie; zawijać do portu

hard (ha:rd) adj. twardy; surowy; trudny; ciężki; ostry; adv. usilnie; wytrwale; ciężko; z trudem; siarczyście

hard by ('ha:rd,baj) adv. blisko;tuż obok; w pobliżu

hard up ('ha:rd,ap) być w kłopotach pieniężnych

hard of hearing (ha:rd,ow'-hieryŋg) adj. głuchawy

harden ('ha:rdn) v. twardnieć; uodpornić; stabilizować

hardheaded ('ha:rd'hedyd) adj. trzeźwy; praktyczny;twardy człowiek

hardhearted ('ha:rd'ha:rtyd) adj. nieczuły; niemiłosierny

hardly ('ha:rdly) adv. ledwie; zaledwie; prawie; z trudem; surowo;chyba nie; rzadko

hardness ('ha:rdnys) s. twardość; wytrzymałość;odporność

hardship ('ha:rdszyp) s. trudność; trudy; męka; znój

hardware ('ha:rdżeer) s. wyroby żelazne;towary żelazne

hare (heer) s. zając;królik

harebell ('heer-bel) s. dzwonek okrągłolistny

hark (ha:rk) v. słuchaj; uważaj; odejdź;słuchaj uważnie

harm (ha:rm) s. szkoda; krzywda; v. szkodzić; krzywdzić

harmful ('ha:rmful) adj. szkodliwy;szkodzący;zadający ból

harmless ('ha:rmlys) adj. nieszkodliwy; niewinny

harmonious (ha:rmounjes) adj. harmonijny;melodyjny;zgodny

harmonize ('ha:rmenajz) s. uzgadniać; harmonizować

harmony ('ha:rmeny) s. harmonia (dźwięków,ludzi);zgoda

harness ('ha:rnys) s. uprząż; v. zaprzęgać:zużytkować(wiatr...)

harp (ha:rp) s. harfa; v. gadać w kółko; grać na harfie

harpoon (ha:'rpu:n) s. harpun;
v. ugodzić harpunem

harrow ('haerou) s, brona; v.
bronować; dręczyć; szarpać;
ranić; pustoszyć; niszczyć

harsh (ha:rsz) adj. szorstki;
żrący; ostry; cierpki; przykry; surowy;nieprzyjemny

hart (ha:rt) s. rogacz (dorosły)(powyżej pięcioletni)

harvest('ha:rwyst) s. żniwa;
zbiory; zbiór; urodzaj; plony; v. zbierać (zboże); zbierać (plony);sprzątać z pól

harvester ('ha:rwyter) s. żniwiarz; żniwiarka (mechaniczna)

has (haez) (on,ona.ono) ma;
zob. have

hash (haesz) s. siekane mięso;
v. siekać;knocić;przemieszać

haste (hejst) s. pospiech

hasten (hejstn) v.przyspieszać;
spieszyć;być szybkim

hasty ('hejsty) adj. pospieszny; prędki; porywczy;niecier-
pliwy

hat (haet) s. kapelusz

hatch (haecz) v. wysiadywać;
wylęgać; wykłuwać; knuć; za-
kreskować; s. wyląg; łuk;
drzwiczki; sluza; kreska

hatchet ('haeczyt) s. toporek

hatchet man('haeczyt,men) s.
człowiek przeprowadzający bote
czystkę(odrabiający brudną ro-

hate (hejt) s. nienawisc;
v. nienawidzieć;nieznosić

hateful ('hejtful) adj. nienawistny;zasługujący na nienawiść

hatred ('hejtryd) s. nienawiść

haughtiness ('ho:tynys) s.pysz-
ność; hardość;zarozumialstwo

haughty ('ho:ty) adj. hardy;
pyszny;zarozumiały;wzgardliwy

haul (ho:l) s. wleczenie; holowanie; ładunek; połów; zysk;
v. wlec; ciągnąć; holować;
wozić; transportować;taszczyć

haunch (ho:ncz) s. biodro z udem

haunt (ho:nt) v. nawiedzać,
s, miejsce często odwiedzane;
melina; spelunka;legowisko

have; had; had (haew; haed;
haed)

have (haew) v. mieć; otrzymać;
zawierać; nabyć; musieć

have-not ('haev,nat) adj. nie-
posiadający; biedny

have on ('haew on) v. mieć na
sobie;być ubranym w

have to do ('haew,tu'du) v. musieć (coś) robić

haven ('hejwn) s. przystań; port;
v. dawać schronienie; wprowadzać do portu

havoc ('haewek) s. spustoszenie

hawk (ho:k) s. jastrząb; packa;
chrząknięcie; v. polować
z jastrzębiem; sprzedawać na
ulicy; chrząkać głosno

hawthorn ('ho:torn) s. głóg

hay (hej) s. siano

haycock ('hejkok) s. stóg siana

hayfever ('hej'fi:ver) s. uczu-
lenie; katar sienny

hayloft ('hej-loft) s. strych
na siano (w stodole etc.)

hayrick ('hejryk) s. stóg siana

haystack ('hejsta:k) s. stóg
siana (w polu, na łące etc.)

hazard ('haezerd) s. przypadek;
traf; ryzyko; v. ryzykować

hazardous ('haezerdes) adj. ryzykowny; hazardowny; niebezpieczny

haze (hejz) s. lekka mgła

hazel ('hejzl) s. leszczyna;
kolor orzechowy

hazel-nut ('hejzl-nat) s. orzech
laskowy

hazy ('hejzy) adj. mglisty;
zamglony; nieco podchmielony

H-bomb ('ejcz bom) s. bomba wodorowa

he (hi:) pron. on

head (hed) s. głowa; łeb; szef;
naczelnik; nagłowek; szczyt;
v. prowadzić; kierować (się)

head over heels ('hed,ouwer'-
hi:ls) do góry nogami; na łeb
na szyję; panicznie;w panice

head or tail ('hed,o:r'tejl)
orzeł czy reszka

headache ('hedejk) s. ból głowy

headgear ('hedgi:r) s. nakrycie głowy;ubiór głowy

heading ('hedyŋg) s. nagłówek

headland ('hedlend) s. przylądek (daleko wysunięty w morze)

headlights ('hedlajts) pl. główne światła samochodu

headline ('hedlajn) s. nagłówek (w gazecie);wiadomość w skrócie

headlong ('hedloŋg) adv. na łeb na szyję; na złamanie karku; na oślep;głową na przód

headmaster ('hedma:ster) s. dyrektor (szkoły)

headphones ('hedfouns) pl. słuchawki(radiowe,gramofonowe)

headquarters ('hed'kło:terz) pl. kwatera główna;główne biuro

headstrong ('hedstroŋg) adj. zawzięty; uparty;bezwzględny

headway ('hedłej) s. postęp

heal (hi:l) v. leczyć; łagodzić; uspakajać;wyleczać się

heal up ('hi:l,ap) v. zagoić

health (hels) s. zdrowie

health resort (hels ry'zo:rt) s. uzdrowisko

healthy (helsy) adj. zdrowy; potężny;spowodowany zdrowiem

heap (hi:p) s. kupa; gromada; v. ładować na stos; obsypywać dużą ilością

hear; heard; heard (hier; he:rd; he:rd)

hear (hier) v. słyszeć; usłyszeć; słuchać; dowiedzieć się

heard (he:rd) zob. hear

hearing ('hieryŋg)s. słuch; posłuch; przesłuchanie; rozprawa;zasięg głosu;słyszenie

hearsay ('hiersej) s. pogłoska

hearse (he:rs) s. karawan

heart (ha:rt) s. serce; odwaga; otucha; sedno;symbol serca

heartbreaking ('ha:rtbrejkyŋg) adj. rozdzierający serce

heartburn ('ha:rtbe:rn) s. zgaga; pieczenie w żołądku

hearth (ha:rs) s. palenisko

heartless ('ha:rtlys) adj. nieczuły; bez serca

heart transplant ('ha:rt,traens¹pla:nt) przeszczepienie serca

hearty ('ha:rty) adj. serdeczny; szczery; otwarty;pożywny;obfity; solidny;dobry;krzepki;rześki

heat (hi:t) s. gorąco; upał; żar; ciepło; uniesienie; pasja; popęd płciowy (zwierząt)

heater ('hi:ter) s. grzejnik; piec

heath (hi:s) s. wrzos; wrzosiec; wrzosowisko

heathen ('hi:zen) adj. pogański; s. poganin. ciemniak

heather ('hedzer) s. wrzos

heating ('hi:tyŋg) s. ogrzewanie

heave; hove; hove (hi:w; houw; houw)

heave (hi:w) v. unosić; dźwigać; podważać; nabrzmiewać; wyciągać; sapać; s. dźwignięcie; przesunięcie

heaven ('hewn) s. niebo; raj; niebiosa

heavenly ('hewnly) adj. niebieski; niebiański; boski

heaviness ('hewynys) s. ciężkość; ocieżałość

heavy ('hewy) adj. ciężki; duży; ponury; zrozpaczony

heavy-handed ('hewy'haendyd) adj. niezgrabny; nietaktowny; bezwzględny

heavy traffic ('hewy'traefyk) ciężki ruch (np. kołowy)

heavyweight ('hewyłejt) s. waga ciężka

hectic ('hektyk) adj. gorący; dziki; niszczący; rozgorączkowany

hedge (hedż) s. płot; żywopłot; ogrodzenie; zapora; ubezpieczenie; v. ogradzać; wykręcać się; ubezpieczać się w spekulacji

hedgehog ('hedżhog) s. jeż; świnka morska

heed (hi:d) v. s. troska; dbałość; uwaga; wzgląd; ostrożność; v. uważać; baczyć

heedful ('hi:dful) adj. uważny; ostrożny

heedless ('hi:dlys) adj. niedbały; nieostrożny; nieuważny

heel (hi:l) s. pięta; obcas; przechył; lajdak; v.dotykać piętą; podbijać obcas;zaopatrywać; przechylać się;tupać obcasem

he goat ('hi:gout) s. kozioł
heifer ('hefer) s. jałówka
height (hajt) s. wysokość;
wzniesienie; wyniosłość;
szczyt;najwyższa granica
heighten (hajtn) v. podnosić,
podwyższać;powiększać etc.
heinous ('hejnes) adj. potworny; ohydny;nienawistny;haniebny
heir (eer) s. spadkobierca;
dziedzic; następca
heiress ('eerys) s. spadkobier-
czyni; następczyni; dziedzicz-
ka (majatku, tytułu etc.)
held (held) zob. hold
helicopter ('helykopter) s.
śmigłowiec; helikopter
hell (hel) s. piekło; psiakrew ! miejsce nędzy i okrucieństwa
hello ('he'lou) excl.: hallo !
helm (helm) s. ster;v.sterować
helmet ('helmyt) s. hełm; kask
help (help) v. pomagać; usługiwac; nakładać (jedzenie)
s. pomoc; pomocnik; robotnik
helper ('helper) s. pomocnik
helpful ('helpful) adj. pomocny; przydatny; użyteczny
helping ('helpyng) s. porcja
(jedzenia);udzielanie pomocy
helpless ('helplys) adj. bezradny; bez pomocy ;słaby
helplessness ('helplysnys) s.
bezradność ;słabość
helter-skelter ('helter'skelter)
adv. na łapu-capu; na łeb na
szyję; s. popłoch; bezładny
pośpiech(w bałaganie)
hem (hem) s. brzeg; obrąbek;
chrząkanie; v. obrębiać; otoczyć; pochrząkiwać; wahać się
hem in ('hem,yn) v. okrążyć;
zamknąć; obrębić
hemisphere ('hemysfier) s. półkula (zachodnia,wschodnia etc.)
hemline ('hemlajn) s. obrąbek
(spódnicy)
hemlock ('hemlek) s. szalej;
cykuta jadowita; drzewo tsuga
hemp (hemp) s. konopie; adj.
konopny (sznur etc.)
hemstitch ('hemstycz) s. mereż-
ka; v. mereżkować (ozdobnie)

hen (hen) s. kura; kwoka; baba
hence (hens) adv. stąd; odtąd;
a więc; przeto; dlatego
henceforth (hens'fo:rs) adv.
odtąd; na przyszłość;od teraz
hen coop ('henku:p) s. kurnik
hen house ('henhaus) s, kurnik
henpecked ('henpekt) s. pantoflarz;adj.będący pod pantoflen
her (he:r) pron. ją; jej; adj.
jej (należący)do niej
herald ('hereld) s. zwiastun;
v. zwiastować; wprowadzać
heraldry ('hereldry) s. heral-
dyka;pompa; ceremonia
herb (he:rb) s. zioło (jednoroczne)
herd (he:rd) s. trzoda; stado;
pastuch; v. iść stadem;zganiać
w stado; paść;popędzać stadem
herdsman ('he:rdzmen) s. pasterz; pastuch
here (hier) adv. tu; tutaj; oto
here you are (,hier'ju:,a:r)
exp.: tu pan ma ! proszę bardzo !
hereafter ('hier'a:fter) adv.
odtąd; poniżej; potem; w życiu pozagrobowym; s, przyszłość; przyszłe życie
hereby ('hier'bay) adv. przez
to; w ten sposób; skutkiem
tego; w pobliżu
hereditary (hy'redytery) adj.
dziedziczny; odziedziczony;
tradycyjny;przekazany dziedzicznie
herein ('hie'ryn) adv. tutaj;
tam że; wobec tego; w tych
warunkach,w tym(rozdziale etc.)
hereof ('hier'ow) adv. tego;
o tym ;w odniesieniu do tego
heresy ('herysy) s. herezja
hereupon ('hiere'pon) adv.
potem; skutkiem tego; o tym
herewith ('hier'łys) adv. ni-
niejszym ;w ten sposób
heritage ('herytydż) s. spuści-
na; spadek; dziedzictwo
hermit ('he:rmyt) s. pustelnik;
odludek;eremita;pustelnica
hero ('hierou) s. bohater
heroic ('hierouyk) adj. bohaterski ;heroiczny;epiczny; bardzo wymowny; podniosły

heroine ('hierouyn) s.bohaterka
heroism ('hierouyzem) s.
bohaterstwo (w czynach i ce-
chach)
heron ('heren) s. czapla
herring ('heryŋg)s. śledź
hers (he:rz) pron. jej
herself (he:r'self) pron. ona
sama; ona sobie; ja sama
hesitate ('hezytejt) v. wahać
się ;byc niepewnym;zatrzymać
się
hesitation (,hezytejszyn) s.
wahanie;być niezdecydowanym
hew; hewed; hewn (hju:; hju:d;
hju:n)
hew (hju:) v. rąbać; ciosac;
kuc; wyrąbywac(ścieżkę etc.)
hewn (hju:n) zob: hew
hey (hej) excl.: hej ! ej że!
heyday ('hejdej) s. pełnia;
rozkwit; świetny nastrój
hi (haj) excl.: hej ! (pozdrowienie) ' cześć! czołem!
hiccup; hiccough ('hykap)
czkawka; v. miec czkawkę
hid (hyd) zob. hide
hidden (hydn) zob. hide
hide; hid; hidden (hajd; hyd;
hydn)
hide (hajd) v. chować; ukrywać;
s. kryjowka; skora (zwierzęca)
hide-and-seek ('hajd,en si:k)
exp.: zabawa w chowanego
hideous ('hydjes) adj. ochydny;
wstrętny ;paskudny;odrażający
hiding ('hajdyŋg)s. kryjówka;
skorobicie ; lanie;manto
hiding place ('hajdyŋg'plejs)
s. kryjówka; melina
hi-fi ('haj'faj) = high-fideli-
ty ('haj fy'delyty) wiernie
odtwarzający dźwięk (aparat)
high (haj) adj. wysoki; wyniosły; silny;cienki(głos)
highbrow ('hajbrau) s. intelektualista;a. intelektualny
high diving('hajdajwyŋg) s.
skakanie z wieży do wody
high jump('hajdżamp) s. skok
wzwyż (w sporcie)
highlands ('hajlend) s. pod-
górze; góry;górzysty kraj
highlights ('hajlajts) pl. głow-
ne punkty (np. programu)

highly ('hajly) adv. wysoko; wysoce; wielce; zaszczytnie
highness ('hajnys) s. wysokość
(tytuł); wyniosłość
high-pitched ('haj'pyczt) adj.
wysoki; ostry; cienki (głos)
spadzisty; stromy (dach)
high-powered ('haj'pałerd) adj.
potężny
high-pressure ('haj'preszer)
adj. wysokiego cisnienia; na-
chalny
highroad ('haj'roud) s. szosa;
główna droga
high-school ('haj'sku:l) s.
gimnazjum; szkoła srednia
high-strung ('haj'strang)adj.
nerwowy; napięty; wrażliwy
high-tide ('haj'tajd) s. przypływ
highway ('haj'łej) s. szosa
highwayman ('haj,łejmen) s.
rozbójnik
hijack ('hajdżaek) v. rabować;
grabić
hike (hajk) v. włoczyć się;
wędrować; wyciągać do góry;
s. wycieczka; podwyżka
hilarious (hy'leerjes)adj.wesoły;
hałasliwie wesoły
hill (hyl) s. górka; pagórek;
kopiec; v. sypac kopiec
hillbilly ('hylbyly) s. pro-
wincjał
hillside ('hyl'sajd) s. stok
hilly ('hyly) adj. pagórkowaty;
górzysty
hilt (hylt) s. rękojeść; garda
him (hym) pron. jego; go; jemu;
mu
himself (hym'self) pron. się;
siebie; sobie; sam; osobiście;
we własnej osobie
hind (hajnd) s. parobek; łania;
adj. tylny; zadni
hinder ('hynder) v. przeszka-
dzac; powstrzymywac
hind leg ('hajnd,leg) s. tylna
noga
hindrance ('hyndrens) s. przeszkoda ; zawada;zawadzanie
hindsight('hajnd,sajt)s.zrozu-
mienie co trzeba było zrobić

hinge (hyndż) s. zawiasa; v.ob-
racać; zależec; zawiesić na
zawiasach;wisieć na zawiasach

hinny (hyny) s. muł (z oślicy
i ogiera)

hint (hynt) s. aluzja; przytyk;
wskazówka; v. napomknąć; dać
do zrozumienia;zrobić aluzję

hinterland ('hynter,laend) s.
zaplecze; daleki teren

hip (hyp) s. biodro; naroże
dachu; chandra;adj.biodrowy

hippie (hypi:) s. niekonformista; adj. zbuntowany przeciw
tradycji (wyobcowany)

hippopotamus (hype'potemes) s.
hipopotam

hire (hajer) s. najem; opłata
za najem; v. najmować; wynajmować; dzierżawić;odnajmować

hire out ('hajer aut) v. wynaj-
mować(się do pracy,na służbę...)

hire purchase ('hajer'pe:rczys)
wynajem - zakup na raty

his (hyz) pron. jego

hiss (hys) v. syczeć; gwizdać;
s. syk; gwizd;głoska sycząca

historian (hys'to:rjen) s.
historyk;historyczka

historic (hys'toryk) adj. histo-
ryczny;sławny w historii

history ('hystory) s. historia;
dzieje; przeszłość (znana)

hit (hyt) s. uderzenie; przytyk; sukces; sensacja; v. uderzyć; utrafić; natrafić; zabić

hit and run ('hyt,en'ran) adj.
uciekający od wypadku (drogowego); walczący podjazdowo;
dorywczy i niepewny

hitman ('hytmen) s. najemny
zabójca;najemny morderca

hit or miss (hyt o:r mys) adv.
na chybił trafił;przypadkiem

hit upon ('hyte'pon) v. natrafić (na coś,na kogoś)

hitch (hycz) s. zacisnięcie;
węzeł; przeszkoda; szarpnięcie;
uchwyt; służba (wojskowa)
v. doczepić; uczepić; pociągnąć; szarpnąć; przywiązać; za
czepić się;ciagnąć szarpiąc

hitchhike ('hycz,hajk) v. jechać autostopem

hitchhiker ('hycz,hajker) s.
jadący autostopem

hither ('hydzer) adv. dotąd,
tutaj;adj. bliżej

hitherto ('hydzer'tu:) adv.
dotychczas; do tej pory

hive (hajw) s. ul; rojowisko;
v. umieszczać w ulu; wchodzić
do ula;zbierać do ula

hoard (ho:rd),v. gromadzić;
zbierać; s. zapas. zbiór; skarb

hoarfrost ('ho: r'frost) s.
szron(na trawie,włosach etc.)

hoarse (ho:rs) adj. zachrypnięty; v. zachrypnąć;mieć chrapliwy
głos

hoax (houks) v. bujać; nabierać; s. bujda; kaczka;kawał

hobble ('hobl) s. pęta; utyka-
nie; v. utykać; kuleć; pętać

hobby ('hoby) s. hobby; pasja
(np. filatelistyka)

hobbyhorse ('hobyho:rs) s.
konik na kiju do zabawy(na biegunach)

hobgoblin ('hob,goblyn) s.
skrzat; chochlik

hobnob ('hobnob) v. być za pan
brat;blisko się zadawać

hobo('haubou) s. włóczęga

hock (hok) s. pęcina; v. zastawić (się) w lombardzie

hockey ('hoky) s. hokej

hoe (hou) s. motyka; graca;
v. gracować;okopywać motyką

hog (hog) s. wieprz; człowiek
zachłanny; v. łapać dla siebie; jechać środkiem; wyginać
łukowato w środku;zagarniać sobie

hoist (hojst) s. dzwig; wyciąg;
v. wyciagać ładunek w górę;
wywieszać(flagę);podciągać do góry

hold; held; held (hould; held;
held)

hold (hould) v. trzymać; posiadać; zawierać; powstrzymywać;
uważać; obchodzić; wytrzymywać; trwać; s. chwyt; pauza;
pomieszczenie; więzienie;
twierdza;silny wpływ;uchwyt

hold back ('hould,baek) v.
powstrzymać; zataić;wahać się

hold on ('hould,on) v. trzymać
się; wytrzymywać;powstrzymać
holdup ('hould'ap) s. zatrzymanie; zator; napad rabunkowy
holder ('houlder) s. właściciel; posiadacz; uchwyt
holding ('houldyng) s. posiadłość; portfel akcji; dzierżawa;uchwyt;ujęcie;trzymanie
hole (houl) s. dziura; nora;
dołek; v. dziurawić; przedziurawić;przekopywać(tunel)
holiday ('holedy) s. święto;
wakacje; urlop:adj.wesoły;ra-
holidaymaker ('holedy,mejker)
s. wczasowicz; letnik; turysta;wycieczkowicz;letniczka
holler ('holer) v. wrzeszczeć;
krzyczeć(po prostacku)
hollow ('holou) s. dziupla;
dziura; kotlina; dolina;
adj. wklęsły; dziurawy; fałszywy; głuchy; pusty; czczy;
głodny;nieszczery;adv.pusto
hollow out ('holou,aut) v.
drążyć;wydrążyć;żłobić
holly ('holy) s. ostrokrzew
holy ('holy) adj. święty
homage ('homydż) s. hołd
home (houm) s. dom; ojczyzna;
kraj; schronisko; bramka;
adj. domowy; rodzinny; krajowy; wewnętrzny; ojczysty
homeless ('houmlys) adj. bezdomny;bez dachu nad głowa
homely ('houmly) adj. swojski;
pospolity; nieładny; prosty;
skromny;niewybredny;niewyszu-
homemade ('houm'mejd) adj.
domowego wyrobu; krajowy
homesick ('houm-syk) adj.
stęskniony za domem rodzinnym;
stęskniony za (czymś swoim)
homesickness ('houm,syknys)
s. nostalgia;tesknota za domem
home team ('houm-ti:m) s. drużyna miejscowa (sportowa)
home trade ('houm-trejd) s.
handel wewnętrzny
homewards ('houm żedz) adv. ku
domowi (ojczyźnie);do domu

homework ('houmżerk) s. zadanie
domowe;odrabianie lekcji
homicide ('homy,sajd) s. zabójca; zabójstwo
honest ('onyst) adj. uczciwy;
prawy; przyzwoity; szczery;
adv. naprawdę
honesty ('onesty) s. zacność;
prawosć; rzetelność; uczciwość
honey ('hany) s. miod;słodycz
honeycomb ('hany,koum) s. (woskowy) plaster pszczeli;
v. dziurawić; przenikać
honeymoon ('hany,mu:n) s. miodowy miesiąc;v.spędzić miodowy miesiąc
honk (honk) s. krzyk gęsi; głos
trąbki, klaksonu; v. trąbić;
(slang; wymyślać)
honorary ('onerery) adj. honorowy (np. urząd);bezpłatny
honor ('oner) s. cześć; uczciwość; cnota; tytuł sędziego;
v. czcić; zaszczycać; honorować
honorable ('onerebl) adj. czcigodny; uczciwy; szanowny; honorowy; zaszczytny;poważany
hood (hud) s. kaptur; kapturek;
maska; buda; v. zaopatrywać
w kaptur; przykrywać
hoodlum ('hu:dlem) s. opryszek;
chuligan;łobuz
hoodwink ('hudżynk) v. oczy mydlić; zmylić;zawiązywać oczy
hoof ('hu:f) s. kopyto; v. kopać; iść; tańczyć;iść pieszo
hook (huk) s. hak; v. zahaczyć;
zakrzywić (sie);złapać (męża)
hoop (hu:p) s. obręcz; v. otaczać obręczą;wykrzyknąć
hooping cough ('hu:pyng-kof) s.
koklusz; krztusiec ,zob.uhooping-
cough
hoot (hu:t) s. hukanie; odgłosy
niezadowolenia; v. hukać; gwizdać; wyć; trąbić;wygwizdać
hooves (hu:wz) pl. kopyta
hop (hop) s. chmiel; skok; po-
tancówka; v. podskakiwać; poderwać (sie); przeskakiwać
hope (houp) s. nadzieja; v.
mieć nadzieję;spodziewać sie;ufać;
żywić nadzieję

hopeful ('houpful) adj, pełen
nadziei; ufny; obiecujący;
rokujący nadzieje

hopeless ('houplys) adj. beznadziejny; rozpaczliwy; zrozpaczony; zdesperowany

horde (ho:rd) s. horda; gromada

horizon (he'rajzen) s. horyzont
widnokrąg; warstwa oznaczona

horizontal (,hory'zontel) adj.
poziomy; horyzontalny; widno-
kręgowy; s. płaszczyzna po-
zioma; poziom równy i płaski

horn (ho:rn) s. rog; trąbka;
syrena; kula (siodła)
v. bóść; przebóść; wmieszać się

hornet ('ho:rnyt) s. szerszeń

horny ('ho:rny) adj. rogowy;
zrogowaciały; rogaty; jak róg

horrible ('horebl) adj. straszny; okropny; szokujący; paskudny

horrid ('horyd) adj. straszny;
ohydny; odrażający; paskudny

horrify ('horyfaj) v. przerażać;
oburzać; cieżko szokować

horror ('horer) s. groza; wstręt;
odraza; przerażenie; dreszcz

horse ('ho:rs) s. koń; konnica;
jazda; kozioł z drzewa

horseback ('ho:rs,baek) s.
grzbiet koński; adv. konno

horsefly ('ho:rs,flaj) s. giez

horsehair ('ho:rs,heer) s.
włosie końskie; sztywna tkanina

horseman ('ho:rsmen) s. jeździec

horse opera ('ho:rs'opere) s.
film kowbojski (nie-realistyczny)

horseplay ('ho:rs,plej) s. ordy-
narna zabawa (brutalna)

horsepower ('ho:rs,pałer) s.
koń mechaniczny= 746 watów

horse race ('ho:rs,rejs) s.
wyścigi konne

horseradish ('ho:rs,raedysh)
s. chrzan; a. chrzanowy

horseshoe ('ho:rs,szu) s. podkowa; a.w kształcie podkowy

horticulture('ho:rty,kaltczer)
s. ogrodnictwo

hose (houz) s. pończochy; wąż do
podlewania (wiedza i praktyka)

hosiery ('haouzery) s. trykotaże;
pończochy

hospitable ('hospytebl) adj.
gościnny; szczodry dla gości

hospital ('hospytl) s. szpital;
lecznica; a. szpitalny

hospitality (, hospy'taelyty)
s. gościnność

host (houst) s. gospodarz; ży-
wiciel; chmara; czereda; tłum

hostage ('hostydż) s. zakład-
nik; zastaw; zakładniczka

hostel ('hostel) s. dom studencki; bursa ;zajazd

hostess ('houstys) s. gospodyni; stewardesa; fordanserka

hostile ('hostajl) adj. wrogi;
nieprzyjemny; antagonistyczny

hostility (hos'tylyty) s. wrogość; stan wojny; ostra opozycja

hot (hot) adj. gorący; palący;
pieprzny; ostry; nielegalny;
świeży; pobudliwy; adv. gorąco

hotbed ('hot,bed) s. inspecty;
wylęgarnia; siedlisko; rozsadnik

hot dog ('hot,dog) s. kiełbaska w bułce; kiełbaska smażona

hotel (hou'tel) s. hotel

hothead ('hot,hed) s. człowiek
zapalczywy; raptus; a. porywczy

hothouse ('hot,haus) s. cieplarnia; oranżeria

hot-pants (,hot'paents) exp.
obcisłe damskie szorty;
vulg.: panna puszczalska

hot water bottle (hot'ło:ter'
botl) s. gorąca butelka

hound (haund) s. ogar; łajdak;
v. tropic; szczuc; podjudzać

hour ('auer) s. godzina; pora

hourly ('auerly) adj. cogo-
dzinny; adv. co godzinę;
ustawicznie; z godziny na godzi-
ne

house (haus) s. dom; zajazd;
teatr; widzowie; v. gościć;
dawać pomieszczenie; mieszkać

housekeeper ('haus,ki:per) s.
najęta gosposia; pomoc domowa

housekeeping ('haus,ki:pyng) s.
gospodarka domowa

housemaid ('haus,mejd) s. pokojówka; pomoc domowa

housewife ('haus,łajf) s.
gospodyni (niepracująca poza
domem)

housework ('haus‚Źe:rk) s. prace domowe;sprzątanie i gotowanie

housing ('hauzyŋg) s. pomieszczenie; kolonia; osłona; pokrywa; czaprak;obudowa

hove (houw) zob. heave

hover ('hower) v, unosić się; kręcić się; byc w niepewności; s. stan niepewności; unoszenie się;wahanie się;przywieranie

how (hau) adv. jak; jak ?sposób

how do you do ('hau,du'ju:du) exp.:dzień dobry !; dobry wieczór ! (jak sie pan(i) ma ?)

how are you ('hau,a:r'ju) exp.: jak sie pan(i) ma ?

how about ('hau,e'baut) exp.: może ?; pozwolisz ? etc.

how much ('hau,macz) exp.: ile ?

how many ('hau,meny) exp.: ile? ilu ? jak wielu?

how much is it ? ('hau,macz'yz, yt) ile to kosztuje ?

however (hau'ewer) adv. jakkolwiek; jednak; niemniej

howl (haul) s. wycie; ryk; v. wyc; wyganiac (gonic)wrzaskiem

howler ('hauler) s. gruby błąd

hub (hab) s. piasta; osrodek; slang: mąż;środek(rozgrywki)

hubbub ('habbab) s. zgiełk;gwar; awantura; wrzawa;tumult

hubby ('haby) s. meżulek (slang)

huckleberry ('hakelbery) s. borówka amerykańska(krzak i jago)

huddle together ('hadl,tu'gedzer) v. przytulac się; tulic sie

huddle up ('hadl,ap) v.skulic się zwinąć się w kłubek

hue (hju:) s. barwa; odcień

hug (hag) s. uścisk; chwyt zapaśniczy; v. ściskac; przyciskac; tulic (sie);uściskac

huge (hju:dż) adj. ogromny

hull (hal) s. łuska; kadłub; v. łuszczyc; godzic w kadłub

hullabaloo ('halebelu:) s. harmider;zgiełk;wrzawa;gwar

hullo (he'lou) excl.: hola! halo!

hum (ham) v. nucic; buczec; mruczec; chrząkac; s. pomruk; chrząkanie; wahanie się; blaga

human ('hju:men) adj. ludzki; s. istota ludzka

humane ('hju:mejn) adj. ludzki; humanitarny ;litosciwy

humanitarian (hju,maeny'teerjen) adj. humanitarystyczny; s. humanitarysta;filantrop

humanity (hju'maenyty) s. ludzkosc; rasa ludzka; cechy ludzkie; dobre uczynki

humble ('hambl) adj. pokorny; uniżony; skromny; v. upokażac; poniżac; poniżyć

humbleness ('hamblnys) s. pokora; bezpretensjonalnosc

humbug ('hambag) s. oszustwo; blaga; bujda; oszust; blagier; v. blagowac; oszukiwac; nabierac;wyłudzac opowiadaniem bredni

humdrum ('hamdram) adj. nudny; banalny; monotonny; s. szarzyzna; banalnosc; nudziarz

humidity (hju'mydyty) s. wilgoc; wilgotnosc(powietrza etc.)

humiliate (hju'myly‚ejt) v. upokarzac; poniżac;martwic

humiliation (hju,:myly'ejszyn) s. upokorzenie; poniżenie

humility (hju'mylyty) s. skromnosc; pokora ducha etc.

humming-bird ('hamyŋg,byrd) s. koliber

humor ('hju:mer) s.humor; nastrój; kaprys; wesołosc; v. dogadzac; zaspakajac; zadowalac; ulegac; dostosowac się do zachcianek etc.

humorous ('hju:meres) adj. śmieszny; pocieszny; pełen humoru; zabawny;komiczny

hump (hamp) s. garb; v. garbic się; wyginac w łuk

humpback ('hampbaek) s. garbus

hunchback ('hancz,baek) s. garbus;garb na plecach

hundred ('handred) num. sto; s. setka;niezliczona ilość

hundredth ('handredt) num. setny; jedna setna

hundredweight ('handred,łejt) s. cetnar angielski

hung (haŋg) zob. hang

Hungarian (haŋ'geerjen) adj.
węgierski ;s. Węgier
hunger ('haŋger) s. głód;
v. głodować; łaknąć; głodzić
hunger strike ('haŋger-strajk)
s. strajk głodowy
hungry ('haŋgry) adj. głodny;
zgłodniały; pożądliwy; ubogi;
jałowy ; nieurodzajny; łaknący
hunt (hant) s. polowanie;
teren łowiecki; v. polować;
gonić; przeszukiwać; szukać
hunter ('hanter) s. myśliwy
hunting ('hantyŋg) s. polowanie; adj. myśliwski
hunting ground ('huntyŋg,graund)
s. teren myśliwski
huntsman ('hantsmen) s. myśliwy; łowca
hurdle ('he:rdl) s. opłotki;
v. poraċ się; skakać przez
płotki; grodzić;przebijać się
hurdler ('he:rdler) s. zawodnik
wyścigów (z płotkami)
hurdle race ('he:rdl,rejs) s.
wyścigi (z płotkami) przez płotki
hurl (he:rl) s. rzut; v. rzucać
hurrah (he'ra:) excl.: hura !
hurray (he'rej) excl.: hura !;
v. krzyczeć hura (z radości etc.)
hurricane ('haryken) n. huragan; orkan tropikalny
hurried ('haryd) adj. pospieszny
hurry ('hary) s. pospiech
hurry up ! ('hary,ap) v. śpiesz
się ! ruszaj się!
hurt; hurt; hurt; (he:rt;
he:rt; he:rt)
hurt (he:rt) v. ranić; kaleczyć;
urazić; uszkodzić; boleć; dokuczać; s. skaleczenie; rana;
szkoda; krzywda; uraz; uszkodzenie ;ból;ujma;ranka
husband ('hazbend) s. mąż;
v. gospodarować oszczędnie;
wydawać za mąż
husbandry ('hazbendry) s. rolnictwo; uprawa; hodowla
hush (hasz) s. cisza; spokój;
milczenie; v. cicho ! sza !;
uciszyć się; milczeć; tuszować (coś);ululać; załagodzić

hush up ('hasz,ap) v. siedzieć
cicho; zatuszować (coś)
husk (hask) s. łuska; v. łuszczyć; wyłuszczać;złuszczać
husky ('hasky) adj. krzepki;
suchy; zachrypnięty; łuszczas-
ty; s. pies eskimoski; język
eskimoski
hustle ('hasl) s. pospiech;
krzątanina; bieganina; popy-
chanie; v. spieszyć się; krzątać się; popychać; pchać się;
szturchać; popędzać; wypchnąć
hut (hat) s. chata; barak; chałupa; v. mieszkać w chałupie
hutch (hacz) s. skrzynia; klatka; domek; v. wkładać coś do
skrzyni;s.kurnik;chlewik;chatka
hybrid ('hajbryd) s. mieszaniec;
adj. mieszany;mieszanego pochodzenia
hydrant ('hajdrent) s. hydrant
hydraulic ('haj'dro:lyk) adj.
hydrauliczny
hydro ('hajdrou) adj. wodo- ;
wodoro-; wodny
hydrocarbon ('hajdrou'ka:rben)
s. węglowodór
hydrochloric acid (,hajdrou'-
klo:ryk,asyd) s. kwas solny
hydrogen ('hajdrydżen) s. wodór
hydrogen bomb ('hajdydżen,bom)
s. bomba wodorowa
hydroplane ('hajdrou,plejn) s.
wodnopłatowiec; ślizgacz
hyena (haj'y:ne) s. hiena
hygiene ('hajdżi:n) s. higiena
hymn (hym) s. hymn; v. śpiewać
hymn :chwalić hymnem
hyphen ('hajfen) s. łącznik;
v. używać łącznika
hypnotize ('hypne,tajz) v.
hipnotyzować
hypocrisy (hy'pokresy) s. hipo-
kryzja ;udawanie cnoty etc.
hypocrite ('hypekryt) s. hipokryta;obłudnik;obłudnica
hypocritical (,hypou'krytykel)
adj. obłudny; hipokryzyjny;
dwulicowy ;udający cnotę etc.
hypodermic (,hajpe'de:rmyk)
adj. podskórny (zastrzyk)

hypothesis (haj'po̱tysys) s.
hipoteza;niesprawdzona teoria
hysterectomy (,histe'rektemy)
s. wycięcie macicy
hysteria (hys'tyerje) s. histeria;wybuch podniecenia
hysterical (hys'terykel) adj.
histeryczny;podlegający histerii
hysterics (hys'teryks) pl.
atak histerii
hysterotomy (,histe'rotemy)
s. operacja macicy
I (aj) pron. ja; dziewiąta litera angielskiego alfabetu
I-beam (,aj,bi:m) s. belka
dwuteówka (stalowa)
ice (ajs) s. lód; lody; v. zamrażać; mrozić; lukrować
Ice Age('ajsejdż) s. epoka lodowa;epoka lodowcowa
iceberg ('ajsbe:rg) s. góra lodowa (na morzu)
ice-cream ('ajskri:m) s. lody
icicle ('ajsykl) s. sopel
ice floe ('ajs-flou) s. kra
icing ('ajsyg) s. lukier
icy ('ajsy) adj. lodowaty
idea (aj'die) s. idea; pojęcie;
pomysł;wyobrażenie; myśl;plan
ideal (aj'diel) adj. idealny;
s. ideał; model doskonały
idealize (aj'dielajz) v. ideali-
zować;wyidealizować
identical (aj'dentykel) adj.
taki sam; identyczny; tożsamoś-
ciowy;zupełnie podobny
identification (ajdentyfy'kejszyn) s. utożsamienie; identy-
fikacja;stwierdzenie tożsamości
identification papers (aj,denty-
fy'kejszyn'pejpers) s. dowód
tożsamości; dowód osobisty
identify (aj'dentyfaj) v. utożsamić; identifikować
identity (aj'dentyty) s. tożsamość; identyczność
identity card (aj'dentyty ka:rd)
s. dowód osobisty
ideological (,ajdye'lodżykel)
adj. ideologiczny
idiom ('ydjem) s. wyrażenie
zwyczajowe; wyrażenie idioma-
tyczne; dialekt;typowy styl

idiot ('ydjet) s. idiota;dureń
idiotic (,ydy'otyk) adj. idiotyczny;bardzo głupi
idle ('ajdl) adj. niezajęty;
bezczynny; leniwy; pusty;
czczy; jałowy; zbyteczny;
v. próżnować; być na wolnym
biegu;być bez pracy;obijać się
idle away ('ajdl̦e'łej) v. marnować (czas);roztrwonić czas
idleness ('ajdlnys) s. bezczynność; lenistwo; próżniactwo;
daremność;bezpodstawność
idol ('ajdl) s. bożyszcze; bałwan;posąg bożka
idolize ('ajdelajz) v. ubóstwiać; uwielbiać; bałwochwalić
idyl ('ydyl) s. sielanka; idyl-
la;opis raju na wsi(w poezji)
if (yf) conj. jeżeli; jeśli;
gdyby; o ile; czy; żeby(tylko)
iffy (yffy) adj. wątpliwy
(slang) gdybowany
igloo ('iglu:) s. eskimoska
chata kopulasta ze śniegu
ignite (yg'najt) v. zapalić
ignition (yg'nyszyn) s. zapłon;
zapalenie; elektryczny zapłon
ignition key (yg'nyszyn,ki:)
s. klucz do zapłonu (w aucie)
ignoble (yg'noubl) adj. nędzny;
podły; haniebny; niecny; marny;
niegodziwy;niskiego pochodzenia
ignorance ('ygnerens) s. nie-
świadomość; ignorancja; nieuctwo; ciemnota;obskurantyzm
ignorant ('ygnerent) adj. nieświadomy; ciemny; bez wykształcenia;zdradzający ignorancję
ignore (yg'no:r) v. pomijać;
lekceważyć; odrzucać;nie zważać
ill (yl) adj. zły; chory; słaby; lichy; s. zło; adv. źle;
nie bardzo ;kiepsko;niepomyślnie
ill-advised ('yled'wajzd) adj.
nierozsądny; nierozważny
ill-affected ('yle'fektyd) adj.
źle usposobiony;nieżyczliwy
ill-bred ('yl'bred) adj. źle
wychowany ;grubiański
illegal (y'li:gel) adj. bezprawny; nielegalny;samowolny;
przeciw prawu i ustawom

illegible (y'ledżybl) adj. nieczytelny;źle napisany(wydrukowa)
illegitimate (,yly'dżytymejt)
adj. bezprawny; nieprawny;
nieprawowity; nieślubny
ill-fated ('yl-fejdyd) adj.
fatalny; nieszczęśliwy;nieszczę
ill-humored ('yl'hju:merd)
adj. w złym humorze
illicit (y'lysyt) adj. bezprawny; niedozwolony;niewłaściwy
illiterate (y'lyteryt) s. analfabeta; adj. niepiśmienny
ill-judged ('yl'dżadżd) adj.
nierozważny; nierozsądny
ill-mannered ('yl'maenerd) adj.
źle wychowany;grubiański
ill-natured ('yl'nejczerd) adj.
zły; złośliwy; opryskliwy
illness ('ylnys) s. choroba
illogical (y'lodżykel) adj.
nielogiczny;nierozsądny
ill-tempered ('yl'temperd) adj.
w złym humorze;zły;kłótliwy
ill-timed ('yl'tajmd) adj. nie
na czasie;niefortunny
ill-treat ('yl'tri:t) v. maltretować; znęcać się(nad kims)
illuminate (y'lju:mynejt) v.
oświetlać; oświecać; uświetniać
illumination (y,lju:my'nejszyn)
s. oświecenie; oświecanie;
uświetnianie;rozjaśnienie
illusion (y'lu:żyn) s. złudze-
nie; iluzja; złuda
illusive (y'lu:syw) adj. złudny; iluzyjny;iluzoryczny;zwodni
illusory (y'lu:sery) adj. złudny; iluzoryczny;zwodniczy
illustrate ('yles,trejt) v.
wyjaśniać; ilustrować
illustration (,yles'trejszyn)
s. ilustracja; ilustrowanie
illustrative ('yles,trejtyw)
adj. objaśniający; ilustru-
jący(przykład,zdarzenie etc.)
illustrious (y'lastrjes) adj.
znakomity; wybitny; sławny
ill will ('yl'łyl) s. niechęć
image ('ymydż) s. wizerunek;
obraz; wcielenie; v. wyobrażać; odzwierciadlać; uciele-
sniać: dawać obraz(wyobrażenie)

imagery ('ymydżery) s. wizerun-
ki; podobizny; gra wyobraźni;
porównanie przez przykłady
imaginable (y'maedżynebl) adj.
wyobrażalny; możliwy;do pomyśle
imaginary (y'maedżynery) a.
urojony; zmyślony;nierzeczywisty
imagination (y,maedży'nejszyn)
s. wyobraźnia; fantazja; urojenie;tworzenie nowych pomysłów
imagine (y'maedżyn) v. wyobrażać sobie;przypuszczać;myśleć
imbecile ('ymby,syl) adj. upośledzony; głupi; niedorozwinięty; cherlawy; s. człowiek
uposledzony; imbecyl(niedorozwi
imitate ('ymytejt) v. naśladować; małpować;imitować;wzorować
imitation (,ymy'tejszyn) s. na-
sladowanie; naśladownictwo;
imitacja;falsyfikat;podróbka
immaterial (,yme'tierjel) adj.
nieistotny; bezcielesny;błachy
immature (,yme'tjuer) adj. niedojrzały;niewyrobiony;niedorosły
immeasurable (y,meżerebl) adj.
niezmierzony; ogromny;bezmierny
immediate (y'mi:djet) adj.
bezpośredni; natychmiastowy;pil-
immediately (y'mi:djetly) adv.
natychmiast; bezpośrednio
immense (y'mens) adj. olbrzymi;ogromny;świetny;kpitalny
immerse (y'me:rs) v. zanurzać;
pogrążać;ochrzcić przez zanużenie
immigrant ('ymygrent) s. imigrant; adj. imigrujący;osadniczy
immigrate ('ymygrejt) v. imigrować;przywędrować;sprowadzać osad
immigration (,ymy'grejszyn) s.
imigracja;urząd imigracyjny
imminent ('ymynent) adj. nad-
chodzacy; groźny;nadciągający;blis
immobile (y'moubajl) adj. nieruchomy;przytwierdzony na stałe
immoderate (y'moderyt) adj.
nieumiarkowany;niepohamowany;nad
immodest (y'modyst) adj. nieskromny; bezczelny; zuchwały
immoral (y'morel) adj. niemoralny;nieetyczny;rozpustny
immorality (ym'e-ral'ety)s.rozpus-
ta: niemoralność

immorality (,yme'raelyty) s.
niemoralnosc;rozpusta
immortal (y'mo:rtl) adj. nie-
smiertelny; wiekopomny
immortality (,ymo:r'taelyty) s.
niesmiertelnosc
immovable (y'mu:webl) adj.nie-
ruchomy; niezmienny; nieczu-
ly; nieugiety;niewzruszony
immune (y'mju:n) adj. odporny;
uodporniony;wolny(od przepisow)
imp (ymp) s. skrzat; diablik
impact ('ympaekt) v. wgnia-
tac; s. zderzenie; uderzenie;
wplyw;wstrzas;kolizja;dzialanie
impair (ym'peer) v. uszkadzac;
oslabiac; nadwyrezac;umniejszac
impart (ym'pa:rt) v. dawac;
udzielac;zakomunikowac
impartial (ym'pa:rszel) adj.
bezstronny; sprawiedliwy
impartiality ('ym,pa:rszy'aelyty) s. bezstronnosc;sprawiedli-
passable (ym'pa:sebl) adj.
nieprzebyty; nie do przebycia
impassive (ym'paesyw) adj.
niewzruszony; obojetny;nieczuly
impatience (ym'pejszens) s.
zniecierpliwienie; niecierpli-
wosc;irytacja(z powodu czegos)
impatient (ym'pejszent) adj.
niecierpliwy; zniecierpliwiony;palacy sie do:podraznieny
impediment (ym'pedyment) s.
przeszkoda; utrudnienie
impend (ym'pend) v. grozic;
zblizac sie;zagrazac(z bliska)
impenetrable (ym'penytrebl)
adj. nieprzenikniony; niedostepny;niezglebiony;nie do prze-
imperative (ym'peretyw) adj.
stanowczy; rozkazujacy; konieczny;naglacy;niezbedny
imperceptible (,ym-pe'rseptebl)
adj. niedostrzegalny;nieuchwyt-
imperfect (ym'pe:rfykt) adj.
niedoskonaly; niedokonczony;
wadliwy; niezupelny;niedokonany
imperial (ym'pierjel) adj.
cesarski; imperialny; do-
stojny;rozkazujacy;majestatycz-
imperialism (ym'pierjelyzem)s.
imperializm(budowanie imperium)

imperil (ym'peryl) v. zagrazac;
narazic na niebezpieczenstwo
imperious (ym'pierjes) adj.
wladczy; naglacy;nakazujacy
imperishable (ym'peryszebl) adj.
niezniszczalny; nieprzemijaja-
cy;trwaly;wieczysty
impermeable (ym'pe:rmiebl) adj.
nieprzemakalny; nieprzenikniony;nieprzepuszczajacy
impersonal (ym'pe:rsenl) adj.
nieosobowy; nieosobisty
impersonate(ym'pe:rsenejt) v.
wcielac; uosabiac; odgrywac
kogos;personifikowac
impertinence (ym'pe:rtynens) s.
niestosownosc; impertynencja;
niewlasciwosc; natrectwo ;nietakt
impertinent (ym'pe:rtynnent) adj.
niestosowny; impertynencki;
bezczelny; natretny;bez zwiazku
imperturbable (,ympe:r'te:rbebl)
adj. niewzruszony; spokojny
impervious (ym'pe:rwjes) adj.
nieprzepuszczalny; niedostepny
impetuous (ym'petjues) adj.
popedliwy; porywczy; gwaltowny
implacable (ym'plekebl) adj.
nieublagalny;nieprzejednany
implement ('ymplyment) s. na-
rzedzie; srodek; sprzet;
v. uzupelniac; urzeczywistniac;
wykonac;uprawomocniac;spelniac
implicate ('ymplykejt) v. uwik-
lac; owijac; wlaczac;wplatac;wmie-
implication (,ymply'kejszyn) s.
uwiklanie; wlaczenie; sugestia
implicit (ym'plysyt) adj. rozu-
miejacy sie sam przez sie;
niezaprzeczalny;domniemany;slepy
implore (ym'plo:r) v. blagac
imply (ym'plaj) v. zawierac
w sobie; miescic; sugerowac;
zakladac;nasuwac wniosek
impolite (,ympo'lajt) adj. nieuprzejmy; niegrzeczny
import (ym'po:rt) s. import;tresc
v. oznaczac; importowac; przy-
wozic z zagranicy;a.importowy
import ('ympo:rt) s. tresc;
znaczenie;waznosc;doniosłosc
importance (ym'po:rtens) s.
znaczenie; waznosc;doniosłosc

important (ym'po:rtent) adj.
ważny; znaczący; doniosły
importation (,ympo:r'tejszyn)
s. przywóz; importowanie
importune (ym'po:rtju:n) v.
dokuczać; żądać natarczywie;
narzucać się;naprzykrzać się
impose (ym'pouz) v. nadawać;
narzucać; oszukiwać; imponować;narzucać;nakładać obowiązek
impose upon (,ym'pouz e'pon)
v. narzucać się komuś;okpiwać
imposing (ym'pouzyng) adj.
imponujący;wspaniały;okazały
impossibility (ym,posy'bylyty)
s. niemożliwość
impossible (ym'posybl) adj.
niemożliwy(do zrobienia,zniesienia)
impostor (ym'poster) s. oszust
(podszywający się);szarlatan
impotence ('ympotens) s. niemoc; zniedołężnienie (płciowe);nieudolność;niesprawność
impotent ('ympotent) s. bezsilny; impotent; nieudolny
impracticable (ym'praektykebl)
adj. niewykonalny;krnąbrny
impregnate ('ympregnejt) v. za-
płodniać; impregnować; nasycać;wpoić;zaszczepić;nasiąkać
impress (ym'pres) v. odcisnąć;
wycisnąć; robić wrażenie;
s. odcisk; odbicie; piętno
impression (ym'preszyn) s. wrażenie; druk; odbicie; nakład
impressive (ym'presyw) adj. robiący wrażenie; uderzający;
podniosły;wstrząsający;frapują
imprint (ym'prynt) v. odbijać;
wpajać; wydrukować; wbijać
w pamięc;wyryć w pamięci
imprint ('ymprynt) s. odbicie;
nadruk; odcisk;piętnc;znak firy
imprison (ym'pryzn) v. uwięzić
imprisonment (ym'pryznment) s.
uwięzienie(kara więzienia)
improbable (ym'probebl) adj.
nieprawdopodobny
improper (ym'proper) adj. niewłaściwy; nieprzyzwoity;zdrożny
improve (ym'pru:w) v. poprawić;
udoskonalić; ulepszać(jakość)

improvement (ym'pru:wment) s.
poprawa; udoskonalenie; wy-
korzystanie(sposobności);poprawa
improvise ('ymprowajz) v. improwizować;sklecić na poczekaniu
imprudent (ym'pru:dent) adj. nierozsądny; nieopatrzny; nierozważny;nieoględny;niebaczny
impudence ('ympjudens) s. bez-
wstyd; bezczelność; tupet
impudent ('ympjudent) adj. bezwstydny; bezczelny;zuchwały;z tupetem
impulse ('ympals) s. impuls;poryw;
popęd;pęd;siła napędowa;bodziec
impulsive ('ympalsyw) adj. im-
pulsywny; porywczy; pobudliwy
impunity (ym'pju:nyty) s. bez-
karność;swoboda od skutków(kary)
impure (ym'pjur) adj. nieczysty; zanieczyszczony
impute (ym'pju:t) v. oskarżać;
przypisywać(zbrodnię;błąd etc.)
in (yn) prep. w; we; na; za; po;
do; u; nie-
in and out ('yn,end'aut) exp.:
na wylot; wchodzić i wychodzić
in a week ('yn,ej'łi:k) exp.: za
tydzień;w ciągu tygodnia
in my opinion ('yn,maj e'pynjen)
exp.: według mnie;moim zdaniem
in order that ('yn.o:rder'daet)
exp.: ażeby;w celu;poto żeby
in pairs ('yn,peers) exp.: parami
in Shakespeare ('yn,Szekspir)
u Szekspira;w sztukach Szekspira
inability (,yne'bylyty) s. niezdolność;niemożność
inaccessible (ynaek'sesybl) adj.
niedostępny; nieprzystępny
inaccurate (yn'aekjuryt) adj.
niescisły; niedokładny
inactive (yn'aektyw) adj. bezczynny;bierny;obojętny;inertny
inadequate (yn'aedykłyt) adj.
nieodpowiedni; niewystarczalny
inadmissible (,yned'mysebl)
adj. niedopuszczalny;nie do przyjęcia
inadvertent (,yned'we:rtent)
adj. nieuważny; niedbały; nierozmyślny;mimowolny;nieumyślny
inalterable (yn'o:lterebl) adj.
niezmienny

inanimate (yn'aenymyt) adj.
martwy; nieożywiony; bezduszny; nieorganiczny

inappropriate,(,yne'prouprjyt)
adj. niewłaściwy;niestosowny

inapt (yn'aept) adj. niezdatny

inarticulate (,yna:r'tykjult)
adj. nieartykułowany; niewyraźny; niemy;słabo mówiący

inasmuch (,ynez'macz) adv.
o tyle; ponieważ; wobec tego;
że; skoro;zważywszy;jako że

inasmuch as (,ynez'macz,aez)
adv. gdyż ;o tyle że;o tyle o

inattentive (,yne'tentyw) adj.
nieuważny; nie uważający

inaudible (yn'o:debl) adj. nies-
słyszalny;nie uchwytny dla ucha

inaugural (yn'no:gjurel) adj.
inauguracyjny

inaugurate (y'no:gjurejt) v.
otwierać uroczyście; inaugurować;uroczyście zapoczątkowywać

inborn ('yn'bo:rn) adj. wrodzony ;przyrodzony;z natury

incalculable (yn'kaelkjulebl)
adj. nieobliczalny;nieprzewi-
dzialny

incapable (yn'kejpebl) adj.
niezdolny; nie będący w stanie

incapacitate ('ynke'paesytejt)
v. czynić niezdatnym; dyskwa-
lifikować;uznać za niezdatnego

incapacity (,ynke'paesyty) s.
niezdolność; nieudolność

incarnate (yn,ka:rnejt) adj.
wcielony; v. wcielać; uciełes-
niać (się);być wcieleniem

incautious (yn'ko:szes) adj.
nierozważny; niebaczny

incendiary (yn'sendjery) adj.
zapalający; podżegający;
s. podpalacz; podżegacz

incense ('ynsens) s. kadzidło

incense (yn'sens) v. rozwścieczać; doprowadzać do szału

incertitude (un'se:rtytju:d) s.
niepewność; niepokój

incessant (yn'sesnt) adj. ustawiczny; bezustanny; stały

incest ('ynsest) s.kazirodztwo
a.kazirodczy

inch (yncz) s. cal (2.54 cm)
v. posuwać cal po calu

incident ('ynsydent) s. zajście;
wydarzenie; incydent; adj. pa-
dający; związany;prawdopodobny

incidental (,ynsy'dentl) adj.
przypadkowy; uboczny;drugorzędny

incidentally (,ynsy'dently) adv.
przypadkowo; ubocznie; nawiasem mówiąc;mimochodem;przy spobności

incinerate (yn'synerejt) v.
spalić; spopielić;palić na popiół

incise (yn'sajz) v. naciać; wyryć;wyrzeźbić;wygrawerować

incision (yn'syżyn) s. nacięcie;
cięcie; cietość; bystrość;östrość

incisive (yn'sajsyw) adj. przenikliwy; ostry; tnący; bystry;
sieczny; zjadliwy;wcinający się

incisor (yn'sajzer) s. siekacz
(ząb)każdy z przednich zębów między kłami

incite (yn'sajt) v. zachęcać;
podburzać;podżegać;namawiać

inclement (yn'klement) adj.
surowy;ostry (klimat etc.)

inclination (ynkly'nejszyn) s.
skłonność; nachylenie;pociąg

incline (yn'klajn) v. mieć
skłonność; pochylać się

inclose (yn'klous) v. ogrodzić;
załaczyć; właczyć;zamknąć

include (yn'klu:d) v. zawierać;
włączać; wliczać(w cene);obejmować

inclusive (yn'klu:syw) adj.
włączony;obejmujący;adv.włacznie

incoherent (,ynkou'hierent) adj.
bez związku; nieskoordynowany

income ('ynkam) s. dochód

income tax ('ynkam,taeks) s.
podatek dochodowy

incoming ('yn,kamyŋg) adj. nad-
chodzący;następujący; przyra-
stający; s. przybycie; dochód

incomparable (yn'komperebl)
adj. niezrównany; nie do porów-
nania; nieporównywalny

incompatible (,ynkem'paetebl)
adj. niezgodny; sprzeczny

incompetent (yn'kompytent) adj.
niekompetentny; nieudolny

incomplete (,ynkem'pli:t) adj.
niezupełny; nieukończony

incomprehensible (yn,kompry'-
hensebl) adj. niepojęty; niezrozumiały

inconceivable (,ynken'si:webl)
adj. niepojęty; nieprawdopodobny; nieprawdopodobny

inconclusive (,ynken'klu;syw)
adj. nieprzekonywujacy; nie-
rozstrzygający;nie decydujący

inconsequent (yn'konsykkent)
adj. bez związku; niekonsekwentny; nielogiczny

inconsiderable (,ynken'syderebl)
adj. nieznaczny; niepokaźny

inconsiderate (,ynken'syderyt)
adj. bezwzględny; nierozważny

inconsistent (,ynken'systent)
adj. niejednolity; niekonsekwentny; niezgodny;bez związku

inconsolable (,ynken'soulebl)
adj. niepocieszony;nieutulony

inconstant (yn'konstent) adj.
zmienny; niestały; nieregularny

inconvenience (,ynken'wi:n jens)
s. niewygoda; kłopot; v. niepokoić; przeszkadzać; sprawiać
kłopot;deranżować

inconvenient (,ynken'wi:njent)
adj. niewygodny; niedogodny;
kłopotliwy; uciążliwy

incorporate (yn'ko:rperejt) v.
jednoczyć; wcielać; zrzeszać
(yn'ko:rperyt) adj. zrzeszony

incorporated (yn'ko:rperejtyd)
adj. zarejestrowany; zalegali-
zowany;wcielony; złączony

incorrect (,ynke'rekt) adj. niepoprawny; nieścisły: błędny

incorrigible (yn'korydżybl) adj.
niepoprawny;nie do poprawienia

increase (yn'kri:s) v. wzrastać;
zwiększać się; pomnażać się;
wzmagać się;rozmnażać się ; s.
('ynkri:s) wzrost; przyrost;
podwyżka;rozrost;mnożenie się

increasingly (yn'kri:syngly)
adv. coraz więcej; coraz bardziej; coraz to; wciąż

incredible (yn'kredebl) adj.
nie do wiary; niewiarygodny;
nieprawdopodobny;nie do pomyślenia

incredulous (yn'kredjules) adj.
nie

incriminate (yn'krymynejt) v.
obwiniać; oskarżać;pomawiać;
objąć (kogoś) oskarżeniem

incubator ('ynkjubejter) s. wy-
lęgarka; inkubator

incur (yn'ke:r) v. narażać się;
ponieść; zaciagać;natknąć się na

incurable (yn'kjuerebl) adj.
nieuleczalny;s.człowiek nieuleczalny

indebted (yn'detyd) adj. dłużny;
zobowiązany: wdzięczny;zawdzięcza-
jacy

indecency (yn'di:sensy) s. nie-
skromność; nieprzyzwoitość

indecent (yn'di:sent) adj. nieprzyzwoity;obrażający moralność

indecision (,yndy'syżyn) s.
chwiejność; niezdecydowanie

indecisiveness(,yndy'sajsywnys)s.
chwiejność; niezdecydowanie

indecisive (,yndy'sajsyw) adj.
nie rozstrzygnięty; niezdecydowany;chwiejny;nie rozstrzygający

indeed (yn'di:d) adv. naprawdę;
istotnie; rzeczywiście; faktycznie;wprawdzie; co prawda;właściwie

indefatigable (,yndy'faetygebl)
adj. niestrudzony; niezmordowany

indefinite (yn'defynyt) adj.
nieokreślony;niewyraźny;nie spre-
cyzowany

indelible (yn'delybl) adj. nie-
zatarty; trwały;nie do zmazania

indelicate (yn'delykyt) adj. niedelikatny; nietaktowny;niestosowny

indemnify (yn'demnyfaj) v. dawać odszkodowanie; zabezpieczać
przed(np. szkodą);powetować

indemnity (yn'demnyty) s. odszkodowanie; zabezpieczenie
przed...;wynagrodzenie

indent (yn'dent) v. naciąć; wy-
ciąć; wyrżnać; zamówić; zawierać umowę; tłoczyć; s. wgłębienie;nacięcie;karbowanie

indent (yndent) s. wcięcie; nacięcie; karbowanie; zamówienie

independence (,yndy'pendens) s.
niezależność; niepodległość;
niezależność materialna

independent (,yndy'pendent) adj.
niepodległy; niezależny (ma-
terialnie);osobny;oddzielny

indescribable (,yndys'krajbebl)
adj. nieopisany; nie do opisania (poza możliwościami opisania)

indeterminate (,yndy'te:rmynyt)
adj.nieokreślony;niewyraźny

index ('yndeks) s. wskaźnik;
indeks; v. umieszczać spi-
sie (indeksie); robić indeks
Indian ('yndjen) adj. indiański;
hinduski ⌐babie lato
Indian Summer ('yndjen'samer)
exp.: słoneczne dni w jesieni;
India-rubber ('yndje'raber) s.
guma (naturalna,elastyczna)
indicate ('yndykejt) v. wskazywać; stwierdzać; wymagać
indication (,yndy'kejszyn) s.
wskazówka; wskazanie; znak
indicative (yn'dyketyw) adj.
oznajmiający; dowodzący
indicator ('yndykejter) s.
wskaźnik; indykator; licznik
indict (yn'dajt) v. oskarżyć
indictment (yn'dajtment) s.
oskarżenie; akt oskarżenia
indifference (yn'dyferens) s.
obojętność ;nieistotność;bła- chose
indifferent (yn'dyfrent) adj.
obojętny;mierny;błachy;neutralny
indigent ('yndydżent) adj.
ubogi; biedny;s.biedak;biedaczka
indigestible (,yndy'dżestebl)
adj. niestrawny ;źle strawny
indigestion (,yndy'dżestczyn) s.
niestrawność
indignant (yn'dygnent) adj.
oburzony (na niesprawiedliwość...)
indignation (,yndyg'nejszyn) s.
oburzenie
indirect (,yndy'rekt) adj; pośredni; okrężny; nieuczciwy
indiscreet (,yndys'kri:t) adj.
nierozważny; niedyskretny
indiscretion (,yndys'kreszyn)
s. nierozwaga; niedyskrecja;
uchybienie(słowem,czynem etc.)
indiscriminate (,yndys'krymynyt)
adj. bezkrytyczny; pomieszany
indispensable (,yndys'pensebl)
adj. nieodzowny; niezbędny;
konieczny;niezastąpiony
indisposed (,yndys'pouzd) adj.
niezdrów; niedysponowany; niechętny;bez zapału;niedomagający
indisposition (,yndyspe'zyszyn)
s. niedyspozycja; niechęć; odraza;dolegliwość;niedomaganie

indisputable (,yndys'pju:tebl)
adj. bezsporny;niezaprzeczalny
indistinct (,yndys'tynkt) adj;
niewyraźny;niejasny;mętny
individual (,yndy'wydjuel) adj.
pojedyńczy; odrębny; s. jednostka; osobnik:okaz;chłowiek
individualist (,yndy'wydjuelyst)
s. indywidualista;individualistka
indivisible (,yndy'wyzebl) adj.
niepodzielny;nieskończenie mały
indolence ('yndelens) s. lenistwo; opieszałość;próżniactwo
indolent ('yndelent) adj. leniwy;opieszały;obojętny;niebolesny
indomitable (yn'domytebl) adj.
nieposkromiony; nieugięty
indoor ('yndo:r) adj. domowy;
wewnętrzny; pokojowy;zakładowy
indoors ('yndo:rz) adv. w domu;
pod dachem ;do domu;do mieszkania
indorse(yn'do:rs) v. potwierdzić (podpisem)
induce (yn'dju:s) v. skłonić;
namówić; powodować; wnioskować;pobudzić;nakłonić;powodować
induct (yn'dakt) v. wprowadzać;
tworzyć; brać do wojska
indulge (yn'daldż) v. pobłażać;
znosić; ulegać; dogadzać; używać sobie ;dawać upust;zaspokajać
indulgence (yn'daldżens) s. do-
gadzanie; nałóg; oddawanie się;
pobłażanie; odpust,uleganie
indulgent (yn'daldżent) adj. pobłażliwy ;ulegający;folgujący
industrial (yn'dastrjel) adj.
przemysłowy (towar,robotnik etc.)
industrial area (yn'dastrjel'
eerje) s. teren przemysłowy
industrial city (yn'dastrjel'
syty) s. miasto przemysłowe
industrialist (yn'dastrjelyst)
s. przemysłowiec
industrialize (yn'dastrjelajz)
v. uprzemysławiać
industrious (yn'dastrjes) adj.
skrzętny; pilny; pracowity
industry ('yndastry) s. przemysł; pilność; pracowitość;
skrzętność;gałąź przemysłu;włas-
ciciele i zarządcy przemysłu

ineffective (,yny'fektyw) adj.
bezskuteczny; niesprawny

inefficient (,yny'fyszent)
adj. niewydajny; niesprawny

inequality (,yny'kłolyty) s.
nierówność; niewystarczalność;
zmienność(krajobrazu);niestałość

inert (y'ne:rt) adj. bezwładny;
ociężały; obojętny; opieszały

inertia (y'ne:rszja) s. inercja; bezwład; ociężałość

inestimable (yn'estymebl) adj.
nieoceniony;bezcenny

inevitable (yn'ewytebl) adj.
nieunikniony; nieuchronny

inexact (,ynyg'zaekt) adj. nieścisły; niedokładny

inexcusable (,ynyks'kju:zebl)
adj. niewybaczalny; nie-
usprawiedliwiony;nie do darowa-
nia

inexhaustible (,ynyg'zo:stebl)
adj. niewyczerpany; nieprzebrany; niestrudzony;bez dna

inexpensive (,ynyks'pensyw) adj.
niedrogi; niekosztowny; tani

inexperience (,ynyks'pierjens)
s. niedoświadczenie;brak wprawy

inexplicable (yn'eksplykebl)
adj. niewytłumaczalny; nie-
wyjaśniony;zagadkowy

inexpressible (,yneks'presebl)
adj. niewysłowiony; niewyra-
żalny;niewymowny

inexpressive (,ynyks'presyw)
adj. bez wyrazu

infallible (yn'faelebl) adj.
nieomylny; niezawodny; niechybny;bezbłędny;zawsze słuszny

infamous ('ynfemes) adj. haniebny; niesławny; hańbiący;podły

infamy ('ynfemy) s. hańba; niesława; podłość;utrata praw obywatelskich

infancy ('ynfensy) s. nie-
mowlectwo; dzieciństwo

infant ('ynfent) s. niemowlę;
dziecko;noworodek;a.dziecinny

infantile ('ynfentajl) adj.
dziecięcy;infantylny;niemowlecy

infantry ('ynfentry) s. piechota (wojsko)

infatuated with (yn'faetjuejtyd
Łyg) adj. szalejący za...;rozko-
chany w;nierozsądnie zakochany

infect (yn'fekt) v. zakazić;
zarazić; zatruwać

infection (yn'fekszyn) s. zakażenie; zarażenie; zaraza

infectious (yn'fekszes) adj. za-
każny; zaraźliwy;infekcyjny

infer (yn'fe:r) v. wnioskować;
zawierać w sobie pojęcie

inference ('ynferens) s. wniosek; konkluzja;domniemanie

inferior (yn'fierjer) adj.
niższy; podrzędny; pośledni

inferior to (yn'fierjer,tu)
adj. ustępujący; gorszy

inferiority (yn,fiery'oryty) s.
niższość;poczucie niższości

infernal (yn'fe:rnel) adj. piekielny; diabelski; szatański

infest (yn'fest) v. nawiedzać;
trapić;być utrapieniem

infidelity (,ynfy'delyty) s.
niewiara; niewierność

infiltrate ('ynfyltrejt) v.
wsiąkać; przesiąkać; przenikać

infinite ('ynfynyt) adj. nieskończony; bezgraniczny; niezliczony; ogromny;bezkresny

infinitive (yn'fynytyw) s. bezokolicznik;adj.nieokreslony

infinity (yn'fynyty) s. nieskończoność

infirm (yn'fe:rm) adj. słaby;
niedołężny;dotknięty niemocą

infirmary (yn'fe:rmery) s.
szpital; lecznica; izba chorych

infirmity (yn'fe:rmyty) s. niemoc; słabość; zniedołężnienie

inflame (yn'flejm) v, zapalić;
rozognić; pobudzać;zagrzewać

inflammable (yn'flaemebl) adj.
zapalny; pobudliwy; palny

inflammation (,ynfle'mejszyn)
s. zapalenie; zaognienie

inflammatory(yn'flaemeto:ry)
adj. podżegający; zapalny

inflate (yn'flejt) v. nadać;
rozdać; powodować inflację

inflation (yn'flejszyn) s.
inflacja; nadymanie; nadmu-
chanie;zwyżka cen

inflect (yn'flekt) v. zginać;
skrzywić; odmieniać;naginać

inflexible (yn'fleksebl) adj.
sztywny; nieugięty;nieelastycz-
inflection(yn'flekszyn) s.
fleksja; modulacja; końcówka;
wygięcie ;nadgięcie;odchylenie
inflict (yn'flykt) v. zadać;
narzucać; zsyłać(na kogoś)
infliction (yn'flykszyn) s.
zadanie (ciosu) narzucanie;nie
przykrość;nieszczęście;strapie-
influence ('ynfluens) s. wpływ
v. wywierać wpływ;oddziaływać
influential (,ynflu'enszel)
adj. wpływowy(polityk etc.)
influenza (,ynflu'enza) s.
grypa; influenca
inform (yn'fo:rm) v. powiado-
mić; nadawać; donosić;ożywić
inform against(yn'fo:rme'genst)
v. donosić na (kogoś)
information (,ynfer'mejszyn)
s. wiadomość; wiedza; objaś-
nienie;informacja;doniesienie
information desk (,ynfer'mejszyn,desk) punkt informacyjny (w banku,hotelu,na wystawie)
information officer (,ynfer'-
mejszyn 'ofyser) oficer in-
formacyjny(w banku etc.)
informative (yn'fo:rmetyw)
adj. objaśniający; pouczający
informer (yn'fo:rmer) s. donosiciel; konfident;konfidentka
infuriate (,yn'fjuerjejt) v.
rozwścieczać: rozjuszać
infuse (yn'fju:z) v. wlewać;
zalewać; zaparzać;dodać(odwagi)
ingenious (yn'dżi:njes) adj.
pomysłowy; dowcipny(pomysł)
ingenuity (,yndży'njuyty) s.
pomysłowość;oryginalność;dowcip
ingot ('yŋgot) s. sztaba
ingratiate (yn'grejszjejt) v.
wkradać się w łaski czyjeś
ingratitude(yn'graetytju:d) s.
niewdzięczność
ingredient (yn'gri:djent) s.
składnik (mieszanki etc,)
ingress ('yngres) s. wejście
inhabit (yn'haebyt) v. zamieszkiwać; mieszkać
inhabitable (yn'haebytebl)adj.
mieszkalny(godny zamieszkania)

inhabitant (yn'haebytent) s.
mieszkaniec; mieszkanka
inhale (yn'hejl) v. wdychać; zaciągać się (dymem);wziewać
inherent (yn'hierent) adj. nieodłączny; właściwy;wrodzony
inherit (yn'heryt) v. dziedziczyć; być spadkobiercą
inheritance (yn'herytens) s.
spadek; spuścizna; dziedzictwo
inhibit (yn'hybyt) v. wstrzymywać; wzbraniać; zakazywać
inhibition (,ynhy'byszyn) s.
zakaz; zahamowanie; wstrzymanie
inhospitable (yn'hospytebl) adj.
niegościnny
inhuman (yn'hju:men) adj. nieludzki; okrutny;brutalny etc.
initial (y'nyszel) adj. początkowy;v.znaczyć własnymi inicjała-mi
initiate (y'nyszjejt) v. zapoczątkować; wprowadzać; zainicjo-
wać; wtajemniczać;s.nowicjusz
initiation (y,nyszy'ejszyn) s.
wprowadzenie;zapoczątkowanie
initiative (y'nyszjetyw) s.
inicjatywa; adj. początkowy
inject (yn'dżekt) v. wstrzyknąć
injection (yn'dżekszyn) s.
zastrzyk;wstrzyknięcie;a.wytrysko-wy
injudicious (,yndżu'dyszes) adj.
nierozważny; nieroztropny
injure ('yndżer) v. zranić;
uszkodzić; krzywdzić; zepsuć
injurious (yn'dżuerjes) adj.
szkodliwy; krzywdzący; obelżywy;przynoszący ujmę;obraźliwy
injury ('yndżery) s. szkoda;
krzywda; rana; uszkodzenie
injustice (yn'dżastys) s. niesprawiedliwość; krzywda
ink (yŋk) s. atrament; tusz
inkling ('yŋklyŋg)s. wzmianka;
podejrzenie; przypuszczenie
ink-pot ('yŋk,pot) s. kałamarz
inland ('ynlend) s. wnętrze
kraju; adj. z głębi kraju;
wewnętrzny; adv. w głębi;
w głąb kraju;w głębi kraju
inlet ('ynlet) s. wstawka; zatoka; wlot; wejście;a.wlotowy
inmate ('ynmejt) s. mieszkaniec;
lokator; współ-(więzień etc.)

inmost ('ynmoust) adj. głęboko
utajony; skryty;najtajniejszy
inn (yn) s. gospoda; oberża
innate ('y'nejt) adj. wrodzony
inner ('yner) adj. wewnętrzny
innermost ('ynermoust) adj.
głęboko ukryty; najskrytszy
inner tube ('yner,tju:b) s.
dętka(samochodowa,rowerowa)
innkeeper ('yn,ki:per) s.
oberżysta;właściciel zajazdu
innocence ('ynesns) s. niewin-
nosc; naiwnosc;prostodusznosc
innocent ('ynesynt) adj. niewinny; naiwny; nieszkodliwy;
niemądry; s. prostaczek;
niewiniątko; głuptas
innovation (,ynou'wejszyn) s.
innowacja;wprowadzanie zmian
innumerable (y'nju:merebl) adj.
niezliczony; bez liku
inoculate (y'nokulejt) s.
szczepic;wpajac;oczkowac rosl1}
inoffensive (,yne'fensyw) adj.
nieszkodliwy; spokojny;obojętny
inpatient ('ynpejszent) s.
pacjent leżący w szpitalu
inquest ('ynkłest) s. śledztwo
inquire (yn'kłajer) s. pytac
się; dowiadywac się; dociekac
inquiry (yn'kłajry) s. badanie;
zasięganie informacji; śledztwo; poszukiwanie;ankieta;wywiad
inquisitive (yn'kłyzytyw) adj.
badawczy; ciekawy;wscipski
insane (yn'sejn) adj. chory
umysłowo;zwariowany;bez sensu
insanity (yn'saenyty) s. obłęd
insatiable (yn'sejszjebl) adj.
nienasycony;niezaspokojony;chc1-
insatiate (yn'sej'szjyt) adj.
nienasycony;niezaspokojony
inscribe (yn'skrajb) v, wpisac;
napisac;umieszczac na liscie
inscription (yn'skrypszyn) s.
napis; dedykacja
insect ('ynsekt) s. owad
insecure (,ynsy'kjuer) adj. niepewny; niezabezpieczony
insensible (yn'sensybl) adj.
nieswiadomy; bez zmysłów;w stanie omdlenia;niedostrzegalny

insensitive (yn'sensytyw) adj.
nieczuły; niewrażliwy
inseparable (yn'seperebl) adj.
nierozłączny;nieodstępny
insert (yn'se:rt) v. wstawiac;
wkładac; s. wkładka; wstawka
insertion (yn'se:rszyn) s. wkładka; wstawka; włożenie; wsta-
wienie;przyczep;przyczepienie
inshore (yn'szo:r) adv. blisko
brzegu; przy brzegu; adj. przybrzeżny; bliski brzegu
inside 'ynsajd) s. wnętrze;
adj. wewnętrzny;adv.wewnatrz
inside (yn'sajd) adv. wewnątrz
inside out ('ynsajd'aut) exp.:
na lewą stronę (np. marynarki)
insight ('ynsajt) s. wgląd;
intuicja;wnikliwośc
insignificant (,ynsyg'nyfykent)
adj. mało znaczący;błachy
insincere (,ynsyn'sier) adj.
nieszczery;zwodny;dwulicowy
insinuate (yn'synjuejt) v. in-
synuowac; podsuwac;sugierowac
insipid (yn'sypyd) adj. mdły;
tępy; bez sensu;głupi;ckliwy
insist (yn'syst) v. nalegac;
nastawac;utrzymywac;obstawac
insist on (yn'syst,on) v. do-
magac się;upierac się;nastawac
insolent ('ynselent) adj. bezczelny;zuchwały;butny;wyniosły
insoluble (yn'soljubl) adj. nierozpuszczalny;nie do rozwiązania
insolvent (yn'solwent) adj. niewypłacalny; s. bankrut;bankrutka
insomnia (yn'somnja) s. bezsen-
nosc (nie normalna)
insomuch (,ynsou'macz) adv.
o tyle; do tego stopnia;tak dale-
inspect (yn'spekt) v. oglądac;
doglądac; miec nadzór;badac
inspection (yn'spekszyn) s.
przegląd; oglądanie; inspekcja;
doglądanie;sprawdzanie;kontrola
inspector (yn'spekter) s. inspektor;nadzorca;kontroler
inspiration (,ynspe'rejszyn) s.
natchnienie ;wdech;wdychanie
inspire (yn'spajer) v. natchnąc;
podsunac; zainspirowac;wdychac

install(yn'sto:l) v. instalować;
wprowadzać na stanowisko
installation (,ynsto:'lejszyn)
s. instalacja; wprowadzenie
na stanowisko;zamontowanie
instal(l)ment (yn'sto:lment)
s. część całości; rata
instance ('ynstens) s. wypadek;
przykład ;v.przytaczać przykład
instant ('ynstent) adj. nagły;
natychmiastowy; bieżący;
s. moment; chwila (szczególna)
instantaneous (,ynsten'tejnjes)
adj. natychmiastowy; momentalny ;zdarzający się w momencie
instantly (yn'stently) adv.
natychmiast; momentalnie
instead (yn'sted) adv. zamiast
tego; natomiast; w miejsce
instead of (yn'sted,ow) adv.
zamiast (kogoś, czegoś)
instigate (ynstygejt) v. podżegać;podjudzać;prowokować
instigator ('ynstygejter) s.
podżegacz;prowokator;poduszczy-ciel
instil(l) (yn'styl) v. wsączać;
wpajać (uczucia etc.);wkraplać
instinct ('ynstyŋkt) s. instynkt;adj.tchnący(czymś);pełen
instinctive (yn'styŋktyw) adj.
instynktowny; odruchowy
institute ('ynstytju:t) s. instytut; v. zakładać; ustanawiać; zarządzać(śledztwo etc.)
institution (,ynty'tju:szyn) s.
instytucja; ustanowienie
instruct (yn'strakt) v. uczyć
instruction (yn'strakszyn) s.
pouczenie; nauka; instrukcja
instructive (yn'straktyw) adj.
pouczający; kształcący
instructor (yn'strakter) s.
nauczyciel;wykładowca;instruktor
instructress (yn'straktrys) s.
nauczycielka ;instruktorka
instrument ('ynstrument) s.
instrument; przyrząd;dokument
insubordinate (,ynseb'o:rdnyt)
adj. niesforny; nieposłuszny
insufferable (yn'saferebl) adj.
nieznośny; nie do zniesienia
insufficient (,ynse'fyszent)
adj. niedostateczny;nieodpowiedni

insulate ('ynsjulejt) v. izolo-
wać;oddzielać;odosabniać
insult ('ynsalt) s. zniewaga;
insult (yn'salt) v. lżyć; znieważać;uchybiać;zelżyć
insupportable (,ynse'po:rtebl)
adj. nie do zniesienia; nieznośny;nieuzasadniony
insurance (yn'szuerens) s.
ubezpieczenie;a.ubezpieczeniowy
insurance policy (yn'szuerens'-
polysy) s. polisa ubezpieczeniowa;polisa asekuracyjna
insure (yn'szuer) v. ubezpieczać
(się);asekurować;zabezpieczać
insurmountable (,ynse:r'maun-
tebl) adj. niepokonany
insurrection (,ynse'rekszyn) s.
powstanie; insurekcja
intact (yn'taekt) adj. nietknięty ;nie uszkodzony
integrate ('yntygrejt) v. scalić; uzupełnić; całkować
integrity (yn'tegryty) s. uczciwość; rzetelność; czystość;
prawość ;niepodzielność
intellect (yn'tylekt) s. rozum;
umysł;rozsądek;wybitne umysły
intellectual (,ynty'lekczuel)
adj. intelektualny; umysłowy;
s. intelektualista;inteligent
intelligence (yn'telydżens) s.
inteligencja; informacja; wywiad;wiadomości;nowiny;informa-sja
intelligent (yn'telydżent) adj.
inteligentny;łatwo uczący się
intelligentsia (yn'tely'dżencja)
s. inteligencja (warstwa kraju)
intelligible (yn'telydżybl) adj.
zrozumiały; jasny;wyraźny
intemperate (yn'temperyt) adj.
nieumiarkowany; bez umiaru
intend (yn'tend) v. zamierzać;
przeznaczać; mieć na myśli
intense (yn'tens) adj. napięty;
usilny; gorliwy;wytężony;uczucio-wy
intensify (yn'tensyfaj) v.
wzmóc; wzmocnić; napiąc;wzmagać
intensity (yn'tensyty) s. inten-
sywność; wzmożenie;natężenie
intensive (yn'tensyw) adj. intensywny; wzmożony ;silny;wzma-
cniający

intent (yn'tent) s. plan; zamiar; adj. uważny; zamierzający; zajęty;pochłonięty;zdecydowany

intent on (yn'tent on) adj. pochłonięty; zajęty czymś

intention (yn'tenszyn) s. zamiar; cel;zamierzenie(czynu)

intentional (yn'tenszenel) adj. umyślny; celowy;zamierzony

inter (yn'te:r) v. grzebać

intercede (,ynte:r'si:d) v. wstawiać się; orędować

intercept ('ynte:rsept) v. przechwycić; przejąć; przerwać; udaremnić; podsłuchać

intercession (,ynter'seszyn) s. wstawiennictwo;orędownictwo

interchange (,ynte:r'czejndż) s. wzajemna wymiana; v. wymieniać się; zmieniać się

intercourse ('ynterko:rs) s. stosunek; obcowanie;spółkowanie

interdict (,ynter'dykt) s. zakaz; v. zakazywać;zabraniać

interest('yntryst),s. zainteresowanie; ciekawość; odsetki; interes;procent;v.zainteresować

interested ('yntrystyd) adj. zaciekawiony; zainteresowany

interesting ('yntrystyŋg) adj. ciekawy; interesujący

interfere (,ynter'fier) v. wtrącać się; wdawać się; kolidować; zakłócać;dokuczać

interfere with (,ynter'fier,łys) v. mieszać się do kogoś

interference (,ynter'fierens) s. wtrącanie się; zakłócenie

interior (yn'tierjer) adj. wewnętrzny; środkowy; s. wnętrze głąb kraju;głąb duszy(serca)

interior decorator (yn'tierjer 'dekerejter) s. architekt wnętrz; sprzedawca mebli

interjection (,ynter'dżekszyn) s. okrzyk; wykrzyknik

interlude (ynter'lu:d) s. przerwa; antrakt

intermediary (,ynter'mi:diery) adj. pośredni; pośredniczacy; s. pośrednik;pośredniczka;pośrednie stadium;pośrednia forma; pośredni produkt; agent

intermediate (,ynter'mi:djet) adj. pośredni; środkowy; średni;s.pośrednik;v.pośredniczyć

intermingle (,ynter'myŋgl) v. mieszać (się); pomieszać (się)

intermission (,ynter'myszyn) s. przerwa;pauza; antrakt

intermittent (,ynter'mytent) adj. przerywany; niemiarowy

intern (yn'te:rn) v. internować; odbywać praktykę lekarską;

intern ('ynte:rn) s. praktykant lekarski w szpitalu

internal ('ynte:rnl) adj. wewnętrzny; krajowy; domowy

international (,ynter'naeszenl) adj. międzynarodowy; s. międzynarodówka; zawody międzynarodowe;zawodnik międzynarodowy

interpose (,ynter'pouz) v. wstawać; wtrącać (się); przerywać

interpret (yn'te:pryt) v. tłumaczyć i objaśniać; interpretować;rozumieć(opatrznie etc.)

interpretation (yn,te:rpry'tejszyn) s. interpretacja; tłumaczenie;sposób zrozumienia

interpreter (yn'te:rpryter) s. tłumacz (ustny)

interrogate (yn'teregejt),v. wypytywać; przesłuchiwać

interrogation (yn,tere'gejszyn) s. przesłuchanie; pytanie

interrogative (,ynte'rogetyw) adj. pytający (np. ton)

interrupt (,ynte'rapt) v. przerywać; zasłaniać (widok)

interruption (,ynte'rapszyn) s. przerwa (w czynności etc.)

intersect (,ynte:r'skt) v. przecinać (się;pokrzyżować)się)

intersection (,ynter'sekszyn) s. przecinanie się; skrzyżowanie

interval ('ynterwel) s. odstęp; przerwa;antrakt;okres(pogody)

intervene (,ynter'wi:n) s. wdawać się; interweniować; zdarzyć sie; zajść;być między(dwoma etc.)

intervention (,ynter'wenszyn) s. interwencja

interview ('ynterwju:) s. wywiad; rozmowa; v. mieć wywiad; widzieć się z kimś (dla wywiadu)

interviewer ('ynterwju:er) s.
przeprowadzający wywiad
intestines,(yn'testynz) pl.
wnętrzności ; jelita
intimacy ('yntymesy) s. zaży-
łość; intymność; poufałe sto-
sunki(płciowe);poufałość
intimate ('yntymyt),adj. zażyły; wewnętrzny; intymny;
v. zawiadamiać; dawać do zrozumienia;s.serdeczny przyjaciel
intimation (,ynty'mejszyn) s.
zawiadomienie; danie do zrozumienia;napomknięcie;znak(czegoś)
intimidate (yn'tymydejt) v.
zastraszyć; onieśmielić
into ('yntu:) prep. do; w; na
intolerable (yn'tolerebl) adj.
nieznośny;nie do zniesienia
intolerant (yn'telerent) adj.
nietolerancyjny; nie znoszący
czegoś (cudzych przekonań etc.)
intoxicate (yn'toksykejt) v.
upić; upajać; odurzać się
intransitive (yn'traensytyw)
adj. & s. nieprzechodni
intrepid (yn'trepyd) adj. nieustraszony ;śmiały;odważny
intricate ('yntrykyt) adj. zawiły ;trudny do zrozumienia
intrigue (yn'tri:g) s. intryga;
potajemna miłość; v. intrygo-
wać; potajemnie utrzymywać
stosunek miłosny; zaciekawiać
introduce (,yntre'dju:s) v.
wprowadzać (coś lub kogoś);
przedstawiać; rozpoczynać; wsuwać; wysuwać; wkładać;zapoznawać
introduction (,yntre'dakszyn) s.
wstęp; wprowadzenie; włożenie;
wsunięcie; przedstawienie
(kogoś);przedmowa;innowacja etc.
introductory (,yntre'daktery)
adj. wstępny; wprowadzający
intrude (,yn'tru:d) v. wpychać
(się); wciskać,(się); wedrzeć
(się); narzucać (się) (komuś)
intruder (yn'tru:der) s. natręt;
intruz; nieproszony gość
intrusion (yn'tr:żyn) s. wcis-
nięcie (się); wepchnięcie (się);
narzucanie (się); wdarcie (się)
w cudze prawa

intuition (,yntju'yszyn) s.
intuicja;przeczucie;wyczucie
inutile (yn'ju:tyl) adj. niepotrzebny; bezcelowy;bezużyteczny
invade (yn'wejd) v. najeżdżać;
wdzierać się; zalewać; owła-
dać; ogarniać; wtargnąć
invader (yn'wejder) s. najezdź-
ca ;okupant
invalid (yn'weli:d) s. chory;
inwalida ;kaleka;człowiek słaby
invalid (yn'waelyd) adj. nieważny ;nieprawomocny
invalidate (yn'daelydejt) v.
unieważniać (prawnie etc.)
invaluable (yn'waeljuebl) adj.
bezcenny; nieoceniony
invariable (yn'weeryebl) adj.
niezmienny;stały;równomierny
invariably (yn'v-eryebly) adv.
niezmiennie;stale;równomiernie
invasion (yn'wejżyn) s. inwazja; najazd; wdarcie (się)
invective (yn'wektyw) s. in-
wektywa; obelga; napaść (słow-
na);obelżywe słowa
invent (yn'went) v. wynaleźć;
wymyślić;zmyślić(coś na kogoś)
invention (yn'wenszyn) s. wynalazek; wymysł; zmyślenie
inventive (yn'wentyw) adj. pomysłowy; wynalazczy
inventor (yn'wentor) s. wynalazca (w nauce,mechanice etc.)
inverse (yn'we:rs) adj. odwrotny; s. odwrotność (czegoś)
inversion (yn'we:rżyn) s. odwrócenie; inwersja; homo-
seksualizm ;wynicowanie
invert (yn'we:rt) v. odwrócić;
przestawić; s. homoseksualista
inverted commas (yn'we:rtyd -
'komes) cudzysłów
invest (yn'west) v. inwestować;
wyposażać; oblegać; obdarzać
investigate (yn'westygejt) v.
badać; prowadzić dochodzenie
investigation (yn,westy gejszyn) s. badanie; dochodzenie; śledztwo;rozpatrzenie;do-
ciekanie
investigator (yn'westygejtor)
s. badacz ;agent(prokuratury)

investment (yn'westment) s.
inwestycja; lokata; oblężenie;osaczenie;obleczenie
invincible (yn'wynsebl) adj.
niepokonany; niezwyciężony
inviolable (yn'wajelebl) adj.
nienaruszalny; nietykalny;
niepogwałcony ;niezniszczalny
invisible (yn'wyzybl) adj.
niewidoczny; niewidzialny
invitation (,ynwy'tejszyn) s.
zaproszenie (pisemne,słowne)
invite (yn'wajt) v. zapraszać;
wywoływać; ściągać; nęcić;
zachęcać; prosic o (radę)
invoice ('ynwois) s. faktura;
v. fakturować
invoke (yn'wouk) v. wzywać;
odwoływac się; wywoływać
involuntary (yn'wolentery) adj.
mimowolny; nieumyślny; bez-
wiedny (czyn,ruch etc.)
involve (yn'wolw) v. gmatwac;
wikłać; wmieszać; komplikować; obejmować; wymagać
invulnerable (yn'walnerebl)
adj. nie do zranienia; nienaruszalny; nie do zdobycia
inward (yn'kerd) adj. wewnętrzny; adv. wewnątrz;w sercu etc.
inwards ('ynkerds) adv. wewnątrz ;w duchu ; w myśli
iodine ('ajoudi:n) s. jod
IOU =I owe you ('ajou'ju:) s.
kwit; skrypt dłużny
irascible (y'raesybl) adj.
gniewliwy; popędliwy; wybuchowy;skory do gniewu
iridescent (,yry'desnt) adj.
mieniący się; tęczowy
iris ('ajerys) s. tęczówka
Irish ('ajerysz) adj. irlandzki;s. Irlandczyk
iron ('ajern) s. żelazo; żelazko;(pistolet; rewolwer;)adj.
żelazny; v. zakuwać; prasować
ironic(al) (aj'ronyk(el)) adj.
ironiczny; drwiący;uczczypliwy.
ironing ('ajernyng) s. prasowa-
nie (bielizna etc.)
ironmonger ('ajern,manger) s.
handlarz wyrobów żelaznych;wła-
ciciel sklepu żelaznego

iron mold ('ajernmould) s.
plama od rdzy
ironworks ('ajernłe:rks) s. huta żelaza ;przetwornia żelaza
irony ('ajereny) s. ironia
irradiate (y'rejdjejt) v. os-
wietlać; naświetlać; oswiecać;
rozjasniać; rozpromienić
irrational (y'raesznel) adj.
nieracjonalny; nierozumny;
niewymierny;s.liczba niewymierna
irreconcilable (y'rekesajlebl)
adj. nieprzejednany; nie dający się pogodzić(z wiarą etc.)
irrecoverable (,yry'kawerebl)
adj. niepowetowany; nie do
odzyskania;stracony bezpowrotnie
irredeemable (,yry'di:mebl)
adj. niewymienny; beznadziejny;nieodwracalny;nieodkupny
irregular (y'regjuler) adj. nieregularny; nierówny; nieporządny; nielegalny;nieprawidłowy
irrelevant (y'relywent) adj.
nieistotny; niestosowny; oderwany; od rzeczy;nie do rzeczy
irremovable (,yry'mu:webl) adj.
nieusuwalny;nie do pokonania
irreparable (y'reperebl) adj.
niepowetowany;nie do naprawie-
nia
irreplaceble (,yry'plejsebl) adj.
niezastąpiony;nie do zastąpienia
irrepressible (,yry'presybl)
adj. niepohamowany;nieodparty
irreproachable (,yry'prouczebl)
adj. nienaganny; bez zarzutu
irresistible (,yry'zystybl) adj.
nieodparty;porywający;gwałtowny
irresolute (y'rezelu:t) adj.
niezdecydowany; chwiejny
irrespective (.yrys'pektyw) adj.
niezależny; adv. niezależnie;
bez względu na...;bez szacunku
irresponsible (,yrys'ponsybl)
adj. nieodpowiedzialny;nieodpowie-
dzialny
irretrievable (,yry'tri:webl)
adj. bezpowrotnie stracony
irreverent (y'rewerent) adj.
lekceważący; uchybiający
irrevocable (y'rewekebl) adj.
nieodwołalny; nie do odwołania
irrigate ('yrygejt), v. nawadniać; przepłukiwać; oświeżać

irritable ('yrytebl) adj.
draźliwy; wraźliwy; nerwowy;
przewraźliwiony;skory do gniewu
irritate ('yrytejt) v. denerwowac; irytowac; draźnic;
rozdraźniac;uniewaźnic prawnie
irritation (,yry'tejszyn) s.
irytacja; rozdraźnienie
is (yz) v. jest; zob. be
island ('ajlend) s. wyspa;
wysepka (na bruku)
isle (ajl) s. wyspa; v. źyc
na wyspie ;zrobic (jak)wyspę
isn't ('yznt) = is not; exp.:
nie jest (w domu etc.)
isn't it ? ('yznt yt) nieprawda ? czy nie prawda?
isolate ('ajselejt) v. odosab-
niac; izolowac;osamotnic
isolated ('ajselejtyd) adj.
odosobniony;osamotniony
isolation (,ajse'lejszyn) s.
odosobnienie; izolacja; wyodrębnienie;osamotnienie
issue ('yszu:) s. wydanie;
przydział; zeszyt; spor; problem; argument; wynik; koniec;
ujscie; wyjscie; wypływ; potomstwo; upuszczenie; dochod;
v. wysyłac; wypuszczac; wydawac; dawac w wyniku; wychodzic; pochodzic ;emitowac
isthmus ('ysmes) s. przesmyk;
międzymorze ;ciesn; węzina
it (yt) pron. to; ono
Italian (y'taeljen) adj. włoski
itch ('ycz) s. swędzenie;
swierzb;chętka; v. czuc swędzenie; swędzic;miec ochotę
item ('ajtem) s. pozycja; punkt
programu; artykuł; wiadomosc;
adv. podobnie; takźe;teź dotyczy
itemize ('ajte,majz) v. wy-
szczegolniac(rachunek,spis)
itinerary (aj'tynerery) s. marszruta; szlak; przewodnik;
adj. podróźny; drogowy
its (yts) pron. jego; jej; swoj
itself (yt'self) pron. się; siebie; sobie; sam; sama; samo
ivory ('ajwery) s. kosc słoniowa;klawisz fortepianu;biel kre-
mowa;adj.z kości słoniowej;biały

ivy ('ajwy) s. bluszcz
j (dźej) dziewiąta litera
angielskiego alfabetu
jab (dźaeb) s. szturchaniec;
dźgnięcie; v. szturchac; dźgac
jack (dźaek) s. lewarek; dźwignia; przyrząd; walet; flaga;
gniazdko elektr.; złącze
jack up ('dźaek,ap) v. podniesc
lewarkiem;wysrubowanie(cen)
jackal ('dźaeko:l) s. szakal;
sługus;harowac za kogos
jackass ('dźaekaes) s. osioł;
duren; balwan;menda;niedojda
jackdaw ('dźaekdo:) s. kawka
jacket ('dźaekyt) s. marynarka;
źakiet; kurtka; okładzina;_ob-
woluta; osłona; v. okrywac; nakładac okładzine;wkładac do teki
jack-in-the-box ('dźaek-yn-dy-
boks) s. figurka wyskakująca
z pudełka;typ ognia sztucznego
jackknife ('dźaeknajf) s.
scyzoryk; nóź składany
jack-of-all-trades ('dźaek,ow-
'o:l,trejds) majster do
wszystkiego;majster klepka
jackpot ('dźaek,pot) s. główna
wygrana; pula
jackscrew ('dźaekskru:) s. lewar srubowy (podnosnik)
jag (dźaeg) s. ostry wystep;
zadarcie; nacięcie; podniecenie; popijawa; zabawa; v. po-
szarpac; postrzepic; ząbkowac
jagged ('dźaegyd) adj. po-
strzepiony;wyszczerbiony;szczerba-
ty
jaguar ('dźaegjuer) s. jaguar
jail (dźejl) s. ciupa; więzienie;v. więzic; wsadzac(kogos)
jam (dźaem) s. tłok; zator; korek; zła sytuacja; v. stłoczyc;
zablokowac; zaciac; zagłuszyc
janitor ('dźaenitor) s. portier;
dozorca;sprzątacz biurowy etc.
January ('dźaenjuery) s. sty-
czen ; a.styczniowy (dzien etc.)
Japanese (,dźaepe'ni:z) adj.
japonski; s.Japonczyk
jar (dźa:r) s. słoj; słoik;
zgrzyt; kłotnia; drganie;
v. zgrzytac; draźnic; wstrzą-
sac; kłócic się ;trzasc;razic

jaundice ('džo:ndys) s. żółtaczka ;v.powodować żażdrość (żółtaczkę)

javelin ('džaewlyn) s. oszczep

jaw (dżo:) s. szczęka; v. ględzic;gadać;wstawiać mowę

jaw-bone ('džo:boun) s. kość
szczękowa; v. nakłaniać słowami (pod presją)

jazz (dżaz) s. muzyka jazzowa;
v. kłamać;adj.zgrzytliwy;krzyk-
liwy,

jazz it up ('džaz,yt'ap) v.
ożywiać; ulepszać (coś)

jay (dżej) s. sójka; dudek;
pleciuga; gaduła (arogancki)

jay-walker ('džej,ło:ker) s.
nieprawidłowo przechodzący
jezdnię ;roztrzepaniec

jealous ('dželes) adj. zazdrosny; baczny (nadzor);zawistny

jealousy ('dželesy) s. zazdrość;
zawiść ;wybuch zazdrości

jeep (dži:p) s. łazik; samochód
terenowy (silnie zbudowany)

jeer (dżier) s. kpina; szyderstwo; drwina; v. drwić; kpić;
wykpiwac (ordynarnie i złośliwie)

jelly ('dżely) s. galareta;
kisiel;v.zgalareciec;robić gala-
retę

jellyfish ('dżelyfysz) s. meduza;człowiek słabej woli

jeopardize ('dżepe,dajz) v. narazić na niebezpieczeństwo

jerk (dże:rk) s. szarpnięcie;
skręt; skurcz; pchnięcie; bzik;
frajer; v. szarpać; targać;
pchnąć; rzucać się;wzdrygać się

jerky ('dże:rky) adj. urwany;
trzesący; bzikowaty;spazmatyczny

jersey ('dże:rzy) s. sweter

jest (dżest) s. żart; dowcip;
zabawa; pośmiewisko; v. żartować; dowcipkować;przekomarzać
się

jester ('dżester) s. błazen;
trefniś; błazen nadworny

jet (dżet) s. strumień; wytrysk;
płomień; dysza; rozpylacz; odrzutowiec; v. tryskać;a.czarny
jak smoła

jet engine ('dżet'endżyn) s.
motor odrzutowy

jet lag ('dżet,laeg) s.ujemny
efekt zmiany sfer czasu na
pasażera samolotu odrzutowego

jet plane ('dżet,plejn) s. samolot odrzutowy;odrzutowiec

jet-propelled ('dżet-pre,peld)
adj. odrzutowy

jet set ('dżet,set) s. złota
młodzież; prominenci

jetty (dżety) s. grobla; molo;
adj. czarny jak smoła

jewel ('dżu:el) s. klejnot;
drogi kamień; v. ozdabiać
klejnotami; osadzać na kamie-
niach(zamontować)

jeweler ('dżu:eler) s. jubiler;właściciel sklepu jubiler-
skiego

jewelry ('dżu:elry) s, klejno-
ty; biżuteria;kosztowności

Jewish ('dżu:ysz) adj. żydowski

jibe (dżajb) v. zgadzać się;
pasować (do czegoś);harmonizo-
wać

jiffy ('dżyfy) s. mig; chwi-
leczka;momencik;skundka

jiggle ('dżygl) v. kołysać;
lekko hustać;wstrząsać zrywnie

jingle ('dżyngl) v. brzękać;
szczekać; dzwonić; s. brzęk;
szczęk; wierszyk(rymy);dzwonek

job (dżob) s. robota; zajęcie;
zadanie; posada; v. pracować;
robić; handlować; wynajmować

job (dżob) v. ukłuć; dzgnać;
dziobnąć; s. dżgnięcie;praca;
dziobnięcie;zadanie;robota;fach

jobless ('dżoblys) adj. bezrobotny ;bez pracy

job-work ('dżobłerk) s. praca
na akord (zob. piece-work)

jockey ('dżoky) s. dżokej;
v. oszukać; nabrać;pchać się na
pozycje

jocular ('dżokjuler) adj. wesoły; żartobliwy;krotochwilny

jocularity (,dżokju'laeryty)
s. wesołość; żartobliwość;
żarty;ktotochwilność;figlarność

jocund ('dżoukend) adj. wesoły

jog (dżog) s. potrącenie; poruszenie; trucht; róg;występ;
v. potrącać; poruszać; przebiedować; biec truchtem;telepać
się

jog-trot ('dżog'trot) s.
trucht;a.monotonny;jednostajny

join (dżoyn) v. łączyć; przy-
łączać (się); przytykać do;
spotykać się;brać udział
joiner ('dżojner) s. stolarz
joint (dżoynt) v. spajać;łą-
czyć; ćwiartować; kantować;
s. spojenie; fuga; złącze;
zestawienie; zawiasa francuska;
część; lokal; melina; a. wspólny; połączony;dzielący się z kims
joint stock ('dżoynt,stok) adj.
akcyjny (bank)
joke (dżouk) s. żart; dowcip;
figiel; v. żartować z kogoś;
dowcipkować;wysmiać:zadrwić
joker ('dżouker) s. żartownis;
dowcipnis; gość; facet; dżo-
ker; pułapka; trudność
jolly ('dżoly) adj. wesoły; miły; podochocony; adv. szalenie;
bardzo; v. przychlebiac; nabierac; zachęcać;mitygować;ugłas-
jolt (dżoult) v. wstrząsać;
podrzucać; s. wstrząs; podrzu-
cenie; szarpnięcie;podskok
jostle ('dżosl) v. rozpychać
(się); roztrącać; szarpać się;
walczyć (z kims); s. pchnięcie;
starcie;szturchnięcie;tłok;ścisk
jot down ('dżot,dałn) v. zapisać napredce;zanotować pospiesz-
journal ('dże:rnl) s. dziennik;
czasopismo; czop;oś w łożysku
journalism ('dże:rnlyzem) s.
dziennikarstwo
journey ('dże:rny) v. podróżować;
s. podróż;jazda;wycieczka
journeyman ('dże:rnymen) s. cze-
ladnik(nauczony rzemiosła)
jovial ('dżouwjel) adj. wesoły;
jowialny;pełen dobrego humoru
joy (dżoj) s. radość; uciecha
joyful ('dżoyful) adj. radosny;
wesoły;zadowolony(bardzo)
joyous ('dżojes) adj.=joyful
jubilant ('dżu:bylent) adj.
triumfujący; rozradowany
jubilee ('dżu:byli:) s. jubileusz; wielka radość;a.jubileuszowy
judge (dżądż) v. sądzić; osadzać;
rozsadzać; s. sędzia; znawca;
znawczyni;człowiek biegły w oce-

judgment ('dżadżment) s.
sąd; sądzenie; wyrok; rozsądek;opinia; ocena; decyzja
judicial (dżu'dyszel) adj. sądowy; sędziowski; bezstronny;
krytyczny;sądownie zastrzeżony
judicious (dżu'dyszes) a. rozsądny;rozumny;wykazujący rozum
jug (dżąg) s. dzbanek; koza;
ciupa; v. gotować; wsadzać do
kozy, ciupy;dusić (potrawkę)
juggle ('dżagl) v. żonglować;
cyganic; robić sztuczki;
s. kuglarstwo;żonglerka
juggler ('dżagler) s. kuglarz;
żongler;oszust;kanciarz
jugglery ('dżaglery) s. kuglarstwo;podstęp;oszukaństwo;żon-
glerka
Jugoslav ('ju:gou'sla:v) adj.
jugosłowianski;Jugosłowianin
juice (dżu:s) s. sok; treść;
benzyna; elektryczność;
v. wyciskać sok; doić
juicy ('dżu:sy) adj. soczysty;
jędrny;barwny;deszczowy etc.
juke box ('dżuk,boks) s. auto-
mat-gramofon(na monety)
July (dżu:laj) s. lipiec
jumble ('dżambl) s. pomieszać;
kotłować; mieszanina; galimatias; bigos;trzęsąca jazda
jumble-sale ('dżambl,sejl) s.
wyprzedaż wysortowanych to-
warów(często dobroczynna)
jump (dżamp) s. skok; sus; podskok; wyskok; v. skakać; podskoczyć; wskoczyć; wyskoczyć;
wyprzedzać; podnosić cenę;się
wykoleić;poderwać się;rzucać
jumper ('dżamper) s. skoczek;
typ sukni (bez rękawów)
jumpy ('dżampy) adj. nerwowy;
zmienny;nierówny;kapryśny
junction ('dżankszyn) s. połączenie; złącze; stacja węzło-
wa; węzeł;skrzyżowanie(dróg)
juncture('dżankczer) s. połączenie; stan rzeczy; krytycz-
na chwila; chwila:przesilenie
June (dżu:n) s. czerwiec
jungle ('dżangl) s. dżungla;
gaszcz zarosli,lian etc.

junior ('dżu:njer) s. junior;
młodszy; student trzeciego
roku (USA);a.młodszy;z młodszych
junk ('dżąnk) s.złom; szmelc;
narkotyki; v. wyrzucać
junkie ('dżąnki) s. narkoman
jurisdiction (,dżurys'dykszyn)
s. wymiar sprawiedliwości;
sądownictwo;zasięg władzy
jurisprudence (,dżurys'pru:-
dens) s. prawoznawstwo
juror ('dżuerer) s. sędzia
przysięgły; ławnik; zaprzy-
sieżony;juror
jury ('dżuery) s. sąd przysięgłych; sąd konkursowy
just (dżast) s. sprawiedliwy;
słuszny; dokładny; adv. wła-
nie; poprostu; zaledwie; przecież; dokładnie; moment wczes-
niej;ściśle;równie;tak samo
just now ('dżast,nał) exp.:
właśnie teraz;przed chwilą
justice ('dżastys) s. sprawiedliwość; słuszność; są-
dzia(pokoju,sadu najwyższego)
justification (,dżastyfy'kejszyn) s. uzasadnienie;
usprawiedliwienie;wykazanie
justify ('dżastyfaj) v. usprawiedliwić; wytłumaczyć; umoty-
wować; uzasadnić;dać dowody
justly ('dżastly) adv. słusznie;
poprawnie;właściwie;sprawiedli-
wie
jut (dżat) s. występ;v.wystawać
jut out ('dżat,aut) v. wystawać;
sterczeć(na zewnątrz);występować
juvenile ('dżu:wynajl) adj.
małoletni; nieletni; s. wyrostek; młodzik;podrostek
juvenile court ('dżu:wynajl,-
,ko:rt) s. sąd dla nieletnich
juvenile delinquent ('dżu:wy-
najl,dy'lynkłent) s. młodociany przestępca
juxtaposition (,dżakstepe'zyszyn) s. zestawienie; bezpoś-
rednie sąsiedztwo(tuż obok)
k (kej)jedenasta litera angielskiego alfabetu
kangaroo (,kaenge'ru:) s. kangur;a.samosądny;nielegalny
kayak ('kajaek)s.kajak;s.kajakowy

keel (ki:l) s. stępka; kil;
v. wywracać do góry stępką
keen (ki:n) adj. ostry; dotkliwy; żywy; cięty; serdeczny;
gorliwy; zapalony; bystry;
przenikliwy; wrażliwy; czuły
keen on ('ki:n,on) adj. palący się do...;czujący miętę
keep; kept; kept (ki:p; kept;
kept)
keep (ki:p) v. dotrzymywać;
przestrzegać; dochować; obchodzić; strzec; pilnować; utrzymywać; prowadzić; trzymać(sie)
powstrzymać sie; mieszkać;
kontynuować; s. utrzymanie;
jedzenie; wikt;umocnienie
keep away ('ki:p,ełej) v. trzymać sie z daleka;odstraszać
keep back ('ki:p,baek) v. powstrzymać; nie zbliżać się
keep down ('ki:p,dałn) v. trzymać w ryzach; tłumić; kulić
się;utrzymywać na niskim poziomie
keep in('ki:p,yn) v. zatrzymywać; nie wychodzić; pozostawać;nie pokazywć się
keep off ('ki:p,of) v. nie dopuszczać; trzymać się z dala
keep on ('ki:p,on) v. kontynuować; iść dalej;nudzić;męczyć
keep on doing ('ki:p,on'du:yng)
v. robić dalej; nie przestawać;nie dawać spokoju;nudzić
keep out ('ki:p, ałt) v. nie
wchodzić; trzymać się na uboczu;nie pozwolić wejść;odpędzać
keep talking ('ki:p'to:kyng)v.
mówić dalej;kontynuować rozmowę
keep time ('ki:p'tajm) v. być
punktualnym;zapisywać czas pracy
keep to oneself ('ki:p,tu'łan-
self) v. trzymać się na uboczu; żyć w odosobnieniu
keep up ('ki:p,ap) v. dotrzymywać; utrzymywać w porządku;
nie dawać isć spać; trzymać
się w dobrym stanie;czuwać
keep up with ('ki:p,ap'łys) v.
śledzić; dotrzymywać (kroku)
keeper ('ki:per) s. opiekun;
dozorca; strażnik; konserwator;
klamra; kotwica magnesu;skobel

keeping ('ki:pyŋ) s. opieka;
zgoda; harmonia;a.do przechowy-
wania
keepsake ('ki:psejk) s. upominek; pamiątka od kogoś
keg (keg) s. beczułka;100 funtów
kennel ('kenl) s. psiarnia;
psia buda; ściek; v. trzymać
w budzie; mieszkać w norze
kept (kept) v. zob. keep
kerb stone ('ke:rb,stoun) s.
krawężnik (ang.) zob. curb
kerchief ('ke:rczyf) s. chustka (na głowę);chustka do nosa
kernel ('ke:rnl) s. jądro;
ziarno;sedno sprawy;istotna rzecz
ketchup ('keczap) s. sos pomidorowy (gotowy) do mięsa
kettle ('ketl) s. kocioł; czajnik; imbryk na herbatę
kettledrum ('ketl,dram) s.bęben-
-kocioł(półkulisty)miedziany
key (ki:) s. klucz; klawisz;
klin; ton; rafa; wysepka;
v. stroic; zamykać kluczem
lub zwornikiem;adj.ważny;kontro-
lujący
keyboard ('ki:bo:rd) s. kla-
wiatura (maszyny do pisania etc.)
keyhole ('ki:houl) s. dziurka
od klucza (w drzwiach etc.)
keynote ('ki:nout) s. nuta
kluczowa ;myśl przewodnia
keystone ('ki:stoun) s. zwornik;zasada;główna część
kick (k;k) s. kopniak; kopnię-
cie; wierzgnięcie; wykop;
strzał; odrzut; skarga; narzekanie; przyjemność; uciecha;
krzepa; miłe podniecenie; opor;
v. kopać; wierzgać; skrzywić
się; protestować; opierać się
kickback ('kykbaek) s. łapówka
za kontrakt;dawanie łapówki
kick downstairs ('kykdałn'steerz)
v. degradować; zrzucać ze
schodów (kopniakiem)
kick-off ('kykof) s. rozpoczęcie
meczu; pierwszy strzał
kick out ('kyk aut) v. wyrzucić;
wykopać ; pozbyć się
kick the bucket ('k;k,dy'bakyt)
v. umrzeć; odwalić kitę; wy-
ciagnąć nogi;wykitować

kid (kyd) s. koźlę; dzieciak;
smyk; młodzik; blaga; bujda;
v. urodzić koźlę; bujać; nabierać; żartować;dowcipkować
kid glove ('kydglaw) s. rękawiczka;adj.galowy;delikatny
kidnap ('kydnaep) v. porywać;
uprowadzać;ukraść dziecko etc.
kidnapper ('kydnaeper) s. porywacz (dziecka;zakładnika etc.)
kidney ('kydny) s. nerka; rodzaj;a.w kształcie nerki
kidney bean ('kydny,bi:n) s.
fasola szparagowa; piesza
kill (kyl) v. zabijać; uśmiercać; wybić; zatrzymać (piłkę,
motor) ścinać (piłkę); s.upo-
lowane zwierzę; zabicie; mord
kill time (,kyl'tajm) v. zabijać czas; marnować czas
killer ('kyler) s. zabójca;
morderca; narzędzie śmierci
kiln (kyln) s. piec do wypala-
nia lub wysuszania cegieł etc.
kilogram(me) ('kylougraem) s.
kilogram;a. kilogramowy
kilometer ('kyle,mi:ter) s. kilometr; a. kilometrowy
kilt (kylt) s. spódniczka męska (szkocka); v. podkasać;
plisować pionowo;s.spódnica
szkocka
kin (kyn) s. rodzina; krewni;
ród; adj. spokrewniony;pokrewny
kind (kajnd) s. rodzaj; jakość;
gatunek; charakter; natura;
adj. grzeczny; uprzejmy;
życzliwy; łagodny;wyrozumiały
kindergarten ('kynder,ga:rtn)
s. przedszkole (do sześciu lat
wieku)
kindhearted ('kajnd'ha:rtyd)
adj. dobrotliwy;współczujący
kindle ('kyndle) v. rozpalić;
rozżarzyć; rozniecać; podniecać;zapalać się
kindly ('kajndly) adj. uprzejmie; życzliwie; adj. dobry;
dobrotliwy; życzliwy;adv.uprzej-
mie
kindness ('kajndnys) s. dobroć;
uprzejmość; łaskawość; życz-
liwość ;życzliwy postępek
kindred ('kyndryd) s. krewni;
pokrewieństwo; adj.pokrewny

king (kyŋg) s. król
kingdom ('kyngdom) s. królestwo;monarchia;świat(roslin etc.)
kingsize ('kyŋgsajz) adj. wielki; duży;krolewskich wymiarow
kingly ('kyŋgly) adj. krolewski
kinsman ('kynzmen) s. krewny;
powinowaty (męszczyzna)
kipper ('kyper) s. sledź wędzony; ryba suszona; v. suszyc;
wedzic i solic; zasuszac(ryby)
kiss (kys) s. całus; v. cało-
wac; pocałowac;lekko dotknąc
kit (kyt) s. przybory; narzę-
dzia; wyposażenie; zestaw;
komplet; torba; bagaż; ceb-
rzyk; kubeł;komplet(narzędzi)
kitchen ('kyczn) s. kuchnia
kitchenette ('kyczynet) s.
kuchenka(mała w kawalerce etc.)
kite (kajt) s. latawiec;v.szybo-
kitten ('kytn) s. kotek
knack (naek) s. spryt; sztuczka; chwyt; dryg; talent
knapsack ('naepsaek) s. plecak
knave (nejw) s. łajdak; łotr;
szelma; walet;naciągacz;kanalia
knavery ('nejwery) s. łajdactwo; szelmostwo;niegodziwosc
knead ('ni:d) v. miesic; gniesc;
masowac;kształcic(charakter)
knee ('ni:) s. kolano;v.klękac
knee breeches ('ni:bryczyz) pl.
spodnie do kolan
kneel; knelt; knelt (ni:l; nelt;
nelt)
kneel ('ni:l) v. klękac
knelt(nelt) zob. kneel
knew (nju:) zob . know
knickerbockers ('nikerbockers)
s. pumpy; krótkie spodnie
spięte pod kolanami
knickknack ('niknaek) s. cacko;
fatałaszek; przysmaczek
knife (najf) s. nóż; v. krajac;
kłuc nożem; zakłuc;zadźgac nożem
knight (najt) s. rycerz; v. nadawac szlachectwo;nobilitowac
knit; knit; knit (nyt; nyt; nyt)
knit (nyt) v. robic na drutach;
dziac; marszczyc (brwi); łączyc; sciągac;powodowac zrosnię-
cie(kosci);spajac(cementem)

knitting (nytyŋg) s. dzianie;
trykotarstwo;dziewiarstwo
knives (najwz) pl. noże; pl.od
knife
knob (nob) s. guzik; guz; gałka; sęk;uchwyt;pokrętło;rączka
knock (nok) s. stuk; uderzenie;
pukanie; stukac; pukac; zapu-
kac; uderzyc; zderzyc; szturchac;zderzyc się
knock down ('nok,dałn) v. powalic; obniżac cenę;rozkręcac
knock out ('nok,aut) v. nokau-
towac; wybijac; wymęczyc
knock over ('nok,ower) v. przewracac; przewrócic
knocker ('noker) s. kołatka na
drzwiach;malkontent;opukiwacz
knot (not) s. węzeł; kokarda;
sęk; zgrubienie; dystans morski 1853 m; v. wiazac; zawiązywac; komplikowac; motac
knotty ('noty) adj. węzłowaty;
sękaty; zawiły; zagadkowy
know; knew; known (nou; nju:;
noun)
know (nou) v. wiedziec; umiec;
znac; móc odrożniac; poznac
know-how ('nouhau) s. umiejętnosc; znajomosc rzeczy
knowingly ('nouyŋgly) adj. swia-
domie; naumyslnie; chytrze
knowledge ('noulydż) s. wiedza;
nauka; znajomosc;zasięg wiedzy
knowledgeable ('nolydżebl) adj.
dobrze poinformowany; mądry
knuckle ('nakl) s. staw palca;
kastet; uderzac koscmi palców
kotow ('kou,tał) = kowtow
kowtow ('koł,tał) v. bic czołem; płaszczyc się; s. ukłon
starochiński czołem do ziemi
Kraut (kraut) adj. szkopski
(niemiecki) ; kapuściany
kudos ('kju:dos) s. nagroda
lub uznanie za znaczne osiągnięcie; sława (slang)
Ku Klux Klan ('kju:,kluks'klaen)
s. rasistowska tajna organizacja w USA przeciw murzynom,
żydom i katolikom
kulak (ku:'la:k) s. zamożny
chłop; kułak

l (el) dwunasta litera alfabetu angielskiego; klauzura; kolanko (rury); kątownik

lab (laeb) s. (slang):laboratorium; a. laboratoryjny

label ('lejbl) s. nalepka; etykieta; naklejka; przezwisko; v. przylepiac etykiety (na coś; komuś);przezywac

labor ('lejber) s. praca; robota; trud; mozół; wysiłek; klasa robotnicza; poród; v. ciężko pracowac; mozolic się; borykac sie; łudzic się; brnąc; opracowac; rozwodzic się; rodzic;szczegółowo opracowywac

laboratory (lae'boretery) s. laboratorium; pracownia

laborious (le'bo:rjes) adj. pracowity; mozolny; wypracowany;ciężko pracujący

labor union('lejber'ju:njen) s. związek zawodowy

laborer ('lejberer) s. robotnik płatny na godzinę(fizyczny)

laborite ('lejberajt) s. członek partii pracy (w Anglii)

lace (lejs) s. sznurowka; sznurowadło; koronka; v. sznurowac; przetykac; koronkowac; urozmaicac; chłostac; zakrapiac (wódkę);młocic;bic;walic

lack (laek) s. brak; niedostatek; v. brakowac; nie miec czegoś;byc bez czegoś

laconic (le'konyk) adj. lakoniczny; zwięzły; treściwy

lacquer ('laeker) s. lakier; v. lakierowac;emaliowac

lad (laed) s. chłopak; chłopiec

ladder ('laeder) s. drabina; v. pruc; rozpruc;puszczac oczka

ladder proof ('laeder,pru:f) adj. nie prujące się (np. pończochy);nie puszczający oczek

laden ('lejdn) adj. obciążony; obarczony;pogrążony(w smutku)

lading ('lejdyŋg)s. fracht; załadowanie; ładunek (statku etc.)

ladle ('lejdl) s. warząchew; czerpak; chochla; v. czerpac; nalewac warząchwią (czerpakiem)

lady ('lejdy) s. pani; dama

lady killer ('lejdy,kyler) s. pożeracz serc niewieścich

ladylike ('lejdylajk) adj. wytworny; zniewieściały

lag (laeg) s. zaleganie; opóźnianie; zwłoka;v. zalegac; wlec się z tyłu; nie nadążac

lag behind ('laeg,by'hajnd) v. pozostawac w tyle;zalegac

lager ('la:ger) s. wystałe piwo

lagoon (le'gu:n) s. laguna

laid (lejd) zob. lay

lain (lejn) zob. lie

lair (leer) s. barłog; legowisko; szałas; v.isc na legowisko

lake (lejk) s. jezioro;a.jeziorny

lamb (laem) s. jagnię; baranina

lame (lejm) adj. kulawy; ułomny; v. okulawic; okaleczyc

lament (le'ment) s. lament; biadanie; v. lamentowac; biadac; opłakiwac; narzekac; ubolewac;zawodzic;byc w żałobie

lamentable ('laementebl) adj. opłakany; godny ubolewania; żałobny;wyrażający ubolewanie

lamentation (,laemen'tejszyn) s. lament; biadanie; lamentacja

lamp (laemp) s. lampa; latarka; kaganek; v. świecic; oświetlac; gapic się;zobaczyc;widziec

lamppost ('laemppoust) s. słup latarniany ;latarnia uliczna

lamp shade ('laempszejd) s. abażur

lance (la:ns) s. lanca; lansjer; lancet; v.kłuc; przebijac lancą lub lancetem; rozcinac

land (laend) s. ląd; ziemia; grunt; kraj; v. wyciągac na ląd; wyładowac; zdobyc (np. nagrodę)

landholder ('laend,houlder) s. właściciel ziemski; dzierżawca

landing ('laendyŋg) s. lądowanie; pomost; przystań; półpiętrze

landing field ('laendyŋg,fi:ld) s. lotnisko polowe ;lądowisko

landing gear ('leandyŋg,gier) s. podwozie(z kołami-samolotu)

landing stage ('laendyŋg,stejdż) s. pomost pływający ; wyładunek

landlady ('laend,lejdy) s.
  właścicielka domu; hotelu
  etc.;gospodyni (pensjonatu)
landlord ('laend,lo:rd) s.
  właściciel domu czynszowego;
  gospodarz odnajmujący pokój
landmark ('laendma:rk) s. punkt
  orientacyjny; słup graniczny
landowner ('laend,oŁner) s.
  właściciel ziemski
landscape ('laendskejp) s.
  krajobraz; v. kształtowac
  teren i ogród (upiększac)
landslide ('laendslajd) s.
  osuwisko; lawina głosów
landslip ('laendslyp) s. osuwisko; obsunięcie się ziemi
lane (lejn) s. tor; uliczka;
  szlak; przejscie; linia ruchu kołowego ;trasa(samolotu)
language ('laengłydż) s. mowa;
  język mowiony i pisany
languid ('laengłyd) s. ospały;
  omdlały; słaby; ociężały; powolny; rozmarzony; tęskny
languish ('laengłysz) v. omdle-
  wac; marniec; ginąc z tęsknoty ;miec wyraz zadumy
languor ('laenger) s. omdlenie;
  osłabienie;ociężałosc; ospa-
  łosc; tęsknota; rozmarzenie;
  powolnosc;brak wigoru;słabosc
lank (laenk) adj, mizerny; wysoki; chudy; wychudzony;
  prosty; gładki ;długi i płaski
lanky ('laenky) adj. wychudzony; wysoki i chudy
lanolin ('laenolyn) s. lanolina
lantern ('laentern) s. latarnia
lap (laep) s. łono; podołek;
  pola; okrążenie; zanadrze;
  dolinka; chlupotanie; lura;
  v. spowijac; otulac; zakładac
  (jak dachówki); wystawac;
  chłeptac; chlupotac;chlupac
lapel (le'pel) s. klapa
  (płaszcza)dochodząca kołnierza
lapse (laeps) s. lapsus; upływ;
  okres; omyłka; v. potknąc sie;
  odstąpic; omylic sie; upłynąc;
  stracic waznosc; minąc; przechodzic;pogrążyc się w stan...

larceny ('la:rseny) s. kradzież
larch (la:rcz) s. modrzew
lard (la:rd) s. smalec; v. szpi-
  kowac; naszpikowywac;ozdabiac
    rcytatami
larder ('la:rder) s. spizarnia
large (la:rdż) adj. wielki;
  rozległy; obfity; hojny
largely ('la:rdżly)adv. znacz-
  nie; hojnie; suto; w dużym
  stopniu; w dużej ilosci;głównie
lark (la:rk) s. skowronek; zabawa; uciecha; v. figlowac;
  żartowac; przeskakiwac
larva ('la:rwa) s. larwa
larynx ('laerynks) s. krtan
lascivious (le'syvjes) adj.
  lubiezny;wzbudzajacy lubieżnosc
lash (laesz) s. bicz; uderzenie;
  nagana; rzęsa; v. chłostac; machac; walic; pędzic; uwiązac
lass (laes) s. dziewczyna;
  dziewczę młoda kobieta
lasso (lae'su:) s. lasso;
  v. chwytac na lasso
last (laest) adj. ostatni; ubiegły; ostateczny; adv. po raz
  ostatni; ostatnio; wreszcie;
  w koncu; v. trwac; wytrzymac;
  wystarczyc; długo słuzyc;
  s. koniec; kres; wytrzymałosc;
  kopyto szewskie ;ostatnie dziecko
last but one ('laest,bat'Łan)
  exp.:przedostatni
lasting ('la:styng) adj. stały;
  trwały ;długo trwały
lastly (la:stly) adv. w koncu;
  na koncu;w konkluzji;ostatecznie
last night ('laest,najt) exp.
  wczoraj wieczór
last name ('laest,nejm) s. nazwisko
latch (laecz) s. zasuwka; rygiel; zatrzask; v. zamykac na
  zasuwkę, rygiel lub zatrzask
latch onto ('laecz,ontu) v.
  uczepic się kogos
late (lejt) adj. & s. pozny;
  spozniony; były; zmarły; adv.
  pozno; poniewczasie; niegdys
lately ('lejtly) adv. ostatnio
later on ('lejter,on) adv.
  pozniej; potem; dalej

lath (laeθ) s. łata; deseczka;
v. pokrywać łatami(do tynkowa-
nia)

lathe (lejz) s. tokarnia; koło
garncarskie; v. toczyć (na
tokarni); obrabiać(na obrabiarce)

lather ('laedzer) s. piana;
mydliny; v. mydlić (brodę);
zapienić (się); v. prać; łoić

Latin ('laetyn) adj. łaciński;
s. łacina; łacinnik

latitude ('laetytju:d) s. szerokość (geograficzna); szerokość poglądów; zakres; roz-
miary; wolność; swoboda (np.
działania); tolerancja

latter ('laeter) adj, drugi;
końcowy; schyłkowy;ostatni

latterly ('laeterly) adv. ostatnio; niedawno; później

lattice ('laetys) s. kratownica; v. kratować;ułożyć w kratę

laudable ('lo:debl) adj. chwalebny ;godny pochwały

laugh (laef) v. śmiać się; za-
śmiać się ;roześmiać się

laugh at ('laef,et) v. wyśmiewać;uśmiać sie(z czegoś)

laugh away ('laef,e'łej) v. zbyć
śmiechem

laugh off ('laef,of) v. obrócić
w żart ;pokryć zmieszanie śmiechem

laughter ('laefter) s. śmiech

launch (lo:ncz) v. puszczać
w ruch; spuszczać na wodę;
miotać; rzucać; zadawać; wydawać; s. szalupa; spuszczenie
na wodę (statku,okrętu,etc.)

launching pad ('lo:nczyŋg,paed)
s. wyrzutnia (rakiet)

launderette (lo:n'dret) s. pralnia samoobsługowa

laundry ('lo:ndry) s. pralnia;
bielizna do prania

laurel ('lorel) s. wawrzyn;
laur; v. wieńczyć wawrzynem

lavatory ('laewetery) s. umywalnia; ustęp; umywalka

lavender ('laewynder) s. lawenda; v. wkładać lawendę w bieliznę ;a. lawendowy

lavish ('laewysz) adj. hojny;su-
ty; rozrzutny; v. nie szczędzić
pieniędzy, miłości etc.)

law (lo:) s. prawo; ustawa; reguła; sądy;posłuszeństwo prawu

lawful ('lo:ful) adj, legalny;
słuszny; prawowity; z prawego
łoża; prawnie uznany

lawless ('lo:lys) adj. bezprawny; łamiący prawo; rozpustny

lawn (lo:n) s. trawnik; murawa

lawsuit ('lo:sju:t) s. proces
(sądowy) ;sprawa sądowa

lawyer ('lo:jer) s. prawnik;
adwokat ;radca prawny

lax (laeks) adj. luźny; nieszczelny; niedbały; nieścisły;
mający rozwolnienie ;wolny

laxative ('laeksetyw) adj.& s.
przeczyszczający (środek)

laxity ('laeksyty) s. luźność;
nieścisłość; niedokładność;
niedbalstwo;rozwiązłość

lay; laid; laid(lej; lejd;
lejd)

lay (lej) v. kłaść; uspokajać;
układać; skręcać (się); zaczać
się; spać z kimś; s. położenie; układ; spanie (z kims);
adj. świecki; laicki; niefachowy; lay- zob. lie

layout ('lejout) s. rozkład;
plan ;założenie; układ

lay out ('lej.aut) v. układać;
projektować; powalić; (slang):
zabić; wydatkować; wyłożyć

lay up ('lejap) v. zbierać;
gromadzić; przechowywać

layer ('lejer) s. warstwa; od-
kład; kura niosąca; zakładają-
cy się;pokład

layman ('lejmen) s. człowiek
świecki; laik

lazy ('lejzy) adj. leniwy;
próżniaczy;ociężały

lead (led) s. ołów; v. pokrywać
ołowiem; obciążać ołowiem

lead; led; led (li:d; led;led)

lead (li:d) v. prowadzić; kierować; dowodzić; naprowadzać;
nasunąć; namówić; dyrygować;
przewodzić; s. kierownictwo;
przewodnictwo; przewaga; prym;
wskazówka ;przykład;powodzenie

leaden ('ledn) adj. ołowiany;
ciężki;ociężały;ponury;szary

leader ('li:der) s. przywódca;
lider; przewodnik; prowadzący
leading ('li:dyng) adj. kierow-
niczy; naczelny; główny;
s. kierownictwo; prowadzenie;
przewodnictwo;przywództwo
leaf (li:f) s. liść; kartka;
pl. leaves (li:wz)
leaflet (li:flyt) s. listek;
ulotka (często złożona)
league (li:g) s. liga; związek;
mila; v. łączyć (się) w ligę
leak (li:k) s. dziura; otwór;
przeciekanie; v. cieknąć;
przeciekać; wyciekać (sekrety);wysączać; zaciekać
leakage (li:kydż) s. przeciekanie (sekretów); wyciekanie
(pieniędzy); rozproszenie
leaky ('li:ky) adj. dziurawy;
nieszczelny; cieknący; niedyskretny;nie dochowujący sekre-tu
lean; leant; leant (li:n; lent;
lent)
lean (li:n) v. nachylać (się);
pochylać (się); opierać(się)
(o coś); adj. chudy; s. chude mięso;nachylenie;skłonność
leant (lent) v. zob. lean
leap; leapt; leapt (li:p; lept;
lept)
leap (li:p) v. skakać; przeskoczyć; s. skok; podskok
leapt (lept) zob . leap
leap-year ('li:pye:r) s. rok
przestępny
learn; learnt; learnt (le:rn;
le:rnt; le:rnt)
learn (le:rn) v. uczyć się;
dowiadywać się;zapamiętać
learned ('le:rnyd) adj. uczony
learner ('le:rner) s. uczący
się; uczeń; uczennica
learning ('le:rnyng) s. nauka;
wiedza; erudicja;umiejętności
learnt (le:rnt) v. zob. learn
lease (li:s) s. dzierżawa;
v. dzierżawić;wydzierżawić
leash (li:sh) s. smycz
least (li:st) adj. najmniejszy
adv. najmniej; w najmniejszym
stopniu; s. najmniejsza rzecz;
drobnostka najmniej ważna

leather ('ledzer)s. skóra; adj.
skórzany; v. pokrywać skóra;
oprawiać w skórę ;sprać(rzemie-niem)
leave; left; left (li:w; left;
left)
leave (li:w) v. zostawiać;
opuszczać; odchodzić; odjeżdżać;
pozostawiać; s. pożegnanie;
urlop; pozwolenie
leaven (lewn) s. drożdże
leaves (li:wz) pl. liście;
zob. leaf
lecture ('lekczer) s. wykład;
nagana; v. wykładać; udzielać
nagany;przemawiać do sumienia
lecturer ('lekczerer) s. wykła-
dowca(w uczelni,klasie etc.)
led (led) zob. lead
ledge (ledż) s. występ; stopień;
półka; gzyms; listwa; rafa
lee (li:) s. strona zawietrzna;
osłona;adj.zawietrzny;osłonięty
leech (li:cz) s. pijawka
leek (li:k) s. por
leer (lier) s. spojrzenie z ukosa; v. łypać okiem znacząco
(chytrze,złośliwie,pożądliwie)
left (left) adj. lewy; adv. na
lewo; s. lewa strona; zob. leave
left-hand ('left,haend) s. lewa
ręka;adj.lewoskrętny;lewostronny
left-handed ('left'haendyd) s.
mankut; adj. leworęki; niezgrabny;wątpliwy;nieszczery
left side ('left,sajd) s. lewa
strona (drogi,samochodu etc.)
leg (leg) s. noga; nóżka; podpórka; odcinek;kończyna;udziec
legacy (legesy) s. spadek;
spuścizna;dziedzictwo;zapis
legal ('li:gel) adj. prawny;
prawniczy ;ustawowy;legalny
legation (li:'gejszyn) s. poselstwo (włącznie z posłem)
legend ('ledżend) s. legenda
legendary ('ledżendery) adj.
legendarny ;tradycyjny
legible ('ledżebl) adj. czytelny ;łatwo czytelny
legion ('li:dżen) s. legion;
legia ;wojsko;wielka ilość;
mnóstwo;tłumy;mnogość

legislation (,ledżys'lejszyn)
s. prawodawstwo; ustawodawstwo

legislative ('ledżysletyw) adj.
prawodawczy; ustawodawczy

legislator ('ledżyslator) s.
prawodawca; poseł do parlamen-
tu (sejmu,senatu etc.)

legitimate (ly'dżytymyt) adj.
ślubny; prawowity; słuszny;
uzasadniony;logiczny;rozsadny

leg-pull ('legpu:l) s. kawał;
żart; sztuczka;naciąganie

leisure ('li:żer) s. wolny czas;
swoboda od zajęc;wolne chwile

leisurely ('li:żerly) adv. swobodnie; bez pośpiechu; adj.
mający czas; spokojny; robiony
w wolnym czasie

lemon ('lemen) s. cytryna;
tandeta;adj.cytrynowy;z cytryn

lemonade ('lemenejd) s. lemo-
niada(z soku cytrynowego etc.)

lend; lent; lent (lend; lent;
lent)

lend (lend) v. pożyczać; użyczać; udzielac

length (lenkg) s. długosć

lengthen ('lenkgen) v. przedłużać; wydłużać(się);podłużać

lengthwise ('lensłajz) adv. adj.
wzdłuż; na długosć

lenient ('li:njent) adj. wyrozumiały; łagodny

lens (lenz) s. soczewka; objektyw ;lupa

lent (lent) s. post; zob. lend

leopard ('leperd) s. lampart

leper ('leper) s. trędowaty;
trędowata

leprosy ('lepresy) s. trąd

less (les) adj. mniejszy; adv.
mniej; s. coś mniejszego;
prep. bez;nie tak dużo(wiele)

lessen (lesn) v, zmniejszac(się);
maleć; pomniejszać

lesser ('leser) adj. mniejszy

lesson (lesn) s. lekcja; nauczka;urywek z Biblji;wykład

lest (lest) conj. ażeby nie; że

let; let; let (let;let;let)

let (let) v. zostawić; wynajmować; dawać; puszczać ; pozwalać

let alone ('let,e'loun) s. zostawić w spokoju; dać spokoj

let down ('let,dałn) v. robić
zawod; spuszczać; opuszczać;
upokorzyć;odmawiac pomocy

let go ('let,gou) v, wypuszczać;
zwalniać; pozwolić odejsć

let know ('let,nou) v. zawiadomić; donieść;powiadomić

let up ('let,ap) v. zelżec;
złagodniec; s. zelżenie

lethal ('li:gel) adj. smiertelny; zgubny;smiercionosny

letter ('leter) s. litera; list;
czcionka; v. drukować; oznaczać literami:kaligrafować

letter-box ('leter,boks) s.
skrzynka pocztowa

letter-carrier ('leter'kaerjer)
s. listonosz

lettuce ('letys) s. sałata (gło-
wiasta);liscie sałaty

leukemia (lju'ki:mje) s. białaczka;leukemia

level ('lewl) s. poziom; płaszczyzna; równina; poziomnica;
adj. poziomy; adv. poziomo;
równo; v. zrównywać; celowac

level crossing ('lewl'krosyng)
s. skrzyżowanie drog (koli-
zyjne)w jednej płaszczyźnie

lever ('li:wer) s. dźwignia;
lewar; v. podważać; podnosic
dźwigiem(lewarem)

levity ('lewyty) s. lekkomyśl-
nosc

levy ('lewy) v. pobierac; nakładać (podatek); s. pobór

lewd (lu:d) adj. zmysłowy; lubieżny;pożądliwy;sprosny

liability (,laje'bylyty) s.
odpowiedzialność; obowiązek;
obciążenie; zadłużenie;ryzyko

liable ('lajebl) adj. odpowiedzialny; podlegający; podatny;
skłonny;narażony;mający widoki

liable to ('lajebl,tu) adj.
skłonny do...;adv.łatwo(zgnije),

liaison (ly'ejzo:n) s. łącznosc;
związek; romans (nielegalny)

liar ('lajer) s. kłamca; łgarz

libation(laj-bej'szyn)s.libacja

libel ('lajbel) s. paszkwil;
oszczerstwo; zniesławienie
(publiczne w piśmie; filmie
etc.);v.zniesławiać

liberal ('lyberel) s. liberał;a.
liberalny; hojny;tolerancyjny

liberate ('lyberejt) v. uwalniać; zwalniać;wyzwalać

liberation ('lyberejszyn) s.
uwolnienie; oswobodzenie

liberator ('lyberejter) s.
oswobodziciel;wyzwoliciel

liberty ('lyberty) s. wolność;
swoboda;nadużywanie wolności

librarian (laj'breerjen) s.
bibliotekarz

library ('lajbrery) s. biblioteka; księgozbiór

lice (lajs) pl. wszy; zob.
louse

license(ce) ('lajsens) s. licencja; pozwolenie; upoważnienie; swoboda; rozpusta;
v. upoważniać; udzielać poz-
wolenia; nadużywać wolności

licensee (,lajsen'si:) s. posiadacz zezwolenia; koncesjo-
nariusz;właściciel licencji

lichen ('lajken) s. liszaj

lick (lyk) s. liźnięcie; odrobina; cios; raz; wybuch;
energia; v. lizać; polizać;
wylizać; bić; smarować

licking ('lykyŋg)s. (slang):
bicie; pobicie; młocka

lid (lyd) s. wieko; powieka;
pokrywa ;nakrywka;przykrywka

lie !. lay ; lain (laj; lej;
lejn)

lie (laj) v. leżeć; s. układ;
położenie;konfiguracja;legowisko

lie 2. lied; lied (laj; lajd;
lajd)

lie (laj) v. kłamać; s. kłamstwo;łgarstwo;fałsz

lie down('laj,dałn) v. kłaść
się;położyć się;nie reagować

lie in ('laj,yn) v. być w poło-
gu; leżeć w (łóżku)

lie over ('laj,ouwer) v. być
odroczonym; zostać przez noc

lieutenant (lef'tenant; lu:te-
nant) s. porucznik

life (lajf) s. życie; życiorys;
zob. pl. lives

life assurance ('lajfe'szuerens)
s. ubezpieczenie na życie

life belt ('lajfbelt) s. pas
ratunkowy

lifeboat ('lajfbout) s. łódź
ratunkowa

lifeguard ('lajfga:rd) s. ratownik

life insurance ('lajf,yn'szuerens) s. ubezpieczenie na życie

life jacket ('lajfdżaekyt) s.
kurta ratownicza;kamizelka ratunkowa

lifeless ('lajflys) adj. bez
życia; martwy;zamarły;wymarły

lifelike ('lajflajk) adj. jak
żywy(człowiek,osoba,stworzenie)

life sentence ('lajf,sentens)
s. kara dożywocia(wyrok)

life-style ('lajfstajl) s. styl
życia; modła życia;sposób życia

lifetime ('lajf,tajm) s. życie; całe życie

lift (lyft) s. dźwig; winda;
przewóz; podniesienie; wzniesienie; v. podnieść; dźwignąć;
podnosić się; kraść; spłacić
(np. dom); kopnąć;buchnąć;awanso-
wać

lift-off ('lyft,of) s. start
lotu (np. rakiety)

ligament ('lygement) s. ścięgno

ligature ('lygeczuer) s. przywiązanie; ligatura; podwiąza-
nie;bandaż;nić chirurgiczna

light; lit; lit (lajt; lyt;lyt)

light (lajt) s. światło; oświetlenie; ogień; adj. świetny; jasny; łatwy; lekki; błahy; słaby; beztroski; niefrasobliwy; lekkomyślny; v.świe-
cić; oświecać; zapalać; ujaw-
nić; poświęcić; rozjaśnić;
przyświecić; zsiadać; wsiadać;
wpaść; wyjechać; adv. lekko

light up ('lajtap) v. zaświe-
cić; rozjaśnić; oświecić

lighten ('lajtn) v. ulżyć; zel-
żyć; oświecać; rozjaśnić się;
błysnąć; błyskać się

lighter ('lajter) s. zapalniczka; latarnik ;lampiarz

lighthouse ('lajthaus) s. latarnia morska

lighting ('lajtyng) s. oswietlenie; oswietlanie

light-minded ('lajt'majndyd) adj. lekkomyslny;roztargniony

lightness ('lajtnys) s. jasnosc; lekkosc; łagodnosc; łatwosc; lekkomyslnosc

lightning ('lajtnyng)s. błyskawica; piorun;a.błyskawiczny

lightning rod ('lajtnyng,rod) s. piorunochron;odgromnik

lightweight ('lajt-łejt) waga lekka; adj. lekkiej wagi; błachy(127 do 135 funtowy boks)

light-year ('lajt,je:r) s. rok swietlny(ok.6x10¹²mil=10x10¹²km.)

lignite ('lygnajt) s. węgiel brunatny; lignit

like (lajk) v. lubiec; upodobac sobie; (chciec); miec zamiłowanie, ochotę; adj. podobny; analogiczny; typowy; adv. podobnie; w ten sam sposob; s. drugi taki sam; rzecz podobna; conj. jak; tak jak;po; w ten sposob; niby to;niczym

like that ('lajk'dzaet) adv. tak; w ten sposob;właśnie tak

likelihood ('lajklyhud) s. prawdopodobienstwo

likely ('lajkly) adj. możliwy; prawdopodobny; odpowiedni; nadający się; obiecujący; adv. pewnie; prawdopodobnie

likeness ('lajknys) s. podobieństwo; podobizna; pozory

likewise ('lajkłajz) adv. także; również; podobno; podobnie;w ten sam sposob;też

liking ('lajkyng) s. sympatia; upodobanie; zamiłowanie

lilac ('lajlek) s. bez; adj. lila; liljowy;blado siny

lily ('lyly) s. lilja;a.jak lilia

lily of the valley ('lyly,ow 'dy,waely) s. konwalia

limb (lym) s. kończyna; konar; brzeg; krawędz;ramie;noga;skrzydło

lime 1. (lajm) s. wapno; v. wapnic; adj. wapienny

lime 2. (lajm) s. lipa; cytrus (dzika cytryna) ;a.cytrusowy

limelight ('lajmlajt) s. swiatło wapienne; swiatło reflektorow; widok publiczny

limestone ('lajmstoun) s. wapien; a. z wapienia

limey ('lajmy) s. (slang):Brytyjczyk (wulg.) zwłaszcza marynarz

limit ('lymyt) s. granica; kres; v. ograniczac; ustalać granic

limitation (,lymy'tejszyn) s. ograniczenie; zastrzeżenie; prekluzja;przedawnienie

limited liability ('lymytyd,laje'bylyty)s. ograniczona odpowiedzialnosc

limp (lymp) adj. wiotki; bez sił; osłabiony; v. kulec; chromac

line (lajn) s. linia; kreska; bruzda; lina; sznur; przewod; granica; zajęcie; zainteresowania; szereg; rząd; linka; v. liniowac; wyscielac; podbic podszewką;służyć za podszewke

lineup ('lajnap) s. uszeregowanie; rząd; ustawianie w rząd

line up ('lajnap) v. ustawić w rząd; uszeregować

lineaments ('lynjements) pl. rysy twarzy;cechy szczegolne

linear ('lynjer) adj. liniowy; linijny; wąski i długi

linen ('lynyn) s. płotno; bielizna; adj. lniany; płocienny

linen closet ('lynen'klozyt) s. schowek na bieliznę

liner ('lajner) s. samolot pasażerski; statek pasażerski

linger ('lynger) v. ociągać się; zwlekac; pozostawac w tyle; marudzic; tkwic; wlec życie

lingerie ('le:nżeri) s. damska bielizna;damskie artykuły bieliżniane

lining ('lajnyng) s. podszewka; podkład; okładzina; zawartość

link (lynk) s. ogniwo; więz; spinka; 20,1 cm; v. połączyc; zczepiac; związać; sprzęgac

links (lynks) pl. wydmy; boisko golfowe ;wydmy piaszczyste

lion (lajon) s. lew ;a.lwi;lwie

lioness (lajonys) s. lwica
lip (lyp) s. warga; brzeg;
ostrze; bezczelne gadanie;
v. dotykać wargami; mruczeć
lipstick ('lypstyk) s. kredka
do warg; pomadka do ust
liquid ('lykłyd) s. płyn;
adj. płynny;niestały;nie ustalony
liquor ('lyker) s. napój alko-
holowy; sok; odwar;bulion
liquorice ('lykorys) s. lu-
krecja
lisp (lysp) v. seplenić; seplenić jak niemowlę;s.seplenienie
list (lyst) s. lista; spis;
listwa; krawędz; v. wciągać na
listę; obramowywać; przechylać (sie); pochylać (się);
s. pochylenie; przechył
listen ('lysen) v. słuchać
usłuchać ;przysłuchiwać się
listen in ('lysen,yn) v. podsłuchiwać ;posłuchać(radia etc)
listen to ('lysen,tu) v. usłuchać kogos (czyjejś rady)
listener ('lysener) s. słuchacz
listless ('lystlys) adj. apatyczny; obojętny; zobojętnia-
ły;bierny(z powodu choroby)
lit (lyt) zob. light
liter ('li:ter) s. litr
literal ('lyterel) adj. literal-
ny; dosłowny; prozaiczny; li-
terowy;rzeczowy(umysł etc.)
literary ('lyterery) adj. literacki;obeznany w literaturze
literature ('lytereczer) s. literatura; pismiennictwo
lithe (lajs) adj, giętki; gibki; łatwo gnący się
litter ('lyter) s. śmieci; pod-
ściółka ; barłog; v. śmiecić;
podścielać; urodzić szczenia-
ki;porozrzucać niechlujnie
litter bin ('lyter,byn) s.
śmietnik ;kosz na śmiecie
little ('lytl) adj. mały; niski;
nieduży; adv. mało; niewiele
little bit ('lytl,byt) adv.
trochę ;bardzo mało;troszeczkę
little one ('lytl,łan) s.
dziecko ;dziecina;dzieciatko

little by little ('lytl,bay'
'lytl) exp. po trochu; stopniowo;po mału;po małutku
live (lyw) v. żyć; mieszkać;
przeżywać; przetrwać; ocalić
live (lajw) adj. żywy; żyjący;
ruchliwy;energiczny;niewyeksplo-
atowany
live on ('lyw,on) v. żyć
z czegoś; żyć czyms
live wire ('lajw'łajer) s.
przewód pod napięciem
livelihood ('lajwly,hud) s.
utrzymanie;środki do życia
lively ('lajwly) adj. żywy;
wesoły; ożywiony; żwawy; gorący;rześki;pełen życia;jaskrawy
liver ('lywer) s. wątroba;
wątróbka ;a.wątroby
livery ('lywery) adj. wątrobia-
ny; chory na wątrobę; opryskliwy; s. liberia; utrzymanie
konia; wynajem (wozów)
lives (lajws) pl. żywotny;
zob. life
livestock ('lajwstok) s. żywy
inwentarz ;zwierzęta domowe
livid ('lywyd) adj. siny;
wściekły ;posiniaczony
living ('lywyng) s. życie;
utrzymanie; tryb życia
living room('lywyn,ru:m) s.
salon; bawialnia; pokój
lizard ('lyzerd) s. jaszczurka
load (loud) s. ładunek; waga;
ciężar; obciążenie; v. ładować; załadować; naładować;
obciążać; nasycać; fałszować
load up ('loud,ap) v. brać ładunek; opychać się
loader ('louder) s. ładowniczy;
maszyna do ładowania
loading ('loudyng) s. ładunek;
ładowanie ;a.ładunkowy(pomost)
loaded words ('loudyd,łe:rds)
s. słowa tendencyjne (nie-
sprawiedliwe)(uwłaszczające)
loaf (louf) s. bochenek; głowa
(cukru); pl. loaves (louvz)
v. wałęsać się;marnować czas
loafer ('loufer) s.
łazik; próżniak ;nierób;wałkoń;
wygodny bucik sportowy

loam (loum) s. gleba ilasta;
ił ;zaprawa gliniana(murarska)

loan (loun) s. pożyczka;
v. pożyczać ; pożyczać

loath (louθ) adj. niechętny

loathe (louθ) v. nienawidzieć;
czuć wstręt

loathsome ('louθsem) adj.
wstrętny; obrzydliwy; ohydny

loaves (louwz) zob. loaf

lobby ('loby) s. przedpokój;
kuluar; v. urabiać senatora
lub posła na czyjąś korzyść
(przekupywać)

lobbyist('lobyst) s. inter-
wencjonalista kuluarowy (często oficjalnie rejestrowany
w USA); lobbyista

lobe (loub) s. płat (np. płucny)

lobster ('lobster) s. homar

local ('loukel) adj. lokalny;
miejscowy;s.oddział związku zaw
dowego

locality (lou'kaelyty) s.okolica
miejscowość; strefa;rejon

localize ('loukelajz) v. umiejscowić; lokalizować

locate ('loukejt) v. umieścić;
znaleźć; osiedlić się

located ('loukejtyd) adj. zamieszkały; umieszczony;znalezio-
ny

location ('loukejszyn) s. położenie; ulokowanie; miejsce
zamieszkania;miejsce zaznaczone

loch (lok) s. jezioro; wąska
zatoka (zwłaszcza w Szkocji)

lock (lok) s. zamek; zamknięcie;
śluza; lok; v. zamykać (na
klucz); przechodzić śluzę

lock in ('lokyn) v. zamykać
(wewnątrz); otaczać (górami etc)

locker ('loker) s. szafka; kabina; skrzynia; schowek

lock out ('lokaut) v. wykluczać;
s. lokaut (lockout)

locksmith ('loksmyś) s. ślusarz

locomotive ('louke,moutyw) s.
lokomotywa; adj. ruchomy

locust ('loukest) s. szarańcza;
akacja

lodge ('lodż) s. chata; loża;
kryjówka; domek myśliwski; nora
v. przenocować; zdeponować;
umieszczać; wnosić (skargę)etc.

lodger ('lodżer) s. lokator

lodging ('lodżyng) s. mieszkanie (tymczsowe,wynajęte etc.)

loft (loft) s. strych; poddasze;chór;v.podbić piłkę golfową

lofty ('lofty) adj. wzniosły;
wyniosły; wysoki;dumny;hardy

log (log) s. kłoda; kloc; log;
dziennik operacyjny (statku;
szybu) v. wycinać drzewa;
ciąć na kłody; wciągać do
dziennika okrętowego etc.

logbook ('logbuk) s. dziennik
pokładowy;książka raportowa

log cabin ('log,kaebyn) s. chata (z belek) (z okrąglaków)

logic ('lodżyk) s. logika

logical ('lodżykel) adj. logiczny;rozumujący poprawnie

loin (loin) s. lędźwie; polędwica; comber;krzyże;biodra

loiter ('lojter) v. marudzić;
wałęsać się; guzdrać; mitrężyć;kręcić się podejrzanie

lol (lol) v. rozwalać się;
opierać się niedbale; wywieszać
(język psa); zwisać

loneliness ('lounlynys) s. samotność;osamotnienie;odludność

lonely ('lounly) adj. samotny

lonesome ('lounsom) adj.
osamotniony; odludny

long (log) adj. długi; długo-
trwały; v. tęsknić; pragnąć
(czegoś); adv. długo; dawno

long ago (,long'egou) adv.
dawno temu;adj.dawno miniony

long before ('long,befor) adv.
dużo wcześniej;znacznie wcześniej

long since ('long,syns) adv.
dawno temu ; od dawna

long distance call ('long'dystans,kol) s. telefon między-
miastowy;rozmowa międzymiastowa

longing ('longyng) s. pragnienie;
tęsknota;ochota;adj.tęskny

long jump ('long,dżamp) s.
skok w dal

longshoreman ('long,szo:rmen)
s. doker; robotnik portowy

long-sighted ('lon'sajtyd) adj.
dalekowzroczny; przewidujący

long spun ('lon'span)a.rozwlekły

long-term ('loŋ'term) adj.
długoterminowy;długofalowy
long-winded ('lon'łyndyd)
adj. gadatliwy; długo mówiący;(koń) ze zdrowymi płucami
look (luk) s. spojrzenie; wygląd; v. patrzec; wyglądac
look after ('luk,a:fter) v. doglądac; opiekowac się(kimś)
look at ('luk,et) v. patrzec
na (kogoś, na coś)
look for ('luk,fo:r)v. szukac
look forwards ('luk fo:rłerds)
v. oczekiwac; cieszyc się
look into ('luk,yntu) v. badac; wglądac
look on ('luk,on) v. przypatry-
wac się;przyglądac się;kibicowac
look out ('luk,aut) v. byc
na bacznosci;wyjrzec;wyszukac
look over ('luk,ouwer) v.
przeglądac;przejrzec
look around ('luk,e'raund) v.
rozglądac się;poszukiwac wzrokiem
look up ('luk,ap) v. szukac;
odwiedzac; patrzec w gorę
looker-on('luker'on) s. widz;
przyglądający się ;kibic
looking-glass ('lukyŋglass) s.
lustro; zwierciadło
lookout ('luk,aut) s. widok;
uwaga; czaty;czujnosc
look out ('luk,aut) v. wyjrzec;
uważac; wyszukac;byc w pogotowiu
loom (lu:m) s. krosna; warsztat
tkacki; v. wynurzac się; zagrażac;grozic;zamajaczyc
loop (lu:p) s. pętla; węzeł;
supeł; v. robic pętlę, kokardę;
podwiązywac;splatac (się)
loophole ('lu:p,houl)s. strzelnica; droga ucieczki (od po-
datkow);wykręt; luka;furtka
loose (lu:s) adj. luzny; roz-
luzniony; obluzniony; wolny;
na wolnosci; rzadki; sypki;
rozwiązły; s. upust; v. luzo-
wac; obluzniac; zwalniac
loosen ('lu:sn) v. rozluzniac
(się); obluzniac (się); roz-
walniac;leczyc zatwardzenie
loot (lu:t) s. łupy; (nadużycia
urzędnika);v.plądrowac;szabrowac

lop (lop) v. obcinac; ciąc; zwisac; plątac się; wałęsac się;
s. scięcie; obcięte (gałęzie)
lop off ('lop,of) v. obciąc
lope (loup) v. biec susami;
pędzic krotkim galopem; s.
krotki galop; sus
lord (lo:rd) s. pan; władca;
magnat; Bog; v. grac pana;
nadawac tytuł lorda
lorry ('lory) s. ciężarowka;
platforma; lora;przyczepa
lose; lost; lost (lu:z; lost;
lost)
lose (lu:z) v. stracic; schud-
nąc; zgubic; zabłądzic; nie-
dosłyszec; spoznic się; prze-
grac; byc pokonanym,pozbawionym
loss (los) s. strata; utrata;
zguba; ubytek;szkoda;kłopot
lost (lost) adj. stracony; zgu-
biony; zob. lose
lot (lot) s. doba; las; losowanie; udział; działka; par-
cela; grupa; zespoł; partia;
sporo; wiele; v. parcelowac;
dzielic; losowac;adv.bardzo dużo
loth (lous) adj. niechętny;
wstrętny;z ciężkim sercem
lotion ('louszyn) s. płyn
(leczniczy)
lottery ('lotery) s. loteria
lotto ('lotou) s. loteryjka
loud (laud) adj. głosny; smrodliwy; krzykliwy; adv. na cały
głos; głosno:w głosny sposob
loudspeaker ('laud'spi:ker) s.
głosnik; megafon
lounge (laundż) v. proznowac;
wylegiwac; łazic; s. lokal;
salonik; hall; włoczęga;
wolny krok;wygodna kanapa
louse (laus) s. wesz; pl. lice
lousy ('lauzy) adj. zawszony;
wstrętny;dobrze zaopatrzony (sl.)
lout ('laut) s. gbur; prostak
love (law) s. kochanie; miłosc;
lubienie; ukochana; ukochanie;
gra na zero; v. kochac; lubic;
byc przywiązanym ;piescic;umizgac
się
love-affair ('lawefeer) s. romans; przygoda miłosna;osobiste
troski w sprawach miłosnych

loveless ('lawlys) adj. niekochany; nie kochający; bez miłości;nie kochany przez nikogo

lovely ('lawly) adj. śliczny; uroczy; rozkoszny;przyjemny(bardzo)

lovemaking ('law,mejkyng) s. zaloty; umizgi; spożkowanie

lover ('lawer) s. kochanek; miłosnik; amator czegos

loving ('lavyng) adj. kochający; s. miłość

low (lou) s. ryk (bydła); ryczeć; adj. niski; niewysoki; słaby; przygnębiony; cichy; podły; mały; adv. nisko; niewysoko; słabo; skromnie; cicho; szeptem; marnie; podle

lower ('louer) adj. niższy; dolny; młodszy; adv. niżej; v. obniżac; zniżac; spuszczac; poniżyc; sciszyc; zmniejszyc; osłabiac; opadac; spadac;ryczeć(jak bydło)

low-grade ('lougrejd) adj. niskoprocentowy; niskiej jakosci;kiepski;tandetny

lowland ('loulend) pl. nizina; adj. nizinny

lowly ('louly) adj. skromny; adv. skromnie;bez pretensji

low-necked('lou'nekyd) adj. dekoltowany (głęboko)

low-pressure ('lou'preszer) s. niskie cisnienie; adj. niskoprężny;pod niskim cisnieniem

low tide ('lou'tajd) s. odpływ (morza)

loyal (lojel) adj. lojalny; wierny(krajowi,ideałom etc.)

loyalty ('lojelty) s. lojalnosc; wiernosc

lozenge ('lozyndż) s. romb; tabletka; pastylka

lubber ('laber) s. niezdara; niedołęga;niezdarny marynarz

lubricant ('lu:brykent) s. smar; adj. smarujący; smarowniczy

lubricate ('lu:brykejt) v. smarowac; oliwic;robic sliskim

lubrication ('lu:brykejszyn) s. smarowanie; oliwienie

ubricity(lu:'brysyty)s.smarownosc;lubieżnosc

lucid ('lu:syd) adj. swiecacy; jasny; błyszczacy; klarowny; przezroczysty; czysty;oczywisty

luck (lak) s. los; traf; szczescie; szczęsliwy traf;powodzenie

luckily ('lakyly) adv. na szczescie; szczesliwie

luckless ('laklys) adj. niefortunny; nieszczesliwy

lucky ('laky) adj. szczesliwy

lucky fellow ('laky'felou) s. szczęsciarz

ludicrous ('lu:dykres) adj. smieszny; nonsensowny; absurdalny;komicznie głupi

lug (lag) v. wlec; pociągac; przytłaczac; s. wleczenie; szarpanie; ucho; uchwyt

luggage ('lagydż) s. bagaż; walizki

luggage carrier ('lagydż'kaerjer) s. bagażowy

luggage rack ('lagydż'raek) s. połka na walizki

luggage slip ('lagydż'slyp) s. kwit bagażowy

luggage van ('lagydż'waen) s. woz bagażowy

lukewarm ('lu:kło:rm) adj. ciepławy; letni; obojętny; oziębły; niezainteresowany

lull(lal) v. ukołysac; uciszyc; usmierzyc; s. cisza; zastoj

lullaby ('lalebaj) s. kołysanka

lumbago (lam'bejgou) s. lumbago; ischias

lumbar ('lamber) adj. lędżwiowy

lumber ('lamber) s. budulec (drewniany); rupiecie; graty; v. zwalac; wycinac; ciężko stąpac; poruszac się ociężale

lumberjack ('lamber'dżaek) s. drwal(przygotowujący do tartaku)

lumber mill ('lambermyl) s. tartak

luminous ('lu:mynes) adj. swietlny; jasny; adj. swiecący; wyjasniający;zrozumiały

lump (lamp) s. bryła; gruda; masa; hurt; guz; niezdara; niedołęga; v. zwalac; gromadzic; dojsc do ładu;zcierpiec;znosic

lump of('lamp,ow) s. kawałek
lump sugar ('lamp,szu:ger) s.
gruda cukru
lump sum ('lamp,sam) s. suma
całościowa
lunar ('lu:nar) adj. księżyco-
wy;mierzony ruchem księżyca
lunar module ('lu:nar,modjul)
s. kapsula do lądowania na
Księżycu
lunatic ('lu:netyk) s. wariat
(chory umysłowo); adj. obłąkany; zwariowany; lunatyk
lunch (lancz) s. obiad (popołudniowy); v. jeść obiad;
gościc obiadem
lunch-hour ('lancz'auer) s.
przerwa obiadowa (w południe)
lung (lang) s. płuco
lunge (landż) s. wypad;
pchnięcie; v. pchnąć; zrobic
wypad;spowodować wypad
lurch (le:rcz) v. opuszczać
w potrzebie; słaniac się na
nogach; przechylac się; s.
nagłe przechylenie się (na
bok);trudna sytuacja
lure (ljuer) s. przynęta; wabik; urok; powab; v. kusic;
nęcic; wabic;przywabiać
lurk (le:rk) v. czaic się;
s. czaty; ukrycie
luscious ('laszes) adj. sło-
dziutki; ckliwy ;soczysty
lush (lasz) adj. bujny; soczysty;miękki i pełen soku
lust (last) s. żądza; lubież-
ność; namiętność; pożądli-
wosc; v. pożądac(namiętnie)
luster ('laster) s. blask; połysk; świecznik; świetność;
v. glansować; wyswiecac
lusty ('lasty) adj. krzepki;
pełen wigoru (młodzieńczego)
lute (lu:t) s. lutnia; glina;
v. lepic gliną;kitować
luxate ('laksejt) v. zwichnąć
(np. nogę)(staw)
luxation (lak'sejszyn) s.
zwichnięcie (nogi w kostce;
stawu biodrowego etc.)

luxurious (lag'żjuerjes) adj.
zbytkowny; luksusowy;zmysłowy
luxury ('lakszery) s. zbytek;
luksus;rozkosz;a.od zbytku
lying ('lajyng) adj. kłamliwy;
zob. lie; s. kłamstwo; adj.le-
żący; zob. lie; s. leżenie;
posłanie;pozycja leżąca
lying-in (,lajyng'yn) adj. położniczy; połogowy; s. połóg
lymph (lymf) s, limfa; szczepionka; wysięk; serum, (czy-
sta woda)
lynch (lyncz) v. zlinczować;s.
linczowanie;zabijanie bez wyroku
lynx (lynks) s. ryś
lyre ('lajer) s. lira
lyric ('lirik) adj. liryczny;
s. słowa piesni; poemat liryczny;tekst piosenki
lysol ('lajsol) s. lizol
m (em) trzynasta litera alfabetu
angielskiego;cyfra rzymska:1000
ma'am (maem) s. pani (madam)
mac (maek) s.nieprzemakalny materiał (płaszcz) mackintosh
machine (me'szi:n) s. maszyna;
machina (polityczna) v. obrabiac maszynowo; adj.maszynowy
machine-made (me'szi:nmejd) adj.
maszynowy; maszynowo robiony
machine-gun (me'szi:ngan) s.
karabin maszynowy
machinery (me'szi:nery) s, maszyneria;maszyneria;aparat
machinist (me'szi:nyst) s, maszynista (np. tokarz)(szwaczka)
macho (ma:czou) s. bardzo męski
mężczyzna (slang)
mack (maek) s. zob. mac
mackintosh ('maekyntosz) s.
zob. mac
mad (maed) adj. obłąkany; szalony; zły; wsciekły; v. doprowadzac do obłędu; byc obłąkanym
madam ('maedem) s. pani; (panienka)(w zwrocie:proszę pani)
madcap ('maedkaep) s. narwaniec
madden ('maedn) v. rozwścieczać;
szalec; wsciekac się;wariować
made (mejd) v. zrobiony; zob.
make (wykombinowany;fabryczny..)

madman ('maedmen) s. wariat;
szaleniec;furiat;obłąkaniec

madness ('maednys) s. obłęd;
obłąkanie; furia; wściekłosc;
wscieklizna;szał;szalenstwo

magazine (maege'zi:n) s. czasopismo; magazynek (na kule);
skład broni dla wojska

maggot ('maeget) s. dziwactwo;
chimera; larwa

magic ('maedżyk) s. magia; adj.
magiczny; działający jak magia

magician (me'dżyszyn) s. czarodziej; magik

magistrate ('maedżystrejt) s.
sądownik; stróż prawa

magnanimous (maeg'neanymes)
adj. wielkoduszny

magnet ('maegnyt) s. magnes

magnetic (maeg'netyk) adj.
magnetyczny; przyciągający

magnificence (maeg'nyfysns) s.
wspaniałosc; swietnosc;
okazałosc

magnificent (maeg'nyfysnt)adj.
wspaniały; okazały

magnify ('maegnyfaj) v. powiększac; potęgowac; wyolbrzy-
miac

magpie ('maegpaj) s. sroka;
gadula

maid (mejd) s. dziewczyna;
dziewka; panna ;służąca

maiden ('mejden) s. dziewczyna;
panna; adj. panienski; dzie-
wiczy; swieży; nowy

maidenly ('mejdenly) adj.
dziewczecy; panienski

maiden name ('mejden,nejm) s.
nazwisko panienskie

mail (mejl) s. poczta; kolczu-
ga; v. wysyłac pocztą

mailbag ('mejl,baeg) s. worek
pocztowy

mailbox ('mejl,boks) s, skrzynka pocztowa

mailman (mejlmen) s. listonosz

mail-order house ('mejlorder,
,haus) s. firma sprzedająca
przez pocztę (z katalogu)

maim (mejm) v. okaleczyc

main (mejn) s. głowny (przewod)
adj. glowny; najważniejszy

mainland ('mejnlaend) s. konty-
nent(w odroznieniu od bliskich
wysp)

mainly('mejnly) adv. głownie;
przewaznie;po większej częsci

main road('mejnroud) s. głowna
droga;głowna szosa

main street ('mejn.stri:t) s.
głowna ulica

maintain (men'tejn) v. utrzymywac (w dobrym stanie); trzymac (pozycję); podtrzymywac;
zachowywac; twierdzic; miec
na utrzymaniu;bronic;pomgac

maintenance ('mejntenens) s.
utrzymanie; utrzymywanie; poparcie; wyżywienie

maize (mejz) s. kukurydza

majestic (medżestyk) adj. majestatyczny

majesty ('maedżysty) s. majestat;godnosc;wielkosc

major ('mejdżer) s. major; pełnoletni; przedmiot kierunkowy
specjalizacji; adj. większy;
głowny; ważniejszy; pełnoletni;
starszy;v.specjalizowac się w stu-
diach

majorette ('mejdżeret) s. tancerka na defiladach i w przer-
wach meczow w USA

majority (me'dżoryty) s.
większosc;a. wiekszosciowy

major road ('mejdżer,roud) s.
droga głowna;ważniejsza droga

make; made; made (mejk; mejd;
mejd)

make (mejk) v. robic; tworzyc;
sporządzac;powodowac; wynosic;
doprowadzac; ustanawiac; stac
się; postanowic etc.

make-believe ('mejk,by'li:w) s.
udawanie; pozory

make off ('mejkof) v. uciec;
uciekac .gwiznąc cos komus

make up ('mejkap) v. uzupełnic;
wynagrodzic; sporządzac; zmonto-
wac; ucharakteryzowac

makeup ('mejkap) s. makijaż;
charakteryzacja; układ (graficzny; stan (kogos,czegos)

make up your mind ('mejk,ap'-
'jo:r,majnd) exp.: zdecyduj się
(czego chcesz, co wolisz, na co
masz ochote,gdzie jedziesz etc.)

maker ('mejker) s. wytwórca;
sprawca; producent; fabrykant;
konstruktor(Maker= Bóg)

makeshift ('mejkszyft) s. namiastka; urządzenie prowizo-
ryczne;adj.prowizoryczny

malady ('maeledy) s. choroba

male (mejl) s. mężczyzna; samiec; adj. męski; samczy;
wewnętrzny; obejmowany

malediction (,maely'dikszyn) s.
przekleństwo; złorzeczenie

malefactor ('maelyfaekter) s.
złoczyńca; zbrodniarz

malevolent (me'lewelent) adj.
niechętny; wrogi

malice ('maelys) s. złośliwość;
zła wola; zły zamiar

malicious (me'lyszys) adj.
złośliwy; zły;powodowany złością

malignant (me'lygnent) adj.
złośliwy; zjadliwy

malnutrition ('maelnju'tryszyn)
s. niedożywienie

malt ('mo:lt) s. słód; v. słodo-
wać;adj. słodowy;zcukrzony

maltreat (mael'tri:t) v. ponie-
wierac; maltretować

mamma (me'ma:) s. mama;gruczoł mlekowy

mammal (me'ma:l) s. ssak;a.ssakowy

man (maen) s. człowiek; mężczyzna; mąż; v. obsadzać (np. zało-
gą); pl. men (men)

manacle ('maenekl) s. kajdany;
v. zakuwać w kajdany

manage ('maenydż) v. kierować;
zarządzać; posługiwać się; obchodzić się; opanowywać; poskramiać; radzić sobie

manageable ('maenydżebl) adj.do
pokierowania (możliwy,łatwy)

management ('maenydżment) s.
zarząd; kierownictwo; dyrekcja;
posługiwanie się; obchodzenie
się ;sprawne zarządzanie

manager('maenydżer) s. kierownik
zarządzający; gospodarz

manageress ('maenydżeres) s.
kierowniczka

mane (mejn) s. grzywa

maneuver (me'nu:wer) s. manewr;
v. manewrować;manipulować

manger ('mejndżer) s. żłób; koryto

mangle ('maengl) s. magiel;
v. maglować; poszarpać; pokale-
czyć; poprzekręcać

manhood ('maenhud) s. męskość;
ludność męska ;wiek męski

mania ('mejnje) s. bzik; obłęd;
mania;zbytni entuzjazm;szał

maniac ('mejnjaek) s. maniak;
szaleniec;adj.umysłowo chory

manifest ('maenyfest) adj. jawny; oczywisty; v. manifestować;
ujawniać; s. manifest okrętowy (szczegółowa lista ładunku)

manifold ('maenyfould) adj.
różnorodny; wieloraki; wielokrotny; v. powielać (tekst)

manipulate (me'nypjulejt) v.
manipulować; umiejętnie; zręcz-
nie pokierować (niesprawiedliwie)

mankind (,maen'kajnd) s. ludzkość; rodzaj ludzki

mankind ('maenkajnd) pl. mężczyź-
ni ;cały rodzaj męski

manly ('maenly) adj. dzielny;
mężny; męski;adv.po męsku

manner ('maener) s. sposób; zwyczaj; zachowanie (się); wychowanie; maniera;procedura;rodzaj

manoeuvre (me'nu:wer) s. manewr;
v. namewrować (pisownia brytyjska)

man-of-war ('maenew'ło:r) s.
okręt wojenny;uzbrojony statek

manor ('maener) s. dwór; rezydencja (w Anglii:duży majatek)

man power('maen,pałer) s. siła
robocza; rezerwy ludzkie

mansion ('maenszyn) s. rezydencja; pałac;duży dwór

manslaughter ('maen,slo:ter) s.
zabójstwo (bez premedytacji)

mantelpiece ('maentlpi:s) s.
gzyms kominka (obramowanie)

manual ('maenjuel) s. podręcznik;
manuał; adj. ręczny;ręcznie zrobiony

manufacture (,maenju'faekczer)
v. wyrabiać; s. wyrób; produkcja; produkt (zwłaszcza masowy)

manufacturer (,maenju'faekcze-
rer) s. wytwórca; producent; rcze
fabrykant;przedsiębiorstwo wytwór-

manure (me'njuer) s. nawóz;
v. nawozić (gnój)

manuscript ('maenjuskrypt) s.
rękopis; adj. ręcznie pisany

many ('meny) adj. dużo; wiele

many-sided ('meny'sajdyd) adj.
wielostronny; wieloboczny;
wszechstronny

map (maep) s. mapa; plan;
v. planować; robić mapę

maple ('mejpl) s. klon

marble ('ma:rbl) s. marmur; kul-
ka do zabawy; adj, marmurowy;
v. marmurkować (np. papier)

March (ma:rcz) s. marzec

march (ma:rcz) s. marsz; v.ma-
szerować

mare (meer) s. klacz; kobyła

margarine ('ma:rdże,ri:n) s.
margaryna

margin ('ma:rdżyn) s. margines;
brzeg; krawędź; nadwyżka;
rezerwa

marine (me'ri:n) adj. morski;
s. marynarka; żołnierz piecho-
ty desantowej (USA)

mariner ('maeryner) s. marynarz;
żeglarz

maritime ('maerytajm) adj. morski

mark (ma:rk) s. marka (pieniądz)
ślad; znak; oznaczenie; nota;
cenzura; cel; uwaga; v. oznaczać; określać; notować; zwracać uwagę

marked (ma:rkt) adj. wybitny;
wyraźny; znaczny

mark out ('ma:rk,aut) v. wyznaczać; wytyczać (np. granicę)

market ('ma:rkyt) s. rynek;
zbyt; targ; v. robić zakupy;
sprzedawać na targu

marketing ('ma:rkytyŋg) s. orga-
nizowanie rynku;handlowanie

market-place ('ma:rkytplejs) s.
rynek; plac targowy

marksman ('ma:rksmen) s. strzelec (doborowy)

marmalade ('ma:rmelejd) s.
marmolada (pomarańczowa)

marmot ('ma:rmet) s. świstak

marriage ('maerydż) s. małżenstwo (skojarzenie);a.ślubny

marriageable ('maerydżebl) adj.
na wydaniu;odpowiedni do małżeństwa

marriage certificate ('maerydż,
,ser'tyfykyt) s. świadectwo
ślubu

married ('maeryd) adj, żonaty;
zamężna; małżeński; ślubny

married couple ('maeryd,kapl)s.&
adj. para małżeńska

marrow ('mearou) s. szpik
(kostny); dynia

marry ('maery) v. poślubić;
udzielać ślubu; ożenić (się)
brać ślub; pobierać się;
wychodzić za mąż

marsh (ma:rsz) s. moczary; bagno;błota;a.bagienny

marshal ('ma:rszel) s. marszałek; mistrz ceremonii; komisarz policji; v. uszykować
(uroczyście); przetaczać wagony;uporządkować;uszykować

marshy ('ma:rszy) adj. bagnisty; bagienny;błotnisty

marten ('ma:rtyn) s.kuna

martial ('ma:rszel) adj. wojenny; wojowniczy; wojskowy

martyr ('ma:rter) s. męczennik; v. zamęczać;zadręczać

marvel ('ma:rwel) s. cudo; cud;
v. podziwiać; dziwić się

marvelous ('ma:rwyles) adj.
cudowny; zdumiewający

mascot ('maesket) s. maskotka

masculine ('maeskjulyn) adj. [1]
męski;płci męskiej

mash (maesz) s. zacier; papka;
mieszanka; v. warzyć; tłuc na
papkę; umizgać się

mashed potatoes ('maeszt,pe'tej-
tous) s. gniecione ziemniaki

mask (ma:sk) s. maska; v. zamaskować; maskować

mason ('mejsn) s. murarz; ka-
mieniarz;v.wymurować;murować

masonry ('mejsnry) s. murarstwo;
obmurowanie;kamieniarstwo

masque (ma:sk) s. maskarada;
pantomima (amatorska)

mass (maes) s. msza; masa; rzesza; v. gromadzić; zrzeszać

massacre ('maeseker) s. masakra; v. masakrować;urządzić rzeź

massage ('maesa:ż) s. masaż;
v. masować ;zrobić masaż
massif ('maesyw) s, masyw
górski
massive ('maesyw) adj. masywny;
ciężki;zwarty;bryłowaty;ciężki
mast (ma:st) s. maszt
master ('ma:ster) s. mistrz;
nauczyciel; pan; gospodarz;
szef; kapitan statku; panicz;
v. panować; kierować; nabywać (np.wprawy);owładnąć
master key ('ma:sterki:) s.
wytrych
masterly ('ma:sterly) adj.
mistrzowski
master of ceremony ('ma:ster,ow-
sere'mouny) s. mistrz ceremonii
masterpiece ('ma:sterpi:s) s.
arcydzieło
mastership ('ma:sterszyp) s.
mistrzostwo; władza; panowanie; zwierzchnictwo
mastery ('ma:stery) s. władza;
panowanie; mistrzostwo
mat (maet) s. mata; v. plątać;
adj. matowy(bez połysku)
match (maecz) s. zapałka; lont;
mecz; dobór; małżeństwo;
v. swatać; współzawodniczyć;
dobierać;dorównywać
matchless ('maeczlys) adj. niezrównany;nie mający równego
matchmaker ('maecz,mejker) s.
swat; swatka;aranżujący mecze
mate (mejt) s. kolega; małżonek;
samiec; pomocnik; łączyć ślu-
bem; parzyć (się); pobierać
się;zadawać mata(w szachach)
material (me'tierjal) s. materiał; tworzywo; tkanka; adj.
materialny; cielesny
maternal (me'te:rnl) adj. macierzyński; matczyny
maternity (me'te:rnyty) s. macierzyństwo;adj.położniczy
maternity hospital (me'te:rnyty
'hospytl) s. szpital położniczy
mathematician (,maetyme'tyszyn)
s. matematyk
mathematics (,maety'maetyks) s.
matematyka

math (maes) s. matematyka
(slang)
matriculate (me'trykjulejt) v.
immatrykulować; zdawać wstępny
egzamin (uniw.);zapisać się na..
matrimony ('maetrymeny) s. małżeństwo;akt ślubu
matron ('mejtren) s. matrona;
kobieta zamężna; (gospodyni)
matter ('maeter) s. rzecz;
treść; materiał; substancja;
sprawa; kwestia; v. znaczyć;
mieć znaczenie;odgrywać rolę
matter-of-fact ('maeter,ow'faekt)
adj. rzeczowy; praktyczny
mattress ('maetrys) s. materac
mature (me'tjuer) adj. dojrzały;
płatny; v. dojrzewać; stawać
się płatnym (np.pożyczka)
maturity (me'tjueryty) s. doj-
rzałość; termin płatności
mauve (mouw) s. kolor różowo-
liliowy ;adj.różowo-liliowy
maw (mo:) s. żołądek; wole
maxim ('maeksym) s. maksyma
maximum ('maeksymem) s. maksi-
mum
May (mej) s. maj,
may (mej) v. być może; might
(majt) mógłby
maybe ('mejbi:) adv. być może;
może być;możliwe że
may I ? ('mej aj) czy mogę ?
may-bug ('mejbag) s. chrabąszcz
mayor (meer) s. burmistrz
maypole ('mejpoul) s. słup do
tańca "gaik", 1-go maja
maze (mejz) s. labirynt; gmatwa-
nina; v. w błąd wprowadzić;
oszołomić;dezorientować;mieszać
mazurka (me'ze:rke) s. mazur;
mazurek
me (mi:) pron. mi; mnie; mną;
(slang): ja
meadow ('medou) s. łąka
meager ('mi:ger) adj. chudy;
cienki; skromny;nie obradzający
meal (mi:l) s. posiłek; grubo
mielona maka;czas posiłku
mealtime ('mi:l-tajm) s. pora
posiłku(ustalona zwyczajem)
mealy ('mi:ly)adj.mączysty;nie-
szczery;słodziutki; oblesny

mean; meant; meant (mi:n; ment; ment)

mean (mi:n) v. myślec; przy- puszczac; znaczyc; s. prze- cietna; srednia; srodek; adj. ubogi; nędzny; podły; marny; skąpy;tandetny;skąpy

meaning ('mi:nyng) s. znacze- nie; sens; tresc; adj. zna- czący;mający zamiar

meaningless ('mi:nynglys) adj. bez sensu; bez znaczenia

meant (ment) przeznaczony; zob. mean

meantime ('mi:n'tajm) adv. tymczasem;w tym samym czasie

meanwhile ('mi:n,hłajl) adv. tymczasem

measles ('mi:zlz) s. odra

measure ('meżer) s. miara; miarka; srodek; zabieg; spo- sób; v. mierzyc; miec roz- miar; oszacowac;byc...wzrostu

measureless ('meżerlys) adj. bezmierny; nieskonczony

measurement ('meżerment) s. wymiar; miara; mierzenie

meat (mi:t) s. mięso; danie mięsne;tresc (książki etc.)

mechanic (my'kaemyk) s. mecha- nik ;rzemieslnik;technik

mechanical (my'kaenykel) adj. mechaniczny

mechanics (my'kaenyks) s. me- chanika

mechanism ('mekenyzem) s. me- chanizm;maszyneria

mechanize ('mekenajz) v. zme- chanizowac

medal ('medl) s. medal

meddle ('medl) v. wmieszac się; wtrącac się w cudze sprawy

mediaeval (,medy'i:wel) adj. sredniowieczny

mediate ('my:djejt) adj. po- sredni; v. posredniczyc

mediator ('my:djejt) s. rozjem- ca; mediator

medical ('medykel) adj. lekar- ski; medyczny

medical certificate ('medykel, ,sertyfykyt) s. swiadectwo le- karskie

medicated ('medykejtyd) adj. leczony; zaprawiony substancją leczniczą

medicinal (me'dysynl) adj. lecz- niczy; lekarski; medyczny

medicine ('medysyn) s. medycyna; lek; lekarstwo; v. leczyc le- karstwami

medieval (,medy'i:wel) adj. sredniowieczny

mediocre ('my:djouker) adj. mier- ny; sredni; przeciętny

meditate ('medytejt) v. obmyslac; rozmyslac; medytowac

meditation (,medy'tejszyn) s. rozmyslanie ;planowanie

meditative ('medytejtyw) adj. zadumany; zamyslony; medyta- cyjny ;kontemplacyjny

Mediterranean (,medyter'rejnjen) adj. srodziemnomorski

medium ('mi:djem) s. srodek; srednia; przewodnik; srodek obiegowy; srodowisko; rozpusz- czalnik; sposób; srodkowa dro- ga; adj. sredni;adv.srednio

medley ('medly) s. mieszanina; pstrokacizna; rozmaitosci

meek (mi:k) s. potulny; łagod- ny; skromny ;bez wigoru

meet; met; met (mi:t; met;met)

meet (mi:t) v. spotykac; zbierac się; gromadzic; isc na kompro- mis; zgadzac się; zaspokajac; s. spotkanie; zbiórka; miejsce spotkania; spotkanie sportowe; zawody(na bieżni etc.)

meet with ('mi:t,łys) v. spot- kac się z (kims);doswiadczyc

meeting ('mi:tyng) s. spotkanie; połączenie się; posiedzenie; zgromadzenie; wiec; zawody; konferencja; pojedynek

melancholy ('melenkely) s. me- lancholia; adj. smutny; melan- cholijny;zasmucający;ponury

mellow ('melou) adj. słodki; miekki; soczysty; uleżały; zła- godzony (wiekiem); łagodny; we- soły; pogodny; podchmielony; dojrzały; miły; swietny; przy- jemny; v. dojrzewac; zmiękczac; uleżec się;łagodniec; łagodzic

melodious (my'loudjes) adj.
melodyjny ;harmonijny

melody ('meledy) s. melodia;
piosenka

melon ('melen) s. melon

melt (melt) s. stop; stopienie;
topnienie; wytop; v. topic;
topniec; roztapiac (się);
rozpuszczac; przetapiac; odlewac; wzruszyc;roztkliwiac

melting point ('meltyng'point)
s. temperatura topnienia

member ('member) s. członek;
człon(odrozniajacy się)

membership ('memberszyp) s.,
członkostwo; przynależnosc;
skład członkowski

membrane ('membrejn) s. błona;
przepona; membrana

memoir ('memła:r) s. pamiętnik;
życiorys;autobiogrfia

memorable ('memerebl) adj. pa-
mietny;znaczny

memorial (my'no:riel) s. pomnik; memorial; petycja; posag (na pamiatke)

memorize ('memerajz) v. za-
pamietywac; uczyc się na pamięc

memory ('memery) s. pamięc;
wspomnienie

men (men) pl. mężczyzni; robot-
nicy; zob. : man

menace ('menes) s. grozba; za-
grożenie; v. grozic; zagrażac

mend (mend) s. naprawa; na-
prawka; reperowac; zaszyc

menial ('mi:njel) s. sługa;
służalec; adj. czarno-robo-
czy; służalczy; służebny

mental ('mentl) adj. umysłowy;
pamieciowy; psychiatryczny;
s. (slang) umysłowo chory

mental hospital ('mentl'hospytl)
s. szpital psychiatryczny

mentality (men'taelyty) s.
umysłowosc; mentalnosc

mention ('menszyn) v. wspominac; wymieniac; nadmieniac;
wzmiankowac; s. wzmianka

menu ('menju:) s. jadłospis

meow (mi:'au) v. miauczec jak kot

mercantile ('me:rkentajl) adj.
handlowy; kupiecki

mercenary ('me:rsynery) adj.
najemny; wyrachowany; s. najemnik; żołnierz najemny

merchandise('me:rczendajz) s.
towar(y); v. handlowac

merchant('me:rczent) s. kupiec;
handlowiec; adj. handlowy;
kupiecki

merciful ('me:rsyful) adj. miłosierny; litosciwy

merciless ('me:rsylys) adj. bezlitosny; niemiłosierny

mercurial (me:r'kjuerjel) adj.
rtęciowy; żywy; bystry; rozgarnięty; zmienny

mercy ('me:rsy) s. miłosierdzie;
litosc; łaska;rzecz pomyslna

mercy killing ('me:rsy'kylyng)
s. eutanazja; zabójstwo z li-
tosci

mere (mjer) adj. zwykły; zwyczajny;nie więcj niż

merely ('mjerly) adv. tylko; jedynie; zaledwie; po prostu

merge (me:rdż) v. roztapiac
(się); zlewac; łączyc (się)

merger ('me:rdżer) s. połączenie; zlanie się; fuzja

meridian (me'rydjen) s. południ-
nik; zenit; szczyt; adj. południ-
niowy; szczytowy

merit ('meryt) s. zasługa; zaleta; odznaczenie; v. zasługiwac

meritorious (,mery'to:rjes) adj.
chwalebny; zasłużony

mermaid ('me:rmejd) s. rusałka;
syrena

merriment ('meryment) s. uciecha; radosc; wesołosc

merry ('mery) adj. wesoły; radosny; podochocony;odswietny;
podchmielony

merryandrew ('mery'aendru:) s.
błazen; trefnis ;wesołek

merry-go-round ('merygou,raund)
s, karuzela

merry-making ('mery,mejkyng) s.
zabawa;uciecha;weselenie się

mesh (mesz) s. siatka; sieć;
układ siatkowy; v. łapac w
sieć; zazebiac;wplatac

mess (mes) s. nieporządek; bałagan; bród; świństwo; paskudztwo; paćka; papka; zupa; bigos; posiłek wspólny; stołówka; wspólny stół; v. zababrać; zapaskudzić; zabrudzic; zabałaganic; pokpic; sfuszerować; obijac się; bawić; dawac jeść (posiłek); stołować się (wspólnie)

mess up (,mes'ap) v. zepsuc; zaprzepaścic; sknocic; zagmatwac;pobrudzic;zabałaganic

message ('mesydż) s. wiadomość; orędzie; morał; wypowiedz; v. komunikowac;podawac;posłac

messenger ('mesyndżer) s. posłaniec; zwiastun

messy ('mesy) adj. kłopotliwy; zapaskudzony; sfuszerowany; brudny etc; upaćkany;niechlujny

met (met) v. zob. meet

metal ('metl) s. metal; v. pokrywac metalem;a.metalowy

metallic (my'taelyk) adj. metaliczny; metalowy;metalurgiczny

meteor ('mi:tjer) s. meteor

meteorology (,mi:tjero'ledży) s. meteorologia

meter ('mi:ter) s. metr; licznik; v. mierzyc;a.metrowy

method ('meted) s. metoda; metodyka; metodycznosc; sposob

methodical (me'todykel) adj. metodyczny;systematyczny

meticulous (my'tykjules) adj. drobiazgowy; szczegółowy; drobnostkowy; pedantyczny

metric system ('metryk'system) s. system metryczny

metropolitan (,metre'polyten) adj. wielkomiejski; metropolitalny; s. mieszkaniec metropolii; metropolita (duchowny)

mew (mju:) v. miauczec;pierzyc się

Mexican ('meksyken) adj. meksykanski;Meksykanin;Meksykanka

miaow (mi:'au) v. miauczec

mica ('maike) s. mika; łuszczyk

mice (majs) pl. myszy; zob.: mouse

micron('majkron)s. mikron

microphone ('majkrefoun) s. mikrofon

microscope ('majkreskoup) s. mikroskop podczas;posrod;między-mid (myd) adj. srodkowy;prep. w;

midday ('myddej) adj. południowy; s. południe

mid summer (,myd'samer) exp. w srodku lata

middle ('mydl) s. srodek; kibic; stan; adj. srodkowy; v. składac w srodku; kopac na srodek

middle aged ('mydl'ejdżd) adj. w srednim wieku

Middle Ages ('mydle'ejdżys) s. sredniowiecze

middle class ('mydl,kla:s) s. klasa srednia; klasa sredniozamożna;a.ze sredniozamożnej klasy

middle name ('mydl,nejm) s. drugie imię

middle sized ('mydl,sajzd) adj. sredniej wielkości; sredni

middleweight ('mydl,łejt) s. waga srednia; adj. sredniej wagi (148 do 160 funtów)

middling ('mydlyng) adj. sredni; przeciętny; adv. srednio

midge ('mydż) s. muszka

midget ('mydżyt) s. karzełek; malenstwo; adj. miniaturowy

midland ('mydlend) s. srodek kraju; adj. leżący w srodku kraju; w głębi kraju

midmost ('mydmoust) adj. leżący w samym srodku;prep.posrod

midnight ('mydnajt) s. połnoc; adj. połnocny; o połnocy

midway ('myd'łej) s. połowa drogi; adv. w połowie drogi

midwife ('mydłajf) s. położna; okuszerka

might (,majt) s. moc; potęga; v. mogłby; zob.: may

mighty ('majty) adj. potężny; adv. bardzo; wielce

migrate ('maj,grejt)v. wędrowac; przesiedlac się

migratory ('maj,gretery) adj. wędrowny(ptak etc.)

mild (majld) adj. łagodny; powolny; potulny; słaby;delikatny

mildew ('myldju:) s. pleśń;
v. pleśnieć;rdzewieć (o zbożu)
mildly ('majldly) adv. łagod-
nie; umiarkowanie;oględnie
mildness ('majldnys) s. łagodnosc; nieostrosc
mile (majl) s. mila; 1,609 km
mil(e)age ('majlydż) s. milaż;
odległość w milach
milestone ('majlstoun) s. kamien milowy
military ('mylytery) adj. wojskowy; pl. wojskowy; wojsko
milk (mylk) s. mleko; v. doic
(krowy); wykorzystac; exploatowac;podsłuchiwac (telefon)
milking machine ('mylkyng,ma'-
'szi:n) s. maszyna do dojenia
milkman ('mylkmen) s. mleczarz
milk shake ('mylkszejk) s. mieszany napoj mleczny
milksop ('mylksop) s. mamin-
synek;fajtlapa;oferma;niedołęga
milky ('mylky) adj. mleczny;
zniewieściały; koloru mleka
mill (myl) s. młyn; huta; fabryka; (1/1000); walcownia;
krawędź ząbkowana; v. mleć;
frezowac; pilsnic; kręcic się
miller ('myler) s. młynarz
millet ('mylyt) s. proso
milliner ('mylyner) s. modniarka; modystka
million ('myljen) num. milion
millionaire('myljeneer) s. milioner
millionth ('myljent) num.
milionowy; jedna milionowa
(część)
milt (mylt) s. mlecz rybi ;
v. zapładniac ikrą
mimic ('mymyk) s. naśladowca;
imitator; v. naśladowac; maż-
powac; adj. naśladowniczy;udany;
mimiczny;zmysłony;fikcyjny
mince (myns) v. siekac; mowic
bez ogrodek; cedzic (słowa);
drobic nogami; s. siekane
mięso; nadzienie mięsne
mincing (mynsyng) adj. mizdrzą-
cy się; afektowany;sztucznie
zachowujący się(wykwintny)

mind (majnd) s. umysł; pamięc;
zdanie; opinia; postanowienie;
zamierzenie; v. pamietac; zwa-
żac; przejmowac się; baczyc;
miec cos przeciwko;byc posłusznym
mind your own business ('majnd;-
jo:'oźn'byznys) pilnuj swego
nosa; nie wtrącaj się
minded ('majndyd) adj. nastawio-
ny na; skłonny do; gotow; gotowy
mindful ('majndful) adj. pomny;
dbały; uważający; troskliwy
mindless ('majndlys) adj. nierozumny; niedbały; nieuważający
mine (majn) pron. moj; moje; mo-
ja; s. kopalnia; podkop; mina;
bomba; v. kopac;.podkopywac;
exploatowac; minowac
miner ('majner) s. gornik
mineral ('mynerel) s. minerał;
adj. mineralny;zawierający mine-rały
mingle ('myngl) v. mieszac się;
przyłączac się (do innych)
miniature ('mynjeczer) s. miniatura; adj. miniaturowy
minimum ('mynymem) s. minimum;
adj. minimalny;najmniejszy
mining ('majnyng) s. gornictwo;
adj. gorniczy; kopalniany
miniskirt ('myny,ske:rt) s. spod-
nica (mini) (b. krotka)
minister ('mynyster) s. duchowny;
minister; v. stosowac; przyczy-
niac się; udzielac; pomagac
ministry ('mynystry) s. dusz-
pasterstwo; kler; duchowienstwo;
ministerstwo; gabinet ministrow;
służba; pomoc;posługa
mink (mynk) s. norka; adj. z norek; z futer norek
minor ('majner) adj. mniejszy;
mało ważny; młodszy; nieletni;
s. człowiek niepełnoletni
minority (maj'noryty) s. mniej-
szosc; niepełnoletnosc
minster ('mynster) s. katedra;
koscioł klasztorny
minstrel ('mynstrel) s. bard;
spiewak przebrany za murzyna
mint (mynt) s. mięta; mennica;
majatek; zrodło; v. bic pieniądze; wymyslac; tworzyc; kuc

minute ('mynyt) s. minuta;
chwilką; notatka; v. szkicować;
protokołować; (maj'nju:t) adj.
szczegółowy;bardzo mały;znikomy

miracle ('myrekl) s. cud;a.cudów

miraculous (my'raekjules) adj.
cudowny ;nadprzyrodzony

mirage ('myra:dż) s. miraż;
fata morgana ;złudzenie wzroko-

mire ('majer) s. muł; błoto;
bagno; v. grzęznąć (w trudnościach); zabłocić się

mirror ('myrer) s. zwierciadło;
v. odzwierciedlać

mirth (me:rs) s. wesołość; radość ;uciecha(pełna śmiechu)

miry ('majry) adj. błotnisty;
mulisty ; bagnisty

mis-(mys) przedrostek: nie; źle;
(błędnie) nie-;źle-

misadventure ('mesed'wenczer)
s. niepowodzenie;zła przygoda

misanthrope ('myzentroup) s.
mizantrop ;wróg ludzkości

misapply ('myse'plaj) v. nadu-
żyć; źle zastosować

misapprehend ('mys,aepry'hend)
v. nie pojąć; źle zrozumieć

misbehave ('mysby'hejw) v. nie-
odpowiednio zachowywać się

miscalculate ('mys'kaelkjulejt)
v. przeliczyć się;przerachować

miscarriage (mys'kaerydż) s.
poronienie; omyłka;niepowodzenie

mischief ('myscryf) s. szkoda;
krzywda; psota; utrapienie;
złośliwość; figiel; figlarność;
licho; szkodnik;bieda;niezgoda

mischievous ('mysczywes) adj.
szkodliwy; niegodziwy; niesforny; niegrzeczny;psotny

misdeed ('mys'di:d) s. przestępstwo; zły czyn(karygodny)

misdemeano(u)r ('mysdy'mi:ner)
s. wykroczenie;złe sprawowanie

miser ('majzer) s. sknera; chciwiec; skąpiec; kutwa

miserable ('myzerebl) adj. nędzny; chory; marny; żałosny

miserably ('myzerebly) adv.
nędznie; marnie; żałośnie

misfortune (mys'fo:rczen) s.
nieszczęście; pech; zły los

misgiving (mysgywyŋg) s. złe
przeczucie; obawa;powątpiewanie

misguide (,mys'gajd) v. wprowadzać w błąd;sprowadzać na manowce

mishap ('myshaep) s. (mały; nie-
poważny) wypadek(niepowodzenie)

misinform ('mysyn'form) v. źle
informować;zwieść z drogi

mislay (mys'lej) v. zatracić;
zob. lay; zagubić;zapodziać

mislead (mys'li:d) v. wprowadzić
w błąd; zob. lead;zbałamucić

mismanage (,mys'maenydż) v. źle
prowadzić;źle pokierować

misplace (,mys'plejs) v. zatracić; położyć; nie na miejscu

misprint (,mys'prynt) v. błędnie wydrukować; s. omyłka druku; błąd drukarski

mispronounce ('myspre'nauns) v.
błędnie wymawiać;źle wymawiać

misrepresent ('mysrepry'zent)
v. przekręcić; błędnie przedstawić ;fałszywie przedstawić

Miss (mys) s. panna; panienka

miss (mys) v. chybić; nie trafić; nie znaleźć; nie dostać;
brakować; tęsknic; zacinać się;
s. pudło; niepowodzenie;
opuszczenie; chybienie

miss out ('mys,aut) v. wypuścić
(słowo); chybić ;nie dostać

missile ('mysajl) s. pocisk; rakieta; adj. nadający się do
rzucania (oszczep;rakieta etc.)

missing ('mysyŋg) adj. nieobecny; brakujący; zaginiony

mission ('myszyn) s. misja; delegacja; v. wysyłać z misją;
zakładać misje ;a.misyjny

missionary ('myszynery) s.
misjonarz ;adj.misjonarski

misspelling ('mys'spelyŋg) s.
błąd ortograficzny

mist (myst) s. lekka mgła;
v. zachodzić parą(mgiełką)

mistake (mys'tejk) s. omyłka;
nieporozumienie; v. pomylić
(się) (co do faktu lub człowieka); źle zrozumieć; mylić się

mistaken (mys'tejken) adj. mylny; błędny ;pomylony;nie mający
zrozumienia sytuacji etc.

mistakenly (mys'tejknly) adv.
błędnie;pomyłkowo;nierozsądnie
Mister ('myster) s. pan, (używane z nazwiskiem); skrót Mr.
(bez nazwiska niegrzecznie !)
mistletoe ('mysltou) s. jemioł-
ka, jemioła;liście jemioły
mistress ('mystrys) s. kochan-
ka; nauczycielka; (myzys) s.
pani; (skrót Mrs); zob.Mister
mistrust (mys'trast) v. podej-
rzewać; nie ufać; s. niedowierzanie; nieufność
misty ('mysty) adj. mglisty;
zamglony;niejasny;nieokreślony
misunderstanding ('mysande r-
staendyng) s. nieporozumienie
misuse ('mys'ju:z) v. nadużywać; źle używać; ('mys'ju:s)
s. nadużycie; złe użycie
mite (majt) s. molik; kruszyna;
drobiazg; grosz (wdowi); ber-
bec;mała sumka pieniędzy
mitigate ('mytygejt) v. koić;
usmierzac; łagodzić; łagod-
niec; ukoić;złagodzić
mitten ('mytn) s. rękawiczka
bez palców; (slang):rękawica
bokserska(zimowa etc.)
mix (myks) v. mieszać; obcować;
współżyć; s. mieszanka; mieszanina; zamieszanie
mix-up ('myks'ap) s. gmatwani-
na; platanina;zamieszanie;bójka
mixed up with ('mykst'ap,łys)
adj. zamieszany (w coś)
mixture ('mykszczer) s. mieszanka; mieszanina;mikstura
moan (moun) s. jęk; v. jęczeć;
lamentować;mówić jęcząc
moat (mout) s. fosa; rów;
v. opasywać fosą
mob (mob) s. tłum; motłoch;
banda; v. napastować; atakować tłumnie;stłoczyć się
mobile ('moubajl) adj. ruchomy;
ruchliwy; zmienne; s. rzeźba-
kompozycja wisząca(abstrakcyj-
na)
mock (mok) v. wykpić; przedrzeźniać; zmylić; stawiać czoło;
żartować z kogoś; s. kpiny;
przedrzeźnianie;naśladownictwo
adj.fałszywy; udany; pozorny

mockery ('mokery) s. kpiny;
śmiech; posmiewisko;pokrzywianie
się
mode (moud) s. sposób; tryb; moda;rzecz modna(lub zwyczajowa)
model ('modl) s. model; wzór; mo-
delka; manekin; v. modelować
moderate ('moderyt) adj. umiarkowany; sredni; s. człowiek umiarkowany (w poglądach etc.)
moderate ('moderejt) v.powściągać;
uspokoić (się);prowadzić(zebranie)
moderation (,mode'rejszyn) s.
umiarkowanie; umiar;spokój
modern ('modern) adj. współczesny;
nowoczesny; nowożytny
modernize ('modernajz) v. unowo-
cześnic (się);modernizować
modest ('modyst) adj. skromny
modesty ('modysty) s. skromność
modification (,modyfy'kejszyn) s.
modyfikacja; łagodzenie z lekka
modify ('modyfaj) v. modyfikować;
zmieniac częściowo; łagodzić
modulate ('modjulejt) v. modulować; regulować; dostosowywać
module ('modju:l) s. moduł; kabina (astronauty)
moist (mojst) adj. wilgotny
moisten (mojsen) v. wilgnąć; zwilżać (sobie usta etc.);wilgotnieć
moisture ('mojszczer) s. wilgoć;
wilgotność;lekkie zamoczenie
molar (mouler) s. trzonowy (ząb)
adj. trzonowy
mole (moul) s. kret; grobla; molo; znamię;brodawka etc.
molecule ('molykju:l) s. molekuła; cząsteczka
molest (mou'lest) v. napastować;
dokuczac; molestować;naprzykrzać
się
mollify ('molyfaj) v. łagodzić;
miękczyć; mięknąc;usmierzać
moment ('moument) s. chwila; moment; waga; znaczenie; motyw;
powod;doniosłość;ważność
momentary ('moumentery) adj.
chwilowy; mijający; lada chwila
monarch ('monerk) s. monarcha;
król;duży motyl tropikalny
monarchy ('monerky) s. monarchia
monastery ('monestery) s. klasztor (głównie męski);miejsce za
mieszkania mnichów (zakonnic)

Monday ('mandy) s. poniedziałek; a. poniedziałkowy

monetary ('manytry) adj. mone-
tarny;pieniężny;walutowy

money ('many) s. pieniądze

money-order ('many,o:rder) s.
przekaz pieniężny

monger ('manger) s. handlarz;
przekupień;kupiec

monk (mąnk) s. mnich

monkey ('manky) s, małpa; v. dokazywać; małpować;wygłupiać sie (ogoniasta)

monkey business ('manky'byznys)
s. małpie figle (dokuczliwe)

monkey wrench ('manky'rencz) s.
francuski klucz (dostosowywalny)

monolog(ue) ('monelog) s. monolog ;a.monologowy

monopolize (me'nopelajz) v.
monopolizować; skupiać na sobie uwagę wszystkich etc.

monopoly (me'nopely) s. monopol

monotonous (me'notnes) adj.
monotonny; jednolity

monotony (me'notny) s. monotonia

monster ('monster) s. potwor;
adj. olbrzymi;potworny;okrutny

monstrous ('monstres) adj. potworny; ogromny;okrutnie zły

month (mant) s. miesiąc

monthly ('mantly) adj. miesięcz-
ny; adv. miesięcznie; s. mie-
siecznik;adv.co miesiac;na mie-siac-wy

monument ('monjument) s. pomnik

moo (mu:) v. ryczeć; s. ryk
(krowy)

mood (mu:d) s. humor; nastrój;
(gram.) tryb;usposobienie

moody (mu:dy) adj. ponury; mający humory;markotny

moon (mu:n) s. księżyc;a.księżyco-na

moonlight ('mu:nlajt) s. światło
księżyca; v. miec kilka posad
równoczesnie

moonlit ('mu:nlyt) adj. oświe-
cony księżycem

moonshine ('mu:nszajn) s. światło księżyca; alkohol pędzony
nielegalnie lub przemycony

Moor (muer) adj. mauretański;
s. Maur

moor (muer) s. otwarty teren łowiecki; wrzosowisko; bagno;
trzęsawisko; v. cumować; umocować;przybijać do brzegu

moorings ('mueryns) pl. kotwica
martwa; miejsca przycumowania

moose (mu:s) s. łoś amerykański

mop (mop) s. szmata do podłóg;
grymas; v. wycierać; zgarniac;
robić miny;spuścić manto

moral ('morel) s. morał; pl.
moralność;adj.moralny;obyczajny

morale (me'rael) s. nastrój;
duch (w wojsku,w narodzie)

morality (me'raelyty) s. moralność; moralizowanie; etyka

moralize ('morelajz) v. umoral-
niać; moralizować

morass (me'raes) s. moczar; bagno;mokradła;grzęzawiska

morbid ('mo:rbyd) adj. chorobli-
wy; chorobowy;niezdrowy;schorzały

more (mo:r) adv. bardziej; wiecej; adj. liczniejszy;dalszy

morel (mo'rel) s. (grzyb)
smardz;psianka;a.psiankowaty

more or less ('mo:r,or'les) adv.
mniej więcej;w przybliżeniu

moreover (mo;'rouwer) adv. co
więcej; prócz tego;nadto;poza tym

morgue (mo:rg) s. morga (na
zwłoki) ; kostnica;a.kostnicy

morning ('mo:rnyng) s. rano;
poranek; przedpołudnie

morose (mo'rous) adj. ponury;
zasępiony;przygnębiony;markotny

morphine ('mo:rfi:n) s. morfina ;a.morfinowy

morsel ('mo:rsel) s. kęs; kąsek;
kawałek; smakołyk; v. dzielić
na kawałki;rozdrabniać;rozparce-lowywać

mortal ('mo:rtl) s. śmiertelnik;
adj. śmiertelny; straszny

mortality (mo;'rtaelyty) s.
śmiertelność;liczba ofjar

mortar 'mo:ter) s. moździerz;
zaprawa murarska; v. tynkować;
kłaść zaprawę; strzelać z
moździerza;zwiazać zaprawa

mortgage ('mo:rgydż) s. hipoteka; v. hipotekować

mortician (mo:r'tyszen) s.
przedsiębiorca pogrzebowy
mortification (mo:rtyfy'kejszyn) s. upokorzenie; umartwia-
nie się;wstyd;gangrena
mortify ('mo:rtyfaj) v. zamierać; ranić (uczucia); upo-
karzać; umartwiać (się);
powściągać;zgangrenować
mortuary ('mo:rtjuery) s. trupiarnia; kostnica;a.pogrzebowy
mosaic (mou'zejyk) s. mozaika;
adj. mozaikowy;mojżeszowy
mosque (mosk) n. meczet
mosquito (mes'ki:tou) s. komar;
moskit;a.moskitowy
moss (mos) s, mech; v. pokrywać
mchem (torfowiskiem)
most (moust) adj. największy;
najliczniejszy; adv. najbardziej; najwięcej; s. najwięk-
sza ilość;maksimum
mostly ('moustly) adv. przeważnie; głównie;po największej częś-
moth (mos) s. cma; mól
moth-eaten ('mos,i:tn)adj.zje-
dzony przez mole;przestarzały
mother ('madzer) s. matka;v.mat-
mother country ('madzer'kantry)
s. ojczyzna;kraj rodzinny
motherhood ('madzer,hud) s. macierzyństwo
mother-in-law ('madzer,yn'lo:)
s. teściowa
motherly ('madzerly) adj. macierzyński
mother tongue ('madzer,tang) s.
język ojczysty
motif (mou'ti:f) s. motyw
(artystyczny);główny temat
motion ('mouszyn) s. ruch; wniosek; stolec; v. kierować skinieniem, znakiem; skinąć na
kogoś znaczącym gestem
motionless ('mouszenlys) adj.
bez ruchu; unieruchomiony
motion picture ('mouszyn'pykczer) s. film ruchomy
motivate ('moutywejt) v. uzasadniać; pobudzać kogoś;zachęcać
motive ('moutyw) s. motyw; podnieta; adj. napędowy;poruszający

motor ('mouter) s. motor; adj.
ruchowy; mechaniczny; samochodowy; v. jeździć; przewozić
samochodem;prowadzić wóz
motorbike ('mouter,bajk) s.
motocykl;rower z motorkiem
motorboat ('mouter,bout) s.
motorówka;łódź motorowa
motorcycle ('mouter,sajkl) s.
motocykl
motorcyclist ('mouter,sajklyst)
s. motocyklista
motoring ('mouteryng) s. jazda
samochodem;automobilizm
motorist ('mouteryst) s. auto-
mobilista; kierowca
motorize ('mouterajz) s. motoryzować;zmotoryzować
mottle ('motl) s. cętka; plamka;
v. cętkować;nakrapiać;upstrzyć
motto (motou) s. motto;dewiza
mo(u)ld (mould) s. pleśń; ziemia;
modła; forma; v. pleśnieć; odlewać; kształtować;urabiać
moulder ('moulder) v. gnić;
pruchnieć; niszczyć się; kruszyć się;zgłupieć;s.odlewacz
mouldy ('mouldy) adj. spleśniały;
zgniły;stęchły;przeżyty;nudny
moult (moult) v. liniec;s.linienie
mound (maund) s. hałda; kopiec
mount (maunt) s. oprawa; podstawa; wierzchowiec; v. stanąć (na);
wsiąść (na konia); podnieść;
wchodzić; oprawić; osadzić; wyposażyć;zmontować;wyreżyserować
mountain ('mauntyn) s. góra; sterta; adj. górski; gorzysty
mountaineer (,maunty'nier) s.
góral; alpinista
mountainous ('mauntynes) adj.
górzysty;olbrzymi;zawrotny
mourn (mo:rn) v. być w żałobie;
opłakiwać;pogrążać się w smutku
mournful ('mo:rnful) adj. żałobny; ponury; przygnębiony
mourning ('mo:rnyng) s. żałoba
mouse (maus) s. mysz; pl. mice
(majs);podbite oko;v.myszkować
moustache (mos'ta:sz) s. wąsy
mouth (maus) s. usta; ujście; wylot;v.mówić przesadnie (patosem)

mouth (moug) v. deklamować;
brać w usta; robić złą minę
mouthful ('mausful) s. pełne
usta; kęs; dźwięk trudny do
wymówienia; powiedzieć do
rzeczy;ważne słowa;dużo czegoś
mouthpiece ('mauspi:s) s. ustnik; rzecznik;kiełzno
mouthwash ('mausłosz) s. woda
do ust;płukanka do ust
move (mu:w) s. ruch; pociągnięcie; krok; zmiana mieszkania;
przeprowadzka; v. ruszać się;
posuwać; przesuwać; postępować; przeprowadzać się; wzruszać; nakłonić; zwracać się;
wnosić;zrobić ruch;działać
move in ('mu:wyn) v. wprowadzać się;wtargnąć   ;wejść
move on ('mu:w,on) v. jechać
dalej; iść dalej;ruszyć(w drogę)
move out ('mu:w,aut) v. wyprowadzać się;wynieść się
movement (mu:wment) s. ruch;
poruszenie; przemieszczenie;
mechanizm; wypróżnienie
movies ('mu:wyz) s. (slang)
kino;film niemy;film
moving ('mu:wyng) adj. ruchomy;
wzruszający; s. przeprowadzka
moving violation ('mu:wyn,waj-
je'lejszyn) przestępstwo drogowe w czasie jazdy (autem)
mow; mowed; mown (moł; młd;
mołn)
mow (moł) v. kosić(trawę)
mower ('młer) s. kosiarz
mown (mołh) v. zob. mow
Mr. (myster) s. pan (używane
z nazwiskiem)
Mrs. (mysyz) s. zamężna pani
(używane z nazwiskiem)
much (macz) adj.& adv. wiele;
bardzo; dużo;sporo;niemało
much too much (,macz'tu,macz)
exp. duźo za dużo; zbyt dużo
mucus ('mju:kes) s. śluz
mud (mad) s. błoto; brud
muddle ('madl) v. nurzać się;
mącić; bełtać; mieszać; brnąć;
wikłać się; s. powikłanie;
trudne położenie ;nieład;zamęt

muddle through ('madl,tru:) v.
przebrnąć;wybrnąć z kłopotów
muddy ('mady) adj. zabłocony;
błotnisty; mętny;v.błocić;mącić
muff (maf) s. zarękawek; fuszerka; fuszer; v. fuszerować
muffle (mafl) v. tłumić; owinąć;
otulić;s.pysk(przeżuwaczy,gryzoni)
muffler ('mafler) s. tłumik;
szal; rękawica bokserska ;szalik
mug (mag) s. dzban; kubek; gęba
mulberry ('malbery) s. morwa
mule (mju:l) s. muł (zwierzę)
mull (mal) v. rozmyślać; pokpić;
sfuszerować; zagrzać i zapra-
wić (np. piwo); s. bałagan;
muslin; przylądek; tabakiera
mullion ('malion) s. pręt; drążek okienny,słupek okienny
multiple ('maltypl) s. wielokrot-
na; adj. wielokrotny ;złożony
multiplication (,maltyply'kejszyn) s. mnożenie ;rozmnażanie się
multiplication table (,malty-
ply'kejszyn tejbl) s. tabliczka mnożenia
multiply ('maltyplaj) v. mnożyć
(się)rozmnażać się;pomnożyć
multitude ('maltytju:d) s. mnóstwo; tłum;pospolstwo;mnogość
mumble ('mambl) s.mruknięcie;
bąknięcie; v. mruknąć; bąknąć;
żuć bezzębnymi dziąsłami;mamrotać
mummy ('mamy) s. mumia; miazga;
brunatny barwik; mamusia
mumps ('mamps) s. (choroba).
świnka; s. zapalenie ślinianki
munch (mancz) v. chrupać ;schrupać
municipal (mju:'nysypel) adj.
miejski; samorządowy; komunalny
municipality (mju:,nysy'paelyty)
s. zarząd miasta ;miasteczko
mural ('mjuerel) s. malowidło
ścienne; fresk ;adj.ścienny
murder ('me:rder) s. mord; mor-
destwo ;v.mordować;paskudzić(rolę)
murderer ('me:rderer) s. morderca
murderess ('me:rderys) s. morder-
czyni
murderous ('me:rderes) adj. morderczy; śmiercionośny

murmur ('me:rmer) s. mrucze-
nie; pomruk; pomrukiwanie;
szmer; szmeranie; sarkanie;
v. mruczec; szmerac
muscle ('masl) s. mięsień;
muskuł ;v. pchac się na siłę
muscle bound ('masl,baund) adj.
z zerwanymi mięśniami
muscular ('maskjuler) adj.
mięśniowy; krzepki; muskularny;wykonany muskułami etc.
muse (mju:z) v. dumac ;s.zaduma
museum (mju:'ziem) s. muzeum
mush (masz) s. papka; kulesza
(z kukurydzy);v.isc po śniegu
mushroom ('maszrum) s. grzyb;
pieczarka polna; dorobkiewicz;
v. zbierac grzyby; rozszerzac
się (jak grzyby po deszczu)
music ('mju:zyk) s. muzyka;
nuty ;konsekwencje postępku(sl)
musical ('mju:zykel) adj. muzyczny; muzykalny; s. komedia
lub film muzyczny
music hall ('mju: zykho:l) s.
teatr rewiowy
musician ('mju:zyszen) s. muzyk (zawodowy)
music stand('mju:zyk,staend) s.
pulpit (na nuty)
musk (mask) s. piżmo
musket ('maskyt) s.muszkiet
muskrat ('mask,raet) s.
piżmoszczur; futro piżmoszczura
Muslim ('muslym) adj. muzułman-
ski; s. muzułmanin
muslin ('mazlyn) s. muslin
musquash ('maskłosz) s. piżmo-
wiec;piżmoszczyr
mussel('masl) s. małż
must (mast) s. moszcz winny;
stęchlizna; szał; v. musiec;
adj. konieczny;nieodzowny
mustache ('mastasz) s. wąsy
mustard ('masterd) s. musztarda
muster ('master) v. musztrowac;
zbierac (się); s. przegląd;
zebranie; zbior; apel;zebrani
muster in ('master,yn) v. za-
ciągac do wojska (powołac)
muster out ('master,aut) v. zwalniac z wojska

musty ('masty) adj. stęchły; za-
plesniały;zbutwiały;przestarzały
mute (mju:t) adj. niemy;v.tłumic
mutilate ('mju:tylejt) v. okaleczyc; psuc;okroic(tekst książki).
mutineer (,mju:ty'nier) s.
buntownik; winny buntu
mutinous ('mju:tynes) s. buntowniczy ; zbuntowany
mutiny ('mju:tyny) s. bunt;v.bun-
mutter ('mater) v. mamrotac; mruczec; szemrac (przeciw); szeptac; pomrukiwac; s. mamrot; pomruk; szemranie; narzekanie
mutton ('matn) s. baranina;a.bara-
mutton chop ('matn,czop) s.
kotlet barani
mutual ('mju:tjuel) adj. wzajemny; wspolny; obustronny;wspolny
muzzle ('mazl) s. wylot lufy;
pysk; kaganiec; v. nakładac
kaganiec (psu;dziennikarzowi etc.)
my (maj) pron. moj;moja;moje;moi
myelitis (,maje'lajtys) s. zapalenie rdzenia pacierzowego
myriad ('myryed) s. krocie; ro-
je; 10.000; miriada; adj. niezliczony; wielostronny
myrrh (me:r) s. mirra
myrtle ('me:rtl) s. mirt
myself (maj'self) pron. ja sam;
sam osobiscie; siebie; sobie
mysterious (mys'tierjes) adj.
tajemniczy;niezgłębiony
mystery ('mystery) s. tajemnica;
tajemniczosc ;misterium
mystify ('mystyfaj) v. wprowadzac w błąd; okrywac tajemnicą
myth (mys) s. mit; postac mi-
tyczna; bajka;mistyfikacja
mystic ('mystyk) s. mistyk;
adj. mistyczny; tajemniczy
n (en) czternasta litera
angielskiego alfabetu
nab (naeb) v. capnąc; złapac;
przydybac;aresztowac;przyłapac
nag (naeg).v. gderac; dokuczac;
dręczyc; s. szkapa;kucyk;konik
nail (nejl) s. gwozdz; pazno-
kiec; pazur; v. przybijac;
utkwic(wzrok); ujawniac(kłam-
przygwozdzic; chwytac   stwo)

naive (na:'i:w) adj. naiwny

naked ('nejkyd) adj. nagi; goły; goła(prawda etc.);obnażony

name (nejm) s. imię; nazwa;
nazwisko; v. nazywac; miano-
wac; wymieniac;naznaczyc(datę)

nameless ('nejmlys) adj. bez-
imienny; nieznany; niesłychany; nieopisany;anonimowy

namely ('nejmly) adv. mianowicie; właśnie;żeby(wyjaśnić)

nanny ('naeny) s. nianka; koza

nanny -goat ('naeny,gout) s.
koza (żywicielka,mlekodajna)

nap (naep) v. drzemac; zdrzem-
nąc się;s.drzemka; meszek;puch;
włos;stroszenie meszku

nape(nejp) s. kark

nappy ('naepy) adj. mocny;
podchmielony; puszysty; v. napój; piwo; półmisek; serwetka

narcosis (na:r'kousys) s. narkoza;uśpienie narkotykami

narcotic(na:r'kotyk) adj.narko-
tyczny; s. narkotyk; narkoman

narrate (nae'rejt) v. opowiadac (coś);opowiedzieć

narration (nae'rejszyn) s. opowiadanie ;opowieść

narrative ('naeretyw) adj. nar-
racyjny; s. opowiadanie

narrator (nae'rejter) n, narrator;opowiadający;opowiadacz

narrow ('naerou) adj. wąski;
ciasny; ograniczony; s. przesmyk; cieśnina; v. zwężac;
ścieśniac; kurczyc się; zmniejszac się; redukowac do...

narrow -minded ('naerou'majndyd)
s. ciasny; ograniczony

nasty ('na:sty) adj. obrzydliwy; wstrętny; nieznośny; groz-
nv: brudny; nieprzyzwoity

nation ('nejszyn) s. naród;
kraj; państwo

national ('naeszenl) adj. narodowy; państwowy; s. członek
narodu; obywatel; ziomek

nationality (,naesze'naelyty)
s. narodowość; obywatelstwo

nationalize ('naesznelajz) v.
upaństwowic; nadawac obywatelstwo (imigrantom etc.)

native ('nejtyw) adj. rodzinny;
krajowy; miejscowy; wrodzony;
naturalny; prosty; s. tubylec;
autochton; człowiek miejscowy

native language ('nejtyw'laengłydż) s. ojczysty język

nativity (ne'tywyty) s. narodzenie

natural ('naeczrel) adj. naturalny; przyrodniczy; przyrodzony; doczesny; fizyczny; przyrodni; pierwotny; nieslubny;
dziki; s. biały klawisz (pia-
nina); kasownik (muzyczny)

naturalize ('naeczerelajz) v.
naturalizowac (się); aklimaty-
zowac (się); robic naturalnym;
przyswajac sobie; pozbawiac
cech nadprzyrodzonych

naturally ('naeczrely) adv. na-
turalnie ;z przrodzenia;oczywiś-
cie

natural-science ('naeczerel'sajens) s. przyroda; nauka przy-
rody; przyrodoznawstwo

nature ('nejczer) s. natura;
przyroda; usposobienie; rodzaj

naught (no:t) s. nic; zero

naughty ('no:ty) adj. niegrzeczny; nieposłuszny; nieprzyzwoity

nausea ('no:sje) s. nudnosc;
mdłość; choroba morska; obrzydzenie; wstręt chęć wymiotowania

nauseating ('no:sjejtyng)adj.
obrzydliwy; przyprawiający
o mdłości ,wymioty etc.

nautical ('no:tykel) adj. ma-
rynarski; morski

nautical mile ('no:tykel,majl)
s. mila morska; 1853 m.

naval (nejwel) adj. morski

naval base ('nejwel,bejz) s.
baza morska (wojskowa)

nave (nejw) s. 1. nawa; 2. piasta (u koła)

navel ('nejwel) s. pępek (ośrodek)

navigable ('naewygebl) adj.
spławny; żeglowny; sterowny;
podatny do żeglugi

navigate ('naewygejt) v. żeglo-
wac; kierowac; (np.balonem)

navigation (,naewy'gejszyn) s.
żegluga;podróż morska;nawigacja

navigator ('naewygejter) s.
żeglarz; nawigator

navy (nejwy) s. marynarka
wojenna;granatowy kolor

nay (nej) adv. nie; nawet; co
więcej; s. sprzeciw

near (nier) adj. bliski; dokładny; v. zbliżać się; adv. blisko; prawie; oszczędnie

nearby ('nier'baj) adj. pobliski; sąsiedni; adv. w pobliżu

nearly ('nierly) adv. prawie;
blisko; oszczędnie;nie całkiem

nearness ('niernys) s. bliskość

nearsighted ('nier-sajtyd) s.
krótkowzroczny

neat (ni:t) adj. schludny;
zgrabny;proporcjonalny

neatness ('ni:tnys) s. schlud-
ność;prostota; porządek; gus-
towność;dobre proporcje

necessary ('nesysery) adj. konieczny; potrzebny;wynikający

necessitate (ny'sesytejt) v.
wymagać; czynić koniecznym

necessity (ny'sesyty) s. potrzeba; konieczność; artykuł
pierwszej potrzeby; niedostatek;los;zrządzenie los

neck (nek) s. szyja; kark;
szyjka; przesmyk;v.pieścić się

necklace ('neklys) s. naszyjnik

neck-tie ('nektaj) s. krawat

nee (nej) z domu (nazwisko
panieńskie)

need (ni:d) s. potrzeba; trudności; bieda; v. potrzebować;
musieć; cierpieć biedę

needful (ni:dful) adj. potrze-
bujący; potrzebny;konieczny

needle ('ni:dl) s. igła;v.kłuć

needless ('ni:dlys) adj. niepotrzebny; zbyteczny;zbędny

needy ('ni:dy) adj. będący
w potrzebie, w biedzie etc.

negate (ny'gejt) s. zaprzeczać;
negować; anulować

negation (ny'gejszyn) s. zaprzeczenie; odmowa; niebyt

negative ('negetyw) adj. przeczący; negatywny; odmowny;
ujemny; s. zaprzeczenie;odmowa;
forma przecząca;wartość ujemna;

negatyw; v. sprzeciwić się;
odrzucać(np. plan)

neglect (ny'glekt) v. zaniedbywać; nie zrobić; s. zaniedbanie; pominięcie; lekceważenie

negligent ('neglydżent) adj.
niedbały; opieszały;nieuważny

negotiate (ny'gouszjejt) v. pertraktować; omawiać; załatwiać;
przezwyciężać;przebić się przez

negotiation (ny,gouszy'ejszyn)
s. pertraktacje; omawianie

Negress ('ni:grys) s. murzynka

Negro ('ni:grou) s. murzyn; adj.
murzyński

neigh (nej) s. rżenie; v. rżeć

neighborhood ('nejberhud) s.
sąsiedztwo; sąsiedzi; okolica

neighboring ('nejberyng) adj.
sąsiedni; sąsiadujący

neither ('ni:dzer) pron. & adj.
żaden (z dwóch); ani jeden
ani drugi; ani ten ani tamten;
conj. też nie;jeszcze nie

neither... nor ('ni:dzer...no:r)
exp. ani,.. ani

neon ('ni:en) s. neon;a.neonowy

neon sign('ni:en,sajn) s. reklama neonowa

nephew ('nefju:) s. siostrzeniec; bratanek

nerve (ni:rw) s. nerw; siła;
energia; odwaga; opanowanie;
zuchwalstwo; tupet; czelność;
v. dodawać sił, odwagi

nervous ('ne:rwes) adj. nerwowy

nervousness ('ne:rwesnys) s.
nerwowość; zdenerwowanie

nest (nest) s. gniazdo; wyląg
v. budować; gnieździć się

nestle ('nesl) v. skulić; stulić się; przytulić się;urządzić
się

nestle down ('nesl,dałn) v.
usadawiać się (wygodnie)

nestle up to ('nesl,ap'tu) v.
przytulić się (do kogoś)

net (net) adj. czysty; netto;
s. siatka; sieć;v. łowić sie-
cią; trafić w siatkę; zarobić
na czysto (na sprzedarzy etc.)

nettle ('netl) s. pokrzywa;
v. parzyć pokrzywą; drażnić;
irytować;docinać(komuś)dopiekać

network ('net,łe:rk) s. sieć
(np. elektryczna)

neurosis (njue:rousys) s. nerwica;zaburzenia psychiczne

neuter ('nju:ter) adj. nijaki;
neutralny; bezstronny; bezpłciowy; s. człowiek bezstronny; rodzaj nijaki

neutral ('nju:trel) adj. bezstronny; neutralny; obojętny;
pośredni; nieokreślony; bezpłciowy; s. państwo neutralne

neutrality (nu'traelyty) s.
neutralność;obojętność

neutralize ('ny:trelajz)v.neutra-
lizować;unieszkodliwiać;zobo-
jętniać

neutron ('nu:tron).s. neutron

never ('never) adv. nigdy;
chyba nie; wcale; ani nawet

nevermore ('newer'mo:r) adv.
nigdy więcej(przenigdy)

nevertheless (,newerty'les) adj.
niemniej; jednak; pomimo tego

new (nju:) adj. nowy; świeży;
nowoczesny;adv.znowu;na nowo

newborn ('nju:,bo:rn) adj. nowo urodzony; s. noworodek

newcomer (nju:'kemer) adj. no-
woprzybyły; s. przybysz

news,(nju:z) s. nowiny; wiadomości; aktualności;zadrzenia

newscast ('nju:z,ka:st) s. na-
dawanie wiadomości

newspaper ('nju:s,pejper) s.
dziennik (gazeta);tygodnik etc.

newsreel ('nju:sri:l) s. kronika filmowa

newsstand ('nju:staend) s.kiosk
z gazetami

new year ('nju:je:r) s. nowy
rok; pierwszego stycznia

New Year's Eve ('nju:,je:rs'i:w)
s. Sylwester(31go grudnia)

next (nekst) adj. następny;
najbliższy; sąsiedni; adv. następnie; potem; z kolei; tuż
obok;prep.obok;najbliżej

next but one ('nekst,bat'łan)
adj. przedostatni

next day ('nekst,dej) exp. na-
stępnego dnia

next door ('nekst,do:r) adj.
(dom) obok; sąsiedni(budynek)

next to ('nekst,tu) prep. obok

nibble at ('nybl,et) v. obgryzać; nadgryzać; brać (przynętę); s. ogryzanie; dziobanie

nice (najs) adj. miły; sympatyczny; przyjemny; uprzejmy;
ładny; wybredny; dokładny

nicely ('najsly) adv. przyjem-
nie; miło; grzecznie; ściśle;
dokładnie; skrupulatnie

nicety ('najsyty) s. delikatność; subtelność; zawiłość;
drobiazgowość; dokładność;
drobny szczegół; małe rozróż-

niche (nycz) s. nisza; v. chować (się)w niszy

nick (nyk) s. karb; otłuczenie;
moment; v, karbować; podcinać;
przecinać; trafić; natrafić;
odgadnąć; oszukać; złapać otłuc

nickel ('nykl) s. nikiel; 5 centów USA: v. niklować

nick-nack ('nyk,naek) = knickknack; ozdóbka;świecidełko

nickname ('nyknejm) s. zdrobnia-
łe imię; przezwisko; v, nazywać
zdrobniale; przezywać

niece (ni:s) s. siostrzenica;
bratanica

niggard ('nyged) s. sknera; adj.
żałujący (czegoś); skąpiący

night (najt) s. noc; wieczór

night cap ('najtkaep) s. kieliszek przed snem; czepek do spania;szklanka wina przed snem

nightclub ('najtklab) s. nocny
lokal (rozrywkowy)

nightgown ('najtgałn) s. damska
koszula nocna;nocny ubiór

nightingale ('najtyngejl) s.
słówik; a. słowikowy; słowika

nightly ('najtly) adv. co noc;
w nocy;adj. nocny; jak noc

nightmare ('najtmeer) s. koszmar; przerażające doświadczenie

night school ('najtsku:l) s.
szkoła wieczorowa

nightshirt ('najtsze:rt) s.
koszula nocna

nighty ('najty) s. koszulka
nocna (dziecinna,kobieca)

nil (nyl) s. nic; zero

nimble ('nymbl) adj. zwinny;
zgrabny;bystry;żywy;żwawy

nine (najn) num. dziewięć;
s. dziewiątka;dziewięcioro

ninepins ('najnpynz) pl. kręgle

nineteen ('najn'ti:n) num.
dziewiętnaście;dziewiętnastka

nineteenth ('najn't:ns) num.
dziewiętnasty;dziewiętnastą część

ninetieth ('najntyys) num.
dziewiędziesiąty

ninety ('najty) num. dziewięć-
dziesiąt;dziewiędziesiątka

ninth ('najns) num. dziewiąty

ninthly ('najnsly) adv. po
dziewiąty (raz)

nip (nyp) v. uszczypnąc; przy-
chwycic; odszczepic; stłumic;
zmrozic; buchnąc; ukrasć; popędzic; poleciec; ucinac;
niszczyc;s.ukąszenie;uszczypnięcie

nipoff ('nypof) v. zemknąc

nipple ('nypl) s. brodawka
sutkowa; smoczek; złącze
gwintowane rury; wzniesienie;
pagórek;bańka;złączka;nasówka

niter ('najter) s. saletra

nitrogen ('najtrydżen) s. azot

no (nou) adj. nie; żaden;
odmowa; adv. nie; bynajmniej;
nic;wcale nie;s.odmowa;sprzeciw

no one ('nou,łan) adj. żaden;
ani jeden; nikt (w ogóle)

nobility ('nou'bylyty) s. szla-
chetnosc; szlachta

noble (noubl) adj. szlachetny;
szlachecki; wspaniały; wielkoduszny; s. szlachcic

nobleman (noublmen) s. szlachcic

nobody ('noubedy) s. nikt;
człowiek bez znaczenia

nod (nod) v. skinąc głową;
ukłonic się; drzemac; przyzwa-
lac skinieniem;byc nachylonym

noise ('nojz) s. hałas; zgiełk;
wrzawa; szum; odgłos; szmer;
v. rozgłaszac cos;rozgłosic

noiseless ('nojzlys) adj. cichy;
bezszelestny;nie hałasliwy

noisy ('nojzy) adj. hałasliwy;
krzykliwy; wrzaskliwy

nomadic ('noumaedyk) adj. wędrowny; koczowniczy ;wędrujący

nominal ('nomynl) adj. nominalny;
imienny; symboliczny:tylko z nazwy

nominate ('nomynejt) v. miano-
wac; wyznaczac; obierac

nomination (,nomy'nejszyn) s.
nominacja

nominative ('nomynetyw) s. mianownik (gram.); ta sprawa(sądowa)

non- (non) prefix nie-; bez-;

nonalcoholic ('non,aelke'holic)
adj. bezalkoholowy

noncommissioned ('nonke'myszend)
adj. bez rangi oficerskiej
(podoficer)

noncommital ('nonke'mytl) adj.
wymijający;nie zobowiazujący(się)

nonconducting ('nonken'daktyng)
adj. nieprzewodzacy

nonconformist ('nonken'fo:rmyst)
dyskontent; niekonformista

nondescript ('nondyskrypt) adj.
nieokreslony; s. człowiek nie-
okreslony(trudny do opisania)

none (non) pron. nikt; żaden;
nic; adv. wcale nie; bynajmniej
nie

nonexistence (,nony'ksystens)
s. niebyt;nie istnienie

nonfiction (,non-'fykszyn) s.
reportaże; opowiesc prawdziwa;
opisy faktów (w dziennikach etc.)

nonsense ('nonsens) s. niedo-
rzecznosc; nonsens; głupstwo

nonskid ('nonskyd) adj. prze-
ciwsliizgowy; nie slizgający
się (samochód, opona etc.)

nonsmoker ('non'smouker) s.
osoba niepaląca; przedział dla
niepalących(w pociągu etc.)

nonstop ('non'stop) adj. bez-
posredni;bez lądowania; bez
postoju; nieprzerwany (lot etc.)

nonunion ('non'ju:njen) adj.
nie należący do związku zawodo-
wego;nie uznający związku zawodo-wego

nonviolence ('non'wajelens) s.
(polityka) bez gwałtów

noodle ('nu:dl) s. makaron; kluska; cymbał; pała; głupek;łeb

nook (nuk) s. kącik; zakątek

noon (nu:n) s. południe

noose (nu:s) s. pętla; stryczek; sidła; lasso; v. usid-
lić; zrobić pętlę

nor (no:r) conj. też nie

norm (no:rm) s. norma;wzorzec;
standard

normal ('no:rmel) adj. normalny; prostopadły; prawidłowy;
s. stan normalny; prostopadła

normalize ('no:rmelajz) v. normalizować; unormować

Norman ('no:rmen) adj. norman-
ski;Normandczyk;Normandka

north (no:rs) adv. na północ;
s. północ; adj. północny

northeast (no:rs'i:st) adj.
północno-wschodni

northerly ('no:rdzerly) adj.
północny; adv. na północ

northerner ('no:rdzerner) s.
człowiek z północnych stanów

northward ('no:rsłerd) adj.
północny; adv. na północ

northwest ('no:rs'łest) adj.
północno-zachodni; adv. na
północno-zachód; s. północny-
zachód

Norwegian (no:rłi:dżen) adj.
norweski ;s.Norweg

nose (nouz) s. nos; węch; wylot; dziób; v. węszyć; pocierać nosem; wtykać nos

nosegay ('nouzgej).s. wiązanka;
bukiet

nostril ('noustryl) s. nozdrze;
chrapy; dziura w nosie

nosy ('nouzy) adj. wścibski;
śmierdzący; aromatyczny; no-
sacz wielki;stęchły;cuchnący

not (not) adv. nie ;ani(jeden)

not a (not ej) adv. żaden

notable ('noutebl) adj. znakomity; sławny; wybitny; s. dostojnik ;wybitny człowiek

notary public ('noutery'pablyk)
s. notariusz

notation (nou'tejszyn) s. znako-
wanie; notacja; symbol

notch (nocz) s. nacięcie; karb;
przełęcz; v. nacinać; karbować; rowkować ;s.krok(dalej)

note (nout) s. nuta; znak; zna-
mie; uwaga; notatka; banknot;
v. zapisywać; zauważać

note down ('nout'dałn) v. zanotować ;zapisywać

notebook ('noutbuk) s. zeszyt;
notatnik ;notes; notesik

noted ('noutyd) adj. znany;
znakomity; wybitny

notepaper ('nout,pejper) s.
papier listowy ;blok

noteworthy ('nout,łe:rsy) adj.
godny uwagi; wybitny ;osobliwy

nothing ('nasyng) s. nic; drobiazg; adv. nic; nie; w żaden
sposób ;bynajmniej nie;wcale nie

nothing but ('nasyng'bat) s.
nic tylko..(coś najlepszego)

notice ('noutys) v. zauważyć;
spostrzec; traktować grzecznie;
powiadamiac; s. zawiadomienie;
uwaga; recenzja ;spostrzeżenie

noticeable ('noutysebl) adj.
godny uwagi; widoczny

notification (,noutyfy'kejszyn)
s. zawiadomienie ;zgłoszenie

notify (noutyfaj) v. zawiadomić

notion ('nouszyn) s. pojęcie;
wyobrażenie; zamiar ;wrażenie

notorious ('nou'to:rjes) adj.
notoryczny; osławiony ;jawny

notwithstanding (,noutłys'staendyng) adv. jednakże; niemniej;
mimo; prep. pomimo(tego) ;mimo

nought (no:t) s. nic; zero

noun (naun) s. rzeczownik

nourish ('narysz) v. żywić;
karmić ;utrzymywać

nourishing ('naryszyng) adj.
pożywny ;pokrzepiający

nourishment ('naryszment) s.
pokarm; pożywienie; żywienie;
karmienie ;żywność; jedzenie

novel ('nowel) s. powieść; opowieść; nowela; adj. nowy; nowa-
torski; osobliwy ;oryginalny

novelist ('nowelyst) s. po-
wieściopisarz

novelty ('nowelty) s. nowość;
innowacja ;oryginalność

November (nou'wember) s. listopad; adj. listopadowy

novice ('nowys) s. nowicjusz;
neofita; początkujący
now (naž) adv. teraz; obecnie;
dopiero co; otóż; a więc;
s. teraźniejszość; chwila
obecna; chwila dzisiejsza
now and again ('naž,ende'gejn)
exp. od czasu do czasu
now and then ('naž,end'dzen)
exp.:nieraz; od czasu do czasu; czasem;co jakiś czas
nowadays ('naže,dejz) adv.
obecnie; dzisiaj; s. obecne
czasy;dzisiejsze czasy
nowhere ('nouhžer) adv. nigdzie; s. niepowodzenie etc.
noways ('noužejz) adv. bynajmniej ; wcale nie
noxious ('nokszes) adj. szkodliwy; niezdrowy (moralnie etc.)
nozzle ('nozl) s. dysza; rozpylacz; dziób; wylot (rury etc.)
nuclear ('nu:kli:er) adj. jądrowy; o napędzie nuklearnym
nuclear fission('nu:kli:er'fyszyn) v. rozszczepienie jądra
nuclear power plant ('nu:kli:-
er'pažer'pla:nt) s. elektrownia atomowa
nuclear reactor ('nu:kli:er,ri:-
'aekter) s. reaktor nuklearny
nucleus ('nu:kljes) s. jądro
nude (nju:d) adj. nagi; goły:
nie ważny (prawnie); s. człowiek nagi; nagość; akt
nudge (nadž) v. trącać lekko;
s. trącenie łokciem
nugget ('nagyt) s. bryłka; złoty samorodek
nuisance ('nju:sns) s. zawada,
naruszenie porządku publiczne-
go; osoba sprawiająca zawadę
null and void ('nal,end'woid)
exp. nieważny; bez znaczenia;
unieważniony;nic, nie zanczący
numb (nam) adj. ścierpły; zdręt-
wiały; odrętwiały; y. drętwieć;
odurzać;paraliżować;zdrętwieć
number ('namber) s. liczba; numer; ilość; v, liczyć; numerować; wyliczać; zaliczać
numberless ('namberlys) adj.
niezliczony; bez numeru

number plate ('namber'plejt) s.
płyta z numerem rejestracji
samochodu;motoru etc.
numeral ('nju:merel) adj. liczbowy; cyfrowy; s. liczebnik;
cyfra (pisana,mówiona etc.)
numerous ('nju:meres) adj. liczny; obfity;liczebny;rytmiczny
nun (nan) s. zakonnica:mniszka
nunnery('nanery) s. zakon żeński
nuptials ('napszels) pl. zaślubiny;gody;wesele;ślub
nurse (ne:rs) s. pielęgniarka;
pielęgniarz; mamka; osłona;
v. pielęgnować; leczyć; opiekować się; żywić; podsycać;
szanować; obejmować; karmić;
pić powoli(piersią) niańczyć
nursery ('ne:rsery) s. pokój
dziecinny; żłobek; przedszkole; ochronka; wylęgarnia;
szkółka (roślin)(drzewek)
nursery school ('ne:rsery'sku:l)
s. przedszkole
nursing bottle ('ne:rsyng'botl)
s. flaszka do karmienia
nursing home ('ne:rsyn'houm)
s. przytułek - lecznica dla
starych i kalekich;dom zdrowia
nut (nat) s. orzech; bzik; dziwak; nakrętka; zakrętka;
v. szukać i zbierać orzechy
nutcracker ('natkraeker) s.
dziadek do orzechów
nutmeg ('natmeg) s. gałka
muszkatołowa
nutria ('nju:trje) s. nutria
(futro);nutrie
nutrient ('nju:trjent) adj.
pożywny; odżywczy ;s.odżywka
nutriment ('nju:tryment) s.
środek odżywczy
nutrition (nju'tryszyn) s. odżywienie; pokarm
nutritious (nju'tryszes) adj.
pożywny; odżywczy
nutshell ('natszel) s. łupka
od orzecha; istota rzeczy;
sama treść(w paru słowach)
nutty ('naty) adj. orzechowy;
pomylony; zbzikowany;dziwaczny
zwariowany;pikantny;zakochany

nuzzle ('nazl) v. wsadzac nos
(w cos); ryc; węszyc; wtulac
się(twarzą w czyjeś ramię)
nylon ('najlon) s. nylon; pończochy nylonowe
nymph (nymf) s. nimfa
nymphomania (,nymfe'mejnia) s.
nimfomania(kobieca żądza miłos-
o (ou) piętnasta litera
angielskiego alfabetu;zero
oak (ouk) s. dąb;a.dębowy
oar (o;r) s. wiosło; v. wiosłowac
oarsman ('o:rzmen) s. wioslarz
oasis (ou'ejsys) s. oaza ;
zielonei żyzne miejsce wsrod
pustynnej okolicy
oat (out) s. owies
oatmeal ('outmi:l) s. owsianka [stwo;świętokradztwo etc.
oath (ous) s. przysięga;przekleń-
obedience (e'bi:djens) s. po-
słuszeństwo
obedient (e'bi:djent) adj. posłuszny
obey (e'bej) v. słuchac; byc
posłusznym (rozsądkowi etc.)
obituary (e'bytjuery) s. nekrolog; adj. posmiertny; żałobny
object ('obdżykt) s. przedmiot;
rzecz; cel; smieszny człowiek;
dopełnienie; v. zarzucac cos;
byc przeciwnym ;sprzeciwiac się
objection (eb'dżekszyn) s. zarzut; sprzeciw; przeszkoda;
trudnosc; wada; niechęc
objective (eb'dżektyw) s. cel;
objektyw; adj. przedmiotowy;
obiektywny;rzeczywisty
obligation (obly'gejszyn) s.
zobowiązanie; obowiązek; obligacja;dług(wdzięczności etc.)
oblige (e'blajdż) v. zobowiązywac; spełniac prosbę
obliging (e'blajdżyng) adj.
uprzejmy; uczynny ;usłużny
oblique (e'bli:k) adj.posredni;
ukosny; skosny; kręty; nieszczery; potajemny;v.isc na ukos
obliterate (e'blyterejt) s. zacierac; zamazywac; wykreslic;
zniszczyc;skasowac (zanczek etc.)

oblivion (e'blywjen) s.
zapomnienie; niepamięc
oblivious (o'blywjes) adj. za-
pominający; niepomny; nieswiadomy; dający zapomnienie
oblong('oblong)adj. podłużny;
s. podłużny przedmiot
obscene (ob'si:n) adj. sprosny;
nieprzyzwoity; niemoralny
obscure (eb'skjuer) adj. ciemny;
skromny; niejasny; ukryty; nieznany; v. zaciemniac; przyciem-
niac; zacmiewac
obsequies ('obsykłyz) pl. pogrzeb
observance (eb'ze:rwens) s. obrzęd; zwyczaj; przestrzeganie;
szacunek;poszanowanie;rytuał
observant (eb'ze:rwent) adj.
uważny; przestrzegający; spostrzegawczy;bystry; czujny
observation (,obzer'wejszyn) s.
obserwacja; spostrzeżenie;
uwaga;spostrzegawczość
observatory (eb'ze:rweto:ry) s.
obserwatorium;punkt obserwacyjny
observe (eb'ze:rw) v. obserwowac;
przestrzegac; obchodzic; zauwa-
żac;wypowiedziec uwagę;zbadac
observer (eb'ze:rwer) s. obserwator;człowiek przestrzegający
obsess (eb'ses) v. opętac; prze-
sladowac;nie dawac spokoju;nawie-
obsession (eb'seszyn) s. obsesja;
opętanie ;natręctwo (myslowe)
obsolete ('obseli:t) adj. przestarzały; szczątkowy;zarzucony
obstacle ('obstekl) s. przeszkoda; zawada
obstetrics (ob'stetryks) s. po-
łóżnictwo
obstinacy ('obstynesy) s. upior
obstinate ('obstynyt) adj. uparty; uporczywy;zacięty;wytrwały
obstruct (eb'strakt) v. tamowac;
zagradzac; zasłaniac; wstrzymywac;wywoływac zator;zawadzac
obtain (eb'tejn) v. uzyskac;
trwac; panowac;obowiązywac
obtainable (eb'tejnebl) adj.
osiągalny (do nabycia etc.);
możliwy do nabycia

obtrusive (eb'tru:syw) adj.
natarczywy; natrętny

obvious ('obwjes) adj. oczywisty; rzucający się w oczy

occasion (e'kejżyn) s. sposobność; okazja; powod

occasional (e'kejżenl) adj.
przypadkowy; okazyjny;
okolicznosciowy; rzadki

Occident ('oksydent) s. Zachod (jako kultura, ekonomia
etc.)-całość geogaficzna

occult (o'kalt) adj. tajemny

occupant ('okjupent) s. mieszkaniec; posiadacz (faktyczny)

occupation (,okju'pejszyn) s.
okupacja; zawod; zajęcie;
zajmowanie;zamieszkiwanie

occupy ('okjupaj) v. okupować;
zajmować (się czyms);zatrudniać

occur (e'ke:r) v. zdarzać się;
przychodzic na mysl; poja-
wiac się;dziac sie;trafic sie

occurrence(e'karens) s. wydarzenie; przypadek;występowanie

ocean ('ouszen) s. ocean;a.ocea-
niczny

o'clock (e'klok) adv. na zegarze;według zegara

October (ok'touber) s. pazdzier-
nik ;a,pazdziernikowy

ocular ('okjuler) adj. oczny;na-
oczny;na oko;okiem;s.okular

oculist ('okjulyst) s. okulista

odd (od) adj. nieparzysty;
dziwny; dziwaczny; zbywający;
pozostały; dodatkowy;od pary

odds (ods) pl. szanse; fory;
nadwyżka; różnica; drobne
szczegóły; spór; nierówność
(w grze);sprzeczność;różnica

odds-and-ends ('ods,end'ends)
exp.: resztki; rupiecie

oddity ('odyty) s. osobliwość;
dziwak;dziwactwo;dziwna rzecz

odor ('ouder) s. odor; won;
ślad; reputacja;sława;posmak

of (ow) prep. od; z; o; w

of Cracow (ow'Krakau) exp.:
z Krakowa(pochodzeniem etc.)

of charity (ow'chaeryry) exp.
z miłosierdzia

off (of) adv. od; z; na boku;
precz; zdala; przy;prep.z dala

offshore (of'szo:r) adv. przy
wybrzeżu ;adj.od lądu(na morze)

offense (e'fens) s. obraza; za-
czepka; przekroczenie ofenzywa

offend (e'fend) v. obrażać; ra-
zic; występować przeciw (np.
prawu);zawinic;wykroczyc

offender (e'fender) s. winowajca ;przestępca;strona winna

offensive (e'fensyw) adj. obraźliwy; drażniący; przykry; cuchnący; zaczepny; s. ofensywa;
postawa zaczepna

offer ('ofer) s. oferta; propozycja (np. slubu); v. ofia-
rowac (się); oswiadczyc (się);
oferowac; nastręczyc się; nada-
rzyc się;występować z propozycją

offering ('oferyng) s. ofiara

office ('ofys) s. biuro; urząd;
obowiązek; służba urzędowania;
posada;funkcja;stanowisko;gabinet

officer ('ofyser) s. oficer;
oficer; policjant; v. obsadzac
kadra; dowodzić; kierowac

official (e'fyszel) s. urzędnik;
adj. urzędowy; oficjalny

officious (e'fyszes) adj. narzucający się; natrętny; gorliwy;
nieurzędowy;nieoficjalny

offish ('ofysz) adj. chłodny;
sztywny; z rezerwą;nieprzystępny

offset (o':fset) s. offsetowy
druk; gałąź; odgałęzienie;
odrosl; potomek; wyrównanie;
kompensata;v.wynagradzać;rozrastać się

offspring ('o:fspryng)s. potomek;
wynik; potomstwo

often ('o:fn) adv. często

oh ! (ou) excl.:och !; ach !

oil (ojl) s. oliwa; olej; ropa;
nafta; farba olejna; v. oliwić;
smarowac; przetapiac;pochlebiac

oilcloth ('ojlklos) s. cerata

oily ('ojly) adj. oleisty;
olejny; tłusty; oblesny;śluzalczy

ointment ('oyntment) s. masc

O.K., okay ('ou'kej) adv. w porządku; tak; adj. b. dobry;
s. zgoda; v. zaaprobować (cos)

old (ould) adj. stary; staroświecki; doswiadczony; były
s.dawne czasy;dawno temu

old age ('ould,ejdż) s. starość
old-age ('ould ejdż) adj. dawny;   stary; starczy
old-fashioned ('ould'faeszend)
   adj. staromodny; staroświecki
old-time ('ould,tajm) adj.
   dawny
old town ('ould,tałn) s. starówka; stare miasto
olive ('olyw) s. oliwka; drzewo oliwne; (kolor) oliwkowy;
   oliwa stołowa
olive-branch ('olywbra:ncz) s.
   gałązka oliwna
Olympic Games (ou'lympyk,gejms)
   pl. igrzyska olimpijskie
ombudsman (om'bu:dz,men) s.
   rzecznik ludu - załatwia skargi na biurokratow
omelet(te) ('omlyt) s. omlet
omen ('oumen) s. omen; wróżba;
   znak ;v. być wróżbą;być znakiem
ominous ('omynes) adj. złowieszczy ; źle wróżący
omission (e'myszyn) s. opuszczenie; zaniedbanie
omit (ou'myt) v. opuszczać;
   pomijać; zaniedbywać
omnipotent (om'nypetent) adj.
   wszechmocny,wszechmogący
omniscient (om'nysjent) adj.
   wszechwiedzący
on (on) prep. na; ku; przy; nad;
   u; po; adv. dalej; przed siebie; naprzód ;przy sobie
on and on ('on,end'on) exp.: coraz dalej;bez końca;wciąż
on demand (,on dy'ma:nd) exp.:
   na żądanie
on the street ('on,dy'stri:t)
   exp.: na ulicy
on to ('ontu) exp. na; do
once (łans) adv. raz; nagle;
   naraz; zaraz; kiedyś; niegdyś;
   dawniej; s. raz; conj. raz;
   gdy; skoro ;od razy;zarazem etc.
one (łan) num. jeden; adj. pierwszy; pojedynczy; jedyny; pewien
   s. dowcip; kieliszek; pron. ten;
   który;ktoś; niejaki;s.jedynka
one Adams ('łan,aedems) exp.: pewien Adams ;niejaki Adams

one day ('łan,dej) exp. pewnego
   dnia; kiedyś;niegdyś
one by one ('łan,baj'łan) adv.
   pojedynczo;jeden za drugim
one antoher (,łan e'nadzer) adv.
   jeden drugiego; wzajemnie
oneself (łan'self) pron. się;
   siebie; sobie; sam; osobiście;
   samodzielnie; samotnie
one-sided ('łan'sajdyd) adj.
   jednostronny
one-up-manship ('łan,ap'-menszyp) s. "wyścig" nerwów
   (w zatargu etc)
one-way ('łan,łej) adj. jednokierunkowy(ruch)
onion ('anjen) s. cebula
onlooker ('onluker) s. widz
only ('ounly) adj. jednyny; jedynak; adv. tylko; jedynie;
   ledwo; dopiero; conj. tylko
   że;coż z tego ,kiedy...
onward ('onłerd) adj. naprzód;
   ku przodowi; adv. naprzód;
   dalej;dalej naprzód
ooze (u:z) v. sączyć się; wydzielać; ciec; s. szlam;
   muł; wyciek; rzadkie błoto
opaque (ou'pejk) adj. nieprzeźroczysty; matowy; mętny;
   niejasny; s. rzecz matowa;
   nieprzezroczysta
open ('oupen) adj. otwarty; rozwarty; dostępny; wystawiony;
   jawny; odsłonięty; wakujący;
   otwarty; wolny; v. otworzyć;
   zwierzyć się; umożliwic; rozpoczynać; rozchylić;udostępnić
open air ('oupen,eer) s. świeże
   powietrze; wolna przestrzeń
opener ('oupener) s. otwieracz
   (np. puszek);przyrząd do otwierania
open-handed ('oupn'haendyd) adj.
   szczodry; hojny
open-hearted ('oupn,ha:rtyd) adj.
   szczery; serdeczny
opening ('oupnyng) s. otwór; wylot; otwarcie; początek; zbyt
   adj. początkowy; wstępny
openly ('oupnly) adv. otwarcie;
   szczerze; publicznie; bez ogródek;po prostu; wprost(powiedzieć)

open-minded ('oupn'majndyd)
adj. z otwartą głowa; bez
przesądów; bez stronny

opera ('opere) s. opera

opera glasses ('operegla:sys) s.
lornetka (teatralna)

operate ('operejt) v. działać;
zadziałać; oddziaływać; pracować; operować (kimś; kogoś);
wywoływać; prowadzić; kierować; obsługiwać;spekulować

operation (,ope'rejszyn) s.
działanie; czynności; operacja;
obsługiwanie; akcja

operative ('oprejtyw) adj. skuteczny; działający; praktyczny; operacyjny;s.pracownik;agent
   mechanik; robotnik; detek-
tyw; agent wywiadu

operator ('operejter) s. operator; pracownik; obsługujący
maszynę; telefonista; kierownik; przemysłowiec; finansi-
sta; spekulant

opinion (e'pynjen) s. pogląd;
opinia; zdanie;zapatrywnie;sąd

opponent (e'pounent) s. przeciwnik; oponent; adj. przeciwny; przeciwległy

opportunity (,oper'tju:nyty)
s. sposobność; okazja

oppose (e'pouz) v. przeciwstawiać; sprzeciwiać się

opposed (e'pouzd) adj. przeciwny;przeciwdziałający

opposite ('epezyt) adj. przeciwny; przeciwległy; odmienny; adv. na przeciwko;na przeciw
s. przeciwieństwo;odwrotność

opposition (,ope'zyszyn) s.
sprzeciw; opor; opozycja;
przeciwstawienie (się); przeciwieństwo;a.opozycyjny

oppress (e'pres) v. przygniatać; uciskać; ciemiężyć;
gnębić; nużyć; męczyć

oppression (e'preszyn) s. ucisk

oppressive (e'presyw) adj.
uciążliwy; dręczący; gnębiciel-
ski; ciężki; duszny;deprymujący

opt (opt) v. wybierac z dwu
alternatyw;optować na rzecz cze-go

optical ('optykel) adj. optyczny; wzrokowy,pomocny w widzeniu

optician (op'tyszen) s. optyk

optimism ('optymysem) s. opty-
mizm;pogodny pogląd na życie

optimize ('optymajz) v. używac
najwydajniej,najsprawniej,

option ('opszyn) s. możnosc wyboru; opcja; wybór; v. wybrac
alternatywę

or (o:r) conj. lub; albo; czy;
ani; inaczej; czyli; s. złoto;
adj. złoty

or else ('o:rels) exp. bo jak
nie..; w przeciwnym razie

oral ('o:rel) adj. ustny; do-
ustny; s. egzamin ustny

orange ('oryndż) s. pomarańcza;
adj. pomarańczowy

orangeade ('oryn'dżejd) s.
oranżada(z pomarańcz,cukru)

orator ('oreter) s. mówca

orbit ('o:rbyt) s. orbita;
oczodół; v. latać w orbicie
(ziemi)(słońca etc.)

orchard ('o:rczerd) s. sad

orchestra ('o:rkystra) s.
orkiestra

ordain (o;r'dejn) v. wyświęcać;
mianować; nakazywać; przeznaczać;zarządzać;nakazać

ordeal (o:r'di:l) s. ciężka
próba; ciężkie doświadczenie

order ('o:rder) s. rozkaz; zlecenie; zarządzenie; przekaz;
porządek; szyk; układ; stan;
zakon; order; obrzęd; zamówienie; zadanie; v. rozkazac; zamawiać; komenderować; zarządzać;
wyswiecać; porzadkować

orderly ('o:rderly) s. posługacz; ordynans; adj. adv.
porządny; czysty; dokładny;
skromny; spokojny; dyżurny

ordinal ('o:rdynl) s. liczebnik
porzadkowy; adj. porządkowy

ordinary ('o:rdnry) adj. zwyczajny; zwykły; przeciętny;
pospolity; typowy; s. rzecz
zwykła,codzienna,pręcietna

ore (o:r).s. ruda; kruszec;
a. kruszcowy;rudowy

organ ('o:rgen) s. narząd;
organ; organy;czasopismo
organic ('o:rgaenyk) adj. organiczny;usystematyzowany
organization (,o:rgenaj'zejszyn) s. organizacja; organi-
zowanie;struktura;zrzeszenie
organize (e'genajz) v. organizować;zrzeszyć;nadawać ustrój
organizer('o:genajzer) s. organizator
orgy ('o:rdży) s. orgia
Orient ('o:rjent) adj. orien-
talny; wschodni;s.Wschód(bliski)
orient ('o:rjent) v. orientować;ukierunkowywać;ustawiać
origin('orydżyn) s. pochodzenie;
poczatek;źródło;geneza
original (e'rydżynel) adj.
oryginalny; początkowy;
s. oryginał; dziwak
originality (e,rydży'naelyty)
s. oryginalność
originate (e'rydżynejt) v. zapoczątkować; powstawać
ornament ('o:rnament) s. ozdoba; v. ozdabiać;upiększać
ornamental (,o:rne'mentl) adj.
ozdobny; dekoracyjny; zdobni-
czy;upiększający
orphan ('o:rfen) s. sierota;
adj. sierocy; osierocony
orphanage ('o:rfenydż) s. sie-
rociniec; sieroctwo
orthodox ('o:tedoks) adj. pra-
wowierny; prawosławny
oscillate ('osylejt) v. drgać;
wahać się; oscylować
ostrich ('ostrycz) s. struś
other ('adżer) pron. inny; drugi; adv. inaczej;odmiennie
otherwise ('adżerłajz) adv.
inaczej; poza tym; skądinąd
ought (o:t) v, powinien; trzeba;
żeby; należy; zobowiazany etc.
ounce (auns) s. uncja; odrobina; lampart;1/16 funta
our ('aur) adj. nasz
ours ('auerz) pron. nasz
ourselves (auer'selwz) pl.pron.
my; my sami;(dla)nas etc.
oust (aust) v. usuwać; wypierać; wyrzucać;wywłaszczać

out (aut) adv. na zewnątrz;
precz; poza; na dworze; poza
domem;nieobecnym(być) etc.
out-and-out (auten'aut) adj.
całkowity; adv. całkowicie
out of ('autow) adv. z; bez;
poza ;nie (modne,rozsądne)
outbalance (aut'baelens) v.
przeważyć;przewyższać
outbid (aut'byd) v. przelicytować;dać więcej (niż inny)
outbreak ('autbrejk) s. wybuch
(np. wojny)(epidemii etc.)
outburst ('autbe:rst) s. wybuch (np. gniewu)(vulkanu)
outcast ('autka:st) s. wyrzutek; wygnaniec; adj. wygnany
outcome ('autkam) s. wynik;
rezultat;konsekwencje
outcry ('autkraj) s. okrzyk;
wrzawa;silny protest
outdoors ('aut'do:rz) adj. na
wolnym powietrzu; s. wolna
przestrzeń;adv.zewnatrz(domu)
outer ('auter) adj. zewnętrzny
outermost ('auter'moust) adj.
najbardziej zewnętrzny
outfit ('autfyt) s. wyposażenie; drużyna; zespół; towarzystwo; zestaw narzędzi; v. wyposażyć; zaopatrywać;wyekwipować
outgoing ('aut,gouyŋg)adj. od-
chodzacy; odjeżdżający; przyjazny;komunikatywny;towarzyski
outgrow (aut'grou) v. przerastać; wyrastać z..; wyrosć(z ro-
outing ('autyng) s. wycieczka(na
otwarte morze,do lasu etc.);wy-
outlast (aut'la:st) v. przetrwać (coś,kogoś);wytrwać dłużej
outlaw ('aut-lo:) v. zakazywać;
wyjmować spod prawa; s. przestępca; banita;notoryczny krymi-
outlet ('autlet) s. wylot; rynek zbytu; wyjście; ujscie
outline ('autlajn) s. zarys;
szkic; v. konturować; szkicować; przedstawiać(plany etc.)
outlive (aut'lyw) v. przeżyć;
przetrwać;wytrwać dłużej
outlook ('autluk) s. widok; pogląd; obserwacja; widoki
(na przyszłość);czaty

outnumber (aut'namber) v. przewyższac liczebnie;być liczniej-
out-of-date (autew'dejt) adj.
przestarzały; niemodny
outpatient ('aut,pejszent) s.
pacjent dochodzący (z domu)
output ('autput) s. wydajność;
wydobycie; moc; produkcja
outrage ('autrejdż) s, gwałt;
zniewaga; v. gwałcić; znieważać;urągać(zdrowemu rozsadko-
outrageous (aut'rejdżes) adj.
wołający o pomstę; bezecny;
gwałtowny;skandaliczny;obrażają-
outright (aut'rajt) adj. całkowity; zupełny; stanowczy; bezpośredni; adv. odrazu; całkowicie; zupełnie; otwarcie
outrun (aut'ran) v. przegonić;
wyścignąć
outside ('aut'sajd) s. okładka;
fasada; strona zewnętrzna; adj.
zewnętrzny; adv. zewnątrz;
oprócz; z wyjątkiem
outside right ('aut'sajd'rajt)
exp. na zewnątrz po prawej
outsider ('aut'sajder) s. człowiek obcy; niewtajemniczony;
laik; obcy zawodnik
outsize ('autsajz) s. wielkość
nietypowa, za duża
outskirts ('aut,ske:rts) s.
krance; kraj; peryferie
outspoken (aut'spouken) adj.
szczery; otwarcie wypowiedzia-
ny, bez ogródek,prosto w oczy
outspread (aut'spred) adj. rozpostarty; rozpowszechniony
outstanding ('autstaendyng)
adj. wybitny; wyróżniający się;
otwarty; niezałatwiony; zaległy; wystający; sterczący
outstretched (aut'streczt) adj.
rozpostarty; wyciągnięty
outward ('autłerd) adj. zewnętrzny; powierzchowny; pozorny;
cielesny; s. strona zewnętrzna;
wygląd zewnętrzny;adv.na zewnątrz
outweigh (aut'łej) v. przeważyć
outwit (aut'łyt) v. przechytrzyć
oval ('ouwel) s. owal; adj.
owalny;owalnego kształtu

oven ('own) s. piekarnik; piec
over ('ouwer) prep. na; po;
w; przez; ponad; nad; powyżej;
adv. na drugą stronę; po powierzchni; całkowicie; od początku; zbytnio; znowu; raz
jeszcze(odrabiać zadanie etc.)
over again ('ouwer,e'gejn) adv.
na nowo; jeszcze raz
over-and-over ('ouwer,end'ouwer) adv. w kółko
overall ('ouwero:l) adj. ogólny; wszystko obejmujący;
pl. s. kombinezon roboczy
overboard ('ouwerbo:rd) adv.
(zaniechać) za burtę (wyrzucić)
overburden (,ouwe'rbe:rden) v.
przeładowywać; s. ciężar po-
kładów (np. nad kopalnią);
nadmiar ciężaru;ciężar warstw
overcast ('ouwerka:st) adj. za-
chmurzony; mroczny; ponury;
obrębiony; v. mroczyć; chmurzyć (się); obrębiać
overcharge (,ouwer'cza:rdż) v.
przeciążać; zdzierać (pieniądze); stawiać za wysokie ceny
overcoat ('ouwerkout) s. płaszcz
overcome (,ouwer'kam) v. pokonać
overcrowd ('ouwer'kraud) s. za-
tłoczyć;przepełniać
overdo (,ouwerdu:) v. przeciążać; przesadzać; przegotowywać;
niszczyć przesadą;robić za dużo
overdraw (,ouwer'dro:) v. wyczerpać (konto); przesadzać;
pisać czeki bez pokrycia
overdue (,ouwer'dju:) adj. zaległy;zapóźniony(pociąg etc.)
overestimate (.ouwer'esty,mejt)
v. przecenić; s. za wysoka
ocena;zbyt duże oczekiwania
overflow (,ouwer'flou) v. przepełniać; przelewać; s. wylew;
przelew;kanał przelewowy etc.
overgrow (,ouwer'grou) v. ob-
rastać; przerastać; rosnąć
nadmiernie;rość zbyt szybko
overhang ('ouwer'haeng) v. zwisać; sterczeć; zagrażać;
s. występ; zwis; nawis (dachu);
występ(skały);zwis(skalny etc.)

overhaul (.ouwer'ho:l) v.gruntownie naprawic; gruntownie zbadac; s. gruntowny remont

overhead ('ouwer'hed) s. wydatki administracyjne; adv. powyżej; na gorze; adj. gorny

overhear (,ouwer'hier) v. usłyszec przypadkiem; podsłuchac

overheat ('ouwerhi:t) v. przegrzac; s. nadmierne goraco; przegrzanie

overjoyed (,ouwer'dżojd) adj. nieposiadajacy sie z radosci

overlap (,ouwer'laep) v. zachodzic na siebie; s. zachodzenie (na siebie)

overload (,ouwer'loud) v.przeładowac;s.nadmierny ciężar; przeciążenie(dachu etc.)

overlook (,ouwer'luk) v. przeoczyc; puszczac płazem; miec widok z gory; nadzorowac; wybaczyc; widok z gory; nadzor

overlord ('ouwerlo:rd) s. suzeren; samodzierżca

over-night ('ouwer'najt) adv. przez noc; poprzedniego wieczoru; adj. nocny; na noc

overpass (,ouwer'oa:s) s.skrzyżowanie wiaduktem; przejazd wiaduktem; v. przecinac; przekraczac; przewyższac; przezwyciężac; pomijac(w koleje etc.)

overrate ('ouwer'rejt) v. przeceniac;spodziewac sie zbyt dużo

overrule (,ouwer'ru:l) v. opanowac; uchylac; odrzucac; unieważniac;zmieniac czyjes postanowienie

overrun (,ouwer'ran) v. najechac; zalewac; przelewac; s. przekraczanie ceny umowionej

overseas ('ouwer'si:z) adv. za morzem; do krajow zamorskich; adj. zamorski

oversee ('ouwer'si:) v. dozorowac; doglądac

overseer ('ouwer'si:er) s. nadzorca

overshadow ('ouwer'szaedou) v. przycmiewac; zacmiewac

oversight ('ouwersajt) s. przeoczenie

oversleep ('ouwer'sli:p) v. zaspac; przespac

overstrain ('ouwer'strain) v. przemęczac; s. przeciążenie; przemęczenie

overtake ('ouwer'tejk) v. doganiac; przeganiac; zaskoczyc

overthrow ('ouwer'grou) v. przewrocic; obalic; pobic; s. obalenie

overtime ('ouwertajm) s. godziny nadliczbowe; adv. nadprogramowa; adj. nadprogramowy; v. przeswietlic; przeeksponowac

overtone ('ouwertoun) s. niedomowienie; sugestia; akcent; głowna nuta

overture ('ouwer,tjuer) s. rozpoczecie rokowan; propozycja; uwertura; v. proponowac

overturn (,ouwer'te:rn) v. wywracac; obalac; s. przewracanie; przewrot;podboj

overweight (,ouwer'łejt) s. nadwaga; dodatkowa waga; otyłosc; adj. ponad normalna wagę

overwhelm (,ouwer'hłelm) v. przygniatac; przywalac; zalewac; rujnowac; ogarniac

overwork ('ouwer'łe:rk) v. przepracowywac sie; przeciążac praca; zmuszac do za ciężkiej pracy; przemęczac sie; s. nadmierna praca

ovulate ('ouwjulejt) v. jajeczkowac; wytwarzac jaja

owe (oł) v.byc winnym; zawdzięczac

owing ('ołyng) adj. dłużny; należny; prep. z powodu; skutkiem

owing to ('ołyng,tu) prep. ponieważ

owl (aul) s. sowa

own (ołn) v. miec; posiadac; przyznawac (się); adj. własny; rodzony

owner ('ołner) s. własciciel

ownership ('ołnerszyp) s. własnosc; posiadanie

ox (oks) s. woł; pl. oxen

oxen ('oksen) pl. wo/y; zob.ox
oxide ('oksajd) s. tlenek
oxidation (oksy'dejszyn) s.
utlenienie; oksydacja
oxidize (oksydajz) v. utleniac
oxygen (oksydżen) s. tlen
oyster ('ojster) s. ostryga
ozone ('ouzoun) s. ozon
p (pi:) szesnasta litera
angielskiego alfabetu
pa (pa:) s. tato
pace (pejs), s. krok; chód;
v. kroczyc; mierzyc krokami;
ustalac rytm kroku; cwiczyc
krok (np. konia); przebywać
(drogę);chodzic(tam i na zad)
pacer ('pejser) s. regulator
rytmu (serca; kroku etc)
pacific (pe'syfyk) adj. spokojny; pokojowy
pacify ('paesyfaj) v. uspaka-
jac; zaspokajac
pack ,(paek) s. pakunek; t/umok;
toboł; stek; sfora; okład;
kupa; v. pakowac; opakowac;,
owijac; st/oczyc; napychac;
objuczyc; zbierac w stado
pack up ('paek,ap) v. spakowac
package ('paekydż) s. pakunek;
paczka
package deal ('paekydż'di:l)
s. przyjęcie złożonej propo-
zycji bez zmian
packer ('paeker) s. pakier;
przedsiębiorca od pakowania
artykułów żywnosciowych; maszyna do pakowania
packet ('kaekyt) s. pakiet;
v. zawijac
packing ('paekyng) s. pakowa-
nie; opakowanie; uszczelka;
okładzina; tampon
packthread ('paektred) s. szpagat
pact (paekt) s. pakt; układ
pad (paed) s. wyściółka; notes;
blok (papieru); bibularz; łapa; podkładka; v. wyściełac;
wywoływac; rozdymac
padding ('paedyng) s. obicie;
wyściółka; podbicie; podszy-
cie; rozwadnianie tekstu

paddle ('paedl) s. wiose/ko
kajakowe; v. wiosłowac
paddock ('paedek) s. wybieg
(koński)
padlock ('paedlok), s. kłodka
v. zamykac na kłodkę
pagan ('pejgen) s. poganin;
adj. poganski
page (pejdż) s. stronnica;
karta; paż; goniec
pagent ('paedżent) s. widowisko
(np. historyczne)
paid (pejd) adj. zapłacony; płatny; zob. pay
pail (pejl) s. wiadro
pain (pejn) s. ból; cierpienie;
trud; starania; v. zadawac ból;
bolec; dolegac
painful ('pejnful) adj. bolesny;
przykry
painless (pajnlys) adj. bezbolesny
paint (pejnt) s. farba; szminka;
v. malowac
paintbrush ('pejntbrasz) s. pędzel
painter ('pejnter) s. malarz
painting ('pejntyng) s. malarstwo; obraz
pair (peer) s. para; parka; sta-
d/o; v. dobierac do pary; stanowic parę
pajamas (pe'dża;mez) pl. piżama
pal (pael) s. kumpel; druh; przyjaciel
palace ('paelys) s. pałac
palate ('paelyt) s. podniebienie
pale (pejl) s. pal; granica; adj.
blady; v. otaczac palami; blednąc; spowodowac blednięcie
pallor ('paeler) s. bladosc
palm (pa:m) s. palma; dłoni;
piedz; v. ukrywac w dłoni; dotykac dłonią
palpitation (,paelpy'tejszyn)
s. palpitacja; mocne bicie serca;kołatanie serca;drżenie;dygota-nie
pamper ('paemper) v. rozpiesz-
czac;przekarmiac;zbyt pobłażac
pamphlet ('paemflyt) s. broszura natury polemicznej na tematy
bieżące, kontrowersyjne etc.

pan (paen) s. patelnia; rondel;
rynka; szalka; panewka; gęba;
kra; v. gotować na patelni;
udawać się; krytykować
pancake ('paen,kejk) s. nales-
nik; adj. płaski
pane (paen) s. szyba; krata;
scianka; płaszczyzna
panel ('paenl) s. tafla; oto-
czyna; płyta; wstawka; tablica (rozdzielcza); komitet;
lista (przysięgłych; lekarzy
etc); czaprak
pang (paeng)s. ostry ból; męka;
wyrzuty (sumienia etc.)
panhandler (,paen'haendler) s.
kwestarz; ksiadz z tacą
panic ('paenyk) s. panika; popłoch; v.wpaśc w panikę; wywoływac panikę ;poddać się panice
pan-Slavism ('paen'sla:wyzem)
s. panslawizm
pansy ('paensy) s. bratek
pant (paent) s. zadyszka;
v. sapać; dyszeć
panther ('paenter) s. pantera
panties ('paentyz) pl. majtki
(damskie)
pantry ('paentry) s. spiżarnia
pants (paents) pl. spodnie; kalesony
panty hose ('paenty'houz) s.
rajstopy; ponczochy z majtkami
pap (paep) s. papka; bzdury;
sutka; brodawka piersiowa
papa ('pa:pe) s. papa; tata
paper ('pejper) s. papier; gazeta; tapeta; rozprawa nauko-
wa; papierowe pieniądze; adj.
papierowy; rzekomy; v. zawinąć
w papier; tapetować
paper-backed ('pejper.baekt)
adj. w papierowej okładce;
kieszonkowe wydanie książki
paper-bag ('pejper,baeg) s.
torba papierowa
paper-hanger ('pejper,haenger)
s. tapeciarz
paper-hangings ('pejperhaengyngs)
pl. tapety
paper-money ('pejper'many) s.
pieniądze papierowe

paper-weight ('pejper,łejt) s.
przycisk
par (pa:r) s. stan równości;
norma
parable ('paerebl) s. przypowieść
parachute ('paere,szu:t) s.
spadochron
parachutist ('paere,szu:tyst)
s. spadochroniarz
parade (pe'rejd) s. parada; pochód; rewia; defilada; popisywać się; obnosić się (z
czymś)
paradise ('paere,dajs) s. raj;
adj. rajski
paragraph ('paere,gra:f) s.
ustęp; odnośnik; notatka;
v. dzielic na ustępy; pisac
notatkę
parallel ('paere,lel) adj.
równoległy; odpowiedni (czemuś)
s. równoległa; równoleznik; porównanie; v. byc równoległym;
kłaść równolegle; zestawiac;
znalezc odpowiednik
paralyze ('paere,lajz) v. pa-
ralizować; porażać
paralysis (pe'raelysys) s. paraliż
paramount ('paere,maunt) adj.
główny; najważniejszy; kapi-
talny; najwyższy
parasite ('paere.sajt) s. pasożyt
parcel ('pa:rsl) s. paczka;
działka; v. dzielic; pakowac
w paczki
parch ('pa:rcz) v. wysuszac
(się); prażyc; cierpiec z
pragnienia
parchment ('pa:rczment) s. pergamin
pardon('pa:rdn) s. ułaskawienie;
przebaczenie; v. przebaczac;
darowac ;ułaskawiac
pardon me ('pa:rdn,mi:) exp.-
przepraszam
pardonable ('pa:rdnebl) adj.
wybaczalny
pare (peer) v. obcinac; obierac; obskrobac

parent ('peerent) s. ojciec;
matka; rodziciel;rodzicielka

parental (pe'rentl) adj. ro-
dzicielski

parenthesis (pe'rentysys) s.
nawias

parentheses (pe'renty,si:z) pl.
nawiasy

parings ('peerynz) pl. łupiny;
obrzynki

parish ('paerysz) s. parafia

parishioner (pe'ryszener) s.
parafianin

park (pa:rk) s. park; postój
samochodów; v. parkować

parking ('pa:rkyng) s. postój
samochodów; parkowanie

parking garage ('pa:rkyng'gae-
ra:ż) s. garaż parkingowy

parking lot ('pa:rkyn,lot) s.
plac parkingowy

parking meter ('pa:rkyn'mi:ter)
s. licznik do płacenia za
parking(na ograniczony czas)

parking ticket ('pa:rkyn'tykyt)
s. mandat karny za złe parkowanie lub za niezapłacenie

parkway ('pa:rkłej) s. cztero-
liniowa szosa, przedzielona
roslinnością

parliament ('pa:rlyment) s.
parlament

parliamentary (,pa:rly'mentery)
adj. parlamentarny

parlo(u)r ('pa:rler) s. salon;
sala; pokój (przyjęć)

parquet ('pa:rkej) s. parkiet;
v. wyłożyć parkietem

parrot ('paeret) s. papuga;
v. powtarzać jak papuga

parsley ('pa:rsly) s. pietruszka; a. pietruszkowy

parry ('paery) v. parować; odpierać; s. odparcie

parson ('pa:rsn) s. proboszcz

parsonage ('pa:rsnydż) s. plebania

part (pa:rt) s. część; ustęp;
udział; rola; strona; przedział (włosów); v; rozchodzić
(sie); rozdzielać; dzielić;
pękać; robić (przedział); wyjeżdżać;adj.mniejszy niż całość

partake (pa:r'tejk) v. brak
udział; dzielić coś z kims;
zob. take

partaken (pa:r'tejkn) v. zob.
partake

partial ('pa:rszel) adj. stronniczy; częściowy; mający słabość do...;nie pełny

partiality (,pa:rszy'aelyty) s.
stronniczość; upodobanie

participant (pa:r'tysypent) s.
uczestnik;adj.uczestniczący

participate (pa:r'tysypejt) v.
brać udział

particle ('pa:rtykl) s. cząstka;
odrobina; partykuła

particular ('per'tykjuler) adj.
szczególny; szczegółowy; specjalny; prywatny; grymaśny
dokładny; uważny; dziwny; nie-
zwyczajny; ostrożny; s. szczegół; fakt

particularity (per,tykju'laeryty)
s. osobliwość; szczegółowość;
drobiazgowość; wybredność

particularly (per,tykju'laerly)
adv. osobliwie; szczególnie

particulars (per'tykjulers) s.
dane osobiste

parting ('pa:rtyng) s. przedzia-
łek (włosów); rozstanie; rozdział; pożegnanie; rozdroże;
zgon

partition (pa:r'tyszyn) s. podział; rozbiór; rozdział; v.
dzielić; przegradzać

partition off (pa:rtyszyn,of)
v. oddzielać

partly ('pa:rtly) adv. częściowo;po części; poniekąd

partner ('pa:rtner) s. wspólnik

partnership ('pa:rtnerszyp) s.
spółka

partook (pa:r'tuk) v. zob. partake

partridge('pa:łrydż) s. kuropatwa

part-time ('pa:rt,tajm) adv.
na niepełnym etacie; na niepełnym czasie;adj.niepełnoeta-
towy

party ('pa:rty) s. partia; przyjęcie towarzyskie; towarzystwo;
grupa;strona; uczestnik;osobnik

pass (pa:s) s. przełęcz; odnoga
rzeki; przepustka; wypad; bilet; umizg; sztuczka; v. przechodzic; mijac; pomijac; zdac;,
przekazac; wymijac; wyprzedzac;
przeprowadzic; przewyzszac;
spedzac; puszczac w obieg; podawac; odchodzic; umierac;
dziac sie; krazyc

pass away ('pa:se,łej) v. odchodzic;umierac

pass by ('pa:s,baj) v. mijac;
pomijac

pass for ('pa:s,fo:r) v. udawac (kogos)

pass out ('pa:s,aut) v. zemdlec;
umrzec; wyjsc

pass round ('pa:s,raund) v.
podawac wkoło (np. gosciom)

pass through ('pa:s,tru) v.
przechodzic (przez, na wskros)

passable ('paesebl) adj. nadajacy sie do przebycia;
(stopien) dostateczny; znosny

passage ('paesydż) s. przejscie;
przejazd; przeprawa; przelot;
upływ; korytarz; urvwek tekstu

passenger ('paesyndżer) s. pa-
sazer; pasażerka

passer-by ('pa:ser'baj) s. prze-
chodzien

passion ('paeszyn) s. namiętnosc;
pasja; Męka Panska; stan bierny

passionate ('paeszenyt) adj. na-
mietny; porywczy; zapalczywy;
zarliwy ;ognisty

passive ('paesyw) adj. biernv:
s. strona bierna

passport ('pa:s,po:rt) s. paszport

password('pa:s,po:rd) s. hasło

past (pa:st) adj. przeszły;
miniony; ubiegły; prep. za;
obok; po; przed; adv. obok;
s. przeszłosc; czas przeszły

paste (pejst) s. pasta; ciasto;
klej maczny; klajster; masa;
makaron; ugerzenie (siang);
v. przylepiac; oblepiac;
obic (kogos)

pasteboard ('pejst,bo:rd) s.
karton; tektura; adj.tekturo-
wy; kartonowy; lichy

pastime ('pa:s,tajm) s. roz-
rywka(po pracy etc.)

pastry('pejstry) s. wyroby cu-
kiernicze; ciastka

past tense ('pa:st tens) s.
czas przeszły (gram.)

pasture ('pa:sczer) s. pastwisko

pat (paet) s. głaskanie; kle-
panie; krążek (np. masła);
v. pogłaskac; poklepac; pochwalic (kogos) adv. trafnie;
w sam raz; adj. trafny; biegły;na czasie;zupełnie własciwy

patch (paecz) s. łata; plama;
skrawek; pólko; zagon; grządka; klapka (na oko); przepaska; v. łatac; załatac; szyc
z łat; sztukowac; naprawic;
skleic; załagodzic

patch pocket ('paecz,pokyt) s.
naszywana kieszen

patchwork ('paecz,łe:rk) s.
łatanina; szachownica

pate (pejt) s. slang: głowa;
łeb; pała;szczyt głowy

patent ('paetnt) s. patent;
v. opatentowac; a. patentowa-
ny; opatentowany;oczywisty

patent ('pejtnt) adj. jasny;
otwarty; oczywisty; chroniony
                              patentem

patent-leather ('paetnt'ledzer)
s. skora lakierowana

paternal (pe'te:rnl) adj. oj-
cowski; po ojcu

paternity (pe'te:rnyty) s.
ojcostwo; pochodzenie po ojcu;
autorstwo (ksiązki,planu etc.)

path (pa:s) s. sciezka; tor;
droga ruchu; zob. paths

pathetic (pe'tetyk) adj. żałosny; smutny; uczuciowy;
wzruszający; rozrzewniający

paths (pa:sz) pl. sciezki; tory;
drogi ruchu

patience ('pejszens) s. cierpli-
wosc; pasjans

patient ('pejszent) adj. cierpliwy; wytrwały; s. pacjent;
pacjentka; chory, chora

patio ('pa:ti:o) s. ogrodek
wewnętrzny; taras

patriot ('pejtryet) s. patry-
jota

patriotic(,paetry'otyk) adj.
patriotyczny

patriotism ('paetrye,tyzem) s.
patriotyzm

patrol (pe'troul) v. patrolo-
wac; s. patrolowanie; patrol

patrolman (pe'troulmen) s. policjant (drogowy USA)

patron ('pejtren) s. klient;
opiekun; patron

patronage ('paetrenydż) s.
opieka; poparcie; klientela;
US rozdawanie posad etc.;
protekcjonalnosc; przywileje;
posady

patronize ('paetre,najz) v. popierac; protegowac; traktowac
protekcjonalnie

patsy ('paecy) s. oferma przez
wszystkich zawsze naduzywana

patter ('paeta) s. stukot; traj-
kot; trajkotanie; gwara; kle-
panie; szybka recytacja; żargon; v. stukac; bębnic; traj-
kotac; klepac (np. pacierze);
odklepywac; kłapac; gadac

pattern ('paetern) s. próbka;
wzor; układ; materiał na suknię lub ubranie (USA); zespół;
cechy charakterystyczne; ślady kul (na tarczy); v. wzoro-
wac; modelowac; ozdabiac wzo-
rami

paunch ('pa:ncz) s. (duży)
brzuch; żołądek krowy

paunchy ('pa:nczy) adj. brzu-
chaty ; z wydatnym brzuchem

pause (po:z) s. przerwa; pauza;
v. robic przerwę; wahac się

pave (pejw) v. brukowac; torowac drogę

pavement ('pejwment) s. bruk;
posadzka; materiał do bruko-
wania

pavement-café ('pejwment'kaefej)
s. kawiarnia ze stolikami na
chodniku

paw (po:) s. łapa; (slang):
tatuś; v. uderzac łapą lub
kopytem; miętosic w łapach;
macac (poufale)

pawn (po:n) s. zastaw; fant;
pionek; v. zastawiac; dawac
w zastaw

pawnbroker ('po:n,brouker) s.
lichwiarz pożyczający pod zastaw; własciciel lombardu

pawnshop ('po:n-szop) s. lom-
bard; sklep zastawniczy

pay; paid; paid (pej; peid;
peid)

pay (pej) v. płacic; zapłacic;
wynagradzac; udzielac (uwagi);
dawac (dochod); opłacac (się)
s. płaca; zapłata; pobory;
wynagrodzenie; adj. płatny
(np. automat telefoniczny);
opłacalny

pay back ('pej baek) v. zwrocic
dług; odpłacac

payday ('pej dej) s. dzień wy-
płaty

pay down ('pej da:n) v. dawac
zadatek; płacic pierwszą ratę
gotowka

pay for ('pej,fo:r) v. płacic
(za cos)

pay in ('pej,yn) v. wpłacac

pay off ('pej,of) v. spłacac

pay out ('pej,aut) v. wydatko-
wac; wypuszczac linę (na statku); wypłacac; płacic

pay up ('pej,ap) v. wyrownywac
(dług); zapłacic

payable ('pejebl) adj. płatny;
dochodowy; opłacający się

payee ('pej'i:) s. odbiorca
płatności

payer ('pejer) s. płatnik

payment ('pejment) s. płatnosc;
wypłata; zapłata

pea (pi:) s. groch; ziarnko
grochu

peace (pi:s) s. pokój; pojednanie; spokój

peaceful ('pi:sful) adj. spokojny; pokojowy

peach (pi:cz) s. brzoskwinia;
wspaniała rzecz, dziewczyna,
człowiek; v. (slang):sypac;
donosic (na kogos)

peacock ('pi:,kok) s. paw;
v. pysznic się jak paw, chodzic
jak paw; paradowac

peak (pi:k) s. (ostry) szczyt;
wierzchołek; daszek (u czapki);
szpic; garb (krzywej)

peak hour ('pi:k'auer) s. godzina szczytu ruchu

peal (pi:l) s. huk; łoskot; bicie w dzwony; huczny śmiech;
zespół dzwonów; v. huczeć;
bic w dzwony; grac (cos) hucz-
nie

peanut ('pi:nat) s. orzeszek
ziemny; drobnostka; a; drobny;
prowincjonalny

pear (peer).s. gruszka

pearl (pe:rl) s. perła

peasant ('pezent) s. chłop;
wieśniak; adj. chłopski

peat (pi:t) s. torf

peat bog ('pi:t'bog) s. torfowisko

pebble ('pebl) s. kamyk; oto-
czak; v. granulowac; obrzucac
kamykami

peck (pek) v. dziobac; wcinac
(jedzenie); dziobnąc; cmoknąc
(męza); stukac; wydziobac;
dłubac; odziobac; v. dziobnięcie; cmok; slad dziobania

peculiar (py'kju:ljer) adj.
szczególny; dziwny; osobliwy;
charakterystyczny;dziwaczny

peculiarity (py'kju:li'aeryty)
s. właściwosc; cecha; osobli-
wosc; dziwacznosc

pedal ('pedl) s. pedał; nuta
pedałowa; v. pedałowac; naciskac pedał; ('pi:dl) adj. pe-
dałowy; nożny

peddle ('pedl) v. sprzedawac po
domach; byc domokrążcą; wydzie-
lac po trochu

peddler ('pedler) s. domokrążca

pedestal ('pedystl) s. piedestał;
podstawa;Vstawiac na piedestał

pedestrian (py'destrjen) adj.
pieszy; przyziemny; prozaiczny;
s. piechur;pieszy człowiek

pedestrian crossing (pu'destrjen'krosyng) v. przejście dla
pieszych; zebra: pasy

pedigree ('pedygri:) s. rodowod;
drzewo genealogiczne

pedlar('peler)s.przekupien;hand-

peek ('pi:k) v. podglądac

peel (pi:l) s. skóra; skórka;
łupa; v. obierac; zdzierac;
łuszczyc się; (slang):rozbierac
(się)

peep (pi:p) v. zerkac; podglądac;
wynurzac (się); wychodzic nie-
postrzezenie

peeping Tom ('pi:pyng,tom) s.
podglądający natręt

peer (pier) s. rowny (komus)
stanem, pochodzeniem etc.

peerless ('pierlys) adj. niezrownany

peevish ('pi:wysh) adj. drazli-
wy; zły; gniewny;zirytowany

peg (peg) s. czop; kołek; zatyczka; szpunt; v. zakołkowac;
przymocowac kołkami

pelican ('pelyken) s. pelikan

pelt (pelt) s. futro; kanonada;
grzmocenie; pospiech; v. ostrzeliwac; obrzucac; obsypywac gradem; rzucac zniewagi; obsypywac
zniewagami; walic

pelvis ('pelwys) s. miednica;
a. miedniczny

pen (pen) s. pioro; kojec; ogrodzenie; schron; (slang):więzie-
nie; v. pisac; układac list;
zamykac w ogrodzeniu

penal ('pi:nl) adj. karny; karalny

penalty ('penlty) s. kara

penalty kick ('penlty,kik) s.
karny strzał (do bramki)

penance ('penens) s. pokuta

pence (pens) pl. grosze; zob.
penny

pencil ('pensl) s. ołowek; ry-
sowac; pisac

pencil sharpner ('pensl'sza:rp-
ner) s. strugaczka do ołowka

pendant ('pendent) s. wisiorek;
proporzec; adj. wiszący; zwi-
sający; nierozstrzygnięty; to-
czący się; do rozstrzygnięcia

pending ('pendyng) adj. niezałatwiony; będący w toku; wisza-
cy; prep.: aż do; podczas

penetrate ('peny,trejt) v. prze-
nikac; przepajac; przedostawac
się przez ;wtargnąc;zanurzyc

penetration (,peny'trejszyn)
s. penetracja; przenikanie;
przenikliwość

pen friend ('penfrend) s. znajomy z listów

penguin ('pengłyn) s. pingwin

penholder ('pen,houlder) s.
piórnik; obsadka; stojak na
pióro

penicillin (,peny'sylyn) s.
penicylina

peninsula(py'nynsjule) s. półwysep

penitent ('penytent) s. żałujący grzesznik; pokutnik; adj.
żałujący; skruszony

penitentiary (,peny'tenszery)
s. więzienie; adj. karany
więzieniem; poprawczy

penknife ('pen.najf) s. scyzoryk

penniless ('penylys) adj. w nędzy; bez grosza

penny ('peny) s. cent; grosz;
pl. pennies ('penyz); Br.pl.
pence (pens)

pennyworth ('penyłe:rs) s. wartość centa; exp. za centa

pension ('penszyn) s. renta;
emerytura; pensjonat; v. wyznaczać pensje; pensjonować

pension off ('penszyn,of) v.
przenosić na emeryturę

pensive ('pensyw) adj. zamyslony

penthouse ('penthaus) s. mieszkanie z ogrodem na szczycie
budynku; przybudówka na dachu

people ('pi:pl) s. ludzie;
ludność; lud; v. zaludniać

pep (pep) s. animusz; werwa;
wigor; adj. ożywiony; wesoły;
dowcipny; dodający animuszu

pep pills ('pep,pyls) pl. pigułki podniecające

pep up ('pep,ap) v. ożywić; dodać animuszu

pepper ('peper) s. pieprz; papryka; v. pieprzyć; kropić;
zasypywać kulami; dać lanie

per (pe:r) prep. przez; za; na;
według; co do;za pośrednictwem

perceive (per'si:w) v. uświadamiać sobie; odczuć; dostrzegać;
spostrzegać

percent (per'sent) s. odsetek;
od sta

percentage (per'sentydż) s. odsetek; procent; od sta

perceptible (per'septebl) adj.
dostrzegalny

perception (per'sepszyn) s.
spostrzeganie; percepcja

perch (pe:rcz) s. okoń; grzęda;
żerdz; pręt; v. siedzieć na
grzędzie; sadzać na grzędzie

percussion (per'kaszyn) s. uderzenie; zderzenie; bicie(bębna)

peremptory (per'emptery) adj.
stanowczy; apodyktyczny; ostateczny; nieodwołalny

perfect ('pe:rfykt) adj. doskonały; zupełny; v. udoskonalić;
wykończyć

perfect tense ('perfykt'tens)
s. gram. czas przeszły dokona-
ny

perfection (per'fekszyn) s.
doskonałość; szczyt; wykończenie; udoskonalenie

perforate ('pe:rferejt) v.
przedziurawiać; dziurkować;
przenikać; przebijać się

perform (per'fo:rm) v. wykonywać; odgrywać; spełniać; występować

performance (per'fo:rmens) s.
przedstawienie; wyczyn; wykonanie; spełnienie

performer (per'former) s. wy-
konawca

perfume ('pe:rfju:m) s. perfuma;
zapach ; (pe'rfju:m) v. perfu-
mować

perhaps (per'haeps, praeps) adv.
może; przypadkiem

peril ('peryl) s. niebezpieczeństwo; ryzyko; v. narazić
na niebezpieczeństwo

perilous ('peryles) adj. niebezpieczny; ryzykowny

period ('pieried) s. okres;
period; menstruacja; kropka;
kres; pauza;miesiączka;a.stylo-wy

periodic (,piery'odyk) adj.
okresowy; periodyczny

periodical (,piery'odykel) s.
czasopismo; periodyk; adj.
okresowy; periodyczny

perish ('perysz) v. zgiąć;
niszczyć; nękać; trapić; gnębić; ginąć (przedwczesną śmiercią)

perishable ('peryszebl) adj.
zniszczalny; s; łatwo psujący się towar

perjury ('pe:rdżery) s. krzywoprzysięstwo; złamanie
obietnicy

perm (pe:rm) s. trwała ondulacja

permanent ('pe:rmenent) adj.
trwały; permanentny

permanent wave ('pe:rmenent,
,łejw) s. trwała ondulacja

permeable ('pe:rmjebl) adj.
przepuszczalny; przenikalny

permission (per'myszyn) s. pozwolenie; zezwolenie

permit (per'myt) s. pisemne
zezwolenie; pozwolenie; v.pozwalać; zezwalać; dopuszczać

perpendicular (,pe:rpen'dykjuler) adj. prostopadły; s, prostopadła; pion

perpetual (per'petjuel) adj.
wieczny; wieczysty; trwały;
dożywotni

persecute ('pe:rsy,kju:t) v.
prześladować

persecution (,pe:rsy'kju:szyn)
s. prześladowanie

persecutor ('pe:rsy,kju:ter) s.
prześladowca

persevere (,pe:rsy'wier) v.
wytrwać

persist (pe'rsyst) v. obstawać;
wytrwać; upierać się

persistence (per'systens); persistency (per'systensy) s. wytrwałość; uporczywość; trwałość

persistent (per'systent) adj. wytrwały; uporczywy; trwały

person ('pe:rson) s. osoba;
człowiek

personage ('pe:rsonydż) s.
osobistość;ważny człowiek

personal ('pe:rsenel) adj. osobisty; robiący osobiste uwagi;
s. wiadomość osobista

personality (,pe:se'naelyty) s.
osobowość; powierzchowność;
postawa; indywidualność; pl.
wycieczki (uwagi) osobiste

personify (pe:r'sony,faj) v.
uosabiać; personifikować

personnel (,pe:rse'n el) s.
personel

personnel manager (,pe:rse'-
'nel'maendżer) s. kierownik
oddziału personalnego; personalny

perspiration (,pe:rspy'rejszyn)
s. pocenie się; pot

perspire (,pe:r'spajer) v. pocić się; wypacać się

persuade (pe:r'słejd) v. przekonywać; namawiać

persuasion (pe:r'słejżyn) s.
perswazja; przekonywanie;
namawianie; przekonanie; wyznanie; wierzenie

persuasive (pe:r'słejsyw) adj.
przekonywujący; s. motyw; pobudka (do czegoś)

pert (pe:rt) adj. śmiały; arogancki; (slang) żwawy

pertain (per'tejn) v. należeć
do czegoś; być właściwym czemuś; odnosić się; wchodzić
w zakres

perusal (pe'ru:zal) s. przestudiowanie; dokładne przeczytanie

peruse (pe'ru:z) v. czytać
uważnie; studiować (np. twarz)

pervade (per'wejd) v. przenikać;
owładnąć; ogarniać; szerzyć się

perverse (per'we:rs) adj. przewrotny; przekorny; wyuzdany

pesky ('pesky) adj. (slang) dokuczliwy; natrętny;cholerny

pessimism ('pesy,myzem) s. pesymizm ;spodziewanie się najgorszego

pest (pest) s. plaga; zaraza

pet (pet) s. faworyt; ulubieniec (np. pies); adj; ulubiony; v. (slang) pieścić; być
w złym nastroju; gniewać się ;
migdalić się; wypieścić

petal ('petl) s. płatek

petition (py'tyszyn) s. petycja; prosba; podanie; v, prosic; wnosic podanie

petrify ('petry,faj) v. zamieniac (się) w kamien; powodowac kostnienie

petroleum (py'trouljem) s. ropa naftowa; olej skalny

pet shop ('petszop) s. sklep zwierzątek pokojowych

petticoat ('petykout) s. halka; spodniczka; kobieta; adj. kobiecy

petty ('pety) adj. drobny

petty cash (,pety'kaesz) s. gotówka podręczna

pew (pju:) s. ławka (kościelna)

pharmacy ('fa:rmesy) s. apteka; farmacja

phase (fejz) s. faza (np. rozwojowa); aspekt

pheasant ('feznt) s. bażant

philanthropist (fy'laentrepyst) s. filantrop

philologist (fy'loledżyst) s. filolog ;lingwista;językoznawca

philology (fy'loledży) s. filologia; językoznawstwo;ligwistyka

philosopher (fy'losefer) s. filozof

philosophize (fy'lose,fajz) v. filozofowac

philosophy (fy'losefy) s. filozofia

phone (foun) s. telefon (slang)

phonetic (fou'netyk) adj. fonetyczny

phon(e)y (founy) adj. fałszywy; udawany; s. rzecz fałszywa; podrabiana;ktos udajacy

photo ('foutou) s. fotka; fotografia; v. fotografowac

photograph ('foute,gra:f) s. fotografia; zdjecie; v. fotografowac

photographer (fe'togrefer) s. fotograf; fotografik

photography (fe'tegrefy) s. fotografia; fotografika

phrase (frejz) s. wyrażenie; zwrot; v. wyrażac; wypowiadac wyrażeniami lub słowami

physical ('fyzykel) adj. fizyczny; cielesny

physician ('fyzyszyn) s. lekarz

physicist('fyzysyt) s. fizyk

physics ('fyzyks) s. fizyka

physique (fy'zi:k) s. budowa ciała; rozwój; wygląd fizyczny;kondycja;siła muskularna

piano (py'aenou) s. fortepian; pianino

pick (pyk) v. wybierac; dorabiac; kopac; krytykowac; dłubac; obierac; zbierac; usuwac; oskubac; wydziobac; krasc; okrasc; s, kilof; dłuto; wybór; czółenko; nitka wątka

pick-off('pyk,of) v. zedrzec; wystrzelac pojedynczo(wrogów)

pick out('pyk,aut) v. wybrac; dobrac; doszukiwac się

pick over ('pyk,ouwer) v. przebierac;wybierac co lepsze

pick up ('pyk,ap) v. podnosic; brac; nauczyc się; zarabiac; odnaleźc; odzyskac; przyjsc do siebie; poznac się; s. adapter; lekka ciężarówka

picket ('pykyt) s. palik; kół; pikieta; posterunek; v. rozstawiac pikiety strajkowe; służyc jako pikieta; zabezpieczac pikietami

pickle ('pykel) s. kiszony ogorek; marynata; kłopot; łobuz; v. marynowac; kisic; wytrawiac

pickpocket ('pyk,pokyt) s. złodziej kieszonkowy; kieszonkowiec

picnic ('pyknyk) s. piknik; majówka; v. brac udział w pikniku, majówce,posiłku na dworze

pictorial (pyk'to:rjel) adj. obrazowy; ilustrowany; malowniczy; malarski; s.(czaso)pismo ilustrowane; ilustracja (trzywymiarowa)techniczna

picture ('pykczer) s. obraz; film; rysunek; rycina; portret; widok; v. odmalowywac; przedstawiac; opisywac; wyobrażac sobie; dawac obraz czegos

picturesque (,pykcze'resk) adj. malowniczy;żywy i przyjemny

pie (paj) s. placek; szarlotka; pasztet; pasztecik;(ptak) sroka

piece(pi:s) s. kawałek; część; sztuka; moneta; utwór; v. łączyc; zeszyc; łatac; naprawiac

piecework ('pi:s,łe:rk) s. robota na akord

pier (pier) s. pomost ładunkowy; molo; falochron; filar (np. mostu)

pierce (piers) v. przewiercac; wnikac; przedziurawiac; przebijac; przedostawac się

piercing (piersyng) adj. przeszywający; ostry; rozdzierający ;przenikający

piety ('pajety) s. pobożnosc

pig (pyg) s. wieprz; swinia; prosię; v. prosic się

pigeon ('pydżyn) s. gołąb; v. oszukiwac

pigeon-hole ('pydżyn,houl) s. przegródka; v. umieszczac w przegródkach

pigheaded ('pyg'hedyd) adj. uparty ; głupi

pigskin ('pyg,skyn) s. swinska skóra; (slang):piłka; siodło

pigtail ('pyg,tejl) s. warkocz

pike(pajk) s. rogatka; dzida; piłka; szpic; ostrze; szczupak

pile (pail) s. stos; sterta; kupa; pal; słup; puszek; meszek; włos; v. układac w stos; gromadzic na kupę;stawiac w kozły

pile up ('pail,ap) v. walic na kupę; s. zwalenie na kupę

piles (pailz) pl. hemoroidy

pilfer ('pylfer) v. ukrasc; zwedzic; buchnac

pilgrim ('pylgrym) s. pielgrzym

pilgrimage ('pylgrymydż) s. pielgrzymka

pill (pyl) s. pigułka; tabletka

pillar ('pyler) s. filar; słup; podpora

pillbox('pylboks)s. bunkier; pudełeczko na pigułki;kapelusz

pillion ('pyljen) s. tylne siodełko (np. na motocyklu)

pillory ('pylery) s. pręgierz; v. stawiac pod pręgierzem

pillow ('pylou) s. zagłówek; jasiek; poduszka; podkładka v. spoczywac; opierac (np. głowę)

pillowcase ('pylou,kejs) s. poszewka

pillow slip ('pylou,slyp) s. poszewka

pilot ('pajlet) s. pilot; sternik; v. pilotowac; sterowac; przeprowadzic

pimp (pymp) s. stręczycielka; alfons; v. stręczyc

pimple ('pympl) s. pryszcz; wągier

pin (pyn) s. szpilka; sztyft; sworzen; kołek; kręgiel v. przyszpilic; przymocowac

pincers ('pynserz) pl. kleszcze; obcęgi

pinch (pyncz) v. szczypac; gniesc; cisnąc; przycisnąc; przyskrzynic; krępowac; dokuczac;doskwierac; podwazac łomem; s. uszczypnięcie; szczypta; łom; (slang) aresztowanie; obława; kradzież

pinch bar ('pyncz ba:r) s. łom (ze stopką)

pine (pajn) s. sosna; ananas; v. usychac

pineapple ('pajnaepl) s. ananas

pinion ('pynjen) s. kółko zębate; wrzeciono zębate; wał przekładni; koniec pióra; lotka v. podcinac (skrzydła); pętac; przywiazywac

pink (pynk) s. różowy kolor; radykał (komunizujacy); goździk; v. urazic do żywego; przekłuwac

pinnacle ('pynekl) s. szczyt; wieżyczka; v. zwienczac; postawic na szczycie; stanowic szczyt

pint (pajnt) s. półkwarcie; 0.47 litra; 1/8 galona

pioneer (,paje'nier) s. pionier; saper; v. torowac drogę

pious (pajes) adj. pobożny

pip (pyp) s. pestka; oczko;
gwiazdka; ziarnko; punkcik;
pypeć; dźwięk gwizdka; v. piszczeć; wykluwać się; pobić;
trafić; postrzelić

pipe (pajp) s. rura; rurka;
przewód; piszczałka; (slang)
łatwizna; drobiazg; v. doprowadzać rurami; włączyć;
połączyć; prowadzić dźwiękiem
fujarki; grać na fujarce;
grać na kobzie; gwizdać; piszczeć

pipeline ('pajp,lajn) s. rurociąg;(slang);informator;
v. przesyłać rurociągiem

piper (pajper) s. kobziarz

pipes (pajps) s. kobza

pirate (pajeryt) s. korsarz;
pirat; statek piracki; maruder; v. grabić; uprawiać kor-
sarstwo; wydawać bezprawnie
(książki)

pistol ('pystl) s. pistolet

piston ('pysten) s. tłok

pit(pyt) s. dół; jama; kopalnia; pestka; v. puszczać do
walki; robić dołki; wkładać
do dołu; wyjmować pestki

piston-stroke ('pysten,strouk)
s. suw tłoka

pitch (pycz) v. rozbijać (obóz);
umieszczać; rzucać; ustawiać;
chwiać się; upaść ciężko; kołysać (na fali); przechylać;
wybierać; ostro pracować;
rzucać się na...; smołować;
s. stopień; najwyższy punkt;
wzniesienie; wzdłużne kołysanie statku· spadek dachu; odstęp między (falami; zębami
kół etc.);skok (uzwojenia,
śruby); smoła

pitcher ('pyczer) s. dzban;
rzucający piłką

piteous ('pytjes) adj. żałosny;
nędzny

pitfall ('pytfo:l) s. pułapka;
wilczy dół

pith (pyg) s. miękisz; rdzeń;
tężyzna; moc; v. wyjmować
rdzeń; przecinać rdzeń w celu
zabijania bydła (w rzeźni etc.)

pitiable ('pytjebl) s. żałosny;
godny pożałowania

pitiful ('pytyful) adj. litościwy;
żałosny; nędzny

pitiless ('pytylys) adj. bezlitosny

pity ('pyty) s. litość; współczucie; szkoda; v. litować się;
współczuć; żałować kogoś

pivot ('pywet) s. czop; oś;
ośrodek ;v.obracać jak na osi

pivotal ('pywetel) s. adj. centralny ;kardynalny;kluczowy;decydu-
jący

placard ('plaeka:rd) s. afisz;
plakat; (ple'ka:rd) v. rozle-
piać plakaty

place (plejs).s. miejsce; miejscowość; plac; ulica; dom; mieszkanie; zakład; krzesło; posada;
v. umieszczać; położyć; ulokować; dać stanowisko; pokładać;
powierzyć; określać

placid ('plaesyd) adj. łagodny;
spokojny

plague (plejg) s. plaga; dżuma;
zaraza; v. dręczyć

plaice (plejs) s. płastuga pospo-
lita

plaid (plaed) s. sukno; pled
w kratę;rysunek w kratę

plain (plejn) adj. wyraźny; prosty; gładki; szczery; płaski;
równy; adv. jasno; szczerze;
s. równina

plain clothesman ('plejn,klozmen)
s. tajny policjant

plaintiff ('plejntyf) s. powód
(zaskarżający); powódka

plaintive ('plejntyw) adj. żałosny; płaczliwy

plait (plejt) s. plecionka; warkocz; fałda; zakładka; v. pleść;
splatać; fałdować

plan (plaen) s. plan; v. planować; zamierzać

plane (plejn) s. płaszczyzna;
równina; poziom; samolot; płat
(skrzydła); strug; wiórnik; gładzik; platan (owoc); v. ślizgać;
ześlizgiwać się; heblować

planet ('plaenyt) s. planeta

plank ('plaeŋk) s. deska; tarcica; punkt programu (polityczne-
go w USA); v.pokrywać deskami

plank down ('plaeŋk,daɪn) v.
wybulic gotówkę
plant ('pla:nt) s. roślina;
fabryka; zakład; wtyczka;
(slang) oszustwo; włamanie;
kant; v. zasadzać; zakładac;
umieszczac; pozorować; ukrywac; wtykac; sadzic(rośliny)
plantation (plaen'tejszyn) s.
plantacja
planter ('pla:nter) s. plantator; maszyna do sadzenia;
skrzynka na kwiaty
plaque (plaek) s. tablica (pa-
miątkowa); odznaka
plaster ('pla:ster) s. tynk;
wyprawa wapienna; przylepiec
v. tynkować; wyprawiac; po-
wlekac; zalepiac; oblepiac
plaster cast ('pla:ster,ka:st)
s. odlew gipsowy; opatrunek
gipsowy
plaster of Paris ('pla:ster of
'paerys) s. gips
plastic ('plaestyk) s. plastyk;
sztuczne tworzywo; adj. plastyczny; giętki
plastics ('plaestyks) s. tworzy-
wa sztuczne
plate (plejt) s. talerz; danie;
płyta; taca; tafla; v. pla-
terowac; opancerzac
platform ('plaet,fo:rm) s.
platforma; podium; trybuna;
rampa; program polityczny
platinum ('plaetynem) s. platyna
platter ('plaeter) s. półmisek
plausible ('plo:zebl) adj. pozornie słuszny, prawdziwy,
uczciwy; obłudnie przymilny
play (plej) s. gra; zabawa;
sztuka; v. grac; bawic się;
zagrac; udawac
play back('plej,baek) v. repro-
dukowac; przegrywac
playboy ('plej,boj) s. lekko-
duch
player('plejer) s. gracz; muzyk; aktor; zawodnik
playful ('plejful) adj. wesoły,
zartobliwy;figlarny; filuterny;
swawolny;rozbawiony;zabawny;
rozbrykany;ożywiony

playground ('plej,graund) s.
boisko; park
playhouse ('plej,haus) s. teatr
playmate ('plej,mejt) s. towarzysz zabaw(dziecinnych,intym-
nych)
play-off ('plejof) s. rozgrywka
poremisowa
play off ('plej.of) v. rozgry-
wac partię poremisową
plaything ('plejtyŋg) s. zabawka
playwright ('plej,rajt) s. dra-
maturg
plea (pli:) s. usprawiedliwienie;
wywod; apel; prośba
plead (pli:d) v. bronic; błagac;
powoływac się
plead guilty ('pli:d'gylty) v.
przyznawac się do winy
pleasant ('plesnt) s. przyjemny;
miły; wesoły
please (pli:z) v. podobac się;
zadowalac
please ! (pli:z) v. proszę
pleased (plizd) adj. zadowolony
pleasing ('pli:zyŋg) adj. przyjemny; miły
pleasure ('pleżer) s. przyjemnosc; adj. rozrywkowy
pleat (pli:t) s. fałda; v. pli-
sowac
pledge (pledż) v. zobowiązywac
(się); zastawiac; s. zastaw;
gwarancja; przyrzeczenie
plenipotentiary (,plenype'tenszery) s. pełnomocnik; adj.
pełnomocny
plentiful ('plentyful) adj. obfity; liczny
plenty ('plenty) s. obfitość;
mnostwo; adv. zupełnie; aż
nadto;adj.obfity;liczny;obszerny
pliable ('plajebl) adj. giętki
pliers ('plajerz) pl. szczypce
plight (plajt) s. trudności;
stan; położenie; przyrzeczenie;
v. ręczyc; dawac słowo
plod (plod) v. mozolic się;
slęczec; s. harowanie; kucie
plod along ('plod,e'long) v.
wlec się;mozolic się;trudzic się
plot (plot)s. osnowa; fabuła;
spisek;dziełka; wykres; mapa;
v.knuc; spiskowac;nanosic na
mapę; planowac; dzielic

plough (plau) s. płùg; v. orać

plow (plau) s. płùg; v. orać

plowshare ('plau-szeer) s.lemiesz

pluck (plak) v. wyrwać; zerwać; szarpnąć

pluck up courage ('plak,ap'karydż) exp.: zdobyc się na odwagę

plucky ('plaky) adj. śmiały; odważny

plug (plag) s. czop; zatyczka; kurek; reklama; świeca (silnika); v. zatykać

plug up ('plag,ap) v. zatkać

plum (plam) s. śliwka; rodzynka; gratka; adv. pionowo

plumage ('plu:mydż) s. upierzenie

plumb (plam) adj. pionowy; zupełny; adv. pionowo; prosto; dokładnie; zupełnie; s. pion murarski; sonda; v. pionować; sondować

plumber ('plamer) s. hydraulik

plumbing ('plambyng) s.instalacja wodociągowo-ściekowa budynku

plume (plu:m) s. pióro; pióropusz; v. ozdabiać piórami; czyścić pióra

plummet ('plamyt) s. pion murarski; v. spadać pionowo

plump (plamp) adj. pulchny; tęgi; stanowczy; otwarty; v. tuczyć; tyć; wypełniac (się); ciężko upaśc; upuścić; rzucić; popierać w wyborach masowym głosowaniem; adv. prosto; nagle; ciężko; s. upadek

plum pudding ('plam'pudyng)s. budyn świąteczny

plunder ('plander) s. grabierz; rabunek; łup; v. pladrować; łupić; grabić

plunge (plandż) v. pogrążać (się) ; zanurzać (się); wpadać; spadać; s. skok do wody; pływalnia

plunk (plank) v. brząkać; wybulić; s. brzęk; adv. z brzękiem; prościutko;v.ciskać;rzucać upaść ciężko;szarpać(struny); strzelić do kogoś;s.sl.:dolar

pluperfect ('plu:'pe:rfykt) adj. zaprzeszły; s. czas zaprzeszły; plusquamperfectum

plural ('pluerel) s. liczba mnoga; adj. pluralny; mnogi

plus (plas) prep. plus; więcej; adj. dodatni; dodatkowy; s. znak plus; dodatek

plush (plasz) s. plusz; adj. pluszowy; okazały

ply (plaj) v. uprawiać gorliwie; używać czegoś; zasypywać (np. pytaniami) ; kursować po...; s. warstwa; grubość; skłonność; pasmo

plywood ('plaj,łud) s. sklejka; dykta

pneumatic (nju'maetyk) adj. pneumatyczny

pneumonia (nju'mounje) s. zapalenie płuc

poach (poucz) v. uprawiać kłusownictwo; grzęznąć; rozrabiać; udeptywac; rozmiękać; gotowac jajko na miękko bez skorupki

poached egg ('pauczt,eg) s. jajko gotowane na miękko bez skorupki

poacher ('pouczer) s. kłusownik

pocket ('pokyt) s. kieszeń; dziura (powietrzna) v. wkładać do kieszeni

pocketbook ('pokyt,buk) s. portfel

pocketknife ('pokyt,najf) s. scyzoryk

pocket money ('pokyt,many) s. kieszonkowe

pod (pod) s. strączek; kokon; stadko; obsada; v. rodzić strączki; łuszczyć; spędzać razem

poem (pouim) s. wiersz ; poemat

poet (pouyt) s. poeta

poetess ('pouytys) s. poetka

poetic (pou'etyk) adj. poetyczny ; poetycki;poetycznie piękny

poetry ('pouytry) s. poezja

pogrom ('pougrem, pe'grom) s. pogrom

poignant ('pojnent) adj.przejmujący; uszczypliwy; cięty; ostry; dotkliwy;wzruszający

point (point) s. punkt; ostry
koniec; szpiczaste narzędzie;
przylądek; kropka; pointa; cecha; sedno; sens; v. zaostrzać;
celować; wskazywać; punktować;
kropkować ;dowodzić;dążyć;pokazywać
point at ('point,aet) v, wycelować; wskazać
point of view ('point,ow'wju:)
s. punkt widzenia
point out ('point,aut) v. wskazywać; uwydatnić
point to ('point,tu) v. wskazać
kierunek (kogoś, coś)
pointed ('pointyd) adj. spiczasty; ostry; cięty; zjadliwy
point-blank ('point'blaenk) adj.
(strzelać) na wprost, bezpośredni; bezceremonialny; bez
ogródek; adv. bezpośrednio;
z bliska; wprost; bez ogródek;
w prostej linii; bez zastano-
wienia się
pointer ('pointer) s. wskaźnik;
wskazówka
poise (pojz) s. równowaga; postawa; swoboda; stan zawiesze-
nia; stan niepewności; v. równoważyć; ważyć w rękach; za-
wisnąć w powietrzu; być przy-
gotowanym do ataku
poison ('pojzn) s. trucizna;
v. truć; zatruć; zakazić
poisonous ('pojznes) adj. trujący; jadowity; szkodliwy
poke (pouk) v. wtykać; wpychać;
szturchać; dłubać; sterczeć;
wtrącać się; plątać
poker ('poułer) s. pogrzebacz;
poker
polar ('pouler) adj. polarny
polar bear ('pouler beer) s.
biały niedźwiedź
Pole (poul) s. Polka; Polak
pole (poul) s. biegun; słup;
żerdź; dyszel; maszt
pole jump ('poul dżamp) s. skok
o tyczce
police (pe'li:s) s. policja;
v. rządzić; pilnować; utrzymywać porządek
policeman (pe'li:smen) s. policjant

police officer (pe'li:s,ofyser)
s. policjant
police station (pe'li:s,stejszyn)
s. komisariat
policewoman (pe'li:s,łumen) s.
policjantka
policy ('polysy) s. polityka
rządzenia; polityka postępowa-
nia; mądrość polityczna; polisa ubezpieczeniowa
polio ('pouljou) s. poliomyeli-
tis (,poliou,maje'lajtis) s.
paraliż dziecięcy; choroba
Haine-Medina
Polish ('poulysz) adj. polski
(język) (obywatel etc.)
polish ('polysz) v. polerować;
gładzić; pochlebiać; nabierać
połysku; s. pasta (do butów);
połysk; politura; polor
polite (pe'lajt) adj. grzeczny;
uprzejmy; kulturalny
politeness (pe'lajtnys) s.
grzeczność; ogłada; kultura;
uprzejmość
political (pe'lytykel) adj.
polityczny
politician (,poly'tyszyn) s.
polityk; politykier
politics ('polytyks) s. polity-
tyka
poll (poul) s. głosowanie; reje-
strowanie głosów; wyniki głosowania; lista; wykaz; lokal
wyborczy; urny wyborcze; ankieta; głowa; tył głowy; obuch
v. oddawać głosy; obliczać
głosy; rejestrować; dostawać
głosy; strzyc włosy; obcinać
rogi
pollen ('polyn) s. pył kwiato-
wy
pollute (pe'lju:t) v. zanie-
czyszczać; skazić
pollution (pe'lju:szyn) s. skażenie; zanieczyszczenie
pomp (pomp) s. pompa
pompous ('pompes) adj. napuszony; nadęty; pompatyczny
pond (pond) s. staw
ponder ('ponder) v. rozważać;
rozmyślać;przemyśliwać;dumać;
zastanawiać się;zadumać się

ponderous ('ponderes) adj.
ciężki; niezgrabny

pontoon (pon'tu:n) s. ponton

pony ('pouny) s. kuc; bryk;
v. odpisywać; ściągać;zrzynać

poodle ('pu:dl) s. pudel(pies)

pool (pu:l) s. kałuża; sadzawka; pływalnia; v. składać się
razem; zbierać się w grupę

poor (puer) adj. biedny; ubogi; lichy; marny; słaby;
kiepski; nędzny; skromny

poorhouse ('puer,haus) s.
przytułek

poorly ('puerly) adv. licho;
kiepsko; skąpo; skromnie;
biednie; ubogo; adj. nie-
zdrów

pop (pop) s. trzask; puknię-
cie; strzał; napój musujący;
lombard; tatuś (slang);
v. strzelać; pukać; nagle wyrzucać; nagle wsadzać; skakać;
wściekać się

popcorn ('pop,ke:rn) s. su-
cha prażona kukurydza

pop in ('pop,yn) v. wskoczyć

pop out ('pop,aut) v. wyskoczyć

pope (poup) s. papież

poplar ('popler) s. topola

poppy ('popy) s. mak

popular ('popjuler) adj, ludowy; rozpowszechniony; popularny (tani)

popularity (,popju'laeryty) s.
popularność

populate ('popjulejt) s. zaludniać

population ('popjulejszyn) s.
ludność

populous ('popjules) adj. ludny; gęsto zaludniony

porch (po:rch) s. weranda; ga-
nek; portyk

porcupine ('po:rkjupajn) s.
jeż; jeżozwierz; kolczątka

pore (po:r) v. rozmyślać; śle-
czeć; wpatrywać się; s. por
(skóry)

pore over ('po:r,ouwer) v. rozmyślać nad czymś;śleczeć (nad
książką);zagłębiać się

pork (po:rk) s. wieprzowina

porous ('po:res) adj. porowaty

porpoise ('po:rpes) s. morswin;
ssak morski

porridge ('porydż) s. owsianka

port (po:rt) s. port; przystań;
otwór; otwór ładunkowy; postawa; trzymanie się; prezentowa-
nie (broni); wino porto; lewa
burta; sterowanie w lewo

portable ('po:rtebl) adj. przenośny; polowy

porter ('po:rter) s. tragarz;
kolejarz od sypialnego wagonu

portion ('po:rszyn) s. część;
porcja; udział; posag; los;
v. dzielić; przydzielać

portion out ('po:rszyn,aut) v.
wydzielać; wyposażać

portly ('po:rtly) adj. dostojny; godny; tęgi; postawny;
okazały

portrait ('po:rtryt) s. portret

pose (pouz) v. pozować; upozo-
wać; stawiać (np. problem);
kłopotać (za pytaniem); s. poza

posh (posz) adj. elegancki; szykowny; v. wyelegantować się

position (pe'zyszyn) s. położenie; stanowisko; postawa;
twierdzenie; umieszczenie;
v. umieszczać; ulokować

positive ('pozetyw) adj. pozytywny; stanowczy; ustanowiony;
zupełny; dodatni; pozytywistycz-
ny; s.znak dodatni; wartość
dodatnia; pozytyw

possess (pe'zes) v. posiadać;
opanować; opętać; przepajać

possessed (pe'zest) adj. opęta-
ny

possession (pe'zeszyn) s. posiadanie; posiadłość; własność;
dobytek;opanowanie

possessor (pe'zeser) s. posiadacz; właściciel

possibility (pose'bylyty) s.
możliwość; możność;ewentualność

possible ('posebl) adj. możliwy; ewentualny

possibly ('posebly) adv. może;
wogóle możliwe; możliwie

post (poust) s. słup; posada;
posterunek; poczta; v. ogłaszać; wywieszać; zalepiać
plakatami

postage ('poustydż) s. opłata
pocztowa

postage stamp ('poustydż,staemp)
s. znaczek pocztowy

postal ('poustel) adj. pocztowy

postal order ('poustel'o:rder)
s. przekaz pocztowy

postcard ('poust,ka:rd) s.
pocztówka

post code ('poust,koud) = zip-
code ('zyp,koud) pocztowy
numer kierunkowy

poster ('pouster) s. plakat

poste restante ('poust'resta:-
nt) s. list lub przesyłka do
odebrania na poczcie

posterity (po'teryty) s. po-
tomność

post-free ('poust'fri:) adj.
wolny od opłaty pocztowej

posthumous ('postjumes) adj.
pośmiertny

postman ('poustmen) s. listonosz

postmark ('poust,ma:rk) s.
stempel pocztowy

postmaster ('poust,ma:ster) s.
naczelnik poczty

post office ('poust,ofys) s.
poczta

post office box ('poust,ofys'-
'boks) s. skrytka pocztowa

postpaid ('poust,pejd) s.
opłata pocztowa z góry uisz-
czona

postpone (poust'poun) v. odłożyć; odroczyć; odwlekać

postscript ('pous,skrypt) s.
dopisek; postscriptum

posture('posczer) s. postawa;
stan; położenie; v. przybrać
postawę; pozować

postwar ('poust'ło:r) adj.
powojenny

posy ('pouzy) s. bukiet

pot (pot) s. garnek; imbryk;
czajnik; nocnik; doniczka;
wazonik;rondel;dzban;kocioł;
kufel;słój;puchar;więcierz;łuza

szklanka; haszysz; v. wsadzać
do garnka; polować; strzelać

potato (po'tejtou) s. ziemniak

potent ('potent) adj. potężny;
skuteczny; jurny

potion ('pouszyn) s. dawka; napój

potter ('poter) s. garncarz;
v. grzebać się; włóczyć się;
łazić

potter about ('poter,e'baut)
v. włóczyć się

potty ('poty) adj. marny; lichy;
błahy; łatwy; stuknięty; pomylony; zbzikowany

pouch (paucz) s. worek; torba;
brzuszysko; ładownica; sakiewka; v, nadawać formę worka;
łykać

poulterer ('poulterer) s.
handlarz drobiu

poultice ('poultys) s. okład;
v. kłaść okład

poultry ('poultry) s. drób

pounce (pauns) s. szpon; nagły
atak z góry; v. rzucać się na
coś; trybować; pumeksować; posypywać (rysunek) proszkiem
(kolorowym)

pound (paund) s. funt (pieniądz;
waga); stuk; tupot; uderzenie;
tłuczenie; walnięcie; ogrodzenie; magazyn; areszt; v.tłuc;
walić; tupać;biegać; więzić;
zamykać

pour (po:r) v. wysypać; posypać; lać; polać; wylać; rozlać;
nalać

pour out ('po:r,aut) v. wysypać;
wylać

pout (paut) v. dąsać się; wydymać; s. wydęcie warg; kwaśna
mina

poverty('powerty) s. bieda;
ubóstwo

powder ('pałder) s. proch; pył;
puder; proszek; v. posypywać;
pudrować; proszkować

powder room ('pałder,ru:m) s.
toaleta damska

power ('pałer) s. potęga; moc;
energia; siła; własność; władza; mocarstwo; v. napędzać;
wspomagać;dostarczać energii

power brake ('pałer,brejk) s.
serwohamulec; wspomagany hamulec

powerful ('pałerful) adj. potężny; mocny

powerless ('pałerlys) adj.
bezsilny

power plant ('pałer,plaent)
s. siłownia

power station ('pałer,stejszyn)
s. elektrownia

powwow ('pał,łał) v. naradzać
się co do taktyki; leczyć;
s. sejmik Indian; odprawa ofi-
cerska; czarownik indiański

practicable ('praektykebl) adj.
wykonalny; możliwy do prze-
prowadzenia

practical ('praektykel) adj.
praktyczny

practice ('praektys) s. praktyka; ćwiczenie; v. praktykować;
uprawiać; ćwiczyć

practise ('praektys) v. = practice

practitioner(praek'tyszener) s.
zawodowiec; praktykujący lekarz

prairie('preery) s. preria

praise (prejz) s. pochwała;
v. chwalić; sławić

praiseworthy ('prejz,łe:rsy)
adj. chwalebny; godny pochwały

pram (praem) s. ręczny wózek

prance (praens) v. stawać dęba;
tańczyć; paradować; hasać;
kazać koniowi stawać dęba

prank (praenk) s. psota; figiel; v. wystroić; popisywać
się

prattle ('praetl) v. paplać;
s. paplanina

prawn (pro:n) s. krewetka;
v. łowić krewetki

pray, (prej) v. modlić się; prosić; błagać

prayer ('prejer) s. modlitwa;
prośba

prayer book ('prejer,buk) s.
modlitewnik; książka do
nabożeństwa

pre-(pri:-)prefix,przed-;z góry

preach (pri:cz) v. głosić; kazać;
wygłaszać

preacher (pri:czer) s. kaznodzieja; pastor

precarious (pry'keeries) s. niepewny; niebezpieczny; dowolny

precaution (pry'ko:szyn) s. przezorność; środek ostrożności

precede (pry:'si:d) v. poprzedzać;
mieć pierwszeństwo

precedence (pry'si:dens) s. pierwszeństwo;nadrzędność

precedent (pry'si:dent) adj.
uprzedni; poprzedzający

precedent ('presydent) s. precedens

precept('pry:sept) s. nakaz;
przykazanie; nauka moralna; reguła

precinct ('pry:synkt) s. okręg
(wyborczy); obręb; granice

precious ('preszes) adj. drogi;
cenny; afektowany; wyszukany;
wspaniały; adv. bardzo; niezwykle

precipice ('presypys) s. przepaść

precipitate (pry'sypytejt) s.
opad; osad; przyspieszać (zdarzenia);skraplać (się); rzucać;
spadać

precipitation (pry,sypy'tejszyn)
s. opady; przyspieszanie; po-
chopność; upadek; strącanie

precipitous (pry'sypytes) adj.
przepaścisty; spadzisty

precis, ('prejsi:) s. skrót; v.
robić skrót

precise (pry'sajs) adj. dokładny; wyraźny; v. precyzować;
wyszczególniać

precision (pry'syżyn) s. precyzja;
dokładność

precocious (pry'kouszes) adj.
przedwczesny; przedwcześnie roz-
winięty; kwitnący

preconceived ('pry:ken'si:wd)
adj. uprzedzony do; powzięty
z góry

predatory ('predetery) adj. łu-
pieżczy; grabieżczy; drapieżny

predecessor ('pry:dyseser) s.
poprzednik; przodek

predetermine ('pry:dy'te:rmyn)
v. z góry ustanowić; z góry
okreslić; z góry zadecydować
predicament (pry'dykement) s,
kłopot; kłopotliwe położenie
predicate ('predy,kejt) v.
opierac się na czyms; łączyc
się z czyms; przypisywać czemus; orzekac o czyms; miescić
pojęcie czegos; ('predykyt) s.
cecha; orzecznik; adj. orzecze-
niowy; dopełnienie orzeczenia
predict (pry'dykt) v. przepowiadac
prediction (pry'dykszyn) s.
przepowiednia
predisposition ('pri:dyspe'zyszyn) s. skłonnosc; predyspo-
zycja
predominant(pry'domynent) adj.
przeważający; panujący; góru-
jący
predominate (pry'domynejt) v.
górowac; przeważać
preface ('prefys) s. przedmowa;
wstęp
prefect ('pry:fekt) s. prefekt
prefer (pry'fe:r) v. wolec;
przekładac; dawac awans
preferable ('preferebl) adj.
lepszy
preferably ('preferebly) adv.
raczej
preference ('preferens) s.
pierwszenstwo; uprzywilejowa-
nie; możnośc wyboru; rzecz bardziej ulubiona, upodcbana
preferment (pry'fe:rment) s.
wybor; awans
prefix ('pry:fyks) s. przedrostek; prefiks; tytuł przed
nazwiskiem; v. umieszczac
przedrostek; umieszczac na
wstępie
pregnancy ('pregnensy) s. ciaza
pregnant ('pregnent) adj. brze-
mienny; doniosły; sugestywny;
płodny ;ciężarna (kobieta)
prejudice ('predżudys) s. uprzedzenie; szkoda; v. uprzedzac się
do kogos; szkodzić (komus);
rozpowszechniac uprzedzenie

prejudiced ('predżudyst) adj.
uprzedzony ;mający uprzedzenie
preliminary (pry'lymynery) adj.
wstępny; przygotowawczy;
s. wstęp
prelude ('prelju:d) s. wstęp;
preludium; v. grac preludium;
dawac wstęp do czegos
premature (,preme'tjuer) adj.
przedwczesny; przedwcześnie
dojrzały
premeditate (pry'medy,tejt) v.
obmyslac; rozważać
premier ('premjer) adj. pierwszy; najważniejszy; premier;
prezes rady ministrów
premises ('premsys) pl. lokal;
obejscie
premium ('pri:mjem) s. nagroda;
premia
preoccupied (pry:'okju,pajd)
adj. pochłonięty; zaabsorbowany
preparation (,prepe'rejszyn) s.
przygotowywanie; przyrządzanie
prepare (pry'peer) v. przygoto-
wywac (się); szykowac (się);
przyrzadzać
prepay ('pry'pej) v. opłacać
z góry
preposition (,prepe'zyszyn) s.
przyimek
prepossess (,pry:po'zes) v.
wpoic; usposobic; natchnąc
prepossessing (pry:po'zesyng)
adj. miły; sympatyczny
preposterous (pry'posteres) adj.
niedorzeczny; absurdalny
prerequisite (pry'rekłyzyt) adj.
& s. (warunek) wstępny; podstawowy
prescribe (prys'krajb) v. prze-
pisac; nakazac; zaordynować
prescribtion (prys'krypszyn) s.
nakaz; przepis; recepta
presence ('presens) v. obecnośc
presence of mind ('prezens,ow'
'majnd) v. przytomnosc umysłu
present ('preznt) s. upominek;
prezent; teraznie jszość; adj.
obecny; niniejszy; teraznie j-
szy;v.stawiac się;nadarzyć się

present tense ('presnt,tens) s.
czas teraźniejszy

presentation (,prezen'tejszyn)
s. przedstawienie; ofiarowanie; podarek; darowanie; przedłożenie

presentiment (pry'zentyment) s.
przeczucie

presently ('prezently) adv.
wkrótce; niebawem; zaraz

preservation (,preze:r'wejszyn)
s. zachowanie; ochrona; zabezpieczenie

preserve (pry'ze:rw) v. zachowywać; chronić; przechowywać;
konserwować; ochraniać;
s. konserwa; rezerwat

preside (pry'zajd) v. przewodniczyć

president ('prezydent) s. prezydent

press (pres) s. prasa; dzienniki; tłocznia; druk; drukania;
nacisk; tłok; ścisk; pośpiech;
v. cisnąć; ściskać; przyciskać;
ciążyć; pracować; naglić; narzucać; wciskać; tłoczyć

press in ('pres-yn) v. wciskać

pressing ('presyng) adj. naglący; natarczywy

pressure ('preszer) s. ciśnienie; napór; parcie

prestige (pres'ty:dż) s. prestiż (szacunek i uznanie)

presumable(pry'zju:mebl) adj.
przypuszczalny

presume (pry'zju:m) v. przypuszczać; wykorzystywać (kogoś);
ośmielać się

presumedly (pry'zju:mydly) adv.
przypuszczalnie

presuming (pry'zju:myng) adj.
zarozumiały

presumption (pry'zampszen) s.
przypuszczenie; założenie;
zarozumiałość

presumptuous (pry'zamptjues)
adj. zarozumiały

presuppose (pry:se'pouz) v.
przypuszczać; zakładać z góry;
stawiać warunek

pretend (pry'tend) v. udawać;
pretendować

pretender (pry'tender) s. pretendent

pretense (pry'tens) s. udawanie;
pozór; pretensja; pretensjonalność

pretension (pry'tenszyn) s.
aspiracje; roszczenie; pretensjonalność; pretensja

preterite ('preteryt) adj.
przeszły; s. czas przeszły

pretext ('pry:tekst) s. pretekst;
pozór;

pretext (pry'tekst) v. wymawiać
się; powoływać się

pretty ('pryty) adj. ładny;
adv. dość; dosyć

prevail (pry'wejl) v. przeważać;
brać górę; przekonać; panować
(np. zwyczaj)

prevalent ('prewelent) adj. panujący; przeważający

prevent (pry'went) v. zapobiec;
powstrzymywać

prevention (pry'wenszyn) s. zapobieganie; środek zapobiegający

preventive (pry'wentyw) adj.
zapobiegawczy; prewencyjny

previous ('pry:wjes) adj. poprzedni; wcześniejszy od...;
przedwczesny; nagły; pochopny

previous to ('pry:wjes,tu) adv.
przed czyms

previously ('pry:wjesly) adv.
wcześniej

prewar ('pri:'ło:r) adj.
przedwojenny

prey (prej) s. zdobycz; łup;
ofiara; v. grabić; trawić

price (prajs) s. cena; koszt;
v. wyceniać

priceless ('prajslys) adv.
bezcenny; nieoceniony

prick (pryk) s. ukłucie;
(wulg.) penis; v. kłuc; przekłuwać

prick up one's ears ('pryk,ap-
'łans,eerz) s. nadstawiac
uszu; postawić uszy

prickle ('prykl) s. kolec;
cierń; v. ukłuc; jeżyć się

prickly ('prykly) adj. kolczasty

pride (prajd) s. duma; pycha;
ambicja; chluba; v. byc dum-
nym z czegos;chełpic' się;pysznić się
się

priest (pri:st) s. kapłan; duchowny

primarily ('prajmeryly) adv.
głownie; przede wszystkim

primary ('prajmery) adj. głowny; zasadniczy; pierwotny;
s. wybor kandydatow (U.S.A.)

primary school ('prajmery,sku:l)
s. szkoła podstawowa

prime ('prajm) adj. pierwszy;
najważniejszy; głowny;v.przygoto-
wać
prime minister ('prajm-'mynyster)
s. premier

primer ('prajmer) s. elementarz;
podręcznik (elementarny)

primitive ('prymytyw) adj. prymitywny; pierwotny

primrose ('prymrous) s. pier-
wiosnek

prince ('pryns) s. książę

princess (pryn'ses) s. księżna;
księżniczka

principal ('prynsepel) adj.
głowny; s. kierownik; zlecenio-
dawca; kapitał sprawca

principality (prynsy'paelyty)
s. księstwo

principle ('prynsepl) s. zasada;
reguła;podstawa;zrodło;składnik

prink (prynk) v. stroic się;
muskac się

print (prynt) s. slad; odcisk;
druk; pismo; fotka; v. wy-
cisnąc; wytłoczyc; wydrukowac;
byc w druku;drukowac się;odbić
printed matter ('prynted'maeter)
v. druki;materiały drukowane

printer ('prynter) s. drukarz

printing ('pryntyng) s. druk;
drukowanie; nakład;a.drukarski

printing ink ('pryntyng,ynk) s.
farba drukarska

printing office ('pryntyn,ofys)
s. drukarnia

prior ('prajer) adj. wcześniejszy; ważniejszy; s. przeor

prior to ('prajer,tu) adv.
przed czyms;wcześniej od czegos

priority ('praj'oryty) s.
pierwszeństwo;starszeństwo

prison ('pryzn) s. więzienie

prisoner ('pryzner) s. więzień

privacy ('prajwesy) s. odosobnienie; samotnosc; utrzymanie
w dyskrecji (tajemnicy); życie
prywatne, intymne, osobiste

private ('prajwyt) adj. prywatny; tajny; ukryty; s. szerego-
wiec;(private parts=genitalia)

private hotel ('prajwyt,hou'tel)
s. pensjonat

privation (praj'wejszyn) s.
prywacja; niedostatek

privilege ('prywylydż) s. przywilej;prawdziwa satysfakcja

privileged ('prywylydżd) adj.
uprzywilejowany;zaszczycony

prize (prajz) v. podważyć; zajmowac; cenic; nagroda; premia;
wygrana; łup;a.kapitalny.v.cenić

prizefighter ('prajz,fajter)
s. zawodowy bokser

prizewinner ('prajz,łyner) s.
laureat; zdobywca nagrody

pro (prou) s. zawodowiec (slang)
adv. za; dla;prep. pro(forma etc.)

probability (proba'bylyty) s.
prawdopodobieństwo;widoki;szanse

probable ('probebl) adj. prawdopodobny;wiarogodny;mający szanse

probation (pro'bejszyn) s. okres próbny; próba;zawieszenie kary
probe (proub) s. sonda; v. sondowac; zagłębiac się;badac w sledz-
twie
problem ('problem) s. problem;
zadanie; zagadnienie;a.problemowy

procedure (pre'si:dżer) s. postępowanie; procedura(sądowa)

proceed (pre'si:d) v. isc dalej;
postępowac;kontynuowac;zaskarżać

proceed from (pre'si:d,from) v.
wychodzic z...;isc dalej z...

proceedings (pre'si:dyngs) pl.
sprawozdanie (z sesji etc.)

proceeds ('prousi:dz) pl. zysk;
dochody;przychód (ze sprzedaży)

process ('prouses) s. przebieg;
proces; postęp; v. obrabiac;
przerabiac; załatwiac; proce-
sowac;poddawać procesowi;mleć

procession (pre'seszyn) s. po-
chod; procesja;kontynuowanie;
prowadzenie dalej;dalszy rozwoj

proclaim (pre'klejm) v. proklamować; ogłaszać; zakazywać;
wskazywać;wprowadzać ograniczenia

proclamation (,prokle'mejszyn)
s. proklamacja; obwieszczenie

procrastinate (pre'kraesty,nejt)
v. zwlekać; odkładać na później

procure (pre'kjuer) v. postarać
się; stręczyć do nierządu

prodigal ('prodygel) adj. marnotrawny; s. marnotrawca;utracjusz

prodigious (pre'dydżes) adj.
niezwykły; cudowny; olbrzymi

prod (prod) v. szturchać; kłuć;
drażnic; popędzać; s. dźgnięcie; bodziec; szpikulec

prodigy ('prodydży) s. dziwo;
cud;genialne dziecko etc.

produce ('produ:s) s. produkty;
plony; wynik; produkcja; wydajność; wydobycie;produkty rolne

produce (pre'dju:s) v. wytwarzać;
produkować; dostarczać; wydobywać; wystawiać; okazywać

producer (produ:ser) s. wytwórca (filmowy); producent

product ('predakt) s. produkt;
wynik; iloczyn;wytwór(natury etc.)

production (pre'dakszyn) s. wytwórczość; wydobycie; produkcja;
utwór;produkty;a.produkcyjny

productive (pre'daktyw) adj.
wydajny; produktywny; produkcyj-
ny; urodzajny; żyzny

profess (pre'fes) v. twierdzić;
zapewniać; udawać; wyznawać;
uprawiać (zawod);być profesorem

professed (pre'fest) adj. jawny;
rzekomy; zawodowy

profession (pre'feszyn) s. zawód; wyznanie; zapewnienie;
oświadczenie;śluby zakonne

professional (pre'feszenl) s.
zawodowiec; adj. zawodowy; fa-
chowy;należący do wolnego zawodu

professor (pre'feser) s. profesor; wyznawca;nauczyciel(tańca)

proficiency (pre'fyszensy) s.
biegłość; sprawność

proficient (pre'fyszent) adj.
biegły; sprawny; s. mistrz;biegły;znający(obcy język);fachowiec

profile ('proufajl) s. profil;
szkic biograficzny; v. przedstawiać z profilu; profilować

profit ('profyt) s. zysk; dochód; korzyść; pożytek; v.
korzystać; być korzystnym;
przydawać się;mieć zyski

profitable (profytebl) adj.
korzystny;intratny;zyskowny

profiteer (,profy'tier) v.pas-
kować; spekulować; s. paskarz;
spekulant(na czarnym rynku etc)

profound (pro'faund) adj. głęboki;gruntowny;s.otchłań

profusion (pro'fju:żyn) s. obfitość; rozrzutność;nadmiar

prognoses (prog'nousi:z) pl.
prognozy; rokowania

prognosis (prog'nousys) s.
prognoza; rokowanie

program ('prougraem) s. program; plan; audycja; przedstawienie; v. planować

progress ('prougres) s. postęp;
bieg; rozwój;kolejne etapy etc.

progress (pro'gres) v. robić
postępy; iść naprzód;być w toku

progressive (pro'gresyw) adj.
postępowy;stopniowy;s.postępo-
wiec

prohibit (pro'hybyt) v. zakazywać; zabraniać

prohibition (,prouy'byszyn) s.
zakaz; prohibicja

project ('prodżekt) s. projekt;
plan;przedsięwzięcie;schemat

project (pro'dżekt) v. projektować; miotać; rzutować; sterczeć; wystawać;wyświetlać(na ek-
ranie)

projection (pro'dżekszyn) s.
rzut; planowanie; projektowa-
nie; rzutowanie; wystawanie;
projekcja; wyświetlanie

projector (pro'dżekter) s.
rzutnik;aparat projekcyjny

proletariat (,proule'teerjet)
s. proletariat;robotnicy przemy-
słowi

prolog ('proulog) s.prolog

prolong (prou'long) v. przedłużać; wydłużać;prolongować(spłaty)

promenade (,promy'nejd) s. przechadzka;przejażdżka; deptak;
promenada; v.przechadzać się

prominent ('promynent) adj. wydatny; wybitny; sterczący; wystający; wyróżniający się;sławny

promise ('promys) s. obietnica;
przyrzeczenie; v. obiecywać;
przyrzekać; zaręczać; zapewniać;robić obietnice;zapowiadać się

promising('promysyng) adj. obiecujący; rokujący nadzieję

promontory ('promento:ry) s.
przylądek; wyrostek

promote (pre'mout) v. popierać;
promować; awansować; (slang)
oszukiwać; kombinować

promoter (pre'mouter) s. organi-
zator:krzewiciel; inspirator

promotion (pre'mouszyn) s. po-
pieranie; ułatwienie; awans;
promowanie; lansowanie

prompt (prompt) adj. szybki;
natychmiastowy; v. nakłaniać;
pobudzać; podpowiadać; sufle-
rować;adv.punktualnie;co do mi-

prompter ('prompter) s. sufler
(w teatrze);podżegacz

promptly ('promptly) adv. natychmiast; z miejsca; bezzwłocznie; punktualnie

prone (proun) adj. leżący twarzą na dół; stromy; skłonny

prong (prong) s. ząb (wideł);
róg; v. kłuć; przebijać;
zaopatrywać w zęby

pronoun ('prounaun) s. zaimek

pronounce (pre'nauns) v. oświad-
czać; wymawiać; mieć wymowę;
wypowiadać się

pronto ('prontou) adv. (slang):
prędko; już;natychmiast;zaraz

pronunciation (pra,nansy'ejszyn)
s. wymowa;zapis fonetyczny

proof (pru:f) s. dowód; próba
(np. złota); sprawdzian; wy-
próbowanie; korekta; próbna
odbitka; adj. odporny; wypró-
bowany;sprawdzony;nieprzemakalny

prop(up) ('prop,ap) v. podpierać; s. podpórka :ostoja;oparcie

propagate ('prope,gejt) v. rozmnażać (się); rozszerzać; propagować; przekazywać

propagation (,prope'gejszyn) s.
rozmnażanie się; propagowanie

propel (pre'pel) v. napędzać;
poruszać; pędzić

propeller (pre'peler) s. śmigło;
śruba (okrętowa)

proper ('proper) adj. właściwy;
własny; przyzwoity

properly ('properly) adv. włas-
ciwie; słusznie; przyzwoicie

property ('property) s. własność;właściwość;cecha;nierucho-
mość

prophecy ('profysy) s. proroctwo

prophet ('profyt) s. prorok;
apostoł

proportion (pre'po:rszyn) s.
proporcja; stosunek; rozmiar;
część; v. dostosowywać; rozdzielać;dawkować;dozować

proportional (pre'po:rsznl) adj.
proporcjonalny (do czegoś)

proposal (pre'pouzel) s. propozycja; projekt; oświadczyny

propose (pre'pouz) v. proponować; przedkładać; zamierzać

proposition (,prope'zyszyn) s.
propozycja; sąd; zagadnienie;
twierdzenie; v. robić nie-
przyzwoite propozycje

proprietary (pre'prajetery) adj.
należący; będący prywatną
własnością; s. właściciel;
własność

proprietor (pre'prajeter) s.
właściciel;posiadacz;gospodarz

propulsion (pre'palszyn) s. napęd; bodziec; popędzanie

prose (prouz) s. proza ;v.nudzić

prosecute ('prosy,kju:t) s. ścigać prawnie; prowadzić (np.
studia) ;nie zaniedbywać;pilno-
wać

prosecution (,prosy'kju:szyn)
s. oskarżenie

prosecutor ('prosy,kju:ter) s.
prokurator; oskarżyciel

prospect ('prospekt) s. widok;
perspektywa; ewentualny klient;
potencjalne złoża; v. przeszukiwać (okolice); próbnie
eksploatować kopalnie; szukać
złota etc.;badać(teren etc.)

prospective (pres'pektyw) adj.
przyszły; ewentualny

prospectus (pres'pektes) s.
prospekt (nowego przedsiębiors-
twa)

prosper ('prosper) v. prosperować; sprzyjać powodzeniu

prosperity (pros'peryty) s.
dobrobyt; powodzenie; kon-
junktura pomyślność

prosperous ('prosperes) adj. mający powodzenie; kwitnący; pomyślny; zamożny

prostate (pros'tejt) s. prostata; gruczoł krokowy

prostitute ('prosty,tu:t) s.
prostytutka; v. prostytuować
(się);adj.wszeteczny;rozpustny

prostrate ('prostrejt) v. powalić (np. ze zmęczenia); adj.
leżący twarzą w dół; powalony;
wyczerpany; bezsilny; kłania-
jący się ;leżący plackiem

protect (pre'tekt) v. chronić;
bronić; ochraniać;zabezpieczać

protection (pre'tekszyn) s. ochrona; opieka; protekcja; list
żelazny; wymuszanie pieniędzy
przez grożenie gwałtem

protective (pre'tektyw) adj.
ochronny;zapobiegawczy

protector (pre'tekter) s. opiekun; protektor; ochraniacz

protest (pro'test) v. protestować; zapewniać;oponować

protest ('proutest) s. protest

protestant ('protystent) s.
ewangelik; protestant

protestation (proutes'tejszyn)
s. uroczyste zapewnienie; protest;zaprotestowanie

protract(pre'traekt) v. przeciągać; przedłużać; wystawiać;
przedstawiać w skali

protrude (pre'tru:d) v. wystawać; wysuwać ;sterczeć

proud (praud) adj. dumny; napa-
wający dumą;piękny;szczęśliwy

prove (pru:w) v. udowadniać;
wykazać (się); uprawomocnić;
poddawać próbie; okazywać się

proverb ('prowe:rb) s. przysłowie ;przypowieść

proverbial (pre'we:rbjel) adj.
przysłowiowy

provide (pre'wajd) v. zaopatrywać; przygotowywać; postarać
się; sprzyjać; postanawiać; zaplanować

provide for (pre'wajd,fo:r) v.
zaopatrywać (dla kogoś)

provided that (pre'wajdyd,daet)
exp.: pod warunkiem że...; o ile

providence ('prowydens) s.
opatrzność; oszczędność; przezorność; skrzętność

province ('prowyns) s. prowincja;
zakres; dziedzina

provincial (pre'wynszel) adj.
zaściankowy; prowincjonalny;
s. człowiek z prowincji

provision (pro'wyżyn) s. klauzula; dostawa; przygotowanie
się; (pl.) prowianty; v. pro-
wiantować; zaopatrywać w żywność;zaprowiantować

provisional (pro'wyżenl) adj.
prowizoryczny; tymczasowy

provocation (,prowe'kejszyn) s.
prowokacja; rozdrażnienie;
podniecenie;spowodowanie

provocative (pro'woketyw) adj.
prowokujący; zaciekawiający;
drażniący;wyzywający

provoke (pre'wouk) v. prowoko-
wać; podniecać; pobudzać; wywoływać; podżegać;jątrzyć

prowl (praul) v. grasować;
s. grasowanie (po łup)

proxy ('proksy) s. zastępstwo;
pełnomocnik

prude (pru:d) s. świętoszka

prudence ('pru:dens) s. rozwaga; roztropność ;ostrożność

prudent ('pru:dent) s. rozważny;
roztropny;ostrożny

prudish ('pru:dysz) adj. pruderyjny;przesadnie skromny

prune (pru:n) s. śliwka (suszona) v. obcinać (np. gałązki);
oczyszczać (z czegoś)

psalm (sa:m) s. psalm

pseudonym ('sju:de,nym) s.
pseudonim;fikcyjne nazwisko

psyche ('sajki:) s. dusza; duch;
umysł (zwierciadło odchylone)

psychiatrist (saj'kajetryst) s.
psychiatra

psychiatry (saj'kajetry) s.
psychiatria

psychological (,sajke'lodżykel)
adj. psychologiczny

psychologist (saj'koledżyst) s.
psycholog
psychology (saj'koledży) s.
psychologia
pub (pab) s. Br., knajpa
puberty ('pju:berty) s. dojrza-
łość płciowa
public ('pablyk) s. publiczność;
adj. publiczny; obywatelski
publication (,pably'kejszyn)
s. opublikowanie; ogłoszenie;
publikacja;wydanie książki
public house ('pablyk,haus) s.
szynk; oberża
publicity (pab'lysyty) s. rozgłos; reklama;a.reklamowy
publish ('pablysz) v. publiko-
wać; wydawać; ogłaszać; rozgłaszać;wydać drukiem
publisher ('pablyszer) s. wydawca; nakładca
publishing house ('pablyszyng,-
haus) s. firma wydawnicza
pudding ('pudyng) s. budyń
puddle ('padl) s. kałuża
puff (paf) v. pykać; sapać; dmuchać; reklamować; pudrować;
s. puszek; pyknięcie; dmuch-
nięcie; blaga reklamowa; pierzyna;kłab dymu;zwój włosów
puff paste ('paf,pejst) s. fran-
cuskie ciasto
puffy ('pafy) adj. dychawiczny;
nadęty; pekaty; napuszony;
otyły; porywisty;dychawiczny
pull (pul) v. pociągnąć; szarpnąć; wyrwać; wyciągać; przeciągać; wiosłować;ściągnać
pull down ('pul,dałn) v. spuścić;
rozbierać (np. budynek); osłabiać;ściągać(store etc.)
pull for ('pul,fo:r) v. popierać
pull in ('pul,yn) v. wciągać
pull off ('pul,of) v. ściągać;
zdobywać;potrafić;zdołać;stapać
pull out ('pul,aut) v. wyrwać;
wycofać; s. wycofanie się
pulley ('puli) s. bloczek; blok
krążkowy; v. podnosić bloczkiem
pullover ('pul,ouwer) s. pulower
pulp (palp) s, miazga; miąższ;
papka; v.rozcierać na miazge

pulpit ('pulpyt) s. ambona; ka-
zalnica;kaznodzieje; kazanie
pulpy ('palpy) adj. papkowaty;
miąższowy
pulsate (pal'sejt) v. tętnić;
pulsować;drgać;trząść się
pulse (pals) s. tętno; puls;
v. tętnić; pulsować
pulverize ('palwerajz) v. proszkować (się); rozpylać; ścierać
w proch;zemleć na proch
pump (pamp) s. pompa; lakierek;
v. pompować;pytać uporczywie
pump gun ('pamp,gan) s. strzelba (do repetowania)
pumpkin ('pampkyn) s. dynia
pun (pan) s. gra słów (dwuznacz-
nych); v. robić kalambury
punch (pancz) s. uderzenie
(pięścią); poncz; przebijak;
krzepa; siła; sztanca; kułak;
rozmach; v. dziurkować; tłoczyć; walić; szturchać
punctual ('panktjuel) adj.
punktualny; punktowy
punctuate ('panktju,ejt) v.
przestankować; przerywać
punctuation (,panktju'ejszyn)
s. interpunkcja
punctuation mark (,panktju'ejszyn ma:rk) s. kropka; znak
przestankowy
puncture ('pankczer) s. przebicie;
punkcja; v. przekłuwać; przedziurawiać;przebić
pungent ('pandżent) adj. kłujący;
ostry; cierpki; zjadliwy; gry-
zący;sarkastyczny;pikantny
punish ('panysz) v. karać;dać bobu
punishment ('panyszment) s. kara;sromotna klezka (na boisku)
pupil ('pju:pl) s. zrenica; uczeń;
wychowanek;małoletni;niepełnolet-
ni
puppet ('papyt) s. kukiełka;
marionetka;a.kukiełkowy;marionet-
kowy
puppet show ('papyt,szou) s. wy-
stępy marionetek
puppet state ('papyt,stejt) s.
państwo marionetkowe
puppy ('papy) s. szczenię; szczeniak; piesek;zarozumialec

purchase ('pe:rczes) s. zakup;
kupno; dźwignia; v. kupić;
okupić;nabywać; podnosić (np.
kotwicę);sprawiać sobie

purchaser (pe:rczeser) s. nabywca; kupujący

pure (pjuer) adj. czysty; zupełny; szczery; niewinny; nie
zepsuty,zwykły;czystej krwi

purgative ('pe:rgetyw) adj. przeczyszczający; s. środek na
przeczyszczenie

purgatory ('pe:rgetery) s. czyściec; adj. oczyszczający

purge (pe:rdż) v. przeczyszczać;
oczyścić; usuwać; dawać na
przeczyszczenie; s. oczyszczenie; czystka; środek przeczyszczający;rafinowanie;klarowanie

purify ('pjuery,faj) v. oczyszczać (się);klarować;rafinować

purity ('pjueryty) s. czystość

purloin (pe:rloyn) v. ukraść;
ściągać;porwać

purple ('pe:rpl) s. purpura;
adj. purpurowy; v. robić purpu-
rowym;robić szkarłatnym

purpose ('pe:rpes) s. cel. zamiar; skutek; decyzja; wola;
v. zamierzać ;mieć na celu;plano-
wać

purposeful ('pe:rpesful) adj.
celowy; znaczący; rozmyślny;
zdecydowany; stanowczy

purposeless ('pe:rpeslys) adj.
bezcelowy; bezsensowny; daremny; próżny(wysiłek etc.)

purposely ('pe:rpesly) adv. naumyślnie; celowo; rozmyślnie

purr (pe:r) v. mruczeć; mrucze-
nie; pomrukiwać;s.pomruk

purse (pe:rs) s. sakiewka; torebka damska; kiesa; nagroda;
v. ściągać (się);marszczyć(czoło)

pursue (per'sju:) v. ścigać; tropić; iść dalej; uprawiać (np.
zawód); działać wg.planu; prześladować; kontynuować; towarzyszyć;spełniać(obowiązek)

pursuer(per'sju:er) s. ścigający;
prześladowca ;dążący do czegoś

pursuit (per'sju:t) s. pościg; pogoń; zawód; zajęcie; rozrywka

pursy (pe:rsy) adj. dychawiczny; wydęty; otyły;ściągnięty

purvey (pe:r'wej) v. dostarczyć;
zaopatrywać; być dostawcą

purveyor (pe:rwejer) s. dostawca

pus (pas) s. ropa

push (pusz) s. pchnięcie; suw;
nacisk; wypad; wysiłek; energia; dryg; bieda; kryzys; zdecydowanie; v. pchać; posunąć;
szturchnąć; nakłonic; dopingować; odpychać; spychać; pomiatać; robić karierę ;ponaglać

push along ('pusz,e'long) v. iść
dalej; ciągnąć się dalej; jechać dalej; spieszyć się

push around ('pusz,a'round) v.
pomiatać kims

pusher ('puszer) s. popychacz;
(uliczny): sprzedawca narkotyków

puss (pus) s. kociak; dziewczyna; (slang: gęba;kot(tygrys)

pussycat ('pusy,kaet) s. kociak;
pliszka; (wulg) narząd płciowy
żeński; ('pasy) adj. ropny

put; put; put (put; put; put)

put (put) v. kłasć; stawiać;
umieszczać; wsadzać; pouczać;
przedkładać; ujmować; wystawiać; dodawać; wlewać; szacować; nakładać; opierać; składać;
narażać; wypychać (np. kule);
zanosić (np. prosby); s. rzut;
adj. nieruchomy(pozostający na
miejscu)

put back ('put,baek) v. przestawić do tyłu;ułożyć z powrotem

put down ('put,dałn) v. położyć;
stłumić;spuscić w dół;zapisywać

put forth ('put,fo:rs) v. wydo-
być; wytężyć(siły);wydawać(pismo)

put off ('put,of) v. odłożyć;
odroczyć ;zbywać;odwieść ;pozbyć
się

put on ('put,on) v. wdziewać;
przybierać; tyć;udawać;dodawać

put out ('put,aut) v. zwichnąć;
zgasić; wytężyć (się); produkować; wydawać;wysunąć(rękę etc.)

put together (,put'tugedzer) v.
łączyć; montować; powiązać;
zbierać(myśli);kojarzyć;zliczyć

put up('put,ap) v. ustawiac;
wywieszac; cierpiec; wetknąc;
schowac;dzwigac do góry;ustawic
putrefy ('pju:try,faj) v.gnic;
ropiec ;ulegac zepsuciu
putrid ('pju:tryd) adj. zgniły;
zepsuty; cuchnący; smierdzący;
wstrętny; obrzydliwy
putty ('paty) s. kit; szpachlów-
ka; v. szpachlowac; zakitowac
putty knife ('paty,najf) s.
szpachla
puzzle ('pazl) s. zagadka; łamigłówka; zakłopotanie;
v. intrygowac; wprawiac w zakłopotanie; odgadnąc; wymyslic
puzzler ('pazler) s. łamigłówka
pyjamas (pe'dża:mez) pl. piżama
pyramid ('pyremyd) s. piramida;
ostrosłup; v. zarabiac na
spekulacji; wznosic (się)
piramidalnie;budowac jak piramide
python ('pajsen) s. pyton
q (kju:) siedemnasta litera
angielskiego alfabetu (q.=kwarta)
quack (kłaek) s. znachor; szarlatan; kwakanie; v. uprawiac
znachorstwo; gadac jak szarlatan; kwakac
quad (kłod) (skrót): s. kwadrat;
czworokąt
quadrangle (kło'draengl) s.
czworokąt
quadruped ('kładru,ped) adj.
czworonozny
quadruple (kło'drupl) adj.
czterokrotny; cztery razy
większy;czterokrotnie większy
quadruplets (kło'dru:plets) s.
czworaczki
quail (kłejl) s. przepiórka;
v. drzec przed czyms
quaint (kłejnt) adj. malowniczy; trochę dziwaczny
quake (kłejk) s. trzęsienie
(ziemi); v. trzasc się (np.
z zimna)(ze strachu etc.)
quaky (kłejky) adj. trzesący
się; grząski
qualification (,kłolyfy'kejszyn)
s. warunek; okreslenie; kwalifikacja; uzdolnienie(do pracy)

qualified ('kłolyfajd) adj. wy-
kwalifikowany; uwarunkowany;
kwalifikujący się
quality ('kłolyty) s. jakosc;
gatunek; własciwosc; zaleta
qualm (kło:m) s. mdłosci; nud-
nosci; obawa; wyrzuty; skrupuły
quandary ('kłondery) s. zakłopotanie; kłopot;dylemat
quantity ('kłontyty) s. ilosc;
wielkosc; hurt; obfitosc
quarantine ('kłorenti:n) s.
kwarantanna; v. izolowac
quarrel ('kło:rel) s. kłótnia;
zerwanie; spor; sprzeczka;
v. kłócic się; sprzeczac się;
zerwac z sobą;robic wyrzuty
quarrelsome ('kłorelsem) adj.
kłótliwy; swarliwy
quarry ('kłory) s. kamieniołom;
kopalnia odkrywkowa; łup; zdobycz; płytka; szybka; v. łamac;
wygrzebywac; wydobywac; exploatowac ;szperac(za wiadomosciami)
quarter ('kło:ter) v. cwiarto-
wac; kwaterowac; rozpłatac;
stacjonowac; s. cwierc; cwiart-
ka; kwadrans; kwatera; 25 cen-
tow (moneta); kwadra; dzielnica;
strona swiata; czynniki wpływo-
we (pl.) sfery(rządzące);kwartal
quarterly ('kło:terly) adj. kwartalny; adv. kwartalnie; s. kwar-
talnik;pismo kwartalne
quartet(te) (kło:r'tet) s. kwar-
tet; czworka
quarto ('kło:rtou) s. format
cwiartkowy
quaver ('kłejwer) s. drzenie
głosu; tryl; v. drzec; drgac;
wibrowac; trelowac
quay (ki:) s. molo;nadbrzeże
queasy ('kłi:zy) adj. przeczulony; mdlejący; grymasny;wrażliwy
queen (kłi:n) s. królowa;królówka
queen bee ('kłi:n.bi:) s. królowa pszczoła
queer (kłir) adj. dziwny; dziwaczny; nieswój; podejrzany; fałszywy; pederasta; v. zepsuc;
wpakowac w złą sytuację; mdlic

quench ('kłencz) v. gasić;
tłumić; nagle oziębiać (metal)

querulous ('kłerules) adj. na-
rzekający; zrzędny;płaczliwy

query ('kłiery) s. zapytanie;
pytajnik; znak zapytania;
v. pytać; kwestionować

quest (kłest) s. poszukiwanie;
śledztwo; v. szukać

question ('kłesczyn) s. pytanie;
zagadnienie; kwestia; wątpli-
wości; v. wypytywać; przesłuchiwać; badać; kwestionować;
pytać się;przeegzaminować

questionable ('kłesczenebl) adj.
wątpliwy (moralnie); sporny;
niepewny; niejasny

question mark ('kłesczyn,ma:rk)
s. znak zapytania

questionnaire (,kłejstje'neer)
s. kwestionariusz

queue (kju:) s. warkocz; ogonek; kolejka; v. czekać
w kolejce;czekać w ogonku

queue up ('kju:,ap) v. ustawiać się w kolejce

quibble ('kłybl) s. kruczek;
v. szukać wykrętów

quick (kłyk) adj. prędki; szybki; bystry; pomysłowy; żywy;
lotny; rudonośny; adv. szybko;
chyżo; v. przyspieszać; ożywiać (się);zwiększać szybkość

quicken ('kłyken) v. przyspieszać; pobudzać; ożywiać się;
wrócić do życia

quickly ('kłykly) adv. szybko;
prędko; z pośpiechem

quickness ('kłyknys) s. prędkość; ostrość

quicksand ('kłyk,saend) s.
grząski piasek

quicksilver ('kłyk,sylwer) s.
rtęć; żywe srebro

quick-tempered ('kłyk'temperd)
adj. porywczy

quick-witted ('kłyk'żytyd)
adj. bystry; rozgarnięty

quid (kłyd) s. funt szterling;
prymka;kawałek do żucia

quiet ('kłajet) adj. spokojny;
cichy; s. spokój; cisza;

v. uspokoić (się); uciszyć
(się);uspakajać;zciszyć;ucichnąć

quiet down ('kłajet dałn) v.
uspakajać;przyciszyć;ucichnąć

quietness ('kłajetnys) s. spokój; cisza;łagodność;skromność

quietude (kłajetju:d) s. spokój (ducha)

quill (kłyl) s. lotka; dutka;
kolec; szpulka; pióro

quilt (kłylt) s. pikowana
kołdra; pikowana narzuta;
v. pikować; watować; robić
kołdry; zszywać;sprawić lanie

quince (kłyns) s. pigwa

quinine ('kłajnajn) s. chinina

quintal ('kłyntl) s. cetnar;
kwintal

quintuple ('kłyntjupl) adj.
pięciokrotny

quintuplets ('kłyntjuplyts) pl.
pięcioraczki

quit (kłyt) v. przestać; odejść;
odjechać; zabrać się; wyprowa-
dzić się; opuszczać; porzucać;
rezygnować; adj. wolny;uwolniony

quite (kłajt) adv. całkowicie;
zupełnie; raczej; wcale

quiver ('kłýwer) s. kołczan;
drżenie; drganie; v. drzeć;
drgać; trzepotać skrzydłami

quixotic ('kłyks,otyk) s. marzyciel w stylu Don Kichota

quiz (kłyz) s. klasówka; egzamin; badanie; przesłuchanie;
kawał; v. egzaminować; badać;
przesłuchiwać'przeglądać;kpić

quota ('kłouta) s. udział;
kontyngent;norma

quotation (kłou'tejszyn) s. cytata: cytowanie; notowanie;
przytaczanie(bieżącej ceny)

quotation marks (kłou'tejszyn,
,ma:rks) pl. cudzysłów

quote (kłout) v. cytować; przytaczać; umieszczać w cudzysło-
wie; notować; podawać kurs;
powoływać się na kogoś

quotient ('kłouszent) s. iloraz

r (a:r) osiemnasta litera
angielskiego alfabetu

rabbi ('raebaj) s. rabin

rabbit ('raebyt) s. królik

rabble ('raebl) s. motłoch

rabid ('raebyd) adj. wściekły; szalony;rozjuszony;rozzłoszczony

rabies ('raebi:z) s. wścieklizna; wodowstręt

raccoon (ra'ku:n) s. pracz pospolity

race (rejs) s. rasa; plemię; szczep; ród; rodzaj; bieg; gonitwa; wyścigi; prąd; kanał; v. ścigać (się); gonić (się); pędzić; iść w zawody

racer ('rejser) s. wyścigowiec

racial ('rejszel) adj. rasowy

racing ('rejsyng) adj. wyścigowy; s. wyścigi; biegi

racist ('rejsyst) s. rasista

rack (raek) s. ruina; zagłada; zniszczenie; koło tortur; wieszak; drabina stajenna; półka; stojak; zębatka; szybki kłus; v. niszczeć; łamać kołem; torturować; cedzić; szarpać; męczyć; dręczyć

racket ('raekyt) s. rakieta; rak; zabawa; hulanka; awantura; hałas; afera; granda; nieuczciwe interesy; kant; v. hałasować; hulać; bumblować; zabawiać się; awanturować się

racketeer (,raeky'tier) s. szantażysta; opryszek; v. szantażować; robić grandę

racoon (re'ku:n) s. szop

racy ('rejsy) adj. typowy; cięty; żywy; dosadny; aromatyczny; pikantny; nieprzyzwoity

radar ('rejder) s. radar

radiance ('rejdjens) s. promieniowanie; blask; promienność

radiant ('rejdjent) adj. promieniujący; promienny; rozpromieniony ;rzucający promienie

radiate ('rejdjejt) v. promieniować (ciepłem, swiatłem etc.)

radiation (,rejdy'ejszyn) s. promieniowanie;zrodło promieniowania

radiator ('rejdy'ejter) s. grzejnik; kaloryfer; chłodnica (samochodowa);radiowa antena nadawcza;radioaktywna substancja wydzielająca promienie

radical ('raedykel) s. pierwiastek; radykał; adj. zasadniczy; radykalny; podstawowy; pierwiastkowy; korzeniowy

radio ('rejdjou) s. radio; adj. radiowy; v. nadawać przez radio :wysyłać drogą radiową

radioactive ('rejdjou'aektyw) adj. radioaktywny; promieniotwórczy

radio set ('rejdjou,set) s. aparat radiowy; odbiornik radiowy

radiotherapy ('rejdjou-'terepy) s. radioterapia

radish ('raedysz) s. rzodkiewka

radius ('rejdjes) s. promień

raffle ('raefl) s. loteria fantowa; rupiecie; v. sprzedawać na loterii; kupować los

raft (raeft) s. tratwa; (slang): mnóstwo; v. spławiać na tratwie; robić tratwę

rafter (raefter) s. krokiew

rag (raeg) s. szmata; łachman; łupek; dachówka; v. (slang): besztać; dokuczać

rage (rejdż) s. szaleć; wściekać się; s. szał; wściekłość; namiętność

ragged (raegyd) adj. szmatławy; obdarty; podarty; poszarpany; kosmaty; zapuszczony; zaniedbany; wadliwy; chropowaty

raid (rejd) s. obława; nalot; najazd; v. urządzać obławę; najeżdżać ;dokonywać napadu

rail (rejl) s. poręcz; szyna; kolej; listwa; erekcja (slang); v. ogradzać poręczami; kłaść szyny; przewozić koleją; drwić; gorzko narzekać ;pomstować

rail in ('rejl,yn) v. przywozić koleją (materiały,towar)

rail off ('rejl,of) v. wywozić koleją (ludzi;towary etc.)

railing ('rejlyng)s. sztachety; ogrodzenie; poręcz;balustrada

railroad ('rejlroud) s. kolej; v. przewozić koleją; przepychać pospiesznie (np.ustawę); (slang) wpakowywać niesłusznie do więzienia

railway ('rejłłej) s. kolej;
tor kolejowy;tor na szynach
railway man('rejłłej,men) s.
kolejarz
rain (rejn) s. deszcz; v. pada
deszcz; spadac deszczem
rainbow ('rejn,boł) s. tęcza
raincoat ('rejnkout) s. płaszcz
nieprzemakalny
rainfall ('rejn,fo:l) s. opad;
ilosc opadów
rainproof ('rejn,pru:f) adj.
nieprzemakalny
rainy ('rejny) adj. deszczowy;
dżdżysty; mokry od deszczu
rainy day ('rejny,dej) exp.
czarna godzina
raise (rejz) v. podnosic;
wskrzeszac; wznosic; wynosic;
hodowac; wychowywac; wysuwac;
wytaczac;wzniecac; zrywac;
wywoływac; budzic; zbierac
(np. fundusze); wydobywac;
przerywac (np. oblężenie);
znosic (zakaz); s. podwyżka
(płac); podwyższenie
raisin ('rejzyn) s. rodzynek
rake (rejk) v. grabic; przegrze-
bac; grzebac; ostrzeliwac
(wzdłuż); obrzucac wzrokiem;
nachylac do tyłu; uganiac się
za zwierzyną; s. grabie; grab-
ki; rozpustnik
rake-off ('rejk,of) s. niele-
galna prowizja;łapówka
rake out ('rejk,aut) v. wygrzebywac; wygarniac (popiół etc.)
rakish ('rejkisz) adj. zgrabny;
rozpustny; hulaszczy;(pozornie)
szybki (okręt)(z wygladu)
rally ('raely) s. zbierac (się);
skupiac (sie); przyjsc do siebie; ochłonac; okrzepnąc; ulegac poprawie (giełda); żartowac
z kogos; s. zbiorka; wiec;
okrzepnięcie; ożywienie walki
bokserskiej; wymiana ciosow;
poprawa (konjunktury)
ram (raem) s. tryk; baran; ta-
ran; tłok; dźwig hydrauliczny;
bijak; v. uderzyc; zderzyc się;
ubijac; wtłaczac; bic taranem;
upychac;ugniatac;najechac;zanu-

ramble ('raemb) v. włoczyc się;
przechadzac się; pnąc się (np.
o bluszczu); mowic bez związku;
odbiegac od tematu;s.wędrówka
ramify ('raemyfaj) v. rozgałę-
ziac (się); odgałęzienie (się)
ramp (raemp) s. rampa; v. rzucac się; stawac na tylnych
łapach;opadac pochyło;szalec
rampart (raempa:rt) s. wał;
szaniec; v. umacniac (szancem)
ran (raen) v. zob. run
ranch (raencz) s. rancho (gospodarstwo hodowlane) v. prowadzic rancho(farmę etc.)
rancher ('raenczer) s. własciciel rancha
rancid ('raensyd) adj. zjełczały (tłuszcz, oliwa etc.)
rancor('raenker) s. uraza; za-
jadłosc; zawziętosc; złosc
random ('raendem) s. na chybił
trafił; adj. przypadkowy;
pierwszy lepszy;nie planowany
rang (raeng)v. zob. ring
range (rejndż) s. skala; zasięg;
rozpiętosc; nosnosc; strzelnica; pasmo; obszar; wędrówka;
pastwisko; piec kuchenny;
s. ustawiac; układac; klasyfikowac; wędrowac; nastawiac teleskop; miec zasięg; wstrzeli-
wac się; ciągnąc się; zaliczac
się;rozciągac się;sięgac;niesc
range finder ('rejndż,fajnder) s.
dalekomierz ; odległosciomierz
ranger (rejndżer) s. strażnik
lesny; policjant; komandos;
wędrowiec;desantowiec etc.
rank (raenk) s. ranga; stan;
stanowisko; v. ustawiac rzędem;
układac; klasyfikowac; zaszere-
gowac; przewyższac ranga; miec
rangę; adj. wybujały; zjełczały;
smierdzący; zupełny; jaskrawy;
obrzydliwy; sprosny;wierutny
ransack ('raensaek) v. przetrząsac; plądrowac;grzebac
ransom ('raensem) s. okup; zwolnienie za okupem; v. wykupic;
zwalniac za okupem
rant (raent)v.deklamowac z patosem;s.tyrada;bombastyczna mowa

rap (raep) v. dać klapsa; stukać; krytykować; s. klaps; kołatanie; nagana; zarzut; skazanie na więzienie; odrobina

rapacious (re'pejszes) adj. drapieżny;chciwy

rape (rejp) s. zgwałcenie (kobiety); zniewolenie; splądrowanie; uprowadzenie; v. gwałcić (kobietę); uprowadzać; plądrować;pogwałcić neutralność

rapid ('raepyd) adj. prędki; szybki; bystry; stromy

rapidity('raepydyty) s. szybkość; bystrość;rwący nurt(rzeki)

rapids ('raepyds) pl. progi (na rzece); wodospad

rapt (raept) adj. zaabsorbowany; zachwycony;urzeczony;oczarowany

rapture ('raepczer) s. zachwyt; uniesienie;wzięcie żywcem do nieba

rare (reer) adj. rzadki; niedopieczony (np. kotlet); na pół surowy;nie dosmażony;adv.rzadko

rarity ('reeryty) s. rzadkość

rascal ('raeskel) s. hultaj; łobuz; adj. hultajski

rascally ('raeskely) adj. hultajski; łobuzerski

rash (raesz) s. wysypka skórna; ulewa; powódż; adj. pochopny; popędliwy; nieprzemyślany

rasher ('raeszer) s. płatek (np. szynki)

rasp (raesp) s. raszpla; pilnik; zgrzytanie; v drapać; skrobać; drażnić; chrapliwie mówić

raspberry (ra:zbery) s. malina

rat (raet) s. szczur; łamistrajk; donosiciel; v. polować na szczury; zdradzać; donosić;zaprzedawać

rats (raets) pl. szczury; bzdura

rate (rejt) s. stopa; stosunek; proporcja; wysokość; poziom; szybkość; cena; stawka; opłata; podatek; stopień; klasa; v. szacować; oceniać; ustalać; zaliczać; opodatkować; zasługiwać; besztać; wymyślać

rate of exchange ('rejt of yks'czejndż) s. kurs wymiany

rate of interest (,rejt of 'yntryst) s. stopa procentowa

rather ('raedzer) adv. raczej; chętniej; dość; nieco; do pewnego stopnia;poniekąd;zamiast

ratify ('raetyfaj) v. zatwierdzać; ratyfikować

ration ('raeszyn) s. przydział; porcja; racja; v. racjonować; sprzedawać na kartki

rational ('raeszynl) adj. rozumny; rozsądny; racjonalny; wymierny;sensowny

rationalize ('raeszyne,lajz) v. racjonalizować; usprawiedliwiać

rattle ('raetl) v. grzechotać; szczekać; brzęczeć; stukać; trzaskać; terkotać; paplać wiersze; s. grzechotanie; terkot; stuk; paplanina; gaduła

rattler ('raetler) s. grzechotnik

rattlesnake ('raetl,snejk) s. grzechotnik

ravage ('raewydż) s. spustoszenie; zniszczenie; v. pustoszyć; niszczyć ;plądrować

rave (rejw) v. bredzić; majaczyć; szaleć; wściekać się; wyć; zachwycać się; v. wrzask; wycie; zaślepienie; przesadna pochwała (entzjastyczna)

raven (rejwn) s. kruk; adj. kruczy; ('raewen) s. grabież; łup; v. pożerać; szukać łupu; mieć szalony apetyt

ravenous ('raewynes) adj. wygłodniały; zgłodniały; żarłoczny; drapieżny

ravine (re'wi:n) s. parów;jar; wąwóz

raving (rejwyng) adj. bredzący; szalony; porywający (np. pięknością); s. atak furii; bredzenie; majaczenie

ravish ('raewysz) v. porywać (kobietę); gwałcić (kobietę)

raw (ro:) adj. surowy; otwarty (np. rana); wrażliwy; nieokrzesany; brutalny; nieprzyzwoity; s. gołe ciało; surówka; v. ocierać (skórę)

ray (rej) s. promień; promyk; (ryba) płaszczka; v. promieniować; naświetlać; prześwietlać wysyłać promienie(światła etc.)

rayon ('rejon) s. sztuczny jedwab

razor ('rejzer) z. brzytwa

razor blade ('rejzer'blejd) s.
żyletka; ostrze brzytwy

re (ri:) prep. w sprawie; tyczy; dotyczy; przedrostek :
znowu; od nowa

reach (ri:cz) v. osiągać; wyciągnąć (np. rękę) dosięgnąć;
dotrzec; docierać; sięgnąć;
s. sięgnięcie; zasięg; połać;
przestrzeń ;pobliże;granice

reach out ('ri:cz,aut) v. wyciągnąć (rękę etc.)

react (ri:'aekt) v. reagować;
oddziaływać; przeciwdziałać

reactor (ri:'aekter) s. reaktor (np. jądrowy)

read; read; read (ri:d; red;
red)

read (ri:d) v. czytać; tłumaczyć; interpretować

read out ('ri:d,aut) v. wydalać kogoś ;wyczytywać

readout ('ri:daut) s. odczyt
wyników komputera

read to ('ri:d tu) v. czytać
komuś

reader ('ri:der) s. czytelnik;
korektor; lektor; czytanka;
wypisy;recenzent(wydawnictwa)

readily ('redyly) adv. łatwo;
chętnie;ochoczo;bez tudu

readiness ('redynys) s. gotowość; pogotowie; obrotność;
ciętość; przytomność umysłu

reading ('ri:dyng)s. czytanie;
oczytanie; interpretacja;
lektura; czytelnictwo; adj.
czytający

readjust ('ri:e'dżast) v. dopasować na nowo

ready ('redy) adj. gotów; gotowy; przygotowany; adv.
w przygotowaniu; gotowy;
v. przygotowywać

ready-made ('redy'mejd) s.
konfekcja; adj. gotowy

ready-to-wear ('redy,tu'łeer)
s. odzież fabryczna pro-
dukcji

real (ryel) adj. prawdziwy;
rzeczywisty; realny; istotny;
prawdziwy;autentyczny;faktyczny

real estate ('ryel,ys'tejt) s.
nieruchomość; realność

realism ('ryelyzem) s. realizm

realistic ('ryelyst) s. adj.
realistyczny

reality ('ty'aelyty) s. rzeczywistość; realizm; prawdziwość

realization (,ryelaj'zejszyn)
s. realizacja; spełnienie;
wykonanie; spieniężenie; uświadomienie sobie

realize ('ry:e,lajz) v. urzeczywistnić; realizować; uprzytam-
niać; zdawać sobie sprawę;
uzyskiwać; zdobywać (majątek)

really ('ryely) adv. rzeczywis-
cie; naprawdę; doprawdy; faktycznie; istotnie

realm (relm) s. królestwo; dziedzina; sfera; zakres

realpolitik (rej'a:lpouly'tyk)
s. polityka egoistyczna

realtor ('ryelter) s. pośrednik
sprzedaży nieruchomości

realty ('ryelty) s. nieruchomość

reap (ry:p) v. żąć; zbierać
plony, owoce pracy etc.

reaper ('ry:per) s. żniwiarz:
żniwiarka

reappear ('ry:e'pier) v. zjawić
się ponownie;znowu ukazać się

rear (rier) s. tył; tyły; ustęp;
v. stawać dęba; hodować; wychowywać; wznosić (się); wybudować;
wystawiać

rear guard('rier,ga:rd) s. tylna
straż

rear-light ('rier,lajt) s. tylne
światło samochodu

rearm ('ry:'a:rm) v. ponownie
uzbrajać

rearmament ('ry:'a:rmement) s.
remilitaryzacja

rearmost (rie:r,moust) adj.
końcowy ;ostatni

rearview mirror ('rier,wju:'-
'myrer) s. (tylne) lusterko
w samochodzie (do sprawdzania
ruchu za samochodem)

rearrange ('ry:erejndż) v.
przestawiać; zmieniać (porządek);poprawić(fryzurę etc.)
rearwards ('rierłedz) adv.
wstecz;ku tyłowi; na tył
reason ('ri:zn) s. rozum; powód; uzasadnienie; motyw; przesłanka; rozsądek; v. rozumować;
rozważać; wnioskować; rozprawiać; przekonywać; dowodzić
reason out ('ri:zn,aut) v.
przemyślać;wrozumować;dociekać
reason with ('ri:zn,łys) v.
przekonywać kogoś
reasonable ('ri:znebl) adj.
rozumny; rozsądny; umiarkowany; słuszny; racjonalny
reassure (,ry:a'szuer) v. zapewniać; upewniać; ubezpieczać
na nowo; uspakajać; przywracać
zaufanie;upewniać na nowo
reassuring (,ry:a'szueryng)
adj. uspokajający
rebate (ry'bejt) s. rabat;
zwrot (części kwoty); v. u-
dzielać rabatu; potrącać (z rachunku);zamortyzować;przytępiać
rebel ('rebel) s. buntownik;
v. buntować się; adj. zbuntowany; buntowniczy
rebellion (ry'beljen) s. bunt;
powstanie
rebellious (ry'beljes) adj.
zbuntowany; buntowniczy; niesforny;oporny;zbuntowany
rebirth (ry'be:rg) s. odrodzenie;odżywanie
re-book ('ry:buk) v. zamawiać
na nowo (program teatralny;
bilety lotnicze etc.)
rebound (ry'baund) s. odbicie;
odskok; rykoszet; v. odskaki-
wać; odbijać (się) (sobie na
kimś)
rebuff (ry'baf) s. ofuknięcie;
odrzucenie; v. ofuknąć; dać
odprawę;odesłać z kwitkiem
rebuild ('ry:byld) v. odbudowywać; przebudowywać
rebuke (ry'bju:k) s. nagana;
v. upominać; łajać
recall (ry'ko:l) v. odwoływać;
przypominać (sobie);wycofywać;
cofać (obietnicę);s.nakaz powrotu

recap ('ry:kaep) s. opona ponownie gumowana; v. ponownie
wulkanizować opony; powtarzać
dla podsumowania
recapture (,'ri:'kaepczer) v.
odzyskać; s. odzyskanie
recede (ry'si:d) v. cofać się;
oddalać sie; maleć; słabnąć
receipt (ry'si:t) s. pokwitowanie; odbiór; recepta
receive (ry'si:w) v. otrzymy-
wać; dostawać; odbierać; przyjmować (np. gości)
receiver (ry'si:wer) s. odbiornik (radiowy); słuchawka (telefoniczna); odbiorca; syndyk;
zarządca upadłości
recent ('ri:snt) adj. niedawny;
świeży; nowy
recently ('ri:sntly) adv. niedawno; świeżo; ostatnio;wspól-
cześnie
reception (ry'sepszyn) s. przyjęcie; odbiór; recepcja
reception desk (ry'sepszyn,desk)
s. biuro do przyjmowania inte-
resantów;portiernia;biuro przyjęć
receptionist (ry'sepszynyst) s.
recepcjonistka; sekretarka
przyjmująca klientów;portier
recess (ry'ses) s. przerwa
(między lekcjami); ferie;
wgłębienie; nisza; wnęka;
v. odraczać; wkładać do wnęki;
robić wnękę;rozjeżdżać się na ferie
recession (ry'seszyn) s. cof-
nięcie; recesja (gospodarcza);
wgłębienie; wnęka:kryzys;zastój
recipe ('rysypy) s. przepis;
recepta
recipient (ry'sypjent) adj. od-
biorczy; s. odbiorca; zdobywca
nagrody; osoba obdarowana
reciprocal (ry'syprekel) adj.
wzajemny; odwrotny; s. odwrotność (w matematyce)
recital (ry'sajtl) s. przedstawienie; opowiadanie; recytacja;
koncert;deklamowanie utworu
recite (ry'sajt) s. recytować
(wiersz); wyliczać
reckless ('reklys) adj. (nie-
bezpiecznie) lekkomyślny;
nieuważający;na oślep;wariacki
brawurowy;szaleńczy;zuchowaty

reckon ('reken) v. liczyć; sądzić myśleć że;polegać na
reckon up ('reken,ap) v. zliczać;zsumować; podsumowywać
reckon with ('reken,łyg) v.
liczyć się (z kimś)
reckoning ('rekenyŋg) s. oblicza-
nie (położenia); rachuba; obrachunek;kalkulacja;rozliczenie
reclaim (ry'klejm) v. odzyskiwać (pod uprawę); użyźniac;
przerabiać odpadki; wyprowadzać z (zaniedbania; błędu
etc.);zażądać zwrotu;dochodzić
recline (ry'klajn) v. kłaść się;
wyciągać się; złożyć (np. głowę);spoczywać poł leżąc
recognition (,rekeg'nyszyn) s.
rozpoznanie; uznanie; pozdrowienie; dowód uznania
recognize ('rekeg,najz) v. rozpoznawać; pozdrowić; uznawać;
przyznawać; udzielać (głosu)
recoil (ry'kojl) v. wzdrygać się;
cofać się; kopać (np. kolbą);
odskoczyć; odbijać; s. odskok;
odrzut; odbicie; wzdrygnięcie
się
recollect (reke'lekt) v. wspomi-
nać; przypominać sobie; zbierać
na nowo;przypominać sobie z trudem
recollection (,reke'lekszyn) s.
wspomnienie; pamięć
recommend (reke'mend) v. polecać;
zalecać;dobrze świadczyć
recommendation(,rekemen'dejszyn)
s. polecenie; zlecenie
recompense ('rekem,pens) v. odpłacać; dawać odszkodowanie;
s. wynagrodzenie; zadośćuczynienie;odszkodowanie;rekompensata
reconcile ('rekensajl) v. godzić
(sprzeczności); zażegnać (spór);
pojednać;pogodzić się
reconciliation (,reken,syly'ejszyn) s. pojednanie; pogodzenie
reconsider (,ri:ken'syder) v.
ponownie rozważyć; reasumować
reconstruct (,ri:ken'strakt) v.
odbudowywać; odtwarzać
reconstruction ('ri:ken'strakszyn) s. rekonstrukcja; odbudowa

record ('reko:rd) v. zapisywać;
notować; rejestrować; zazna-
czać; nagrywać; s. zapiska;
archiwum; rejestracja; dokument; przeszłość (czyjaś); pamięć o kimś; nagranie; rekord
recorder (ry'ko:rder) s. re-
gistrator; aparat zapisujący;
pisak;pisarz archiwista
record holder ('reko:rd,houlder)
s. rekordzista; mistrz
recording ('reko:rdyŋg) s. nagranie (płyta)
record player ('reko:rd,plejer)
s. adapter
recourse (ry'ko:rs) s. ucieka-
nie się (ratunek)
recover (ry'kawer) v. odzyskać;
nadrabiać; powetować sobie;
uzyskać; przywracać; wyzdrowieć;
ochłonąć; przyjść do siebie
recovery (ry'kawery) s. odzyskanie (pozycji); wyzdrowienie
poprawa (gospodarcza)
recreation (,rekry'ejszyn) s.
rozrywka; zabawa; odtworzenie
recruit (ry'kru:t) s. rekrut;
poborowy; v. werbować; uzupełniać (stan zatrudnienia)
rectangle ('rektaeŋgl) s.
prostokąt; a.prostokątny
rectify ('rektyfy) v. prostować
(np. błąd); poprawiać (np.
plan); usuwać (np. nadużycia)
rector ('rekter) s. proboszcz;
rektor
rectory ('rektery) s. probostwo
recur (ry'ke:r) v. powtarzać
się; przypominać (się); nawiązy-
wać do czegoś (wielokrotnie)
recurrent (ry'karent) adj. po-
wracający; nawracający
red (red). adj. czerwony;
s. czerwień; lewicowiec; komunista;radykał (skrajny);forsa(sl.)
red-bait('redbejt) v. oskarżać
o komunizm (USA)
red-blooded('red,bladyd) adj.
męski; krzepki;jurny
redden ('reden) v. zaczerwie-
nić się;zarumienić się
reddish ('redysz) adj. czerwo-
nawy

redeem (ry'di:m) v. wykupywać;
okupywać; wybawiać; zbawiać;
odkupić; zamienić;kompensować
redemption (ry'dempszyn) s.
wykup; okupienie; odkupienie;
wybawienie;umorzenie;zbawienie
red-handed ('red'haendyd) adj.
splamiony krwią; exp. na gorącym uczynku
red letter day ('red'leter dej)
s. dzień specjalny; dzień
świąteczny
redouble (ry'dabl) v. podwoić
(się); zwijać się
reduce (ry'dju:s) v. zmniejszać (się); chudnąć; redukować; ograniczać; obniżać; dostosować; sprowadzać; doprowadzać; rozcieńczać; osłabiać;
odtleniać; wytapiać
reduction (ry'dakszyn) s.
zmniejszenie; redukcja; obniżka; sprowadzenie; dostosowanie; odtlenianie; wytapianie
reed (ri:d) s. trzcina; słoma;
fujarka; strzała; płocha
tkacka; stroik (muzyczny)
reeducation ('ry:edju'kejszyn)
s. przeszkolenie ponowne
reef (ri:f) s. rafa; skała podwodna; ref; v. refować
reek (ri:k) s. odor; para; dym;
v. śmierdzieć; parować; dymić;
wędzić; ociekać (krwią)
reel (ri:l) s. szpula; cewka;
rolka; chwianie się; kręcenie
się; v. nawijać; odwijać; rozwijać; recytować; chwiać się;
zataczać się; kręcić się; dostawać zawrotu głowy; dawać zawrót
głowy;zachwiać się na nogach
reel off ('ri:l,of) v. odwijać
reel up ('ri:l,ap) v. nawijać
reelect (ri:y'lekt) v. ponownie wybierać
reenter ('ri:'enter) v. ponownie wchodzić (w posiadanie etc.)
reentry ('ri:'entry) s. ponowne wejście;rewindykacja
re-establish (,ry:ys'taeblysz)
v. ponownie: zakładać; ustanawiać; ustalać; wprowadzać

refer (ry'fe:r) v. odsyłać; po-
wiązywać; skierować; odwoływać;
cytować; odnosić się; dotyczyć;
powoływać się
referee (refe'ri:) s. sędzia
sportowy; rozjemca; v. sędzio-
wać
reference ('refrens) s. odsyłacz; odnośnik; odwoływanie
się; aluzja; informacja; referencja; stosunek; związek;
wzgląd;przelotna wzmianka
reference book ('referens,bu:k)
s. tekst podręczny;podręcznik
reference library ('referens
laj'brery) s. biblioteka podręczna naukowo-informacyjna
refill (ry:'fyl) s. ponowne;
napełnienie; wypełnienie; nowy
zapas; v. ponownie napełniać,
wkładać,zapełniać etc.
refine (ry'fajn) v. oczyszczać;
rafinować; wysubtelniać; rozprawiać subtelnie
refinement (ry'fajnment) s.
rafinowanie; wyrafinowanie;
subtelność; wytworność
refinery (ry'fajnery) s. rafineria
reflect (ry'flekt) v. odbijać;
odzwierciadlać; rozmyślać; zastanawiać się; krytykować;
przynosić (zaszczyt; ujmę)
reflection (ry'flekszyn) s. odbicie; odzwierciedlenie; odbicie światła; zarzut; rozwaga;
namysł;wzmianka;pomysł;wstyd
reflex ('ry:fleks) s. odruch;
refleks; odbicie; odzwierciedlenie; adj. refleksyjny; odbity; wygięty; v. poddawać
refleksom; wyginać wstecz
reflexive (ry'fleksyw) adj.
odbijający; pełen zadumy;
refleksyjny
reform (ry'fo:rm) v. reformować;
poprawić; usuwać; ulegać refor-
mie; s. reforma; poprawa
reformation (,refer'mejszyn) s.
reformacja; poprawa
reformer (ry'fo:rmer) s. refor-
mator(moralności,warunków etc.)

refract (ry'fraekt) v. załamywać światło;wyginać promień światła

refractory (ry'fraektery) adj. oporny; uporczywy; krnąbrny; odporny; ogniotrwały

refrain (ry'frejn) v. powstrzymywać się; s. refren

refresh (ry'fresh) v. odświeżyć; wzmacniać; pokrzepiać

refreshment (ry'freszment) s. odpoczynek; wytchnienie; odświeżenie; zakąska

refrigerator (ry'frydże,rejter) s. lodówka; chłodnia

refuel ('ry:'fjuel) v. zaopatrzyc w paliwo; dodać paliwa

refuge ('refju:dż) s. schronienie; azyl;przytułek;v.schronić się

refugee (,refju'dżi:) s. zbieg; uchodźca; uciekinier

refund (ry'fand) s. zwrot; spłata; v. zwracać pieniądze

refusal (ry'fju:zel) s. odmowa; prawo opcji; wbijanie do oporu

refuse (ry'fju:z) v. odmawiać; odrzucać; adj. odpadowy; s. odpadki; rupiecie

refute (ry'fju:t) v. zbijać (np. twierdzenie)

regain (ry'gejn) v. odzyskać; wrócić (do zdrowia)

regard (ry'ga:rd) v. spoglądać; zważać; uważać; dotyczyć; s. wzgląd; spojrzenie; szacunek; uwaga;pozdrowienia;ukłony

regarding (ry'ga:rdyng) prep. odnośnie;co się tyczy;w sprawie

regardless (ry'ga:rdlys) adv. w każdym razie; adj. nie zważający; bez względu (na kłopoty etc.);nie licząc się(z wydatkami)

regard of (ry'ga:rd,ow) exp. co się tyczy; w sprawie etc.

regent ('ri:dżent) s. regent; opiekun; członek zarządu

regime (ry'żi:m) s. ustrój; reżym; tryb życia; system; rządy

regiment ('redżyment) s. pułk; zastęp; v. organizować; koszarować; wcielać do pułku

region ('ri:dżen) s. okolica; sfera; rejon; obszar; dzielnica

register ('redżyster) v. rejestrować; zapamiętywać; wysyłać polecony list; prowadzić rejestr; wstrzeliwać się; wyrażać minami

registered letter ('redżysterd, ,leter) s. list polecony

registration (,redzys'trejszyn) s. rejestracja; meldunek; ilość zarejestrowana

regret (ry'gret) s. ubolewanie; żal; v. żałować czegoś

regrettable (ry'gretebl) adj. godny ubolewania

regular ('regjuler) adj. regularny; stały; zawodowy; poprawny; przepisowy; s. regularny (żołnierz; ksiądz etc.); stały gość; wierny partyjnik

regularity (,regju'laeryty) s. regularność; systematyczność

regulate ('regjulejt) v. regulować;przystosowywać do wymogów

regulation (,regju'lejszyn) s. przepis; regulowanie; adj. przepisowy; zwykły

rehearsal (ry'he:rsel) s. próba; powtarzanie

rehearse (ry'he:rs) v. odbywać próbę; powtarzać

reign (rejn) v. panować; władać; s. władza; panowanie

rein (rejn) v. kierować wodzami; trzymać na wodzach

reins (rejns) pl. wodze

reindeer ('rejn.dier) s. renifer

reinforce (,ri:yn'force) v. wzmocnić;popierać;dodać sił

reject (ry'dżekt) v. odrzucić; odpalić; zwracać; ('rydżekt) s. wybrakowany towar; niezdatny do wojska;coś odrzuconego

rejection (ry'dżekszyn) s. odrzucenie; odmowa; wybrakowany towar;oblanie studenta;odkosz

rejoice (ry'dżojs) v. radować; cieszyć się; weselić się

rejoicing (ry'dżojsyng) s. radość;uradowanie;adj.uradowany

rejoin ('ri:dżoyn) v. ponownie łączyć (się); zestawiać połamane części; odpowiadać na zarzut

relapse (ry'laeps) s. nawrot;
pogorszenie; v. ponownie popadać; zapadać z powrotem

relate (ry'lejt) v. opowiadać;
referować; łączyć się

related (ry'lejtyd) adj. bliski;
spokrewniony; spowinowacony;
związany;pokrewny;powinowaty

relation (ry'lejszyn) s. sprawozdanie; opowiadanie; stosunek; związek; pokrewieństwo;
powinowactwo; krewny

relationship (ry'lejszynszyp)
s. stosunek; pokrewieństwo;
powinowactwo;zależność

relative ('reletyw) adj.
względny; stosunkowy; podrzędny; zależny; dotyczący;
adv. odnośnie; w sprawie;
s. krewny; zaimek względny

relax (ry'laeks) v. odprężać
(się); osłabnąć; rozluźniać
się; łagodnieć; odpoczywać

relaxation (,ry:laek'sejszyn)
n. odprężenie; odpoczynek;
rozrywka; złagodzenie

relay(ry'lej) s. bieg rozstawny; wzmacniacz;v.przekazywać;
zmieniać (tor);kłaść na nowo

relay race (re'lej,rejs) s.
bieg rozstawny; bieg sztafe-
towy

release (ry'li:z) v. wypuszczać; uwalniać; zwalniać;
s. zwolnienie; uwolnienie;
puszczenie (do druku); spust;
wyzwalacz;wypuszczenie(filmu)

relent (ry'lent) v. łagodnieć;
mięknąć;dać się wzruszyć

relentless (ry'lentlys) adj.
nieugięty; bezlitosny; nieprzejednany;nieustępliwy;srogi

relevant ('relewent) adj.
istotny; trafny; na miejscu;
należący do rzeczy

reliability (ry,laje'bylyty) s.
rzetelność; solidność; pewność

reliable (ry'lajebl) adj. pewny; solidny; rzetelny

reliance (ry'lajens) s. zaufanie; otucha

reliant (ry'lajent) adj. ufny
w siebie;liczący na kogoś;zależ-
ny od czegoś

relic ('relyk) n. zabytek; relikwia;pozostałość;resztka

relief (ry'li:f) n. odprężenie;
ulga; urozmaicenie; zapomoga;
pomoc; zmiana (np. warty);
płaskorzeźba;uwypuklenie

relieve (ry'li:w) v. nieść pomoc, ulgę; ulżyć (sobie);
oddać mocz; ożywić; zmieniać
wartę; zluzować; uwypuklić
(na tle czegoś);uwydatnić

religion (ry'lydżyn) s. religia;
obrządek; wyznanie; zakon

religious (ry'lydżes) adj. pobożny; religijny; zakonny;
s. zakonnik; zakonnica

relinquish (ry'lynkłysz) v. porzucać; wyrzekać się czegoś;
zaniechać; zrzekać się; rezygnować; wypuścić coś z rąk

relish ('relysz) s. smak; posmak;
przyprawa; przysmak; urok; zamiłowanie; v. smakować w czyms;
czynić smaczniejszym; przyprawiać; mieć dobry smak; być
przyjemnym;dodawać smaku

reluctance (ry'laktens) s. niechęć; opór(magnetyczny);wstręt

reluctant (ry'laktent) adj. niechętny; oporny

rely on (ry'laj,on) v. polegać
na czyms lub kims ;liczyć na

remain (ry'mejn) v. pozostawać

remains (ry'mejns) pl. pozosta-
łości; resztki; przeżytki;
zwłoki; szczątki

remainder (ry'mejnder) s. reszta; pozostałość; remanent

remand (ry'maend) v. odsyłać
(do niższej instancji lub więzienia); s. odesłanie do
więzienia; człowiek odesłany
z powrotem

remark (ry'ma:rk) v. zauważyć;
zrobić uwagę; s. uwaga

remarkable (ry'ma:rkebl) adj.
wybitny; godny uwagi

remedy ('remydy) s. lekarstwo;
środek; rada; v. leczyć; za-
radzać ;naprawiać

remember (ry'member) v. pamiętać;
przypominać; pozdrawiać; modlić
się za kogoś;mieć w pamięci

remembrance (ry'membrens) s.
wspomnienie; pamiątka; pamięc; pozdrowienie;ukłony

remind (ry'majnd) v. przypomi-
nac coś komuś;przypomnieć

reminder (ry'majnder) s. przypomnienie; upomnienie; ponaglenie;ktoś przypominający

reminiscent (,remy'nysnt) adj.
przypominający; wspominający;
pełen wspomnień

remiss (ry'mys) adj. niedbały;
ospały; niechlujny

remit (ry'myt) s. przekazywać
(pieniądze); darować (dług);
odpuszczać (grzechy); odsyłać; przywracać; łagodzić;
łagodnieć; słabnąc

remitance (ry'mytens) s. przesyłka pieniężna; wypłata

remnant ('remnent) s. resztka;
pozostałość; ślad czegoś

remodel (ry'modl) v. przerabiać; odnowić; przemodelować

remonstrate ('remenstrejt) v.
protestować

remorse (ri'mo:rs) s. wyrzuty
sumienia; skrupuły

remorseless (ri'mo:rslys) adj.
bezlitosny ;nie skruszony

removal (ry'mu:wl) v. usunięcie; przeprowadzka

remove (ry'mu:w) v. usuwać;
przewozić; zdejmować; przeprowadzać się; opuszczać;
s. przeprowadzka; odległość;
stopień;oddalenie

remover (ry'mu:wer) s. usuwacz
(plam); środek do usuwania

renaissance (ry'nesens) s. odrodzenie;renesans;a.renesansowy

rend; rent; rent (rend; rent;
rent)

rend (rend) v. drzeć; targać;
wydzierać; urągać; rozdzierać

render ('render) v. uczynić;
zrobić; oddawać; okazywać;
składać; wydawać; płacić; odpłacać; oczyszczać; wytapiać;
tynkować; s. odpłata (np.
w naturze); pierwsza warstwa
tynku

rendezvous ('ra:ndy,wu:) s.
randka; umówione spotkanie;
miejsce spotkań

renew (ry'nu:) v. odnawiać; ponawiać; wznawiać; odświeżać;
prolongować

renewal (ry'nu:el) s. odnowienie (np. kontraktu)

renounce (ry'nauns) v. zrzekać
się; zrezygnować; wyrzekać się;
wypowiadać; odstępować; nie-
uznawać

renovate (ry'nowejt) v. odnowić;
naprawić

renown (ry'naun) s. sława; rozgłos; pogłoska

renowned (ry'naund) adj. sławny

rent 1. (rent) v. zob. rend

rent 2. (rent) s. komorne;
czynsz; renta; najem; rozdarcie; szczelina; rozłam; parów;
v. wynajmować; dzierżawić; pobierać czynsz; być wynajmowanym

rental ('rentl) s. czynsz; komorne; wypożyczanie; adj. czynszowy

rental agency ('rentl'ejdżensy)
s. biuro wynajmu (narzędzi;
mieszkań etc)

rent free ('rent'fri:) adj.
wolny od opłaty czynszowej

repair (ry'peer) v. pójść;
uczęszczać; naprawiać; reperować; remontować; powetować;
wynagrodzić; s. naprawa; remont; stan

repair shop (ry'peer,shop) s.
warsztat naprawy

reparation (repa'rejszyn) s.
naprawa; remont; odszkodowanie

repartee (repa:r'ti:) s. ripos-
ta; cięta odpowiedź; odcina-
nie się

repay (ry:'pej) v. spłacić;
zwrócić; wynagrodzić; odwza-
jemnić się; oddać

repeat (ry:'pi:t) v. powtarzać
(się); repetować; odbijać się;
robić powtórkę; robić ponownie;
odtwarzać; s. powtórka; powtórzenie; powtórne zamówienie
a.powtórny;wielokrotny

repel (ry'pel) v. odpierać;
odrzucać; odtrącać; budzić
odrazę,niechęć, wstręt etc.
repent (ry'pent) v. żałować
repentance (ry'pentens) s.
skrucha; żal
repentant (ry'pentent) adj.
żałujący; pełen skruchy
repetition (,repy'tyszyn) s.
powtórzenie; powtórka
replace (ry'plejs) v. zastępować; zwracać; oddawać; umieszczać z powrotem; przywrócić;
wymienić
replacement (ry'plejsment) s.
zastępstwo; zastępca; zastąpienie; wymiana (części)
replenish (ry'plenysz) v. ponownie napełniać; wypełniać;
uzupełniać
replay (ry'plej) v. ponownie
rozgrywać; ('ry:plej) s. ponowna rozgrywka
reply (ry'plaj) v. odpowiadać;
s. odpowiedź
report (ry'po:rt) v. opowiadać;
meldować; dawać sprawozdanie;
zdawać sprawę; pisać sprawozdanie; referować; s. raport;
sprawozdanie; komunikat;
opinia; huk; wybuch; pogłoska
reporter (ry'po:rter) s. dzien-
nikarz; sprawozdawca; reporter
repose (ry'pouz) s. odpoczynek;
spokój; v. odpoczywać; spoczywać; polegać; opierać; pokładać
represent (,repry'zent) v.
przedstawiać; reprezentować;
wyobrażać; grać (kogoś)
representation (,repryzen'tejszyn) s. przedstawicielstwo;
reprezentacja; przedstawienie;
wyobrażenie
representative (,repry'zente-
tyw) adj. przedstawiający;
reprezentujący; wyobrażający;
s. przedstawiciel; reprezentant (poseł na sejm)
repress (ry'pres) v. tłumić;
hamować; powstrzymywać; po-
skromić

reprieve (ry'pri:w) v. zawieszać; odraczać; dawać odroczenie; s. odroczenie; darowanie,
zmiana kary (śmierci)
reprimand ('reprymaend) v. karcić; udzielać nagany; s. nagana
reproach (ry'proucz) v. robić
wyrzuty; wymawiać; s. wyrzut;
zarzut; wymówka
reproachful (ry'prouczful) adj.
pełen wyrzutu
reproduce (,rypre'du:s) v. odtwarzać;reprodukować; rozmnażać; wznawiać
reproduction (,ri:pre'dakszyn)
s. reprodukcja; rozmnażanie
się; płodzenie
reproof (ry'pru:f) s. nagana
reprove (ry'pru:w) v. ganić
reptant ('reptent) adj. pełzający
reptile ('reptajl) s. gad; płaz;
gadzina; adj. pełzający; ga-
dzinowy
republic (ry'pablyk) s. republika; rzeczpospolita
republican (ry'pablyken) adj.
republikański; s. republikanin
repugnance (ry'pagnens) s. odraza; niechęć; niezgodność;
sprzeczność
repugnant (ry'pagnent) adj.
odrażający; oporny; sprzeczny;
niezgodny
repulse (ry'pals) v. odpierać;
odrzucać; odtrącać; s. odparcie; odrzucenie; odmowa
repulsive (ry'palsyw) adj. odrażający; wstrętny; odpychający;budzący odrazę
reputable ('repjutebl) adj.
szanowany; zaszczytny
reputation (,repju'tejszyn) s.
reputacja; sława; dobre imię
repute (ry'pju:t) s. reputacja;
sława; v. uważać za coś
request (ry'kłest) s. prośba;
życzenie; żądanie; zapotrzebowanie; v. prosić o pozwolenie;
upraszać ;poprosić o przysługę
require (ry'kłajer) v. żądać;
nakazywać;wymagać;być wymaganym

required (ry'kɫajerd) adj.
obowiązkowy;wymagany;żądany
requirement (ry'kɫajerment) s.
wymaganie; zadanie; potrzeba
requisite ('rekɫyzyt) adj. wy-
magany; s. rzecz konieczna,
potrzebna; rekwizyt
requisition (,rekɫy'zyszyn) s.
zadanie; nakaz; zapotrzebowanie; v. wydawać zapotrzebowanie; zapotrzebowywać; rekwiro-
wać;zarządać dostaw
requite (ry'kɫajt) v. odwzajemniać się;wynagradzać;zemścić się
rescue ('reskju:) v. ratować;
wybawiać; odbijać z więzienia;
s. ratunek; odbicie z więzienia; odebranie przemocą
research (ry'se:rcz) s. poszukiwanie; badanie
researcher (ry'se:rczer) s. badacz (naukowy etc.);badaczka
resemblance (ry'zemblens) s.
podobieństwo
resemble (ry'zembl) v. być po-
dobnym (z wyglądu)
resent (ry'zent) v. czuć urazę
resentful (ry'zentful) adj.
urażony;obrażony;zawzięty
resentment (ry'zentment) s.
uraza;złość;oburzenie;obraza
reservation (,rezer'wejszyn) s.
zastrzeżenie; zarezerwowanie;
miejsce zarezerwowane; rezerwat (np. indiański); rezerwa;
zapas;ograniczenie
reserve (ry'ze:rw) v. odkładać;
zastrzegać; zarezerwować;
s. rezerwa; zapas; rezerwat;
zastrzeżenie; warunek
reserved (ry'ze:rwd) adj.zare-
zerwowany; powściągliwy; pełen rezerwy;z rezerwą;zastrzeżo-
ny
reservoir ('reserwła:r) s.
zbiornik; zbiór; pokład kopalniany; v. składać w zbiorniku
reside (ry'zajd) v. mieszkać;
tkwić;spoczywać w;osadzać się
residence ('rezydens) s. miejsce zamieszkania; pobyt (stały)
residence permit ('rezydens,-
per'myt) s. prawo pobytu

resident ('rezydent) s. stały
mieszkaniec; adj. zamieszkały;
umiejscowiony;zamieszkujący
residue ('rezydju:) s. reszta;
pozostałość;reszta spadkowa
resign (ry'zajn) v. zrzekać się;
wyrzekać się; godzić się z losem
resignation (,rezyg'nejszyn) s.
dymisja; zrzeczenie się; wyrzeczenie się;pogodzenie się(z losem)
resigned (ry'zajnd) adj. zrezyg-
nowany;w stanie spoczynku
resin ('rezyn) s. żywica; v. zaprawiać żywicą
resist (ry'zyst) v. opierać się;
stawiać opór; być odpornym;
powstrzymywać się
resistance (ry'zystens) s. opór;
sprzeciw; wytrzymałość; odporność; opornica;a.oporowy
resistant (ry'zystent) adj. odporny; opierający się; s. coś
lub ktoś odporny,opierający się
resolute ('rezelu:t)adj. rezolutny; śmiały; zdecydowany
resolution (,rese'lu:szyn) s.
uchwała; postanowienie; rezo-
lucja; śmiałość; rozłożenie;
rozwiązanie;rozkład(sił)
resolve (ry'zolw) s. postanowienie; decyzja; stanowczość;
v. rozkładać; rozwiązywać;
uchwalać; decydować; postanawiać; usuwać;przemieniać;skłaniać
resolved (ry'solwd) adj. zdecydowany; śmiały
resonance ('resnens) s. oddźwięk;
odgłos ; rezonans
resonant ('reznent) adj. rezonu-
jący; rozbrzmiewający
resort (ry'zo:rt) v. uciekać się;
uczęszczać; s. uzdrowisko;
uczęszczanie; ucieczka; ucieka-
nie się; ratunek; wyjście
resort to (ry'zo:rt,tu) v. uciekać się do...
resound (ry'zaund) v. rozbrzmiewać; odbijać; opiewać; obiegać;
wypowiadać się;odbijać się echem
resource (ry'so:rs) s. zasoby;
środki; bogactwa; zaradność;
pomysłowość;zasoby naturalne

resourceful (ry'so:rsful) adj.
zaradny; pomysłowy
respect (rys'pękt) v. szanować; dotyczyć; zważać;
s. wzgląd; szacunek; poważanie;związek;łaczność;pozdrowie-nia
respectable (rys'pektebl) adj.
chwalebny; godny szacunku;
poważny; pokaźny
respectful (rys'pektful) adj.
pełen szacunku
respectfully (rys'pektfuly)
adv. z poważaniem; z uszanowa-
niem
respecting (rys'pektyŋg) prep.
odnośnie do...
respective (rys'pektyw) adj.
odpowiedni;poszczególny
respectively (rys'pektywly)
adv. odpowiednio; każdemu
z osobna;kolejno
respiration (,respy'rejszyn)
s. oddech; oddychanie
respite ('respajt) s. wytchnienie (krótkie); odroczenie;
v. odraczać (stracenie); przynosić (krótką) ulgę
resplendent (rys'plendent) adj.
błyszczący silnie;jasny
respond (rys'pond) v. odpowiadać; reagować; być czułym
respondent (rys'pondent) adj.
odpowiadający; wrażliwy;
s. pozwany; obrońca
response (rys'pons) s. odpowiedź; odzew; reakcja; oddźwięk;odezwanie się
responsibility (rys,ponse'bylyty) s. odpowiedzialność
responsible (rys'ponsebl) adj.
odpowiedzialny (wobec; przed)
rest (rest) s. odpoczynek;
spokój; przerwa; przestanek;
podpórka; pomieszczenie;
schronienie; reszta; v. spoczywać; odpoczywać; dawać odpoczynek; uspokoić; być spo-
kojnym; podpierać się; polegać
restaurant ('resterent) s. restauracja ;jadłodajnia
restful ('restful) adj. spokojny; uspokajający;wypoczęty

restless ('restlys) adj. niespokojny; bezsenny;niesforny
restlessness ('restlysnys) s.
niepokój ;zniecierpliwienie
restoration (,reste'rejszyn) s.
odnowienie; rekonstrukcja; restytucja; odtworzenie
restore (rys'to:r) v. przywracać; uleczyć; odnawiać; restau-
rować; restytuować; zwracać;
rekonstruować; odtwarzać
restrain (rys'trejn) v. powstrzymywać; powściągać; krępować;
ograniczać;trzymać w ryzach
restraint (rys'trejnt) s. skre-
powanie; uwięzienie; zamknięcie w szpitalu psychiatrycznym;
wstrzemięźliwość; umiar
restrict (rys'trykt) v. ograniczać do; zamykać w (granicach)
restriction (rys'trykszyn) s.
ograniczenie
rest room('rest,rum) s. ustęp;
toaleta
result (ry'zalt) s. rezultat;
wynik; v. wynikać; dawać w wyniku;wypływać;pochodzić
result in (ry'zalt,yn) v. kończyć się na
resultant (ry'zaltent) adj. wy-
nikający;(np. siła) wypadkowa
resume (ry'zju:m) v. wznawiać;
ponownie podejmować; obejmować;
zajmować; odzyskiwać; ciagnąć
dalej; streszczać;odzyskać
resumption (ry'zampszyn) s.
wznowienie; odzyskanie; podjęcie
na nowo;powrót do czegoś
resurrection (,reze'rekszyn) s.
odżycie; zmartwychwstanie;
wskrzeszenie;wznowienie(zwyczaju)
retail ('ri:tejl) s. detal; adj.
detaliczny; v. sprzedawać de-
talicznie; szczegółowo opowiadać ;adv.detalicznie;a.detaliczny
retailer (ri:'tejler) s. sklepikarz; detalista; plotkarz
retain (ry'tejn) v. zatrzymywać;
zapamiętywać; zgodzić (do pracy);zachowywać(tradycje)
retaliate (ry'taeliejt) v. od-
wzajemniac się; brać odwet

retaliation (ry,taely'ejszyn)
s. odwet;zemsta;odpłata

retell ('ri:'tel) v. ponownie
opowiedziec;powtorzyc

retention (ry'tenszyn) s. zatrzymanie (np. moczu); zdol-
nosc zatrzymywania; pamięc

retinue ('retynu:) s. orszak;
swita;czeladz;poczet(dostojnika)

retire (ry'tajer) v. wycofywac
(się); isc na spoczynek;
pensjonowac;s.sygnał odwrotu

retired (ry'tajerd) adj. emery-
towany; ustronny;odosobniony

retirement (ry'tajerment) s.
przejscie w stan spoczynku;
ustronie; odosobnienie; wy-
cofanie(weksla);odwrót

retort (ry'to:rt) v. odpłacac
się; odcinac się; odparowac;
ripostowac; s. retorta; ri-
posta; odwet; odwrócenie
(oskarżenia); cięta odpowiedz

retrace (ry'trejs) v. odtwo-
rzyc; przypomniec sobie; badac początek   (1)

retrace (ry:'trejs) v. ponownie liniowac; kopiowac   (2)

retract (ry'traekt) v. cofnąc
się; odwołac; chowac się;
wciagac(sie)(pazury)

retreat (ry'tri:t) v. cofac
się; s. odwrót; wycofanie się
w zacisze; kryjówka; odosobnienie; przytułek;ustronie

retribution (,retry'bju:szyn)
s. odpłata; kara; nagroda

retrieve (ry'tri:w) v. odzyskac; powetowac; odszukac; ura-
towac; uprzytomnic sobie;
aportowac; s. odzyskanie; od-
szukanie; powetowanie; urato-
wanie;ruch wsteczny(powrotny)

retrospect ('retrespekt) s.
spojrzenie wstecz; rozważanie
przeszłosci; v. rzucac okiem
wstecz; nawiązywac do (przeszłosci);patrzyc w przeszłosc

retrospective('retrespektyw)
adj. retrospektywny; działający wstecz;z mocą retroaktywną

return (ry'te:rn) v. wracac;
przynosic dochód;złożyć(zeznanie)

obracac w..; oddawac; odwzajem-
nic; odpowiedziec; wybrac;
s. powrot; nawrot; dochód;
zysk; zwrot; rewanż; sprawozdanie (np podatkowe)

return flight (ry'te:rn,flajt)
s. lot powrotny

return ticket (ry'te:rn,tykyt)
s. powrotny bilet

reunification ('ri:ju:nyfy'kejszyn) s. ponowne zjednoczenie

reunion ('ri:'ju:njen) s. zjazd;
ponowne połączenie; zebranie

revaluation (ri:'waelju'ejszyn)
s. ponowna ocena; przewartoscio-
wanie(po ponownej ocenie)

revaluate (ri:'waelju:'ejt)v,
ponownie ocenic; przewartoscio-
wac(dom w celach podatkowych)

revamp (ry:'waemp) v, przerabiac; reorganizowac; rewidowac;
okapowac (buty);odnowic

reveal (ry'wi:l) v. ujawniac;
objawiac; odsłaniac; s. rama
okna w karoserii

revel ('rewl) s. zabawa; hulanka; v. hulac; używac sobie

revelation (,rewy'lejszyn) s.
ujawnienie; objawienie; odsłonięcie; rewelacja;odkrycie

revenge (ry'wendż) s. zemsta;
msciwosc; v. pomscic; zemscic
się(za zniewage,krzywde etc.)

revengeful (ry'wendżful) adj.
msciwy

revenue ('rewy,nu:) s. dochód
(z podatków)

revenue office ('rewy,nu:'ofys)
s. urząd podatkowy (finansowy)

revere (ry'wier) v. czcic;
odnosic się z czcia

reverence ('rewerens) s. czesc;
szacunek; wielebnosc

reverend ('rewerend) adj. czcigodny; wielebny; s. duchowny

reverse (ry'we:rs) s. odwrot-
nosc; rewers; tył; niepowodzenie; wsteczny bieg; adj. odwrotny; przeciwny; wsteczny;
v. odwracac; zmieniac kierunek; obalac (np. przepis)

reverse gear (ry'we:rs,gier) s.
wsteczny bieg(w samochodzie)

reverse side (ry'we:rs,sajd)
s. odwrotna strona

review (ry'wju:) v. przegląda-
dać; pisać recenzje; przeglądać w myśli; dokonywać prze-
glądu; s. recenzja; przegląd;
rewia;ponowny przegląd

reviewer (ry'wju:er) s. recenzent; krytyk

revile (ry'wajl) v. wyzywać;
wymyślać; przezywać

revise (ry'wajz) v. przejrzeć;
zrewidować; przerabiać

revision (ry'wyżyn) s. rewizja;
przejrzane wydanie; przeróbka

revival (ry'wajwel) s. ożywienie; odżywanie; powrót do życia;powrót do stanu użyteczności

revive (ry'wajw) v. wskrzeszać;
przywracać do życia; wznawiać;
ożywiać; odżywać; wracać do
przytomności

revolt (ry'woult) s. bunt;
powstanie; v. buntować się;
wzdrygać się; mieć odrazę;
budzić odrazę

revolution (,rewe'lu:szyn) s.
obrót; rewolucja

revolutionary (,rewe'lu:sznry)
adj. rewolucyjny; s. rewolucjonista

revolutionist (,rewe'lu:szynyst)
s. rewolucjonista

revolutionize (,rewe'lu:szn,ajz)
v. zrewolucjonizować; wywoływać rewolucje

revolve (ry'wolw) v. obracać;
krążyć; obracać się; obmyślać

revolving (ry'wolwyng) adj.
obrotowy

reward (ry'Żo:rd) s. nagroda;
wynagrodzenie; v. wynagradzać

rheumatism ('ru:metyzem) s.
reumatyzm; gościec stawowy

rhubarb ('ru:ba:rb) s. rabarbar;
(slang):kłótnia

rhyme (rajm) s. rym; rymować się

rhythm ('rytm) s. rytm

rhythmic ('rytmyk) adj. rytmiczny; miarowy

rib (ryb) s. żebro; żeberko;
wręga; v. żeberkować; nabierać;
wyśmiewać;droczyć się;płytko orać

ribbed(rybd)adj.żebrowany

ribbon ('ryben) s. taśma; pasek; strzęp; wstążka; v. drzeć
na strzępy, paski; ozdabiać
wstążką;wić się wstęgą

rice (rajs) s. ryż

rich (rycz) adj. bogaty; kosztowny; suty; obfity; tuczący;
pożywny; soczysty; mocny (zapach); pełny; tłusty (np. pokarm); pocieszny (zdarzenie)

riches ('ryczyz) pl. bogactwo;
bogactwa

richness ('rycznys) s. bogactwo;
pełnia

rick (ryk) s. stóg; v. ustawiać
w stogi; stawiać stóg

rickets ('rykyts) s. choroba
angielska; krzywica; rachityzm

rickety ('rykyty) adj. chwiejny; koślawy; rachityczny

rid; rid; ridded (ryd; ryd;
'rydyd)

rid (ryd) v, uwalniać się od...;
oczyszczać się; pozbywać się

ridden ('rydn) zob. v. ride

riddle ('rydl) s. zagadka;
v. zadawać zagadki; mówić za-
gadkami; rozwiązywać zagadki

ride; rode; ridden (rajd; roud;
'rydn)

ride (rajd) v. pojechać; jechać (też statkiem); jeździć;
tyranizować; wozić; nosić;
dokuczać; s. przejażdżka; jazda; nabieranie (kogoś); droga

rider ('rajder) s. jeździec;
dżokej; dodatek; poprawka;
klauzula; ciężarek przesuwany;
nasadka;poprawka na dokumencie

ridge (rydż) s. grzbiet (też
góry; krawędź; kalenica; pasmo górskie; wał; skiba; grobla; v. pokrywać skibami; robić
krawędzie; marszczyć

ridicule ('rydy,kju:1) v. wyśmiewać się; s. kpiny

ridiculous (ry'dykju:les) adj.
śmieszny; bezsensowny

riding ('rajdyng) s. konna jazda; adj. jadący;do konnej jazdy

rifle (rajfl) s. karabin; gwin-
tówka; gwint;strzelec; v.gwin-
tować (lufę); strzelać;ogra-
bić; okraść; pokrzyżować

rift (ryft) s. szczelina; różnica zdań; v. rozszczepiać
się ;pęknąc;popękać
rig (ryg) v. zaopatrywać; klecić; montować; stroić; robić
kanty; manipulować ceny;
s. sprzęt (wiertniczy); wóz
z koniem; kostium; machlojka
right (rajt) adj. prawa; prawy; poprawny; prawoskrętny;
prosty (też kąt); właściwy;
słuszny; dobry; odpowiedni;
prawidłowy; w porządku; zdrowy; adv. w prawo; na prawo;
prosto; bezpośrednio; bezzwłocznie: dokładnie; słusznie; dobrze; s. prawa strona;
prawo; dobro; słuszność;
sprawiedliwość; pierwszeństwo;
v. naprostować; naprawić;
sprostować; odpłacać; mścić;
usprawiedliwiać
right ahead ('rajt,e'hed) exp.
wprost ;na wprost;przed siebie
right away ('rajt,e'łej) exp.
zaraz ;natychmiast;już teraz
righteous ('rajtszes) adj.
sprawiedliwy; prawy ;słuszny
rightful ('rajtful) adj. słuszny; sprawiedliwy; prawowity;
należny z prawa;prawy
right-hand ('rajt,haend) adj.
praworęki; położony na prawo
right-handed ('rajt-'haendyd)
adj. praworęczny; dostosowany
do prawej ręki; idący wg.ru-
chu zegara; obracający się
w prawo (gwint etc.)
right of way ('rajt,ow'łej)
exp.: prawo pierwszeństwa na
drodze; prawo przejazdu; grunt
pod drogą (kolej)(pod szosą etc.)
rightist ('rajtyst) s. prawico-
wiec; adj. prawicowy
rightly ('rajtly) adv. spra-
wiedliwie; słusznie; poprawnie; właściwie;na miejscu
rigid ('rydżyd) adj. sztywny;
nieugięty; surowy;nieustępliwy
rigor ('ryger) s. rygor; surowość; zesztywnienie
rigorous ('rygeres) adj. surowy; rygorystyczny

rim (rym) s. brzeg; krawędź;
obręcz; powierzchnia wody
(przy żeglowaniu); v. robić
krawędz; posuwać wzdłuż kra-
wędzi;dawać oprawę(do okularów)
rimple ('rympl) v. marszczyć
rind (rajnd) s. kora; łupina;
skórka; v. zdzierać korę
ring (ryng) s. pierścień; obrączka; kółko; koło; zmowa;
szajka; słój; arena; ring
(bokserski); v. otaczać; kołować; krając w kółko
ring; rang; rung (ryng; raeng;
rang)
ring (ryng) v. dzwonić; dźwięczeć; brzmieć; rozbrzmiewać;
wydzwaniać; telefonować; wybijać czas na zegarze kontrolnym;
sprawdzać monetę dźwiękiem;
s. dzwonek; dzwony; dźwięk;
brzęk; telefonowanie
ring off ('ryng,of) v. skończyć
rozmowę telefoniczną
ring the bell ('ryng,dy'bel) v.
dzwonić (do drzwi etc.)
ring up ('ryng,ap) v. wybijać
kwotę (na kasie rejestracyj-
nej);zatelefonować(do kogoś)
ringleader ('ryng,li:der) s.
prowodyr; herszt
rink (rynk) s. ślizgawka; tor
jazdy na wrotkach; boisko do
gry w kule
rinse (ryns) v. płukać; s. wy-
płukanie
rinse out ('ryns,aut) v. wypłukać;przepłukiwać
riot ('rajot) s. zgiełk; zamęt; rozruchy; bunty; rozpusta; hulanka; rozprężenie;
orgia; v. buntować się; robić
rozruchy, zamieszki; hulać;
używać sobie;uprawiać rozpustę
riotous ('rajetes) adj. buntowniczy; rozpustny; hulaszczy;
hałaśliwy; bujny;oporny;niesfor-
ny
rip (ryp) v. odrywać; zrywać;
łupać; rozpruwać; piłować
wzdłuż; pękać; pędzić; s. roz-
prucie; rozpustnik; hulaka;
szkapa; rzecz nie warta nic;
wir;wzburzona powierzchnia wody

ripe (rajp) adj. dojrzały
ripen ('rajpn) v. dojrzewac;
przyspieszac dojrzewanie
ripeness ('rajpnys) s. dojrza-
łość
ripple ('rypl) s. zmarszczki
(na wodzie); fale (na włosach);
falowanie; grzebien do lnu;
v. marszczyc; falowac; roz-
czesywac; rozwodzic się
rise; rose; risen (rajz; rouz;
'ryzn)
rise (rajz) v. podniesc się;
stanac; ustawac; powstawac;
buntowac się; wzbierac; wzbi-
jac się; wzmagac sie; spros-
tac; s. wschod; wznoszenie
sie; podwyżka; wzrost; powodzenie; poczatek; stopien
risen ('ryzn) v. zob. rise
riser (rajzer) s. osoba wstaja-
ca; pionowy przewod (też rura);
podstawka stopnia (na schodach)
rising ('rajzyng) s. wzniesienie; powstanie; zmartwychwstanie; bąbel; pryszcz; zaczyna-
nie ciasta; adj. podnoszący
się; wzrastający;wschodzący
risk (rysk) s. ryzyko ; niebezpieczenstwo; v. narażac się;
ryzykowac;ponosic ryzyko
risky ('rysky) adj. niebezpieczny; ryzykowny;pikantny;drastyczny
rite (rajt) s. obrządek; obrzed
(slubny);rytuał
rival ('rajwel) s. rywal; wspoł-
zawodnik; v. rywalizowac
rivalry ('rajwelry) s. rywalizacja; współzawodnictwo
river ('rywer) s. rzeka
riverboat ('rywer,bout) s. statek rzeczny;łodz rzeczna
riverside ('rywer,sajd) s.
brzeg rzeki
rivet ('rywyt) s. nit; v. nito-
wac; utkwic; przykuc
rivulet ('rywjulyt) s. rzeczuł-
ka;mały strumien;mały potok
road (roud) s. droga; kolej;
reda; v. topic
road hog ('roud,hog) s. pirat
drogowy (lekceważący przepisy)

road map ('roud,maep) s. mapa
drogowa;mapa samochodowa
roadside ('roud,sajd) s. bok
drogi; adj. przydrożny
roadsign ('roud,sajn) s. znak
drogowy
roam (roum) v. włóczyc się;
s. włóczęga; wędrowka
roar (ro:r) v. ryczec; huczec;
s. ryk; huk(armat);ryk(smiechu)
roars of laughter ('ro:rs,ow-
'lafter) exp. wybuchy smiechu
roast (roust) v. piec; opiekac;
przypiekac; wypalac; osmieszac;
krytykowac ostro; s. pieczen;
pieczenie; kpiny; krytyka
ostra; adj. pieczony
roast beef ('roust,bi:f) s.
pieczen wołowa
roast meat ('roust,mi:t) s.
pieczone mięso
rob (rob) v. grabic; rabowac;
ograbic; pozbawiac (czegos)
robber ('rober) s. rabus
robbery ('robery) s. rabunek
robe (roub) s. podomka; suknia;
szata; płaszcz kąpielowy; toga; v. przyodziewac;przyoblekac
robin ('robyn) s. drozd; rudzik
robot ('roubot) s. robot
robust ('roubast) adj. krzepki;
trzezwy; szorstki; hałasliwy;
ciężki;silny; mocny
rock (rok) s. kamien; skała;
forsa; kołysanie; taniec
(rock and roll); pl. kostki
lodu w napoju; v. kołysac się;
bujac się; hustac się; wstrzą-
sac; wypłukiwac piasek; płukac (się);a.kamienny;skalisty
rocker ('roker) s. biegun; łyżwa holenderka
rocket ('rokyt) s. rakieta;
v. wznosic się
rocket power ('rokyt'pałer) s.
napęd rakietowy
rocketry ('rokytry) s. bron
rakietowa; technika rakietowa
rocking chair ('rokyng,czeer)
s. krzesło na biegunach
rocky ('roky) adj. skalisty;
chwiejny;kamienisty;skalny

rod (rod) s. pręt; drąg; rózga;
wędka; (pręt = 5.029 m)

rode (roud) v. zob. ride

rodent ('roudent) s. gryzoń

roe (rou) s. sarna; łania;
ikra we wnętrzu ryby;sperma ryby

rogue (roug) s. łobuz; łajdak;
psotnik; słoń samotnik

roguish ('rougysz) adj. psotny;
figlarny; łobuzerski

role (roul) s. rola

roll (roul) s. rólka; zwój;
zwitek; rulon; bułka; rożek;
spis; wykaz; rejestr; lista;
wokanda; wałek; walec; wałek;
kołysanie (się);,werbel; huk;v.
toczyć; wałkować; tarzać;
grzmieć; dudnić; rozlegać się;
zataczać beczkę; toczyć koło;
kręcić; obracać; wymawiać "r";
rozwałkowywać ;wałkować

roll up ('roul,ap) v. zawinąć
(rękawy); kłębić się; pod-
jeżdżać; skumulować (się)

roller ('rouler) s. wałek; rolka; kółko; długa tocząca się
fala ;narzędzie do wałkowania

roller coaster ('rouler'kous-
ter) s. kolejka wysokogórska;
wesołe miasteczko

roller-skate ('rouler'skejt) s.
wrotka

rolling mill ('roulyŋ,myl) s.
walcownia

Roman ('roumen) adj. rzymski

romance (rou'maens) s. romans
średniowieczny; powieść miłosna; sprawa miłosna; adj. romański; v. romansować; koloryzować; przesadzać;pisać romanse

romantic (rou'maentyk) adj. romantyczny; s. romantyk

romp (romp) s. urwis; zbytki;
swawole; figle; igraszki;
v. figlować; dokazywać; uganiać; łatwo wygrać (wyścigi)

rompers ('rompers) pl. kombinezon do zabawy dla dziecka

roof (ru:f) s. dach; v. pokrywać dachem

roof over ('ru:f,ouwer) v. pokrywać dachem

rook (ruk) s. gawron; szuler;
wieża (w szachach); v, ograć;
oszukać; zdzierać skórę

room (rum) s. pokój. miejsce;
mieszkanie; izba; wolna przestrzeń; sposobność; powód;
v. dzielić pokój lub mieszkanie;mieszkać lub odnajmować pokój

room-mate ('rum,mejt) s. współ-
mieszkaniec; współlokator

roomy ('rumy) adj. przestronny;
obszerny

roost (ru:st) s. grzęda; v. siedzieć na grzędzie

rooster (ru:ster) s. kogut

root (ru:t) s. korzeń; nasada;
podstawa; istota; źródło; sedno;
pierwiastek; v. posadzić; za-
korzenić; ryć; szperać; wygrzebywać; popierać; dopingować

root out ('ru:t,aut) v. wykorze-
niać; wyrywać z korzeniami

rope (roup) s. sznur; powróz;
lina; stryczek; v, związać;
przywiązać; łapać na lasso;
ogradzać sznurami; ciągnąć na
linie; przyciągać; zdobywać;
obśliznąć

rope off ('roup,of) v. ogradzać
linami

rose (rous) s. róża; kolor różowy; rozetka; v. zaróżowić;
zob. rise

rosy ('rouzy) adj. różowy

rot (rot) s. zgnilizna; rozkład;
zepsucie; głupstwa; brednie;
motylica; v. gnić; butwieć;
rozkładać się

rotary ('routery) adj. rotacyjny;
obrotowy

rotate ('routejt) v. obracać
(się); kolejno zmieniać (się);
wirować ;adj.kółkowy

rotation (rou'tejszyn) s. ro-
tacja; ruch obrotowy; obracanie
(się); płodozmian; ciągła wymiana; kolejne następstwo

rotor ('router) s. wirnik

rotten ('rotn) adj. zgniły; zepsuty; zdemoralizowany; lichy;
kiepski; marny;chory na moty-
licę ;do niczego;do chrzanu

rotund (rou'tand) adj. okrągły; zaokraglony; szumny; przysadkowaty

rough (raf) adj. szorstki; chropowaty; ostry; nierówny; wyboisty; nieokrzesany; brutalny; drastyczny; cierpki; nieprzyjemny; nieociosany; surowy; gruby; burzliwy; gwałtowny; hałaśliwy; ciężki; pobieżny; przybliżony; prymitywny; wstępny; szkicowy; adv. ostro; szostko; grubiańsko; z grubsza; s. nierówny teren; stan naturalny – nieobrobiony; hacel;hulıgan; v. być szorstkim; szorstko postępować; hartować (się); jeżyć (się); burzyć (się); szlifować z grubsza; pasować z grubsza; obrabiać z grubsza; szkicować; przebiedować; ujeżdżać (konia); robić coś z grubsza; podkuwać hacelami

roughness ('rafnys) s. szorstkość; grubiaństwo; chamstwo

rough-neck ('rafnek) s. członek obsługi szybu; łobuz; brutal; chuligan

round (raund) adj. okrągły; zaokrąglony; kolisty; okrężny; tam i nazad; kulisty; sferyczny; adv. wkoło; kołem; dookoła; prep. dookoła; s. koło; obwód; kula; obrót; krąg; bieg cykl; ciąg; zasięg; seria; objazd; obchód; runda; zaokrąglenie; pasmo (np. trudności); przechadzka; v. zaokrąglać; wygładzać; okrążyć; obchodzić; opływać

round off (,'raund,of) v. zaokrąglać

round out (,'raund,out) v. zaokrąglać się; tyć

round up ('round,ap) v. spędzać (bydło)

round-up ('round'ap) s. spędzanie bydła

roundabout ('raundebaut) adj. okrężny; s. rondo; karuzela

round trip ('raund,tryp) s. podróż tam i nazad

rouse (rauz) v. pobudzić; wzniecać; ruszyć; ożywiać; podsycać; wyrywać; wypłoszyć; obudzić się; otrząsnąć się

roustabout ('rauste,baut) s. robotnik portowy; robotnik przemysłu naftowego

route (ru:t) s. droga; trasa; marsz; szlak

routine (ru:'ti:n) s. rutyna; tok zajęć

rove (rouw) v. wałęsać się; błądzić wzrokiem; łowić; skręcać włókno; s. niedoprzęd

rover ('rouwer) s. wędrowiec; włóczęga; korsarz; pirat

row (roł) s. szereg; rząd; jazda łodzią; v. wiosłować

row (rał) s. zgiełk; hałas; kłótnia; bójka; burda; nagana; bura; v. besztać; pokłócić się

row-boat ('roł,bout) s. łódź wiosłowa

rower ('rołer) s. wioślarz

rowing boat ('rołyngbout) s. łódź wiosłowa

royal ('rojel) adj. królewski

royalty ('rojelty) s. królewskość; honorarium autorskie

rub (rab) v. trzeć; potrzeć; wytrzeć; wycierać; głaskać; nacierać; s. tarcie; nacieranie

rub down('rab,dałn) v. nacierać;wcierać

rub in ('rab,yn) v. wcierać; wytykać

ruh off ('rab,of) v. zetrzeć

rub out ('rab,aut) v. wymazać

rubber('raber) s. guma; masażysta; pl. kalosze; v. pokrywać gumą; odwracać (głowę)

rubberneck ('raber,nek) s. ciekawski; turysta; gapa

rubber plant ('raber,plaent) s. kauczukowa roślina

rubbish ('rabysz) s. śmieć; gruz; tandeta; nonsens; brednie; głupstwa; bzdury

rubble ('rabl) s. gruz; rumowisko skalne; kamień łamany

ruby ('ru:by) s. rubin

rucksack ('ruksaek)s. plecak

rudder ('rader) s. ster

ruddy ('rady) adj. rumiany; czerstwy; czerwony; v. rumienic się

rude (ru:d) adj. szorstki; niegrzeczny; ostry; surowy; prosty; pierwotny; nagły; gwałtowny; krzepki

ruff (raf) s. kołnierz; kreza; batalion; bojownik; bicie atutem; v. przebić atutem

ruffian ('rafjen) s. zbój; łotr

ruffle ('rafl) s. kreza; żabot; mankiet koronkowy; kłopot; zamieszanie; marszczenie; v. marszczyć (powierzchnię); rozwiewać; rozczochrać; nastroszyć; wzburzyć (się)

rug (rag) s. pled; kilim; dywan

rugby ('ragby) s. (sport) rugby

ruin ('ruyn) s. ruina; v. rujnować (się); zniszczyć (się)

rule (ru:l) s. przepis; prawo; reguła; zasada; rządy; panowanie; postanowienie; miarka; linijka; v. rządzić; panować; kierować; orzekać; postanawiać; liniować

rule out ('ru:l,aut) v. wykluczać

ruler ('ru:ler) s. władca; liniał; linijka

rum (ram) s. rum; adj. dziwny

rumble ('rambl) v. dudnić; grzmieć; turkotać; s. huk; grzmot; dudnienie; tylne miejsce w pojeździe na bagaż lub służącego

ruminant ('ru:mynent) adj. przeżuwający; s. przeżuwacz

rummage ('ramydż) s. szperanie; przetrząsanie; wyprzedaż resztek; v. grzebać; przetrząsać

rumor ('ru:mer) s. pogłoska; słuchy; v. puszczać pogłoski

rump (ramp) s. zad; kuper; comber; kadłub

rumple ('rampl) v. zmiąć; zmiętosić; mierzwić; czochrać

run; ran; ran (ran; raen; raen)

run (ran) v. biec; biegać; pędzić; spieszyć się; jechać; płynąć; kursować; obracać się; działać; funkcjonować; pracować; uciekać; zbiec; prowadzić; toczyć się; wynosić (sumę); rozpływać się; łzawić; głosić; spotykać; narzucać się; molestować; zderzyć się; sprzeciwiać się; wpaść etc.; s. bieg; przebieg; bieganie; rozbieg; rozpęd; przebieg; passa; sekwens; okres; seria; ciąg; dostęp; wybieg; pastwisko; zjazd; tor

run about ('ran,e'baut) v. biegać tu i tam; s. wędrowiec; adj. wędrowny

run across ('ran,e'kros) v. spotkać przypadkowo

run after ('ran,aefter) v. gonić

run away ('ran,e'łej) v. uciekać; ponieść

run down ('ran,dałn) v. przejechać; wyczerpać; wytropić

run in ('ran,yn) v. wpaść na...; dotrzeć

run off ('ran,of) v. uciekać; recytować; drukować

run out ('ran,aut) v. skończyć się; wygasnąć; wydrukować

run over ('ran,ouwer) v. przejechać; przepełniać

run up ('ran,ap) v. dobiec; dojść do..; dodać; wysrubować; s. dochodzenie do celu

rung (rang) s. poprzeczka; szczebel; szprycha; v. zob. ring

runner ('raner) s. goniec; biegacz; posłaniec; woźny; akwizytor; łopatka; obsługujący maszynę; chodnik; przemytnik; płoza; łożysko ślizgowe; wałek

running ('ranyng) adj. bieżący; biegający; będący w biegu; cieknący; ropiejący; w ruchu; ruchomy; ciągły; nieustanny; pochyły; nieprzerwany; s. bieg; wyścig; kandydowanie; funkcjonowanie; ropienie; kierownictwo

running board ('ranyng,bo:rd)
s. stopien; pomost
runway ('ran,łej) s. bieżnia
(do łądowania); tor (jezdny)
rupture ('rapczer) s. złamanie;
zerwanie; przepuklina; v.
przerywac; zrywac; poderwac
się (miec przepuklinę)
rural ('ruerel) adj. wiejski
ruse (ru:z) s. podstęp
rush (rasz) v. pędzic; poga-
niac; ponaglac; rzucac się na
cos; przeskakiwac; wysyłac
pospiesznie; zdobywac szturmem; zdzierac (pieniądze);
słac sitowiem; s. pęd; ruch;
pospiech; napływ; atak; intensywny popyt; sitowie
rush hour ('rasz,auer) s. godzina szczytu; chwila uderze-
nia
Russian ('raszyn) adj. rosyjski ;s.Rosjanin
rust (rast) s. rdza (zbożowa)
v. rdzewiec ;niszczyc się
rust-eaten ('rast.i:tn) adj.
zardzewiały
rustic ('rastik) adj. wiejski;
prostacki; s. wiesniak; prostak
rustle ('rasl) v. szelescic;
krasc bydło; krzątac się;
s. szelest
rusty ('rasty) adj. zardzewiały; zaniedbany; wyszły z wprawy ;podniszczony
rut (rat) s. koleina; bruzda;
utarty szlak; rutyna; nawyk;
rowek; wyżłobienie; ruja;
b-kowisko rykowisko
ruthless ('ru:tlys) adj. bezlitosny; bezwzględny; niemiłosierny
rutted ('ratyd) adj. rozjeżdżo-
ny; wyjeżdżony
rutty ('raty) adj. wyjeżdżony
rye (raj) s. żyto; żytniówka
rye whisky (raj,hłysky)
szkocka żytnia wódka
s (es) dziewiętnasta litera
alfabetu angielskiego
's skrót: is, has, us

saber ('seiber) s. szabla; pałasz; v. ciąc; ranic; scinac
sable ('sejbl) s. sobol; czern;
adj. czarny;sobolowy(z futer)
sabotage ('saebeta:ż) s. sabo-
taż; v. sabotowac
sabre ('sejber) s. szabla; zob.
saber
saccharin ('saekeryn) s. sacharyna
sack (saek) s. worek; torebka;
sak; luźny płaszcz; plądrowa-
nie; v. pakowac do workow;
zwalniac z pracy; plądrowac
sacrament ('saekrement) s. sakrament
sacred ('sejkryd) adj. poświęco-
ny; nienaruszalny
sacrifice ('saekryfajs) s. ofiara; wyrzeczenie (się); v. ofia-
rowywac; poświęcac; wyrzekac
się w zamian za cos innego
sacrilegious (,saekry'lydżes)
adj. świętokradzki
sad (saed) adj. smutny; bolesny;
posępny; ponury; okropny
sadden ('saedn) v. zasmucac (się);
posmutniec
saddle ('saedl) s. siodło;
v. siodłac; obarczac; wkładac
ciężar (komuś)(na kogos)
sadness ('saednys) s. smutek
safe (sejf) adj. pewny; bezpieczny; s. schowek bankowy;
kasa pancerna; spiżarnia
wietrzona; (slang); kondon
safeguard ('seifga:rd) v. ochra-
niac; zabezpieczac; gwarantowac;
s. zabezpieczenie; gwarancja
safety ('sejfty) s. bezpieczeństwo; zabezpieczenie; bezpiecznik ; adj.dający bezpieczeństwo
safety belt ('sejfty,belt) s.
pas bezpieczeństwa (np. w samochodzie)
safety lock ('sejfty,lok) s. zamek bezpieczeństwa
safety pin ('sejfty,pyn) s.
agrafka
safety razor ('sejfty,rejzer) s.
maszynka do golenia się żyletka-
mi (które się wymienia po użyciu)

safety-valve ('sejfty,waelw)
s. klapa bezpieczeństwa; zawór bezpieczeństwa

sag (saeg) v. obwisać; zwisać;
wyginać (się); przechylać się;
spadać w cenie; s. zwis; wygięcie; spadek (ceny)

sagacity (se'gaesyty) s. rozwaga; mądrość; roztropność;
bystrość

said (sed) v. zob. say

sail (sejl) s. żagiel; podróż
morska; żaglować; kroczyć okazale; sterować okrętem; bawić się modelem statku

sail-boat ('sejl,bout) s. żaglówka

sailing-ship ('sejlyng,szyp) s.
statek żaglowy

sailor ('sejlor) s. żeglarz;
marynarz

saint (sejnt) s. & adj. święty

sake (sejk) s. czyjeś dobro;
wzgląd

salad ('saeled) s. sałata

salary ('saelery) s. pensja;
pobory; wynagrodzenie

sale (sejl) s. sprzedaż; wyprzedaż

saleslady ('sejls'lejdy) s.
sprzedawczyni

salesman ('sejlsmen) s. sprzedawca

salesmanager (,sejls'maenydżer)
s. kierownik działu sprzedaży

saliva (se'lajwa) s. ślina

sallow ('saelou) adj. ziemistv;
blady; żółtawy; v. dawać żółtawy odcień; s. iwa (wierzba)

sally ('saely) s. wypad; wycieczka z oblężenia; docinek
(cięty)

sally out ('saely,aut) v. wyruszać w podróż

salmon ('saemen) s. łosoś; adj.
łossiowy; łososiowego koloru

saloon (se'lu:n) s. bar; szynk;
sala (zabaw); salon (na okręcie)

salt (so:lt) s. sól; adj; słony; v. solić

saltcellar ('so:lt,seler) s.
solniczka

salt-free ('so:lt,fri:) adj.
bezsolny;pozbawiony soli

salty ('so:lty) adj. słony

salutation (,saelju:'tejszyn)
s. pozdrowienie; przywitanie

salute (se'lu:t) s. pozdrowienie; salutowanie; honory wojskowe; salwa (powitalna);
v. pozdrowić; powitać; salutować; odbierać defiladę; przejść
przed kompanią honorową

salvation (sael'wejszyn) s.
zbawienie; ratunek; wybawienie

salve (sa:w) v. natrzeć; złagodzić; uspokoić; s. maść; balsam

same (sejm) adj. ten sam; taki
sam; jednostajny; monotonny;
adv. tak samo; identycznie;
bez zmiany; pron. to samo

sample ('sa:mpl) s. próbka;
wzór; v. próbować; dawać próbki

sanatorium (,saene'to:rjem) s.
sanatorium

sanctify ('saenkty,faj) v.
uświęcać; poświęcać

sanction ('saenkszyn) v.
usankcjonować; s. sankcja

sanctuary ('saenkczuery) s.
przybytek; azyl

sand (saend) s. piasek; v. posypywać piaskiem; obrabiać papierem ściernym

sandal ('saendl) s. sandał; rzemyk; v. wkładać sandały; przywiązywać rzemykiem

sandwich ('saendłycz) s. kanapka;
sandwicz; v. wkładać (między)

sandy ('saendy) adj. piaskowy;
piaskowego koloru

sandy beach ('saendy,bi:ch) s.
plaża

sane (sejn) adj. zdrowy na umyśle; rozsądny; normalny

sang (saeng) v. zob. sing

sanitarium (,saeny'teerjem) s.
sanatorium

sanitary ('saenytery) adj. higieniczny; zdrowy

sanitary napkin ('saenytery
'naepkyn) s. podpaska higieniczna

sanitation (,saeny'tejszyn) s.
higiena; kanalizacja; urządzenia sanitarne

sank (saeŋk) v. zob. sink

Santa Claus (,saenta'klo:z)
s. Dziadek Mróz; Święty Miko-
łaj

sap (saep) s. żywica; sok; głupiec; kujon; nudziarstwo; sa-
pa; podkopywanie; v. wyciągać
soki; usuwać biel z drzewa;
podkopywać; podmywać; kopać
sapę

sappy('saepy) s. soczysty; pełen wigoru; energiczny

sarcasm ('sa:rkaezem) s. sar-
kazm

sardine (sa:r'di:n) s. sardynka

sash (saesz) s. szarfa; rama
okienna do pionowego suwania
okien; v. instalować ramy
okienne

sash window('saesh'łyndou) s.
suwane okno

sat (saet) v. zob. sit

Satan ('sejtn) s. szatan

satchel ('saeczel) s. torba
z rzemieniami na plecy

satellite ('saete,lajt) s. satelita

satin ('saetyn) s. atłas; adj.
atłasowy; v. satynować (papier)

satire ('saetajer) s. satyra

satirize ('saety,rajz) v. wy-
kpiwać; wyśmiewać; satyryzo-
wać

satisfaction (,saetys'faekszyn)
s. zadowolenie; satysfakcja;
spłacenie długu ;zaspokojenie

satisfactory (,saetys'faektery)
adj. zadawalający; odpowiedni

satisfy ('saetys,faj) v. zaspokoić; uiścić; spełnić; zadowalać; odpowiadać; przekonywać

Saturday ('saeterdy) s. sobota

sauce (so:s) s. sos; kompot;
v. przyprawiać jedzenie; na-
gadać komuś ;stawiać się

saucebox ('so:s,boks) s. impertynent ;zuchwalec

saucepan ('so:spen) s. patelnia; rondel

saucer ('so:ser) s. spodek

saunter ('so: nter) s. przechadzka; przechadzać się; chodzić
powolnym krokiem

sausage ('sosydż) s. kiełbasa

save (sejw) v. ratować; oszczędzać; zachowywać pozory; zbawiać;
uniknąć; zyskiwać (czas); prep.
oprócz; wyjąwszy; poza; pominąwszy; conj. że; poza tym;
chyba że; z wyjątkiem

save for a car ('sejw,fo:r'ej-
,ca:r) exp.: oszczędzać na samochód

saver ('sejwer) s. osoba oszczę-
dzająca; przedmiot oszczędzający
(np, czas)

saving ('sejwyŋg) adj. zbawienny;
oszczędny; prep. wyjąwszy

savings-bank ('sejwyŋz'baenk) s.
kasa oszczędności

savior ('sejwjer) s. zbawca;
zbawiciel

savor ('sejwer) s. smak; aromat;
powab; v. mieć smak; pachnieć;
smakować; nadawać smak

savory ('sejwery) adj. smaczny;
apetyczny; smakowity; pikantny;
aromatyczny

saw; sawed; sawn (so:; so:d;
so:n)

saw (so:) v. zob. see; piłować;
s. piła

sawdust ('so:,dast) s. trociny

sawmill ('so:,myl) s. tartak

Saxon ('saeksn) adj. saksoński;
saski ; s. Sas

say; said; said (sej; sed; sed)
v. mówić; powiedzieć; odprawiać; twierdzić

sayso ('sejso) s. rozkaz; powiedzenie; ostatnie słowo

saying ('sejyŋg) s. powiedzonko;
powiedzenie

scab (skaeb) s. strup; parch;
świerzb; łamistrajk

scaffold ('skaefeld) s. rusztowanie; platforma; estrada; szafot; v. stawiać rusztowanie

scaffolding ('skaefeldyŋg) s.
rusztowanie

scald (sko:ld) v. oparzyć; wy-
parzyć; pasteryzować; s. opa-
rzenie

scale (skejl) s. skala; podziałka; układ; drabina;
szalka; łuska; kamien nazębny;
v. wyłazic; wdzierac się;
mierzyc (podziałką); ważyc;
łuszczyc; łuskac; złuszczac
się

scale down ('skejl,dałn) v.
zmniejszac (proporcjonalnie)

scale up ('skejl,ap) v. po-
wiekszac (proporcjonalnie)

scales ('skejls) pl. waga

scalp ('skaelp) s. skalp; skora na głowie; v. oskalpowac;
złosliwie krytykowac

scan (skaen) v. badawczo przeglądac; skandowac; miec rytm

scandal ('skaendl) s. skandal;
zgorszenie; oszczerstwo;
plotki

scandalous ('skaendeles) adj.
skandaliczny; gorszący;
oszczerczy

Scandinavian (,skaendy'nejw-
jan) adj. skandynawski

scant (skaent) adj. skąpy;
ograniczony; ledwo wystarczający; niedostateczny

scapegoat ('skejp,gout) s. kozioł ofiarny

scar (ska:r) s. blizna; szrama;
wyrwa; urwisko; v. pokiereszowac (się); zablizniac się

scar over ('ska:r,ouwer) v.
zabliznic

scarce (skeers) adj. rzadki;
niewystarczający

scarcely ('skeersly) adv. zaledwie; ledwo; z trudem;
z trudnością

scarcity ('skeersyty) s. niedostatek; niedobor; brak

scare (skeer) s. popłoch; panika; strach; v. nastraszyc;
przestraszyc; siac popłoch

scare away ('skeere,łej) v.
odstraszac

scarecrow ('skeer,krou)s.
straszydło; strach na wroble

scarf (ska:rf) s. szalik;
chustka na szyję; szarfa

scarfs (ska:rfs) pl. styk;
złącza

scarlet ('ska:rlyt) s. szkarłat;
adj. szkarłatny

scarlet fever ('ska:rlyt,fi:wer)
s. szkarlatyna ; płonica

scarp (ska:rp) s. skarpa; urwisko

scarred (ska:rd) adj. poznaczo-
ny bliznami; poszarpany

scarves (ska:rwz) pl. zob.scarf;
chusty na szyję; szarfy etc.

scathing ('skejzyng) adj. kostyczny; zjadliwy; niszczący

scatter ('skaeter) v. rozpra-
szac (się); rozsypywac; roz-
rzucac; rozwiewac; posypywac;
rozpierzchnąc (się)

scavenge ('skaewyndż) v. czyscic; oczyszczac; wyrzucac spa-
liny; byc zamiataczem ulic

scene (si:n) s. scena; miejsce
zdarzeń; widowisko; widok; obraz; awantura publiczna

scenery (si:nery) s. widok;
krajobraz; dekoracje sceniczne

scent (sent) v. węszyc; wiet-
rzyc; wydawac zapach; s. zapach; nos (węch); perfumy

sceptic ('skeptyk) s. sceptyk;
adj. sceptyczny ;powątpiewający

sceptical ('skeptykel) adj.
sceptyczny;powątpiewający we wszystko

schedule ('skedżul) s. rozkład
jazdy; wykaz; zestawienie; tabela; taryfa; harmonogram; lista; plan; v. planowac; wciągac
na listę ;naznaczac wg. planu

scheme (ski:m) s. intryga; podstęp; plan

scholar ('skoler) s. uczony;
stypendysta; uczen ;student

scholarship ('skolerszyp) s.
poziom naukowy; stypendium;
erudycja ;systematyczna wiedza

school (sku:l) s. szkoła; katedra; nauka; ławica; adj. szkolny; v. szkolic; kształcic; nauczac; wycwiczyc; tworzyc ła-
wicę ;karcic; sprawdzac naukę

schoolboy ('sku:l,boj) s.
uczen

schoolgirl ('sku:l,ge:rl) s.
uczennica

schooling ('sku:lyŋg) s. nauka;
szkolenie; wykształcenie
schoolmaster ('sku:l,ma:ster)
s. kierownik szkoły
schoolmate ('sku:l,mejt) s. kolega szkolny
school of driving ('sku:l,ow-
'drajwyŋg) s. nauka jazdy
(samochodem)
schooner ('sku:ner) s. skuner;
szklanka na piwo
science ('sajens) s. wiedza;
nauka; umiejętnosc
scientific ('sajentyfyk) adj.
naukowy; umiejętny
scientist ('sajentyst) s. uczony; przyrodnik; naukowiec
scissors ('syzez) s. nożyce;
nożyczki
scoff (skof) v. szydzić; kpić;
drwić; s. posmiewisko; szyderstwo; kpiny; drwiny
scold (skould) v. besztac;
skrzyczec; obrugac; łajać;
złorzeczyc; s. jędza; sekutnica; megiera
scone (skon) s. placek trójkątny z jęczmiennej mąki
scoop (sku:p) v. zaczerpnąć;
wygarnąc; wybrac; s. czerpak;
szufelka; chochla; kubeł; sensacyjna wiadomosc
scooter ('sku:ter) s. skuter;
hulajnoga
scope (skoup) s. zasięg; zakres;
dziedzina; meta; sposobnosc;
możliwosc
scorch (sko:rcz) v. spalić;
przypiekac; przypalac; dopie-
kac; wypłowiec; pędzic samochodem jak szalony; s. poparzenie
score (sko:r) v. zdobyc (punkt);
podkreslic; zanotowac; zapisac;
wygrac; osiągnąc; strzelic
bramkę; s. ilosc (zdobytych
punktów lub bramek); zacięcie;
rysa; znak; dwadziescia
scorn (sko:rn) s. lekceważenie;
wzgarda; v. lekceważyc; gar-
dzic; odrzucac z pogardą
scornful ('sko:rnful) adj. pogardliwy (i zagniewany); odrzuca-
jący z gniewem i pogardą

Scot (skot) adj. szkocki
Scotch (skocz) adj. szkocki
scot-free ('skot'fri:) adj.
cały; nietknięty; niezraniony;
gratis; bezpłatny
scoundrel ('skaundrel) s. kanalia; łotr
scour ('skauer) v. podmyc; szorowac; przepłukiwac; poszuki-
wac; grasowac; przetrząsac;
s. podmycie; przemywanie;
przepłukiwanie
scout (skaut) s. harcerz; zwia-
dowca; v. isc na zwiady; robic
rekonesans
scoutmaster ('skaut,ma:ster)
s. harcmistrz
scowl (skaul) v. chmurzyc się;
patrzec spode łba; groznie
patrzec; s. zła mina; grozne
spojrzenie; krzywa mina
scramble ('skraembl) s. ubija-
nie się; gramolenie się; do-
bijanie się; robienie jajeczni-
cy; v. ubijac się; gramolic się;
dobijac się; robic jajecznicę
scrambled eggs ('skraembld,egs)
s. jajecznica
scrap (skraep) s. szmelc; odpadki; skrawki; wycinki; bójka; v. wyrzucac na szmelc; odrzucac; wycofac; bic się
scrape (skrejp) s. skrobanie;
tarapaty; szurnięcie; ciułanie;
drasnięcie; v. skrobac; drasnąc;
ciułac; szurnąc
scrape off ('skrejp,of) v. ze-
skrobac
scrape out ('skrejp,aut) v. wyskrobac
scrape together (skrejp,tu'gedzer) v. uciułac
scrap iron ('skraep,ajern) s.
złom żelazny
scrappy ('skraepy) adj. niejednolity; bez związku; frag-
mentaryczny
scratch (skraecz) s. drasnięcie;
zadrapanie; rozdarcie; skrobanie; linia startu; adj. do pisania (np. brulion; brulionowy);
v. drapac (się); zadrasnąc;
gryzmolic; wydrapac; wykreslic

scream (skri:m) s. krzyk; pisk;
gwizd; kawał; v. krzyczec
przenikliwie; śmiac się hałasliwie i histerycznie

screech(skri:cz) s. zgrzyt;
pisk; skrzypienie; v. zgrzytac; piszczec; skrzypiec

screen (skri:n) s. zasłona; osłona; siatka na komary; ekran;
sito; siewnik; filtr (swiatła)
v. zasłaniac; osłaniac; zabezpieczac; wyswietlac; przesie-
wac; sortowac; badac; przesłu-
chiwac; filmowac; izolowac

screw (skru:) s. sruba; prope-
ler; smigło; zwitek; wyzyskiwacz; dusigrosz; (slang):sto-
sunek płciowy; v. przysrubo-
wac; wyduszac; naciskac; wykrzywiac; zabałaganic; obracac się; (slang):spółkowac;
wkopac (kogos) ;oszukac

screwdriver ('skru:,drajwer) s.
srubokręt; wodka z sokiem poma-
rańczowym

scribble ('skrybl) s. gryzmoły;
bazgranina; v. gryzmolic;
bazgrac; pisac naprędce

script (skrypt) s. rękopis;
scenariusz

scripture ('skrypczer) s. Pismo Swięte

scroll (skroul) s. zwitek;
krzywa; spirala

scrub (skrab) s. zarosla; zagajnik; karłowate drzewo; pętak; niepozorny człowiek; szo-
rowanie; v. szorowac; oczyszczac;adj.lichy;marny;maławy

scruple ('skrupl) s. skrupuł;
v. wahac się; miec skrupuły

scrupulous ('skru;pjules) adj.
sumienny; dokładny; skrupulatny; pedantyczny

scrutinize ('skru:tynajz) v.
badac szczegółowo

scrutiny ('skru:tyny) s. dokładne badanie

scuff (skaf) s. włoczenie nogami; wytarte miejsca; v. powłoczyc nogami; wycierac; roz-
rzucac; porysowac ;musnąc;ze-
drzec;zdzierac;szurac

scuffle (skafl) s. włoczenie nogami; szamotanie się; utarczka;
bojka; v. szamotac się; bic się;
powłoczyc nogami;szurac;zaszurac

sculptor ('skalpter) s. rzezbiarz

sculpture ('skalpczer) s. rzezba;
v. rzezbic

scum (skam) s. szumowiny; v.
zbierac szumowiny; wytarzac

scurf (ske:rf) s. łupiez;strup;par-
chy

scurvy ('ske:rwy) s. szkorbut;
adj. podły; nędzny

scuttle ('skatl) s. wiaderko;
szybka ucieczka; właz; v. pędzic; uciekac; robic dziury
w dnie; zatapiac

scuttlebutt ('skatelbat) s. kadz;
pogłoska

scythe (sajz) s. kosa; v. kosic

sea (si:) s. morze; fala

sea breeze ('si:'bri:z) s. wiatr
od morza

seafarer ('si:,feerer) s. żeglarz;
podróżnik morski

seafood ('si:fu:d) s. potrawy
morskie (ryby; skorupiaki)

sea gull ('si:gal) s. mewa

seal (si:l) s. foka; futro foki;
uszczelka; zagadka; plomba;
pieczątka; piętno; znak; v. polowac na foki; uszczelniac; płom-
bowac; pieczętowac; zalakowac

seal up ('si:l,ap) v. zaplombowac; uszczelnic; zamknąc; zalakowac; zapieczętowac

sea level ('si:,lewl) s. poziom
morza

sealskin ('si:lski:n) s. futro
z fok

seam (si:m) s.szew; rąbek; pokład; blizna; szpara; szczelina; v. łączyc szwami; pękac;
pokiereszowac

seaman ('si:men) s. marynarz;
żeglarz

seamstress ('semstrys) s.
szwaczka

seaplane ('si:,plejn) s. hydroplan

seaport ('si:,po:rt) s. port
morski

sea-power ('si:,paŕer) s. potęga morska

search (se:rcz) s. poszukiwanie; badanie; szperanie; rewizja; v. badać; dociekać;
szukać; przetrząsać; rewidować

searching ('se:rczyng) adj.
badawczy; przenikliwy

seashore ('si:,szo:r) s. wybrzeże; brzeg morski

seasick ('si:,syk) adj. chory
na morską chorobę

seaside ('si:'sajd) s. wybrzeże morskie

season ('si:zn) s. pora roku;
pora; sezon; v. zaprawiać;
przyprawiać; okrasić

seasonable (si:znebl) adj. stosowny; odpowiedni; właściwy na
porę roku; w porę

seasonal ('si:zenl) adj. sezo-
nowy

seasoned ('si:znd) adj. zaprawiony; wdrożony; przyprawiony;
pikantny; wystały

seasoning ('si:znyng) s. przyprawa

season ticket ('si:sn'tykyt) s.
abonament; karta wstępu; bilet (np. na serię przedstawień)

seat (si:t) s. siedzenie; ławka;
krzesło; miejsce siedzące;
siedlisko; siedziba; gniazdo;
v. posadzić; usadowić; wybierać (do sejmu); siąść; osadzić

seat belt ('si:t,belt) s. pas
ochronny w samolocie lub samochodzie; pas beapieczeństwa

seaward ('si:ŀerd) adv. ku
(otwartemu) morzu; adj. skiero-
wany ku morzu

seaweed ('si:ŀi:d) s. wodorost

seaworthy ('si:,ŀe:rsy) adj.
zdatny do podróży morskiej
(m.in. wodoszczelny)

secession (sy'seszyn) s. secesja; oddzielenie się

seclude (sy'klu:d) v. odosab-
niać (się)

secluded (sy'klu:dyd) adj. odosobniony

seclusion (sy'klu:żyn) s. odosobnienie; ustronie; zacisze

second ('sekend) adj. drugi;
wtorny; powtórny; ponowny; za-
stępczy; zapasowy; drugorzędny;
v. poprzeć; sekundować; s. sekunda; moment; chwila; drugi;
sekundant; delegat; zastępca

secondary ('sekendery) adj.
drugorzędny; wtórny; pochodny

secondary school ('sekendery-
,sku:l) s. szkoła średnia

second floor ('sekend,flo:r) s.
pierwsze piętro

secondhand ('sekend,haend)
adj. z drugiej ręki; używany

secondly ('sekendly) adv. po
drugie

second-rate ('sekend'-rejt)
adj. drugorzędny; lichy; kiepski

secrecy ('si:krysy) s. tajemnica; skrytość; dyskrecja

secret ('si:kryt) adj. tajny;
tajemny; sekretny; skryty;
ustronny; dyskretny; s. tajemnica; sekret; pl. wstydliwe
części ciała

secretary ('sekretry) s. sekretarz; sekretarka; sekretarzyk

secretary of state ('sekretry-
,ow'stejt) minister spraw
zagranicznych USA

secrete (sy'kri:t) v. wydzielać;
ukrywać

secretion (sy'kri:szyn) s. wydzielina; wydzielanie; ukrycie

section ('sekszyn) s. część;
wycinek; etap; oddział; grupa;
dział; ustęp; paragraf; sekcja;
przekrój; żelazo profilowe;
przedział; drużyna robocza;
v. dzielić na części; robić
przekrój

sector ('sekrer) s. wycinek;
odcinek

secular ('sekjuler) adj. świecki; wiekowy; stuletni; s.
ksiądz świecki

secularize (,sekjulerajz) s.
sekularyzować

secure (sy'kjuer) v. zabezpieczać (się); umacniać; uzyskiwać; zapewniać sobie; adj;
spokojny; bezpieczny; pewny

security (sy'kjueryty) s. bezpieczeństwo; zabezpieczenie;
pewność; zastaw; papier wartościowy; zbytnia ufność

sedan (sy'daen) s. samochód
4-osobowy

sedate (sy'dejt) v. uspokajać
(lekarstwami); adj. spokojny;
opanowany; zrównoważony

sedative ('sedetyw) adj. & s.
(środek) uspakajający, nasen-
ny

sediment ('sydyment) s. osad;
nanos; (skała osadowa)

seduce (sy'du:s) v. uwodzić

seduction (sy'dakszyn) s. uwo-
dzenie; pokusa; poneta; powab

seductive (sy'daktyw) adj. kuszący; necący

sedulous ('sedjules) adj. pilny; skrzętny; staranny; skwapliwy

see; saw; seen (si:, so:,si:n)

see (si;) v. zobaczyć; widzieć;
ujrzeć; zauważyć; spostrzegać; doprowadzić; odprowadzić;
zwiedzać; zrozumieć; odwiedzać; przeżywać; dożyć; uważać; zastanawiać się; dopilnować

see off ('si:,of) v. odprowadzać

see out ('si:,aut) v. odprowadzić do drzwi

see through ('si:,tru:) v.prze-
prowadzić do końca; doczekać
się końca

see to ('si:,tu) v. troszczyć
się o...

seed (si:d) v. obsiewać; obsypywać się; zasiewać; wybierać;
s. nasienie; zarodek; plemię

seek; sought; sought (si:k;
so:t; so:t)

seek (si:k) v. szukać; starać
się; chcieć; zadać; nastawać;
usiłować; próbować; przetrząsać; dążyć

seek out ('si:k,aut) v. odszuki-
wać; wykrywać

seem (si:m) v. zdawać się; robić
wrażenie; okazywać się; mieć
wrażenie

seeming (si:myng) adj. pozorny;
widoczny

seemingly ('si:myngly) adv. na
pozór; widocznie

seemly ('si:mly) adj. właściwy;
przyzwoity

seen (si:n) v. zob. see

seep (si:p) v. sączyć się; wyciekać

seesaw ('si:so:) s. huśtawka
(na desce); adj. wahadłowy;
huśtawkowy; s. huśtać się; wahać się; adv. (poruszać czymś)
do góry i na dół

segment ('segment) s. odcinek;
segment; v. podzielić na części

segregate('segry'gejt) v. oddzielać; segregować

segregation ('segry'gejszyn) s.
oddzielenie; segregacja

seize (si:z) v. uchwycić; złapać; zrozumieć; owładnąć; sko-
rzystać; zaciąć się; zatrzeć
się; zablokować się

seizure ('si:zer) s. zagarnięcie;
zawładnięcie; zajęcie; napad;
atak apopleksji; zatarcie; za-
blokowanie ;atak drgawek

seldom ('seldem) adv. rzadko;
z rzadka

select (sy'lekt) v. wybierać;
wyselekcjonować; adj. wybrany;
doborowy; ekskluzywny

selection (sy'lekszyn) s. wybór;
dobór; selekcja

self (self) prefix. samo; auto-
matycznie; s. jaźń; osobowość;
własne dobro; pl.selves (selwz)

self-acting ('self'aektyng) adj.
samoczynny

self-command ('self,ke'ma:nd) s.
spokój; panowanie nad sobą;
opanowanie

self-confidence ('self,konfydens)
s. pewność siebie; tupet

self-conscious ('self'konszes)
adj.nieśmiały; zażenowany

self-control ('self,ken'troul)
s. zimna krew; opanowanie

self-defense ('self,dy'fens) s.
samoobrona

self-employment ('self,ym'plojment) samozatrudnienie

self-government ('self'gawen-
ment) s. samorząd; autonomia

self-interest ('self'yntryst)
s. interesowność; własne dobro

selfish ('selfysz) adj. samolubny; egoistyczny

self-made ('self'mejd) adj.
przez samego siebie osiągnięty

self-possessed ('self,pe'zest)
adj. opanowany; spokojny

self-reliant ('self,ry'lajent)
adj. na sobie polegający

self-respect ('self,rys'pekt) s.
poczucie własnej godności

self-righteous ('self'rajczes)
adj. nadmiernie pewny siebie

self-service ('self'se:rwys) s.
samo-obsługa

sell; sold; sold (sel; sould;
sould)

sell (sel) v. sprzedawać; za-
przedawać; sprzeniewierzyć;
wykiwać; mieć zbyt; być na
sprzedaż; wyprzedawać

sell out ('selaut) v. wyprzedawać

seller ('seler) s. sprzedawca

selves (selwz) pl. zob. self

semblance ('semblens) s. pozór;
podobieństwo

semen ('si:men) s. nasienie

semicolon ('semy'koulen) s.
średnik

semifinal ('semy'fajnl) s. pół-
finał

senate ('senyt) s. senat

senator ('seneter) s. senator

send; sent; sent (send; sent;
sent)

send (send) v. posyłać; wysyłać;
nadawać; transmitować; wystrze-
liwać; sprawiać; wywoływać

send away ('send,e'łej) v. odprawiać; wypędzać

send for ('send,fo:r) v. zawołać; zamawiać; kazać przynieść

send in ('send,yn) v. posłać;
nadesłać

send off ('send'o:f) v. wysyłać;
odprowadzać (np. na lotnisko);
pożegnać kogoś (na stacji)

sender ('sender) s. nadawca;
nadajnik (np. radiowy)

send-off ('send'o:f) s. pożegnanie

senior ('si:njer) adj. starszy
(np. rangą); s. starszy człowiek; senior; student ostat-
niego roku

sensation (sen'sejszyn) s. wrażenie; doznanie; uczucie; sensacja

sensational (sen'sejszenl) adj.
sensacyjny; wrażeniowy

sense (sens) s. zmysł; poczucie; uczucie (np. zimna); świadomość (czegoś); rozsądek;
znaczenie; sens; v. wyczuwać;
czuć; rozumieć

senseless ('senslys) adj. bez
sensu; nierozumny; nieprzytomny

sensibility(,sensy'bylyty) s.
wrażliwość

sensible ('sensybl) adj. rozsądny; świadomy; przytomny;
wrażliwy; odczuwalny; pozna-
walny; sensowny

sensitive ('sensytyw) adj.
wrażliwy; delikatny

sensual ('senszuel) adj. zmysłowy (też seksualnie)

sensuous ('senszues) adj. zmysłowy (nie seksualnie)

sent (sent) v. zob. send

sentence ('sentens) s. zdanie;
powiedzenie; wyrok; sentencja;
v. wydawać wyrok; skazywać

sentiment ('sentyment) s. sentyment; uczucie; opinia; zdanie;
życzenie; sentymentalność

sentimental (,senty'mentl) adj.
uczuciowy; sentymentalny

sentimentality (,senty'ment'aelyty) s. uczuciowość; czułost-
kowość; sentymentalność

sentry ('sentry) s. posterunek;
wartownik

separable ('seperebl) adj. roz-
łączny

separate ('seperejt) v. rozłączyć; rozdzielić; oddzielić;
oderwać; odseparować (się);
odgrodzić; rozszczepić;

separate ('sepryt) adj. odrębny;
oddzielny; osobny; indywidualny; poszczególny

separation (,sepe'rejszyn) s.
separacja; rozdzielenie; oddzielenie; rozłączenie

September (sep'tember) s.
wrzesien

septic ('septyk) adj. septyczny;
zakazny

sepulcher ('sepelker) s. grób;
v. składać do grobu

sequel ('si:kłel) s. ciąg dalszy; wynik; następstwo

sequence ('si:kłens) s. następstwo; kolejność; porządek;
progresja

serene (sy'ri:n) adj. pogodny;
spokojny; s. spokojne morze;
pogodne niebo etc. v. rozpogodzić

sergeant ('sa:rdżent) s. sierżant

serial('sierjel) a. seryjny;
periodyczny; kolejny; odcin-
kowy

series ('sieri:z) pl. seria;
szereg; rząd

serious ('sierjes) adj. poważny

sermon ('se:rmen) s. kazanie;
nagana

serpent ('se:rpent) s. wąż

serum ('sierem) s. surowica

servant ('se:rwent) s. służący;
sługa; służąca; urzędnik
(państwowy)

serve (se:rw) s. służyć; odbywać służbę (też kadencję;
praktykę etc.); nadawać się;
obsługiwać; podawać; sprzedawać;
dostarczyć; wręczyć; potrakto-
wać; postępować; spełniać
fukcje; sprawować urząd; odbywać karę (więzienia); zaserwo-
wać

service ('se:rwys) s. służba;
obsługa; praca; urząd; zaopatrzenie; instalacja;
uprzejmość; grzeczność; przysługa; pomoc; użyteczność;
nabożeństwo; serw; serwis
(stołowy); wręczenie; v. doglądać; naprawić; kryć (sami-
ce)

serviceable ('se:rwysebl) adj.
pożyteczny; użyteczny; praktyczny; wygodny; mocny; trwały

service-station('se:rwys-'stejszyn) s. stacja obsługi
i sprzedaży benzyny

session ('seszyn) s. posiedzenie; siedzenie; półrocze

set; set; set (set; set; set)

set (set) v. stawiać; ustawiać;
wstawić; urządzić; umieszczać;
przykładać; nastawiać; osadzać;
wbijać; wyznaczać; ustalać;
sądzić; nakrywać; składać;
wysadzać (czyms); ścinać się;
okrzepnąć; adj. zastygły; nieruchomy; zdecydowany; stały;
ustalony; s. seria; garnitur;
skład; komplet;zespół; grupa;
szczepek; zachod: ustawienie;
układ; twardnienie; gęstość;
rozstęp; oszalowanie

set at ease ('set,et'i:z) v.
uspokoić

set-back ('setbaek) s. pogorszenie; nawrót; zahamowanie

set free ('set,fri:) v. uwolnić

set off ('set,of) v. uwydatnić;
wyodrębnić; wystrzelić; wysadzić; wywołać; wyruszyć; wyjeżdżać

set out ('set,aut) v. wystawiać;
ozdabiać; wykładać; wyruszać;
zacząć się

set to ('set,tu) v. zabierać
się (do czegoś)

set up ('get,ap) v. ustawiać;
zakładać; zaczynać; zaopatrywać; rościć; wysuwać; przywracać; podnosić; założyć; podawać
się (za kogoś)

settee (se'ti:) s. kanapa; sofa

setting ('setyŋg) s. otoczenie; oprawa; ułożenie; układ; inscenizacja

settle (setl) v. osiedlić (się); umieścić (się); uregulować; osadzić (się); ustalić; rozstrzygnąć; zapłacić (dług); zamieszkać; usadowić (się); uspokoić (się); zawierać (umowę); układać (się)

settle down ('setl,dałn) v. ustatkować się; osiedlić się; zabrać się do czegoś

settlement ('setlment) s. osiedle; osada; kolonia; osiadanie; sedymentacja; załatwienie; rozstrzygnięcie; ustalenie

settler ('setler) s. osadnik; kolonista

set-up ('set,ap) s. postawa; układ; drużyna; dodatki do alkoholu; (slang):ukartowane zawody; łatwa sprawa

seven ('sewn) num. siedem; s. siódemka

seventeen ('sewn'ti:n) num. siedemnaście; s. siedemnastka

seventh ('sewent) adj. siódmy

seventy ('sewnty) num. siedemdziesiąt; s. siedemdziesiątka

sever ('sever) v. odrywać; odłączyć; zrywać; urywać; rozchodzić się

several ('sewrel) adj. kilku; kilka; kilkoro

severe (sy'wier) adj. surowy; srogi; ostry; dotkliwy; bolesny; zacięty

severity (sy'weryty) s. surowość; srogość; ostrość; zaciętość; ciężki stan

sew; sewed; sewn (sou; soud; soun)

sew (sou) v. szyć; uszyć

sewage ('sju:ydż) s. ścieki

sewer ('suer) s. kanał ściekowy; v. kanalizować

sewer ('souer) s. osoba szyjąca

sewerage ('su:erydż) s. kanalizacja; system kanalizacyjny

sewing ('souyŋg) s. szycie

sewing-machine ('souyŋgme,szi:n) s. maszyna do szycia

sewn (soun) v. zob. sew

sex (seks) s. płeć

sex appeal('sekse'pi:l) s. atrakcyjność płciowa; seksapil

sexton ('seksten) s. grabarz

sexual ('sekszjuel) adj. seksualny; płciowy

Sejm (sejm) s. sejm

shabby ('szaeby) adj. brudny; skąpy; odrapany; wytarty; nędzny; podły

shack (szaek) s. buda; szałas; dom

shack up ('szaek,ap) v. spędzać noc z kimś (slang)

shackle ('szaekl) s. kajdany; klamra; pęta; v. zakuwać; szczepiać

shade (szejd) s. cień; odcień; abażur; stora; pl. ustronie; piwnica na wino; v. zasłaniać; zamroczyć; cieniować

shadow ('szaedou) s. cień (czyjś); v. pokrywać cieniem; śledzić kogoś

shady ('szejdy) adj. cienisty; nieczysty; mętny

shaft (szaeft) s. drzewce; trzon; strzała; promień; wał; trzonek; dyszel; szyb

shaggy ('szaegy) a. włochaty; krzaczasty

shake; shook; shaken (szejk; szuk; szejken)

shake (szejk) v. potrząsać; uścisnąć dłoń; grozić (palcem); wstrząsać; drżeć; dygotać; s. dygotanie; dreszcze; drżenie; potrząsanie

shake-up ('szejkap) s. otrząśnięcie (się); czystka (slang)

shaky ('szejky) adj. drżący; rozklekotany; słaby; zachwiany; chwiejący się

shale (szejl) s. łupek

shall (szael) v. będę; będziemy; musisz; musi; muszą (zrobić)

shallow ('szaelou) s. mielizna; adj. płytki; powierzchniowy; v. spłycać; płycieć; obniżać poziom (wody)

sham (szaem) adj. fałszywy;
oszukańczy; sztuczny; udawany; symulowany; upozorowany;
s. poza; symulowanie; symu-
lant; pozor; udawanie; v.uda-
wać, symulować

shambles ('szaemblz) pl. jatki; rzeź

shame (szejm) s. wstyd; v.wsty-
dzić się

shame on you ! ('szejm,on'ju:)
exp.: wstydź się !

shameful ('szejmful) adj. sromotny; haniebny

shameless ('szejmlys) adj. bezwstydny; bezczelny

shampoo (szaem'pu:) s. szampon;
mycie głowy szamponem; v. myć
szamponem

shank (szaenk) s. goleń; trzonek; uchwyt

shape (szejp) v. kształtować;
rzeźbić; modelować; formułować; wyobrazić; s. kształt;
kondycja; postać; zjawa; widmo; model

shaped ('szejpt)adj. ukształto-
wany

shapeless('szejplys) adj. bezkształtny; nieforemny; niezgrabny

shapely ('szejply) adj. kształtny; foremny; zgrabny

share (szeer) s. udział; należ-
na część; lemiesz; v. rozdzielić; dzielić (się); podzielać;
brać udział

share-holder ('szeer,houlder)
s. akcjonarjusz

shark (sza:rk) s. rekin

sharp (sza:rp) adj. ostry; bystry; pilny; wyraźny; chytry; do-
minujacy; inteligentny; adv.
punktualnie; szybko; biegiem

sharpen ('sza:rpen) v. ostrzyć;
temperować; obostrzyć; za-
ostrzyć

sharpener ('sza:rpner) s. temperówka; narzędzie do ostrze-
nia

sharpness ('sza:rpnys) s, ostrość; bystrość; chytrość; pilność

sharp-witted ('sza:rp'łytyd)
adj. bystry; dowcipny; rozgarnięty

shatter ('szaeter) v. gruchotać; roztrzaskać; niweczyć;
szarpać

shave; shaved; shaven (szejw;
szejwd; szejwn)

shave (szejw) v. golić (się);
oskrobać; strugać; s. golenie;
musnięcie

shaven (szejwn) v. zob. shave

shaving ('szejwyng) v. golenie;
skrobanie; wiórkowanie; s.
wiór

shawl(szo:l) s. szal

she (szi:) pron. ona

sheaf (szi:f) s. snop; wiązka;
wiązanka; plik; pl. sheaves
(szi:wz)

shear; sheared; shorn (szier;
szierd; szo:rn)

shear (szier) v. ścinać; uci-
nać; ostrzyc; s. ścinanie; pl.
nożyce (shears)

sheath (szi:s) s. pochwa; futerał; powłoka; prezerwatywa

sheaves (szi:wz) pl. od sheath

shed (shed) s. szopa; buda;
v. zrzucać; strącać; pozbywać
(się); pogubić; ronić; przelewać (krew); wydzielać; promieniować

sheep (szi:p) pl. owce

sheep dog ('szi:p,dog) s. owczarek

sheepish ('szi:pysz) adj. bojaźliwy; nieśmiały; zakłopota-
ny; zbaraniały; ogłupiały

sheer (szier) v. schodzić z kur-
su; skręcać nagle; adj. zwykły;
jawny; czysty; zwyczajny; stromy; prostopadły; pionowy;
przejrzysty; przewiewny; lekki;
adv. zupełnie; pionowo; stromo

sheet (szi:t) s. arkusz; prześcieradło; gazeta; tafla; obszar; warstwa; v. pokrywać
prześcieradłem; okrywać brezen-
tem

sheet iron ('szi:t,ajren) s.
blacha stalowa

shelf (szelf) s. półka; rafa;
mielizna; pl. shelves (szelwz)

shell (szel) s. łupina; skorupa; powłoka; osłona; łupina;
pancerz; muszla; szkielet;
łuska; pocisk; granat; gilza;
v. ostrzeliwać z armat; wyłus-
kiwać

shellfish ('szel,fysz) s. sko-
rupiak; mięczak

shelter ('szelter) s. schronienie; ochrona; osłona; v. chronic; osłaniać; udzielać schro-
nienia; zabezpieczać

shelve (szelv) v. odkładać (na
półkę; wkładać do szuflady;
opadać (wzdłuż stoku)

shelves (szelwz) pl. zob.shelf

shepherd ('szeperd) s. pastuch;
pasterz; y. paść; (pilotować)
prowadzić

shield (szi:ld) s. tarcza;
osłona; v. osłaniać; ochraniać

shift (szyft) v. zmieniać (np.
biegi); przesuwać; przełączyć;
zwalić; s. przesunięcie; zmiana; szychta; wykręt; wybieg

shiftless ('szyftlys) adj. niezaradny

shifty ('szyfty) adj. zmienny;
fałszywy; chytry

shilling ('szylyng) s. szyling

shin (szyn) s. goleń; v. kopać
w goleń

shine; shone; shone (szajn;
szon; szon)

shine (szajn) v. zabłyszczeć;
zajaśnieć; oczyścić na połysk;
s. jasność; blask; (slang):
granda; awantura; sympatia

shingle ('szyngl) s. gont; szyld;
wywieszka; kamyk; v. pokryc
gontami; krótko ostrzyc

shingles ('szynglz) pl. półpa-
siec

shiny('szajny) adj. błyszczący;
wypolerowany

ship (szyp) s. okręt; statek;
samolot; v. załadować; zaokre-
towac; posyłać

shipment ('szypment) s. załadunek; przesyłka; fracht

shipowner ('szyp,ołner) s. armator

shipping ('szypyng) s. flota
handlowa; żegluga; załadunek;
usługi żeglugowe; przesyłka;
adj. spedycyjny; okrętowy

shipping company ('szypyng'kampeny) s. firma okrętowa; armator

shipwreck ('szyp,rek) s. rozbicie statku; v. ulec rozbiciu;
spowodować rozbicie statku;
rozbić się

ship-wrecked('szyp,rekt) s. rozbitek

shipyard('szyp,ja:rd) s. stocznia

shire ('szajer) s. hrabstwo
(powiat)

shirk (sze:rk) v. uchylać się;
wymigiwać się; s. nierób; wy-
migiwacz

shirt (sze:rt) s. koszula

shirt sleeves ('sze:rt,sli:wz)
pl. rękawy od koszuli; bez
marynarki; adj. prosty; domowy

shit (szyt) v. wulg.: srać;s.gów-
no

shitty ('szyty) adj. wulg.: za-
srany

shiv (szyw) s. majcher (slang)

shiver ('szywer) v. drżeć;
trząsc się; rozbijać się w kawałki; s. dreszcz; kawałek

shock (szok) s. wstrząs; cios;
uderzenie; starcie; porażenie;
czupryna; kopka; v. wstrząsać;
gorszyć; oburzać; porazić

shock absorber ('szok-eb,so:r-
ber) s. tłumik drgań; amorty-
zator

shocking ('szokyng) adj. okropny; wstrętny; skandaliczny;
oburzający; niestosowny

shoddy ('szody) adj. tandetny

shoe (szu:) s. but; półbucik;
trzewik; okucie; podkowa;
nakładka (hamulca); obręcz;
nasada; v. obuwać; podkuwać

shoe; shod; shod (szu:, szod,
szod)

shoehorn ('szu:,ho:rn) s. łyżka do butów; wzuwacz

shoelace ('szu:,lejs) s. sznurowadło

shoemaker ('szu:,mejker) s. szewc

shoestring ('szu:,stryŋg) s. sznurowadło; bardzo mały kapitał

shoeshine ('szu:,szajn) s. czyszczenie butów (na połysk)

shone (szon) v. zob. shine

shook (szuk) v. zob. shake

shoot; shot; shot (szu:t; szot; szot)

shoot (szu:t) v. strzelić; wystrzelić; zastrzelić; rozstrzelać; zrobić zdjęcie; nakręcić film; mknąć; przemknąć; spłynąć; rwać; kiełkować; s. pęd; kiełek; polowanie; progi; plac zwozu śmieci

shooter ('shu:ter) s. strzelec; rewolwer

shooting ('shu:tyŋg) adj. mknący; pędzący; strzelający

shooting gallery ('shu:tyŋg,gaelery) s. strzelnica

shooting-star ('shu:tyŋg,sta:r) s. spadająca gwiazda

shooting-party ('shu:tyŋg,pa:rty) s. wyprawa łowiecka; polowanie

shop (szop) s. sklep; pracownia; warsztat; zakład; v. robić zakupy

shopkeeper ('szop,ki:per) s. kupiec; sklepikarz

shoplifter ('szop,lyfter) s. złodziej sklepowy

shopping center ('szopyŋg,senter) s. skupisko sklepów; ośrodek zakupów

shopping mall ('szopyŋg,mol) s. skupisko sklepów wzdłuż krytej hali ;pasaż handlowy

shop window('szop'łyndoł) s. wystawa

shore (szo:r) s. brzeg; wybrzeże; podpora; v. podpierać; podstęplowac

shorn (szo:rn) v. zob. shear

short (szo:rt) adj. krótki; niski; zwięzły; oschły; niecały; niewystarczający; adv. krótko; nagle; za krótko; s. skrót; zwarcie; pl. szorty

shortage ('szo:rtydż) s. brak; niedobor; deficyt

short circuit ('sho:rt'se:rkyt) s. krótkie spięcie; zwarcie

shortcoming ('sho:rt'kamyŋg) s. wada; niedociągnięcie; brak; niedobor

shorten ('szo:rtn) v. skracać

shorthand ('szo:rthaend) s. stenografia

shortly ('szo:rtly) adv. wkrótce; niebawem

shortness ('szo:rtnys) s. krótkość; niedobor

shorts ('szo:rts) pl. szorty; kalesony (krótkie)

shortstory ('szo:rt,sto:ry) s. nowela

short-sighted ('szo:rt'sajtyd) adj. krótkowzroczny; nieprzewidujący

short-term ('szo:rt'term) adj.. krótkoterminowy; krótkotrwały

short-winded ('szo:rt'łyndyd) adj. zasapany; krótko mówiący

shot (szot) v. zob. shoot; ładować broń; s. strzał; pocisk; śrut; zastrzyk; docinek; adj. mieniący się

shotgun ('szotgan) s. dubeltówka; śrutówka; strzelba

should (szud) v. tryb warunkowy od shall

shoulder ('szoulder) s. ramię; plecy; łopatka; pobocze; v. brać na ramię; rozpychać się

shout (szałt) s. krzyk; okrzyk; wrzask; v. krzyczeć; wykrzykiwać

shove (szaw) v. popychać; posuwać (coś); s. pchnięcie

shovel ('szawl) s. łopata; szufla; v. przerzucać łopatą lub szuflą

show; showed; shown (szou; szoud; szoun)

show (szou) v. pokazywać; wskazywać; s. wystawa; przedstawienie; pokaz

show around ('szou,e'raund) v.
oprowadzać

show off ('szou,o:f) v. popisywać się; paradować; starać się
imponować

show up ('szou,ap) v. demaskować; zjawiać się; ukazywać się

show business ('szou'byznyz)
s. przemysł widowiskowy

shower ('szałer) s. tusz; prysznic; przelotny deszcz; grad;
stek; przelotnie kropić; obsypywać; oblewać

shower bath ('szałer,ba:t) s.
tusz; prysznic

shown (szołn) v. zob. show

showy ('szoły) adj. ostentacyj-
ny; okazały

shrank (szraenk) s. zob. shrink

shred (szred) s. strzęp; v.
ciąć na strzępy

shrew (szru:) s. złośnica; sekutnica; sorek

shrewd (szru:d) a. przenikliwy
(np. obserwator)

shriek (szri:k) v. wrzeszczeć;
piszczeć; rechotać; s. wrzask;
pisk; gwizd (ostry)

shrill (szryl) adj. ostry;
przenikliwy; przeraźliwy;
v. rozlegać się przenikliwie;
adv. przenikliwie

shrimp (szrymp) s. krewetka;
karzełek; v. łowić krewetki

shrine (szrajn) s. przybytek;
relikwiarz; v. umieszczać
w przybytku

shrink; shrank; shrunk (szrynk;
szraenk; szrank)

shrink (szrynk) v. kurczyć (się)
wzbraniać (się) wzdrygać się;
s. kurczenie się; (slang):psy-
chiatra

shrinkage ('szrynkydż) s. kurczenie się; ubytek na wadze

shrivel ('szrywl) v. kurczyć
(się)

Shrovetide ('szrouwtajd) s. os-
tatki; zapusty

Shrovetide Tuesday ('szrouwtajd'tju:zdy) s. tłusty wtorek

shrub (szrab) s. krzew; krzak

shrubbery ('szrabery) s. krzaki

shrubby ('szraby) adj. krzaczasty

shrug (szrag) s. wzruszenie ra-
mion; v. wzruszyć ramionami

shrunken ('szrankn) v. zob.
shrink

shudder ('szader) s. dreszcz;
(slang):nudziarz; v. zadrżeć;
wzdrygać się

shuffle ('szafl) v. wlec się;
powłóczyć; kręcić; tasować;
mieszać; s. krok suwany; krętactwo; tasowanie (kart); wleczenie się; szuranie

shun (szan) v. unikać; wystrze-
gać się, s, baczność; uwaga

shut; shut; shut (szat; szat;
szat)

shut (szat) v. zamykać (się);
przytrząsnąć; adj. zamknięty

shut down ('szat,dałn) s.
zamknięcie; wstrzymanie pracy;
v. zamykać; kłaść koniec; zasłaniać; (o zakładzie) stanąć

shut up ('szat,ap) v. pozamykać;
zamknąć gębę; zamilknąć; bądź
cicho; wulg.:stul pysk!

shutter ('szater) s. okiennica;
zasłona; migawka; regulator
organów; v. zamykać okiennice

shy (szaj) adj. płochliwy;
wstydliwy; nieśmiały; nieufny;
ostrożny; skąpy; szczupły;
v. płoszyć się; stronić; rzucać; s. rzut (w coś)

shyness ('szajnys) s. skromność;
nieśmiałość

shyster ('szajster) s. chytry
(polityk) bez zasad; adwokat-
krętacz

sick (syk) adj. chory; znudzony; chorowity; skażony zaraz-
kami; chorobowy

sickbed ('sykbed) s. łóżko
chorego; łoże boleści

sick benefit ('syk'benefyt)
s. zasiłek chorobowy

sicken ('sykn) v. zaczynać cho-
rować; wywoływać obrzydzenie;
brzydzić (się)

sickle ('sykl) s. sierp

sick leave ('sykli:w) s. zwolnienie lekarskie; urlop chorobowy

sickly ('sykly) adj. chorowity;
słabowity; niezdrowy; choro-
bliwy; ckliwy

sickness ('syknys) s. choroba;
wymioty; nudności

sick room ('syk-ru:m) s. izba
chorych; pokój chorego

side (sajd) s. strona; adj.
uboczny; v. stać po czyjejś
stronie

side by side ('sajd,baj'sajd)
exp.: obok siebie; jeden przy
drugim

side arms ('sajda:rmz) pl. broń
boczna (np. szable)

sideboard ('sajdbo:rd) s. kredens

sidecar ('sajd,ka:r) s. przyczepa do motocykla

sided ('sajdyd) adj. stronny;
mający strony

side dish ('sajd,dysz) s. przystawka

side-kick ('sajdkyk) s. (slang):
kompan; pomagier

sideroad ('sajd,roud) s. boczna
droga

side line ('sajd,lajn) v. odsuwać na bok; zapobiegać

sidewalk ('sajd-ło:k) s. chodnik; trotuar

sidewalk café ('sajdło:kaefej)
s. kawiarnia na chodniku

sidewards ('sajdłedz) adv. bokiem; w bok

sideways ('sajdłejz) adv. bokiem;
na poprzek; adj. boczny

side with ('sajd,łys) v. brać
czyjąś stronę

siege (si:dż) s. oblężenie

sieve (syw) s. sito; rzeszoto;
przetak; v. przesiewać

sift (syft) v. przesiewać; przebierać; oddzielać; prószyć;
posypywać

sigh (saj) s. westchnienie;
v. wzdychać

sight (sajt) s. wzrok; widok;
celownik; przeziernik

sighted ('sajtyd) adj. spo-
strzeżony

sightly ('sajtly) adj. dający
dobry widok; miły; przyjemny

sight seeing ('sajtsi:yng) s.
zwiedzanie; adj. turystyczny

sight seeing tour ('sajtsi:yng-
,tu:r) s. zwiedzanie z wycieczką; wycieczka krajoznaw-
cza

sightseer ('sajtsi:er) s. turysta; zwiedzający

sign (sajn) s. znak; omen; godło; napis; wywieszka; szyld;
skinienie; oznaka; objaw;
slad; znak drogowy; hasło; odzew; v. znaczyć; naznaczyć;
podpisać; skinąć

sign up ('sajn,ap) v. zapisywać
się

sign out ('sajn,aut) v. wypisywać się

signal ('sygnl) s. sygnał; znak;
v. sygnalizować; zapowiadać;
dawać znak

signature ('sygnyczer) s. podpis; sygnatura; klucz

signature-tune('sygnyczer,tju:n)
s. oznaczenie tonacji

signboard ('sajnbo:rd) s. wywieszka; szyld; godło

signet ('sygnyt) s. sygnet;
pieczątka; v. pieczętować

significance (syg'nyfykens) s.
wyraz; ważność; znaczenie

significant (syg'nyfykent) adj.
istotny; znaczący; doniosły;
znamienny; ważny

signification (syg'nyfykejszyn)
s. znaczenie

signify ('sygnyfaj) v. znaczyć;
mieć znaczenie; oznaczać; za-
znaczać

signpost ('sajn,poust) s. drogowskaz

silence ('sajlens) s. milczenie;
cisza; v. nakazywać milczenie;
cicho !

silencer ('sajlenser) s. tłumik

silent ('sajlent) adj. milczący; cichy; małomówny

silk (sylk) s. jedwab; adj. jedwabny

silken ('sylkn) adj. jedwabny; jedwabniczy

silky ('sylky) adj. jedwabisty

sill (syl) s. próg; podkład; parapet

silly ('syly) s. głupiec; adj. głupi; ogłupiały

silver ('sylwer) s. srebro; v. posrebrzać; adj. srebrny; srebrzysty

silvery ('sylwry) adj. srebrzysty

similar ('symyler) adj. podobny; rzecz podobna

similarity (,symy'laeryty) s. podobieństwo

simmer ('symer) v. wolno gotować (się); burzyć się wewnątrz; s. gotowanie na wolnym ogniu

simple ('sympl) adj. prosty; zwykły; naturalny; szczery; naiwny; głupkowaty; zwyczajny

simplicity (sym'plysyty) s. prostota

simplification (,symplyfy'kejszyn) s. uproszczenie

simplistic ('symplystyk) adj. zbyt upraszczający

simplify ('symplyfaj) v. uprościć; ułatwić

simply ('symply) adv. po prostu

simulate ('symjulejt) v. udawać; naśladować

simultaneous (symel'tejnjes) adj. równoczesny; jednoczesny

sin (syn) s. grzech; v. grzeszyć

since (syns) adv. odtąd; potem; conj; skoro; ponieważ; od czasu jak

sincere (syn'sier) adj. szczery

sincerely (syn'sierly) adv. szczerze

sincerity (syn'seryty) s. szczerość

sinew ('synu:) s. ścięgno

sinews ('synu:s) pl. muskulatura; siła; moc

sinewy ('synuy) adj. muskularny; mocny

sing; sang; sung (syng; saeng; sang)

sing (syng) v. śpiewać; wyć; zawodzić; bzykać; świstać; opiewać; s. śpiew; świst

singe (syndż) v. opalać; osmalać

singer (synger) s. śpiewak

single ('syngl) adj. pojedynczy; jeden; samotny; szczery; uczciwy; s. bilet w jedną stronę; gra pojedyncza; v. wybierać; wyróżniać

single out ('syngl,aut) v. wybierać

single-handed ('syngl'haendyd) adj. adv. w pojedynkę; na własną rękę; samodzielny; samodzielnie

single room ('syngl'ru:m) s. pojedynczy pokój

single ticket ('syngl'tykyt) s. bilet w jedną stronę

singles bar ('syngls,ba:r) s. bar dla samotnych

singular ('syngjuler) adj. osobliwy; niezwykły; pojedynczy; liczba pojedyncza

singularity (,syngju'laeryty) s. osobliwość; niezwykłość; niezwykły człowiek

sinister ('synyster) adj. zbrodniczy; złowieszczy; lewy

sink; sank; sunk (synk; saenk; sank)

sink (synk) v. zatonąć; zatopić; zagłębić (się); opuścić; obniżyć; pogrążyć; zanikać; zmaleć; wykopywać; ukrywać; wyryć; zainwestować; amortyzować; s. zlew; ściek; bagno zepsucia

sinking ('synkyng)s. uczucie mdłości (np. z przerażenia)

sinner ('syner) s. grzesznik

sip (syp) s; łyk; popijanie; v. popijać

sir (se:r) s. pan; v. nazywać panem; exp.: proszę pana !

sirloin (se:rloyn) s. polędwica

sister (syster) s. siostra

sister in law ('syster yn,lo:)
s. szwagierka

sit; sat; sat (syt; saet; saet)
sit (syt) v. siedziec; przesia-
dywac; usiąsc; zasiadac; obra-
dowac; leżec; pozowac

sit down ('syt,dałn) v. usiąsc

sit up ('syt,ap) v. wyprosto-
wac się siedząc; czuwac;
usiąsc prosto

site (sajt) s. miejsce; plac
(np. budowy); położenie;
v. umieszczac

sitting ('sytyng) s. posiedzenie; sesja

sitting-room ('sytyng,ru:m) s.
bawialnia; salon

situated ('sytjuejtyd) adj.
umieszczony; stojący; usytuo-
wany

situation (,sytu'ejszyn) s. położenie; posada; sytuacja

six (syks) num. szesc; s. szost-
ka

sixteen ('syks'ti:n) num. szes-
nascie; s. szesnastka

sixth (sykst) num. adj. szosty;
s. jedna szosta

sixthly ('sykstly) adv. po
szoste

size (sajz) s. wielkosc; numer;
format; klajster; krochmal;
rzadki klej; v. sortowac wg
wielkosci; oceniac wielkosc;
nadawac się; krochmalic; usz-
tywnic klejem

sized-up ('sajzd,ap) adj. oce-
niony (co do wielkosci, siły
lub ważnosci)

sizzle ('syzl) v. skwierczec;
s. skwierczenie

skate (skejt) s. łyżwa; wrotka;
płaszczka; szkapa; pętak; pa-
tałach; v. slizgac się; jeż-
dzic na wrotkach

skater ('skejter) s. łyżwiarz;
wrotkarz

skeleton ('skelytn) s.szkielet

skeptic ('skeptyk) adj. sceptyczny; s. sceptyk

sketch ('skecz) s. szkic; skecz;
zarys; v. szkicowac ;przedstawic
w ogolnych zarysach(w krotkich
słowach);robic wstępny rysunek

sketch block ('skecz,blok) s.
szkicownik

sketchbook ('skecz,bu:k) s.
szkicownik

ski (ski:) s. narta; wyrzutnik
bomb; v. jezdzic na nartach

skid (skid) s. deska; płoza;
podporka; klin hamowniczy;
poslizg; zarzucenie; v. slizgac się; zarzucac; umieszczac
na płozach; hamowac

skier ('ski:er) s. narciarz

skiing ('skiyng) s. narciarstwo; jazda na nartach

ski lift ('ski lyft) s. wyciąg narciarski

skill ('skyl) s. zręcznosc;
wprawa

skilled ('skyld) adj. wykwali-
fikowany; wykonany fachowo

skillful ('skylful) adj. zręczny; wprawny

skillet (skylyt) s. patelnia;
(slang): draka

skim (skym) v. zbierac (smie-
tankę); szumowac; przebiegac
wzrokiem; puszczac po powierzchni; szybowac; s. zbieranie;
mleko zbierane; adj. zbierany

skimmer ('skymer) s. warzęchwa;
cedzidło

skimp (skymp) v. skąpic

skimpy (skympy) adj. skąpy; za
mały; niewystarczający

skin (skyn) s. skora; skorka;
cera; szawłok; (slang):oszust;
v. zdzierac skorę; pokrywac
naskorkiem; sciągac z siebie

skin-deep('skyn'di:p) adj.
powierzchowny

skindiver ('skyn'dajwer) s.
płetwonurek

skindiving ('skyn'dajwyng) s.
sportowe nurkowanie (z płetwami)   skora i kosci

skinny ('skyny) adj. chudy ;

skip (skyp) v. skakac; przeskakiwac; odskakiwac; pomijac;
(slang):uciekac; s. skok;
przeskok; kapitan sportowy

skipper ('skyper) s. szyper;
kapitan statku; skoczek; kapitan drużyny

skirt ('ske:rt) s. spódnica;
poła; wulg.:kobietka; przepona; brzeg; v. jechać brzegiem;
obchodzić; leżeć na skraju
skit ('skyt) s. skecz; satyra;
mnóstwo
skoal (skoul) excl.:na zdrowie!
skull (skal) s. czaszka
sky (skaj) s. niebo; klimat
skyjack ('skaj,dżaek) s. porwanie samolotu w locie; v. porwać samolot w locie (uprowadzać)
skyjacker ('skaj,dżaeker) s.
pirat powietrzny
skylark ('skajla:rk) s. skowronek; v. dokazywać; swawolić
skylight ('skajlajt) s. okno
dające górne światło; okno
w suficie
skyscraper ('skaj.skrejper) s.
drapacz chmur
skywards ('skajłerdz) adv.
ku niebu
slab (slaeb) s. płytka; v. krajać na płytki (kromki)
slack (slaek) adj. luźny; wolny; rozlazły; opieszały; ospały; leniwy; niedbały;
v. zluźniać; zwalniać; popuszczać; zaniedbywać; gasić (np.
ogień); s. luźna część; lenistwo; zastój; bezczelność;
miał węglowy ;zwis;impertynencja
slacken (slaeken) v. rozluźniać
(się); zwalniać; poluźniać
(się); popuszczać; zaniedbywać; gasić (np. wapno)
slacks (slaeks) pl. (luźne)
spodnie
slain (slejn) zabity; zob.slay
slake (slejk) v. gasić (np.
wapno); wywierać (np.zemstę)
slam (slaem) v. zatrzasnąć (się)
(slang) krytykować ostro; pobić; s. trzaśnięcie; ostra
krytyka; ciupa
slang (slaeng) s. gwara; żargon;
slang; adj. gwarowy; żargonowy;
v. nawymyślać komuś
slangy (slaengy) adj. gwarowy
slant (sla:nt).s. pochyłość;
skos; tendencja; punkt widze-

nia; spojrzenie; adj. ukośny;
v. iść skośnie; pochylać (się);
odchylać (się); być nachylonym
slap (slaep) s. klaps; plasnię-
cie; v. plasnąć; dać klapsa;
uderzyć; narzucić; adv. nagle;
prościutko; regularnie
slapstick ('slaep,styk) s. laska
arlekina; błazeńska komedia
slash (slaesz) v. pokiereszo-
wać; przeciąć; hłostać; smagać;
walić; ciąć; s. cięcie; szrama;
przecięcie; wyrąb; odpadki
drzewne; porosłe (krzakami) moczary
slate(slejt) s. łupek; dachówka
łupkowa; tabliczka do pisania;
lista (kandydatów w USA); v.po-
krywać dachówkami; umieszczać
na liście kandydatów; łajać;
wymyślać; krytykować
slate pencil ('slejt'pensl) s.
rysik
slattern ('slaete:rn) s. brudas;
flejtuch; kocmołuch
slaughter ('slo:ter) v. rżnąć;
zabijać; wymordować; s. ubój;
rzeź; masakra
Slav (sla:w) adj. słowiański
slave (slejw) adj. niewolniczy;
s. niewolnik; v. harować
slavery ('slejwery) s. niewol-
nictwo
slay; slew; slain (slej; slu:,
slejn) v. zabić; uśmiercać
sled (sled) s. sanie; v. wozić
saniami
sledge hammer ('sledż-haemer)
s. oburęczny młot
sleek (sli:k) adj. gładki; uli-
zany; v. gładzić; wygładzać
sleep; slept; slept (sli:p;
slept; slept)
sleep (sli:p) v. spać; spoczywać; dawać nocleg; s. sen;
spanie; drzemka
sleep off (sli:p,of) v. ode-
spać wtyczka (szpiegowska etc.)
sleeper ('sli:per) s. człowiek
śpiący; dźwigar; potencjalny
przedmiot rozgłosu;truteń;leń
sleeping-bag ('sli:pyng,baeg)
s. śpiwór

sleeping car ('sli:pyng,ca:r)
s. wagon sypialny

sleeping partner ('sli:pyng-
'pa:rtner) s. cichy wspólnik

sleeping pill ('sli:pyng,pyl)
s. pigułka nasenna

sleepless ('sli:plys) adj. bezsenny

sleepwalker ('sli:p,ło:ker) s.
lunatyk

sleepy ('sli:py) adj. śpiący

sleet (sli:t) s. słota; deszcz
ze śniegiem; gołoledź

sleeve (sli:w) s. rękaw; tuleja; łuska; nasadka; tuba;
zanadrze

sleeved ('sli:wd) adj. z rękawami

sleigh (slej) v. saneczkować
(się); jechać saniami

slender ('slender) adj. wysmukły;szczupły; wiotki; nikły;
skromny; niewielki; słaby

slept (slept) v. zob. sleep

slew (slu:) v. zob. slay

slice (slajs) s. kromka; płatek;
plasterek; kawałek; łopatka
kuchenna; v. krajać na kromki;
kawałki etc. przecinać; wiosłować; wyjmować łopatką

slick (slyk) adj. gładki; tłusty; oślizgły; miły; pociągający; pierwszorzędny; adv. gładko; prościutko; s. tłusta plama (na morzu); szerokie dłuto

slicker ('slyker) s. gładki
płaszcz od deszczu; oszust

slid (slyd) v. zob. slide

slide (slid; slid (slajd; slyd;
slyd)

slide (slajd).v, suwać (się);
sunąć (się); ślizgać (się);
s. ślizganie się; suwak; pro-
wadnica ślizgowa; poślizg;
przeźrocze; zrzutnia

slide rule('slajd,ru:l) s. suwak logarytmiczny

slight (slajt) adj. wątły; niewielki; drobny; skromny; nieznaczny; v. lekceważyć;
s. lekceważenie

slim (slym) adj.szczupły; wysmukły; słaby; (slang):chytry;
v. wyszczuplać; odchudzać (się)

slime (slajm) s. szlam; muł;
śluz; płynna smoła ziemna;
v. zamulać; odmulać; zwilżać
(np. śliną)

slimy (slajmy) adj. mulisty;
zamulony; obleśny; oślizgły

sling; slung; slung (slyng;
slang; slang)

sling (slyng) s. proca; rzut;
pętla (np. do ładowania dźwigiem); temblak; rzemień do
strzelby itp. v. rzucać;
strzelać z procy; podnosić na
pętli; zawieszać na (np. rze-
mieniu)

slinger ('slynger) s. procarz

slinky ('slynky) adj. ukradko-
wy; (slang):mający ruchy węża

slip; slipped; slipped (slyp;
slypd; slypd)

slip (slyp) v. poślizgnąć (się);
wyśliznąć (się); ześliznąć
(się); popełnić nietakt; zrobić błąd; przepuścić (np.okaz-
je); wymknąć się; zerwać się;
zapomnieć; spuszczać (np. ze
smyczy); s. poślizg; potknięcie; pomyłka; błąd; przemówienie się; zsuw; halka; świstek
(papieru); pochylnia

slip off ('slyp,of) v. zdejmować; rozbierać się; ześlizgiwać się; spadać

slip on ('slyp,on) v. wdziewać

slip out ('slyp,aut) v. wymknąć się

slip up ('slyp,ap) s. błąd; za-
chwianie się; przemówienie się;
zsuw; ślizg; v. zrobić błąd;
pomylić się; potknąć się

slipper ('slyper) s. pantofel

slippery ('slypery) adj. śliski; niebezpieczny; ryzykowny;
nieuczciwy; nieczysty; drażliwy; delikatny; wykrętny;
chytry

slit; slit; slit (slyt; slyt;
slyt)

slit (slyt) v. rozszczepić;
rozedrzec wzdłuż; s. szpara;
szczelina; rozcięcie,
slobber ('slober) s. ślina; roz-
czulenie; v. oślinic się; roz-
czulic się
slogan ('slougen) s. slogan;
hasło; powiedzonko (np. rekla-
mowe)
sloop (slu:p) s. slup (łódź)
slop (slop) v. rozlewać; przepełniać płynem; rozpryskiwać;
s. kałuża; brudna woda; pomyje; lura
slop over ('slop,ouwer) v.
przelewać się przez wierzch
slope (sloup) s. pochyłość;
spadek; nachylenie; spadzis-
tość; stok; skarpa; zbocze;
pochylnia; v. być pochylonym;
miec nachylenie; nachylac;
pochylac; wałęsac się; łazi-
kować
sloping (sloupyng) adj. pochyły; skosny
sloppy ('slopy) adj. błotnisty;
pochlapany; zaniedbany; rozlazły; ckliwy
slot (slot) s. szczelina; rozcięcie; trop; ślad; v. roz-
ciąć; nacią́c; wyżłobic
sloth (slous) s. lenistwo; le-
niwiec
slot-machine ('slotme,szi:n)
s. (grający lub sprzedający)
automat na monety
slouch (slaucz) s. przygarbie-
nie; niedbała postawa; wałkoń;
v. garbic się; iśc ociężale;
opuszczac rondo kapelusza
slough (slau) s. bagno; trzęsawisko
slaugh (slaw) v. leniec; zrzu-
cac skórę
sloven ('slawn) s. niechlujny;
brudas; flejtuch; fuszer;
partacz
slovenly ('slawnly) adj. niechlujny; partacki
slow (slou) adj. powolny; nie-
gorliwy; nieskory; opieszały;
leniwy; tępy; nudny; adv. wolno; powoli

slow down ('slou,dałn) v. zwalniać; przyhamować
slow-motion ('slou'mouszyn) s.
zwolnione tempo; w zwolnionym
tempie
slowworm ('slou,łe:rm) s. padalec
sluggish ('slagysz) adj. ospały; leniwy; powolny
sluice ('slu:s) s. śluza; ściek;
rynna; v. puszczac wodę (ze
stawu etc). spłukiwać; zalewać; chlusnąć; spływac ze
śluzy
slums (slamz) s. dzielnica nędzy
slumber ('slamber) v. spac lekko; drzemac; s. sen; drzemka;
spokój; bezczynność
slung (slang) v. zob . sling
slush (slasz) s. chlapa; odpadki tłuszczowe; smar; fundusz
z odpadków; tajny fundusz na
przekupstwo; v. opryskac; wysmarowac; pokrywac zaprawą
slut (slat) s. flejtuch; kocmołuch; plucha; pinda; szmata;
flądra; suka
sly (slaj) ad. szczwany; chytry;
filuterny
slyboots ('slajbu:ts) s. urwis;
spryciarz; chytrus (udający
głupiego)
smack (smaek) s. posmak; odrobina; trzask; mlasnięcie;
cmoknięcie; klaps; jednomasz-
towiec; v. cmokac; strzelac
z bata; dac w pysk; oblizywac
(wargi)
smacking ('smaekyng) adj.
zgrabny; raźny; mocny (wiatr)
small (smo:l) adj. mały; drobny; niewielki; skromny; ciasny;
nieliczny; nieznaczny; małostkowy; adv. drobno; na małą ska-
lę; cicho; s. drobna rzecz;
mała częsc
small change ('smo:l,czejndż)
s. drobne (pieniądze)
small hours ('smo:l,auers) pl.
bardzo wczesne ranne godziny
smallish ('smo:lysz) adj. ma-
ławy

small of the back ('smo:1,ow-
'dy,baek) s. krzyże
smallpox ('smo:1,poks) s. ospa
smart (sma:rt) adj. dotkliwy;
cięty; zreczny; żwawy; dowcipny; szykowny; zgrabny; elegancki; v. piec; palić (np.
w oczy); cierpieć; szczypać;
parzyć; odczuwać boleśnie;
pokutować
smart aleck ('sma:rt,alek) s.
Jędrek-mędrek
smash (smaesz) v. rozbić; rozwalić; roztrząskać; zmiażdżyć;
potłuc; palnąć; rozgromić;
upadać; zbankrutować; ścinać
piłkę
smashing ('smaeszyŋg) adj. nadzwyczajny; niezwykły
smattering ('smaeteryŋ) s. znajomości po łebkach; wiedza
powierzchowna
smear (śmier) v. osmarować;
zasmarować; wlepić komuś sma-
ry; s. plama; smar
smell; smelt; smelled (smel;
smelt; smeld)
smell (smel) s. węch; woń; zapach; odor; smród; v. pachnieć; tracić; mieć zapach;
śmierdzieć; mieć powonienie;
obwąchiwać; czuć zapach;
zwietrzyć; zwąchać; poczuć
smelt (smelt) v. sob. smell;
stapiać; wytapiać (metal);
s. stynka (ryba)
smile (smajl) v. uśmiechać się;
s. uśmiech
smite; smote; smitten (smajt;
smout; 'smytn)
smite (smajt) v. uderzać; porazić; powalić; zabić; nękać;
karać; oczarować; s. cios;
uderzenie;s próbą
smith (smyŝ) s. kowal
smithy (smyŝy) s. kuźnia
smitten ('smytn) v. zob.smite
smock (smok) s. chałat; kitel;
v. ubierać chałat; ozdabiać
rysunkiem szachownicy
smog (smog' s. mgła zanieczysz-
czona dymem (Londyn,Los Angeles)

smoke (smouk) s. dym; palenie;
papieros; v. dymić; kopcić; wykurzać; wyjawiać; wykadzać; oka-
dzać; okopcić; uwędzić; przypa-
lać; palić (tytoń)
smoke-dried ('smouk,drajd) adj.
wędzony
smoker ('smouker) s. palący; pa-
lacz
smoking ('smoukyŋg) s. palenie
(tytoniu)
smoking car ('smoukyŋg,ka:r) s.
wagon dla palących
smoking compartment ('smoukyŋg-
kaem,pa:rtment) s. przedział
dla palących
smoky ('smouky) adj. dymiący;
przydymiony; zadymiony; okopcony
smolder ('smoulder) v. tlić się;
s. tlenie się; dym
smooch (smu:cz) v. brudzić; walać; całować się; ściskać się;
migdalić się
smooth (smu:ŝ) adj. gładki; spokojny; łagodny; v. gładzić; łagodzić; adv. gładko; s. wygła-
dzenie
smooth down ('smu:ŝ,dałn) v.
wygładzić; uspakajać (się)
smother ('smadzer) v. stłumić;
stłamsić; obcałowywać; zatuszować; okrywać
smudge (smadż) v. poplamić; za-
brudzić; s. plama; kleks; brud
smuggle ('smagl) v. przemycać
smuggler ('smagler) s. przemytnik
smut (smat) v. poplamić; s. brud
z sadzy; sprośności; tłuste
kawały; śnieć
smutty ('smaty) adj. sprośny;
brudny od sadzy
snack (snaek) s. zakąska
snack bar ('snaek,ba:r) s. bufet; bar
snafu (snae'fu:) v. zabałaganić;
s. bałagan (slang)
snail (snejl) s. ślimak
snake (snejk) s. wąż; v. wić
się; wlec (za sobą);pełzać jak
wąż;przybierać kształt węża

snap (snaep) v. łapać zębami;
warczeć; błysnąć; urwać; złamać; chwytać; zapalić się do;
przerwać szorstko; poprawić
się; mieć się na baczności;
zatrzasnąć (się); strzelać
z bicza; pstryknąć; sfotogra-
fować; spiesznie załatwiać;
machnąć ręką lekceważąco;
s. ugryzienie; warknięcie;
trzask; zatrzask; dociskacz;
zdjęcie; rzecz łatwa; adj.
prosty; łatwy; doraźny; nagły

snap bolt ('snaep,boult) s.
zatrzask u drzwi

snap fastener('snaep,fa:sner)
s. zatrzask

snappish ('snaepysz) adj.
zgryźliwy; kostyczny

snappy ('snaepy) adj. zgryźliwy; kostyczny; żwawy; prędki

snapshot ('snaepszot) s. zdjęcie migawkowe; strzał na chybił trafił

snare (sneer) v. usidlać; łapać w sidła; s. sidła; pułapka

snarl (sna:rl) s. warknięcie;
plątanina; v. warczeć; plątać (się); zaplątać; robić
zator

snatch (snaecz) v. złapać;
wyrwać; s. złapanie; urywek;
strzęp; mig

sneak (sni:k) v. chyłkiem zakradać się; przemykać się;
zerkać; zwiać; s. podły
tchórz

sneakers ('sni:kers) pl. trze-
wiki; trampki

sneer (snier) v. uśmiechać się
szyderczo; kpić; drwić; s.
szyderstwo; szydercze spojrzenie

sneeze (sni:z) v. kichać;
s. kichnięcie

sniff (snyf) v. prychać; pociągać nosem; krzywić się na
coś; powąchać; obwąchać; zwąchać; wyczuć; s. prychnięcie;
pociągnięcie nosem

sniffle ('snyfl) s. katar; po-
ciąganie nosem; v. pociągać
nosem

snipe (snajp) s. bekas; strzał
z ukrycia; v. z ukrycia: strzelać; trafić, zabić

sniper ('snajper) s. strzelec
wyborowy; strzelec z ukrycia

snivel ('snywel) s. śluz z nosa;
biadolenie; udawanie; v. smarkać się; skamleć; biadolić;
płakać; rozczulać się

snob (snob) s. człowiek wywyższa-
jący się

snoop (snu:p) v. myszkować;
wścibiać nos; s. szpicel

snoop around ('snu:p,e'raund)
v. przemyszkowywać; szpiegować

snooze ('snu:z) s. drzemka;
v. drzemać; zdrzemnąć się

snore (sno:r) v. chrapać; s.
chrapanie

snort (sno:rt) v. parskać;
s. parsknięcie

snout (snaut) s. ryj; pysk; morda; wylot

snow (snou) s. śnieg; (slang):
kokaina; heroina; v. ośnieżyć;
śnieg pada; zasypać śniegiem;
pobić na głowę; omamiać

snowball ('snoubo:l) s. kula
śnieżna; v. bić się śniegiem;
rosnąć jak lawina

snow blindness ('snou'blajndnys)
s. śnieżna ślepota

snowdrift ('snou'dryft) s. zas-
pa śnieżna

snowdrop ('snoudrop) s. śnie-
życzka

snow job ('snou,dżob) s. naciąganie pochlebstwami

snow-white ('snou'hłajt) adj.
śnieżnobiały

snowy ('snoły) adj. śnieżny;
śniegowy

snub (snab) v. ofuknąć; dać po
nosie; traktować lekceważąco;
nagle zatrzymać; adj. perkaty;
zadarty nos; s. bura; ofuknięcie;ostra odprawa;afront;ucie-
ranie nosa komuś;przywodzenie
kogoś do porządku

snuff(snaf) s. tabaka; proszek
do zażywania przez nos; zapach;
opalony koniec knota; v. zażywać tabakę; pociągać nosem;
czyścić koniec knota
snug (snag) adj. przytulny;
wygodny; ukryty; v. tulić się;
zrobić przytulnym
snuggle ('snagl) v. przytulić
się
so(sou) adv. tak; a więc; w ta-
kim razie; a zatem; też; tak
samo; bardzo to; także; excl.:
to tak ! no, no !
so far ('sou fa:r) adv. jak
dotąd ; jak do tej pory
soak (souk) v. moczyć (się);
nasycać (się); przenikać; namoknąć; (slang):wyciągać (od
kogoś) pieniądze; mocno uderzyć; s. moczenie (się); woda
do moczenia; popijawa; zastaw
soap (soup) s. mydło; pochleb-
stwo; wazelinowanie się (komuś) v. mydlić (się); po-
chlebiać; adj. mydlany; myd-
larski
soap box ('soup,boks) s. skrzynia od mydła; mównica (np.
uliczna). v. przemawiać na
ulicy, w parku etc.
soap opera ('soup'opere) s.
(popołudniowe) przedstawienie
radiowe lub telewizyjne pełne
małżeńskich kryzysów, tragedii,
cierpień, płaskiej czułostko-
wości i melodramatycznych za-
kończeń
soar (so:r) v. wznosić się;
osiągać wyżyny; iść w górę
(np. ceny)
sob (sob) v. łkać; szlochać;
s. łkanie; szloch
sober ('souber) adj. trzeźwy;
wstrzemięźliwy; stateczny;
zrównoważony; rzeczowy; poważny; spokojny; v. trzeźwieć;
wytrzeźwieć; wytrzeźwiać ;
otrzeźwieć; opanować się
sober up ('souber,ap) v. wytrzeźwieć
sober-minded ('souber,majndyd)
adj.stateczny; zrównoważony

so-called ('sou-ko:ld) adj.
tak zwany
soccer ('soker) s. piłka nożna
sociable ('souzebl) adj. towarzyski; przyjacielski; gro-
madny; stadny
social ('souzel) adj. społeczny; socjalny; s. zebranie
towarzyskie
social democrat ('souszel'de-
mekraet) s. socjaldemokrata
socializm ('souszelyzem) s.
socjalizm
social security ('souszel-
sy'kjueryty) s. ubezpiecze-
nia społeczne
socialist ('souszelyst) s.
socjalista; adj. socjalistycz-
ny
social worker ('souszel'łerker) s. pracownik społeczny;
pracownik urzędu opieki spo-
łecznej
socialize ('souszelajz) v.
upaństwowić; uspołecznić
social welfare ('souszel,łel-
feer) s. opieka społeczna
society (so'sajety) s. towarzystwo; społeczeństwo; społeczność; spółka (np. akcyj-
na)
sock (sok) s. skarpetka; cios;
szturchaniec; v. cisnąć w kogoś; uderzyć; walnąć; adv.
prosto (np. w nos)
socket ('sokyt) s. oprawka;
oczodół; zębodół; gniazdko;
wydrążenie
sod (sod) s. darń; darnina;
wulg.: skurwysyn; sodomita
sofa ('soufe) s. kanapa; sofa
soft (soft) adj. miękki; delikatny; przyciszony; łagodny;
słaby; głupi; wygodny
soft drink ('soft,dryŋk) s.
napój bezalkoholowy
soft goods ('soft,gu:ds) pl.
tekstylia
soften ('softn) v. zmiękczyć;
osłabić; złagodzić; złagod-
nieć; zmięknąć
soil (sojl) s.gleba; rola; ziemia; brud;plama; v.zabrudzić;
powalać; poplamić;wysmarować

sojourn ('sedże:rn) s. pobyt;
v. przebywac; zatrzymywać (się)

sold (sould) v. sprzedany; zob.
sell

soldier ('souldżer) s. żołnierz
najemnik; adj. żołnierski;
v. służyc w wojsku

sole (soul) s. podeszwa; podwa-
lina; zelówka; stopa; spodek;
sola; adj. jedyny; wyłączny

solemn ('solem) adj. solenny;
uroczysty; poważny

solicit (se'lysyt) v. prosić;
zwracac się (o cos); nagabywać; ubiegać się; zwracać (np.
uwagę)

solicitor (se'lysyter) s. radca prawny; akwizytor; agent
firmowy

solicitous (se'lysytes) adj.
pragnący; troszczący się o...;
niepokojący się

solicitude (se'lysytju:d) s.
troska; pieczołowitość;
troskliwość

solid ('solyd) adj. stały; masywny; lity; trwały; mocny;
rzetelny; solidny; ciało stałe; bryła

solidarity ('soly'daeryty) s.
solidarnosc

solidity (so'lydyty) s. masyw-
nosć; trwałość; rzetelność

soliloquy (se'lylekły) s. monolog; mówienie do siebie

solitary (so'lytery) adj. samotny; odosobniony; odludny;
pojedynczy; wyjątkowy; adj.
pustelnik; odludek; samotnik

solitude ('solytju:d) s. samot-
nosć; osamotnienie; odludne
miejsce

solo ('soulou) adj. adv. w pojedynkę; adj. jednoosobowy;
s. solo

soloist ('soulyst) s. solista

soluble ('soljubl) adj. rozpuszczalny; możliwy do rozwiązania

solution (so'ljuszyn) s. rozczyn; roztwor; rozwiązanie
(problemu)

solve (solw) v. rozwiązywać
(np. problemy)

solvent ('solwent) adj. wypłacalny; rozpuszczający; s.
rozpuszczalnik

somber ('somber) adj. mroczny;
ciemny; posępny; ponury

some (sam) adj. jakis; pewien;
niejaki; nieco; trochę; kilku;
kilka; kilkoro; niektorzy;
niektore; sporo; niemało; nie
byle jaki; adv. niemało; mniej
więcej; jakies; pron.: niektorzy; niektore; kilku; kilka

some more ('sam,mor) exp.: nieco
więcej

somebody ('sambedy) pron. ktos;
s. ktos ważny

someday ('samdej) adv. kiedys

somehow ('samhał) adv. jakos;
w jakis sposób

someone ('samłan) pron. ktos;
s. ktos

somersault ('samerso:lt) s.
salto; koziołek

something ('samsyng) s. cos;
cos niecos; ważna osoba; adv.
trochę; nieco; (slang):co się
zowie

sometime ('samtajm) adj. były;
adv. kiedys; swego czasu

sometimes ('samtajmz) adv. niekiedy; czasem; czasami

someway ('sam,łej) adv. jakos

somewhat ('samhłot) adv. nieco;
do pewnego stopnia; niejaki

somewhere ('samhłe:r) adv.
gdzies

son (san) s. syn

song (song)s. piesn; spiew

song-bird ('songbe:rd) s. ptak
spiewający

song-book ('songbuk) s. spiew-
nik

sonic ('sonyk) adj. dźwiękowy

sonic boom ('sonyk,bu:m) s.
grzmot samolotu przekraczają-
cego szybkość dźwięku

son-in-law ('san,ynlo:) s. zięć

sonnet ('sonyt) s. sonet

soon (su:n) adv.wnet; niebawem;
wkrótce; zaraz; niedługo

sooner ('su:ner) adv. wcześniej; adj. chętnie

soot (sut) s. sadza; kopeć; v. brudzić sadzą; użyźniać sadzą

soothe (su:z) v. uspakajać; uciszać

sooty ('suty) adj. okopcony; zakopcony; czarny jak sadza

sophisticated (se'fystykejtyd) adj. wyszukany; wyrafinowany; wymyślny; doświadczony

sophomore ('sofemo:r) s. student drugiego roku

sorcerer ('so:rserer) s. czarownik; czarodziej

sorceress ('so:rserys) s. czarodziejka

sorcery ('so:rsery) s. czary

sordid ('so:rdyd) adj. brudny (np. zysk); nikczemny; podły; skąpy

sore (so:r) adj. bolesny; drażliwy; wrażliwy; dotkliwy; dotknięty; złoszczący się; zmartwiony; adv. srodze; bardzo; akrutnie

sore throat ('so:r,trout) s. zapalenie gardła; anßina

sorrow ('sorou) s. zmartwienie; żal; smutek ; narzekanie; v. martwić się; boleć za...

sorrowful ('sorouful) adj. smutny; zmartwiony; przykry

sorry ('so:ry) adj. żałujący; zmartwiony; przygnębiony; nędzny; marny

sorority (se'ro:ryty) s. korporacja studentek (w USA)

sort (so:rt) s. rodzaj; gatunek; sorta; v. sortować

sortie ('so:rty) s. wypad wojskowy; lot bojowy

so-so ('sou-sou) adj. taki sobie; adv. tak sobie

sought (so:t) v. zob. seek

soul (soul) s. dusza

soulless (soulys) adj. bezduszny

sound (saund) s. dźwięk; ton; szmer; cieśnina wodna; pęcherz pławny; sonda; v. dźwięczeć;

brzmieć; grać (na trąbce); bić na alarm; głosić; opukiwać; wymawiać; zabierać głos; chwalić się; sondować; zanurzać się do dna

soundless ('saundlys) adj. bezdźwięczny

soundproof ('saundpru:f) adj. dźwiękoszczelny

soundwave ('saundłejw) s. fala dźwiękowa

soup (su:p) s. zupa

sour ('sauer) adj. kwaśny; skwaszony; cierpki; v. kisnąć; kwasić się; zniechęcać się

source (so:rs) z. źródło

south (saus) adj. południowy; z. południe; adv. na południe

southeast ('saus'i:st) s. południowy wschód; adj. południowo-wschodni; adv. na południowy wschód

southern ('sadzern) adj. południowy; s. południowiec

southernmost (,sadzern'moust) adj. najbardziej na południe

southwards ('sausłerdz) adv. ku południowi; na południe

southwest ('saus'łest) s. południowy zachód; adj. południowo-zachodni; adv. na południowy zachód

southwesterly ('saus'łesterly) adj. południowo zachodni

souvenir ('su:venier) s. pamiątka

sovereign ('sawryn) s. suweren; władca; adj. suwerenny; wyniosły; najwyższy

sovereignty ('sawrenty) s. suwerenność; zwierzchnictwo; najwyższa władza

Soviet ('souwjet) adj. sowiecki; radziecki

sow; sowed; sown(sou; soud; soun)

sow (sou) v. siać; zasiewać; posiać

sow (sau) s. maciora; koryto odlewnicze

sown (soun) v. zob. sow

spa (spa:) s. zdrojowisko; zdrój mineralny; (USA) sport zdrowotny za opłatą

space (spejs) s. przestrzeń;
miejsce; obszar; odstęp; okres;
przeciąg (czasu); chwila;
v. robić odstępy; rozstawiać

spacecraft ('spejs,kra:ft) s.
pojazd międzyplanetarny

spaceship ('spejs,szyp) s. statek międzyplanetarny(kosmiczny)

space suit ('spejs;sju:t) s.
kombinezon międzyplanetarny

spacious ('spejszes) adj. przestronny; obszerny

spade (spejd) s. łopata; v. kopać łopatą

spades (spejdz) pl. piki (w kar-
tach)

spadework ('spejd-łe:rk) s.
praca przygotowawcza

span; spanned; spanned (spaen;
spaend; spaend)

span (spaen) v. zob. spin; sięgać (np. przez rzekę); rozciągać się (np. nad rzeką); obejmować (pamięcią); mierzyć pię-
dzią; posuwać się stopniowo;
łączyć brzegi; s. piędź; rozpiętość; przeswit; przęsło;
przeciąg (czasu) zasięg; roz-
ciągłość; para; zaprzęg

spangle ('spaengl) s. świecidełko; błyskotka; v. pokrywać
świecidełkami; błyszczeć świecidełkami

spangled ('spaengld) adj. pokryty (świecidełkami)

Spanish ('spaenysz) adj. hiszpański

spank ('spaeŋk) s. klaps; v. dawać klapsa; popędzać klapsami;
iść kłusem

spanking (spaeŋkyŋg) s. skorobicie; lanie; adj. chyży; zamaszysty; silny; solidny; świetny; adv. bardzo (slang)

spanner ('spaener) s. ścięgno
(mostu); klucz do nakrętek
gąsienica miernikowa

spare (speer) v. oszczędzać; zaoszczędzić; odstępować; obywać
się; zachować; przeznaczać;
szanować (uczucia); szczędzić;
a. zapasowy; oszczędny; skromny;

drobny; szczupły; wolny (np.
czas) s. część zapasowa; koło
zapasowe

spare time ('speer,tajm) s.
wolny czas

spare tire ('speer,tajer) s.
koło zapasowe

sparing ('speeryŋg) adj. oszczędn-
ny; wstrzemięźliwy

spark (spa:rk) s. iskra; zapłon;
wesołek; zalotnik; v. iskrzyć
się; sypać iskrami; zapalać się;
dawać początek; zalecać się
grać galanta

spark plug ('spa:rk,plag) s.
świeca samochodowa (zapłonowa)

sparrow ('spaerou) s. wróbel

sparse (spa:rs) adj. rzadki;
z rzadka; rozsiany; szczupły

spasm ('spaezem) s. skurcz;
spazm; napad (kaszlu)

spastic ('spaestyk) adj. skur-
czowy; spazmatyczny; chory na
paraliż kurczowy

spat (spaet) v. zob. spit;
kłócić się; dawać klapsy; składać jaja (przez ostrygi); s.
jaja mięczaków; kłótnia;
klaps; lekki cios

spatial ('spejszel) adj. przestrzenny

spawn (spo:n) s. ikra; skrzek;
nasienie; v. składać (ikrę;
skrzek); wylęgać się; płodzić;
zasiewać grzybnię

spayed (spejd) adj.(samica)
z usuniętymi jajnikami; bez-
płodna: wytrzebiona

speak; spoke; spoken (spi:k;
spo:k;'spoken)

speak (spi:k) v. mówić; przemawiać; szczekać na rozkaz; grać;
sygnalizować do statku

speak out ('spi:k,aut) v. wypowiadać (się); mówić otwarcie;
mówić głosno

speak up ('spi:k,ap) v. wypowie-
dzieć się bez osłonek

speaker ('spi:ker) s. mówca;
głosnik; marszałek sejmu; przewodniczący

spear (spier) s. dzida; włócznia; oszczep; kopia; oscien;
zdzbło; v. przebijac dzidą;
kłuc; wystrzelic w górę

spearhead ('spierhed) s. ostrze dzidy; czołówka; v. prowadzic; byc na czele

special ('speszel) adj. specjalny; wyjątkowy; osobliwy;
dodatkowy; nadzwyczajny;
s. dodatkowy autobus; nadzwy-
czajne wydanie; reklamowa
dzienna znizka ceny w sklepie

specialist ('speszelyst) s.
specjalista

speciality (,speszy'aelyty)
s. specjalnosc; specjalna
cecha

specialize ('speszelajz) v.
wyspecjalizowac (się); wy-
szczególniac; precyzowac;
rozniczkowac(się); ograniczac
(się)

specially ('speszely) adv.
specjalnie; szczególnie

specialty ('speszelty) s.spec-
jalnosc; specjalizacja

species ('spi:szi:z) s. gatunek; rodzaj; postac czegos

specific (spy'syfyk) adj.
okreslony; wyrazny; gatunkowy;
charakterystyczny; specyficzny

specify ('spesyfaj) v. wyszcze-
gólniac; precyzowac; konkrety-
zowac; sporządzic specyfika-
cję

specimen ('spesymyn) s. okaz;
przykład; wzor; typ; próba;
numer okazowy

spectacle ('spektekl) s. widowisko

spectacles ('spektekls) pl. okulary

spectacular (spek'taekjuler)
adj. widowiskowy; efektowny;
sensacyjny; okazały; s. film
widowiskowy "wielki"

spectator ('spektejter) s.
widz

speculate ('spekjulejt) v.
spekulowac; rozmyslac nad..;
rozwazac

speculation (,spekju'lejszyn)
s. spekulacja; domysł; rozmyslanie

sped (sped) v. zob. speed

speech (spi:cz) s. mowa; prze-
mowienie; język; wymowa; przemowa

speechless ('spi:czlys) adj.
(chwilowo) niemy; oniemiały;
(slang): pijany (kompletnie)

speed; sped; sped (spi:d; sped;
sped)

speed (spi:d) v. pospieszyc;
popędzic; pędzic; odprawic;
kierowac spiesznie; popierac
(np. sprawę); s. szybkosc;
prędkosc; bieg

speedboat ('spi:dbout) s.
slizgacz

speed limit ('spi:d,lymyt) s.
ograniczenie szybkosci

speedometer (spi'domyter) s.
szybkosciomierz

speed up ('spi:d,ap) v. przy-
spieszyc; s. przyspieszenie

speedy ('spi:dy) adj. szybki

spell; spelled; spelt (spel;
speld; spelt)

spell (spel) v. przeliterowac
(poprawnie); napisac ortogra-
ficznie; znaczyc; mozolnie
odczytywac; sylabizowac; zaczarowac; urzec; dac (wytchnienie); odpoczywac; zaczarowac;
pracowac na zmiany; s. chwila
pracy; chwila; okres; pewien
czas; zaklęcie; czar

spellbound ('spel baund) adj.
zaczarowany; urzeczony;
oczarowany

spelling ('spelyŋg) s. pisownia

spelt (spelt) v. zob. spell

spend; spent; spent (spend;
spent; spent)

spend (spend) v. wydawac (np.
pieniądze); spędzac (czas);
zuzywac (się); wyczerpywac;
tracic (np. siły); składac
ikrę

spent (spent) v. wyczerpany;
wydany; zob. spend

sperm (spe:rm) s. sperma; nasienie męskie

spew (spju:) v. wypluwać; wymiotować; wyrzucać z siebie

sphere (sfier) s. kula; globus;
ciało niebieskie; sfera (np.
działalności)

spice (spajs) s. wonne korzenie;
pikanteria; v. przyprawiać
korzeniami; dodawać pikanterii

spicy ('spajsy) adj. korzenny;
zaprawiony korzeniami; aromatyczny; pikantny; nieco nieprzyzwoity; elegancki; żywy;
ostry

spider (spajder) s. pająk

spike (spajk) s. ćwiek; bretn-
al; kolec; gwóźdź do szyn;
szpic; ostrze; fanatyk religijny; kłos; v. przymocowywać
gwoździami; zaostrzać końce;
ranić kolcami; zagważdżać
armatę; zaprzeczać pogłoskom;
odpierać; zakrapiać alkoholem;
wspinać się na słup ostrymi
okuciami(na butach)

spiky ('spajky) adj. kolczasty;
wydłużony; ostro zakończony;
fanatyczny religijnie

spill; spilled; spilt (spyl;
spyld; spylt)

spill (spyl) v. rozlewać (się);
rozsypywać (się); uchylać żagiel z wiatru; wyśpiewać; wygadać (się); powiedzieć
wszystko; popsuć sprawę; s.roz-
lanie; rozsypanie; ilość roz-
lana; ilość rozsypana; odłamek;
zatyczka; upadek; fidybus do
zapalania świec

spilt (spylt) v. zob. spill

spin; spun; span (spyn; span;
spaen)

spin (spyn) v. snuć; prząść;
kręcić (się); puszczać bąka;
toczyć na tokarni; łowić ryby
na błyszczkę; zawirować;
s. kręcenie (się); zawirowanie;
ruch wirowy; przejażdżka; korkociąg (w locie)

spinach ('spynycz) s. szpinak

spinal column ('spajnel'kolem)
s. stos pacierzowy;kręgosłup

spinal cord ('spajnel'ko:rd)
s. rdzeń kęgowy

spindle ('spyndl) s. wrzeciono;
oś; wał; 14400 jardów lnu;
15120 jardów bawełny; v. mieć
kształt wrzecionowaty

spine ('spajn) s. kręgosłup;
grzbiet; cierń

spinning mill ('spynyŋg,myl)
s. przędzarnia

spinster ('spynster) s. stara
panna

spiny ('spajny) adj. ciernisty;
kolczasty; trudny

spiral ('spajerel) s. spirala;
adj. spiralny; v. poruszać się
spiralnie; szybko isc w górę
(np. ceny); nadawać kształt
spirali

spire ('spajer) s. iglica; hełm
wieży; zwój; spirala; ostry
szczyt; szpic; pęd; v. strzelać w górę; nakładać hełm na
wieżę

spirit ('spyryt) s. duch; intelekt; umysł; zjawa; odwaga;
nastawienie; nastrój; v. zachęcać; ożywiać; rozweselać; zabierać (potajemnie)

spirits ('spyryts) s. spirytus;
alkohol

spirited ('spyrytyd) adj. ożywiony; z werwą; napisany
z zacięciem

spiritual ('spyryczuel) adj.
duchowy; duchowny; natchniony;
s. murzyńska pieśń religijna

spit; spat; spat (spyt; spaet;
spaet)

spit (spyt) v. pluć; zionać;
splunąć; wypluć; lekceważyć;
fuknąć; parsknąć; mżyć; kropić; pryskać; nadziewać na rożen; s. plucie; ślina; parska-
nie; mżenie; jaja owadów; rożen; językowaty półwysep;
głebokość łopaty

spite (spajt) s. złość; uraz;
złośliwość; v. zrobić na złość;
in spite of= wbrew; pomimo

spiteful ('spajtful) adj. złośliwy; mściwy

spittle ('spytl) s. plwocina;
ślina

splash (splaesz) v. chlapać;
pryskać; plusnąć; rozpryskać;
upstrzyc; s. rozprysk; plusk;
zakropienie; plamka; sensacja

splash down ('splaesz,dałn) v.
wodować; s. wodowanie

spleen (spli:n) s. śledziona;
przygnębienie; splin; złość

splendid ('splendyd) adj.
wspaniały; świetny; doskonały

splendor ('splender) s. wspaniałość; przepych, blask

splint (splynt) s. łupek; szyna; patyk; kość piszczelowa;
v. wstawiać w szyny złamaną
kość

splinter ('splynter) s. drzazga;
odłamek

split; split; split (splyt;
splyt; splyt)

split (splyt) v. łupać; pękać;
rozszczepiać (się); dzielić;
oddzielać (się) odchodzić;
s. pęknięcie; rozszczepienie;
rozdwojenie; odejście

splitting ('splytyŋg) adj. roz-
sadzający; ostry; gwałtowny

splutter ('splater) v. pryskać;
opryskać; mówić bezładnie;
s. pryskanie; szybka gadanina;
zgiełk

spoil; spoilt; spoiled (spojl;
spojlt; spojld)

spoil (spojl) v. psuć (się);
zepsuć (się); (slang): krasc;
sprzątnąć; przetrącić

spoils (spojls) pl. łupy (też
w polityce)

spoilsport ('spojl'spo:rt) s.
psujący zabawę

spoilt ('spojlt) v. zob.spoil

spoke (spouk) v. zob. speak;
s. szczebel; szprycha

spoken ('spoukn) v. zob. speak

spokesman (spouksmen) s. rzecznik

sponge (spandż) s. gąbka; wycior; tampon; pieczeniarz; pasożyt; v. myć gąbką; chłonąć;
łowić gąbki; wyłudzać; wsysać;
pasożytować

sponger ('spandżer) s. pasożyt;
pieczeniarz (slang)

sponge cake ('spandż'kejk) s.
biszkopt

spongy ('spandży) adj. gąbczasty

sponsor ('sponser) s. patron;
organizator; gwarant; ojciec
chrzestny; v. wprowadzać; być
gwarantem; popierać; opłacać
(np. program telewizyjny)

spontaneous (spon'tejnjes)
adj. spontaniczny; samorzutny;
naturalny; odruchowy

spook (spuk) s. zjawa; duch;
upiór

spool (spu:l) s. cewka; rolka;
szpulka; nawijać na (rolkę
etc).

spoon (spu:n) s. łyżka; v. czerpać (łyżką); durzyć się w kims

spoon out ('spu:n,aut) v. drążyć; nabierać

spoon-fed ('spu:n,fed) adj. roz-
pieszczony; łyżką karmiony

spoonful ('spu:nful) s. łyżka
czegoś

spore (spo:r) s. zarodnik;
v. wytwarzać zarodniki

sport (spo:rt) s. sport; zawody;
zabawa; rozrywka; sportowiec;
(slang): człowiek dobry, elegancki, lubiący zakładać się;
v. bawić się; uprawiać sport;
obnosić się z czyms; popisywać się; wyśmiewać się

sportive ('spo:rtyw) adj. żartobliwy

sportsman ('spo:rtsmen) s.
sportowiec; myśliwy

sporty ('spo:rty) adj. (slang):
sportowy; krzykliwy (ubiór);
modny

spot (spot) s. plama; skaza;
kropka; cętka; plamka; miejsce;
lokal; odrobina; punkt; dolar;
krótkie ogłoszenie; v. plamić
(sie); umiejscowić (np. zepsucie); poznawać; wyróżniać;
rozmieszczać; adj. gotowy;
gotówkowy; dorywczy

spotless ('spotlys) adj. bez
skazy

spotlight ('spotlajt) s. reflektor szczelinowy; v. rzucać światło (na coś)

spout (spaut) s. wylot; rynna;
wylew; dziobek; strumień;
pochyłe koryto; v. wyrzucać
z siebie płyn; tryskać;
chlusnąć; recytować

sprain (sprejn) s. bolesne
wykręcenie (nie zwichnięcie);
v. wykręcić

sprang (spraeng) v. zob.
spring

sprat (spraet) s. szprotka
(śledź); v. łowić szproty

sprawl (spro:l) v. rozwalać
się; gramolić się; rozłazić
się; rozrzucać; być rozrzu-
conym; s. rozwalenie się;
rozłażenie się; rozkrzewia-
nie się

spray (sprej) s. rozpylony
płyn; krople z rozpylacza;
płyn do rozpryskiwania;
spryskiwacz; grad (kul); gałązka; v. opryskiwać; rozpryskiwać (się)

spread; spread; spread (spred;
spred; spred)

spread (spred) v. rozpościerać (się); rozszerzać (się);
posiać; rozsmarowywać; rozkładać; pokrywać; nakrywać;
rozklepywać; s. rozpostar-
cie; rozpiętość; zasięg;
szerokość; pasta; narzuta;
(slang: smarowidło na chleb

sprig (spryg) s. gałązka;
latorośl; młokos; szyft;
v. ozdabiać gałązkami

sprightly ('sprajtly) adj. żywy; dziarski; wesoły

spring; sprang; sprung (spryng;
spraeng; sprang)

spring (spryng) v. skakać;
sprężynować; wypłynąć; puścić
pędy (pąki); zaskoczyć; spowodować wybuch; paczyć się;
puszczać oczko; pękać; s.wios-
na; skok; sprężyna; źródło;
zdrój; prężność; adj. wiosenny; sprężynowy; źródlany

springboard ('spryng,bo:rd)
s. trampolina; odskocznia

springtime ('spryngtajm) s.
wiosna

sprinkle ('sprynkl) v. posypać;
pokropić; s. deszczyk

sprint (sprynt) s. krótki bieg;
krótki zrywny wysiłek; v.biec
na krótki dystans

sprinter (sprynter) s. sprinter;
biegacz krótkodystansowy

sprout (spraut) s. pęd; odrośl;
v. puszczać pędy; wyrastać

spruce (spru:s) s. świerk;
smrek; adj. elegancki; schludny; v. stroić się

sprung (sprang) v. zob. spring

spun (span) v. zob. spin

spur (spe:r) v. pogardliwie odtrącać; pospieszyć; popędzać;
s. odtrącenie z pogardą

sputter ('spater) v. pryskać
(śliną); bełkotać; s. pryskanie; plwociny; bełkot

spy (spaj) s. szpieg; tajniak;
szpiegowanie; v. szpiegować;
wybadać; czatować; wypatrzeć

squabble ('skłobl) s. sprzeczka; sprzeczać się

squad (skłod) s. oddział; grup-
ka; (lotny) patrol; wóz patro-
lowy; v. formować grupki

squall (skło:l) s. szkwał; kłopot; wrzask; v. wiać gwałtownie; wrzeszczeć

squander ('skłonder) s. marno-
trawstwo; v. trwonić; marno-
trawić

square ('skłeer) s. kwadrat;
czworobok (budynków); plac;
kątownik; węgielnica; adj.
kwadratowy; prostokątny; prostopadły; uporządkowany; zupełny;
uczciwy; v. robić kwadratowym
prostym; podnosić do kwadratu;
płacić (dług); adv. w sedno;
rzetelnie; wprost

squash (skłosz) v. ubijać (się);
gnieść (się); miażdżyć;
s. miazga; tłok; rodzaj tenisa;
napój owocowy; mała dynia

squat; squat; squat (skłot;
skłot; skłot)

squat (skłot) v. kucac; przycupnąć; nielegalnie koczowac
na gruncie; adj. przysadzisty;
niski; szeroki; s. osoba przy-
sadzista; kucki

squeak (skłi:k) v. piszczec;
skrzypiec; mowic piskliwie;
(slang): zdradzac (sekrety);
sypac; przepychac się z trudnością; s. pisk; trudne osiągnięcie czegos

squeal (skłi:l) v. piszczec;
kwiczec; (slang): awanturowac
się; sypac; wydawac (kogos);
s. pisk; kwik; sypanie (kogos, czegos)

squeamish ('skłi:mysz) adj.
wybredny; pruderyjny; przesadny; wrażliwy

squeegee ('skłi:dżi:) s. przyrząd w kształcie litery T do
usuwania wody z mytych szyb

squeeze (skłi:z) v. sciskac;
wyciskac; wygniatac; wciskac;
odciskac; sciesnic; s. ucisk;
nacisk; odcisk; tłok; scis-
nięcie

squeezer ('skłi:zer) s. wy-
ciskacz (soku)

squid (skłyd) s. przynęta
z mątwy; kałamarnica (ryba)

squint (skłynt) s. zez; ukosne
spojrzenie; zerknięcie; skłonność; v. mrużyc oczy; wysiłac
wzrok; zezowac; skłaniac się;
adj. zezowaty; zerkający

squirm (skłe:rm) v. wic się
(z bolu); płonąc (ze wstydu);
kręcic się niespokojnie;
s. skrecanie się

squirrel ('skłó:rel) s. wiewiórka

squirt (skłe:rt) v. strzykac;
tryskac; s. strzykawka; struga; pętak

stab (staeb) v. dzgnąć; pchnąc;
ugodzic; ranic; s. pchnięcie;
dzgnięcie; rana kłuta

stability (ste'bylyty) s.sta-
łosc; statecznosc; stabil-
nosc; równowaga

stabilize ('stejbylajz) v.
ustalac; stabilizowac

stable ('stejbl) s. stajnia;
stadnina; v. trzymac konie
w stajni; adj. stały; stanowczy; trwały

stack (staek) s. stóg; stos;
sterta; komin; kupa; v. układac w stogi; ustawiac w kozły;
układac podstępnie przeciwko
komus

stadium('stejdjem) s. stadion;
faza; stadium (czegos)

staff (staef) s. laska; drzewce; sztab; personel; adj.
sztabowy; v. obsadzac persone-
lem

stag (staeg) s. rogacz; jeleń;
samotny meżczyzna

stage (stejdż) s. scena; stadium; etap; rusztowanie; pomost; postój; v. wystawiac;
odegrac (sztukę); urządzac;
inscenizowac; adj. teatralny;
sceniczny

stagecoach ('stejdż-koucz) s.
dyliżans

stage-manager ('stejdż'maenydżer) s. reżyser

stagflation ('staegflejszyn)
s. stagnacja, rosnące bezrobocie i inflacja jednoczesnie

stagger ('staeger) v. zataczac
się; wahac się; chwiac się;
układac w zygzak lub w odste-
pach; porażac; s. układ skosny; zachodzący na siebie w od-
stępach lub zygzakowaty; zataczanie się; pl. zawroty głowy

staggering ('staegeryng) adj.
przerażający; oszałamiający;
rozbrajający

stagnant ('staegnent) adj. za-
stały; stojący; będący w za-
stoju

stain (stejn) v. plamic (się);
brudzic; szargac; barwic; ko-
lorowac; farbowac; drukowac
tapety; s. plama;barwik; bej-
ca do drzewa

stained ('stejnd) adj. zabar-
wiony (np. szkło)

stainless ('stejnlys) adj. nierdzewny (stal); nieskalany

stair (steer) s. stopień; pl.
schody

stair case ('steer,kejs) s.
klatka schodowa

stair way ('steerłej) s. schody

stake (stejk) s. słup; słupek;
kołek; palik; stawka; kowa-
dełko blacharskie; v. przy-
twierdzać kołkami; wytaczać;
przywiązywać do słupa; stawiać na coś

stake out ('stejk,aut) v.
wziać pod obserwację; wyznaczać granicę

stake-out ('stejkaut) s. zasadzka (slang)

stale ('stejl) adj. stęchły;
nieświeży; zwietrzały;
czerstwy; przestarzały;
v. czuć nieświeżym

stalk (sto:k) v. kroczyć; podkradać się; podchodzić; s.(majestatyczny) chód; podkrada-
nie się; podchodzenie; wysoki komin; łodyga; nóżka (kie-
liszka)

stall (sto:l) v. działać opóź-
niająco; zwlekać; przewlekać;
kręcić; zwodzić; przetrzymy-
wać; dławić motor; utykać;
grzęznąć; trzymać bydło w obo-
rze; zaopatrywać w przegrody
s. stajnia; obora; stragan;
kiosk; przegroda; komora
(w kopalni); (slang): trik;
kruczek

stallion ('staeljen) s. ogier

stalwart ('sto:lłert) s. bojownik partyjny; adj. dzielny;
krzepki; stanowczy

stammer ('staemer) v. jąkać się;
s. jąkanie się

stamp (staemp) v. stemplować;
wytłaczać; tupać; kruszyć;
wbijać (w pamięć); przylepiać
znaczki pocztowe; s. stempel;
pieczątka; znaczek; piętno;
cecha; pokrój; tupnięcie; ubijak do kruszenia (rudy)

stanch (staencz) v. tamować
krwotok; adj. wierny; stały;
krzepki; szczelny

stand; stood; stood (staend;
stud; stud)

stand (staend) v. stać; stanąć;
wytrzymać; znosić; przetrzymać;
zostać; utrzymywać się; stawiać
opór; znajdować się; być; postawić; (slang): płacić; s. stanie;
stanowisko; stojak; trybuna;
postój; łan; ława dla świadków;
unieruchomienie; umywalka

stand back ('staend,baek) v.
stać w tyle; zachowywać rezerwę

stand by ('staendbaj) v. popierać; być w stanie pogotowia

stand off ('staend,of) v. cofać
się

stand-off ('staend,of) s. nie-
rozegrana (równowaga sił)

stand out ('staend,aut) v. wyróżniać się; kontrastować;
wytrwać

stand up ('staend,ap) v. wstawać; powstawać; stawać w obro-
nie; nie ustępować; stawiać
czoło

standard ('staenderd) s. sztandar; norma; miernik; wzorzec;
wskaźnik; stopa (życiowa);
próba; słup; podpórka; adj.
znormalizowany; normalny; typowy; przeciętny; wzorcowy;
klasyczny; literacki (język)

standardize ('staenderdajz) v.
normalizować; dostosowywać do
normy; mierzyć wzorcem; porów-
nywać z wzorcem

standing ('staendyng) adj. stojący; na pniu; pionowy; stały;
s. stanie; stanowisko; znaczenie; poważanie; reputacja;
czas trwania

standing room ('staendyng,ru:m)
s. miejsce stojące

standoffish ('staend'ofysz) adj.
nieprzystępny; trzymający się
z dala

standpoint ('staend,poynt) s.
punkt widzenia; punkt obserwacyjny

standstill ('staendstyl) s. zastój; przerwa; martwy punkt;
unieruchomienie

stank (staenk) v. zob. stink

star (sta:r) s. gwiazda; gwiazdor; gwiazdka; v. ozdabiać gwiazdkami; być gwiazdorem; adj. gwiezdny; występujący w głównej roli

starboard ('sta:rberd) s. prawa burta; v. sterować na prawo

starch (sta:rcz) s. skrobia; sztywność; krochmal; v. nakrochmalić; (slang):siła

starchy ('sta:rczy) adj. nakrochmalony; skrobiowaty; sztywny

stare (steer) v. patrzeć; gapić się; wpatrywać się; zwracać uwagę; s. nieruchomy wzrok; wytrzeszczone oczy; zagapione spojrzenie

stare at ('steer,aet) v. gapić się na...

stark (sta:rk) adj. sztywny; zupełny; czysty; wierutny; ponury; posępny; adv. zupełnie; całkowicie

starling ('starlyng) s. szpak

starlit ('sta:rlyt) adj. gwiaździsty; oświetlony gwiazdami; wygwieżdżony

starry ('sta:ry) adj. gwiaździsty; usiany gwiazdami; promienny; marzycielski; rozmarzony

stars-spangled ('sta:r-spaengld) adj. usiany gwiazdami (flaga USA)

start (sta:rt) v. zacząć; ruszyć; startować; zerwać się; podskoczyć; wyruszyć; zabierać się; uruchamiać; obsuwać; rozpoczynać; wszczynać; s.początek; start; wymarsz; poderwanie się; obsunięcie się; zdobywanie przewagi

starter ('sta:rter) s. starter; rozrusznik; startujący zawodnik; pierwsze danie; kierownik ruchu

startle ('sta:rtl) v. zaskoczyć; zaniepokoić; podrywać; wzdrygać się; przestraszać;

s. zaniepokojenie; poderwanie się

startling ('sta:rtlyng) adj. sensacyjny; zdumiewający; niepokojący

starvation (sta:r'wejszyn) s. głód; głodowanie; głodzenie; przymieranie głodem

starve (sta:rw) v. głodować; zagłodzić; przymierać z głodu, zimna; łaknąć; zmuszać (głodem, brakiem)

stash (staesz) v. (slang): chować na potem; s.schowanie; schowek

state (stejt) s. państwo; stan; zajęcie; parada; pompa; ceremoniał; stan prac; adj. państwowy; stanowy; uroczysty; paradny; formalny; v. stwierdzać; wyrażać; określać; wyrażać (też symbolami)

state department ('stejt,dy'-'pa:rtment) w USA ministerstwo spraw zagranicznych

stately ('stejtly) adj. uroczysty; okazały; adv. uroczyście; okazale

statement ('stejtment) s. wyrażenie; twierdzenie; sprawozdanie; wyciąg; oświadczenie; deklaracja; zeznanie

state room ('stejt,rum) s. prywatny pokój; kabina; przedział

state side ('stejt,sajd) adj. amerykański; w stanach

statesman('stejtsmen) s. mąż stanu

statesmanship ('stejtsmenszyp) s. rozum polityczny

static ('staetyk) adj. statyczny; nieruchomy

station ('stejszyn) s. stacja; stanowisko; stan; pozycja życiowa; godność; punkt; stacja telewizyjna; radiowa, etc.

stationary ('stejsznery) adj. niezmienny; stały; nieruchomy; pozycyjny

stationmaster ('stejszyn,ma:-ster) s. naczelnik stacji

station wagon ('stejszyn,łaegn)
s. samochod typu kombi
statistics (ste'tystyks) s.
statystyka
statue ('staeczu:) s. posąg
statute ('staetju) s. ustawa;
prawo; statut; nakaz
staunch (sto:ncz) v. tamować
krwotok; tamponować; adj. oddany; wierny; zagorzały
stay; stayed; staid (stej;
stejed; stejd)
stay (stej) s. pobyt; zwłoka;
odroczenie; opóźnienie; zawieszenie; podpora; wanta;
zatrzymanie; przerwa; wytrzymałość; v. zostać; przebywać;
wytrzymać; odraczać; kłaść
kres; zaspakajać (głod)
stay away ('stej,ełej) v.
trzymać się z dala
stay up ('stej,ap) v. nie siadać
stay with ('stej,łys) v. mieszkać u kogoś
stead (sted) s. miejsce; na
miejsce; pożyteczność
steadfast ('sted,fa:st) adj.
stały; nieruchomy; niezachwiany; niewzruszony; mocny;
pewny
steady ('stedy) adj. mocny;
silny; pewny; stały; rzetelny;
rowny; stateczny; excl.: powoli ! prosto ! naprzod ! stoj!
v. dawac rownowagę; odzyskiwać
rownowagę; s. podpora; (slang):
ukochany
steak (stejk) s. stek; befsztyk; płat (np. mięsa)
steal; stole; stolen (sti:l:
stoul; stoulen)
steal (sti:l) v. kraść; wykraść;
wejść ukradkiem; zakradać się;
skradać się; s. kradzież;
rzecz ukradziona; rzecz ku-
piona prawie że za darmo; dar-
mocha (slang)
stealth (stels) s. tajemni-
czość; ukradkowość
stealthy ('stelsy) adj. ukrad-
kowy; tajemny

steam (sti:m) s. para; v. parować; dymić; płynąć pod parą;
gotować w parze; umieszczać
pod parą
steam up ('sti:m,ap) v. zamglić
(się); zajść mgłą lub parą
steamer ('sti:mer) s. parowiec
steamship ('sti:m,szyp) s. parowiec
steel (sti:l) s. stal; pręt
stalowy; adj. stalowy; ze
stali; v. pokrywać stalą; kar-
tować
steelworks ('sti:l,łe:rks) s.
stalowania
steep (sti:p) v. moczyć się;
rozmiękczać; impregnować; pogrążyć się; rozpijać się;
adj. stromy; nieprawdopodobny;
wygórowany; przesadny
steepen ('sti:pn) v. nagle
podnosić ceny; robić stromym
steeple ('sti:pl) s. strzelista
wieża; ostra wieżyczka
steer (stier) v. sterować; kierować; prowadzić; s. wskazówka; młody wół na mięso
steering wheel ('stieryng,hłi:l)
s. kierownica; koło sterowe
stem (stem) s. pień; łodyga;
szpulka; trzon; trzonek; nóżka; v. pochodzić; tamować; powstrzymywać; iść pod prąd;
zwalczać
stench (stencz) s. smród; odor;
fetor
stenographer ('stenegraefer) s.
stenograf; stenografistka
step (step) s. krok; stopień;
takt; szczebel; schodek;
v. stąpać; kroczyć; iść; tan-
czyć; podnosić; wzmagać; przyciskać nogą; mierzyć (krokami)
stepchild ('step,czajld) s.
pasierb
stepfather ('step,fa:dzer) s.
ojczym
stepmother ('step,madzer) s.
macocha
stereo ('steriou) s. stereoskop;
dwugłosnikowe radio-adapter;
adj. stereofoniczny

sterile ('sterajl) adj. wyjałowiony; jałowy; sterylny;
bezpłodny

sterilize ('stery,lajz) v. wy-
jałowic; wysterylizowac

sterling (,ste:rlyŋg) s. pieniądz pełnowartosciowy; adj.
solidny; niezawodny

stern (ste:rn) adj. surowy;
srogi; s. rufa; zad; zadek;
tył; posladki

sternness ('ste:rnys) s. suro-
wosc; srogosc

stew (stu:) v. gotowac; dusic
(się); martwic się; wkuwac
się; s. potrawa duszona; kłopot; staw na ryby

steward ('stu:erd) s. zarządca;
ekonom; kelner; v. zarządzac;
byc stewardem

stewardess ('stu:erdys) s.
stewardesa

stewpan ('stu:,paen) s. rondel; garnek

stick; stuck; stuck (styk;
stak; stak)

stick (styk) v. wtykac; przekłuwac; kłuc; wbijac; zaryna-
nac; przyklejac; naklejac;
utkwic; utknąc; ugrzęznąc;
przyczepiac (się); trzymac
się (tematu); oszukiwac;
s. pałka; patyk; laska; kij;
tyczka; żerdz

stick out ('styk,aut) v. wystawiac; sterczec; zadac

stick to ('styk,tu) v. trzymac się (tematu); przylepiac

stick up, ('styk,ap) v. terro-
ryzowac (bronia); brac w obro-
nę; podnosic; przeciwstawiac
się

sticky ('styky) adj. lepki;
kleisty; grząski; parny;
(slang): marny; nieprzyjemny

stiff (styf) adj. sztywny;
twardy; kategoryczny; zdręt-
wiały; "słony"; wygorowany;
trudny; ciężki; silny;
s. (slang): trup; umrzyk;
niedojda; włoczęga; facet;
pedant

stiffen ('styfn) v. usztywniac;
podniesc (wymagania); zgęszczac;
zesztywniec

stifle (stajfl) v. dusic (się);
tłumic; przygaszac; tuszowac

stile (stajl) s. przełaz; kołowrot; pionowa rama drzwi

still (styl) adj. spokojny; cichy; nieruchomy; martwy (przedmiot); milczący; adv. jeszcze;
jednak; wciąż; dotąd; niemniej;
mimo to; v. uspokoic (się); uciszyc; destylowac; s. destylar-
nia (też wodki)

stillness ('stylnys) s. cisza;
spokoj; bezruch

stilt (stylt) s. szczudło

stilted ('styltyd) adj. na
szczudłach; nienaturalny;
sztuczny; na wspornikach

stimulant ('stymjulent) s. bodziec; podnieta; alkohol;
srodek podniecający; zachęta;
adj. pobudzający

stimulate ('stymjulejt) v. po-
budzac; zachęcac

stimulating ('stymjulejtyŋg)
adj. podniecający; pobudzający

stimulation ('stymjulejszyn)
s. podnieta; zachęta; podniecenie

stimulus ('stymjules) s. bodziec;
zachęta; podnieta

sting; stung; stung (styŋg;
staŋg; staŋg)

sting (styŋg) v. kłuc; parzyc;
kasac; szczypac; palic; rwac;
gryzc; s. żadło; ukłucie; poparzenie; piekący bol; uszczyp-
liwosc; zjadliwosc

stingy ('styndży) adj. skąpy

stink; stank; stunk (styŋk;
staeŋk; staŋk)

stink (styŋk) v. cuchnąc; smier-
dziec; zasmradzac; wyganiac
smrodem; (slang): poczuc smrod
s. smrod

stipulate ('stypjulejt) v. za-
żądac; uwarunkowac; zastrzegac
w umowie

stir (ste:r) v. ruszac; poruszac;
grzebac; mieszac; wzniecac; podniecac; s. poruszenie; podniecenie; ruch; (slang): więzienie

stirrup ('styrep) s. strzemię;
pociągiel; okucie do wspinania się

stitch (stycz) s. szew; ścieg;
oczko; kłucie; v. szyc; zaszyc; zeszywac

stoat (stout) s. gronostaj; v.
zaszywac niewidocznym ście-
giem

stock (stok) s. zapas; zasób;
bydło; pien; strzon; kłoda;
łożysko; ród; rasa; surowiec;
kapitał udziałowy; akcje giełdowe; obligacje; wywar; v. zaopatrywac; zagospodarowac; za-
rybiac; miec na składzie;
adj. typowy; seryjny; w stałym zapasie; repertuarowy

stockade(sto'kejd) s. palisada;
częstokół; obóz

stockbroker('stok,brouker) s.
makler giełdowy

stock exchange ('stok,eks'-
'czejndż) s. giełda

stockholder('stok,houlder) s.
akcjonariusz; udziałowiec

stocking ('stokyŋg) s. ponczo-
cha

stocky ('stoky) adj. krępy

stock market ('stok-'ma:rkyt)
s. giełda

stole (stoul) v. zob. steal;
s. stuła; etola

stolen ('stouln) v. zob. steal

stolid ('stolyd) adj. obojętny;
flegmatyczny

stomach ('stamek) s. żołądek;
brzuch; apetyt; ochota;
v. jesc; przełykac (obelgę);
znosic

stone (stoun) s. kamien; głaz;
skała; pestka; adj. kamienny;
v. ukamieniowac; obkładac
(mur) kamieniem; wyjmowac
pestki; upijac (się) na umór

stonewall ('stoun-ło:l) v. od-
mówic zaciekle jakiejkolwiek
kooperacji

stoneware ('stoun-łeer) s. naczynia kamionkowe

stony ('stouny) adj. kamienny;
kamienisty; skamieniały;
pestkowy

stood (stud) v. zob. stand

stool (stu:l) s. stołek; sedes;
taboret; stolec; klęcznik; podnóżek; pniak puszczający pędy;
wabik; v. puszczac pędy

stoop (stu:p) v. schylac się;
ugiąc się; poniżyc się; raczyc;
garbic się; s. pochylenie;
przygarbione plecy; weranda;
taras (przy domu)

stooping ('stu:pyŋg) adj. przy-
garbiony

stop (stop) v. zatrzymywac;
powstrzymywac; wstrzymywac;
zatykac; zaplombowac; zagrodzic;
zablokowac; zamknąc; zaprzesta-
wac; niedopuscic; stanąc; prze-
stac; exp.:przstan ! stój !
dosyc tego !; s. zatrzymanie
(się); stop; postój; przystanek; zatkanie; zator; zatyczka;
zderzak; ogranicznik

stop by ('stop,baj) v. wstąpic
do kogos na chwilę

stopover ('stop'ouwer) s. zatrzymanie się w podróży

stoppage ('stopydż) s. wstrzymanie; zatrzymanie (się); zatwardzenie

stopper ('stoper) s.korek; zatyczka; v. zatykac; umocowac
liną

stopping ('stopyŋg) s. plomba
(w zębie); zatrzymanie; zatkanie

storage ('sto:rydż) s. skład;
przechowywanie; magazynowanie

store ('sto:r) s. zapas; sklep;
skład; mnóstwo; składnica;
v. magazynowac; miescic w sobie; zaopatrywac; wyposażac

store up ('sto:r,ap) v. zama-
gazynowac; zachowac

storehouse ('sto:rhaus) s.
skład; magazyn; skarbnica; kopalnia

storekeeper ('sto:r,ki:per) s.
sklepikarz; kupiec

storey ('sto:ry) s. piętro

storeyed ('sto:rjed) adj. pięt-
rowy (angielska pisownia)

storied ('sto:rjed) adj. pięt-
rowy

stork (sto:rk) s. bocian

storm (sto:rm) s. burza; wichura; sztorm; zawierucha; szturm; v. szaleć (burza etc.) wpaść do pokoju; wypaść z pokoju (jak burzą); rzucać gromy; szturmować; brać szturmem

stormy ('sto:rmy) adj. burzliwy; zwiastujący burzę

story ('sto:ry) s. opowiadanie; opowieść; powiastka; historia; bajka; anegdota; gawęda; zmyślanie; nowela; piętro

story teller ('sto:ry,teler) s. gawędziarz; kłamczuch

stout (staut) adj. dzielny; krzepki; gruby; s, mocny np. porto (wino); mocne piwo; tęga osoba

stove (stouw) s. piec (też kuchenny); cieplarnia; v. zob. stave; hodować w cieplarni

stow (stou) v. wypełniać; układać szczelnie; mieścić; wsuwać; chować; przesłać (slang)

stow away ('stou,e'łej) v. jechać na gapę

stowaway ('stouełej) s. pasażer na gapę

straggling ('straeglyng) adj. sporadyczny; rozpościerający się; rzadki

straight (strejt) adj. prosty; bezpośredni; celny; szczery; otwarty; rzetelny; zwykły; s. prosta linia; prosty odcinek (toru); adv. prosto; wprost; na przełaj; po prostu; pod rząd; należycie; nieprzerwanie; ciągiem

straightaway ('strejt,ełej) adv. natychmiast ;bez zwłoki

straight ahead ('strejt,ehed) adv. na wprost

straighten ('srejtn) v. wyprostować(się); poprawić (się)

straightforward (strejt'fo:rłerd) adj. łatwy; jasny; prosty; prostolinijny; szczery; uczciwy

strain (strejn) v. prężyć; naprężać; naciągać; wytężać; odkształcać; nadużywać; nadwerężać; przeciążać; robić gwałtowne wysiłki; cedzić; przecedzać; s. naprężenie; napięcie; obciążenie; przemęczenie; zwichnięcie; nadwerężenie; wysiłek; odkształcenie; rasa; odmiana; rys

strainer ('strejner) s. sito; sączek; cedzidło; rozciągacz; napinacz

strait (strejt) v. ścieśniać; być w trudnościach

straited circumstances ('strejtyd,ser'kamstenses) s. kłopoty pieniężne

straiten ('strejtn) v. zbiednieć; zubożeć

strait jacket ('strejt'dżaekyt) s. kaftan bezpieczeństwa

straits (strejts) pl. cieśnina morska; kłopoty finansowe; braki czegoś

strand (straend) s.skręt; zwitek; pasmo; nitka; warkocz; sznur; rys; kosmyk; brzeg; plaża; v. splatać; osadzać na mieliźnie; osiąść na mieliźnie

strange (strejndż) adj. obcy; dziwny; niezwykły; nieznany; niewprawny

stranger ('strejndżer) s. obcy; nieznajomy; człowiek nieobeznany; exp.:panie tego !

strangle ('straengl) v. dusić; trzymać za gardło; zadusić

strap (straep) s. rzemień; pasek; rzemyk; taśma; uchwyt; rączka; chłosta; bicie; v. na pasku umocowywać; ostrzyć; bić paskiem; zalepiać plastrem

strategic (stre'ti:dżyk) adj. strategiczny

strategy ('straetydży) s. strategia; taktyka

straw (stro:) s. słoma

strawberry ('stro:bery) s. truskawka

stray (strej)v. zabłądzić; zabłąkać się; schodzić na manowce; s. zbłąkane zwierzę; dziecko bez opieki; adj.zabłąkany

strays (strejs) pl. zaburzenia
atmosferyczne (np. w radiu)
streak (stri:k) s. smuga; pasek; pasmo; prążek; rys;
pierwiastek;passa; v. ryso-
wac paski, prążki; błyskawicznie poruszać się; wpadać
nagle dokąds
streaky ('stri:ky) adj. prążko-
wany; w paski; zmienny; nie-
rowny (slang)
stream (stri:m) s. strumien;
potok; rzeka; struga; prąd;
v. płynąc (strumieniami);
ociekać; tryskać; powiewać
street (stri:t) s. ulica
streetcar ('stri:tka:r) s.
tramwaj
strength (strenkθ) s. moc; siła; stężenie; natężenie;
ilość; skład (ludzi)
strengthen ('strenkθn) v.
wzmocnic (się); wzmagac; dać
przewagę
strenuous (strenjues) adj.
męczący; żmudny; mozolny; wy-
teżony; zawzięty; pracowity;
energiczny; silny
stress (stres) s. nacisk; akcent; napór; wysiłek;
v. kłasc nacisk; podkreslac;
naciskać
stretch (strecz) s. naciągać
(się); naprężać; napinać; nad-
uzywac; przeciągać; rozciąg-
gać (się); ciągnac się; się-
gac; powiesic (kogos) s. napięcie; rozciąganie; przeciąganie się; nadużycie; połać;
okres służby; przeciąg czasu;
prosty odcinek toru; (slang):
pobyt w więzieniu
stretcher ('streczer) s. nosze
strew; strewed; strewn (stru:,
stru:d; stru:n)
strew (stru:) s. posypać; roz-
rzucić; porozrzucać
strewn (stru:n) v. zob. strew
stricken (stri:ken) v. zob.
strike; adj. dotknięty; nawie-
dzony; rażony; udreczony
stride; strode; stridden
(strajd; stroud; stridn)

stride (strajd) v. kroczyc;
przekroczyc; stać okrakiem
(nad czyms); s. krok; rozkrok
strife (stajf) s. spór; walka;
wspołzawodnictwo
strike; struck; stricken (strajk;
strak; strykn)
strike (strajk) v. uderzac; bic
(monetę); walic; kuc; wykrze-
sac; zapalic (zapałkę); natra-
fic; zastrajkowac; porzucac
robotę; chwytac (przynętę);
s. strajk; strychulec; wybicie
monety; natrafienie (żyły, np.
złotodajnej); chwycenie przy-
nęty; nieudane uderzenie palan-
tem; zwalenie wszystkich kręgli
naraz
strike off ('strajk off) v. od-
rapywac; scinac; wykreslac;
drukowac kilka egzemplarzy
strike out ('strajk,aut) v.
uderzac na odlew; zacząc; ukuc;
wymyslic
striker ('strajker) s. strajku-
jący; młotek (w dzwonku)
striking ('strajkyŋg) adj.
uderzający
string; strung; strung (stryŋg;
straŋg; straŋg)
string (stryŋg) v.zawiązac;
przywiązac; zaopatrzyc w struny; stroic; napinac; podniecac;
powiesic kogos; ciągnąc się
(klej); obwieszac; s. sznurek;
szpagat; powroz; sznurowadło;
tasiemka; cięciwa; struna;
żyła; włokno; rząd; stek
(głupstw)
strip (stryp) v. obdzierac;
ogałacac; obnażać; zdzierac;
rozbierac (się); wydobyc do
końca; scierac (gwint); ciąc
na paski; s. pasek; skrawek;
seria komiksow
strip-tease ('strypti:z) s.
rozbieranie się na scenie
stripes (strajps) pl. paski;
prążki; naszywki; chłosta;
cięgi
striped ('strajpt) adj. pa-
siasty; w pasy

strive; strove; striven
('strajw; strouw; strywn)
strive (strajw) v. starać się;
usiłować; dążyć; borykać się;
zwalczać
striven ('strywn) v. zob.strive
strode (stroud) v. zob. stride
stroke (strouk) s. uderzenie;
cios; cięcie; raz; porażenie;
ciąg; pociągnięcie (pióra);
rys; kreska; ruch (wiosła);
wysiłek; suw; skok (tłoka);
takt; głaskanie; v. znaczyć;
przekreślać; nadawać tempo;
głaskać; ugłaskać
stroke of luck ('strouk,ow'lak)
exp.: los szczęścia
stroll (stroul) v. przechadzać
się; spacerować; wędrować;
s. przechadzka
stroller ('strouler) s. space-
rowicz; włóczęga; aktor
wędrowny; wózek (dziecięcy)
strong (strong) adj. mocny;
silny; będący w liczbie...;
mocarstwowy; potężny; trwały;
solidny; wyskokowy; przekonywujący; ordynarny
strongbox ('strong,boks) s.
sejf; kasa ogniotrwała
strongroom ('strong,rum) s.
skarbiec
strove (strouw) v. zob.strive
struck (strak) v.zob. strike
structure ('strakczer) s. budowa; struktura; budowla; wiązanie; splot; v. nadawać
kształt
struggle ('stragl) v. szarpać
się; szamotać się; walczyć;
usiłować; s. walka;borykanie
strum (stram) v. rzępolić;
brzdąkać; s. brzdęk; brzdąkanie
strung (strang) v. zob. string;
adj. napięty
strut (strat) v. kroczyć ma-
jestatycznie; rozpierać;
s. krok majestatyczny; zastrzał; rozpora
stub (stab) s. pniak; korzeń;
resztka; niedopałek; grzbiet

(biletu); v. karczować; gasić (papierosa)
stubble ('stabl) s. rżysko;
ściernisko; twardy zarost
stubborn ('stabern) adj. uparty
stuck (stak) v. zob. stick
stud (stad) s. sworzeń; gwóźdź;
guz; trzon; słup; rozporka;
ogier; stadnina; v. nabijać
(np. gwoździami; guzami);
usiewać czyms; być rozsianym;
podpierać (słupami)
student ('stu:dent) s. student;
badający coś; znawca czegoś
studio ('stju:djou) s. studio;
pracownia
studio couch ('stju:djou,kaucz)
s. tapczan
studious ('stu:djes) adj. pilny; staranny; dbały; wyszukany
study ('stady) s. pracownia;
gabinet; nauka; przedmiot nauki, starań, troski, zadumy,
marzenia; v. badać; studiować;
dociekać; uczyć się
stuff (staf) v. napychać; opychać (się); tuczyć (się); fa-
szerować; wpychać; wkuwać;
s. materia; materiał; glina;
rzecz; rupiecie (brednie)
stuffing ('stafyng) s. nadzienie; farsz; nadziewka; wyściółka
stuffy ('stafy) adj. zatęchły;
duszny; ciężki; nudny; zatka-
ny (nos); (slang): ważny;
tępy; skwaszony; zły; purytań-
ski
stumble ('stambl) v. potykać
(się); utykać; natknąć się;
zawahać (kogoś); mieć skrupuły; czuć się dotkniętym;
s. potknięcie się
stumblebum ('stambl,bam) s.
(slang): zawalidroga; próżniak
stump (stamp) s. pniak; głąb;
kikut; ogarek; resztka; niedopałek; kulas; krzykactwo; agitacja (polityczna); kuć; klocek;
przysadkowaty człowiek; v. karczować; obcinać; zdumieć (się);
agitować; wyzwać kogoś; chodzić na protezie

stun (stan) v. ogłuszyć; oszołomić; s. oszołomienie (uderzenie hukiem)

stung (stang) v. zob. sting

stunk (stank) v. zob . stink

stunning ('stanyng) adj. nadzwyczajny; szlagierowy; ka-
pitalny

stupefy ('stu:pyfaj) v. ogłu-
piać; odurzać; wprawić
w osłupienie

stupid ('stu:pyd) adj. głupi;
odurzony; nudny; s. głupiec

stupidity ('stu:pydyty) s.
głupota; głupstwo

stupor ('stu:per) s. osłupienie; odurzenie; apatia

sturdy ('ste:rdy) adj. krzepki; dzielny; solidny; s. motylica

stutter ('stater) v. jąkać (się)
s. jąkanie się

sty (staj) s. chlew; burdel;
jęczmień (w oku); v. żyć w
chlewie; trzymać w chlewie

style (stajl) s. styl; maniera;
sposób; fason; wzór; kształt;
rylec; szyjka; tytuł; nazwa;
format; wskazówka; v. formować stylowo; określać mianem

stylish (stajlysh) adj. szykowny; stylowy; wytworny

suave (sła:w) adj. gładki; łagodny; uprzejmy

subdivision (,sabdy'wyżyn) s.
dzielnica (miasta; osiedla);
podział

subdue (seb'du:) s. ujarzmiać;
poskramiać; przyciszać; tłumić; łagodzić; podbijać

subject ('sabdżykt) s. podmiot;
przedmiot; temat; treść; tworzywo; (sab'dżekt) motyw;
poddany; osobnik; v. podporządkować; ujarzmić; podbić;
narazić; poddać czemuś; adj.
poddany; uległy; podległy;
narażony; podatny; podlegający; ujarzmiony; adv. pod warunkiem; z zastrzeżeniem;
z uwzględnieniem czegoś

subjective('sabdżektyw) adj.
subiektywny; podmiotowy

subjunctive mood (seb'dżanktyw,
,mu:d) s. tryb warunkowy

sublime (se'blajm) adj. wzniosły; wyniosły; podniosły

submachine-gun ('sabme'szi:ngan)
s. (automatyczny) pistolet maszynowy

submarine (sabme'ri:n) s. łódź
podwodna

submariners (sabme'ri:ners) pl.
załoga łodzi podwodnej

submerge (seb'me:rdż) v. zalewać; zatapiać; zanurzać (się);
zakrywać

submission (seb'myszyn) s.
uległość; poddanie się; przedłożenie (opinii)

submissive (seb'mysyw) adj.
uległy

submit (seb'myt) v. poddawać
(się); przedkładać

subnormal (sab'no:rmel) adj.
niżej normy; cofnięty w roz-
woju

subordinate(se'bo:rdnyt) adj.
zależny; podporządkowany;
s. podwładny; (se'bo:rdnejt)
v. podporządkowywać

subordinate clause (se'bo:rd-
nyt,klo:z) s. zdanie podrzędne

subscribe (seb'skrajb) v. za-
prenumerować; podpisywać (np.
obraz); pisać się na coś; dawać na cel

subscribe for (seb'skrajb,fo:r)
v. zapisywać się na (nową)
książkę

subscribe to (seb'skrajb,tu) v.
abonować gazetę

subscriber (seb'skrajber) s.
abonent; człowiek popierający

subscription (seb'skrypszyn) s.
prenumerata; przedpłata; pod-
pisanie; zgoda pisemna; podpis dołączony

subsequent ('sabsykłent) adj.
następny

subsequently ('sabsykłently)
adv. następnie

subside (seb'sajd) v. klęsnąć;
opadać; osadzać się; osiadać;
uspokajać się

subsidiary (seb'sydjery) adj.
pomocniczy; subsydiowany (zależny); s. pomocnik

subsidiary company (seb'sydjery'kampeny) s. firma zależna
od innej firmy

subsidize ('sabsydajz) v. za-
siłkować; zasilać; opłacać;
przekupywać

subsidy ('sabsydy) s. zasiłek
(państwowy); subwencja; danina

subsist (seb'syst) s. istnieć;
egzystować; utrzymywać się
przy życiu; żyć czyms

subsistence (seb'systens) s.
utrzymanie; istnienie

substance ('sabstens) s. istota; treść; sens; sedno; substancja; znaczenie; rzeczywistość; majątek

substandard (sab'staenderd)
adj. poniżej poziomu; ordynarny (język)

substantial (sab'staenszel)
adj. materialny; rzeczywisty;
solidny; zasadniczy; ważny;
bogaty; wpływowy; konkretny;
treściwy

substantive ('sabstentyw) adj.
rzeczywisty; niezależnie
istniejący; zasadniczy; poważny; rzeczownikowy; wyrażający
istnienie; s. rzeczownik

substitute ('sabstytut) s. namiastka; zastępca

substitution (,sabsty'tuszyn)
s. zastępstwo; zastąpienie

subtitle ('sabtajtl) s. pod-
tytuł; napis na filmie

subtle ('sabtl) s. subtelny;
delikatny; cienki; rzadki;
chytry; bystry

subtract (sab'traekt) v. odejmować

suburb ('sabe:rb) s. przedmieście

suburban ('sabe:rben) adj.
podmiejski

subway ('sabłej) s. kolejka
podziemna

succeed (sek'si:d) v. mieć po-

wodzenie; udawać się; następ-
pować po kims

success (sek'ses) s. powodzenie;
sukces; rzecz udana; człowiek
mający sukces

successful (sek'sesful) adj.
udały; mający powodzenie

succession (sek'seszyn) s. następstwo; kolej; kolejność;
sukcesja; spadkobiercy; szereg

successive (sek'sesyw) adj.
kolejny

successor (sek'seser) s. następca; dziedzic; spadkobierca

succumb (se'kam) v. ulegać (po-
kusie); poddawać się; umierać

such (sacz) adj. taki; tego
rodzaju; pron. taki; tym podobny

suck (sak) v. ssać; korzystać;
wyzyskiwać; wchłaniać; wciągać;
(slang): nabierać; dać się nabrać; podlizywać się komus;
s. ssanie; wciąganie; (slang):
łyk

suckle ('sakel) v, karmić piersią; dawać piers; ssać piers

suckling ('saklyng) s. osesek;
młode w okresie ssania

sudden ('sadn) adj. nagły

sudden death ('sadn,det) s.
nagła śmierć; rozstrzygnięcie
w następnej rozgrywce

suddenly ('sadnly) adv. nagle;
raptowanie; nieoczekiwanie

suds (sadz) pl. mydliny; (slang):
piwo

sue (su:) v. skarżyć; zaskarżać;
pozywać; upraszać; ubiegać się

suede (slejd) s. zamsz

suet ('su:yt) s. łój; adj. ło-
jowy

suffer ('safer) v. cierpieć;
ucierpieć; ścierpieć; doznać
(czegoś); zostać straconym

suffer from ('safer,from) v.
być chorym(na coś)

sufferable ('saferebl) adj.
znosny

sufferer ('saferer) s. cierpiący

suffice (se'fajs) v. wystar-
czyć

sufficiency(se'fyszensy) s. wy-
starczająca ilość; zapasy

sufficient (se'fyszent) adj.
dostateczny; wystarczający

suffix ('safyks) s. przyrostek

suffocate ('safokejt) v. udusić; zadusić

sugar ('szuger) s. cukier; słodkie dziecko; (slang): forsa;
v. słodzić

sugar-cane ('szugerkejn) s.
trzcina cukrowa

suggest (se'dżest) v. sugerować; proponować; nasuwać; podsuwać; poddawać (myśl)

suggestion (se'dżestszyn) s.
sugestia; wskazówka; myśl;
poddawanie; podsuwanie; ślad
(czegoś)

suggestive (se'dżestyw) adj.
przypominający; nasuwający
(myśl). dwuznaczny

suicide (,su:y'sajd) s. samobójstwo; samobójca; v. popełnić samobójstwo

suit (su:t) v. dostosować; odpowiadać; służyć; wybrać; być
odpowiednim; zadowalać; pasować; s. garnitur; ubranie;
komplet; skarga; proces;
prośba; zaloty; staranie się;
zestaw

suit yourself ('su:tjor,self)
exp.:rób co chcesz

suitable ('su:tebl) adj. właściwy; stosowny; odpowiedni

suitcase ('su:tkejs) s. walizka

suite (sli:t) s. świta; orszak;
szereg; zestaw (mebli);
apartament; garnitur; komplet;
suita

suitor ('su:ter) s. zalotnik;
petent; pretendent; strona;
konkurent

sulfate ('salfejt)s. siarczan;
v. zakwaszać; zamieniać na
siarczan

sulfur ('salfer) s. siarka;
v. siarkować

sulk (salk) v. być w złym humorze; s. zły humor; człowiek
w złym humorze

sulky ('salky) adj. w złym humorze; ponury; s. jednokonny
dwukołowy wózek

sullen ('salen) adj. ponury;
posępny; flegmatyczny; powolny

sulphur ('salfer) s. siarka;
v. siarkować

sultry ('saltry) adj. parny;
duszny; gwałtowny; gorący;
namiętny

sum (sam) s. suma; w sumie; rachunek; v. dodawać; zbierać;
podsumowywać

sum up ('sam,ap) v. dodawać;
zbierać; podsumowywać

summarize (,'samerajz) v.
streszczać; zbierać; podsumowywać

summary ('samery) s. streszczenie; skrót; adj. pobieżny;
doraźny; krótki

Summer ('samer) s. lato;
v. spędzać lato

Summer resort ('samer ry'so:rt)
s. letnisko

Summer school ('samer,sku:l)
s. szkoła w lecie, w czasie
wakacji

summit ('samyt) s. szczyt

summon ('samen) v. wzywać
(oficjalnie); zdobywać się(na
odwagę)

summons ('samens) pl. wezwanie
urzędowe; v. doręczać wezwanie urzędowe

sun (san) s. słońce; v. nasło-
neczniać (się)

sunbath ('sanba:s) s. kąpiel
słoneczna

sunbathe ('sanbejg) v. opalać
się

sunbeam ('sanbi:m) s. promień
słońca

sunburn ('sanbe:rn) s. opalenizna

Sunday ('sandy) s. niedziela

sundial ('sandajel) s. zegar
słoneczny

sundries ('sandryz) s. różności;
rozmaitości
sundry ('sandry) adj. różny;
rozmaity
sung (sang) v. zob. sing
sunglasses (san,gla:sys) pl.
okulary od słońca
sunk (sank) v. zob. sink
sunken ('sanken) v. zob. sink;
adj. zapadnięty; zatopiony;
podwodny
sunny ('sany) adj. słoneczny
sunny side up ('sany,sajd ap)
exp.: jaja sadzone
sunrise ('san-rajz) s. wschód
słońca
sunshade ('sanshejd) s. parasol
od słońca
sunset ('sanset) s. zachód
słońca
sunshine ('sanszajn) s. blask
słońca; pogoda. wesołość
sunstroke ('sanstrouk) s. porażenie słoneczne
sup (sap) s. łyk; v. częstować
kolacją; zjeść kolacje; pić
małymi łykami
super ('su:per) adj. pierwszorzędny; wspaniały; kwadratowy;
prefix: nad-; prze-; s. statysta; nadzorca; szlagier;
przebój (filmowy); najlepszy
gatunek
superabundant ('su:per,e'bandent) adj. nadmierny; przebo-
gaty
superb (se:'pe:rb) adj. wspaniały
super-duper (,su:per-'du:per)
adj. (slang): b. dobry; luksusowy; bardzo elegancki
superficial (,su:per'fyszel)
adj. powierzchowny; powierzchniowy
superfluous (su'pe:rflues)
adj. zbędny; zbyteczny
super-highway (su'per-hajłej)
s. (m.in. 4-pasmowa) autostrada
superhuman (,su:per'hju:man)
adj. nadludzki

superintend (,su:peryn'tend)
v. nadzorować; doglądać; kierować
superintendent (,su:peryn'tendent) s. nadzorca; dozorca;
nadinspektor
superior (su:'pierjer) adj.
wyższy; nieprzeciętny;
pierwszorzędny; przewyższa-
jący; lepszy; nadęty; wyniosły;
s. zwierzchnik; przełożony;
starszy rangą
superiority (su:,pie:ry'oryty)
s. wyższość
superlative (su:'pe:rlatyw)
adj. najwyższy; s. szczyt;
superlatyw; stopień najwyższy
superman ('su:permen) s. nadczłowiek
supermarket ('su:per'ma:rkyt)
s. supersam; duży sklep samo-
obsługowy (żywnościowy)
supernatural (,su:per'naeczerel) adj. nadprzyrodzony
supernumerary (,su:per'nju:me-
ryry) adj. nadliczbowy; nie-
etatowy; statysta
superscription (,su:per'skrypszyn) s.napis u góry; nadpis;
adres; napis
supersede (sju:per'si:d) v.
zastąpić; wypierać; zajmować
miejsce
supersonic (,su:per'sonyk)
adj. ultradźwiękowy; ponad-
dźwiękowy
superstition (su:per'styszyn)
s. zabobon; przesądy
supervise ('su:perwajz) v.
nadzorować; doglądać
supervisor ('su:perwajzer)
s. inspektor; nadzorca
supper ('saper) s. wieczerza;
kolacja
supple ('sapl) adj. giętki;
gibki; v. stawać się gibkim
supplement ('saplyment) s.
dodatek; uzupełnienie;
v. uzupełniać
supplementary ('saplymentery)
adj. dodatkowy; uzupełniają-
cy

supplication (,saply'kejszyn)
s. błaganie; prosba

supplier (se'plajer) s. dostawca

supply (se'plaj) s. zapas;
aprowizacja; zaopatrzenie;
dostarczenie; dostawy; kredyty; podaż; dopływ; zasilanie;
v. dostarczac; zaopatrywac;
zaradzic; zastępowac

support (se'po:rt) s. utrzymanie; podtrzymanie; podpora;
poparcie; pomoc; wspornik;
dźwigar; rama; łożysko; podłoże; ostoja; v. podtrzymywac; utrzymywac; podpierac;
popierac; wytrzymywac; znosic; tolerowac

suppose (se'pouz) v. przy-
puszczac; zakładac; sądzic

supposed (se'pouzd) adj. domniemany; przypuszczalny;
rzekomy

supposedly (se'pouzdly) adv.
rzekomo; przypuszczalnie

supposition (sape'zeszyn) s.
przypuszczenie; domniemanie

suppress (se'pres) v. tłumic;
zgniatac; znosic; zatrzymywac (krwawienie); usuwac;
taic

suppression (se'preszyn) s.
stłumienie; zgniecenie;
zniesienie; usunięcie; prze-
milczenie; zatajenie

suppurate ('sapjurejt) v. ropiec

supremacy (se'premesy) s.
zwierzchnictwo; przewaga; najwyższa władza; supremacja

supreme (se'pri:m) adj. najwyższy; doskonały; ostateczny

surcharge (se:r'cza:rdż) s.
nadpłata; nadmierny ciężar;
dodatkowy ciężar; opłata (kar-
na); przeładowanie; v. ścią-
gac opłatę podatkową; nakładac grzywnę; przeładowac;
przedrukowac (znaczek)

sure (szuer) adj. pewny; niezawodny; niemylny; bezpieczny;
exp.:napewno !; zgadza się !

adv. z pewnoscią; pewnie; napewno; niezawodnie; niechybnie

sure enough ('szuer,y'naf) adv.
faktycznie

surely ('szuerly) adv. pewnie;
z pewnoscią

surety ('szuerty) s. ręczyciel;
gwarancja; zabezpieczenie;
kaucja; pewnosc

surf (se:rf) s. (łamiące się)
fale przybrzeżne

surface (se:rfys) s. powierzchnia; v. wypływac na powierzch-
nie; wykanczac powierzchnię

surfboard ('se:rfbo:rd) s. pojedyncza (deska); narta wodna;
v. jezdzic na desce na falach
ku brzegowi

surfriding ('se:rf,rajdyng) v.
zjeżdżac z fal ku brzegowi

surge (se:rdż) s. gwałtowny
impuls; fala uskokowa; falowanie; fala; v. nagle wzbierac;
drgac; popuscic; kołysac;
hustac; zeslizgiwac się

surgeon ('se:rdżen) s. chirurg

surgery ('se:rdżery) s. chi-
rurgia; operacja; sala opera-
cyjna

surgical ('se:rdżykel) adj.
chirurgiczny

surly ('se:rly) adj. grubianski;
zgryźliwy

surmise ('se:rmajz) s. domysł;
v. domyslac się czegos

surmount (ser'maunt) v. pokony-
wac; wychodzic na (górę);
przechodzic przez; pokrywac;
wznosic się

surmounted by (ser'mauntyd baj)
adj. pokonany przez

surname ('se:rnejm) s. nazwisko;
przydomek; (se:r'nejm) v.
przezywac; nadawac przydomek

surpass (se:r'paes) v. przewyższac; przechodzic (oczekiwania)

surpassing (se:r'paesyng) adj.
nieprzescigniony; niezrównany

surplus (se:r'plas) s. nadwyżka; nadmiar; superata;nadwyżka
produkcyjna; wartosc dodatkowa;
adj. stanowiący nadwyżkę;nadwyżko-
wy; zbywający

surprise (ser'prajz) s. niespodzianka; zaskoczenie; zdziwienie; v. zaskoczyc; zdziwic; zmuszac; złapac na gorącym uczynku; adj. nieoczekiwany; niespodziewany

surprised (ser'prajzd) adj. zaskoczony; złapany na gorącym uczynku

surrender (se'render) s. poddanie się; wyrzeczenie się; v. poddawac się; oddawac się; wyrzekac się czegos

surround (se'raund) v. otaczac; okrążac

surroundings (se'raundyŋgs) pl. otoczenie

survey (se:r'wej) s. przegląd; oględziny; inspekcja; pomiary; plan (topograficzny); opis; ankieta; statystyka; v. przeglądac; robic pomiary; wymierzac; oglądac

surveying (se:r'wejyŋg) s. miernictwo

surveyor (se:r'wejer) s. mierniczy; inspektor celny

survival (ser'wajwel) s. przeżycie; przeżytek

survive (ser,wajw) v. przeżyc; dalej życ

survivor (ser'wajwer) s. człowiek pozostały przy życiu

susceptible (se'septybl) adj. wrażliwy; drażliwy; podatny; dopuszczający

suspect (sęs'pekt) v. podejrzewac kogos; ('saspekt) adj. podejrzany

suspected (ses'pektyd) adj. podejrzany

suspend (ses'pend) v. zawiesic; powstrzymac (się chwilowo)

suspended (ses'pendyd) adj. zawieszony w czynnosciach

suspenders (ses'penders) pl. podwiązki; szelki

suspense (ses'pens) s. niepewnosc; zawieszenie; nierozstrzygnięcie

suspension (ses'penszyn) s. zawieszenie; zawiesina; wstrzymanie

suspension bridge (ses'penszyn,brydż) s. wiszący most

suspicion (ses'pyszyn) s. podejrzenie; v. podejrzewac

suspicious (ses'pyszes) adj. podejrzany; nieufny

sustain (ses'tejn) v. podtrzymywac; dzwigac; cierpiec; doznawac; ponosic; potwierdzac; utrzymywac; uznawac (słusznosc)

sustenance ('sastynens) s. pożywienie; utrzymanie

swab (słob) s. wycior; wacik chłonący; scierka na kiju; gamon; epoleta; v. wycierac; scierac; wuszorowac

swab up ('słob,ap) v. wytrzec; swagger (słaeger) v. parądowac; dumnie chodzic; chełpic się; pysznic się;odstraszyc; nakłaniac strachem

swallow ('słolou) v. połykac (np. zniewagę); przełykac; dac się nabrac; odwołac (słowa); s. przełykanie; łyk; kęs; przełyk; jaskółka

swam (słaem) v. zob. swim

swamp (słomp) s. bagno; v. zalewac; pochłaniac; przysłaniac; grzęznąc

swampy (słompy) adj. bagnisty; błotnisty

swan (słon) s. łabędz

swap (słop) v. zamieniac (się); wymieniac (się); s. zamiana; wymiana

swarm (sło:rm) s. mrowie; mnostwo; roj; v. roic (się); wyroic; obfitowac (w cos); wspinac się; wdrapywac się

swarthy ('sło:rty) adj. sniady; smagły

swathe (słejz) v. spowijac; s. zawinięcie; bandaż

sway (słej) v. kołysac (się); chwiac (się); zachwiac (się); rządzic czyms; władac; s. chwianie się; władza

swear; sware; sworn (słeer; sło:r; sło:rn)

swear (słeer) v. przysięgac; poprzysiąc

sweat (słet) s. poty; pot; harówka; v. pocić się; pracować ciężko; (slang): harować; szwejsować; fermentować; wyswiechtywać monety; wydzielać (żywicę)

sweat out (słet,aut) v. wypacać (się); (slang): ciężko pracować; wyduszać z kogoś coś; wyciągać pieniądze szantażem; wyciągać odpowiedzi torturami; odsiadywać więzienie

sweater ('słeter) s. sweter; wyzyskiwacz robotników

sweatshop ('słet,szop) s. zakład wyzyskujący robotników

sweatshirt ('slet,sze:rt) s. koszula trykotowa

Swedish ('słi:dysz) adj. szwedzki

sweep; swept; swept (słi:p; słept; słept)

sweep (słi:p) v. zamiatać; wymiatać; zmiatać; oczyszczać; wygrywać (np. wszystkie medale); porywać (słuchaczy); przewalić się przez coś (burza; wichura; powódź); ogarniać; obejmować; rozciągać się; sunąć uroczyście; ślizgać się; śmigać; zwalać (kogoś z nóg); ostrzeliwać; etc. s. zamiatanie; zdobycie; zagarnięcie; ogołocenie; śmieci; śmignięcie; machnięcie; zasięg; robienie zakrętu; etc.

sweeper ('słi:per) s. zamiatacz; zamiataczka; zmiotka

sweeping ('słi:pyng) adj. szeroki; wspaniały; rozległy; daleko idący

sweepings ('słi:pyngs) pl. śmieci

sweepstake ('słi:pstejk) s. wyścigi; loteria; nagroda (zbiorowa) w wyścigach

sweet (słi:t) adj. słodki; przyjemny; miły; rozkoszny; dobrze osłodzony; deserowy; melodyjny; świeży; łagodny; zakochany

sweeten ('słi:tn) v. słodzić; osładzać; stawać się słodkim; (slang): zwiększać stawkę; zwiększać zastaw

sweetheart ('słi:t-ha:rt) s. ukochana; ukochany

sweetness ('słi:tnys) s. słodycz

sweetpea ('słi:tpi:) s. groszek pachnący

swell; swollen; swelled (słel; słoulen; słeld)

swell (słel) v. puchnąć; wzdymać (się); nadymać (się); wydymać (się); rozdymać; wzbierać; wzrastać; potęgować się; s. wydęcie; zgrubienie; nabrzmienie; wzbieranie; wzburzona fala (morze); (slang): wytworniak; gruba ryba

swelling ('słelyng) s. spuchlizna; wzdęcie; obrzęk; wezbranie (rzeki)

swept (słept) v. zob. sweep

swerve (słe:rw) s. odchylenie; zboczenie; v. zbaczać; odchylać (się)

swift (słyft) adj. prędki; rączy; chyży; żywy; s. nawijak przędzy; traszka; jaszczurka; jerzyk

swiftness ('słyftnys) s. prędkość; chyżość

swim; swam; swum (słym; słaem; słam)

swim (słym) v. płynąć; przepływnąć; pływać (w wyścigach); pławić; ociekać czymś; unosić się na powierzchni; iść z prądem; kręcić się (w głowie); s. pływanie; nurt (życia); woda (do pływania); głębia; pęcherz pławny

swimmer ('słymer) s. pływak

swimming ('słymyng) s. pływanie

swimming pool ('słymyng,pu:l) s, pływalnia

swimming suit ('słymyng,sju:t) s. kostium kąpielowy

swindle (słyndl) s. oszustwo; v. oszukiwać

swine (słajn) s. świnia

swing ; swung; swang (słyng;
słang;słaeŋg)

swing (słyng) v. huśtać (się);
kołysać (się); wahać (się);
bujać (się); machać; wywijać;
przerzucać (się) na coś; porywać (za sobą); pociągać
(za sobą); s. huśtanie (się);
kołysanie (się); ruch wahadłowy; zmiana pracy; objazd (te-
renu); rytm; przerzucanie się;
kołyszący chód; taniec (swing)

swing bridge ('słyng,brydż) s.
most wahadłowy

swing door ('słyng,do:r) s.
drzwi wahadłowe

swing wheel ('słyng,hłi:l) s.
koło rozpędowe (zamachowe)

swirl (słe:rl) s. wir; wirowanie; skręt; lok; v. wirować;
kręcić się; unosić się (wiru-
jąc)

Swiss (słys) adj. szwajcarski

switch (słycz) s. pręt; zwrotnica; przekładnia; wyłącznik;
przełącznik; kontakt; śmignięcie; v. bić prętem; machać;
wyrywać; zmieniać; przełączać;
włączać; rozłączać (się); wyłączać (się); włączać (np.
światło)

switch off ('słycz,of) v. wyłączać

switch on ('słycz,on) v. włączać

switchboard ('słyczbo:rd) s.
tablica rozdzielcza; łącznica
(telefoniczna etc.)

swollen ('słoulen) v. zob.swell
adj. opuchnięty; wzdęty;
wezbrany

swoon (słu:n) v. zemdleć; omdleć; zamierać; s. omdlenie

swoop down on ('słu:p,dałn on)
v. zaatakować z góry; runąć
na coś

swoop up ('słu:p,ap) v. porywać; s. spadnięcie; porwanie

swop (słop) v. zamieniać; wymieniać; s. zamiana; wymiana

sword (so:rd) s. pałasz; szpada;
miecz; szabla; bagnet (slang)

swore (sło:r) v. zob. swear

sworn (sło:rn) v. zob. swear;
adj. zaprzysiężony; przy-
sięgły

swum (słam) v. zob. swim

swung (słaŋg)v. zob. swing

sycamore ('sykemo:r) s. jawor;
klon; figowiec

syllable ('sylebl) s. sylaba;
zgłoska

symbol ('symbel) s. symbol;
v. symbolizować

symbolic (,sym'bolyk) adj.
symboliczny

symbolism ('symbelyzem) s.
symbolizm

symmetric (sy'metryk) adj. symetryczny

symmetry ('symytry) s. svmetria

sympathetic (,sympe'tetyk) adj.
współczujący; życzliwy; sympatyczny; współbrzmiący;
s. współczulny; łatwy do za-
hipnotyzowania

sympathize ('sympetajz) v.
współczuć; mieć zrozumienie;
sympatyzować z kims

sympathy ('sympety) s. współczucie; solidarność; sympatia

symphony ('symfeny) s. symfonia

symptom (sympten) s. symptom

synagogue ('synegog) s. bożni-
ca; synagoga

synchronize ('synkrenajz) s.
działać równocześnie; synchronizować; pokazywać jednakowo
(czas); uzgadniać (zegary)

synonym ('synenym) s. synonim

synonymous (sy'nonymes) adj.
równoznaczny z czyms

syntax ('syntaeks) s. składnia

synthesis ('syntysys) s. synteza

syntheses ('syntysi:s) pl. syn-
tezy

synthetic (syn'tetyk) adj.
sztuczny; syntetyczny

syphilis ('syfylys) s. kiła; sy-
filis

syringe ('syryndż) s. strzykawka; v. strzykać (wodą)

syrup ('syrep) s. syrop

system ('systym) s. system

systematic (,systy'maetyk) adj. systematyczny

t (ti:) dwudziesta litera alfabetu angielskiego

tab (taeb) s. patka; wieszak (przyszyty); język (buta); naszywka; języczek; ucho; przywieszka; rachunek; kontrola; pilnowanie; v. prowadzić ewidencję; tabelować; zaopatrywać w (języczek lub ucho etc.)

table ('tejbl) s. stół; stolik; tablica; tabela; tabliczka (np. mnożenia); płyta; płaskowyż; blat; v. kłaść na stole; odraczać (na długo); wciągać na agendę; adj.stołowy

tablecloth ('tejbl,kloß) s. obrus

tableland ('tejbl-laend) s. płaskowyż

tablespoon ('tejbl-spu:n) s. łyżka stołowa (do zupy)

tablespoonful ('tejblspu:nful) s. pełna łyżka (pół uncji)

tablet ('taeblyt) s. tabletka; tabliczka (do pisania)

taboo (te'bu:) s. tabu; v.zakazywać; adj. zakazany

tacit ('taesyt) adj. milczący; cichy; niemy

taciturn ('taesyte:rn) adj. małomówny

tack (taek) s. gwóźdź tapicerski; papiak; pluskiewka; fastryga; kurs (polityki); taktyka; stan lepki; prowiant; żywność; jedzenie: v. przyczepiać; przybijać (lekko); fastrygować; zmieniać kurs; lawirować; hałasować

tackle ('taekl) s. zestaw przyborów (do łowienia, golenia); wielokrążek; takielunek; złapanie i trzymanie; v. zewrzeć się; borykać (się); złapać i trzymać; zmagać (się); brać się do czegoś (ostro); umocowywać; porać (się)

tacky ('taeky) adj. lepki; niemodny; marny

tact (taekt) s. takt; wyczucie; dotyk

tactful ('taektful) adj. taktowny

tactics ('taektyks) pl. taktyka

tactile ('taektajl) adj. dotykowy; dotykalny

tactless ('taektlys) adj. nietaktowny

tad (taed) s. berbeć

tadpole ('taedpoul) s. kijanka

tag (taeg) s. skuwka; etykieta; kartka; strzęp; przywieszka; znaczek tożsamości; marka; mandat karny (pisany); ucho; igliczka; wieszadło (przyszyte); błyszczka; dodatek; morał; frazes; banał; cytat; refren; ogon; zabawa w gonionego; v. przyczepiać: skuwkę; kartkę; znaczek, markę; ucho; wieszadło, igliczkę, ogon; dawać: mandat karny, morał, bawić się w gonionego; tańczyć odbijanego; wymierzać wyrok; przeznaczać; włóczyć się za kimś; dołączyć do czegoś

tail (tejl) s. ogon; tył; koniec; tren; poła; pośladki; buńczuk; warkocz; świta; cień (chodzący za kimś); v. dodawać ogon; obrywać ogonki; śledzić (krok w krok); zamykać pochód

tailcoat (,tejl'kout) s. frak

taillight ('tejl,lajt) s. tylne światło (wozu)

tailor ('tejler) s. krawiec; v. szyć odzież

tailor-made ('tejlermejd) adj. uszyty na zamówienie

tail wind ('tejlłynd) s. wiatr w plecy

taint (tejnt) s. skaza; zaraza; plama; v. plamić; kazić; zepsuć; plugawić

taintless ('teintlys)adj. bez skazy

take; took; taken (tejk; tuk; 'tejkn)

take,(tejk) s. brać; wziąć; łapać; chwytać; zdobywać (twierdzę); zajmować (miejsce); rezerwować; zażywać; pic; jeść; odczuwać; rozumieć; pojechać; notować; zrobić (zdjęcie); zadać sobie (trud); dostawać (napadu); przyjmować (radę; karę; etc.); mierzyć swoją temperaturę; godzić się(na traktowanie); nabierać (połysku); isć (za przykładem) s. połow; zdjęcie; wpływy (do kasy)

take along (,tejke'long) v. zabrać ze sobą

take down ('tejk,dałn) v.zdejmować; rozmontowywać

take-in ('tejk'yn) s. oszukanie; naciąganie

take off ('tejk,of) v. rozbierać; kasować; małpować; wystartować; odjąć; usunąć

takeoff (tejkof) s. start; skok; skocznia; karykatura; parodia; naśladowanie; odbicie; lista materiałów

take out (tejk aut) v. podejmować (poza domem); wyprowadzać; wynieść;wyrywać; wykupić; odjąć; oddzielić

takeover ('tejkouwer) s. opanowanie firmy przez manipulacje giełdowe lub finansowe

take over (,'tejk,ouwer) v. przejmować (firmę); przyjmować (obowiązki);dominować

take up (,'tejk,ap) v. ponosić; wchłonąć; wziąć (miejsce); zacząć (uczyć się); zadawać się;brać;zciesniać; besztać

taken ('tejkn) v. zob. take; adj. zabrany; porwany; zdobyty; nabrany; oszukany

talc(taelk) s. talk; v. posypywać talkiem

tale (tejl) s. opowiadanie; plotka; wymysł

talent ('taelent) s. talent (do czegoś); dar; uzdolnienie

talk (to:k) v. mówić; rozmawiać; plotkować; namawiać;

s. rozmowa; dyskusja; pogadanka; plotka: gadanie; mowa

talkative ('to:ketyw) adj. rozmowny; gadatliwy

talk-to ('to:k,tu) s. bura

tall (to:l) adj. wysoki; (slang): nieprawdopodobny

tall talk ('to:l,to:k) s, przechwałki

tallow ('taelou) s. łój; v. tuczyc; smarować łojem

talon ('taelen) s. szpon; pazur; rygiel; łapa ludzka; palec

tame ('tejm) v. oswajać; poskramiać; ujarzmić; okiełzać; łagodzic; przytłumić; upokorzyć

tamper ('taemper) s. ubijak; v. majstrować; manipulować; zmieniać coś nielegalnie

tan (taen) s. opalenizna; kolor (brązowy) brunatny; kora garbarska; v. garbować; opalać się (na słoncu); brązowiec; wyłoic komus skóre

tangent ('taendżent) adj. styczny; s. styczna; szczegół oderwany; zmiana tematu (od rzeczy); zmiana kierunku rozmowy

tangerine (taendże'ri:n) s. mandarynka

tangle ('taengl) s. plątanina; v. plątać (się); wikłać (się); (slang): pobic się z kims

tank (taenk) s. tank; zbiornik; cysterna; czołg; (slang): więzienie; v. nabierać do zbiornika; (slang): popić sobie

tankard ('taenkerd) s. kufel

tanner ('taener) s. garbarz

tantalize ('tae ntalajz)v. dręczyć (zwodną) nadzieją; łudzic

tantrum ('taentrem) s. napad złości

tap (taep) v. stukać; odszpuntować; napocząć; robic punkcje; naciąć; ciągnąć sok; wykorzystywać; gwintować; podsłuchiwać (telefon); s. czop; szpunt; kurek; zawór; gwintownik; zaczep; odczep

tape (tejp) s. taśma; tasiemka;
tasiemiec; (slang): wódka;
v. wiązać tasmą (przylepcem);
mierzyć; (slang):oceniać kogoś

tape measure ('tejp,meżer) s.
miara na taśmie (krawiecka)

taper ('tejper) s. stopniowe
zwężanie (się); stożek; ubytek; osłabianie; stoczek;
świeczka

taper off ('tejper,of) v. zwężać się stopniowo; cichnąc
stopniowo; kończyć się spi-
czasto

tape recorder ('tejp-ry,ko:r-
der) s. magnetofon

tape recording ('tejp;ry,ko:r-
dyng) s. nagranie na taśme

tapestry ('taepystry) s. go-
belin; arras; v. zdobić go-
belinami

tapeworm ('tejpłor:m) s. soliter; tasiemiec

tar (ta:r) s. smoła; dziegieć;
ter; v. smołować; terować

target ('ta:rgyt) s. cel;
obiekt; tarcza strzelnicza;
v. kierować do celu; celować;
ustalać cel

tariff ('taeryf) s. cło; taryfa; cennik; c. clic wg
taryfy; układać taryfę celną

tarnish ('ta:rnysz) v. mato-
wieć; przyćmiewać; brudzić
(się); brukać (się); tracić
połysk; s. matowienie; skaza

tart ('ta:rt) adj. cierpki;
zgryźliwy; s. ciastko owoco-
we; (slang): kurewka

tartan ('ta:rten) s. materiał
w kratę szkocką

task ('taesk) s. zadanie
(specjalne); lekcja zadana;
przedsięwzięcie; v. wyznaczać zadanie; wystawiać na
próbę; rugać

taskforce ('taesk,fo:rs) s.
oddział (grupa) do specjalne-
go zadania

taskmaster ('taesk,ma:ster)
s. nadzorca (kontrolujący wykonanie zadania)

tassel ('taesel) s. kutas; kitka; v. ozdabiać kutasami; kit-
kami

taste (tejst) s. smak; gust;
posmak; zamiłowanie; v. smakować; kosztować; czuć smak;
mieć smak; doznawać (czegoś)

tasteful ('tejstful) adj. gustowny; w dobrym smaku

tasteless ('tejstlys) adj. bez
gustu; bez smaku

tasty ('tejsty) adj. smakowity;
smaczny

ta-ta (tae'-ta:) exp. do widzenia; pa ! pa !

tattoo (te'tu:) v. bębnić palcami; tatuować; s. capstrzyk; ta-
tuaż

taught(to:t) v. zob. teach

taunt (to:nt) v. urągać; wymyślać komuś; zwymyślać kogoś;
s. urąganie; wymyślanie; adj.
wysoki (np, maszt)

taut (to:t) adj. napięty; naprężony; w dobrej formie; w dobrym
stanie

tax (taeks) s. podatek; wysiłek;
ciężar; obciążenie; v. opodatkować; obarczać; obciążać; nadwerężać; sprawdzać; wymagać
wysiłku; zarzucać coś

taxation (taek'sejszyn) s. opo-
datkowanie

tax collector ('taekske,lekter)
s. poborca podatkowy

taxi ('taeksy) s. taksówka;
v. jechać taksówką;wieźć taksówką

taxidriver ('taeksydrajwer) s.
taksówkarz

taximeter ('taeksy,mi:ter) s.
licznik (w taksówce); takso-
metr

taxpayer ('taeks,pejer) s. podatnik

tax return ('taeks,ry'te:rn)s.
podatek (zapłata ze sprawozda-
niem)

tea (ti:) s. herbata; herbatka;
podwieczorek; v. pić i częstować herbatą

teabag ('ti:baeg) s. woreczek
papierowy z herbatą

teach; taught; taught (ti:cz;
to:t; to:t)

teach (ti:cz) v. uczyc (się);
nauczac; wykładac

teacher (ti:czer) s. nauczyciel

teacup ('ti:kap) s. filiżanka
na herbatę

teakettle ('ti:,ketl) s. imbryk; czajnik

team (ti:m) s. zespół; drużyna; zaprzęg; v. zaprzęgac;
jeździc zaprzęgiem

team up ('ti:map) v. łączyc
się razem (do pracy etc.)

teamwork ('ti:młe:rk) s. praca zespołowa

teapot ('ti:pot) s. mały czajnik

tear; tore; torn (teer; to:r;
to:rn)

tear (teer) v. drzec; targac;
rwac; kaleczyc; wydrzec (rane)
pedzic; s. dziura; rozdarcie;
wybuch pasji; kropla; łza;
(slang) hulanka

tearoom ('ti:ru:m) s. herbaciarnia

tease (ti:z) v. draznic; nudzic; s. dokuczanie; nudziarstwo

teat (tyt) s. cycek (wulg.-ko-
biecy)

technical ('teknykel) adj.
techniczny; formalny; spekula-
cyjny

technician ('teknyszyn) s.
technik

technique (tek'ni:k) s. technika malowania, rzezby etc.

tedious ('ti:dies) adj. nudny

teem (ti:m) v. roic sie; obfitowac; opróżniac; wylewac

teen (ti:n) s. szkoda; zgryzota

teens (ti:nz) pl. wiek 12 do
18 lat

teeny ('ti:ny) adj. malenki

teeth (ti:s) pl. zęby; zob.
tooth

teethe (ti:s) v. ząbkowac

teetotaler (ti:'toutler) s.
abstynent

telegram ('telygraem)s. telegram

telegraph ('telygra:f) s. telegraf

telephone ('telyfoun) s. telefon; v. telefonowac

telephone booth('telyfoun,bu:s)
s. kabina telefoniczna

telephone call('telyfoun,ko:l)
s. rozmowa telefoniczna

telephone directory ('telyfoun,
dyrektory) s. książka telefoniczna

telephone exchange ('telyfoun-
eksczendż) s. centrala telefoniczna na zagranice

telephone kiosk ('telyfoun-
kiosk) s. kiosk telefoniczny

teleprinter ('tely,prynter) s.
dalekopis

telescope ('telyskoup) s. teleskop

teletypewriter (,tely'tajpraj-
ter) s. dalekopis

televise ('telywajz) v. nadawac przez telewizję

television ('telywyżyn) s. telewizja

television set('telywyżyn,set)
s. telewizor; odbiornik telewizyjny

televisor ('telywajzer) s.
telewizor

tell;told; told (tel; tould;
tould)

tell (tel) v. (o kims; o czyms):
mowic; opowiadac; powiedziec;
wskazywac; pokazywac; kazac;
poznac; sprawdzic; policzyc;
poznawac; wiedziec; doniesc;
oskarżyc; skarżyc; miec znaczenie; odbijac się na kims;
odrożniac

teller ('teler) s. narrator;
kasjer; liczący głosy

telltale ('teltejl) s. plotkarz; okolicznosc ostrzegaw-
cza; wskaznik odchylenia
(steru); aparat sprawdzający,
ostrzegawczy; adj. ostrzegawczy; wymowny

temper ('temper) s. usposobienie; humor; gniew; złosc; domieszka;mieszanka; stan; har-
townosc; v.łagodzic; hartowac

temperament ('temprement) s.
temperament; usposobienie;
skala temperowana; temperatura skali

temperance ('temperens) s.
umiarkowanie; powściągliwość;
obstynencja; wstrzemięźliwość

temperate ('temperyt) adj.
umiarkowany; powściągliwy;
wstrzemięźliwy

temperature ('tempereczer) s.
temperatura; ciepłota

tempest ('tempyst) s. burza;
v. zaburzać

tempestuous (tem'pestjues) adj.
burzliwy

temple ('templ) s. świątynia;
skroń; ucho od okularów; rozciągacz tkacki

temporal ('temperel) adj. doczesny; czasowy; skroniowy;
s. kość skroniowa

temporary ('temperery) adj.
chwilowy; tymczasowy

tempt (tempt) v. kusić; nęcić

temptation (temp'tejszyn) s.
pokusa; kuszenie

tempting ('temptyŋg) adj. ponętny; nęcący; kuszący

ten (ten) num. dziesięć; s.
dziesiątka

tenacious (ty'nejszes) adj.
wytrwały; nieustępliwy; trwały; wierny; czepny; ciągliwy;
mocny; spoisty

tenant ('tenent) s. lokator;
dzierżawca; v. zamieszkiwać;
dzierżawić

tend (tend) v. skłaniać się:
zmierzać; służyć; doglądać;
obsługiwać

tendency ('tendensy) s. skłonność; tendencja

tender ('tender) adj. delikatny; miękki; kruchy; wrażliwy;
czuły; niedojrzały; młody;
młodociany; uważający; dbały; łamliwy; drażliwy; wy-
wrotny; v. oferować; przedło-
żyć; założyć; s. oferta; środek płatniczy; dozorca; tender; statek pomocniczy-za-
opatrzeniowy

tenderloin ('tenderloyn) s.
polędwica

tenderness ('tendernyss) s. czułość; dbałość; delikatność

tendon ('tenden) s. ścięgno

tendril ('tendryl) s. wąs; wić

tenement house ('tenymenthaus) s.
dom czynszowy

tennis ('tenys) s. tenis

tennis court ('tenys'ko:rt) s.
kort tenisowy

tense (tens) s. czas (np. przyszły) adj. naprężony; napięty

tension ('tenszyn) s. naprężenie;
napięcie; prężność

tent (tent) s. namiot

tentacle ('tentekl) s. macka;
czułek

tenth (tens) adj. dziesiąty

tenthly ('tensly) adv. po dzie-
siąte

tepee ('ti:pi:) s. namiot indiański (stożkowy)

tepid ('tepyd) adj. letni; ciepławy; bez zapału

term (te:rm) s. okres; czas
trwania; przeciąg; semestr; kadencja; termin; wyrażenie;
określenie; kres; v. określać;
nazywać

terms (te:rms) pl. warunki
(kontraktu, porozumienia) stosunki wzajemne

terminal ('te:rmynel) adj. końcowy; terminowy; ostateczny;
s. zakończenie; końcówka;
uchwyt; końcowa stacja

terminate ('te:rmynejt) v. skończyć; zakończyć; kończyć (się);
ograniczać; upływać; rozwiązywać (umowę); ustawać; wygasać;
upływać; wymawiać pracę

termination (,te:rmy'n ejszyn)
s. koniec; wypowiedzenie (pracy); wygaśnięcie; zakończenie;
końcówka

terminus (te:rmynes) s. końcowa stacja; kres; koniec; granica

termite ('te:rmajt) s. termit

terrace ('teres) s. taras; terasa; ulica wzdłuż zbocza;
v. robić terasy

terraced ('terest) adj uformo-
wany w terasy

terrible ('terybl) adj. straszliwy; straszny; okropny

terrific ('te'ryfyk) adj. przerażający; (slang): fantastyczny; pierwszej klasy

terrify ('teryfaj) v. przerażać

territorial (,tery'torjel) adj.
terytorialny

territory ('teryto:ry) s. obszar; rejon; (terytorium bez
praw stanu np. w USA)

terror ('terer) s. terror;
przerażenie; postrach

terrorize ('tereraiz) v. siac
strach; przerażać; terroryzo-
wac

test (test) s. proba; sprawdzian; test; egzamin; odczynnik; skorupa; v. sprawdzać;
poddawac próbie; oczyszczać
(metal)

testament ('testement) s.
testament

testify ('testyfaj) v. swiadczyc; dawac swiadectwo; za-
swiadczac; poswiadczac

testimonial (,testy'mounjel)
s. swiadectwo (moralnosci);
polecenie; nagroda w uznaniu
zasług

testimony ('testymouny) s.
swiadectwo

testy ('testy) adj. draźliwy;
popędliwy; pobudliwy

tetanus ('tetenes) s. teżec

text (tekst) s. tekst

textbook ('tekstbuk) s. podręcznik

textile ('tekstail) s. tkanina; adj. tkacki; tekstylny

texture ('tekszczer) s. budowa; tkanina; struktura;
tkanie

than (dzaen) con. aniżeli; niż;
od

thank (taenk) v. dziękowac;
s. podziękowanie; dzięki

thank you ('taenkju:) exp.:
dziękuję

thank you very much ('taenkju:-
'wery,macz) exp.:bardzo dziękuję

thankful ('taenkful) adj.
wdzięczny; dziękczynny

thankless ('taenklys) adj. niewdzięczny

thanks ('taenks) pl. podziękowanie; dzięki

Thanksgiving Day ('taenksgy-
wyng,dej) s. dzien swięta
dziękczynienia (USA)

that (daet) adj. & pron. pl.
thouse (dzous); tamten; tam-
ta; tamto; ten; ta; to; ow;
owa; owo; pl. tamci; tamte;
ci; te; owi; owe; adv. tylu;
tyle; conj. że; żeby; aby;
skoro

thatch (taecz) s. strzecha;
v. pokrywac strzechą

thaw (tso:) s. odwilż; rozkroch-
malenie się; v. tajać; odtajac;
taje; jest odwilż

the (przed samogłoską dy; przed
społgłoską de; z naciskiem dy:)
przyimek okreslony rzadko
kiedy tłumaczony; ten; ta; to;
pl. ci; te; ten własnie , etc.
adv. tym; im...tym

theater ('tieter) s. teatr;
kino; widownia; amfiteatr

theatrical (ti:aetrykel) adj.
teatralny; sceniczny; aktorski

theatricals (ti:'aetrykels) pl.
przedstawienie (amatorskie)

theatrics (ti:'aetryks) s.
sztuka teatralna

thee (di:) archaiczna forma;
ty używana przez kwakrów

theft (teft) s. kradzież

their (dzeer) zaimek; ich

theirs (dzeers) zaimek dzier-
zawczy: ich

them (dzem) przypadek zależny
od: they , (np.: im; nimi;
nich)

theme (ti:m) s. temat; zadanie;
wypracowanie

themselves (dzem'selwz) pl.oni
sami; one same

then (dzen) adv. wtedy; wówczas;
po czym; potem; następnie; później; zatem; zaraz; poza tym;
ponadto; conj.a więc; no to;wo-
bec tego; ale przecież; adj.ow-
czesny;s.przedtem;uprzednio;
dotąd; odtąd;

theologian (tie'loudźjen) s.
teolog

theology (tie'oledźy) s. teologia

theoretic(al) (tie'retyk-el)
adj. teoretyczny

theory (tiery) s. teoria

therapy (terepy) s. leczenie;
terapia

there (dźeer) adv. tam; w tym;
co do tego; oto; własnie; potem; tędy; dlatego; z tego;
na to; s. ta miejscowość; to
miasto; to miejsce

thereabout ('dźeerebaut), adv.
w tych stronach; gdzieś tam
mniej więcej; coś około tego

thereafter ('dźeera:fter) adv.
póżniej; odtąd

there are (dźeer'a:r) exp.: są

thereby ('dźeer'baj) adv. przez
to; w ten sposób; skutkiem
tego

therefore ('dźeer,fo:r) adv.
dlatego; zatem więc

therein (,dźeer'yn) adv. w tym;
w nim; w niej

there is (,dźeer'ys) exp.: jest

thereupon ('dźeer,e'pon) adv.
skutkiem tego

therewith (,dźeer'łys) adv.
tym; z tym; w następstwie tego

there you are (,dźeer'ju:,a:r)
exp.: proszę; tu jest to !
tu pan to ma ! etc.

thermometer (ter'momyter) s.
termometr

thermos ('termos) s. termos

these (di:z) pl. od this

thesis ('ti:sys) s. teza; praca dyplomowa; pl. theses
('ti:syz)

they (dźej) pl. pron. oni; one
(ci; którzy)

they say (dźej sej) exp.:podob-
no (mówią)

thick (tyk) adj. gruby; gęsty;
zbity; rzęsisty; stłumiony;
niewyraźny; mętny; ponury;
tępy; ochrypły; (slang): blat-
ny; spoufalony; s. gruba część;
duren; głup tas; adv. gęsto;
grubo; ochryple; tępo

thicken ('tykn) v. pogrubiać
(się); zagęszczać (się)

thicket ('tykyt) s. gaszcz;
gęstwina

thickness ('tyknys) s. grubość;
warstwa; gęstość

thief (ti:f) s. złodziej;
pl. thieves (ti:ws)

thigh (taj) s. udo

thimble ('tymbl) s. naparstek;
końcówka (metalowa liny)

thimbleful ('tymblful) s. odrobina; naparstek

thin (tyn) adj. cienki (sos;
głos etc). rzadki; szczupły;
słaby (kolor. etc.); (slang):
paskudny; v. rozcieńczać;
szczuplić; przerzedzać (się)

thine (tajn) sob. thy; stara
forma: twój; twoje

thing (tyng) s. rzecz; przedmiot;
uczynek; coś; krzyk mody; warunek; urojenia; przywidzenia;
pl. zwierzęta; rzeczy; odzież;
ubrania; ruchomości; sytuacja;
konjunktura:wszystko; nieruchomości; głupstwa

think; thought; thought (tynk;
'to:t; 'to:t)

think (tynk) v. myśleć; pomyśleć;
zastanawiać się; rozważać; rozmyślać (się); wymyślić; wyobrażać sobie; uważać za; mieć zdanie; mieć za; zapomnieć (rozmyślnie); mieć na myśli (rozwiązywać; etc.

think over ('tynk'ouwer) v. przemyśliwać; zastanawiać się

think up ('tynk,ap) v. wymyślać;
wykombinować; rozwiązać

third (te:rd) adj. trzeci

third degree (,te:rd dy'gri:)
exp.: trzeci stopień (przesłuchi-
wania na policji - głupi, przykry i męczący)

thirdly ('te:rdly) adv. po trzecie

third party (,te:rd'pa:rty) s.
strona trzecia; osoby trzecie

thirdrate ('te:rd'rejt) adj.
trzeciorzędny

Third World ('te:rd'Æe:rld) s.
trzeci swiat (poza Europą,
Chinami, Indią oraz Ameryką)
thirst ('te:rst) s. pragnienie;
żądza; v. pragnąc
thirsty ('te:rsty) adj. spragniony; żądny; suchy; wyschnię-
ty; (slang): ciężki
this (tys) adj. & pron. pl.
these (ti:z) ten; ta; to; tak;
w ten sposob; tyle; obecny;
bieżący; adv. tak; tak daleko; tyle; tak dużo
thistle ('tysl) s. oset
thorn ('to:rn) s. kolec; ciern;
krzak cierniowy; v. kłuc;
drażnic
thorny ('to:rny)adj. kolczasty;
ciernisty; drażliwy
thorough (terou) adj. dokładny;
zupełny; całkowity; sumienny;
adv. na wskros; na wylot
thoroughbred ('te:rou,bred)
adj. rasowy; czystej krwi;
s. koń rasowy
thoroughfare ('te:rou,feer)
s. arteria komunikacyjna;
przejazd; ulica
thoroughly (te:rouly) adv. zupełnie; dokładnie; całkowicie;
na wskros; sumiennie; gruntownie
those (douz) pl. od that
thou (dau) biblijne: ty
though (tou) conj. chociaż;
chocby; gdyby; adv. jednak;
pomimo tego; przecież
thought (to:t) v. zob. think;
s, mysl; namysł; zastanowienie
się; pomysł; oczekiwanie; rozwaga; zamiar; pl. zdanie; pogląd; odrobina;troszkę
thoughtful ('to:tful) adj. zamyslony; zadumany; rozważny;
uważający; dbały; uprzejmy;
(oryginalnie) myslący
thoughtless ('to:tlys) adj.bez-
myslny; nieuważający; nierozważny
thousand ('tauzend) num.tysiąc
thousandth ('tauzendt) adj.
tysięczny

thrash (traesz) s. młocic; walic; bic; prac; dyskutowac;
s. młocenie; walenie
thrashing (traeszyng) s, młocka;
lanie
thread (tred) s. nic; nitka;
przędza; sznurek; wątek; żyłka;
krok (sruby); zwojnik (nici);
gwint; v. nawlekać (igłę);
przetykac; nacinąc gwint (swoj-
nik); przepychać się
threadbare (tredbeer) adj. wytarty; wyswiechtany; wyszarza-
ły
threat (tret) s. grozba; po-
grozka
threaten ('tretn) v. grozic;
zagrażac; odgrażac się
threatening ('tretnyng) adj.
grożący; zagrażający; groźny
three (tri:) num. trzy; s.trój-
ka
threefold ('tri:fold) adj.
potrójny
threescore ('tri:sko:r) num.
szescdziesiąt
threestage ('tri:stejdż) adj.
trójfazowy; trzystopniowy
thresh (tresz) v. młocic; roz-
trzasac; obgadac szczegołowo;
omowic gruntownie; s. młocka
thresher ('treszer) s. młockarnia
threshing ('treszyng) s. młocenie
threshing machine ('treszyng,me-
'szi:n) s. młockarnia
threshold ('treszould) s. próg
threw (tru:) v. zob. throw
thrice (trajs) adj. trzykrotnie
thriftless (tryftlys) adj. rozrzutny
thrifty (tryfty) adj. oszczędny; rozrastający się; kwitnący
thrill (tryl) v. przejmowac
(sie); drgac; s. dreszcz;
dreszczyk; drganie; powiesc
sencacyjna; szmer (serca)
thriller (tryler) s. dreszczowiec; powiesc sensacyjna (kry-
minalna); sztuka sensacyjna;
opowiesc sensacyjna

thrilling (trylyŋg) adj. podniecający; przejmujący; sensacyjny

thrive; throve; thriven
(trajw; trouw; trywn)

thrive (trajw) v. dobrze: rosnąć, chować się, rozwijać się,
miewać się, kwitnąć, prosperować

thro(tru:) = through

throat (trout) s. gardło; szyja; wlot; gardziel; wąskie
przejście; v. żłobić; żłobko-
wać; mówić gardłowo

throb (trob) v. pulsować; drgać;
bić; tętnić; rwać; s. pulsowa-
nie; drganie; bicie serca;
dreszcz; warkot maszyny

thrombosis (trom'bousys) s.
skrzep

throne (troun) s. tron; v. tro-
nować; wprowadzać na tron

throng (tro:ng)s. tłum; tłok;
rzesza; masa; v. tłoczyć się;
zatłaczać; napierać na

throstle (trosl) s. drozd;
przędzarka

throttle ('trotl) s. gardziel;
dławik; przepustnica; zawór
dławiący; v. dusić; regulować
dławikiem

through (tru:) prep. przez; po-
przez; po; wskroś; na wylot;
ze; z; skutkiem; na skutek;za;
dzięki; z powodu; adv. na
wskroś; na wylot; adj. przelo-
towy; bezpośredni; skończony
(np. życiowo)

throughout ('tru:,aut) prep. po-
przez; przez cały; od początku
do końca; wszędzie; całkowicie;
adv. na wskroś

throw (trou) v. zob. thrive

throw; threw; thrown (trou;
tru:, troun)

throw (trou) v. rzucać; ciskać;
zarzucać; zrzucać; skręcać;
powalić; narzucać; modelować
na kole; odrzucać; marnować;
s. rzut; ryzyko; szal; narzuta;
uskok

throw up ('trou,ap) v. wymiotować; rzucać w górę; podrzucać

thrown ('troun) v. zob. throw

thru (tru:) = through

thrum (tram) v. rzępolić; bębnić; robić z nitek; odcinać
luźne nitki; s. brzdąkanie;
odcięta nitka; krajka

thrush (trasz) s. drozd; choroba strzałki kopyta końskiego;
pleśniawka

thrust; thrust; thrust (trast;
trast; trast)

thrust (trast) v. wpychać;
wsadzać; wtykać; wrazić; pchać
(się); przepychać się; wysuwać (się); szturchać; przebijać; wepchnąć; narzucać (się);
wtrącać (się); zadawać pchnięcie; pchnąć; s. pchnięcie;
dzgnięcie; wypad; wypchnięcie;
nacisk; siła : napędu, ciągu,
pędu; zrzut; parcie; uwaga;
przytyk

thud (tad) s. łomot; łoskot
(głuchy); v. łomotać; upadać
z łoskotem

thug (tag) s. bandyta; zbir

thumb (tam) s. kciuk; duży palec; władza (domowa); talent
ogrodniczy; zasada (praktycz-
na); v. kartkować; brudzić
palcami; niszczyć; walać; grać
niezgrabnie; prosić o podwiezienie; wyprosić (gestem)

thumb a lift (tam a lyft) v.
prosić o podwiezienie (autostopem)

thumbtack ('tam-taek) s. pi-
neska; pluskiewka

thump ('tamp) s. grzmotnięcie;
v. grzmocić; walić; iść ciężko

thunder ('tander) s. grzmot;
burza; grom; piorun; v.
grzmieć; rzucać gromy; pioru-
nować; miotać (groźby)

thunderstorm ('tander-sto:rm)
s. burza z piorunami

thunderstruck ('tander-strak)
adj. rażony piorunem; oszołomiony

Thursday ('te:r-zdej) s. czwartek

thus (tas) adv. tak; w ten sposób; tak więc; a zatem

thus far ('tas,fa:r) adv. jak dotąd

thus much ('tas,mach) adv. tyle

thwart (tło:rt) v. udaremnic; pokrzyżowac; psuc szyki; adj. poprzeczny; przeciwny; niepomyślny; s. poprzeczna ławka wioslarska

thy (taj) pron. twój; twoje; zob. thine

tick (tyk) s. kleszcz; tykanie; moment; wsyp; kredyt; sprawne działanie; v. tykac; kupowac na kredyt; sprzedawac na kredyt (slang); ustalac sprawne działanie

tick away ('tyke'łej) v. znaczyc tykaniem

tick off ('tykof) v. odliczac; besztac; odfajkowac

ticker ('tyker) s. telegraf; zegarek; serce (slang)

ticket ('tykyt) s. bilet; kwit; znaczek; wywieszka; lista kandydatów (USA); v. zaopatrywac w bilet, etykietkę; umieszczac na liście kandydatów

ticket office ('tykyt'ofys) s. kasa biletowa

tickle ('tykl) v. łaskotac; łechtac; swędzic; rozsmieszac; bawic; cieszyc; s. łaskotanie; łechtanie; swędzenie

tidal wave ('tajdelłejw) s. olbrzymia fala przypływu skutkiem trzęsienia ziemi

tide (tajd) n. przypływ & odpływ morza; fala; okres; v. przypływac falą; płynąc z falą; wybrnąc

tidy ('tajdy) adj. schludny; czysty; niemały; spory; s. zbiornik na odpadki; pokrowiec na mebel; v. oporządzic; sporządzac; oporządzac (się); porządkowac

tie (taj) v. wiązac; zawiązac;

przywiązac; łączyc; sznurowac; remisowac; zawrzec ślub; unieruchomic; s. węzeł; krawat; podkład kolejowy; próg; remis; sznur; rozgrywka; półbucik

tie up ('taj,ap) v. zawiązywac; unieruchamiac

tier (tier) s. piętro; rząd; węzeł; zwój; kondygnacja; rzecz wiążąca; fartuszek; v. spiętrzac się (też warstwami)

tiger ('tajger) s. tygrys; jaguar; kugar; zawadiaka; pracujący zapamiętale

tight (tajt) adj. zacisnięty; mocny; zwarty; szczelny; spoisty: obcisły; wąski; nabity; wstawiony; zalany; skąpy; niewystarczający; silny; mocny; uparty; adv. zwarcie; ciasno; szczelnie; obcisle; mocno; silnie

tighten ('tajtn) v. zaciskac (się); uszczelniac; napinac (się)

tightfisted ('tajt-,tystyd) adj. sknera; kutwa

tight fitting ('tajt-fytyŋg) adj. obcisły; opięty

tightrope ('tajt-roup) s. lina akrobatyczna

tights (tajts) pl. trykot baletnicy, akrobaty etc.; w Anglii rajstopy

tigress ('tajgrys) s. tygrysica

tile (tajl) n. dachówka; kafelek; dren; (slang): cylinder; v. pokrywac dachówkami; wykładac kaflami (płytami)

till (tyl) prep. aż do; dopiero; dotychczas; aż; dopóki nie; dotąd; v. uprawiac (ziemię); s. szufladka na pieniądze; kasa podręczna

tilt (tylt) s.przechylenie ; przechył; nachylenie; natarcie kopią; plandeka; daszek; v. przechylac (się); nachylac (się); nacierac kopią; (pełnym) pędem leciec; zaopatrywac w daszek timber ('tymber) s. drzewo; budulec; drewno; belka; wręga; las; charakter; v. zaopatrywać w budulec; podpierać belką

timberland ('tymber'laend) s. obszar lasu budulcowego

timberwork ('tymber:łe:rk) s. konstrukcja drewniana

timber yard ('tymber,ja:rd) s. skład (drzewa) budulca

time (tajm) s. czas; pora; raz; takt; v. obliczać czas zużyty; ustalać czas; wybierać czas; robić we własciwym czasie; nastawiac (przyrząd); regulować (zegar); synchronizować; harmonizować; trzymać takt; excl.: czas ! (zamykać lokal etc.)

time and again ('tajm end,e'gen) exp.: ciągle; ustawicznie

time bomb ('tajm,bom) s. bomba zegarowa

time is up ('tajm'ys,ap) exp.: koniec (zabawy; rozmowy etc)

timely ('tajmly) adv. na czasie; w porę; adj. aktualny; odpowiedni; własciwy; punktualny

timetable ('tajm,tejbl) s. rozkład jazdy, zajęć etc.

timeless ('tajmlys) adj. wieczny; ponadczasowy (niekończący się)

timid ('tymyd) adj. niesmiały; bojazliwy

timidity (ty'mydyty) s. bojazliwosc

timorous ('tymeres) adj, bojazliwy

tin (tyn) s. cyna; blacha; puszka blaszana; blaszanka; folia cynowa; pieniądze; adj. cynowany; blaszany; dziadowski (kubek); v. cynować

tinfoil ('tynfojl) s. folia metalowa; cynfolia; staniol

tinge (tyndż) s. odcien; lekkie zabarwienie; v. zabarwiać lekko

tingle ('tyngl) s. mrowienie; swierzbienie; kłucie; v, czuc kłucie; mrowienie; kłuc

tinkle ('tynkl) v. dzwonic; brzęczec;(siusiac) s. dzwonienie

tinned (tynd) adj. cynowany

tinopener ('tyn,oupner) s. otwieracz puszek (narzędzie)

tint (tynt) s. odcien;zabarwienie; v. zabarwiac

tinware ('tynłeer) s. wyroby blaszane

tiny ('tajny) adj. drobny; malusienski; malutki

tip (typ) s. koniec (np. palca); koniuszek; szczyt; zakonczenie; skuwka; okucie; napiwek; poufna informacja; wiadomosc; rada; wskazówka; trącenie; przechylenie; skład smieci; v. wykanczac koniec; okuwac; przechylac (sie); wazyc; przewracac (się); dac napiwek; informowac (poufnie); trącać lekko; dotykac; uderzac ukosem (piłkę); przewazac

tip off ('typ,of) v. ostrzegac

tip-off ('typof) s. poufne ostrzeżenie (informacja)

tipster ('typster) s. człowiek udzielajacy poufnych informacji (o wyscigach etc.)

tipsy ('typsy) adj. podchmielony; pijany; chwiejny; niepewny

tiptoe ('typtou) s. koniec palca u nogi; v. chodzic na palcach; adv. na palcach (u nóg)

tire ('tajer) v. męczyc (się); nudzic (się); nakładac obręcz, oponę; przystroic; s. obręcz; opona; stroj

tired ('tajerd) adj. znęczony; znużony; znudzony

tireless ('tajerlys) adj. niestrudzony

tiresome ('tajersem) adj. męczący; nudny

tissue ('tyszu:) s. tkanka; tkanina; siatka; bibułka

tissue paper (tyszu:,pejper) s. bibułka; papier toaletowy; papier płótnowany tit (tyt) s. sikora

tit for tat ('tyt,fo:r taet) exp.:wet za wet

titbit ('tytbyt) s. smakołyk

titilate ('tytylejt) s. łechtać

title ('tajtl) s. tytuł; nagłowek; napis; tytuł rodowy; tytuł prawny; prawo; czystość złota w karatach

titled ('tajtld) adj. utytułowany

titter ('tyter) v. chichotać; s. chichot

tittle-tattle ('tytl-'taetl) v. robić granki; s. plotkowanie

to (tu:; tu) prep. do; aż do; ku; przy; w stosunku do; w porównaniu z; w stosunku jak; stosownie do; dla; wobec; względem; za (zależnie od ustaleń zwyczajowych)

toad (toud) s. ropucha

to and fro ('tu:end,rou) exp.: tam i z powrotem

toast (toust) s. grzanka; toast; v. robić granki;wznosić toast

tobacco (te'baekou) s. tytoń

tobacconist (te'baekounyst) s. sprzedawca wyrobów tytoniowych

toboggan (te'bogen) s. saneczki; v. sankować się; spadać (ceny)

today (te'dej) adv. dzisiaj; dziś; s. dzień dzisiejszy

toddle ('todl) v. dreptać; drobić nóżkami; s. drobienie nóżkami; dreptanie; pędrak

toddler ('todler) s. pędrak; berbeć

to-do (te'du:) s. zamieszanie; rwetes

toe (tou) s. palec u nogi; nosek; szpic; stopa wału (tamy); występ z przodu; przednia część kopyta; hacel; dno odwiertu; v. kopnąć; cerować palec u pończochy; podporządkować się; stawać na starcie; stosować się do linii (też partyjnej); ukośnie wbijać gwoździe; krzywo chodzić (palcami zbyt do wewnątrz lub na zewnątrz)

toffee ('tofi) s. karmelek

toffy ('tofy) s. karmelek (śmietankowy)

together (te'gedzer) adv. razem; wspólnie; naraz; równocześnie

toil (tojl) s. znój; mozół; trud; mozolić się; trudzić się; harować

toilet ('tojlyt) s. ustęp; toaleta; ubranie; adj. toaletowy

toilet paper ('tojlyt,pejper) s. papier toaletowy

toils (tojlz) s. sidła; matnia

token ('toukn) s. znak; dowód autentyczności; symbol; pamiątka; żeton; bon; adj. symboliczny; niewiążący

told (tould) v. zob. tell

tolerable ('tolerebl) adj. znośny; nienajgorszy; dosyć zdrowy

tolerance ('tolerens) s. tolerancja; luz; wyrozumiałość

tolerant ('tolerent) adj. tolerancyjny; wyrozumiały; tolerancki

tolerate ('tolerate) v. znosić; tolerować; cierpieć

toleration (,tole'rejszyn) s. znoszenie; tolerancja; tolerowanie

toll (toul) s. opłata (np. telefoniczna); myto: mostowe; drogowe; miejski podatek; trybut; danina; dzwonienie; v. uiszczać opłatę; wydzwaniać; dzwonić jednostajnie; wabić (zwierzynę)

toll bar ('toulba:r) s. szlaban

tollgate ('toulgejt) s. rogatka wjazdowa na płatny most lub autostradę

tomato (te'mejtou) s. pomidor

tomatoes (te'mejtouz) pl. pomidory

tomb (tu:m) s. grób; grobowiec; v. pochowanie

tombstone (tu:m-stoun) s. kamień nagrobny; nagrobek

tomcat ('tom'kaet) s. kocur
tomorrow (te'mo:rou) s.& adv.
jutro
ton (tan) s. tona (2000 funtów)
(slang): mnóstwo
tone (toun) s. ton; normalny
stan (np. ciała; organizmu);
brzmienie; v. stonować się;
stroic; harmonizować
tone down ('toun,dałn) v. zła-
godzic; stonować
tongs (tonz) s. szczypce;
kleszcze; obcęgi
tongue (tan) s. język; mowa;
ozor; v. dotykać językiem;
łajać; mleć językiem
tonic ('tonyk) adj. wzmacnia-
jący; elastyczny; krzepiący;
s. środek tonizujący
tonight (te'najt) s. dziś wie-
czor; dzisiejsza noc; adv.
dziś wieczorem; gwara: ubieg-
łej nocy; wczoraj wieczór
tonnage ('tanydż) n. tonaż;
opłata od tony ładunku
tonsil ('tonsel) s. migdałek
tonsillitis (,tonsy'lajtys)
s. zapalenie migdałków
tony (touny) adj.(slang):szy-
kowny
too (tu:) adv. tak; także; ponadto; do tego; zbytnio; zanadto; zbyt; za; na dodatek;
też
took (tuk) v. zob. take
tool (tu:l) s. narzędzie; obrabiarka; v. obrabiać;
oporządzać
tool up ('tu:l,ap) v. oprzyrzą-
dzać
tools (tu:ls) pl. przybory;
sprzęt
tooth (tu:s) s. ząb; pl. teeth
(ti:s) v. uzębiać; wcinać zęby; ząbkować; szczepiać zębami trybów
tooth ache ('tu:s ejk) s. ból
zęba
tooth brush ('tu:s,brasz) s.
szczotka do zębów
toothless('tu:slys) adj. bezzębny

toothpaste ('tu:spejst) s. pasta do zębów
toothpick ('tu:spyk) s. wykałaczka
top (top) s. wierzchołek; czu-
bek; szczyt; wierzch; powierzchnia; góra; bociane gniazdo;
przykrywka; bąk; fryga; adj.
wierzchni; zewnętrzny; górny;
wyższy; najwyższy; szczytowy;
maksymalny; v. nakrywać; wień-
czyc; uwieńczać; przewyższać;
stanowić wierzch; osiągnąć
szczyt; ścinać szczyt; przeskoczyc (przez coś); położyć
kres; mierzyc wysokość; wznosic się
topaz ('toupez) s. topaz
topic ('topyk) s. temat (rozmowy)
topple ('topl) v. przechylać;
wywracać
topple down ('topldałn) v.
przewrócić
top secret (,topsi:kryt) adj.
ściśle tajny
topsy-turvy ('topsy'te:rwy)
adj. do góry nogami; v. przewracać do góry nogami; s. rozgardiasz; bałagan; galimatias
torch (to:rcz) s. pochodnia;
znicz; kaganek; palnik (do
lutowania etc.)
tore (to:r) v. zob. tear
torment ('to:rment) s. męka;
udręka; (to:r'ment) v. męczyć;
dręczyc
torn (to:rn) v. zob. tear
tornado (,to:r'nejdou) s. trąba
powietrzna; tornado
torrent ('to:rent) s. potok
(rwacy); ulewny deszcz; burza
torsion ('to:rszyn) s. skręt;
skręcanie
tortoise ('to:rtes) s. żółw
(słodkowodny)
torture ('to:rczer) s. tortura;
meka; v. torturować; męczyć;
dręczyc; wykręcać; przekręcać

tosh (tosz) s. bzdury; brednie; banialuki

toss (to:s) v. rzucać się;
podrzucać; zarzucać; podnosić;
niepokoić; kłopotać; przewracać się (w łóżku); podbijać
(piłkę); wypaść z pokoju;
kołysać się na boki; s. rzut;
losowanie; upadek (z konia)
toss about (,to:s e'baut), v.
przewracać się (po czymś)
toss up ('to:s,ap) v. przewracać; grać w orła i reszkę
toss-up ('to:sap) s. 50%
prawdopodobieństwa; orzeł
czy reszka ?;rzecz wątpliwa
total ('total) a. ogólny; zupełny; całkowity; totalny;
kompletny; v. zliczać; wynosić ogółem; (slang): niszczyć
całkowicie (np. samochód
w wypadku)
totalitarian (tou,taely'tear-
jen) adj. totalitarny; tota-
listyczny; s. totalista
totter ('toter) v. chwiać się;
zataczać się; s. chwianie
się; zataczanie się (dziecka)
touch (tacz) v. dotykać; stykać (się); wzruszać (się);
poruszać (coś); brać; wydobywać; zabarwiać;lekko uszka-
dzać; cechować; mierzyć; retuszować; rabnąć kogoś na
pieniądze (slang); s. dotyk;
dotknięcie; pociągnięcie;
odrobina; kontakt; lekka (choroba); rys; nuta (np.złości);
obmacywanie;cecha; probierz;
naciąganie na pieniądze(slang)
touch down ('tacz,dałn) v. lądować;uzyskiwać 6 punktów
touchdown (taczdałn) s. lądowanie;gol w futbolu(6 punktów)
touching ('taczyng) adj. wzruszający; rozrzewniający; adv.
odnośnie (do czegoś)
touchy ('taczy) adj. drażliwy;
obraźliwy; przewrażliwiony
tough (taf) adj. twardy;trudny;
ciężki; łobuzerski; adv. trudno; s. człowiek: trudny, twardy; łobuz; chuligan

tour (tuer) s. objazd; wycieczka; tura; przechadzka; służba
(wojskowa); v. objeżdżać; ob-
wozić
tourist ('tueryst) s. turysta;
klasa turystyczna
tourist-agency ('tueryst'ejdżensy) s. biuro podróży
tournament ('tuernement) s.
turniej
tousle ('tauzl) v. szarpać;
mierzwić; czochrać; targać;
s. rozczochrane włosy;rozczo-
chranie
tow (tou) v. holować; ciągnąć;
s. holowanie; lina holownicza;
przedmiot holowany; włókna
lniane; paździory
towards (to:rdz; 'tołerdz) prep.
ku; w kierunku; dla; w celu;
na (coś)
tow-boat ('taubout) s. holownik
towel ('tauel) s. ręcznik;
v. wycierać ręcznikiem
tower ('tauer) s. wieża; wznosić (się); sterczeć; wzbijać
się
town (tałn) s. miasto
town councilor (,tałn'kaunsyler)
s. radny miejski
town hall ('tałn,ho:l) s. ratusz
towrope ('touroup) s. lina
holownicza
toy (toj) s. zabawka; cacko;
v. bawić się; cackać się; robić niedbale; flirtować (też
np. z pomysłem)
toxic ('toksyk) adj. trujący;
jadowity
trace (trejs) s. ślad;postronek;
drążek przekaźnikowy; v. iść
śladami; kopiować rysunek;
przypisywać czemuś; wytyczać;
nakreślać; kreślić
track (traek) s.tor; koleina;
ślad; trop; bieżnia; rozstaw
kół; v. śledzić; tropić; zostawiać ślady; zabłocić; zawalać; zakładać tor; mieć
rozstęp kół; ciągnąć liną
z brzegu

track down ('traek,dałn) v.
wytropić; wyśledzić; schwytać

track and field events ('traek-
,end-fi:ldy'wents) s. lekkoatletyka

track events (traek y'wents)
s. biegi; zawody na bieżni

traction engine (traekszyn-
endżyn) s. lokomotywa; pociągowy motor; traktor

tractor ('traekter) s. ciągnik;
traktor

trade (trejd) s. zawód; zajęcie;
rzemiosło; handel; wymiana;
klientela; branża; kupiectwo;
v. handlować; wymieniać; frymarczyć; przewozić towary;
kupczyć; przehandlować

trademark ('trejd,ma:rk) s.
znak ochronny; v. przybijać
znak ochronny; rejestrować
znak ochronny

trader ('trejder) s. handlowiec;
statek handlowy; spekulator
giełdowy

trade-union ('trejd'ju:njen)
s. związek zawodowy

trade unionist ('trejd'ju:n-
jenyst) s. działacz związku
zawodowego

tradition (tre'dyszyn) s. tradycja

traditional (tre'dyszynel) adj.
tradycyjny

traffic ('traefyk) s. ruch(kołowy, pasażerski,towarowy,
telegraficzny, telefoniczny,
drogowy, etc.); v. handel
czyms; frymarczyć; kupczyć

traffic island ('traefyk-aj-
lend) s. wysepka na jezdni

traffic jam('traefyk-dżaem)
s. zator ruchu

traffic lights ('traefyk-
lajts) pl. semafory uliczne

traffic regulation ('traefyk,re-
gju'lejszyn) s. przepisy ruchu

traffic sign ('traefyk,sajn)
s. znak drogowy

traffic-cop ('traefyk,kop) s.
policjant ruchu (drogowego)

tragedy ('traedżydy) s. tragedia

tragic ('traedżyk) adj. tragiczny

tragical ('traedżykel) = tragic

trail (trejl) v. pociągnąć (się);
powlec (się);holować; wlec (się)
pozostawać w tyle; iść za tro-
pem; ścigać; wydeptywać (ścieżkę); nosić (karabin poziomo
przy boku); s. szlak; ścieżka;
trop; ogon; smuga; struga;
bruzda; koleina

trailer ('trejler) s. przyczepa
(do samochodu); przyczepa to-
warowa, mieszkalna, turystyczna, etc.; maruder; pnąca (się)
roślina

train (trejn) v. szkolić; kształcić; przyuczać; wytresować;
ćwiczyć (się); trenować (się);
kierować na kogoś (np. wzrok);
wlec; s. pociąg; tren; ogon;
sznur; szereg; następstwo;
orszak; świta; porządek; wątek;
łańcuch

trainer ('trejner) s. trener;
instruktor; samolot szkolny

training ('trejnyng) s. zaprawa; trening; ćwiczenie; szkolenie

trait (trejt) s. cecha

traitor ('trejtor) s. zdrajca

tram (traem) s. tramwaj

tramp (traemp) v. stąpać; włóczyć się; wędrować pieszo;
iść pieszo; s. włóczęga;tramp;
wędrowiec; statek (nieregular-
nej żeglugi)

trample ('traempl) v. deptać

trance (tra:ns) s. trans; uniesienie; ekstaza

tranquil ('traenkłyl) adj. spokojny

tranquility ('traen'kłylyty) s.
spokój

tranquilize ('traenkłylajz) v.
uspokajać

tranquilizer ('traenkłylajzer)
s. środek uspakajający

transact (traen'saekt) v. załatwiać; pertraktować; przeprowadzać

transaction (traen'saekszyn)
s. transakcja; przeprowadze-
nie sprawy; pl. sprawozdania
naukowe; rozprawy

transalpine (traens'aelpajn)
adj. transalpejski

transatlantic (traenzet'laentyk) adj. transatlantycki

transcend (traen'send) v.
przewyższać; prześcignąć;
górować

transcribe (traens'krajb) v.
nagrywać na taśmie; przepi-
sywać

transcript ('traenskrypt) s.
kopia; transkrypcja

transfer (traens'fe:r) v.
przemieścić; przenieść (się);
przewozić; przekazać; s.prze-
niesienie; przewóz; przedruk;
przekaz; przelew; odstąpienie

transferable (traens'fe:rebl)
adj. przenośny

transform (traens'fo:rm) v.
przekształcić; zmienić postać

transformation (,traensfer'-
'mejszyn) s. przekształcanie;
przeobrażenie

transfuse (traens'fjuz) v.
przelać; przetoczyć (krew)

transfusion (traens'fjużyn) s.
transfuzja

transgress (traens'gres) v.
naruszyć; zgrzeszyć

transgression (traens'greszyn)
s. naruszenie; grzech; wykroczenie

transgressor (traens'greser)
s. grzesznik

transient ('traenzjent) adj.
przechodni; przejeżdżający;
przelotny

transistor (traen'syster) s.
tranzystor

transit ('traensyt) s.przejazd;
przelot; przewóz; tranzyt;
teodolit

transition (traen'syszyn) s.
przejście; zmiana

transitive ('traensytyw) adj.
przechodni

translate (traens'lejt) v. przetłumaczyć; przełożyć

translation (traens'lejszyn)
s. tłumaczenie; przekład

translator (traens'lejter) s.
tłumacz

translucent (traenz'lu:sent)
adj. przeświecający; pół-
przezroczysty

transmission (traenz'myszyn) s.
przekładnia; transmisja

transmit (traenz'myt) v. przekazywać; nadawać; transmitować

transmitter (traenz'myter) s.
nadajnik; przekaźnik

transparent (traens'peerent)
adj. przezroczysty

transpire (traens'pajer) v. pocić się; wyparować; okazywać
się; zdarzyć się

transplant (traens'pla:nt) v.
przeszczepiać; przesadzać;
s. przesadzanie; przeszczep

transport (traens'po:rt) v.
przewozić; zachwycać; s.prze-
wóz; zachwyt; uniesienie

transportation (,traenpo:r'tejszyn) s. przewóz; transport;
deportacja; zesłanie

trap (traep) s. pułapka; potrzask; sidła; zasadzka; podstęp; syfon; skała wylewna;
(slang): jadaczka; pl.:manatki;
v. złapać w pułapkę; zaopatrywać w pułapkę; zatrzymywać
(w czymś); przykrywać czapra-
kiem; puszczać rzutki

trap-door ('traep'do:r) s.
drzwi zapadowe; zapadnia

trapeze (tre'pi:z) s. trapez

trapper ('traeper) s. traper;
myśliwy; zastawiający pułapki;
nadzorca szybów powietrznych
w kopalni

trappings (traepyngz) s.ozdoby;
strój ozdobny; czaprak

trash (traesz) s. śmieci; ru-
pieci; tandeta; odpadki; bzdury; hołota; v. obdzierać (z
liści, gałązek)

travel ('traewl) v. podróżować
(też za interesem); poruszać
się (części maszyny); przesuwać się; biec (w terenie);
przechodzic (oczami po czyms);
poruszać się żwawo; błądzic;
s. (daleka) podróż; ruch (po-
jazdów); suw (maszynowy);
przesunięcie

travel agency ('traewl'ejdżensy)
s. biuro podróży

traveler ('traewler) s. podróżnik; wodzik nitkowy; komiwojażer

traveler's check ('traewlers,-
,czek) s. z góry wykupiony
czek do użytku w podróży

traveling bag ('traewlyng,baeg)
s. torba podróżna

traverse (trae'we:rs)v. przecinać; przesuwać na bok; przechodzic; omawiać; pokrzyżować;
zaprzeczyc formalnie; nakiero-
wywac (działo); obracać (się)
jak na osi

travesty ('traewysty) s. trawe-
stia; parodia; v. trawestować;
parodiować

trawl (tro:l) s. włók; włók;
tral; niewód; sieć - worek do
holowania;v,ciągnąc niewód; ło-
wic niewodem, włókiem, wędką
ciągnioną za łodzią

trawler ('tro:ler) s. trawler

tray (trej) s, taca; szufladka
(też wkładowa)

treacherous ('treczeres) adj.
zdradziecki; niebezpieczny;
zdradliwy; zawodny; perfidny

treachery ('treczery) s. zdrada; zdradzieckość; zdradliwość;
perfidia

treacle ('tri:kl) s. syrop; melasa; sok (drzewny)

tread; trod; tro(den), (tred,
trod; 'trodn)

tread (tred) v. deptać; stąpać
(po czyms); nadepnąc; tłoczyc;
wdeptywać; iśc (ścieżką); wydeptać (ścieżkę) ; gniesc;
s. stąpanie; krok; podnóżek;

guma opony dotykająca jezdni;
szyna; bieżnik; podeszwą (dotykająca ziemi); stopień

treadle ('tredl) s. pedał;
v. pedałować

treadmill ('tredmyl) s. kierat
(cylindryczny ze stopniami)

treason('tri:zn) s. zdrada

treasure ('treżer) s, skarb;
v. zaskarbiac; cenic; strzec
skarbu

treasure up ('treżer,ap) v.
przechowywać jak skarb

treasurer ('treżerer) s. skarbnik

treasury ('treżery) s. urząd
skarbowy; skarbnica

Treasury Department ('treżery,-
,dy'pa:rtment) s. ministerstwo
skarbu (USA)

treat (tri:t) v. traktować; po-
traktować; obchodzic się z
kims; uważać kogos za; brać
coś (za żart); leczyc coś; poddawać działaniu; pertraktować;
fundować (komus); s. przyjęcie;
uczta; majówka; poczęstunek;
zabawa; przyjemnośc; rozkosz

treatise ('tri:tys) s. traktat;
rozprawa

treatment ('tri:tment) s. traktowanie; leczenie

treaty ('tri:ty) s. traktat;
układ; umowa

treble ('trebl) adj. potrójny;
wysoki; ostry; przenikliwy;
sopranowy; s. sopran; wysoki
dźwięk; v. potrajać (się)

tree (tri:) s. drzewo; forma;
kopyto; rama siodła; belka;
nadproże; krokiew; szubienica;
v. zapędzić (na drzewo); wsa-
dzic (na kopyto)

treeless ('tri:lys) adj. bez-
drzewny

tree-trunk ('tri:,trank) s.
pien roślina trójlistna;

trefoil ('trefojl) s. koniczyna trójlistna;adj.trójlistny

trellis ('trely) s, krata; altana; v. kratować winorosl;
nadawać formę kraty

tremble ('trembl) v. trząść
się; drzeć; dygotać; s.drże-
nie; drżączka
tremendous (try'mendes) adj.
straszny; olbrzymi
tremor ('tremer) s. drżenie;
drganie; trzęsienie (ziemi)
tremulous ('tremjules) adj.
drżący
trench (trencz) s.rów; okop;
bruzda; cięcie; rów strzelec-
ki; v. kopać rów; okopywać
się; kłaść do rowu; żłobić;
ciąć; przecinać; podkopywac
się; graniczyc
trench up ('trencz,ap) v.
wdzierac się (bezczelnie)
w cudze (prawa etc.)
trend (trend) s. dążność; ogól-
na tendencja; ogólny kierunek;
v. dążyć; mieć tendencję;
kształtowac się; ciągnąc się
trespass ('trespas) v. wdzierac się w cudze; nadużywac;
naruszac; wykraczac; grze-
szyc; v. przekroczenie; wykroczenie; grzech; szkoda wy-
rządzona na cudzym terenie
trespasser ('trespaser) s.
człowiek naruszający przepisy,prawo (czyjeś)
tress (tres) s. warkocz; v.za-
platac warkocz
trestle ('tresl) s. kozioł;
kobylica; most filarowy
trial ('trajel) s. próba; proces sądowy; zmartwienie; zawody eliminacyjne; adj. próbny; doswiadczalny
trial and error ('trajel end'-
'erer) exp.: chaotyczne próby
(w nieznane)
triangle ('trajaengl) s. trójkąt
triangular (traj'aengjular) adj.
trójkątny
triangulate (traj'aengjulejt)
v. mierzyc (trójkątami) przy
pomocy triangulacji
tribe (trajb) s. plemię; szczep
tribunal (traj'bju:nl) s. try-
bunał; sad

tribune ('trybju:n) s. trybuna;
mównica; gazeta; trybun (ludu)
tributary ('trybjutery) adj.
pomocniczy; płacący daninę;
haracz; s. dopływ; kraj płacący daninę
tribute ('trybju:t) s. haracz;
danina
trick (tryk) s. podstęp; chwyt;
sztuczka; sposób; nawyk; maniera; psota; fortel; (slang):
dziecko; dziewczynka; v. oszu-
kac; okpic; wyłudzic; płatać
figla; zawodzic; zaskakiwac
trick up ('tryk,ap) s. wystroic
trickle ('trykl) v. sączyć (się);
przeciekac; przesączyc; puszczac ciurkiem; kroplami;
s. struga (mała)
tricky ('tryky) adj. podstępny;
chytry; sprytny; trudny; zawiły; zręczny
tricycle ('trajsykl) s. rower
na trzech kołach
trifle ('trajfl) s. drobiazg;
drobnostka; błachostka; bagatela; odrobina; głupstewko; byle
co; stop cyny i ołowiu; biszkopt z kremem; v. nie brac po-
ważnie; poflirtowac; baraszko-
wac; paplac; bagatelizowac
trifling ('trajflyng) adj. płochy; błachy; znikomy
trigger ('tryger) s. spust;
cyngiel; zapadka; v. pociągac
za spust; wyzwolac; dawac początek; zaczynac (akcję)
trill (tryl) s. trel; wibrująca
spółgłoska; v. wymawiac z wi-
bracją; trząść głosem; trelowac; wymawiac wibrująco
trillion ('tryljen) = USA billion ('byljen) num. trylion
trim (trym) v. oporządzac;
usuwac niepotrzebne (gałęzie;
tłuszcz etc.); przybierac (li-
stwą; tasmą etc); rozkładać
poprawnie ładunek; poprawiac
(opinię); byc oportunista;
zmyc komus głowe; dac komus lanie; wyprowadzic w pole; besztac; rugac; s. stan; forma;

nastrój; gotowość; porządek;
strój; ozdoby; listwy; taśmy;
wstążki do poprawienia wyglądu; dekoracja wystawy; oporzą-
dzenie; obcięcie; równowaga
lotu; wyposażenie wnętrza
(np. samochodu, domu etc,)
adj. schludny; porządny;
uporządkowany; wysprzątany

trimming ('trymyŋg) s. ozdoby;
uporządkowanie; przystrzyżenie;
garnirowanie

trimmings ('trymyŋgs) s. zrzyn-
ki i obrzynki z przybierania;
dodatki do potraw; obcinki

Trinity ('trynyty) s.Trójca Św.

trinket ('trynkyt) s. ozdóbka
(na sukni); świecidełko;
błahostka

trip (tryp) s. podróż; wycieczka; jazda; trans narkomana;
potknięcie; podstawienie nogi;
zgrabny krok; wyzwalanie za-
padkowe lub wychwytowe; błąd;
pomyłka; v. potknąć się; iść
lekkim krokiem; drobić nóżkami;
tańczyć (lekko); pomylić się;
podstawiać nogę; złapać na błędzie; wyzwalać; odczepiać kotwicę; przesuwać wychwytem kot-
wicowym; obracać reje; spuszczać nagle część maszyny

tripe (trajp) s. flaki (też potrawa); byle co; paskudztwo;
lichota

triple (tripl) adj. potrójny;
s. potrójna ilość; trójka;
v. potrajać (się)

triplets ('tryplyts) pl. trojacz-
ki

tripod ('trajpod) s. trójnóg;
statyw

triumph ('trajemf) s. triumf;
v. triumfować

triumphal (traj'amfel) adj.
triumfalny

triumphant (traj'amfent) adj.
zwycięski; triumfalny

trivial ('trywiel) adj. trywialny; błahy; płytki; banalny;
znikomy

trod (trod) v. zob. tread

trodden ('trodn) v. zob. tread

trolley car ('troly car) s.
tramwaj; wywrotka (wóz)

trombone (trom'boun) s. puzon

troop (tru:p) s. grupa; gromada; trupa teatralna; rota;
pół szwadronu; s. iść gromadą;
gromadzić się; formować w ro-
ty (pułk)

trophy ('troufy) s. trofeum

tropic ('tropyk) adj. podzwrotnikowy; tropikalny; s. zwrotnik

tropical ('tropykel) adj. tropikalny; gorący; namiętny

trot (trot) s. kłus; trucht;
bryk (szkolny); (slang): biegunka

trouble ('trabl) s. kłopot;
zmartwienie; zaburzenie; niepokój; trud; dolegliwość; fatyga; bieda; awaria; uszkodzenie; defekt; v. martwić (się);
dręczyć (się); dokuczać; niepokoić (się); kłopotać (się)

troublesome ('trablsem) adj.
kłopotliwy

trough (trof) s. koryto; rynna;
rów (też między falami); niec-
ka; łęk; synklina

trouser leg ('trauserleg) s.
nogawka

trousers ('trauzez) pl. spodnie

trousseau (tru:sou) s. wyprawa
(ślubna)

trout (traut) s. pstrąg; v. ło-
wic pstrągi

truant ('tru:ent) s. wagarowicz;
opuszczający pracę; adj. próż-
niacki; wałęsający (się); v.
chodzić na wagary; opuszczać
pracę

truce (tru:s) s. rozejm; zawieszenie broni

truck (trak) s. ciężarówka;
taczki; wózek; podwozie na kołach; lora; drobne towary; warzywa; wymiana; interes; śmieci; brednie; stosunki z kimś;
v. przewozić wozem; ładować na
wóz; wymieniać się z kimś; obnosić towar; utrzymywać stosunki z kimś

truck farm ('trak,fa:rm) s.
gospodarstwo warzywne
trudge (tradż) s. trudny marsz;
v. trudzić się marszem; odbywać z trudem drogę
true (tru:) adj. prawdziwy;
wierny; ścisły; dokładny; praw-
domowny; czysty; faktyczny;
szczery; lojalny; dobrze do-
pasowany; s. prawda; właściwe
położenie; v. regulować; wyre-
gulować; adv. prawdziwie; dokładnie; exp.:to jest prawda !
truly ('tru:ly) adv. prawdziwie;
dokładnie
true-blue ('tru:blu:) adj. bez-
kompromisowy; prawdziwie oddany
trump (tramp) s. atut; as; zuch;
złoty człowiek; trąba; v. bić
atutem; roztrąbić
trump up ('tramp,ap) v. wyssać
z palca; zmyślać (zarzuty);
preparować (zarzuty)
trumpet ('trampyt) s. trąbka;
dźwięk; trębacz; v. grać na
trąbie; trąbić; roztrąbić
truncheon ('tranczen) s. pałka
policjanta; buława marszałka
trunk (trank) s. pień; trzon;
tułów; tors; kadłub; główny kanał; główna linia; trąba słoniowa; kufer; bagażnik;
pl. spodnie (krótkie)
trunk line ('trank-lajn) s.
linia międzymiastowa (też telefoniczna w Anglii)
trunk road ('trank-roud) s.
szosa główna
truss (tras) s. wieżba; wspornik;
kratownica; wiązanie dachowe;
wiązka (siana); pas przepukli-
nowy; v. związać (np. dach);
przywiązać; wieszać (zbrodnia-
rza)
trust (trast) s. pewność; zaufanie; wiara; nadzieja; kredyt;
opieka; powiernictwo; trust;
v. zaufać; mieć zaufanie; ufać;
wierzyć; polegać (na pamięci
swojej etc.) powierzać; kredytować

trustful ('trastful) adj. ufny
trusting ('trastyng) adj. ufny;
pełen zaufania
trustworthy ('trast,łe:rty) adj.
godny zaufania; pewny
truth (tru:s) s. prawda; prawdziwość; rzetelność
truthful ('tru:sful) adj. prawdo-
mówny; prawdziwy (np. opis)
truths (tru:sz) pl. prawdy
try (traj) v. próbować; wypróbować; sądzić; sprawdzić; kosztować; doświadczyć; starać się;
męczyć; s. próba. usiłowanie;
wysiłek
trying (trajyng) adj. przykry;
męczący; nieznośny; irytujący;
ciężki
try on ('traj,on) s. przymierzać
try out ('traj,aut) v. wypróbo-
wywać
T-square ('ti:,skłeer) s. węgielnica
tub (tab) s. balia; ceber; kadź;
wanna; kąpiel; łódź terningowa
(wiosłowa); oszalowanie;
v. wsadzać do wanny; prać;
szalować
tube (tju:b) s. rura; wąż; dętka; tubka; tunel (kolei pod-
ziemnej); v. zamykać w rurze;
zaopatrywać w rury; nadawać
kształt rury
tuberculosis (tjube:rkju:lou-
sys) s. gruźlica
tuck (tak) v. wtykać; wsuwać;
podwijać; zawijać (rąbek);
otulać; zbierać w fałdy; obrębiać; schować; (slang): pa-
łaszować; wcinać; wieszać
(skazańca); s. fałd; fałda;
obręb; koncha
tuck in ('takyn) v. otulać
(w łóżku)
tuck up ('tak,ap) v. podkasać
Tuesday ('tju:zdy) s. wtorek
tuft (taft) s. pęk; pęczek;
kisć; kępa; kitka; brodka;
pikowanie; v. robić pęki; dawać pęki; rosć pękami; pikować

tug (tag) v. ciągnąc (z trudem)
holowac; wciągac; s. holownik;
gwałtowne pociągnięcie

tug-of-war ('tag,ow łor) s.
przeciąganie liny (próba sił;
zawody);zażarta walka o przewagę

tuition (tju'yszyn) s. czesne;
nauczanie; lekcje (płatne)

tulip ('tju:lyp) s. tulipan

tumble ('tambl) v. upasc; zwa-
lic (się); potknąc się; zataczac się; kołysac się; hustac
się; wywalic się; gramolic się;
rzucac się; biegac na oślep;
cisnąc; zwichrzyc; (slang):
kapowac; isc do łóżka; v.zwa-
lenie; pobicie rekordu; upadek;
sztuka akrobatyczna; bałagan

tummy ('tamy) s. żołądek;
brzuch (dziecka)

tumor ('tu:mer) s. tumor;
obrzęk; guz; nowotwor

tumult ('tu:malt) s. zgiełk;
wrzawa; tumult; podniecenie;
zaburzenie

tumultuous ('tu:altjues) adj.
burzliwy; podniecony; hałasliwy

tun (tan) s. beczka; kadz (252
galonow); v.wlewac do beczki;
przechowywac w beczce

tuna ('tu:na) s. tunczyk

tune (tu:n) s. melodia; nastroj;
harmonia; v.stroic; dostroic;
harmonizowac; nucic

tune in ('tu:n,yn) v. nastawiac
(radio etc.)

tune up ('tu:n,ap) v. nastrajac
(np. motor)

tunnel ('tanl) s. tune;; nora;
v. przekopywac tunel, korytarz,
norę; przekopywac się

turbine ('te:rbyn) s. turbina

turbot ('te:rbet) s. skarptur-
bot (ryba)

turbulent ('te:rbjulent) adj.
wzburzony; burzliwy; gwałtowny;
buntowniczy

turf (te:rf) s. torf; darn;
v. pokrywac darniną; (slang):
drałowac (piechotą)

Turk (te:rk) adj. turecki

turkey ('te:rky) s. indyk;
v.mowic bez ogrodek

Turkish ('te:rkysz) adj. turecki

Turkish bath ('te:kysz,ba:s)
s. parowka; kąpiel parowa;
łaznia

turmoil (te:rmojl) s. zamieszanie; zgiełk; niepokoj; podniecenie

turn (te:rn) v. odwrocic (się);
odkręcic (się); przekręcac
(się); skrecac (się); zwracac
(sie); odwracac (się); odpierac
(atak); napadac; zmieniac się;
nawracac (się); popełniac
(zdradę); stawac się (np. kato-
likiem); wyswiadczac; obracac;
kierowac; robic skręt; wyprawiac; odprawiac; toczyc (na
kole); puscic w ruch; okazac
się; zdarzac się; zwolnic; wyganiac; wyrzucac etc.
s. obrot; kolej; z kolei; po
kolei; tura; zakręt; zwrot;
skręt; punkt zwrotny; przełom;
kształt; forma; przechadzka;
transakcja; wstrząs; atak;
przysługa; numer (popisowy);
kolejnosc; postępowanie wobec
kogos

turn away ('te:rn,e'łej) v. odwracac się od; porzucic

turn back ('te:rn,baek) v. za-
wrocic (z drogi)

turn down ('te:rn,darn) v. odmowic; przyciszac; odrzucac

turn off ('te:rn,of) v. zakrę-
cic (kurek); skrecic; wyłączac
(swiatło); odprawic

turn on ('te:rn,on) v. puszczac
(wodę); włączac (swiatło); od-
kręcac (kurek)

turn out ('te:rn,aut) v. wyrzucac (za drzwi); wyrabiac; zwalniac (z pracy)

turn over ('te:rn'ouwer) v. odwracac; rozważac; miec obrot;
wydawac (policji);przekazywac

turn round ('te:rn raund) v.
przekręcac; odwracac; zmieniac
przekonania ;przekabacic

turn to ('te:rn,tu) v. zabrać
się (do czegoś)

turn up ('te:rn,ap) v. odwracać;
zawinąć (rękawy); podkręcać;
przychodzić; zgłosić się;
przytrafić (się)

turncoat ('te:rn,kout) s. zdrajca

turning point ('te:rnyng,poynt)
s. punkt zwrotny

turnip ('te:rnyp) s. rzepa

turnout ('te:rnaut) s. stawienie się; ilość obecnych;ekwipunek

turnover ('te:rn,ouwer) s. zmiana; kapotaż; przewrócenie; placek; przemieszczanie (ludzi,rzeczy)

turnpike ('te:rn,pajk) s. kołowrot; rogatka;autostrada(płatna)

turnstile ('te:rnstajl) s. koło-
wrot(do wchodzenia pojedynczo)

turnup ('te:rnap) s. traf; za-
mięszanie; część wywrócona;
coś podwiniętego; podwinięcie

turpentine ('te:rpentajn) s.
terpentyna; v. terpentynować;
zbierać terpentynę

turret ('te:ryt) s. wieżyczka;
imak wielonożowy

turtle ('te:rtl) s. żółw (morski)

turtledove ('te:rtl,daw) s.
turkawka

tusk (task) s. kieł; ząb (u bro-
ny); v. bość; kłuć; rozdzierać
kłami

tutor ('tu:ter) s. nauczyciel
prywatny; korepetytor; opiekun
(studentow); v. uczyć kogoś;
mieć opiekę nad kimś; powściągać
(się); być korepetytorem; uczyć
się pod nadzorem nauczyciela

tutorial ('tu:terjel) adj. wychowawczy; opiekuńczy

TV (ti:wi:) s. telewizja

tuxedo (tak'si:dou) s. smoking
(USA)

twang (tłaeng) s. brzęk (struny);
mówienie przez nos; v. brzęczeć;
rzępolić; brzdąkać; mówić przez
nos

tweed(tłi:d) s. materiał wełniany lub wełniano-bawełniany z
szorską powierzchnią

tweet (tłi:t) s. ćwierkanie;
v. ćwierkać

tweezers (tli-zez) s. szczypczyki (kosmetyczne itp.)

twelfth (tłelfs) adj. dwunasty

twelve (tłelw) num. dwanaście;
s. dwunastka

twentieth ('tłentyjes) adj.
dwudziesty

twenty (tłenty) num. dwadzieścia; s. dwudziestka

twice (tłajs) adv. dwa razy;
podwójnie; dwukrotnie

twiddle ('tłydl) s. obracanie;
v. kręcić; obracać; przebierać palcami; próżnować

twig (tłyg) v. zrozumieć; po-
łapać się; spostrzec; zauważyć; rozpoznawać; s. gałązka;
rożdżka czarodziejska

twilight ('tłajlajt) s. zmrok;
półcień; półmrok; zmierzch

twin (tłyn) s. bliźniak; adj.
bliźniaczy; v. rodzić się jako bliźnięta; łączyć (się)
ściśle ze sobą

twin-engined ('tłyn'endżynd)
adj. dwumotorowy

twinkle (tłynkl) v. migotać;
błyszczeć; mrugać; s. migotanie; błysk; mrugnięcie

twirl (tłe:rl) v. wirować;
kręcić (się); s. wirowanie;
kręcenie się; zakrętas; piruet

twist (tłyst) v. skręcać (się);
zwijać (się); zwichnąć (się);
zawirować; wykrzywiać (twarz);
przekręcać; pokręcić (się);
wić (się); powikłać (się);
tańczyć (twista); wykręcać;
przewijać się (przez tłum)
s. skręt; szpagat; przędza;
lina (skręcona); splot; obrót;
przekręcenie (znaczenia);
zwichnięcie; skłonność;
strucla

twitch(tłytcz)v. szarpać; wyrwać; wydrzeć; wykrzywić (się);
poruszyć się gwałtownie;
s. skurcz; szarpnięcie;pociag-
nięcie(za rękaw);drgawka; tik;
drganie(powieki);spazm;kurcz

twitter ('tłyter) v. ćwierkać;
świergotać; chichotać; drżeć
(ze strachu etc.); s. świergot; chichot; podniecenie;
zdenerwowanie

two (tu:) num. dwa; s. dwójka

two-bit ('tu:byt) adj. tandetny;
marny; (slang): wart 25 centów;
rzecz mała; rzecz bez znaczenia

twofold ('tu:fould) adj. podwójny; adv. podwójnie; dwojako

two-piece ('tu:pi:s) adj. dwu-
częściowy

two stroke ('tu:,strouk) adj.
dwutaktowy; dwusuwowy

two-way ('tu:,łej) adj. dwukie-
runkowy (np. ruch); dwutorowy;
dwuwartosciowy

type (tajp) s. typ; wzor; przykład; symbol; klasa; okaz;
czcionka; kaszta (drukarska);
v. pisać na maszynie; ustalać
typ; symbolizować; wyznaczać
role

typewriter('tajp,rajter) s. maszyna do pisania

typhoid ('tajfoyd) adj. tyfusowy; s. tyfus; dur brzuszny

typhoon (taj'fu:n) s. tajfun;
burza (morska) w układzie
wielkiego wiru

typhus ('tajfes) adj. tyfusowy

typical ('typykel) adj. typowy;
charakterystyczny

typify ('typyfaj) v. uosabiać;
stanowić typ; zapowiadać

typist ('tajpyst) s. maszynistka

tyrannical (ty'raenykel) adj.
tyranski

tyrannize ('tyrenajz) v. tyranizować

tyranny ('tyreny) s. tyrania

tyrant ('tajerent) s. tyran

tyre ('tajer) s. opona; obręcz;
v. nakładać oponę (obręcz)

u (ju:) dwudziesta pierwsza litera alfabetu angielskiego

ubiquity (ju'bykłyty) s. wszech-
obecność

U-boat ('ju:bout) s. łódź podwodna (niemiecka)

udder ('ader) s. wymię

ugly ('agly) adj. brzydki; paskudny

uhlan ('u:la:n) s. ułan

ulan ('u:la:n s. ułan

ulcer ('alser) s. wrzód

ultimate ('altymyt) adj. ostateczny; ostatni; koncowy; podstawowy; s. ostateczny wynik;
podstawowy fakt

ultimatum (alty'mejtem) s. ultimatum

umbrella (am'brela) s. parasol

umpire ('ampajer) s. sędzia
sportowy; rozjemca; v. sędzio-
wać; rozstrzygać jako arbiter

unabashed ('ane'baeszt) adj.
niespeszony; niezmieszany;
nie zbity z tropu

unabated ('an,e'bejtyd) adj.
niesłabnący; niezmniejszony

unable ('an'ejbl) adj. niezdolny; nieudolny

unacceptable ('ane'kseptebl)
adj. nie do przyjęcia

unaccountable ('ane'kauntebl)
adj. niewytłumaczony; niezrozumiały; dziwny; nie
tłumaczący się nikomu

unaccustomed ('ane'kastemd)
adj. niezwykły; nie przyzwyczajony

unacquainted ('ane'kłejntyd)
adj. nie obznajomiony

unaffected (,ane'fektyd) adj.
niekłamany; naturalny

unanimous (ju'naenymes) adj.
jednogłosny

unapproachable (,ane'prouczebl)
adj. niedostępny; niezrównany

unarmed ('an'a:rmd) adj. bezbronny; nie uzbrojony

unashamed ('an,e'szejmd) adj.
bezwstydny

unassisted ('an,e'systyd)adj.
nie wspomagany

unassuming ('an,e'sju:myng)
adj. skromny; bezpretensjonalny

unauthorized ('an'o:terajzd)
adj. nieupoważniony

unavoidable ('an,e'wojdebl) adj.
nieunikniony; niechybny

unaware ('ane,e'řeer) adj.nie-
świadomy; niepoinformowany

unawares ('ane'řeerz) adv.nie-
świadomie; znienacka; niespo-
dziewanie ;nic nie wiedząc

unbalanced ('an'baelensd) adj.
niezrównoważony

unbar ('an'ba:r) v. odryglowáć

unbearable (an'beerebl) adj.
nieznośny; nie do wytrzymania

unbecoming ('an,by'kamyŋg)adj.
niestosowny; niewłaściwy;
nieodpowiedni; nietwarzowy

unbelievable (,anby'li:webl)
adj. niewiarygodny; nieprawdopodobny

unbelieving (.anby'li:wyŋg)
adj. niewierzący; niedowierzający

unbending ('an'bendyŋg) adj.
nieugięty; niezłomny

unbiased ('an'bajest) adj.
bezstronny

unbidden ('an'bydn) adj. nieproszony

unborn baby ('an'bo:rn'bejby)
adj. przyszłe dziecko; nie-
urodzone (jeszcze) dziecko

unbounded (an'naundyd) adj.
bez granic; bezgraniczny

unbroken (an'brouken) adj.
nieprzerwany; niezbity; nie
ujeżdżony (koń)

unbutton ('an'batn) v. odpiać;
rozpiąć (sie)

uncalled-for (an'ko:ld,fo:r)
adj. niewłaściwy; niezasłużony;
niczym nie usprawiedliwiony

uncanny (an'kaeny) adj. niesamowity

uncared-for ('an'keerd,fo:r)
adj. porzucony; zaniedbany

unceasing (an'si:syŋg) adj.
bezustanny; nieprzerwany

uncertain (an'se:rtn) adj. niepewny; wątpliwy

unchallenged (an'chaelyndżd)
adj. niekwestionowany

unchangeable (an'chejndżebl)
adj. stały; niezmienny

unchanged (an'chejndżd) adj.
niezmieniony

unchecked (an'czekt) adj. niepowstrzymany; niepohamowany;
nieposkromiony

uncivil ('an'sywyl) adj. niegrzeczny; nieuprzejmy; nieokrzesany; grubiański

uncivilized ('an'sywylajzd)
adj. dziki; niecywilizowany;
barbarzyński

uncle ('ankl) s. wujek; stryjek

unclean ('an'kli:n) adj. nieczysty; plugawy; sprośny

uncomparable ('an'komperebl) adj.
nieporównywalny

uncommon ('an'komen) adj. niezwykły; rzadki; adv. niezwykle;
nadzwyczaj

uncommunicative ('an-ke'mju:ny-
ketyw); adj. małomówny; skryty;
niekomunikatywny

uncomplaining ('an-kem'plejnyŋg)
adj. cierpliwy; nienarzekający

unconcern ('anken'se:rn) s,
beztroska; niefrasobliwość;
obojętność

unconcerned ('anken'se:rnd) adj.
obojętny; niefrasobliwy; beztroski

unconditional ('an-ken'dyszynl)
adj. bezwarunkowy

unconfirmed ('an-ken'fe:rmd) adj.
nie potwierdzony

unconscious ('an'kouszes) adj.
nieprzytomny; zemdlony; nieświadomy; s. podświadomość

unconsciousness ('an'konszesnys)
omdlenie; nieprzytomność

unconstitutional ('an,konsty'-
'tju:szynl) adj. niezgodny
z konstytucja

uncontrollable ('an,kon'troulebl)
adj. nieposkromiony; niepohamowany

unconventional ('an-ken'wenszynl)
adj. niekonwencjonalny; oryginalny

unconvinced ('an-ken'wynst) adj.
nieprzekonany

unconvincing ('an-ken'wynsyŋg)
adj. nieprzekonywujący

uncouth (an'ku:s) adj. nieokrzesany; niezręczny; niezgrabny

uncover (an'kawer) v. odkryć;
demaskować

uncultivated ('an'kaltywejtyd)
adj. nieuprawny; leżący odłogiem; niekulturalny

uncultured ('an'kalczerd) adj.
niewykształcony; niekulturalny

undamaged ('an'daemydżd) adj.
nieuszkodzony

undecided ('an-dy'sajdyd) adj.
niezdecydowany; niepewny;
nieokreślony; nierozstrzygnięty

undefined ('andy'fajnd) adj.
nieokreślony; mglisty

undeniable (,andy'najebl) adj.
niezaprzeczalny

under ('ander) prep. pod; poniżej; w; w trakcie; zgodnie
z; z; adv. poniżej; pod spodem; adj. spodni; niższy;
dolny; podrzędny; podwładny

underbid ('ander'byd) v. zob.
bid; składać niższą ofertę
w przetargu

undercarriage ('ander,kaerydż)
s. podwozie

underclothes ('ander;klousz)
pl. bielizna

underclothing ('ander-klousyng)
s. bielizna

underdeveloped (ander,dy'welept) adj. zacofany; nie wywołany poprawnie; niedorozwinięty

underdone ('ander'dan) adj.
półsurowy; niedogotowany

underestimate (,ander'estymejt)
v. niedoceniać; za nisko
oszacować

underfed ('ander'fed) v. niedożywiony

undergo (,ander'gou) v. zob. go;
doznawać czegoś; przechodzić
coś; doświadczyć; poddawać się
(operacji)

undergraduate (,ander'graedjuit)
s. student bez stopnia bachelor

underground ('ander,graund) adj.
podziemny; zaskórny; tajny;
s. kolej podziemna; ruch oporu;

adv. (,ander'graund)pod ziemią;
skrycie; tajnie

undergrowth ('ander-grous) s.
poszycie (lasu)

underline ('anderlajn) v. podkreślać; s. podkreślenie; podpis pod ilustracją; zawiadomienie (u spodu afisza teatralnego) o następnej sztuce

undermine (,ander'majn) v. podkopywać (zdrowie etc.) podmywać (brzegi etc.)

undermost ('andermoust) adj.
najniższy

underneath (,ander'ni:s) adv.
pod spodem; poniżej; na dole;
pod spód

underpass (,ander'pa:s) s.
przejazd poniżej poziomu (w
skrzyżowaniu bezkolizyjnym)

underpay ('ander'pej) v. za mało płacić

underprivileged ('ander'prywylydżd) adj. upośledzony

undershirt ('andersze:rt) s.
podkoszulek

undersigned ('ander'sajnd) adj.
(niżej) podpisany

undersized ('ander'sajzd) adj.
zbyt mały; małego wzrostu

under soil ('ander,sojl) s.
podglebie

understaffed ('ander'sta:ft)
adj. mający zbyt mały personel

understand; understood; understood (,ander'staend; ander'-
stud; ,ander'stud)

understand (,ander'staend) v.
rozumieć; domyślać się; orientować się; znać; wywnioskować;
wiedzieć jak; umieć dobrze

understandable (,ander'staendebl) adj. zrozumiały

understanding (,ander'staendyng)
adj. pełen zrozumienia; s. zrozumienie; warunek; (wyższa)
inteligencja; porozumienie;
rozum

understatement (,ander'stejtment) s. zbyt skromne wyrażanie się; niedomówienie

undertake (,ander'tejk) v.zob.
take; przedsiębrać; podejmować się; ręczyć; zobowiązywać się do czegoś; być przed-
siębiorcą pogrzebowym
undertaker (,ander'tejker) s.
przedsiębiorca pogrzebowy
undertaking (,ander'tejkyng) s.
przedsięwzięcie; zobowiązanie;
obietnica; przyrzeczenie;
przedsiębiorstwo pogrzebowe
undervalue (,ander'waelju:) v.
niedoceniać; za nisko szacować
underwear ('anderłeer) s. bielizna
underwood ('ander,łu:d) s. poszycie (lasu)
underworld ('ander,łe:rld) s.
podziemie; świat podziemny;
pl. antypody
underwrite ('ander-rajt) v.
zob. write; zakontraktować
(ubezpieczenie); podpisać(się);
wydawać (polisę ubezpieczenio-
wą); zobowiązywać się
underwriter ('ander-rajter) s.
ajent ubezpieczeniowy
undeserved (,andy'ze:rwd) adj.
niezasłużony; niesłuszny
undesirable (andy'zajerebl)
adj. niepożądany; niedogodny;
s. człowiek niepożądany
undeveloped (andy'welopt) adj.
nierozwinięty; niewywołany
undies (andyz) pl. bielizna
(damska i dziecięca)
undignified (an'dygnyfajd) adj.
niegodny; bez godności
undiminished (an'dymynszt) adj.
niezmniejszony
un-disciplined (an'dysyplind)
adj. niezdyscyplinowany; nie-
karny
undisputed (,andys'pju:tyd)
adj. bezsporny; niezaprzeczony
undisturbed ('andys'te:rbd) adj.
niezakłócony
undo; undid; undone ('an'du;
'an'dyd, an'dan)
undo ('an'du:) v. robić nieby-
łym; unieważniać; usuwać;
niszczyć; rujnować; rozpakować;

rozwiązać; otwierać; rozpinać;
przekreślać
undreamt-of ('an'dremt,ow)
adj. nieprawdopodobny; nie do
pomyślenia; niesłychany
undress (an'dres) v. rozbierać
(się); odbandażowywać; s. negliż; zwykłe ubranie
undressed (an'drest) adj. nie
przyrządzony; chropowaty; nie
opatrzona (rana); rozebrany
undue (an'dju:) adj. przesadny;
nadmierny; postronny; niewłaściwy; jeszcze niepłatny (np.
rachunek)
undutiful (an'djutyful) adj.
nieobowiązkowy
uneasy (an'i:zy) adj. niespokojny; niepokojący; nieswój;
zażenowany; nieprzyjemny;
krępujący; budzący niepokój
uneducated (an'edjukejtyd)
adj. niewykształcony; bez
wykształcenia
unemployed (an'emplojd) adj.
bez pracy; bezrobotny; nie-
wykorzystany; nie zużytkowany
unemployment (an'emplojment)
s. bezrobocie
unendurable ('anyn'djuerebl)
adj. nie do zniesienia
unenviable ('an'enwjebl) adj.
nie do pozazdroszczenia
unequal ('an'i:kłol) adj. nie-
rowny; nie na wysokości (zadania)
unequaled ('an'i:kłold) adj.
niezrównany
unequivocal ('any'kływokel) adj.
niedwuznaczny; wyraźny; jasny
unerring ('an'e:ryng) adj.
nieomylny; niezawodny
uneven ('an'i:wen) adj. nieparzysty; niejednolity; nie-
rowny
uneventful ('an,y'wentful)
adj. nieurozmaicony; spokojny;
jednostajny
unexpected ('anyks'pektyd)
adj. niespodziewany; nieoczekiwany
unfailing (an'tejlyng) adj.
niezawodny; niewyczerpany

unfair (an'feer) adj. niesprawiedliwy; krzywdzący; nieuczciwy; nieprzepisowy

unfaithful (an'fejgful) adj.
niewierny; wiarołomny; nieścisły

unfamiliar ('anfe'myljer) adj.
nieznany; nieobznajomiony;
obcy

unfashionable ('an'faeszenebl)
adj. niemodny

unfasten ('an'fa:sn) v. odczepić (się); odpiąć (się); od-
wiązywać (się); odryglować
(się); rozluźnić (się)

unfavorable ('an'fejwerebl)
adj. niepomyślny; nieżyczliwy;
niesprzyjający; nieprzychylny

unfeasible (an'fi:sebl) adj.
niewykonalny

unfeeling (an'fi:lyng) adj.
bez uczucia; bez serca; okrutny

unfinished ('an'fynyszt) adj.
niewykończony; niedokończony

unfit ('an'fyt) adj. nie nadający się; niezdatny; niezdolny; nieodpowiedni; v. czynić
niezdolnym do czegoś

unflappable ('an'flaepebl) adj,
nie do wytrącenia z równowagi

unfold ('an'fould) v. ujawniać
(się); rozwijać (się); otwierać; odsłonić

unforseen ('an'fer,si:n) adj.
nieprzewidziany; niespodziewany

unforgettable ('an-fer'getebl)
adj. pamiętny; niezapomniany

unforgiving ('an-fer'gywyng)
adj. niewybaczający; nieprzejednany

unforgotten ('an-fer'gotn)adj.
niezapomniany

unfortunate (an'fo:rcznyt) adj.
niefortunny; pechowy; niepomyślny; nieszczęśliwy

unfortunately (an'fo:rcznytly)
adv. niestety; nieszczęśliwie

unfounded (an'faundyd) adj.
bezpodstawny

unfriendly (an'frendly) adj.
nieprzyjazny; nieprzychylny

unfurnished (an'fe:rnyszt) adj.
nieumeblowany

ungainly (an'gejnly) adj. niezdarny; niezgrabny

ungenerous (an'dżeneres) adj.
małostkowy; nie szczodry

ungentle (an'dżentl) adj. nie-
łagodny

unget-at-able ('anget'aetbl)
adj. niedostępny (slang)

ungovernable (an'gawernebl)adj.
dziki; niesforny; krnąbrny;
nieopanowany

ungraceful (an'grejsful) adj.
niewdzięczny; nieuprzejmy

ungrateful (an'grejful) adj.
niewdzięczny

unguarded ('an'ga:rdyd) adj.
niebaczny;nieopatrzny; nierozważny; niestrzeżony

unhappy (an'haepy) adj. nieszczęśliwy; pechowy; zmartwiony;nieudany

unharmed ('an'ha:rmd) adj. nietknięty

unharness ('an'ha:rnys) v. wyprzęgać; zdejmować zbroję; etc.

unhealthy (an'helsy) adj. niezdrowy

unheard-of (an'he:rd,ow) adj.
niesłychany; niebywały; nieprawdopodobny

unheeded (an'hi:dyd) adj. niezauważony; niedostrzeżony

unheeding (an'di:dyng) adj. nieuważający; niedostrzegający

unhesitating (an'hezytejtyng)
adj. nie wahający się

unhoped-for (an'hopt,fo:r) adj.
niespodziewany; nieoczekiwany

unhurt (an'he:rt) adj. nieuszkodzony; bez szwanku

unicorn ('ju:nyko:rn) s. jedno-
rożec; jednoróg

unification (,ju:nyfy'kejszyn)
s. zjednoczenie; zcalenie;
ujednolicenie

uniform ('ju:nyfo:rm) adj.
jednolity; równomierny; jednostajny; s, mundur; uniform

uniformity ('ju:ny'fo:rmyty)
s. jednolitość; jednostajność;
ujednolicenie;ujednostajnienie

unilateral ('ju:ny'laeterel)
adj. jednostronny

unimaginable (any'maedżynebl)
adj. nie do pomyslenia

unimaginative (any'maedżynejtyw)
adj. bez wyobraźni; bez polotu

unimportant ('anym'po:rtent)
adj. nieważny; błahy; mało
ważny

uninhabitable('anyn'haebytebl)
adj. nie do mieszkania; nie
do życia

uninhabited ('anyn'haebytyd)
adj. niezamieszkały

uninjured ('an'yndżerd) adj.
bez szwanku; nie uszkodzony;
bez obrażeń

uninspired ('anyn'spajerd) adj.
banalny

unintelligible ('anvn'telydżebl)
adj. niezrozumiały

unintentional ('anyn'tenszynl)
adj. mimowolny; nie zamierzony

uninteresting ('anyn'terestyng)
adj. nudny; nieciekawy; nie-
interesujący

uninterrupted ('anyn'teraptyd)
adj. nieprzerwany; ciągły;
bezustanny

uninvited ('anyn'wajtyd) adj.
nieproszony

uninviting ('anyn'wajtyng) adj.
nie zachęcający; odpychający;
nieapetyczny

union ('ju:njen) s. połączenie;
złącze; łączność; związek;
zjednoczenie; małżeństwo; zgoda; łącznik; złączka; godło

unionist ('ju:njenyst) s.
związkowiec; zwolennik związku

union Jack ('ju:njen'dżaek) s.
flaga angielska

unique (ju:'ni:k) adj. wyjątkowy; jedyny; niezrównany

unisex ('ju:ny'seks) adj. styl
(wyrobów) do użytku obu płci;
odzież, przybory toaletowe,
zakład fryzjerski etc.

unison ('ju:nyzn) adj. zgodnie
(razem)

unit ('ju:nyt) s. jednostka;
zespół

unite (ju:'najt) v. łączyć; jednoczyć; zjednoczyć

united (ju:'najtyd) adj. połączony; zjednoczony; łączny

unity ('ju:nyty) s. jedność
(czasu, miejsca, działania, etc);
jednostka; jednolitość; harmonia; zgoda

universal (ju:ny've:rsel) adj.
powszechny; ogólny; uniwersalny

universe ('ju:nyvers) s. wszechświat; świat; ludzkość; kosmos

university (,ju:ny'wersyty) s.
uniwersytet; wszechnica; uczelnia

unjust ('an'dżast) adj. niesprawiedliwy

unkempt ('an'kempt) adj. nie-
uczesany; rozczochrany; niechlujny

unkind (an'kajnd) adj. niedobry;
okrutny

unknown ('an'noun) adj. nieznany;
niewiadomy

unlace ('an'lejs) v. rozsznurować

unlawful ('an'lo:ful) adj. bezprawny; nielegalny

unlearn ('an'le:rn) v. oduczać
(się); zob. learn

unless (an'les) conj. jeżeli
nie; chyba że

unlike ('an'lajk) adj. niepodobny; odmienny; prep. odmiennie;
inaczej; w przeciwieństwie

unlikely (an'lajkly) adj. nieprawdopodobny; nieoczekiwany;
nie rokujący

unlimited (an'lymytyd) adj.
nieograniczony; bezgraniczny;
dowolny

unload ('an'loud) v. rozładowy-
wać; zrzucać ciężar

unlock ('an'lok) v. otwierać
zamek; otworzyć

unlocked ('an'lokt) adj. otwarty; niezamknięty

unlooked-for (an'lukt,fo:r)
adj. nieoczekiwany; niespodziewany; nieprzewidziany

unloosen ('an'lu:sn) adj. rozluźniony; rozwiązany; rozsznu-
rowany

unlucky (an'laky) adj. pechowy; niefortunny; niepomyślny;
nieszczęśliwy

unmanageable (an'maenydżebl)
adj. niesforny; krnąbrny

unmanly (an'maenly)adj. znie-
checający; odbierający odwagę; adv. zniechecająco

unmarried (an'maeryd) adj. nieżonaty; niezamężna

unmistakabe ('anmys'tejkbl)
adj. niewątpliwy; wyraźny;
niedwuznaczny

unmoved ('an'm:wd) adj. niewzruszony

unnatural (an'naeczrel) adj.
sztuczny; nienaturalny;
wbrew naturze; nienormalny

unnecessary (an'nesysery)
adj. zbędny; zbyteczny; niepotrzebny

unnoticed ('an'noutyst) adj.
niezauważony; (pominięty)

unobtainable ('anęb'tejnebl)
adj. nie do nabycia(otrzyma-
nia)

unobtrusive ('aneb'tru:syw)
adj. skromny; dyskretny; nie
narzucający się

unoccupied ('an'okjupajd) adj.
wolny; nie zajęty

unoffending ('ane'fendyng)
adj. nieszkodliwy; (niewinny)

unofficial ('ane'fyszel) adj.
nie urzędowy; nieoficjalny

unpack ('an'paek) v. rozpako-
wywać (się)

unpaid ('an'pejd) adj. niezapłacony; (bezinteresowny)

unparalleled(an'paereleld)adj.
niezrównany; niespotykany;
bezprzykładny; niesłychany

unpardonable (an'pa:rdnebl)
adj. niewybaczalny

unperceived (an'per'si:wd)
niespostrzeżony

unperturbed ('an-per'te:rbd)
adj. spokojny; nie zaniepokojony; nie przejmujący się

unpleasant (an'plezent) adj.
nieprzyjemny; przykry; niemiły

unplug (an'plag) v. odczopować;
wyciągnąć z kontaktu

unpolished ('an'polyszt) adj.
niewyczyszczony; niewygładzony

unpopular (an'popjuler) adj. m.
niepopularny; niemile widziany

unpopularity ('an,popju'laeryty)
s. niepopularność; złe przyjęcie

unpractical ('an'praektykel) adj.
niepraktyczny; nierealny

unpracticed (an'praektyst) adj.
nie wypraktykowany; niewprawny

unprecedented (an'presydentyd)
adj. bezprzykładny; bez pre-
cedensu; niesłychany

unprejudiced (an'predżudyst)
adj. bezstronny; nie mający
przesądów

un-premeditated ('anpry:'medy-
tejtyd) adj. bez premedytacji;
nienaumyślny

unprepared ('anpry'peerd) adj.
nieprzygotowany; nieprzyrzą-
dzony

unprincipled (an'prynsepld) adj.
bez skrupułów; niegodziwy

unproductive (an'prodaktyw) adj.
niewydajny; nie wytwórczy;
niepłodny;

unprofitable (an'profytebl) adj.
niepopłatny; niekorzystny; nie-
rentowny

unprovided-for ('an-pre'wajdyd-
,fo:r) adj. niezabezpieczony;
bez środków do życia

unqualified ('an'kłolyfajd) adj.
niewykwalifikowany; bez kwali-
fikacji; niesprecyzowany; nieograniczony (np. zaufanie)

unquestionable (an'k'esczynebl)
adj. bezsporny; niewątpliwy

unquestioned (an'k'esczynd)
adj. niezaprzeczony; niepytany

unreasonable (an'ri:znebl),adj.
nierozsądny; niedorzeczny; wygórowany (w cenie)

unrefined ('anry'fajnd) adj.
niesubtelny; niewyrafinowany;
niewykształcony

unreliable ('anry'lajebl) adj.
niepewny; niesolidny

unreserved ('anry'ze:rwd) adj.
otwarty; szczery; bez zastrze-
zeń; całkowity; niezarezerwo-
wany

unresisting ('anry'zystyŋg)
adj. nieodporny; nieopierają-
cy się

unrest ('an'rest) s. niepokój;
zamieszki; niepokoje

unrestrained ('anrys'trejnd)
adj. niepowstrzymany; niepohamowany; nieopanowany

unrestricted ('anrys'tryktyd)
adj. nieograniczony; (niedostępny)

unrip ('an'ryp) v. porozpruwac

unripe ('an'rajp) adj. niedojrzały

unrivaled (an'rajweld) adj.
niezrównany; bezkonkurencyjny

unroll ('an'roul) v. rozwinąć
(zwój; rolkę)

unruffled (an'rafld) adj. niezmącony; niezakłócony; zachowujący równowagę

unruly (an'ru:ly) adj. niesforny

unsafe ('an'sejf) adj. niepewny;
ryzykowny; niebezpieczny

unsanitary ('an'saenytery) adj.
niehigieniczny; szkodliwy;nie-
zdrowy

unsatisfactory ('an,saetys'faektery) adj. niezadawalający;
niedostateczny

unsatisfied (an'saetysfajd) adj.
niezadowolony; niezaspokojony

unsavory ('an'sejwery) adj.
niesmaczny; przykry

unscrew('an'skru:) v. odsrubo-
wac; rozsrubowac; odkręcic
(gwint)

unscrupulous ('an'skru:pjules)
adj. bez skrupułów; niegodziwy

unseen (an'si:n) adj. nie widziany; niewidoczny

unselfish (an'selfysz) adj.bez-
interesowny

unsettled ('an'setld) adj. za-
burzony; zakłócony; nieustalo-
ny; niezapłacony; rozstrojony

unshaven (an'szejwn) adj. nie-
ogolony

unshrinkable (an'szrynkebl)
adj. nie kurczący się (w praniu)

unshrinking (an'szrynkiŋg) adj.
nie wahający się; nie wzdry-
gający się

unskilled (an'skyld) adj. niewprawny; niewykwalifikowany

unskilful (an'skylful) adj.
niewprawny; niezręczny

unsociable (an'souszebl) adj.
nietowarzyski

unsocial (an'souszel) adj. nie-
socjalny; niespołeczny

unsolvable (an'salwebl) adj.
nierozwiązalny; nierozpuszczalny

unsolved (an'solwd) adj. nie-
rozwiązany; nierozpuszczony

unsophisticated (,anso'fystykejtyd) adj. prosty; naturalny; prawdziwy

unsound (an'saund) adj. niezdrowy; sprochniały; słaby;
niepewny; ryzykowny; błędny;
niesolidny

unspeakable (an'spi:kebl) adj.
niewypowiedziany;nie do opisania

unspoiled (an'spojld) adj.
niezepsuty; nierozpieszczony
(dziecko)

unspoken ('an'spouken) adj.
nie mówiony (np. prawo)

unspoken-for (an'spoukn;fo:r)
adj. niezamowiony

unspoken-of (an'spoukn) adj.
nie omawiany

unstable (an'stejbl) adj. niepewny; chwiejny;niezrównowa-
żony

unsteady (an'stedy) adj.
chwiejny; chwiejący się; niezdecydowany; nieustabilizowany;
zmienny; niepewny

unstressed ('an'strest) adj.
nieakcentowany; niepodkreslony;
nieobciążony

unsuccessful ('an-sek'sesful)
adj. nieudany; bez powodzenia;
nieudały; nie mający powodzenia; bezowocny

unsuitable ('an'sju:tebl) adj. niewłaściwy; niestosowny; nieodpowiedni

unsure (an'szuer) adj. niepewny; zawodny

unsurpassed ('an-ser'pa:st) adj. nieprzescigniony; niezrownany

unsuspected ('an-ses'pekyd) adj. (zupełnie) niepodejrzany

unsuspecting('an-ses'pektyng) adj. nieczego nie podejrzewający

unsuspicious ('an-ses'pyszes) adj. ufny; niepodejrzliwy

unthinkable ('an'tynkebl) adj. nie do pomyslenia; nieprawdopodobny

unthinking ('an'tynkyng) adj. bezmyslny

untidy (an'tajdy) adj. niechlujny;niestaranny; rozczorrany; zaniedbany; nie posprzątany

untie(an'taj) v. rozwiązywać (się); rozsupłać; uwalniać (się) z więzów; usuwać (trudności)

until (an'tyl) prep. & conj. do; dotychczas; dopiero; aż

untimely (an'tajmly) adj. nie w porę; przedwczesny; nie na czasie; wczesny; adv. przedwcześnie; w nieodpowiedniej chwili

untiring (an'tajeryng) adj. niezmordowany

unto ('antu:) prep.= to; do; ku; aż do

untold (an'told) adj. niewypowiedziany; nieprzeliczony

untouchable (an'taczebl) adj. niedotykalny

untouched (an'taczt) adj. nietknięty; nieskazitelny; nieczuły

untried (an'trajd) adj. niewypróbowany

untroubled (an'trabld) adj. spokojny; beztroski

untrue ('an'tru:) adj. nieprawdziwy; fałszywy; niewierny; sprzeniewierzający się

untrustworthy ('an'trast,łe:rsy) adj. niegodny zaufania; niepewny

untruth ('an'tru:s) s. nieprawda; kłamstwo

unused ('an'ju:zd) adj. nie używany; nie przyzwyczajony; nie stosowany

unusual (an'ju:żuel) adj. niezwykły; wyjątkowy

unutterable (an'aterebl) adj. niewysłowiony; niewypowiedziany

unvarying (an'weery-yng) adj. jednostajny; nieurozmaicony; nie zmieniający (się)

unvoiced (an'wojst) adj. bezgłosny; bezdzwięczny

unwanted (an'łontyd) adj. niepożądany; niepotrzebny; zbędny; zbyteczny

unwarranted ('an'łorentyd) adj. nieusprawiedliwiony; bezpodstawny

unwholesome ('an'houlsem) adj. niezdrowy; szkodliwy

unwilling ('an'łylyng) adj. niechętny

unwind ('an'łajnd) v. zob.wind; rozwijać (się); odprężać (się); (slang): odpoczywać sobie

unwise ('an'łajz) adj. niemądry; nieostrożny; nieroztropny

unworthy (an'łe:rsy) adj. niegodny; niegodziwy; niewart; niezasługujący; ujemny

unwrap ('an'raep) v. rozwijać (się); rozpakować; odsłonić (się); odwijać (się)

unyielding ('an'ji:ldyng) adj. nieustępliwy; twardy; nieugięty

up (ap) adv. do góry; w górę; w zwyż; w górze; wyżej; na; tam (gdzie); na górze; wysoko; wyżej; aż (do); aż (po); na (piętro); pod (górę); v. podnosić; zrywać się; podbijać (cenę); zaczynać

up-and-about ('apend,ebaut)
exp.:(znowu) na nogach (po
chorobie)

up-and-coming ('ap,end'komyŋg)
exp.;(slang): obiecujący;
rzutki; przedsiębiorczy (człowiek)

up-and-doing ('ap,end'duyŋg)
exp.:(slang): czynny; ruchliwy

up-and-up ('ap,end'ap)być uczciwym
up to('ʋp,tu)adv.aż do pogodny
upbeat('apbi:t)adj.optymistyczny;

upbringing (' p,bryŋgyŋg) s.
wychowanie; wychowywanie

uphill ('ap'hyl) adj. wznoszą-
cy (się); stromy; trudny;
uciążliwy;.adv. stromo; pod
górę; w górę

upholster (ap'houlster) v.
obijać (meble); wyścielać;
pokrywać; urządzać

upholsterer (ap'houlsterer)
s. tapicer; dekorator

upholstery(ap'houlstry) s.
tapicerstwo; meble wyścielane

upkeep ('apki:p) s. utrzymanie;
koszty utrzymania szanie się

upmanship('apmen,szyp)s.wywyż-
upon (e'pon)prep.=on; na; po
upper ('aper) adj. wyższy; górny; wierzchni; s. przyszwa

uppermost ('aper,moust) adj.
najwyższy; adv. na górze; na
górę

uppish ('apysh) adj. zadziera-
jący nos do góry (slang)

upright ('ap'rajt) adj. wypro-
stowany; prosty; uczciwy; prawy; adv. pionowo; s. pionowy
słup; podpora; pianino; pozycja pionowa

uprising (ap'rajzyŋg) s. powstanie; wstawanie

uproar ('ap,ro:) s. zgiełk;
wrzawa; harmider; tumult

upset ('apset) v. zob. set;
przewracać (się), pokonywać;
wzburzać; rozstrajać; rozku-
wać; pogrubiać; skręcać; rozklepywać; s. wywrócenie (się);
porażka; podniecenie; zaburzenie; rozstrój; niepokój;

bałagan; sztanca do kucia

upside-down ('apsajd'dałn)adv.
do góry nogami; do góry dnem;
adj. odwrócony do góry nogami

upstairs ('ap'steerz) adv. na
górę; na górze

upstart ('ap-sta:rt) s. par-
wenjusz

upstream ('ap'stri:m) adv. pod
prąd; w górę rzeki

uptight ('ap'tajt) adj. (slang);
napięty; naprężony (nerwowo)

up-to-date ('ap-tu-'dejt) adj.
bieżący; nowoczesny

upwards (apʋerdz) adv. w górę;
ku górze; na wierzch; wyżej;
powyżej (czegoś)

uranium (ju'rejnjem) s. uran

urbane (e:r'bejn) adj. grzeczny; układny; wytworny

urchin ('e:rczyn) s. ulicznik;
urwis; łobuz; smyk; jeżowiec;
jeżak; czesak

urge (e:rdż) v. poganiać; popędzać; ponaglać; przyspieszać; nalegać; pilić; namawiać; s. pragnienie; impuls;
tęsknota; pociąg; bodziec

urge on ('e:rdż,on) v. namawiać
na cos

urgent (e:rdżent) adj. pilny;
naglący; gwałtowny; natarczywy; nalegający

urine ('jueryn) s. mocz; uryna

urn (e:rn) s. urna

usage ('ju:sydż) s. zwyczaj;
praktyka; obchodzenie (się);
używanie (zwrotów, języka po-
prawnego)

use (ju:s) s. użytek; używanie;
użycie; posługiwanie; zastosowanie; pożytek; korzyść; zwyczaj; praktyka; obrządek; przyzwyczajenie; v. używać; korzystać; wykorzystać; zużywać; zużyć; wyczerpać; traktować;
obejść się; mieć zwyczaj

used (ju:zd) adj. przyzwyczajony; używany; stosowany

useful ('ju:zful) adj. użyteczny;
pożyteczny; dogodny; wygodny;
(slang):doskonały; sprawny;
biegły; zdolny

useless ('ju:zlys) adj. niepotrzebny; bezużyteczny; zbyteczny; bezcelowy; nieużyteczny; do niczego

use up ('ju:s,ap) v. zużyć
(wszystko); wyczerpać (np.
pracą

usher ('aszer) s. odźwierny;
woźny; bileter; rozprowadza-
jący na miejsca (w kinie;
w kościele etc.) v. wprowadzac; zapoczątkować

usher in ('aszer,yn) v. wprowadzać do

usherette (,asze'ret) s. bi-
leterka (rozprowadzająca)

usual ('ju:zuel) adj. zwykły;
zwyczajny; normalny; zwyczajowy; utarty

usually ('ju:żuely) adv. zwykle; zazwyczaj

usurer ('ju:żerer) s. lichwiarz

usury ('ju:żury) s. lichwa

utensil (ju'tensyl) s. sprzęt;
naczynie; narzędzie

utility (ju'tylyty) s. pożytek;
użyteczność; firma dostarcza-
jąca gaz, elektryczność lub
wodę ludności w USA

utilize ('ju:tylajz) v. zużytkować; spożytkować; wykorzystać

utmost ('atmoust) adj. najwyższy; ostateczny; skrajny; największy; najdalszy; ostatni

utter ('ater) adj. całkowity;
zupełny; kompletny; skończony; skrajny; ostatni; v. wydawać (głos); powiedzieć; wy-
powiedzieć (hasło itp.); wyrażać; wystawiać (czeki); podrabiać (np. dokumenty); puszczać (w obieg)

utterance ('aterens) s. wypowiedz; wymowa; wyrażenie;
zeznanie; oświadczenie

uvula ('ju:wjula) s. języczek
miękkiego podniebienia

v (wi:) dwudziesta druga litera
alfabetu angielskiego

vacancy ('wejkensy) s. wolne
mieszkanie; wolne pokoje mote-
lowe; wakans; próżnia; pustka;
bezczynność

vacant ('wejkent) adj. pusty;
próżny; wolny; wakujący;bez-
czynny; bezmyślny; obojętny

vacate (we'kejt) v. opróżniac;
opuszczać; unieważniać

vacation (we'kejszyn) s. wakacje
ferie; opróżnienie; zwolnienie
(mieszkania); ewakuacja

vaccinate ('waeksynejt) v.
szczepić

vaccination ('waeksynejszyn)
s. szczepienie

vaccine ('waeksi:n) s. szczepionka

vacuum ('waekjuem) s. próżnia

vacuum bottle ('waekjuem'botl)
s. termos

vacuum cleaner ('waekjuem'kli:-
ner)s. odkurzacz

vacuum flask ('waekjuem,fla:sk)
s. termos

vagabond ('waegebond) adj.
włóczęgowski; wędrowny;
s. włóczęga; nierób; próżniak

vagary ('wejgery) s. kaprys;
chimera

vague (wejg) adj. niejasny; niewyrazny; nieokreślony; nieuchwytny; niewyrazny; wymijający; niezdecydowany

vain (wejn) adj. próżny; zarozumiały; czczy; pusty; gołosłowny; daremny; bezcelowy

valance ('waelens) s. krótka
podłużna zasłona (światła);
rodzaj adamaszku

vale (wejl) s. dolina; pożegnanie; excl.;żegnajcie !

valerian (we'lerjen) s. waleria-
na

valet ('waelyt) s. służący;
v. usługiwać

valiant ('waeljent) adj. dzielny;
s. zuch

valid ('waelyd) adj. słuszny;
ważny; uzasadniony

valley ('waely) s. dolina; koryto fali; wewnętrzny kąt płaszczyzn dachu

valor ('waeler) s. dzielność

valuable ('waeljuebl) adj.
wartościowy; cenny; kosztowny;
s.(pl)kosztowności;biżuteria

valuables (,waljuebls) pl.
kosztownosci

valuation (,walju'ejszyn) s.
oszacowanie; cena

value ('waelju:) s. wartosc;
cena; stopien jasnosci barwy
(w obrazie); v. szacowac; cenic; oceniac

valueless (,waelju:lys) adj.
bezwartosciowy

valuer ('waelju:er) s. taksa-
tor

valve (waelw) s. zawor; wentyl;
klapa; zastawka

van (waen) s. kryty woz (cię-
żarowy); czoło armii; v. przewozic krytym wozem; badac rudę pukaniem

vane (wejn) s. chorągiewka (od
wiatru); łopatka śmigła;
brzechwa bomby; skrzydło wiatraka

vanilla (we'nyle) s. wanilia

vanish ('waenysz) v. znikac;
zanikac

vanity ('waenyty) s. proznosc;
pycha; marnosc; czczosc; toaleta; zrodło proznosci; rzecz
bez wartosci

vanitycase ('waenyty,kejs) s.
kosmetyczka

vantage ('waentydż) s. korzyst-
na pozycja; przewaga (w tenisie)

vaporize ('wejporajz) v. wypa-
rowac; zamieniac sie w pare

vapor (wejpor) s. para; mgła;
v. parowac; ględzic

vaporous ('wejperes) adj.
mglisty; zamglony

variable ('weerjebl) adj. zmienny; niestały; s. zmienny wiatr

variance ('weerjens) s. rozbieżnosc; niezgodnosc

variant ('weerent) s. odmiana;
wariant; adj. odmienny; rozny

variation (,weery'ejszyn) s,
zmiana; odmiana; wariant;
wariacja

varicose vein ('waerykous,wejn)
s. żylak

varied ('waeryd) adj. roznorodny;
rozny; urozmaicony

variety (we'rajety) s. rozmai-
tosc; urozmaicenie; roznorod-
nosc; wielostronnosc; teatr
rozmaitosci; kabaret; szereg;
odmiana

various ('weerjes) adj. rozny;
rozmaity; urozmaicony; wiele;
kilka; kilkakrotnie

varnish ('wa:rnysz) s. pokost;
politura; werniks; polewa;
v. pokostowac; werniksowac

Varsovian (wa:r'souwjen) adj.
warszawski; s.warszawiak

vary ('weery) v. zmieniac (się);
urozmaicac; roznic się; nie po-
dzielac zdania

vase (wejz) s. waza; wazon

vat (waet) s. zbiornik; kadz;
cysterna

vault (wo:lt) s. sklepienie;
podziemie; piwnica; grobowiec;
skok o tyczce; v. przesklepiac;
osklepic; przeskoczyc; skoczyc
o tyczce

vaulting horse ('wo:ltyng,ho:rs)
s. kozioł (przyrząd gimnastyczny)

veal(wi:l) s. cielęcina

vegetable ('wedżytebl) s. jarzyna

vegetarian (,wedży'teerjen) adj.
jarski; s. jarosz; wegetarianin

vegetate ('wedżytejt) v. wegeto-
wac; rosnac

vehemence ('wi:ymens) s. gwał-
townosc; porywczosc; wybucho-
wosc

vehement ('wi:yment) adj. gwałtowny; porywczy; wybuchowy

vehicle ('wi:ykl) s. pojazd;
srodek; narzędzie; przymieszka
do farby

veil (wejl) s. welon; woalka;
wstąpienie do klasztoru; zasłona (maska); chrypka; v. zasłaniac; ukrywac

vein (wejn) s. żyła (też złota);
usposobienie; natura; nastroj;
wena; v. żyłkowac

velocity (wy'losyty) s. szybkosc

velvet ('welwyt) s. aksamit;
delikatna skórka; (slang);
zarobek; forsa; adj. aksamit-
ny

venal ('wi:nl) adj. sprzedajny

vend (wend) v. sprzedawać

vender ('wender) s. (uliczny)
sprzedawca; automat do sprzedaży

vending machine ('wendyng,me'-
'szi:n) s. automat do sprzedaży

venerable ('wenerebl) adj.
czcigodny; wielebny

venerate ('wenerejt) v. czcić

venereal (wy'njerjel) adj.
weneryczny; chory wenerycznie;
przeciwweneryczny; płciowy

Venetian blind (wy'ni:szyn,-
,blajnd)s. żaluzja (wenecka)

vengeance ('wendżens) s. zem-
sta; pomsta

venison ('wenzn) s. dziczyzna

venom ('wenem) s. jad

venomous('wenemes) adj. jadowity

vent (went) s. odwietrznik;
wentyl; otwór wentylacyjny;
rozcięcie w tyle marynarki;
ujście; upust; v. dawać upust
czemuś; wyładowywać (złość);
rozgłaszać; wietrzyć; wiercić
otwór wentylacyjny

ventilate ('wentylejt) v.
wentylować; wietrzyć; prze-
dyskutować

ventilator ('wentylejtor) s.
wentylator; wietrznik

ventriloquist (wen'trylokłyst)
s. brzuchomówca

venture ('wenczer) s. ryzyko;
stawka; spekulacja; impreza;
interes; próba; v. odważać
się; ośmielać się; ryzykować;
śmieć; narazić się

veranda (we'raende) s. weranda

verb (we:rb) s. czasownik;
słowo

verbal ('we:rbel) adj. ustny;
słowny; werbalny; czasownikowy

verdict ('we:rdykt) s. wyrok;
werdykt; osąd; orzeczenie

verdure ('we:rdżer) s. zieleń

verge ('we:rdż) s. skraj; brzeg;
krawędź; v. graniczyć; zbliżać
się; chylić się; skłaniać się;

verge on ('we:rdż,on) v. graniczyć

verification (,weryfy'kejszyn)
s. uwierzytelnienie; sprawdzenie

verify ('weryfaj) v. sprawdzać;
potwierdzać; udowadniać

vermicelli (we:rmy'sely) s. cienki makaron

vermiform appendix (we:rmy'fo:rm
e'pendyks) s. ślepa kiszka;
wyrostek robaczkowy

vermin ('we:rmyn) s. robactwo;
świat przestępczy

vernacular (we:r'naekjuler) adj.
rodzimy; miejscowy; krajowy;
s. gwara; język rodzinny; do-
sadne powiedzenie

versatile ('we:rsetail) adj.
wszechstronny

verse (we:rs) s. wiersz; strofa

versed ('we:rst) adj. doświadczony; wprawiony (w czyms)

version ('we:rżyn) s. wersja;
przekład; przekręcenie macicy

vertebra ('we:rtybre) s. krąg

vertebrae ('we:rtybri:) pl.
kręgi

vertical ('we:rtykel) adj. pionowy; szczytowy; s. pionowa
płaszczyzna; linia

very ('wery) adv. bardzo; absolutnie; zaraz; własnie; adj.
prawdziwy; sam; skończony(drań)

vessel ('wesl) s. naczynie; pojemnik; statek; okręt

vest (west) s. kamizelka; v. nadawać; przekazać; przysługiwać
komuś; przypadać komuś; odziewać w szaty; przykrywać ołtarz

vestry ('westry) s. zakrystia

vet ('wet) s. weterynarz

veteran ('weteran) s. weteran

veterinary ('weterynery) s.
weterynarz

veto ('wi:tou) s. weto; v. zakładać weto

vex (weks) v. złościć; dręczyc; dokuczać

vexation (wek'sejszyn) s. dokuczanie; drażnienie; zniecierpliwienie; irytacja; udręka; przykrość; zaniepokojenie

vexatious (wek'sejszes) adj. dokuczliwy; irytujący; przykry; nieznosny

via ('waje) prep. przez; wia

vibrate (waj'brejt) v. zadrgać; zadrzeć; oscylować; wprawiać w drganie lub ruch wahadłowy

vibration (waj'brejszyn) s. drganie; drżenie; wibracja; oscylacja; ruch wahadłowy

vibrator (waj'brejter) s. wibrator; oscylator

vicar ('wyker) s. wikary; wikariusz; zastępca

vice (wajs) imadło; zacisk; rozpusta; występek; nałog; narow; wada; v. zaciskać w imadle

vice versa ('wajsy'we:rsa) adv. odwrotnie

vicinity (wy'synyty) s. sąsiedztwo; pobliże

vicious ('wy'szes) adj. błędny; występny; złośliwy; wadliwy; zepsuty; dokuczliwy; narowisty; rozpustny

victim ('wyktym) s. ofiara

victor ('wykter) s. zwycięzca

victorian (wyk'to:rjan) adj. wiktorjański

victorious (wyk'to:rjes) adj. zwycięski

victory ('wyktery) s. zwycięstwo

victuals ('wytlz) s. prowianty; wiktuały

video ('wydjou) s. telewizja; adj. telewizyjny

view (wju:) v. oglądać; rozpatrywać; zbadać; zapatrywać się; s. obejrzenie; spojrzenie; wizja; zasięg wzroku; widok; przegląd umysłowy; pogląd; zapatrywanie; intencja; zamiar; cel; ocena

viewer ('wju:er) s. widz (telewizyjny etc.)

viewpoint ('wju:,pojnt) s. punkt widzenia; zapatrywanie

vigil ('wydżyl) s. czuwanie; wigilia

vigilance ('wydżylens) s. czujność; bezsenność

vigilant ('wydżylent) adj. czujny

vigor ('wyger) s. krzepkość; tężyzna; rzeskość; energia; siła; moc

vigorous ('wygeres) adj.krzepki; mocny; jędrny; energiczny

vile (wajl) adj. podły; nędzny; marny

village ('wylydż) s. wieś

villager ('wylydżer) s. wiesniak (raczej nieokrzesany)

villain ('wylen) s. łajdak; łotr; nikczemnik; łobuziak

villainous ('wylenes) adj. łajdacki; niegodziwy

villainy ('wyleny) s. łajdactwo

vim (wym) s. tężyzna

vincible ('wynsybl) adj. przezwyciężalny

vindicate ('wyndykejt) v. oczyszczać z zarzutu, oskarżenia, podejrzenia; rehabilitować; usprawiedliwiać; bronić; dochodzić; dowodzić

vindication (,wyndy'kejszyn) s. obrona; windykacja; usprawiedliwienie: oczyszczenie się (z zarzutu); rehabilitacja

vindictive (wyn'dyktyw) adj. mściwy; karzący

vine (wajn) s. winna latorosl; winorosl

vinegar ('wynyger) s. ocet; v. kwasić

vineyard ('wynjerd) s. winnica

vintage ('wyntydż) s. rocznik wina; winobranie; robienie wina; model (roczny)

violate ('wajelejt) v. gwałcić; zgwałcić (kobietę)

violation (,waje'lejszyn) s. pogwałcenie; zgwałcenie; gwałt; zbeszczeszczenie; naruszenie (też praw ruchu) violence ('wajelens) s. gwałtowność; gwałt; przemoc

violent ('wajelent) adj. gwałtowny; niepohamowany; wściekły

violet ('wajelyt) s. fiołek; adj. fioletowy (np. promień)

violin (,waje'lyn) s. skrzypce

violinist (,waje'lynyst) s. skrzypek

viper ('wajper) s. żmija

virgin ('we:rdżyn) s. dziewica

virginity (we:r'dżynyty) s. dziewictwo

virile ('wyrajl) adj. męski

virility (wy'rylyty) s. męskość; wiek męski; cechy męskie

virtual ('we:rczuel) adj. zasadniczy; właściwy; faktyczny; prawdziwy; rzeczywisty

virtually ('we:rczuely) adv. rzeczywiście; faktycznie; praktycznie biorąc

virtue ('we:rczju:) s. cnota; prawość; czystość; skuteczność; siła; moc

virtuoso (,we:rczju'ouzou) s. wirtuoz; miłośnik- znawca sztuki

virtuous (,we:rczjues) adj. cnotliwy; prawy

virulent ('wyrulent) adj. jadowity; złośliwy; zjadliwy

virus ('wajeres) s. wirus; jad (chorobowy)

visa ('wi:za) s. wiza; v. wiza; v. wizować

viscosity (wys'kosyty) s. lepkość; kleistość

visibility (wyzy'bylyty) s. widoczność

visible (wyzybl) adj. widoczny; wyraźny; widzialny

vision ('wyżyn) s. widzenie; wzrok; wizja; dar przewidywania; v. okazywać wizję; mieć wizję

visit ('wyzyt) v. odwiedzać; wizytować zwiedzać; nawiedzać; karać; udzielać się; gawędzić; s. wizyta; odwiedziny; pobyt

visitor ('wyzyter) s. gość; przyjezdny; zwiedzający; inspektor

vista ('wysta) s. perspektywa; wizja; widok

visual ('wyżjuel) adj. wzrokowy; optyczny

visualize ('wyżjuelajz) v. wyobrażać sobie; uwidaczniać; uzmysławiać

vital ('wajtl) adj. witalny; życiowy; żywotny; zasadniczy; śmiertelny

vitality (waj'taelyty) s. żywotność; żywość

vitamin ('wajtemyn) s. witamina

vivacious (wy'wejszes) adj. żywy

vivacity (wy'waesyty) s. żywość

vivid ('wywyd) adj. żywy

vivify ('wywyfaj) v. ożywiać

vivisection ('wywysekszyn) s. wiwisekcja

vixen ('wyksen) s. liszka; lisica; jędza

vixenish ('wyksenysz) adj. jędzowaty

vocabulary (wou'kaebjulery) s. słownik (specjalny); słownictwo

vocal ('woukel) s. samogłoska; adj. głosowy; wokalny; głośny; natarczywy

vocalist ('woukelyst) s. śpiewak; wokalista

vocation (wou'kejszyn) s. zawód; zamiłowanie; powołanie; skłonność

vogue (woug) s. moda; popularność

voice (wois) s. głos; dźwięk samogłoskowy; strona (czasownika); v. wymawiać; wyrażać; dawać wyraz czemuś; wymawiać dźwięcznie; udźwięczniać; pisać partie głosowe do muzyki; stroić

void (woid) s. próżnia; pustka; adj. próżny; pusty; pozbawiony czegoś; wolny od czegoś; wakujący; nieważny; v. unieważniać; wydalać; wypróżniać (się); oddawać (mocz)

void of ('woid,ow) exp.: bez

volatile ('woletyl) adj. lotny;
ulatniający się; zmienny
volcano (wol'kejnou) s. wulkan
volley ('woly) s. salwa; potok;
odbicie (piłki); wolej;
v. dać salwę; wypuszczać salwę; podawać wolejem; miotać
potokiem (przekleństw);lecieć
salwą; odbijać w locie
volleyball ('woly,bo:l) s.
siatkówka
volt (woult) s. wolt (elektr.)
wolta; v. robić woltę
voltage ('woultydż) s. napięcie
prądu; woltaż
voluble ('woljubl) adj. gładki;
potoczysty; ze swadą
volume ('wolju:m) s. tom; objętość; masa; ilość; pojemność;
rozmiar; siła
voluntary ('wolentery) adj.
ochotniczy; dobrowolny; wolą
kontrolowany; spontaniczny;
samorzutny; s. specjalny wyczyn z wyboru sportowca; gra
solo na organie
volunteer ('wolentier) s. ochotnik (bezpłatnie pracujący);
v. robić z własnej ochoty;
zgłaszać się na ochotnika;
podejmować coś dobrowolnie;
być ochotnikiem
voluptuous (we'lapczues) adj.
zmysłowy; lubieżny
vomit ('womyt) v. wymiotować;
wyrzucać; pobudzać do wymiotów; s. wymioty; środek wymiotny
voodoo ('wu:du:) s. wiara w
czary; czarownikv.zaczarować
voracious (we'rejszes) adj.
żarłoczny
voracity (we'raesyty) s. żarłoczność
vote (wout) s. głos; głosy;
głosowanie; prawo głosowania;
uchwała; wotum (zaufania);
v. głosować; uchwalać; orzekać; uznawać powszechnie za
coś
vote down ('wout,dałn) v. odrzucać w głosowaniu

voting paper ('woutyng'pejper)
s. kartka wyborcza
vouch (waucz) v. ręczyc; gwarantować; potwierdzać; zapewnić
voucher ('wauczer) s. dowód
kasowy
vouch for ('waucz,fo:r) v. ręczyć za kogoś
vouch safe (waucz'sejf) v. (łaskawie) raczyć
vow (wau) s. ślub (też zakonny);
przymierze; v. przysięgać;
ślubować; składać śluby
vowel ('wałel) s. samogłoska
voyage ('wojydż) s. podróż
(statkiem)
voyager ('wojedżer) s. podróżnik
vulcanize ('walkenajz) s. wulkanizować
vulgar ('walger) adj. ordynarny;
wulgarny; prostacki; gminny;
pospolity; powszechny
vulgarity (wal'gaeryty) s.
wulgarność; wyrażenie wulgarne
vulnerable ('walnerebl) adj.
czuły; wrażliwy; mający słabe
miejsce; narażony na cios; poddatny na zranienie; niezabezpieczony
vulpine ('walpajn) adj. lisi;
przebiegły; chytry   szakal
vulture ('walczer) s. sęp;(slang)
vulturine ('walczeryn) adj. sępi
w ('dablju:) dwudziesta trzecia
litera alfabetu angielskiego
wabble ('łobl) v. (slang); rozklekotać; roztrząsnąć; rozchwiać;
s. rozchwianie; rozklekotanje;
wack (łaek) s. (slang); oryginał;
dziwak
wacky ('łaeky) adj.(slang):
zwariowany;zdziwaczały; nieobliczalny
wad (łod) s. tampon; wałek (zwinięty); wata (w uszach); przybitka naboju w strzelbie;
(slang): forsa; plik (banknotów);
v. zatykać (tamponem); watować;
przybijać (nabój); wypychać;
zwijać w wałek
wadding ('łódyng) s. watowanie;
watolina; wata; wełna (do utykania); podkład; przybitka

waddle ('łodl) v. chodzic kołysząc się w biodrze jak kaczka; s. kaczy krok,

wade (łejd) y. brodzic; brnąc; przechodzic w bród; brodzenie

wafer ('łejfer) s. wafel; opłatek; naklejka urzędowa (pieczątkowa); v. zapieczętowywac naklejką

waffle ('łofl) s. wafel z ciasta naleśnikowego

waft ('łaeft) v. popychac (lekko); posuwac; posyłac (całusa); przepędzac; unosic (w powietrzu). s. śmignięcie skrzydła; powiew; podmuch; tchnienie; przelotne uczucie; smuga (światła)

wag (łaeg) v. kiwac (ogonem); poruszac się; wahac się; chodzic tam i spowrotem; merdac

wage (łejdż) s. płaca; zarobek; zapłata; v. prowadzic (np. wojnę)

wage earner ('łejdż,e:rner) s. człowiek zarobkujący

wages ('łejdżyz) s. zapłata

wager ('łejdżer) s. zakład; v. zakładac się o cos

wagon ('łaegen) s. ciężki wóz (kryty); lora; wóz policyjny; furgon

wail (łejl) v. zawodzic; lamentowac; opłakiwac; v. zawodzenie; lament; płacz

wainscot ('łejnsket) s. boazeria; ozdobne obicie scian drzewem

waist (łejst) s. talia; stan; pas; kibic; stanik; środokręcie; zwężenie

waistcoat ('łeiskout) s. kamizelka

wait (łejt) v. czekac; oczekiwac; czyhac; czatowac; czaic się; obsłużyc; obsługiwac kogos; s. czekanie; oczekiwanie; zasadzka; czaty

wait at table('łejtettejbl) v. usługiwac przy stole

waiter ('łejter) s. kelner

wait on('łejton) v.obsługiwac

waiting (łejtyng) s. czekanie; oczekiwanie; wyczekiwanie; zasadzka

waiting list (łejtyng,lyst) s. lista kolejnosci (kandydatów, klientów)

waiting room(łejtynrum) s.poczekalnia

waitings (łejtyns) pl. kolędnicy

waitress (łejtryss) s. kelnerka

wake; woke; woken (łejk; łouk; łoukn)

wake (łejk) v. obudzic (się); nie spac; pobudzic; rozbudzic; wzbudzic; wskrzesic; czuwac przy (zwłokach); s. niespanie; czuwanie przy zwłokach; kilwater; fala w ślad za statkiem (motorówka); ślad (po kims, po czyms)

wake up ('łejk,ap) v. obudzic (się); ocknąc się; oprzytomniec; zdawac sobie sprawę; zbudzic

wakeful ('łejkful) adj. czuwający; bezsenny; czujny

waken ('łejkn) = woken (łouken) v. zob. wake

waken ('łejkn) v. zbudzic; obudzic; ożywiac; wzbudzic; wskrzesic (np. zmarłego)

walk (ło:k) v. isc; przechadzac się; chodzic; kroczyc; isc stępa; jechac stępa; wejsc; zejsc; s. chód; krok; przechadzka; spacer; marsz; deptak; aleja; odległosc przebyta

walk about ('ło:ke,baut) v. włóczyc się; łazic

walk along ('ło:ke,long) v. chodzic sobie

walk away ('ło:ke,łej) v. odchodzic; (w zawodach): łatwo wygrywac

walk back ('ło:k,baek) v. wracac

walk down ('ło:k,dałn) v. schodzic

walk in ('ło:k,yn) v. wchodzic

walk off ('ło:k,of) v. odchodzic; zniknąc; ulotnic się (z czyms)

walk out ('ło:k,aut) v. wyjsc; opuscic

walk over ('ło:k,ouwer) v. wygrywac łatwo; traktowac pogrdli-wie

walk up ('ło:k,ap) v. podejsc; wejsc na gorę

walker ('ło:ker) s. piechur

walkie-talkie ('ło:ky-'to:ky) s. przenosny, mały odbiornik- nadajnik radiowy

walking (ło:kyng) s. chodzenie; marsz; wycieczka piesza; adj. chodzący; wędrowny

walking papers ('ło:kyn'pejpers) pl. zwolnienie z pracy na pismie

walking stick ('ło:kyng,styk) s. laska

walking-tour ('ło:kyng,tu:r) s. wycieczka piesza; zwiedzanie piechotą

walk-out ('ło:kaut) s. strajk

walk-over ('ło:k-over 'ło:k-ouwer) s. walkower (sport)

wall (ło:l) s. sciana; mur; przepierzenie; wał; v. obmurowac

wall in ('ło:l,yn) v. otaczac

wall up ('ło:,ap) v. zamurowac

wallboard ('ło:l,bo:rd) s. licówka (sciany)

wallet ('łolyt) s. portfel

wallop ('łolep) v. walic; łoic; prac; pobic na głowę; galopowac; łazic ciężko i niezgrabnie; s. wyrżnięcie (cios); galop; ruch ciężki i niezgrabny

wallow ('łolou) v. tarzac się; kłębic się; kołysac się; s. tarzanie się

wallpaper ('łol,pejper) s. tapety; v. tapetowac

Wall Street ('łolstri:t) s. osrodek finansowy (USA)

walnut ('ło:lnat) s. orzech włoski

walrus ('ło:lres) s. mors

waltz ('ło:ls) s. walc; v.tan-czyc walca; (slang): ruszac się żwawo

wan (łon) adj. blady; wybladły; blednąc

wand (łond) s. laseczka; pałeczka; pręt; buława

wander ('łonder) v. wędrowac; błądzic; błąkac się

wanderer ('łonderer) s. wędrowiec

wane (łejn) v. zanikac; gasnąc; s. zanik

wangle ('łaengl) v. (slang): wycyganic; wyłudzic; sfałszowac; s. krętactwo; kant

want (ło:nt) s. brak; potrzeba; niedostatek; niedopatrzenie; bieda; nędza; v. pragnąc; chciec; brakowac; potrzebowac; pożądac

wanted ('ło:ntyd) adj. poszukiwany

wanting ('ło:ntyng) adj. brakujący; kiepski; niedokładny; pozbawiony; nie na poziomie; słaby na umysle; prep. bez; mniej;przy braku

want in ('ło:nt,yn) v. chciec wejsc

wanton ('łonten) adj. złosliwy; krzywdzący; bez powodu; bezmyslny; samowolny; bezczelny; nieokiełzany; wyuzdany; lubieżny; bujny; zbytkowny; s. lubieżnik; lubieżnica; v. oddawac się rozpuscie; używac sobie; swawolic; rosc bujnie; trwonic; psocic; figlowac; bawic się

want out ('ło:nt,aut) v. chciec wyjsc

war (łor) s. wojna; v. wojowac; zawojowac

warble ('łorbl) v. nucic; jodłowac; s. nucący głos; nucona piesn; guz od siodła na grzbiecie konia; guz wywołany larwą gza bydlęcego

ward (ło:rd) s. dzielnica; cela; sala; oddział; podopieczny; opieka; kuratela; postawa obronna; parada; straż; v.odparowywac (cios); odsuwac (niebezpieczenstwo);umieszczac na oddziale

ward off ('ło:rd,of) v. odparowywać cios; odsuwać (zagro-
żenie)

warden ('ło:rdn) s. dyrektor
więzienia; dozorca; nadzorca;
gatunek twardej gruszki

warder ('ło:rder) s. strażnik
więzienny; posterunek; buława

ward heeler('ło:rd,hi:ler) s.
naganiacz partyjny

wardrobe ('ło:droub) s. garderoba; szafa na ubranie

ware (łeer) s. towar; wyrób;
ceramika; v. uwaga na coś;
trzymać się z dala od czegoś;
excl.: strzeż się !

warehouse ('łeerhaus) s. magazyn; składnica; dom składowy;
v. magazynować; składować

warm (ło:rm) adj. ciepły; świeży (trop); bliski znalezienia;
zadomowiony (na posadzie);
zamożny

warm up ('ło:rm,ap) v. ożywiać
(się); podgrzewać (się); ogrzewać (się); rozgrzewać (się)

warmup ('ło:rmap) s. ćwiczenia
rozluźniające (przed zawodami
etc); zagrzanie się

warmth ('ło:rms) s. ciepło;
serdeczność; zapał

warn (ło:rn) v. ostrzegać;
przypominać; wzywać; zapowiadać; uprzedzać

warn against(ło:negejnst) v.
ostrzegać przed czymś

warning ('ło:rnyng) adj. ostrzegawczy; s. ostrzeżenie; przestroga; znak ostrzegawczy;
wypowiedzenie (posady)

warp ('ło:rp) v. wypaczyć (się);
zwichrować (się); wykrzywić
(się); spaczyć (się); przyholo-
wywać do miejsca utwierdzenia
liny lub łańcucha; użyźniać
(przez zalewanie osadem);
s. spaczenie; wypaczenie; osnowa; szew skośny; lina holownicza; osad

warrant ('łorent) v. uspraweie-
dliwiać; uzasadniać; gwarantować; s. upoważnienie; gwarancja;

nakaz prawny (aresztu; rewizji,
etc). pełnomocnictwo dla ad-
wokatów; patent starszego pod-
oficera (USA)

warranty ('łorenty) s. gwarancja; poręka; rękojmia; podstawa; usprawiedliwienie; upoważnienie; dokument sądowy

warren ('ło:ryn) s. królikarnia

warrior ('ło:rjor) s. wojownik;
żołnierz; adj. wojowniczy

wart (ło:rt) s. brodawka; ku-
rzawka

wary ('łeery) adj. ostrożny

was (łóz) v. zob. be

wash (ło:sz) v. myć (się); prać;
prać (się); oczyszczać; zraszać; lekko barwić; lawować;
umyć się; sunąć; płynąć z
pluskiem; płukać (rudę);
s. mycie; pranie; płyn (czyszczący); fale; plusk; pomyje;
lura; wypłukane miejsce w ziemi; ględzenie; zaburzenie wody za statkiem; zaburzenie powietrza za samolotem; ziemia
na tacy zawierająca złoto; pod-
mywanie przez fale; mielizna;
kanał wyżłobiony przez wodę;
mielizna naniesiona wodą; la-
wowanie; cienka warstwa metalu;
kilwater; ślad wodny

wash away ('ło:sze,łej) v. spłukać; zmyć; unosić

wash down ('ło:sh,dałn) v. zmywać strumieniem wody; popić
jedzenie

wash off ('ło:sh,of) v. odeprać;
wymywać

wash out ('ło:sh,aut) v. wypłu-
kiwać (się) (z pieniędzy etc.)

wash up ('ło:sh,ap) v. zmywać
naczynia; wymyć się

wash and wear ('ło:sz,end'łeer)
s. bielizna i odzież gotowa
do noszenia po praniu bez pra-
sowania

washbowl ('ło:sz,boul) s.mied-
nica; umywalka; umywalnia

washcloth ('ło:sz,clos) s. zmy-
wak; szmatka do zmywania

washer ('ło:szer) s. uszczelka;
podkładka; maszyna do prania

washing ('łoszyŋg)s. mycie;
pranie; przemywanie; woda
z prania; popłuczyny; wypłukane złoto; wypłukany żwir;
bielizna do prania

washing machine ('ło:szyŋg,me
szi:n) s. pralka; maszyna do
prania

washing powder ('ło:szyn'pałder) s. proszek do prania

washing up ('ło:szyŋg,ap) v.
obmycie się

washleather ('ło:sz,ledzer) s.
ircha; zamsz

washout ('ło:szaut) s. zapad-
nięcie się; podmycie; (slang):
klapa; niepowodzenie

washtub ('ło:sztab) s. balia

washy ('ło:szy) adj. wodnisty;
rzadki; blady; cienki; wypło-
wiały

wasn't = was not

wasp (łosp) n. osa; (slang):
biały-anglosaksonin-protestant

waspish ('łospysh) adj. zjadliwy; cienki w pasie (jak
osa)

wastage ('łejstydż) s. strata;
zużycie

waste (łejst) adj. pustynny;
pusty; nieużyty (ziemia);
opustoszały; wyludniony; leżący odłogiem; zużyty; niepotrzebny; zbyteczny; odpadowy; v. pustoszyć; psuć; niszczyć (się); stracić (też zabić); zmarnować; ginąć; zużywać (się); zapuscić; zaniedbać;
s. pustynia; marnowanie; trwo-
nienie; zniszczenie; ubytek;
zużycie: odpady; bezmiar (np.
wody); zaniedbanie; marno-
trawstwo

waste away ('łejst,e'łey) v.
marnieć

wasteful ('łejstful) adj. rozrzutny; marnotrawny

wastepaper basket ('łejst-pej-
per-ba:skyt) s. kosz na śmieci

waste pipe ('łejstpajp) s. rura
odpływowa; rura ściekowa

waster ('łejster) s. marnotrawca; zepsuty materiał; artykuł
wybrakowany; nicpoń

watch (ło:cz) s. czuwanie; pilnowanie; czaty; czujność; wach-
ta; zegarek; miec się na baczności; oczekiwanie na coś;
wygladanie czegos; v. czuwać;
oczekiwac; czatować; pilnować;
opiekować się; uważać; mieć
na oku; mieć się na baczności;
wyglądać czegos; obserwować;
szpiegować; przyglądać się;
patrzyć; oczekiwać sposobności;
śledzić

watch out ('ło:czaut) v. uważać;
strzec się; uwaga !; uważaj !

watchdog ('ło:czdog) s. pies
podworzowy

watchful ('ło:czful) adj. czujny; baczny

watchmaker ('ło:cz,mejker) s.
zegarmistrz

watchman ('ło:czmen) s. stróż;
dozorca

watchtower ('ło:cz,tauer) s.
strażnica; wieża strażnicza

watchword ('ło:człe:rd) s.
hasło; slogan

watch your step ('ło:cz,jo:r'-
'step) exp.: uważaj !; pilnuj
się !

water (ło:ter) s. woda; wysięk;
przypływ; odpływ; pl. zdrój;
wody lecznicze; ocean; morze;
jezioro; rzeka; v. polewać;
podlewać; pokropić; poić; isć
do wodopoju; nawadniać; rozwadniać; rozcieńczać; skrapiać;
łzawić się; ślinic się

water anchor ('ło:ter'aenker)
s. kotwica dryfująca

water blister ('ło:ter,blyster)
s. pęcherzyk z wodą

waterborne ('ło:ter,born) adj.
przenoszony lub przekazywany
przez wodę

water bottle ('ło:ter,botl) s.
karafka; manierka

water brush ('ło:ter,brasz) s.
zgaga

water but ('ło:ter,bąt) s.
zbiornik na deszczówkę

water-cart ('ło:ter,ca:rt) s.
beczkowóz

water closet ('ło:ter'klozet)
s. ustęp

watercolor ('ło:ter'kaler) s.
akwarela

water cool ('ło:ter,ku:l) v.
chłodzić wodą

water course ('ło:ter,ko:rs)
s. strumień; rzeka ; kanał

watercress ('ło:ter,kres) s.
rzeżucha wodna

water-cure ('ło:ter,kjuer) s.
kuracja wodna

water-dog ('ło:ter,dog) s. pies
myśliwski aportujący z wody;
(slang): amator pływania, etc)

water down ('ło:ter,dałn) v.
rozwadniać

waterfall ('ło:ter,fo:l) s.
wodospad

waterfowl ('ło:ter,faul) s.
ptactwo wodne

waterfront ('ło:ter,frant) s.
wybrzeże; doki; dzielnica
portowa

watergap ('ło:ter,gaep) s.
przełom rzeki

water gate('ło:ter,gejt) s.
śluza

water gauge('ło:ter,gejdż) s.
wodowskaz; licznik wodny

water-glass ('ło:ter,gla:s) s.
szklanka; naczynie; kubek;
szklany wodowskaz; przeziernik podwodny

water hammer ('ło:ter,haemer)
s. silny wstrząs wywołany na-
głym zatrzymaniem wody w rurze

water hen ('ło:ter,hen) s. kur-
ka wodna

water hole ('ło:terhol) s. stojąca woda (w suchym łożysku
rzeki); wodopój

water ice ('ło:ter,ajs) s. sor-
bet

watering place ('ło:teryng-
plejs) s. wodopój; kąpielisko;
zdrojowisko

waterless ('ło:terłys) adj.
bezwodny; pozbawiony wody

water lily ('ło:ter,lyly) s.
grzybień biały; lilia wodna

water level ('ło:ter'lewl) s.
poziom wody

waterline ('ło:terlajn) s.
linia zanurzenia statku

waterlogged ('ło:ter,logd) adj.
przesycony wodą

watermain ('ło:ter,mejn) s.
główna rura wodociągów

waterman ('ło:termen) s. przewoźnik; wioślarz

watermark ('ło:terma:rk) s.
znak wodny; wodowskaz; v. robić znak wodny

watermelon ('ło:ter,melen) s.
arbuz; kawon

water meter('ło:ter'mi:ter) s.
wodomierz; licznik wodny

water mill ('ło:ter,myl) s.
młyn

water mocassin ('ło:ter,mokesyn)
s. żmija wodna w USA

water motor ('ło:ter'mouter) s.
motor wodny

water plane ('ło:ter'plejn) s.
hydroplan

waterpower ('ło:ter'pałer) s.
siła wodna; prawo do używania
wody

water pot ('ło:ter,pot) s.ko-
newka; polewaczka

waterproof ('ło:ter,pru:f)
adj. nieprzemakalny; v. robić
nieprzemakalnym

water-rat ('ło:ter,raet) s.
szczur wodny

water rate ('ło:ter,rejt) s.
opłata za wodę; cena wody

waterscape ('ło:ter,skejp) s.
krajobraz morski

watershed ('ło:ter,szed) s,
dział wodny; (slang): ważna
granica

water-ski ('ło:ter,ski:) s.
narta wodna

water spout('łó:ter,spaut) s.
trąba wodna; rynna pionowa
water supply ('łó:terse,plaj)
s. zaopatrzenie w wodę; sieć
wodociągowa
water table ('łó:ter,tejbl) s.
poziom (w ziemi) wody zaskor-
nej
watertight ('łó:ter,tajt)
adj. wodoszczelny
water tower ('łoter,tauer) s.
wieża cisnien
water wave ('łó:ter,łejw) s.
ondulacja wodna
waterway ('łó:ter,łej) s.
droga wodna; kanał; rzeka
spławna
waterwheel ('łó:ter,hłi:l) s.
koło (młynskie) wodne
water witch ('łó:ter,łycz) s.
różdżkarz
waterworks ('łó:ter,łe:rks) s.
wodociągi; fontanna
watery ('łó:tery) adj. wodnisty;
zalzawiony; śliniący się; wro-
żący deszcz
watt (łot) s. (electr.) wat
waul (ło:l) v. miałczec ostro
i przeciągle
wave (łejw) s. fala; falistość;
ondulacja; pokiwanie ręką;
gest ręką; v. falowac; ondulo-
wac; machac do kogos
wave away ('łejwe'łej) v. odprawiac machnięciem ręki
wave back ('łejw,baek) v. przy-
woływac (spowrotem) machnięciem ręki
wavelength ('łejw,lenks) s.
długosc fali
wave meter('łejwmi:ter) s. falo-
mierz
waver ('łejwer) v. zachwiac(się);
zamigotac; byc niezdecydowanym;
załamywac się; drzec; zawahac
sie; kołysac sie; trzepotac
sie;schwianie (się)
wavy ('łejwy) adj. falisty; sfa-
lowany; drżący; migocący;
karbowany
wawl ('łó:l) v. wrzeszczec jak
kot

wax (łaeks) s. wosk; adj. woskowy; v. woskowac; stawac się
waxen ('łaeksn) adj. woskowy;
miękki jak wosk
wax paper ('łaeks'pejper) s.
papier woskowy
waxwork ('łaeksłe:rk) s. figura woskowa; v, modelowac
z wosku
waxy ('łaeksy) adj. woskowy;
woskowaty; (slang): wsciekły;
zły; okrutny
way (łej) s. droga; szlak;
trakt; przejscie; wolna droga;
odległosc; kierunek; strona;
sposob; zwyczaj; bieg; tok;
sens; stan; położenie
way back (łej baek) adv. dawno
temu; daleko w tyle; dawno
waybill ('łejbyl) s. list
przewozowy; fracht
wayfarer ('łej,feerer) s. pod-
rożnik (pieszy)
waylay (łejlej) v.zob. lay;
zaskoczyc kogos; czyhac na
kogos; czatowac
way of life ('łej ow,lajf) s.
styl życia; sposob życia
way-out ('łej,aut) s. wyjscie;
rozwiązanie; adj. (slang):
nadzwyczajny; nadzwyczaj;
dobrze zrobiony; nadzwyczaj
zdolny; (zob.: far-out)
wayside ('łej,sajd) s. skraj
drogi; adj. przydrożny
way station (,łej'stejszyn) s.
przystanek
-ways (łejz) (przyrostek)
w taki sposob (np:sideways)
wayward ('łejłerd) adj.,prze-
wrotny; uparty; kaprysny;
nieobliczalny; chimeryczny
we (łi:) pron. my
weak (łi:k) adj. słaby
weaken ('łi:kn) v. osłabiac;
słabnąc; rozcienczac
weak-kneed ('łi:kni:d) adj.
słaby
weakling ('łi:klyng) s. sła-
beusz; cherlak; człowiek słaby; adj. słaby

weakly ('łi:kly) adj. słabowity; adv. słabo

weak-minded ('łi:k,majndyd) adj. słaby na umyśle; słabego charakteru

weakness (łi:knys) s. słabość; słabostka

wealth (łels) s. bogactwo; dobrobyt

wealthy ('łelsy) adj. bogaty

wean (łi:n) v. odłączać od piersi; oduczac; odrywać

weanling ('łi:nlyng) s. dziecko świeżo odsunięte od piersi

weapon ('łepon) s. broń

wear; wore; worn (łeer; ło:r; ło:rn)

wear (łeer) v. nosić; chodzić w czyms; ścierać się; wycierać się; żłobić; zacierać się; przechodzić; mijać; zdzierać; nużyć; męczyć; wyczerpywać; długo trwać; długo służyć; s. noszenie; rzeczy noszone; moda; zużycie; wytrzymałość

wear away ('łeer,e'łej) v. zużywać; wlec się

wear off ('łeer,of) v. zetrzec (się); zacierać (się); mijać

wear on ('łeer,on) v. wlec się

wear out ('łeer,aut) v. zdzierać (się); wyczerpywać (się)

wearing ('łeryng) adj.przeznaczony do noszenia na sobie

wearisome ('łerysem) adj. męczący; nużący; nudny

weary ('łery) adj. zmęczony; znużony; znudzony; męczący; nużący; nudny; v. męczyć; nudzić; naprzykrzać się; uprzykrzać sobie

weasel ('łi:zl) s. łasica

weather ('łedzer) s. pogoda; adj. atmosferyczny; odwietrzny; pogodny; v. zwietrzać; okrywać się patyną (śniedzią)

weather-beaten ('łedzer,bi:tn) adj. zaharowany; skołatany przez burze

weather-bound ('łedzer,baund) adj. zatrzymany przez pogodę (statek)

weather bureau ('łedzer,bjuerou) s. instytut meteorologiczny

weather chart ('łedzer,cza:rt) s. wykres meteorologiczny

weathercock ('łedzer,kok) s. chorągiewka na dachu; kurek na dachu; człowiek niestały

weather forecast ('łedz,fo:rka:st) s. komunikat meteorologiczny

weather vane ('łedzer,wejn) s. wiatrowskaz; chorągiewka na dachu

weave; wove; woven (łi:w; łouw; łouwn)

weave (łi:w) v. tkać (tkaninę); knuć (spisek); układać (intrygę; opowiadanie) spleść; splatać; zajmować się tkactwem

weaver ('łi:wer) s. tkacz

weaving ('łi:wyng) s. tkactwo

web (łeb) s. tkanina; sztuka (materiału); stek (kłamstw); pajęczyna; błona (nietoperza); tkanka łączna; usztywnienie

wed (łed) v. zaślubiać; łączyć się; pobrać się; adj. zaślubiony

wedded ('łedyd) adj. zaślubiony; ślubny; oddany (sprawie)

wedding ('łedyng) s. ślub; wesele; adj. ślubny; weselny

wedding ring ('łedyng,ryng) s. obrączka ślubna

we'd (łi:d) = we had; we would; we should

wedge (łedż) s. klin; trójkatny kawałek (tortu); golfowy kijek z klinowym zakończeniem; v.klinować; zaklinować; rozklinować; łupać

wedge in ('łedż,yn) v. wpychać (się); wcisnąć (się)

wedge off ('łedż,of) v. wypychać (się)

wedlock ('łedlok) s. małżeństwo

Wednesday ('łenzdy) s. środa

weed (łi:d) s. chwast; zielsko; cygaro; (slang): chuchro; cherlak; mizerak; szkapa; v. pielić; odchwaszczać

weeder ('łi:der) s. pielnik; wypielacz

weed grown ('łi:dgroun)adj.
zachwaszczony

weed out ('łi:d,aut) v. wypie-
lać; usuwać

weeds ('łi:ds) pl. krepa żałobna; strój żałobny

weedy ('łi:dy) adj. zachwaszczony; chudy; wysoki

weed killer ('łi:d,kyler) s.
trucizna na chwasty

week (łi:k) s. tydzień

weekday ('łi:kdej) s. dzień
powszedni

weekend ('łi:kend) s. niedziela oraz części wolne
soboty i poniedziałku;
v. spędzać weekend

week in-week out ('łi:k,yn-
'łi:k,aut) adv. exp.: co tydzień

weekly ('łi:kly) adj. tygodniowy; adv. tygodniowo; s.
tygodnik

weep; wept; wept (łi:p; łept;
łept)

weep (łi:p) v. płakać; opłakiwać; zapłakać; lamentować;
cieknąć; wyciekać; ociekać;
s. płacz; cieknięcie

weeper ('łi:per) s. płaczek;
płaczka; welon żałobny; krepa żałobna

weep away ('łi:pe,łej) v. wy-
płakać się

weeping willow ('łi:pyng,ły-
lou) s. wierzba płacząca

weep for joy ('łi:p-fo:r-dżoj)
v. płakać z radości

weep out ('łi:p,aut) v. powiedzieć z płaczem

weigh (łej) v. ważyć (się);
rozważać; mierzyć; równoważyć;
podnosić (kotwicę); s. waże-
nie

weigh in ('łej,yn) v. ważyć
(boksera; dżokeja przed zawodami)

weigh out ('łej,aut) v. wywa-
żyć człowieka przed zawodami

weigh up ('łej,ap) v. rozważyć

weigh upon ('łej,apon) v. przygniatać; ciążyć na kims

weight (łejt) s. ciężar; waga;
obciążenie; ciężarek; odważnik;
przycisk; grubość (odzieży);
znaczenie; doniosłość; odpowiedzialność; v. obciążać; pogrubiać sztucznie tkaninę

weight lifting ('łejt lyftyng)
s. (sport) podnoszenie ciężarów

weightless ('łejtlys) adj. lekki;
bez ciężaru

weighted-with(łejyd,łys) adj.
obarczony (np. wiekiem)

weighty ('łejty) adj. ciężki;
ważki; doniosły; ważny; poważny ; przekonywujący; rozważony;
przemyślany

weir (łier) s. jaz; grobla

weird (łierd) adj. niesamowity;
tajemniczy; nadprzyrodzony;
dziwny; dziwaczny; s. los

welcome ('łekem) exp.: witaj !
witajcie ! s. powitanie; adj.
mile widziany; mający pozwolenie; mogący korzystać; v. powitać; witać (z radością)

weld (łeld) v. spawać (się);
spajać; zespalać; zgrzewać;
s. spoina; spawanie; spojenie;
miejsce spojenia

welder ('łelder) s. spawacz;
spawarka; przyrząd do spawania

welfare ('łelfeer) s. dobro;
dobrobyt; powodzenie; pomyślność; szczęście

welfare-state ('łelfeer'stejt)
s, panstwo o bardzo wysokich
świadczeniach społecznych

welfare-work ('łelfeer,łe:rk)
s. praca społeczna; społecz-
nictwo; praca dobroczynna

well; better; best (łel; beter;
best) adv. dobrze; lepiej; najlepiej

well (łel) s. studnia; otwór
wiertniczy; odwiert; źródło;
klatka (schodowa); adv. dobrze;
należycie; porządnie; mocno; so-
lidnie; szczęśliwie; całkiem;
wyraźnie; łatwo; lekko; słusznie; adj. dobry; zdrowy; zadawalający; pomyślny; w porządku;
exp.: dobrze ! a więc ?

well-balanced ('łel'baelenst)
adj. zrównoważony

well-behaved ('łelby'hejwd)
adj. dobrze wychowany

well-being ('łel'bi:yŋg)s.
dobrobyt; powodzenie; po-
myślność

well-born ('łel'bo:rn) adj.
dobrze urodzony

well-bred ('łel'bred) adj.
rasowy; dobrze wychowany

well-connected ('łel'konektyd)
adj. dobrze skoligacony

well-disposed ('łeldys'pouzd)
adj. życzliwie usposobiony

well done ('łeldan) exp.:
brawo ! dobrze zrobione !

well-fed ('łelfed) adj. dobrze
odżywiony

well-founded ('łelfaundyd)
adj. uzasadniony

wellhead ('łel'hed) s. źródło

well-heeled ('łel'hi:ld) adj.
slang): forsiasty (ma forsę)

Wellingtons ('łelyŋtenz) s.
buty z wysokimi holewami
(też z gumy)

well-informed ('łel-ynfo:rmd)
adj. dobrze poinformowany;
wykształcony

well-intended ('łel-'yntendyd)
adj. dobrze pomyślany

well-judged ('łel-'dżadżd) adj.
rozsądny; roztropny; dobrze
pomyślany

well-knit ('łel'nyt) adj.
zwarty; dobrze zbudowany;
jędrny

well-known ('łel'nołn) adj.
dobrze znany

well-meant ('łel'ment) adj.
zrobiony w najlepszej intencji

well-nigh ('łel'naj) adv. nieledwie; o mało co; o mało nie

well-off ('łel'o:f) adj. dobrze sytuowany; zamożny

well point ('łel'poynt) s. rura
do usuwania wody podskórnej
(przed kopaniem)

well-read ('łel'red) adj.
oczytany

well-sinker ('łel'syŋker)s.
studniarz

well-spoken ('łel'spouken) adj.
uprzejmy; pięknie mówiący;
dobrze powiedziany

wellspring (łel'spryŋg)s.
źródło

well-timed ('łel'tajmd) adj.
na czasie; odpowiedni

well-to-do ('łel-te'du:) adj.
zamożny; dobrze sytuowany

well-wisher ('łel'łyszer) s.
sympatyk

well-worn ('łel'ło:rn) adj.
wytrwały; wyświechtany; oklepany; dobrze noszony

welsh (łelsz) adj. walijski;
s. wykręcanie się od płacenia;
v. uciekać nie zapłaciwszy,

welter ('łelter) v. falować;
tarzać się; s. falowanie;
powódź; zamęt; kolos; silne
uderzenie

wench (łencz) s. dziewucha;
ulicznica; v. latać za dziew-
kami

Wendish (łendysz) adj. łużycki

went (łent) v. zob. go

wept (łept) v. zob. weep

were (łe:r) v. zob. be

we're (łier) = we are

werewolf('łe:rłuf) s. wilkołak

west (łest) s. zachód; adj.
zachodni; adv. na zachód; ku
zachodowi

westerly ('łesterly) adj. zachodni; adv. na zachód

western ('łestern) adj. zachodni; pochodzący z zachodu

westward ('łestłerd) adj. zachodni; ku zachodowi; na zachód

wet (łet) adj. mokry; wilgotny;
zmoczony; przemoczony; słotny;
deszczowy; dżdżysty; (slang):
w błędzie; s. wilgoć; wilgotność; trunek; v. moczyć (się);
zwilżać; zraszać

wet nurse ('łet,ne:rse) s.
mamka; v. karmić

wether ('łedzer) s.skop (ka-
strowany baran)

wet through ('łet'tru:) v.
przemoczyć (na wylot)

we've (łi:w) = we have

whack (hłaek) v. walić; grzmocić; (slang: dzielić się
czyms; s. walnięcie; trzas-
nięcie; (slang): część; próba;
stan (rzeczy)

whacker ('hłaeker) s. kolor

whacking ('hłaekyng) adj. kolosalny

whale (hłejl) s. wieloryb;
rzecz wspaniała; v. polować
na wieloryby; (slang): bić

whale-boat ('hłejl,bout) s.
łódź do połowu wielorybów;
łódź strażnicza; ratunkowa

whalebone ('hłejlboun) s, fisz-
bin

whale-fin ('hłejlfyn) s. fisz-
bin

whale-oil ('hłejl,ojl) s. tran
wielorybi

whaler ('hłejler) s. statek do
połowu wielorybów

whammy ('hłaemy) s. (slang):
urok (rzucony na kogoś)

whang (hłaeng) s. grzmotnięcie;
huczenie; v. walić; grzmocić;
huczeć

wharf (hło:rf) s. przystań (wy-
ładunkowa); nabrzeże; v. cumować do wyładunku; wyładowywać
w przystani

wharves (hło:rfs) pl. nabrzeża
wyładunkowe

what (hłot) adj. jaki; jaki
tylko; ten; ktory; ten...co;
taki... jaki; tyle.., ile;
pron. co; to co; coś;
excl.:co ? czego ? jak to !

what about ('hłote,baut) exp.:
a co z... ?; co powiesz o...?

whatever (hłot'ewer) adj.
jakikolwiek; pron. cokolwiek;
wszystko co; co tylko; bez
względu; obojętnie co

what for ('hłotfo:r) s. (slang):
bura; lanie; exp.: za co ?

what next ('hłot,nekst) exp.:
co dalej ?

whatnot ('hłotnot) s. etażerka;
cacka; (slang): cokolwiek;
obojętnie co; wszystko

whatsit ('hłotsyt) s. jak się
to nazywa; ten (przedmiot)

whatsoever ('hłotsou'ewer) adj.
jakikolwiek by; cokolwiek by;
co tylko by; pron. wszystko
co tylko

wheat (hłi:t) s. pszenica

wheaten ('hłi:tn) adj. prze-
niczny

wheel ('hłi:l) s. koło; kółko;
ster; kierownica; v. obracać
(się); wrocić (się); prowadzić
taczki (rower); wozić taczkami
etc.

wheelbarrow ('hłi:l,baerou) s.
taczki

wheel chair('hłi:l,czeer) s. fotel na kółkach

wheeler-dealer ('hłi:ler,di:ler)
s. cwaniak; politykier

wheelwright ('hłi:lrajt) s.
kołodziej

wheeze ('hłi:z) v. sapać; s. sa-
panie; (slang): dowcip; komunał

wheezy ('hłi:zy) adj. sapiący;
zasapany

when (hłen) adv. kiedy; kiedyż;
wtedy; kiedy to; gdy; przy;
podczas gdy;
s. czas (zdarzenia)

whenas (,hłen'aez) conj. kiedy;
podczas gdy

whence (hłens) adv. & conj. skąd

whenever ('hłenewer) adv. kiedy
tylko; skoro tylko

whensoever ('hłensou'ever) adv.
skoro tylko; skądkolwiek

where (hłeer) adv. & conj. gdzie;
dokąd

whereabout ('hłeere'baut) adv.
gdzie ?

whereabouts ('hłeere'bauts) adv.
zważywszy; gdzie;mniej więcej;
s. miejsce zamieszkania;(pobytu)

whereas('hłeer'aez) conj. podczas
gdy

whereat ('hłeer,et) conj. podczas
gdy

whereby ('hłeer,baj) adv. po
czym ? po kim ? po ktorym; za
pomocą którego? jak?ktorym

wherefore('hłeerfo:r) adj.
dlaczego; dlatego; z tego
powodu

wherefrom (hłeer'fro:m) adv.
skąd; z czego

wherein (hłeer'yn) adv. w czym;
w ktorym

whereof (hłeer'ow) adv. z czego; z którego

whereon (hłeer'on) adv. na
czym; na ktorym

wheresoever (,hłeersou'ever)
adv. wszędzie by; dokądkolwiek
by; gdzie tylko by

whereupon (,hłeere'pon) adv.
na czym; po czym

wherever (,hłeer'ever) adv.
dokądkolwiek; wszędzie; gdzie
tylko

wherewith (,hłeer'łyz) adv.
(z) czym ?

wherewithal (,hłeerły'so:l) s.
potrzebne srodki (fundusze,
przybory)

whet (,hłet) v. naostrzyc;
zaostrzyc (też apetyt);
s. ostrzenie; zakąska

whether ('hłedzer) conj. czy-
czy; czy tak, czy owak

whetstone ('hłet,stoun)s. oseł-
ka; kamien szlifierski

whey (hłej) s. serwatka

which (hłycz) pron. ktory; co;
ktoredy; dokąd; w jaki (sposób)

whichever (hłycz,ewer) adj.
ktorykolwiek; jaki; każdy...
jaki; ktory tylko; pron.
ktorykowiek; każdy

whichsoever (,hłyczsou'ewer)
adj. pron. = whichever (z naciskiem)

whiff (hłyf) s. powiew; podmuch; tchnienie; zapach; dym;
lekki wybuch gniewu; v. dmu-
chac; dymic; palic; lekko
wiac

while (hłajl) s. chwila; pewien czas; po chwili; niebawem; wkrotce; conj. podczas
gdy; jak długo; dopóki; poki;
natychmiast; chociaż co prawda

while ago ('hłajl'egou) adv.
(nie)dawno

while away ('hłajle'łej) v.
spedzac czas; skracac sobie
czas

whim ('hłym) s. kaprys; zachcianka; fantazja; fanaberia;
kołowrot gorniczy

whimper ('hłymper) v. piszczec;
kwilic; skomlec; skowyczec;
s. kwilenie; skowyt; skamlanie

whimsical ('hłymzykel) adj.
kapryśny; dziwaczny; cudaczny

whimsy ('hłymzy) s. kaprys

whim-wham('hłymhłaem) s. cacko

whine ('hłajn) v. skomlec; ję-
czec; powiedziec jękliwie;
s. skomlenie; jęk

whip (hłyp) s. bat; bicz; pomocnik; woznica; naganiacz;
uderzenie biczem; bita smietana; v. chłostac; zacinac (batem); ubijac (smietanę); sma-
gac; przyrządzac na prędce;
zwyciężyc; zakasowac (kogos);
owijac; windowac; smigac;
zbierac; wyjechac (pospiesznie)

whip in ('hłyp,yn) v. zapędzac
batem

whip off ('hłyp'o:f) v. zerwac
cos; czmychnąc z czyms

whip on ('hłyp'on) v. popędzac
batem

whip out ('hłyp,aut) v. wyciąg-
nąc błyskawicznie

whip round ('hłyp,raund) v. odwrocic się znienacka

whip together ('hłyp te'gedzer)
v. zganiac batem; zwalac na
kupę; montowac na gwałt

whipped cream ('hłypt'kri:m) s.
bita smietana

whipper-snapper ('hłyper'snae-
per) s. chłystek; smarkacz

whipping boy ('hłypyng,boj) s.
kozioł ofiarny (chłopak chło-
stany za innego)

whipping top ('hłypyng,top) s.
bąk do podbijania

whippy (,hłypy) adj. giętki;
elastyczny

whipsaw (,hłyp'so) s. wąska
piłeczka; v. ciąć piłką;
wygrać podwojnie; pobic podwojnie

whipstock (,hłyp'stok) s. biczysko

whirl (hłe:rl) v. kręcic (się);
wirowac; zawirowac; porywać
w wir; s. wirowanie; ruch
wirowy; wir; (slang): próba
(czegos)

whirlpool ('hłe:rl'pu:l) s.
wir

whirlwind ('hłe:rl'łynd) s.
trąba powietrzna; wir po-
wietrzny

whirlybird (hłe:rly'be:rd) s.
helikoper (USA)

whirr (hłe:r) v. furgotac;
warkotac; s. furgot; warkot
(maszyny)

whisk (hłysk) s. wiechec;
smignięcie; trzepaczka (do
jajek etc.); miotełka;
v. otrzepac; odpędzac; pory-
wac; szybko odwozic; przywo-
zic; czmychac; wymachiwac;
smigac

whisk away ('hłyske'łej) s.
strzepnąc; przewiezc lotem
strzały; czmychnąc

whiskers ('hłyskers) pl. baki;
bokobrody; wasy

whisky ('hłysky) s. (wodka)
whiskey

whisper ('hłysper) v. szeptac;
mowic cicho; szmerac; szelescic; s. szeptanie; szmer

whistle ('hłysl) v. gwizdac;
swistac; zagwizdac; s. gwizdanie; gwizd; swist; gwizdek;
gardło

whistle away ('hłysle'łej) v.
pogwizdywac sobie

white (hłajt) adj. biały; bezbarwny; blady; czysty; niepokalany; uczciwy; rzetelny;
niewinny; s. biel; biały (człowiek); białko; białe wino

white coffee (hłajt'kofi) v.
kawa z mlekiem

white-collar('lajt,koler) adj.
zajęci biurowo(urzędnicy etc.)

white elephant (hłajt'elyfent)
s. towary wybrakowane; buble

white collar worker ('hłajt,ko-
ler łerker) s. pracownik
umysłowy

white frost ('hłajt'fro:st) s.
szron

white-headed ('hłajt'hedyd) adj.
siwowłosy

white heat (hłajt'hi:t) biały
żar

white lie (hłajt'laj) s. kłamstwo; wykręt towarzyski

white paper ('hłajt,pejper) s.
oficjalna publikacja wykazują-
ca, że rząd ma zawsze rację
(USA)

whiten ('hłajtn) y. wybielac;
pobielac; bielic; zbieleć

whiteness ('hłajtness) s. biel

whitewash (,hłajt'łosz) s.
wapno; wybielanie czegos lub
kogos; v. wybielac; wymywac
na czysto; uniewinnic; uspra-
wiedliwic; pobic na sucho
(na zero)

Whitsuntide ('hłajtsntajd) s.
Zielone Swięta

whittle down ('hłytl,dałn) v.
strugac; zestrugac; wystrugac;
obstrugać

whity ('hłajty) adj. białawy

whizz (hłyz) s. swist; (slang):
mistrz; rzecz wspaniała;
v. swistac; suszyc

who (hu:) pron. kto; ktory

whodunit (hu:danyt) s. (slang):
"kryminał"; powieść detekty-
wistyczna

whoever (hu:'ewer) pron. ktokolwiek

whole (houl) adj. cały; pełnowartosciowy; zdrowy; s. całość

wholehearted ('houl'ha:rtyd)
adj. serdeczny; szczery

whole hogger ('houl'hoger) s.
człowiek idący na całego

whole length ('houl'lenks) s.
(portret) w całości

wholesale ('houl,sejl) s. hurt;
handel hurtowy; adj. hurtowy;
masowy; adv.hurtem; masowo

wholesaler ('houl,sejler) s.
hurtownik

wholesale trade ('houlsejl-
,trejd) s. handel hurtowy

wholesome ('houlsem) s. zdrowy;
zdrowotny

whole-time ('houltajm) adj.
pełno-etatowy (czasowy)

whole-wheat ('houl'hłi:t) adj.
pełno-ziarnisty (chleb)

who'll (hu:l) = who shall;
who will

wholly ('houly) adv. całkowicie

whoom (hu:m) pron. kogo ?
zob. who

whoop (hu:p) s. okrzyk (wesoły
np.)

whooping ('hu:pyng) adj.(slang):
ogromny

whooping cough ('hu:pyn,kof)
s. koklusz

whore (ho:r) s. wulg.: kurwa;
dziwka; v. kurwić się; gonić
za dziwkami

whorelet ('ho:rlyt) s. wulg.:
kurewka

whose (hu:z) pron. & adj. czyj;
czyja; czyje; którego

why (hłaj) adv. dlaczego; czemu;czemuż; dlatego; własnie;
s. przyczyna; powod; exp.: jak
to ! własnie ! patrzcie;
no wiesz !;no to co !

why so ('hłaj'sou) adv. dlaczego

wick (łyk) s. knot; tampon

wicked ('łykyd) adj. niegodziwy; niedobry; frywolny; paskudny; złosliwy; zły; nikczemny

wickedness ('łykydnys) s.
nikczemnosc; niegodziwosc

wicker basket ('łyker,ba:skyt)
s, pleciony kosz

wicker chair (łyker,czeer) s.
plecione krzesło

wicket (łykyt) s. furka; kołowrot; okienko kasowe; bramka;
cel; drzwi na pół wysokości
(otworu)

wide (łajd) adj. szeroki; rozległy; szeroko otwarty; ob-

szerny; wielki; pokazny; znaczny; duży; daleki; szeroko otwarty; adv. szeroko; z dala
(od czegos)

wide-awake ('łajde,e'łejk) adj.
czujny; rozbudzony; bystry;
z szeroko otwartymi oczami

widen ('łajdn) v. poszerzyc;
rozszerzac

wideness ('łajdnys) s. szerokosc;
rozległosc; bezmiar

wide-open (,łajd'oupen) adj.
szeroko otwarty

widespread (,łajd'spred) adj.
rozprzestrzeniony; szeroko
rozpostarty

widow ('łydou) s. wdowa; v. wdowiec

widower ('łydouer) s. wdowiec

width (łyds) s. szerokosc

wife (łajf) s. żona; pl. wives
(łajwz)

wig (łyg) s. peruka; v. zaopatrywac w peruke

wild (łajld) adj. dziki; dziko
rosnący; gwałtowny; wsciekły;
szalony; burzliwy; rozwichrzo-
ny; pustynny;zdziczały; rozwydrzony; fantastyczny; nierealny; podniecony; s. pustynia;
dziki teren; adv. na chybił
trafił

wildcat ('łajld,kaet) adj. porywczy; awanturniczy; nadzwyczajny (np. pociąg); s. żbik;
szyb naftowy na nowym terenie;
awanturnicze przedsiębiorstwo;
spekulacja; samotna lokomotywa;
porywcza osoba; v. szukac nafty na niesprawdzonych terenach

wilderness(łajldernys) s.
pustynia; puszcza; odludzie

wildfire (,łajld'fajer) s.
błyskawicznie rozprzestrzenia-
jący się ogien; ogien grecki;
błędny ognik

willful('łylful) adj. rozmyslny;
umyslny; zamierzony; swiadomy;
samowolny; uparty

will (łyl) s. wola; testament;
siła woli; v. postanowic; zarządzac; zapisywac (w testamencie)
zmuszac; chciec

willing (,Ɫylyŋg) adj. skłonny
(cos zrobic); chętny; pełen
dobrej woli

willow ('Ɫylou) s. wierzba

willowy (Ɫyloɫy) adj. smukly;
gibki; giętki; obfitujący
w wierzby

will power ('Ɫyl,paɫer) s.
siła woli

willy-nilly ('Ɫyly'nyly) adv.
chcąc nie chcąc

will you ? ('Ɫylju:) exp.: czy
zrobisz; czy zechcesz ?; czy
obiecasz ?

wilt (Ɫylt) v. więdnąc; opadać;
oklapnąc; powodować zwięd-
nięcie; opadac z siɫ; s. więd-
nięcie; osłabienie; depresja

wily (Ɫajly) adj. chytry

win; won; won (Ɫyn; Ɫon; Ɫon)

win (Ɫyn) v. wygrywac; zwy-
ciężac; zdobywać; zarabiac;
osiągać; pozyskac; przedostac
się; przezwyciężać; s. wygrana; zwycięstwo

win over (Ɫynouwer) v. pozyskac sobie; przekonac

wince (Ɫyns) v. skrzywić się
(z bólu) drgąc; s. drgnięcie;
skrzywienie

winch (Ɫyncz) s. korba; wyciąg; kołowrot; v. podnosic;
wyciągac kołowrotem lub korbą

wind; wound; wound (Ɫajnd;
Ɫaund; Ɫaund)

wind (Ɫajnd) v. nawijac; zwijac; zwinąc; owinąc (się);
wic (się); zakończyc
(Ɫynd) s. wiatr; podmuch; oddech; dech; zapach; puste
słowa; gadanie; v. trąbic;
dąc w róg; przewietrzyc;
zwietrzyc; poczuc; zmęczyc;
dac wytchnąc

windbag (Ɫyndbaeg) s. czczy
gaduła

windfall ('Ɫynd fo:l) s.
gratka; owoc zrzucony wiatrem

winding (Ɫajndyŋg) adj. kręcony; kręcący się

winding-stairs (Ɫajdyŋ steers)
s. kręcące się schody

wind-instrument (Ɫynd,ynstru-
ment) s. intrument dęty

windlass (Ɫyndles) s. wyciąg;
kołowrot

windmill ('Ɫynmyl) s. wiatrak

wind off (Ɫajnd,o:f) v. odwinąc
(się)

wind up (Ɫajnd,ap) v. nakręcać
(zegar); kończyc (mowę; zamykac zebranie)

window ('Ɫyndou) s. okno; okienko

window dressing ('Ɫyndou,dres-
syŋg) s. dekoracja wystawy
sklepowej

windowpane ('Ɫyndou,pejn) s.
szyba okienna

window shade ('Ɫyndou,szejd)
s. żaluzja

window shopping ('Ɫyndou-
szopyŋg) v. oglądac wystawy
(a nie kupowac)

window-sill ('Ɫyndou,syl) s.
parapet

windpipe ('Ɫynd,pajp) s. tchawica

windshield ('Ɫyndszyld) s.
szyba ochronna (przednia) w
samochodzie

windshield wiper ('Ɫyndszyld-
'Ɫajper) s. wycieraczka
szyby ochronnej

windy ('Ɫyndy) adj. wystawiony
na wiatr; wietrzny; gadatliwy

wine ('Ɫajn) s. wino

wineglass ('Ɫajngla:s) s. kieliszek do wina

wine-press ('Ɫajnpres) s. wy-
tłaczarka do winogron

wing (Ɫyŋg) s. skrzydło; ramię
kulisa; dywizjon; lot;
v. uskrzydlac; przewozic na
skrzydłach; przeleciec (przez
cos); leciec; szybowac

wing commander ('Ɫyŋg-ke,ma:n-
der) s. dowodca dywizjonu
lotnictwa (podpułkownik)

wink ('Ɫyŋk) s. mrugąc (na kogos); przymykac oczy; s.mrug-
nięcie

winner ('Ɫyner) s. zdobywca nagrody; człowiek wygrywający;
laureat

winning ('łynyŋg) s. otwór do
wydobywania węgla; adj. ujmujący; zwycięski

winning post ('łynyŋg,poust)
s. meta

winnings ('łynyŋgs) pl. wygrana

winsome ('łynsem) adj. ujmujący; pociągający

winter ('łynter) s. zima; adj.
zimowy; v. zimować

winter crop('łynter,krop) s.
ozimina

winterize ('łynterajz) v. dostosowywać, przygotowywać do
zimy

wintry ('łyntry) adj. zimowy;
chłodny; obojętny

winy ('łajny) adj. podchmielony; winny

wipe (łajp) v. wycierać; ocierać; ścierać; wymazać; za-
machnąć się; s. starcie; wy-
tarcie; bicie

wipe away ('łejpe,łej) v. wycierać; wymazać

wipe off ('łajp,o:f) v. zetrzeć (plamę etc.)

wipe out ('łajp,aut) v. wytrzeć; wymazać; wyniszczyć;
zgładzać

wipe up ('łajp,ap) v. wytrzeć
(podłogę etc,)

wire (łajer) s. drut; przewód;
telegram; kabel; struna metalowa; sidła; v. drutować;
zadrutować; złapać (w sidła);
założyć przewody (w domu);
zatelegrafować; ciągnąć za
sznurki zakulisowe

wire cutter ('łajer,kater) s.
szczypce do cięcia drutu

wire haired ('łajer,heerd)
adj. ostrowłosy (pies)

wireless ('łajerlys) adj. radiowy; bez drutu

wireless set ('łajerlys,set)
s. radio

wire netting ('łajer,netyŋg)
s. siatka druciana

wire-pulling ('łajer,pulyŋg)
s. używanie protekcji; wpły-
wów

wire rope ('łajer,roup) s. lina
stalowa

wiry ('łajery) adj. twardy; żylasty; muskularny; druciany

wisdom ('łyzdem) s. mądrość

wisdom tooth ('łyzdem.tu:s) s.
ząb mądrości

wise (łajz) s. sposób; adj. mądry; roztropny

wiseacre ('łajz,ejker) s. mądra-
la; medrek

wise after('łajz,a:fter) adj.
mądry po...

wisecrack ('łajzkra:k) s. dowcip-
na uwaga; v. robić dowcipy

wise guy('łajzgaj) s. nadęta
wielkość

wise saw('łajzso:) s. przysłowie

wish (łysz) v. życzyć (sobie);
pragnąć; chcieć; s. pragnienie;
życzenie; chęć; powinszowanie;
ochota; rzecz upragniona

wishbone ('łyszboun) s. kość
widełkowa (ptaków)

wish for ('łysz fo:r) v. życzyć
sobie (np. pogody)

wishful ('łyszful) adj. pragnący

wishful thinking ('łyszful-
tynkyŋg) s. pobożne życzenie

wish well ('łysz,łel) v. dobrze
życzyć

wishy-washy ('łyszy,łoszy) adj.
bez treści; wodnisty; lurowaty

wisp (łysp) s. wiązka; garść;
pęczek; kosmyk; wstęga (dymu)

wistful ('łystful) adj. smutny;
zadumany; pełen tęsknoty

wit (łyt) s. umysł; rozum; dowcip; człowiek dowcipny; inteligencja; olej w głowie

witch (łycz) s. czarownica;
czarodziejka; v. zaczarować;
oczarować

witchcraft ('łycz.kra:ft) s.
czary; czarnoksięstwo

witch doctor ('łycz,dakter) s.
czarownik; znachor

witchery ('łyczery) = witchcraft

witch hunt('łyczhant) s. tro-
pienie czarownic; polityczne
głosne śledztwo (propagandowe)
w celu udowadniania działalności wywrotowej

with (łyg) prep. z (kims; czyms)
u (kogos); przy (kims); za pomocą); (stosownie) do; (cierp-
liwosc) dla

withdraw (łys'dro:) v. zob.
draw; cofac (się); wycofywac
(się); odwołac (cos); ode-
brac (ze szkoły); odsuwac
(zasłonę)

withdrawal (łys'dro:el) s.
wycofanie

wither ('łydzer) v. powodowac
wiednięcie, usychanie; zabi-
jac (spojrzeniem); usychac;
usuwac się (w cien itp)

withers ('łydzers) pl. kłęby
(u konia miedzy łopatkami)

withhold (łys'hould) v.zob.
hold; wstrzymywac; odmawiac;
wycofac

within (łys'yn) adv. wewnątrz;
w domu; u siebie; w (czyms);
w duchu; do wnętrza; w obrę-
bie; w odległosci (np. mili);
w ciągu (np..dnia); w zasięgu (wzroku); s. wnętrze

without (łysaut) prep. bez;
poza; na zewnatrz; adv. na
zewnatrz; poza domem; s. strona zewnetrzna

withstand (łys'staend) v. zob.
stand; opierac się; przeciwstawiac sie; byc wytrzymałym;
wytrzymywac

witling ('łytlyng) s. dowcipnis

witness ('łytnys) s. swiadek;
widz; swiadectwo; v. byc
swiadkiem; swiadczyc (też
podpisem)

witness box ('lytnys,boks) s.
miejsce dla swiadka w sądzie
(USA)

witness stand ('łytnys,staend)
s. miejsce dla zeznawania
w sądzie (USA)

witticism ('łytysyzem) s. złosliwy dowcip; dowcipkowanie

witty (łyty) adj. dowcipny

witty at someone's expense
('łyty et'somłans,yks'pens)
exp.: dowcipny cudzym kosztem

wives (łajwz) pl. żony; zob.
wife

wiz (łyz) s. (slang): znawca;
mistrz; rzecz wspaniała

wizard ('łyzerd) s. czarownik;
czarodziej; adj. czarodziejski;
(slang): wspaniały

wo (ło:u) exp.: prrr (na konia,
żeby stanął)

wobble ('łobl) v. chwiac się;
ruszac się chwiejnie; chodzic
chwiejnie; jechac kołysząc się;
mowic drżąco; grac drżąco (me-
lodię); drgac; wahac się; byc
niezdecydowanym

wobbler ('łobler) s. człowiek
chwiejny

wobbly (łobly) s. chwiejący
się; chwiejny

woe (łou) s. nieszczęscie

woebegone ('łoubi,go:n) adj.
nieszczęsny

woeful ('łouful) adj. bolesny;
żałosny

woke (łouk) v. zob . wake

woken (łoukn) v. zob. wake

wolf (łulf) s. pl. wolves
(łulvz); wilk; (slang): kobieciarz; v. żrec; pożerac; połykac jak wilk; polowac na
wilki

wolf down ('łulf,dałn) v. pożerac jak wilk

wolfcall ('łulf,ko:l) s. (slang):
gwizdanie na kobietę (z po-
dziwem, zaczepką etc.)

wolf-cub ('łulf,kab) s. wilczek;
wilczę; młodszy harcerz

wolf-dog ('łulfdog) s. wilczur

wolfhound ('łulfhaund) s.
wilczur rosyjski lub alzacki

wolfish ('łulfysz) adj.wilczy

wolf skin('łulf'skyn) s. wilcza
skora (na podłoge etc.);
wilczura (okrycie)

wolf whistle('łulfhłysl) =
wolfcall

wolverene (,łulve'ri:n) s.
rosomak; mieszkaniec stanu
Michigan

woman ('łumen) s. pl. women
('łymyn); kobieta; baba; żona; v. mówić per "kobieta";
umieszczać między kobietami

woman doctor ('łumen'dakter)
s. lekarka

womanhood ('łumenhud) s. kobiety; kobiecość (dojrzała)

womanish ('łumenysz) adj. bab-
ski; zniewieściały

womanize ('łumenajz) v. ba-
bieć; niewieścieć; gonić za
kobietami

womankind ('łumen,kajnd) s.
kobiety; ród niewieści

womanlike ('łumen,lajk) adj.
kobiecy

womanly ('łumenly) adj. kobiecy

womb (łu:m) s. macica; łono;
żywot

women (łymyn) pl. zob, woman

womenfolk ('łymynfouk) =
womankind

won (łan) v. zob. win

wonder ('łander) s. zdumienie;
cud; v. dziwić się; być ciekaw; zastanawiać się

wonderful ('łanderful) adj.
cudowny

wonderland ('łanderlaend) s.
kraina cudów (czarów)

wonderment ('łanderment) s.
zdziwienie; zdumienie

wondering ('łanderyng) adj.
zdumiony; niedowierzający

wonderwork ('łanderłe:rk)
s. cud

wonder-worker ('łanderłe:rker)
s. cudotwórca

wonder-working ('łanderłe:rkyng)
adj. sprawiający cuda

wondrous ('łandres) adj. cudowny; adv. cudownie

wont; wont; wonted (łont;
łont; łantyd)

wont (łant) v. przyzwyczajać;
mieć zwyczaj; s. zwyczaj;
przyzwyczajenie

won't (łount) = will not

wonted ('łantyd) adj. zwykły

woo (łu:) v. zalecać się (do
kobiety): umizgać się; ubiegać
się; namawiać do czegoś

wood (łud) s. drzewo; drewno;
lasek; pl; lasy; puszcza;
v. obsadzać drzewami; dostarczać drzewo

woodbine ('łudbajn) s. powój
wonny; wiciokrzew pomorski

woodblock ('łudblok) s. drzeworyt (do odciskania)

wood carving ('łudka:rwyng) s.
drzeworytnictwo

woodchuck ('łudczak) s. świstak

wood coal ('łudkoul) s. węgiel
drzewny

woodcock ('łudkok) s. słomka

woodcraft ('łudkra:ft) s. znajomość lasu

woodcraftsman ('łudkra:ftsmen)
s. myśliwy; traper

woodcut ('łudkat) s. drzeworyt

woodcutter ('łudkater) s.
drwal; drzeworytnik

wooded ('łudyd) adj. lesisty;
zalesiony

wooden ('łudn) adj.drewniany;
tępy

wood engraver (,łudyn'grejwer)
s. drzeworytnik

wood engraving(,łudyn'grejwyng)
s. drzeworytnictwo

wooden head ('łudn,hed) s. głupiec

woodland ('łudlaend) s. las;
lesisty okręg; adj. lesisty
leśny

woodman ('łudmen) s. drwal;
leśnik

wood notes('łudnouts) s. dźwię-
ki lasu

woodpecker ('łud,peker) s. dzięcioł

wood pulp ('łud,palp) s. miazga
drzewna

woodruff ('łudraf) s. marzan-
na (wonna)

woodshed ('łud,szed) s. drwal-
nia; drewutnia

woodsman ('łudsmen) s. mieszkaniec lasu; drwal

wood sorrel('łudserel) s. szcza-
wik zajęczy

woodsy (łudzy) adj. leśny

wood wind ('łud,łynd) s.(dęty)
instrument drewmiany

woodwork (łudłe:rk) s. wyroby
drzewne; części drewniane (np.
ramy okien etc.); drewniana
część budowy; budowa drewniana; stolarka; ciesiołka

woody ('łudy) adj. lesisty;
drewniany

wooer ('łu:er) s. zalotnik

woof (łu:f) s. wątek

wool (łul) s. wełna (czesana,
strzyżona, zgrzebna); czupryna; włosy (wełniste); owcze
runo; wełniane rzeczy

wool-bal ('łulbo:l) s. kłębek
wełny

woolen ('łuln) adj. wełniany;
s. wyrób wełniany

wool fat ('łulfaet) s. lanolina

woolfell, ('łulfel) s. barani-
ca; skóra owcza

woolgathering ('łul,gaedzeryng)
adj. głupio rozmarzony (roztargniony); s. głupie marzy-
cielstwo

woollen ('łulyn) adj. wełniany;
pl, tkanina wełniana

woolly ('łuly) adj. wełnisty;
oschły (głos); mętny umysł;
nie soczysty; mączasty;
włókniasty (owoc); zamazany;
(slang): surowy i niekulturalny; s. wełniana odzież; (slang):
owca

wooly ('łuly) = woolly

woozy ('łu:zy) adj. (slang):
wstawiony; otumaniony; nie-
zdrow

word,(łe:rd) s. słowo; wyraz;
słówko; komplement; przechwał-
ka; obelga; mowa; wieść; rozkaz; adv. ustnie; słownie;
adj. słowami wyrażony; v. wyrazić; redagować; sformułować;
ubierać w szatę słowną; przybierać w słowa

wordage ('łe:rdydż) s. ilość
słów

word-blind('łe:rd,blajnd) adj.
niezdolny do rozumienia pisma

wordbook ('łe:rd,buk) s. słownik

wording ('łe:rdyng) s. ujęcie,
wyrażenie słowami

wordplay, ('łe:rd,plej) s.
gra słów

word-splitter('łe:rd,splyter)
s. pedant słowny

word-splitting ('łe:rd,splytyng)
s. sofistyka; dzielenie włosa
na czworo

wordy ('łe:rdy) adj. rozwlekły;
gadatliwy; słowny (wojna słów)

wore (ło:r) v. zob. wear

work ; worked; worked (łe:rk;
łe:rkt; łe:rkt)

work (łe:rk) s. praca; robota;
zajęcie; energia; zadanie;
dzieło; utwor; uczynek;
pl. fabryka; huta; fortyfika-
cje; ozdoby; v. pracować;
działać; funkcjonować; skutkować; oddziaływać; wywoływać;
sprawiać; wymuszać; kazać
robić; prowadzić; obsługiwać;
poruszać (motor); posuwać (się);
przesuwać (się); wprawiać w
(pasję); nadawać kształt;
przeprowadzać przez coś; obrabiać; urabiać (się); wyszy-
wać; robic robótkę; (slang):
wykorzystywać (znajomości);
drgać; burzyć; falować; fermentować; trzeszczeć (statek);
źle działać (maszyna); wyczerpać się; odrabiać; wypracować;
wytwarzać; uzyskiwać z trudem;
podniecać (się) stopniowo; za-
znajamiać się z czyms; mieszać
w całość; dokazywać (cudów);
wywierać (wpływ); urabiać; fa-
sonować; exploatować (kopalnie itp.)

work away ('łe:rke,łej) v.
pracować zawzięcie

work in ('łe:rkyn) v. pasować;
wprowadzać cos

work off ('łe:rko:f) v. pozbywać się czegos

work on ('łe:rkon) v. pracować dalej

work out ('łe:rkaut) v. przeprowadzać; realizować; obliczać; rozwiązywać; wyczerpywać; wyeksploatować; skończyć; wynosić (w sumie)

work up ('łe:rkap) v. pod-
niecać(się); doprowadzać
(się); opracowywać; wyrabiać;
rozwijać; wspinać się; podnosić (się)

workable ('łe:rkebl) adj.
możliwy (do obróbki, uprawy
etc.); opłacalny; wykonalny;
realny; możliwy do przeprowa-
dzenia; w stanie używalności

workaday ('łe:rkedej) adj.
codzienny; roboczy; powszedni

work-basket ('łe:rk,ba:skyt)
s. koszyk z robótką

workbook ('łe:rk,buk) s. podręcznik ze wskazówkami;
dziennik pracy

workbox ('łe:rkboks) s. pudełko z przyborami do szycia

workday ('łe:rkdej) adj.
dzień roboczy; dzień powszedni

worker ('łe:rker) s. pracownik;
robotnik

workhouse ('łe:rk,haus) s.
dom poprawczy; przytułek

working ('łe:rkyng) adj. pracujący; pracowniczy; roboczy;
praktyczny; działający; czynny; ruchomy; powszedni;
s. praca; robota; działanie;
ruch; roboczodniówka; obróbka

working capital ('łe:rkyng -
kaepytl) s. kapitał obrotowy

working knowledge ('łe:rkyng-
'nolydż) s. wiedza praktycz-
na

working-class ('łe:rkyng'-
kla:s) s. klasa robotnicza

working day ('łe:rkyngdej)
s. dzień pracy

working hours ('łe:rkyng,au-
ers) s. godziny pracy

working load ('łe:rkyng,loud)
s. ciężar użyteczny; nośność

workingman ('łe:rkyng,men) s.
robotnik

working pressure ('łe:rkyng,pre-
szer) s. ciśnienie robocze

workless ('łe:rklys) adj. & s.
bezrobotny

worklike ('łe:rklajk) adj. dobrze wykonany; dobrze nasta-
wiony do pracy

workman ('łe:rkmen) s. pl.
workmen ('łe:rkmen); robotnik
(fizyczny); fachowiec

workmanship ('łe:rkmanszyp) s.
wykonanie; jakość wykonania;
faktura; twór

work of art ('łe:rk-ow,a:rt) s.
dzieło sztuki

workout ('łe:rkaut) s. trening;
zaprawa; danie komuś szkoły

workroom ('łe:rk'rum) s. pracownia

works council ('łe:rks'kansl) s.
rada zakładowa

workshop ('łe:rkszop) s. pracownia; warsztat; zakład; posiedzenie

workshy ('łe:rkszaj) s. próżniak

worktable ('łe:rktejbl) s.
biurko

workup ('łe:rkap) s. podniecenie (się); powalanie podczas
druku

workwoman ('łe:rkłumen) s. pl.
workwomen ('łe:rkłymyn) ; robotnica; pracownica fizyczna

world (łe:rld) s. świat; ziemia; kula ziemska; sfery; masa; mnóstwo; zatrzęsienie czegoś; bezmiar; wielka ilość
adj. światowy

worldling ('łe:rldlyng) s.
człowiek oddany sprawom doczesnym

worldly ('łe:rldly) adj. światowy; ziemski; doczesny

worldminded ('łe:rld'majndyd)
adj. oddany sprawom doczesnym

world old ('łe:rld,old) adj.
stary jak świat

world power ('łe:rld'pałer)
s. potęga światowa; wielkie
mocarstwo

world-series ('łe:rld'sieri:z)
s. mistrzostwa palanta
(baseball) USA

world-war ('łe:rld'łor) s. wojna światowa

world-weary ('łe:rld'łeery)
adj. zmęczony życiem

world-wide ('łe:rld,łajd) adj.
światowy

world wise ('łe:rld,łajz) adj.
obyty; doświadczony

worm (łe:rm) s. robak; robaczek; glisda; dżdżownica;
gwint; zwojnik; śruba (nie
ostra); wężownica; v. wkradać się; wykradać; czołgać
się; wyciągać(tajemnice z
kogoś); czyścić (zwierzę)
z robaków; czyścić (grządkę)
z robaków

wormcast ('łe:rm,ka:st) s.
gleba wydalana przez dżdżow-
nicę

worm-eaten ('łe:rm,i:tn) adj.
robaczywy; stłoczony przez
robaki; (slang); przestarzały

worm-fishing ('łe:rm,fyszyn)
s. łowienie ryb na robaki

worm gear('łe:rm,gier) s.
przekładnia ślimakowa

wormhole ('łe:rm,houl) s.
dziura wygryziona przez roba-
ka

wormseed ('łe:rm.si:d) s.
rośliny stosowane przeciw
robakom

worm wheel ('łe:rm,hłi:l) s.
koło przekładni ślimakowej

wormwood ('łe:rm,łud) s. pio-
łun;(też) przykrość

wormy ('łe:rmy) adj. robaczywy

worn (ło:rn) v. zob. wear;
adj. używany; noszony; pomarszczony

worn-out ('łó:rn,aut) adj. zużyty; zniszczony; wynoszony

worried ('łe:ryd) adj. zatros-
kany; zaniepokojony

worriment (łe:ryment) s. zmartwienie

worrisome (łe:rysem) adj. trа-
piący; lubiący się martwić

worry (łe:ry) v. dręczyć (się);
martwić (się); trapić (się);
zadręczać; zamartwiać; naprzykrzać (się); narzucać (się);
napastować; kąsać; szarpać zębami; s. zmartwienie; troska;
kłopot; kąsanie (zdobyczy przez
psa)

worry along ('łe:rye,long) v.
uporać się z trudnościami

worry dawn ('łe:ry,dałn) v. połykać łapczywie

worry out ('łe:ry,aut) v. rozwiązać z wysiłkiem (np. problem)

worse (łe:rs) adj. gorszy (niż:
bad; evil; ill); podniszczony;
słabszy; bardziej chory;
s. coś gorszego; to co najgor-
sze; najgorszy stan; najgorszy
wypadek; v. pogarszać się;
adv. gorzej; bardziej

worsen ('łe:rsn) v. pogorszyć
(się)

worship ('łe:rszyp) s. cześć;
kult; uwielbienie; nabożeństwo;
bałwochwalstwo; v. czcić;
wielbić; uwielbiać; brać udział
w nabożeństwie

woshipful ('łe:rszypful) adj.
pełen czci; czcigodny

worship(p)er ('łe:rszyper) s.
czciciel

worst (łe:rst) adj. najgorszy;
s. coś najgorszego; najgorszy
wypadek; adj. najgorzej; najbardziej; (slang); bardzo
v. pokonać; wziąć nad kims górę; zadać klęskę; pobić

worsted ('łustyd) adj. czesan-
kowy; s. kamgarn; przędza wełniana czesana; czesanka

worth (łe:rs) s. wartość; cena;
adj. wart; opłacający się

worthless ('łe:rslys) adj. bezwartościowy

worth reading ('łe:rs'ri:dyng)
adj. wart czytania

worth seeing ('łe:rs'si:yng)
adj. wart widzenia

worthwhile ('łe:rshłajl) adj.
wart zachodu; opłacający się

worthy ('łe:rɛy) adj. godny;
wartościowy; poczciwy;
s. godny człowiek; wybitny
człowiek (też żartem)

would (łud) v. zob. will
(forma warunkowa)

would be ('łud,bi:) adj. rzekomy; niedoszły; adv. rzekomo;
niby to

wound (łu:nd) s. rana; v. ranić; zob. v. wind

wounded ('łu:ndyd) adj. ranny;
urażony

wove (łouw) v. zob. weave

woven ('łouwn) v. zob. weave

wow (łau) (slang): s. szlagier;
świetna rzecz; v. mieć powodzenie; wywoływać zachwyt
excl.: au !;cudownie !

wrack (raek) s. = wreck (age);
chwasty morskie wyrzucone na
brzeg; używane na nawóz

wraith (rejs) s. sobowtór;
cień (duch)

wrangle ('raengl) s. kłótnia;
burda; v. kłócić się; (slang):
pilnować koni

wrangler ('raengler) s. kłótnik;
pastuch koński (kowboj)

wrap; wrapt; wrapt (raep;
raept; raept)

wrap (raep) v. zawijać; owijać;
zapakowywać; spowijać; otulać
się; okrywać (się); zachodzić
na siebie; s. szal; chusta;
okrycie

wrap up ('raepap) v. owijać
(się); pakować

wrapper ('raeper) s. opakowanie; opaska; obwoluta; bande-
rola; papierek; bibułka; osłona; podomka (damska); pako-
wacz

wrapping ('raepyng) s. opakowanie

wrapping paper ('raepyng pejper) s. papier do pakowania

wrapt (raept) v. zob. wrap

wrasse (raes) s. (ryba) wargacz

wrath (ra:s) s. gniew; oburzenie

wrathful (ra:sful) adj. gniewny

wreak (ri:k) v. wywierać (zem-
stę); dawać upust; wyładować
(gniew)

wreath(ri:s) s. wieniec

wreathe (ri:z) v. wieńczyć; wić
się; splatać; spowijać; pleść
się; kłębić się (dym etc.)

wreck (rek) s. ruina; wrak;
rozbicie się (np.statku); katastrofa; szczątki (np. na wodzie); zniszczenie; rozbitek
życiowy; kaleka; wypadek;
v. rozbić (pojazd); zniweczyć
(nadzieje); burzyć; być roz-
bitym; spowodować rozbicie;
zrujnować; mieć wypadek

wreckage ('rekydż) s. rozbicie;
szczątki; gruzy

wrecked ('rekt) adj. rozbity;
zniszczony; zepsuty

wrecking company ('rekyng'kampeny) s. przedsiębiorstwo
rozbiórki budynków

wrecking service ('rekyng'se:r-
wys) s. przewóz zepsutych samochodów

wrecker ('reker) s. sprawca wypadku; ciężarówka (z dźwigiem)
do przewozu zepsutych samochodów; kierowca przewożący ze-
psute samochody; przedsiębiorca rozbiórki budynków; przedsiębiorca wydobywania zatopio-
nych statków; człowiek kradnący
szczątki statku; szkodnik; roz-
bijacz małżeństwa

wren (ren) s. strzyżyk

wrench (rencz) s. gwałtowne
skręcenie; ukręcenie; szarpnięcie; wykręcenie; zwichnięcie; przekręcenie (faktów);
ból (rozstania); klucz maszynowy; klucz nasadowy; klucz
nakrętkowy; v. szarpnąć;
skręcić; wykręcić; zwichnąć
(nogę); przekręcać(fakty);
ukręcać

wrench open ('rencz'oupen) v.
odkręcic; otwierac; odsrubo-
wywac
wrench off ('rencz,o:f) v. wy-
rywac; wykręcic; ukręcic
(głowę)
wrest (rest) v. wykręcac; wy-
rywac; przekręcac (fakty);
wydobywac zeznania; s. wykręcanie; wyrywanie; klucz
do strojenia (harfy)
wrest from ('restfrom) v. wyrwac komus
wrestle ('resl) v. mocowac
się; zmagac się; borykac się;
walczyc; s. zapasy; walka
wrestler ('resler) s. zapasnik
wrestling ('reslyng) s. za-
pasnictwo
wrestpins ('rest,pynz) pl. koł-
ki na struny fortepianowe
wretch (recz) s. nieszczęsnik;
biedaczysko; biedak; nędzarz;
łajdak; łotr; nikczemnik
wretched ('reczyd) adj. nie-
szczęsliwy; pechowy; biedny;
nędzny; marny; fatalny;
ochydny; wstrętny; nadzwyczajny (łotr)
wrick (ryk) v. lekko zwichnąc;
nadwyrężyc; s. zwichnięcie;
lekkie naderwanie
wriggle ('rygl) v. wic się;
wkręcac (się); kręcic; wy-
winąc się; s. ruch wijący
się; wicie
wriggle along ('rygle'long)
v. posuwac się wijąc
wriggle in ('rygl,yn) v. wkręcac się
wriggle out ('ryglaut) v. wykręcac się
wright (rajt) s. robotnik;
tworca
wring; wrung; wrung (ryng;
rang; rang)
wring (ryng) v. wyzymac; wykręcac; ukręcic (łeb); przekręcac (słowa); sciskac (serce); usciskac (rękę); wymoc
(cos na kims); zniekształcic;
s. wyzymanie; uscisk; scis-
kanie; wyżęcie; wycisnięcie;

wringer (rynger) s. wyżymaczka
wrinkle ('rynkl) s. zmarszczka;
fałda; zmarszczenie; (slang):
ciekawy pomysł; rada
v. marszczyc (się); byc pomar-
szczonym; zmiąc (się)
wrinkle up ('rynklap) v. po-
marszczyc
wrinkly (rynkly) adj. pomarszczony
wrist (ryst) s. przegub; ruch
ręki w przegubie
wristband ('rystbaend) s. mankiet u koszuli
wristwatch ('ryst,łocz) s.
zegarek na rękę
writ (ryt) s. nakaz pisemny;
prawny
writ for ('ryt,fo:r) s. rozpi-
sanie (wyborow)
write; wrote; written (rajt;
rout; rytn)
write (rajt) v. pisac; napisac;
zapisac; wypisac; komponowac;
wstawiac (czek); spisywac;
sławic (piórem)
write back ('rajt,baek) v. od-
pisywac (komus)
write down ('rajtdałn) v. spisywac; notowac; okreslac (ujem-
nie)
write home ('rajt,houm) v. pisac do domu
write-in ('rajt,yn) v. wpisy-
wac; dopisywac
write-off ('rajt,of) v. odpisy-
wac (na straty); pisac na
prędce
write out ('rajt,aut) v. wypi-
sywac; sporządzac
write-up ('rajt,ap) v. zapisywac; opisywac; przesadnie szacowac; pochwalic
writer ('rajter) s. pisarz;
niżej podpisany; powiescio-
pisarz
writhe (rajs) v. wic się (z bolu); cierpiec (zniewagę);
skręcac się (ze wstydu)
writing ('rajtyng) s. pismo;
utwor; artykuł; pisanie;
pismiennictwo; sztuka pisania;
praca literacka;napisana rzecz

writing desk ('rajtyng,desk)
s. biurko; pulpit

writing ink ('rajtyng,ynk)
s. atrament

writing paper ('rajtyng,pej-
per) s. papier listowy; papier do pisania

writing table ('rajtyng,tejbl)
s. biurko

written ('rytn) v. zob.: rite;
adj. pisany

wrong (ro:ng) adj. zły; niewłaściwy; błędny; nie w porządku; mylny; niekorzystny;
niesprawiedliwy; s. zło; wykroczenie; krzywda; wina; pomyłka; grzech; strata; niesprawiedliwość; v. skrzyw-
dzić; niesłusznie posądzać;
być niesprawiedliwym;
adv. mylnie; niewłaściwie;
błędnie; źle; zdrożnie; nie-
korzystnie

wrongdoer ('ro:ng'du:er) s.
krzywdziciel; grzesznik;
winowajca

wrongdoing ('ro:ng'duyng) s.
nadużycia; wykroczenia;
grzechy; przestępstwa

wrongful ('ro:ngful) adj.zły;
krzywdzący; niesprawiedliwy;
bezprawny

wronghead ('ro:ng'hed) v.
przekręcać (słowa etc.)

wrongheaded ('ro:ng'hedyd)
adj. uparty; przewrotny

wrote (rout) v. zob. write

wroth (ro:g) adj. gniewny

wrought (ro:t) v. zob. work

wrought iron ('ro:t'ajern)
s. kute żelazo

wrought-up ('ro:t,ap) adj.
napięty; zdenerwowany

wrung ('rang) v. zob. wring

wry (raj) adj. krzywy; okrzy-
wiony

wryneck ('rajnek) s. zastrzał
szyi; kręcz karku

wynd (łajnd) s. (kręta) uliczka

x (eks) dwudziesta czwarta litera angielskiego alfabetu;
rzymska cyfra 10; niewiadoma

xenon ('zenon) s. ksenon

xenophobia (,zene'foubje) s.
ksenofobia

Xmas ('krysmes) = Christmas

x-ray ('eks'rej) adj. rentge-
nowski; v. prześwietlać; robić
zdjęcie rentgenowskie

x-ray diagnosis ('eks'rej,da-
jeg'nouzys) s. rozpoznanie
rentgenowskie

x-ray examination ('eks'rej-
yg'zaemynejszyn) s. badanie
rentgenowskie

x-ray picture ('eks'rej'pykczer)
s. zdjęcie rentgenowskie

x-rays ('eks'rejs) pl. promienie rentgenowskie

xylem ('zajlem) s. drewno

xylophagous (zaj'lofeges) adj.
drzewożerny

xylophone ('zylefoun) s. ksylo-
fon

y (łaj) dwudziesta piąta litera
angielskiego alfabetu

yabber ('jaeber) v. gadać

yacht (jot) s. jacht; y. płynąć
jachtem; urządząc wyścigi jach-
towe

yachting ('jotyng) s. sport
żeglarski

yak (jaek) s. jak; (slang): gadanie; śmiech; v. gadać; śmiać
się

yap (jaep) v. ujadać; (slang);
paplać; s. ujadanie; paplanina;
krzykacz; jadaczka

yard (ja:rd) s. jard (91.44 cm);
podwórze; dziedziniec; v. umieszczać w ogrodzeniu

yarn (ja:rn) s. włókno; przędza;
historyjka; v. opowiadać histo-
ryjki

yawn (jo:n) v. ziewać; ziąć; zionąć; s. ziewnięcie; ziewanie

ye (ji:) pron. wy (biblijne)

yea (jej) adv. tak; s. głosowanie "tak"

yeah (jej) (slang): tak; excl.:
tak !;nie wierzę !

year (je:r) s. rok

yearly ('je:rly) adj. roczny;
coroczny; adv. corocznie;
s. rocznik;adv.raz na rok

yearn (je:rn) v. tęsknić

yeast (ji:st) s. drożdże; ferment; piana; v. fermentować; pienić (się)

yell (jel) v. wrzeszczeć; s.wrzask; dopingowanie

yellow ('jelou) adj. żółty; (slang): tchórzliwy; zawistny; żółty z zazdrości; n. żółty kolor; żółtko; v. żółknąć; powodować zółknięcie

yelp (jelp) s. skowyt; v. skowyczeć

yeoman ('joumen) s. podoficer marynarki; (dawniej) wolny chłop

yep (jep) adv. (slang): tak

yes (jes) adv. tak; v.potakiwać

yesterday ('jesterdy) adv. & s. wczoraj

yet (jet) adv. & conj. dotąd; jeszcze do tej pory; na razie; jak dotąd; jednak; ani też; mimo to

yew (ju:) s. cis

Yiddish (jydysz) s. język żydowski

yield (ji:ld) v. wydawać; dawać; rodzić; przynosić; oddawać (się); porzucać; ustępować; s. plon; zysk; wydajność

yielding (ji:ldyng) s. wydajność; adj. ustępliwy

yogurt ('jouguert) s. jogurt

yoke (jouk) s. jarzmo; v. zaprzęgać; nakładać jarzmo; (slang): zaskakiwać (przechodnia) w celu rabunku

yolk (jouk) s. żółtko; rodzaj łoju

yonder ('jonder) adj. & adv. tam dalej; tamten

you (ju:) pron. ty; wy; pan; pani; panowie; panie

you'd (ju:d) = you would; you had

you'll (ju:l) = you shall; you will

young (jang) adj. młody; młodzieńczy; młodociany

youngster ('jangster) s. dziecko; młodzik

your (ju:r) adj. twój; wasz; pański

you're (jo:r) = you are

yours (juers) pron. twój; wasz; pański (z poważaniem)

yourself (,juer'self) pron. ty sam

yourselves (,juer'selvz) pron. wy sami

youth (ju:s) s. młodość

youths (ju:dz) pl. młodzież; młodzieniec

youthful ('ju:sful) adj. młody; młodzieńczy

youth-hostel ('ju:s'hostl) s, schronisko młodzieżowe

you've ('ju:w) = you have

Yugoslav ('ju:gou'sla:w) adj. jugosłowiański

z (zi:) dwudziesta szósta litera alfabetu angielskiego

zany ('zejny) adj. pocieszny; błazenski; s. błazen; głupek

zeal (zi:l) s. gorliwość

zealous ('zeles) adj. gorliwy

zebra ('zi:bre) s. zebra; (slang): mulat; adj.pręgowany

zebra crossing ('zi:bre'krosyng) s. pasami znaczone przejście jezdni dla pieszych

zenith ('senit) s. zenit; szczyt (sławy)

zero ('zierou) s. zero; v. ustawiać na zero; brać na cel

zest (zest) s. smak; pikanteria; rozkosz; zamiłowanie; v. dodawać pikanterii

zigzag ('zygzaeg) s. zygzak; adj. zygzakowaty; adv. zygzakiem

zinc (zynk) s. cynk; v. cynkować

zip (zyp) s. świst; wigor; v. śmigać; gnać; zapinać zamek błyskawiczny

zip code ('zyp,koud) s. numeracja pocztowa miejscowości

zipper ('zyper) s. zamek błyskawiczny

zippy ('zypy) adj. żywy; zgrabny
zloty ('zlouty) s. złoty (pieniądz polski); adj. golden
zodiac ('zoudjaek) s. zodiak
zombie ('zomby) s. bóg-pyton;
(slang); bałwan; tuman
zone (zoun) s. strefa; zona; v.
opasywać; dzielić na zony

zoo (zu:) s. ogród zoologiczny
zoology (zou'oledży) s. zoolo-
gia
zoom (zu:m) v. buczeć; wzlatywać;
wzbijać się szybko; śmigać;
s. poderwanie (samolotu);
soczewka zbliżająca w aparacie
do filmowania oraz w aparacie do
fotografowania

Appendix

ABBREVIATIONS – SKRÓTY

a.	– attribute	– przydawka
adj.	– adjective	– przymiotnik
adj. f.	– adjective feminine	– przymiotnik żeński
adj. m.	– adjective masculine	– przymiotnik męski
adj. n.	– adjective neuter	– przymiotnik nijaki
adv.	– adverb	– przysłówek
am.	– American	– amerykański
chem.	– chemistry	– chemia
conj.	– conjunction	– spójnik
constr.	– construction	– budowa
etc.	– and so on	– i tak dalej
excl.	– exclamation	– wykrzyknik
expr.	– expression	– wyrażenie
f.	– substantive feminine	– rzeczownik żeński
gram.	– grammar	– gramatyka
hist.	– history	– historia
hyp.	– hyphen	– łącznik
indecl.	– indeclinable	– nieodmienny
inf.	– infinitive	– bezokolicznik
m.	– substantive musculine	– rzeczownik męski
m.in.	– among others	– między innymi
n.	– substantive neuter	– rzeczownik nijaki
num.	– numeral	– liczebnik
part.	– particle	– partykuła
pl.	– substantive plural	– rzeczownik liczba mnoga
poet.	– poetry	– poezja
polit.	– politics	– polityka
p.p.	– past participle	– imiesłów czasu przeszłego
prep.	– preposition	– przyimek
pron.	– pronoun	– zaimek
s.	– substantive	– rzeczownik
sb.	– somebody	– ktoś
slang	– slang	– gwara, żargon
v.	– verb	– czasownik
vulg.	– vulgarity	– ordynarność
wg	– according to	– według
W.W. II	– World War II	– druga wojna światowa
zob.	– see	– zobacz

<u>SAY IT IN POLISH</u>!

POLISH CONVERSATIONS FOR TRAVELERS TO POLAND
WITH COMPLETE PRONUNCIATION GUIDE AND WITH A
DETAILED DESCRIPTION OF POLISH FOOD

1
Excuse me, where is the passport control?

Przepraszam, gdzie jest kontrola paszportowa?
pshe-pra-sham, gdźhe yest kon-tró-la pash-por-tó-va

The passport control booth is straight ahead.

Kontrola paszportowa znajduje się tam na wprost.
kon-tró-la pash-por-tó-va znay-dóó--ye śhäñ tam na vprost

Your passport, please.

Proszę o pański paszport.
pró-shäñ o päñ-skee pásh-port

Here is my passport.

Oto mój paszport.
o-to mooy pásh-port

2
Thank you, your visa is in order.

Dziękuję, pańska wiza jest w porządku.
dźhän-kóó-yäñ, päñ-ska veé-za yest v po-zhóẃnd-koo

Could you tell me where to exchange my money vouchers?

Czy mógłby pan mi powiedzieć gdzie mogę zrealizować kwit wymiany?
chi móögw-bi pan mee po-vyé-dźhech gdźhe mó-gäñ zre-a-lee-zó-vach kveet vi-myá-ni

Money exchange is inside on your right.

Wymiana waluty jest wewnątrz po prawej stronie.
vi-myá-na va-lóó-ti yest vév-nóẃntsh po prá-vey stro-ñe

Thank you.

Dziękuję,
dźhän-kóó-yäñ

3
Please, exchange my voucher.

Proszę zrealizować mój kwit wymiany.
pró-shäñ zre-a-lee-zó-vach mooy kveet vi-myá-ni

I would like to exchange a fifty-dollar bill.

Chciałbym wymienić banknot pięćdziesięciodolarowy.
khćháw-bim vi-myé-ñeech bank-not pyäñćh-dźhe-śhäñ-cho-do-la-ró-vi

Here is your exchange receipt.

Oto pański dowód wymiany.
o-to päñ-skee dó-voot vi-myá-ni

Here is your money.

Oto pańskie pieniądze.
o-to päñ-ske pye-ñóẃñ-dze

Thank you.

Dziękuję panu.
dźhän-kóó-yäñ pá-noo

4
Please, remember that you will need your exchange receipt later during your stay in Poland.

Proszę pamiętać że dowód wymiany będzie panu potrzebny później, w czasie pobytu w Polsce.
pró-shäñ pa-myäñ-tach zhe dó-voot vi-myá-ni bäñ-dźhe pá-noo po-tsheb-ni póóźh-ñey, v chá-śhe po-bí-too v póls-tse

I am glad you told me that.

Dziękuję że pan mi to powiedział.
dźhän-kóó-yäñ zhe pan mee to po-vyé-dźhaw

Have a good time.

Życzę przyjemnego pobytu.
zhí-chäñ pshi-yem-né-go po-bí-too

Thank you, where are the customs?

Dziękuję, gdzie jest odprawa celna?
dźhän-kóó-yäñ, gdźhe yest odprá-va tsel-na

5

You will find the customs near
the exit.

Odprawa celną jest przy wyjściu.
od-prá-va tsel-na yest pshi víy-sh-
choo

I'll see you later.

Do widzenia.
do-vee-dzé-ňa

Here is my baggage.

Oto mój bagaż.
ó-to mooy bá-gazh

Do you have anything to declare?

Czy ma pan coś do oclenia?
chi ma pan tsosh do o-tslé-ňa

No I have only personal items.

Nie,   mam tylko rzeczy osobiste.
ňe,   mam tíl-ko zhé-chi o-so-beés-te

6

Please, open this suitcase!

Proszę otworzyć tą walizkę!
pró-shaň ot-vó-zhich town va-leéz-kaň

What is in this package?

Co jest w tym zawiniątku?
tso yest v tim za-vee-ňównt-koo

Small gift- toy for a child.

Mała zabawka, podarunek dla dziecka.
ma-wa za-báv-ka, po-da-roó-nek dla
dźéts-ka

You may close your suitcase.

Może pan zamknąć walizkę.
mó-zhe pan zámk-nównch va-leéz-kaň

What do you have in this bag?

Co ma pan w tej torbie?
tso ma pan v tey tór-bye

7

Mainly small personal things and
magazines and a book.

Głównie drobne rzeczy osobiste, cza-
sopisma i książkę.
gwoóv-ňe drob-ne zhé-chi o-so-beés-te
cha-so-peés-ma ee kshównzh-kaň

Thank you, you may proceed.

Dziękuję, może pan iść.
dźáň-koó-yaň, mó-zhe pan eesh-ch

Porter, please, take my luggage
to a taxi.

Bagażowy, proszę zanieść mój bagaż
do taksówki.
ba-ga-zhó-vi, pró-shan zá-ňeshch
mooy bá-gazh do tak-soóv-kee

Here   you are.

Proszę, to dla Pana.
pró-shaň, to dla pa-na

8

I want to go to the Hotel Forum.

Chcę jechać do hotelu Forum.
khtsaň yé-khach do kho-té-loo fó-rum

Do you know where it is?

Czy pan wie gdzie to jest?
chi pan vye gdźhe to yest

Of course!

Oczywiście!
o-chi-veésh-che

Do you speak English?

Czy pan mówi po angielsku?
chi pan moóvee po an-ǵél-skoo

I speak a little English;
please, speak slowly.

Mówię trochę po angielsku; proszę
mówić powoli.
moóv-yäň tró-khaň po an-ǵél-skoo;
pró-shaň moó-veech po-vó-lee

9

How far is it to the hotel?

Jak daleko jest do hotelu?
yak da-lé-ko yest do kho-té-loo

Almost half an hour's ride, about
ten kilometers.

Prawie pół godziny jazdy, około dziesięciu kilometrów.
pra-vye poow go-dzhée-ni yáz-di, o-kó-
wo dzhe-śhāñćh kee-lo-mét-roov

How much is the fare?

Ile kosztuje przejazd?
ée-le kosh-tóo-ye pshe-yazd

The fare is a hundred fifty zl.

Opłata za przejazd wynosi sto pięćdziesiąt złotych.
o-pwa-ta za pshe-yazd vi-nó-śhee sto
pyáñćh-dźhé-śhownt zwó-tikh

Please get in.

Proszę wsiadać.
pro-śhāñ vśha-daćh

10

Here is your money!

Proszę, to dla Pana.
pro-śhāñ, to dla pa-na

Keep the change.

Proszę zatrzymać resztę.
pro-śhāñ za-tshi-maćh resh-tāñ

I like your service, how can I
reach you again?

Jestem zadowolony, jak można pana
znaleźć?
yés-tem za-do-vo-ló-ni, yak mózh-na
pá-na zná-leźhćh?

My telephone number is two zero
zero thirty.

Mój numer telefonu jest dwa zero
zero trzydzieści.
mooy nóó-mer te-le-fó-noo yest dva
zé-ro zé-ro tshi-dźéśh-chee

11

Please, write your number here.

Proszę mi ten numer tu zapisać.
pró-śhāñ mee ten nóó-mer too za-pée-
saćh

Thank you very much.

Dziękuję bardzo.
dźhāñ-kóó-yāñ bár-dzo

Goodbye.

Do widzenia.
do-vee-dzé-ńa

I have a reservation here.

Mam tu rezerwację.
mam too re-zer-vá-tsyāñ

What is your name?

Jak Pana nazwisko?
yak pá-na naz-veés-ko

12

My name is Jimmy Karter.

Nazywam się Jimmy Karter.
na-zí-vam śhāñ dzhí-mi Kár-ter

I have a room for you.

Mam dla pana pokój.
mam dla pá-na pó-kooy

Please register.

Proszę się zarejestrować.
pró-śhāñ śhāñ za-re-yes-tró-vaćh

You can pick up your passport
tomorrow.

Może pan odebrać paszport jutro.
mo-zhe pan o-déb-raćh pásh-port
yóót-ro

Porter, room two zero two for
Mister Karter.

Portier, pokój dwa zero dwa dla
pana Karter'a.
pór-tyer, pó-kooy dva zé-ro dva
dla pá-na Kar-té-ra

13

The room is on the third floor.

Pokój jest na trzecim piętrze.
pó-kooy yest na tshé-cheem pyáń-tshe

Let us take the elevator.

Pojedźmy windą.
po-yédźh-mi veén-dǒwñ

After you, madam.

Pani pierwsza.
pá-ñee pyérv-sha

Press the button, please.

Proszę przycisnąć guzik.
pró-shañ pshi-chees-nówñch goó-źheek

Open the door, please.

Proszę otworzyć drzwi.
pró-shañ ot-vó-zhich dzhvee

14

Let us go left then right.

Chodźmy na lewo a potem na prawo.
khóch-mi na lé-vo a pó-tem na prá-vo

Here is the bath and here is the
closet.

Tu jest łazienka a tu jest szafa.
too yest wa-źhén-ka a too yest shá-fa

The telephone is beside the TV set.

Tu jest telefon obok telewizora.
too yest te-lé-fon ó-bok te-le-vee-zó-ra

Press this button for the maid.

Proszę przycisnąć ten guzik aby wezwać pokojowa.
pró-shañ pshi-chees-nówñch ten goó-
źheek á-bi véz-vach po-ko-yó-vǒwñ

Here is your key.

Oto pański klucz.
ó-to páñ-skee klooch

15

Please, show me the soap and the
towels.

Proszę mi pokazać mydło i ręcznik.
pró-shañ mee po-ká-zach míd-wo ee
ráñch-ñeek

May I have my suit dry cleaned
here in the hotel?

Czy mogę oddać moje ubranie do pralni chemicznej tu w hotelu?
chi mó-gäñ ód-dach mó-ye oo-brá-ñe
do, prál-ñee khe-meéch-ney too v kho-
te-loo

I want my shoes shined.

Chciałbym mieć wyczyszczone buty.
khcháw-bim myech vi-chish-chó-ne
boó-ti

May I have my suit
pressed.

Chciałbym mieć wyprasowane ubranie.
khcháw-bim myech vi-pra-so-vá-ne
oo-bra-ñe

16

I would like to have my shirts
washed.

Chciałbym mieć koszule wyprane.
khcháw-bim myech ko-shoo-le vi-prá-ne

When is the restaurant open?

Kiedy jest retauracja otwarta?
ké-di yest res-taw-ráts-ya ot-vár-ta

The restaurant is open from
7 a.m. till 11 p.m.

Restauracja jest otwarta od siódmej
rano do jedenastej wieczorem
res-taw-ráts-ya yest ot-vár-ta od
shódh-mey rá-no do ye-de-nás-tey vye-
chó-rem

Would you like to eat?

Czy chciałby Pan coś zjeść?
chi khcháw-bi pan cosh zyeść

I am hungry.

Jestem głodny./yés-tem gwód-ni/

17

Is there a swimming pool in this hotel?

Czy jest w tym hotelu basen kąpielo-wy?
chi yest v tim ho-té-loo bá-sen kówn-pye-ló-vi

Yes, there is a swimming pool in the basement.

Tak, basen kąpielowy jest w podziem-iu.
tak, bá-sen kówn-pye-ló-vi yest v pod-źhém-yoo

The swimming pool is open from six a.m. till ten p.m.

Basen kąpielowy jest otwarty od szóstej rano do dziesiątej wieczorem.
bá-sen kown-pye-ló-vi yest ot-vár-ti od shoós-tey rá-no do dźhe-shówn-tey vye-chó-rem

18

Let us go to the restaurant.

Chodźmy do restauracji.
khóch-mi do res-taw-ráts-yee

Let me make reservations.

Pozwól mi zrobić rezerwacje.
póz-vool mee zró-beech re-zer-váts-ye

May I reserve a table for three for dinner at 8 p.m. today.

Chciałbym zarezerwować stół na trzy osoby na obiad dziś o ósmej wieczorem.
khcháw-bim za-re-zer-wó-wach stoow na tshi o-só-bi na ob-yad dźheesh o oós-mey vye-chó-rem

Good evening, sir.

Dobry wieczór panu.
dob-ri vyé-choor pá-nu

Follow me, please.

Proszę iść za mną.
pró-shan eeshch za mnówn

19

Here is the menu.

Proszę, jadłospis.
pró-shan, yad-wós-pees

Which waiter serves at this table?

Który kelner obsługuje ten stół?
ktoó-ri kél-ner ob-swoo-goó-ye ten stoow

What do you wish?

Co pan sobie życzy?
tso pan só-bye zhí-chi

What kind of cuisine do you have?

Jaki rodzaj kuchni tu prowadzicie?
yá-kee ro-dzay kookh-ñee too pro-va-dźheé-che

Polish traditional and general European.

Polską tradycyjną i ogólną europej-ską.
pól-skówn tra-di-tsíy-nówn ee o-goól-nówn e-oo-ro-péy-skówn

20

What are the consommés Polish style?

Jakie są polskie zupy?
yá-ke sówn póls-ke zoó-pi

Polish consommés are traditional-ly seasoned beef or chicken broth.

Polskie rosoły z wołowiny lub kury są tradycyjnie przyprawiane.
pól-ske ro-só-wi z vo-wo-veé-ni loop koó-ri sówn tra-di-tsíy-ke pshi-pra-vyá-ne

Consommé with raw egg yolk.

Rosół z żółtkiem.
ró-soow z zhoówt-kem

Consommé with salty biscuit.

Rosół z diablotką.
ró-soow z dyab-lót-kówn

Consommé in a cup.

Rosół w filiżance.
ro-soow w fee-lee-zhán-tse

21

Polish soups cooked of bones and
served with sour cream.

Polskie zupy gotowane na kościach i
podawane z kwaśną śmietaną.
pól-ske zoó-pi go-to-va-ne na kósh-
chakh ee po-da-ya-ne z kvásh-nówn
shmye-tá-nówn

Polish beet-root soup with stuffed patties with meat or mushrooms.

Barszcz podany razem z pasztecikami
z mięsem lub grzybami.
barshch po-dá-ni rá-zem z pash-te-
chee-ká-mee z myán-sem loop gzhi-bá-
mee

Polish barley kasha soup.

Krupnik.
kroóp-ñeek

Yellow cheese soup with browned
butter, flour and sour cream

Neapolitańska z żółtego sera.
ne-a-po-lee-tán-ska z zhoow-té-go sé-
ra

22

Polish mushroom and noodle soup.

Zupa z grzybów suszonych z lanym cias-
tem.
zoó-pa z gzhi-boof soo-shó-nikh z lá-
nim chás-tem.

Polish style tomato soup with
rice.

Zupa pomidorowa z ryżem.
zoó-pa po-mee-do-ró-va z ri-zhem.

Vegetable soup.

Zupa jarzynowa.
zoó-pa ya-zhi-nó-va

Pea and smoked ham soup.

Zupa grochowa na wędzonce.
zoó-pa gr-khó-va na van-dzówn-tse

Sour cabbage soup.

Kapuśniak.
ka-poósh-ñak

23

Potato soup with browned butter
and flour.

Zupa ziemniaczana.
zoó-pa zhem-ña-chá-na

Cauliflower soup.

Zupa kalafiorowa.
zoó-pa ka-la-fyo-ró-va

Fermented meal soup with browned
bacon.

Żur z wędzonką.
zhoor z ván-dzon-kówn

Fermented meal soup with browned
sausage.

Żur z kiełbasą.
zhoor z kew-ba-sówn

Polish-Jewish bean soup with
noodles.

Zupa fasolowa po żydowsku.
zoó-pa fa-so-ló-va po zhi-dós-koo

24

Asparagus soup.

Zupa szparagowa.
zoó-pa shpa-ra-gó-va

Chicken soup with mushrooms.

Zupa z kury z grzybami.
zoó-pa z koó-ry z gzhi-bá-mee

Duck soup.

Zupa z kaczki.
zoó-pa z kách-kee

Goose soup.

Zupa z gęsi.
zoó-pa z gán-shee

Minced liver soup.

Zupa z wątroby.
zoó-pa z vówn-tró-bi

Lobster soup.

Zupa z homara.
zoó-pa z kho-má-ra

25
Barley soup with mushrooms.

Zupa jęczmienna z grzybami.
zoó-pa yañch-myén-na z gzhi-bá-mee

Calf's brain soup.

Zupa z móźdżku cielęcego.
zoó-pa z moózhj-koo che-lãñ-tse-go

Fish soup.

Zupa rybna.
zoó-pa ri-bó-va

Turtle soup.

Zupa żółwiowa.
zoó-pa zhoow-vyó-va

Bread soup with egg.

Zupa chlebowa.
zoó-pa khle-bó-va

Onion soup.

Zupa cebulowa.
zoó-pa tse-boo-ló-va

26
Lemon soup with rice.

Zupa cytrynowa z ryżem.
zoó-pa ci-tri-nó-va z ri-zhem

Caraway seed soup.

Zupa kminkowa.
zoó-pa kmeen-kó-va

Tart sorrel soup with eggs.

Zupa szczawiowa z jajkami.
zoó-pa shchav-yó-va z yay-ká-mee

Lentil soup with ham.

Zupa soczewicowa z szynką.
zoó-pa so-che-vee-tsó-va z shín-kowñ

Spring vegetable soup.

Zupa z młodych jarzyn.
zoó-pa z mwo-dikh ya-zhin

Mixed vegetable soup.

Zupa jarzynowa.
zoó-pa ya-zhi-nó-va

27
Dill pickle soup.

Ogórkowa zupa z koperkiem.
o-goor-kó-va zoó-pa z ko-pér-ḱem

Chesnut broth with vegetables.

Zupa orzechowa.
zoó-pa o-zhe-khó-va

Ukrainian barshch with Polish
sausage.

Barszcz ukraiński z polską kiełbasą.
Barshch oo-kra-eéñ-skee z pol-skówñ
kél-ba-sowñ

Fermented beetroot for barshch.

Kwas.
kvas

Clear barshch with mushrooms.

Czysty barszcz z grzybami.
Chís-ti barshch z gzhi-bá-mee

Polish barshch with sour cream.

Polski barszcz ze śmietaną.
pól-skee barshch ze shmye-tá-nówñ

28
Lenten barshch with mushrooms.

Barszcz postny z grzybami.
barshch póst-ni z gzhi-bá-mee

Zhoor on sour rye bread.

Żur na zakwaszonym chlebie.
zhoor na za-kva-shó-nim khlé-bye

Oatmeal soup with Polish sausage.

Zupa wielkanocna na kiełbasie.
zoó-pa vyel-ka-nóts-na na kél-ba-she

Oatmeal soup with salami.

Zupa wielkanocna na salami.
zoó-pa vyel-ka-nóts-na na sa-lá-mee

Beer soup with sour cream.

Zupa piwna ze śmietaną.
zoó-pa peév-na ze shmye-tá-ñówñ

Pumpkin soup with rice.

Zupa z dyni z ryżem.
zoó-pa z dí-ñee z ri-zhem

29
Vegetable broth with egg yolk.

Rosół jarzynowy z żółtkiem.
ró-soow ya-zhi-nó-vi z zhoówt-ḱem

Rice soup with onions.

Zupa ryżowa z cebulą.
zoó-pa ri-zhó-va z tse-boó-lówn

Vegetable soup with browned flour.

Zupa jarzynowa zasmażana.
zoó-pa ya-zhi-nó-va za-sma-zhá-na

Vegetable soup with sour cream.

Zupa jarzynowa ze śmietaną.
zoó-pa ya-zhi-nó-va ze shmye-tá-nówn

Kashoobyan vegetable soup.

Zupa kaszubską.
zoó-pa ka-shoób-ska

Milk soup with kasha.

Zupa mleczna z kaszą.
zoó-pa mlech-na z ka-shówn

30
What cold soups do you serve?

Jakie zimne zupy można dostać?
Yá-ḱe zeém-ne zoó-pi mózh-na dós-tach

Buttermilk soup with vegetables.

Chłodnik.
khwód-ńeek

Barshch and cucumber soup.

Zupa ogórkowa na barszczu.
zoó-pa o-goor-kó-va na barsh-choo

Apple soup with sweet cream.

Zupa jabłkowa.
zoó-pa yabw-kó-va

Blackberry soup with sour cream.

Zupa ożynowa ze śmietanką.
zoó-pa o-zhi-nó-va ze shmye-tán-kówn

Raspberry soup.

Zupa malinowa.
zoó-pa ma-li-nó-va

31
Cold almond soup.

Zimna zupa migdałowa.
zheém-na zoó-pa meeg-da-wó-ya

Plum soup with sour cream.

Zupa śliwkowa.
zoó-pa shleev-kó-va

Fruit soup with milk and eggs.

Zupa owocowa.
zoó-pa o-vo-tsó-va

Milk soup with vanilla.

Zupa waniliowa.
zoó-pa va-ńeel-yó-va

Cold tomato soup.

Chłodna zupa pomidorowa.
khwód-na zoó-pa po-mee-do-ró-va

Raspberry soup with wine

Malinowa zupa z winem.
ma-lee-nó-va zoó-pa z veé-nem

32
What additions to soups are available?

Jakie dodatki do zup można dostać?
Yá-ḱe do-dát-kee do zoop mózh-na dós-tach

Potato dumplings.

Kluski ziemniaczane.
kloós-kee zhem-ña-chá-ne

Potato balls in bread crumbs.

Krokiety osmażane.
kro-ḱé-ti os-ma-zhá-ne

Polish style meat stuffed ravioli.

Uszka nadziewane mięsem.
oósh-ka na-dźhe-vá-ne myáń-sem

Polish ravioli with mushrooms.

Uszka z grzybami.
oósh-ka z gzhi-bá-mee

33
Polish patties with meat.

Paszteciki z mięsem.
pash-te-chéekee z myáń-sem

Polish patties with mushrooms.

Paszteciki z grzybami.
pash-te-chee-kee z gzhee-bá-mee

Egg balls with grated cheese.

Krokiety z jajka.
kro-ké-ti z yáy-ka

Stuffed cucumbers.

Nadziewane ogórki.
na-dźhe-vá-ne o-góor-kee

Dumplings with meat.

Pierożki z mięsem.
pye-rózh-kee z myáń-sem

Dumplings with chicken.

Pierożki z kurą.
pye-rózh-kee z kóo-równ

34
What are the Polish fish dishes?

Jakie są polskie potrawy rybne?
yá-ke sówn póls-ke po-trá-vi rib-ne

Cod with horseradish sauce.

Dorsz w sosie chrzanowym.
dorsh w só-she khzha-nó-vim

Stuffed pike.

Szczupak faszerowany.
shchóo-pak fa-she-ro-vá-ny

Boiled pike with horseradish sauce.

Gotowany szczupak z sosem chrzanowym.
go-to-vá-ny shchóo-pak z só-sem
khsha-nó-vim

Baked pike with horseradish sauce.

Pieczony szczupak z sosem chrzanowym.
pye-chó-ni shchóo-pak z só-sem
khsha-nó-vim

35
Haddock fillet in batter.

Łupacz w cieście.
wóo-pach w chésh-che.

Carp in jelly.

Karp w galarecie..
Karp w ga-la-ré-che

Carp in grey sauce.

Karp a szarym sosie.
Karp w sha-rim só-sie.

Carp with red cabbage.

Karp w czerwonej kapuście.
karp w czer-vó-ney ka-póosh-che

Carp Jewish style.

Karp po żydowsku.
Karp po zhi-dóv-skoo

Carp in mushroom sauce.

Karp w sosie grzybowym.
karp w só-she gzhi-bó-vim.

36
Baked pike with anchovies.

Pieczony szczupak z sardelami.
pye-chó-ni shchóo-pak z sar-de-lá-mee

Pike Jewish style.

Szczupak po żydowsku.
shchóo-pak po zhi-dóv-skoo

Perch with white wine.

Okoń na białym winie.
ó-koń na byá-wim veé-ńe

Perch with hard boiled eggs.

Okoń z jajkami na twardo.
ó-koń z yay-ká-mee na tvár-do

Broiled perch with mushrooms.

Okoń z rożna z grzybami.
ó-koń z rózh-na z gzhi-bá-mee

Stewed eel in wine.

Duszony węgorz w winie.
Doo-shó-ni váń-gosh v veé-ńe

37

Sole in white wine.

Sola w białym winie.
só-la v bya-wim veé-ñe

Stewed sole with tomatoes.

Duszona sola z pomidorami.
doo-shó-na só-la z po-mee-do-rá-mee

Minced cod balls in tomato sauce.

Zrazy mielone z dorsza w sosie pomidorowym.
zrá-zi mye-ló-ne z dór-sha v só-she
po-mee-do-ró-vim

Fried herring in bread crumbs.

Smażony śledź w bułce tartej.
sma-zhó-ni śhledźh v boów-tse tár-tey

Minced cod cutlet.

Kotlet mielony z dorsza.
kót-let mye-ló-ni z dór-sha

38

Fillet of sole with grated cheese.

Filet z soli z tartym serem.
feé-let z só-lee z tár-tim sé-rem

Fillet of flounder with grated
cheese.

Filet z flądry z tartym serem.
feé-let z flównd-ri z tár-tim sé-rem

Trout with parsley.

Pstrąg z pietruszką.
pstrówng z pyet-roósh-kówn

Fricassee of fish with grated
cheese.

Potrawka z ryby z tartym serem.
po-tráv-ka z rí-bi z tár-tim sé-rem

Cod steamed with vegetables.

Dorsz parzony z jarzynami.
dorsh pa-zhó-ni z ya-zhi-ná-mee

39

Salmon in jelly.

Łosoś w galarecie.
wó-sosh v ga-la-ré-che

Salmon with stuffing.

Łosoś nadziewany.
wó-sosh na-dźhe-vá-ni

Sturgeon with sour cream.

Jesiotr z kwaśną śmietaną.
Ye-śhotr z kvaśh-nówn śhmye-tá-nówn

Lobster with sour cream.

Homar ze śmietaną.
khó-mar ze śhmye-tá-nówn

Oyster cakes with mushrooms and
grated cheese.

Krokiety z ostryg z grzybami i z
tartym serem.
kro-ké-ti z óst-rig z gzhi-bá-mee
ee z tár-tim sé-rem

40

What are your meat specialities?

Jakie są tu dania mięsne?
Yá-ke sówn too dá-ña myáñs-ne

Here is the menu.

Proszę, jadłospis.
pró-shań, yad-wó-spees

Veal cutlets in mushrooms and
white wine.

Kotlety cielęce z grzybami w białym
winie.
kot-lé-ti che-lán-tse z gzhi-bá-mee
v byá-wim veé-ñe

Veal with paprika.

Cielęcina z papryką.
che-lań-cheé-na z pap-ri-kówn

Pounded veal chops with Bechamel.

Bite zrazy cielęce z Beszamelem.
Beé-te zra-zi che-lań-tse z be-sha-
mé-lem

41

Pounded veal stewed with onion.

Bite zrazy cielęce duszone z cebulą.
bée-te zrá-zi che-láń-tse doo-szó-ne
z tse-bóo-lówn

Fried minced veal patties.

Paszteciki z siekanej cielęciny.
pash-te-chée-kee z she-ká-ney che-
láń-chée-ni

Veal patties with sour cream.

Paszteciki cielęce ze śmietaną.
pash-te-chée-kee che-láń-tse ze
shmye-tá-nówn

Veal roast with garlic.

Pieczeń cielęca z czosnkiem.
pyé-cheń che-láń-tsa z chósn-kem

Stuffed veal cutlets.

Nadziewane kotlety cielęce.
na-dzhe-vá-ne kot-lé-ti che-láń-tse

42

Veal brain cutlets.

Kotlety z mózgu cielęcego.
kot-lé-ti z móoz-goo che-láń-tsé-go

Veal steak.

Stek cielęcy.
stek che-láń-tsi

Fried veal liver.

Smażona wątroba cielęca.
sma-zhó-na vówn-tro-ba che-láń-tsa

Pounded veal chops.

Bite zrazy cielęce.
bée-te zra-zi che-láń-tse

Veal chops with mushroom sauce.

Zrazy cielęce w sosie grzybowym.
zrá-zi che-áń-tse w só-she gzhi-bó-
vim

43

Pot roast of beef.

Pieczeń wołowa, duszona.
pyé-cheń vo-wó-va, doo-shó-na

Cooked beef with horseradish
sauce.

Wołowina gotowana z sosem chrzanowym.
vo-wo-veé-na go-to-vá-na z só-sem
khsha-nó-vim

Pot roast with sour cream.

Pieczeń wołowa ze śmietaną.
pyé-cheń vo-wó-va ze shmye-tá-nówn

Pot roast with mushrooms.

Pieczeń wołowa z grzybami.
pyé-cheń vo-wó-va z gzhi-bá-mee

Beef steak with horseradish.

Befsztyk z chrzanem.
béf-shtik z khshá-nem

44

Simmered beef Radecki style with
mushrooms.

Duszona wołowina Radeckiego z grzybami.
doo-shó-na vo-wo-veé-na ra-dets-ké-
go z gzhi-bá-mee

Maet loaf with sour cream.

Rolada mięsna ze śmietanką.
ro-lá-da myáńs-na ze shmye-tán-kówn

Meat loaf Cracov style.

Rolada mięsna po krakowsku.
ro-lá-da myáńs-na po kra-kóv-skoo

Stuffed roast husar style

Pieczeń wołowa po husarsku.
pyé-cheń vo-wó-va po hoo-sár-skoo

Boiled beef with horseradish
sauce

Sztuka mięsa z sosem chrzanowym.
shtóo-ka myáń-sa z só-sem khsha-nó-
vim

45

Steak Tartare.

Befsztyk po tatarsku.
béf-shtik po ta-tár-skoo

Meat loaf stuffed with eggs.

Klops nadziewany jajkami.
klops na-dźhe-vá-ni yay-ká-mee

Meat loaf stuffed with sausage.

Klops nadziewany kiełbasą.
klops na-dźhe-vá-ni kél-ba-sówn

Meat loaf with sour cream sauce.

Klops w sosie śmietanowym.
klops v só-śhe śhmye-ta-nó-vim

Meat loaf with mushrooms.

Klops z grzybami
klops z gzhi-bá-mee

Goulash meat stew.

Gulasz.
goó-lash

46

Beef tongue with carrots.

Ozór wołowy z marchewką.
o-zoor yo-wó-yi z mar-khév-kówn

Fried tongue.

Ozór smażony.
o-zoor sma-zhó-ni

Beef chops with onion.

Zrazy wołowe, z cebulą.
zrá-zi vo-wó-ve z tse-boó-lówn

Cooked tongue, browned in horseradish sauce.

Ozór zapiekany w sosie chrzanowym.
o-zoor za-pye-ká-ni w só-śhe
khsha-nó-vim

Cooked beef, browned in horseradish sauce

Sztuka mięsa zapiekana w sosie
chrzanowym.
shtoó-ka myáñ-są za-pye-ká-na w
só-śhe khsha-nó-vim

47

What pork products do you have?

Jakie wyroby masarskie można tu dostać?
vá-ke vi-ró-bi ma-sár-ske móżh-na
too dós-tach?

We have a great variety of Polish
trditional pork products.

Mamy urozmaicony wybór polskich tra-
dycyjnych wyrobów masarskich,
má-mi oo-roz-ma-ee-tsó-ni vi-boor
pól-skeekh trą-di-tsiý-nikh vi-ro-
boof ma-sár-skeekh

Lean ham smoked and cooked.

Chuda szynka wędzona gotowana.
khoó-da shin-ka vǽñ-dzo-na go-to-vá-
na

Pork ribs cooked with vegetables.

Żeberka wieprzowe gotowane z jarzynami.
zhe-bér-ka vyep-shó-ve go-to-vá-ne
z ya-zhi-ná-mee

48

Pork loin cutlets.

Kotlety schabowe.
kot-lé-ti skha-bó-ve

Ground pork cutlets.

Kotlety wieprzowe mielone.
kot-lé-ti vyep-shó-ve mye-ló-ne

Pounded ham cutlets.

Bite kotlety z szynki.
beé-te kot-lé-ty z shin-kee

Cold cooked ham.

Szynka gotowana na zimno.
shiń-ka go-to-vá-na na źheém-no

Pork chops.

Zrazy wieprzowe.
zrá-zi vyep-shó-ve

Stewed pork chops.

Zrazy wieprzowe duszone.
zrá-zi vyep-shó-ve doo-shó-ne

49
Minced pork chops with rice.

Siekane zrazy wieprzowe z ryżem.
she-ká-ne zrá-zi vyep-shó-ve z
rí-zhem

Pounded minced lean pork chops-
royal bitki.

Bite zrazy wieprzowe po królewsku.
bee-te zrá-zi vyep-shó-ve po kroo-
lév-skoo

Lean pork meat balls with
anchovies

Krokiety wieprzowe z sardelami.
kro-Ké-ti vyep-shó-ve z sar-de-la-mee

Sauer cabbage with pork ribs.

Żeberka wieprzowe z kiszoną kapustą
zhe-bér-ka vyep-shó-ve z kee-shó-nówn
ka-poós-tówn

Roast loin of pork.

Schabową pieczeń wieprzowa.
skha-bó-va pyé-cheń vyep-shó-va

50
Ham baked in dough.

Szynka pieczona w cieście.
shín-ka pye-chó-na v chésh-che

Young pork liver.

Wątróbka wieprzowa.
vównt-roób-ka vyep-shó-va

Pork brain cutlets.

Kotlety z mózgu wieprzowego.
kot-lé-ti z moóz-goo vyep-sho-vé-go

Pork brain Polish style.

Mózg wieprzowy po polsku.
moózg vyep-shó-vi po póls-koo

Pork goulash.

Gulasz wieprzowy.
goó-lash vyep-shó-vi

Stuffed piglet.

Prosię nadziewane.
pro-shań na-dzhe-vá-ne

51
Spare-ribs stewed with kohlrabi.

Żeberka wieprzowe duszone z kalarepą.
zhe-bér-ka vyep-shó-ve doo-shó-ne z
ka-la-ré-pówn

Ground pork chops with tomato
sauce

Mielone zrazy wieprzowe w sosie pomidorowym.
mye-ló-ne zrá-zi vyep-shó-ve v só-she
po-mee-do-ró-vim

Smoked sausage with onion sauce.

Kiełbasa wędzona w sosie cebulowym.
kéł-ba-sa vến-dzó-na v so-she tse-
boo-ló-vim

Sausage served hot.
Kiełbasa na gorąco.
kéł-ba-sa na go-równ-tso

Franks served hot.
Parówki na gorąco.
pa-roóv-kee na go-równ-tso

52
Pig's foot jelly.

Golonka gotowana.
go-lón-ka go-to-vá-na

Pork kidneys with groats.

Nerki wieprzowe z kaszą.
nér-kee vyep-shó-ve z ka-shówn

Baked bacon.

Boczek pieczony.
bó-chek pye-chó-ni

Pork meat loaf.

Klops z wieprzowiny.
klops z vyep-sho-veé-ni

White pork sausage with onion.

Kiełbasa biała z cebulą.
kel-ba-sa byá-wa z tse-boó-lówn

53
How about lamb?

Czy jest baranina?
chi yest ba-ra-ńeé-na

Lamb roast with sour cream.

Pieczeń barania ze śmietaną.
pyé-cheń ba-rá-ńa ze śhmye-tá-nówn

Lamb roast with garlic.

Pieczeń barania z czosnkiem.
pyé-cheń ba-rá-ńa z chósn-kem

Roast lamb shoulder.

Łopatka barania pieczona.
wo-pát-ka ba-rá-ńa pye-chó-na

Fricassee of lamb.

Potrawka z baraniny.
po-tráv-ka z ba-ra-ńeé-ni

Lamb shish kebab with bacon.

Szaszłyk barani z boczkiem.
sháśh-wik ba-rá-ńee z bóch-kem

54
Pounded lamb chops.

Bite zrazy baranie.
beé-te zrá-zi ba-rá-ńe

Lamb chops with grated cheese.

Zrazy baranie z tartym serem.
zrá-zi ba-ra-ńe z tár-tim sé-rem

Marinated lamb with Polish
sausage.

Marynowana baranina z polską kiełbasą
ma-ri-no-vá-na ba-ra-ńeé-na z pols-
kówn kel-ba-sówn

Lamb chops with mushrooms.

Zrazy baranie z grzybami.
zrá-zi ba-rá-ńe z gzhi-bá-mee

Lamb cooked with cabbage.

Baranina gotowana z kapustą.
ba-ra-ńeé-na go-to-vá-na z ka-
poós-tówn

55
Cooked lamb with onion sauce.

Baranina gotowana z sosem cebulowym.
ba-ra-ńeé-na go-to-vá-na z só-sem
tse-boo-ló-vim

Cooked lamb shoulder.

Łopatka barania gotowana.
wo-pát-ka ba-rá-ńa go-to-vá-na

Ground lamb cutlets.

Kotlety baranie mielone.
kot-lé-ti ba-ra-ńe mye-ló-ne

Lamb brisket cutlets.

Kotlety z mostka baraniego
kot-lé-ti z móst-ka ba-ra-ńé-go

Lamb stewed with vegetables.

Baranina duszona w jarzynach.
ba-ra-ńeé-na doo-shó-na v ya-zhí-na

56
Lamb-veal-beef meat balls in
dough.

Kołduny zawijane w cieście.
kow-doó-ni za-vee-yá-ne w chéśh-ch

Lamb stewed with tomatoes.

Baranina gotowana z pomidorami.
ba-ra-ńeé-na go-to-vá-na z po-mee-
do-rá-mee

Lamb and beans.

Baranina z fasolą.
ba-ra-ńeé-na z fa-só-lówn

Lamb stewed with potatoes.

Baranina gotowana z ziemniakami.
ba-ra-ńeé-na go-to-vá-na z żhem-
ńa-ká-mee

Calf's liver, veal, and pork
meat loaf with bacon, eggs and
mushrooms.

Pasztet.
pásh-tet

57

Tripe with soup bone and
vegetables.

Flaki.
flá-kee

Liver pudding.

Pasztet z wątroby.
pásh-tet z vówn-tró-bi

Chopped liver and pork with groats.

Kiszka.
keésh-ka

Sour cabbage with diced pork,veal,
beef, ham,sausage and mushrooms.
stewed, then fried.

Bigos.
bée-gos

Black pudding.

Krwawa kiszka.
krvá-va keésh-ka

58

What poultry dishes do you
recommend?

Jakie potrawy z drobiu pan poleca?
Yá-ke po-trá-vi z drób-yoo pan
po-lé-tsa

Chicken Polish style cooked with
vegetables and chopped mushrooms.

Kurczę po polsku.
koór-chań po póls-koo

Chicken fricassee.

Potrawka z kury.
po-tráv-ka z koó-ri

Fricassee of giblets.

Potrawka z podróbek.
po-tráv-ka z po-droó-bek

Chicken in dill sauce.

Kurczak w sosie koperkowym.
koór-chak v só-she ko-per-kó-vim

59

Chicken stuffed with pea puree.

Kurczę nadziewane z puree z groszku.
koór-chań na-dźhe-vá-ne z pee-re z
grósh-koo

Chicken stewed with pepers.

Paprykarz z kurcząt.
pap-rí-kash z koór-chówńt

Roast stuffed chicken.

Pieczone kurczę nadziewane.
pye-chó-ne koór-chań na-dźhe-vá-ne

Baked chicken with sour cream.

Kurczę pieczone ze śmietaną.
koór-chań pye-chó-ne ze shmye-tá-nów

Caesar's chicken with mushrooms.

Kurczę po cesarsku z grzybami.
koór-chan po tse-sárs-koo z gzhi-
bá-mee

60

Chicken stewed with tomatoes.

Kurczę duszone z pomidorami.
koór-chań doo-shó-ne z po-mee-do-
rá-mee

Chicken breast cutlets.

Smażone kotlety z piersi kury.
sma-zhó-ne kot-lé-ti z pyér-shee
koó-ri

Chicken cutlets with mushrooms.

Kotlety z kury z grzybami.

Chicken livers with rice and
cheese.

Wątróbki z kurczęcia z ryżem i serem.
Vówn-troób-kee z koor-chań-ćha z
rí-zhem ee se-rem

Fricasse of pigeons with nuts.

Potrawka z gołębi z orzechami.
po-tráv-ka z go-wań-bee z o-zhe-khá-
mee

61

Baked stuffed turkey with cranberries.

Pieczony nadziewany indyk z żurawinami.
pye-chó-ni na-dźhe-vá-ni een-dik z zhoo-ra-vee-ná-mee

Minced turkey cutlets.

Siekane kotlety z indyka.
she-ká-ne kot-lé-ti z een-di-ka

Fried chicken.

Kurczak pieczony.
koór-chak pye-chó-ni

Duck stewed with cabbage and apples.

Kaczka duszona w kapuście z jabłkami.
kách-ka doo-shó-na v ka-poósh-che z jabw-ká-mee

Roast goose.

Pieczona gęś.
pye-chó-na gáñsh

62

Fried goose liver.

Smażona gęsia wątróbka.
sma-zhó-na gań-sha vown-troób-ka

Goose with liver stuffing.

Gęś z nadzieniem wątrobianym.
Gáñsh z na-dźhé-ñem vown-tro-byá-nim

Goose baked with apples.

Gęś pieczona z jabłkami.
Gañsh pye-chó-na z yabw-ka-mee

Duck baked with apples.

Kaczka pieczona z jabłkami.
kách-ka pye-chó-na z yab-ka-mee

Partridge baked in bacon.

Kuropatwa pieczona w słoninie.
koo-ro-pát-va pye-chó-na v swo-ñée-ñe

Roast venison.

Pieczona dziczyzna.
pye-cho-na dźhee-chiz-na

63

Roast venison with sour cream.

Dziczyzna pieczona w śmietanie.
dźhee-chíz-na pye-chó-na v shmye-tá-ñe

Pounded venison chops with wine.

Bite zrazy z dziczyzny w winie.
Beé-te zra-zi z dźhee-chíz-ni v veé-ñe

Pounded venison cutlets.

Bite kotlety z dziczyzny.
Beé-te kot-lé-ti z dźhee-chíz-ni

Fried minced venison patties.

Paszteciki z siekanej dziczyzny.
pash-te-chée-kee z she-ká-ney dźhee-chíz-ni

Fricassee of hare.

Potrawka z zająca.
po-tráv-ka z za-yóẃn-tsa

64

Hare meat loaf with onions and bacon.

Pasztet z zająca.
pásh-tet z za-yóẃn-tsa

Fricassee of rabbit.

Potrawka z królika.
po-tráv-ka z kroo-leé-ka

Rabbit hunting style.

Marynowany królik po myśliwsku.
ma-ri-no-vá-ni kroó-leek po mish-leév-skoo

Marinated wild duck stewed.

Dzika kaczka.
dźheé-ka kách-ka

Marinated wild goose with olives.

Dzika gęś z oliwkami.
dźheé-ka gáñsh z o-leev-ká-mee

65

Baked marinated deer haunch in sour cream Polish style.

Udziec sarni w śmietanie po polsku.
oó-dźhets sár-ñee w śmye-tá-ñe po póls-koo

Boar ham stewed and baked.

Pieczeń duszona z dzika.
pye-cheń doo-shó-na z dźheé-ka

Marinated boar cutlets.

Kotlety z dzika.
kot-lé-ti z dźheé-ka

Venison meat loaf.

Pasztet z dziczyzny.
pásh-tet z dźhee-chíz-ni

Fricassee of venison.

Potrawka z dziczyzny.
po-tráv-ka z dźhee-chíz-ni

66

What sauces do you have?

Jakie ma pan sosy?
yá-ke ma pan só-si

Let us start with the hot sauces.

Zacznijmy od sosów gorących.
zach-neéy-mi od só-soof go-równ-tsikh

White sauce.

Sos mleczny.
sos mléch-ni

Cheese sauce.

Sos serowy.
sos se-ró-vi

Horseradish sauce.

Sos chrzanowy.
sos khsha-nóvi

67

Mushroom sauce.

Sos grzybowy.
sos gzhi-bó-vi

Dried mushroom sauce.

Sos z grzybów suszonych.
sos z gzhí-boof soo-shó-nikh

Dill sauce with sour cream.

Sos koperkowy ze śmietaną.
sos kop-er-kó-vi ze śmye-tá-nówn

Tomato sauce with sausage.

Sos pomidorowy z kiełbasą.
sos po-mee-do-ró-vi z kél-bá-sówn

Tomato sauce with sour cream.

Sos pomidorowy ze śmietaną.
sos po-mee-do-ró-vi ze śmye-tá-nówn

Onion sauce.

Sos cebulowy.
sos tse-boo-ló-vi

68

Polish egg sauce.

Polski sos jajowy.
pól-skee sos ya-yo-vi

Polish gray sauce.

Polski szary sos.
pól-skee shá-ri sos

Raisin sauce with wine.

Sos rodzynkowy z winem.
sos ro-dzin-kó-vi z veé-nem

Mustard sauce.

Sos musztardowy.
sos moosh-tar-dó-vi

Pickle sauce.

Sos ogórkowy.
sos o-goor-kó-vi

Anchovy sauce.

Sos sardelowy.
sos sar-de-ló-vi

69

There are many good Polish cold sauces.

Jest wiele dobrych polskich zimnych sosów.
yest vyé-le dóo-rikh póls-keekh źheém-nikh só-soof

Tartare sauce.

Sos tatarski.
sos ta-tár-skee

Beet sauce.

Ćwikła.
chveék-wa

Mayonnaise sauce.

Sos majonezowy.
sos ma-yo-ne-zó-vi

Mayonnaise sauce with wine.

Sos majonezowy z winem.
sos ma-yo-ne-zó-vi z veé-nem

70

Vegetables served Polish style:

Jarzyny podane po polsku.
ya-zhí-ni po-dá-ne po póls-koo

Polish potato dishes.

Polskie dania ziemniaczane.
póls-ke dá-ña źhem-ña-chá-ne

Browned mashed young potato pies.

Smażone placki z młodych gniecionych ziemniaków.
sma-zhó-ne pláts-kee z mwó-dikh gñe-chó-nikh źhem-ñá-koof

Cabbage and onion dish.

Kapusta gotowana z cebulą.
ka-póos-ta go-to-vá-na z tse-hóo-lówn

Sour beans dish.

Fasola na kwaśno.
fa-só-la na kváśh-no

71

Green peas.

Zielony groszek.
źhe-ló-ni gró-shek

Asparagus dish.

Szparagi.
shpa-rá-gee

String beans.

Szparagowa fasola.
shpa-ra-gó-va fa-só-la

Beet dish.

Buraczki.
boo-rách-kee

Brussels sprouts.

Brukselka.
brook-sél-ka

Kohlrabi dish.

Kalarepa.
ka-la-ré-pa

72

Peas and carrots.

Marchewka z groszkiem.
mar-khév-ka z grósh-kem

Horseradish sauce.

Sos chrzanowy.
sos khsha-nó-vi

Spinach with eggs.

Szpinak z jajkami.
shpeé-nak z yay-ká-mee

Broccoli with butter.

Brokuły z masłem.
bro-koó-wi z maś-wem.

Turnips and potatoes on bacon.

Brukiew po mazursku.
broó-kev po ma-zóor-skoo.

Browned turnips with bacon.

Brukiew zasmażana.
broó-kev za-sma-zhá-na

73

Turnips with carrots on bacon.

Brukiew z marchewką.
broó-kev z mar-khév-kõwñ

Turnips with tomato sauce.

Brukiew w sosie pomidorowym.
broó-kev w só-she po-mee-do-ró-vim

Browned beets with vinegar.

Zasmażane buraki z octem.
zas-mazhá-ne boo-rá-kee z óts-tem

Beets with rhubarb.

Buraki z rabarbarem.
boo-rá-kee z ra-bar-bá-rem

Onion stew on bacon.

Cebula duszona.
tse-boó-la doo-shó na

Pumpkin with potatos on bacon.

Dynia po mazursku.
dí-ña po ma-zoór-skoo

74

Pumpkin with Polish pickles.

Dynia z kiszonymi ogórkami.
dí-ña z kee-sho-ní-mee o-goor-ká-mee

Beans in tomato sauce.

Fasola w sosie pomidorowym.
fa-só-la w só-she po-mee-do-ró-vim

Cauliflower in sour cream sauce.

Kalafior w sosie śmietanowym.
ka-láf-yor w só-she shmye-ta-nó-vim

Cauliflower with bread-crumbs.

Kalafior z bułeczką tartą.
ka-láf-yor z boo-wéch-kõwñ tár-tõwñ

Cauliflower with cheese in
Béchamel sauce.

Kalafior z serem w sosie beszamelowym.
ka-láf-yor z sé-rem w só-she be-sha-me-ló-vim

75

Polish style shredded cabbage with
bacon and onion.

Kapusta szatkowana z cebulą na boczku.
ka-poós-ta shat-ko-vá-na z tse-boó-lõwñ na bóch-koo

Cabbage with apples and sour
cream.

Kapusta z jabłkami ze śmietaną.
ka-poós-ta z yabw-ká-mee ze shmye-tá-nõwñ

Browned cabbage with apples.

Kapusta zasmażana z jabłkami.
ka-poós-ta za-sma-zhá-na z yabw-ká-mee

Sour shredded cabbage with browned
onion.

Kiszona szatkowana kapusta z zasmażaną
cebulą.
kee-sho-na shat-ko-vá-na ka-poós-ta z zas-ma-zhá-nõwñ tse-boó-lõwñ

76

Browned white cabbage with
tomatoes.

Kapusta biała zasmażana z pomidorami.
ka-poós-ta byá-wa zas-ma-zhá-na z po-mee-do-rá-mee

White cabbage chunks with potato.

Biała kapusta "parzybroda".
byá-wa ka-poós-ta pa-zhi-bró-da

Red cabbage browned with apples.

Kapusta czerwona zasmażana z jabłkami.
ka-poós-ta cher-vó-na zas-ma-zhá-na z yabw-ká-mee

Sour cabbage with peas.

Kapusta kiszona z grochem.
ka-poós-ta kee-shó-na z gró-khem

Sour cabbage with mushrooms.

Kapusta kiszona z grzybami.
ka-poós-ta kee-shó-na z gzhi-bá-mee

77
Sour cabbage shredded and boiled.

Kapusta kiszona "parzonka".
ka-poós-ta kee-shó-na pa-zhón-ka

Cabbage rolls with mushrooms.

Gołąbki z grzybami.
go-wównb-kee z gzhi-bá-mee

Cabbage rolls with minced pork.

Gołąbki z mięsem.
go-wównb-kee z myáń-sem.

Carrot and potato chunks
Mazovian style.

Marchew po mazursku.
már-khev po ma-zoór-skoo

Carrots browned with butter and
flour, Polish style.

Marchew zasmażana.
már-khev za-sma-zhá-na

78
Carrots with turnips with
marjoram, Polish style.

Marchew z brukwią.
már-khev z broók-vyówn

Carrots with kohlrabi dish.

Marchew z kalarepą.
már-khev z ka-la-ré-pówn

Browned tomatoes Polish style.

Pomidory osmażane.
po-mee-dó-ri os-ma-zhá-ne

Tomatoes stuffed with pickles.

Pomidory nadziewane mizerią.
po-mee-dó-ri na-dźhe-vá-ne mee-zér-yówn

Tomtoes stuffed with mixed
vegetable salad.

Pomidory nadziewane sałatką.
po-mee-dó-ri na-dźhe-vá-ne
sa-wát-kówn

79
Tomatoes with cheese and chives
filling.

Pomidory z serem i szczypiorkiem.
po-mee-dó-ri z sé-rem ee shchi-pyór-kem

Tomatoes stuffed with rice and
mushrooms.

Pomidory nadziewane ryżem i grzybami.
po-mee-dó-ri na-dźhe-vá-ne ri-zhem ee gzhi-bá-mee

Tomatoes with meat filling.

Pomidory nadziewane mięsem.
po-mee-dó-ri na-dźhe-vá-ne myáń-sem

Tomatoes in batter.

Pomidory w cieście.
po-mee-dó-ri- v ćhéśh-će

Meat stuffed tomatoes with sour
cream.

Nadziewane pomidory ze śmietaną.
na-dźhe-vá-ne po-mee-dó-ri ze śhmye-tá-nówn

80
Celery fried in batter.

Selery smażone w cieście.
se-lé-ri sma-zhó-ne v ćhéśh-će

Celery stewed in wine.

Selery duszone w winie.
se-lé-ri doo-shó-ne v vée-ñe

Baked cucumbers stuffed with
mushrooms and onions.

Pieczone ogórki nadziewane grzybami
z cebulą.
pye-chó-ne o-goór-kee na-dźhe-vá-ne
gzhi-bá-mee z tse-boó-lówn

Asparagus with grated cheese.

Szparagi z tartym serem.
shpa-rá-gee z tár-tim sé-rem

Asparagus with sour cream.

Szparagi ze śmietaną.
shpa-rá-gee ze śhmye-tá-nówn

81
Browned leeks.

Pory zasmażane.
pó-ri za-sma-zhá-ne

Leeks with butter.

Pory z masłem.
pó-ri z más-wem

Artichokes boiled.

Karczochy gotowane.
kar-chó-khi go-to-vá-ne

Artichokes stewed.

Karczochy duszone.
kar-chó-khi doo-shó-ne

Artichokes with wine.

Karczochy z winem.
kar-chó-khi z veé-nem

Baked stuffed artichokes.

Pieczone nadziewane karczochy.
pye-chone na-dźhe-vá-ne kar-chó-khi

82
Stuffed red peppers.

Nadziewana czerwona papryka.
nadźhe-vá-na cher-vó-na pap-rí-ka

Baked stuffed yellow peppers.

Pieczona nadziewana żółta papryka.
pye-chó-na na-dźhe-vá-na zhoów-ta
pap-rí-ka

Stuffed green peppers.

Nadziewana zielona papryka.
na-dźhe-vá-na źhe-ló-na pap-rí-ka

Spinach with sour cream.

Szpinak z kwaśną śmietaną.
shpeé-nak z kvásh-nówn shmye-tá-nówn

Fried spinach patties.

Smażone paszteciki ze szpinaku.
sma-zhó-ne pash-te-chee-kee ze shpee
ná-koo

83
Early spinach with butter.

Szpinak wczesny z masłem.
shpeé-nak vchés-ni z más-wem

Spinach and radishes with sour
cream sauce.

Szpinak z rzodkiewką w sosie śmietanowym.
shpeé-nak z zhod-kév-kówn v só-śhe
shmye-ta-nó-vim

Spinach with grated Parmesan.

Szpinak z tartym parmezanem.
shpeé-nak z tár-tim par-me-zá-nem

Spinach with mushroom sauce.

Szpinak w sosie grzybowym.
shpeé-nak v só-śhe gzhi-bó-vim

Green peas with mushroom.

Groszek z grzybami.
gro-shek z gzhi-bá-mee

84
Potato pancakes Polish style.

Smażone placki ziemniaczane.
sma-zhó-ne pláts-kee żhem-ńa-chá-ne

Boiled potatoes with parsley.

Gotowane ziemniaki z pietruszką.
go-to-vá-ne żhem-ńá-kee z pyet-roósh-
kówn

Mashed potatoes.

Ziemniaki tłuczone.
żhem-ńá-kee twoo-chó-ne

Fried potatoes.

Ziemniaki smażone.
żhem-ńá-kee sma-zhó-ne

Early potatoes with dill and
butter

Młode ziemniaki z masłem i koprem.
mwó-de żhem-ńá-kee z más-wem ee
kóp-rem

85

Baked potatoes.

Ziemniaki pieczone.
Żhem-ña-kee pye-cho-ne

Potatoes stewed with onions and
bacon.

Ziemniaki duszone po "szewsku".
Żhem-ña-kee doo-sho-ne po shév-skoo

Fried potato balls.

Smażone krokiety ziemniaczane.
sma-zho-ne kro-Ké-ti Żhem-ña-cha-ne

Potato balls with mushrooms.

Krokiety ziemniaczane z grzybami.
kro-Ké-ti Żhem-ña-cha-ne z gzhi-ba-mee

Potato pancakes with onions.

Placki ziemniaczane z cebulą.
pláts-kee Żhem-ña-cha-ne z tse-boo-lówn

86

Potato-milk mix pancakes.

Ziemniaczane placki parzone.
Żhem-ña-cha-ne pláts-kee pa-zho-ne

Potato and eggs with sour cream
casserole.

Zapiekane ziemniaki z jajkami i śmietaną.
za-pye-ká-ne Żhem-ña-kee z yay-ká-mee
ee shmye-tá-nówn

Potato and eggs with mushroom
sauce casserole.

Zapiekane ziemniaki z jajkami i sosem grzybowym.
za-pye-ká-ne Żhem-ña-kee z yay-ká-mee
ee so-sem grzi-bó-vim

Potatoes stuffed with meat.

Ziemniaki nadziewane mięsem.
Żhem-ña-kee na-dżhe-vá-ne myáñ-sem

87

Potatoes stuffed with mushrooms.

Ziemniaki nadziewane grzybami.
Żhem-ña-kee na-dżhe-vá-ne gzhi-bá-mee

Potatoes stuffed with grated
cheese.

Ziemniaki nadziewane tartym serem.
Żhem-ña-kee na-dżhe-vá-ne tár-tim
sé-rem.

Stewed potatoes with barley and
sour cream.

Ziemniaki duszone z jęczmieniem i
kwaśną śmietaną.
Żhem-ña-kee doo-sho-ne z yáñch-mye-
ñem ee kvásh-nówn shmye-tá-nówn

Potato noodles stuffed with meat.

Pyzy.
pí-zi

Potato and cheese noodles.

Kluski ziemniaczane.
kloós-kee Żhem-ña-cha-ne

88

Potato and milk puree.

Ziemniaki przecierane z mlekiem-purée
Żhem-ña-kee pshe-che-ra-ne z mlé-Kem

Potato salad with smoked fish.

Sałatka z ziemniaków z rybą wędzoną.
sa-wát-ka z Żhem-ña-koof z ri-bówn
vañ-dzo-nówn

Potato salad with onion.

Sałatka z ziemniaków z cebulą.
sa-wát-ka z Żhem-ña-koof z tse-boó-
lówn

Potato salad with chives and dill.

Sałatka z ziemniaków ze szczypiorkiem
i koprem.
sa-wát-ka z Żhem-ña-koof ze shchip-
yór-Kem ee kóp-rem

Potato salad with celery.

Sałatka z ziemniaków z selerem.
sa-wát-ka z Żhem-ña-koof z se-lé-rem

89
Potato salad in egg sauce with
lemon and wine.

Sałatka z ziemniaków w sosie jajowym.
sa-wát-ka z żhem-ńá-koof v só-she
ya-yó-vim

Potato salad with eggs and
mushrooms.

Sałatka z ziemniaków z grzybami.
sa-wát-ka z żhem-ńá-koof z gzhi-bá-
mee

Potato salad with apples and
capers.

Sałatka z ziemniaków z jabłkami i z
kaparami.
sa-wát-ka z żhem-ńá-koof z yabw-ká-
mee ee z ka-pa-rá-mee

Potato salad with anchovies.

Sałatka z ziemniaków z sardelami.
sa-wát-ka z żhem-ńá-koof z sar-
de-lá-mee

90
Red beet salad with horseradish.

Ćwikła.
Chyeék-wa

Herring salad with mustard.

Sałatka śledziowa z musztardą.
sa-wát-ka śhle-dźhó-va z moosh-tár-
dówn

Herring salad with mayonnaise.

Sałatka śledziowa z majonezem.
sa-wát-ka śhle-dźhó-va z ma-yo-né-
zem

Jellied lobster salad

Sałatka w galarecie z homara.
sa-wát-ka v ga-la-ré-che z kho-má-ra

Royal salad with herring.

Królewska sałata ze śledziem.
kroo-lév-ska sa-wá-ta ze śhle-dźhem

91
Cauliflower salad with mayonnaise.

Sałatka z kalafiora z majonezem.
Sa-wát-ka z ka-la-fyó-ra z ma-ya-né-
zem

Mixed cooked vegetable salad.

Mieszana sałatka jarzynowa.
mye-shá-na sa-wát-ka ya-zhi-nó-va

Asparagus tips salad.

Sałatka szparagowa.
sa-wát-ka shpa-ra-gó-va

Jellied vegetable salad.

Sałatka jarzynowa w galarecie.
sa-wát-ka ya-zhi-nó-wa w ga-la-ré-che

Tomato and grated onion salad.

Sałatka pomidorowa z cebulą.
sa-wát-ka po-mee-do-ro-va z tse-boó-
lówn

92
String bean salad.

Sałatka z fasoli szparagowej.
sa-wát-ka z fa-só-lee shpa-ra-gó-vey

Sardine salad with mustard.

Sałatka z sardynek w musztardzie.
sa-wát-ka z sar-dí-nek w moosh-tár-
dźhe

Vegetable salad with tomatoes.

Sałatka jarzynowa z pomidorami.
sa-wát-ka ya-zhi-nó-va z po-mee-do-
rá-mee

Sliced fruit salad with wine.

Sałatka owocowa z winem.
Sa-wát-ka o-vo-tsó-va z veé-nem

Onion salad with tarragon.

Sałatka z cebuli z estragonem.
sa-wát-ka z tse-boó-lee z es-tra-
gó-nem

93

What are the Polish mushroom dishes?

Jakie są polskie potrawy grzybowe?
ya-ke sown pols-ke po-tra-vi gzhi-bo-ve

Minced mushroom cutlets.

Siekane kotlety grzybowe.
she-ka-ne kot-le-ti grzi-bo-ve

Stuffed mushrooms.

Grzyby nadziewane.
gzhi-bi na-dzhe-va-ne

Mushrooms stewed in sour cream.

Grzyby duszone w śmietanie.
gzhi-bi doo-sho-ne w shmye-ta-ne

Marinated mushrooms.

Grzyby marynowane.
gzhi-bi ma-ri-no-va-ne

94

May I see the list of your dairy dishes?

Czy mógłbym zobaczyć listę potraw z nabiału?
chi moogw-bim zo-ba-chich lees-tan po-trav z na-bya-woo

We have a list of dairy dishes right here.

Tutaj właśnie mamy listę potraw z nabiału.
too-tay vwash-ne ma-mi lees-tan po-trav z na-bya-woo

Stuffed eggs.

Jajka nadziewane.
yay-ka na-dzhe-va-ne

Scrambled eggs with ham.

Jajecznica z szynką.
ya-yech-nee-tsa z shin-kown

Scrambled eggs with chives.

Jajecznica ze szczypiorkiem.
ya-yech-nee-tsa ze shchi-pyor-kem

Scramble eggs with sausage.

Jajecznica z kiełbasą.
ya-yech-nee-tsa z kew-ba-sown

Scrambled eggs with tomatoes.

Jajecznica z pomidorami.
ya-yech-nee-tsa z po-mee-do-ra-mee

Eggs sunny side up.

Jajka sadzone.
yay-ka sa-dzo-ne

Soft boiled eggs in a glass.

Jajka na miękko w szklance.
yay-ka na myank-ko v shklan-tse

Soft boiled eggs in an egg cup.

Jajka na miękko w kieliszku.
yay-ka na myank-ko v ke-leesh-koo

96

Poached eggs.

Jajka w koszulkach.
yay-ka v ko-shool-kakh

Poached eggs in a sauce.

Jajka w koszulkach w sosie.
yay-ka v ko-shool-kakh v so-she

Poached eggs in sour cream.

Jajka w koszulkach w śmietanie.
yay-ka v ko-shool-kakh v shmye-ta-ne

Egg cutlets.

Kotleciki z jaj.
kot-le-chee-kee z yay

Omelette.

Omlet naturalny.
om-let na-too-ral-ni

Omelette with spinach.

Omlet ze szpinakiem.
om-let ze shpee-na-kem

97

Omelet with peas.

Omlet z groszkiem zielonym.
óm-let z grosh-kem zhe-ló-nim

Omelet with cauliflower.

Omlet z kalafiorem.
om-let z ka-la-fyó-rem

Omelet with ham.

Omlet z szynką.
óm-let z shín-kówn

Hard boiled eggs.

Jaja na twardo.
yá-ya na tvár-do

Eggs in a horseradish sauce.

Jaja w sosie chrzanowym.
yá-ya v só-she khzha-nó-vim

Egg noodles with ham.

Kluski na jajach z szynką.
Klóos-kee na yá-yakh z shín-kówn.

98

Egg noodles with poppy seed.

Kluski na jajach z makiem.
klóos-kee na yá-yakh z má-kem

Noodles with cheese and milk.

Kluski z mlekiem i serem.
klóos-kee z mlá-kem ee se-rem

Noodles with cottage cheese.

Kluski z białym serem.
klóos-kee z byá-wim se-rem

Baked noodles.

Kluski pieczone.
klóos-kee pye-chó-ne

Polish ravioli with cheese.

Pierogi leniwe z serem.
pye-ró-gee le-ñee-ve z se-rem

Ravioli with Cracov kasha.

Pierogi z kaszą krakowską.
pye-ró-gee z ka-shówn kra-kóv-skówn

99

Pancakes with sour cream.

Naleśniki ze śmietaną.
na-lesh-ñeé-kee ze shmye-tá-nówn

Pancakes with cottage cheese.

Naleśniki z białym serem.
na-lesh-ñee-kee z byá-wim se-rem

Pancakes with yeast and sour
cream.

Bliny.
bleé-ni

Pancakes with jam.

Naleśniki z dżemem.
na-lesh-ñeékee z je-mem

Polish dumpling with prunes.

Knedle ze śliwkami.
knéd-le ze shleev-ká-mee

100

Polish dumplings with plum.

Knedle z rodzynkami.
knéd-le z ro-dzin-ká-mee

Polish dumplings with apricots.

Knedle z morelami.
knéd-le z mo-re-lá-mee

Polish dumplings with cherries.

Knedle z czereśniami.
knéd-le z che-resh-ña-mee

Polish dumplings with cream of
wheat.

Knedle z grysikiem.
knéd-le z gi-sheé-kem

Boiled browned flour with bacon.

Prażucha.
pra-zhóó-kha

101

I have heard about the Polish gourmet desserts.

Słyszałem o polskich przysmakach deserowych.
swi-shá-wem o póls-keekh pshi-smá-kakh de-se-ró-vikh.

Would you like to look at the list of our desserts?

Czy chciałby pan popatrzeć na spis naszych deserów?
chi khcháw-bi pan po-pá-tshech na spees ná-shikh de-sé-róof

I would really like to.

Z chęcią.
z kháń-chówń

Here you can make your selection.

Z tego może pan wybrać.
z té-go mó-zhe pan vi-brach

Thank you.
Dziękuję.
dźháń-koó-yáń

102

Raisin pudding.

Budyń rodzynkowy.
boó-diń ro-dzin-kó-vi

Vanilla pudding.

Budyń waniliowy.
boó-diń va-ńeel-yó-vi

Almond pudding.

Budyń migdałowy.
boó-diń meeg-da-wó-vi

Nut pudding.

Budyń orzechowy.
boó-diń o-zhe-khó-vi

Milk pudding.

Budyń mleczny.
boó-diń mlech-ni

Cheese pudding.

Budyń z sera.
boó-diń z se-ra

103

Chocolate pudding.

Budyń czekoladowy.
boó-diń che-ko-la-dó-vi

Wine pudding.

Budyń winny.
boó-diń veén-ni

Chestnut pudding with fruit.

Kasztanowy budyń z owocami.
kash-ta-nó-vi boó-diń z o-vo-tsá-mee.

Bread pudding with sour cream.

Budyń chlebowy ze śmietaną.
boó-diń khle-bó-vi ze śhmye-tá-nówń

Potato pudding.

Budyń ziemniaczany.
boó-diń źhem-ńa-chá-ni

Rice pudding.

Budyń z ryżu.
boó-diń z rí-zhoo

104

Cranberry pudding.

Budyń z żurawin.
boó-diń z zhoo-rá-veen

Rum pudding with raspberries.

Budyń na rumie z malinami.
boó-diń na roó-mye z ma-lee-ná-mee

Sherry pudding with cherries.

Budyń na winie z czereśniami.
boo-diń na vee-ńe z che-resh-ńá-mee

Frozen pudding with apricots.

Mrożony budyń z morelami.
mro-zho-ni boó-diń z mo-re-lá-mee

Apricot compote /stewed/.

Kompot morelowy.
kóm-pot mo-re-ló-vi

Stuffed apple compote.

Kompot z nadziewanych jabłek.
kóm-pot z na-dźhe-va-nikh yab-wek

105

Orange and apple compote.

Kompot z pomarańcz i jabłek.
kóm-pot z po-má-rańch ee yáb-wek

Strawberry compote with wine.

Kompot truskawkowy z winem.
kóm-pot troos-kav-kó-vi z veé-nem

Rhubarb compote.

Kompot z rabarbaru.
kóm-pot z roo-bar-bá-roo.

Pear compote.

Kompot z gruszek.
kóm-pot z groó-shek

Blueberry compote.

Kompot z czarnych jagód.
kóm-pot z chár-nikh ya-goot

Marinated cherry compote.

Kompot z marynowanych czereśni.
kóm-pot z ma-ri-no-vá-nikh che-résh-ñee

106

Melon stuffed with berries.

Melon nadziewany jagodami.
mé-lon na-dźhe-vá-ni ya-go-dá-mee

Pears in wine sauce.

Gruszki w sosie winnym.
groósh-kee w só-she veén-nim

Pears in rum.

Gruszki w rumie.
groósh-kee v roó-mye

Stuffed peaches.

Brzoskwinie nadziewane.
bzhos-kveé-ñe na-dźhe-vá-ne

Strawberries with sour cream.

Truskawki ze śmietaną.
troos-káv-kee se śhmye-tá-nówn

Fresh fruit salad.

Surówka owocowa.
soo-roóv-ka o-vo-tsó-va

107

Baked apples.

Pieczone jabłka.
pye-chó-ne yáb-ka.

Sour milk jelly.

Galaretka z kwaśnego mleka.
ga-la-rét-ka z kvaśh-né-go mlé-ka

Fried fruit juice jelly.

Galaretka ze smażonych soków owocowych.
ga-la-rét-ka ze sma-zhó-nikh só-koof o-vo-tsó-vikh

Currant jelly.

Galaretka porzeczkowa.
ga-la-rét-ka po-zhech-kó-va

Boiled apple jelly.

Galaretka jabłkowa.
ga-la-rét-ka yab-kó-va.

108

Cooked cherry jelly.

Galaretka z wisien gotowanych.
ga-la-rét-ka z veé-shen go-to-vá-nikh.

Raw raspberry jelly.

Galaretka surowa malinowa.
ga-la-rét-ka soo-ró-va ma-lee-nó-va

Sour cream souffle.

Suflet śmietanowy.
soóf-let śhmye-ta-nó-vi

Coffee souffle.

Suflet kawowy.
soóf-let ka-vó-vi.

Tea souffle.

Suflet herbaciany.
soóf-let kher-ba-ćhá-ni

Lemon souffle.

Suflet cytrynowy.
soóf-let tsi-tri-nó-vi

109
Wheat grain and honey dessert.

Kutia.
koót-ya

Apple soufflé.

Suflet jabłkowy.
soóf-let yab-kó-vi

Apple slices in batter.

Krajane jabłka smażone w cieście.
kra-yá-ne yáb-ka sma-zhó-ne v chésh-che

Grated carrots and apples.

Marchewka tarta z jabłkami.
mar-khév-ka tár-ta z yap-ká-mee

Coffee layer cake.

Tort kawowy.
tort ka-vó-vi

110
Chocolate layer cake.

Tort czekoladowy.
tort che-ko-la-dó-vi

Almond and strawberry layer cake

Tort migdałowo truskawkowy.
tort meeg-da-wó-vo troos-kav-kó-vi

Nut layer cake.

Tort orzechowy.
tort o-zhe-khó-vi

Chestnut cake.

Tort kasztanowy.
tort kash-ta-nó-vi

Cheese layer cake.

Tort serowy.
tort se-ró-vi

Round coffee cake.

Babka.
báb-ka

111
Poppy seed roll.

Makownik.
ma-kov-ñeek

Fried cookies Polish style.

Chrust = Faworki.
khroost = fa-vór-kee

Yeast batter balls fried.

Pączki.
pówñch-kee

Cherry stuffed batter balls.

Pączki z wiśnią.
pówñch-kee z veésh-ñówñ

Batter balls with preserved
rose petals.

Pączki nadziewane konfiturą z róży.
pówñch-kee na-dźhe-vá-ne kon-fee-toó-równ z roó-zhi

112
Creamed apples.

Mus jabłkowy.
moos yab-kó-vi

Creamed strawberries.

Mus truskawkowy.
moos troos-kav-kó-vi

Lemon cream.

Krem cytrynowy.
krem tsi-tri-nó-vi

Strawberry cream.

Krem truskawkowy.
krem troos-kav-kó-vi

Chocolate sweet sauce.

Słodki sos czekoladowy.
swód-kee sos che-ko-la-dó-vi

Sweet cream sauce.

Krem śmietanowy.
krem śhmye-ta-nó-vi.

113

Almond sauce.

Sos migdałowy.
sos meeg-da-wo-vi

Apricot sauce.

Sos morelowy.
sos mo-re-lo-vi

Raspberries sauce.

Sos malinowy.
sos ma-lee-no-vi

Vanilla sauce.

Sos waniliowy.
sos va-ñeel-vo-vi

Fruit juice sauce.

Sos na soku owocowym.
sos na so-koo o-vo-tso-vim

Fruit sauce.

Sos owocowy.
sos o-vo-tso-vi

114

What kind of appetizers do you have?

Jakie państwo macie zakąski?
ya-ke pañs-tvo ma-che za-koẃn-skee

Stuffed eggs Polish style.

Jaja faszerowane po polsku.
ya-ya fa-she-ro-va-ne po pols-koo

Stuffed eggs with sauce.

Jaja faszerowane z sosem.
ya-ya fa-she-ro-va-ne z so-sem

Eggs stuffed with ham.

Jaja faszerowane szynką.
ya-ya fa-she-ro-va-ne z shin-koẃn

Eggs stuffed with herring.

Jaja nadziewane śledziem.
ya-ya na-dźhe-va-ne śhle-dźhem

115

Eggs in horseradish sauce.

Jaja w sosie chrzanowym.
ya-ya v so-śhe khzha-no-vim

Eggs in mustard sauce.

Jaja w sosie musztardowym.
ya-ya v so-śhe moosh-tar-do-vim

Marinated mushrooms.

Grzyby marynowane.
gzhi-bi ma-ri-no-va-ne

Marinated herring.

Śledzie marynowane.
śhle-dźhe ma-ri-no-va-ne

Herring in sour cream.

Śledzie w kwaśnej śmietanie.
śhle-dźhe v kvaśh-ney śhmye-ta-ñe

Canapés Polish style.

Wybór kanapek.
vi-boor ka-na-pek

116

Browned onion and mushroom ravioli.

Pierożki.
pye-rozh-kee

Chicken pâté.

Pasztet z kury.
pash-tet z koo-ri

Pork pâté.

Pasztet z wieprzowiny.
pash-tet z vyep-sho-vee-ni

Venison pâté.

Pasztet z dziczyzny.
pash-tet z dźhee-chiz-ni

Cod fish pâté.

Pasztet z dorsza.
pash-tet z dor-sha

Smoked meat (and fish) plate.

Wędliny.
waṅd-lee-ni

117
Refreshments.

Napoje orzeźwiające.
na-pó-ye o-zheźh-vya-yówn-tse

Rhubarb beverage.

Napój z rabarbaru.
ná-pooy z ra-bar-bá-roo

Cranberry beverage.

Napój z żurawin.
na-pooy z zhoo-rá-veen

Honey beverage.

Napój z miodu.
ná-pooy z myó-doo

Mint beverage.

Napój z miety,
ná-pooy z myán-ti

Linden flower beverage.

Napój z kwiatu lipowego.
ná-pooy z kvyá-too lee-po-vé-go

118
Hot drinks.

Napoje gorące.
na-pó-ye go-równ-tse

Black coffee.

Czarna kawa.
chár-na ká-va

Coffee with milk.

Biała kawa.
byá-wa ká-va

Coffee with cream.

Kawa ze śmietanką.
ká-va ze śhmye-tán-kówn

Tea.

Herbata naturalna.
her-bá-ta na-too-rál-na

Cocoa.

Kakao.
ka-ká-o

119
Retail of alcoholic drinks.

Wyszynk.
vi-shink

Bison vodka.

Żubrówka.
zhoo-bróov-ka

Rye vodka.

Żytnia wódka.
zhít-ña vóod-ka

Choice vodka, grain vodka.

Wódka wyborowa.
vóod-ka vi-bo-ró-va

Caraway seed vodka.

Kminkówka.
kmeen-kóov-ka

Rowanberry vodka.

Jarzębiak.
ya-zhánb-yak

120
Sweet, after dinner vodkas.

Słodkie wódki.
swód-Re vóod-kee

Apricot vodka.

Wódka morelowa.
vóod-ka mo-re-ló-va

Orange vodka.

Pomarańczówka.
po-ma-rań-choóv-ka

Lemon vodka.

Cytrynówka.
tsi-tri-nóov-ka

Peppercorns, vanilla, honey vodka.

Krupnik.
kroóp-ñeek

Sweet sedge vodka.

Ajerówka.
a-ye-roóv-ka

121
Wine brandy.

Winiak.
vée-ñak

Cherry cordial.

Wiśniówka.
veesh-ñóóv-ka

Plum brandy.

Śliwowica.
shlee-vo-veé-tsa

Golden vodka.

Złota woda.
zwó-ta vó-da

Eggnog vodka.

Ajerkoniak.
a-yer-kó-ñak

Mead,honey wine.

Miód pitny.
myood peét-ni

122
Beer.

Piwo.
peé-vo

Light beer.

Jasne piwo.
yás-ne peé-vo

Dark beer.

Ciemne piwo.
chém-ne peé-vo

Hot beer with egg yolks.

Gorące piwo z żółtkami
go-równ-tse peé-vo z zhoowt-ká-mee

Malt liquor.

Piwo słodowe.
peé-vo swo-dó-ve

Hot wine with cloves.

Gorące wino z goździkami.
go-równ-tse veé-no z gozh-dzhee-ká-mee

123
Operator, how do I make a telephone call outside the hotel?

Proszę mi powiedzieć jak się mogę połączyć z miastem?
pró-shañ mee, po-vye-dzhech yak shañ
mó-gañ po-wówn-chich z myás-tem

Please, dial nine and then the
number you want.

Proszę nakręcić dziewiątkę a potem
numer panu potrzebny.
pró-shañ na-kañ-cheech dzhev-yównt-
kañ a pó-tem nóó-mer pá-noo po-tshéb-
ni

University, may I help you?

Uniwersytet, słucham.
oo-ñee-ver-si-tet, swoó-kham

Extention seven two one, please.

Proszę o wewnętrzny siedem dwa jeden.
pró-shañ o vev-nántsh-ni shé-dem dva
ye-den

124
Good morning, may I talk to Mr.
Barski ?

Dzień dobry, czy mogę mówić z panem
Barskim?
dźheñ dób-ri, chi mó-gañ móó-veech
z pá-nem Bárs-keem

Barski speaking, who is calling?

Mówi Barski, kto przy telefonie?
móó-vee bárs-kee, kto pshi te-le-fó-ñe

This is Jimmy Parker.

Przy telefonie Jimmy Parker.
pshi te-le-fó-ñe Jimmy Parker

Oh, how nice to hear from you.
Where are you now?

Jak to miło cię usłyszeć. Gdzie jesteś?
yak to meé-wo chañ oo-swi-shech.
gdźhe yés-tesh

I am in the Hotel Forum.

Jestem w hotelu Forum.
yés-tem v kho-té-loo fó-room

125

What is your room number?

Jaki masz numer pokoju?
yá-kee mash. nóó-mer po-kó-yoo

My room number is two zero two.

Mam pokój numer dwa zero dwa.
mam pó-kooy nóó-mer dva zé-ro dva

Are you free this morning?

Czy masz czas dziś rano?
chi mash. chas dźheesh. rá-no

Yes, I am free.

Tak, jestem wolny.
tak, yés-tem vól-ni

Could we get together for a few minutes?

Czy moglibyśmy spotkać się na parę minut?
chi móg-lee bísh-mi spot-kach śhań na pá-rań mee-noot

126

Fine.

Bardzo dobrze.
bar-dzo dób-zhe.

I would like to invite you to my appartment or I can come to your hotel.

Chciałbym cię zaprosić do mego mieszkania, albo mogę przyjść do twojego hotelu.
khćháw-bim ćhań za-pró-śheech do mé-go myesh-ká-ńa, ál-bo mó-gań pshiyśhch do tvo-yé-go kho-té-loo

Since I do not know my way around, could you come to the hotel?

Ponieważ nie znam miasta, czy mógłbyć przyjść do hotelu?
po-ńe-vazh. ńe znam myás-ta, chi móogw-bish. pshiyśhch do kho-té-loo

With pleasure.

Z przyjemnością.
z pshi-yem-nóśh-chówń

127

I shall be at your hotel at ten thirty a.m.

Będę u ciebie w hotelu o dziesiątej trzydzieści.
bań-dań oo ćhéb-ye v kho-té-loo o dźhe-śhówń-tey tshi-dźhéśh-chee

I can not wait to see you, Ed.

Nie mogę się doczekać żeby cię zobaczyć Edziu.
ńe mó-gań śhań do-ché-kach zhé-bi ćhań zo-bá-chich. e-dźhoo

I shall see you soon, Jimmie.

Zobaczymy się wkrótce, Jimmie.
zo-ba-chi-mi śhań vkroót-tse, Jimmie

Hello, room two zero two.

Halo, pokój dwa zero dwa?
khá-lo, pó-kooy dva zé-ro dva

Yes indeed, Parker speaking.

Tak jest, mówi Parker.
tak yest, móó-vee pár-ker

128

Mr. Barski is waiting for you in the hotel coffee shop.

Pan Barski czeka na pana w kawiarni hotelowej.
pan bárs-kee ché-ka na pá-na v kav-yár-ńee kho-te-ló-vey

Thank you, please, tell him that I shall come down shortly.

Dziękuję, proszę mu powiedzieć że zaraz przyjdę.
dźhan-kóó-yań, pró-shań moo po-vyé-dźhech zhe zá-raz pshiy-dań

Good morning Ed, I am glad you came.

Dzień dobry Edziu, cieszę się że przyszedłeś.
dźheń dób-ri é-dźhoo, ché-shań śhań zhe pshi-shéd-wesh

I am glad to see you again, Jimmie.

Miło mi cię znowu zobaczyć, Jimmie.
meé-wo mee ćhań znó-voo zo-bá-chich, Jimmie

129

It must be nearly ten years since
we were in school together.

Prawie dziesięć lat minęło od czasu
kiedy studiowaliśmy razem.
prá-vye dźhé-śhanćh lat mee-náń-wo od
chá-soo ke-dí stoo-dyo-va-leéśh-mi
rá-zem

Yes, the time is really flying.

Tak, czas rzeczywiście leci szybko.
tak, chas zhe-chi-veéśh-che lé-ćhee
shíb-ko

I am glad you came to Warsaw.

Cieszę się że przyjechałeś do Warszawy.
ćhe-shan śhan zhe pshi-ye-khá-weśh do
var-shá-vi

Let us sit down.

Usiądźmy.
oo-śhówhdźh-mi

130

You might find the Polish coffee
rather strong, so you might want
a lot of cream.

Polska kawa może ci się wydawać zbyt
mocna, tak że może będziesz chciał
sporo śmietanki.
póls-ka ká-va mó-zhe ćhee śhań vi-da-
vaćh zbit móts-na, tak zhe mó-zhe
bań-dźhesh khćhaw spó-ro śhmye-tan-kee

I would love to try the Polish
coffee.

Bardzo chciałbym spróbować polskiej
kawy.
bár-dzo khćháw-bim sproo-bó-vaćh póls-
key ká-vi.

Strong coffee might help you recover from jet lag.

Mocna kawa może ci pomóc przystosować się do zmiany godzin.
mats-na ka-va mo-zhe ćhee po-moots
pshi-sto-so-vaćh śhan do zmya-ni
go-dźheen

131

Miss, would you give us two small
black coffees?

Proszę dwie małe czarne kawy.
pró-shań dwye má-we chár-ne ká-vi

Would you like anything else?

Czy panowie pozwolą coś jeszcze?
chi pa-nó-vye poz-vó-lówń tsośh
yésh-che

No, thank you.

Nie dziękuję.
ńe dźhań-koó-yáń

Jimmie, my wife and I would like
to have you for dinner tonight.

Jimmie, zapraszamy cię na kolację
do nas dziś wieczór.
Jimmie, za-pra-sha-mi ćháń na kola-
ts-yan do nas dźheeśh vye-choć-

That is a splendid idea.

To wspaniały pomysł.
to vspa-ńá-wi pó-misw

132

Janka can not wait to meet my old
school friend.

Janka nie może się doczekać żeby poznać mego starego przyjaciela ze studiów.
yán-ka ńe mó-zhe śhań do-che-kaćh zhe-
bi póz-naćh mé-go sta-ré-go pshi-ya-
ćhe-la ze stoód-yoof

Edward, you have to help me overcome the language and custom gap.

Edward   musisz mi pomóc radzic sobie
z różnicami w mowie i zwyczajach.
Ed-vard   moó-śheesh mee pó-moots rá-
dźheećh sób-ye z roozh-ńe-tsá-mee v mó-
vye ee zvi-chá-yakh

You are smart, Jimmie, to notice
this gap.

To dowcipnie z twojej strony że zauwa-
żyłeś tę różnicę.
to dov-ćheép-ńe z tvó-yey stró-ni zhe
za-oo-va-zhi-weśh tań roozh-ńeé-tsań

133

I remember how you used to ask
me about such things in America.

Pamiętam jak o takie rzeczy pytałeś
mnie w Ameryce.
pa-myáń-tam yak o tá-ke zhé-chi pi-
tá-wesh   mńe v a-me-rí-tse

Now we have a chance to talk
about them in Poland.

Teraz mamy okazję porozmawiać o nich
w Polsce.
té-raz má-mi o-káz-yáń po-roz-máv-
yach o ńeekh v póls-tse

I notice that people in Poland do
not use the family name with the
word mister as we do in America.

Zauważyłem że w Polsce nie używa się
nazwiska ze słowem pan, tak jak to
robi się w Ameryce.
za-oo-ya-zhí-wem zhe v póls-tse ńe
oo-zhi-va śhań naz-veés-ka ze swó-
vem pan, tak yak to śhań ró-bee y
a-me-rí-tse

134

You are right.

Masz rację.
mash ráts-yáń

In Poland it sounds unpleasantly
official to use the family name
with the word mister.

W Polsce używanie nazwiska ze słowem
pan brzmi zbyt oficjalnie.
v póls-tse oo-zhi-vá-ńe naz-veés-ka
ze swó-vem pan bzhmee zbit ofee-tsyál-
ńe

In America it is impolite to call
anyone mister without using his
family name.

W Ameryce jest niegrzecznie mówić do
kogoś per pan i jednocześnie nie wymieniać jego nazwiska.
v a-me-rí-tse yest ńe-gzhéch-ńe móo-
veech do kó-gosh per pan ee yed-no-
chéśh-ńe ńe vi-mye-ńach yé-go naz-
veés-ka

135

In a conversation in Poland the
words Mister, Mrs   are
used without the family name.

W Polsce w rozmowie słowa pan, pani
są używane bez nazwiska.
v póls-tse v roz-mó-vye swó-va pan,
pá-ńee   sówn oo-zhi-va-ne
bez naz-veés-ka

How do you say politely in Polish
Please, pass me the coffee.

Jak się grzecznie mówi po polsku:
Proszę podać mi kawę.
yak śhań gzhéch-ńe móo-vee po póls-
koo : pró-shań pó-dach mee ká-vań

Your expression is correct.

Twoje wyrażenie jest poprawne.
tvó-ye vi-ra-zhé-ńe yest po-práv-ne

It depends on who is being
addressed.

Zależy z kim rozmawiasz.
za-lé-zhi z keem roz-máv-yash

136

Miss, could you pass me the
coffee?

Czy mogłaby pani podać mi kawę?
chi mog-wá-bi pa-ńee pó-dach mee
ká-vań

Waiter, could you pass me the
coffee?

Czy mógłby pan podać mi kawę?
chi móogw-bi pan pó-dach mee
ká-vań

Little girl, could you pass me
the coffee?

Dziewczynko, czy mogłabyś podać mi
kawę?
dźhev-chín-ko, chi mog-wá-hiśh pó-
dach mee ká-vań

Little boy, could you pass me
the coffee?

Chłopczyku, czy mógłbyś podać mi
kawę?
khwop-chí-koo, chi móogw-biśh pó-
dach mee ká-vań

137

The Polish word "pan" is used
like English "you","Mister" and
"Sir"

Polskie słowo "pan" używa się jak w
angielskim "you", "Mister" i "Sir".
póls-ke swó-vo pan oo-zhi-va śhãn
yak v an-ģéls-keem you, mister ee sir.

I hope that these tips will help
me make a good impression at the
dinner party.

Mam nadzieję że te wskazówki pomogą
mi zrobić dobre wrażenie na przyjęciu u ciebie.
mam na-dźhé-yãn zhe te vska-zoóf-kee
po-mó-gõwn mee zró-beech dób-re vra-
zhé-ñe na pshi-yãñ-choo oo ćhéb-ye

What are some other typical
Polish customs?

Jakie są inne typowe polskie zwyczaje?
yá-ke sõwn eén-ne ti-pó-ve póls-ke
zvi-chá-ye

138

Cut flowers are always an acceptable gift in Poland.

W Polsce bukiet kwiatów jest zawsze
dobrze widziany.
v póls-tse boó-ket kvyá-toof yest záv-
she dób-zhe vee-dźhá-ni

In Poland the guest may compliment
the hostess directly about her beauty,
her dress or her cooking.

W Polsce gość może wprost mówić komplementy pani domu o jej urodzie, jej
sukni czy też jej gotowaniu.
v póls-tse gośhćh mó-zhe vprost moó-
veech kom-ple-mén-ti pá-ñee dó-moo o
yey oo-ró-dźhe, yey soók-ñee chi tezh
yey go-to-yá-ñoo

In America we usually tell the
husband about the beauty and the
elegance of his wife.

W Ameryce my zwykle mówimy mężowi o
piękności i elegancji jego żony.
v a-me-rí-tse mi zvik-le moo-veé-mi
man-zhó-vee o pyãñk-nóśh-ćhee ee e-le-
gánts-yee yé-go zhó-ni

139

What about table manners in
Poland?

Jakie są polskie zwyczaje przy stole?
yá-ke sõwn póls-ke zvi-chá-ye pshi
stó-le

The guest of honor sits at the
head of the table.

Gość honorowany zasiada na pierwszym
miejscu.
gośhćh kho-no-ro-vá-ni za-śhá-da na
pyérv-shim myéys-tsoo

In the family the lady of the
house sits at the head of the
table.

W rodzinie.pani domu zasiada na pierwszym miejscu.
v ro-dźheé-ñe pá-ñee dó-moo za-śhá-da
na pyérv-shim myéys-tsoo

The host pours the drinks.

Pan domu nalewa napoje.
pan dó-moo na-lé-va na-pó-ye

140

The guest of honor is the first
to be served.

Gościowi honorowanemu podaje się jedzenie jako pierwszemu.
gosh-ćhó-vee kho-no-ro-va-né-moo po-
dá-ye śhãn ye-dzé-ñe yá-ko pyerv-shé-
moo

In the family the lady of the
house serves herself first.

w rodzinie pani domu pierwsza nabie-
ra sobie jedzenie.
v ro-dźheé-ñe pá-ñee dó-moo pyérv-sha
na-byé-ra sób-ye ye-dzé-ñe

Everybody takes as much food as
he is sure to eat.

Każdy bierze tyle jedzenia ile zje.
kázh-di byé-zhe tí-le ye-dzé-ña eé-le
zye

That makes sense.

To jest słuszne.
to yest swoósh-ne

141
In Poland, it is considered impolite to leave a quantity of food
on one's plate.

Tak, w Polsce nie należy do dobrych
manier zostawiać jedzenie na talerzu.
tak, v póls-tse ńe na-lé-zhi do dób-
rikh má-ńer zos-táv-yach ye-dzé-ńe na
ta-lé-zhoo

In Poland you may use your fork
with either your right or your
left hand.

W Polsce można używać widelca prawą
lub lewą ręką.
v póls-tse mózh-na oo-zhí-vach yee-
dél-tsa prá-vówn loob lé-vówn rań-kówn

Most Americans hold the fork in
their left hand while cutting
food, then transfer the fork to
their right hand for placing food
in their mouths.

Amerykanie jedzą widelcem tylko prawą
ręką.
a-me-ri-ká-ńe ye-dzówn vee-dél-tsem
til-ko pra-vówn rań-kówn

142
It is funny how these habits
differ.

Ciekawe jak się zwyczaje różnią.
che-ká-ve yak śhań zvi-chá-ye roózh-
ńówn

I hope I will remember what you
have told me.

Mam nadzieję że zapamiętam co mi po-
wiedziałeś.
mam na-dzhé-yan zhe za-pz-myáń-tam
tso mee po-vye-dzhá-weśh

What time should I arrive?

O której godzinie powinienem przyjść?
o któ-rey go-dzhée-ńe po-vee-ńé-nem
pshiy:śhch

You are invited for seven p.m.

Jesteś zaproszony na siódmą wieczorem.
yés-teśh za-pro-shó-ni na śhoód-mówn
vye-chó-rem

143
However, the guests are usually
fifteen minutes late.

Zwykle goście spóźniają się piętnaś-
cie minut.
zvík-le góśh-che spoozh-ńá-yown śhań
pyant-náśh-che meé-noot

That gives the hostess an extra
quarter of an hour.

To daje pani domu dodatkowy kwadrans.
to dá-ye pá-ńee dó-moo do-dat-kó-vi
kvád-rans

It is not polite to be much more
than fifteen minutes late.

Nie jest uprzejmie spóźniać się więcej niż kwadrans.
ńe yest oo-pshéy-mye spoózh-ńach śhań
vyáń-tsey ńeezh kvád-rans

That is good to know.

To dobrze wiedzieć.
to dób-zhe vyé-dzhech

144
In America at dinner parties we
try to avoid discussing politics
religion and women.

W Ameryce na przyjęciu unikamy rozmów
o polityce, religii i kobietach.
v a-me-ri-tse na pshi-yáń-choo oo-ńee-
ká-mi róz-moof o po-lee-ti-tse, re-
leég-yee ee ko-byé-takh

Is there such a custom in Poland?

Czy jest taki zwyczaj w Polsce?
chi yest tá-kee zvi-chay v póls-tse

In Poland conversation starts
light and then turns to more serious subjects.

W Polsce rozmowa zaczyna się lekko a
potem zwraca się do poważniejszych
tematów.
v póls-ts roz-mó-va za-chí-na śhań
lék-ko a pó-tem zvrá-tsa śhań do po-
vazh-ńéy-shikh te-má-toof

You have to be tactful.

Musisz być taktowny.
moó-śheesh bich tak-tóv-ni.

145

Your Polish ladies seem most attractive.

Polskie kobiety wydają się bardzo interesujące.
póls-ke ko-bye-ti vi-dá-yówn shań bár-dzo een-te-re-soo-yówn-tse

Polish woman have a reputation for selecting clothes to enhance their best features.

Polskie kobiety znane są z dobrego doboru twarzowych sukienek.
póls-ke kob-yé-ti zná-ne sówn z dob-ré-go do-bó-roo tva-zhó-vikh soo-Ké-nek

Yes, I have not seen anybody walking around in hair curlers.

Tak, nie widziałem nikogo na ulicy w papilotach.
tak, ńe vee-dźha-wem ńee-kó-go na oo-lee-tsi v pa-pee-ló-takh

146

You have good sight-seeing weather today.

Masz dziś dobrą pogodę do zwiedzania.
mash dźhee-sh dó-brówn po-gó-dán do zvye-dzá-ńa

I would like to go on a general tour of the capital, first.

Chciałbym naprzód ogólnie zwiedzić stolicę.
khćháw-bim ná-pshoot o-góól-ńe zvyé-dźhee-ćh sto-leé-tsän

You can join a guided tour here at the hotel.

Możesz przyłączyć się do wycieczki z przewodnikiem tu w hotelu.
mó-zhesh pshi-wówn-chićh śhän do vi-ćhéch-kee z pshe-vod-ńeé-Kem too v kho-té-loo

That is convenient.

To wygodnie.
to vi-góod-ńe

147

The "Orbis" travel agency handles the tours here at the hotel.

Agencja "Orbis" tu w hotelu załatwia sprawy wycieczek.
a-génts-ya ór-bees too v kho-té-loo za-wat-vya sprá-vi vi-ćhé-chek

I hope they do have English speaking guides.

Mam nadzieję że mają przewodników mówiących po angielsku.
mam na-dźhé-yän zhe má-yówn pshe-vod-ńeé-koof moov-yówn-tsikh po an-géls-koo

Most guides speak English.

Większość przewodników mówi po angielsku.
vyáńk-shoshćh pshe-vod-ńeé-koof moó-vee po an-géls-koo

Let us go to "Orbis".

Chodźmy do "Orbisu".
khodźh-mi do or-beé-soo

148

"Orbis" is located between the coffee shop and the florist.

"Orbis" znajduje się między kawiarnią i kwiaciarnią.
ór-bees znaj-doó-ye śhän myáń-dzi ka-vyár-ńówn ee kvya-ćhár-ńówn

Good morning.

Dzień dobry.
dźheń dóo-ri

May I help you?

Czym mogę służyć?
chem mó-gän swoo-zhićh

I would like to go on a sight-seeing tour this afternoon.

Chciałbym dziś po południu zwiedzać z wycieczką.
khćháw-bim dźhee-sh po-po-woód-ńoo zvye-dzać z vi-ćhéch-kówn

149

There are seats on the Wilanów tour and on the Żelazowa Wola tour.

Są miejsca na wycieczkę do Wilanowa i do Żelazowej Woli.
sown myéys-tsa na vi-chéch-kan do vee-la-nó-va ee do zhe-la-zó-vey vó-lee

Which tour is more interesting?

Która wycieczka jest ciekawsza?
któo-ra vi-chéch-ka yest che-káv-sha

That depends on you.

To zależy od pana.
to za-lé-zhi od pá-na

The tour to Żelazowa Wola is longer.

Wycieczka do Żelazowej Woli jest dłuższa.
vi-chéch-ka do zhe-la-zó-vey vó-lee yest dwoózh-sha

150

Żelazowa Wola is the birthplace of Chopin.

Żelazowa Wola jest miejscem urodzenia Szopena.
zhe-la-zó-va vó-la yest myéys-tsem oo-ro-dzé-ña sho-pé-na.

Wilanów palace belonged to King John III Sobieski, the Supreme Commander of the Allied Christian Army at Vienna in 1683.

Pałac wilanowski należał do króla Jana trzeciego Sobieskiego, naczelnego wodza zjednoczonej armii chrześcijańskiej pod Wiedniem w tysiąc sześćset osiemdziesiątym trzecim roku.
pá-wats yee-la-nóv-skee na-lé-zhaw do króo-la yá-na tshe-ché-go so-byes-ké-go, na-chel-né-go vó-dza zyed-no-cho-ney árm-yee khshe-sh-chee-vań-skey pod vyéd-ñem v ti-shównts shé-sh-ch-set o-shem-dzhe-shówn-tim tshé-cheem róo-koo

151

Wilanów palace is one of the best examples of the Polish baroque.

Pałac wilanowski jest jednym z najlepszych przykładów polskiego baroku.
pá-wats yee-la-nóv-skee yest yéd-nim z nay-lép-shikh pshi-kwá-doof pols-ké-go ba-ró-koo

I would like to go on the Wilanów tour first.

Chciałbym naprzód pojechać na wycieczkę do Wilanowa.
khcháw-bim ná-pshood po-yé-khach na vi-chéch-kãñ do vee-la-nó-va

Your tour starts at two p.m.;here is your ticket.

Pańska wycieczka wyrusza o drugiej po południu; oto pański bilet.
pań-ska vi-chéch-ka vi-róo-sha o droó-gey po po-woód-ñoo, ó-to páń-skee beé-let

152

The ticket costs 200 zloties.

Bilet kosztuje dwieście złotych.
beé-let kosh-toó-ye dvyésh-che zwó-tikh

I have a thousand zloty bill.

Mam banknot tysiąc-złotowy.
man bánk-not ti-shownts zwó-to-vi

Your change: 800 zloties.

Pańska reszta: osiemset złotych,
páń-ska resh-ta: o-shém-set zwó-tikh

Does "Orbis" handle the air tickets?

Czy "Orbis" załatwia bilety lotnicze?
chi ór-bees za-wátv-ya bee-lé-ti lot-ñée-che

No, the air tickets are handled by "Lot".

Nie, bilety lotnicze załatwia "Lot".
ñe, bee-lé-ti lot-ñée-che za-wát-vya lot

153

"Orbis" handles bus and railroad tickets and sight seeing tours.

"Orbis" załatwia bilety kolejowe i autobusowe oraz zwiedzanie.
ór-bees za-wát-vya bee-lé-ti ko-le-yó-ve ee aw-to-boo-só-ve ó-raz zvye-dzá-ńe

Where is the "Lot" office?

Gdzie jest biuro "Lotu"?
gdźhe yest byóo-ro ló-too

The "Lot" office is on the second floor.

Biuro "Lotu" jest na drugim piętrze.
byóo-ro ló-too yest na dróo-geem pyáńt-she

Thank you.

Dziękuję.
dźhań-koo-yáń

154

Good morning to you.

Dzień dobry pani.
dźheń dób-ri pa-ńee

May I help you?

Czym mogę służyć?
chim mo-gáń swoó-zhich

I have an open return ticket on the Polish airline "Lot".

Mam bilet z otwartą datą powrotu na polskie linie lotnicze "Lot".
mam bée-let z ot-vár-tòwñ dá-tòwñ po-vró-too na póls-ke leéń-ye lot-ńeé-che lot

May I see your ticket?

Czy mogę zobaczyć pański bilet?
chi mo-gáń zo-bá-chich páń-skee bée-let?

155

When would you like to fly back?

Kiedy chciałby pan lecieć z powrotem?
ké-di khćháw-bi pan le-ćhech z po-vró-tem

I would like to fly in two weeks.

Chciałbym lecieć za dwa tygodnie.
khćháw-bim le-ćhech za dva ti-gód-ńe

I will check the Saturday flight.

Sprawdzę lot w sobotę.
správ-dzáń lot v so-bó-tàñ

The Saturday flight is sold out.

Sobotni lot jest wyprzedany.
so-bót-ńee lot yest vi-pshe-dá-ni

There are several passengers wait-listed for this flight.

Jest kilku pasażerów na liście oczekujących (zwolnień miejsc) na ten lot.
yets keél-koo pa-sa-zhé-roof na leéśh-che o-che-koo-yówñ-tsikh zvól-ńeñ na ten lot

156

I would like to have confirmed flight reservations.

Chciałbym mieć potwierdzoną rezerwację lotu.
khćháw-bim myech po-tvyer-dzó-nòwñ re-zer-váts-yáñ ló-too

Friday and Sunday flights still have a few seats available.

Piątkowy i niedzielny lot mają po kilka wolnych miejsc.
pyówñt-ko-vi ee ńe-dźhél-ni lot má-yòwñ po keél-ka vól-nikh myeysts

I will take the Friday flight.

Polecę w piątek.
po-le-tsan v pyówñ-tek

Fine, here is the confirmation of your departure.

Dobrze, oto potwierdzenie pańskiego odlotu.
dób-zhe o-to pot-vyer-dzé-ńe pańs-ké-go od-ló-too

157
Have a pleasant flight.

Życzę przyjemnego lotu.
zhi-chán pshi-yem-né-go ló-too

Thank you and good-bye.

Dziękuję i do widzenia.
dźhan-koó-yán ee do vee-dzé-ña

It's going to rain.

Deszcz będzie padał.
deshch ban-dźhe pá-daw

You need an umbrella.

Potrzebny jest Panu parasol.
po-tshéb-ni yest pá-noo pa-rá-sol

I ought to buy an umbrella.

Powinienem kupić parasol.
po-vee-ñé-nem koo-peech pa-rá-sol

Let's go to the store.

Chodźmy do sklepu.
khódźh-mi do skle-poo

158
Excuse me.

Przepraszam.
pshe-pra-sham

Do you have an umbrella?

Czy ma pani parasol?
chi ma pá-ñee pa-rá-sol

Certainly, sir.

Tak jest, proszę pana.
tak yest, pró-shán pá-na

I want the black umbrella.

Proszę o ten czarny parasol.
pró-shán o ten chár-ni pa-rá-sol

Do you need a raincoat?

Czy jest Panu potrzebny płaszcz
przeciwdeszczowy?
chi yest pá-noo po-tshéb-ni
pwashch pshe-cheev desh-chó-vi

159
Yes, I need a raincoat.

Tak, potrzeba mi płaszcza od deszczu.
tak, po-tshé-ba mee pwash-cha od désh-
choo

What size?

Jaki wymiar?
yá-kee vim-var

Please try this on.

Proszę ten spróbować.
pró-shán ten sproo-bó-vach

It doesn't fit.

Nie pasuje mi.
ñe pa-soó-ye mee

Let's try a larger size.

Spróbujmy o numer większy.
sproo-boóy-mi o noó-mer vyáñk-shi

160
I don't like the color.

Kolor mi się nie podoba.
kó-lor mee śhán ñe po-dó-ba.

What color do you like?

Jaki kolor panu odpowiada?
yá-kee kó-lor pá-noo od-po-vyá-da

I want a gray coat.

Chciałbym szary płaszcz.
khcháw-bim shá-ri pwashch

What about this one?

Jak się panu ten podoba?
yak śhán pá-noo ten po-dó-ba

This suits me fine.

Ten mi odpowiada.
ten mee od-po-vyá-da

Very good.

Bardzo dobrze.
bár-dzo dób-zhe

161
We have suits on sale.

Mamy ubrania na wyprzedaży.
má-mi oo-brá-ña na vi-pshe-dá-zhi

I have heard that the Polish tailors are very good.

Słyszałem że polscy krawcy są bardzo dobrzy.
swi-shá-wem zhe póls-tsi kráv-tsi sówñ bár-dzo dób-zhi

I would like to buy a jacket made in Poland.

Chciałbym kupić marynarkę uszytą w Polsce.
khcháw-bim koó-peech ma-ri-nár-kañ oo-shi-tówñ v póls-tse

Do you prefer wool or cotton?

Czy woli pan wełnę czy bawełnę?
chi vó-lee pan véw-nañ chi ba-véw-nañ

162
I want a brown cotton jacket.

Chciałbym mieć brązową marynarkę z bawełny.
khcháw-bim myech brówñ-zó-wówñ ma-ri-nár-kañ z ba-véw-ni

I am sorry, sir.

Niestety nie mamy.
ñe-sté-ti ñe má-mi

Where is the sales lady?

Gdzie jest sprzedawczyni?
gdźhe yest spshe-dav-chí-ñee

How much is this dress?

Ile kosztuje ta suknia?
eé-le kosh-toó-ye ta soók-ña

4000 zloties.

Cztery tysiące złotych.
chté-ri ti-shówñ-tse zwó-tikh

163
That is very expensive.

To jest bardzo drogo.
to yest bár-dzo dró-go

Where are the blouses and the sweaters?

Gdzie są bluzki i swetry?
gdźhe sówñ bloóz-kee ee svét-ri

Where are the shirts and the skirts?

Gdzie są koszule i spódnice?
gdźhe sówñ ko-shoó-le ee spood-ñeé-tse

We have many hats on sale.

Mamy wiele kapeluszy na wyprzdaży.
má-mi vyé-le ka-pe-loó-shi na vi-pshe-dá-zhi

These are very cheap.

Te są bardzo tanie.
te sówñ bár-dzo tá-ñe

164
Do you like these ties?

Czy podobają się panu te krawaty?
chi po-do-bá-yówñ shañ pá-noo te kra-vá-ti?

Are they rayon?

Czy są ze sztucznego jedwabiu?
chi sówñ ze shtooch-né-go yed-váb-yoo

They are silk.

Są z jedwabiu.
sówñ z yed-váb-yoo

Do you have a jewelry department.

Czy macie dział jubilerski?
chi má-che dźhaw yoo-bee-lér-skee?

A jeweler is across the street.

Jubiler jest po drugiej stronie ulicy.
yoo-beé-ler yest po droó-gey stró-ñe oo-leé-tsi

165
May I show you some watches?

Czy mogę panu pokazać zegarki?
chi mó-gãñ pá-noo po-ka-zach ze-gár-kee

I am looking for a diamond ring.

Chciałbym kupić pierścionek z bry-
lantem.
khcháw-bim koó-peech pyerśh-chó-nek
z bri-lán-tem

Do you handle signet rings?

Czy sprzedajecie sygnety?
chi spshe-da-ye-che sig-né-ti

Yes, we also have an engraving
service.

Tak, mamy też rytownictwo.
tak, má-mi tezh ri-tov-ñeéts-tvo

That is very good.

To bardzo dobrze.
to bár-dzo dób-zhe

166
Your driver's license, please.

Proszę o pańskie prawo jazdy.
pró-shan o páns-ke pra-vo yáz-di

You have a flat tire.

Pan ma przebitą dętkę.
pan ma pshe-bee-tõwn dént-kãñ

I need gasoline.

Potrzebuję benzyny.
po-tshe-boó-yãñ ben-zi-ni

Where is a gas station?

Gdzie jest stacja benzynowa?
gdźhe yest státs-ya ben-zi-nó-va

Let's change the oil.

Zmieńmy oliwę.
zmyéñ-mi o-leé-vãñ

There is the garage.

Tam jest garaż.
tam jest gá-razh

167
How far is it to Warsaw?

Jak daleko jest do Warszawy?
yak da-lé-ko yest do var-shá-vi

Which road goes to Cracov?

Która droga prowadzi do Krakowa?
któó-ra dró-ga pro-vá-dzhee do Kra-
kó-va

Do not drive so fast.

Nie jedź tak szybko.
ñe yedźh tak shíb-ko

The road is good.

Droga jest dobra.
dró-ga yest dób-ra

The road is very steep.

Droga jest bardzo stroma.
dró-ga yest bár-dzo stró-ma

168
I want to rent a car.

Chciałbym wynająć samochód.
khcháw-bim vi-ná-yõwñch sa-mó-khoot

How much does it cost to rent it?

Ile kosztuje wynajęcie samochodu?
eé-le kosh-toó-ye vi-na-yáñ-che
sa-mo-kho-doo

Twenty dollars per day.

Dwadzieścia dolarów dziennie.
dva-dźheéśh-cha do-lá-roof dźhén-ñe

Which car do you like?

Który samochód panu się podoba?
któó-ri sa-mó-khoot pá-noo śhãñ po-
dó-ba

I like this blue Fiat.

Podoba mi się ten niebieski Fiat
po-dó-ba mee-śhãñ ten ñe-byés-kee fyat

169

Let us go to write the rental contract.

Chodźmy spisać kontrakt wynajmu.
khóźh-mi spee-sach kón-trakt vi-náy-moo

For how many days?

Na ile dni?
na eé-le dńce

Do you want complete insurance?

Czy chce pan pełne ubezpieczenie?
chi khtse,pan péw-ne oo-bez-pye-ché-ńe

I need a road map.

Potrzebna mi jest mapa samochodowa.
po-tshéb-na mee yest má-pa sa-mo-kho-dó-va.

You start with a full tank.

Zaczyna pan z pełnym bakiem.
za-chí-na pan z péw-nim bá-ńem

170

What town are we in?

W jakim mieście jesteśmy?
v yá-keem myéśh-che yes-téśh-mi

You are in Poznań.

Jesteście państwo w Poznaniu.
yes-téśh-che páńs-tvo v poz-ná-ńoo

No parking.

Zakaz postoju.
zá-kaz pos-tó-yoo

Please don't close the window.

Proszę nie zamykać okna.
pró-sháń ńe za-mí-kach ók-na

Be careful.

Proszę uważać.
pró-sháń oo-va-zhach

The motel is on the next corner.

Motel jest na następnym rogu.
mó-tel yest na nas-táńp-nim ró-goo

171

I do not understand any Polish.

Wcale nie rozumiem po polsku.
vtsá-le ńe ro-zoóm-yem po póls-koo

I understand a little Polish.

Rozumiem trochę po polsku.
ro-zoóm-yem tró-kháń po póls-koo

I speak little Polish.

Mało mówię po polsku.
má-wo moóv-yáń po póls-koo

Please, speak slowly.

Proszę mówić powoli.
pró-sháń moó-veech po-vó-lee

Are you from America?

Czy jesteście państwo z Ameryki?
chi yes-téśh-ńe páńs-tvo z a-me-ri-kee

Yes, we are from America.

Tak jesteśmy z Ameryki.
tak, yes-téśh-mi z a-me-ri-kee

172

Where is the railroad station?

Gdzie jest dworzec kolejowy?
gdźhe yest dvo-zhets ko-le-yó-vi

It isn't near by.

Nie jest blisko.
ńe yest bleéz-ko

Where is the bus stop?

Gdzie jest przystanek autobusowy?
gdźhe yest pshi-stá-nek aw-to-boo-só-vi

Does this bus go to the railroad station?

Czy ten autobus dojeżdża do dworca kolejowego?
chi ten aw-tó-boos do-yéźh-dzha do dvór-tsa ko-le-yo-vé-go

How much is the fare?

Ile kosztuje bilet?
eé-le kosh-toó-ye beé-let

173

Do you want a one way or a round trip ticket.

Czy chce pan bilet w jedną stronę czy powrotny?
chi khtse pan beé-let v yed-nówn stro-nāñ chi po-yrót-ni

Do you have a time table?

Czy ma pani rozkład jazdy?
chi mᵃ pá-ñee róz-kwad yáz-di

What time does the train for Gdańsk leave?

Kiedy odjeżdża pociąg do Gdańska?
Ké-di od-yezh-dzha po-chówñg do gádñ-ska

Please tell me where to get off.

Proszę mi powiedzieć gdzie mam wysiąść?
pró-shāñ mee po-vye-dźhech gdźhe mam vi-shówñshch

174

What time does the train from Lublin arrive?

Kiedy przyjeżdża pociąg z Lublina?
Ké-di pshi-yézh-dzha po-chówñg z loob-leé-na

Is this seat occupied?

Czy to miejsce jest zajęte?
chi to myéys-tse yest za-yāñ-te

No, please sit down.

Nie, proszę usiąść.
ñe, pró-shāñ oó-śhówñshch

Please, open the window.

Proszę otworzyć okno.
pró-shāñ ot-vó-zhich ók-no

Please, close the window.

Proszę zamknąć okno.
pró-shāñ zámk-nówñch ók-no

175

No smoking.

Nie palić. = Palenie wzbronione.
ñe pá-leech= pa-lé-ñe vzbro-ñó-ne

I would like to smoke a cigarette.

Chciałbym zapalić papierosa.
khcháw-bim za-pá-leech pa-pye-ró-sa

Do you have a cigarette?

Czy ma pan papierosa?
chi ma pan pa-pye-ró-sa

Do you have matches ?

Czy ma pan zapałki?
chi ma pan za-páw-k ee

Do you see the sign "no smoking"?

Czy widzi pan napis "palenie wzbronione"?
chi veé-dźhee pan ná-pees "pa-lé-ñe vzbro-ñó-ne"

176

Please write it down.

Proszę zapisać.
pró-shāñ za-peé-sach

Do you have a pen?

Czy ma pan pióro?
chi ma pan pyoó-ro

I lost my pen.

Zgubiłem moje pióro.
zgoo-beé-wem mo-ye pyoo-ro

Do you have a pencil?

Czy ma pan ołówek?
chi ma pan o-woó-vek

Here is pencil and paper.

Oto ołówek i papier.
ó-to o-woó-vek ee pá-pyer

Thank you.

Dziękuję.
dźhāñ-koó-yāñ

177

Are you sick?

Czy źle się pan czuje?
chi zhle shañ pan choo-ye

I am sick at my stomach.

Jest mi niedobrze.
yest mee ñe dob-zhe

I am nauseated.

Mam nudności.= Nudzi mnie.
mam nood-nósh-chee=noo-dzhee mñe

Please call the doctor.

Proszę wezwać lekarza.
pró-shañ véz-vach le-ká-zha

How do you feel?

Jak się pan czuje?
yak shañ pan choo-ye?

I have a stomach ache.

Boli mnie żołądek.
bó-lee mñe zho-wówñ-dek

178

You must stay in bed.

Musi pan pozostać w łóżku.
móó-shee pan po-zós-tach v woozh-koo

Do you feel better?

Czy czuje się pan lepiej?
chi choo-ye shañ pan lé-pyey

I feel much better.

Czuję się dużo lepiej.
choo-yañ shañ dóó-zho lé-pyey

I have a headache.

Boli mnie głowa.
bó-lee mñe gwó-va

You can get headache pills at the "Ruch" news-stand.

Może pan dostać proszki na ból głowy w kiosku "Ruchu".
mó-zhe pan dós-tach prósh-kee na bool gwó-vi v kyós-koo roó-khoo

179

Headache pills and aspirin are available at "Ruch" news-stand.

Pastylki od bólu głowy i aspirynę można dostać w kiosku "Ruchu".
pas-tíl-kee od bóó-loo gwó-vi ee as-pee-ri-nañ mózh-na dós-tach v kyós-koo roó-khoo

"Ruch" news-stands also sell some basic cosmetics, shaving supplies etc.

Kioski "Ruchu" również sprzedają niezbędne artykuły kosmetyczne, przybory do golenia etc.
kyós-kee roó-khoo roóv-ñezh spshe-dá-yówñ ñez-bánd-ne ar-ti-koó-wi kos-me-tích-ne, pshi-bó-ri do go-lé-ña et-tsé-te-ra

Polish drugstores sell medicines only.

Polskie apteki sprzedają wyłącznie lekarstwa.
póls-ke an-té-kee spshe-dá-yówñ vi-wówñch-ñe le-kárs-tva

180

What do you call the cosmetics supply store?

Jak się nazywają sklepy z kosmetykami?
yak shañ na-zi-vá-yówñ sklé-pi z kos-me-ti-ká-mee

"Drogeria" is the Polish word for a cosmetics supply store.

Polskie słowo na sklep z kosmetykami jest "drogeria".
póls-ke swó-vo na sklep z kos-me-ti-ká-mee yest dro-gér-ya

I want to buy some toothpaste.

Chciłbym kupić pastę do zębów.
Khchów-bim koó-peech pás-tañ do záñ-boof

I also need a tooth brush.

Potrzebuję również szczoteczkę do zębów.
po-tshe-bóó-yañ roóv-ñezh shcho-tétch-kañ do záñ-boof.

POLISH—ENGLISH PHONETICS

POLISH VOWELS

Schematic ellipse of the tip of the tongue positions

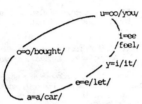

u=oo/you/
i=ee /feel/
o=o/bought/
y=i/it/
e=e/let/
a=a/car/

Polish nasalized vowels:
A, ą /ćwh/ one nasalized sound
E, ę /ăn/ two sounds:
short "a" and nasalized "n"

dąb /dołmp/   kęs /kańs/
wąs /vołns/   gęś /gańsh/

POLISH CONSONANTS

UNVOICED	VOICED	NASALS
p	b	m
t	d	n
k and ǩ	g and ǧ	ń and ni
f	w /v/	/ń/
s	z	
ś /śh/	ź /źh/	GLIDES
sz /sh/	ż /zh/	r /flut-
c /ts/	dz	tered/
ć /ćh/	dź /dźh/	j /y/
cz /ch/	dż /j/	ł /w/
h and ch= = /kh/		

NOTE: A trace of the sound "ee" as in "feel" is typical in softening of Polish consonants as in: "kie","gie","pie","bie","mie",and "wie" in the phonetic notation:"ǩ" "ǧ","pye","bye","mye" and "vye". The softened consonant is followed by vowel "e" /as in "let"/, without which it is impossible to pronounce.

SPEECH ORGAN DIAGRAM

for Polish consonants not used in the English language

"dź","dzi"/dźh/ and "ć","ci"/ćh/ air compressed behind lips and teeth then suddenly released /ex-plosives/;
"ź","zi"/źh/ and "ś","si"/śh/ air flow with continuous friction /fricatives/;
In each case the tip of the tongue is at the tooth ridge.

POLISH SOUND "R"

is fluttered and may be pronounced alone like Scottish "R"

Mouth is slightly open; tip of the tongue is raised; it vibrates on exhailing impulse and strikes the toothridge; sides of the tongue touch back teeth. Tongue does not glide as far as needed to pronounce the English "R". DWG. OF SPEECH ORGANS BY PROF. JERZY STARCZEWSKI

BY IWO CYPRIAN POGONOWSKI

SAMOGŁOSKI ANGIELSKIE

Schematyczna elipsa pozycji języka dla dwunastu samogłosek angielskich /wymowa amerykańska/.

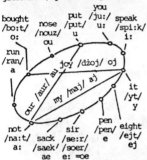

```
                        you
bought          put /ju:/  speak
/bo:t/   nose /put/ u:  /spi:k/
o:       /nouz/   u        i:
         ou
run                              it
/ran/      joy /dżoj/ oj       /yt/
a                                y
    our /aur/ au
         my /maj/ aj
                              pen
not          sir        pen /pen/ eight
/na:t/  sack /se:r/     e       /ejt/
a:   /saek/ /soer/              ej
     ae   e: =oe
```

Trzy podstawowe dwugłoski angielskie: diphtongs /'dyftons/ są zaznaczone wewnątrz elipsy

SPÓŁGŁOSKI ANGIELSKIE

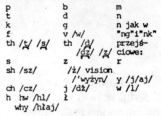

Bezdźwięczne	Dźwięczne	Nosowe
p	b	m
t	d	n
k	g	n jak w
f	v /w/	"ng"i"nk"
th /t/ /s/	th /d/	przejś-
	/dż/ /z/	ciowe:
s	z	r
sh /sz/	/ż/ vision	
	/'wyżyn/	y /j/aj/
ch /cz/	j /dż/	w /l/
h hw /hl/	ł	
why /hłaj/		

Uwaga: Często spółgłoski angielskie dźwięczne na końcu słowa są wymawiane dźwięcznie / w przeciwieństwie do polskich, które na końcu słowa wymawia się bezdźwięcznie/.

ANGIELSKI DŹWIĘK "TH"

struny głosowe

angielska spółgłoska "th" "sepleniona", koniec i przód języka szeroko spłaszczony, widzialny między zębami; ciągły przelot powietrza między zębami i wargami.

Bezdźwięczna: thank /taenk/
bath /ba:s/
Dźwięczna: they /dzej/
those /douz/
bathing /bejzyng/

ANGIELSKI DŹWIĘK "R"

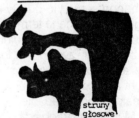

struny głosowe

Angielska spółgłoska "r": usta nieco otwarte; koniec języka uniesiony wklęsłym podgięciem ku tyłowi, nie dotyka podniebienia; boki języka dotykają zębów; wymowa możliwa tylko w przejściu od lub do samogłoski. Dźwięk angielski spółgłoski "r" przypomina lekkie rżenie.

Glossary of Menu Terms

Polish cuisine is made for hospitality. It abounds in wonderful hors d'oeuvres, fragrant soups, delightful dishes produced with subtle skill and care integrating native traditions and adaptations from other lands. Polish desserts and sweets are unusually good. They never fail to delight Poles and tourists. There is an abundant variety of very tasty Polish bakery products. Polish cuisine includes distinctive seasonal menus for spring, summer, autumn and winter. Examples of Polish food served in quality restaurants are listed in this glossary of menu terms.

A unique item of daily diet is the Polish bread or "chleb." It is always sold in loaves, has a substantial body and a delicious crust. Fresh Polish bread is bought and consumed daily.

Breakfast or "sniadanie" is served from 6:30 until 10 A.M.; dinner or "objad" is served from 1 until 3:30 P.M.; supper or "kolacja" is served from 6 until 9 P.M. Cafes serve good coffee topped with whipped cream during the day and late into the evening. A small serving of strong coffee is called "pol-czarnej" (half-cup of black).

A variety of excellent pastries are served in the "kawiarnia" (cafe) or "cukiernia" (pastry shop). Food is served in the "restauracja" (restaurant).

"Jadłospis" (menu) will list:
"przystawki" (apetizers);
"zupy" (soups);
"dania" (main courses) including:
"dania miesne" (meats),
"dania jarskie" (vegetarian courses),
"ryby" (fish),
"drób" (poultry or other birds),
"wedliny" (smoked meats and fish,
also pates),
"jarzyny" (vegetables),
"sałatki" (salads)
"desery" (desserts) which may include:
"owoce" (fruits),
"kompoty" (compotes),
"ciastka" (cakes),
"torty" (multi-layer torts)
"lody" (ice cream).
Menus will also list:
"napoje" (beverages)
"zakaski" (snacks, usually
served with vodka).

"Przystawki" (Appetizers)

"grzyby marynowane" (marinated mushrooms)
"jajka faszerowane po polsku" (stuffed
eggs Polish style)
"jajka faszerowane z sosem" (stuffed eggs
with sauce)
"jajka faszerowane szynka" (eggs stuffed
with ham)
"jajka w sosie chrzanowym" (eggs in
horseradiash sauce)
"jajka w sosie musztardowym" (eggs in
mustard sauce)
"krokiety z jajka" (egg balls with grated
cheese)
"pierozki" (browned onion and mushroom
ravioli)
"pierozki z miesem" (dumplings with meat)
"sledzie marynowane" (marinated herring)
"sledzie w smietanie" (herring in sour
cream)

"<u>Zakaski</u>" (Snacks, Usually With Vodka)

"wybór kanapek" (canapes Polish style
                      many different snacks)

"<u>Sniadanie</u>" (Breakfast)

"boczek" (bacon)
"bułka" (white bread or roll)
"chleb" (bread made in loafs)
"masło" butter)
"ser bialy" (farmer's cheese)
"ser zółty" (cheese, melted)
"jajka na mieko" (soft boiled eggs)
"jajka po wiedeńsku" (soft boiled eggs
with butter)
"jajka sadzone" (fried eggs, sunny
side up)
"jajecznica" (scrambled eggs)
"szynka" (ham)
"konfitury" (preserves)
"mleko" (milk)
"dżem" (jam)
"miód" (honey)
"naleśniki z dżemem" (pancakes with
jam)
"omlet" (omlette)
"sok z czarnej porzeczki" (black
currant juice)
"sok jabłkowy" (apple cider)
"sok pomarańczowy" (orange juice)

"<u>Objad</u>" (Dinner, 1.00-3.30 P.M.)
"<u>Kolacja</u>" (Supper, 6.00-9.00 P.M.
            lighter meal served with
            the same manu as dinner)

"Zupy Gorace" (Soups Served Hot)

"rosól" (comsomes or broth of
traditionally seasoned beef or chicken)
"rosół z zoltkiem" (consome with a raw
egg yolk)
"rosół z diablotka" (consome with salty
biscuit)
"barszcz z pasztecikiem" (beet-root
soup)

"barszcz ukraiński z polska kiełbasa"
(Ukrainian barshch with Polish sausage)
"barszcz zabielany" barshch with sour
cream)
"kapuśniak" (sour cabbage soup)
"krupnik" (barley kasha soup)
"zupa grzybowa" (mushroom soup)
"zupa pomidorowa z ryzem" (tomato
soup with rice)
"zupa jarzynowa" (vegetable soup)
"zupa grochowa na wędzonce" (pea
and smoked ham soup)
"zupa ziemniaczana" (potato soup)
"zupa chlebowa" (bread soup with egg)
"zupa cytrynowa z ryzem" (lemon soup
with rice)
"zupa kminkowa" (caraway seed soup)
"zupa szczawiowa z jajkami" (tart
sorrel soup with eggs)
"zupa ogórkowa z koperkiem" (dill
picle soup)
"żurek" (sour soup)

"<u>Zupy Zimne</u>" (Cold Soups)

"chłodnik" (cold barshch with cream)
"zupa jabłkowa" (apple soup)
"zupa ogórkowa na barszczu" (barszcz
and cucumber soup)
"zupa owocowa" (fruit soup)

"<u>Dania Miesne</u>" (Main Meat Courses)

"baranina" (lamb)
"befsztyk po tatarsku" (Tartar
steak)
"bigos" sour cabbage with diced pork,
veal, beef, ham, sausage and
mushrooms; stewed, then fried
"bite kotlety" (pounded cutlets)
"bite zrazy cielęce" (pounded veal
chops)
"boczek pieczony" (baked bacon)
"chuda szynka" (lean ham)
"chude mieso" (lean meat)
"cielecina z papryka" (veal with
paprica)

"duszona wołowina z grzybami"
(simmered beef with mushrooms)
"flaki" (tripe)
"golonka gotowana" (pig's foot
jelly)
"gulasz" (goulash, meat stew)
"gulasz wieprzowy" (pork goulash)
"kiełbasa" (sausage)
"kiełbasa wedzona" (smoked
sausage)
"kiszka" (sausage of chopped liver
and pork with groats)
"klops" (meat loaf)
"kłoduny) (meat balls in dough)
"kotlet" (cutlet)
"krokiety" (meat balls)
"królik marynowany" (marinated rabbit)
"krwawa kiszka" (black pudding)
"łopatka barania" (lamb shoulder)
"marynowana baranina" (marinated
lamb)
"mielone mięso" (ground meat"
"mózg wieprzowy" (pork brain)
"ozór wołowy" (beef tongue)
"parówki na gorąco" (franks served
hot)
"pasztet" (calf's liver, veal and
pork meat loaf with bacon, eggs and
mushrooms)
"pasztet z watroby" (liver pudding)
"pieczeń barania" (lamb roast)
"pieczeń wolowa duszona" (pot roast
of beef)
"potrawka z baraniny" (fricassee of
lamb)
"prosię nadziewane" (stuffed piglet)
"rolada mięsna" (meat loaf)
"schab" (loin)
"schabowa pieczeń" (roast loin)
"siekane zrazy" (minced chops)
"smazone mięso" (fried meat)
"szaszłyk" shish kebab
"szynka" (ham)
"szynka gotowana" (cooked ham)
"szynka gotowana, na zimno" (cold
cooked ham)

"sztuka miesa" (cooked beef)
"watróbka" (liver)
"wedzone mieso" (smoked meat)
"zeberka" (ribs)
"zrazy baranie" (lamb chops)
"zrazy wieprzowe" (pork chops)

"<u>Drób</u>" (Poultry, Ducks and Geese)

"kura" (hen or chicken)
"kurczak" (spring chiken)
"kurcze pieczone" (baked chicken)
"kaczka" (duck)
"gęs" (goose)
"gołąb" (pigeon)

"indyk" (turkey)
"bazant" (pheasant)
"nadziewany indyk" (stuffed turkey)
"paprykarz z kurcząt" (chicken
stewed with pepers)
"potrawka z kury" (chiken
fricassee)
"smazone kotlety z piersi kury"
(chicken brest cutlets)

"<u>Dziczyzna</u>" (Venison)
"dzika gęs" (wild goose)
"dzika kaczka" (wild duck)
"kuropatwa" (partridge)
"pasztet z dziczyzny" (venison meat
loaf)
"pieczona dziczyzna" (roast venison)
"potrawka z zająca" (fricassee of
hare)
"sarnina" (deer meat)
"udziec sarni" (deer haunch)
"zając" (hare)

"<u>Dania Jarskie</u>" (Vegetarian courses)

"<u>Dania Rybne</u>" (Fishes)

"dorsz w sosie chrzanowym"
(cod with horseradish sause)

"gotowany szczupak z sosem chrzanowym"
(boiled pike with horseradish sause)
"jesiotr z kwaśną śmietana" (sturgeon
with sour cream)
"filet z soli z tartym serem" (fillet
of sole with grated cheese)
"karp" (grain fed carp)
"karp w galarecie" (carp in jelly)
"losos w galarecie" (salmon in jelly)
"okon na bialym winie" (perch on
white wine)
"okoń z rozna z grzybami" (perch
broiled with mushrooms)
"potrawka z ryby z tartym serem"
(fricassee of fish with grated cheese)
"pstrąg z pietruszka" (trout with
parsley)
"szczupak pieczony z sardelami"
(baked pike with anchovies)
"szczupak po zydowsku" pike Jewish
style
"węgorz duszony w winie" (eel stewed
in wine)

"<u>Jarzyny</u>" (Vegetables)

"brokuly" (broccoli)
"brukiew" (turnips)
"buraczki" (beat dish)
"buraki z rabarbarem" (beets with
rhubarb)
"brukselka" (Brussels sprouts)
"chrzan" (horseradish)
"cebula" (onion)
"dania ziemniaczane" (potato dishes)
"dynia" (pumpkin)
"fasola" (beans)
"groszek" (green peas)
"kalafior" (cauliflower)
"kalarepa" (kohlrabi)
"kapusta" (cabbage)
"karczochy" (artichokes)
"kiszona kapusta" (sour cabbage)
"marchewka z groszkiem" (carrots
with peas)

"młode ziemniaki" (early potatoes)
"placki zemniaczane" (potato pies
or pancakes)
"pomidory" (tomatoes)
"szparagi" (asparagus)
"szparagowa fasola" (string beans)
"szpinak" (spinach)
"ziemniaki smażone" (fried potatoes)
"ziemniaki tłuczone" (mashed potatoes)

<u>"Sałatki"</u> (Salads)

"ćwikła" (red beet salad with
horseradish)
"mieszana sałatka" (mixed salad)
"sałatka jarzynowa" (vegetable salad)
"sałatka owocowa" (fruit salad)
"sałatka pomidorowa" (tomato salad)
"sałatka śledziowa" (herring salad)
"sałatka w galarecie" (jellied salad)
"sałatka z cebuli" (onion salad)
"sałatka z ziemniakow" (potato salad)

<u>"Deser"</u> (dessert)

"babka" (round cofee cake)
"budyń" (pudding)
"budyń czekoladowy" (chocolate pudding)
"chrust" (Polish fried cookies)
"galaretka porzeczkowa" (currant
jelly)
"gruszki w rumie" (pears in rum)
"kompot" (compote)
"kompot morelowy" (apricote compote)
"kutia" (wheat grain and honey
dessert)
"lody" (ice cream)
"lody waniliowe" (vanilla ice cream)
"lody czekoladowe" (chocolate ice
cream)
"makownik" (poppy seed cake)
"mus jabłkowy" (creamed apples)
"paczki" (cherry stuffed batter
balls)

"suflet kawowy" (cofee souffle)

"Napoje Orzezwiajace" (Refreashments)

"Napoje gorace" (Hot drinks)

"biała kawa" (coffee with cream)
"czarna kawa" (black coffee)
"herbata" (tea)
"kakao" (cocoa)
"mleko" (milk)
"surówka owocowa" (fresh fruit salad)
"truskawki" (strawberries)

"Napoje Alkocholowe" (Alcoholic
Drinks)

"ajerkoniak" (eggnog vodka)
"ajerowka" (sweet sedge vodka)
"ciemne piwo" (dark beer)
"cytrynowka" (lemon vodka)
"jarzębiak" (rowanberry vodka)
"jasne piwo" (light beer)
"kminkowka" (caraway seed vodka)
"krupnik" (peppercorns, vanilla,
honey vodka)
"miód pitny" (mead, honey wine)
"morelowka" (apricot vodka)
"piwo" (beer)
"piwo słodowe" (malt liquor)
"pomarańczówka" (orange vodka)
"śliwowica" (plum brandy)
"winiak" (wine brandy)
"wiśniówka" (cherry cordial)
"wódka" (vodka)
"wódka wyborowa" (choice grain vodka)
"wyszynk" (retail of alcoholic drinks)
"złota woda" (golden vodka)
"żubrowka" (bison grass wodka)
"zytnia wódka" (rye vodka)

Note: please, see pages 346-373 for
conversations about Polish food,
with a complete pronunciation guide.